L. BLANKENSHIP

This book is a work of fiction. All the characters and events portrayed in this book are ficticious, and any resemblance ro real people or actual events is purely coincidental.

DISCIPLE OMNIBUS

Edited by Debra Doyle and Jon VanZile at Editing for Authors
Cover artwork by Alejandro Martínez
Maps by The Cabil
Cover design by The Cabil
Published by The Cabil

discipleofthefount.blogspot.com/

ISBN: 978-0-9914477-8-7
First edition.

Also by L. Blankenship

Novels/Novellas

Disciple, Part I
Disciple, Part II
Disciple, Part III
Disciple, Part IV
Disciple, Part V
Disciple, Part VI

Fire's First Kiss
Discple Omnibus

Hawks & Rams
(available from Dreamspinner Press)

Anthologies

The Battle of Ebulon

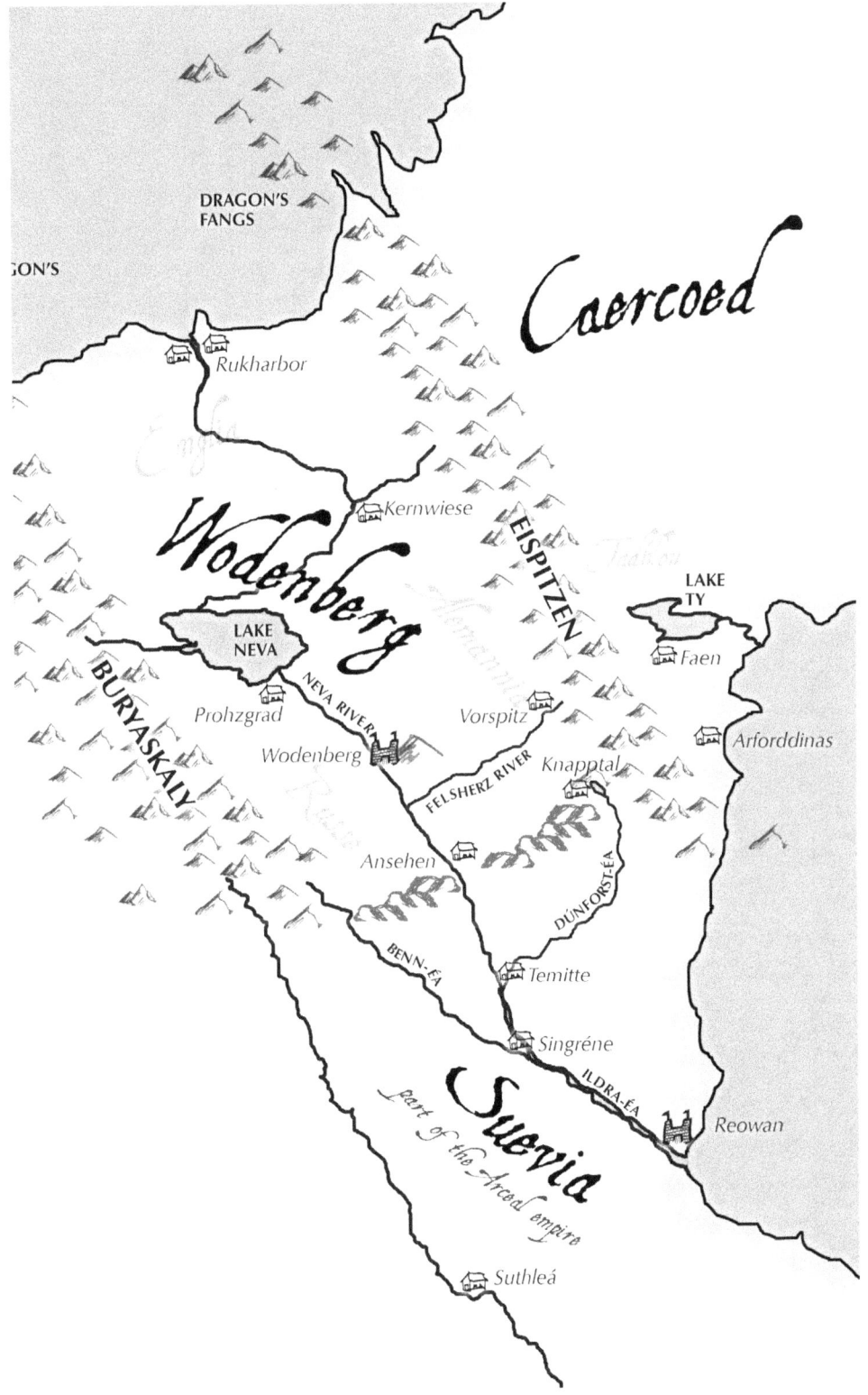

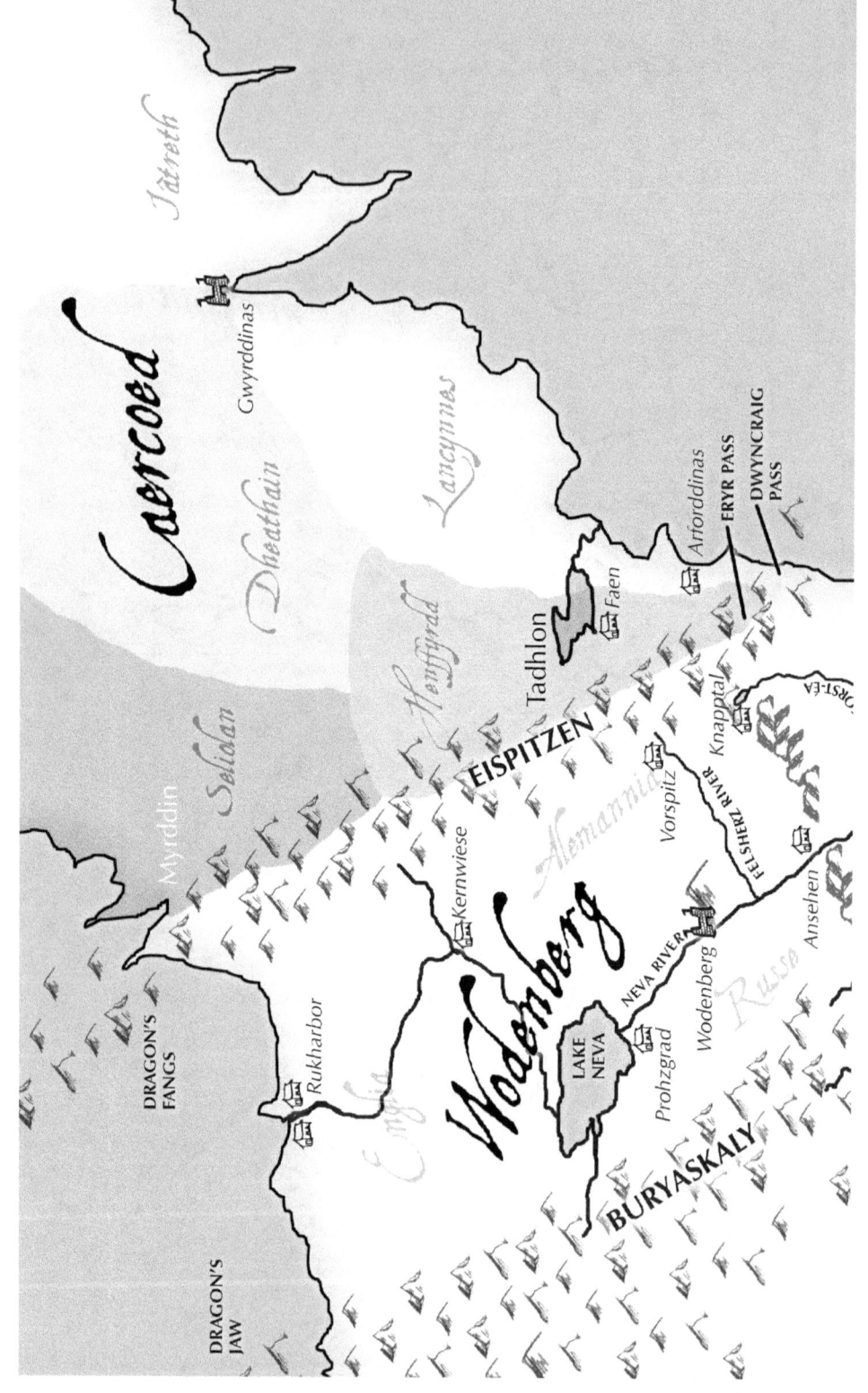

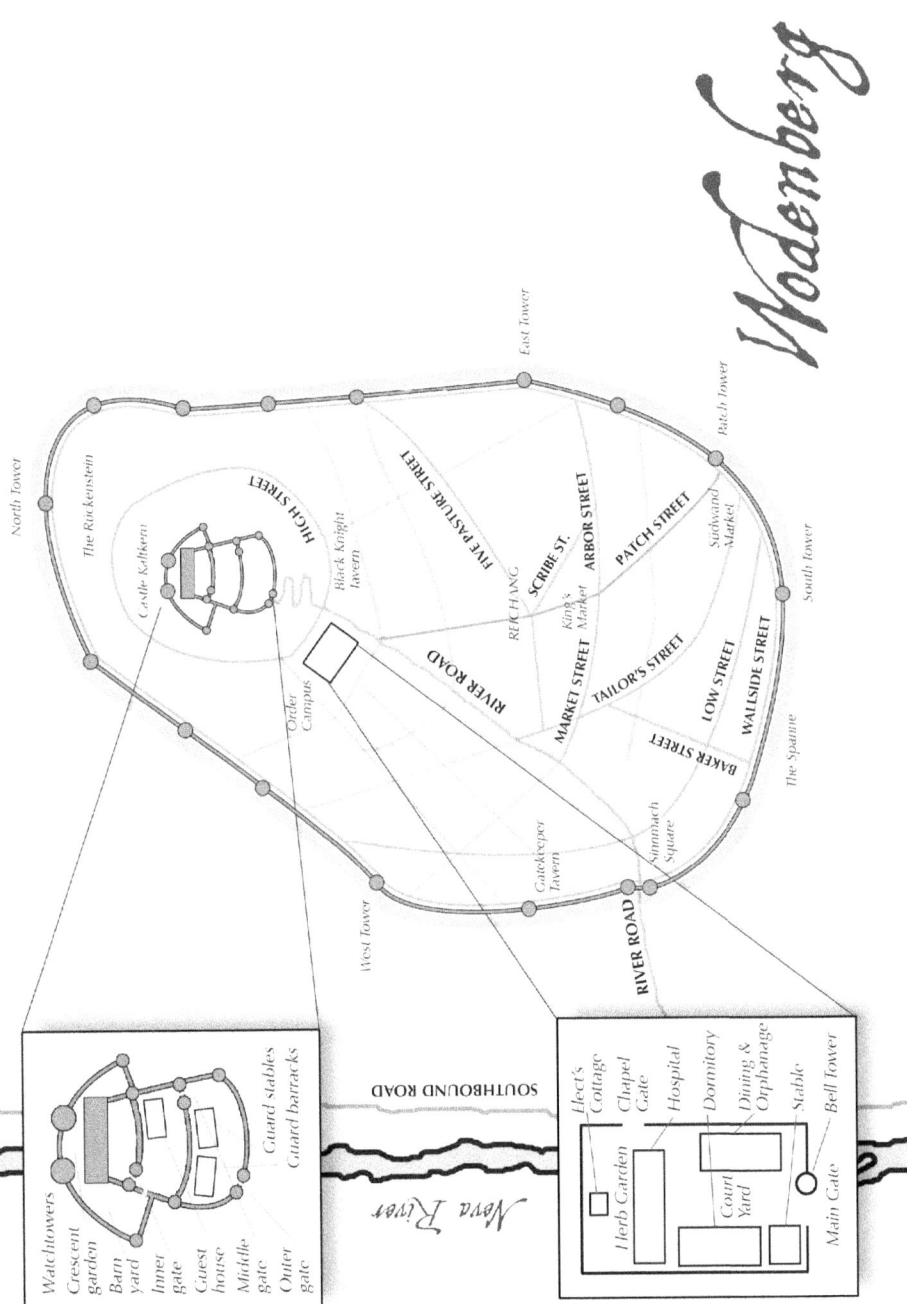

Wodenberg

North Tower

The Rackenstein

Castle Keltkern

HIGH STREET

Order Campus

Black Knight Tavern

FIVE PASTURE STREET

REICHANG

SCRIBE ST.

King's Market

MARKET STREET

TAILOR'S STREET

BAKER STREET

RIVER ROAD

Gatekeeper Tavern

West Tower

RIVER ROAD

Sunnmach Square

ARBOR STREET

PATCH STREET

Südwand Market

LOW STREET

WALLSIDE STREET

The Spanne

South Tower

Patch Tower

East Tower

SOUTHBOUND ROAD

Neva River

Watchtowers
Crescent garden
Barn yard
Inner gate
Guest house
Middle gate
Outer gate
Guard stables
Guard barracks

Hect's Cottage
Chapel Gate
Hospital
Dormitory
Dining & Orphanage
Stable
Bell Tower
Herb Garden
Court Yard
Main Gate

DISCIPLE, PART I
for want of a piglet

CHAPTER 1

"You couldn't sleep either?"

At the whisper, I looked up from struggling to lace my boots with trembling hands. My master stepped into my dormitory room, adding his lamp's light to my candle.

"Why must I dress as a boy?" I whispered back. Perhaps I was not so buxom, but I doubted I'd fool anyone. "This makes little sense."

"Patience." Master Parselev placed his lamp on my writing-table and checked my packed bags. "They're gathering at the chapel already. None of us got much sleep, it seems."

The straw mattress creaked when I stood, boots laced and the woolen hose sagging between my thighs. I ran my fingers around my waist, under my layered cotes, to check the drawstring. "Are these right, Master?" I'd strung the hose and braies together as best I could guess and as memory was my Blessing I had no excuse for failing. Men's underthings weren't much concern to me — if I saw such, or more, it was while the man lay bleeding on the surgery table.

"If they stay up, it's right. Good. This too." He slung a heavy felt cloak across my shoulders and pinned it on. The hood buried my face in shadows; my blonde braid, even wrapped around my head, would give me away.

I asked, "Master, this journey will be long, won't it?" Parselev had given me more clothes than I'd ever owned to pack in those bags. All heavy winter woolens, too. "Shouldn't you go, then?"

He looked down at me, mouth quirking to one side. Master was a greybeard, said to be over a hundred years old, but his kir kept his eyes bright and his face lightly creased. I had only been his apprentice two years. Surely I could not be ready for this.

"It must be you, Kate," was all he said. He carried one of my bags, and I took the other.

Wreathed in breath-clouds, we crossed the Order's campus. Low on the horizon, the slim, waxing crescent of the Shepherd hung golden, all seven of his Flock scattered in the sky behind him. He gave the only hint that dawn was coming. The cloak kept me marvelously warm, even in the chilly breeze. No frost this morning, not yet, but it was only a few weeks off.

Master un-bolted the side gate and led me to the door of the Grand Chapel. Horses waited on the grass, many horses chewing at their bits and shaking their heads, most of them with knights in the saddles. The knights' black tabards, worn over suits of mail, had a white horse embroidered on the right shoulder and two gold stars on the left, marking them knights and Prince's Guard as well. Kite shields and bucket helms hung on their saddles, in easy reach.

Several of the horses stood with empty saddles, collectively held by a couple of pageboys, and that gave me pause. I'd never been on a horse; I was only a peasant girl. But it could not be so awful, I told myself, so I gripped my cloak a little tighter and followed Master Parselev inside.

My new boots rang too loudly in the empty chapel, and when I slowed to lighten my step I fell behind. Only one lamp burned on the high table before the icons, and its light was mostly blocked by those gathered below the two steps. Faces were cast in shadow as they turned toward us — all looming in the dim light, some cloaked like me, others not — and I knew none of them. I kept my head down as I joined my master before them, glad the hood hid my face.

"Not ready, Elect?" one asked, his voice low but strong. "Who's this?"

"My apprentice will safeguard the travelers," my master answered. "She has —"

"What?" The man stepped closer, his shoulders blocking out the light.

"Majesty, she's my finest student." Parselev put up a hand when the stranger reached for my hood.

My knees trembled as the word echoed in my head. Majesty. I stood before the king of Wodenberg. Wobbling a bit, I dropped to one knee in obeisance, fist pressed to my heart. The king yanked off my hood while I stared at the flagstone floor, pulse pounding.

"This girl?" the king demanded. "You trust a mere disciple with this mission?"

"Absolutely. Saint Qadeem and I have discussed it, and we agree. Do we not, Master?"

"We are in agreement, Wilhelm." I felt kir blossom nearby, like a candle flaring to life in a dark room, and my own kir stirred in my chest. He was here, no doubt, my master's master. Our saints appeared and spoke to us on solstices, and I knew that silken, lilting voice. My saint, the one who'd Blessed me with perfect memory and marked me as his disciple. Kings and now saints in the chapel, and me just a peasant-born apprentice. I didn't dare budge.

"You know what rides on this mission," King Wilhelm said.

"And know well," Saint Qadeem replied. "Accord her the proper rank of a physician and let her take her place. Kate?"

I hesitated, even then. "M'lord?"

Gently, "Stand up, Kate Carpenter."

Hands clenched on the felt cloak, I managed to rise and risked a glance at the high table before the icons of the Mother and the Father. All three saints were there, jolting cold terror through my veins. Qadeem sat in the middle, olive-skinned and exotic as his voice. His kir-lit eyes glittered black as midnight. I could see nothing else.

He spoke with a faint, kind smile. "It's not the Saint-day announcement and not the celebration feast that a new physician deserves. But once it's done it's done. I ask believing that you will not fail me, Kate. Do you accept the duties and the burdens of Physician as my disciple?"

Even though my voice quavered, I raised my chin. "I am honored to."

———————————✝———————————

King Wilhelm put a strong hand on my shoulder and charged me with the care of those assigned to this mission. It so stunned me that I stared up at him, forgetting myself, for a moment. Then he patted me, heavy as a brick, and stepped away.

The three saints came down from the high table to lay hands on their disciples and say a few words. Saint Woden went to the two cloaked men who wore swords — they were surely his disciples. Saint Aleksandr the craftsman spoke to the two others briefly, clasping each by the hand. Qadeem went first to one of Aleksandr's disciples.

I stood alone for a moment; the king and an armed woman had drawn Master Parselev aside. Her black tabard, over the mail, bore four gold stars and captain's brasses; someone had told me the captain of the King's Guard was a woman. She studied me and I fidgeted with my cloak.

I was a newly minted physician and an honorary knight as well. My master and saint thought me ready to serve the kingdom. Surely she'd been as eager, once. I would do my duty, whatever my saint asked.

A light hand on my shoulder. Saint Qadeem was not so tall, I realized as I turned, and not so broad-shouldered. I'd never been so near to him. His hair was as inky black as his eyes

Part I: For Want of a Piglet

and his hands deft when he straightened my cloak. They warmed my cheeks when he cupped my face briefly, and kir tingled into me through his touch. It swirled and settled in my chest, soothing and cheering.

With a crisp nod, he pulled my hood back up.

No more needed saying to me, it would seem. Though I wanted to ask him why.

My new companions — those in the cloaks like me, I had to guess — strode out to where the horses waited. I followed, my eyes feeling dry but I still could not blink as I stood looking at the horses. They looked back, breath billowing around their heads. The four hooded men chose their mounts and swung up into the saddles, one of them pausing again to speak quietly with the king and the captain of the guard.

"Kate, I put this together for you." Master Parselev emerged last from the chapel with a bulging messenger bag in his hand. He passed it too me by the strap, and for all its bulk it wasn't heavy. "Well stocked for first aid. Charms, too."

"Where are we going? How far? We'll be home before the frost, won't we?"

"Your leader will tell you soon enough. For now, keep your hood up." My master smiled, but it thinned under his worry. "Onto the horse with you." He turned and saw that one of my new companions waited with two horses' reins in hand.

"I've never been on a horse."

"Pal, then," the man said, turning to the horse on his right. "I'm Ilya, m'lady. Ilya Rabskov."

"I'm Kate Carpenter."

"Dame Kate," my master corrected. I must've looked bewildered, because he reminded me, "You've been knighted by the king. Dame Kate."

Ilya showed me how to wedge my foot in the stirrup and helped boost my rump up into the saddle. While he checked that my other foot was well in, he told me, "Just let Pal follow the others. He won't give you any trouble."

I heard a whistle and twisted in the saddle to see the two knights — armed, mailed, though I didn't catch the insignia on their tabards — tap their horses to a trot. Our third companion rode after. Pal's ears pricked up and he seemed glad to follow. Ilya was quick to mount up and join me.

I glanced back toward the chapel as the twenty-odd knights of the Prince's Guard fell in behind. Master Parselev, the king, and the captain of the King's Guard watched us go, hard to spot in the chilly shadows of dawn.

———————————✕———————————

Our two leaders took us out of the Order by the main gate and we rode down River Road at a quick walk.

"Ther Boristan Tolstyev," the third of our party introduced himself. "Glad to meet you, Dame Kate. Took you by surprise, did they?" He was Russe, like Ilya: thick-handed, barrel-chested, on the rusty side of blond. Honest, sober faces, and the Ther's bearded as well.

"Easy, easy," Ilya said, reaching over to tug on Pal's reins for me. "Don't squeeze. He'll think you want him to run."

From the height of a saddle, I wouldn't want to go any faster down a slope like River Road's. It was all I could do to cling to Pal. "Mother's mercy, no," I breathed. I already rocked far too much, it seemed.

Pal slowed a bit, though we'd gotten closer to the pair in the lead. My pulse eased enough to answer Ther Boristan. "Yes, a surprise. Master Parselev brought me a whole wardrobe and Ter Holly helped me pack last night. That was the first I—"

The tallest horse, the grey, slowed alongside me until the rider's stirrup knocked against mine. The knight's hood, pulled deep, shadowed his face completely. Pointing to the two men, our leader said, "Keep your voices down. We're eastbound to reinforce Baron Eismann against the harriers Arcea's sent across the Wall. That's all you need say to anyone. And you." The finger turned to me and his tone sharpened. "Not a word." At a tap, the grey stepped ahead to the lead.

His black tabard, under the cloak, bore the royal sigil, a full Shepherd moon silhouetting Mount Woden. Only the king and the prince wore it. Stung, I set my teeth on my lower lip. Kings, saints and princes. My mother would never believe this, if I lived to tell it.

Ilya leaned over to put my hands on the saddle horn, which improved my stability without squeezing Pal with my knees. I was grateful for that much.

Even so early, on a dew-laden morning, wagons and riders plied River Road. The Shepherd's thin crescent faded into the strengthening dawn and the small Flock moons turned from ivory to gold. Wodenberg's city gate stood open and we rode through with hardly a glance from the armsmen on duty. True to its name, River Road sloped onward through the grassy Spanne that ringed the city wall, and the foulburg below, to the Neva. The water rippled, languorous, as the early ferry crept its way along the guide-rope.

We turned onto the Southbound Road and wove through a cluster of wagons stacked with sheaves of oats. The sliver of the Shepherd signaled the start of the Grain Moon and the harvest in earnest. The rumbling hooves of the Prince's Guard held many eyes as we passed, but knights a-horse were not so uncommon, these days.

Arcea's harriers troubled the southlands; I'd heard the stories as much as anyone. There'd been little good news since the disaster at Ansehen a moon and a half ago. Master Parselev had taken me to assist him in the surgery — my first trial by fire, and the same for many young knights. It had been a terrible battle. Arcea had sent an elect, a kir-mage who ranked just below the saints themselves, and King Wilhelm spent many lives to break through the enemy line. With Saint Woden's aid, the elect was killed.

The earthquake called up in the final duel destroyed Ansehen. The castle and the gates that barred the Southbound Road cracked and tumbled. I had seen it myself.

Without their elect, and suffering losses thanks to the prince's cavalry charge, Arcea's army withdrew. The word was that their general swore to return in the spring. Arcea was a huge empire, and had armies and elect to spare.

Wodenberg's knights and infantry had paid heavily, too, and ours was a far smaller kingdom.

My thoughts trailed off, though, as we hurried past inns and taverns and wagon yards. Soon the buildings thinned out, spread by small pastures at first and then stone-walled oat fields. I'd been born in Wodenberg city and never been further than the river's shore. But still our leader rode on, silent and cloaked.

Pal's easy walk and the warm sun lulled me, even in the saddle. Ilya had passed me a trail biscuit and a waterskin to wash it down. We'd picked up to a canter for some distance, and I'd nearly fallen for not knowing what to do, but Ilya caught me, Father bless him, and helped me get the rhythm. I caught sight of the earthwork fortress where the Felsherz met the Neva as we turned off the Southbound Road onto an eastbound branch. After the terror of cantering wore off, the sleep I'd missed put me in a doze until a sharp whistle jerked me awake.

A column of black smoke marred the blue sky, freshly sprung from somewhere on the road ahead.

A Guard with captain's brasses on his epaulettes had joined the prince and the second knight of our company at the head of our party. The captain twisted in his saddle and shouted back, "Brauer, escort them!" while pointing at Ther Boristan, Ilya and me. Then they were off at a canter and the mass of Prince's Guard flowed around me for a moment. Pal perked up and wanted to run too, but I pulled on the reins. Maybe too hard; he fretted a bit, tossed his head.

"Easy on him," Ilya told me.

The horses kicked up dirt in pulling away from us. Sergeant Brauer and his squad of five stood with us on the road. The men shielded their eyes against the morning sun.

"Is it Gabel?" one of the squad asked.

"I'd bet it," Brauer answered. "Got some stones on them, to raid this close to the city."

"M'lord'll straighten them on that," another knight said. After a few heartbeats of watching the smoke climb, he said, "Must be worse in the hills if we're reinforcing Baron Eismann."

We rode in at a walk and when we reached Gabel there were only a handful of dead Arceal soldiers and a half dozen Prince's Guard securing the town square after the fight. The smoke came from the fields south of the small town — a handful of houses, an inn, a tavern and an Orderhaus — and it thinned as we watched.

I swung down from Pal's saddle, slipped and fell on my butt in the dust. But I was up again, with a wince, and digging in my medicine bag as I trotted over to a pair of wounded peasant men. A shallow slash on one man's arm had already clotted, so I only washed the wound and then held a cleansing charm over it.

The carved bit of wood held a knot of kir; with my mind, I picked the bound charm loose and its kir unfolded. Warm glow poured down onto the wound, calling up the man's own kir with its light. The injury had torn his kir's colorful whorls, but not badly. Once the wound was cleansed, I bandaged him. His older companion had a sprained elbow; I felt the joint to be sure it was no worse than that, and told him to drink some willow tea if it hurt so much.

By how he smirked, he'd only wanted an excuse to have my hands on him.

A shadow fell over us and the peasant startled, then dropped to one knee with his fist against his chest. I stepped back, myself, from the grey horse as it pranced close, mouthing its bit and puffing.

"I thought I told you to keep quiet."

I squinted up at the crown prince. I'd seen him at a distance, riding beside the king, and with my memory Blessing that was all I needed. Wodenberg had only one prince, and it was well known that the queen had sworn she'd die before she let the king touch her again.

A good thing that Prince Kiefan was so easy to look at, then, golden-haired and grey-eyed, Blessed as few were and still unwed at eighteen.

Stern glares were his stock in trade, it seemed. Like his father.

"These men were wounded," I said, then wanted to take it back as he towered over me. But then I steadied, sure that I was right. "How can I treat patients without speaking?"

M'lord leaned down from the saddle. "A squad of reinforcements doesn't need a physician at all, let alone a young girl. Keep quiet."

Fear stiffened my spine, kept my eyes on his black, shiny-new riding boot in the stirrup. "M'lord," I murmured, to accept the command. My mind whirled, though, flickering through Master Parselev's every word; he'd said I must go, Saint Qadeem had agreed, surely there could be no mistake…

The prince's horse still fidgeted, full of energy from the charge. Prince Kiefan tapped him and trotted off toward Sergeant Brauer and the growing cluster of Guard. "Fire's under control," the prince announced. "We're off."

I was quick to tie my medicine bag shut and climb back onto Pal as the party began to trot out of the little town. Tight muscles in my thighs protested, but with a hard heave and a boost on the rump from Ilya — bless him for not smirking — I was in the saddle.

CHAPTER 2

Some ways past Gabel, the prince whistled and turned his grey off the road. Pal followed the horses a few steps to stop near a well and a long trough dug into the ground. The stone walls lining the road made room for our party and even the two dozen Guard behind us. "Rest and water the horses," our leader commanded, easily swinging down from his saddle.

In a moment, I was the last one a-horse. Working one foot free, I picked myself up and swung but a muscle sharply protested, making me lose my balance and scrabble at the saddle as I fell. My ankle twisted in the stirrup and jammed before I landed. One leg in the air, I got up as far as my elbows before the pressure on my ankle stopped me.

I had my free foot down and was trying to lift myself with that and one hand, reaching for the stirrup, when boots came running.

"Father's beard, did you fall? Are you hurt?" Strong arms scooped me up and he hoisted me against his shoulders. He smelled of oiled mail and leather. "Wedged in there good," the knight said as I reached for my stirrup.

Pal shifted to back away and the knight clicked his tongue a few times. Pal's ears straightened and he stood still. My rescuer pried my boot free, thankfully, and I put both feet down.

"Thank you, sir...?"

He'd let his hood down and thrown his cloak's shoulders back; the open sun bleached his hair to palest blond and his eyes matched the sky. He'd been Blessed by Saint Woden — two ridges of grey horn erupted at his hairline and cut across his crown. Scar tissue hemmed the line between scalp and Blessing like a fingernail cuticle. Between the ridges, his knight's crest was long enough to tie in a flaxen pig tail but the rest was only grown back enough, since Ansehen, to color his scalp. All the knights shaved their heads down to a crest the eve before battle, and many kept that bit of a tail even if they never rode again.

His tabard had a sergeant's single brass ring knotted on each epaulette to mark his rank in the Prince's Guard. His sword, hanging from a double-wrapped belt, barely cleared the ground by his foot.

"Anders," he supplied. "Sir Anders Bockmann." He had an infectious smile, too. With a glance around at the empty road, the oat fields, and the mild commotion at the well, he sketched a bow. "Dame Kate, a pleasure to meet you even if you were upside-down at the time. Not broken?"

I checked. "Only a little twist." I'd skinned the heels of my hands, and brushed the dirt out of the scrapes.

"First time on a horse? Walk a bit." Anders gestured at the space around the well. "Stretch your legs before they knot up."

I had to agree. "They're sore already." My hood had slipped a bit and I pulled it back up as I took a few steps. My ankle hitched a little, but I kept going.

Anders walked with me. "Riding's more work than it looks."

"But easy enough for you, if you know horses so well. Or only Pal? That was a command, wasn't it, the…?" I clicked in imitation.

He nodded. "Hold," he translated. "Bockmann horses, all, to get us to Vorspitz." Turning, Sir Anders whistled short and sharp and some two dozen horses looked toward him, ears perked. But then the first bucket of well water was tipped into the trough and they jostled to drink.

I kept walking, circling the watering-stop. Prince Kiefan stood holding the well's rope as the massive bucket drained. He tracked us, a faint frown marring his brow. I pulled my hood further up, ears burning, and continued. He'd told me not to speak. Twice.

"You're limping a bit," Sir Anders said. "Are you sure it's not sprained? Here, I know a sprain from a break."

He indicated the field's stone wall and I leaned against it. Sir Anders had my boot and wool sock off in a moment and stroked both hands up my foot. My bones shifted a little, pinching the corner of my mouth. By how he checked my ankle, he did know a thing or two. And it might be a mild sprain but it was no break.

"No, I'm sure you're not a horse," he said, flashing me a grin.

I couldn't help a chuckle. His thumb massaging my instep was nice, too. "Checking my soundness?" I asked, quietly.

"Can't have you foundering—"

Sir Anders' head jerked hard as the prince appeared behind him; there must've been a cuff across the head, too quick to see. Then Sir Anders was eye to eye with the prince, both tensed and sharp, before I could gasp in surprise. Speed Blessings on both of them, and now that Sir Anders was half turned away I could see how his horn ridges joined and continued as one down the back of his head. They followed his spine down neck, betwixt shoulders, all the way to —

I couldn't see that part, of course, under his clothes. We'd had knights on the operating table often enough during the Ansehen battle that I'd seen most of their secrets. Admittedly, the thought of these two knights in less than full mail and winter cloaks made for a distracting thought.

Prince Kiefan spat something, and it took my Blessing a moment to recognize and point me toward the translation. It was Arceal, something to the effect of, "Keep your eye on the mission and not her."

Sir Anders bowed, curtly, and went to help see to the horses.

My pulse jittered as the prince spared me a glance. "Keep your hood up and quiet," was all he said.

———————————✕———————————

I sat in my saddle, sweating under the felt, holding my tongue. Despite the strange, dramatic morning in the Grand Chapel and the harriers at Gabel, this day had turned stiflingly dull.

The road delivered us to the Felsherz River, which crossed the broad valley from the eastern Eispitzen mountains to join the Neva River. Clusters of a few houses around a tavern and an Orderhaus cropped up on the roadside every now and then. We kept riding even though people came out to see us. Cantered through, even.

Prince Kiefan let us rest often enough, but didn't speak or even wave when we passed vegetable wagons or knots of harvesters scything the fields. Sir Anders and Ther Boristan and Ilya handled that. They chattered along for hours about horses and riding gear, happy as magpies. The Prince's Guard rode at the rear, in orderly lines.

Part I: For Want of a Piglet

I kept quiet, as ordered.

Since Prince Kiefan had spoken some Arceal, I closed my eyes and reviewed my lessons in that language. Because Saint Qadeem Blessed me with memory at twelve, I could recall any moment of any day in perfect clarity. My horn ridges weren't so pronounced as a knight's speed or anticipation Blessing, but the two grey nubs at my hairline were easy to spot. The rest barely peeked through my hair.

The saints chose their disciples for their own reasons. Odd, true, for Saint Qadeem to choose a peasant girl, but I'd been duly sent up to the Order's main campus for two years of reading and writing lessons. Languages had come later, after Master Parselev plucked me from the ranks of memory-Blessed students and apprenticed me. Odder, that, and there'd been some feathers ruffled over it. The Elect chose from the ranks of other physicians' apprentices — advanced students of worthy skill. Not some Englic peasant who could barely read. But elect and saints were never wrong in their choices. Not to be questioned, in the end.

Maybe someday I could ask Saint Qadeem why, if I dared.

The sun was low and the lone mountain, Woden, cast its long shadow. No question who owned this broad valley; Woden stood alone. Its city, Wodenberg, lying on its southern flank, was only a smudge in the distance. The castle, perched on the low sub-peak, caught the afternoon light.

A good stretch past another village, we came to a cistern in the stream's bank. Prince Kiefan chose the trodden-flat apron around the cistern's trough for a campsite and both Ilya and Ther Boristan set to unpacking our saddlebags. The prince began drawing water for all the horses, as he had each time we'd stopped.

Sour he might be, but he didn't turn up his nose at labor.

I landed on my feet from the saddle but a twinge in my ankle still made me wince. Then I tried to walk and found my thighs and butt had fused into one solid knot. Or so it felt. On Sir Anders' advice, I'd hobbled around whenever I was off Pal, but now I was reduced to mincing my way to the campfire circle where Ther Boristan was setting up his firewood.

Trees lined the quick-running river. Ilya hobbled to and fro to bring armfuls of branches. He suffered as much as I from the day's ride but he declined help from any of the Guard. Ther Boristan arranged kindling under his careful stack of wood. Pinching his thumb and two fingers together, he reached down to let his hand hover just over the clump of dry grass he'd tented with twigs. I felt a little kir move, echoing from him as he focused. A glow rose to his fingertips and gathered into a twinkle of light. Snapping his fingers, he dropped the spark charm onto the kindling. The grass caught, flames chewed up the twigs merrily and the fire was soon crackling.

I stopped Ilya when he stood up with a wince after watching the fire start. "You'll be quicker if you let me unknot those cramps," I said. "And I know you're suffering too, Ther."

"Would you have kir for both of us?" Ther Boristan asked.

"I've made no charms today," Ilya said, extending his right hand as if to shake, "but I'm no physician. Take mine and use it for yourself. I'll manage as I am." He was charm-handed. A single nub of horn broke the skin on the back of his right hand, where he could give his kir to someone else if he did not use his day's worth.

"No, I'll have some willow bark once he boils water," I said.

"I'll drink it," Ilya said. "Truly, Dame Kate, I'll be well. I've ridden before, simply not often. More than the two of you, likely."

I gave in. "Thank you. Let me see to Ther Boristan first. May I?"

Boristan stood stiffly from the campfire. "What do you require, m'lady?"

It was something of a reach, but I slipped my hand under the collars of his layered cotes at the back of his neck. Then I called my kir and it welled up warm in my chest. It tingled down my arm as I sent it along, and its glow rose on my hand as it gathered. Answering, Ther Boristan's kir rose to the light from inside him. It spun in little whorls and ripples of color across his skin, visible despite his clothes thanks to my hand on him.

In living flesh, kir took shape and danced in slow, deliberate patterns. Meridians carried fresh kir to the dances and helped orchestrate. Where flesh broke, the pattern was interrupted. Where kir was pinched or knotted, the flesh felt pain without a wound.

I sent my kir down Ther Boristan's spine, his prime meridian, and my gaze went with it. His kir tangled and stumbled where the muscles were tense and overworked. With a little focus, I smoothed them out. Like combing out your hair, the tangles fought it but I loosened them till they came free. As the whorls unknotted, the muscles relaxed and the pain faded.

"Mustn't tell your wife of Dame Kate's studying your ass," Ilya said with a smirk.

I think Ther Boristan blushed, under his beard. "Is that why you declined?"

"She'd be angry if she learned." Ilya nodded. "Now for yourself," he said to me, holding out his hand again.

I laid my palm on Ilya's charm-node and kir tingled, tickled, through my skin and up my arm. Sending it down my spine, I combed it through my own knotted kir. It put up a bit of struggle and I had to go carefully, finding the larger tangles and twisting them loose. Little by little, they came free.

"Much better." I smiled. "Now, what can I do while the water boils?"

They sent me to unpack the bedrolls while Ther Boristan cooked for just the few of us. The Guards saw to their own, though I think they grew jealous as the mouth-watering scent developed. Ilya dutifully drank the bitter willow bark tea to ease his own aches the simpler way. The horses jostled around Sir Anders, as he had the feedbag of oats, and he spoke to them in clicks and whistles as he portioned out their dinners. When it came to our own meals, I was handed a trencher, a handsome wooden trencher, covered with pan-cooked potatoes and cabbage and salt pork. I started to pass it on, but the others already had theirs. It was all for me.

I was hungry enough to lick it clean. It was stunningly delicious. Ther Boristan only shrugged. "My wife lets me cook," he admitted. "That gives her more time to weave."

The sky darkened overhead as I helped clean up. Five of the Flock moons were high in the sky and a sixth was rising. The seventh, the shy one called Love, would not be back until the Shepherd waned. Puffy clouds caught the last light as the sun fell below the western mountains. When I crossed my legs by the stone-ringed campfire again, the shadows were thickening in earnest.

My bedroll tempted me. But something more important had stewed me all day. Prince Kiefan had told me to be quiet and I had. None of this had been my plan, or anyone's other than my master and Saint Qadeem, but obeying had come easily enough. More than simply being the prince, he carried himself like an alerted tomcat. Both the knights did. Sir Anders could break that illusion with one of his easy grins, but on Prince Kiefan it only made me think of the stories I'd heard after the battle at Ansehen. Of the cavalry charge he'd led, and that on the battlefield his Blessings made him unstoppable.

"Majesty?" I had to know. "May I ask something?"

Across the fire, Prince Kiefan glanced at me. "You may. But 'Sir Kiefan,' not 'majesty.' Not out here."

"This can't be to deliver reinforcements, can it?" Once I started, I couldn't help saying it all. "Even if the prince went himself, he wouldn't bring a Ther and a physician's apprentice. And why leave before dawn, hoods pulled up and silent?"

I'd thought he'd glare or snap but he only watched, eyes measuring me. I'd let my braid down, for the night, and wrapped it around my hand as I waited. Sir Anders, sitting beside him, raised his eyebrows when the prince glanced at him sidelong.

Prince Kiefan — Sir — said, "Baron Eismann sent word that the lamia have been growing bolder of late. Coming down from the kir fount on Himmelbaum and taking sheep. Children, too. We're to lead a hunt of them before the snows get too deep and the lamia get any hungrier. Do you know about them?"

Monsters. They haunted the Winter Wood, in children's tales. "Only what stories say. Are they so dangerous as the monsters Arcea sent to invade us?"

"Centaurs are made things," Sir Kiefan said, "Saint Woden told us. Forged by Arcea's saints from men and horses. Lamia are animals — raised on the waters of a kir fount, but only animals. The kir makes them powerful. Clever."

When he paused, I asked, "As kir makes the Blessed powerful?"

"I've never hunted lamia. Baron Eismann wrote that a physician is prudent to bring. Lamia are cunning and cruel. He'll advise us as best he can." His voice dropped as his thoughts strayed, and it seemed he left much unsaid.

"But why must I hide? Why bring Ther Boristan? Surely they have Thers of their own."

He fixed me with a steady look and spoke slowly. "We meant to bring the Elect, but lacking him — this is no place for a girl that's not discipled to Saint Woden. So keep your hood up. We're hunting lamia. That is what you've been told."

My head cocked, on reflex, weighing that. There was more to come, I didn't doubt. "Yes, m'lord," I responded, quietly. "I see."

I thought I saw the corner of his mouth pick up a little, at that.

Ther Boristan rode with a book open in his hands, and I tapped Pal until he ambled up alongside. Ther sketched on the blank page with a piece of charcoal wrapped in linen. He noticed me and, with a smile, tipped it for me to see. It was Sir Kiefan, caught looking away and his Blessing's ridges rising fierce and sharp through the down of regrowing hair. His braided knight's crest swung as if he'd turned abruptly.

Leaning close, I whispered, "It's a good likeness."

Ther Boristan shrugged, humble. "Blessings fascinate me. Especially those few with multiple Blessings. To think we've two of them here — I couldn't help trying a sketch. I hope you don't mind if I sketch you? The memory Blessing's uncommon, too."

Fortunately, Sir Anders and the prince were absorbed in conversation, safely ahead of us. I could disobey a little. I murmured, "I wouldn't mind. What about your Blessing? Saint Qadeem spoke to you, I saw." Ther had nothing on his head, nor his hands, so I thought he must have the strength Blessing, which was easy to conceal. That was one of Saint Aleksandr's Blessings, though, as well as Saint Woden's. Not Saint Qadeem's at all.

Boristan offered his hand to me. "Craft-handed, m'lady. It barely shows. Both Saint Qadeem and Aleksandr have been kind to me."

I felt his fan of bones and knuckles -- oversized, true, now that I touched them -- and sure enough, the ridges lurked below his skin. "No surprise your sketch is so true, then."

Ilya slowed down on the other side, curious. He nodded when Ther Boristan showed him the sketch. "So serious," Ilya said, of it. "He does smile sometimes, truly."

"Does he?" Ther Boristan commented, for me.

"M'lord does smile. I've worked in the castle long enough to see it for myself. Heard a laugh, even. When His Majesty isn't on hand, the prince isn't much different from any other young knight. More serious, perhaps."

"His Majesty's serious indeed."

"He keeps Prince Kiefan close under his wing," Ilya said, his humor fading. But then he grinned again. "Many a maiden wishes he didn't, that's the Father's own truth. But he's a good prince. Never puts on airs, like some nobles do."

I kept to a murmur, leaning toward Ilya. "You work in the castle?"

"Oh, yes, always have. Since Papa let me tag along with him to the stables. Started me in the scullery and I picked up a bit here, a bit there. Whatever's needed around the courtyard, I'm your man."

"On hunting trips, too?"

Ilya nodded. "The hounds know me well. Nearly got myself gored by an elk, one hunt, up on Lake Neva. Majesty gave me a bonus for that, while I was laid up from the trampling. Very kind of him."

Boristan had gotten in a few more lines on his sketch, adding Kiefan's shoulder. "Have you been on hunting trips?" I asked him.

"Me? No, never. Since I took vows, I'm either home or at the Order. The abbot wants me on hand." When I nudged for more, he said, "I've been his secretary going on ten years now."

As I thought it, I said, "They must trust you."

"He's trusted me with private things, now and then. Things not to be spoken of."

A trustworthy servant and a trustworthy secretary. "Sir Anders must be worthy too."

Both men looked at Sir Anders' back when I said that, and hesitated. It was Ilya who said, "Sir Anders earned his place on the Prince's Guard at the jousting tournament. He rode beside m'lord at Ansehen, in the charge against the centaurs. In the saddle, true, he's a worthy knight."

"I saw enough of what they did to knights, in the surgery with Master Parselev," I said. As I thought of my teacher, I stumbled back across the question from that morning in the Chapel. "You expected the Elect to come with you."

Neither of them wanted to answer that. "I don't think anybody expected you," Boristan said. "A young girl like you? On a hunt? Folk would talk. No surprise he told you to keep quiet."

"I doubt it's a hunt." My voice dropped further. "Why did Sir Kiefan set a watch overnight? The Guard had their own watch, and surely that's enough. Do they set watches on hunts?"

Ilya answered. "To guard against wolves and bears. M'lord said it was to set the habit."

"Have you ever hunted lamia? Does one watch for them?"

"They're looking," Boristan murmured.

I glanced up, right into Sir Kiefan's eyes. A hot blush on my cheeks, I tugged on Pal's reins until he sidled away from Ther Boristan's horse.

I said nothing and let Pal trail a little behind the group until we stopped to eat at noon. Trail biscuit in hand, I walked while the horses drank from the trough at another cistern. Though today was better than yesterday, it was more an achy shuffle than a walk.

The valley spread out behind us, now clearly lower and gentler than the hills we'd been riding up and down all morning. Mount Woden still towered in the distance, its flanks dark with forest, its peak naked stone. On the road ahead of us, forested hills climbed fast and ascended into the cloudbank shrouding the Eispitzen mountains.

"Were you gossiping?" Sir Kiefan stood a few feet away, chewing on his trail biscuit as he watched me.

I was struck dumb for a heartbeat, under those chilly grey eyes. "Appreciating Ther Boristan's art, m'lord. Then Ilya told us about hunts."

A nod. "Ilya's served on several hunts with us."

"He said you set watches, on hunts, against wolves and bears."

The prince stepped closer. "True enough. And oat fields crawl with wolves and bears, as everyone knows."

"It did seem odd, m'lord."

"What does the Elect's apprentice know of setting watches?" he asked, drawing closer still. I looked away from his stern eyes, swallowing. The biscuit crumbled in my grip.

"How long have you been apprenticed?"

"Two years, m'lord."

"Where were you born?"

"In Wodenberg. On Engl Street."

I could smell horses and leather on him. A bit of sweat from hoisting buckets of water. The prince said, "Your parents are un-Blessed."

For that, I braved his eyes to be sure he saw my honesty. "My father and mother both swore to Saint Aleksandr, m'lord."

"And they raised a girl who won't keep quiet and keep her nose to herself."

"A timid physician is of little use, Master Parselev taught me."

A moment passed. I held my eyes on his, mostly. The scar tissue around the foremost nubs of his Blessing kept drawing me upward — silvery, raised spider-legs as if there'd been more that didn't quite surface. He took a step back. "We'll reach Vorspitz today. Can you hold your peace until tonight?"

"I'll burst for all my questions, m'lord," I replied.

Sir Kiefan was walking away, but he turned on his heel to say, "That would be curious to see, I think," and then kept going.

CHAPTER 3

The promise of answers helped me hold my peace through the day's ride and then dinner at Baron Eismann's own table in his keep's great hall. His wife and daughter served us themselves, with gracious smiles and no questions why I was counted among this hunting party. Little was said at all, in truth, until the Baroness took a steaming charger of apple strudel from a servant outside the hall and carried it to the table. I regretted eating so much of the venison pie, but was determined to have some of the strudel once the scent hit me.

"I've given you my two best huntsmen," Baron Eismann began, as he leaned on the table with both elbows. Sir Kiefan had declined to take the baron's seat at the head of his own table in his own hall, and Eismann had insisted that the prince sit at his right. "They've been as high as any man who's gone up Himmelbaum and Starknadel and lived to tell of it. Move quick, don't hunt, and the lamia may let you pass."

Bjorn and Ulf Waldgrun — cousins — had joined us for dinner and, after polite introductions, sat silently. Sir Kiefan had presented me as "his physician" and they'd given me a moment's measurement. From archers Blessed with hawk's eyes, that was something. Whatever color their eyes had been, they were golden now and crowded out the whites so their pupils could gape wide in dim light. Archers blinked rarely, letting a near-transparent inner eyelid do the job most often. Both were ten years and more my elder, Ulf seemingly sewn from grizzled leather by Father Duty's strong hands. Bjorn, the younger of them, smiled more but all about him was spare and sober.

Baron Eismann paused as his wife poured mugs of spiced, Arceal tea; I picked mine up as soon as she finished, wanting a taste of the exotic brew. Black tea was pricy enough, and Master Parselev rarely opened his box of spiced leaf.

"What knowledge can I give you as well, m'lord?" the baron asked.

"Do you see many Suevi in Vorspitz?" Sir Kiefan asked in reply. "Arceal merchants?"

It wasn't what Eismann expected, by how he frowned and stroked his grey-shot beard. "Here? It's a hard day's ride to Knapptal. And your grandfather saw to it that the pass is well watched, m'lord. How could Suevi reach Vorspitz?"

The Empire of Arcea had conquered Suevia, the land below Wodenberg's broad mountain valley, in the days when Kiefan's grandfather ruled. Arcea had been content to let Suevia and Wodenberg continue trading as neighbors for near fifty years. Then, over the summer, they'd sent an army of Suevi and kir-forged Arceal monsters to our southern border.

"Whatever smuggling there may be is of no consequence now," Sir Kiefan said, leaning toward the baron on one elbow. "The secrecy of this mission is of utmost importance. Must I watch my back all the way up the mountain? Through the pass? Arcea must not know we've tried for an alliance with Caercoed."

We were going through the Eispitzen? I'd caught a glimpse of the mountains in the afternoon, when the cloudbank lifted. Trees were barely turning for autumn here, but above was ice and snow. I managed to swallow the bit of strudel in my mouth, but suddenly didn't want any more.

Eismann, after leaning back and frowning, said, "There are a few Suevi who come this far. The King knows of them — they bring news from the Queen's kin. One brought a warning a week ago, and has already gone back."

"The word of their army massing at Temitte?" Kiefan grimaced. "Their harriers were bold enough to raid within an afternoon's ride of Mount Woden. Next year will be hard."

Temitte was the nearest Suevi city to our southern border.

I looked at the portion of strudel on my trencher, my stomach sinking under dread. The golden apples and pastry, cloaked in honey, glistened, trying to tempt me. While I considered one more bite, a warm head laid itself on my thigh. I sat at the end of the bench, and one of the baron's hunting hounds looked up at me with sad brown eyes. He licked his greying chops and stared longingly at my portion of strudel.

Across from me, Bjorn whispered, "Old Ritter's always glad to help, if you're full."

Tearing off a piece of the pastry, I gave it to Old Ritter and he hurried off. At the other end of the table, Sir Kiefan said, "Tell me what you know of the land beyond the mountains."

Eismann took another sip of his tea. "If any of us have reached Caercoed, they have not returned. Better to ask the Englic or the Suevi what they know of it." The baron's eyes fell squarely on me, the only Engl at the table.

"I was born in Wodenberg, m'lord," I said. "My father was never a sailor, nor any of his kin."

"A hunting party found the remains of a group lost years before," the baron went on. "They'd reached the far side of the pass and glimpsed a vast, green land. The archer saw smoke from villages in the distance. Then they were caught in a blizzard for days. Their food ran out as they struggled to cross back. Lamia finished them off, but did not touch the book the Ther had written in."

"A green land in winter?" Sir Anders broke his silence.

"The party went late in the Warm Moon."

Summer. Early, but full summer. Mother have mercy.

"The pass over Starknadel is the lowest in Wodenberg," Baron Eismann said, "but the snows never thaw. The pass is never easy — and the Grain Moon has begun in earnest. To be plain, m'lord, you should not go that way. South, over the smugglers' trails, then turn north in Suevia through one of their lower passes, and you might still beat the winter if you ride hard."

Kiefan hadn't eaten much of his strudel either, but the baron's daughter refilled his mug. Old Ritter laid his head on my thigh again, and let me scratch his soft ears.

"Whatever risk Starknadel offers, there's no chance of capture by Arcea," Kiefan replied. "No chance I'll be used as a hostage against my father."

"There's wisdom in that, m'lord, but sending you both?" The Baron included Sir Anders, on his left, with a glance.

Sir Anders? My brows crept together.

"The saints were clear. If there's to be an alliance, there's to be a marriage, and I am the heir. All they named to this party are here, in obedience. If the mountain keeps me, my eldest nephew has time to earn the job." That with a sidelong look.

"Your nephews are fine boys, m'lord, but we'd rather have you for king."

In the silence that followed, the wind rose and fell outside the baron's manor house. The heavy, split logs held without creaking, sound and warm. Far off, though, a clear high note lingered after the wind. Was it a woman's voice? A child's? A second joined it, a slightly lower note. Then a third, weaving up and down. A shiver tickled my spine.

The baron took no notice, nor did half the table. "They say it's a land of amazons," Sir Anders said.

Ther Boristan had stopped eating when the distant singing began. "Like Saint Woden's disciples?"

"In their own way. Twin saints rule there, twin women, and the men call cooking and diaper-changing a good day's work," Anders replied.

Boristan laughed, but hushed himself. "It must be a strange land. Where do the stories come from?"

"Merchants who've been to Temitte and seen traders from Caercoed. Strange, perhaps, but surely a land ruled by women could not be unpleasant."

"Their men must do more than cook, if they've held their southern passes against Arcea," Sir Kiefan said, and drained his tea again. "Hardly a day's work, changing diapers."

Anders chuckled. "Said by one who's never been handed a little sister to watch. I thanked the Father the day I was claimed for a stableboy."

Old Ritter whimpered, having been so patient, and I paid him with a bigger piece of strudel. The keening voices still rose and fell in the distance, drowned out by the occasional gust of wind. Ther Boristan finally asked, "Who could be out singing at night, m'lord?"

Baron Eismann seemed surprised. "That's the lamia, Ther."

I was given the smallest of the guest rooms as my own, and the men shared the others. My boots had hardly been off in two days, and when I sat on the mattress and unlaced them it took some two-handed wiggling to get them loose and then some peeling for the wool socks. The floor was chilly under bare feet, but no worse than my dormitory room at the Order. The baron's daughter had said she'd return with a hot water bladder for my bed.

I got up to shut my door. Glancing down the hall — I was at the end — I saw her, lamp in hand, leaning against the wall opposite Sir Anders. They spoke too quietly to hear, but she

Part I: For Want of a Piglet

laughed at something he said and played at sassing back with one fist on her generous hip. He laughed in return.

Anders shifted to put his hand to the wall beside her and lean on it. She turned her nose away, haughty, but spoiled the effect with a smile. He caught her chin with two fingers and turned her back for a kiss.

I felt a blush rise on my face. I pushed the door shut but couldn't help lingering with one eye at the shrinking crack.

The baron's daughter stepped around him and he turned, leaned against the wall where she'd been. She took a few steps, looked back, and then kept walking. After a few moments, Sir Anders followed.

I never did get that hot water bladder.

———————————✕———————————

I slept in my woolen cote and tried to pretend it was a proper shift but it barely reached the middle of my thighs. My feet were cold all night. Next morning, it was back into the rest of the boy clothes. The too-big hose still sagged and the garters for my wool stockings at home would've fixed that but no, men had to do things their own way. Run them all the way to your waist and lace them together with your braies — or, I had found out, men could string them separately so they didn't drop everything when they only needed to pee.

The things you learn on the road.

Not being built for that sort of convenience, I assembled a clean set of clothes while sitting on the straw mattress and dressed. I pulled the heavier, looser surcote on over my cote, fussing with the long sleeves to get them all evenly settled together. There'd been time before dinner, thankfully, for me to comb out my hair and re-braid it. Wrapping the braid around my head again, I picked up my wooden hairpin and secured braid to braid at the base of my skull.

The baroness fed us as much breakfast as we would eat. The seven of us — now that we had two woodsmen and left behind the Prince's Guard to reinforce the baron's soldiers — sat around the kitchen table and cleaned out bowls of oatmeal, apples, fried potatoes, eggs, whatever she gave us. Old Ritter wanted to know if I needed help. I didn't.

M'lady was so kind in calling me Physician Carpenter and overlooking my table manners that my throat choked shut when she slipped me a packet of horehound lozenges. The Baroness smiled at my thanks and promised to pray the Mother watch over us.

Afterwards, there was last-minute packing to see to — fresh provisions from the kitchen, and new gear that Bjorn and Ulf brought. Instead of our horses, we met two shaggy ponies in front of the stables. The larger of them, Acorn, could look me in the eye if he held his head high enough. Puck didn't care to try. The stable master caught Sir Anders checking the ponies' hooves and took offense, setting off an argument until Baron Eismann and Sir Kiefan arrived to break it up.

Bjorn managed the packing of the baggage and the messenger bags he handed out. I already had the medicine bag that Master Parselev had given me, though I'd hardly used it yet. Bjorn gave me a couple trail biscuits tied in a kerchief to keep with the bandages and charms — "For emergencies," he said — and a small water skin on a baldric. The little eating knife on my belt was not sufficient, apparently, and he changed it for a double-edged blade as long as my hand.

"What could I do with a dagger?" I asked. Aside from slice myself open.

"You never know what you'll need," Bjorn said.

There were thrummed mittens and wool gloves and a snug cap to be packed in my bag, too. Overnight, the maids had stitched fur linings into our hoods and our cloaks. They gave me three extra cloak pins. There had been a hint of frost before the sun rose, but it wasn't cold enough to endure the sunshine. Not cold enough for all this new gear, or for the heavy blanket rolls the men added to the ponies' loads on top of coils of rope and oilskin tarps, the cuts of smoked meat and sacks of oats. There was some debate over how much the ponies would need and how much we'd eat. And how long we'd be out there.

Sir Kiefan and Anders had traded their mail suits for lighter, boiled-leather breastplates worn over their surcotes. We had swords and bows, spare quivers and daggers, shovels and an iron-bound pry-bar that could bash a man's head in.

We were ready for trouble in the unknown. Expecting it, maybe. Beyond the baron's stockaded keep, the Eispitzen were free of clouds for now. Though the sun rose behind them, their brilliant white snow carried the morning light. Forests ascended from below, black in the mountains' shadow, but the trees couldn't climb far against the creeping blanket of winter that lived on the slopes and descended every year.

And the saints had sent us to cross through it.

"You won't be saddle-sore tonight," Sir Anders said, catching up to me after a short trip behind a tree. The road was one wagon wide and the cleared shoulders only a few feet more than that, so it was a quick diversion even with a pony trailing him. Anders led Puck, who had declined to have his reins tied to Acorn so Ilya could lead both ponies.

"No, but this is nearly as steep as River Road."

And had been all morning. We walked in half-shade under trees dotted with yellow leaves, the first thoughts of autumn. I had slowly fallen near the back of our party, but Ulf still brought up the rear. Or so I thought; he was only there half the times that I looked. Neither woodsman seemed worried, as yet, so the lamia could not be close by. The Felsherz ran quick and foamy from pool to pool and each had a clot of fishers' cottages on its shores. Shepherds' folds, too. We were not so deep in the forest, yet.

"You and Elect Parselev were at the quartermaster's pavilion the evening we laid camp at Ansehen, weren't you?"

I blinked, pulled from my musings. On cue, that memory passed through my mind. "Yes. An extra wagon of hay and oats turned up at the infirmary instead of our sleeping tents. Master wanted to show me the proper channels to go through with the quartermaster's staff."

He chuckled, at that. "So you got my missing feed."

"Your missing feed?"

"I'm master of the horse for the Prince's Guard," Anders said. "I was there about a wagon of hay and oats as well. A shame we didn't happen to meet then, we could have cleared it up quickly."

It had been a chaotic pavilion, or seemed so to me, all managed under the hawk's eyes of the duchess of Prohzgrad. To find Sir Anders in it, I had to comb through a still moment of my memory to find him. I hadn't noticed one more mail-clad knight in a black tabard, even if it did have two gold stars on it for the Prince's Guard.

"You saw me there?" I asked. "In all that confusion?"

He infected me with another one of his smiles. "I always notice a pretty face. Even in a crowded room."

There wasn't much to say to that, so I said, "I only caught a couple glimpses of you. Duchess Vysokova was in a dark mood, by all the shouting."

"M'lady was not pleased by how many things had gone wrong. I saw you beside the Elect and thought you must be that apprentice there's been a fuss about. Prettier than I expected."

"What did you expect?" What had 'pretty' to do with apprentices?

"Perhaps I didn't expect, exactly. The fuss I'd heard had been over older students being passed by in favor of some Englic peasant girl." Sir Anders took on a stuffy, disgruntled voice as he went. "Outrageous. A fourteen-year-old peasant? Chosen by the elect when she can barely read?"

I couldn't help a grimace. "I read well enough. I studied hard, those two years."

"I don't doubt it," Sir Anders said. "If they'd known you were pretty to boot, they'd have been doubly outraged. There." He tucked a black-eyed susan under my braid, just by my ear. As I'd been glaring at the pebbly dirt road, I didn't see the bright yellow coming and flinched at first.

My father and mother had told me I was pretty, now and then. It rarely came up when there was so much studying to do and so many patients to see to.

"I saw you after the battle," Sir Anders said, voice a little lower now that he walked closer by me. "A friend was in the infirmary with a gash in his side, and I tracked him to there. You were trying to feed one of the worse-off men. Barely conscious and twitching, but you kept trying to get some soup into him. I thought it a touching scene. Compassionate."

He looked me in the eye and it sounded likely enough. Except… "After the battle? That afternoon?"

A moment's thought. "I believe so. I hauled Viktor out of there and was back in time for dinner. Late afternoon."

I had to say, "I was in the surgery with Master Parselev until full dark. That wasn't me you saw."

His turn to echo. "In the surgery?"

"There was a late ambulance of knights from the king's attack."

"Are you sure? She wore her hair braided up, like you."

"You don't think I misremember, do you?" I tipped my head toward him an inch or two. He was tall enough that he ought to have a good view of my Blessing in any case.

That quieted him. There were several women with blonde hair long enough to braid and wrap. I usually let my braid hang free, as I wasn't wed yet. "It's not so odd to confuse me with one of the Ters," I said, to excuse him in an honest mistake.

Anders frowned, and then a burst of open sun made him squint as well. When we reached a patch of shade, he looked over at me. "Still, I was glad to see you again at the chapel that morning. A touch of kindness will do the journey well."

That late ambulance had been full of broken bones on men who'd survived lying or crawling for hours on the field. As we'd been out of charms, and kir, and even my master exhausted by then, it had been a great deal of blood and screaming. The saw and the cauterizing iron had been needed. Little kindness to speak of, at a glance.

"If you'd fallen from your horse and come to me with both leg bones jutting from your flesh, you might think differently."

Sir Anders said nothing after that, and I let my pace slow as my ankles were aching. He didn't seem to notice, and then a whistle from up ahead marked that we were stopping to rest. A small branch in the road led down to the Felsherz.

As Puck walked by, he reached with his lips and plucked my black-eyed susan to eat. I chuckled under my breath. A far better use for the poor flower.

———————————⊹———————————

Evening light clung to the mountain peaks well after darkness fell on our camp. Their glowing slopes peeked through the high canopy when the lodgepole pines swayed in the high-up wind of winter drawing breath. I sat on a tarp eating ham pan-fried with cabbage and onions, stuffed into half a round of bread. The grease, soaked into the crust, kept me from stopping until it was gone. Ther Boristan, across the fire from me, wrote and sketched in his book. I'd volunteered to clean up after dinner so he would have time. Ilya brought the ponies back from their drink at the stream.

The song began with one note, again, high and pure and far more human than any monster had a right to sound. Two more voices joined in, then a third.

We all looked up, breath billowing before our faces, the quiet chat about horses between Sir Anders and Bjorn dropping.

"They're higher up, near the kir fount," Ulf said, after listening to the song. "Not likely to stalk us tonight, but we should set a watch all the same, m'lord."

"For wolves and bears?" Ilya asked.

Ulf shook his head. "Lamia drive out wolves and bears. They'll brook no competition in their forest from animals. Or humans."

CHAPTER 4

Saint-day began with frost. We'd slept atop one tarp and under another, each wrapped in a bedroll and laid alongside each other like sausages. As I had no watch duty, by morning I was in the middle of the sausage-line and had to crawl out on all fours when I woke. Ilya always drew the last watch and always began by stoking up the fire and checking the oats left cooking overnight in a spider-legged pot over the coals. When I saw him busy, I knew it was close enough to morning to get up.

Sir Anders settled beside me when the porridge was ready and passed me the maple syrup bottle with a smile. I added a dollop and passed it on to Ulf.

"You wake early," Anders said, between spoonfuls of oatmeal. "You left half of me cold when you climbed out."

"Was that you?" We all looked about the same when wrapped up. "You were up soon enough after me."

"Chills keep me awake — they get into my bones and then I'll be sore all morning. I wasn't going to get any more sleep, so I had to follow before the cold crept in." He even added a melancholy sigh.

Master Parselev had a keen eye for the health of anyone standing before him; he said it was a sense I'd learn with time. I couldn't claim to have too much yet, but Sir Anders wasn't ill-fed or consumptive. "Do you want me to believe you're so fragile? The master of horse for the Prince's Guard?"

That got me a wry smirk, so I guessed I'd scored a hit.

Then there was the cleaning up and the repacking to see to and we were underway by the time sun peeked into the forest. Our woodsmen knew a good place to set the next camp, they said, atop a waterfall where there'd be a clear view of the valley. And we'd get there by noon, in time for the Saint-day washing and the disciple's dance.

"If we keep a good pace, we'll be there with time to spare," Ulf said. "And it's far enough from the kir fount that we won't draw the lamia."

We parted from the road — more a trail, in truth, since we'd passed through a tiny village yesterday — and climbed a slope that gave way to bald rock near the top. The Felsherz tumbled a few dozen feet onto rocks; at the top, it lay in a flat pool. Shorter, denser evergreens had replaced the lodgepole pines over the morning's walk and from here we saw just over their heads. The sun above was warm, once I was in it, and I pulled my hood back.

Hills fell away into golden prairie, and far in the distance the western mountains rose jagged and grey. Through the middle of the basin, the Neva River twisted southward toward its falls on Wodenberg's southern border. Mount Woden stood alone by the river. Its peak cut through the belly of a foolish puff of cloud as it passed over. That was one of a flock of clouds rolling eastward toward us, still some distance off.

"Weather changes quickly up here," Bjorn reminded us. "Clear one moment, ice or snow the next. And the river's fed by snowfields — ice cold, so take care. It'll nip you to buds, in washing, and kill you if you fall in."

I braved the pool first, bathing by halves. Men's clothes were good for that, I had to allow. In a dress, I'd have to strip entirely. Each of the men took a turn behind the hanging blanket at the shore, and we all went shivering to the fire to warm. Once Ther Boristan had the stew simmering, he went to wash last. In returning, he began the gathering song, which drew Sir Anders back from the ponies and the woodsman from hanging the tarp.

Ther Boristan took a moment to compose himself, and said, "I don't often give the homily, so I'll be brief. Saint-day so far from home is strange for most of us. Though we met only a few days past, we are as much a community of disciples as in our own Orderhäuser. We are answering the call of Father Duty and we've traveled under his protection thus far. Mother Love has kept the weather fair and the road clear for us." With a glance over his shoulder at the clouds, he added, "Pray she keeps it as fair as she can. Even though we're far from home, we will obey the instructions of those children the Father and the Mother sent to guide us: our saints. Saint Qadeem bids us wash, Saint Aleksandr bids us eat as a community, and Saint Woden bids us dance."

It took a moment for us to get all boots and socks off, and spread out around the fire. Boristan checked the stew.

Ther began with slow, careful stretches, held long to loosen our joints. Gently, at first. Then the poses progressed into deeper muscles, required more flexibility. Boristan did not push us so hard as some Thers; I could manage these, at least in part. And sidelong, I tracked the others. My eyes kept creeping to Sir Kiefan.

From stretching we moved into balance and focus, where I often wobbled and had to settle for the less intense poses. Ilya was with me in that, I was secretly glad to find. Ulf and Bjorn had all the focus of hunting hawks, and stood firm when even Ther Boristan and the knights began to waver.

Came the strength movement, which Kiefan and Sir Anders took with ease, and my legs were already crying for rest. Perhaps Boristan's were as well, for he eased up at last and didn't lead us to some of the toughest strength poses. I was sweating and breathing in time with my pulse when we finally stood, on both feet with palms pressed together, at the end.

"Thank you," Ther Boristan said with a bow. "Don't stray far. I'll call when the stew is ready."

I cast about for some chore to do, and thought of the work my master had given me for the journey. Ulf and Bjorn caught my eye, though, odd in their caution approaching me.

"Dame Kate," Ulf said, "you're the Elect's apprentice? And were at Ansehen?" When I nodded to both, the elder archer continued. "It's said the Elect stole Margrave Schutze back from the Shepherd. Did you see that?"

"The margrave was not dead." I was quick to correct him. "It was a mortal wound, yes, but the Shepherd didn't have him yet."

This drew Ilya, and Ther Boristan left off stirring the stew to listen. Sir Kiefan and Anders hesitated on the verge of starting sword drills a few yards from the campfire. "Tell us of it?" Ilya asked. "I heard it said, too, that the margrave died on the field. Or so most thought, until he walked into the command pavilion."

"He was in Vorspitz half a moon ago, but wouldn't speak of it," Bjorn said. "I told Johanna he couldn't have been dead — the Shepherd can't be cheated — but none of our garrison were at Ansehen. Please, m'lady?"

I settled by the campfire, cross-legged, and called up the memory to give them the truth.

Master Parselev's surgery, at Ansehen, was sectioned off from the main infirmary by canvas walls. We had kettles boiling just outside, for cleansed water, and cauterizing irons in the fire. The day had run long, already, through a stream of ambulance wagons bringing dozens of wounded from the battlefield. We stood catching our breath betwixt arrivals, drinking cups of water and washing what we could. In the general noise, I didn't hear more hooves riding up to the infirmary pavilion.

One Ther and a knight burst through the tent flap, carrying a travesty between them. My cup hand was suddenly empty and my shoes wet. They had the patient by a shoulder and knee apiece and I had no idea who he was. I could only see the length of four-inch sapling stake rammed through his ribs.

"No help for the dead!" Parselev shouted over their voices, putting up a hand.

"M'lord, please! He lives!" The knight — a lieutenant, by the brass rings on his epaulettes — heaved his burden onto the surgery table. "He's my lord, sir, please! Margrave Schutze!" The stake's sharpened end scraped on the table and its movement tore a weak cry from the man. The margrave. They rolled him on his side, the Ther putting a hand on the bloody end of the stake to hold it steady.

My master touched the patient, calling up his kir. His mouth pursed, tight. To the lieutenant, "You. Your day's kir?"

He blinked. "I have much of it. If you need it, take it." He held out his hand.

Only the charm-handed could give their kir, or so I thought. But Master Parselev gave him a sharp look and even I could feel the force he sucked the kir out with. It arced from the knight's hand to my master's chest in a golden strand. The lieutenant's knees buckled and I ducked under his arm to steady him. He dropped to his knees, gasping for breath. His tabard was soaked in blood; wetness seeped into my dress.

"Hold him," Master told the Ther who'd helped carry Schutze in. My master put his hand on the margrave and looked to Ter Biya, who aided him in surgery. She had a strength Blessing. "Biya, pull the stake. And Kate? Don't look away."

The margrave was ashy grey, barely breathing. Biya put both hands on the cruel stake and checked it with a little twist. Then she bit her lip, pulled with her Blessing strength, and it slid out red, ragged, scraping on bone. Gore splattered. Screams ripped out too, but they were sucked down into silence as kir blossomed in my master's hand, spinning up from his palm in knots of green and gold. I could feel it flowing through him, it was so clear and strong. The kir twisted, tightening down, stars igniting in the misty stuff until the whole mass of it lit with a flash, brilliant as the sun. Stars spun around the sun in my master's hand and scattered, confused, when he threw the mass of kir into the margrave's chest.

It landed on him in heavy ripples, like a cloak, and his body clenched. Kir patterns flooded the wound, pulling the flesh with them. The stars chased after, each strike sending out ripples of green and smoothing the kir's dance.

The world released the breath it held.

I wobbled at the suddenness, and my hand fell on the lieutenant's sweaty hair. He glanced up, startled, and hastily let go of my waist. I hadn't noticed him clutching me, either. He left me half covered in blood from his tabard. The Ther fell to his knees, letting the margrave drop onto his back. Biya already sat on the grass, the stake in her hands, her eyes calmly closed.

Master Parselev and I alone stood, in the room. Margrave Schutze breathed, unconscious, as the Ther straightened him on the table. Through the hole in his armor and gambeson, a purple bruise on the mended flesh roiled to a stop before my eyes.

"That lesson must wait, I'm afraid," my master told me with a thin smile. "Let's hope the king isn't brought in as well. A cup of water, please, Biya? Ther, take the patient out to a pallet. Lieutenant? You served your lord well today. I'll tell him that myself."

The lieutenant bowed, still on his knees. "Elect, I…"

"Stay with him now. He may wake before dark."

Scrambling to his feet, the lieutenant followed the Ther and his lord. Parselev took a fresh cup that Biya offered him and drank deeply as another Ther carried in the next wounded knight.

My story earned me thanks and a few questions, but after that my audience melted away to their chores, scouting, and sword drills. It left me with little to do, so I hunted through my bags on Puck's back and dug out the book Master Parselev had entrusted to me. I hadn't known why, when I was packing, but now it was clearer. It was a philosophy text that I was partway through already. As it was written in Arceal, it was a struggle for me to work through the language. Arceal was a strange, jumbly tongue, not like Alemannic or the Englic I spoke at home with my parents.

I hadn't known how I could manage to read any more without my teacher. Now I had two knights on hand who had to know some Arceal. And if this Caercoed kingdom sent merchants to Temitte, they must speak Arceal themselves. I had both a reason to keep learning and the means, if I could find a way to ask one for help. Perhaps Sir Anders, if he could be weaned off the teasing and the flowers.

I settled cross-legged by the fire again to read.

A few words in, the crash of steel in the forest caught my ear. Both knights dashed into the campsite clearing, Anders leading by a few steps and pivoting into the prince's unprepared guard. My eyes could hardly catch Kiefan's block and counter-stab and Anders' tumble to one side that came up on his feet and ready as if he'd planned the whole thing.

They were far enough off that I only heard a mutter of what they said. By mutual agreement, they paused a moment to catch their breath and then started a new line of practice. Slow, at first, like the disciple's dance, swinging and blocking with the flats of their swords. When the pattern began again, they moved to half speed.

At full speed, I found I followed it clearly and could pick out the individual poses even as they blended together. But then they shifted into Blessing speed and it all became a frightening, blurry tangle that kept going far too long for the one series of moves. With a louder crash, one of them fell and they were on the ground scattering dry pine needles until they abruptly froze. Anders pinned Kiefan, a knee on his chest, arm drawn up to hold the sword-tip to the prince's throat.

I'd forgotten to breathe.

Sir Kiefan heaved up and threw Anders off like a blanket, proof of his strength Blessing. The prince brushed needles from his woolens, apparently unconcerned.

"The king should let you compete in the joust," Sir Anders said, on the edge of my hearing. "It would make for a more challenging tournament."

"We can't have any accidents."

Anders laughed. "But if it's a fool's quest across the Eispitzen, you're first in line."

Kiefan shot him a look. "Call the saints fools at your peril."

Anders seemed less than worried. Sheathing his sword, he went to his water skin for a drink. I'd forgotten all about my book in watching the duel, I realized, and searched for my place on the page.

"You brought a book?"

My finger on my place, I glanced up as Sir Kiefan crouched beside me. "Master Parselev wanted me to finish it. The dialogues about logic, if nothing else. It's to help me learn Arceal as well."

He leaned to look, braided knight's crest hanging free. "May I?" he asked, and took the book from me. Keeping a finger on my page, he checked through it. "Oh, I remember this. d'Ovio Alain, isn't it? I read 'On fear and love' from this. Father didn't give me time for any of the other dialogues."

"I'm partly through 'On proof' and I'm to read 'On reason and clarity' as well. Master Parselev didn't mention 'On fear and love.'"

"It's about ruling. Whether a ruler should strive to be loved or feared. I don't suppose a physician would have much need of that. Unless one should fear one's physician." Sir Kiefan said that with a smile as he handed the book back. Ilya was right; he did smile sometimes.

It nearly distracted me from replying. "No, love is far better for physicians. Trust. Honesty."

"Ah, honesty." Kiefan settled cross-legged beside me. "To be honest, I wanted to read 'On reason and clarity.'"

"To be honest, I'll be too slow in getting through it."

He considered. "I've spoken Arceal a bit. Perhaps I could help?"

Our eyes met and my mind was struck dumb by the thought of being tutored by the prince of Wodenberg. "I'm sure you could," I managed to say.

"Though I've never had reason to teach anything. Haven't had time for a squire, even."

I bowed my head. "Your honesty is appreciated."

"Well, you are my physician now," he said, and then pressed his mouth shut as if he hadn't expected that.

It hit me, too, that I was sole physician to half a dozen strangers now. "I should've asked Master Parselev for your history," came out of my mouth unbidden.

"He didn't tell you about the headaches, then," he said, his voice dropping to near a mutter.

A snowflake landed on the open book. Fat, slow flakes tumbled down, swirling when a breeze wandered by. Boristan, at the fire, said, "They didn't jest. I didn't smell snow coming."

I closed the book, asking Sir Kiefan, "You have headaches?"

He was looking up at the snow, but he nodded as he stood. "Ilya, we'll need to shelter the fire. Where's Bjorn and Ulf?"

"Just gone to look about, m'lord."

Then Kiefan was helping Ilya unpack another tarp for our shelter and I noted the headaches to ask him about later. Bjorn and Ulf came hallooing through the thickening snow soon after. They'd seen proof of lamia, both nearby and only a few days old.

CHAPTER 5

Snow still fell when Ilya shook me awake in the middle of the night. The patter of flakes on the overhead tarp blended with anxious whispers and sharp coughs. A pony puffed nearby and hooves shifted.

"Ulf says stay close," Ilya whispered in my ear. "Get the bedroll off and flat so nobody trips. Careful of Acorn, he's right here."

I blinked and rubbed at my eyes and a whiskery horse nose nudged my cheek. Acorn shifted away as I struggled out of my bedroll and to my feet. I put my arm over his neck for balance as I kicked the heavy blanket off and tried to spread it flat. Puck snorted, close by too.

The fire, half sheltered by our tarp lean-to, had lowered to glowing coals. Ulf and Sir Kiefan stood on the far side with their backs to it, one with bow and nocked arrow, the other with sword in hand. Kiefan asked something of the woodsman and he muttered a reply. Beyond them, the black forest waited, crusted by a layer of snow that glowed blue when moonlight fought through thin patches of the clouds. Tumbling flakes kept up a quiet patter as we all fell silent, even the ponies.

Fear drove off the lethargy of waking so late, but there was nothing to see in the clusters of squat pine trees and thickets. Ulf and Kiefan moved a few steps apart, tense and alert. I wanted to ask what was wrong.

Lantern eyes lit up beyond the fire, paced by, and vanished. A shape moved across a snow-laden pine branch. That coughing sound came again, from the moving shadow, and it was answered from behind me.

Ilya, holding Acorn's bridle beside me, whispered, "Mother Love, we're surrounded."

I sidled closer to the middle of the tarp, though it meant letting go of the solid mass of the pony. Ther Boristan stood holding Puck. A few steps out from that side of the lean-to, Bjorn faced the forest with bow and arrow ready. Beyond him, another pair of eyes caught the light.

"I could stoke up the fire," Ilya raised his voice to a murmur.

Ulf answered, as he was closest. "They're not afraid of fire. Whatever you do, stay together. Stand and fight."

I looked over Puck's rump, and Sir Anders stood watch on that last side with his sword in hand. A snow-covered bush there offered a clear backdrop for the form that stalked across it. The lamia were perhaps the size of a hunting hound, if bulkier in the shoulders. Their tails ran long and hairless, and lashed like a cat's.

I felt around in the dark mass of bedrolls and found my medicine bag. With it on, I was a little more useful. I'd taken my dagger off for the night, but I'd be little help with it.

A bit of wind drove the snowflakes in my face for a moment, then they fell back. The lamia stalked their circle around our smaller circle and coughed to each other in little patterns. Snow slowed its pace, and the moonlight strengthened. I watched along with Ulf and Ilya and Acorn, all of us shifting on our feet.

The lamia went still and silent. Ulf's bow rose as he drew his arrow halfway.

Snarling, a lamia charged from the trees. One long bound and the shadow split into two, one diving across Ulf's sights and drawing his bow, the other angling straight on into Anders. Puck shimmied back with a whinny, yanking Boristan off his feet. A second bound and the lamia threw itself under one blur of steel but the second blur as Anders twirled Blessing-fast caught the beast low in the spine. It screamed, far too human. Puck and Acorn wove and fought to get free, and someone's rump knocked me down. Hooves stomped all around me; I scurried under a pony's belly, only to stop short when movement on the snow yanked my eyes up. Four paws broke the white as the lamia angled toward me, the vulnerable one on the ground, and fangs caught the moonlight a moment before an arrow took the monster in the neck. It crashed from a full run.

Then, nothing. The ponies snorted and stamped, but after a few low whistles and clicks from Sir Anders they settled. Snowflakes kept pattering, definitely slower now. We waited.

In the distance, though not so far as I'd like, a lamia sang. A second joined it, cycling from louder to softer and back. Further away, a third note answered.

Ulf and Bjorn returned their arrows to their quivers. "They're done, m'lord," Ulf told Sir Kiefan. "They're reporting in to their lords."

"They won't return?" Kiefan returned to the fire, sword lower.

"Not tonight."

He surveyed the forest again. "They were testing our strength."

Ulf nodded. "They know what bows are, and they'll remember who has one."

"We killed two. Will that weaken them?"

"They hunt and lair in small groups, but there's always some master in the distance answering songs."

Sir Anders kicked the one he'd killed and lifted a paw with the point of his sword. "Any chance we'll get back to sleep?"

Bjorn laughed. "It takes cool blood to sleep after that. You're entitled to keep its teeth, since you killed it. They bring luck."

———————×———————

"Have you seen the kir fount on Mount Woden?" I asked Boristan as we walked through the mist. Last night's snow had melted quickly, but the vapors lingered around our ankles.

"Nobody goes to the fount itself but the saints," he answered. "It's near the peak. But I've been near enough to the Pool, with the abbot, to feel its kir. Through stone walls, it's so strong."

Soon after we packed up camp and set out, I'd felt a faint tingle over my heart. As we followed the shrinking Felsherz up, it strengthened. Even though I was tired after lying awake most of the night, the draw of the kir kept my feet moving. "Stronger than this?"

"You can feel it already?"

I looked back at him, surprised. "You can't?"

Boristan smiled. "You must be sensitive, m'lady." As we trudged on, he added, "As Master Parselev chose you for an apprentice, that should be no surprise."

We'd been put in the middle of the party, along with Ilya and both the ponies, so that a woodsman and a knight could guard us ahead and behind. The only noises in the forest were birdcalls and snow sliding off pine boughs.

The two dead lamia had been strange even in daylight. They were wolves raised on the kir-rich waters of the fount, Ulf had said. Their skulls had lengthened, their skin thickened to leathery hide over their hindquarters and their rat-tails grew long. The remaining fur on their forequarters was harsh, and a spiny crest rose between their shoulder blades. Even slack and dead, something about their eyes and face recalled a human's. There was a structure to it, a hint of cheekbones, despite the lupine muzzle and the fangs.

A few blows with the pry-bar and the menfolk had pulled out all of the monsters' fangs as prizes. Bjorn had shown me the distinct serrations that distinguished lamia's teeth from wolves'. Fakes were common enough, he'd said.

We followed the trail around tangles of rock and tree trunks that avalanches brought down during the winter. Young pines sprang up eagerly in the path of a slide, but even the older trees were small now. Brambles grew thick and close to the path, catching on my felt cloak. Topping one last rise, we clustered for a moment within view of a reed-lined pond. The stream, all that was left of the Felsherz, gushed out of it and down the slope. A heron took off from the cattails, heavy grey-blue wings thumping as it rose.

Ulf held up an arm and turned to remind us, "Stay together. The fount's just off the north side."

I could have told him that by how it tugged at me. The trees on the north side grew taller, thicker, and as the trail led us up I could see how they'd twisted in growing. Not content with that, they'd also coiled over as if bending to drink from the fount.

Puck's head was up, ears forward, and he actually hurried ahead as we approached. "Now I feel it," Boristan said, perking up himself. "Just a little fount, but it's still kir."

The near-human shriek from my left paralyzed me and the reeds on my right exploded. Puck shrilled and knocked me to the muddy ground as he bolted. Boristan stumbled and a black mass of crest and fangs and whipping tail tackled him. My feet scrabbled and I lunged up, off balance and blank-minded. The lamia's snarl sounded just behind me, far louder than any shouts. I ran, blind. The monster galloped after me, roaring, and it landed on my back like a falling wagon. Crusty snow in my face, blood in my mouth, a thousand pounds of snarling heat pinning me down.

A crash and a yell and the lamia landed on its shoulder beside me. Instantly, it was up and lunging and I was scrambling to my feet again. Growling and screaming — the scream human for sure. I swung around to see the lamia shake Bjorn hard and rip a mouthful from his bicep. Blood, a kir fount of its own. The gushing scarlet etched on my eyes clear as day. I kept running.

Trees scratched at me as I careened through them. Three lunging steps and I glimpsed the lamia, this time, looked it right in its leaf-green eyes as it tackled me. I screamed. Its hot breath, stinking of carrion, and the teeth —

Light flashed on metal and the hideous head fell on me, spasming and drooling. Its hot blood splashed my scrunched-tight face. A hand grabbed my arm and pulled me from under the beast's dead weight. I hit my rescuer's warm side, threw my arms around his waist and clutched. His arm wrapped across my shoulders. His chest pumped, breathing hard, and he twisted in my grip, shifting his crouch, to look for more trouble.

My face was against his cloak; I wiped my eyes clear on it. His sword drew a straight, bright line across the jumbled mass of autumn-gold shrubs around us. His breathing slowed. Kiefan spared a glance at me. "Hurt?"

I shook my head. He stood, bringing me along by the shoulders, and let his sword drop to a lower guard. I found my feet and his arm loosened.

In the distance, a shout. "M'lord?"

"Here!" he called back, turning toward the pond.

"Bjorn," I breathed, remembering; breaking loose, I pushed past a young pine and cast about. "Bjorn?" I called. Silence. Past a second tree, I found the blood — sprayed droplets on golden leaves, a long stain on the ground. Bjorn's bow lay nearby, and a few loose arrows.

Kiefan came up beside me. "Here!" he called again, and I heard someone approaching.

Ulf came on the scene from the other side, and stopped short for a moment. Then he grimaced and knelt to pick up the bow.

"Can you track them?" Kiefan asked.

Cords rose on Ulf's neck. He covered his hawk's eyes with one hand and fought with his answer for long heartbeats. "We can't leave the others long enough," he said eventually. "And all we'll find will be pieces."

My throat knotted too tight to speak.

Kiefan put a hand on Ulf's shoulder. Voice thick with emotion, "He died defending us. The Shepherd will give him a place of honor."

Ulf held his tongue and avoided looking at me when he stood.

The six of us regrouped at the kir fount while the lamia sang in the distance. It was a little pool between the thick roots of pines, fed by a spring at the deep end that burbled in a little fountain. The water glowed warmly, in the shade, and threw off bits of rainbow where it tumbled. The moment I laid eyes on it, I was thirsty. We humans dipped handfuls from wherever we could — Anders hopped across for more room — and even just a mouthful soothed and strengthened. The ponies shoved their way up to the little creek that ran down to the pond and drank from that.

After slaking our thirst, Ther Boristan said a few words for Bjorn, our brother disciple who we had known only a short time, but now owed much to. I kept my eyes on the toes of my boots, wiping away guilty tears.

Then there were wounds to see to while the men filled all the water skins from the spring. I cleaned Boristan's gash with plain water and, taking another gulp of kir, laid my hand on his wound. The lamia's fang had sliced across his collarbone, tearing wool and flesh alike and laying the bone bare. Bjorn's arrow had found the beast's heart a moment later.

I called the fresh kir up and it came, rising in a warm tingle in my chest and flowing along my arm to my hand. It drew up the disrupted patterns of kir in Boristan's wound until I could see them clearly. Lines and whorls of colorful kir moved through his flesh, through all flesh, in a set pattern. Wounds and illness disrupted the patterns, and though the body would work to repair its patterns the process was slow.

From my Blessed memory, I took the correct pattern for skin and muscle in a simple area such as the collarbone. Flicks and twists with my mind shaped my kir to match the memory. My charm flooded down onto the wound, overwhelming it, and the flesh responded. The gash knit together into a red weal.

"Thank you, Dame Kate," Boristan said, checking it as best he could. "Heal the wool, too?"

I shook my head. "I haven't studied cloth."

"Perhaps I'll have a chance to do it myself."

Ilya's bite, on his calf, was more serious. When Acorn bolted along with Puck, Ilya had run after both ponies and been pulled down by a lamia. Ulf's arrow had taken it between the eyes. Anders had held three of the monsters off our pack-laden ponies when they'd been pinned between the pond and the stream's headwaters. One lamia was dead and the other two had run.

Rolling up Ilya's hose to his knee, I prodded the half-dozen half-crusted tooth marks. They still bled a little. He bit his lip and hissed through his teeth. I had seen a dog bite like this, a year ago, and Master Parselev had put my hand on his so I could see how he mended the patterns. I took another drink of kir and called it up. The muscles of a calf were far more complex; a meridian shot through the bundles of whorled kir, and the disruption the fangs had caused put up a fight.

As I worked, the frozen instant of Bjorn under the lamia's jaws, his muscle tearing, flashed past my eyes. A damaged knot of kir slipped out of my focus and danced away, jostling its neighbors and unsettling their dance. Ilya tensed with a curse as the jostle propagated in a ripple, knocking whorls together and tangling some. I countermanded it with more kir and the proper pattern, but it was spreading outside the part I'd seen under Master Parselev's guidance.

Grabbing a water skin, I took another swallow of kir and put my spare hand on Ilya's other, unhurt calf. Using that for reference, I halted the spreading damage. I combed through Ilya's tangled kir again, careful, and checked the patterns against his other calf. It took longer than it should have, and he'd found a stick to clench in his hands for when it hurt.

"I'm sorry," I told him, rolling down his hose over the lingering bruises, "I didn't mean to be so sloppy."

He managed a smile. "Still better than limping and slowing us all down, m'lady."

Puck, poor Puck, had a wound on his flank but Anders knew how to use a simple blood-stop charm and had already seen to it. I put my hand on the scabs and merely cleansed it to be sure it would heal quickly. For a moment, I glimpsed an entirely different dance of kir in the pony's heavy muscle. His skin shivered under my hand as it lingered there, remembering how Puck had spooked last night when the lamia charged. An echo of my own fear raised gooseflesh on my arm.

"Careful, he doesn't like that," Anders said, taking my hand from the pony's flank. "He's still a bit skittish after the bite."

I glanced up at him, mind far away, and I felt a blush rise on my cheeks. "I'm sorry, Puck," I whispered, and turned away.

"Are we ready?" Kiefan asked, striding down the half-assembled line with one hand on his sword. "Do we have all the ponies? And will we not let them bolt next time? There are pageboys in the castle with a better grip."

Ilya's face went white. "M'lord, I'm sorry," he blurted, dropping to one knee as Kiefan passed. "I let the fount distract me, m'lord. It won't happen again."

Kiefan stopped to hear the apology, then looked to me with a sharp glare like those he'd used on the first day.

It was a cold knife through my chest. I'd run. After all the orders to stay together, I'd bolted like a foolish pony. And Bjorn had suffered for it. He was dead now, when he'd been pointing out signs of elk and naming birdcalls this morning.

My eyes brimmed with tears that knocked loose at a blink. My failure, when I'd been charged with their care. I tried to whisper, "It won't happen again."

It didn't quite get out. Kiefan stepped closer, brows raised.

The lamia's green eyes as it pounced filled my mind. It wasn't half as bad as the blood spraying loose while Bjorn screamed. I focused on Kiefan's eyes and told him, "It will not happen again."

His head cocked, but then he acknowledged it with a nod, turned and gestured to Ulf and Boristan at the front. We walked on, past the burbling kir fount and its happy twinkle, up the steep hillside beyond the pond.

After the horrors of the surgery during the disaster at Ansehen, my master had taught me a trick of my Blessing. Something like a charm, a self-healing. While my feet moved and my hands held Puck's bridle — I'd taken him from Anders without a word — I dragged up each panic-fueled moment of the ambush and studied it. There were lessons in each one.

Kir patterns, anatomy, physiology. Details about the lamia, such as the faint stripes on their forelegs. I looked at each bit of information and named it.

Once studied and put away, like blankets in trunks, those memories would behave themselves and come when called. Only when called. Though in dreams they slipped from their trunks, sometimes.

It was best done while lying in bed, but I had to keep up. Puck was very patient with me even though I kept leaning on him. I wasn't entirely aware of the others, but it seemed that they checked on me, concerned, and Ther Boristan said something about this happening to physicians. He walked with me, after that.

When I closed my eyes for a long moment, letting it all slide away, and then looked over at him, Boristan's brows rose. "Are you with us?"

I nodded. "Thank you. I needed to put it away."

Even though I had topped off with kir, I was tired. And that night there was little sleep to be had. The lamia stalked around our camp, keeping the horses jittery, for hours after dark fell. When the near half-moon Shepherd and his four Flock finally vanished behind clouds and it began snowing, the lamia left us in peace.

<hr />

The morning passed in silence; for hours, nobody wanted to speak. But then Anders grew impatient when we had to turn at a steep, rocky hillside and look for a gentler slope to climb up. Even in the afternoon sun, the snow underfoot wasn't melting and I know the chill was getting into my fur-lined boots by then, if not everybody else's.

"At this pace we'll miss the jousting tournament, if not the Solstice," he declared, throwing his hands up. "I'll lose my title by forfeit — and I'd rather be unhorsed by a green squire than that!"

Ilya called back over his shoulder, "You won me three crescents last year, Sir Anders."

Anders gestured back. "You'll win a dozen when I make it three years in a row."

"Nobody's ever done it, m'lord."

"Just you tell everyone you heard me swear I'd do it."

"Are you swearing, then?"

"By the Father's bloody —" Anders' volume dropped off suddenly when he remembered me, beside him. "— sword?"

I chuckled, knowing what he'd meant to say. "I've heard worse than that, sir."

"A maiden's heard worse than 'by the Father's bloody balls?'" He feigned outrage. "I'd never think physicians were so coarse."

"I might have even met some bloody balls while working the surgery."

He chuckled. "It's amazing where you find bloodstains after a fight like Ansehen."

"You're the tournament champion, then? Twice over?"

Anders dipped a quick bow. "At your service, m'lady."

"I hadn't realized it was you. I never saw your face, and everyone called you the Green Knight." Those cool, clear days at the beginning of the Hunter's Moon came back easily; the knight in the dark green tabard who unhorsed every opponent he faced, then fought them to a yield on foot. Repeat champions were rare, at the great joust — knights came from all over the kingdom to compete. They made their reputations, and their whole careers, in just a few days.

"The Green Knight?" Anders frowned. "Everyone in the pavilion knows my name."

Oh. "I've never been to that side of the field, m'lord." The tall, flag-bedecked pavilions at the joust were for the lords and ladies. I had been enjoying a rare day off with my family on the peasants' side of the field.

Part I: For Want of a Piglet

He smirked, caught in another mistake with me. "You've taken so easily to noble rank, m'lady, that I forgot. I hope you found the tournament thrilling?"

"We cheered ourselves hoarse," I said. "There are few days off, for apprentices, and it was thrilling indeed. Though I winced whenever a knight took that tumble off his horse and feared he'd break his neck. It must be harrowing to be a knight's wife at the joust. Save for yours."

It was a fair joke, and we both chuckled at it. Anders drifted a little closer, as we walked, and said, "No lady for a simple knight errant, though."

I found that hard to swallow; a handsome knight and twice champion, unwed? "A betrothed?"

He still shook his head. "What father would want a son with only a sword and a horse to his name? I'm sure you've done better yourself."

That touched a nerve. "No, I'm not wed. Or betrothed, not anymore."

"Anymore? What man would decline the apprentice of the Elect? Not only a fool, he's blind as well." Anders' eyes narrowed with a sly smile. "There must be a story there. A love story?"

I only shook my head and said nothing. When I last saw my father, we'd argued about my betrothal again. And then he had died at Ansehen, taken by fever when he should've been safe from swords and arrows. I would never make peace with him on how the betrothal had fallen apart. That fight haunted me still.

Anders' smile faded. "Did I offend? I didn't mean to."

"No, it's nothing you said." I clutched my cloak shut with one hand, to keep from fidgeting, and nearly tripped on a twisted little pine. The trees weren't much more than bushes now, the forest giving way to heath. My feet were cold and starting to dampen, too, from the snow soaking in.

Anders tried to touch my shoulder, getting closer still. "You're troubled. Don't say you aren't."

It was kind of him, but I shook him off and angled away. "My feet are cold."

He chuckled again. "If you need warming, just say the word."

That only soured me further. I quickened my stride and headed up the line past Acorn and Ilya and Boristan. At the front, Kiefan led. Ulf scouted the forest ahead, as he often did. I fell into Kiefan's pace at a polite distance, focusing on the rocks and fallen branches we had to navigate. No path to follow, up here. It had ended at the kir fount. This was barely a game trail through the brush.

The corner of my eye caught Kiefan looking at me, sidelong. After a time, he said, "Sir Anders has that effect on people."

"Does he think of anything but foolishness?"

Kiefan shrugged. "Not from what I hear. This is the most time I've spent with the man, in truth."

It was a day to learn oddities, it seemed. "You don't know the man, but trusted him enough for this mission?"

"The saints named him, as they did me. Putting all else aside, Sir Anders is one of our best knights. It rankles many, you can believe that."

That made me think of their sparring on Saint-day. The prince of Wodenberg had three Blessings, I had heard — speed, anticipation, and strength — and was the only disciple so blessed. Anders had only the first two. "He bested you in your skirmish."

"True. Rare that I meet a knight who can, though I think I saw a weakness in his guard… well, in any case, little time for sword training of late. Or reading." Pausing, he looked at me afresh and asked, "What of your reading? If there's some part of that Arceal you have questions about, I'm sure you can quote it to me."

I smiled and he echoed it. "True, I can. And there are a few parts I meant to ask about."

CHAPTER 6

I woke, even in the bedroll sausage-row, from the chill cutting through my blanket and cloak when the wind spun up to a howl. There was nothing to see but blue-white snow all around, and that was driving into my eyes. There had been no trees when we made camp, and the roofing tarp was far lower this time; when I sat up to rub my eyes, my head brushed the oilskin.

The wind shifted the snow away. I peered toward where the campfire had been and saw only shadows and blizzard. The ponies, tethered near the lean-to and wearing their blankets, were one mass huddled together against the storm. No sign of the fire, so what light there was had to be some sort of dawn.

As I watched, another form emerged from the driving snow. Kiefan crawled under the tarp on all fours, shedding flakes as he went. To me, "Good morning," and he shook Ilya by the shoulder. Sleepy noises came from under Ilya's fur-lined hood and blanket.

"Time for your watch, near as I can tell," Kiefan said. While Ilya muttered his way awake, Kiefan added, "If you're going out, don't go further than the other side." He indicated the tall bush that the upper edge of the tarp was tied to. The lower edge had been staked to the rocky ground. "Anyone gets lost in this and we'll need all Qadeem's wits to find them."

Ilya rolled over and lifted himself up on his hands. "Snowing?"

"And the fire died. You'll need a charm to get it going, if at all. Wake us at the usual time, or your best guess, and we'll see how the storm looks then."

"Can't walk in this, m'lord," Ilya commented as he crawled out of the sausage-row.

Kiefan spread out the bedroll that Ilya left behind, over the sleeping neighbors, and climbed into the spot before the wind stole all its warmth. When he pulled the ends around himself, I helped him get his feet covered. He shot me a tired smile before he pulled his hood deep over his head. "Maybe we'll get a little extra sleep out of this."

We did. The storm whistled and howled long after light came. We ate trail bread and used one of the heating charms we'd brought to melt a pot of snow to drink. We'd save the water from the fount until we needed it. We huddled around the heating charm until its kir ran out.

Then in half the time I'd ever seen a storm end, the blizzard was picked up and carried off by a stiff, icy blade of wind. The tarp rattled under the blast, smacking me through my bedroll and cloak. Sunlight glowed on the oilskin. The wind eased.

The sun was high and winking through fast-moving clouds as we struck camp — nearly noon, and Ulf urged us to be quick. The snow was ankle deep, powdery, and carried on the persistent breeze. I walked alongside Acorn, my hood up, mittens on, cloak pinned shut to my waist. Once out in the sun and walking, I warmed up and the day was clear and beautiful, in truth, though the breeze kicked up to a wind and threw snow in our faces every so often.

We stopped early to rest, and I was glad to. I brushed snow off a rock and sat to catch my breath. Without trees, the snow was a brilliant sheet laid over the slopes around us. I shaded my eyes and tried to look back, but we'd come around the shoulder of a hill and the valley was gone. Ahead a lumpy expanse of white rose until a sharp line of blue sky took over. In some places dark rock jutted, too vertical for snow to cling to. High up, the peaks loomed around us.

Kiefan checked on Puck and Anders, and in walking back paused to look up with me. "Ulf tells me that is Himmelbaum," he said, pointing back toward a snowy peak. Northeasterly, ahead of us still, "That's Starknadel. The pass goes over his flank."

"And where is this?" I pointed at my feet.

"The eastern side of Himmelbaum. Ready to walk?"

"It feel that we only just stopped."

"Ulf says we need to cross the valley while the wind is low. And this is as low as it gets."

My cloak swirled around my legs and the breeze pulled open the gaps between my cloak pins. We crunched across miles of snow, and if it was a valley I could hardly tell. The white hid all clues, and the sun washed out any lingering details when he emerged from the clouds. When I saw Ulf, his hawk's eyes were irised down to pinpricks of black. He scouted out a crevice in the rock, one with a ring of stones and a little ash still inside. It was deep enough for us and the horses, and sheltered enough that the snow hadn't filled it in.

"I wanted to be sure we found this camp," Ulf said. "In the spring, the snow melts a bit here and we hunt mountain sheep before they shed their winter coats. They supplied the pelts." He put a gloved hand to the lining of his hood.

"Glad that we did, it's a good site," Kiefan said, and coughed. "Glad we found it early, I was nearly forced to call another rest stop."

"Saps a man's strength, this cold," Ulf told him, patting him on the shoulder. "Call a rest whenever you need to, m'lord. And take a sip of kir, that's why we filled all the skins."

The morning sun had gotten a few rays in underneath the leading edge of the storm, then disappeared. We'd retreated to the safety of the crevice, out of the rising wind. The ponies seemed just as happy to have Ilya and Anders unload the baggage again. Blankets on, they idly licked the green lichen off the rocks while we kept the fire going with the last of Boristan's firewood.

We talked about hot summer days while the blizzard screamed.

Kiefan said that in the summer Dame Aleksandra, captain of the King's Guard, drilled him with sword and shield, in full mail and padded gambeson until sweat blinded him. "She called for cups of pickle brine," he said. "I thought she'd gone mad, but one taste and I downed the cup. Then I begged for more."

Ilya talked of the forge in the castle's barn-yard and pumping its bellows while the smith heated iron. Anders had a story about chasing a mischievous colt for miles in the middle of the Summer Moon.

When they came to me, I had no summer story worthy. The men expected I would tell them something about picking flowers in sunny fields on lazy summer days, and I got a good laugh from that. The laugh made me dizzy and then I started coughing. Ilya passed me the skin of fount water and I took a sip. The kir eased the cough and the creeping chill.

Ulf had brought a pack of cards and we played several games, brushing stray snowflakes away and coughing now and then. Boristan left to relieve himself and when he returned he was red in the face, breathing a bit hard for just a short walk and back.

"Do you feel ill?" I asked. "Feverish?"

He laughed. "I'm too cold to feel feverish."

Still, I put my hands on his face. "A little, perhaps."

"Your hands are cold."

True enough. I rubbed them together and put my mittens back on. The fire died in the afternoon but it was too soon for another of the heating charms. We kept playing cards until the shadows deepened. The blizzard raged on, and the snow outside grew deep. The wind skirled along the mouth of the crevice and carved the bank's inside slope into a smooth wave.

Once it was dark, Boristan triggered a heating charm to thaw out trail biscuits and heat some water to make bergamot tea. I was surprised they'd brought a little box of it in the baggage, but it was comforting to wrap my hands around a warm mug and sip.

Though we hadn't walked at all, I was still tired enough to sleep. The stone was just as cold as the previous night. We huddled close, and didn't bother making anyone stay up on watch.

When light returned, the snow had slowed. It was even falling almost straight down. Ulf went out to climb higher for a look, and came back a long while later with bleeding hands. "Slipped on the rock," he said while I dug out a cleansing charm from my medicine bag. "The clouds are breaking up, so let's head out."

The charm was bound to a wooden cameo of Mother Love. Ulf cupped his hands under it and I focused on the kir knotted up inside it. I imagined squeezing the knot and felt it give. The cameo glowed faintly and the kir dripped onto Ulf's wounds, banishing putrefaction from the flesh. My master had told me I would understand the why of that, someday; for now, I did it for knowing cleansed wounds healed faster.

"Thank you, m'lady. Just bandage them up and all's well. Save your kir."

I crashed into Acorn's rump before I realized we had stopped, bounced off, and landed on my butt in the knee-deep snow. The jostle set off another round of coughing, and that knocked my sore head around too much. I'd meant to get up, but the throbbing convinced me to stay down.

At the pony's other end, Ilya plopped down in the snow too, chest heaving. Another stop to rest, thank the Mother. My feet were numb and the damp crept in despite my oiled leather boots. Head throbbing, I tipped back and lay on the powdery snow. My eyes fell shut. Perhaps I could get a little sleep before Kiefan started us marching again. Perhaps…

"Dame Kate? Are you hurt?" Kiefan landed on his knees beside me, pulling my hood open.

Startled, I batted his hand away and half sat up. "No, no, I'm sorry. Only tired and sore and…" I pulled off my mitten before it got to my forehead. The headache needled out from the foremost nubs of my Blessing, and kneading them helped.

"Headache? Me too. Take a drink, it helps." Kiefan offered the skin of kir-water.

I pulled the stopper and drank. "You said that Master Parselev wouldn't have told me about headaches? Your headaches?"

There was a tightness around his grey eyes and a crease in his brow, I could see now that he was close. "There are larger things to worry about," he said. "Frostbite. Storms."

The sky overhead was as blue as if clouds did not exist.

"You worry about the storms and I'll worry about the frostbite. And your headaches. They strike often?"

"Often enough. But since we left the city, not a one until we were snowed in."

"Does Master Parselev give you something or use kir?"

"I don't trouble the Elect with my headaches, most of the time. Don't trouble yourself with them either. One more sip and it's Anders' turn." He indicated the water skin.

"If you won't trust me with the truth, I'm no use as a physician." I took one more sip.

Kiefan considered that for a moment, and glanced toward Ilya who watched as he lounged in a snowbank. In Arceal, the prince murmured, "It's unwise for a leader to be weak. If there's a private moment, ask again."

That would have to do for a promise. I passed the skin back and he carried it down the line to Sir Anders, who seemed to have fallen straight into a nap the moment he sat down. Kiefan lightly cuffed him and held out the skin.

A bit of wind was all the warning we got; icy needles crackled on my cloak and a curtain of snow swept through the pass. All but the rocky slope an arm's reach away disappeared. Acorn stopped. The wind rose further, whistling, then shrieking. I put my hands on Acorn's packs and pulled myself between the pony and the stone wall, slogging through the unbroken snow as best I could. I got as far as his shoulder and threw my arm over to hug him. I met Ilya's arm, there, as he'd done the same from the other side.

My head pounded as the wind wailed on and on. My throat was dry from panting, but I couldn't stop. I scooped up a mouthful of snow to eat.

The wind's voice trembled. Then it dropped, and the pelting ice slowed. Sun broke through and the squall pushed down the pass. The curtain of snow lifted as quickly as it had fallen.

I looked across Acorn's neck at Ilya. He laughed, shaking his head. "Do we get a moment's rest?"

"Can you see Kiefan?" Rock blocked my view, and I wasn't tall enough to lean over the pony.

"Boristan's lying down," he said, and took a seat in the snow. "M'lord should take another rest, he's been breaking trail all day."

Acorn shook his head, scattering ice crystals. I pulled myself to the pony's rear and stepped back into the narrow lane of trodden snow. Behind us, Anders was sitting too, Puck's reins in his hand. My mouth was cold from eating snow, but my throat was drying out again. I picked up another bite from a fresh snowbank.

"Dame Kate! Kate!"

At Kiefan's call I shuffled around Acorn, nearly stepped on Ilya's feet, and trotted up the line. Boristan tried waving me off with a mittened hand, but Kiefan tugged his arm down. "I'll be well. Just a few minutes to rest," Ther said as I crouched down beside both of them. "All I need is a few minutes."

Kiefan only tugged Boristan's hood back so the sunlight hit his face. He was pale, far too pale, and gasping for breath. I put my fingers to his throat and his heartbeat raced in his veins.

"He tried to stand and fell," Kiefan said.

"Just a moment's dizziness." Boristan tried to wave that off too. "I'm tired. We all are. Who can sleep well on cold stone?"

Ulf arrived from somewhere ahead. He'd been helping break the trail, to guess by his snow-plastered cloak. He breathed hard, but his color was much better than Boristan's. "We must press on," he said. "We're near the top of the pass, and well beyond where anyone's lived to tell of it."

Boristan clutched Kiefan's shoulder. "Help me, then," he rumbled, trying to heave himself up. Kiefan picked him up easily and held on when Boristan tried to stand alone.

"Can you break the trail a while more?" Kiefan looked to Ulf, who nodded. "Ilya! Up!"

I wasn't so sure it was merely fatigue. It looked like an illness, and we all had it. Cold, dry air and we were a small group in close quarters... I had seen how typhus fever rippled through the army as we marched to Ansehen. On cue, my chest tightened and I coughed as I started walking again. My pulse picked up and throbbed around my Blessing. A frown settled onto my face as my feet slogged on through the snow. I wished I'd found a walking stick while the forest was still with us. I wished —

"M'lord!" Ilya called. "M'lord, stop! Sir Anders!"

Kiefan turned and I did too. There was a thump as Boristan returned to the snowdrift and Kiefan trotted past, flicking a hand at me to follow. My leaden feet quickened and I followed his trail around Acorn, through fresh snow, back onto the path.

Puck stood unmoved, mouthing at his bit, connected to a dark mass in the snow by two reins. "Anders!" Kiefan yanked him up roughly and he startled to life. "He's bleeding!"

I arrived in time to see the bright smear of blood on Anders' lip as he wiped it away. His hood had fallen back and he was the same ashy pale as Boristan. Breath rapid and shallow. I checked his pulse and it was high.

"I dozed off, that's all," he protested. "Dozed off and another fucking nosebl —" A coughing attack cut him off.

"We spent all day lazing around camp yesterday," Kiefan said, "and you doze off out here?"

By the crease in his brow, Anders had a headache too. "The snow's more comfortable," he managed to retort.

"Kate, do whatever you must," Kiefan said, stepping back. "Whatever you can."

I hesitated. "Boristan's worse off," I murmured.

A glare. "Ther Boristan can't hold off three lamia at once. Can you heal this or not?"

I looked at Anders, sitting there pressing his knuckles to his bleeding nose and heaving deep breaths. Kneeling in the snowdrift beside him, I put my hands on his cheeks — scratchy with four days' flaxen stubble — and called up my kir. Tingling warmth rose to my chest, and even that far off I felt an echo in Anders' kir. Not surprising he'd be sensitive, given his double Blessing. His eyes fell shut and he leaned into my hands with a weary sigh.

Kir glowed in my hands and my patient's colorful whorls came to the surface. I focused on their dance, my own eyes closing as well to clearly see the full structure of his chest. Slow and weak, the whorls turned rather than spun. A persistent wobble in one of his meridians caught my mind's eye. I knew that one from studying the pneumonia patients in the Order's hospital — it joined the lungs to the heart and the prime meridian along his spine.

My hand slipped under Anders' cloak, under his layered woolens to press against his breastbone and he startled with a hiss. Then, a weak laugh. "You could warn a man, ice-hands!"

The contact made it easier to focus on his lungs, where the kir should be strong and vital. Stronger than what I saw. Peering close, I saw no competing kir pattern, as in an illness. Nothing attacking, only the sluggishness of heavy congestion. Strange. Nothing in my memory could advise me.

Still, I could help; my master had shown me how to clear the lungs. "Take a deep breath and hold it," I told him.

I wove my kir into a mesh and drew it through both of his lungs. The phlegm, as it was not a living thing or part of Anders' pattern, peeled away and I scooped it upward. The body's urge to be rid of it came on fast and strong, so one must be quick. Anders twisted over, heaving, and got most of it out in a mass. A second hard retch and he spat in the snow.

His kir strengthened and his meridian steadied. When I opened my eyes, his color was better. A bit of his smile was back, after he wiped his mouth. His arm looped around my hips and pulled me to his chest.

"If the rest of you needs warming, m'lady, I'd be glad to repay you for the kindness," Anders told me with a teasing smile.

"Here?" I cast a glance at the snowbanks, the pony, and more importantly the other five of our party watching. I was quick to extricate my warmed hand from under his cotes. No need to dwell on the muscles under there.

"If m'lady insists."

He did let me go when I pried at his hand, but I told him, "You've been kind enough to me thus far, Sir Anders, though you make it hard to remember that. Couldn't you simply be the good knight who untangled me from the stirrup that first day?"

His teasing smile dropped. There had been a nerve to hit in there, unexpectedly. More soberly than I had expected, Anders inclined his head. "My apologies, Dame Kate."

My new name had settled in, but it still didn't fit. "My name is Kate," I said, looking to Kiefan to include him in this. And I raised my voice so the rest of my audience would hear. "Majesty was kind to give me a title, but I'm only Kate. I'm not anyone's m'lady. Certainly not after you've all seen me tripping over these damn braies in the bushes."

Dizziness struck when I stood, and I nearly fell over. Kiefan caught me. "Bring that kir-water," he called to Ilya. "So was it a fever, D — Kate? Pneumonia?"

"No, I've seen pneumonia often enough. It's not." I stood on my own and he let me. "I don't know what it is. Ulf said it was the cold, but it's something about the cold here in the pass."

<hr />

They strung tarps from the rock to make camp. Kiefan had to hammer pitons in, as he had the strength Blessing to make quick work of it. But so late in the day, he had little kir left. He clung to the bare rock when the wind whipped his cloak into a flag, pausing with the hammer in hand as he set his spine against the blast. The next blow he struck had half the strength, but he beat at the stone until the pitons were set. Then he stumbled to the little knot of Boristan and me, letting Ilya tie down the tarps around us.

We took Kiefan in, between us, swaddled him in our wool and fur. I hardly had a chance to think it was the prince who clutched me close for warmth. Boristan had us both in his bear hug until the shivering eased.

The ponies were glad enough to huddle with us in the windbreak even though it rattled and thumped under the air's fist. Whether it was a storm or merely snow blown up in the gale, it was impossible to tell. And perhaps it didn't matter.

Bundled together in blankets, in the dim light, I checked feet and hands for frostbite. The kir-water skin was getting light, but a few sips gave me enough to thaw out sluggish kir in a few sets of toes. I was leery of seeing a damaged pattern slip my control when there was little kir handy, but it seemed to help. The hairiest of the feet put in my hands was hardly even cold. I almost laughed. "Whose is this?"

"Me," Ulf said, his other end off in the shadowy mass of us.

"Did you glue wool to your feet, or is this the usual?"

They all chuckled. "Wife says I'm half wolf," he answered, doubly a joke as he was named for the beast. "Threatens to put me out in the kennel if I'm not polite enough for human company. That's how I know it's time for another hunt."

CHAPTER 7

"It's sleet," Ulf reported, and that was that.

Despite all the walking and fatigue, our appetite ran low. We dozed in our windbreak — the wind had lowered, thankfully, though the rain splattered loudly on the tarp — without breakfast and ate only a little at noon. Anders hauled himself up to unpack oats for the ponies and returned as exhausted as if he'd walked all day.

"We've another two days of oats, at full rations," he told Kiefan, and dropped back into his slot in the sausage row. "The sooner we get them to grass, the better."

Kiefan sat at the outside end of the row, pretending to be untouched by fatigue or headache. He nodded. "Soon as it lifts, we'll go. I don't want to lose this day any more than you."

But we did. I unpacked my Arceal book and sat beside Kiefan, closest to the light, reading and asking him to translate some of the more tangled passages. At one part, Anders spoke up, in the language, and explained an especially odd phrase.

"It's something they say when they think you're lying, but they don't want to insult you," he said. "They have quite a few of those."

"And how would you know of that, Anders?" Boristan asked, in Arceal, and managed a chuckle before breaking into a cough.

He smiled. "There may have been a few horses involved in a deal."

"How often have you been to Temitte?" Kiefan asked.

"Only a few times, and as part of the Kaufmanns' caravan. I wouldn't say I speak Arceal well, but if there's swearing to be done I can hold my own."

Still, I made good progress on my reading. The sleet finally stopped too late in the afternoon to strike camp, and we had to spend a second night in that crowded, cold lean-to, coughing and sore. Boristan wheezed in his sleep as if he had pneumonia, but it still was not. The blanket of clouds finally broke after dark and the Shepherd filled the valley with light. The Grain Moon was three-quarters full and five of the seven Flock were scattered across the sky.

I said, in Arceal, "Shepherd, gather your Flock."

"Shepherd, though I stray you call me home." Kiefan continued the nursery song, in translation, looking up at the sky with me. Beyond the moons, the stars lay thick on the sky's blanket.

"Shepherd, lead your lambs back to hearth," I finished. We sat quietly and I looked over my shoulder at the sausage-row of men. Still in Arceal, I asked, "Will you tell me about your head pain?"

"Headaches." He supplied the word. "I have headaches. There's nothing more to it than that."

"Often?" A shrug. "But you must have told the Elect about them." Parselev was the royal family's own physician.

Kiefan looked out at the narrow, snow-covered valley. We were up on a shoulder, following a trail of rock instead of walking on the snowfield below. The wind cut hard, down the center. He said, "If I can't shake it, it builds over days. When it's too much, the Elect sees to it."

"How do you shake it? Willow bark?"

"A few days' peace. Sometimes a quiet ride up to Prohzgrad will do it. At worst, a bottle of brandy."

I considered that. "A quiet ride up to the mountains?"

"I don't know when I'd gone so long without one, until the blizzards began."

"Blizzards," I echoed. That was a new word, in Arceal. Kiefan corrected my pronunciation. "Is the headache bad now?"

"I can hold out."

We watched the Shepherd and the Flock until I dozed off sitting up. Excusing myself, I crawled back to wrap myself in my bedroll and join my wheezing, snoring companions.

———————✕———————

I had taken Acorn from Ilya so that he and Boristan could lean on each other as they walked behind the pony. Ther did most of the leaning, in truth. He was still deathly pale. I kept looking behind to be sure that Anders was still leading Puck, too.

When I turned forward after one such check, Ulf was breaking the path out front and Kiefan followed to widen it. The crust of sleet had frozen solid overnight, and fought even a man's weight before breaking.

Kiefan simply dropped, limp.

I blinked, and then fear stabbed me. I ran, pulling Acorn up to a trot. "Ulf, stop! Stop!"

My master's training guided my hands. I rolled Kiefan over, put my fingers to his throat to find his heartbeat, then brushed snow from his nose and mouth. His pulse was high, his breath fast and shallow like us all. He shook his head, muttering, and squinted in the light.

"I'm all right," he tried to claim. "Let me up."

"No. Don't argue with me." I took his head in both hands, thumbs on the initial nubs of his Blessing, and called my kir. His surged back, glad to answer.

Unwinding headaches was one of the first healing charms taught to apprentices. One didn't need to know the proper pattern for kir in the mind — there was none. All minds were different. A tangle of kir whorls and maybe a meridian caught in the mess was the usual culprit for a headache.

Kiefan's kir was knotted, hard and tight, around the meridians that sprang from his Blessing. He'd been shrugging this off for days? I'd never seen kir bound so firmly. I squeezed the knots, as one would an object-bound charm, but they didn't respond. Pressing a knuckle in with a twist, I felt one loosen. I reached for a second knot, did the same, and knew I didn't have enough kir to force all of them open. They were tough little nuts to crack.

He'd used half his day's kir, as it was nearly noon, and in my mind's eye the remainder hovered nearby in a glowing mist. Nearer than it should, in truth, as if it wanted to help. Mentally, I put out a hand and it flowed up eagerly. I picked the knots open one by one and the whorls tumbled out, confused and weak. The last of Kiefan's kir washing over them helped restart their spinning dance.

When I opened my eyes, fatigue fell on me like another cloak. They'd all clustered around to watch, sitting in the snow.

"Is he well?" Boristan asked. "You took longer, it seemed."

"I believe he is," I answered. Kiefan's eyes were open, under my hands, I realized. My thumbs were still on the roots of the two horn ridges that broke his scalp. I wiped away drops of melted snow, there.

"That's where they start," he murmured up at me.

"Did I get all the pain?" I asked. "You were full of knots."

Kiefan's smile was tired and thin. "That was amazing. How'd you use my kir? I'm not charm-handed."

Only charm-hands could donate their kir, unless one were Elect. "It wanted to help," I said. "Let Ulf and Ilya break the path today, for a change."

Anders took the chance to interrupt. "If you're not going to cuddle afterwards, we should keep going."

That got him two glares, which he laughed off. Ilya passed us the kir-water. The skin was light in my hands; I only took a sip and gave it back.

For once, we woke to the same weather we'd slept with. That alone brightened the day. Before we struck camp, I spent my kir on Anders' re-growing congestion and then took Ilya's through his charm-hand. That I spent on Boristan, and he perked up considerably after a lung-clearing — though he did complain that my hands were cold when I put one on his chest.

It was only more snow to look forward to, but we went in good spirits. The shoulder path lowered toward the snow that filled the valley. We met with rockslides from seasons past and picked our way through the rubble where we could. It took a little digging, at one point, and a heating charm to melt the ice that held the mass of gravel together.

But the happiest moment, by far, came in the afternoon as we forged through the calf-deep snow at what seemed to be the bottom of the valley. The shelf we'd followed through the pass had given out for good, but the snow had been knee deep up there. From up ahead, we all heard Ulf shout, "M'lord! Come see!"

He'd been scouting ahead now that the snow was shallowing. We followed his trail at a trot through a jumble of hillocks of rock and snow, finding him at last on the edge of a flat sheet as big around as my father's cottage. And we all heard it. Running water.

A frozen pool, that flat sheet, and a creek burbled out from underneath to run downhill. Its ice-crusted path led us, cautiously, down a ragged stone slope and around one last berm of avalanche rubble. There we stopped, stunned by the view.

The rock ran level for a hundred feet or so, more or less flat, and simply ended. We crept toward the edge, leaving the ponies behind, and sat within a few feet of the cliff. It fell away, as did the suicidal stream, far enough to make me dizzy when I peeked over. Ice glittered on the granite face below.

It was the view of Caercoed that held us there. Pine-forested piedmont gave way to a forest aflame in full autumn glory. Gold, orange, and red hills rolled north and east, interrupted by lakes here and there. On the shore of the near lake, a dark smudge of a village had pushed back the forest. From the center of the village rose a single, scarlet-cloaked tree in a gentle spiral, arms thrown wide as if in a dance.

"Tree's three hundred feet if it's an inch," Ilya said.

Ulf pointed into the distance. "There's another one, another village. I can make out three or four more, in the distance. The forest gives way to prairie, it looks like, but the trees still mark villages."

I could just make out a taller red head in the sea of gold and orange. The rest hazed into the distance, unless you had hawk's eyes.

"And there's the start of your grass, Anders." Ulf pointed closer. "Tomorrow afternoon, if we can find a way around this cliff."

When we turned, the ponies were already licking the lichen off the nearest rocks. We set camp behind the rocks and Kiefan assigned watches for the night again. I was glad just to wash my face in liquid water, even if it was ice cold.

The third day after we found the cliff, I clung to Puck's back as Anders led him down a slender trail. My fever had been high enough, that morning, and I'd coughed out enough phlegm, that Kiefan had picked me up and put me on the pony. I hadn't fought it much. Puck's saddle wasn't meant for riding, but I wobbled along with two handfuls of the blanket and saddlebags on either side to fall against. Anders kept a close eye; he'd wanted to tie me down.

Addled as I was, I felt Puck stop, take a few more steps to come alongside Acorn, and stop again. The men clustered in front of the ponies, muttering and looking ahead. I craned my neck enough to see a small pond and a clearing, through the thick screen of gold and orange leaves.

"Archers in the trees, I'm sure of it," Ulf said. "Well camouflaged. They've waited all day, I'd bet."

"They saw our campfires these past nights." Kiefan looked toward the clearing. "And since we stopped short of their ambush, they must know we suspect." A pause. "We didn't come to start a fight."

"Why are they in the trees, if not to kill us?" Ulf asked.

"Armed strangers wandering your forest? What would Baron Eismann do?" Anders asked.

"Saint Woden told me they knew we're coming," Kiefan said.

Boristan put a hand on our prince's shoulder. "Let me go in first, m'lord. Maybe they'll talk."

Kiefan grimaced, but nodded and stepped aside. Ther Boristan walked into the clearing, hood down, cloak behind his shoulders, and hands open. Stopping to cough up phlegm and spit a couple times, he followed the path to the well-worn patch at the pond's edge. He nearly got there before an arrow hissed into the ground beside his foot.

"Stay where you are!"

The accent was strange, but it was Arceal. Boristan stopped.

"Where 'tis you travel from?"

Ther answered in kind. "We came through the Eispitzen, by Starknadel's pass, from Wodenberg. Our saints charged us with finding the land of Caercoed. Have we found it?"

There was a pause. "Your leader must present and disarm."

Boristan looked back. Kiefan shifted his cloak over his shoulders and strode into the clearing, unbuckling his sword belt as he went. Sheathed blade in hand, he spread his arms wide. He'd started wearing the boiled leather breastplate again after the cliff, but aside from that he looked the part of a traveler.

"Name yourself."

"Kiefan Weissberg, Blessed knight of the Trinity, prince and heir to the kingdom of Wodenberg. I seek an alliance with the High Crowns of Caercoed against our mutual foe, the empire of Arcea."

A single word, and an arrow hissed. I saw only a flash of steel and a broken arrow tumbling to the grass. Kiefan spun his sword over his hand and pointed up into the trees. Where the shot had come from, I assumed. "Does Caercoed fire on the unarmed, then?" he asked.

"Legends must be put to test, must they not?"

Kiefan returned his sword to the sheath and spread his arms again. "So how should I test the legend of the amazons across the mountains?"

I didn't see the huntress until she stepped into the sun; her mottled cloak matched the shadows, her leather jerkin the tree trunks. A glimpse of short golden skirt had stood in for autumn leaves, over dark hose. She carried a bow, but un-nocked the arrow and returned it to her quiver.

The other half dozen archers who emerged did not, though.

"Peace-bond your weapons and we shall take you to —" and she used a long, bumpy word I didn't know. "Be welcome in Tadhlon of Caercoed."

'Tay-lon,' it sounded like to my ear. I leaned toward Anders to ask, "Who are we being taken to?"

"It's a noble rank, something like a margrave," he answered. "The Margraves Gwatcyn."

"Captain Mohra Fionmaen." She introduced herself to Kiefan with a bow. "Is your companion well enough to ride? We've horses." The captain indicated me with a nod.

"She can ride double. How far is it?"

"Come noon tomorrow, we reach Faen, where soft beds and mulled cider await the weary."

I dissolved into the hot bath. Fire crackled on the washroom's hearth, heating another kettle of water if I wanted it, and noontime sun slanted through the gap in the curtained window. The clay tub was long and deep enough for me to lie in, if I folded up my knees, and I let myself slide to the bottom with my hair fanning out around me.

Near two weeks' sweat had crusted in places I didn't want to dwell on. We hadn't tried to wash on the Saint-day in the mountain pass, or even stopped for a disciple's dance. Now I picked at pimples and scrubbed with the coarse brush the maid had left me. The soap was lovely and smelled of rosewater.

When my maid, Anwyl, returned, I had gotten a layer of skin off and felt far more human. She wrapped me in a towel and squeezed out my hair into the tub, then pulled its plug and let it drain. Though she didn't speak any Arceal, she pointed me toward the fresh clothes I'd brought to the washroom and wanted me to dress.

After far too long dressing as a man, I was glad to slide into my light woolen shift and pull the drawstring neck close before tying it. While far warmer than the pass, it was still an autumn day here. My yellow dress, fitted more loosely and its neckline a broad, flat-hemmed scoop, went over my shift. Simply feeling skirts around my ankles again was a relief, despite that my dress was nothing like what the Caer ladies wore.

They wore straight-seamed, billowing tunics and tied them with a sash just under the breasts. The hem might be near their ankles, it might be at their knees, or just to their thighs, and worn over knit hose. Anwyl's tunic was knee long, and she wore hose as well. Her brown hair was twisted up in a simple bun and pinned.

Once my wet hair was wrapped in a small towel, she ushered me out of the washroom. Then I saw why; there was a line for the bath. As the washroom was just off the kitchen and its massive fireplace, so Kiefan and Anders and Ther Boristan waited on a bench next to one of the tables, watching the margrave's household chop and knead and roast. The girls who ought to be working were snapped at every few minutes for being distracted by the three strangers in the room, and every maid who hurried through stole an appraising glance.

The master of the kitchen, Aed, who was the margraves' husband, was not amused.

Anders said, "Hold on, I thought Kate was in the bath? Who's this, then?"

I know I blushed, and they chuckled, and Anwyl shooed me along back to my room upstairs. There, on the bed, she gestured for me to keep toweling my hair while she brought a small tea tray to my bedside table. When she lifted the lid to check the tea, it smelled wonderful and just like the blend Master Parselev preferred. All tea came from Arcea, so it might well be the same.

Anwyl picked up the comb and I untangled the towel from my hair, letting it fall down my back. When she only stood there, I glanced up, asking, "Is something wrong?"

Her eyes were fixed on my head, on my Blessing. She started to reach out with the comb, but hesitated and withdrew.

Nobody in Caercoed had a Blessing, from what I'd seen. As strange as it was for us to see women here, women there, only a scattering of men, we had to be far stranger to them.

I tried to look reassuring when I smiled. "Don't worry," I said, though she couldn't understand. "It only looks strange. You can touch it, don't be afraid." I took her empty hand and brought her fingers to one of the nubs, let her feel the cuticle where the ridge jutted up out of my scalp. "You have goats in Caercoed, don't you? Sheep? See how it feels like a lamb's horn nub?"

It took a moment, but Anwyl gently pressed. Maybe she'd been afraid the comb would tear the skin, as if it were a wound. Then she ran her fingers along the bumps, feeling how smooth and solid they were. Nothing to fear. I smiled with her as she said something, looking relieved, and then she sat down behind me to comb my hair.

I sipped a cup of tea, glad for its soothing warmth. A healer had visited me last night, after I'd been carried up to bed on arrival, and my fever and congestion had ebbed. The tea scalded some lingering phlegm from my throat. And though my hair was nearly long enough to sit on, Anwyl made short work of combing it out — far faster than my little sister, who couldn't stop chatting when she combed my hair. Anwyl began plaiting it without asking, some sort of braid far more complicated than I ever did, but I let her finish and tie the tail with a bit of cord.

There was a well not far inside the manor's gatehouse, with troughs for animals to drink and rough-hewn, sturdy benches. From my window, I watched water carriers line up buckets on the bench and one girl drew the water while the others took the filled ones, moved empties up the line, and hauled away when they had a matching pair.

Most importantly, the benches were in the sun whereas my room was a little dim for reading.

I tried to explain to Anwyl, but in the end she followed me and didn't entirely understand until I sat down and opened my book. Then she gestured to ask me to stay there. "Yes," I said, one of a few words of Caer I had picked out. I indicated my book and then the sun overhead.

That satisfied her and she went to see to other duties.

The manor's gate was ironbound wood, and the gatehouse a square tower on either side connected by a walk. Granite walls swept off in either direction, broadly encircling the tall manor and its outbuildings. The squad of guards at the gate noted all who passed through, but that was not too much excitement, it seemed. I caught them watching me a few times.

Kiefan sat down beside me, smelling of rose soap. Freshly clean-shaven, as well, he'd slicked his golden knight's crest flat between his Blessing ridges to his collar. He wore a black surcote embroidered with the royal sigil, a full Shepherd moon silhouetting Mount Woden, in snowy white.

He looked at me as long as I looked at him. "I must apologize. It had slipped my mind that you likely wear dresses most of the time."

"I'm glad to be out of cotes and hose. You men can keep them."

He smiled, watching the bustle of the gate-yard. "It's not so different from Baron Eismann's manor."

Chickens scattered as a wagon rumbled through, laden with firewood. Swirling dust picked out rays of afternoon sun. "Even with so few men?" I asked. "And those few in the kitchen?"

"It's strange," he allowed. "I'd heard the stories, but thinking of knights is one thing. I squired with Captain Aleks, after all, and she's been captain of the King's Guard for years. No man would dare question her strength or courage. One doesn't think that a land of amazons would be a land of carpenter women as well."

He gestured at the scene across the way, where a wagon minus one wheel was parked on blocks next to an open-sided hut. There, the carpenter carved new spokes for the broken wheel. She worked one stave with a draw-knife while shouting instructions to her apprentice, who cut more from a maple log.

"Why wouldn't there be carpenter women?" I asked. Bolder, "Why must men do everything? Women work as hard, speak as well, learn as quickly."

Some would laugh at that, but Kiefan only shrugged. Looking at my book, he said, "They do learn as quickly. I thought it ambitious of the Elect to give you such a book, but you soon proved otherwise."

I echoed the smile that crept out as he told me that. "I did?"

And for a moment, I almost thought he turned a bit shy when he looked away. "You're quite unexpected, Da — Kate." He corrected himself. "You asked to be Kate, so as you wish."

"I also wish you to tell me, next time, about your headache before your kir gets so tightly knotted." When he shrugged that off, I told him, "Master Parselev warned me about men like you."

Kiefan tried to appear wounded by that.

"Men who won't admit to pain," I said, "until they drop like a sack of potatoes on a snowy mountain pass. A few minutes could've put them right earlier, but no, they must press on."

He looked down at his hands, cracking his knuckles. "I'm the best heir Father has," he murmured. "I must be ready. My sister married Duke Seagrace and there are those who think my nephews unfit to stand in line to the crown. Will and Gerhardt are only boys, as well. And cousin Adalrich's crippled now..." His voice fell off further as he fidgeted.

"I regret that."

Kiefan frowned. "You? How — you were in the surgery." I nodded. "Adalrich said he owed an apology to the Elect for his language. You were out of pain charms?"

"So late in the day, none had the focus left for even a spark charm. Sir Adalrich needed three to hold him down, so it fell to me to amputate."

A nervous laugh. "You cut his foot off."

I nodded. "I'm sure it was only the pain that made him say such things."

"He hardly ever raises his voice."

"And had to be tied to his pallet to keep him from trying to walk, the next morning. That was when Master Parselev gave me the warning." I paused to check the memory. "He did say that all the king's kin were prone to it."

Kiefan turned serious again. "Leaders must pay their dues."

"You push yourself too hard." He started to brush that off too, and I said, "I know, it's better too hard than too little. But you're no use to anybody dead, either. I'm not going to tell anybody you get headaches. Saint Qadeem's rule honor-binds me."

Kiefan relented a little. "Next time, then. Shall we begin the second dialogue?" He pointed to my book, still open but barely read. We spent the rest of the sunlight sitting by the well, but only got through a few paragraphs. Our conversation wandered far and wide, and my thoughts slipped away every time his hand brushed mine.

CHAPTER 8

Mohra, the captain who had brought us to the margraves, collected us in a sitting room off the main hall as she'd told us she would. We six were clean and presentable, by then. She wore a uniform much like what the gate guards wore, a short version of the Caer tunic in beige, bound with a red leather belt at her waist rather than a sash under her breasts. The belt was for her sword. Her hair, it turned out, was short as a boy's.

"The Gwatcyns wish a dinner with you," she said, "ere the Crowns' Elect arrives. Likely, 'twill be on the morrow. They wish to welcome you as guests ere you are emissaries of your kingdom. There shall be no state questions, they wish me to tell you, merely curiosity. Bear in mind the family speaks Arceal passably well, even the boys — m'ladies do not believe in ignorance. Should you need a difficult translation, I will be at hand."

I wished I'd had a nicer dress to wear, not my old yellow thing with the ragged hem. A margrave was between a baron and duke in rank — far too polite a company for a peasant girl. I sidled closer to Ulf, who looked nearly as uncomfortable. Ilya and Ther Boristan knew more of such folk, and waited unruffled.

"No need to hide," Ilya whispered, nudging me closer to Kiefan and Anders. "His Majesty knighted you."

I nodded, as it was true, and took that step. But I clenched my hands together behind my back.

The ladies arrived and the Captain introduced them as Margraves Leix and Lorcana Gwatcyn of Tadhlon. At a glance, they were twins and dressed alike as well in full-length gowns of pale blue. M'lady Leix Gwatcyn served as a captain-general in the Crowns' army and had a square-shouldered air about her. M'lady Lorcana smiled more. Both ladies wore their grey-streaked hair and faint crow's-feet with dignity and grace, and kindly acknowledged my attempt at a curtsy and the menfolk's bows.

It was when the daughters arrived, Aifric and Esgwen, that gave me pause. They came running down the hall outside chattering until a man's voice sharply stopped them. Half composed, they stepped into the drawing room door, pink-cheeked and fighting down giggles. They were twins as well, dark hair cut short like Mohra's, short-skirted and looking to be twelve or thirteen.

"'Tis well we could have one meal together ere the elect rides in," m'lady Leix said, in Arceal, as a maid handed out teacups. "Please, Captain, introduce our guests."

She began with our prince, then his guardsman and then, to my surprise, his physician. Lorcana said with a smile, "Healing is a lofty art in Caercoed. Is it so in Wodenberg?"

I curtsied again. "The highest calling of Saint Qadeem's disciples, m'lady."

"Surely it made your mother proud."

I could say, honestly, "My mother was proud, yes."

M'lady Lorcana's blue eyes narrowed, catching me. "But who was not proud?"

Everyone who understood Arceal watched me now, with curiosity. Especially Kiefan. I felt a blush creeping into my cheeks, but there was no helping the truth. "My father did not want me —" I began, but didn't know the word in Arceal. "Taught? By my master, in an agreement?"

Mohra supplied the word. "Apprenticed."

"'Twas your father who opposed?" M'lady Lorcana weighed that. "But did not prevent, else you would not be here."

"The piglet died," I said.

"A piglet?" Leix chuckled when she said it. "How did a piglet sway your father?"

"Father brought me home from the Order after my first two years of study, even though the Elect wanted me for his apprentice. An apprentice is for five years, so when I finish I will be nineteen. To be unwed at nineteen, even as a physician…" From the faint lines in their brows, the margraves didn't quite see why that troubled my father. I risked a glance at Kiefan, but he studied his tea. Anders and Boristan were translating for Ulf and Ilya. "I am only an Englic peasant girl, m'ladies. Father arranged my betrothal to a blacksmith and clinched it with a sow piglet for my dowry. But she took ill and died when the snows came early. For want of a piglet, my Father signed the apprentice papers and I went back to the Elect."

M'lady Lorcana smiled. "How far along?"

"Two years, m'lady."

"You must be a bright star, to be trusted with such so young."

My blush deepened. Thankfully, attention passed from me to continue the introductions. Ther Boristan of the Order, woodsman Ulf and manservant Ilya were presented in turn. "Be welcome at our table, no matter how humble your roots," Lorcana told them and Kiefan translated. "You've crossed dire mountains and there will be no offense taken tonight. 'Tis a saga to tell, surely, Prince Kiefan?"

"It was a difficult journey, and we were glad to see trees again after so many days of snow and ice. And to hear wolves howl rather than lamia singing."

Aifric and Esgwen perked up at that. "'Tis lamia across the mountains?" one asked.

"Do you have them here too?"

"In the northern lands. A wonder your little ponies outran such beasts." The girl jabbed that at Anders, who only smiled.

"Our ponies are as valiant as ten horses," he replied. "They didn't even trouble themselves to run."

In the drawing room door, the margraves' husband Aed — whose husband? both? — cleared his throat and offered a slight bow. "Dinner is prepared," he announced. "'Tis an honor for my son Tiarnan and I to serve."

I wondered, for a moment, if the son had a twin too but no, only one boy about my age was in evidence in the dining room. Pale, delicate, and his hair was so dark it was nearly black. Tiarnan saw the guests to the table, and his father escorted the margraves and the daughters. The former were seated at the head of the broad table, the latter at the foot, and we guests in between. We each had a fine-glazed porcelain plate waiting for us, a matching cup, and a wooden spoon besides. The table was well lit by candelabras and evening light through the windows.

In our Alemannic, Kiefan asked, "What was that about the ponies?"

Anders sat across the table. "I checked on them, to be sure of their treatment. And I may have been looking at the other horses when the twins discovered me." He grinned. "I nearly had a chance to see their swordsmanship. They're fierce defenders of their favorite horses."

Kiefan stood and caught both girls' eyes with a shallow bow. "If my guardsman troubled you or your horses, m'ladies, I apologize."

I believe it was Aifric who fought down a laugh and Esgwen who stood and answered. "'Twas only a startle, sir. Though your guardsman was nosy as a horse-trader."

"Perhaps because I am a horse-trader, now and then. Most often a trainer of warhorses," Anders said.

That got them off and talking about horses, particularly with m'lady Leix who rode warhorses herself in the Crowns' army. As they talked, I ate by turns a bowl of potato soup and a plate-full of roasted chicken with greens. The dagger I had carried and eaten with through the trip suddenly seemed far too large and awkward. I tried to copy Kiefan's table manners by watching him sidelong.

The conversation subsided a few minutes when the apple-and-raisin tarts arrived and cups of brandy were poured. "Needs must ask," m'lady Leix said while Tiarnan cut and served slices of tart, "of the obvious, dear guests. Stories told by far-ranging caravans of horned men tend to put one in a mind of a man's natural horn." She chuckled at that along with my companions; I turned some shade of pink. "But I see 'tis not a mere turn of phrase. What 'tis that does such violence to your profile, Prince Kiefan? To look at it, I'd think 'twas painful."

"Blessings are bestowed without pain, m'lady. Once Blessed and claimed by a saint, we know our purpose in the kingdom. Some for war, some for wisdom, some for building," Kiefan said, reciting what we were all told as children.

"An alliance of three saints — a rare thing. Qadeem was one, you said?"

"Qadeem for wisdom, Aleksandr for craft, and Woden for war."

M'lady Leix paused in taking a bite of apple tart. "Saint Woden? Of Wodenberg."

"And the city of the same name, on the slopes of Mount Woden."

"Puts his mark on everything, does he? Aught else?"

"He is my grandfather, some times over," Kiefan said.

That was well known, that the royal family was descended from Saint Woden, but when Kiefan said it I happened to be watching Anders splash a little of the brandy onto his apple tart. And I remembered what Baron Eismann had said about sending both... claimants to the crown? Now that Anders was cleaned up and out of that deep-hooded cloak, I suddenly saw a bit of the resemblance. He was a little older, lighter in the hair and bluer-eyed, but he and Kiefan shared a jawline and cheekbones.

Everyone said that the queen hated the king because of the bastard son that'd come after her two princes died. Before Kiefan.

Anders leaned back in his chair with his doctored slice of tart. He wore his uniform, a black tabard embroidered with the cavalry sigil, for knighthood, two golden stars for the Prince's Guard, and a brass ring knotted on each epaulette to indicate a sergeant's rank. Jousting champions were always promoted to the Guard, and he'd won it twice.

Kiefan had said the saints assigned Anders to the mission, and he hardly knew him. Why?

I had lost track of the conversation with the margraves, but m'lady Leix managed to catch my ear. "You mean to say that all your people are Blessed? There are no laypeople, no disciples?"

Ther Boristan answered. "We are all disciples, m'lady. We are all part of the kingdom, we are all bound to the cause of the Trinity."

Lorcana said, "But not all have the gift of kir. In Caercoed, as in many places, only those who prove sensitive are discipled by saints. Of those, the stronger rise to the rank of blessed and perhaps on to elect."

"Some Blessings are greater than others," Boristan offered. "I have only a minor Blessing, myself, but I receive my due share of kir and use it to serve the saints."

That seemed to be a new point. "Your due share?"

"Yes, daily, for my Blessing. And if I don't require it, I can use it in a charm."

The margraves' eyes tracked across each of us, newly wary. "'Tis quite an arrangement your Trinity has, dear guests," m'lady Lorcana said, in low tones. "If you are all so blessed, there must be so many elect that you could hardly need the aid of Caercoed."

That deepened the silence. The answer itched in my mouth, but I didn't think it my place to speak. It was Kiefan who said, quietly, "Wodenberg has only one elect for the moment. Elect Parselev, Dame Kate's master."

Another long moment passed, and Leix broke the silence. "I do apologize, dear guests, for I promised no questions of weight tonight. 'Twould seem that we should arrange for sparring, for I've heard from my guards that they're eager to see how such knights handle a sword. And if the woodsman is willing, 'twill be archery as well."

"Tomorrow is Saint-day," Boristan said, "and there'll be training for certain. We missed a Saint-day, up in the pass, so we'll all be following instruction this week." With a stern look, he repeated that for Ulf and Ilya. "Washing, disciple's dance, and all." They muttered a bit for having to wash again so soon, but it was half-hearted.

"Fortunate, then, Elect Tannait will be here tomorrow," Lady Leix said. "She'll wish to see these war Blessings at use."

I, for one, was glad for the chance to stretch in the disciple's dance.

We drew an audience in the gate-yard. M'lady Leix and her daughters watched, as did several squads of guards from the barracks and as many housemaids as could sneak away from their duties. Caercoed had no Blessings, no Saint-day and no disciple's dance — when Captain Mohra told me as much, I had to wonder just what the Caer saints gave their people.

After the dance ended, wooden swords and round shields were brought. I sat on a bench outside the kitchen with the captain to watch the audience as they watched the knights. Aifric and Esgwen wore their own wooden training swords and stared, rapt. Two littler sisters had come out to watch, too, a pair of six-year-old girls. Twins.

I had to ask. "Mohra, I noticed that… oh, your pardon," I began to apologize; I had been in the wrong language.

She only smiled. "'Tis long enough now that I've picked up your tongue," she said in Alemannic. "We have Blessed of our own, in Caercoed."

"How many do you speak?"

"Arceal, Suevi, Ryu and now — what do you call this?"

"Alemannic."

"Ah. Not so different from Suevi. I speak Englic, too," Mohra said, switching again. "Could have a truly private conversation. You're Englic, yes? By your name, I thought you were."

"Yes, but I only speak Englic at home," I said, lowering my voice. Ther Boristan and Ilya weren't far away. "It's not used in Wodenberg."

Mohra nodded. "Few Englic ships make the north crossing, the old timers say, since Wodenberg took you." But she returned to Alemannic. "What 'tis you meant to ask?"

I indicated the margrave and her daughters. "The ladies are twins. As are Aifric and Esgwen. The two little ones as well? Are twins so common, here?"

A laugh escaped her. "All girls are twins in Caercoed. Saint Conbarre and Saint Sabh bestowed it on us."

"Twins as well."

"Naturally."

"Is your twin a captain also? Blessed with languages?"

She shook her head. "She's a disciple and sees to her market stall. Our husband keeps house and raises our girls."

I wanted to ask about that too, but Kiefan and Anders finished their training forms and began their sparring. M'lady Leix and some of the officers shouted out requests in specific swordsman's terms. The two men stripped off their surcotes, as the afternoon was growing warm, and faced off in their closer-fit, plain wool cotes. At first, neither used his speed Blessing and they merely showed off their swings and jabs and blocks. But then they shifted into a true blur and held it longer than I'd seen before. Wood cracked on wood, on flesh, and when they slipped out of speed both their chests heaved. They circled, guards high, and Anders lunged in to set them off again.

Leix leaned to the nearest of her officers to ask something; the woman only shook her head. The skirmish lapsed out of Blessing speed when Kiefan stumbled back from a hard jab to the shoulder, gritting his teeth. I didn't see the counter-strike, nobody did, but Anders' sword skittered away on the packed dirt and he shook his arm with a grimace.

"No need to truly disarm me," he said, loud enough to carry.

"M'lady, Captain?"

Tiarnan Gwatcyn stood in the kitchen door. He took a few steps toward us, fidgeting with his hands until he clasped them behind his back. The knee-length surcote he wore looked old-fashioned, to me, and the apron over it was streaked with flour. "Think you that they'll want some tea? Or perhaps ale? Once they end their… swordplay?" he asked.

"Mayhaps you should take a sword and try it yourself, m'lord. You're sure to know what they'll want then." Captain Mohra smiled, teasing.

Even the lightest touch of pink showed, on Tiarnan's pale face. But he was handsome enough, in his quiet way. "'Twould be foolishness, Captain. M'lady, would you care for tea?" That with a smile that had to fight its way out.

"Tea would be very kind of you," I said, managing a smile back. First knights and princes, now a margrave's son offering me tea. Stranger and stranger.

"Oh, 'tis no trouble. Not for a master of the healing arts."

"I'm hardly a master."

Tiarnan was quick to shake his head. "On such a journey through the Iawyr? When you faced lamia? I've mended but a few fevers, splinted a broken bone — I cannot imagine, m'lady. I would tremble in my boots."

"I did some of that myself."

"Surely you…" Tiarnan trailed off when he looked in the direction the captain jerked her chin. He closed his mouth, pressed it in a thin line.

Kiefan had the practice sword across his shoulders and gripped in both hands, using it to casually massage a muscle or two as he crossed the yard toward us. He didn't say a word, he merely took an extra step closer to Tiarnan to make it clear the margrave's son had to look up to meet the prince's gaze. Not a glare, not a twitch in Kiefan's face, but Tiarnan looked away quickly and retreated into the kitchen.

I didn't notice that until he was half gone, and felt a twinge of sympathy. "He was asking if we'd like some tea."

Kiefan stretched both arms up and back, sword for a spacer between his hands, and his joints crackled a bit when he let go, swung the wooden blade down. "Tea? Water would be enough."

Mohra chuckled and leaned close to my ear to whisper, in Englic, "Lucky girl, to draw that one's jealousy."

My mind stumbled over that. Kiefan said, "Pardon, Captain?"

"How does one train at such speeds?" she asked him, instead of answering. "And how long does a day's kir last, spending it on speed?"

"One trains at ordinary speeds and the mastery carries over. The second's for me to know and my enemies to fear."

I felt a tickle, a faint shiver in my kir, and I would have thought little of it if Kiefan and Captain Mohra had not both looked toward the gate with me. "Do you feel that?" I asked.

"Must be the Elect," Kiefan said.

"Yes, 'tis." The captain stood and called to m'lady Leix, then at an order trotted toward the gatehouse.

Anders wandered over to my bench as well. "What chance of getting a drink of water while they prepare, do you think?"

I chuckled as I got up. "If he hadn't been frightened off, we might've had some." I went to the kitchen door and leaned in.

Tiarnan looked up as he turned out a lump of dough from its rising bowl. The mass deflated as it landed. "M'lady?"

"Might we have some water, rather than tea?" The words were strange in my mouth, asking a gentle-born man for something so plain. But he obliged, and still had time to knead down his dough, return it to its rising, and join us in the gate-yard before the Elect arrived.

Four riders trotted in, but my eyes went to Elect Tannait the moment she was in view. She was a small woman, when she alit from the saddle, but she let her kir draw eyes and hold them. It was nothing so obvious, not the kir fount's glittering or glow, merely a warmth under my breastbone and an inability to overlook her. Master Parselev usually wrapped his kir away, and said it was a good trick to know when you wanted to go unnoticed.

She went first to Leix and Lorcana, accepted their bows and kiss of fealty on her hand. The Elect wore her hair loose and it shone steel-grey in the sun, but her face was ageless like my master's. She walked directly to the six of us next, not waiting for the margraves' introductions, and looked up at Kiefan with narrowed green eyes. She didn't say a word as she went to each of us.

I meant to look her in the eye, when my turn came, but kir moved, plucked mine in my chest and it answered like a bell. My breath caught. It bloomed white in my mind's eye, singing out a few clear, strong notes. The blossom subsided but the chord hung in the air. Elect Tannait could hear it, I didn't doubt, but nobody else seemed to. A tiny nod was all she gave me, and moved on.

I'd felt that once before. Elect Parselev had done it, bit his lower lip a moment, and said I would be his apprentice.

Ilya, last to be inspected and the most nervous of us, was the one she said something to. Captain Mohra stepped up quickly and translated, "She asks why you came here."

That bewildered the poor man. "I came to serve m'lord. M'lady."

Another question, which Mohra translated as, "'Twas your free will?"

"Of course, m'lady."

She asked the same of Ulf, who answered, "I was asked to lead m'lord through the mountains, and was honored to."

Boristan said, in turn, "The abbot told me Saint Qadeem wished me to keep a book of the mission, and I was honored to."

The Elect went to Anders next, and asked her question. "This sounded better than haying—"

A slender vine of green kir shot from the Elect's hand and cut him off with a firm grip on his jaw. Her eyes narrowed. I saw him swallow and look away from the elect's eyes.

"My saint ordered it."

She said, "You might have refused."

Anders stared into the distance and held his silence. She waited. Her grip on his jaw tightened. A wince twitched at the corner of his eye, but still he said nothing.

Tannait coiled her kir away and moved on to Kiefan. "It was my duty," he said.

She measured him for an extra moment, but did not ask about free will. Then it was my turn. "My master sent me," I answered, before she asked.

Her kir-vine grabbed my jaw, strong as any man's hand. I tensed — it was an honest answer, I knew. Tannait asked, in Arceal, "Why was it you?"

The answer bubbled up, called by her tight grip. For a moment, I hesitated, but saw no reason not to answer. "Master said it must be me."

Tannait nodded. "'Tis an interesting bouquet your saints send." She beckoned the margraves closer, to include them in what she said next. "'Tis the saints' business that brings us here. They have their own concerns and have made their own arrangements. 'Tis for us to manage the remainder. Questions on both sides, no doubt, that it falls to us to ask and answer. The first of these: how many elect does Wodenberg bring?"

Kiefan answered. "One."

That surprised her. "One? Not ten? How many Blessed?"

"All of us."

Tannait nodded. "I see. 'Tis a wager of a different sort. You bear the most of these — Blessings — what are they?"

"Anticipation, to know my enemy's attack before he swings. Speed, to strike before he does. And strength."

Her head cocked. "How strong?"

Kiefan took his practice sword in both hands — fine, strong oak, thick as my wrist — and snapped it like a twig. Then he took the two pieces in his hands and broke them together. They resisted only a heartbeat. The margraves' eyes went wide for a moment, then recovered.

Tannait only smiled. "Please, dear guests, continue your sparring for us. Leix, find us your best swords to join in. Do you have a Blessed in your guard? I trust these knights are too polite to embarrass them."

———————————×———————————

There were many questions over the next two days, as the Grain Moon waned. I was privy to some of the meetings, and some of them Kiefan told us about while we sat around the kitchen fire after dinner. The kitchen fell quiet after all was cleaned up, and the Gwatcyns withdrew with Elect Tannait to their private den and their own fireplace to share their own thoughts.

Little had been said, at home, about the state of Wodenberg's army after Ansehen. I knew we left a broad field covered in dead men, but it wasn't for a physician's apprentice to know what that meant. Killing Arcea's elect had cost the kingdom thousands of lives, none of them easily replaced. Arcea, though, was a vast empire with lakes of kir and a host of elect to channel it through. Their elect's last attack had destroyed much of the fortifications on Wodenberg's southern border and our first line of defense was little more than an inconvenience now, as the raiders at Gabel had proven.

We had a kingdom of Blessed, fearsome on the field, but only one elect — and him a healer.

Caercoed had held off Arcea's armies at the two southern mountain passes that bordered Suevia, and knew the empire's power well. They had fought the same kir-forged monsters that Arcea's saints produced. Caercoed understood, and they were even impressed that we had faced an even number of Arceal and won, however narrowly. Caercoed used its strategic advantage of the passes, its defensive engineers' wits, and its strong elect to win against Arcea's monsters.

"Our Trinity has kept to themselves, Elect Tannait said," Kiefan told us, swirling the brandy in his glass. "And being good neighbors, Caercoed's saints did not press the matter as there was little contact across the Eispitzen. Arcea conquered Suevia fifty years ago and then had to see to its own southern border. Now they are turning their eyes north again and seeing the kir founts in Wodenberg. Wanting them.

"Our weakness is how close the fount on Mount Woden is to our border. The battle at Ansehen weakened our southern army. Father sent orders to Duke Seagrace late in the Summer Moon: collect the northern reserves and come south. Progress reports have been good and they'll march from Rukharbor in the spring, soon as they can, but armies are slow. Even cavalry. Arcea will swarm the fallen wall and arrow for Wodenberg. Any aid Caercoed can give to slow them, or hamper the siege they will lay on the city…"

There were stories of Arcea's sieges on cities in Suevia. Terrible stories. We sat in silence after that.

Anders had gained a pair of demanding students of horsemanship, in the margraves' daughters, and excused himself to bed each night after a quick drink. Kiefan would excuse himself soon after, and if a headache was twisting its way into his skull he took my hand and kissed it. I would put my palm on his cheek for a moment, enough time to pinch out the tangles of kir before they tightened into knots.

Kiefan would smile, and that always made me smile. I went to bed warmed by a few sips of brandy and the feel of his lips on my hand.

CHAPTER 9

"Yes, needs must. 'Twill be a traditional Caer interrogation, as Dame Kate is a woman. No harm will come to her," m'lady Leix told Kiefan. "Most likely, we'll be home ere midnight. Needn't wait up."

He shot a troubled glance at me, mittened and cloaked and waiting at the great hall's door between Captain Mohra and Elect Tannait. "There's little Kate could tell you that I cannot, m'lady. Whatever this interrogation is —"

"—'tis not for boys," she told him, with a pointed look. "If you worry on trust, consider that I trust you in easy reach of my husband and children." Turning, she gestured me out the door.

I looked back to Kiefan to be sure, and he nodded. Horses waited outside, held by Anders rather than one of the stable-girls. He gave me a boost up that I didn't entirely need, and while pretending to check my stirrup he jammed a sheathed knife between my boot and calf. As if I could fend off all my escorts with it.

Still, he was sincere when he whispered, "Be careful."

We rode out of the gate and down into the town of Faen, on the shores of the lake they called Ty. The last gloaming shone on clouds' bellies and the first stars twinkled in the blackening blue. Even in the gathering dark, the Mother Tree glowed red, rising over Faen with her arms thrown wide. The ladies led me under her broad canopy, and a red leaf fell near my hand. I caught it, tucked it away with a glance at the heavy branch above.

The tavern's sign was a maple leaf and a golden crown. A girl took our horses and I followed Leix and Lorcana into the main room. The voices within paused a moment when the door let in a gust of chilly air, but then they recognized the margraves and welcomed us with a cheer and raised steins. A waitress put down her tray of drinks to take our cloaks, smiling and bobbing a curtsy.

Elect Tannait put her arm across my shoulders and announced something that got another cheer. Half a dozen guardswomen who'd been lounging with their boots on the largest table quickly cleared out. I looked to Captain Mohra for a translation as I was steered toward a chair.

"She only told them 'tis to be an interrogation. Don't get many, here. Don't worry, Dame Kate."

I landed in a chair at the table. The tavern was warm, well lit and full of smiles; it smelled of mutton soup and autumn ale. The waitresses wore knee-length gowns, woolen hose, and kept their necklines sensibly high. Despite what m'lady Leix had said earlier, a man brought out a pair of small glasses and a large bottle of clear liquid. He put one glass before the margrave as she sat opposite, one before me, and the bottle in the center of the round table. He spared me a kind smile through a close-cropped brown beard. The tavern's patrons settled down again, dragging tables and chairs to a polite distance to watch.

I thought it was m'lady Leix opposite me, and glanced to her twin to check. But they were dressed identically, down to their hair tied back in buns, and I couldn't be sure at first. Elect Tannait picked up the bottle from the center and pulled the stopper.

Captain Mohra pulled up a chair beside me to translate. "These are the rules: both sides drink, the subject answers a question. If 'tis a worthy answer, the subject may ask a question."

The elect filled both glasses and stoppered the bottle. "What sort of questions?" I asked the captain.

She nodded to my shot. "Drink and see."

It was cool in my hand and smelled like the triply-distilled spirits Master Parselev bought from a Russe merchantman and tucked away on a shelf in his office. The margrave — I matched the streak of grey by her ear to Leix's face, thanks to my Blessing — drank hers in one swallow.

Pressure touched my temples again and I glanced at the elect. She raised an eyebrow. Her kir-vine turned my head toward the glass. Our audience chanted one word, low and growing, that didn't need translating. The shot bumped against my lips and I drank. The stuff seared my throat.

M'lady Leix asked, in Arceal, "Surely you're not the sole apprentice in Wodenberg. Or your master the sole physician. How 'tis that he sent you, rather than one of them?"

One glass of the spirit felt like a whole stein of ale at once. It didn't give me the answer, though. "He said only that it must be me, m'lady. Nothing else. Even my saint, when they saw us off, said nothing of why. Only that he believed I wouldn't fail." The memory of Saint Qadeem's dark eyes was a sudden weight on my shoulders. He expected me to succeed. I hadn't even known what to succeed at.

"And you did not fail."

"I failed when the lamia ambushed us. I ran, and Bjorn died for defending me."

"Still, you've given a good answer. Ask your question," Leix said.

"About what?" I looked to Captain Mohra, who'd been handed a stein of ale by a waitress.

"Anything," she answered.

I thought I'd hold them to that. "Why did you want to question me alone?"

"Needs must have the truth of your menfolk's ways," m'lady Leix answered, as if it were a simple thing.

Elect Tannait filled our glasses again. M'lady drank hers without hesitating. I looked at the glass, wondering what they'd ask next. The pressure returned to my temples, prodding me, and I drank.

"If 'tis right, I ken you're sixteen now, Dame Kate, and were fourteen when your father wished you wed. How 'tis your father didn't wish you the honor of apprenticing to your kingdom's only elect?"

Father had told me why, at the top of his lungs, when the piglet died. "He wanted me safe." It made my throat thicken, to remember that fight. He'd thought I'd murdered the piglet, at first. "He was right, I suppose. Nothing safe in crossing the Eispitzen."

That got a murmur of agreement from the audience when Captain Mohra translated. Leix said, "Ask your question."

A glow was creeping into my chest, and it wasn't kir. "Would it be different, were I Caer?"

"Most certainly. 'Twould be an honor for any daughter to be apprenticed of an elect. At any age. If Aed said aught 'gainst it, I'd consider, but…" m'lady Leix shook her head.

"A father's will means nothing?"

It was a second question, but she answered while the Elect poured. "Fathers are for kisses and sweets. The mother who bore you knows the truth of life." Leix picked up her shot for a toast in Caer, then repeated it for me in Arceal. "To hearth and home and the boys who keep them warm."

That sounded nice enough, I had to admit, and toasted along with the guards.

Her next question was, "This husband you'd have had — 'twould have allowed you to study?"

I had seen it happen often enough with other apprentices to answer. "Perhaps. I might have gotten another year before falling pregnant." My fluxes hadn't come until I was nearly fifteen. "After that, what time is there? Half Mother's luck, in being a midwife, was having an eldest daughter at home while she was seeing to deliveries."

M'lady beckoned for more. "I'm only a peasant girl. Gentle-born wives may study more, if there's a wetnurse for their babies. Servants to cook dinner." Thinking of the morning in the Chapel, I mused, "The king may have knighted me, but I've little to my name but my Blessing."

She was nodding now. "You play this game well, Kate. Ask your question."

"Husbands, in Caercoed," I began, and had to think a moment. The question slipped away in the warm haze, then circled back. "Whose husband is m'lord Aed?"

A grin. There was a bit of pink on m'lady's cheeks, perhaps from the drink, perhaps not. "Why, 'tis our husband. We courted him, each in our way, we came to love him, we married him. 'Tisn't always thus. Had we not agreed, one of us might've taken him as consort instead."

"Consort? Leaving one sister unwed? How…?"

"Our brother Oisin is a consort. Crown Ceelin's very fond of him, and he's given her fine princesses. Crown Ciara's kind, but isn't so inclined. She has her own lovers."

Elect Tannait unstoppered the bottle for a fourth time, held it up and began to sing. The audience immediately joined in, leaping up from their chairs to dance in time with the rollicking tune. Captain Mohra swept me up by the elbow and I was spinning, tripping, trying to regain my feet. She didn't let me fall. I went on a complete circuit of the table and I had almost caught up as the song drew to a finish. The last note was held a long time, with laughter, and then I had only a moment's glimpsed warning before she leaned over and kissed me.

Not a chaste kiss.

And she deposited me in the chair again, my knees gone wobbly. The Caers all picked up their steins and cheered, then drank. My glass was full again and m'lady... I tipped my head, frowning. She was picking up her glass, raising it to me, and then drinking.

Kir-vines nudged me, pulling my eyes to the Elect. Drink. The glowing green kir sprouting from her hand unsettled my stomach a moment but I was playing the game well, Leix said. I couldn't be harming the mission. I emptied the glass.

"You're peasant-born, Dame Kate — we have none, in Caercoed, but 'tis common in Suevia. Arcea keeps slaves. What means it in Wodenberg?"

"I must obey my lord," I said. She beckoned for more. "Whatever my lord commands, unless it goes against a greater lord, I must obey. My father obeyed Duke Seagrace and came to Wodenberg as part of his retinue. He helped build m'lord's manor in the city, helped furnish it. Father was a master carpenter, and m'lord was pleased with his work." That gave me some pride. Father had always been proud of it.

Then I realized Captain Mohra was translating, as I'd lapsed into Alemannic. "Your pardon, m'lady," I said, my face catching fire. "I forgot myself."

"'Tis no concern," Leix said. "Should m'lord order you to his bed, must you obey?"

That made me blink. I'd never so much as met Duke Seagrace. "M'lord?"

"Your Prince Kiefan, say."

Though my face still burned, a shiver ran down my spine at the thought. The kiss Mohra had given me, from Kiefan...? My pulse rose.

Beside me, she chuckled and leaned toward one of the guardswomen to whisper something. The other grinned, a wicked glint in her eye, and agreed.

I found the answer, while part of my mind was still caught on kisses. "The Mother's discipline binds us, m'lady. No lord should ask, and any maiden should refuse. But m'lord might bargain with her father. Contribute to her dowry, to maintain her marriage-worth after. Any good man would do so."

A hush had fallen on the room when I finished. "Would you be weddable?" Leix asked.

"Most any girl is. It's only a question of who. But Father is dead, and I'm a Physician now." I sat straighter in my chair. "I have my virtue and I'm still weddable even without that damn piglet."

"You certainly are."

Elect Tannait poured me another drink as I leaned back in the chair. I watched the clear spirit splash out, thinking of the kir fount and its glow, how its sparkle cut the light into rainbows. Captain Mohra handed her empty stein to a waitress and declined a fresh one. My lips still felt that kiss, as did my tongue.

"Why did you kiss me?" I asked.

She smiled. "'Tis what you do at the end of the song. Want another?"

My face had only just cooled and it heated back up. "I only ask because it was so... different."

"Never been kissed, even?" Apparently, that was amazing. "I'm glad I fixed that, then."

"I kissed Harold, once," I said in my own defense. "He stole one. I let him."

"If you get through this and the next, we'll sing again." She smirked and indicated my full glass. I turned back to it and I was listing. Or else the table was. Gripping the rim in both hands, I straightened us both.

"You're doing very well, Kate," M'lady... she didn't have the grey streak by her ear. M'lady Lorcana said. She held up her glass. "You're being a great help."

She drank, so I had to. I could barely taste it anymore.

"Five days you've been our guest now. Do you think a wedding 'twixt Caercoed and Wodenberg could be happy? Could your Prince Kiefan wed one of ours?"

I leaned back in my chair again. Five days. I had watched m'lord Aed and Tiarnan run their house and kitchen, precise in their expectations but kind when need be. Never had I eaten so well or so much. My shift was getting snug. A chuckle burbled up out of my warm glow, jiggled me in my seat. "Don't expect him to cook, m'ladies," I managed to say.

They chuckled, and there were some comments in Caer and laughs.

"What?" I asked, looking toward one of the speakers. "What?"

Captain Mohra told me, "Only that they'd be willing to cook, if one of those knights waited in bed."

"Dame Kate." Lorcana pushed through the mirth. "Do you think the Caer too different, too... wild, to be wives? In Wodenberg."

"Wild?" I echoed.

"Some have said that."

I looked to the uniformed guards again, their boots on the tables, not minding that their braies showed where their hose ended. That they wore braies at all would be odd, in Wodenberg. "Saint Woden does claim some women for knights, m'lady. The captain of the King's Guard is Dame Aleksandra — I haven't heard her family name. Ask Kiefan, he told us that she squired him. And that no man can question her courage."

We didn't drink again, but we sang the song in any case. I tried to get out of my chair for the dance, but fell against the table and Mohra caught me. She put me back in the chair and kissed me again at the end. Then she helped me out to a horse and into the saddle, and rode close beside me while the margraves spoke with Elect Tannait.

I hadn't realized that saddles were so slippery. The captain had to keep a grip on my arm.

The guards at the gate welcomed us back. My eyes hung half-shut, by then, and it was a good thing my horse stopped along with the others. I leaned on Mohra; she was solid and warm.

"Catch her?" she asked, and I blinked as she slid away. I flailed but fell only a little, into a pair of strong arms. The stirrups caught on my feet and I kicked at them.

"Hold still," Anders told me, shifting me higher on his shoulder, and the stirrups were pulled off my boots. "You have the horses, Tana? Doesn't look like this one should try walking."

"I can walk," I protested, swinging my feet down to try it. A few steps went well enough, but then one foot tripped on the other and Anders caught me.

As he half-carried me, by the arm and waist, toward my room Anders told me, "My little sister came home this drunk, once. I helped her sneak in, but then she threw up. Feeling anything like that?"

"I feel great," I said, lolling against his shoulder. "I'm supposed to sneak? I don't think we're sneaking."

"Well, nobody here can thrash us for getting drunk. No need to sneak."

My room was at the top of the stairs, at the beginning of the hall. The sight of my bed made me tired. "I've never been so drunk. Didn't even mind when Mohra kissed me."

"I'm sorry I missed that." The lamp in the hall cast a slice of warm light through my room, enough to stand in while Anders pulled back the covers.

I caught myself leaning too far and stumbled against the wall. Bed seemed like an eminently sensible idea, suddenly. "You're right, I should go to bed. But I should tell Kiefan what happened."

"You can tell him in the morning." Anders held out a hand. "Get some sleep first."

His hand was strong and warm when I took it, used it to steady myself as I crossed the floor. Then I remembered, "I should take my dress off," and started to pull my hems up.

"Don't worry about that now," he told me. "You're tired. Get in bed."

It was a nice, warm bed. M'lord Aed had laid on plenty of quilts and wooly blankets. The straw stuffing was fresh, I could tell by the scent when I fell onto it. I started to climb in and realized my boots were on. And what was stuck in my boot. "Your knife," I said, and lifted my leg up to get it.

Anders intercepted my hand, took the little knife, tugged my foot down and pulled my skirts back over my bare knees. "Got it. And your boots."

He untied them and loosened the laces. Nobody ever took my boots off for me, before. "You see? Like I said, you can be kind. Without all that foolishness."

Anders' voice dropped. "You're not making it easy."

From the door, Kiefan said, "I'll make it easy for you." He leaned against the sill, partly blocking the lamplight, arms crossed over the silhouetted moon on his chest. "You keep your hands where I can see them."

My boots slid off, one at a time. "And what's it to you, where my hands are?" Anders asked. "You can't be jealous of how quickly I got into her skirts. Unless…" He trailed off as he stood. I pulled my feet up before they got cold, and grabbed at the covers. "Unless you want her."

"Leave her alone. And go."

Anders stepped past him through the doorway, trading glare for glare. Kiefan put his hand on the latch and drew the door shut as he went, lip pulled under his teeth as he looked back at me.

"The Crowns' courier did bring word from Castle Adhalon," Leix told us. "She winters there, at Arforddinas."

She put her finger on the map spread on the table, on the coastal city nearest the southern tip of Caercoed. Below Arforddinas, the mountains and then Suevia. Kiefan had laid out our map of Wodenberg so that the Eispitzen overlapped Caercoed's Iawyr — as the two lines of mountains were one and the same. The margraves' town of Faen lay nearly due east of Vorspitz.

"They reaffirm 'tis my judgment where Tadhlon's forces march in the spring. I did neglect to tell you our brother Oisin is Crown Consort. When they were but princesses, the Crowns were as our younger sisters."

Leix had brought us all to this office, even Ilya and Ulf, who'd been working as handymen to keep busy. Ther Boristan sat scribing in his book, as he had at all the meetings, and m'lady Lorcana did the same. I stood by the table with hands clasped, not sure what my part was, studying the Caercoed map and trying to work out the place names through the fancy script. The pounding in my head had eased a bit after a trencher of eggs and three cups of tea, but it was still hard to focus.

"The Crowns don't wish to meet?" Kiefan asked.

She shook her head. "Winter Court is hip-deep in plots and intrigue. To toss you in would be less than kind. Fortunate for Wodenberg, then, that Dame Kate answered so well last night and I'm partial to killing monsters. Are we to cross through your pass, Prince Kiefan? 'Twill be dangerous, come spring. Avalanches."

"There's a smuggler's trail," Kiefan said, pointing out the very southeastern corner of Wodenberg. "Our border here is steep hills, and guarded. If you push through your southern pass early and hook north, it will get you to Wodenberg. Though the danger may be equal. I'll write you a letter of introduction and give you some names — which must be guarded closely." He paused until Leix nodded in agreement. "My mother the Queen is Suevi, the last of their royal blood after Arcea's slaughter. There are those who will help, in Suevia, but they do it at peril of their lives."

"Why a letter of introduction? Come yourself. Be welcome to winter here."

"We leave soon as we can," Kiefan said, which caught everyone's ear.

A shiver shot down my spine, the echo of far too many days in that snow.

"The Grain Moon's waning fast, m'lord," Boristan said.

"All the more reason. The Leaf Moon won't be any warmer on Starknadel. The word must get to Baron Eismann and Margrave Schutze to redistribute their reserves. And to watch the smuggler's trail for your soldiers. They can see you safely over, if need be." Kiefan paused a moment. "And I must take the word to my father."

Leix pointed out, "'Twould be a pleasant surprise, riding to your city's relief with Caer knights."

I was only across the table, and I barely heard Kiefan murmur, "Father hates surprises." Louder, "I'm honored by your offer of hospitality, m'lady, but I must go."

Her grimace seemed honest enough. Leix exchanged a worried look with her sister. "'Tis only the marriage to discuss, then. The Crowns have their consort and their heirs. The princesses are too young for such things, but there's others. Duchesses of age."

"I'm sure a suitable marriage will be the simplest of the matters," Kiefan said.

"We'll speak more on it in the spring. At your feast table." Leix smiled.

CHAPTER 10

Leave-taking needed another day of preparation. I'd recharged my blood-stops and cleansers; Ulf and Ilya had done the same with the warming charms. Puck and Acorn had enjoyed their week's sleep and good grazing, Anders reported.

Not even the autumn Equinox could keep Kiefan from beginning the trip home. The Gwatcyn's gate-yard was decked with banners for tomorrow's festival and the kitchen ran full tilt baking and roasting. We were squeezed down to a cluster around the end of one table to drink our brandy, that final evening.

Still, we had that chance to clear out our few grievances, as one ought to at Equinox. When light and dark balanced, one should balance one's accounts with the community. But most of our personal accounts waited at home; the mountain pass had bound us in close camaraderie, and we easily said all we needed to say. Quiet followed.

I only sipped my brandy, still wary after the interrogation's headache. Kiefan sat at the table end closest to the fire, writing on a sheet of fine linen paper. We watched him finish with his signature. "This is for my father," he said, folding it. "Should anything happen, it's this bag that must be put in my father's hands." It was a plain enough leather shoulder bag. Kiefan added the letter to its contents. "It's all here: Ther Boristan's book, letters from the Crowns and the margraves, a draft of the treaty. The list of marriage prospects. All of it."

"It's true, then? You'll have to marry one of these — ladies?" Ulf asked.

Kiefan buckled the bag's flap tightly. "It's hardly a matter of wanting." Bringing it with him, he joined us at the hearth and reclaimed the glass of brandy he'd left on the mantle. He took a deep breath of its fumes, then sipped.

"They're good enough shots with a bow, m'lord, and their crossbows are impressive. M'ladies have been fine hostesses and I'd be glad enough to visit. But these brassy girls for wives?"

I had seen Ther Boristan's diagrams of the crossbows in his book. Ulf said they were powerful, and that was enough explanation for me.

"It's hardly a sacrifice, in comparison to what I asked of those who followed my charge at Ansehen," Kiefan replied. Sadness lingered around his mouth. "I only ask my marriage be peaceful. Mother Love knows that's eluded the king and queen."

Ilya spoke up in the quiet that followed. "They weren't always so angry. It was your brothers dying that drove them apart."

Ulf said, "We all grieved for the little princes, m'lord."

My eyes wandered to Anders, but he only studied his brandy. Even if it were true that he was the king's bastard son, it was hardly his fault. He'd had no say in the matter.

"We've an early morning," Kiefan said to break the silence. "Thank the Mother for your warm bed, tonight." As the other four made agreeing noises, he turned to me. "Kate?"

I let him take my hand and kiss it. When I put my hand to his cheek and called up my kir, I didn't see any tangles in him. "You've a headache? I don't see any…"

He put his hand over mine, pressed it with his eyes shut. "I wanted your touch."

The melancholy in his voice pinched my heart. "You only have to ask," I murmured.

Kiefan's fingers combed into my loose hair and drew me into a kiss, gentle and chaste but slow to part. I confess I tensed in surprise, held my breath. But my heart pounded.

"I didn't want to risk Starknadel without having done that," he whispered, near my lips. When my eyes opened, there was a faint smile on him.

The margrave's question flashed through my memory. Should m'lord order you to his bed — as if he would need to order, after the hours we'd spent studying d'Ovio Alain's dialogues together. My hand, which had fallen to his shoulder, trembled and I took it back. I knew what happened to girls with neither dowry nor virtue, despite my spirit-bolstered claim during the interrogation.

"M'lord, you know Father Duty's teachings," Ther Boristan said, perhaps a bit louder than need be. "A moment's fun is a poor trade for a lifetime's happiness. Not only yours — hers."

I looked, and they were all watching. Boristan frowned, Ulf seemed amused, Ilya's mouth was pursed and uncertain. Anders merely drained his glass of brandy and said, "I'm off to enjoy that warm bed."

"It's only a good-night kiss, Ther," Kiefan said, letting me go. To me, warmly, "Good night."

And he melted me all over again. I wanted another kiss, I wanted his arms around me. They thought the Caer were brassy? I was only a peasant girl, but dared to moon over a prince.

I murmured, "Good night. M'lord."

Next evening, though, I put the lesson Captain Mohra had given me to good use. And I did surprise him, though only for a moment and then his tongue was quite able to match mine. My skin throbbed where his hands had landed on my waist; I felt the pressure even through my layered boy's cotes. He'd seen me to the little lean-to I shared with the captain and another Caer, and they were waiting back at the campfire. I'd taken my leave a little early in hopes of precisely this moment of privacy.

"Good night," Kiefan murmured, lingering at close range for a tantalizing moment.

I hadn't realized my hands were trembling until his found them, squeezed them. That gave him pause, and I took the chance to try to swallow the tightness in my throat.

"I don't mean to frighten you," he whispered, shifting away.

The truth spilled out of me. "I'm frightened of myself."

Kiefan squeezed my hands again as he took a full step back. His mouth pulled to the side and he wanted to say something more, I was sure, but he slipped away instead. He left me alone with wild daydreams to dispel as best I could.

Captain Mohra saw us up the hill as far as the frozen spring, two easy days on horseback with her squad cooking and setting up shelter for us. Frost sparkled every morning on the leaf-littered ground. The trees' flame-painted cloaks thinned.

Two days without another good-night kiss. My blood cooled a little, aided by a conveniently timed lecture Ther Boristan gave on Father Duty's lessons of discipline. I read a little more of my master's book and Kiefan helped translate, both of us on best behavior.

A mushy crust of snow had reached the bottom of the cliff face, and thickened as we rode up to the spring. At the top, the spring took some finding, lost as it was under snow and too frozen to flow anymore. I recognized the rocks near it. Captain Mohra doubted me, at first, for the scattered rubble all looked much the same.

"You remember the rocks?" Kiefan asked, a bit puzzled as well.

"When Ulf called us down, we stopped at the edge here," I said. Checking my memory, I pointed to two boulders that seemed to have noses and eyebrows. "Those didn't have any snow on them. There was a blue jay on the taller one." The bright flash of feathers had caught my eye.

He tipped his head now, curious. "What else do you remember?"

I checked my memory again. "Your cloak was sodden about a handspan from the hem. When you took a handful of water and drank, you noticed how thick the stubble on your chin was. Then Puck nosed you aside to get some water himself."

"I hadn't known you saw so much detail."

"I remember everything I see," I said. It was simple as that.

"And smell? Feel?"

"Yes."

Kiefan paused a moment. Voices called us to dinner at the campfire, and we started across the gravelly snow. "So when you cut off Adalrich's foot, you remember…"

"Everything, yes."

"What he said?"

"Why wouldn't I?"

"It sounded like what people say when they've forgotten," Kiefan said. "You remember taking — an axe?"

"Saw. Master Parselev had cut much of the flesh off, but then Sir Adalrich punched our orderly, put him down hard. Master had to help keep him on the table. I was the last free pair of hands. Fortunate that I'm a carpenter's daughter." I thought it amusing enough for a smile, but the prince looked a little pale.

"I still have nightmares of the charge, and it's only a handful of clear moments when I try to think of it. I doubt I could stand to have anything more," he said.

"My memories can be put away," I told him. "Like folded blankets. But I do have nightmares, now and then."

In the morning, we left the Caers to strike their camp and continued up the snowy slope. Ulf led, somehow finding the trail through ankle-deep snow — I knew it was the same we'd come down by, largely — and I fell into a dogged rhythm with my feet.

The first snowstorm hit us that afternoon.

We lost three days to storms, and hours to passing squalls. I only noticed the wind when it eddied for a moment, dropped enough that when it rose again it was a fresh knife across my face. My nose bled as I gasped for air, and froze more than clotted. We all coughed and panted and slogged as best we could through thigh-deep snow.

Kiefan helped me wash the blood from my face, using his bare hands to melt the snow. Then a kiss, just a quick, chaste one. I stared at him a moment, but he only nodded and said, "Good night."

Once we were up on the shoulder ledge again, against the stone face, Kiefan broke the path for us. I followed, leading Puck, and Anders behind me with Acorn. Ulf and Ilya took turns half-carrying Ther Boristan at the rear.

The nights were dark and frigid, and all seven Flock moons could not provide much light while the Shepherd waned to a sliver. Every night, we bundled up together with a heating charm in the blankets at our feet. I did what I could to clear the congestion, ease the head-aches, spending all my kir and whatever Ilya could give me through his charm-hand Blessing. I got a little good-night kiss each evening, but exhaustion kept them brief. We didn't have flasks of kir to ease the journey, this time, though the Caer did give us what extra charms they could.

"To think the saints chose us for this," Ther Boristan said. The wind screamed, thumping the tarps against our bodies, and horizontal snow poured by our windbreak. "I thought them kind. Saints Aleksandr and Qadeem, that is. Saint Woden always seemed a stern master, to me."

Anders snorted, which started his cough.

"He is," Kiefan said for him. "Are they kind, then? The others?"

"You've a strength Blessing, m'lord, that's a claim by Saint Aleksandr," Boristan said.

"Not in my case. And here, not strong enough even with the Blessing."

"Nobody could ask you to be stronger," Boristan said, but at that Kiefan laughed until he coughed.

When he got his voice back, he said, "You haven't met my father? Was a time I thought he and Saint Woden agreed beforehand which Blessings I'd get. They have me so well cor-ralled."

Ther seemed puzzled to have to explain. "No, the saints make their own choices. They know which Blessings fit you best."

Another harsh laugh. "I studied, when I learned about the Blessings, I read every book I could lay hands on. I learned Russe and Arceal and asked Mother to teach me Suevi. Believ-ing that if I was ready, if I was smart enough..." Kiefan trailed off, clamping his mouth shut. "Child's dreams," he said. "Nothing more. Born yoked to the plow, so best to put my shoul-der to it."

He said no more and after a time the conversation turned to home. The storm blew itself through the pass late in the day and we dug ourselves out as best we could with our two shov-els. Blinding sun beat on the fresh snow for a short time before the shadows gathered. We ate a cool dinner of Caer trail bread, full of walnuts and bits of dried apple.

When I got my kiss good-night, I whispered, "You wanted Saint Qadeem to choose you."

He hesitated; it was something of a blasphemy. But Boristan's even wheezing marked that he'd dozed off, and Ilya's snore was unmistakable. The rest likely couldn't hear. "Yes. I wanted it even more, after. I hardly saw a book for all the sword training and jousting. Even asked —" Kiefan's voice dropped further, though I was huddled close. "I asked him why."

"You questioned Saint Woden?" I nearly tripped over the words in surprise.

"No — Mother have mercy!" He chuckled, and coughed a little. "I asked Saint Qadeem."

"What did he say?"

"That four Blessings would have been too much." Kiefan was lost in the memory, for a moment. "Said he would've been proud to have me. It was kind of him, I suppose."

"Saint Qadeem doesn't say things idly, Master Parselev told me."

Kiefan's mouth twitched to one side. "Still, if I'd been Blessed with memory, or with master-craft, or even just craft-handed, as Ther Boristan is, I would be better for it, I think."

It seemed a strange thing to say. "You hate the sword?"

"No. There's a grace, when my kir melds the speed and anticipation to the strength and the flow of it — but since I woke from my Blessing and found the sword was my destiny, there's not been one day I'd want to treasure."

That saddened me. Since my Blessing, studying at the Order had changed my entire world. They sent me home a few times a year and I was ashamed at how my feet dragged on leaving and flew in returning. My parents' little hut, which had been so cozy and safe, now reminded me of the hungry winters and threadbare clothes when there'd been little work for my father. "I wished for the heat-sight Blessing," I admitted, "when I was little. I thought I'd be a better cook with it. But now I wouldn't want anything but memory."

"If you'd gotten any other Blessing, I'd never have met you," he said. "Perhaps I'll have to admit to my headaches, if it's you who heals them."

My heart quivered in my chest, at that. "I might not see you again, otherwise."

"You'll see me again," Kiefan murmured, sounding half-asleep.

I wasn't so sure, and the more I thought on it as he drifted off, the more I doubted it. The ache of that kept me awake.

CHAPTER 11

The second day after, we stopped early to set up camp and all grinned as we did it. Ilya trotted off as fast as his coughing let him while Ulf unloaded the tarps and Anders found a place to tether the ponies.

Under the snow, the lumps around us were juniper and stunted spruces. The branches Ilya found were wet, but Boristan had enough kir for a fire-spark. "At least I can be some use," he said with a smile, stoking the flames carefully with grass and leaves. The branches caught slowly, smoking. Boristan coughed and had to turn away. "May not be cooking with this soon," he managed to add.

"Smoke is what we need," Kiefan said, watching the column rise off the little fire. The sky was clear, for now. "Smoke for a hawk-eye in Vorspitz to spot."

It was enough to melt some snow, bring it to boil and make some tea. Boristan was too weak to do more than manage the fire; I took the big skillet and cut up some potatoes to fry with a bit of ham. Below us, the forest rose up and blocked much of the view, but in the purple distance I could see Wodenberg's western mountains. The afternoon sun settled itself behind them as I cooked. I thought I saw a silver curve of the Neva River, out there.

Home. My eyes misted and I had to put the pan down to wipe them.

Dinner was simple but heavenly. The men praised my cooking until I laughed myself into a coughing fit. Since we ate early, I had enough light to clean the pan by, and stood wiping it dry at the fire while Ilya told us about his young daughter's coming birthday.

I saw Ulf cock his head, and both the ponies look up from grazing on tough mountain grass. "Bring them in! Close to the fire!" He scrambled toward the leads, tied to a stubby spruce tree.

Boristan, energized by the meal, hauled himself up to help. "I'll get Acorn."

Anders got up too. "Don't strain —"

Ragged snarls tore into camp and the ponies squealed. Dark forms streaked by and two hit Boristan full on. A glimpse of sword and shouting and the pain of the skillet hitting my foot knocked me back to sense. Screaming, and not just mine. Boristan's feet, kicking, dragged through the snow away from me and I leaped on them. I caught one ankle in both hands and threw my weight against it.

Two lamia had him, one per arm, shaking him, blood spraying, as he shrieked. One beast planted its paws and pulled. The other lunged at me and I let go on reflex, threw myself back from its yellowed fangs with a scream.

The lamia burst in half, innards spilling free; the second stumbled from the sudden freedom and then ran with its prize as if Boristan weighed nothing. I fell backward, through the campfire. Kiefan slipped from Blessing speed for half a second to keep from tripping on the monster he'd killed and was struck from behind, thrown down. That one didn't stop, it ran over him and caught Boristan's thrashing ankle, helped its pack-mate drag.

Ilya caught me, pulled me clear of the flames before my woolens caught. He hollered and I heard teeth snap. Then Kiefan was there, between us and two more lamia, bloody sword ready. Boristan's wails, fading with distance, spiked to a ragged scream that faltered and choked into horrible silence.

"Behind us, m'lord!"

Kiefan spared a glance over his shoulder and I looked too. Three more circled, across the fire. Their spiny hackles flexing, ratty tails lashing, they paced to and fro, eyes fixed on me and Ilya.

I gasped, "Where're the ponies? Anders and Ulf?" No sign of them but churned snow and the ends of broken leads on the spruce.

One lamia lunged, teeth snapping, but danced back quickly when Kiefan swung around the fire. Ilya had his dagger out and shifted up to his feet. His hands shook, but he pointed the blade toward the monsters. My chest heaving, head spinning, I fumbled for my own knife and clenched my hand on it. Useless, to me, but it was something.

It dragged into an impasse. The lamia circled us, teeth bared. One tried a dash at Ilya but Kiefan swooped around in a blur and the beast's ear went flying as it tried to dodge. With a squeal it fell back. Then another feinted on the other side and Kiefan was there too.

My breath slowed enough that I swallowed and said, "They mean to wear you down."

"It'll take longer than they think," Kiefan growled, loud enough to tell them all.

Five lamia pinned us down at the fire. The shadows deepened. They darted at Ilya, at me, to make Kiefan spend his kir. Over and over. One got too bold and took a slash across the shoulder. It hobbled into the dark and five became four. But they kept at it.

We heard a shout and an arrow took one beast through the neck. The rest scattered, snarling, and Kiefan rallied with a yell. He wasn't using speed anymore, but they kept well clear of his sword as they fled. Kiefan chased them only a few steps and stopped, swaying on his feet.

Puck's eyes showed whites as he followed Ulf toward the fire; the pony's lead was tied to his belt. A few steps behind, Anders trotted across the clearing and turned to check behind them. Every line on him showed fatigue, the same as Kiefan. Worn down.

I saw the lamia charge from the brush and screamed, throat ragged. Anders' sword spitted one and its impact knocked him down. A second's teeth flashed. Third lamia leaped from the shadows to join in. Kiefan raced across the gap, roaring fury, and the third one kept running. The second broke off and fled too, before our prince's blade was in range.

Ilya rushed to help. I untied Puck from Ulf so he could circle the campfire, arrow nocked and ready. His quiver was half empty, I glimpsed. "Shot that many of them? How many are there?"

His jaw was clenched grimly. "Not all hits. Lamia know about bows."

Ilya put Anders down by the fire and he toppled onto his back, coughing fit to bring a lung up. Blood streaked his sleeve. The boiled leather breastplate had split in two places, at the shoulder, from a pair of punctures.

"He's bleeding," Ilya told me. "His shoulder."

Passing him Puck's reins, I opened my medicine bag. While I knelt beside him, Anders levered himself into sitting up and the effort set him coughing again. His breastplate had stymied half the bite; the other two fangs had torn his left shoulder. I took a blood-stop charm and squeezed it over the wound. The kir unfolded and did its work.

Then I got his cloak off and pulled his cotes aside to see to the rest, as blood-stops did only one thing. I cleansed the bite and asked, "Who else is hurt?"

Kiefan turned toward the fire and I saw his breastplate was gouged with parallel claw stripes. "None of this blood's mine."

Ulf said, "Nothing that needs kir, on me. Just a bandage or two."

"Ilya, give me your kir so I can clear his lungs too," I said, reaching.

"Wait!" Kiefan looked to Ulf. "They're not singing. Will they attack again? How many are left?"

Ulf grimaced. It was true, the lamia weren't singing. "They might. Lamia sing when the hunt's done. As for how many — I wouldn't guess, m'lord. Sometimes we see a dozen at once, but there always seem to be more. We come up here to kill what we can when they get too bold, and we retreat before we lose anybody."

"Save the kir. If they return, I'll need it." Kiefan heaved a sigh. "They've tapped me out."

Anders only twitched a little when I hooked my needle into his flesh. The gashes needed a few stitches of catgut to close them. As I sewed, Ilya asked, "What happened to Acorn?"

I felt Anders tense under my hands. "They hamstrung him. Went for his belly. I cut his throat myself — I wouldn't see an animal eaten alive like that. Let alone a friend." His voice was rough, and he coughed to clear his throat.

"Half our supplies gone," Kiefan muttered.

"Only two days to Vorspitz," Ulf said. "Day and a half if we push hard. If they push hard to reach the fount, perhaps we'll meet them sooner."

Kiefan considered the campfire. "Will they push hard?"

"No secret the lamia will try for weak prey. Especially weak men."

I cut my thread free and Anders sidled his torn cotes back onto his shoulder. Reaching under both layers, I laid my hand on his sweat-slicked chest. "Hope I'm not cold," I murmured, near his ear, and he tried to chuckle. When I called up my kir to clear his lungs, he leaned back against me with a sigh. His kir was tapped out, too, by how little of an answering echo I felt. It took three hard heaves to cough out all his phlegm into the snow, and a little blood came too.

"They took our weakest," Kiefan said, and tensed, spotting something in the darkness. "They're watching still."

"Weakest are taken first." Ulf turned to check on what Kiefan had seen. "Two of them there, yes. It's happened before, to other hunting parties. They whittle away till the strongest is exhausted. Alone. Sometimes that one makes it home, though."

Kiefan's hand went to the leather bag of documents he wore opposite his sword.

I'd never been awake, before, when my day's kir came. At midnight the lamia circled our camp, eyes reflecting the moons and the dim coals the fire had fallen to. Kiefan circled opposite them. Anders and Ulf switched off in joining him. Ilya and I leaned back to back, loosely wrapped in bedrolls, and tried to doze. The lamia would mock-charge, snarling and snapping, just enough to frighten Puck and jolt us all awake. Then they would peel off and meld with the blue snow-shadows.

The day's ration of kir blossomed in my chest, refreshing as a whiff of baking bread to the hungry. We all straightened, we all sighed.

"The saints are with us," Ilya said.

Ulf wasn't as impressed. "With us themselves would be a greater help."

"We're given Blessings to endure trials like these." Kiefan shot a stern glare across the fire at Ulf. "Don't ask Saint Woden to give quarter. He will not."

"As well he's not my saint, then," Ulf returned. "Any who'd care to lend their hand would be welcome, now."

We all glanced up at the cloudy sky, knowing the tales of saints dropping in unexpected. But there was nothing to see.

I caught what sleep I could, the rest of the night. When I saw the Shepherd rising, a thick rind and well before dawn, it confirmed that we'd been gone all the Grain Moon and four days into the Leaf Moon already. I dozed again, longer this time, and woke when Ilya moved to get up. Dawn caught on high, feathery clouds over us. Anders and Ulf stood watch and Kiefan slept, finally, by the fire. The lamia had melted away sometime after moonrise.

Ilya and I packed up what there was of the camp, quietly as we could though Kiefan slept sound as the dead. Anders woke him with a shake, and slipped back Blessing-fast when Kiefan's sword shot up.

"We'll make the fount by noon," Ulf said. "We should skirt it, keep going."

Kiefan still had dark circles under his eyes. "We need the kir. One skin of it could make all the difference."

"They'll be waiting."

"Can you swear they'll leave us be if we skirt the fount?"

Ulf looked away from the challenge. "No, m'lord."

"Then we make the fount by noon."

Clouds thickened overhead and the frost lingered well past dawn. Winter advanced down the mountainside at night, was pushed back by sunny days but left crusts of snow under the pines. We walked without speaking, Ulf ahead and the knights behind, Ilya and I with Puck in the middle. I had to watch my feet, as my tired mind wandered and missed the tree roots or jutting rocks in the trail. My ankles throbbed from stumbling. My back ached from sitting all night.

And they followed us, a rustle off to one side, a whuffed breath on the other. Puck's ears swiveled to and fro and at first he startled every few minutes, as raw-nerved as any of us. Well before noon came, he merely plodded on, exhausted.

The trail led down a rocky slope that was tricky for a pony. I took Puck's reins and Ilya leaned against his chest to counter-brace and we got him down the first few feet. The fount's pond was in sight and I could feel the kir tugging at me. Puck was looking at it, too, ears perkier than they'd been all morning. He slipped a little and slid against Ilya's weight.

Anders came down a steeper part quickly, sword in hand. "I'll brace his other side."

Ulf stood at the bottom with bow ready, scanning a half-circle. It was only the motion that warned me; they came silently this time, from opposite sides. My scream was entirely too slow. An arrow took one; the other knocked Ulf to the ground.

I was thrown down on the rocks and agony clamped onto my arm. It dragged me like a doll, despite my thrashing against its wiry fur, despite grabbing at whatever passed by. The beast shook me and my shoulder cracked.

That instant it paused to shake, a hand grabbed my ankle and pulled so hard the lamia spun around on my arm despite its claws scrabbling for purchase. A blur of steel and the monster screamed. Kiefan spun around over me, straddling, blade slicing a wide, challenging circle. Lamia fell back on either side, snarling, and he snarled back.

"Come on, you fucking cowards!"

My head spun from the pain and his voice hazed out. Hands dragged me, this time. Blood pulsed under my grip as I clutched my wounded right arm. A hand pried at mine, forced it off. I felt kir pour onto my agony and the distinctive clench and twist of a blood-stop working on my flesh.

"Kate!" Ulf shook me. "Kate, we need you! Ilya needs you!"

The haze parted a little. I had half a heartbeat to glimpse the underside of a grandfather tree's torn-up roots and the shelter it gave us. "Kate, it's Ilya," Ulf told me, pulling me up to sitting. "They tore him bad."

"Use a…" I wobbled, a little dizzy. When I tried to raise my right hand, all I got was pain.

"The charm couldn't stop it."

That jolted me clearer. Ilya lay just beside me, in a spreading puddle. I pulled my medicine bag over my hip and groped in it left-handed. His arm, at the elbow, was a ragged tear that bone peeked through. Blood gushed in time with his racing pulse, slowed by the blood-stop but still draining him.

Too much for a charm, yes, they'd punctured the artery. For all my time in the battle-field surgery, we'd gotten no bleeders like this. They all died on the grass they fell to. I didn't have a memory to call up for this, I realized with a stab of fear.

My hand found another blood-stop, pulled it out. Ilya looked up at me, tear-streaked, eyes crinkled in pain, hissing breath through his teeth. He was pale and weak from lost blood, and still bleeding. I was the only one who could help him.

Tucking the charm under my ring and pinkie fingers, I called my kir to my hand. Ilya's patterns responded, weak and stumbling, his meridian thready. In the raw meat of his arm, my thumb and index finger found the broken artery near the meridian and I pinched it shut.

At a nudge, the blood-stop charm unknotted and this was something I wasn't sure I could do. I focused the charm solely on the one artery, and funneled its kir onto a small clump of whorls with the memory of a freshly cauterized amputation to shape it.

I thought I smelled a bit of singe, but that may have been the memory.

When I let go, the seal held. Ilya's meridian still wavered, above the wound, and below the gash it faded. He'd lose the arm. I couldn't stop that, and I couldn't finish that job either. Not until I could get the hatchet.

Ilya still gasped for breath, terribly pale, his eyes unfocused. I found his pulse in his clammy throat, racing but weak. He'd lost a lot of blood.

"Water!" I looked for Ulf, for anyone, but they stood in a ring, holding off the lamia. Puck was a few steps away, too exhausted to care. One of our water skins lay on the dirt, too — mine, in fact. I tried to get up, got a fresh stab of pain from my own wound that made my head spin, and crawled on my knees instead. Dragging it back, I pulled the stopper with my teeth.

Ilya coughed when I poured water into his mouth, but he swallowed some. He swatted at me, or tried to, and moaned in pain. I saw the charm-hand nub on him and grabbed at his wrist. He tried to shoo me off, but I leaned across and caught him. His day's kir was unspent, I could feel it through his Blessing.

I lost my balance, one-handed, and fell across his broad, heaving chest. "Get off!" he gasped. "Can't breathe… can't…"

Master Parselev had saved a few men who'd come close to dying on the table. Even once the wounds were closed, the lack of blood could kill a man. He hadn't shown me how he'd done it, not in detail, but Ilya didn't have long. I tugged at his kir and it came, rushing out of his Blessing into my arm in a warm glow. My own damaged kir surged as the flood passed through, and I clenched my teeth against the pain.

I remembered the densely packed, dancing whorls of healthy blood flow and poured both Ilya's kir and my own into him.

His body shuddered under me the same moment as I felt my pain slip through my focus, twisting the charm. I grabbed after the kir as it slid from me, its new pattern askew. Caught a handful or two that was still mine, pulled it back. But the tainted charm splashed into Ilya and maimed his patterns, multiplied by a double dose of kir.

He screamed, throwing me off with another convulsion. Ilya clawed at his chest with his good arm, wounded limb feebly scrabbling at the dirt, as I tried to stop him. Ilya was too strong for me to stop him from scratching himself. The charm, set in its faulty pattern, struck his weakened meridians and they sputtered.

I couldn't see for a moment, and then the tears gushed out and the sight of him shuddering with pain cording his throat was too much. With the little kir I had left, I put my palm to his head and struck. Clumsy as a hammer, but it knocked him out.

Ilya went limp, passing out of pain's reach. His voice trailed off as his breath ran out, then turned to a hoarse gurgle in his throat. Still glowing with kir, the meridians around his heart faltered. I bit my lip as I watched my patient, companion, and friend die from my fumbling. I burned it into my memory, tear-blurred, anguished and all.

"Kate?" Kiefan asked, from behind me. "What happened?"

I covered my face with both hands and sobbed.

CHAPTER 12

Lamia lounged by the kir fount, drinking when they pleased and taking turns circling our windfall. A tall pine's roots had torn up a little hollow when it fell, and a smaller fallen tree alongside provided us a bit of low wall.

The sparkling kir and its siren call made my throat all the drier. I had run out of tears after killing Ilya. I could hardly bring myself to speak at all. Somehow, they still trusted me to hold Puck's reins, in the elbow of the roots and the tree trunk. My right bicep pounded under my torn sleeve. Ulf had cut off my layered woolens and I'd wiped the clotted tooth marks with witch hazel. He'd bandaged me. I could move my hand a bit, but kept it tucked in my belt for warmth.

"Two arrows left," Ulf said. "Lost the rest when they knocked me down." He'd used a blood-stop on himself and bandaged his own bites. Wise not to let me try anything, I supposed.

"Save them. Sundown's still a mile off." Kiefan said, intent on the fount.

"There's ten of them, m'lord. It would be suicide."

"They could finish us now, if they wished."

A moment's silence, and then Ulf said, "They're better fed."

I closed my eyes, seeing Boristan dragged off again. And poor Acorn.

Kiefan said, "But they won't let us go."

"No."

Three lamia charged our windfall with more snarls and Kiefan swept Ulf back with one arm. Anders was half a step ahead, counter-charging, and the two knights drove back two of the beasts. The third raced in closest and angled its charge at the last moment, leaping up onto the low tree trunk and running its length, snapping at Puck's head as it passed.

Puck spooked back with a scream and reared. I lost his reins and saw only hooves above me; cringing, I crawled and was nearly hit when Puck came down. The pony dropped his head and I saw teeth; I flinched back under his feet. The men yelled. Puck shrilled and kicked — he'd had enough of all this and who could blame him. I wrapped my arm around my head and looked for an opening, some chance to get out from under his hooves.

Anders caught his bridle; Puck lunged to bite and Anders slapped his palm flat on the pony's forehead, square on his little white star. Kir moved, I felt it. Puck froze, head lifting, ears perked, eyes locked on his. Anders nodded to the pony and took his hand away. Puck whuffed and mouthed his bit. Anders started unbuckling the packs.

I crawled out and stood. Kiefan and Ulf looked as puzzled as I.

And it was an excellent chance to attack us again; two lamia took it, and Kiefan swung around on one of them. It peeled off with a snarl. The second got closer, made to take the same route along the tree trunk as its pack-mate, but Puck lunged with his teeth bared. The lamia spooked, this time, fell off to the outside and scrambled away.

Anders patted the pony's shoulder.

"Could've charmed him earlier," Kiefan said.

"Never did that before," Anders replied, getting the tarp roll off Puck. "You need a horse de-wormed, I know that one. Never tried charming before. He needs the weight off, though. Looks like we're staying here tonight in any case."

———————————✕———————————

No fire. No camp. The overcast sky blanketed us in shadows quickly as the sun set, and the fount's glow was soon the strongest light under the trees. I wrapped my cloak tight around myself, and sat atop one of the bedrolls we had left. Should the final attack come, being bundled up was no safer than trying to run. Better to not be tangled in a blanket, better to run and be pulled down. A quicker death, perhaps.

What would they tell my mother?

"Kate?" Kiefan's hand found my arm and he knelt beside me. I clasped his hand as the other touched my cheek, cupped it to be sure where I was for a kiss. Then he whispered, "We'll survive this night. And I hope you forgive me for Ilya, someday."

I breathed a bitter laugh. "Forgive you? I'm the one who failed him."

"We should've skirted the fount. You should not have had to overreach yourself."

I stroked his scratchy cheek. "Anything might have happened. You can't say there was no chance he'd be bitten, out here. It was my fault."

He hugged me and I felt a moment's safety; then he went back to the front line.

I sat alone. Ulf had his dagger, and leaned against the sloping tree-trunk to watch for flank attacks. Puck stood guard with him, biting at any lamia who came near. They didn't care to let him succeed. Kiefan and Anders took to letting the mock-charges get far closer before reacting, and killed a couple more lamia thus. The harrying slowed, then.

Pain ground out of my bitten arm, my sprained shoulder. I could feel the swelling, with my left hand, but the joint was still sound. My bandage needed checking, but would have to wait. I focused on clenching my right hand in a fist, wincing and gritting my teeth through the jolts and jabs.

With no moons to track the night's progress, I don't know how much I slept. Puck dozed on his feet and I suspect the men did too.

Sometime before dawn, it began to snow. Wind breathed through the pines' high branches. Flakes pattered down steadily. Snow caught the sparkling kir fount's light and made a misty glow of it.

The silence was nearly peaceful.

"Have you seen any?" Kiefan asked.

Anders jerked awake, I think, on his feet. "No, no sign."

"Only the snow," Ulf said. "Not much night left."

"Give Puck his breakfast, he'll need it. Kate, something for the rest of us?"

There was trail bread aplenty, and cold ham. We drank some water from one of the skins.

"And this is what happens next," Kiefan said as he brushed crumbs from his hands. "Kate takes the documents and some food. She rides Puck. Anders, can you charm him to run till they're safe or he drops?"

Quietly, Anders said, "Don't need a charm for that."

My throat was too tight to speak as Kiefan continued. "We attack. We show these animals what they should be afraid of. And we make an opening for Puck to get through. Ulf? You shoot from up there." He jerked his chin toward the crown of the windfall's roots. "Are we agreed?"

I squeezed out a tiny, "No?"

"You're the smallest. Puck can run the fastest. Would d'Ovio Alain disagree with my logic?" Kiefan asked, referring to the book we'd studied together.

"Don't…" I had packed away my memories of Ther Boristan screaming as the lamia tore at his arms, but I could still picture it all too clearly. Kiefan, Anders, Ulf.

Kiefan hung the leather bag on my shoulder. Ulf put some bread in my medicine bag. I hugged him, and he said something kind, and then I hugged Kiefan longer, tighter. He had to pry me off.

Anders stood with Puck, and dawn was clearly here. The snow had paled to nearly white. He put me on the pony and threw a rope around my waist, then Puck. "Just to be sure," he told me, softly. "Hang on tight. Stay low, there may be branches. I told Puck what I could — horses see things differently. If he stops and you're off the path, find running water and follow it down."

Puck's back put me a little taller than Anders; I caught him with my good arm and hugged him too. He gave me a quick squeeze back and said, "Don't tell anyone you did that."

It seemed ludicrous, given the moment. "I can hug my friends if I wish."

Anders started to tease in return, there was enough light to see that, but it died in his mouth. He only looked at me as he tightened the rope's knots. Then he turned to Kiefan. "Ready?"

"Shepherd, guide my sword."

The lamia clustered around the fount, watching. Kiefan and Anders took deep breaths, crouching to run, steeling their nerves; my hands shook around handfuls of Puck's mane. With a yell, they charged. At Blessing speed, they were halfway to the fount before the lamia could believe their eyes.

The boldest pack-mates answered the charge, and the snow swirled in the wake of two of the saints' Blessed carving through fur and bone.

"Go, Kate! Go!" Ulf shouted.

I kicked Puck hard and he sprinted across the fresh powder. He galloped toward the water, cut right through a gap I barely saw and passed between the pond and the fount. I glimpsed furious green eyes as lamia turned to give chase. One leaped up at the pony's shoulder and an arrow thumped into the monster's neck.

Puck ran into the pines. I threw myself down and gripped his neck as best I could with both arms. Two lamia raced alongside us, on either side, and one suddenly crashed in a shriek and a glimpse of fletching.

Needled branches scratched at me, then vanished. I forced my eyes to open and risked looking up. Puck loped alongside the stream, down the forest path we'd followed up to the fount weeks ago. The way twisted, but wasn't so steep as above the pond. The pony still leaped now and then over little drops and I rattled against him each time.

When he landed, the last lamia slammed into his rump. Claws caught on my cloak and teeth sank in as the beast lost its balance. Puck stumbled, whinnying, and bucked. I yanked at my cloak pins as the lamia's weight dragged at my neck and got them free as it choked me. Puck kicked again as the beast fell, taking my cloak along, and the pony bolted. I checked over my shoulder; the lamia lost a few moments scrambling out of my cloak, and chased. Puck pulled away, though, across a brief flat stretch. He puffed out even clouds of breath.

Puck threw me against his neck when he braked hard, skidded, and I nearly lost my grip. Then the kir hit, like a curtain, and as the pony slid to a stop I was slack-jawed and casting about for the source. Behind me, the lamia shrieked a challenge as it all but sat on its rear to stop.

A massive cougar, all rippling golden hide and hazy kir, charged past Puck up the hill. The cat roared in reply and a bright fist of kir smashed the lamia into a red cloud. The cougar leaped up onto a jut of rock and pirouetted, tail slinging wide for balance, to look back.

When his kir-lit golden eyes met mine, I knew he wanted me to follow. I kicked Puck, and he obeyed.

I heard, behind us, more horses and men's shouts. As Puck galloped back upstream I twisted to look. They were a dozen, maybe more, wearing a mix of forest green surcotes and black military tabards and carrying strung bows. They saw me, and Puck, and their shouts got louder. I waved and pointed up the hill, tried to yell back but they couldn't have heard me.

Puck crested the last rise and veered toward the pond. We broke some sort of stalemate and the nearer lamia turned, hackles bristling. Kiefan shouted, "Kate, no!" from beyond the fount and I spotted him, back-to-back with Anders. My mind couldn't grasp why there was a lamia against Anders' leg, in the moment I had before the circling beasts rushed him. The weaker one. And the nearer ones charged Puck. Where was the cougar?

With a hiss, an arrow took one lamia down mid-gallop. The scouting party thundered up and the lamia routed before the onslaught. I turned Puck, kicked him, and we circled tight around the pond, crossed the fount again to reach the two knights first. I sawed at the rope that held me and nearly fell off in haste.

Kiefan snatched me in a brief, rib-creaking hug, and I was babbling at him. "Are you hurt? Let me see. Are you bleeding? Anders?"

One lamia had died with its jaws locked on Anders' thigh, at the knee. His strength drained along with the focus of combat, leaving him a rag doll; Kiefan caught him. Blood dripped from Anders' sword arm as his blade fell.

"Get it off him. Then to the fount," I said, untying my medicine bag.

Kiefan wedged his fingers between fangs and yanked, ripping the lamia's lower jaw off clean. Anders toppled flat as blood gushed free. Bright, arterial spurt stained the grass, sinking my hopes with it. But Kiefan was already dragging him to the fount, and getting help from a rescuer with captain's brasses. I followed.

The kir fount's little pool was barely ankle deep and its diamond glitter quickly shifted to ruby. No time for doubts, nor mistakes. Anders was dying before my eyes. I sat beside him in the kir-water, slopped up a mouthful from the clearer side by the spring, and held his wound in the fast-running flow. Surrounded by raw kir, Anders' whorls and patterns came up strong and colorful, stumbling and broken as they were. The torn meridian pulsed bright as he bled, and I reached into the ripped flesh. My fingers found the artery and pinched it.

My memory raced through all of my surgeries, the handful of medical books, all my master had told me, for what to do. How to fix, not just cauterize. And my mind cleared, calmed, as the fount's kir moved through me. With my other hand, I traced the continuation of the meridian up from his ankle and dug into the wound. Somewhere outside my focus, they were holding Anders down while he screamed.

Both ends of the broken artery in my fingers, I pinched and — they couldn't meet, could they? Torn as they were? I tugged, feeling the kir move around me and into the flesh, coaxed with little massaging circles, and found my pinched fingers touching. The reunited meridian pulsed, weak and stuttering for lack of blood. His skin had gone deathly pale; I called on my kir… my kir?

Around me, brilliant tendrils arced up from the fount, traced across me briefly, and fell back. I called again, and a few more shot out to answer. No surprise I felt buoyant and alert; I brimmed with power.

Blood. Do it right, this time. I focused on Anders' meridian, on his artery and the blood inside, and shaped the kir to match its rushing, whirling pattern. Poured it into him. All of it. It felt like wind, or rushing water, that funneled down to a pinprick at the tips of my fingers and into his artery.

A ragged gasp, and Anders lurched up. Then he wobbled and fell back against Kiefan.

I blinked, dazed by how much I'd spent. A lot of kir made less blood than I'd have thought. The pool's light was gone, its twinkle dulled — though not lost entirely. I could feel kir creeping back into the spring, when I called to it. It would be some time before it was strong again.

"Pull him out. I'll stitch the rest," I said.

"M'lady," the captain breathed, eyes wide. "The Shepherd had him. You —"

From my bag, I dug out a blood-stop and tossed it to Kiefan. "For his arm. Do you need one?" I reached for needle and catgut, and a cleansing charm.

Anders' kir patterns still glowed clearly from the washing, making the job of matching torn edges easier. Someone stuffed a blanket under his head and Kiefan left us both to confer with the captain. I sewed carefully, matching grain to grain as I had when a peasant's hatchet had slipped onto his calf while chopping wood. Anders' knuckles gripped white on his cloak.

I ought to have given him a knock-out. Still failing, even in success. "I'm sorry," I told him.

He laughed, and the tension rolled out of him for a moment. "I'm alive," he said. "I'm the last one you'll need to apologize to."

CHAPTER 13

They found Ulf. What the lamia left of him.

"Just a few dozen yards off," the woodsman reported, gesturing past the roots of the grandfather tree. "He put up a good fight, it looks. Followed a blood trail and found one of them half-dead with his knife in its side."

We all looked up as a second archer passed by, hauling a dead weight: the lamia. Blood darkened its fur, and the final arrow quivered from the dragging.

"Men're wrapping him up to bring. Something to bury, that's good. Something for his wife and the boys." The woodsman nodded.

"I'll speak to Baron Eismann," Kiefan said, voice low as he tracked the dead lamia. "His widow, and Bjorn's, will be looked after."

Two armsmen picked up Ilya's blanket-wrapped body from the hollow we'd sheltered in. My throat tightened, again. They carried him to their own pack horse, slung him over and followed that with ropes.

I stood in the eye of all their activity — seeing to the dead, collecting lamia fangs, filling water skins at the fount — reluctant to move. They asked nothing of me, in any case. I was still full of kir, but the sleepless night and healing Anders left me brain-weary. Unfocused. After the long day's battle at Ansehen, I'd felt this and my master had warned me not to try any charms. Having felt kir slip my fingers, I knew why now.

Two more men came from the brush, carrying a tarp wrapped and tied around — too small a bundle. Too thin. And despite the oilskin, it dripped. My stomach twisted, thinking of those two arrows that had helped me escape. But at least we could bring Ulf home.

"Did you see the cougar?" I asked Kiefan, as we rode down the trail.

"Cougar?" He frowned. "Here? Ulf said lamia drive out any competition."

"I saw a cougar on the trail. A lamia had chased us down, and the cougar destroyed it. When he looked at me, I had to follow — and he was leading the scouts."

"He was, m'lady," the captain put in. "If I may." He slowed his horse from a few steps ahead of us, twisting in his saddle.

"You followed a cougar up this trail?" Kiefan frowned.

The man breathed a laugh, shaking his head. "When a cat walks into your camp during last watch and tosses your bow to you, m'lord, you snap to attention. I'll swear to Father Duty he had a man's hands, when he did it. Not a one of us hasn't heard the stories — Saint Aleksandr can wear a cougar's skin when he pleases — but we never thought to see it. Yes, we followed him, and glad we did."

I'd heard more of Saint Aleksandr the craftsman, castle-builder, bridge-raiser, but I had no reason to doubt the captain. "We're in his debt, then," I said.

Kiefan nodded at that. "But I never saw the cougar. Only you riding up, Kate. You stopped my heart for a moment."

"Father Duty must've been watching. You've barely a mark on you," I said. Some tooth-scratches on his forearms, a few sore spots, and nothing more. His woolens had suffered, but not his skin.

He had no answer for it. "They didn't lack in trying."

We rode for Vorspitz as quickly as the horses could manage. I'd wanted Anders carried on a litter for the trip, so as not to worsen his wound, but he'd refused and Kiefan wanted to be home as quickly as we could. Anders rode tied to one of the scouts — and he hadn't much liked that either, but the grumbling had stopped once the riding worsened his pain.

We made good time and pushed on past dark to reach the town. Baron Eismann waited at his gate, lantern in hand, to greet us. I was so exhausted I nearly fell from the saddle; a stable-boy caught me. Soon as my feet touched the ground, I saw Eismann's physician crossing the gate-yard at a run.

I knew her face, and she knew mine; we all had Saint Qadeem's memory Blessing. Anders lay groggy against his scout's back, and needed careful untying and pulling down. I could smell the blood on his bandage as soon as they laid him on a blanket. The physician put a hand on him, called his pattern, and told the men to wait when they began to pick him up.

Putting my hand by hers, I saw the damage too. "He tore the stitches."

"Men." She pursed her mouth and wove her kir into a charm. The top layer of muscle was worst off — and he'd torn the skin's stitches too. Anders hissed through his teeth as his flesh shifted under the charm.

"I'll re-stitch his skin," I said, reaching into my bag.

"Let me help. You're worn to a shade," she said, through her focus on the charm. "Did he… was his meridian torn? You mended that before he bled out?"

I nodded. Her brows rose and she nodded slowly. "Small wonder the Elect apprenticed you."

The men stood waiting; I could re-stitch Anders inside, with a lamp at hand. When the physician gestured for them to carry him in, I stood along with her. The weight of my bag on my right shoulder, so I could reach in with my left, twisted a sharp breath out of me.

Her hand touched me, called my pattern. "You should've told me," she chided. "Come inside. They've kept some mulled cider on the fire. Let me dull that so you can sleep, at least."

Across the gate-yard, as I went, I saw Kiefan and Baron Eismann looking at Ther Boristan's notebook from the document bag. Then Kiefan closed it with a nod, and the Baron gave a few orders to the captain at hand. They followed us inside. I hoped, for a moment, Kiefan might stop, ask about Anders or me — but they strode on with business to see to. Plans to make.

As they should. I pressed my lips together and looked away. Kiefan was the prince, after all. I had a patient to see to.

I sipped a cup of mulled cider as I re-stitched and re-bandaged, and then a maid led me straight to bed. I dropped onto the mattress fully clothed and instantly slept.

A hand shook me awake far too early. "The sooner we leave, the sooner we're home," Kiefan said.

He was right, but I couldn't help a wince as I sat up; my shoulder stabbed pain at the least weight on it. My eyelids were made of lead. And another day's —

Kiefan kissed my cheek. I turned toward him, startled, as he leaned back. His mouth twisted to one side, for a heartbeat. "Word's been sent to my father. We're expected," he murmured, and stood.

I nodded and got up.

Kiefan took the baron aside again over breakfast. I wolfed down eggs and bread and cheese while the physician checked on Anders again. I had my days' ration of kir, and could charm my shoulder a little more. Enough that it wouldn't pain me all day. It needed a fresh bandage, too. The physician strengthened the stitches in Anders' thigh, but it was too large a wound for her to mend entirely. She didn't think he should ride.

There wasn't much that could stop him once he was full of breakfast, though. I followed Anders into the stable and hugged Puck good-bye around his thick neck. He was more interested in the apple that Anders had smuggled out for him, and I would have understood if Puck had been glad to see us leave without him.

Eismann sent a small escort of the Prince's Guard with us and we changed horses at each village along the way. The frosty morning warmed nicely, but the trees were turning to gold and red. Fields were now half-harvested and stacks of oats stood drying.

Ahead, Mount Woden loomed, snow-capped already, the city on its flank wreathed in chimney smoke. On the jutting promontory, the pale granite castle perched with watchtowers craning to take in the entire broad valley. A little downslope, the neatly arrayed roofs of the Order's campus reminded me of the routine I'd be back to soon enough: patching up patients in the hospital, preparing medicines, studying my master's books, eating in the common hall.

I stole a look at Kiefan, riding a little ahead with his eyes fixed on the castle towers. His home.

I gripped my reins tighter, casting my eyes down with a heavy heart.

DISCIPLE, PART II
winter's fools

CHAPTER 1

I'd slept for a thousand years, the ache in my joints told me, and I could have slept another thousand.

When I opened my eyes, Elect Parselev sat at the writing desk near my trundle bed, the tuft at the end of his quill bobbing as he wrote. Late morning light slashed across the spacious guest bedroom. I hadn't seen much of the room when the housemistress brought me in by candle light and pulled out the trundle for me. Now the pine walls glowed in the sunlight, warm and reassuring after the cold blues of the snow.

Parselev glanced over when I sat up; his smile flushed out fans of crow's-feet around his brown eyes. He put down his pen and capped his jar of ink.

"Tell me everything, Kate."

I told him everything: the lamia, the strange sickness in the mountain pass, Kiefan's headaches, the threat of frostbite. He wanted to know Caercoed's answer and I recited m'lady Leix's words from my memory Blessing. She would bring her Tadhlon Guard to our aid, come spring, and Prince Kiefan would seal the alliance by marrying a Caer duchess. I described the hard journey back through the pass, the harrying, Ther Boristan's awful death and my failure with Ilya.

My voice fell to a strangled whimper, halfway through that part.

Parselev let me recover. "Thus, your tears at the gate."

Last night, I'd ridden up River Road a half dozen paces behind a lieutenant carrying a lantern and shouting, "Make way! The prince!" For the first time, I'd climbed to the very top of River Road and passed through the outer gates of Castle Kaltkern. The king had been waiting for us, as had Elect Parselev and squads of servants. The confusion and noise had fallen away, though, when I saw a lone woman with a candle searching through our riding party, asking questions with hope in her face.

Kiefan had taken her to the wrapped body tied to the spare horse.

"I tried to replenish his blood," I said to Parselev, "but my focus slipped. My own wound tainted the charm. I only gave him pain as he died."

"But you tried it."

"It seemed simple enough." I tugged the blankets up around my chin with a shiver. I sat cross-legged on the straw mattress in only my boy's cote and braies. My master's shoulder bag sat on the rumpled main bed, where he'd slept, and I hoped it contained a fresh shift and dress for me.

"Whenever you spin substance from kir, a great deal of it is needed. Far greater than what results. I checked Sir Anders, and I see you must've worked the charm out for yourself."

I told him about the kir fount and Anders' torn artery, and how I had joined the ends of the artery together. How the kir had arced up when I called, and rushed through me like wind. When I finished, Parselev was nodding and stroking his grey beard as he did when he was pleased.

"And that is why you had to go with them, Kate." Then he twitched his shoulders. "One reason, of several. Need spurs growth. And success is the greatest source of confidence. Even a gifted student might never realize that they can work out healing charms on their own, and shy away from challenges. You know that in your bones now." My master smiled and waved a finger vaguely in the air. "Call kir, as you would a patient's pattern. Tell me what you sense."

I cocked my head. He finished his cup of tea while I waited, trying to detect any tug of kir in my chest — as I'd felt at the lamia's fount. Nothing. Taking a deep breath, I called with all my strength.

My own kir rippled in answer. In my mind's eye, a warm green light echoed back my call from where Elect Parselev sat. And I felt a distant answer, as a tingle against my breastbone.

"That is the Pool," Parselev said. "Good."

"You know that I could feel that?"

A nod. "I felt it shift when you called. It's deep inside the castle, well hidden. You've grown more sensitive and stronger as well — excellent. When we're elbow-deep in wounded this spring, you will need it."

My chin jerked up at that. There had been talk of evacuating most of the Order's campus to keep the students safe when Arcea's army marched on the city.

Parselev lowered his voice. "Need spurs growth. Whatever happens, I will be here in Wodenberg if Arcea lays siege to us, and I mean to have you here with me. You are no longer my apprentice, you are a physician in service of the Order. I want you here as my assistant, not shuffled off to some frostbitten village Orderhaus that needs a physician. I haven't had as strong a student in twenty years, and I mean to see you bloom to your fullest — but," and he raised a hand to further emphasize his point, "but you must stand your ground and bloom on your own. Which you won't if you allow the others to bully you."

He'd said such things before, because for my first year of apprenticeship I had let the older students foist their scutwork onto me. They were my betters, and I was only a peasant girl, and it had seemed natural enough. Master had needed to sit by me, my second year, to be sure I stitched every patient he assigned, rather than find me later changing sheets or emptying chamber pots. I could boil bandages and scrub tools with the best of the nursemaid Ters, after all the practice I'd had.

I shivered again, imagining they would send me to a village buried in snow as deep as the mountain pass we'd slogged through. "I won't, Master."

"No longer your master, Kate." He gave me one of his stern looks to reinforce that. Then he asked, "Do you have other questions on what you saw during your journey?"

I took a moment, during which he collected the handful of papers he had spread out on the desk. "Kiefan's headaches," I said. "Prince Kiefan, I mean to say. I've never seen such tightly knotted kir. And he works even through the pain?"

"Our dear prince," my teacher said, tucking the papers into his letter wallet, "suffers from a recurring affliction. I have seen a scattering of such, in my time, and I've traced the headaches to a flaw in the prime meridian's roots which causes the kir to tangle. The tangles catch on his two adjacent Blessings and, when emotions run high, swiftly develop the tight knots you observed."

"There's no way to repair the flaw?"

"There has been no injury to the prime meridian, as the flaw is inherited, in many cases, from one's bloodline. And it's not for anyone to say how a person's mind should be, whatever you might hear otherwise." Parselev stood, with his letter wallet, and lapsed out of his lecturing tone. "I'll let you dress — your clothes are in the bag there. You have a patient to see to, do you not?"

I nodded, but had to ask. "Surely His Majesty couldn't hide such headaches for his entire life?"

He hesitated before answering. "You're my student and I am physician to the royal family. You will be attending to them as well, so in confidence I will tell you that it's the Queen who also suffers a flawed meridian and the headaches — a fact I did not learn until she'd lived here nearly five years, lest you think the prince exceptionally stubborn. Now, I'll see if I can find us some breakfast. Meet me in the hall or down in the kitchen."

———✦———

Castle Kaltkern lay in rings, its keep and watchtowers on the promontory's peak. From the gatehouse on the innermost wall, the castle's road dropped steeply into an herb garden, wound past a few fruit trees, and then led past the guesthouse Parselev and I had roomed in.

We followed the road outward through the gatehouse in the second ring. I looked up as we walked under the portcullis, wondering at the lattice of iron.

Down another slope we walked into the bustle of the royal stables and the broad yard inside the third, outermost ring. Four wagons stacked high with ale barrels stood in the yard, their lead teamster arguing with a man in servant's blacks about the tally and why it was short. The other teamsters lounged on their wagons, waiting for leave to drive up to the castle proper.

Tucked against the wall, past the stables, was the royal guardsmen's barracks. King, queen and crown prince had their own guard, each with castle duties to see to.

As Parselev and I strolled past the ale wagons, a pageboy in messenger's red sprinted past us, calling for a horse. A stablehand led one out by the reins and the page vaulted into the saddle with ease. At a kick from the boy, the horse burst off at a canter through the outer gatehouse, hoofbeats echoing off the deep walls.

He nearly collided with two horses trotting in. The man leading the way twisted in his saddle to shout after the racing pageboy. By the crest of brown hair between his Blessing ridges, the man was a field-proven knight, and by the fur-lined, dark green cloak he was titled too — and by how his lean, bearded face darkened, he was furious. He dismounted before the stablehand could catch his bay's bridle, and fumed toward the stables, shouting for Schwartzman. He didn't stay to see his lady off her horse.

She dismounted with ease, though, green skirts and all, and nodded thanks to the stablehand. Then she spotted my teacher and me, well across the gate yard. Parselev stopped.

"M'lady, it's good to see you well," he called.

"It's kind of you to remember, Elect." She crossed to us at a brisk walk, smiling. The morning sun, just full over the castle walls and flooding the yard, shone on flaxen hair netted up in a dark crespine. I didn't doubt that as a girl she'd been beautiful and kind; she still was, though now seasoned by years. A few lines had gathered around her eyes, but they still twinkled with spirit. And I recognized her smile. "This must be your apprentice?"

Parselev presented me with a sweep of his hand. "My student only, as she's been graduated by Saint Qadeem himself. Dame Kate Carpenter, physician. Kate, the Baroness Rossweide, Frida Bockmann."

Anders' mother. I curtsied, thankful I was back in skirts to do it properly. "M'lady, I'm honored."

"A pleasure to meet you, Physician Carpenter. I suppose we are at the same purposes," m'lady Frida said, with a glance toward where her husband had vanished into the stables. "Is he well? His message was too brief." She walked toward the barracks and Parselev fell into step beside her. I trailed them, hands clasped.

"Ask his physician," my teacher said, turning to me as he walked.

Frida's brows shot up, startled. "Your pardon, Physician. They dragged you up the Eispitzen for this lamia hunt?"

That was the story we were to tell, if any asked about the mission across the mountains to Caercoed. "The Elect knew it would be excellent training for me," I said. "Anders should recover without trouble, m'lady. Sir Anders, I mean to say."

We paused at the sill of the barracks' double doors, which stood open on this fine autumn morning. She smiled with a familiar wry twist. "He said as little in his message. And if you spent the whole moon a-hunting, little wonder if you're on familiar terms. My son, please, Lieutenant." That last to the officer, who snapped to attention, fist over his heart, beside the duty ledger's table inside the door. "I believe you have him here. Sir Anders Bockmann?"

"He's asleep in the Prince's Guard room, m'lady. I'll fetch him —"

"No mind, sir, I can manage that much. See to your work. Which room?"

Once we had directions, we climbed the spiraled stone stairs. Parselev put a hand on my shoulder to slow me. "Let a mother see her son first," he murmured.

So we lagged a bit behind her along the hallway. M'lady Frida paused at the door to listen — this late in the morning, the upstairs was empty — and pressed the latch. She leaned to look, then stepped inside.

"Is it true Anders is the king's son?" I whispered.

"You didn't know?" Parselev asked, but then answered himself. "It's of little matter to us, in the Order. Yes, to the gossips' joy, he is. He is also a fellow disciple of the saints, sworn to their service."

I couldn't help thinking of the tall, lean Baron Rossweide, with grey-touched brown hair and beard, as he strode across the gate yard. Then, the king I had seen last night: blonde-bearded, built for the heavier muscle that he still carried despite being many years the Baron's elder. The resemblance was more than the jawline that I had noticed earlier; Anders' whole frame matched the king's.

Near the door, I stopped and waited without looking in.

"I came with your father," Frida said, inside, "but he got no further than the stables."

Anders snorted. "You could've come alone. I have no father."

Her tone steeled. "You'll both be fools if you cast away all your good years over a few head-buttings. He'll take you on as a trainer if you'll only mind the manners I know I taught you. Room and board and working with the horses. Don't try to pass that off as a fleeting fancy to me. You love those horses."

"Trading one hayloft for another," he muttered.

"Will and Ein miss you. And nobody's safe near Nipper. Bring this wound of yours home and recover your strength. Though I must admit you look well — it must be only a slight injury? Why has your physician has come to check on you, then?"

Parselev, on cue, pushed the door open. M'lady Frida sat on the foot of Anders' cot and he sat cross-legged under the blankets. The other cots stood empty and neatly made. His tabard, mail, and gambeson were thrown over a small chest against the wall; he wore only his off-white wool cote and braies.

"Come to check on me? There's nothing to see."

"Let your physician be the judge of that. Show us this trifling wound, then," his mother said, standing up from the cot.

I took her seat as Anders kicked the covers off his right leg. He wore full-length braies, against the cold, and rolled one leg up above his knee. Browned blood stained the bandage. I shooed his hands away and unknotted it myself.

"Eismann's physician told you not to ride," I said.

"I wasn't about to come home tied to a saddle." He leaned back against the pillow and the wall, content to let me unwind the bandage.

"If you tore those stitches and the wound's set, you'll have a limp."

He didn't answer that as I pulled the stained cloth free of the wound. The lamia had latched onto Anders' thigh just above the knee and had shaken him as it died, leaving a matched pair of gashes as long as my hand. My top stitches, done in plain wool thread, looked as rushed as I had been in making them.

"Those — are no minor wound," m'lady Frida said, voice low. "Anders, what happened?"

I laid my palm against his skin between the wounds and called his kir. His meridian pulsed strong and clear, and most of the wound was beginning to knit, hurried along by the healing charms. But patches of kir that followed their own dance were strung through his whorls. Left on their own, they'd become abscesses.

"One lamia got under my guard and put his fangs in me. Locked his jaws and I couldn't get the bastard off even dead. Then I heard the scouting party arrive, and…" He shrugged it off with a shake of his head.

"And?" Frida's tone sharpened.

"And here I am."

Sharp enough to cut, she said, "Don't you try to dodge — "

"The Shepherd's shadow fell on me." Anders turned harsh. "I felt his culling knife on my throat. And like a fool, I begged the Mother and Father for one more chance. Swore on my Blessings to both of them." He raked a hand through his hair, pressed the heel of his palm against the ridges of striated horn that jutted through.

His mother turned to me, her sky-blue eyes bright with pain. "What happened?"

He'd left off the part where the lamia had harried us for two nights. He'd likely run out of kir and that was how the beast got under his guard. But I stuck to the question of the wound. "He lost too much blood while I repaired his meridian. The Shepherd nearly took him."

Her knees wobbled and she sank to the floor, green skirts puffing out as if to catch her. She held Anders' free hand to her cheek and whispered, "Mother Love, thank you… thank you, Saint Qadeem, for your disciple."

I worked through the clotted lines of kir and the young abscesses in his wound. By how he winced, he felt me undoing the damage his day's ride had done to the interior stitches. I didn't have enough kir to repair it all, but I did enough that he wouldn't have a limp.

"I will need to check the wound again and remove these stitches," I said, tapping the wool threads. "In a week or so."

"Come by whenever you wish, Physician," m'lady Frida said, wiping her eyes. "Be welcome in my house whenever you wish a good meal."

From the door came a new voice. "What did you swear?"

Parselev waited just inside the sill. Beside him stood the Baron Rossweide with arms folded.

Anders heaved a sigh. "To the Discipline. To submit to their Discipline."

The baron snorted at that. "You haven't the stomach for either of their Disciplines. That much is clear from the past few years. Culling knife, indeed."

"I'll keep my word."

Another snort. "Your mother wants you home to heal. You won't be under my roof a moment longer unless you earn your keep — and keep for that damn horse of yours."

"I'll be in the training yard at dawn, then," Anders said, his voice gone cold. "Once I've seen to duties here."

"You do that." Turning on his heel, the Baron stalked out.

"The Father's Discipline would go far toward mending bridges between you," m'lady Frida said. "And the Mother's…"

"I was a fool to swear." Anders shook off her hand and leaned out to reach for his gambeson. "I've the Guard's horses to check."

Parselev spoke up. "And debriefing with the King's Council and a funeral tonight."

"Let me bandage that." I put a hand on his wounded knee to stop him, digging through my medicine bag with the other.

Anders pulled the padded tunic to the side of the bed, but waited for me to wrap him back up. "Me, at the King's Council? That will be interesting. If I don't turn up at Ilya's funeral, don't expect to find my corpse."

"Does Krepkin know you're wasting the day walking me about, or did you slip away?" I asked as we climbed the castle road.

Parselev chuckled as we passed under the inner gatehouse, waving to the armsmen standing watch. "It will do him well for me to vanish now and then. The exercise will loosen his mind. Perhaps his joints as well. Meantime, I must observe my student's progress, the better to know what you are ready to learn. And to assure myself that you have come to no harm."

Castle Kaltkern rose above its curtain wall, seamless and smooth; carved from the mountain itself by Saint Aleksandr's craft, they said. Its central keep and two wings embraced the castle yard, and the watchtowers loomed behind like guardsmen. Only arrow slits pierced the ground floor walls, but higher up granite ram's heads framed the windows. Along the rooftop, the crenellations ran like heavy, square teeth — even striated and a little off-true like real teeth. Saints' whimsies could turn odd.

"Harm?" My mind had caught that much, while I stared up at the castle. Parselev had healed my lamia bite and my sprained shoulder. Only faint scars and tender patches remained.

"Aside from your wounds." When I still frowned, he said, "You spent a moon afield with half a dozen men, Kate. Sir Anders, in particular. Some will believe he seduced you."

"Anders has only treated me with kindness," I said. As he led me through the ironbound door at the end of the west wing — closest to the gate — I lowered my voice. "I can swear on my virtue to the Father himself."

Parselev nodded and spoke quietly as well. "I trust you — and stole no peeks when I healed you. There will be questions, though. Be ready for them."

"Krepkin." I could predict that much.

The King's Guard occupied the foremost room inside, and they directed us down the central hall toward the kitchens. We passed offices and a laundry, and stepped aside for housemaids with armloads of dishes. Then the scent of roasting meat caught my nose.

Parselev asked one of the maids, in passing, "Is Herr Lauter in the kitchen?"

She called back over her shoulder, "No, but Wenda is, m'lord."

"Lauter is the chamberlain," Parselev said for my benefit as we walked deeper into the delicious aroma. "He'd know if the King's Council expects you yet. But Wenda will know as well."

The hall emptied into the kitchen. There, an array of tables structured the confusion of vegetables, shanks of meat, basins of bread dough, and the tubs of dirty pots and pans, as well as the servants elbow-deep in peeling, chopping, kneading and scrubbing. My eyes went straight to the deep hearth, though, and the spitted geese roasting over the fire. The smell of their onion-laced drippings, as the cook basted them, set my mouth to watering.

"Wenda! Kate, this is Wenda Stark, the castle housemistress. My student, the physician Dame Kate Carpenter. Will the Council call for her soon?"

My stomach growled, intent on the geese, but I pried my gaze off them to meet the housemistress. She wore the plain black woolens of the castle servants and a kerchief tied over her bundled hair. Her brown eyes surveyed me, quick and sharp. "You're the physician, then? Went a-hunting monsters?" A *tsk* at that. "Tougher than you look. Good. They've about wrung Kiefan out, I think, so bring her along."

The platter on the table, a slab of wood big enough to be a tabletop itself, was buried in cold beef roast, bread, cheese and apples. Wenda hoisted it up so easily, she had to have a strength Blessing under her dress. She snagged the pitcher of small beer in her other hand, and led the way.

Through a side door, the housemistress led us into the central keep. Its ground floor was one vast receiving hall inside the double front doors; empty, then, its furniture pushed against the walls, chandeliers unlit, the hanging banners too hard to see in the dim light. From the great hall, a broad stone staircase curved upward. Its balustrade began with a seated stone bear that watched the front doors. I dared pet its head, as if it were a dog, and trailed my hand along the polished granite banister as we climbed.

At the top of the stairs, the King's Council door stood open, letting through the sunlight from the chamber's south-facing windows. A knight stood on either side of the door, their shields slung across their backs, their tabards bearing four gold stars on the right shoulder for the King's Guard.

"You declined that hospitality and risked the pass again?" the king asked as we gained the first floor.

"Schutze will be on alert in Knapptal come spring," Kiefan answered. "If he pins down the Caercoed soldiers, believing them in league with Arcea, it would make the entire mission futile."

"You could've met these Crowns yourself and further grounded the alliance. You could have seen your marriage options and sounded out the most advantageous offers."

Kiefan stood with his back to the open door, hands clasped behind him, a black shadow of wool and well-scuffed riding boots. A fireplace, crackling just enough to keep a kettle hot, stood between the two sun-drenched windows and King Wilhelm, fourth of that name, sat in a heavy-carved chair with his back to the fire. The other chairs, describing something of a circle, held only a few other men. The one at the king's right, though, was Saint Woden himself.

"My people are preparing for war this winter, and I would prepare with them," Kiefan said. His fingers, wrapped around each other, clenched.

The king glowered under the simple gold band he wore for a crown. "I told you to take no risks."

"It was a risk to send me at all."

It was Saint Woden who crooked two fingers to call Wenda into the room. "There will always be risks," he said, putting a hand on the king's arm. "Let's eat and then move on."

Wenda put the platter on the table — a massive slab of dark-stained oak — where a lone secretary scribbled, attended by stacks of papers and books. She plowed aside a couple of tomes with the platter's carved rim. Parselev followed her and I trailed him, my feet a little slow and my hands finding the end of my braid, at the small of my back, to twine in my fidgety fingers.

"Mechdan, good to see you." Saint Woden came to clasp my teacher's hand with a nod. I dropped to one knee, fist to my breastbone. Then, Mother have mercy, he turned to me. "And your apprentice?"

"Kate Carpenter, m'lord. Student, now that she's a physician."

A pair of fingers, hard as iron, hooked under my chin and tipped my head up to meet his gaze.

If I hadn't known him, Saint Woden would've been another broad-shouldered knight of seasoned years but yet un-greyed. One with some slight resemblance to the king — ashy blond, bearded, blue eyes in a sternly chiseled face. But when he looked at me, I felt a pluck and my kir rang like a bell, blooming from my chest in a brief, bright flower. The chord it sounded hung in the air, so clear and yet going so un-noticed. My third sounding, and still I startled at it.

It earned me a nod from the saint, though. "And did this Englic apprentice live up to Qadeem's confidence, Kiefan?"

Kiefan had not so much as relaxed, yet, in the center of the room. But he turned his head, and light caught on the silver band he wore. "She kept us well through ice and storm and stole a man back from the Shepherd. I know we will be in good hands when she attends to the Elect's duties here in the castle."

"True, she's ready enough to aid me in that," Parselev said. The Elect was physician to the royal family and often the castle staff as well. "If Majesty is willing to have her?"

Wenda offered Saint Woden a plate of beef and cheese on bread, doused with gravy. He took it and returned to his chair as she brought a second plateful to the king. He looked up from leafing through Ther Boristan's notebook and glanced me up and down as he accepted the food.

"I've always preferred you to your apprentices, Elect. I'm sure the queen would say the same."

"Kate earned my trust on the mission, Father, and is not trust between a physician and patient vital?" Kiefan asked.

Wenda had a third plate ready in hand. To serve by ranking, it ought to be Kiefan's, but as he still stood at attention she had to wait with him for the king's leave. His Majesty glanced up and waved toward some empty chairs and a side table. "Sit. Eat, all, and let me read. Trust — true, that's what it is. Mechdan's said as much, often enough. Do you mean to decline the Elect's care?"

"Respectfully, m'lord," Kiefan said, turning to bow to the Elect, "I trust Kate with my life."

Parselev accepted that with a nod. "Majesty, I will always attend you and the queen when you call. I will leave the rest to my student."

CHAPTER 2

Ilya's body lay curled up on the high table, his arms gently tied to hold his knees to his chest. A woolen shroud secured with antler-carved pins wrapped him up snug and tidy. I had to admire the shroud's design of chunky-horned rams rendered in natural white and brown wool, interspersed with crescent moons on a black field. Traditional and dignified.

I lifted the corner of the shroud just to see his face one more time, two days dead now and pallid. His slack face had turned hollow around his eyes. Tucked between his knees and his chest, a small drawstring sack held little gifts from his family to go with him to the Shepherd's Hearth.

With a guilty glance toward his wife and toddling daughter, I laid the shroud back.

Ilya's head pointed toward a small, separate votive table on which a carved icon of the Father and one of the Mother stood looking toward him. They were old-style icons — the Father was a Ram and the Mother a Ewe, who taught us, their Flock of lambs, how to be found worthy when the Shepherd came for us. Most these days preferred icons of a human Father and Mother. Whatever form they took, it was the Shepherd who called us home from the summer pastures for the eternal winter. Or banished us to the Winter Wood, if he did not find us worthy.

Before the icons stood a small sigil of Wodenberg's trinity, carved from fine granite: an anvil with a book open upon it and a sword laid across the book. An array of scented candles burned, to mask any ill odors. Three more bags of grave gifts lay before the icons and the sigil, each marked with a name: Ther Boristan, Ulf, and Bjorn Waldgrun. The Grand Chapel's graveyard had a place for the lost dead and the gifts their family or friends wanted to send.

I clapped my hands three times and asked the Father and Mother to speak for the dead, though the four of them hardly needed it. The Shepherd couldn't have found them unworthy.

Then I retreated with a sigh. The funeral feast was laid out in the dining room on the ground floor of the east wing — smaller than the great hall, but large enough for the dozens of servants and family who came to wish Ilya a farewell. Funeral feasts were communal meals, like Saint-day dinners, the tables along two walls were steadily filling with the guests' dishes under housemistress Wenda's direction. The two roasted geese had just arrived from the kitchen and awaited carving. We lacked only our hostess, who had so swiftly arranged this feast and the handsome shroud for Ilya. That was further proof of what a good servant he'd been to the Queen's household.

I had succeeded in holding the Council's attention all afternoon with my detailed descriptions of Caercoed, especially the attention of the steward who was memory-Blessed as Parselev and I were. The king and Duke Vysokov listened as well, but Saint Woden took his leave after a little time and crooked a finger to Kiefan to follow. "Best not have lost your edge," was all he said.

Parselev had sent me to rest after my long questioning, then stayed to speak with the Council himself. I hadn't expected to doze off, but it was easy enough. I had no idea where my teacher was now; one of the housemaids had fetched me for Ilya's funeral. I drifted through the bustle of his fellow servants, returning kind smiles and nods but a stranger all the same.

"Goodfolk, attend!"

The sharp announcement brought us all around to the door as Queen Mercia Weissberg of Wodenberg, born the Aethlings-dóhtor of Suevia, entered, flanked by two handmaids. I dropped to my knee in obeisance along with the servants. The lady swept by, the train of her black gown trailing on the floor and her fine black veil light enough to cloud behind her. Since her two sons had died, she'd worn only black, in mourning. Her simple gold crown was the only touch of warmth I glimpsed on the drawn face under the dark tint of the long veil. Sorrows had put silver in her sandy hair and hard lines around her mouth.

Queen Mercia went to the high table and laid a hand on Ilya's shrouded shoulder. We all stood as she said whatever quiet words she had for him. Then she turned to his wife. His little girl threw herself against her mother's leg, hiding in her skirts. Whatever the queen said then, Ilya's wife burst into tears and tried to put on a brave smile, but it trembled.

The queen turned to the rest of us. "Goodfolk, our family is a little smaller today. Let's remember Ilya Rabskov as we share this meal, and then bring him to his resting place together."

That was the signal for us to move on the tables of food and for the pages to begin handing out steins of autumn ale. I made sure to catch one of those as they passed by; Majesty served a fine, apple-based ale. While I sipped, the clot of guests gathered food from the tables, then fell to talking and eating on their feet rather than moving off to sit. Queen Mercia drifted among them, greeting and chatting, but while they were quick to curtsy or bow in respect, they averted their eyes from her and didn't say more than they needed. Her face hardly wavered from a thin, sad concern, and I began to wonder if she truly saw the people before her.

"Have you paid your respects yet?" Anders asked beside me, nearly startling the ale out of my hands.

"Yes, just a moment ago."

"Watch for me, as I do?" Anders took a step toward the high table.

"Watch for you?"

"I'll only be a moment, then gone." He took another step and I moved to follow. "I need to apologize," Anders said, turning to Ilya at the table, "for that lamia getting past me and biting him. They played me, that time, as if they'd sparred with me before and knew what to do."

I glanced across the crowd at the tables but saw nothing of note. "I apologized for the charm I bungled. He died... I should've..." I tugged the corner of the shroud a little further over Ilya's head, to hide him.

Anders met my eye. "You did what you could, I'm sure."

"I could've done better. Your wound was far worse, and yet here you are."

"It was those ice-cold hands of yours that woke me. Drifting off to sleep and —" He jerked awake, with a teasing smirk. To Ilya, he said, "You didn't suffer those, at least. May a warm Hearth await you, friend." As he turned away, Anders said to me, "That ale looks —"

"Get out of my house."

Queen Mercia's quiet, seething words all but threw me back against the high table in a fright. Anders straightened under her harsh gaze, losing all trace of mirth. She faced him with arms folded, hands pale and spidery on the black, pinning him with her eyes though he had several inches' height on her.

"You are not to be in my house," she said. "Ever."

"I was summoned by the Council, Majesty," Anders said, his eyes fixed on the far wall.

"You were not summoned to this feast. Odile, call my guard to remove this vermin."

One of her handmaids grabbed her skirts and ran for the door.

Anders' eyes flicked after her and I risked a glance, too. Kiefan stood aside in the doorway to let the maid by and walked in.

"I came to wish a friend farewell," Anders told the queen.

"Speak again and I'll have you whipped."

"Mother, don't make this day any worse for Gudrun and her daughter," Kiefan said, stepping between the two of them. "She's lost her husband and nobody wishes his memory tarnished by a poor funeral. My guard has his duties to see to and he won't trouble you any further."

Shifting her focus to Kiefan, Queen Mercia's face gentled at last. Then she *tsked*, softly, reaching for his collar where the golden tail of his knight's crest brushed. "Grown so wild, on your hunt."

"Pay it no mind, Mother."

The tips of her cool steel claws re-emerged, in her voice. "I trust you will save my guard the trouble of dealing with that creature," she said, and turned away.

"You'd best go," Kiefan said. "I'll have no say if she sees you again."

"My apologies, Ilya." Anders looked over his shoulder and spat the words. "I've tainted your memory."

Kiefan's tone soured. "You do Kate no favors by standing beside her, either. Go."

With a snort and a dark frown, Anders stalked to the far door and slipped out a few moments before a knight wearing three gold stars on his tabard, for the Queen's Guard, appeared in the other door with Odile the handmaid. Kiefan gestured to the Guard, a curt flick of one hand, and the knight nodded but crossed the room to check with the Queen as well.

"You survived the Council?" Kiefan asked me. He stepped away from the high table, toward the votive where the icons watched over Ilya.

"Yes. If you were there all morning, they must have been gentle with me."

"It's nothing new for me to report to the Council. Father was no more disappointed than usual." I thought the faint frown on his brow might be a headache, though. "You've said your farewell?"

"Yes, I've been here — well, I had no place else to be. The Elect wished to speak to the Council and I haven't seen him since then."

"I said mine when they laid him out this morning," Kiefan said. "There's food, but…" He turned to check on his mother, whose face had kept the dark frown Anders had put there. The servants were quick to scatter now to the tables to sit at a safe distance and eat. The queen guarded the remaining food, it seemed, her two handmaids back in their places.

How she still mourned her two sons was no secret, and that she'd said she'd die before the king touched her again was well known. There'd been other rumors, never spoken above a whisper, that the queen's mind had broken after the deaths, the bastard, and the bitter duty that had created the third prince. I thought of what my teacher had said of Her Majesty suffering from a flawed meridian, and those terrible headaches.

Still, Anders had only meant to say good-bye to Ilya. It was cruel to deny anybody that.

Kiefan leaned close to my ear, breath prickling the fine hairs on my neck. "Come, I want to show you something."

Kiefan led me down the east wing hall and opened a door onto a narrow, straight stair that took us downward. The lamplight from the hall quickly dimmed as we descended, and his hand found mine. My breath caught for a heartbeat, at that.

"A few more steps, and turn," he said, and sure enough when we turned the corner a lamp burned in the wall sconce. Another hallway, windowless and cool, brought us to an ironbound door in the wall. He put his hand on the latch and it clicked open.

Evening sunlight and birdsong trickled into the hall. I'd lost track of time in napping and waiting for the funeral, but it was near sunset now. Outside the door, Kiefan stepped down onto a flagstoned cloister walk and gestured for me to watch the drop when I did the same.

He still held my hand. No voices, nobody nearby to see us. I swallowed a nervous lump in my throat, wondering where he meant to take me. And what he meant to do there. Surely I didn't have to worry whether anyone would hear me scream… was there anything he could do that I'd need to?

My cheeks warmed.

Slim pillars held up a graceful stone arcade. Between them, we walked onto frost-burnt grass. A gnarled apple tree, leaves golden and half fallen to the ground, stood ringed by a waist-high juniper hedge. Beyond, the castle wall rose sheer and seamless. To either side, the watchtowers bulged from its face and spiked up like smooth horns. I had to crane my neck to find the tips, and in doing spotted the catwalks that connected each tower to the roof of Castle Kaltkern. The garden lay below the keep, hemmed in by saint-cut cliffs on both sides.

A crescent garden, I saw now. To either side, more fruit trees dropped their leaves, and the rose bushes had gone bare for the winter, but the juniper hedges held their green. Under the central apple tree waited a broad wooden bench. By my hand, still warm in his grip, Kiefan led me toward it and a tangle of hopes and fears snapped tight around my heart.

He didn't sit, though. He stood under the tree and looked up. "Sometimes I can get some quiet here," he said. "When Mother isn't seeking solitude herself."

I looked up, too, into golden leaves and dark branches. Blue, beyond. "It must be lovely in the spring." I could imagine the trees hazed by white blossoms.

"And in the summer, when the roses are out, the scent hangs like a fog between the walls."

He still held my hand. My nerves eased, I sidled closer to his shoulder. He smelled of sweat, under his layered woolens. "You spent the afternoon at swordplay?"

He nodded, bringing his gaze down to me. "I thought he would send for the captain, but Woden tossed me a sparring sword himself. I nearly dropped it when he chose one and stood at guard."

"You sparred with a saint?"

Kiefan shook his head, disbelieving it himself. "I saw him spar with Captain Aleks, once. She said it was her most valuable lesson."

"You lived to tell. You didn't ask him to give you quarter?" I risked a smile.

A chuckle. "He gave none, that's true. I won't know how many bruises I have until morning, I'm sure." He tugged out the collar of his cote to feign checking inside. "We spoke about the lamia, and he told me I was using my kir to keep their teeth off me despite the close quarters. The beginnings of a kir-shield. With training, I'll be able to control it more."

"We all learned something out there." I looked up as a chilly breeze sent a few more leaves spinning from the branches and caught a wince on Kiefan's brow. "Are you hurt? A headache?"

"A little."

I knew what that meant. I put my hand on his fresh-shaven cheek and turned his head toward me to call his kir. It glowed in answer, revealing a few tangles on his meridian, but I got no further in checking him.

Kiefan leaned over and kissed me, wrapping me in both strong arms. Coaxed my mouth open to spar with his tongue. He left me breathing harder with my palm still on his face.

I combed my fingers over the ridges of his Blessing at the back of his neck and pulled him down for another. His arms tightened on me. His lips made their way to my throat and his tongue tracing the hollow there stabbed a shiver into my spine. My pulse surged.

With a hard breath, he buried his face against my neck and squeezed me till I squeaked. I clung to his shoulders, my feet lifted an inch off the ground. He held me warm and safe, despite the cold breeze.

"You must come to Prohzgrad with us," he said against my neck. "Cure me with a kiss each night."

I swallowed a sudden lump. "You're going away?" I managed to ask through his grip.

He loosened, letting my feet back to the grass, but still held me. "Father must see the duke's war preparations," he said, meaning Duke Vysokov. "Then, north to Kernwiese and Rukharbor. Home in time for the jousting tournament. If the snow holds off, we ride south to Ansehen to seal the plans with Adalrich."

It shouldn't have been a surprise. Not even taking on my teacher's duties at the castle could earn me a chance to see him. "Parselev said I must be here to finish my training."

Kiefan put his forehead to mine, his silver band of a crown skin-warm and Blessing nubs pressing me beside my own. "Write to me. I'll send letters and tell the messenger to wait for your answer."

"My writing is awful." I only had a few years' practice.

"Do it. Write anything. And be sure to seal it against prying eyes."

"I could try writing in Arceal."

"I'll set tutoring you as one of my duties."

That pinched my heart. "You have so many duties. Your father, the kingdom…"

"Blessed, bound and sworn to Father Duty."

"And you'll marry for duty as well."

That silenced us both for a moment. "Yes," Kiefan said, a rough edge to his voice. "And you'll marry too."

Speaking it stung all the worse. My eyes blurred and cleared a bit when a tear escaped down my cheek. "Someday," I whispered.

"If it's what you wish. Saint Qadeem — some of his disciples forswear marriage."

I had never thought of taking that path. "I want a home. A family." I leaned away from Kiefan, looking down. "A husband and… kisses."

He followed, aiming for my mouth, and I shrank back. Kiefan froze, worry driving off the warmth in his eyes. His arms slid from around me, down both of mine to catch my hands in his as a last resort.

Too true, all of it. We would both marry, and it couldn't be to each other. Friendship was the best we could hope for, and more kisses would only promise the impossible. I asked, "Why did you ever kiss me, if…?"

He hesitated. "I only wanted to kiss who I pleased. Not for duty. Of all the girls I've kissed, there's only few I truly wished to." Kiefan let that hang for a heartbeat, and I wanted him to do it again if there'd been so few. "I thought for sure you'd slap me."

A surprised chuckle burst out of me. "Who slapped you for a kiss?"

Sheepish, he looked away. "One of the maids. Mother warned them well not to let me overstep my honor."

"Poor prince," I murmured, laying my hand to the likely cheek in sympathy.

Sure as a charm, he kissed me again but I pushed away. Or meant to, as I might as well try to push the mountain away.

"Don't." It came out a whimper. "Don't lie to me."

Kiefan let me go. "Never, Kate."

Stepping backward, I wobbled and hugged myself as the breeze skirled through the apple tree again. "Don't make me think we could…"

I couldn't finish. I couldn't bear to look at him standing under the apple tree with eyes downcast. Turning, I walked back to the door under the columned arcade. The iron latch was frigid and heavy; I struggled a moment as it sucked the warmth from my hands.

Kiefan reached past me and lifted it. He pulled it open. "I'm sorry," he said, voice low. "You are right, of course. I shouldn't make promises I cannot keep."

I stepped up into the hall, out of the breeze. "And neither should I."

He let me lead the way, by memory, up the stairs and along the hall. Voices from the funeral feast carried; they were singing now, which was a good sign. They'd be carrying Ilya to the graveyard by the Grand Chapel soon. I stepped into the doorway and saw Parselev standing with the Queen, listening and nodding gravely. From the castle, I'd return to the Orderhaus and my room in the dormitory; in the morning, it would be back to my routine. Back to the cold shoulders and disdain of gentle-born physicians and apprentices.

On the sill, I turned to Kiefan. "I'll try to write letters if you do."

CHAPTER 3

Elect Parselev kept an office under the eaves. It owned the entire loft, had no walls, no door, only steep steps climbing from the kitchen below. The cottage was small, built at the back of the medicinal herb garden behind the hospital and up against the Order's campus wall. He and Ter Heima needed little, though. She only needed the kitchen and he only needed space for the stacks of books and his collection of herbs, extracts, seeds, roots, spare charms, strings of desiccated fungus, mortars and pestles, bottled elixirs, all the detritus of an elect's lifetime. He knew where everything was, of course, as did I after two years. But much as I loved my teacher like another father, the man could not put anything back where he found it.

I spent my first morning home sorting it all out as it ought to be. Ter Heima never set foot in the office save to bring him meals — she slept downstairs in the curtained bed by the fireplace. Some mornings, Parselev was asleep there, too, but he did not seem to sleep much.

"Elect says to stop ruining his office and come see the new patient."

Artem, one of the orphanage boys, had climbed the stair only high enough to set his chin on the office floor. I slid the last book in my hand into its shelf slot and said, "I'm not ruining it. Where should I meet him?"

"Invalids' floor. He says come quick."

I dusted my hands off; the job wasn't done, but it was an improvement. I shouldered my medicine bag. "Is Heima's bread done?" I'd been suffering the scent of it baking for too long.

He grinned. "It's cooling on the table."

Heima was washing laundry outside. Artem and I both stole a piece of bread on our way out. Artem ran with his prize. I trotted across the herb garden to the hospital's rear door. Inside, the central hallway separated the surgery rooms on one hand, curtained spaces for private examinations on the other. In the center, a broad staircase was wide and gently curved enough to carry stretchers up; we had pulleys rigged, as well, to lift heavier things straight up to the invalids' floor.

The cots lay on the floor, heads to the outside walls. Our handful of patients occupied the cots nearest the fireplace at each end of the hospital, men at one, women at the other. My teacher sat beside a cot with a small occupant. One of the Ters, Holly, had the child's mother by the elbow and was steering her toward the fireplace where chairs and a small table waited, likely to ply her with tea.

"Our first dire pneumonia," Parselev said as I settled on my knees beside the cot. It was a little boy, brown-haired, trembling and wheezing under the blankets. "Two days' travel to get him here. The town physician wouldn't have been able to heal him for a week — the mountain villages always suffer winter scourges earliest and he's hard pressed already."

The boy was lucky to have well-off parents; his mother's cloak was fur-lined, her dress embroidered, and she'd been able to leave her home for the journey. In the countryside, physicians who could only manage a few charms were all the people had. Preference went to the most ill, the worst wounded, so far as the physician's ration of kir stretched each day. After that, they had herbs, stitches and bandages. Those who could, came to the Elect — who could heal near anything.

"When were his lungs last cleared, then?" I asked. The boy's breath ran fast and shallow, his face pale. I remembered Ther Boristan, collapsed on the snow and nearly the same color as the drifts.

"His mother says he hasn't been. It's for you to decide the severity of his illness and the course of action, all without expending your kir."

The elect raised a finger, as I had a habit of doubting him when he said such things. But this time, it did not sound so outlandish.

"You've seen patterns rise when you give them kir. You can read the illness in their dance." He could read my face, too, because next he asked, "But must you give kir, to bring the patterns up?"

I flicked through my memories from the mission, looking close at the timing. "The whorls appeared when I held my kir over the skin, before I released it," I said. I hadn't noticed, and I'd energized them to bring their colors up stronger.

"I told you some time ago I could deduce anyone's health at a glance. Casting charms without touch is an elect's ability — you've strengthened a great deal but not enough for that. Still, you can call this boy's patterns up as you called the fount."

The boy was perhaps eight, too young for a Blessing or a daily kir ration, but obviously that meant nothing. I put my palm on the patient's forehead. The call was a thrum of desire in my chest. I felt an echo in the boy and faint colors traced over his skin, then vanished. I closed my eyes and called again, this time tapping the memory of Kiefan's kiss under the apple tree. Like a week's hunger, that desire had hollowed me out.

And the kir answered in equal strength, bright and clear. The boy's sluggish meridians, the antagonizing patterns in his chest, all were easy to read. So was the twist in his ankle bone. "He's club-footed," I said.

Parselev smiled. "You pass the test. Your verdict?"

"I could clear his lungs. Or I could disperse the illness. Or correct that ankle. Perhaps some of the first two, if I had more —"

"Elect. We must speak." Krepkin stood at the foot of the cot, heavy silver brows knit together over his knife-edged nose. His memory Blessing ridges had driven back his hairline, I often thought, so they could dominate his age-thinned scalp.

Parselev spared only a glance. "In your turn, Stannis. Would you ask the mother and Ter to return?"

Krepkin's mouth worked a bit, annoyed to be sent on an errand when he was the senior-most physician aside from the elect, but he continued down the invalids' row. Parselev did not even look to see if he obeyed; he laid a hand on the whimpering boy's forehead and hushed him.

"You've drawn free kir from charm-hands," Parselev said. "You drew free kir directly from the fount. Did you say you also tapped the prince's when you dealt with his headache? Good. The next step is to call the kir from a disciple to use for your own purposes — not only on its owner. Frau, do you have your day's kir still?"

The boy's mother, hurrying over, bobbed a curtsey. "Yes, m'lord Elect." Her moment of confusion resolved into eagerness. "Can it help? Anything I can do, I will."

"I will require your kir, yes. Please sit."

She did, her fur-lined burgundy cloak pooling along with her walnut-brown skirts. "But I'm not charm-handed?"

"No matter. While it may feel alarming, don't try to hold your kir when I call it. There's nothing to fear, whatever you see."

Ter Holly was charm-handed, but she only clasped her hands behind her back. Lessons such as this were common enough. Krepkin stood beside her, watching; in truth, all the patients who could sit up to see were craning their necks.

To me, Parselev said, "You recall the margrave at Ansehen. This boy isn't so near death's door, ill as he is. You'll see this more clearly, now that you've handled a fair-sized charm as you did at the fount. Watch closely. And hold onto your kir."

I put my hand atop his, on the boy's forehead, and imagined my fist clenched around the kir in my chest. Parselev spread his other hand, took a deep breath and all our eyes were drawn to his palm as the moving kir prickled up our gooseflesh. Bright tendrils snaked up from the elect's hand, twisting around, tiny stars spitting out and spiraling back in as it wrapped. From the mother's heart, kir arced to the sphere in a glittering bolt, tracing across the surface. It grew, whirled, tightened, and through my contact with Parselev's hand I could see the structure that he spun it into — the dance of strong, clear lungs and straight bones, fueled by enough kir to destroy any antagonizing patterns.

He slung the charm at the boy's chest and it splashed, shooting out ripples heavy as felted wool. The boy's kir blazed, burning clear of its taints, the congealed phlegm in his lungs turning fluid and rising up his throat. The trailing stars skittered down his leg, mending his club foot with a jerk. He twitched under our hands, his breath gurgling into a cough, and then spat up the congestion onto the pillow.

My breath sighed out of me. I'd held without thinking.

Faintly, from the bed: "Mama?"

Her eyes were tired now, maybe a little sunken, but she threw herself onto the cot and clutched her son in her arms.

Parselev leaned back to give her room, then rose to his feet with the slimy pillow in his hand. "Tea?" he asked Ter Holly as he passed it to her. She hurried back to the fireplace. He sighed as he stood, and I heard his joints crackle as if he were as old as he looked. I jumped up, meaning to help, but he held up a hand to stop me.

Krepkin was less impressed. "A few pains of age suit you," he said.

"Don't envy." Parselev shook out one leg and folded his arms across his chest.

"You've not greyed a hair since I was the girl's age." Krepkin said that with a twitch of his lip in my direction.

Krepkin had never thought much of me — I was too young and too low-born, though it seemed my chief crime was being Englic. As he was master of the Order's hospital, this had led to some trouble. His disdain marked me, and the other physicians and apprentices tended to follow his lead. He had trained many of them, over the years, and was second only to Parselev in commanding their respect.

Ter Holly brought tea for all and handed a mug to me with a smile, which I returned. There were a few of us Engls in the Order, and more turned up each year to take vows or as their Blessings brought them to study here. That annoyed Krepkin too, no doubt.

"How is it I only now hear of this hunt of the prince's?" Krepkin asked.

Parselev stepped away from the patient's bed and walked, slowly, toward the central stairs. Krepkin and I followed on either side, him with a flash of irritation at me.

"Meinrad is in his fifth year and far more skilled," he said. "Why is it you're always passing the lad over for this slip of a girl? He's as able as any physician here."

"Saint Qadeem and I agreed that Kate should go," Parselev said, and took a sip of his tea as if that settled it.

"You agreed to saddle a hunting party with a half-taught —"

That pricked my voice from me. "I was no hindrance to the party. Prince Kiefan has said I kept them well. Is his word enough for you?"

Krepkin's bushy brows fluttered. "Kept them well, oh? A girl alone in the forest with young men? For a full moon and some?"

My face burned.

"Do you doubt our prince's honor?" Parselev's tone was mild, but the question dangerous.

"The prince's, not at all. The honor of a bastard and adulterer, I doubt completely."

"Nevertheless, Physician Carpenter," the elect said, emphasizing my rank, "will be attending to my duties in the castle, save for attending to the king and queen. The prince was well satisfied with her abilities and there is no more to discuss."

"It would be wiser to see if her abilities haven't led to rendering her unfit for such duty." Krepkin spat the words.

"Sir," I shot back at him, "if you doubt my virtue, see for yourself." I took a step ahead and held out my hand to him, stopping the entire walking discussion. I knew the man disliked me, but such slander was too much. If I were gentle-born, if I had knights for brothers, he'd never dare.

When he drew up stiffly and only glared, I added a barb of my own. "Or would reading my pattern be too much work for you?"

Parselev's hand landed on my shoulder and steered me away as Krepkin's face reddened. "Insults are unbecoming," he murmured as we reached the head of the stair. "Stannis is no fool. Don't make him one in anger."

"He slandered me! And Anders too — how's he not a fool, slandering the champion of the joust?"

"Cool your head." We stopped at the stair. The elderly physician followed us, mouth set in a grimace. As he drew closer, Parselev told him, "Kate's word that she isn't pregnant is sufficient. So long as duty keeps her here, she will be my student and a Physician, due the respect of her rank. Do I make myself clear?"

Krepkin's grimace twisted and he averted his eyes. "As you say, Elect."

"I will be in the dining hall. That charm took a bite out of me. Kate, come. A little more discussion before I see the wreckage you've made of my office."

My stomach growled too, but I couldn't help rolling my eyes before I followed him.

"You missed the equinox!"

I stood in the final pose of the disciple's dance, centered over my feet, hands pressed together, eyes closed, feeling more relaxed and clear than any of the days since I arrived home. Even if my ankles throbbed from the work of the full dance.

I cracked an eye open. "Hold your focus until Ther gives us leave," I hissed back, but I couldn't help smiling.

"You were ever the good girl." Coming from Alice, that was a poke in the ribs rather than praise.

She was right, though, about Equinox. What story I ought to tell, if our mission was merely a hunting party, I didn't know. Perhaps we'd roasted a fresh-killed boar for a proper feast in the forest.

Alice had joined me in the back row of the disciple's dance a little late, falling in with a grin and a wink and saying nothing. When Ther gave us leave to go, she threw her arms around my shoulders for a hug.

"You vanished without a word — for shame!"

I hugged her back, my dearest friend even after our roads parted ways years ago. We'd lived three doors from each other, just two more Englic peasant girls. One blonde, one brunette. One seeming the good girl, the other — well, Alice had her reasons.

"I got no warning myself," I said, speaking in Englic as she did. "They simply put me on a horse and it was all I could do to hang on."

"A horse? Oh, well, m'lady." Alice waved a hand about her head airily, hanging on me by one arm across my shoulders. Then she turned more serious. "Did you achieve balance this equinox? All matters leveled and equaled? I made a real try of it. All my patrons had settled accounts with me on that morning and in turn I settled some of my debts."

"You must've cleared some?"

We crossed the courtyard as the dancers dispersed. There was a bench under the lone maple tree, as good a place as any to talk. "Two. It's becoming far too complicated. I'm in need of an accounts-keeper, but that would be another debt," Alice said, tossing her brown braid over her shoulder. She sat down, rubbing the two dark spots on her forehead, one above each eye. She'd been discipled by Saint Aleksandr and given the Blessing of heat vision. As she was a couple years my elder, she'd been Blessed first and swiftly become a good cook afterward. I had wanted the same Blessing in hopes it would improve my skills.

She flashed another smile, always so pretty on her. "Perhaps I should take one as a patron."

There was sadness behind it, though. Her debts had hounded her for years now. I tried to shift the subject. "Who threw the equinox celebration?"

"No, no talk of Arbor Street. You, Kate. You were in the castle? You? Standing before the queen? Beside Sir Anders Bockmann?" Alice grew more amazed as she went. "It's a miracle you're alive."

I tried to shrug it off. "I survived a lamia's teeth in me — what other fangs should I fear?"

That was news, by how wide her blue eyes went. "It's true you were in this hunting party the prince took up the mountains?"

I nodded.

"It's true that's where Sir Anders disappeared to, all Grain Moon?"

I nodded again and Alice's eyes turned sly.

"Oh, Kate."

For almost a whole day, I'd avoided this wearisome obsession. "Oh, nothing, Alice."

"No." She put a hand on my arm. "No, no, no. I'll allow that you don't have much to compare to, so listen to your elders." Taking a breath, she imparted wisdom to me: "It would be unfair to judge other men by him. We should all thank the lady who trained Sir Anders in bed — I can give you her name."

I wilted on the bench, hid my reddening face in both hands. Silently, I thanked the Mother that nobody nearby understood Englic. At wit's end, I turned to her with both hands raised. "I did not —" and froze. "You know Anders?"

She tipped her head, brows crowding her Blessing spots toward her hairline. "Do I know the dearest friend of Herr Theo Kaufmann, heir to a richer estate than half the barons of Wodenberg and the beating heart of any worthy party?" Alice dropped back to a faint smirk. "All the girls on Arbor Street know Herr Kaufmann and Sir Anders. You should hear the stories."

I put up a hand to fend them off.

"So add to them." She beckoned for more.

"He was kind and honorable," I said. "Flirty, yes. To the point of annoyance. But I did not share a bed with him." I doubted the bedroll-bundled sausage row counted in that tally; there'd been enough layers of wool to disguise any morning eagerness the men might've suffered.

"Yet you're on familiar terms?" Alice arched one brow, referring to how I'd left off his rank.

"After weeks knee-deep in snow? I call him a friend. No more."

She considered that, mouth pursed. "You're brave to defend him."

I spread my hands, at a loss. "I only tell the truth. He fought off lamia to protect us, he put himself at grave risk to see me to safety — and took a wound for it, nearly a mortal wound. I can't speak ill of him."

Alice considered that, too. "Most do speak ill of him, and they have their reasons. That story that went around, just before my troubles started? The story of a squire caught abed with his knight's wife? The knight dragged him into the street and beat him half to death before the City Guard stopped it."

That had been some three years ago, when I was first learning to read at the Order. "I heard a little of that."

"The seneschal allowed a duel, at the knight's demand. Anders was barely on his feet from the beating. The crowd turned out meaning to see an adulterous squire slaughtered. Saint Woden himself came to watch it."

"But he won."

"And won knighthood from his saint on the spot. Anders spared the knight's life on condition he wouldn't divorce his wife. That word was kept, but she hung herself from a rafter within two moons. Sir Anders' career has been grist for the gossip mill ever since. Be careful around him, Kate. That mill will grind you up too."

"And all the girls thank this lady?"

Alice grimaced. "We light a candle and ask the Shepherd to show mercy. She was one of us, before she wed."

We sat under the maple tree, warmed by the sun but chilled by the Shepherd's shadow. Trying to steer us back to kinder topics, I asked, "You might wed a knight, then, and escape Arbor Street?"

She smiled. "It would be a bit of luck."

"Anders, even?" I strayed closer to teasing.

Alice chuckled, but it was melancholy. "That would have to be love — a disgraced, disinherited knight? Even if he is champion of the joust? My patrons are kind enough, but I doubt any would propose. Now, Herr Kaufmann, if I could lure him away from Süssie... that man pays his debts."

"You have enough to eat, though? Despite your debts?" She wore a green dress that had been fitted close in the bodice, but it hung a bit loose now, despite her generous curves. The embroidery around the high neck was fine and expensive, and necessary to maintain her image. I knew she came to the Saint-day communal meals without a dish sometimes, and I knew it ground at her to do it.

"I am well enough, Kate, don't worry. But could I ask a favor?"

"Anything."

"I saw Magda when I came to help bathe the children this morning. She's coughing and has a bit of fever. Could you see her?"

I'd do anything for Alice's little girl. "Of course."

CHAPTER 4

The captain was right; it wasn't far. If you were on horseback.

The split rail fence was just as he described it, and the gate onto the small yard stood open. The Bockmanns' two-floor house of split boards and thatched roof stood at square angles to a barn of equal size. A couple acres of pasture also ranged inside the rail fence's embrace. Baron Rossweide's property lay on the east side of Wodenberg, where the slope ran gentler, within sight of the city wall. It was as proper and tidy as any of the baronial city homes on the east side, intent on guarding its honor and reputation.

As I walked into the yard, the clanging of metal on metal in the near pasture drew my ear. A grey-dappled horse cantered the length of the grass and swung around tight at a silent command from the full-armored knight on his back. I reached the rail fence and leaned over the top as the knight began his run through the array of man-high stacks of hay bales, each topped with a battered helmet. The stallion cornered tightly as the knight struck each helmet from its bale, always hitting with the added power of the outside of the turn.

One, two, three bales beheaded, and at the last someone leaped up with a sword and a yell. I jumped, nearly tripping on my own feet, but the stallion didn't spook. He lunged at the attacker with ears pinned back. The swordsman threw himself aside, more falling out of the way than dodging. The stallion swung around for a second try, but his knight drew him up by the reins.

The failed swordsman rolled up to his feet easily, dusting off his green and brown woolens. The knight tapped his horse to a quick step; I'd been spotted. I held my ground as the stallion slowed to a stop alongside me, prancing in place for a moment and eyeing me with his lips peeled back from his teeth.

Anders pulled off the great helm — an iron bucket, really, with an eye-slit and a few vents in the back — and set it on the saddle's pommel. His knight's crest, tied in a little tail, hung wet despite the cool air. The rest of his hair had grown in enough to hide his sweating scalp, despite how flaxen he was. "What brings you out here, Kate?"

"Captain Rytsarova put the City Guard through its paces to gauge its war-readiness," I said. "Her testing left two broken bones, half a dozen sprains and a concussion."

He grinned. "If that was all she did, she was in a kind mood. Your master sent you here, too? Alone?"

"I'm here for your stitches. It's been a week."

"And they itch like hell. I meant to call at the Orderhaus, but Nipper here has been a lazy boy. Watch his teeth."

I jerked my hand from the top rail as Anders tugged the horse's head back.

"Don't I get an introduction?" The swordsman stood with his blade's tip — a wooden practice sword, I saw now — on the grass, his other fist on his hip.

Anders waved a gloved hand. "Oh, that's my stableboy, don't —"

The stableboy slapped Nipper's flank with the sword and the horse jolted away with a snort. He reached across the fence to take my hand and touch a kiss to my fingers. "Wilhelm Bockmann, m'lady."

"Physician Kate Carpenter," I said, and bobbed a curtsy out of habit. And blushed. He was about my age, and a younger version of Baron Rossweide. One that smiled more — Frida's smile, and Anders', I recognized it. No ridges broke his warm brown hair, so I guessed he might have a strength Blessing.

"Watch out!"

Will ducked aside and Nipper missed biting his ear. Nobody was safe near the horse, just as the baroness had said.

"My stableboy can put Nipper up while those stitches come out," Anders said, and tapped his horse toward the gate and the barn.

"Squire," Will told me, to correct Anders. "Meet us at the gate?"

There, Anders dismounted and handed the stallion off to Will, then invited me into the barn with a sweep of his arm. The light was dim, despite the doors at both ends standing open, but I made out a double row of stalls, many with horses looking out, and the cavernously high rafters overhead where the hay had been lofted. The smell of leather and horse manure hung in the air with the hay dust.

A door to the side led directly into the house's kitchen. Warm bread drove back the barn's smells as the door swung open. M'lady Frida looked up from the kettle on the fire. Beside the hearth, a pregnant young lady sat sewing and a five-year-old girl played with her rag dolls.

"Boots," the baroness said first, pointing at Anders sternly. To me, "Physician Kate, isn't it? The Elect's student? So good to see you again — come! Warm up."

Anders put the boot scraper by the door to use. I crossed the room, between the two trestle tables, to take the hands m'lady Frida offered. She leaned in to peck me on one cheek.

"You're kind to remember me, m'lady," I said, taking my yellow dress's skirt in hand and curtsying as politely as I could.

"Have you come to check on Anders? You must stay for dinner."

"Yes, for his stitches. And I don't mean to impose, m'lady. This won't take long and I can be home before —"

She stopped me there. "You must stay for dinner."

I bowed my head, yielding. I stole a glance toward the pregnant woman who still worked at her seams, but she wasn't introduced. I could guess she wasn't Anders' sister; her round face didn't fit the family, and her bundled-up hair was rusty red. The little girl had retreated under the chair, watching me with cautious eyes.

Metal clanked on one of the trestle tables; one table was for preparations to cook, and was covered with bowls and chopped vegetables, the other stood bare but for the great helm Anders had tossed down. He unbuckled his sword belt and laid the sheathed blade on the table as well. "How much more do you want off?" he asked, with a teasing flick of his brows.

"Only so much as is needed," his mother answered for me. "No need to distress Sasha in her condition."

The mail leggings had their own belt under the tunic, apparently, and the iron slithered down quickly enough. Anders sat on the bench to get them off, then started unlacing his boots.

"I've a stronger stomach than that," Sasha said, knotting her thread. "Is this a new scar for you, then, Anders?"

"Not that I meant to take up collecting, but likely enough." Quilted gambeson legs were next, the unbleached wool tinted by the mail's oil.

"Kate said it was nearly the death of him," Frida told Sasha. "She saved his life, so she will always be welcome here."

"Of course, m'lady."

The barn door opened again as Anders pulled off the gambeson legs. Will made a face as he stepped in. "Father's beard, you stink."

"You didn't brush Nipper down that fast."

"For all I've been hearing of this mortal wound, I've seen no proof," Will said, scraping his boots clean. "Wore thin your welcome in Kaufmann's loft, more likely."

I still stood by the baroness, watching the pile of gear on the table grow. "It was a mortal wound, m'lord," I said. "He took all the skill I had."

Frida put a hand on my arm. "No need for titles, here. Except Reinhardt, perhaps."

"Bring the lamp over," Anders said. The window onto the front yard was mullioned glass but the sky outside was clouded. Will took the lamp from the preparation table and brought it over to peer at the wound.

That was my cue to join them. Anders sat with his foot on the bench, braie leg hiked up past his knee again. His half-brother held the lamp closer. The two red weals stood out against Anders' skin, through the dusting of blond hair.

"Lamia did that?" Will asked. "Must've been a bastard."

I sat on the bench and unpacked my small knife, tweezers, and a cleansing charm. Sasha took her turn eyeing the wound, and the little girl followed her lead. The child was brave enough to trace her finger along one weal.

"Scary, isn't it?" Frida asked. "You should thank Kate for healing Anders so well. This is Fridhilde, my youngest. We call her Hilly."

Hilly bobbed a little curtsy and murmured something that might have been a thank you. They all watched me cut and tweeze out the wool threads, jerking them from the half-healed skin. Anders did a fair job of ignoring the pain, but there were a lot of stitches. After I cleansed it all with the charm, I asked, "Do you have the bandage that he's supposed to be wearing? We'd be out a year's supply in no time if we didn't chase them down."

Sasha went to find it. I unrolled a boiled-clean one from my medicine bag and wrapped Anders up. His wound was healing well enough, inside, where the catgut stitches would bond with the flesh. I used a little kir to squash out a small discordance.

Then he put the gambeson legs back on for warmth, shucked off the mail tunic to unload all his armor onto his squire, and went to see to Nipper's grooming himself. Will collected the gear from the table and carried it into the barn.

"Not only alive, but un-maimed," Frida said, watching the door shut behind them. "Sit with me, Kate, have some tea. Dinner's at sundown."

That wasn't too far off, but we finished a pot of tea in the time we had. Frida quickly sussed from me that my mother was a midwife and that had been my first training; I put a hand on Sasha's belly and called her patterns up. The child whirled within her, entwined and yet separate, a storm of healthy kir. "The baby will come partway through the Bitter Moon," I told her, as she wasn't sure how far along she was.

"I don't know what we'll do without you, Sasha. Especially with the trouble coming in the spring." Frida had taken up her embroidery as we sat by the fire. "Midwinter's no time to be searching for a new maid. Is that Reinhardt?"

The clatter of hooves in the barn was the baron riding in, as it turned out. When he swept into the kitchen with a swirl of dark green cloak, Frida re-introduced me as the physician who had saved Anders' life. That didn't carry much weight with him, but he kissed my hand politely when I curtsied. He took the high-backed chair at the end of the empty table and unpacked a ledger book from the satchel slung at his side.

Dinner waited a little to give their third son a chance to get home; Ein, as the younger Reinhardt went by, was a pageboy at the castle. Though only ten, he was a sober-faced replica of his father. We all sat down to dine at last on the rich venison stew in the kettle and warm bread with butter and cherry preserves.

Amid his brown-haired siblings, Anders was even more the cuckoo's chick in the nest. He sat beside his mother at the foot of the table, as Will took the place at his father's right hand. Disgraced and disinherited, Alice had said. Anders had told me, on the mountainside, that he had only a sword and a horse to his name. Perhaps that part hadn't been foolishness after all.

Sasha kept our steins full of small beer and brought out the second loaf when the first was devoured. There was no talk, and I was glad to clean my bowl of stew, until m'lord Reinhardt finished his meal.

"The reports on the harvest look good," he said, sitting back in his chair with his stein. "The haying goes well, too. Will, I want you and Anders moved out to the manor before Saint-day to see to the final training of those dozen warhorses. Riker's got his hands full and we can't bring them up here. The pastures are too small."

"I'm entered in the king's joust," Anders said, with a frown. "It's less than a fortnight off, now."

"Which is where we'll be peddling those dozen fresh mounts. Those that aren't spoken for. Bring them with you when you ride out, and then take your place in the melee."

"Competitors are gathering already — I need to be at the Black Knight some nights to hear the news. And to be the news as well."

Reinhardt's face hardened. "You will not be out carousing at those parties of your friends' and coming home to this house drunk. You'll go to the manor and hone your edge there, after an honest day's work."

"I need the measure of my competitors." Anders' voice rose a notch. "And they need mine. Half the battle's won in intimidation."

Hilly slid off the bench across from him, climbed into her mother's lap and curled under her arm.

"After what happened last year, you will not humiliate me again." The baron drove the words into the trestle table with one finger as he spoke.

Frida stood up from the table, Hilly on her hip, and turned away. Sasha began to clear the table, her face a calm mask. I was tempted to follow Frida, but the argument riveted me to the bench.

"If the word of a few gossip-snipes is worth more than mine, it hardly matters where I am. They invent stories whole cloth!"

"Do you claim the queen is a liar, now?"

"Oh, the queen —?"

"Your insolence to her is an affront to my house!"

Insolence? A heartbeat's silence. "M'lord," I said, and all eyes snapped to me. "Do you mean what was said at Ilya's funeral?"

I threw him for a moment, by how he glowered. M'lord Reinhardt waved a hand to dismiss certainty. "Soon as he rode in from the hunt, he was troubling Her Majesty. She's laid simple rules and you see fit to ignore them." His temper regathered toward Anders.

"Sir, I was there. He only wanted to say good-bye to our friend Ilya, and the queen threatened to have him whipped." I clenched my hands under the table to hold my ground against the glare the baron threw. He wasn't so stern as the queen, though. Not so cold.

Anders, across the table, stared as if I'd begun spouting madness.

"I will not have my name associated with anything troubling the royal family," m'lord Reinhardt said, tapping the table again. "I do a great deal of business with the castle and I mean to keep it. If Anders wishes to live under this roof, he'll mind his manners and do nothing to harm the Rossweide name. My apologies, Physician, for stooping to argue while you're a guest at my table. I take matters of honor quite seriously."

That last he threw as a barb at Anders, but got no response.

Bidding farewell to the dead was allowed to any who knew the departed, by the Mother's and Father's teachings, so I still did not see any fault on Anders' part. I hadn't come here to argue on that, though, and I didn't wish to upset m'lady Frida any further. Best to take my leave. "I only wished the facts laid straight on the matter, m'lord." I stood from the bench and picked up my medicine bag. "Thank you for the meal, m'lady Frida. It was delicious. I should be on my way home."

She turned, wiping at her eyes to hide the tears. "Can we see you —?"

"It isn't far, and it isn't so cold. Please don't trouble yourself."

Bag over my shoulder, I fixed my eyes on the barn door and strode out. Once out in the soft rustling of horses shifting on their hay, it was safe to sprint through the barn's gate.

Outside, the evening's last birdsongs held off the hush of night. The blue sky deepened into star-scattered black above, the only remnant of the sun a ruddy glow in the west. Opposite, the full Shepherd rose to meet the three most faithful of the seven Flock moons: Strength, Kindness, and Courage. Taking a deep sigh, I pulled my wool shawl from my medicine bag and wrapped it around my neck and shoulders. My breath billowed; it would be a hard frost tonight, but I'd survived colder on Starknadel's slopes.

The way should be simple enough, straight across to River Road and uphill to the Order's front gate. I folded my arms across my chest to settle a hand in each armpit and set to a determined walk. The road was empty already and the baronial houses, sheltered behind fences and widely spaced, gave little light. As well the Shepherd shone full and my belly was full of a nice, warm dinner.

Hooves tapped up from the distance behind me. I didn't think much of it, as I was well to the side of the street, until they slowed on drawing near. I slowed as well, looking over my shoulder. Nipper puffed at me.

"I believe you're heading my way, m'lady," Anders said, tugging his horse's nose away from me.

"To the Order?"

He nodded and offered me a hand up, slipping his foot from the stirrup. When I hesitated, he said, "Yes. I'll take the Father's Discipline, as I swore to."

"And the Mother's?"

"If she'll give me the means to do so."

I took his hand and put one foot in the stirrup. It was too long for me, of course, but Anders hauled me up and advised on how to hook my knee over the pommel. It wasn't so easy as riding in boy's clothes, and if I'd been daintier I might've objected to how much adjusting it took.

"Lean on me, not his neck. Hang on."

He was the only thing to hang on to, his cloaked shoulder and his sword belt at least. Nipper walked briskly, unfazed by all of this.

"Did m'lord send you back to sleeping in haylofts?" I asked.

"We'll speak on it afterwards. It will give Mother time to reason with him."

The Father's Discipline ran four weeks, testing obedience, ability to serve and no little bit of stamina. Burlap clothes, cold stone floors and table scraps were what the Father's Dogs had to look forward to as they learned his Discipline. Most of all, it was a lesson in humility, the Father taught. All taking the vows of Ther or Ter were subject to it. So were all squires seeking knighthood from Saint Woden. And anyone could take the Discipline to prove their worthiness or clear a debt of honor. In the stories, heroes became Father's Dogs to prove their love — or to be free of it.

The tournament was only two weeks off, though. "Will you be able to compete, if you're submitting to Discipline?"

"Abbot Bruder won a tidy purse betting on me, last year. He'd love to be first to feed the mill with news of my training."

"They'll run you ragged."

"Sunup to sundown. There will be time to practice — always squires among the Dogs, before the tournament, who mean to be fresh-knighted and make a name for themselves. So there will be eyes on me as well. And there'll be no question of how honorably I spend my days." He nearly spat the last few words.

I had little to say to that, and focused on keeping my balance as Nipper clopped across Wodenberg toward River Road and home.

CHAPTER 5

Elect Parselev wrote a letter at his desk while I sat in the spare chair and read the book he'd handed me. His office was cool despite the beam of sunlight through the window under the south-facing eaves, but smelled pleasantly of drying bergamot and mint. I sat with legs crossed on the seat, leaning over the book and tracing my finger across the words as I worked them out. Parselev had written it himself, years ago, and he had sketched illustrations in the generous margins. His work was as fine as any craft-hand's.

"Did you see these starving people yourself?" I asked.

His quill stopped scratching. His voice was quieter than I expected when he answered. "I did."

"Was it a drought?"

There was no indication of who the people were, or where; he merely described the stages of starvation as they manifested in flesh and kir. The few faces included were ordinary enough, though I saw no Blessings.

"When Arcea conquered Suevia, miles of crops were burnt and grain stores captured or destroyed. Without food and without seed for the spring, no drought was needed. Arcea was little inclined to aid a people who had fought them so hard. Or to allow Wodenberg to aid them. I made those observations during a diplomatic mission to Temitte."

My gaze lingered on the black ink sketch of a man's bony hand with the kir whorls overlaid in red. I wondered how much would be lost in the spring, for a moment. "Arcea left them to starve? My parents never spoke of starving after Wodenberg conquered Englia."

"Our wish was to incorporate Englia, not to rape it. Saint Ethmund was slain, yes, but the people were not left helpless as the Suevi were."

Ethmund had been the saint of Englia; my parents had spoken of him often enough. "Surely the Suevi elect still defended their people?"

"A saint is more than a leader and protector. He is the link between the founts of his kingdom and his people. When Saint Seaxneat was killed, every elect, blessed and disciple was left with only what kir they had or what they could draw from others. Arcea's elect and the saints they sent to murder him, however, had the empire's kir to tap, and they took ownership of Suevia's founts as well. She lost her saint, her saint's royal bloodline, her elect, many of the blessed as well… and the goodfolk starved. They will do no less, here. Now, I need to finish this letter."

My gaze crept to him, as he inked his pen, and my heart quavered in my chest. Arcea would murder him, if they could. Kiefan. Anders, for the king's bastard was Woden's blood too. Would they kill me, for being the Elect's student?

A little while later, there was a voice at the front door downstairs. "Is the Elect at home, Ter?"

"He's in his office."

Boots on the stairs brought up a Russe messenger, broad-faced, dusty from the road, carrying a satchel slung across his chest. "M'lord." After a quick bow, he opened his bag. "Messages for you from His Majesty the King and His Grace, Duke Vysokov. Physician Mudrysky as well."

These were a sheaf of folded parchments, some sealed with ribbons and generous dollops of wax. Parselev took them and slid a letter-knife under the seal of the least ornate.

"Are you the Elect's student, Dame Kate Carpenter?" the messenger asked next.

Blinking, I nodded. He reached in his satchel and handed me a folded sheet of plainer linen paper, sealed with white beeswax. My name was above the seal, in a quick, sure hand. Kiefan had written.

"I'm to wait for your reply. When should I expect it?"

"Whatever for? These are reports," Parselev said, glancing up from his papers.

"For the fraulein's." The messenger looked to me. When I sat there casting about for an answer, he said, "There will be messages from the castle to return to his Majesty's retinue by tomorrow, noon. If I'm ordered to go at once, it will overrule the prince's request."

I would think of something to write by then. "It will be ready at noon."

"I will stop on my way out, then. M'lord, by your leave?" Parselev nodded and with another bow the messenger was gone.

Then my teacher cast a glance at the letter in my hands. "The prince?"

"He's tutoring me in Arceal, still." I turned it over, brushing my fingers over the smooth fibers and then across my name. His hands had touched this…

"Oh?"

I glanced up when the Elect said no more than that. His raised brows knocked my voice down small. "May I go?"

He nodded. I left the book in the chair and trotted out of the cottage, crossed the herb garden and returned to my room in the dormitory. Snapping out a spark charm, I lit the candle and sat on my bed, wrapped in my blanket against the chill, to read.

Kiefan had found another volume of d'Ovio Alain's essays in the duke's library in Prohzgrad and had asked to borrow it. He copied in a couple of sentences from one essay and pointed out a few unusual words of the Arceal. He'd written in Alemannic, aside from those parts, and I lingered over his clean pen strokes with a pang of jealousy.

Mine were always jagged and clotted with ink. Pens were unruly things, spitting and splitting and the smudgy ink got everywhere. Under my hands, that was.

They were northbound, now, across Lake Neva and further north to Kernweise. Toward the bottom, he said that others complained about the cold but he hadn't noticed it yet. There was no wind to speak of. That brought a smile to my face, despite that he meant the icy knife we'd been under in the mountain pass.

Then there was a little gap, as if he'd stopped to think, and a single line.

"I wish you were here."

And then just his name, no title, no rank.

My eyes blurred and I folded the paper away.

Our saints wanted no masses of refugees fleeing northward ahead of the Arceal army, and no hordes of helpless packed into the city walls should the enemy lay siege. Thus, there was a plan to move, to evacuate, rather than flee. The livestock and wagonloads of grain driving north were meant to deprive the enemy army of easy living off our land; we would also leave them no peasants to slaughter or women to rape.

The Leaf Moon was well off full, and wagons rumbled up the Southbound Road carrying the year's oats, wheat, and potatoes from south to north. Flocks and herds were on the move, too, away from Arcea's coming army. Here in the hospital, we saw teamsters who got kicked by cart oxen, who sprained themselves by carrying too much, or who spent the night drinking and fell down the stairs. That had only been one man, thus far, but Krepkin said there were sure to be more.

It fell to the Order to arrange much of this through the village chapels, and it fell to the Order's physicians to serve both our people and our armies.

"All first through third-year apprentices and their masters will accompany the Queen's sortie when it departs after the spring equinox," Parselev said, standing at the head of the tables we'd pushed together to seat all who'd been called to the general meeting. "They will take what supplies they can carry, but no more. Our main concerns are the maintenance of the hospital here and the staffing of the infirmary in Duke Seagrace's army."

"Surely that Englic duke can staff his own infirmary." Krepkin neatly summarized the murmur that rippled around the tables.

Parselev held up a folded letter. "Bridewell has explained his shortage at length and he will be sending as many physicians as he can. This will be a fine opportunity to earn distinction in service."

"Bridewell's been claiming a shortage for nigh on five years now. Is there no native talent in these Englic fishermen? Or have they no spine for the training?"

Physician Ada Brauer, sitting beside Krepkin, answered him. "Low-blooded, still, after Majesty's campaign burned off what nobility there was."

I clenched my jaw and sipped my tea through my teeth. A few fifth-year apprentices were nominated for early graduation and placement in the army infirmary. The names of some free-lance physicians, who maintained shopfronts in the city and took no apprentices, were brought up as well. Many new-minted physicians spent some years thus before returning to the Order to teach or to apply for higher training with the Elect.

"Of course, there's our newly graduated Englic physician," Krepkin said, pouring himself a fresh cup of tea from the pot on the nearby service. "I'm sure Carpenter would feel quite comfortable among her own people."

There were a few supportive voices.

"As there will be a substantial Russe contingent in the army, I am sure you would be quite comfortable among them as well," I said. "It's a fine opportunity for you and your fifth-year apprentice." I tipped my head toward Meinrad, who sat at his master's elbow. His ears pinkened under the attention.

"Indeed, a fine opportunity for any fifth-year." Krepkin put his emphasis on the number. "As you haven't completed your third year yet, by rights you should be among the Queen's sortie. You would be able to attend to the royal family, then, as the Elect was so eager to promote you to that post."

Parselev stepped in. "I will be here in the city to attend to His Majesty, as will Kate."

"You're sending the younger students north because there will be no time for explaining or lecturing in the midst of war, true? No lives to risk on inexperience." Ada Brauer looked around the tables for agreement and found it. "Why keep this second-year apprentice?"

"I assisted my master in the surgery at Ansehen," I said.

"You saw a few arrow-shot scouts one afternoon and aided with true battlefield wreckage for a single day." Krepkin dismissed my work with a wave of his hand. "Arcea will likely be at us from the spring equinox until the autumn. We need physicians that can be trusted alone, under such pressure. Who can manage raw volunteer nurses and orderlies."

My mind multiplied the carnage of one day at Ansehen by six moons. "I can pull my weight. I already have," I said, but it felt weak in my mouth.

"The prince's little hunting trip?" Brauer asked. "How many wounded did you treat? How dire? How many did you lose? Four years ago you walked through the Order's gate not knowing which end of a quill to write with, so I'll keep my doubts about your supposed talents — if it please m'lord the Elect."

I looked to Parselev. He met my eyes, expectant, then gave me a nudge. "Who else trusts your talents?"

My memory flicked to the chapel on the morning the mission began, and my saint's dark eyes as he smiled at me. "It was Saint Qadeem who offered me the post of physician, so question his choice as you wish."

That shut her mouth, for now. I scanned the tables and saw a few physicians willing to meet my gaze. The apprentices in attendance, mostly older than I, fidgeted and looked away. I'd stolen the place they'd all worked long years to earn, as Parselev's student, and while they'd put that aside when it came to work, they wouldn't do a hair more than that.

"The saints may see talent," Krepkin said after a sip of tea, "but there is still the issue of experience and maturity. The Englic campaign lasted moons and took its toll in more than blood."

"Kate will prove herself up to the challenge," Parselev said. "There will be patients over the winter and volunteers to train. The king's joust will offer another chance for her to prove herself. She will pull her fair share as any other physician here."

There were doubtful faces, but no answers to that. I set my teeth on my lip, not entirely sure how I would prove my teacher right.

"Let us move on to the supplies."

The letter I'd sent with the Russe messenger, before the general meeting, had told Kiefan how glad I was to hear of the new d'Ovio book and a little about my assignment to read Parselev's book on starvation. Also, I'd written about the drunk teamster.

I wished I'd had more interesting things to say.

Kiefan's second letter came in the satchel of a messenger as flaxen-haired as Anders. The man spoke with an odd accent and he first passed another handful of reports to Parselev, then gave me one folded letter sealed with white wax.

The royal party had lingered a few days at a Russe baron's manor and the king had been sufficiently impressed, and Duke Vysokov had spoken well enough of him, that it had been decided it was time the prince had a squire. Gregor Malyshev, the baron's second son.

"Gregor had no say in it," Kiefan wrote, "and neither did I. He's had his anticipation Blessing for two years but hasn't learned to focus through it — he's distracted and clumsy.

Smart enough, thank the Father, and well mannered, but awkward. It's not his fault and it's not for me to blame him for this. I only hope I can teach him one thing or another. Taking a squire was farthest from my mind, of late.

"Gregor found the d'Ovio book among my gear and asked of it. He was curious until I said the text was Arceal, and d'Ovio was an Arceal scholar of centuries past. Then he dropped the book as if it might bite, and I saw him speaking with his father, to one side, as we took our leave. This drew my father's attention and it was a few words between them. Father knows I read d'Ovio, of course, but few else do and I hadn't mentioned the new book. Father is not fond of surprises. Nor of having to speak anything but ill of Arcea.

"It did not sit well with our Guard. The extra bruises they gave me in sword-drills are not so difficult as the doubt in their eyes. They don't see the perspective that d'Ovio's given me — or that you've given, in reading with me.

"I know you would never doubt me over a book, Kate. That's been a comfort. And thank you for writing about the Elect's book. Mother never wishes to speak about Suevia, unless it's of her father."

They had just arrived in Kernweise when Kiefan wrote, and then it would be on to Rukharbor on the Englic coast. I sat with the letter in my hands, thinking of all my parents had told me of Englia and wishing I could see it with Kiefan. I could tell him all those stories, and he'd likely be glad to hear them.

Longing gnawed at me, wishing I'd been able to go with him as he'd wanted.

"Carpenter!" From the top of the stairs, Ada Brauer waved me over. I might have ignored her, but she stood with a woman wearing a sword on a double-wrapped belt. Her brown cloak was thrown back over her shoulders and she wore her black tabard over plain cote and hose like any man.

I didn't need to see the four gold stars on her tabard or the captain's brasses on her epaulettes to recognize Captain Rytsarova of the King's Guard. She wore her knight's crest long and braided, hanging free to her waist. Thanks to her dark brown hair, her three moons' regrowth since shaving her scalp for battle at Ansehen looked nearly ordinary, if too short for a lady. She watched me approach, her arms folded.

"The captain asks for a physician on hand while she tests the Father's Dogs," Brauer said. "Elect sent you to the Guard when they called, didn't he?"

"Yes, I've some experience with m'lady's handiwork," I said.

Brauer caught the barb about my experience, and glared. "You're physician to the castle. Do your duty." Finished with the issue, she walked away.

The captain snorted. "Aleksandra Rytsarova, King's Guard." She offered a hand.

I clasped it, as men did. "Dame Kate Carpenter, physician."

"Indeed." She turned and started down the stairs. I had thought she'd say more, and was a few steps behind when she spoke again. "I won't be so hard on the Dogs. Unless they need it."

"What brings you to the Order at all?" I asked, trotting to catch up as she strode out of the hospital. "The Father's Discipline is Sir Eindan's —"

"The tournament's only a week off." She cut me off in answering. "There's a great deal of interest in the competitors this year, and you've three on hand."

We crossed the courtyard to the five burlap-robed subjects of the Discipline, the Father's Dogs, and nearly a dozen younger boys, all under grizzled Sir Eindan's watch. Two of the Father's Dogs were squires preparing for knighthood, being seventeen or eighteen and considered ready by their masters. Saint Woden would see them tested and decide if they were worthy of the rank, or if they would instead be armsmen. Two Dogs were applicants to the Order, enduring the Discipline to prove their readiness to take the oath of service and be called Ther and Ter — one was a woman. And the fifth was Anders, though nobody should speak of him by name while he was a Dog.

The dozen boys were twelve and thirteen, freshly Blessed with speed or anticipation and sent to the Order to learn the basics of the sword because their peasant-born fathers could not teach them. Gently-born boys picked up wooden swords much younger, and often were ready for squiring by the time they were Blessed.

The Father's Discipline emphasized obedience, self-control, and teaching; it wasn't unusual to see the Father's Dogs giving lessons to the current crop of boys in Sir Eindan's stead. Or to see them mucking out toilets, turning compost piles, and standing ready as porters by the gate in all weather. They were to be nameless, unseen, hooded and silent.

"Eyes front!" Sir Eindan gestured for the boys to fall back in a circle, and they were quick to obey. Two of the Dogs went with them. "This's a rare treat for you, getting to see Dogs learn a thing or two. Captain Rytsarova will even do it without her Blessings, but blink and you'll miss it all. You think I've been riding your asses about stance and centering? Now you'll see why. It keeps you alive in a fight."

Trading her blade for a training sword, Captain Aleksandra pointed to one of the younger Dogs and flicked the other two away. "You last," she said, pointing the wooden blade at Anders.

The two squires acquitted themselves respectably, so near as I could tell, against the seasoned Captain. True to her word, she neither tapped her kir nor broke any bones; even without her Blessings, I could see her skill after a few exchanges. She dealt sharp raps on limbs out of alignment and drew an off-center squire into fumbling, but when the second Dog got in a hit on her thigh she nodded crisply.

"Good. You saw how proper alignment let him use his strength in the attack?" She directed that to the audience, and got a few nods back. "Watch. Again, Dog."

They repeated the sequence for the boys, slower, and the Captain traced out the strong, balanced line from the squire's feet to the wooden sword. It was as eye-opening for me as for the boys.

Captain Aleksandra nodded to the squire. "Good. Catch your breath. Now, you."

She pointed to the last of the Father's Dogs. Anders took the wooden sword from the dismissed squire and spun it around in his hand lightly.

"I've laid my bets on the tournament," the Captain said, settling into what Sir Eindan identified as a high forward guard. "Let's see what you'll bring this year."

I watched the initial flurry, but then Sir Eindan waved me over to look at the squire's wrist. I could feel the bones were a little off, and smoothed his kir so it wouldn't knot further. Until I finished, I heard only Sir Eindan's comments on the skirmish along with the occasional whack or curse. They were still dancing when I looked up.

Anders deflected a thrust and the Captain slipped in close. I heard a fist land, then an elbow and a hard crack that sent him stumbling back, hand on his mouth. The audience didn't like that, but fell silent as she swooped in and put Anders fully on the grass.

"All's fair," she said, letting her sword rest on his chest, "when it's your life or his." When he tried to sit up, she pressed harder. "Yield."

"I'm at m'lady's mercy," Anders said, with a lisp. She let him up enough to wiggle a tooth free. "And a great help you've been for the tournament."

"I never said my money was on you."

"Water?" I asked, kneeling down beside him. Anders was spitting out blood. "Let me see."

He put the tooth in my hand. "Do you know that charm?"

I didn't, but after a look at the slow, strong patterns of kir around his jaw and a quick rinse of the gushing blood, I slipped the tooth back into place and dropped a small charm onto its roots to make it match its mate across the jaw. It seemed to take.

"If that loosens again, I'll try something stronger," I told him, voice low.

Captain Aleksandra snorted. "I did you a favor, Sir Anders — lose the tooth, draw fewer dancing partners and focus on your training."

"It'll keep me off the dance floor a week," he muttered, pressing on the lump that was already growing. I swatted his hand away. "Thank you, m'lady," he said, with a wincing smile, then stood and brushed himself off.

"Drills!" Sir Eindan announced. He described the series of moves they were to practice and tapped Anders' shoulder with his wooden blade. "Since you got these correct enough, oversee them. You other Dogs report to Ther Ivor for duty."

My second letter to Kiefan had been to sympathize about d'Ovio. His writings were assigned to most of the physicians' apprentices, partly to learn Arceal for the purpose of reading anatomical texts, and there were discussions of his ideas from time to time.

Those discussions were among fourth and fifth-year apprentices, though. Parselev had given me the book early, as he did in all things concerning me. I was not made welcome in discussions, and I also had not read some other books to which the apprentices often referred. Thus, there'd been nobody for me to talk to before Kiefan agreed to tutor me. I was eager to start this new d'Ovio book with him.

I also wrote a little about proving my worth to the physicians over the winter. Without giving names, I admitted that I had my doubts about changing their minds. The Elect had put me in charge of the tournament infirmary for the first day, during the general melee, to give me a chance to lead on my own.

The royal messenger was Englic, this third time — pale, freckled and hawk-nosed. He trailed slushy boot-prints from the first crust of snow that had fallen that morning. His accent was thick and I think he was glad to find someone who spoke his tongue.

Kiefan wrote about Rukharbor, the Englic city on the northern coast. Duke Seagrace had been a perfect host, he said, full of stories about the sea and the kir-bred rukhs that soared above the coast hunting seals. Kiefan's older sister, both princess and duchess, kept them warm and fed, and her two sons followed Kiefan like ducklings.

She had, he confided, changed in becoming a wife and mother. When he'd been little and she already blooming into womanhood, a younger brother tagging at her heels during banquets and dances had been something to foist off onto the housemistress. Now, she'd actually consented to dance with him once he'd obliged every other gentle-born maid at the court.

The duke's family was coming south with the king and a contingent of knights for the tournament. They'd stay the winter and meet the duke's army when it marched south. Kiefan had watched some of the Englic knights jousting in the snow — ankle deep already, for snow always came early on the coast — and picked up a training sword with a few. The duke's knights were talented enough to represent him well, Kiefan judged.

He hoped to see me at the joust, though not for being in the infirmary. He'd bring the book of d'Ovio's essays, which he hadn't started reading yet.

I set my teeth on my lower lip, mentally hunting for a block of time in the four days of the tournament that I could get away, and wondering if I could even find Kiefan in the bustle and noise.

CHAPTER 6

I heard shouting and trumpets and went to the infirmary's open front flaps with the rest to see the royal procession arrive. The King's banner, its stark white moon silhouetting a black Mount Woden, rippled in the breeze a few steps ahead of the Russe black bear on red, the Alemanni elk on white, and the Englic white rukh on divided blue and grey. His Majesty rode at the head of the parade, arm raised to acknowledge the cheer from the crowd. A subtle tug of kir pulled my gaze to the three riding with him, though; the saints attended all of the king's jousts. I struggled to find Kiefan in the stream of riders as they milled before the three gaily bedecked pavilions.

Two days ago, this had been a mown hayfield that smelled of dry grass and the coming snow. Now it smelled of leather, oiled mail, manure and wood smoke. The pavilions had been set up along one long side of the jousting field and the goodfolk congregated on the other, leaving the short sides for the competing knights to use. And for the infirmary.

"They'll be starting soon enough," Brauer snapped, herding us back into the infirmary. "No use gawping at the king. Saint Qadeem will be here to see the quality of our discipleship. Holly! That kettle had better be a-boil. Liese, get those blankets on the cots. And Carpenter. Aren't you to be mistress of all this?"

Soured in trying one more time to spot Kiefan, I turned away and stalked across our little infirmary toward the surgery at the back. Parselev had reminded all of them to defer to me and taken his leave to sip tea in the Queen's private pavilion on the far side of the jousting field. Brauer tailed me like a hound, giving orders before I could and countermanding those that I did.

"There's no need to harry them," I told her, stopping at the pinned-up flap in the canvas wall that sectioned off the surgery. "Our Ters are no fools and they have the trainees well in hand."

"Keep on them or you'll find they're lying about with nothing ready," she said. "Wasting time on the lightly wounded when there's worse to be seen to."

Through the open front, I glimpsed the wagon we'd brought to act as an ambulance. "You'd best see the ambulance is in order, then, and make sure they waste no time when they go to clear the field."

A hundred knights and more descended on the city late in the harvest season for the king's great joust. Many came after winning a summer tourney in a village somewhere. Some were ringers in the pay of rich patrons with wagering strategies. Freshly knighted squires came to try for the prizes — more of those this year, I'd heard it said, to fill the ranks after Ansehen. To winnow the crowd, the tournament began with a grand melee. After each pass, the field would be cleared of the fallen.

I had never enjoyed watching this stage; my mother and father had agreed, and we'd only come to see the later days of the tournament when the knights jousted one on one.

Our infirmary looked directly onto the field, and the view filled rapidly with warhorses' rumps and knights' backs. Squires darted across the rear of the line, swapping out lances and adjusting stirrups at the last moment. The horses shifted and snapped at each other, packed in tighter than they'd like. Grey and black and chestnut tails in a row, and their riders all alike in grey mail, many wearing black military tabards as well. A scattering of brown, though and…

I thought to look for dark green, then, for Anders. But I spotted two, at least. It wasn't an uncommon color.

"Knights of Wodenberg!" Saint Woden's voice carried on a ripple of kir from the royal pavilion at the center of the field's sideline. "Let honor be served in this tournament, first of all. We compete as brothers, not enemies — there will be enemies aplenty come spring. Fall as you may and think it no shame, for it is an honor simply to stand in this line ready to serve Father Duty. Among you ride future elect of Wodenberg!" Saint Woden raised a fist for a cheer, and got it. "I've not had a bound elect in twenty years, so do not doubt that I'm watching you. There shall be two passes with lances. There shall be combat on horseback and then combat on foot. The last thirty-two standing advance to the next round. Use only the blunt lances and training blades provided. Use only your own skill and strength. No Blessings and no kir."

I felt it before I saw it; I don't know how even the dullest mind could miss the kir draining from a hundred men at once. It rose from the crowd of knights, rippling up in folds of green and gold. Stars condensed in the haze as it arched overhead, twisting slowly into a thick spiral. Once gathered, the glittering mass split in three and arrowed down to its master saints.

In a blink it knotted and vanished, and my mind reeled for a moment as from a quick shot of brandy burning behind my nose.

The horses shifted in their line, some starting to jitter. They waited for the trumpet.

It must look grander from the sidelines. The pavilions would be full of lords and ladies in colorful finery, taking in the sport over refreshments. Kiefan would sit beside his father, surveying the lines, discussing something of royal concern about knights and war. The sun would shine on horse's hides and men's armor, picked out in rays by their billowing breath.

I walked out to see, not much caring what Brauer thought or whether the Ters watched with me. Flags snapped in the breeze, atop the pavilions. The tips of the raised lances swayed in a row overhead. Horse tails swished, impatient.

Trumpets blared and half the warhorses sprang forward into a run. The remainder tore up the earth under knights' spurs. Lances lowered one by one as they pounded across the grass.

"I can't watch," one of the Ters said, beside me.

Master said a doctor must not look away, so I did not.

The impact tore across the ragged line in a cloudburst of splintered wood. Horses crashed against each other, shoulders striking shoulders and knocking both askew. Some plunged to the ground, hooves flailing, their knights a tangle of limbs and helms. Riderless mounts ran loose past the line. And, somehow, dozens of knights still a-horse and alive slowed their mounts as they reached our end of the field. Some even still carried lances.

"Ambulance!" I shouted, startling the driver out of his reverie. Brauer stood on the grass watching the charge. "Go with them, Brauer," I called. "See they don't waste their time."

If she was so eager for efficiency, let her see to it.

Our first wounded knight rode up to the infirmary clutching his shield arm, and there was no more watching the tournament. Orderlies caught the knight as he swung from the saddle and set to undressing him. I put a hand on his face and called up his kir.

"Broken collarbone," I said. "Ter Liese? Take him."

A lance striking the shield just so sent the rim into the collarbone and upper ribs. Sometimes the shoulder took the blow and popped out of joint. Now and then, an upper arm broke.

Those were common wounds, and those men could ride to us. When Brauer returned with the first wagonload of the most seriously wounded, I touched each one and brought up their kir to show me their injuries. One, a leg broken in three places. The second, crushed ribs and bleeding inside. The third's prime meridian along his spine was a jumble of shards from the waist down, as if he had been made of pottery when he fell from his horse.

"Runner! Fetch the Elect!" I shouted. We could not help the third. "Him, to the surgery." I pointed at the second. "Ter Holly: three blood-stops evenly spaced, and splint." That for the first, gesturing at his ruined leg. Brauer and the ambulance were already gone for more. Orderlies carried the two wounded in on blankets. "Watch him and wait for the Elect," I told the orderlies ready to pick up the third. Thankfully, the man was unconscious.

In the surgery, Ter Biya had already used a knockout charm on my patient. His mail shirt was off and his gambeson untied down the front, revealing a plain cote streaked with sweat. "Get just that off," I told them, pointing at the gambeson tunic. They left off unbuckling his mail hose.

I collected the charms and blades I needed while they shucked him. His breath was rapid and shallow, his skin turning pallid from lack of air. Slicing open the side of his cote, I called up his kir again to place the breaks and the wound precisely. The curve of his ribs was interrupted by a hard line of broken bone, and under the skin patterns whirled and pooled, muscling in on the delicate dance of his neighboring lungs. Lines feeding into his prime meridian from the lungs wavered, weakened.

A little incision and the blood gushed out, dark and lumpy. When it dropped to a mere drip, I hooked my finger in the cut and fished out a clot. Kir glowed brighter and stronger in his lungs as the pooled mass drained. "Bandages," I said, reaching for the blood-stop I'd picked. When the blood truly slowed to drops, I squeezed the charm and let it fall onto the patient's ribs. Inside, the bleeding stopped.

If I had kir left — unlikely as that was — at day's end, I could see that his ribs would heal true, but that was a simple thing and several of us could manage it. I spent a cleansing charm on my incision and pressed the bandage to it.

"We'll see to him," Ter Biya said, putting her hand over mine. "Go sort the next load."

I heard the ambulance pulling up in the front. At the surgery's door, I saw two riders jump down from the wagon bed. One was Brauer and one — the two Thers by the shattered knight glanced up as the second's shadow fell on them. They scuttled back on their knees, bowing.

Saint Qadeem merely looked at the shattered knight; my memory supplied the impossible jumble of his prime meridian that my saint must be seeing. Kir welled up, small but so strong I could feel it across the tent and then growing until every head in the infirmary turned toward our saint. Light gathered in m'lord's palm, bright and golden as a miniature summer sun. Kneeling, he laid the kir down with one sweep of his hand, as if clearing the heap of shards away.

And that was all; the knight startled awake and sat up. Saint Qadeem stood and brushed his hands off on the dun cloak he wore over dark woolens. He spotted me across the infirmary and I remembered to drop to one knee, put my fist to my heart in obeisance. A rustle spread across the tent as those who could, did likewise.

"Please continue," our saint said. "See to the wounded and pay me no mind."

I had to walk past him, to the ambulance, but a few moments of checking kir and triage set my mind back in place. From the wagon, I put broken bones in others' care and saw to a dislocated shoulder myself. I spared a little charm to re-knit the worst of the damage to the joint.

The shattered knight climbed to his feet on the arm of a Ther and declined a cup of water in favor of tracking down his horse.

The field was finally clear, so the remaining knights set to littering it again. While they drew up on their opposite sides and prepared, I took a deep breath and approached Saint Qadeem, who'd taken a cross-legged seat on one of the empty cots.

"Thank you for coming, m'lord," I said, kneeling again. "I didn't mean to inconvenience you."

"I have a surfeit of kir today," he said, "and Mechdan has duties to see to. No inconvenience. Ah, there they go again." I risked a glance at him as the galloping of hooves caught his ear.

Nobody in Wodenberg had olive brown skin, or hair and beard so black. In profile, he sent my memory to my father's carved rukh finials for the duke's manor — sleekly polished, yet sharp. Qadeem's clothes seemed plain, but were finely woven, and his cloak was lined in snowy white ermine. In the distance, wood and horseflesh crashed. He turned back, caught me looking. His eyes were dark as his hair. Not the common blue, not brown, but black.

My questions were obvious, I suppose. "Yes," he said, "my homeland is far away. And long ago. Go, they've made more work for you. Mechdan will want to know how you've managed."

My teacher would hear it from the saint himself; that added speed to my feet.

———————————⟶×——————————

Next morning, I was grateful to still have the fur-lined felt cloak I had worn through the mountain pass. I wrapped it close against the wind when I left the infirmary tent. Flags and banners lashed as the wind peaked, then ebbed.

A quick-work fence delineated the jousting lane in the tournament field. Fresh combatants at either end checked their horses, their supply of lances, and their armor one last time before mounting up. I scanned my memory for the announcement of their names, but neither was Anders. The eliminations had started at dawn and would go till sundown, or however long it took to halve the thirty-two.

The crowd on the grass, recovering from the cold gust of wind, roused a cheer as one knight climbed into the saddle.

Parselev and I had discussed yesterday's events at length while checking on the patients still in our care. There had been the matter of a misplaced box of knockout charms. And the angry baron whose son had lain waiting for care while a more serious wound was seen to. I had done a fair job, my teacher said, and would improve. Now the infirmary was in the hands of Krepkin's apprentice and I had the remaining morning to myself. I would have charge again in the afternoon, but I hoped to steal a few moments of smiles and wit before plowing past Brauer's sour face again.

Squires handed up great helms to their knights; the one nearest me wore a red silk kerchief threaded through the rear vents and knotted. A lady's token. It billowed when he kicked his mare into a full charge, lowering his lance across the horse's neck toward the oncoming knight's shield.

I turned my feet toward the pavilions and tried not to watch the two ride toward each other. I meant to keep my eyes on the king's pavilion, in the center, but I couldn't help looking just before the knights hit. Both struck, one's lance snapping in three, the other's holding firm. One was thrown back against his horse's rump but held on, then dragged himself upright in the saddle as he tossed his lance down.

"Your business, Fraulein?"

The closest pavilion was Duke Seagrace's and knights of his own guard stood at the entrance. The accent on the older knight, who'd spoken, was not too thick but I answered them in Englic nonetheless. "I am Elect Parselev's student, Dame Kate Carpenter, and I am expected by the prince. Do you know if he is in the pavilions?"

I might have circled around to the king's pavilion, but behind the line of pavilions ran dozens of smaller tents and tethering lines for horses and latrines and cooking areas and light fences of split rail to cordon it all off. Far simpler to find my way through.

"You must be a local," the older knight said in Englic. "Where's your family hail from?"

My father had told us many times. "Stoneham-on-Ebb."

The knight nodded and twisted around to lean through the flap door. "Steward, a young miss here. Says she's the Elect's student."

A woman lifted the flap and gestured me inside. The lady was stout, no taller than me, and wore a grey dress with a white wimple and veil as married Englic women did. The small nubs of a memory Blessing peeked out from under the veil along with a little blonde hair. She looked me up and down and asked, "Dame Kate Carpenter? M'lord hoped to meet you. I am his steward, Hope Dunlea. Come."

M'lord? I gripped the strap of my medicine bag, glad for its steadying weight. All attention was on the tournament outside; most of the audience sat in a line of camp chairs where the tent wall would have been. We went unnoticed behind their backs as the same pair of knights laid into each other with swords, their horses circling and prancing.

On a low couch sat a lady in blue so light I thought of the snows of Starknadel, her wimple and veil dyed to match and embroidered with scarlet roses. She noticed me as the steward leaned to whisper to the man on the couch beside her. She wore a plain band of silver under the veil.

I dropped into obeisance to the princess. "Majesty," I murmured.

She dipped her chin as her husband rose from the couch to meet me. Like his banner, his surcote was divided blue and grey, the white rukh caught in a fierce plunge with bloodied talons outstretched. The fine embroidery picked out each feather in its wings.

"Duke Tomas Seagrace of Rukharbor," Steward Dunlea said. "Dame Kate Carpenter, physician, daughter of Edward Carpenter of Stoneham-on-Ebb."

My duke was not so tall, not so handsome as some, but his smile was easy and warm. An anticipation Blessing broke through his auburn hair and marked him as Woden's disciple. "I remember Edward Carpenter," he said, putting out his hand. I took it and dropped to one knee, meaning to make obeisance, but he tugged me to my feet instead, which reminded me I wasn't a peasant any longer. A simple curtsy was correct, now. "Your father cut some fine furnishings to grace my manor in Wodenberg, and has served the household there ever since. Please give him my best wishes, next you see him."

"I wish I could, m'lord," I said, still a bit flustered. "He was taken by the Shepherd soon after the battle at Ansehen. He always spoke highly of you, m'lord."

A frown twisted his brow and his hand tightened on mine. "I am sorry to hear that. Truly sorry." He switched to Alemannic to say, "The king's taken two subjects from me, then, Kiefan?"

My heart stumbled in my chest when he stood, trying to fight a smile at my surprise. "Only one was intentional. My father apologizes for — requisitioning Kate without your leave, but time was of the essence."

He'd been sitting in a chair to the side of the sofa the entire time. I'd glimpsed the ginger-haired squire standing behind the chair, but the princess had stolen my attention away.

"Knighted, yes. I am sure she took it well in stride." Duke Seagrace let my hand go at last. "I hear you have served the crown well. That you've represented Englia well."

"I've tried to, m'lord."

The duke's voice softened, blending into the clatter of swords outside and returning to Englic. "You know how they think of Engls, in Wodenberg. Do not forget that you serve for us all, when you serve the king."

I bowed my head. "M'lord."

"Your graciousness in the matter is kind, my father noted," Kiefan said, circling behind the duke to join us. "I thank you as well. It will not become a habit."

Duke Seagrace was not so old, either, I saw when he twisted a smile back at Kiefan. Not thirty yet. "I trust you will see it does not. I thought I'd sussed out all the odd habits Gisella brought —" He let the herald cut him off when the names of the next contesters were announced.

The princess Gisella twisted around with an eager smile. "It's Pirra!"

"Your pardon," the duke said to Kiefan, then included me with a glance. "I must see this match. Please stay and watch with us, Physician. Kiefan, you've wagered on Pirra, yes?"

"I look forward to collecting, too. She will compete again tomorrow, I'm sure."

But Kiefan didn't move toward his chair while the duke sat beside his wife. I wasn't sure what he intended, for a moment. Then Kiefan took a step back from the line of chairs, gesturing with an open hand to his squire, who still had his eye on him. With a slight nod, the boy turned toward the jousting field.

"That's Gregor," Kiefan said, voice low. "His father's barony is on the north side of Lake Neva."

"You haven't the time for a squire, you said." I kept my voice low too. We retreated another step.

"I don't. We managed a lesson or two in Rukharbor, between inspecting the troops Tomas has assembled and going over the records. I even saw the city a little — the whale carved into the hillside above the city, if nothing else. Have you seen it?"

The rear of the pavilion was arranged for dining at long tables, and a maid tended a fire pit to maintain the supply of hot tea. At the back, a door flap hung loose and belled now and then in the wind.

"Seen it?" I nearly laughed. "I've only been to Ansehen and Vorspitz, outside this city."

Still, his eyes were bright as he described it, and I hung on his words. "The hill is a thick meadow, and the carved lines are filled with chalk from the cliffs. It's a massive thing, arched like a bow, and there are white patches on its head."

"Keto," I said. "He brings good fortune. He's always watched over Englia."

"Tomas said nobody knows who carved it."

"It was Saint Ethmund, I was told."

That gave him a moment's pause. "Perhaps not what you'd tell the king who led the conquering army," he said. "I'd have thought he would trust me to hear the truth."

My hand reached for his, at that. He caught it and squeezed. Wanted to pull me closer, I could see it in how his eyes sharpened, and though I wanted that too I let go. Had to let go. I couldn't look at him, and couldn't let the silence tempt me either.

"You found a book, you told me in your letter," I said.

"Yes." He shifted to the new subject gratefully. "Vysokov suffered a fire, not long ago, and some books were damaged. I found them laid out for the chamberlain to see what could be salvaged. I noticed the title of the essay — 'On Truth' — and d'Ovio's style on an open page. I brought it with me…"

Kiefan gestured toward the doorflap; we had stood in front of it for some time already. The promise of a new book put a smile on my face. "It wasn't badly damaged?" I asked.

He held the flap open for me and led the way through the bustle outside. Preparations for the mid-day meal were in full roll, and we darted through it all as we went. "Singed a bit,"

Kiefan said. "It was doused with water, but it's dried now. A bit fragile, perhaps. I wrapped it well for the journey."

We angled across, into the area behind the King's pavilion, and the bustle fell away as we entered a cluster of smaller tents. Kiefan nodded to the knight standing watch as we passed — he was one of the Prince's Guard.

"Hold the flap for me," Kiefan said, stopping at one of the tents. The grey-cast canvas and the shade of the pavilion made for a dim interior, so I stood outside letting a bit of light in to help. He knelt down to untie a saddlebag and dug out a cloth-wrapped bundle. I'd never seen inside such a tent, before. Behind him, on the camp bed, his mail was laid out in pieces, the great helm and spurs with them, and a dark red tabard. His sword and shield leaned against the frame. The tabard struck me as odd. He wore black, usually, with the king's sigil.

When he stood with the bundled book, I caught a wince. "A headache?" I asked. "Do you need —?"

I reached for him again, meaning to check his kir, but Kiefan handed me the book instead. "I am well enough, for now."

I took the book, but shot him a frown as well. He smiled and looked away, caught.

"Truly, Kate, I am well enough. I would not lie to my physician. Or to you."

He joined me just outside the door as I untied the bundle, and he tossed the cloth back inside when I got it free. "Are these all new essays in this book?"

"I leafed through and saw several new titles. But I haven't read any yet. I decided to wait when I came to one..." Kiefan faded into uncertainty, then, and I looked up from the page I'd opened to. His grey eyes had lost their smile, and that sank my heart. But he finished, voice low. "I found one titled 'On Love and Fidelity' and thought we could start with that. Forgetting, for a moment, what passed in the garden."

Sitting with him by a fire, warm and indoors rather than under a storm-beaten tarp, sharing an essay and the questions it posed — longing tore at me. "There wouldn't be time, even if we could read it together," tumbled out of my mouth. "They already think me an upstart peasant girl foisting some scam on the Elect. Whenever they look for me, I must be busy and sure."

"Who?"

I shook my head. "I can prove myself."

"Kate —"

"I will prove myself," I said. I tried to hand the book to him. "Perhaps after... Arcea is turned back?"

"Take it," Kiefan said. "Read and remember it, and we can talk as I read it. You can return it at the Solstice banquet, if not sooner."

My brows took flight on their own. "The banquet?"

"You're physician to the castle. You'll be expected," he said.

"Me?" My voice faded, still disbelieving.

"Yes, you." A bit of a smile tucked up the corner of his mouth. His fingers nearly stroked my cheek before he caught himself, clenched that hand in a fist. "I insist. You must return the book to me for Solstice. And we must get back before we're missed."

We both regretted that, but it was true enough.

CHAPTER 7

Brauer assigned me to the ambulance, on the fourth and final day of the tournament, for revenge. I sat in the wagon bed, leaning against the sideboard, and let the morning sun warm my cloak. Our ambulance driver Borhardt had parked on the far side of the jousting field, right where the boundary fence that held the crowd back ended. I had a prime view.

The last day of the tournament drew the biggest crowd. It was also a Saint-day and so the peasants called it a full day's laziness and turned out in droves to see the best fights of the whole contest. The thirty-two had been halved to sixteen on the second day, then again to eight the morning of the third day, then cut to four in the afternoon, and it was now time to finish the job.

Two jousts in the morning, and then the last after the disciples' dance and community feast. There might be some bathing, as it was part of the Saint-day obligations, but it tended to go overlooked in this hayfield.

My mother had walked down from Engl Street with my two younger brothers and sister, and my uncle and his family, and had arrived in the evening. She'd appeared in the infirmary, hands clasped and reluctant to let her Englic accent embarrass her. Thankfully, Ter Holly had found her before any of the apprentices took notice.

In the knot of Englic peasants, at the skirts of the commoners' camp, I'd hugged all my kin and tried not to say where I'd vanished to on Equinox. Over a simple dinner of oat-bread and potatoes with a little cheese, Mother had told me the word had come down to the Street that Duke Seagrace's Engls were to move north before the Hunter's Moon ended. He'd given instructions for his people to evacuate to a small town outside Prohzgrad.

Mother wanted to petition the duke, while he was here in Wodenberg, to allow her and a handful of others to return to Englia. Perhaps even to Stoneham-on-Ebb.

She'd kept asking me if she should, and I had no answer for that until I saw that she wanted my leave to go. Then, I had told her how Parselev meant for me to be here through the war, how I'd been given charge of the infirmary, and that seemed to settle her mind. Mother had objected when I told her I'd send the bruns the Order would owe me this moon, but I kept after her until she agreed. Since I was a physician in their service, the Order paid me — largely in food and shelter, but there were a few bruns left each moon after deducting the cost of those. I'd been sending the little bronze coins to my mother, for I knew each one would help feed my siblings a bit better.

She'd asked if I wanted anything from home, but didn't seem surprised when I said no. Mother had reminded me of the neighbors who'd be staying, who could recommend a good husband from Engl Street when the Elect gave me leave to marry. I doubted it would be so simple, but I'd smiled and nodded and kissed my mother good-bye. As I'd walked back to the infirmary, the twinges of regret had begun.

Now, I wanted to be sitting with her in the crowd, sipping small beer and watching the joust without the least care which of the knights fell. But Brauer had charge of the infirmary today and the ambulance was my post. And Anders was one of the four remaining knights, so neither of my wishes would come true.

Anders' contest would be later in the morning. I watched Dame Pirra Seagrace and her squire tighten the last few straps of her gear after Saint Woden had drained the jousters of their day's kir. She was a cousin of the duke's and had as striking a head of auburn hair as m'lord — and a full mane of it, as she'd not yet served in the battlefield, and thus had no knight's crest. When she put on the great helm, she might have been a slightly built man for all her sex showed under the mail and gambeson. To her helmet's rear vents, she'd tied a trio of squirrel tails. I wondered if they were a token from some gentleman. She took her first lance and raised it to salute the crowd; they cheered in return.

Her opponent, on the other end of the field, was Sir Adal Rytsarov — who must be some relation to Captain Aleksandra Rytsarova of the King's Guard, and that was certainly a fine pedigree as well. Though as the knights prepared for their first pass, I overheard some disagreement about that.

Borhardt had struck up a conversation with a knot of men about the wagering on this last day's contests, in which they shared a great interest. They had already worked over Anders' chances of winning a third tournament at length. Then the subject changed. "Dame Pirra I heard about," Borhardt said. "She rode down with the duke and trained a week in the city. Who's this Sir Adal?"

"Yesterday, I thought for sure he was a ringer for the Silnyovs," one of the others answered. "They've cheated before and raked in tidy wagers. But he should've thrown his fight by last evening."

"They wouldn't dare put a ringer in the last day, would they?" another asked.

"Could they?" Borhardt seemed to think it unlikely. "Wouldn't Saint Woden pick him out?"

"Master of all ringers, if he is." The first man turned to Borhardt. "You're in the infirmary — has this Sir Adal been by for healing? He's taken some solid hits."

My wagon driver shrugged. "She might know. She's a physician." He turned the question to me.

"Not that I've heard," I said, after a skim of my memory. "But I haven't heard every knight named, who's been in the infirmary. Can you describe him?"

None of them could, though. The trumpet blast ended the talk. Dame Pirra spurred her black stallion and he burst off with a snort, tearing up clods. She dropped her lance into place, pinning it snug under her arm, as he neared a gallop. Sir Adal charged to meet her in the middle.

Lances smashed and flew in pieces, and Dame Pirra slammed back against her saddle under the blow. She bounced up straight, though, and threw her broken lance away. Sir Adal did the same as his bay slowed to a lope at our end of the field. His squire, racing to catch up, skidded to a halt and held up the second lance as the warhorse swung a wide turn.

He caught and hefted it under his arm one-handed, which earned a louder cheer from the crowd. Sir Adal wore no lady's favor on his helm, and no family crest on his dark red tabard. I wondered if the Rytsarovs had a crest. The cheering grew to a roar as both horses circled back to the jousting line and sped up again. Lance points dropped into line as they went.

My memory flashed to the camp bed in Kiefan's tent and the plain, dark red tabard.

My blood ran cold for an agonizing heartbeat.

They hit, the same sharp crack of lance on shield, and I saw them both waver in their saddles. Both recovered. Both drew swords and rode to meet on the same side of the central fence line.

It couldn't be Kiefan. The king didn't let him compete in the tournament and hadn't even wanted him on the field at Ansehen. Kiefan had told us that story while we were storm-bound. Red was a common enough color for a knight to wear, especially a Russe. Knights came from all over the kingdom for the tournament, arriving as late as the evening before. Nobody had ever heard of most of them, and wouldn't again after unless they did well.

There'd been a spare tabard in Kiefan's tent. Perhaps it was his squire's — Gregor was Russe.

But I clenched my cloak with whitened knuckles.

Dame Pirra was quick, even without her Blessings, and her stallion nimble. She circled Sir Adal, getting in two blows and ducking under a swing. His bay twisted around and took a nip at the black, but the stallion danced away. At a spur, Sir Adal chased and they crashed shield to shield, jabbing around the edges for weak spots.

Blunted swords. They were only blunt sparring swords and it wasn't Kiefan, I told myself.

Sir Adal shoved harder, urging his bay to plow against the black, and Dame Pirra tipped, fought to hang on, then tumbled from her saddle. The crowd's voice surged as she hit, rolled, and came up on her feet with only a mild wobble. She dove to grab her sword from the grass and then whistled to her horse. The black broke away and trotted toward her squire. She took a high guard, shield raised to catch blows from above.

Sir Adal backed his bay a few steps from her and dismounted. It was the honorable thing to do, and the audience duly applauded. Dame Pirra charged the moment he put one foot to the grass and the applause vanished into a roar. The crowd loved bold fighters. He got his shield up in time but had to retreat before her attacks, deflecting and dodging.

I was on my knees and craning over the sideboard for a clear view as they moved. How he shifted the advantage, I didn't see, but she stumbled back from a hard blow and the tables clearly turned. He had both height and weight on her, and his heavy blows forced her back another step. After another, Dame Pirra sidestepped his swing entirely and jogged backward several yards with her shield up. She slapped her blade against it, the noise all but lost in the crowd's.

Sir Adal chased, shield poised for a crash, and I glimpsed her planting her feet in a crouch in the moment she had before knocking his blade away and diving under his full hit on her shield. She dipped and rose and their shields scraped across each other in a horrible shriek, but she sent him over her shoulder and tumbling.

I cringed behind my hands.

She was up and after him as he landed, flailing for control and twisting badly off-balance. A blow hit, metal on metal, and Sir Adal fell on his knees, swinging around wide — I saw his blade connect with the back of her knee and couldn't have heard it, but I knew the bones snapped.

The crowd's voice broke, at her collapse, and then recovered. Sir Adal lunged up to stand over her and slide the edge of his sword under her helm to lie against her neck. He stood there, chest heaving, as the crowd roared. I thought my ears would burst, or my heart.

"Our first finalist is decided." Saint Woden's voice cut through the din. "Sir Adal Ryt-sarov, prepare yourself well for this afternoon. Dame Pirra Seagrace, rise if you can and approach the pavilion."

Sir Adal saluted the pavilion, put up his sword, and offered her his hand; she accepted and hauled herself up. They hung on each other to get to the King's pavilion, she hobbling on one leg, he limping. There would be a prize awarded to the defeated, and the honor of meeting both the saints and the King. And the Prince.

I didn't have a clear sight, but Kiefan had to be standing beside his father.

Dame Pirra shook off aid and hobbled the last few steps on her own, lifting her helm. Sir Adal fell back, his squire met him — it was not Gregor, I noted — and ducked under his arm to help. I tracked them as they limped into Duke Vysokov's pavilion and disappeared.

"Think she'll let us carry her over to the infirmary?" Borhardt asked with a grin. "She's a feisty one."

He clucked the cart horse up to a walk as Dame Pirra turned and hoisted her prize to salute the crowd. Traditionally, knights who reached the penultimate round earned a sword in a fine scabbard and belt set with stones — this year, handsome aqua-blue beryl on black leather. She handed it to her squire as I slid off the back of the wagon.

"Let me see that," I said in Englic as I knelt on the grass. "Don't put your weight on it. Lean on the wagon."

"Thank the Mother," she said, between gritted teeth, and leaned.

Her knee was a ruin. I knew that before I even saw her kir. Reaching up, I took her bare hand and through that contact made a thorough survey of the snapped meridian, the broken bones and the wild tumble of loose blood. With my other hand, I dug in my medicine bag for a blood-stop and poured its charm onto her knee. I didn't have enough kir to completely heal her, but I called it up into my hands. It rose in a haze, congealing into an egg-sized knot bright as a candle in a black room.

A tiny thing, compared to what Saint Qadeem had called to heal the shattered knight.

I set the bones in their proper alignment, pieced together her kneecap loosely, sketched the tendons' structure and eased much of the swelling. The clotting blood fought me, in particular, but broke into smaller clumps at least. Brauer would be able to finish the job.

"May we give you a ride?" I asked, looking up.

Her jaw and nose were a little too long to be pretty, but it was a strong enough face to match her spirit. "Do I need to go? It feels better. Just splint it up."

"Go. Physician Brauer will finish the job."

Dame Pirra put out an arm and her squire was there to help her limp toward the infirmary. Borhardt chuckled and called, "A fine fight, m'lady — you'd have killed him three times before he got that first blow in." She raised a fist to agree with that.

I climbed to my feet, a little heavier without my kir. And as I thought it, with a jolt a dose of new kir hit me. Startled, I turned toward the pavilion. Saint Qadeem nodded to me from his seat on the royal dais. I curtsied in return.

Someone tugged on my sleeve. "Dame Kate?" the page asked as I turned again. "That squire wishes to speak to you. It's urgent."

At the corner of Duke Vysokov's pavilion stood Kiefan's ginger-haired squire, Gregor.

"M'lady, there's a knight in need of a physician," Gregor murmured. "Can you help?"

I was right. I had to steady myself with a deep breath. "Where is he?"

Gregor led me out the back of the pavilion and wove through the bustle behind. Eventually we approached Kiefan's tent and passed between two knights whose tabards bore two gold stars for the Prince's Guard.

Captain Aleksandra waited by the flap. Gregor said, "She came," when we neared, but the captain put out a hand to stop me as he passed on into the tent. Her blue eyes narrowed.

"You'll be bound to a secret, if you step inside, and I'll have your measure first," she said.

"I'm bound to keep all that my patients tell me in confidence, Captain," I said. "And I guessed —"

The tent flap pulled aside. "Aleks, let her be," Kiefan said, voice low and strained.

Without easing her scrutiny of me, she said, "Wiser to call the Elect. And wiser not to be seen, sir."

He hobbled closer to the opening, his voice picking up an edge. "I'll be seen by the physician I trust most. The one I call a dear friend."

Captain Aleksandra's head turned, brows arching. "How dear a friend?"

"A friend only. I know my duty. Now let her in."

The sidelong glance he threw me, though — his melancholy tightened my throat. Kiefan turned to hobble back to his camp bed and Gregor was there to help. Captain Aleksandra pursed her mouth to the side, considering me, and held the flap open to let me in.

Kiefan dropped onto the cot, creaking its frame. He was already shucked of his armor and gambeson, and held one leg out straight as he settled. Free of the boot, the ankle was already swelling. He still breathed hard, from the pain, and a touch of sweat lined his brow.

A second knight in captain's brasses knelt to unlace Kiefan's other boot quickly. Captain of the Prince's Guard, though I didn't know his name. "Set the gear to dry," he snapped at Gregor, pointing. "Bring his clothes. And water! He must be ready for table before noon!" The captain's voice rose as the squire ran to obey.

They meant to send Kiefan back as if nothing had happened. They were lying to the king, the saints, and the entire crowd. "Why?" was all I could ask.

He looked up from under his brows, heavy with pain. "Kate…"

"You could've fallen, you could've broken your neck —"

"It's only blunted —"

"Break your neck and there's no saving you!" I waved an arm toward the jousting field, where it had happened on the second day — a young knight killed for sport.

The prince's captain said, voice low, "M'lady, anything you ask. Only heal him and say nothing."

Anything? That put a sour twist in my throat. "And if I ask he take no more wounds?"

"Kate, please. I must walk." He fixed me with those grey eyes, pleading, and my shoulders wilted.

"Don't ask me to lie to the king and the saints."

Captain Aleksandra said, "Out us now and you ruin the entire tournament. Wilhelm would call it all off. Knights build their careers on how they place here, and that's all lost if the king declares the joust invalid. Don't dash the hopes of a hundred as well."

I knelt on the grass and put my hands on Kiefan's bare foot. The red swelling darkened in streaks under the skin. On the nubs of his ankle, a crescent of gray horn broke the skin through thick cuticle, marking the anchoring of his strength Blessing on the bone. Squeezing in search of the damage, I felt the heavy cords of the Blessing alongside the muscles. When his kir surged up at my call, they were a lattice of additional meridians through his calf, up his leg, through all his muscle.

The ankle wasn't broken, but he'd torn one tendon and strained the rest. The interwoven muscles and their bindings were complex, and I went slowly in determining which patterns were damaged. I used his other ankle for reference.

Meanwhile, Gregor returned with a bundle of clothes and above me they pulled off Kiefan's sweat-soaked cote to better clean him up for the charade. I couldn't help stealing a peek, but it was the splay of bruises in ugly purple across his left shoulder that caught my eye. He massaged the flesh with a wince and I heard a joint click as he stretched.

"Just the ankle," Captain Aleksandra reminded me, with a narrowed eye.

Even with the strength Blessing to aid him, Kiefan had worked up a fair cording of muscle. Nubs of horn broke his skin where the extra meridians skimmed close to the surface at elbows and breastbone. I pried my eyes off and back to my work. Tendons were not difficult, individually, so I addressed them individually with small charms.

"Will Dame Pirra recover?" he asked as he wiped down with a wet towel.

"She will," I said.

"That was a fine fight she put up," the Prince's captain said.

"I want her on my Guard."

"I'm sure you can lure her away from Seagrace," Captain Aleksandra said. "Was Charmer any trouble for you?"

"Better than yesterday. Still, if only I could've ridden Pip."

I didn't notice they'd paused until the last tendon re-knit. I glanced up at them, all watching me. "Pardon?"

"He needs to get all that sweaty wool off," Captain Aleksandra told me, and waited again.

I'd seen men and women undressed for surgery, and one's kir did not include clothing. I hadn't been so prying as to call Kiefan's full pattern without cause, but even so it took a few heartbeats for me to grasp that I was, in their eyes, an innocent maiden.

And even so, part of my mind fumbled for an excuse to stay. There wasn't one. "I need kir," I muttered, honestly enough, and climbed to my feet. "There must be a charm-hand about?"

I stepped outside long enough to catch a passing stablehand carrying a bale of hay. He put out his charm-hand and I drained him. I was a little disappointed to find Kiefan up and already re-dressed in black hose and cote when I returned. He leaned on his injury carefully.

"Sit." I still needed to break up the swelling. "Your father will find out in the end," I said as I combed through the tangled kir. "You can't keep your helm on forever."

"If the last duel's been decided, he can say what he likes." Kiefan leaned back on the cot, lounging. "One way or the other, that's all that matters."

The last of the tangle gave way, and I pulsed the remainder of my kir toward the bruising in his shoulder. It loosened a little, which would ease the pain.

"If Sir Anders lays a sword on you," Captain Aleksandra said, "the queen would gladly see him executed for it."

"If I face him I'd best win, then."

"Would she?" I asked.

The captain shrugged. "Her Majesty sets her mind to peculiar things."

"You wouldn't risk his life for — glory? Would you? After facing down the lamia together?" I didn't want to believe that. I rose from the grass.

Kiefan's voice was low, but strong. "I will prove myself to my father. To all the knights."

"He deserves better. And you deserve better than having to lie to your father and the saints. There must be a way they could to allow —"

He was on his feet, hand on my arm. "Kate, if you love me at all, say nothing. Please."

My mind tripped on his words and reeled for balance. He was close enough to kiss. But his eyes were sharp and wary, and dear friends could talk of loving each other without kissing. I had to fight a sudden tightness in my throat.

"I'll say nothing," I murmured. "And I'll feel every hit you take."

His wariness melted. "I'm sorry to make you worry."

I turned away before the urge to kiss him got any stronger. "I must report to the infirmary," I said, and found the loose flap out of the tent.

I was too dazed to do more than return to the infirmary and restock my kir from one of the charm-handed orderlies. Brauer snapped at me to get back out before the second duelist fell, and I shuffled back into the weak sunlight.

Borhardt loaded the knight into the ambulance once Anders was done with him. I found two cracked ribs from the fall he'd taken from his horse and checked his head for any bleeding inside the skull. He'd put up a good fight until Nipper took a bite from his horse's flank and spooked the poor thing. A few moments of distraction were enough for Anders to unseat him and he'd landed hard.

The crowd had wanted something more dramatic, but settled for the juicy morsel of Anders within reach of a third championship.

As one of the Father's Dogs for another week yet, he was still subject to the Order and was kept at the their pavilion deep in the goodfolks' side of the field. The abbot had been easy to talk into letting one of the Dogs compete; he was a betting man, and now had the benefit of intimate information on the favorite.

They were setting up long tables for the communal meal and clearing an area for the disciple's dance. Thanks to Ter Holly's directions, I found my way to the abbot's tent and finally spotted Nipper tethered nearby. Will had his tack off and was brushing him down quickly; he happened to see me and waved.

The doorflap was pinned open, as the day had finally warmed, and I heard Anders as I entered.

"— disciple's dance going on four days now. I'll not be doing more. The only dance offer I'd take now would involve a lady in need of undressing."

"You'll take a seat at table," the abbot said, wagging a finger at Anders. "Make yourself presentable, Dog." Though a small man, he'd left the infantry at the rank of captain-general and wouldn't hesitate to back up his threats.

Anders pulled his mail tunic off over his head and said, "I could as soon lie under the table and gnaw the bones," through the iron rings. He spotted me as he got it off and sorted it back into the shape of a cote. "Kate, what brings you here?"

I'd seen how his shoulder hitched in the dis-armoring. "You need some cold hands," I said, crossing the sparse tent to slip a hand under the close neck of his gambeson.

"If m'lady insists." He tipped his head, puzzled, but didn't feign a wince.

"Are you hurt?" the abbot asked. "You said you were well."

"Don't change your bet," Anders told him. "I'm well enough."

His left shoulder had swollen under the lance strikes, and couldn't take much more punishment before tearing. Bruises strung along his ribs to match the rim of his shield. On his right, a deep bruise ran in a straight line just below his ribs, the spreading tendrils of the damaged kir reaching into his gut.

"As well as a beaten dog," I said, trying to fix him with a stern look.

He answered with one of his infectious smiles. "I gave as well as they did."

I used my kir to disperse the swelling in his shoulder and loosen the bruise on his side. Anders' breath caught as I combed through the tangled kir. Still, he asked, "What brings you, though?"

"It should be a fair fight, should it not?"

He chuckled. "Not if I had my say." Then, after a moment's thought, "Sir Adal was limping — you've healed that? What do you know of him?"

I watched a clump of whorls work free, nudging them back into their dance. Then I answered. "He is determined to prove himself."

"As are we all." Anders set his mouth in a grim line.

CHAPTER 8

My teacher found me sitting alone with a trencher of shepherd's pie gone cold before me, too heartsick to eat.

"You were not so troubled by the tournament last year," he said, fishing a pickle from the brine jar on the table.

"Last year I only set bones and changed bandages."

"And all knights were strangers."

For a moment, I feared he knew. But then I saw the larger meaning in what he said. "I know they're not so different from me, now."

Parselev nodded as he crunched his pickle. "And you've looked the Shepherd in the eye. Sometimes you've cheated him. Sometimes he's cheated you. Have you eaten anything?"

I had stuck a spoon in the mashed potatoes and fidgeted, but forgotten it. "Not since breakfast."

"Have a pickle. You will not be able to go all summer without eating." He plucked one out for me. "This is what Krepkin meant when he spoke of maturity."

"And what you meant by not looking away."

"Yes. Now come and stand behind me as my squire, and don't look away."

I dutifully ate the pickle while I followed. It was better than I expected. I thought Parselev meant to stand at the front of the infirmary, but he led me toward the pavilions. The Englic guardsmen held the door flaps open for us and bowed. Likewise, the King's Guard welcomed us into the center pavilion.

The king's table held more a feast than a communal meal, and nobody's appetite suffered here; the leg of venison had been cut to the bone and the bread trenchers thrown down for the dogs bore only scraps. Empty serving dishes cluttered the table.

"You have not met Saint Aleksandr," Master Parselev said, putting a hand on my elbow. "You should. M'lord?"

Saint Aleksandr turned, a stein of autumn bock in one hand, scratching a hound's head with the other. Though as large a man as Woden, his laugh lines dispelled any sternness. He'd been dark-haired, but had streaks of grey to complement the age in his green eyes. When Parselev introduced me, I dropped to one knee in obeisance but he took my hand to draw me back up. My hand felt dwarfed by his — stone-hard, rimmed with calluses, yet deftly analyzing my structure with a few touches. He said nothing until he'd taken his measure of me.

"Kate Carpenter. Good to meet you at last." His smile was kind, too.

"M'lord." How he knew of me… my mind balked at the thought of saints discussing me, of all people in the kingdom.

"Qadeem, your elect is here." Woden's voice carried even without kir; he stood on the dais, among the various chairs, with the king at his side. The saint drained his stein and ended with a frown on his face. "The sooner there are more elect, the better. We've been askew far too long. Arcea will use it to their advantage," he said.

"No-one can force a flower to bloom." Qadeem had gone unnoticed, wrapped in his dust-colored cloak despite the sunny afternoon. He moved to take his seat on the dais, accepting a stein of autumn bock as he went.

Woden snorted. "We're in need of steel flowers, this time. Let's check our garden again." He gestured broadly for all to sit, and took his own chair in the middle of the dais.

I trailed after my teacher, keeping my mouth firmly shut. The captain took her post behind the king's shoulder. His Majesty sat on Woden's right hand, Saint Aleksandr on his left. The hound, and a second, flopped down under Saint Aleks' chair. Qadeem already occupied the fourth chair, on the King's other side. Off the dais, Parselev settled into a seat beside our saint.

"Where's Kiefan?" The king twisted to check the table, where servants were still clearing. "He wouldn't miss this."

"The trumpets will remind him," Woden said, and signaled the master of ceremonies. A moment later, the fanfare played to call the final pair of knights to their joust.

Still, the king shifted in his seat. "He should've returned by now."

Captain Aleksandra put a hand on his shoulder. "I'll find him."

"Thank you."

I clenched my jaw as I watched her trot out the back. Then I glanced to Parselev, but he leaned toward Qadeem to discuss something in low tones.

They came, a knight in dark red and a knight in dark green, one riding a bay and the other a vicious dappled grey. Anders rode a lap around the jousting fence, great helm raised, when he was introduced as a knight of the Prince's Guard and twice champion. Kiefan rode with his helm on and raised his lance when his false name and pedigree were read.

Woden stood, welcomed all, and made certain both knights were drained of kir. I clenched my hands behind my back, looking from one to the other. Anders laughed at something Will said as he put on the helm and then took his first lance. On the other side, Kiefan adjusted the plain red shield on his arm and leaned over to tell the boy helping him something.

My stomach twisted in a knot.

The hooves began and I did not look away. From this vantage, the jousters flashed in from either side, lances flat and steady, and were gone in a crack of wooden thunder. I followed Kiefan, saw him toss aside the broken lance to grab the pommel. Anders shook his shield arm, numbed by the blow.

Nipper cornered tight, barely giving Anders time to grab the second lance, and accelerated with teeth bared. The second hit broke both lances, pieces flying so hard that one thwacked into the canvas overhead.

The crowd's cheer picked up a notch; nobody wanted a knight unseated in the jousting passes, not this late in the tournament. They wanted swordplay.

Kiefan urged his bay — Charmer, the captain had said — in tight again to crash against Anders' shield and shove. Nipper pushed back, snapping at the bay and then at Kiefan. Nipper's teeth on his mail sleeve distracted Kiefan a moment and Anders got in a strike on his helm. That shifted the fight and put Kiefan on the defensive. Nipper took advantage, too, lunging into Charmer's flank and bullying him into circling his rump away. The bay danced sideways to get room; Kiefan easily deflected Anders' parting swing.

Nipper's ears pinned back and he kicked Charmer square in the shoulder, just by Kiefan's knee. The bay squealed and stumbled. Nipper lunged after, teeth-first, and Kiefan had to grab the reins when Charmer spun away with his eyes rolling. A bad nip on the rump and Charmer bucked with another shrill squeal.

My nails dug into my skin when Kiefan fell. The crowd gasped as Charmer's hooves came down around him and the horse burst into a run. Rolling over, Kiefan found his sword and came up on his knees looking for Anders and Nipper.

Anders circled around tight and Nipper charged. Kiefan gained his feet in time to sidestep the horse's teeth and deflect the hard sword blow with his shield. The wood rang. Dirt clouded up as Nipper swung about and bore down again for a second hit. Kiefan wobbled back a step under the force.

"Dismount!"

"Why give up his advantage?" Parselev asked in return. I hadn't realized I had said it aloud.

On the third pass, Kiefan swung early and it was Nipper who squealed, his head knocked hard aside. His speed carried him, though, and Anders' sword connected with Kiefan's helm in passing. I saw red on Nipper's grey hide and gasped; skin had broken across his muzzle and bled. He jolted and wanted to bolt, eyes rolling, but Anders put his sword hand against his horse's neck and steadied him enough to swing down from the saddle.

"The prince! The prince!"

The rising cry tore my eyes back. Kiefan's helm lay on the ground, dented from the blow, and he hauled himself back to his feet. His golden knight's crest hung loose between his Blessings. Anders hesitated a few yards short, raised his helm.

"No! No, this ends now!" The king was on his feet, arm raised in command. "No further!"

The crowd opposite us faltered, its volume dropping.

"This tournament is over!"

A hand landed on the king's shoulder and flung him back into his chair like a child, tumbled him backward over it and half off the dais to boot.

"Sit down," Woden thundered, kir-fueled voice ripping through all else. A heavy cloak of kir fell loose around him, searingly strong and tiny suns twinkling in its folds. "The crown will pass to your son and you cannot stop that. Cling to that crown, deny him his strength, and you mark yourself as weak. If you choose weakness, you will learn your proper place!"

Silence. I couldn't breathe for shock. King Wilhelm lay gaping up at his saint, stunned.

"I cannot bury a third son." The raw pain in the king's voice tightened my throat.

Woden loomed over the fallen old man. "I have buried all my children. This will be your place, then." That with a finger pointed in judgement.

It was Saint Aleksandr who stepped between them, letting his own kir fall visible as if he'd been wearing it all along. Eyes locked, not a word was said as whole constellations swirled around the two of them. And fainter, closer to me, I felt more kir shift like water under a crust of ice. Qadeem watched the scene with deceptive calm; I could see an intense knot of kir shifting between his brown fingers.

Woden turned back to the jousting field and issued his command. "Continue."

Both the knights — and the crowd — didn't dare breathe until the kir cloaks faded and tucked neatly away.

"If neither of you wishes the title, we'll find two who will fight for it!" Woden retook his seat.

That spurred Anders; he let his helm drop in place and charged the last few yards.

Captain Aleksandra, helping the King up from the ground, caught my eye and I offered my hand to help but he shook his head. His face was set grim under his greying beard. He'd never looked old, to me, until that moment. Old, or weak.

I set my teeth on my lower lip, muddled by fears and confusion. Anders and Kiefan fought on the grass, without Blessing speed, without the polite forms they'd used in sparring that Saint-day I first saw them. They shoved and stabbed and snarled at each other. And were evenly matched, I knew from having watched a dozen duels over the last few days. It was a question of stamina now.

Anders lunged inside Kiefan's guard and slammed his helm against Kiefan's bare head. I couldn't help a wince of pain and bit my lip as Kiefan tumbled back with a wild swing. He had to be knocked out, he couldn't — but he thrashed and tried to crawl backwards. Anders put his sword to Kiefan's neck.

The crowd re-found its full volume, at that. Woden rose from his seat again, fist raised in salute to announce the victor.

Kiefan grabbed his blade and lunged up, tackling Anders. They rolled and thrashed and Anders kicked him away, pulled off his helm and threw himself atop Kiefan, ready to beat him down with the iron bucket. The crowd surged forward to see, shocked but eager.

"Enough. His sword was at your throat, Kiefan. You've earned full honors for spirit, but there will be another day to fight. Both of you have done me proud today."

Anders' chest heaved as he found his feet. Kiefan was slower to roll over onto his knees, hanging his head. I watched him as Saint Woden crossed the grass; Kiefan didn't look up, didn't offer an obeisance. He pulled his mail gloves off and pressed one hand against a lump so red I could see it from where I stood.

Woden offered him a hand up. Kiefan dared glare at it, but accepted. The saint told him something and put the hand on his shoulder. Kiefan nodded and stalked off the field still dark as a thundercloud.

I shifted, wanting to follow. "Let him go," Parselev said, from his chair. "I'll see to the head wound. You see to our champion."

For days afterward, I wished I'd gone after Kiefan. I could've healed that awful lump, unknotted the headache he'd surely gotten, and repaired whatever hurt the fall from the horse had done. I could've hugged him, maybe, comforted him. Surely there would've been a moment alone, perhaps in his tent, for a hug.

And if for a hug, then for a kiss as well. If for a kiss...

Nights were cold enough that I had taken up sharing a bed with Hannah, a craft-handed Englic girl training as a secretary. I lay awake, back-to-back with her, mind lost in what could happen after a hug and a kiss. Or what could've happened under the apple tree, if I'd been bolder. I tormented myself with daydreams, but didn't dare do anything about the throbbing between my thighs for fear of disturbing Hannah.

But no, Parselev mended Kiefan and sent me to check on the thrice-named champion. Anders needed more healing the morning after his celebration than before, in truth. The abbot thought a Dog should suffer for his foolishness, but I took pity and cleared most of the sickness. Not all. Ten days later, his Discipline finished and some bridges mended with the Baron Rossweide, Anders rode out of the Order on Nipper as he ought to be — smiling and trading teasing jabs.

Meantime I wrote Kiefan a letter, as I didn't leave the Order's campus for days on end, to apologize for not being his physician after the joust as he had wanted. He wrote back that same day to tell me he hadn't been fit for polite company the rest of that afternoon and if a pack of lamia had attacked him he would have been glad for the fight.

That set off a torrent of letters between us. Kiefan wrote to me when he rode out with a company of knights to answer reports of Arceal raiders still attacking villages along the southern border. He told me of small towns half emptied by the planned evacuations, of granaries stripped down to one winter's supply, of pastures standing empty after flocks were butchered and smoked for jerky. The reports of raiders had been true enough; the knights fell upon two dozen Suevi soldiers in a patch of forest and cut them down.

"I took an arrow," Kiefan wrote, "but not deeply. Captain Rostislav," — of the Prince's Guard — "cut it out quickly and I've been careful to keep the wound clean as you showed us in the mountains."

Still, I worried and wrote to him about the signs of an abscess. His next letter told me that a village physician had seen to it and he would be home in the castle soon. When he returned, he wrote that his father had given him charge of seeing to the evacuation of all who were to leave the city before Arcea's army came. I told him how I'd gotten word from my mother that she and my siblings and my uncle's family had reached their assigned winter camp near Prohzgrad, and I was glad to know they'd be safe. Winter illnesses trickled in as the Hunter's Moon waxed toward full, and we were kept to using herbs and nurse-care to heal them. The Elect would still mend a grave wound or heal the desperately sick, but all spare kir went into charging charms for the spring.

Kiefan and I lamented the stone walls between us and the conversations made impossible by them. I looked through a few of d'Ovio's essays, but without my tutor it seemed pointless. In one letter, Kiefan wrote that several calls for me to treat illness in the castle, including one of his terrible headaches, had brought some other physician instead. That was the letter I took to Parselev.

<hr />

"Carpenter's welcome to assist in the hospital," Krepkin said when presented with the letter during the weekly meeting, "but honors on the order of attending the royal family should be earned with time and service, not handed out as honeycakes."

Brauer, her arms folded firm, nodded as he spoke. "One moon on a hunt is no equal to years of experience."

"Did you find fault in how she managed the infirmary during the grand melee?" Parselev inquired.

"It was an acceptable trial run," Krepkin said.

"Then you agree the Elect of the kingdom perhaps knows whereof he speaks, in wishing his student trained to leadership?"

My teacher, having read the complaint and shown them Kiefan's signature at the bottom, passed the scrap of paper back to me. I was glad to have it; they were all precious.

"If she has time to be trading letters with the prince, she'll never be trained properly," Krepkin muttered as he tracked the handoff. "Discipline comes with time as well."

"Especially for those who come to it late," Brauer added.

"If you doubt that I'm up before the sun and working long past, the kitchen staff can vouch for me," I said, especially to her. "I haven't sat at a proper meal since the tournament. The Elect gave me responsibility for attending to the castle, but when they send for me another doctor goes in my stead? I cannot trust the physician of the floor to direct castle messengers correctly, it seems."

During the day, Brauer was the physician of the floor and oversaw the assignment of duties. I had been dutifully changing sheets and feeding invalids and charging charms. The head nurse had asked me to take her shift a few times, I was so reliable.

Parselev said, "If you're overwhelmed, Brauer, I can move that duty to the gatekeeper. In fact, I think I will until I am sure you can manage it. Kate, be sure the gatekeeper knows where you can be found."

"Elect, I send the most able physician at hand when Carpenter is not available," Brauer said.

"When am I not available?"

Krepkin cut in. "When are you off writing these letters? And what business do you have writing letters to the prince?"

"From that one, I gather that Kate is still studying d'Ovio Alain's philosophy and the prince assists in translation," Master Parselev said. "There is no harm in that."

I thanked the Mother that it hadn't been a letter full of our complaints and frustrations. I resolved anew to keep reading.

"High language for such as her to tackle."

"Enough, Stannis."

"Enough? How many Engls within our walls is enough?"

Parselev's voice sharpened further. "The campaign is long over, the Engls are our sworn brothers and Kate was not even a twinkle in her father's eye when it all happened. Enough."

The old man glowered under his thick eyebrows and held his peace resentfully. He shuffled away muttering to Brauer and her sympathetic ear; she nodded as they went.

My teacher sighed. "And what else do you and the prince discuss?"

I drew a breath and held it, looking up from my seat at him.

Parselev gave me a chiding look. "Sergeyev's mentioned he must order more paper, as you've burned through the store of it. And I saw a messenger pass through the campus without even asking after me."

My cheeks warmed. "I'm sorry, sir, I didn't mean to use so much paper. We talk of… everything, or near enough. As my penmanship improves, my writing shrinks." I offered that as some solace. "I've gotten a great deal of practice."

That got me half a smile. "That much is good. Of the rest, Kate — I know how rare it is to find someone to talk of everything with. Truly. You know who he is, though. You know he will never be yours."

I looked away, to the floor. He was right. Parselev said no more of it, and gathered up the tea service to return to the kitchens. I sat staring at Kiefan's letter in my hands. I had these bits of paper and my perfect memories of him. Memories of his sword ready to fight off lamia for me. Memories of kisses and tight hugs, of wanting more but letting go. It wasn't entirely true that he would never be mine. I had… little scraps.

Precious little scraps.

"How is it that you and Krepkin disagree so much about me? You say I have talent and he does not?"

I had the chance to ask a few days later, while sitting in my teacher's office going over correspondence from physicians all over the kingdom. They had been talking of the year's newly Blessed and the talent they saw or didn't see.

Parselev's office was chilly, now that the Shepherd waned and the Flock gathered behind his back, even with warmth rolling up from Heima's kitchen below. The Hunter's Moon had already brought some flurries, and there would be more once the Snow Moon began. I wore my woolen shawl and the gloves from the mission while reading through the letters.

He weighed his answer, then put down his quill and set the lid on his ink pot. I knew I was in for a lecture.

"Stannis cannot see your talent. That is not willful blindness. It is mere fact. He has never been very sensitive to kir or to potential and there is nothing to be done about it. The ability to read potential in others requires a level of ability that's been lacking for far too long. These letters," he held up a few, "speak much about the hunt for new elect which is ever more on our minds of late. Wodenberg has lain fallow for many years, and we all hope the crop will come in time." Master put the letters down, neatened the stack. "This is a skill you will need, and now's as good a time as any. Heima? Could you come up?"

"A moment," she called back, and I heard bowls clattering. "Do you want tea?"

"No, only a little time."

She came up soon after, wiping her hands on her apron. Heima was round-faced, round-bodied, and smiling while she hummed to herself. "Why do you need my time, then?"

"To illustrate." Parselev took her hand in his, turning it to show her charm-hand nub. "Heima, my wonderful Heima, without whom I would starve, freeze and go naked —"

"Such a silver-tongued old fox," she warned me with a wink.

"Saint Aleksandr gave her a charm-hand, the simplest of the Blessings. Take her other hand and mine."

I obeyed.

"I'm going to sound you, dearest," he said.

Through their hands, I felt the tiny hook of kir flick from Parselev and pluck at Heima's heart like a bowstring. Her kir bloomed in response like a candle flaring to life, giving off one brief, high-pitched note, and as quickly faded back to quiescence.

"Saint Woden did that to me," I said. "At the King's Council. And Elect Tannait."

"Yes, and that was another reason we sent you, Kate. Woden is a nosy one. Always checking. However, when he sounded you your response was longer, lower-pitched and far more complex."

That was true. "What does it mean? He did not even touch me to do it."

Parselev kissed Heima's hand, first. "Thank you, that's all." As she left, he answered, "Breaking the need to touch when casting charms is the hallmark of the elect and the sainted. Little else can be said for sure of the progress of kir-mages, but mark that well. Now, first try sounding me and describe what you hear. Then I will explain further."

I faced him on my chair, took both his dry, lean hands in mine, and closed my eyes to focus. The Elect's kir was a mass in his core, a warm glow in my mind's eye. I took a moment to call my own kir and try to shape it in a hook. Crooking my index finger helped. It held the shape, so I reached through my master's hand and imagined plucking his kir's surface.

The low chord that belled out knocked my eyes open, and the bloom of his kir peaked so brightly that it forced me to squint. Chord was too small a word for it, for there were too many notes. His sounding hung in the air, sinking into my bones, and faded slowly. "Can't Heima hear that?"

"However loud, only the sensitive can hear it," he said. "Your observations?"

Stringing together Heima's sound, my own at Woden's plucking, and the Elect's, I spun out a list. "It seems high notes progress to low notes smoothly with skill? My own tone was close to the middle between you and Heima. However, in length mine was much like yours. Our tones and the number in the chord differed too, though it seemed some notes were the same. Your kir came up much brighter than either of ours as well."

"The brightness relates only to what kir I have at the moment. As one's skill develops, one can hold more and one tends to hoard it, I'll confess. I may tap the Pool whenever I need to, but were I drained I'd be dimmer than Heima was. All else relate to the subject's talents with kir, their mastery and their potential — but not so simply as one might hope. We do share notes, as you heard, for we share a talent for healing. Recall when I first sounded you, at your evaluation after basic instruction here. Compare that to Woden's sounding. Your pitch has dropped noticeably, due to your training."

I had been not a little frightened and confused, that day of my evaluation, for not knowing what a sounding was or why I'd made such a noise that nobody seemed to hear.

"And be honest, Kate, your chord lingers longer than mine." My teacher smiled as he said it.

"You should sound me, and tell me for sure," I said, not wanting to turn a suspicion into arrogance.

He did it then, without touching my hand, and it made me jump in my chair. How long the chord echoed unsettled me, somewhere around my gut. True, it did hang longer.

"A word of caution — do not try sounding Woden the next time he does it."

"He's nosy, but can't be nosed back?" I said it before thinking, and thought the answer was clear enough. It would be presumptuous to pry.

But that wasn't what my master said. "You saw what he did in the pavilion. He answers challenges as swiftly and more severely." Parselev shifted the subject, though. "The saints read soundings, and they use them to gauge what Blessings best fit. That's a tricky alchemy. Both tone and complexity may shift with time and experience, but one's sustain generally does not. That was what caught my ear, the first time I sounded you. That was why I apprenticed you over all the objections. You will go far, Kate. You are part of the harvest from the fallow field."

He looked me in the eye, forceful and sincere, and I couldn't hold his gaze. It was too unsettling to think I had more of something than my teacher. But still, I had to ask, "Why didn't you tell them, then? Wouldn't they have agreed instead of complaining?"

"Nothing can be said for certain about how quickly even the most gifted will bloom, if at all." Then he said again, "If at all. There are traditions that come down from the ancients, and there's a wisdom to them. The disciples of saints may be ranked by their current strength, but potential is not spoken of. It is for the safety of the student while they are at their weakest — still buds on the vine. Perhaps this sounds foolish here in Wodenberg, isolated as we are and different as our traditions are, but do not doubt that the number and quality of our gifted is as much a matter of war as the number of our knights.

"The saints bestow Blessings on all and this encourages even the least gifted to master a spark charm or mend torn fabric. In other lands, the laypeople cannot do even that. Our saints both push our people to reach beyond their innate gifts and mask our true strength behind the single face of 'Blessed.' That was the clever twist that Qadeem brought with him to the Trinity.

"I am the only elect — true enough, since Prince Wolfgang's death. But there are buds on the rose. Were we using traditional ranks, I would place you among the truly blessed. New to it, and with more to learn, but blessed. Stannis, by the same measure, is only a disciple but do not forget the value of experience. He harps on it for a reason. He can squeeze three charms from the kir of two and you would do well to learn what you can from him.

"Now. Resist the urge to sound all you meet. It's rude. D'Ovio Alain wrote an essay titled 'On the Obligations of the Discipled' which you should read. Are you reading the book that Duke Vysokov owns, or has a new copy been found? It's part of that collection. We'll discuss this more."

CHAPTER 9

"M'lady? Physician Kate?"

I looked up from tucking the blankets snug under the cot, to make sure the young patient didn't kick them off so quickly. The squire calling me trotted across the invalids' floor from the staircase, his hood falling back in the jostling. His bright ginger hair gave him away.

"You're Physician Kate?" Gregor asked, breathing as if he'd run all the way from the castle. Puppy-soft as he looked, I wasn't sure if he could manage such a thing.

"We've met before," I said. "At the joust."

"Yes, m'lady. But." He gasped one last deep breath and slowed down. "But m'lord is very specific. Has been since I brought the wrong physician. He sent me to bring you, m'lady. Right away."

"Let me get my cloak," I said.

While it grew colder toward the end of the Hunter's Moon, little snow had fallen. Kiefan and his father had gone south to see to the preparations on our border, and one letter had come for me. Only one, speaking of how Kiefan missed me and chiding me a little to read so I had something to ask about. When I'd answered, I had committed Parselev's assignment to my memory for later reading, carried the book to the castle to await Kiefan's return, and I had much to write about the obligations of the discipled. I'd needed a second piece of paper.

There'd been no reply. The Hunter's Moon had gone dark and turned to the first crescent of the Snow Moon, and still no reply came even though the king and prince were back in Castle Kaltkern. Surely Wenda the housemistress had brought him the book as soon as he arrived home. Had he nothing to say? Waiting had become agony.

Gregor saw me into the saddle first, then swung up behind me. The poor horse did its best to canter up the steep slope to the castle, then had to drop to a trot to carry us through the three gates. It was puffing and blowing clouds in the cold air by the time we arrived. The late afternoon sun lay against the castle walls and the innermost yard fell mostly into shadow, chill and grey. Gregor led me straight inside, leaving the horse to the stableboy.

Across the great hall and up the grand staircase we climbed, toward the King's Council room. I slowed, realizing the squire hadn't said why I was needed.

"Is it an illness, Gregor? Another cracked ankle?" My only call to the castle, while Kiefan was away, had been when a maid slipped on the back stairs and took a bad tumble. They'd had her laid out in the kitchen to wait for me.

Gregor stopped at the closed Council door and put a finger to his lips. I reached the top of the stairs at last — it was high and the steps steep — and heaved a weary sigh. Under my cloak, I loosened the ties on my medicine bag. If it were, Mother Love help me, the king or the queen taken ill, I had best be ready.

The latch clicked open. Gregor leaned in. "M'lord?" he called, softly. "Physician Kate is here."

"If it's not her, I'll take you back out in the practice yard and see you've enough bruises to remember."

I came to the door. Gregor shot me a worried glance as if I might still be the wrong one. "It's me, Kiefan."

There was a fire laid in the grate. One of the chairs had been pulled over to face it. Otherwise, the room was empty and dim. Kiefan straightened in the chair, twisting, at my voice. "Thank the Mother," he said, voice softening. "Thank you, Gregor. Go and see to your chores."

With a click, the door latched behind me. I laid my cloak on the massive Council table, then set my medicine bag atop it. Kiefan stood, draining the cup in his hand, and met me halfway across the room. He took my hand and kissed it, our old signal, and I put my palm to his cheek. I could smell the brandy on his breath.

"You're drinking?"

"I wasn't sure he'd bring you," he murmured. "After the day it's been, I needed the edge off."

His kir had knotted harder than ever; ridges of pain mirroring his Blessings, spidering out deep into his mind.

"What happened? You haven't been so bad since the mountain pass," I said, voice falling to a murmur too. Noise had to hurt. And light. Thus, this empty, dim room and its faint must of books.

Kiefan laid his hand on mine, pressed it to his cheek. "A fight, brewed over several days by way of handmaids and pageboys. My mother and father avoid each other, but still find ways to argue. Today the breaking point was reached, as always happens, and it fell to me to make peace, as it always does."

I worked one knot loose and a few whorls of kir spilled free. He blinked, feeling it, and touched a kiss to the heel of my hand.

"Father thinks me so talented at negotiations. I learned it all by brokering between him and mother."

With one knot loose, the second and third came a little quicker. The brandy might have loosened them a bit, as well. I made good progress until my kir began to run out. Kiefan had a little, but must have used the rest in sparring with Gregor. I drew on it to do what I could.

"I hope your journey was not so bad," I said, keeping my voice low.

"Aside from being far from you…" he said, and let that hang for a long moment. I'd gotten another knot undone before he spoke again. "In truth, I've been miserable since Ilya's funeral."

"Miserable?" I focused on his eyes, and fell into them. His fingers threaded in mine, against his cheek, and squeezed. My voice shrank to almost nothing. "You too?"

He kissed me, wrapped his arms around me, and I was lost. I tasted brandy in his mouth. Kiefan let me go for a moment to look me in the eye again. "You don't have a healing charm for this?" he whispered.

"Where does it hurt?"

He drew my arm from around his neck and put my hand over his heart, thumping hard under his black cote. My fingers crept up to the neck and tugged it down what little it could go. I used it to pull him back for another kiss, a slower one with plenty of time to breathe between skirmishes. Kiefan's hands returned to my back, stroked down my spine inch by inch to my hip. My breath caught when he gripped me by the butt, pulling me on tiptoe against him. Knocked off the kiss a little, I nuzzled against his cheek and inhaled a deep lungful of the lavender soap he'd shaved with.

Settling back onto my feet, I cuddled against his neck. Kiefan hugged me tight and I wrapped my arms around his ribs to squeeze back.

"You missed me?" he barely whispered.

"Yes."

"But in the garden…" His hand found my braid and coiled it over his palm. "You didn't want me to kiss you."

"I didn't want you to lie to me," I said, trying to squeeze my heartache out against his chest. But his grip was loosening and his voice was sinking into melancholy. I couldn't stop that, couldn't kiss him and pretend he would ever be mine to comfort.

"I'd be lying if I said I didn't want to kiss you." Kiefan's hands settled on my hips, and mine found his sword belt to hold on to. "There's no charm against this, is there?"

I gripped the leather belt with both hands. There'd been a few girls he'd wished to kiss, he'd said in the garden. "Surely you've recovered from worse than…"

"This?" Kiefan shook his head. "Nothing like this."

"Even if I had the charm," I said, but couldn't admit I wouldn't want to use it. "I'm out of kir."

A brief kiss. "More medicine, then," he squeezed in before another. He picked me up by the butt, and sat me on the table. It barely noticed me, for being so solid.

A few inches higher, now, he nuzzled my chin aside to kiss my neck, trace his tongue along my throat, and my pulse throbbed along the trail. I still had one hand on his belt, and pulled him to the edge of the table. Spread my knees to get him closer. His lips brushed across my collarbone at the neck of my shift where it peeked from under my dress, and my skin prickled with gooseflesh.

This. I'd remember this all my life…

Kiefan's hand stroked over my breast, then gathered up the scant handful. His other hand did the same as he kissed me again. He tweaked my nipples through the layers and my breath caught at the jolt.

He met my eyes and took a deep breath. Leaving my breasts, he set both hands on both my knees, atop my layered skirts.

"Kate, stop me now if you mean to."

My crotch throbbed against the table, my heart pounded in my chest, and he thought I could merely tell him to stop. When he could, in truth, be mine for a little while and then forever in my memory. I whispered back, "I don't mean to."

Another kiss, deep and hungry, and the hands on my knees worked my skirts up, shifted onto the bare skin underneath. The calluses on his fingers left tingles across my thighs under his touch.

I made his breath catch, for once, when I sent my free hand searching and found, below his belt, something hard and eager. He rumbled against my mouth when I stroked it. For a moment, my resolve wavered but the little whimper he made when I squeezed him eased my nerves.

I tipped back when he leaned over me, though it meant letting go of him. Kiefan nipped at my breast through my dress in parting, then scooted my rear further onto the table and climbed up on his knees after me. I bumped against a stack of books in crawling backwards, and that set off giggles and a pile of paper went slithering. The books teetered and fell alongside me, smelling of leather and dust. Kiefan nudged them aside with one hand as he settled onto the other elbow, over me.

"Perfect," he murmured, smiling as he stroked that hand along my thigh to work my skirts up to my waist.

He was perfect, too, his blonde knight's crest hanging free and long enough that he had to flick it over to one side before he kissed me. He lay on me warm, not too heavy, grinding his hips against mine. It was only a matter of untying his braies and in doing that my fingers tangled in his for a moment down there. I wanted to feel a cock, after Alice had told me so

132   Part II: Winter's Fools

much about them. Soft skin, yes, on clenched muscle. My touch squeezed another rumbly groan out of him and he shifted closer.

It took a little hunting to find what we wanted. The moment's pain twisted a whimper through my teeth.

"Are you hurt? Did I — ?" He eyes turned worried and he began to sit up, but hesitated when I combed my fingers into his crest.

"No more than any maiden."

Kiefan's eyes closed and his forehead touched mine, Blessing to Blessing. "Oh, Kate…"

I kissed him. His next thrust made me whimper again, not in pain but it sounded like it.

"Gently," he murmured, lips against mine, and took a slower pace. "Gently."

Slow and gentle drowned my brain in a spinning haze, as I lay there on a sheaf of parchment notes, gripping handfuls of his cote near the small of his back. Lulled me with our shared breaths, tantalized me with the little catches in our throats. Kiefan kissed me and fucked me and when his breath turned harsher, when the bliss crept up into his eyes to overwhelm the control — he pulled out with a rough gasp and caught himself in his hand. He curled against me, moaning through clenched teeth, as he came. Then relaxed, letting his head rest on my chest.

Kiefan held up his hand and the firelight caught on a streak of blood amid the other wetness. He shifted for a better look at the situation. What he saw had him up on his knees. "Kate, please — you're not hurt?"

I didn't care to move, too languid to worry much. But I propped up on my elbows and he pulled me the rest of the way up.

"It's no worse than a little moon's flux. Haven't you seen blood before?"

"I've never wanted to see it there." Kiefan considered his hand, now a mess of fluids and he had nothing to clean it with. Then he noticed how close I was and leaned closer for a kiss. "Never want to see it on you."

I smiled and kissed him back. "Don't you know who I was apprenticed to?"

His tongue probed into my mouth and I leaned closer, sighing —

A brief knock and the door opened, letting in a slice of light. "Kiefan? The queen is —" The woman froze, spine stiffening, on the sill.

Kiefan pushed my knees together and turned me away from the door. "Wenda, shut the —"

The bang of its slamming cut him off, and as I twisted Wenda stormed across the room to slap him square across the face. By how he caught himself on the table, she'd put some of her strength Blessing into it.

"What would make you such a fool! I could as easily been Her Majesty!" the housemistress hissed. "After what it cost Duscha…" She trailed off as she eyed me, my loose blonde braid, my memory ridges. "You're not one of mine."

"And who are you to slap him?" I frowned, reaching for his hand against his jaw. He intercepted me and put my hand aside.

"The one who's cleaned up worse messes than this." Wenda added a stern glare at each of us. Kiefan took his hand from the table, leaving a sticky print behind, as he shifted toward the edge. She nodded at the mark. "They told you that much, at least. Off, both of you. The queen means to apologize," and Wenda drew that out, "for calling you cruel as the king — and this is how I find you. How long's this fancy been —?"

Kiefan's boots thumped on the floor and he towered over the housemistress. "It's no fancy. I love her."

My heart tripped, in my chest, as I put my feet over the side of the table. Questions about Duscha fled my brain.

Wenda sighed and pulled her mouth to one side. "Your mother won't give one pip," she said, tilting her frown up at him. "She'll only see your father in you — or Prince Wolfgang. There's good reason she guards you!" The housemistress scolded him with one finger, as well. "And you know what it will do to her. Clean your hand, here... you, m'lady? Your pardon, I've forgotten your name." She pulled up her shift from under her skirt to wipe Kiefan's hand clean with the ease of a mother, throwing a glance at me.

My brain fumbled for words. "Kate Carpenter."

"The Elect's student," she said with a nod. "From the hunt. And the letters." Wenda leaned over the table and wiped the handprint with her sleeve. "We must smuggle you out, clean and proper. Do you need anything for that?"

I was still throbbing from the lovemaking and a bit dazed by what Kiefan had said, but that was fading fast. Off the table, I smoothed my skirts down and saw no bloodstains seeping through. "I'm well enough."

"I'll divert the queen." Wenda poked Kiefan high in the chest as he settled his cote over his re-tied braies. Her voice fell to a growl. "You'll break this girl's heart." With another side-long glance at me, "I've heard this story before."

"I'd sooner die," he told her.

"You'll wish for it, if Majesty catches you." Wenda pointed at him as she went to the door. Kiefan leaned against the table as the latch clicked open. She looked to either side before she left, closing the door behind herself.

I crept around the table, reaching for Kiefan's hand, hoping for a hug. I got it, warm and close and safe. Another breath of lavender and warm wool.

I had to ask. "If Her Majesty catches you? Us?"

He took a deep breath. "I know what they say about my mother," he said. "I know they say her mind broke, after she caught my father with the baroness. And after what he had to do to... get me. She had to be watched, for years, lest she hurt herself."

My stomach sank, hearing that, and I remembered her sad smile from Ilya's funeral. "Broken minds can heal, the Elect says," I whispered.

"She — caught me with one of the housemaids. The spring before this past. Duscha."

It stung, a little, but I flicked it away. On the heels of talk of broken minds, the words turned darker in my head. "And?"

"I haven't seen her since. Wenda won't tell me what became of her. After that, my kisses earned slaps."

Of all the disquieting details tied up in that, the one I asked about was, "Only one house-maid?"

"Only one." He paused a moment, then grimaced. "She was pretty, nothing more. She was nothing like you." He put his forehead to mine. "I was rougher on her than I meant to be. Blessings don't always wait for you to think before they take hold. If I seemed to worry..."

I leaned against him, warm in his arms where I wanted to be. "I'm not fragile." He was mine, now, if only... though he'd said... my heart ached for swelling, trapped in my chest. My voice fell back to a whisper. "I love you, too."

His grip tightened, for a long moment, breathing deep and ragged, and the ache drained from me. Then we had to part. We had to open the door.

I had the rest of my shift with the patients and then my laundry to see to. The queen expected him. Kiefan walked with me down the front stair, his hands clasped behind his back. "I'm sorry I didn't answer your letter," he said. "I will, though. Wenda brought me the book, but I've had little time for reading."

"You'll call for me if you sprain anything else in sparring?" I raised my voice as a page passed us on the steps.

Kiefan shot me an amused smile. "Gar! Fetch a courier for Kate." He pointed to one of the pages sweeping the floor around the main doors and the boy sprinted to obey. To me, "I could claim I called you for that. But if I sprained anything sparring with Gregor, I'd have to do it myself. Even mother would see through that excuse."

"Then call me for the least headache," I said as we crossed the great hall. "Call me — well, if you wish to see me again." My feet slowed, fear chilling me. There must be something to bring me to the castle —

"Solstice," Kiefan said as I thought it. "Come for Solstice."

My concentration was completely ruined, that week.

I wallowed in daydreams until a charm slipped away from me and my patient convulsed under my hands. The phlegm I'd wrung from his lungs stuck in his throat, choked him, and his face went white, then blue, while I yelled for a nurse and her charm-hand. Pulling her kir, I thrust it into the man's chest and he heaved out the whole slimy mass at once, with a little blood to boot. He sucked in a huge breath and hoarsely screamed.

"It's not required to be gentle with the patients, but it's polite," was what my teacher said of that.

Over the days, my mind cleared. In letters, Kiefan and I worked through my assigned reading and into another essay. The supply master began to give me smaller pieces of cheaper paper, still complaining about how much I was using.

A week after that, I was called from stoking the fire under the brandy still. Someone had come to see me. I hesitated, knowing I couldn't leave the still unattended for long. It was a bad choice of time to visit.

"Where is he now?" I asked Artem, who'd been sent to find me.

"At the gate."

That was odd, if it was Kiefan. "Bring him to the courtyard and I'll be there."

I refilled the coolant water tank as high as I could and checked the fire again before trotting out of the shack. I slung my cloak around me as I went through the dormitory and out its front door and into the courtyard. I looked for Kiefan or maybe Gregor to be standing...

Anders had brushed the snow off the bench under the maple tree and paced slowly to and fro on the clean wood. His horse, a roan mare, stood tied to a low tree branch. He turned at the end of the bench and spotted me as I recognized him.

"Anders?"

"Kate." He hopped down into the snow, cloak belling.

"You're back for more Discipline?" I tried to tease him. His stint in the Father's Discipline had ended weeks ago, and I hadn't seen him since.

He laughed at that. "There was a matter of a few palfreys for the Order. And the matter of the Solstice banquet at the castle."

"What of it?" I folded my arms under my cloak.

"You're the castle's attending physician, so you're expected at the Solstice. The Elect will be there also, but he has a lady for company already. It's wise of him to do so. When the banquet guests get their teeth into an unescorted lady — or knight, for that matter — they will pair the unfortunate up with the most awkward dance partners in hopes of starting a romance."

"Oh?" I considered what little I knew of the castle's Solstice banquet; Alice was always glad to tell me the scandalous stories churned out by the rumor mill. Dancing did always come up. "They'll saddle some poor knight with me for a dance partner?"

"If you don't have one to fight them off."

I could bring it up in my next letter to Kiefan, I thought. Dancing with him would give us an excuse to talk. Perhaps slip away…

Anders shifted closer while I stood inattentive. "The Prince's Guard are expected to be on hand at the castle for the Solstice," he said, as if it were entirely by coincidence. "The officers are invited to the feast as well."

"They invite you to the castle? But what of the queen?"

"Her Majesty makes her appearance and withdraws to a private meal with her guests — she dislikes His Majesty even more than she does me. We need only be in the great hall for the banquet. The true party is out by the bonfire in any case. However, the matchmakers will be in force everywhere."

"If I cower under the table, I'm sure I can escape their notice," I said to tease him. "Or I can easily pass as a housemaid." I indicated my humble brown dress.

He paused only a moment to find his counter-tease. "You'll have to contend with the dogs, under the table."

"True. Some of them Father's Dogs, I'm sure."

Anders smirked; it was a good barb. "Indeed. So if we're to spend the Solstice under a table, at least it will be in good company. I could offer you a ride to the castle at the very least. On a fine palfrey fit for a lady."

My turn to smirk. "If only I were a lady."

He *tsked* me. With a bow and a formal sweep of his arm, he asked, "Physician Kate, may I have the honor of escorting you to the Solstice celebration? I will fend off all matchmakers for merely the price of a dance and a little dinner conversation."

"A dance? Only one?"

"More as m'lady wishes, of course."

"Only if the lords are partial to 'Ducks in the Mud,' sir. I'm hopeless on the dance floor."

"By sunrise, the band will be playing 'Ducks in the Mud' and anything else they can think of."

I shook my head. "Bring me home after midnight. There will be lessons in the morning." Though that did remind me… "Midnight."

Anders' brows rose. "You must've earned good luck, at last year's Solstice."

Good luck came from a kiss at moonrise, the night of winter Solstice. Last year, I had been at the bonfire on Engl Street, and gotten kisses from my mother and father. That was fair enough, but all knew that it ought to be a lover's kiss.

Surely Kiefan would be glad to…

"We'll all be needing some luck this year," Anders said, as I'd been silent so long. "But luck can't be stolen, so all I ask is fair warning if I must get my luck elsewhere."

Could I steal a moment with Kiefan for a kiss? I nodded, lost in thought.

"I will come for you at sunset, bring you home after the midnight moonrise. Unless m'lady changes her mind."

I didn't think that likely.

After the disciple's dance, I took Alice's head in my hands and called up my kir to dispel her three-day-old black eye. The partly-healed bruise and the lingering swelling resisted me more than a fresh one would; her kir patterns had settled into a partly-righted dance and weren't so confused as in a new wound. Still, I could hurry it along.

"That should be gone by the Solstice," I said, passing my thumb over the lingering yellow and purple when I finished. "You can prowl for a new patron."

Alice nodded. "I hope this one," she said, gesturing at her eye, "receives his dis-invitation in time. You should come to our celebration. Eat at the castle but then bring Anders down to Arbor Street and join us. If you're determined to be seen with him, be seen by all."

"Kate!" Heima called from the rear door of the Great Chapel — Saint-day had moved indoors with the snow's arrival. "Our fitting! Quick, before dinner!"

Alice grabbed me by both hands. "You have a fitting? Which seamstress? You're to have a Solstice dress?"

"Parselev said I must be presentable and not confused with the maids." Anders would be sure to tease me about that, but I smiled in spite of myself.

"Well, hurry before dinner!" Still gripping my wrists, Alice all but dragged me across the Chapel. Heima laughed at the sight and was glad to meet my old friend as we went to join the seamstress in my teacher's cottage.

Frau Schneider and her apprentice had the dresses laid out on the kitchen table along with pins and measuring tapes and bits of charcoal. She and Alice knew each other well, and chatted about the other gowns being made for the Solstice while Heima and I changed.

My new shift, bleached as bright as snow, seemed a good fit to me but Frau Schneider pinned the bodice seams even snugger. Instead of a drawstring neck like my other two shifts, this one had a flat neckline that scooped rather lower than I was accustomed to.

I fussed it up a little higher and she set it right again. "Your shoulders aren't back here," she said.

As the seamstress and her apprentice worked, Alice sat at the table and watched. "Don't worry about keeping warm," she added. "That's what he's there for."

Frau Schneider chuckled as she checked the set of the waist and pinned it snug from there to my hips. "Do you have an escort, Physician Kate?"

"Sir Anders Bockmann," Alice answered for me; I hadn't told her, but perhaps it was no surprise that she knew.

"Oh, well, then we'll add a layer of mail to this as well."

"Kate insists he isn't all bad," Heima said. The apprentice worked more slowly at pinning Heima's shift, arranging pleats under her more generous bosom.

Below the hips, my shift fell in folds. Schneider took a piece of charcoal and drew a line down my back to mark the opening in the shift for lacings, then took my hand in hers to set the cuffs. She arranged each into a peak across the back of my hand and, while pinching the fabric tight in her fingers, used kir to meld it to itself. Other seams would be stitched so they could be adjusted later, but my arms weren't likely to lengthen.

"I know the stories can't all be true, but I wouldn't want him eyeing my daughter," she said as she worked. "Take care, fraulein. Don't let him get you alone in a room. Any young man, for that matter — you're a pretty enough girl."

My mind flicked to Kiefan, in the Council chamber, and the taste of brandy on his tongue.

"Don't let him get too much beer in you," Heima said, interrupting my memory. That hadn't been an issue, though. It had only been a taste, and then his mouth had moved to my neck...

"And don't let him sample the wares for free," was Alice's contribution. I slipped a bit of my lip between two teeth, shooing the memory away. She continued. "You're not a toy of his, so don't let him slip past the bargaining table. Sweet talk means nothing." Alice wagged a finger at me — she knew whereof she spoke.

Kiefan hadn't sweet-talked me. And what was I to bargain for — money? I was no whore. He loved me. He'd said it himself. And nobody in the cottage knew anything of this, so I shooed it away again and turned my mind to Anders. "I think I've weaned him off sweet-talking me," I said. "You know I've never been one for that."

"Now the dress." Frau Schneider picked up a golden cloud and shook it out into a gown.

I blinked, looking at it. "It didn't look so thin before." But, obedient, I put my arms up and she poured it onto me.

"It's a nice, lightweight linen so you can wear it with a linen shift for summer Solstice."

Alice chuckled. "Or, in the right circumstances, with nothing at all."

Frau Schneider pretended not to hear. "This came out such a nice shade of honey — your hair looks two shades lighter next to it."

Its sleeves belled out wide at the wrist, too impractical for anything but a party. The neckline sank lower still than my shift's, and the white daisies had already been beaded along that seam. The sides hung nearly straight, hardly shaped at all, and the skirt trailed on the floor.

"I'll add a braided white belt here," Frau Schneider said, checking the fit at my hips and folding in a little pleat on either side. Kneeling, she began to pin the hem. "What shoes will you wear?"

I had no answer; I was still sliding the gauzy stuff between my fingers. My white sleeves glowed through the linen. "I only have these shoes. Or my boots."

As she had a good view of the shoes, Frau Schneider said, "That would be a shame."

"I'll bring it up with Mechdan," Heima said.

I stroked the linen dress with my teeth on my lower lip, not quite believing still that I'd have a new dress just for a banquet. Kiefan wouldn't be able to recognize me.

And I wouldn't force him to bargain for love, not when the saints would tell him who to marry. When the Elect declared my training complete and I was ready to take a betrothal... surely there would be a man who could replace...

"You truly call Sir Anders a friend, Kate?" Alice asked. "Did you hear of the celebration after he won the tournament?"

"It's no concern of mine," I said, mind distant.

"The rumor mill wasn't sure how to grind his stint in the Father's Discipline. But now all are wondering how he'll manage the Mother's. There's many girls who'd play his little games, but with no dower to his name and no inheritance to come? The tournament might be a simpler feat."

Heima said, "If he took a Ther's vows, he'd have honor and the stipend. Make a better catch of himself."

Alice tipped her head. "Serving the Order doesn't seem his way, precisely."

"He did well enough training the boys. Sir Eindan had no complaints."

Frau Schneider stood and put aside her remaining pins. "This will be lovely," she declared, surveying her work on me. "A white veil to top it off would be precious. So pretty on a young maiden. Let me help get it off in one piece..."

I was glad to bunch it up over my head; my cheeks warmed a bit, probably pinkened, as the warm haze of lying in Kiefan's arms touched me again.

CHAPTER 10

The fresh snow was ankle-deep by Solstice, and the smell in the air warned of more. That decided me on what my feet should wear.

Anders stood holding four horses when we crossed the gate yard to meet him. Elect Parselev had my hand in his left, Heima's in his right, and as we went the cold breeze knifed through my gold linen and white wool alike, picking up my unbraided hair. I shifted my trusty felt cloak over my shoulders and its fur lining slid across the linen.

But Anders' eyes had already locked on me, and it seemed he couldn't tear them away. I expected a wink or a smirk or some little flirt, but none came. That grew unsettling as we approached. He couldn't, in fact, look away until my teacher cleared his throat.

"It's only because Kate has spoken so well of you," he told Anders, "that I'm trusting you with her. Keep her as safe as on your mission."

Anders bowed low, hand on his sword. "On my honor, Elect, I will not allow any harm to come to her." When Parselev released my hand, Anders took it and kissed my knuckles. He cut a dashing figure himself, in dark Rossweide green and a snow-white cote that showed its snug sleeves inside the wider green ones. Atop it all he wore his black tabard with new lieutenant's brasses strung onto the epaulettes. His twice-wrapped sword belt and the sheath were finely carved and set with golden beryl.

"Your champion's sword?" I asked.

"Yes. I fear I'll actually need it, now." Finally, a flirty smirk from him and we were back on familiar footing. "This's Mustard, he's Mother's palfrey. She insisted I bring him for you."

"You must have three of those swords now." I climbed up and took a moment to settle myself sidesaddle with one knee hooked over the pommel.

"They fetch a nice pile of coin, I've found." He paused, noticing my snow-streaked boots under my layered skirts, and laughed. "Good. You can run while I hold the wolves off."

"The wolves?"

He swung up into his palfrey's saddle. "You'll be drawing more than matchmakers, in that dress."

The heap of wood for the midnight bonfire waited in Castle Kaltkern's second ring. Monsters built of bundled oat-straw stood in attendance to be burnt in effigy: lamia, rukhs, Arceal centaurs and minotaurs. The guest house, just behind, was well lit and alive inside with revelers.

We rode up to the inner gate, though, and into the castle yard, where a smaller bonfire crackled and shot up sparks into the darkening sky. Sleek clouds blotted out half the stars when I looked up, and in the distance, high above, the peak of the mountain shone green and twinkled like a candle in a breeze. The saints lit the fount each winter Solstice, to call back the sun.

I could feel a faint tug of the mountain's kir at my chest, even miles off.

"You feel it too?" Anders asked, looking up with me. "I see it every year, but this's the first I've felt it. Careful, the flagstones are icy." He put up his hands to help me. I unhooked my knee and slid off into his grip. Anders said a few words to the stableboy who took the two horses by the bridle.

The double doors into the great hall stood wide open to let out the welcoming light. The castle yard had clotted with guests, some under the pavilion tent pitched before the west wing, many clustered around the fire. From under their dark cloaks came peeks of rich colors, glints of gold and jewels, and a few black military tabards as well. The guests circulated like lazy whorls of kir.

My heart sank. There were far too many to merely spot Kiefan through. I would be lucky to see him at all, even given the advantage that he was sure to draw attention. How would he find me in all this?

Parselev and Heima were already off to see to their greetings. I was to join them at the Elect's table for the feast, but until then I was to see to my own obligations as my master had sketched them out for me.

Those were a problem themselves. "We're to greet our hosts," I said, even though Anders surely knew that. "Their Majesties?"

"I'm to report to my captain," he said, holding out his hand to request mine. "After that, the saints are our hosts as much as their Majesties." I put my hand in his and he carried it, at formal shoulder height, as we went.

The captains were easy to find; one apiece for the King's, Queen's and Prince's Guard, they stood close by the fire co-ordinating both the current watch and those off-duty for the Solstice. Anders gave his captain a curt nod, fist to his chest. I curtsied, guessing at how low it should be.

"Sir Rostislav Loshadsky, captain of the Prince's Guard. Dame Kate Carpenter, physician and student of the Elect." Anders introduced me, not knowing I'd briefly met the captain in Kiefan's tent.

"Physician Carpenter, yes. We were grateful for your discretion, for so long as it mattered. Anders, keep a low profile. Her Majesty would still love an excuse." Sir Rostislav nodded to us both, which amounted to dismissal.

"Discretion?" Anders frowned as we moved deeper into the crowd. "You — you knew who Sir Adal was. And you didn't warn me?"

"Warn you? Why?"

"Going blind into — do you know what the punishment for striking the crown's heir is?"

My memory tallied up the blows I had seen, but... "Surely Kiefan's been struck in training."

"You owe me a second dance for putting my life at risk."

"I put your —?"

"At five lashes per hit?"

We had been steering toward the end of the line that snaked out of the pavilion, where the saints stood meeting the guests. I got out a few more syllables of objection before a voice interrupted.

"Anders!"

He turned, spotted the caller, and changed our course upstream rather than down. "A bit of luck," he told me.

The man who'd called Anders met him with a hearty cuff and wrapped that arm across Anders' shoulders. He was tall enough to do that easily, but still there was a softness about him, something buttery, and it wasn't only the color of his hair. His red cloak was lined with mink and the rich brocade of his cote was shot with gold thread. Enough gems glittered on his cloak pin and belt that had I not known better, I'd have thought him a prince.

"Theobald Kaufmann, tedious bean-counter and disreputable gentleman, please meet Dame Kate Carpenter, the brilliant physician and renowned student of our singular Elect."

"M'lady," Herr Kaufmann said, bowing over my hand, "I trust you know better than to listen to this muck-raking stableboy. Consider me your servant."

Anders twisted to look over his friend's shoulder and said, "He's got a wife, too, tucked somewhere in his purse."

Herr Theo shrugged to dislodge Anders and waved that idea off. "Brynhilde's occupied. Brilliant physician, you said? Impossible. Too pretty."

Still, on his other side I glimpsed the back of a lady whose gown sparkled with glass beads. Her hair was bundled up in a gold-wire crespine and topped with a slender diadem; I saw it glitter as she turned, at hearing her name, away from her knot of friends. A thin glance and a dismissive nod were all Anders and I were worth, apparently.

"M'lord's very kind," I said, suspecting Theo would be a duelist of wit.

"How do you do it?" he asked Anders. "It's criminal how you monopolize the supply of interesting girls."

"It's all the knightly sword-swinging and prancing about. Try it some time."

Theo shook his head. "Not when they were laying such long odds on you through the first two rounds." He thumped Anders in the ribs with one fist. "You're good as gold, friend, even at three to two in the final."

I glanced up and down the line in vague hope of a familiar face, but no luck.

"And you spent it all on the party afterward."

"Waking on Arbor Street with a girl in each arm? Worth every brun."

Near the bonfire, I spotted a parting in the guests and a dipping as they dropped in brief obeisance. Firelight danced, impossibly, on black. I leaned away from the line to see.

The queen wore black, of course, but it twinkled in spiraling patterns. Her veil had been folded back for the occasion, and her simple gold band replaced by a crown studded with rich blue and green tourmaline. Without the veil, I could see how Duchess Seagrace resembled her mother, and how the queen's beauty had withered under the burden of her grief.

She smiled, though, when Kiefan touched a kiss to her hand. He shone, too, his cote's white sigil and the oversized cloak pin of silver and lamia fangs glittering on their black field. The cloak was lined in white, another stark contrast. His only touches of color were the amethysts set in his silver crown.

With them came a cluster of musicians with lutes, drums, and flutes, who set down their stools before the fire and began to prepare their instruments. Another stool was put out for the queen, who took the seat with slow dignity. Kiefan bowed to take his leave, and turned to request the hand of a young lady in dark blue.

My stomach twisted as she curtsied to accept. The jewels at her neck, the rich embroidery on her bodice, and the dark blue itself were all marks of nobility even before her grace and brilliant smile came into play. She was near as tall as him, slender as a birch save for the generous bosom. Her warm brown hair hung loose under a gauzy white veil pinned beneath a tiara of braided ribbons and silk flowers.

So pretty on a young maiden.

A hand caught mine. Anders handed me a small cup. "Theo won't talk about money any further," he promised. "Will you rejoin us?"

I took a swallow, tearing my eyes away from Kiefan and the girl. It was mulled cider wine, thank the Father.

"How did you meet Anders?" Theo asked, a cup of his own in hand.

"We were in the prince's hunting party."

"Oh, that?" His brows shot up. "You're the one claiming —" With a sidelong look to Anders, Theo left that hanging.

"I should think you know him well enough to believe me."

His eyes narrowed. "I also know him well enough to suspect. You are the one, then, who helped him acquire that new set of scars. Impressive work."

"Suspect what, sir?"

Theo drained his cup and shrugged. We had made our way to the head of the line and needed to form up to be presented; Anders took my hand again, and Theo turned to take his wife's.

"Dame Kate Carpenter," he told her, of me. "The Elect's student. Kate, Brynhilde. My wife."

Frau Brynhilde leaned a bit to eye me again. From this angle, I could see the first bulge of a pregnancy on her. She couldn't have been more than a year my elder; Theo was of an age with Anders.

But then we stepped forward toward the saints and dropped to our knees. I caught vague boredom as it slipped from Qadeem's face and my nerves fluttered when he smiled in my direction.

"Your horse, Sir Anders? How is he?" It was Saint Aleksandr who spoke, however.

"Well, m'lord," Anders said with a bow. "Recovered from his wound and eager for spring to come. I've been working with him as you suggested and it's going well."

When we moved on, out from under the pavilion, Theo asked about that. "You know everything about horses. What did the saint suggest?" When Brynhilde let go of his hand to rejoin her clique, he nodded in her general direction.

"It wasn't so much about the horse, it was a matter of…" Anders let that hang a moment, then waved it off. "Let's see what dance the band begins with." That, to me.

"But the queen will see —"

Anders smiled. "I'm not in her house yet."

<hr/>

It was not "Ducks in the Mud." Anders did his best to show me the steps as we went and I did my best not to trip over my feet. Still, I retreated to the edge of the audience and took another cup of cider wine when the music ended. The band quickly turned over into another song.

"Dance with whomever you like," I told him when he started to offer more lessons. "I won't stray far."

There was, in fact, a lady in a pale green dress drifting toward us. She was quick to swoop in and claim Anders for the dance, and as they went she cast an analytical, suspicious eye on me. I hadn't the least idea who she was nor any need to know; the mulled wine was pleasantly warm in my mouth and now I could watch for Kiefan.

He danced with the lady in blue, and as it was a square dance Duke Seagrace and his wife the princess filled the other two spots in their square. When Kiefan traded partners with the duke, his sister said something that made him smile. She laughed at his reply. His smile lingered when he swapped back to the lady in blue.

I finished the cup of wine in one pull.

"Kate?" A hand touched my arm. M'lady Frida Bockmann smiled when I turned. "So good to see you again."

"I'm glad to see you're well, m'lady," I said and bobbed a curtsy.

She was lovely in Rossweide green, like Anders, layered over white. Her flaxen hair was netted in white as well. Her necklace of golden beryl beads glittered in the firelight. "I hope Mustard behaved well for you on the ride up. When Anders said he'd learned you didn't have an escort for Solstice, I didn't want him putting you on one of our youngsters."

"Mustard was a gentleman. Thank you for loaning him."

"You're here with the Elect? Your master?"

I explained that I still studied with Parselev, but I was a physician and not an apprentice.

"I had thought you still had some years of training. You must have done well to earn your title so quickly — and now you must be considering your prospects sooner than expected."

"My prospects outside medicine?" I had few aside from it, it seemed to me.

"Certainly. Any lady may seek a husband, but the advantage is ever with the young in that field. Your father must be quite busy helping you judge your suitors." Frida expected me to answer, but then was quick to add, "Unless, of course, you plan to forswear marriage and devote yourself to the Order."

"No, I don't mean to forswear marriage," I said, and my voice dropped a bit as I continued. "I would like a husband, of course, a family, but... my father's dead and I don't have any..."

My eyes slid back toward Kiefan, in the dance, and a needle of despair pricked me.

"I'm so sorry, Kate, I didn't realize your father was gone." Frida took my free hand in hers. "I didn't mean to remind you of that."

"You couldn't have known, m'lady."

"But you still have many options open to you, even so. You must've thought of what you're looking for in a husband?"

Intellect. Wits and a warm smile. Gentle hands, even though they were calloused.

"The coming war has me focused elsewhere," I said, in apology. "There's so much to prepare in time for the Queen's sortie. The Order will be all but empty once they're gone, and we're still to be a hospital."

Frida's smile turned to alarm. "You can't mean you're staying in the city?"

"It's the Elect's wish and my own," I said.

"Frida!"

A lady joined us, then a second, and Frida fell to telling them I was no longer an apprentice. This sent the conversation into marriage prospects, and I began to realize that I had fallen in with the very matchmakers that Anders had warned me of. By then, the next song had already begun and while they could not foist me onto some misfortunate dance partner, they were soon narrowing down their list of victims.

They had decided I required a husband wise enough to value my worth as a physician and well enough off to let me pursue that calling. Another lady was drawn in to advise on the list of likely widowers. Frida, bless her, began to mount a counter-argument, claiming I'd be happier with someone closer to my own age. The plans were shifting out of her hands, though. Of the names that came up, it took me a moment to suss out that one was Theo Kaufmann's own father.

The dance ended, but I had lost sight of both Kiefan and Anders. I stood on tiptoes and craned for any sign of them.

"Mother, thank you for watching Kate for me." Anders swooped in from the side to kiss Frida's cheek. "I didn't mean to leave her alone so long."

"You shouldn't neglect her so," she said, turning stern. "Get this poor girl into the next dance."

I was glad enough to take his hand and be pulled out of that closing trap. The matchmakers tracked me as I escaped, like vultures.

"You thought I spoke in jest, didn't you." Anders steered me toward a half-square forming up for the next dance.

"Not entirely, but…"

"Exaggerated, perhaps."

"Yes."

"I won't let Mara steal me again."

———————————✕———————————

Trumpets called us into the great hall for dinner. The twin fireplaces and ranks of candelabras lit the array of banners and trophies hung upon the walls; all of the lords of Wodenberg were represented, along with the torn flags of defeated enemies and their broken weapons. Most prominent were the Arceal standards taken during the battle at Ansehen a few moons past. A few racks of elk antlers filled in the edges. Garlands of evergreen scented the warming air.

The cold was shut outside at last and the cloaks came off to let the court's colors blossom in full. I draped mine over my arm and felt small, me with my simple dress and my hair falling loose — practically a banner to the matchmakers that I was unwed, but Heima had said I looked lovely that way. Still, I was tracked as I crossed the great hall with Anders carrying my hand and I thought perhaps it was my plainness, or because they knew I was only a peasant girl, or, most likely, that they all still thought me Anders' current conquest. Perhaps they were surprised he hadn't moved on yet.

Anders and I found our way to the Elect's table, which stood near the high table toward the staircase end of the great hall. There, I met more of Saint Qadeem's disciples than I had even suspected existed: Krepkin and a few physicians were there, true, but also stewards to the king and the dukes, high-ranking secretaries, master artisans, and military engineers. It was that last with whom Anders fell to talking; they were well into the topic of cavalry and defensive ditches when order was called for.

The king and queen stood together behind the high table and greeted all of their guests. Each of the saints said a few words about the coming year; Saint Woden made a point of clapping a hand on the king's shoulder and reminding us all how he'd conquered Englia and would lead us well against Arcea. Saint Aleksandr told us we had altered the southern half of Wodenberg to minimize the damage Arcea could do and deny them easy pickings. Qadeem spoke of how war was sure to provoke the blooming of new elect.

The abbot gave the usual homily on the transition of the sun to the Ewe's horns to lead the Flock through winter and spring — Mother Love, who taught us to show love and kindness to each other through the long, cold winter and the spring planting. At the summer solstice, the sun would return to the Ram — Father Duty, when we saw to our obligations to the kingdom and the hard work of the harvest in autumn. This year the obligations would come early with Arcea's army, and we would spend summer Solstice mourning the dead. He told us to celebrate, then, the lives we had now.

Toasts were drunk to the health of their Majesties and to victory, and to half a dozen other things while the first course arrived. I nearly finished the stein of double bock that had been waiting beside my trencher. The queen withdrew for her private meal with her friends and Kiefan settled down beside the king.

And the lady in blue sat beside Kiefan, with a smile. The high table's pages brought her a tea service, rather than double bock, and she daintily poured a cup for herself while Kiefan leaned away to hear a story that Duke Vysokov was telling further down the table. As the lady set the teapot down, her eyes slid across the room, over the tables filled by knights and officers of the Guard. They tracked across to the Elect's… and caught on Anders. Her head tipped as her brows rose. She sipped her tea.

Only my eyes moved, in glancing at him beside me. Anders leaned back in his chair and took another swallow of double bock as a page spooned greens onto each trencher along the table.

"Do you know that lady in blue?" I ventured. I wasn't sure if he'd seen her take note of him.

"Did she find me?" he asked in return, but didn't wait for an answer. "Her name is Kleelinde Vollmann."

My memory found the name in a lesson about the kingdom's noble houses. "Margrave Vollmann of Kernweise?"

"His daughter. A leading contender for the queen's crown, so far as most know. A kind and beautiful maiden. So far as most know."

Mid-sip of bock, that caught my ear. When I looked to Anders, he only smiled and finished his stein. He made me ask. "Which of those isn't she?" I doubted it was 'beautiful.'

He put out his stein for a refill with a shake of his head. "I'm not playing the grand game tonight."

When I looked back to the high table, Kleelinde and Kiefan were chatting, but by how their eyes wandered neither took much interest in the topic. There was little excuse for me to approach the high table during the feast. He had a lady to escort, as well. To kiss at midnight. I stared down at a tiny, roasted pigeon a servant spooned onto the bed of sautéed greens on my trencher, frowning as I wrestled with excuses and tossed them away as implausible.

The feast had only just begun, though, and winter Solstice was a very long night. There would be more dancing after the food, and more chances to talk. Perhaps I could dance with the prince — I had gotten better at the steps on the second time through with Anders' help. I straightened in my seat and began to listen to Duke Vysokov's steward, who was discussing the library fire that the d'Ovio book had survived. I thumbed the little bird's breast meat off the bone and popped it in my mouth. Then I washed it down with beer, as my stein had been refilled.

Englic fish came after the pigeon, accompanied by pickled vegetables, then beef and potatoes wrapped in pastry and cheese sauce. All of it was delicious, and through all of it I never ran low on double bock. We at the Elect's table never ran low on conversation, either, and partway through the feast our saint joined us to discuss coding systems for royal messages.

Anders leaned back from the table a bit and focused on finishing his meat before the pages came to clear the course away. "You've been keeping up well," he said, with a nod to my half-full trencher. "Ran out of room at last? Best to stop now and get in a few bites of the sweets."

"I need to find a toilet," I said, and stood up from the bench. Or tried to; my head spun and I wobbled.

"Gently." Anders caught my arm and steadied me.

In sitting so long, I hadn't noticed the effect of the beer. I hung onto his arm until I got both feet over the bench, and with a bit of recovered balance headed off in search of a toilet. One of the maids pointed me toward the closest, between the great hall and the kitchens. I had to wait in line, but it was a great relief. My head a little clearer, I returned.

My trencher had been replaced by a clean one bearing a small tart of strawberry preserves topped with crushed hazelnuts. Trays of sliced apples and cheese had arrived, and my stein was gone. Anders was pouring me a cup of brandy from a white porcelain decanter.

"I had to defend your tart," he told me sidelong. "Most of them are pear — there were a few attempts at theft." My cup full, he added a dash of brandy to his own tart.

"I saw you do that in Caercoed."

He smiled. "Tricky not to add too much. You don't want it dripping." Reaching back, he poured a little onto mine.

He was right, and it was delicious.

CHAPTER 11

When the servants began to clear the tables toward the wall, Anders had gone in search of the toilets and I was without a dance partner. I lingered near the bench and my cloak, keeping a sharp eye out for matchmakers. They circled, at a distance, as did a few knights in King's Guard tabards. I couldn't pick out m'lady Frida, or I would've risked her protection.

Kiefan had been drawn aside by his sister, who now had one of her young sons falling asleep on her shoulder and looked to be saying her good-nights along the high table. M'lady Kleelinde traded eyes with a knight of the Prince's Guard, then cast a glance my way. In search of Anders, no doubt; by how her eyes slid past me, I was below her notice.

The prince needed a new dance partner; m'lady Kleelinde could have her grand game and welcome to it. The band was checking the tune on their lutes by the fireplace and would be starting soon. I fidgeted with the braided leather belt that sat on my hips, trying to think of how to approach the high table. How in the world did men make this seem easy?

I took a few steps, still uncertain, and was intercepted.

"I apologize for being so dull earlier, m'lady." Theo caught one of my hands in his and put a cup of brandy against my palm. "I'm sure you had more important concerns than wagering, during the tournament. You must've been worried Anders would break his fool neck."

Startled, I said the first thing I could think of. "Someone did break his neck, this year. I worried, true, but about Anders?" My shoulder twitched.

Theo's brow creased. "So you do claim immunity to his charms, then? I had heard a rumor of someone claiming that. A girl who was on the prince's hunting trip. I thought surely there couldn't have been a girl on such a thing but you were their physician, weren't you?"

"Yes."

"To both?"

I'd misplaced the other question already, but quickly found it. "If his flirting is the sum of his charms, then I suppose I am immune."

He had a sly smile, this Theo Kaufmann, to go with his butter-rich, velvet-lined, gold-shot... I took a sip of the brandy in my hand and considered this friend of Anders'. Alice's words bobbed up in my memory, that he was heir to a greater fortune than some lords of Wodenberg had.

"Of course a physician would be. Anders is witty enough, but he's never read a book that I know of. You want something more intellectual. Something more... polished?"

Kiefan and half the top-tier guests stepped aside as two manservants picked up the high table to move it back. Theo wasn't unpleasant, but he was standing between me and my proper dance partner.

"Your pardon, I'm…"

I started to step around him, though my feet were a little slow to respond, and Theo caught my arm. He didn't pull, but turned me and moved to keep in line. "Surely he warned you about the matchmakers. The band's only waiting for leave to begin." Theo glanced toward them and I looked; the musicians had their eyes on the king and Kiefan, who were standing with brandy cups and talking intently with the duke. "Better to pick your own dance partner."

Theo's hand slipped down my white under-sleeve to my hand. I hadn't noticed how close he was, either.

"I did pick, sir," I said, though my voice came out smaller than I wanted. I took my hand from his.

"Leave her be." From behind me, Anders reached to block Theo when he moved to touch me again.

He shot Anders a wry look. "You leave her alone like this, and she's likely to be snatched up. You've seen the looks she's been drawing."

"She's not part of the game."

Theo's voice lowered. "Don't play righteous with me. You've got her tipsy enough to tumble right over. Even money says you promised to take her home after moonrise — and you've plans for that midnight kiss. Well enough, then. One dance is all I meant to steal, and better me than…" He gestured vaguely at the other side of the hall, where an array of men were watching all too alertly.

Anders' arm wrapped around my shoulders and I wasn't sure, for a heartbeat, if he was safety or more danger. "No game, no hunting tonight," he repeated, slower.

Theo threw up a hand. "You brought the easy prey, don't blame the dogs for catching the scent. And don't claim you've no taste for it yourself, of a sudden." He shook his head, frowning. "You're the only one who could find a rose in a shit-hole like Engl Street. Don't play shocked if all assume you'll be plucking it."

"Stick to the roses on Arbor Street. Süssie's waiting for you."

I backed up against Anders' chest, putting my free hand on his arm; of the two of them, I trusted him. Still, my heart shivered in my chest, wondering what sort of wolves and prey were usually loose on the Solstice and whether a peasant girl like me had any business being here.

"This'll be on your balance sheet." Theo noted it with one raised finger, and went in search of a dance partner. The band was starting to play. I had half a mind to point him toward m'lady Kleelinde.

Anders stroked a finger across my warm cheek. "How much've you been drinking?"

I looked for someplace to put my brandy cup down. He took it and handed it to a passing pageboy. "My stein never emptied — I don't know," I said. "Too much, I suppose."

"It's a good time to slow down. They'll bring tea, if you ask. A dance or two would help clear your head." Anders steered us out of the way as the dancing began, though. "Midnight's still a distance off, and I will take you home as you asked. On my honor, Kate," he said when I tensed under his arm, and he let me go when I leaned away. "On my honor, I will take you home and I only want to talk about — a few things. Only to talk."

That made my head tip — and spin a little — in curiosity. "Then we will talk," I said.

One of his infectious smiles broke out and he kissed my hand. "A dance to clear your head, then? You were improving, I noticed." It almost sounded like a tease, when he said it.

"Let me visit the toilet again. I'll be back in time for the next song."

With a nod, he released my hand.

I started toward the same toilet near the kitchen, but the line had mushroomed and looked far too long. For a time I fidgeted at the end, and then walked back toward the great hall. Sure enough, I met a maid with a tray of empty brandy bottles returning from there. I asked if there were another toilet and she hesitated, glanced at the long line, and took pity on me.

Her directions sent me back across the great hall to a discreet doorway under the main staircase. The hall behind it was dimly lit by oil lamps in sconces. That light was enough to find the second door on the right. As the maid said, there was small room there filled with spare chairs, stacks of folded draperies, shelves bearing incomplete tea sets and spare candles. I took one of those and lit it with a spark charm. In the back of the room, a narrow door sectioned off a toilet.

I'd been about to burst from all the beer and brandy. Too much. Tea sounded like just the thing to clear my head, I decided as I finished. Before midnight, I meant to talk to Kiefan. Though how he hadn't found an excuse to...

Two steps out of the toilet, someone grabbed my candle and a hand clapped over my mouth. I screamed, muffled, and was pulled against a broad chest.

"Kate, it's me. It's me."

Heart racing, I collapsed against Kiefan. The hand on my mouth shifted to hug me across my shoulders. I gasped, "You almost killed me."

"I'm sorry." His lips touched my cheek.

Then he blew out the candle. I turned, in the dark, and found his mouth for a real kiss. Kiefan stepped me back and pressed me against a stone wall, pinned me full-body for more kissing and his hands petting over my curves. His cote was sleek silk under my hands, worked with tiny beads on the chest sigil. That oversized cloak pin tried to scratch my arms when I clung to his neck.

He tasted like pears and brandy. Wood smoke clung to his hair. I raked my fingers through it, under his silver crown, and kissed his smooth-shaven cheek, then inhaled a lungful of him. I caught a trace of that lavender soap again, and it made my heart ache.

Kiefan hugged me, nuzzled into my loose hair. I wondered what he smelled on me.

"Come upstairs," he murmured.

Right here was where I wanted to be. "What's upstairs?"

"My room." His tongue flicked my earlobe. "I said I would go down to the bonfire to meet up with Gregor for the rest of the night. Come upstairs." His voice dropped to a whisper. "I want you."

I shivered in his arms. I put my hands on his face and kissed him again. My pulse throbbed under my whole skin. "I don't mean to stop you," I whispered.

His hand gripped mine. Opening the door, he checked the hall and led me further down. It ran the whole length of the east wing — the same hall that we'd slipped through to find the garden — and turned at the end through an archway. Kiefan stopped with me behind him, arm held straight to keep me there, but I glimpsed the guardsmen at the stair.

"Face the wall until I pass," he told them.

Booted feet scraped on stone and Kiefan pulled me around the corner. The oil lamps on the walls lit the staircase well, and there would've been no slipping past the two King's Guard who stood on the landing. They had both turned toward the wall, though. I looked back as we climbed, and neither of them even stole a peek. The second floor landing was empty and we climbed on to the third floor. The stairs continued toward a hatchway and the roof, but Kiefan led me into a twin of the first floor hallway. Again, he kept me behind his back with one arm.

Shuttered windows pierced the outside wall, but they were covered by white woolen drapes to keep out the cold. The only light came from lamp sconces. Past Kiefan, I glimpsed doors off this hall, two of them, each with a pair of guards.

He stopped at the first. "Face the wall until I pass. I am not to be disturbed."

"Sir," one said, to acknowledge, as they turned.

Behind the door was a sitting room, lit only by a splash from the hall before the door shut, but Kiefan swept me into the adjoining room. Dim firelight, here. My feet landed on a carpet and he closed his bedroom door.

It was fur under my boots, a huge swath of dark fur. The fireplace was at my back, its low coals casting only a dim, red light on the wardrobe standing to one side and on the bed before me. The mattress stood on a frame, not on the floor, and was piled with wooly blankets and more furs.

Kiefan dropped a log on the coals and it crackled. In a heartbeat, the dry wood began to catch and cast a bit more light. His arms wrapped around me from behind, hands cupping my breasts together. I leaned back against him with a whimper, my hands sliding over his.

"It's cold. Get in bed," he whispered, and nipped my ear.

"I'll need a ladder." I'd never seen a bed so high off the ground.

He breathed a laugh, scooped me up, and tossed me onto it. I landed and slid on the unmade rolls of blankets, sank into the mattress — without a sound. No crinkle of straw or hay. I managed to right myself and looked around at the thing. A good layer of furs, yes, but it was mostly mattress. Silent and softer than snow.

Kiefan leaned his sword against the wall and tossed off his crown as if glad to be rid of it. He bent over to unlace his boots and I thought to do the same for my own. My fingers were clumsy on the ties, though. He kicked his off first and grabbed mine at the ankle, pulled.

"You wore boots under that?"

"Why wouldn't I?"

Under my boots I'd worn my simple woolen stockings. Kiefan's hands followed them up my legs, under my skirts. He climbed onto the bed to caress further up my thighs. "A girl glowing white in amber, a little string of daisies around her neck?" He traced a finger over my beaded neckline. "A delicate, innocent maiden… wearing boots that slogged through the teeth of the Eispitzen?" His mouth hovered over mine. "Only you, Kate."

His lips were more intoxicating than any brandy. "Not a maiden anymore."

"No. Mine, now."

"Was it truly only a piglet?" Kiefan asked.

I lay cuddled against his side, head on his shoulder, tracing one fingertip down the low ridge that his strength Blessing raised along the center of his breastbone. I wanted every inch of him, every line and crease, burned into my perfect memory.

"It was only the dead piglet that sent me back to the Order."

"Did you want to marry him?"

My hand wandered lower, to the first short hairs that would lead me from his navel downward… Kiefan's hand intercepted mine, pinned it against his stomach.

His lips against my forehead, he murmured, "M'lady is a demanding mistress."

I smirked and leaned into the touch. "I liked Harold. He was a blacksmith's apprentice, and he loved the work. Father wanted a good match for me and Harold was a good match. For a carpenter's daughter."

Kiefan let a moment pass before prodding me. "But?"

Wood shifted in the fireplace, settling, and the light dimmed. "Few peasant-born can read," I said.

"The finer points of d'Ovio's 'On Love and Fidelity' go un-noticed?"

"I didn't love him, if that's what you're after." I propped myself up on one elbow, meaning to get a more thorough kiss if he didn't want my hand wandering yet. "No more than you loved that maid."

"I didn't love the maid. Or the lecture she earned me. Or..."

He picked up his head to kiss me. I leaned over him, climbed up onto my hands so I could pin him down on the pillow as he had me. He put up a good defense with his tongue, admittedly, and his tweak on my nipple made me squirm.

I smiled, but prodded him back. "Or?"

"Or when a squad of King's Guard took me out drinking at the Black Knight, and happened to fall to talking of the finer points of — controlling Blessings. In bed. They meant to smuggle me down to Arbor Street. I think I would have melted into the ground from humiliation if word of that got out."

My hair fell in a messy blonde curtain; I combed it to one side with my fingers. "You've been to Arbor Street?"

The time it took him to speak was answer enough. "Once. She was — well, it went well enough but I saw no reason to go back."

Alice talked about her work, sometimes just to make me blush but she'd also answered many questions. "What are the finer points of controlling Blessings, then?"

His hand nudged my hip up and I slid a leg across his waist. On all fours over him, I leaned in for another kiss while his hands petted up over my hips, my waist, found my breasts again. He kneaded them together, urged me further up so he could kiss them, then suckle. My grip tightened on the pillows as my mind took a lazy spin on the eddies of pleasure. When he let me go, I started to shift off him but his hands stopped me.

"No, stay," he whispered. "Stay. I'll show you."

I woke swaddled in warmth, sunk in the feather mattress with Kiefan's arm over my waist, spooned up to him under wool quilts. A contented purr sighed though my throat. My eyes cracked open.

Cold blue light, filtered through the white window drapes, supplanted the dim coals in the fireplace. An ironbound chest stood under the window, silently enduring the indignity of the tangle of golden and white dress that had been flung on it. With a smile, I curled my arm over Kiefan's. His grip on me tightened and he shifted closer with an inquisitive noise. I answered with another purr and guided his hand up my stomach.

A shout from outside jolted my eyes open: "Majesty! M'lord doesn't wish to be disturbed!"

Blankets covered my head, muffling half of that, but I heard the bedroom door open. Kiefan scrambled from beside me. "Mother! What in the saints' name —"

"What? How can you ask that? The morning watch has changed already." I curled up under the blankets, pulse rising. The queen paused a moment. "And you question me? You'll freeze — put something on. How late were you out at the bonfire? If that captain of yours brought you home and let you sleep naked in this cold, I'll have..."

Her voice had grown a little clearer; perhaps she was closer. I didn't dare move, eyes fixed on a thin spot in my cover where light fought its way through the layers.

"Mother —"

She snarled. "You've a girl in here! You! After all I've given you!" The blankets tugged and I snatched at them; I heard a struggle. The queen shrieked, words half lost in her rage. "All my agony and you replace me with a whore!"

"Guard!"

I pulled the blankets tight over my head and the queen screamed at the proof I was there, but her voice was fading into the front room.

"Fetch her captain!"

The bedroom door was kicked shut, muffling her cries as they fell into wailing. My hands trembled as I clutched the blankets. Her mind had broken, and they always said it with a sad shake of the head. How much could a woman be asked to bear, losing her sons and her place in the king's bed, then dragged back into it? This Duscha, the housemaid Kiefan had been caught with, if the queen had flown into a rage at her…

For a moment, the queen's sobbing grew louder and the door clicked shut again. My heart froze in terror, ears straining to hear through the covers. Footsteps?

"M'lady, quickly." A soft voice, nearby, then a hand on me.

I peeked out.

Housemistress Wenda nodded, with a grimace. "There you are. Up."

I sat up enough to look toward the door. Quiet had fallen, on the other side. Wenda went to the two windows and pulled their drapes. "Is Her Majesty…?"

"She' hasn't suffered such a fit in years, but we all know what to do," she said. She picked up my gown from the trunk and sorted it till she found the shoulders.

Kiefan slipped back in, wearing only his braies. Three red scratches streaked across one shoulder. He cast me a melancholy glance as I sidled to the edge of the bed. "The captain will see that she's watched," he told Wenda, his voice low.

"I'll see she gets her tea. Fresh linens," Wenda ordered, pointing.

Turning, Kiefan shucked off the braies and sat on the bed. I caught a view of the Blessing ridge down his spine that my fingers had found grooves in to hang on by, last night. And a glimpse of his butt.

Wenda clucked at me and shook out my shift by the shoulders. But then she winked as she laid it on the blankets beside me. "Dress quickly. The king will be looking for you — and Saint Woden. We must get you both out before you're further missed."

I took my shift and pulled it over my head, then slid off the mattress to wiggle it down. The lacings had been loosed roughly, in the hurry last night, and my hands were still trembling. "Could you?" I asked, turning.

She pulled them tight with precise jerks. "Get your shoes on, don't mind the gown. Kiefan, you were at the bonfire past moonrise and Captain Loshadsky poured you into bed. You likely aren't clear on when, though."

"Perhaps Mother thought I ranged too far afield in drinking with the Guard, last night," Kiefan said, behind me.

"Down to Arbor Street, perhaps." Wenda nodded. "That could give her a fit. It will do for the rumor you didn't sleep alone, as well — that's afoot already. You may trust your Guard, but men gossip near as much as women."

I found my stockings and pulled them on, tied the garters, then circled the bed for my boots. Kiefan took a black surcote from his wardrobe and pulled it on over his white cote and hose. The housemistress picked up his beaded silk finery from the floor, setting off its sparkles in the sunlight.

"I'll see to things here," she said, tossing it on the bed. My gown was over her shoulder. She watched us a moment, hands on her hips. "Will you hear my advice, Kiefan?"

He looked up from pulling his socks on. "Of course."

She doubted that, by the crease in her brow. "Don't do this again."

Kiefan's arms folded. "You said yourself I've earned —"

"You've been a good boy all your life, and Mother Love knows you've been the only ray of sun in this castle for far too long. Steal a dalliance if you must, and if it's love —" She raised one hand to fend that off and continued. "Mother have mercy on you both. But take greater care. The queen has her reasons to guard you. Don't draw her anger to Dame Kate as you did to Duscha."

I laced one boot up, wondering if he would ask, and he did. "What became of her?"

"Last I saw her, she was flogged bloody and I washed her wounds. She returned to her family on the riverbank and as her father lost his appointment to bring up fish twice a week, I heard no more. Though a girl's body was fished off the stones at Sevropor a moon later. But that happens, now and then, and the eels had had their way with her."

I nearly lost my balance, second boot half on, in looking up at Kiefan. Waking warm in his bed pulled me one way; fear pulled the other.

"She won't harm you." His arm caught me across the shoulders and pulled me up straight. "I was the one that caused her fit. She mistook me for Father, she was so taken by it." He flicked his hand at the scratches, with a grimace. "I'm the one who did her harm and I'll pay whatever blood's required. I won't let Mother or anyone else harm you, Kate. I love you. I need you." His hand stroked my hair back, fingers combing through a few tangles.

Me. My throat tightened and I leaned into his hand; Kiefan hugged me close.

"It's not blood and it's not Kate," Wenda said with a grimace. "Not even that your mother caught you here. She didn't come here alone last night." She pointed at me.

"Anders?" Fear jabbed me again.

"Left, finally, but it took some doing — and a great deal of hushing lest the saints catch wind anything was amiss." The housemistress' grimace became a stern glare at Kiefan. His lip had crept under his teeth. "Should Saint Woden catch you dallying… you know why m'lord Wilhelm was king and not Prince Wolfgang. Despite that the prince was Woden's bound elect."

Kiefan's voice was low. "My father's discipline. His obedience to duty."

"Someday, Woden must choose between you and your own brother. Don't make all your mother's suffering worthless, on that day. Both of you, be careful. Now, hurry."

When my boots were on, Wenda passed the folded gown to me. In the sitting room outside, my cloak lay across a chair. That, I bundled up in, hid under the hood, and was slipped out while the guards looked away.

Kiefan's words were still caught on my ear and wouldn't let go. He loved me; he needed me.

My dormitory hall was empty and quiet; all the students who could had gone home for Solstice. I trotted with my gown clutched to my chest, hood still deep on my head, thinking of my plain brown dress that I could pull on over this shift. If I rolled up the long, pointed sleeves, they wouldn't give me away. Comb my hair quickly and find a bite to eat before —

A few steps from my door, I tripped and fell hard onto my hands and chest. The thing I'd stumbled on scrambled up to his feet.

"Kate? Mother's mercy, where were you?"

I turned on my butt, on the stone floor, and stared up at Anders with a slack jaw. He snatched me up, put me on my feet and took in my shift, the dress on the floor, all of me in a glance. He was still in his uniform, under his cloak, and the dark green from last night.

"You slept here?" came out of my mouth.

"I had no place else to look for you. You weren't lost in the halls or fallen down a staircase or left crying in a closet — you hadn't gotten out into the crescent garden or up the stairs, you hadn't gone back out to the pavilion so far as I could tell. I'd never thought you fool enough to go out in a snow squall without your cloak, but you weren't at the bonfire either. Or in the guest house. Or lying in an alley along River Road…"

His hands, after adding emphasis to the story, returned to my arms and squeezed. My heart had sunk to the cold floor and frozen there while I watched the frustration flail across his brow. I had no reason I could give, and no excuse could suffice. Nothing.

"Are you hurt?"

I swallowed. "No."

"If Theo laid a finger on you, Father help me but I'll —"

I shook my head. "No."

"What happened?"

My mouth opened, but I had no words. I closed it. There was nothing I could tell him, and he had every right to be angry. Though in truth he seemed more worried than angry.

I took a deep breath and picked up my gown, which broke off his hold on my arms. "Nothing you need worry about. I'm sorry that I caused you such trouble, and I'm in your debt for taking such concern for me." I said that with as steady a voice as I could manage, then pushed my door open and tossed the gown onto my humble straw bed. I swung the door behind me to close it, but it struck something solid.

"I gave my word no harm would come to you."

"And no harm came to me." I turned to face him, as well as shame would let me. "I'm sorry for causing you so much trouble. I truly am. I wasn't thinking of you, that's all it was. You didn't have to waste your night searching, or sleep on a cold floor waiting for me."

Something in my words tipped his worry into misery.

"Mustard's in the gatehouse stable…" I added, increasingly at a loss for words.

Anders stood there, his hand on my door, his mouth in a grim line and summer-sky eyes gone chill. I cast about for some scrap to offer him.

"I owe you that dance I never returned for. Collect on it whenever you wish. And —" My memory cut me off by bringing up those last moments before I abandoned him. "You wanted to talk?"

His jaw shifted. When he spoke, I barely heard him. "Don't trouble yourself, m'lady."

He pulled the door shut hard as he left. I heard his boots fade down the hall.

I sat down on my bed with a heavy sigh, sure I couldn't ever look at him again without being crushed by guilt. Or at the queen, for fear she'd know it was me in Kiefan's bed. Or Kiefan, for… temptation? I heaved another sigh, sinking my face into my hands. The warmth of his feather bed, his arms, might have only been a dream if it weren't for my memory.

And my memory reminded me of last night, parsing out what had been a hazy blur of kisses and nips and slithering skin on skin, of moans and gasps and… heat inside me, as his hands tightened on my hips to grind deeper. He'd meant to pull out. Most of the times, he had.

Mother had told me of women who fell pregnant despite that. My nerves had been so stretched, yesterday, in worrying about seeing Kiefan at all, that I hadn't thought of a pessary. That he'd steal me away for the whole night was too wild a dream to cross my mind.

Mother had told me which herbs one could call one's blood with — widow's tea, she'd called it — and that they were not a certainty, either. But so long as I took care with the dose, it was simple enough. Standing, I took my brown dress from the low shelf and pulled it on. There was a jar of the dried leaves on Parselev's shelf and it was not wax-sealed.

CHAPTER 12

The first signs of scarlet fever in the orphanage turned up that afternoon. Nearly every winter, something struck the children — fevers, pneumonia, measles — and this winter was all the worse for having to save our kir. By the first Saint-day of the Bitter Moon, all the littlest ones had it, including Alice's daughter Magda. We brought our herbs to the orphanage floor, above the kitchens, and gave them teas and kept their fevers down with snow compresses.

I took one of the three doses of widow's tea, was late in getting the second — and didn't remember the third until after a long shift of keeping fevers down. I lay on my bed, next to sleeping Hannah, and tried to reason myself into walking to the kitchen to stoke the fire, boil water, and make tea. Instead, I called up my body's whole pattern.

All was as I should be. I had seen babies ready to be born, their kir storming bright in the mother's womb, younger ones small as ducklings, even as small as my thumb when the pregnancy was only a few moons old. How small would a fresh-made baby be?

One blink, and it was morning. And the orphans needed me.

Parselev assigned me to watch Krepkin as he went to the worst-off of the children, doling out tiny, precise charms to ease their illness and stretch his kir as far as he could. In truth, it was fascinating to learn and I swallowed enough of my anger to admit as much to him.

He muttered a bit, but accepted my words.

The widow's tea I'd taken gave me a few spots of blood, but nothing like my usual — though in truth, I hadn't been myself since the mission. My flux hadn't come during the journey, and being a virgin I hadn't worried much. It had come eventually, but my rhythm was lost and I hardly knew when to expect it anymore.

I was dreading those three days of cramps and weakness soon enough; Brauer rode out to the garrison's encampment on the north slope to be their physician. They were re-training the local reserves and apparently that couldn't be done without sprains, knocked heads, or getting anybody frostbit. I took over her post as physician of the floor under Krepkin's still-skeptical eye.

Even with my memory Blessing, keeping track of the nurses, orderlies, apprentices, patients, and the handful of physicians took all my wits. With the snow growing deeper, the ill and injured didn't reach us until they were half under the Shepherd's shadow. Only my teacher had kir to spare, for he could draw from the Pool, and each evening he began with the worst off and healed until his focus wavered. Standing by his side, I learned a great deal of frostbite and revitalizing near-frozen flesh that was still attached to the living.

Each day, I sank my daily kir into charging charms: blood-stops, knockouts, and cleansers. Parselev made new ones, as he was able — only he and Saint Qadeem could, in the entire kingdom. We had hundreds of them, but the fight at Ansehen had taught us that however many we had, there would not be enough for the whole summer. In time, we had charged every last one and hoarded them away.

The Bitter Moon was as good as its name, from its first day. None of our orphans died of scarlet fever, but it took Parselev's healing in some cases. Snow, deep and bright, blanketed mountain and city alike and muffled all but the hollow voice of the wind. When I woke sweating, seeing lamia in the shadows, Hannah muttered and rolled over beside me. Maybe others feared the war coming in the spring, but I was haunted by monsters.

Of the many gatherings to plan for both the Queen's sortie with the main body of city evacuees and the anticipated siege, the largest came just before the Bitter Moon reached full. The dining hall was the only space where all could meet at once, and the tables were of great help to the secretaries who scribbled notes as fast as the reports were given.

I was there as Parselev's student, though my tired head buzzed with the shifting states of the patients on the invalids' floor and those orphans still suffering scarlet fever. I sat with my hands around a nice, warm mug of tea while the rumble of voices swirled through the dining hall.

All parts of the Order's campus were represented, and the city-dwelling free-lance physicians besides. The army had sent officers to report on both the military and the supply aspects of the Queen's sortie. Civilian mercantile interests had come to confer with both the Order and the officers. It made for a great deal of bergamot tea and oat-cakes and talking.

Krepkin sat down beside me with his own mug. "A sensible enough idea, Carpenter," he said, wrapping his knot-knuckled hands around it.

We'd hammered out a willingness to communicate facts to each other, over the weeks, and little by little civility was starting to creep in. "Ther Ivor brews a good cup of tea."

"That he does."

Parselev, with some kir to strengthen his voice, called for order and the noise settled.

"I need to learn that charm," I said. Krepkin snorted.

The litany of preparations began with the Order's orphanage and staff, then progressed to the hospital. Parselev announced the duty assignments: Brauer and the free-lance physicians would bolster the infirmary in Duke Seagrace's army, and the younger students and their teachers would go with the Queen to serve any wounded during her journey. The Elect would remain in the city to head the hospital with Krepkin as his right hand. I would be physician of the floor and attend the castle in support of Parselev.

"Are there any objections?" My teacher turned to Krepkin, brows raised.

Only a shake of his head answered. Krepkin focused on taking another sip of tea.

"Thank you, sir," I felt obligated to say as the announcements moved on.

"Keep your nose to the grindstone. We'll put an edge on you yet."

The reports worked their way through the merchant representatives, talking of emptied grain silos and warehouses, oxen and wagons. Next came the officers and the readiness of the City Guard, the garrison, the local reserves. My mind began to wander. The Equinox would come late in the Slush Moon, and the Queen's sortie left the next day. Perhaps there would be a chance to see Kiefan at the festival — if there were one, up at Castle Kaltkern. Surely I would be called there before —

"The City Guard's knights have been found wanting in their horsemanship." Anders' voice jolted me back into the room. "At Captain Rogen's request, in a few weeks I will be refreshing their memory out at the winter camp. My apologies to the hospital if I fill their beds too quickly."

He got a chuckle from most of the room. Anders stood in the middle of the cluster of black tabards, just one more blonde head and easy to miss. I slouched on the bench a little, looking away before there was any danger of meeting his gaze.

"Concerning the requests to Baron Rossweide from various of you," Anders said, pointing to a few faces, "the answer is that save for warhorses sold at the tournament or otherwise spoken for, he's been fully requisitioned by the king's army and cannot supply any hooves to the city."

That got some grumbles. The reports moved on to supply lines. After all had spoken, more specific issues began to separate the meeting into clumps; the winter camp's commanding officer came to our table to speak to Parselev about a possible case of typhus.

I felt a chill at that news. My father had died of typhus after Ansehen, in the back of a wagon with a hand of other sufferers. It had been too far in the hot summer sun to even bring him home, and he'd shared a grave just off the Southbound Road.

My sigh rattled the congestion in my chest and I coughed, then took a sip of tea. It was too cool now to loosen the phlegm, though.

"Your cough sounds deep," Krepkin said. The officer had moved on and Parselev was dictating further notes to one of the craft-handed secretaries.

"It does seem to be settling in." I tried to clear my throat and coughed a bit more. "Perhaps I can get this freshened. That would help." I got up from the bench with my mug.

"Physician, heal yourself," the old man told me.

I shook my head. "Brauer sent up a night watchman with three frozen toes."

With a grumble, Krepkin put a hand on my arm and pulled himself up. "Don't waste tea on pneumonia," he said, falling into his lecturing tone. "To do the most good, a physician must first tend to his own health. Now, watch. One precise charm will turn the tide in your favor."

My kir rose up bright and colorful at Krepkin's call, whirling strong save for around my congested lungs and...

Breath stopping, I looked down at what I could see only in my mind's eye. Between my hips, a tiny, star-bright knot of kir.

My flux wasn't late.

"You little slut," Krepkin hissed. He flung my arm away. "Parselev thinks he can train manners into a pig fresh from the mud — what can anyone expect from coarse peasant blood? And Englic to boot." His voice rose with the heat in my face. "No respect for the Father or Mother, nothing but lies and dishonor to the Order, to the Elect, to our Saint!"

Heads were turning. "I never lied," I hissed back, panic clawing at my throat. "I've never dishonored —"

The old man's voice kept rising. "I'll see you're put on Arbor Street with the rest of the —"

My hand went to his throat, skin to skin, and all I could think was to silence him. His kir surged up at my call, twisted into a bright blade of light and stabbed his prime meridian. Krepkin stiffened, watery eyes flaring wide, and gasped in pain. His heart stuttered, sending kir whorls tumbling like leaves in wind.

"Stop!" A larger hand landed on mine and a greater will overrode the spreading chaos. Kir flowed, so strong I could see it ripple around Krepkin. The strength of it knocked me back a step, head spinning. The old man blinked, wobbled on his feet, and stumbled into the hands of a secretary.

There was a moment of stunned silence. My master looked down at me, bewildered. I felt my kir pulse up at his bidding, telling my secret again. I took another step back and bumped against the bench, landed heavily on it. Krepkin knew, Parselev knew, and I had... I had just...

"She —!" Krepkin pointed, lunging up from the helpful hands. "You all saw it, she —"

Kir knotted in Parselev's hand and flashed out a green sphere of light. The other voices in the room vanished as if a door had slammed shut.

"— tried to kill me! The little whore!"

I stared at my own trembling hands, still trying to grasp what I had almost done to a fragile old man. "I only meant to —" Dead was silent, and I'd wanted him silent. I hugged myself and the tremble spread into my guts. Over, it was all over now. I'd almost murdered my senior physician.

"You thought you could only heal?" Parselev shot me a chiding glance. "We'll speak on that."

The hush sphere enveloped the three of us and part of the table, its surface a thin green glow. Outside, half the men gathered in varying degrees of confusion and concern. Mouths moved, but I heard no voices.

Parselev raised his hand again and kir arced from one of the officers, through the sphere, curved around my master's hand and shot off again with a crackle. Parselev crooked his fingers and a moment later Anders was hauled, splayed and off-balance, into the sphere, by the green vine of kir. He was dumped on the floor and the vine shot back to Parselev.

He closed his eyes a moment, and for a heartbeat we waited. "Leave us," he announced, kir-strengthened, and apparently that was heard outside the sphere. Ther Ivor, who'd come out of the kitchen at the commotion, took charge of dispersing the audience.

"All these theatrics over another Englic backstabber?" Krepkin folded his arms across his chest. "She's played us for fools, Parselev."

That cut through my muddle of fear and despair. "I did not!"

"Rutting under the shelter of the Order is an insult to Saint Qadeem and the Mother!"

My eyes blurred, the memory of my saint's trust a stab between my ribs. Whatever words I had choked into sobs and then coughing.

"Peace, Stannis. Sir Anders, not a word. Kate?"

Parselev's hand gripped my shoulder gently. The phlegm in my throat came loose and I took a trembling breath. I had to be stronger than this; I risked a look up and wiped my eyes. Anders stood biting his lower lip, gripping his elbows. Krepkin glowered under his bushy brows. The Elect stood over me, brown eyes more worried than angry — but angry, no doubt of that.

"Did he rape you, Kate?"

The question was so absurd that I blinked and fumbled for an answer. "No."

"Truly?"

"Truly. I —" My mouth twisted shut again. My fist pressed against my gut, against the evidence. Pregnant. Unbidden, memories from Kiefan's bed flickered past my eyes.

"Of course she wasn't," Krepkin said. "She'd have come crying if she had." He turned away.

"Stannis! Say nothing. This will be resolved," Parselev said.

Krepkin hesitated, his foot already put through the sphere's rim. "Slim chance there's any true solution," was his opinion, and he stalked away.

"Do you know how hard she's worked?" Parselev's voice turned low and angry. His hand left my shoulder as he strode to Anders, whose spine stiffened as the Elect's accusations rolled out. "Do you know what your bit of fun is going to cost her? It never crossed your mind, did it, you only thought to souse her up for a tumble when you gave your word on her safety!"

"Tumble her? I haven't even kissed —" Anders' voice dropped mid-sentence and he stared at me, past Parselev's shoulder.

He knew. A fresh, icy cloak of fear dropped onto me. I shook my head, a terrified little tremble.

My teacher clapped a hand to Anders' face and seethed: "On your life, did you do this?"

Kir rippled. Sudden pain curled Anders' lip and he tore the hand from him. "No! Shepherd strike me if I lie."

They glared at each other. Then Parselev said, "But you know who. Tell me and I'll stick him to his honor to do right by her."

I had to salvage this, somehow. My heart trembled and I rose, weak-kneed, trying to find my voice and something that would fix this. Krepkin could call me whatever he wanted; one night in the prince's bed didn't make me a whore, no matter how soundly he'd fucked me. I wouldn't let a sour old man harry me out.

"He can't," Anders said. "His hand's already been promised, and by the saints themselves."

Parselev heaved a sigh as he turned toward me. My voice came out tiny, half strangled by my knotted throat. "Master, please don't send me away. I don't care what names they call me. I can be strong, I can work as hard as you want but please…"

He was shaking his head. "It's not as simple as names."

"Nobody needs to know. It's just a little knot; it can be undone, can't it…?"

"Kate." He crossed the gap to me in two long steps, putting his hands on my shoulders. "Kate, stop and think. Clear your head. Do not be a frightened peasant girl — you are a physician and a Blessed of Saint Qadeem. If you run panicking to the first thing that crosses your mind, that truly would be an insult to him."

"But there's only sending me home to my mother, or…" I whined, my own words tearing at me. Back to cold and hunger and lampless, book-less nights.

A little shake brought my eyes back to Parselev's. "I've had this conversation many times, with many frightened girls. I've seen this story play out. Sometimes well. Sometimes badly. Often, a mixed bag — as happened twenty years ago." That with a sidelong glance toward Anders. "Take heart from what became of Baroness Rossweide, Kate. There are many paths to choose from."

I knew it would be true enough, though it was strange to think, that m'lady Frida might have come to the Elect in tears when she realized she was pregnant by the king. My head cleared a little in wondering what had been said.

"She could stay?" Anders asked.

"No. An unwed pregnant girl kept in a besieged city would be an affront to both the Mother and the Father. Both duty and love oblige me to send her with the Queen's sortie to greater safety. But even so, there are choices to make."

"I can stay in the Order. I don't have to be down at the city walls," I said.

"There will be disease," Parselev said, counting them off, "there will be fire, there may well be hunger, and if Arcea breaches the city wall there will be fighting in the streets. Anyone with a drop of royal blood in them will be sought by Arcea — they will not spare infants or the pregnant."

"She faced most of those dangers here as your student," Anders said.

"There was only her life and her duty to the kingdom. Now the child is part of her duty to the kingdom as well — to contribute new lambs. And this one may have a claim to the crown." My teacher sat on the bench beside me, taking my hand in his. "Go with the Queen, be safe, parlay your worth as a physician and your proof of fertility into a good marriage. If I live, I'll seek you out when it's safe to return."

If he lived? "But you said I need to be here. That you need me here to learn and blossom — all that talk of the fallow —?"

"You are a Blessed disciple of Saint Qadeem." Parselev held up a hand to cut me off. "Don't speak of anything more. And do not ask for allowances, as it will only draw attention to you. Arcea's attention. You carry Woden's blood, that is trouble enough. Go to Prohzgrad."

My gut wrenched at the thought of leaving Wodenberg again, remembering only snow and lamia though I knew Prohzgrad would be far safer. "This is my home, and I mean to help protect it. I don't want to leave."

Parselev took a slow breath. "Of course you don't. If you — lost the baby, you'd be well before spring. But Krepkin's not likely to keep his mouth shut and he'll be free with his venom on you. Word would reach all ears, in time. We must have a story of who the father was — not you," to Anders, "and not Kiefan. None of Woden's blood. He'll not take kindly to undoing one of his line — especially so close to the crown. Convince all that you crept off with some other man, and endure the slander. I know it won't stop you from outshining every student here, Kate, but come time to talk of marriage it will be a mark on your name. Did you want to marry?"

I nodded. That all seemed a thousand miles away, but I could still see it.

"Rukharbor needs strong physicians and nobody there would know your story."

My mouth twisted again; I was an Engl, true, but Rukharbor would be as strange as Prohzgrad.

"This is ludicrous," Anders said, throwing up his hands. "Kate, I can see to it that you stay here as long as you like, and that old windbag won't be able to say one word against you." He gestured toward the other side of the room.

The dining hall outside the sphere had emptied, save for one small knot of men around a secretary. They were looking through some papers and paying us no mind. Krepkin lingered on the fringes of that group, watching us.

Parselev stroked his beard and looked to me, brows raised.

Confused, I asked Anders, "What do you mean?"

"I accepted the Father's Discipline, as I swore I would. I would accept the Mother's as well, but Baron Rossweide has washed his hands of me, Woden isn't likely to put a crown on my head, and that leaves precious few marriage options. I can't offer you much but as husband and wife, we would answer to the Mother and Father in our own right. The Elect would have no duty to send you away. We choose how to serve, as befits us. And I say we stay, you with the Elect as you should be, through the siege and whatever comes with it. What you do, where your affections lie…" He slid that aside with one hand. "You've called me your friend. A marriage is what you make of it — and marriages have survived on less than friendship."

Anders looked away while he said it, and he shifted on his feet as my brain tried to absorb that. He paced across the breadth of the hush sphere.

"How do you think I'd go to your bed when I love him?" I asked. A bit of anger gathered, but was shot through with confusion. "You think me a whore, too? Or to be taken advantage of?"

He bristled for a moment. "You think I would force a woman into my bed?"

His tone brought up a bristle or two on me, as well. "No. Thus, I ask you to explain. How am I not in my husband's bed, if we are married?"

That put him back to fidgeting. "Be in your husband's bed only when you wish it."

When? Perhaps on a cold winter's night, and if I trusted his hands to mind themselves… "And still be your wife? Even if that's to be never?"

"If you'll grant me the same freedom," Anders said, risking a glance as he paced.

Alice's story of the knight's wife flicked back to my mind, and what he'd implied of Kleelinde Vollmann. "I shall not ask where you spend your nights."

"Likewise, then."

Still, I had to press a little more. "As a friend, I trust you, but on your honor, Anders — you'll not expect me in your bed?"

Eyes on the floor, he nodded. "On my honor, Kate."

"Could such a marriage work?" I hoped Parselev had an answer.

He took a deep breath. "I've seen enough of them to know they can stray far from what the Mother lays out in her teachings and still obey in spirit. They can still bring strength and healthy children to the community. Do that, and the rest is for the two of you to decide. I'll not give advice or criticism, with my history."

I pressed my hand against my stomach, knowing what the pregnancy would bring and what the child would need; learning midwifery from Mother and helping with my siblings had taught me that. I knew I could raise a healthy child, so long as I was not huddled cold and hungry in a peasant cottage, alone, dismissed from the Order, or shipped off to a strange city where I had no footing.

I needed to be here, to continue my training with Parselev and to face the coming war with Arcea. War and fire in the streets of my home, in addition to a baby, were frightening, true. But the king had an army, Duke Seagrace had an army, we had three strong saints, and Caercoed was coming to aid us. I didn't doubt that Wodenberg would survive. I knew I could not do more to aid my home than to stay here to heal the wounded, and I meant to do all I could.

"Will you still have me as a student?" I looked to my teacher to be sure.

Parselev stood from the bench. "In truth, I would not have you anyplace else. A child does not alter your talents, only how quickly you master them. I do not doubt that you will have lifetimes, Kate, to master them, but I will not have you falling prey in the meantime for being ill-prepared."

That was far more than I'd expected. "Prey?"

A sober nod, arms folded across his chest. "Kir-mages play a deadly game, whether they wish to or not. Arcea is bringing the game to our door, so you must be ready — it's good that you attempted a Shepherd's knife, even if on Stannis. If you're willing to take Sir Anders' offer, then so be it."

Anders' offer brought more than a bed. As a carpenter's daughter, I'd expected a craftsman for a husband, or some manner of trade. Someone who could provide a leak-free roof and steady meals, plus a few bruns for other necessities. Of me, cooking, crafting — I'd thought I would be a midwife, as Mother was — housekeeping, and babies would be required. I could still do much of that, in addition to healing, and Anders was a knight. He was a craftsman of a sort, if warhorses were something crafted.

Married, we'd both be bound to the Mother's Discipline and secure in our obligation to the kingdom to create a good home for the baby. We'd be as respectable as we could be, with a child that wasn't...

"Everyone will think the baby's yours," I said as I realized it, turning back to Anders.

"The Elect assumed it was my doing — I doubt anyone will outsmart him." He risked a look at me. "Is my proposal worthy, m'lady? Should I make it on one knee?" The corner of his mouth risked a teasing dimple.

That was the first ray of light in this dark afternoon. I nodded, but I said, "I should ask Kiefan."

"Ask? I'm not marrying him."

Parselev touched my hand again. "You should tell Kiefan about the child and this arrangement, not ask. And not alone."

"Call him down," Anders said. "You've the authority, Elect. I'll see that he listens."

CHAPTER 13

A runner went to the castle. Anders and I waited in Parselev's cottage, in the kitchen before the fire, and he went upstairs to rummage through his papers. Heima cared for the orphans during the day, so the fire had settled low. I stoked it a little and put a kettle on.

"So you have nothing to your name, as you said that day in the mountains?" I asked when the silence had been wearing along for some time.

"Near enough. My uncle inherited Kaltgrasen when my grandfather died. Will is heir to Rossweide, unless Ein proves better. The king has been too ashamed to even look me in the eye, all these years. All I have I earned myself or owe to my mother." Anders sat at the table idly rearranging the bowl of eggs Heima had left there. He shot a smile toward me, sidelong. "Mother will love you forever, for this. She'll dote on the baby."

That needled me. "It would be a lie."

"The baby's still blood kin of mine. Let her dote. It makes her happy." Anders turned an egg in his fingers, considering it. "I owe her happiness."

"Why?"

He shrugged. "Ask on any street corner and you'll hear enough stories."

"Why would I want stories? You said they invent them whole cloth."

The egg's shell clinked as Anders replaced it. I wanted more, to hear the truth from him, but a knock at the door was Kiefan arriving at last. Gregor stood in the knee-deep snow behind him, but was dismissed back to the hospital to warm up once Kiefan took in me and Anders and Parselev descending the stair slowly. The prince stepped into the little kitchen and shut the door, pushing back his hood and dropping clots of snow on the floor.

"Your message said the matter is urgent, Elect?" Kiefan asked.

"It is, but I am only here to advise." My teacher sat down on a low step and looked to me.

Following his eyes, Kiefan looked too. I drew a deep breath and crossed to take his hand; the squeeze he gave mine did more to strengthen me than he could know. "I'm pregnant," I murmured, and called up my kir.

Kiefan's breath caught when he saw the star in my belly. He crushed me tight in his arms, whispering, "I'm sorry, I'm so sorry — to fail you —" He kissed my forehead. "Can you forgive me?"

"I love you," I whispered back. His grip kept me from bursting into tears again.

He exhaled hard and loosened his arms, took my hands in his. "You had to tell the Elect," he said, voice steadying, "but why is Anders here?"

I looked Kiefan in the eye and said, "I have agreed to marry him."

His hands tightened on mine in shock. "No." It was a simple statement. "Don't, Kate, you don't have to."

"Because you'd sooner let your child bear the mark of a bastard?"

Anders' venom startled me as much as Kiefan; I felt him tense through his grip on my hands. I looked toward Anders, at a loss for words.

"You know nothing of what that child faces," he said.

Kiefan's hands slid away as he took a step toward Anders. "You think you've been wronged? Whose shadow have you lived in, then? Who gnawed out your mother's heart and left scraps for her own son? I will not abandon Kate or our child."

"Because Saint Woden will let you keep a mistress, though he denied your father? Or is that only the story that's told to excuse him? No, surely Saint Woden will give you quarter in this. You know what he thinks of the weak." Anders sat at the table with arms folded, the sharpness of his eyes matching the anger in his words.

"Are you calling me weak?" Kiefan's voice shot a chill down my spine.

"Better than a fool for thinking your Caercoed brides will share you. You saw what they expect of husbands."

"I don't need marriage advice from a bastard."

I heard only the clatter of the bench and steel scratching across steel. Kir flooded the kitchen and bodies thumped against walls in a crash of pottery and tipped furniture. I stumbled against the kitchen door, putting my back to it as I tried to catch up with Blessing-sped knights. Parselev flicked his hand and the kir withdrew into his palm. Kiefan and Anders, backs slammed high to opposite walls, dropped onto their feet with bared swords still in hand.

The kitchen table, having tipped far enough to lose all its crockery and the eggs, started to fall entirely over. I lunged, but my master caught it first with his kir. We both set it upright.

"I advise we discuss this in a manner more worthy of Mother Love and Father Duty," he said. "Kate, please continue."

Neither sheathed their sword, but the two knights looked to me.

"Anders and I will not share a bed," I told Kiefan. "He won't ask where I spend my nights and I won't ask where he spends his. That was why I agreed."

"You trust him on this?"

"He gave me his word." When Kiefan's brow furrowed at that, I said, "Did he not swear to keep you safe, when he joined the Prince's Guard? Did he fail in that, on the mission?"

He couldn't say no but he didn't want to agree either, by how he glared across the room at Anders. Kiefan leveled his blade at Anders' heart. "Swear to me, on your life, this marriage will go unconsummated. If you touch her, if you ever hurt her in the least way — I will kill you myself."

"Pardon, which of us won the tournament?"

Kir surged again and Kiefan raised his free hand as he stopped himself, already halfway across the kitchen on Blessing speed. Anders, on the other side, kept his blade at a low guard, tracking Kiefan closely.

"You cannot make demands —" my teacher said.

"How can I be a prince of Wodenberg, and stand by —" Kiefan's shout cut short, whether from rage or pain, as he pointed at me. Raw, weak, he tried again. "I have never asked anything for myself."

Parselev told him, firm and quiet. "The saints' Blessings bear a price."

"Tell me how to quit my bonds, and I will!" Kiefan watched the Elect for an answer. My own throat knotted in sympathy for him. "If I must leave it all, if I could… and if Kate would come with me… the crown has its claimants." Kiefan threw his free hand up, toward Anders.

"No, you're welcome to it," Anders was quick to say.

"Hush." Parselev raised one hand, and silence followed. His gaze had sunk into the distance, but now snapped back to Anders, then Kiefan. "You have been betrothed to Caercoed, Kiefan, and you will not dishonor your saints or your kingdom. You've seen the thousands willing to die to keep Arcea from murdering you. You will not dishonor them."

The weight of that fell on Kiefan, and I felt it touch me too. I reached for his hand as I crossed the kitchen; our fingers twined together. Kiefan's forehead touched mine with a heavy sigh. My throat was too knotted to speak. I hoped my grip was tight enough to say how much I wanted to be his extra strength.

Kiefan took a deep breath. Straightened, his hand still clutching mine. "You. Swear." He pointed at Anders again, with the sword. "You will not touch her."

Anders met his gaze, calm and steady. "My word's sufficient for Kate. If she wishes you to enforce it, do what you must. Till then, see to your own marriage."

Anders fetched me, a few afternoons after that day, when the weather cleared enough to ride across the city to the Rossweide house. He brought Mustard for me to ride, and the palfrey picked his way smoothly through the fresh layer of snow and ice. Dry powder, churned up by the hooves, billowed and glittered behind us. A few brave souls out clearing the drifts from their doors stopped their shoveling to wave as we passed.

At Anders' whistle, the barn door opened for us and we rode in, trailing snow. Will pushed the door shut and the light faded down to only covered lanterns and stray beams through chinks. The horse-scented dimness was all but black, after the brightness outside. I slid down from Mustard with an ease that surprised me, and kept my hand on the palfrey as my eyes adjusted.

"Go in and warm up," Anders said, brushing the snow off his own horse's legs. "I won't be long." He gestured toward a lantern hung by the kitchen door.

When Frida heard it open and turned, her face lit up in surprise. "Kate? Now, why wasn't I warned you were coming? Mercy, I don't even have the kettle on."

Still, she crossed the room with her arms open to hug me and kiss my cheek. Little Hilly trailed after her and reached up for a hug and kiss, too.

"Thank you," I told Hilly when she asked me to sit by the fire. "I didn't mean to surprise you both. I thought Anders had told you I was coming."

Frida shrugged as she crossed back to the fireplace. "He didn't. Though he's certainly welcome to bring you. I only wish he had so I'd have more than gratin and bread on the fire. I'm a fair hand, but in truth it was Sasha's cooking that kept my guests happy."

The chair by the fire stood empty but for a sewing basket. Hilly led me toward it by my hand. "Is she well?"

"Oh, yes, thank the Mother. She and her daughter are quite well." When the door opened again, she turned with fists on her hips. "Anders! You didn't warn me there'd be a guest for dinner."

He checked his boots for manure and came to kiss Frida on the cheek as Will scraped his own boots clean. "I'm sorry, Mother. I wanted this to be a surprise."

"Dragging the poor girl through the snow for gratin and bread is more a surprise for her, I think." Frida turned to put the kettle on the fire.

"There was something else," he said. When he checked that Will was ready, and waited for her to turn back, I knew what the surprise was. We had our two witnesses.

Anders dropped gracefully to one knee and took my hand, putting a small cloth bundle in my palm. Looking up, his pale knight's crest hanging loose to one side, he asked, "Kate would you honor me with your hand in marriage? I would swear my fealty to you, before the Mother and the Father."

With a solemn nod, I said, "I would gladly do the same."

He rose for the brief kiss to seal the betrothal and Frida caught us both in her arms with a happy cry. I felt her tears on my cheek when she kissed me and my own guilt blurred my eyes. My heart swelled against my breastbone, feeling safe for the first moment since Krepkin found me out. Putting my arm around Frida, I hugged back and tried to ignore how she had me half pressed against Anders as well.

"Open it, open it!" Frida let me go enough to urge me toward the cloth bundle. She poked Anders in the shoulder. "You said it was nothing — something you were saving! Don't you ever lie to me."

"I would never, Mother," he said as I worked off the ribbon tied around the bundle.

A bit of jewelry was traditional for a betrothal gift; it was a necklace strung with smoky quartz beads and a matched pair of lamia fangs bound in gold wire. Frida took it from my hands and I gathered up my hair so she could knot the cord around my neck. The teeth sat high on my breastbone, smooth and deadly. My arm twinged in remembered pain around my scars.

Frida wiped at her eyes and hugged me again. "Thank you, thank you, you don't know how happy I am, how long I've prayed..." She sighed. "Let me get Reinhardt. He'll never believe me!" Frida chuckled as she let me go.

She left us standing in front of the fire, I with my fingers on the quartz beads at my neck. A smile lingered on Anders' face, an honest one with no teasing in it. It suited him.

"I wouldn't believe Mother either, if I hadn't seen it." Will crossed from the barn door with his hand out, clasped Anders' and added a quick hug. For me, a kiss on the cheek. "Too late for second thoughts now — Mother's had you in her sights since she first laid eyes on you."

That sounded true enough. "She was asking what I look for in a husband, at the Solstice."

"You should've held out a year or two. You could've been the next baroness Rossweide," Will said with a grin.

Anders swiped a cuff at him, but he ducked. "She'll find you one, give her time."

A small hand tugged at mine, and Hilly pointed at the boiling kettle. I thanked her for telling me and shifted it off the fire. She and I made tea, then, and when Frida returned with m'lord Reinhardt we sat down at the table with fresh cups.

I had come to discuss the dowry and dower; it was a short conversation. Still, the baron being a thorough man, pen and paper were fetched and everything written down.

My dowry was only a few linens that I had sewn before I received my Blessing and began studying. I had a few bruns that the Order owed me, all that was left of my per-moon stipend after they deducted the cost of my food and the dormitory room.

Anders' dower was not so poor as he thought. His sword was the one he'd won for his first tournament championship, its jeweled sheath sold and replaced with a plain one. Likewise, his mail and helm had come with the title. Nipper, as a foal, had been his Blessing-day gift. The warhorse's tack and the rest of Anders' knightly gear had come from selling his second set of tournament prizes. He was in the process of selling this year's set of armor and the beryl-inlaid sword he'd worn at Solstice.

"Oh, and you must have my mother's rings," Frida said, hopping up from the bench. She trotted up the stairway in the corner of the kitchen.

"Will you keep me on as a trainer?" Anders asked while she was gone.

"We'll see how things lie, come autumn," m'lord Reinhardt replied. "Frida will want you to go with her to her brother's holdings — are you expected in the Queen's sortie?"

That was aimed at me. "No, I'm staying with the Elect."

His dark brows shot up. "You? Here?"

"Yes, sir," I said, and left it at that.

"At least you'll be near each other," the baron said as Frida's footsteps returned from upstairs. "If things go badly, if you're widowed, I'll give you a good price for Nipper if he survives. And I'll see the rest of the dower is sold fairly as well."

A warhorse wasn't good for much but war, and expensive to keep. Still… "We can speak further on that, if we need to," I said. M'lord's pen paused when his brows perked, at that, but he crossed out the part that he'd already written.

Frida, returning to the table, heard that and put her finger to the table next to her husband as she told him, "And Kate will be welcome in this house so long as I'm drawing breath."

M'lord Reinhardt yielded that without a fight and began to write it down. Frida opened a small box and laid two gold bands inscribed with whorls, one large, one small, before Anders.

"Those were worn by your grandparents," she said, sitting down. "Mother left them to me, as the eldest. Try them on. I'll have them adjusted if they don't fit."

Anders passed me the smaller one and I turned it in my fingers, feeling the chisel of the carving. They were in an old style, the spirals squared off rather than smooth. I slipped it slowly onto my left hand and it caught on my second knuckle. M'lady must have been small, or more likely her hands weren't so coarsened by work.

I pulled it off and gave it back to Anders.

There had been a wedding each Saint-day since the Solstice; the next one was no exception. The exception, that week, was that when the disciple's dance ended Alice still had not arrived. When Ther gave the orderly array of dancers on the Great Chapel floor leave to begin setting up the community wedding feast, I joined in.

The groom was a student of the city's master blacksmith and the bride came from a merchant family in the middle tier of the city. Her family flooded the Chapel. He had come from a small town and had only distant relatives here, but they came to help him and his bride set up the tables and decorate with garlands and golden ribbon.

I spread a tablecloth and smoothed its wrinkles. The bride placed the centerpiece, a handsome spray of fragrant pine and bright holly tied with ribbon — green and gold, the colors of fertility and prosperity. She was all smiles, and the silk roses braided in her hair echoed the excited blush in her cheeks. My hand went to my necklace to fidget, stomach twisting at the thought of next week and my own wedding.

A hand grabbed my elbow and tugged; when I turned, the darkening bruise around Alice's eye dropped my jaw. "Again? What happened?" It was fresh, I could see. I put my hand to her cheek and called up her kir. "Was it the same patron?"

Alice brushed my hand off, too angry to let me help. "Why do I have to hear about you from the rumor mill, now? I'm not good enough to tell me first?"

"I would've told you before the dance, had you been here." I reached for her again and she swatted at me; I caught her hand and worked through that.

"You were the first I told," she said. "I trusted you."

When Alice first feared she was pregnant, she'd come to me because my mother had taught me all the signs. The potter's son who'd sweet-talked her into bed had denied his part at first and set off a scandal. When he finally confessed, his father had been honorable enough to contribute a couple silver crescents to Alice's dowry.

Alice's father being a drunkard, that money hadn't lasted long. Came winter and lean days, Alice had gathered her few belongings and walked up to the Order to ask for shelter. Which they gave, for a price that she was to work off. That had been the first debt of many, for her, and turning tricks on Arbor Street had seemed the quickest way to pay them. At first.

Magda was two, nearly three now, and an adorable little orphanage ward. Alice visited her as often as she could.

"I didn't know I was pregnant until a physician tried to clear my congestion," I said, lowering my voice. "If I had found out myself, I would have told you first."

"You." Alice cocked her hip, frowning at me. "You didn't know you were pregnant."

I blushed. "Not every woman suffers morning sickness."

"Father Duty needs to mete some justice on you, then." Alice hadn't been able to keep her food down for weeks. A smile crept through her frown and she said, "I could not believe my ears when Borrik made his rounds. You, of all people, marrying Sir Anders Bockmann. Sampled the wares, then? You must've cast the Mother's own charm on him."

Krepkin was as much a gossip as all of Arbor Street, it seemed. He'd taken the news of my betrothal with a sour face, and had scrutinized my necklace with a grumble about how most lamia fangs were fakes. I'd nearly showed him my scars to prove I knew exactly how genuine they were. But the old man had said no more about my fitness for hospital duty. He could content himself with tutting over my sampling the wares, for all it mattered to me.

I smoothed out the tangling kir in Alice's bruise before answering her. While I worked, she lowered her voice and asked, "Are you sure you want to marry him? He's been playing seduction games for years — that may be a hard habit to break. Theo Kaufmann's been married a year now but he's still a cornerstone of Arbor Street."

The red lingered, but wouldn't darken. "Anders' games aren't my concern. Did another patron hit you?"

She grimaced. "No, it was Ludmilla. She's impatient about the money we'll need to hire our security detail if the city's besieged. I can't get any more credit to pay my share. No share, no place on Arbor Street. No Arbor Street, lower pay and more fists. I've no other prospects."

"As good a cook as you?" I caught her hand, squeezed it. "Haven't you been feeding your patrons? That would keep them —" I paused when the idea hit me. "Would you be a housemaid?"

Alice considered. "In the right circumstance."

"Baroness Rossweide needs a housemaid who can cook. I can put in a good word. Meet her when you're my bride's maid?"

Alice smiled, finally.

CHAPTER 14

Castle Kaltkern's training yard stood at the far end of the crescent garden, tucked into a pocket made by three high walls. The staircase at the end of the wing went down from the ground floor, as well as up, and a simple door let me out into the foot-pounded yard. In midwinter, it wasn't much more than ice-crusted snow and a scattering of training dummies; racks of wooden training swords waited just inside the door, along with a stack of well-beaten shields.

Gregor slumped with a sigh of relief at the sight of me. I soon knew why he hadn't been sent to fetch me; it was his elbow that had a crack in the bone. It was already swelling badly.

"And you force him to continue?" I spared Kiefan a frown as I combed through Gregor's tangled patterns.

"With my other arm," Gregor muttered. "M'lady."

Kiefan stood fidgeting with his sparring sword. "It's nothing I haven't suffered," he said. "One must focus through the pain, sometimes."

I bandaged Gregor's elbow tightly, and made a rough sling of another bandage. "That will need checking," I told him. "Come to the hospital in a week. Bring the bandages back."

A nod from Kiefan excused the squire from further practice, and he set about putting away their gear. Kiefan tossed him his sparring sword and put out a hand to me. "Come and warm up?"

I hadn't seen him since he made his demands of Anders. No word, no letters. The silence had worn at me, filled me with questions, but now the sight of him drove those from my mind, and left only a gnawing worry I couldn't put words to.

But I took his hand, and he led me up the stairs — though at the first landing, in the shadows midway between the lamps at each floor, Kiefan pinned me to the wall with a kiss. For a heartbeat I stiffened in surprise, and then I melted. Pressed, full-body, despite the cold stone, my worry eased.

Kiefan broke off the kisses, gently, and whispered. "Don't do this. Don't marry him." His fingers combed into my loose hair. "I won't abandon you, as my father did the baroness."

"But I cannot stay, without the safety of —"

"I can keep you safe."

He had so many duties already. "You've the whole kingdom to keep safe."

The outside door closing, below, cut off his answer. Gregor's boots scuffed on the stone floor as he followed the corridor below into the castle's depths. Above us, voices echoed down the stairwell. We were well cloaked in the shadows, but I recognized the king's voice and my grip tightened on Kiefan's arms. I meant to push him away, but he didn't budge. He looked up toward the voices, the faint light catching on his silver prince's band. The voices, and footsteps, climbed the stairs above us.

Kiefan's hand found mine. "We'll tell my father."

He strode for the steps, meaning to bring me; I planted my feet, leaned against his pull. "No, don't —" He was strong, though, and dragged me to the bottom step before he paused.

"Kate —"

"And what will he say?" It burst out of me, in despair. I twisted my wrist in his hand. He let me go, taking a breath to object. I asked, first, "Will he decline an alliance with Caercoed, for you?"

"There are —" Kiefan lowered his voice back to a forceful whisper and he dropped off the steps close to me. "There are other candidates. Vysokov has a daughter nearly old enough for marrying. Once she's knighted."

My stomach twisted at the thought of laying thin pleas before the king and Saint Woden. "The saints gave their word. We're not to make liars of them, we're to be strong and serve. I need to serve." My teacher and my saint trusted me, and failing them would leave me broken. I never doubted Kiefan understood that, and felt the same of his own duty.

"And skulk in the shadows, stealing kisses?" Kiefan leaned close, as if to kiss me again. "I need you, Kate, to be strong."

My heart tore, at that.

"Woden can be reasoned with," he said.

That moment in the pavilion flashed through my memory. "He threw the king down and called him weak, for fearing you'd be hurt in the joust."

"He isn't cruel. He's harsh, but the need is great." Kiefan grimaced, looked away. His own words turned against him, in that. The need for him to marry in alliance was great.

True, but it hurt all the same. "The Mother tells us to cast our seeds wisely," I murmured. "To nurture them in one garden. You'll have princes and princesses to —"

He pressed the breath from me, against the wall, cut me off with a kiss. "I cannot lose you, Kate," he whispered, fierce with pain, against my mouth. "Please."

"You won't." That was all I could choke out. I raked my fingers over his Blessing ridges, over his braided knight's crest. A hard swallow cleared my throat a little. "Anders gave his word. I won't be lost. I won't."

A pause. Our breath, harsh with the agony of it, was the only sound. Then Kiefan whispered, "Do you love him?"

That was easy, after all else. "He's my dear friend. No more."

Kiefan hugged me, rib-creakingly tight. Pressed his face against the curve of my neck. I squeezed hard as I could in return, tears creeping out through my lashes. It took many heartbeats for it to ease, but in the end he let me go. Kissed me once more.

And then had to see me out.

———————✕———————

The last Saint-day of the Bitter Moon dawned dimly, through low clouds that threatened snow. Lamps were lit to supplement the grey light from the Chapel's glazed windows.

I despaired halfway through the disciple's dance; my concentration was lost to the grinding worry in my gut. After falling out of a balance pose, I sighed and sat down on the Chapel floor with my head in my hands. It was all too much. I wished my father were here to tell me if I was being a fool. I wished mother were here to lay the impossible out in sensible, easy steps to take, as she always did. But father was dead and mother had gone north with all my family.

I wished the piglet had never died. But then I took that back.

Alice knelt and wrapped her arms around my shoulders, shushed me. The tears welled up and tumbled off my lashes. She let me cry on her shoulder, one hand gently stroking my loose hair. This would be the last day I'd wear it unbound, in public.

"I'm jealous of you, did you know?" she whispered, which wrung another handful of tears from me. "You've always made it look so simple." As the disciple's dance moved from the balance phase into strength, Alice said, "Let's get you dressed."

As my bride's maid, she had laid out my Solstice gown and brought her perfumes. I let her and Heima prepare me in my teacher's kitchen, from bathing to dressing to braiding up my hair in green ribbons. They debated what combination of scents to put on me, finally settling on attar of lilac and a little rosewater.

The Great Chapel was half ready when I returned, and I helped to keep my hands busy. Alice had invited those who'd remained on Engl Street, and they'd all come with food and smiles to wish me well. The hospital nurses had left Krepkin with a skeleton staff for the afternoon, with Parselev's blesisng. Frida and the gentle-born Rossweides were taking all we goodfolk wonderfully in stride. I was hugged and kissed two dozen times while trying to cut trenchers from a big loaf of Ther Ivor's black bread.

Nobody asked where Anders was, which was just as well — I had no idea. I hadn't seen him since last morning.

The Chapel was nearly finished when I crept away to the toilet. I sat and tried to breathe evenly, tried to reassure myself. Anders would keep his word. Not because of Kiefan's threat, but because he'd treated me honorably thus far. I had combed through my memories closely to be sure.

When I slipped out, Alice was just coming to look for me. "My stomach's tied in knots," I said, which was true enough, and returned to the Chapel with her.

The decorations were set, the community feast laid out, and still no groom. I took my post before the high table on the dais at the head of the Chapel, where the abbot stood leafing through his book of homilies. Behind the high table and its cushioned chairs for the saints, candles illuminated the full-body icons of the Mother and the Father. Between them, our trinity's symbol, life-sized: an anvil, a book laid open on it and a sword placed across the book. One took marriage fealty before both, and was held to them by both.

Alice, in her embroidered green dress, joined me. "If we must send a search party, I have some ideas where," she murmured near my ear.

The doorman opened the double portal, just then, to the grey day outside, and a rumble of hooves and voices poured in with the chill. I glimpsed horses and black tabards, outside, and then the door was filled by a cloaked figure who pulled off his leather gloves as he came. Anders unpinned his cloak and stopped to give it to Frida, with a kiss for her cheek, on his way to the high table. Theo Kaufmann was two steps behind, his groom's man, and then came the two dozen Prince's Guard. All in black tabards, swords, riding boots and clinking spurs — even Theo, though his insignia was the supply division's white wheel rather than the cavalry's horse.

Anders stepped up to the high table with a final jingle of spurs and flourished a bow to apologize. He looked freshly laundered and shaven, at least. His mother had wanted to trim his hair, but he meant to let it grow until the knights' cresting ceremony before they rode to war.

I had to admit, I liked how he raked the shaggy, flaxen stripe between his Blessing ridges over to the left.

With a song to gather the Flock, our ceremony began. The abbot lectured us on our obligation to take the mantles of Mother Love and Father Duty to teach our children, and how we echoed our own giving to the kingdom and receiving protection from it in giving to and being protected by our family.

I swore to my acceptance of these duties, united in purpose and affection with my husband. My voice quavered a little and I had to swallow. Anders hesitated a moment, but took the oath as well.

He knelt, fist on his heart, to offer me his fealty. The fear in his eyes for the moment before I accepted pinched at my heart but steadied my hand. I put the wedding band on his finger.

Then I knelt, said the same words, and tried to look him in the eye. My nerves wouldn't let me, though I came close. The matching band slipped onto my finger easily.

I stood and kissed him, as brief a touch as for our betrothal, and it was done.

Who cheered first, I don't know, but the Guard broke out in applause and the rest followed. I turned to look at the faces, picking out those I knew by their smiles. The mothers, teary-eyed. Parselev with his arm around Heima, his constant worries lifted for the moment.

And by the Chapel door, arms folded over a plain black tabard, eyes downcast, Kiefan.

My hand was still in Anders'; it tightened.

Alice hugged me, then Frida, then Heima, and by the time I looked back to the door Kiefan was gone. There was a feast to see to, though I didn't know if I could eat anything.

The crowd moved to attack the food and, in particular, the roasted whole hog that m'lord Reinhardt had contributed as his gift. There was some talk of how to carve it properly and swords were drawn at first, but Parselev waved them away.

"I haven't done this trick in years, so stand back," he told us all, with a broad sweep of his arms. "Tidy, it isn't. Heima?"

Parselev touched her hand and took her kir. Then he turned to the roasted hog, which lay on its own cart with an apple in its mouth, nicely browned and still hot from the spit. The beast weighed as much as I, or more. He raised his hand toward it and kir glowed in his fingertips. The glow strengthened into five bright points.

The hog lay there. We all looked from one to the other, expectant.

It was too quick to see, at the time; Parselev twisted his wrist with a flick and the five points shot out at the hog. The whole beast heaved up off the cart, flying to pieces as it went, and all that flesh spiraled around a tight orbit and landed in a fair approximation of where it had been before. Only now, the meat, bones and the stuffing of onions and apples in the abdomen were cleanly apart.

That got an astonished cheer, and then we fell upon it ravenously. There was a halo of grease around the cart, though, and that made the work a bit hazardous.

My meal began with the many swallows of dark winter stout required for all the toasts to health and prosperity. I had to sing along with the Englic wedding songs and hope that nobody realized we were invoking a blessing from Ethmund, the long-dead Englic saint. The afternoon flew, and the stout soothed me enough to eat some of the delicious pork and the potato pasties that couldn't be found off Engl Street. Somebody had brought a tray, bless them.

Theo, doing his duty as the groom's man, stood and announced that the sun was setting. The whole Prince's Guard was up off their benches with a cheer, at that, and called for the horses. Beside me, Anders stood and offered me his hand. I took it and stood as well.

He leaned over to tell me, "The Black Knight. Theo insisted on paying."

I smiled, nodded, and my stomach tied itself back in a knot despite the stuffing I'd put in it. A marriage must be consummated before nightfall, by tradition. Often in the couple's own bed, but any would do. Since my condition was common knowledge, at least there would be no calls for proof of my maidenhood.

Cloaks wrapped back on, farewells kissed — Alice winked at me with a smirk — and the front doors opened again on a gate yard full of warhorses. Nipper stood at the chapel steps, Will Bockmann holding his bridle tight.

The blanket of clouds had thickened, and fat white flakes drifted down. The muddy, crusty old snow in the gate yard was frosted with fresh white.

Anders swung into the saddle and pulled me up onto his lap. I clung to him, straddling the pommel, as best I could when Nipper stepped up to a broad, even stride. The mounted Guardsmen followed, whooping and hollering to draw well-wishes from the houses we rode past.

I only looked up at the falling snow, the grey overhead, and glimpsed a band of rich orange sky to the west where the clouds gave out. Both of us were wrapped in dark cloaks, on a grey dapple warhorse in the snow, the only splash of color my amber dress.

The Black Knight tavern and inn, the finest in the city of Wodenberg, stood on High Street. They expected us; they had put up clusters of holly and gold ribbon, and had a row of filled steins lined up on the bar for the Guard. The barkeep, the band, and the patrons greeted us with a hearty cheer and a toast.

But none of that was for us; Anders swept me up in his arms and I hid my face against his shoulder as he carried me upstairs. Theo shouted, behind us, that he should know where the master suite was by now, and laughter from the common room echoed up the stairwell.

"Pay him no mind," Anders said.

On the upper landing, he let me down and opened the door. The fire in the hearth crackled and I went to it with hardly a glance to the rest of the fine room. I held out my hands to its warmth, pretending that was why my hands were trembling.

He would honor the agreement. He would.

I jumped when Anders unpinned my cloak. He took it off my shoulders, shaking the snow from the hem, and went to hang it up. I stayed at the fire, watching the flames play across the flat face of a split log. The clink of Anders' spurs tracked him across the room and back in slow, even steps.

"Do you want anything to drink?" he asked, voice low. I shook my head, not sure if I could speak. "Pardon me a moment."

I turned from the fire, curious, as he crossed to the door, silently drawing his sword as he went. Pausing with his hand on the latch, he yanked it open with a yell and lunged out; surprised shouts outside from half a dozen eavesdroppers turned into laughs and a scramble of boots to escape.

"I could hear you louts breathing through the fucking door!" Anders shouted in parting as they thundered back down the stairs. He slammed it for good measure.

By Engl tradition, the bride's maid and the groom's man stood guard outside the door but no such luck here. I couldn't help a smirk at the little ambush, though, and tried to hide it with my hand. He caught me and smiled too as he sheathed the sword. My mirth faded as he crossed the room again and I turned back to the fire. My fingers laced between each other and twisted.

"You smell like spring." Anders was close by my shoulder. "After all the winter we've lived through this year, I think I'd forgotten."

I smiled in spite of my nerves. "It will be nice to be warm again. Wartime or not."

His breath prickled my neck; he'd leaned closer. "We could do anything, here, and nobody needs ever know."

My heart stumbled in my chest.

"Anything could happen."

That was closer to what I feared; Anders could throw me down on the bed and nobody would stop him. I said, "I know you're true to your word."

"You trust me?"

"When I was drunk, you put me to bed untouched. You sat me on Puck and helped cover my escape. When I abandoned you at Solstice, you spent the night fearing I lay dead in an alley. And you made sure to give your mother a betrothal to cry over." I turned my head enough to meet his gaze. "I trust you."

We looked at each other for several heartbeats, and I didn't know what to make of his expression. There was a sadness to it, but that was only part.

In the common room below, the flutist and drummer had started playing and feet were thumping. "You owe me a dance," Anders said, tipping his head toward the door. "I think I'll collect that." My eyebrows rose, surprised. He said, "You're pregnant, so they'll be gentle with their ribbing for our quick return. A few dances, or whenever you tire, then come back up and take the bed. I'll stay longer and lay down the cloaks on the hearth."

"I can stoke up the fire before I go to bed so you don't freeze."

Anders smiled. "I'm expected at the training camp in the morning, to whip those City Guard into shape. I'll be freezing soon enough."

"You won't be put on watch?" When he shook his head, I was glad for that much. "All our frost-bitten are watch-men. Keep warm." My voice dropped a bit. "Don't fall sick."

He inclined his head. "Home in a moon's turning, m'lady. Shall we dance?"

I learned the steps to another dance, that night, and stayed longer than I expected. When I woke in the morning, Anders had already gone.

DISCIPLE, PART III
embers on the wind

CHAPTER 1

"This time, you never wrote back," Kiefan said as we climbed the stairs toward the castle roof.

My feet stopped and I frowned, my entire spool of thought rolling away. A tangle of letters whisked through my memory until his last one sifted out. No, I hadn't answered his letter from before the Slush Moon reached full. Mother had always said that being pregnant scattered her mind, but I'd had no idea how badly. If not for my Blessing, I'd be entirely useless, of late. "I meant to. There was so much to do for the Queen's sortie, and so much still to do."

"Were you in balance, else-wise, for Equinox?" When he glanced back and saw that I'd fallen behind, he trotted down to put his arm around me — as he did every time. I shook him off with a smile. I could manage some stairs.

One ought to balance one's life — clearing debts, mending relationships — twice a year, when night and day reached their balance as well. There was still no peace I could make with Krepkin, even though I'd managed both the invalids' floor and my teacher's daily lessons since the end of the Bitter Moon.

I'd been dubious when Parselev told me I would represent the hospital at the weekly status meeting in the King's Council chamber in addition to my duties. A choice between seeing Kiefan or taking a midday meal in the dining hall would not have been difficult two moons ago, but a little kir-storm was growing between my hips and I was ravenous.

Still, it was my duty, so I came and gave the Elect's report. Then, tried not to stare at the dark surface of the Council chamber table and remember how gentle Kiefan had been, that first time.

Near the end of the meeting, Housemistress Wenda had carried in a platter of cold ham, bread, and sauerkraut. Another maid had followed with pitchers of the last of the winter bock. I could've kissed them both.

We reached the top of the stairs and turned the corner. As I hadn't answered, Kiefan asked, "They must've allowed you time to eat at the festival?"

I chuckled as we crossed the third floor. Leaning against the wall at the base of the next flight, I paused to answer. "Yes, I stole a little honeycake yesterday. And spent the eve stitching gashes in the heads of drunken knights. Anders told me of your little ritual before battle, but I'd thought you'd have the sense to finish the shaving before you began the drinking."

He frowned. "No army barber should take a drink, when shaving crests. There weren't any Guard among the wounded, were there?"

"No. I do wonder how many knights hide scars under their hair, though."

By tradition, the ritual shaving of the knight's crest began with the lowest ranked of the squad — the most likely to have virgin scalps — and progressed upward. The last to be shaved were, often, the most drunken and most likely to forget where the barber's scalpel was. Despite the fact that he'd have been last of those shaved in the Prince's Guard, Kiefan's crest was as precise as any I'd seen today. He'd been left with the stripe of blonde hair between the ridges of his Blessing, and the rest shaved down to the skin. He'd braided his growing tail afresh; it had added another inch or so over the winter, and hung just below his shoulders. His ridges looked all the fiercer now, for having the scarred line where they had pushed up through his scalp laid bare. And the band of silver he wore for a crown was all the easier to spot.

He'd been marked by the saints as ready to defend the kingdom with all he had. Saint Woden had given leave for all the knights in the city and the mustered armies to shave and maintain their crests during the invasion — for they might be called on to fight at any moment.

He led the way up and I followed, but my little pause hadn't rested me as much as I'd hoped. Kiefan stopped, quickly dropped back a step. "Have you been well?"

"Well enough. Only tired."

His arm slipped around my waist. "Why didn't you say —"

I shooed him off. "I can climb some stairs." My own weakness irritated me, along with the absent-mindedness.

"Kate —" He touched a kiss to my temple, as we were alone here. "Please."

I leaned against his lips, the warmth easing my frustration. I wrapped my arm around his and let him help that much. Else he'd carry me up bodily, or do something equally foolish.

Above, the trapdoor to the roof was a rectangle of white clouds on blue. A tolerably warm shaft of sun reached down the stair; this late in the Slush Moon, it still frosted most nights but the days grew warmer. When we emerged, a cool cross-breeze awaited us and I shivered when it brushed across my neck. I wore my hair braided, rolled into a bun and skewered with a bone pin, now that I was a married woman. There'd been a crespine among my wedding gifts, and an Englic wimple and veil too, but I hadn't settled on which to wear.

"The prince! Attend!"

The King's Guards along the wall turned at the call and dropped to one knee with fists pressed to their hearts. "To your duty," Kiefan told them with a nod. "Lieutenant, how's the view from the watchtowers?"

"If you've hawk eyes you can see Temitte, m'lord." He gestured at the two watchtowers in the castle's outer wall. The catwalk to the western tower opened through the crenelated wall nearby. Though the catwalk had its own walls, it looked a long, dangerous way to the door and a longer climb to the top.

"You can see Seagrace's army from here," Kiefan said, pointing toward the western-most wall. That breeze wandered past again and my hand went into my medicine bag for my wool shawl.

The jagged, tooth-like merlons were high as Kiefan's head, but the crenels between were easy enough to lean through. I looked straight down onto a small barn and its yard, snugged between the castle and its wall. The pigs in the sty were mere lumps in their mud. Beyond the wall, the western side of Wodenberg clung to the steeper part of the mountain's slope in a jumble of thatched roofs. It wasn't far to the city wall, on this side of the castle.

On my left, southward, the city spread out. Northward, a saddle of rock connected the castle's promontory to Mount Woden. That saddle was called the Rückenstein, and it was full of barracks for the City Guard and a company of infantry. The city wall looped around it, studded with towers, to guard Castle Kaltkern's back, and outside the wall the terrain ran rough and bare. Too thin for trees or farming. Sheep dotted what grass there was.

Mount Woden, outside the city and its foulburg, was a wild thing under a deep pine blanket. The forest gave way where the slope gentled out to the north and west, and those muddy fields were covered now with a layer of dingy white tents and a haze of campfire smoke. The tents seemed to run for miles.

"Seagrace's army will swing around the eastern side of the mountain so that the sortie has the road to themselves," Kiefan said, pointing me leftwards toward the Southbound Road where it ran alongside the Neva River.

The Queen, her Guard, and the main body of evacuees had started out that morning. Parselev had judged her well enough for it, after recovering from her fit, and had lectured me at length on why one could not simply heal a mind's thinking. She'd spent the winter in either her suite or the frozen crescent garden, plied with soothing teas and Kiefan's company whenever he could escape his duties.

The head of her procession had made good progress, but it was a large convoy with many slow wagons, families and livestock. It spilled off the Southbound Road wherever it could, into the half-frozen mud.

"The river isn't flooding too badly?" I asked. I could see the speed of it in the foaming eddies and an occasional loose chunk of ice.

"The river-men think the water will run fast but not get too much higher. My mother should reach Prohzgrad late tomorrow, though the rest of them will take longer." Kiefan raised his arm a little higher, toward a dark smudge on the other side of the river and an expanse of blue beyond it. "That's Prohzgrad, on the shores of Lake Neva. There's a bridge there, at the root of the river. Saint Aleksandr built it long ago, the Russe say. It was one of his first feats as a saint."

The wind came up again and I pulled my shawl closer around my neck. I shifted behind the merlon with a shiver. Kiefan straightened off the stone, glanced across the castle roof at the guards, and put an arm around me. His black woolens had caught some warmth from the sun, and I couldn't help snuggling in his grip for a moment. The guards largely watched the south and east, and we were further shielded from view by the little guard-house in the middle of the west wing's roof. There was a matching one on the east wing — and three catapults, so fresh-made their wood was still golden.

Kiefan's hand slid onto my belly. "You could've been rid of the child and never told me. My mother always said a man should be honored if a woman will carry his child. She was always so angry at Father, I thought it another of her complaints. But now… I wish you'd gone to Prohzgrad," he murmured, close to my ear. Then he squeezed me tighter and kissed my cheek.

"I can wish you safe in Prohzgrad all I please, but I know you won't be. You or Anders. I have my duty as much as either of you." I put my hand on his, and he loosened his grip.

I meant to do my part, whatever Krepkin or anyone else thought, for saints and kingdom. I wouldn't ask Kiefan or Anders to do any less, however much I dreaded the risk. None of us wanted this duty, but it must be done. The enemy had brought this to us. We only acted in self-defense.

The south wall drew my gaze. "Can you see Arcea's army? Is that why the Guard are clustered over there?"

I crossed the long roof, weaving my way to an empty crenel facing south-eastward. Wodenberg's city wall looped out, here, across a gentler slope, and the foulburg ran further. The Southbound Road and the Neva continued, joined by the river Felsherz flowing from the Eispitzen mountains. Its headwaters were at the lamia fount, where we'd made our last, harried stand against the beasts and nearly lost Anders. At the ford across the Felsherz, the earthwork fortress had been bolstered with taller, ringed walls.

"My father will ride for Ansehen within a week," Kiefan said, beside me again. I could pick out the half-ruined castle at Ansehen, but only just. It was thirty miles and some away, and a smoky haze blanketed the town. "The southern army is camped there already. Nine thousand men, or thereabouts. We have those, Seagrace's army, and the reserves once spring planting's done — if no enemy ships brave the Englic shoals. And Schutze's border guard on the southeast. This is the largest gathering of men that Wodenberg has ever seen."

"How many?"

"Thirty thousand. Maybe thirty-five." He took a breath. "We believe Arcea massed seventy in Temitte. That fifty of those are marching northward."

"You'll have nineteen at Ansehen, though."

"They'll reach it before Seagrace does. Father will hold them as long as he can, and fall back to the Felsherz."

Parselev would go with the king, taking the infirmary tents, near all the ambulance wagons and some of my best staff. Our newly trained nurses and orderlies were improving, but still needed me to keep all running smoothly. I would be staying for that, though I felt a pull to go with my teacher.

"Will you be there too?" I asked.

"I'm to see the last of the evacuations are orderly, and to see to the supply lines." Kiefan grimaced. "Thousands uprooted and moved. Near a third of our fields will lie fallow this year. Thousands dead and thousands more to die. For ownership of three founts."

I looked up at the mountain, still brilliant under snow. The natural, if steep, slope was broken by a tall collar of sheer, vertical granite that the saints had raised long ago to protect the fount at the top. Wind picked up snow above the collar and streamed a tail from the sharp peak. Our three saints lived up there, we were all told, but I couldn't see how.

The second of Wodenberg's founts sprang from the cliffs above Rukharbor. Sea eagles drank from it and grew into rukhs, as wolves drank from the third, small fount in the Eispitzen and became lamia.

"We protect our saints, our saints protect us." I quoted d'Ovio Alain, on that. "Else we'd be at the mercy of any passing kir-mage."

"Promise me you'll stay at the hospital. Away from the fighting."

"Only if you'll promise the same," I said, and looked to him for it. There would be no promise, I knew. Only hope and worry. "I need to be back for afternoon rounds."

Kiefan saw me down the stairs and out to the gatehouse, my hand in his whenever we were alone. On the stairwell he turned and kissed me, said nothing but stroked back a few of my stray hairs with his callused fingers. My heart quivered at the worry in his eyes, welling up from wherever he kept it locked away when there was duty to see to. It pulled tears to mine, something else that was coming easier to me since the little one took root.

"Don't make me cry," I whispered.

I collected stoneware jars from the rear shelves in Parselev's library. Each was sealed at the neck with wax, the symbol painted on the lid denoting infusion of goldenrod or cinquefoil or alum-root. I took only those that could slow bleeding or cleanse a wound, and nested them into a straw-filled box.

My teacher sat at his desk, leafing through his stacks for blank sheets of paper and parchment to bring. Once we were done, Heima and I would see him out to the king's party. We'd join in singing Mother Love's benediction to the men, so they would know how we loved and trusted them in what they must do for Father Duty.

The thought set my teeth on my lip, in worry. "Shouldn't I go with you?" I asked. The question had been rattling around my head for days.

Parselev neatened one stack. "No, you're physician of the floor here. Krepkin needs you, though he's not likely to admit it." Collecting his blank sheets, he stood and packed them into his letter wallet.

I knelt down to wiggle one more jar of cinquefoil into the box.

"Kate." I looked up. His mouth was set in a grim line, between his grey mustache and beard. Voice tight, he said, "I have not fought your battles for you because you must learn to fight for yourself. You must make your own mistakes and you must repair them. As in Krepkin's case. I hope — if it seemed I thought little of you…"

I stood, too, and a bit of straw in my hand became something to bend and worry. I'd wished for his protection, sometimes, and only gotten advice. A few words of praise, precious for being rare. Another question haunted me more, though. "You aren't disappointed in me?"

"No." He breathed a laugh. "No, Kate. I wish you hadn't fallen pregnant, but I don't doubt you'll manage." Taking a deep breath, he crossed the office to hand me the letter wallet so he could pick up the box of jars. "If I do not return, Kate, this is to be yours — the books, the cottage — so long as you do not put Heima out of her home."

My mouth fell open a moment when he went to the stairs, as casual as if I already knew this. "You'll be in the infirmary. Behind the battle. As at Ansehen," I said, to be sure I was right.

"That was only two days. I will be as much a target in the field as Saint Qadeem will," Parselev said as he descended.

I followed. King Wilhelm rode out at noon, escorted by his Guard. Parselev and Saint Qadeem would ride with him. Saint Aleksandr had been given charge of the northern half of the kingdom and Woden would remain on the mountain.

"But you're a healer," I said. "And so is Qadeem — he's no saint of war."

"No saint is merely one thing. Nor any elect." Parselev put the box on the kitchen table. Heima had two bags packed with his clothes waiting there. An assortment of tools, medical and otherwise, lay in neat lines, freshly cleaned and ready to bundle up. My teacher heaved a deep breath and looked me in the eye. His voice lowered. "If Saint Qadeem should die — or any of the saints, or if Arcea should reach the fount atop the mountain — I will certainly be dead as well, and you must run, Kate."

When I took a breath to object, he lowered his brow further to stop me.

"The people will need your gifts. And your child's royal blood to rally behind, should we lose the king in battle. And, Father Duty forbid, Kiefan as well. Anders has shown no ambition for the crown, but he has the blood and the leadership for it to fall to him next. Wish it or not. How that will fare…" Parselev grimaced. "All I taught you of kir-shields and the Shepherd's knife, you'll need in self-defense," he said.

I had slaughtered four chickens and a sheep for the Order's Equinox celebration, and done it with only a touch — far cleaner than the clumsy stab I'd made at Krepkin. A quick slice with a tight-twisted crescent of kir to their prime meridian, at the base of the skull, and they collapsed silently. All kir-blades were called the Shepherd's knife because they left no mark on the body and such deaths were blamed on the Shepherd culling his Flock. Parselev said the name was more properly kept for the larger, saint-cast blades that devastated battlefields.

Shields had not come so easily to me. Parselev had taken to flicking small things at me with his little kir-vines, but half of them hit me. I couldn't get the kir to knot properly and hold the charm strong and stable. Internal charms like healing never needed knots; they weren't meant to last.

The trapdoor to the root cellar was open. Heima set two jars of strawberry preserves on the kitchen floor and climbed up. Parselev paused until she had closed the trap with a thud.

"At Ansehen, when Saint Woden slew the Arceal Elect," Parselev said, voice low, "you felt the shockwave of kir released. You were sensitive enough for that. In the moment of death, there is a chance for the killer to harvest the charms of the dying. If the killer is able is to call the victim's core to him, that is. The harvest is the knowledge and skill coded in the kir's whorls."

"Saints can harvest from elect, then?"

"And from fellow saints. Elect harvest saints. Elect harvest each other. An ambitious Blessed can try to stick a knife in a young, drunk elect outside the Black Knight one evening, meaning to become one himself. An elect reeling from the harvest of a saint, struggling to fledge into a saint himself…" Parselev stopped himself and took a deep breath. "Vulnerable as a butterfly fresh from its cocoon. It's a deadly power game that saints must play. Even those that seem gentle, like Aleksandr and Qadeem. Don't forget that, Kate."

"But I'm only a blessed, you told me."

"With much potential. Should you face an elect, claim your due."

It seemed ludicrous, that I could kill and harvest an elect. I tried to picture my teacher standing over a corpse with bloodied hands. That didn't sit easy, either. "Have you — harvested?"

He looked away, bit his lip. "Yes. I've killed two elect, and the first gave me many of the knife and shield charms I've shown you. Those saved me, when the second attacked." Then he set the lid on the box and tacked it shut with a few hammer taps. "Some tally their kills and wear them proudly. I did what I must. We are both healers first, you and I, but never forget that others will want your skill for themselves."

"I won't forget."

He smiled. "I know. Practice your shields. Read that book I showed you and try spinning some ropes before attempting knots again. When I return, we'll speak on it more."

"Yes, when you return," I said, and could manage a smile for that.

Some days later, I took a deep breath to steel my anger before I struck one quick knock on the unlatched door and threw it open without waiting for leave. Inside, Krepkin turned from the pegboard that served as a staff schedule, a frown knitting his bristly brows together. With him were his apprentice Meinrad and two of the senior orderlies, both older men and neither Englic. Good.

"Wachmann was to charm the broken leg last night, not the typhus." I let my anger harshen the words, but kept well away from anything Krepkin might call screeching. He'd trained me well, in his snide, dismissive way. "Now the bone's another day set and still misaligned. Are you determined to see the man limp the rest of his life?"

Krepkin heaved a sigh. "If such a charm is below you, m'lady, I can piece it together once it's re-broken."

"You told Wachmann to see to the typhus when I had told him otherwise," I said, fighting not to grind my teeth. "The priority list for charms is for the physician of the floor to arrange. Is it not?"

He turned back to the pegboard and hung the last name tag of the few staffers we had left. "I hardly need a broody hen to tell me how my hospital's run."

"Wachmann said he acted on your instructions. Which are unbiased, I'm sure, by the fact the broken leg belongs to an Englic knight. You wouldn't be so petty." I spat that well enough to get the sarcasm across. The old man all but ignored any Engl, since he'd turned on me, and that irked me far worse than any words. "How is it a mild case of typhus outweighs a lifetime's crippling, sir? Do please teach me."

I folded my arms across my chest.

"If you'll excuse us —"

"You fear they'll disagree?" I cut Krepkin off in dismissing the orderlies and Meinrad.

Krepkin's spine straightened and he likewise folded his arms. "They've duties to see to, rather than listening to your hysterics."

My gut was twisting into knots, but I turned my head toward our audience. "Am I screaming and raving?"

The senior orderlies, there to work out the schedule for the next few days, were good enough men but they wouldn't disagree with Krepkin. They averted their eyes. Meinrad, though no friend of mine, was known by the nurses to slip a little kindness to victims of Krepkin's biases — mostly Englic children whose tears went ignored. Meinrad knew how to keep his mouth shut and keep up appearances, however, and he didn't answer me.

"I expect as your condition progresses these fits will become more serious," Krepkin said.

"You've no reasons at all. You mean to simply over-rule me as the whim takes you."

"I'll over-rule you as the need presents itself. This is my hospital, still."

"And I am physician of the floor," I said. "You mean to undercut my authority despite that I've run the floor smoothly since Solstice."

"Undercut you? You managed that yourself by landing on your back." He took a step toward me. "You've chosen your road, so attend to it. And the fruits of your labors." Krepkin jerked his chin at me, at my belly.

I'd been an apprentice here when Ada Brauer was pregnant with her child, though. "Did you tell Brauer as much? Was there need to over-rule her throughout her pregnancy, as she wasted physicians' kir on mild illnesses? She was physician of the floor until her eighth moon — she ordered me off my duties and set me to scrubbing the floor often enough. And she returned two moons after she delivered."

"She'd proven herself far worthier than you." Krepkin's brow furrowed and his voice tightened. And he took another step so I'd have to tip my head up to keep eye contact.

It was a fight to keep my voice steady. The rage wanted to hiss through my teeth. "By hiring a wet-nurse to care for her baby? Or simply in that she's Alemanni?"

"Ask again when your mind's crushed under the carnage of war."

"Any less will be disappointing, after all I've heard."

A grin split Krepkin's hard mouth, and then a harsh laugh. "You're such a fool, child."

"Is the Elect a fool, too, for giving me the post?"

He shot me a shrewd look, too smart to bite that bait. "When you've known him nigh on fifty years, you'll see things differently. Get out of my office. All of you."

CHAPTER 2

As the King's Guard were gone to Ansehen, and the Queen's Guard to Prohzgrad, Castle Kaltkern fell into the hands of the Prince's Guard. Captain Rostislav Loshadsky was as good an officer as any, but he had only two dozen to do the job of fifty and there existed a long-standing disdain for the thought of letting mere City Guards stand watch on the castle walls. They were too prone to dozing at their posts and falling off the walls when drunk.

Thus, the Master of Horse for the Prince's Guard had charge of the castle stables with only his squire and brother, Will, to help oversee the stable-hands. I hadn't seen Anders at all while he drilled knights at the winter camp. Now, he took Alice's space beside me at the Saint-day disciple's dance when he could. She had left with m'lady Rossweide as her new housemaid, bound for Kernweise and Frida's family's lands. M'lord Bockmann was posted on his baronial lands with his garrison, as a hedge against Arceal squads venturing too far north.

I might also see Anders on my way out of the castle after the weekly status meeting and mid-day meal.

The castle stables held more horses than the barn at the Rossweides' city home, and these were a mix of courier palfreys, wagon drays, and a handful of warhorses. The first two came and went daily as messages were dispatched and supply wagons moved; as the barn doors were so often open, the stables smelled less of hay and horses than they should. The warhorses belonged to the royal family. Nipper was there because he would only let Anders or Will touch him.

Or Saint Aleksandr. I paused in the open barn doorway to let my eyes adjust and saw the saint first. He stood in the open gate of Nipper's stall with his hands on the stallion's head, stroking and murmuring. Aleksandr wore only a single light cote, even though it wasn't so warm yet, and woolen braies.

Weekly, the saint arrived at the castle for his own debriefing in the morning, and left in the afternoon. I hadn't expected to see him in the stables, but who was I to know a saint's priorities? And if he wished to go about in only under-clothes, well, saints generally did as they pleased. He was a broadly built Russe, bearded and near furry enough that he might not feel a chill.

"Not to worry, though," Saint Aleks said as I approached. "Of all an animal's talents, smell is the one you have the most to learn of. Sharp ears, sharp eyes, even flying — all simpler, on the whole, than the nuances of scent." He spotted me, and lines crinkled around his eyes when he smiled.

"It was something like being thrown into a river," Anders said from inside the stall. He brushed Nipper's dappled coat with long, smooth strokes as he spoke. I leaned against the sill of the stall, arms crossed, but he didn't see me at first. "Drowning, of a sudden."

"When did you try it?"

Anders circled around Nipper's rump, noticed me and grinned. "In the evening, after seeing he was bedded down. He didn't startle so badly, this time. I'd thought it would be simpler when all was quiet, but the rush of it nearly knocked me on my ass."

Saint Aleksandr chuckled. "You did it rightly, then. It's worth mastering, so keep at it. With practice, all things grow easier. Is that a new friend?"

He flicked a finger toward a grey tomcat lying on the narrow rail atop the divider between Nipper's stall and the next. The cat seemed to think it a perfectly good place to nap. Anders glanced as he hung up the brushes.

"Yes, he's decided I'm worthy. At last. He even let me see his kir, for a moment."

"An excellent animal to study. I doubt you thought horses and cats were anything alike."

Anders nodded. "He set me straight on that, among other things."

Saint Aleks stepped back from the stall, beckoning us both as he went. I was glad to follow and hear more. "With practice, one will also learn how to learn quickly. The similarities and the differences between the skills of different animals become clear," he said.

Anders latched the stall gate as we followed the saint toward the sunlight outside. I was still trying to think of similarities between cat and horse, piqued by the riddle. Perhaps the ears?

"When you've fully learned the kir patterns and know their function, you find the form itself is the least of your difficulties," Saint Aleksandr continued. "A barn cat is too small a thing for a man, of course, but having learned from a cat in my youth it was a quick thing to learn the manner of a cougar. Fortunate, since they do not suffer fools lightly."

My memory flicked back to that last, awful day of our mission. "You were the cougar on the path, m'lord? Thank you." That last lamia could've killed Puck and then me, but the mys-

Part III: Embers on the Wind

terious cougar had struck it down and led me — and the woodsmen riding to our rescue — to save Kiefan and Anders at the little fount.

He smiled, nodded. We stepped out into the gatehouse yard, under a pleasantly warm sun. "It's easiest to become something of similar size. A large cougar. A small bear. A truly enormous dog, at times." He pulled off his cote as he spoke and handed it to Anders. The saint was a big, barrel-chested man, as most Russe were, and his brown hair was sprinkled with grey. "I've managed a horse, now and then — something of a pony, though. A wild boar, now that's a good form. Quick, powerful. But this is my favorite, I must confess."

Saint Aleks dropped his braies, but my eyes were on his arms as he spread them; I had glimpsed this once before and didn't want to miss a moment. Fat white quills rose through his skin as his fingers lengthened, and when the quills had stabbed out two hands'-widths they unfurled into brown-and-cream barred feathers. Row by row, they broadened, shivered into lapped layers, and a sparkling green haze of kir wisped between each.

In the rukh's face, there was still a trace of him, despite the hooked black beak and the staring, golden eyes. He rose on his hind legs — and legs they were, like a cat's hindquarters, complete with near-human hands bigger than my own and retractable black talons — and stepped off his puddled clothing. He crouched again, and was still a good five feet tall. Saint Aleks winked.

With a cat's powerful leap, the rukh launched over our heads and threw out wings that blocked the sun. I glimpsed a barred tail as my eyes winced shut against the sudden wind, and felt the thrust of kir that helped hoist the massive raptor into the air. A few pumps of his wings and he cleared the castle wall, coasted a moment and soared on an updraft to circle northward.

Anders and I watched the rukh shrink into the distance. "Maybe someday," he murmured, with a shake of his head.

"You want to fly?" I asked, with a smile. "It looks exhilarating."

His eyebrows rose. "Perhaps you should ask him about it."

"He's not my saint, though. How is it you know him?"

Anders turned back to the stables and led the way to another stall. "When I was a boy, he came by f— the baron's stables now and then. I only knew that he told me things, not about how to keep horses or handle them, but how they think. He told me I could find their pains, or the worms in their guts, if I tried. I was sure I'd come home from my Blessing-day as his disciple."

I glanced up at his Blessing ridges, speed and anticipation combined, bare now though a sheen of flaxen stubble was coming in. He'd tied his knight's crest into a little pigtail that stood straight back, as if at guard. "Did you ever ask why?"

"He said that they all claim us, in their way."

It seemed that I was the only one who hadn't asked a saint why, yet. Still, the words stuck in my mind. "They all claim us." Saint Aleks had a wealth of interesting things to say.

"All these years, all Saint Woden's said to me is 'Well done,' more or less, at the end of the tournament. I've never felt a need to say more, myself. The man looked me in the eye when he spoke, at least, unlike the one beside him." Anders let himself into one of the stalls and whistled two notes to the courier palfrey when it looked up from its hay. "Must've been the saints who wanted me here, in the castle, all those years I was a page. Mother Love knows nobody else did. This's the first I've ever been able to walk the gate-yards without one eye over my shoulder."

He glanced up at me, in saying that, as he took a hoof pick from his belt. Then he bent to run his hand along the gelding's foreleg. The palfrey shifted on his feet, then stepped away. With a couple clicks of his tongue, Anders followed and stroked again. This time, the horse offered its hoof for checking.

"Soon as I've a chance, I'll be out of here. Out of the Guard, too, when the chance comes to resign. I can serve the saints as well in Rossweide's garrison, or wherever you…" He paused in picking dirt out of the hoof and looked up again. "He's been stopping by every week, Saint Aleks. Checking on me, I suppose. What brings you?"

"Ter Holly is worried you're neglecting me," I said. I leaned against the stall door to watch as he continued, intrigued by the process of grooming all four hooves. "No sign of you the first moon after our wedding. Then you visited for one Saint-day but missed the next."

"Tell her I was tending a colicky horse and thrashing the stable-boy responsible."

"I will, then, when I tell her I saw you today."

Anders focused on his work until he let the last hoof go and straightened with a grin. "You should go back with a little straw in your hair, to keep up appearances. If that's the only reason you stopped by."

My mouth twisted to one side for a moment, but I had to admit, "I'll likely be back, if Saint Aleksandr stops here each week. I could watch him shape-shift daily and not tire of it, and I never knew his charms were so interesting. Did you mean that you used Nipper's kir, when you were speaking of smells?"

"Imitated it, in a way. I've tried it with ears a few times. I use his to check the charm's pattern, and then lay it over my own. It's a tremendous — sharpening. As if I was hearing so much all along but didn't know it." Anders leaned against the gate beside me. "Not simple to explain. Perhaps that's why Saint Aleks only says that I could do this or that, but leaves it to me to try."

"So you tried to imitate Nipper's nose?"

"And it was as overwhelming as the first time my speed Blessing took hold."

That piqued another question I'd long wanted to ask. "What's that like? How do you see it?"

"You don't." Anders paused as the grey tomcat came walking, tail up, along the top of the stall gates between us. He scratched the cat's ears as he continued. "You'd best know what you want your hands to do, because it's done before you see it. It's why squires are drilled so hard in striking sequences. They're long enough, even at speed, that you've time to think of your next move."

The cat arched his back, purring, under Anders' hand. His tail lashed as he leaned into another good scratch. To be brave, and because his grey fur looked so soft, I petted the tomcat along his spine. He was silky indeed.

"Should I expect you on Saint-day, then?"

Anders clicked the gate's latch open and the cat jumped down, trotted away. I had places to be, as well. "The Order's disciple's dance is easier, the meal's better — and the company is a welcome change." That with a smile to me. I echoed it. "May I?"

He'd seen me home to Parselev's cottage, where I had moved in with Heima to keep warm on chilly nights, after the Saint-day meal, and then ridden back to his cot in the castle barracks. We hadn't spoken much, but the quiet had been comfortable. Pleasant, after all the demands of the invalids' floor. Maybe this time we could talk further about Saint Aleks' lessons.

"Of course," I said.

Once we were settled in the King's Council chamber, the next week, Kiefan nodded to Captain Rostislav and the messenger was called into the room. He paced to the center of the open circle of chairs, snapped to attention and saluted with fist over his heart. On one shoulder of his black tabard, he wore the white, crossed swords of the armsmen; on the other, a blue square behind a yellow maple leaf. He was Englic, Blessed with speed ridges, and a

Part III: Embers on the Wind

lieutenant by the brasses on his epaulettes. The woman just behind him, in a tabard with the same insignia, was a sergeant.

Saint Woden nodded, accepting their salutes. Kiefan sat at the saint's right hand, and he'd seen that I got the chair on his other side. So that I would be close to the fire, Kiefan had said. Saint Aleksandr never sat, at Council meetings; he paced slowly with one hand on his chin, seeming deep in thought. The officers and city officials who made the rest of the Council watched closely, eager for news. There'd been little since Arcea smashed through Ansehen's earthquake-broken gates and set fire to the town. King Wilhelm had been on the retreat, last we heard for certain.

"Give your report, Lieutenant Burrbreak," Woden said.

Despite two saints and a prince in the room, the lieutenant was so composed that I didn't doubt he could take command in a heartbeat if he must. And despite that his Alemannic was heavily accented, his report was clear and sure.

"Three days past, the king's army forded the Felsherz and took up post in the earthworks at Flussbock. M'lord Saint Qadeem and his engineers destroyed the wagon ford behind us. We were well prepared when Arcea attempted to cross yesterday."

He went into particulars about the attack; I had been in the hospital, but I'd run outside in time to see Saint Qadeem's kir-flare peak in the cloud-dotted sky and begin to fall. We'd all heard the crack of thunder, seen a hand of lightning bolts tear from Mount Woden's peak toward the Felsherz.

"Your strike, m'lord," Burrbreak said, bowing his head to Saint Woden, "caught a full company of Suevi armsmen in the water. Their elect and saints had slowed the river with kir-walls, and they meant to cross above the rocky rapids. So many died that they choked the water further, despite that the kir-walls broke and freed the river."

Aleksandr muttered something that must have been in Russe.

"How many saints?" Woden asked, voice low.

"Saint Qadeem is sure of one, and two crafter elect."

Word was that there'd been proof of two battle elect, as well, during the fighting at Ansehen. Four elect and a saint, at least… yet our two saints hardly flicked an eye in surprise. The rest of us in the Council dared not murmur in worry, if they showed none.

Burrbreak went on. "Arcea sent a second company across the rocks, across the dead. We were ready for them, m'lords, and we killed all those who remained after Saint Qadeem broke the bridge of them." He reported on casualties; the king, Duke Seagrace, and my saint were all well. Burrbreak took a folded and sealed letter from the pouch on his sword belt and dropped to one knee. "M'lord the duke wished me to deliver this with my report, m'lord."

Woden rose, took it, and opened it. He glanced at the kneeling lieutenant. "Do you know what this says?"

"No, m'lord."

Saint Woden read it. "Lieutenant Burrbreak commanded the squad nearest the Arceal crossing-point, and despite the speed and ferocity of the attack by the Fifteenth Light Division, the lieutenant held an unfortified stretch of common riverbank until relief could come to his aid." Woden paused, glanced at the officer, but the man kept a sober face. "Lieutenant Burrbreak took severe wounds but continued to command until overcome by loss of blood. His sergeant, Staffwright, pulled him from the water when he would have drowned and dragged him to safety. He only lives today by the skill of Elect Parselev."

The sergeant dropped into obeisance when the saints looked to her. Staffwright seemed rather younger than the lieutenant — though both must've been near thirty — and wore her hair in the same martial cut: cropped close but for a patch atop her head. She had an anticipation Blessing.

Woden folded the letter. "Seagrace makes some requests of what to do with you. Did you present yourself for knighthood?"

I could've answered that, given the lieutenant's name. "No, m'lord, I hadn't the learning for such as that."

"Order-trained, after your Blessing?"

A nod. Burrbreak would be a farmer's name, in Englia, or perhaps a shepherd.

"Family?"

"Yes, m'lord, my wife and three boys. A fourth on the way."

"May Mother Love grant you a daughter," Woden said, taking his seat again. "Your wife will be glad you'll draw a captain's salary now. We must equip you as one, as well."

Both Engls wore simple, boiled-leather breastplates. Burrbreak's looked like it was missing a chunk, by how his tabard hung over it. Saint Aleksandr gestured for both armsmen to stand, and put out his hand. "Your sword."

Burrbreak drew and surrendered it at once. The saint considered it; even I could see the nicks and scratches. I felt a twitch of kir. A flood of it poured into the blade, till it glowed green, then brilliant gold. Saint Aleks pinched two fingers on one edge, at the hilt, and with a smooth flick of his arm threw off a white-hot star from the point. The mended edge shone. He did the same for the other side. Lightly, he tossed the sword from hand to hand, brow furrowed, and flicked it. More sparks fell, dying to cinders before they reached the floor.

"A fair blade," he said as the sword dimmed, became an ordinary thing again. "Better, now."

It looked perfect, so far as I could see, when Aleksandr passed the hilt to the lieutenant. The saint reached for the sergeant's weapon and she handed it over. With that battered old thing in hand, he grimaced and shook his head. "Give this woman something decent from the armory."

"Along with mail shirts and new brasses for this captain and his lieutenant," Saint Woden added. "Rest on the crown's hospitality tonight, and return to your posts tomorrow."

Captain Rostislav took charge of the two officers and saw them out. Saint Aleksandr kept the sergeant's unacceptable sword, leaning it against the wall by the hearth. There were more reports after that: of Suevi scouts caught roving the southlands, of what our own Rangers had spied of the enemy. Arcea's army still flooded up the Southbound Road from Suevia, through burned, ruined Ansehen, all the way to the banks of the Felsherz. Thousands of centaurs, minotaurs, Arceal and Suevi knights, armsmen, and archers.

My heart sank; Parselev would have to stand against four elect, to aid Saint Qadeem.

Theo Kaufmann gave the quartermaster's report on our supply lines. That was dull going, and I rested my chin on my hand, elbow on the chair's arm. I had seen a dead centaur, after the first battle of Ansehen last year. Such a massive thing, draped in armor…

"What's wrong?"

Kiefan murmured the same question that Anders had asked on Saint-day, and I gave him the same answer. "I hope Elect Parselev returns well and soon."

I wished my teacher safe, but I also wanted his presence to support me. I still found my charm priority board with its bed numbers re-arranged, though Meinrad had taken to discreetly consulting me when he faced conflicting instructions. My nurses did as Krepkin told them, but after finishing what I had assigned. The orderlies were less united, but generally got word to me when their schedules suddenly changed.

Physician Wachmann had been Krepkin's apprentice, years ago, and I couldn't rely on him for anything. So be it.

As for me, I relied on Ther Ivor to cross the herb garden and knock on the cottage door to wake me before dawn when he started the morning's bread. He and I shared a pot of strong tea and eggs on toast, and then I was physician, nurse, and orderly combined until I stole some time to eat at noon. Sometimes a little sleep, too. Then straight on past dark.

"They run you ragged? Still?" Kiefan's hand inched near mine, on his chair's arm, but Woden was too close by to risk a touch.

"The meal will help."

When that finally came, the scent of it made my stomach grind; warmed beef with gravy, potatoes, and spring greens. Housemistress Wenda and her maid Gudrun had brought pitchers of beer as well, and much as I wanted some I had to decline. Beer was making me so belchy, now, that I would stop all conversation in the Council chamber if I had more than a sip.

Kiefan sent Gudrun to fetch me a pot of tea quickly, before the short meal ended.

"My mother suffered the same," I told him as we walked up to the castle roof for our weekly view of the southlands. "Beer, she could avoid, but cabbage caused trouble as well. It will ease, if all goes the same for me."

He had his arm snug around me, and I'd given in to leaning on him so he wouldn't carry me up. As the stairwell was empty, he kissed my cheek. "I could assign a support squad to the hospital. Would that earn you more sleep?"

I grimaced, in truth, at the thought of having to train a few dozen new hands to hospital duty. "It would be worse, sadly. I've settled in well enough with my work, now — it's only that — those monsters. I saw one, after Ansehen."

Breezes caught the wisps from my wrapped braid and blew them in my eyes when we reached the roof. Fat clouds scudded overhead, thicker and greyer than they'd been this morning. Rain coming.

"They bleed the same as men," Kiefan said, squeezing my hand in his.

The guards on the roof saluted, then politely turned away and paid us little mind. I led the way to our usual crenel and looked south. The Felsherz and Neva glittered as the sun broke through the clouds for a moment, then faded to dull silver again.

My fingers fidgeted on the smooth face of the stone, remembering the dead centaur and yet seeing the lamia pulling poor Ther Boristan away from me. Parselev said Arcea's monsters were made things, not mere animals, and had this on the authority of Saint Qadeem himself. Both hoped to capture one alive and inspect its kir — such mergings of men and beasts were masterworks of flesh-forging. How so many were made was only one question they had.

Kiefan's hand settled on mine, hidden by the crenel. His voice lowered. "Fearsome as the monsters are, it's their elect and saints that are more dangerous."

"Four of them, already," I murmured. "And only my teacher…"

"He faces them with Saint Qadeem."

"But he never fought, at Ansehen."

Kiefan nodded. "The Elect's a gentle man. My father told me he's never sought a fight, but he'll do what he must. He's a bound elect and he will defend us."

"And the army's end hasn't yet arrived." My gaze crept back to our southern border. Forty thousand enemies on our land, the tally stood at, and another ten to come.

Parselev had sent me a letter without saying a word about that. He'd included a few Arceal arrows so that we could all see the barbs they used, and sketches of the centaurs and minotaurs. All that had come with a wagonload of worsening typhus patients. Seagrace's army had brought more sickness.

They were massive, Arcea's monsters. The horse parts of the centaurs were equal to any of our warhorses, and the men were heavy-boned bruisers. And no man could be merged with a bull — even just its head and hooves — without becoming near as strong as one. They all wore lamellar cuirasses and helms, and carried weapons sized to fit them.

Still, it was the reports of how many arrows it took to fell one that stuck in my mind. Our Blessed archers rarely missed vitals, and they hated the monsters' stubbornness.

"You fought centaurs at Ansehen?" I murmured, looking to Kiefan. "Your charge saved the king, they said. You've killed them."

His hand was still on mine; his fingers shifted to thread between mine. "I've killed them. They're only men and horses."

"Is it true that arrows don't stop them?" Centaurs would still charge with two and three arrows in their torsos, each good for a kill on an ordinary man.

"They bleed the same and their guts are the same color," Kiefan said. "No need to dwell on it, Kate."

He kissed my hand, and I wished I could simply put my worries from my mind.

CHAPTER 3

Saint Aleksandr must have already flown, by the time I reached the stables' main door. Iron scraped on the stone floor as a stable boy shoveled manure and old hay into a wheelbarrow. At the far end, Anders led a bay gelding out into what sunlight there was. My feet picked up a little energy at the sight and I trotted the length of the barn to catch up.

He knelt by the bay with a dull wooden scraper in hand, inspecting the horse's legs. I must've caught his eye; he glanced up as I slowed to a quick walk at the barn door.

"Did I miss him?"

"He was needed up on the coast. He only stopped to ask if I'd tried again. I asked how tricky flying is and he laughed," Anders said. Peering closer, he flicked the scraper across the gelding's leg, his hand underneath to catch. The slim, long-legged horse shifted his weight, cocking one hind foot off the stone paving.

I leaned over Anders' shoulder. "What is it?"

He scraped again, then picked with thumb and finger. Standing, he showed me a few yellow specks in his hand. "Botflies are out. All the messenger mounts coming up from Felsherz have nits on them. Likely all the warhorses do too, and they'll all have worms come summer."

I barely touched one nit, but it stuck to my finger. "You know a charm for that, you said." I tried to flick it off a couple times, but then simply crushed the thing.

"Yes. I'm not the only one, either, but it needs the better part of a day's kir. That'll be difficult to spare." Anders stepped around the horse and knelt again to check his other foreleg. "Does it take so much to de-worm a man?"

"Not at all. I know several elixirs that can do the job. Aren't there any for horses?"

The bay snuffed about my shoulders and face. He had soulful brown eyes, a white blaze and a ragged black forelock. I reached out a hand slowly, not wanting to startle him.

"One can persuade a man to drink something nasty far easier than a horse," Anders said from below. "All things equal, the charm's both quicker and more thorough."

The bay let me stroke his warm, soft nose, and ducked his head so my hand was on the crown of his head. So I scratched there. Anders stood with a few more nits in hand.

"How many horse charms do you know?" I asked. "I know that blood-stops and cleansers work on them, but I haven't heard of others."

He scraped the nits to the stone and stepped on them. "Given those two, horses do well enough. As with Kit, here — he's favoring his hoof, you see?" Anders coaxed the bay into lifting the rear hoof he'd cocked, to show me. "He came in with a stone, and bled a little when I pried it out. Washed him with witch hazel, since we don't have any charms, and I've kept one eye on it. He should be well soon enough. But he's bottom of the courier roster now, when he could be at the top. Kit's a good runner."

There was some crusty clot near the rim of the hoof and I knew enough about clots even though the rest looked strange indeed. Gently, I touched the wound, my hand brushing his in passing. "That shouldn't be any harder to heal than on a person," I said. "Though as I need to ration my kir I'd likely do the same as you."

"True, it's only a little thing." Anders let Kit put his hoof down.

Through the outer gate rode a boy in a courier's red tabard, on a roan horse. Kit perked up as they trotted by, and Anders caught his halter before the bay got any ideas about following. He tugged at the horse, taking a step toward the barn, but Kit ignored him at first.

"Come," he said, and gave three little clicks. Kit tracked the roan trotting toward the middle gate, still ignoring him. "Not one of ours," Anders said, meaning Baron Rossweide's. "He doesn't know the code. Can physicians heal a broken leg? Completely, from fresh break to whole?"

I nodded. "Parselev can. If it's a simple crack then most physicians can manage it — or charm it part way at least. Thus, we see that it's properly aligned, no shards straying in the flesh, and once begun it will heal cleanly and quickly. It needn't be done right away, either. A break can keep a day or two, so long as the bleeding's not severe."

The roan finally disappeared through the middle gate and Kit reluctantly let Anders lead him toward the barn. "A horse's broken leg must be made entirely whole," he said, "or so close that he can walk on it. I've never heard of the Elect trying it, though."

"He may have. I've never heard of a worming charm used on a man, but he may have tried that too."

"Never?"

I shrugged. "Worms are too big for cleansing charms. Too complex. How does one kill the thing inside without harming the owner?" As I said it, I had to frown while trying to work that out. "Do they have prime meridians that you cut? Did you learn kir-blades so young?" Parselev had said it was a charm a knight might learn, if he were truly gifted. They bound it to their sword, to cut through kir-shields.

Anders only smiled. He unlatched Kit's stall and led him inside. While unbuckling the halter, he said, "Show me how to charm a broken leg and I'll show you how to de-worm." And he threw a quick grin as well.

I echoed it, but folded my arms to hide a little frustration. "It's a difficult charm to master. Especially without a memory Blessing." A broken leg was no simple thing; its own strength made it difficult to goad into movement, and the marrow at the core whirled in tight, complex patterns.

The halter in hand, he leaned across the latched stable gate so I could hear him ask, softly, "You think I'm not up to the challenge?"

He leaned close. I drew breath to reply, but something about the teasing question in his eyes and his closeness stopped me. My answer would have been 'no,' with a 'but' appended… and he was sure to ask about that as well. What it was, I couldn't put my finger on. He was no simpleton. But.

And so close, smelling of leather and honest work.

My memory rescued me. Theo Kaufmann had said, at Solstice, that Anders had never read a book. Likely true, though I didn't doubt Anders could. Could read as much, understand as much, if he wanted to, as... Kiefan.

Kiefan, who'd only been kept from attacking Anders by my teacher.

My cheeks warmed a bit; I retreated a step. "I'll see you on Saint-day," I said, instead. And kept retreating. Anders watched me go with a curious, unsettling twist to his smile.

When Saint-day arrived, I had been bed-bound two days with typhus. We suffered much from the soldiers Parselev sent — they arrived with lice if not fleas, reeking fit to stun a horse — despite our best efforts to contain the mess. I had asked the gatekeeper if they could possibly set up a kettle of boiling water to dunk patients in as they arrived. He'd nearly taken me seriously. For a moment, I'd nearly been serious. In the end, we kept those soldiers in the dormitory, along with their filth. I was ashamed to see it, but two of every three were Englic.

One by one, the Ters took to their beds with fevers and rashes. Thers as well. When Ther Kop, who had a heat-sight Blessing, warned me I looked feverish, I followed the advice Krepkin kept repeating; I saw to my own health and stayed abed the next morning. Heima watched me well. The fever blurred my memory and I caught only slivers of those two days when she woke me to drink or eat or helped me to the outhouse. The third day, I knew that Anders brought me a bread trencher from the communal meal and sat with me a while, but whatever we spoke of was smeared out.

I woke in the afternoon, clearer and cooler. The trencher of potatoes, cabbage and mutton waited, and when Heima saw I was awake she set about warming it. I climbed out of bed and changed my sweat-soaked shift for my clean one. With my wool shawl wrapped around my shoulders, I moved to the table and ate, wincing as I found all the aches in my joints. The rash on my chest was fading, under my shift.

Closing my eyes, I called up my kir patterns and saw my baby whirling strong and safe inside me. His — her? — prime meridian shone brightly, the other meridians less so but clear. Tiny, but perfect. I saw a twitch, too, though I couldn't feel it, and I smiled while I stroked my belly.

Strengthened, and as there was a little sunlight still reaching in through the un-shuttered windows, I climbed the stair to Parselev's office. The book he'd wished me to read, and that I hadn't yet had a moment to crack open, was a tattered thing on the shelf of books that he lent often. All were worn and stained, their wooden covers scratched and their bindings weak.

Downstairs, I sat on the bench under the open window and leaned against the wall as I read. Heima brought her sewing and worked quietly, long in the habit of not interrupting a reader. Especially one as slow as me.

Kir could be shaped; I had learned that in trying to stab Krepkin and in slaughtering chickens with a little Shepherd's knife. The kir in my core had molded like clay in my hands, when I shaped it. I'd felt it run like water, too, and rush like wind, and I'd asked Parselev what kir was.

"Heat. Strength. Raw life force, perhaps. If you suss it out, kindly tell me," he'd said, and smiled.

His book began by listing the substances that kir had been compared to — many I had thought of, and more I had not. For these lessons, he wished me to think of kir as wool.

I glanced across the bench, to where Heima sat hemming the armholes of her woolen dress after removing the sleeves for the summer. Mother had taught me spinning, and a little knitting, before I'd been discipled. I knew something of wool.

Part III: Embers on the Wind

The vines, tendrils, ropes, what-have-you, of kir that Parselev had used to fetch Anders into the hush-sphere, to part him and Kiefan even at Blessing speeds in this very kitchen, had been spun with the same pinching twitch I'd used on wool. The sketch of a drop spindle and its thread set my fingers to sliding over each other.

Once spun, these vines of kir could push, grasp, pull, throw, or lash like a whip. They could also maintain the contact between a charm and its caster, reducing the need to knot the charm off to keep it stable. Keeping a charm on a stalk would transmit a portion of any blows it took into the caster — a drawback when it was a kir-shield.

Flicking through the rest of the book, I found more pictures. One in the back caught my eye in particular; it was simple, just a man's hand sketched in strong black lines. But from the smallest fingertip ran a red line slender as spider's thread. Curious, I stopped to read that page.

Parselev wrote that he was only an elect, not a saint, but he had now and then glimpsed the disciple's-bond that tied each of us to our saint. It was finer spinning than he could manage, and seemed to have no limits to its range. Our daily ration of kir moved through that thin line. Parselev's own binding to Saint Qadeem was, and he gave a picture of this as well, a much heavier thread anchored in the palm of his hand. It was a far more complex bond, he wrote.

But said no more than that. I knew that elect were always bound to saints — or ought to be — and some stories made it sound like slavery. Others said little. Rogue, unbound elect were dangerous things, all agreed. Villains.

A knock at the door startled me. Heima went to open it, and dropped into a low curtsy as she stepped aside to let Kiefan in. "Majesty, what brings you?" she asked.

"I heard Kate was —" He scanned the room, finding me by the window and smiling when he saw the book in my hands. I stood, closing it. "I didn't mean to interrupt."

My eyes were tired after so much work. "I was nearly done."

"I heard you were sick abed — thank the Mother that you aren't."

"My fever's broken. No need for you to trouble yourself." Though I was glad he had.

"But she's not entirely well yet," Heima said, crossing to the hearth. "Tea, m'lord?"

"After you took such care of us out on the mountain, it's no trouble. And yes, please," he answered Heima with a nod. Kiefan held up a covered jar that he'd carried in his far hand. "That will go well with these."

My brows rose, curious. "Those?"

He smiled. A few steps to the kitchen table, and he set the earthenware jar down. "Housemistress Wenda helped me steal them, when I told her you'd fallen sick."

I drifted toward the table, slowed by my aches but too intrigued to stay away. "You've been reading all afternoon," Heima told me, with a stern look. "You should lie down. I'll bring you the tea and —"

Kiefan set the jar's lid on the table. I saw what was inside the same moment she did, and I scooted to the bed quickly, willingly, bringing Parselev's book with me. I sat up against the headboard and threw the blankets across my waist and crossed legs.

Fresh strawberries were a rare thing, for a peasant girl.

While Heima poured two mugs of tea, Kiefan shook out a generous handful of the strawberries into a bowl. He took the mugs by their handles in one hand and the jar in the other. "I served at table," he said, when Heima's breath caught. "As any pageboy does."

Her eye fell on the bowlful of bribe he left behind, and she sat down with a smile. Poured herself a mug of tea as well.

Kiefan passed me my tea with fair grace, and sat down on the mattress at my feet. I picked the topmost strawberry from the jar and bit into it. Sweet. Bright. Near as big as my thumb — the best of the crop, surely.

"Does she know Arceal?" Kiefan asked in that tongue, with a glance toward Heima. He took a strawberry too.

"No." I ate a second. I wanted them all, now that I'd gotten a taste, but I fought down the urge to grab the whole jar.

"What are you reading?"

I told him about kir-spinning, showed him Parselev's pictures. Kiefan hadn't tried such a thing; Saint Woden had been drilling him on shields and blades. A sword with a kir-blade added to its edge would break any kir-shield and cut into its owner. We worked our way through the strawberries, and finished our tea. I didn't miss that Kiefan let me eat most of them.

The door creaked when it opened, and Heima threw me a glance. She left the door just ajar and I heard her feet on the path outside. I murmured, "She's going to the outhou —"

Kiefan's mouth caught mine. He tasted sweet. His hand cupped my neck, his thumb at the corner of my jaw. I did the same, and felt a little invisible stubble under my palm. And I wanted to pull him closer, wanted to think we had time to... but Heima wouldn't be gone long. I broke off the kiss with a sigh. He touched one more to my lips, gentle and light.

"Is the baby well? Are you?"

I nodded. Kiefan slipped a hand under the blankets and found my little swelling. Four moons along, or so, and I was beginning to show. He pushed the covers aside and leaned down to touch a kiss to my belly.

"The enemy's coming," he said, "but I will defend you to my last breath."

I shuddered at the thought of what Kiefan's last breath would mean, remembering my teacher's warnings, and I hugged him. He squeezed me, stroking my hair, until we heard Heima's footsteps on the path.

"Here she is," Saint Aleksandr said when I walked into the stables. He sent the two stable boys back to their chores as I approached.

"A quick lesson in telling a horse's age," the saint explained as he stroked Nipper's nose. "Though this one's teeth are something we all see too much of. You've encouraged him too much, I think."

That, to Anders at Nipper's other end. "When other horses hesitated at the sight of centaurs, he charged straight for them," Anders said. "He'll be worth his weight in silver next spring, as a stud."

"Let's see you do it, then," Saint Aleks said to him.

"You waited for me? How kind of you." I was doubly glad, now, that I hadn't lingered at the meeting for further discussion of how steeply the price of food was rising. I leaned far enough into the open stall to see Anders coming around Nipper's rump. He took Saint Aleks' place, and his handful of the stallion's halter, at the gate.

"He wanted to." The saint gestured at Anders.

Who feigned an indifferent shrug, then pretended to check the buckles on the halter. "On the heels of last week's talking, I thought you might like to see it."

"See what?"

"Horse-sense," Saint Aleks said. "Will you try smell, or hearing?"

Anders stroked Nipper's neck, close by his head. "Hearing. It's coming easier to me now."

"That would be interesting," I agreed.

The horse's ears twitched, as if uncertain about this. Anders' hand slowed in its petting and his eyes closed as he focused his attention. I felt a faint ripple as his kir twisted into a charm. The little knot wasn't strong enough for me to pinpoint, but I knew it was nearby. Curious, I wished I could touch his hand and see its structure, but it would be rude to interrupt.

Saint Aleksandr leaned close to my ear and whispered, "Whatever happens, don't laugh. He likely doesn't know."

That piqued my curiosity even further. Being so close, I felt a tiny echo as Anders called Nipper's kir-patterns and the horse shifted, puffed out a breath. Small movement tugged my eyes back to Anders' ear, and the bit of a point developing at the top. I drew a sharp breath and held it. The point lengthened and his ear cupped around into a leaf shape, just like Nipper's. It even acquired a bit of velvety grey dapple, I could see when it swiveled outward.

I covered my open-mouthed grin with my hand, and was glad I did because he opened his eyes. Fighting the grin down wasn't easy, but I twisted it into a pursed mouth and tried to look skeptical.

Anders tipped his head, ears twitching again. "Quit gossiping and get back to work, you two!"

The stable boys' shoveling re-started, at the other end of the barn.

"Is it well knotted?" Saint Aleks asked. "Not trying to unravel?"

Anders nodded. "I found another place to tie it to me, last I tried this. Seems sturdier now."

Saint Aleks nodded and reached, silently asking. Anders took his hand from Nipper to clasp the saint's and have his work checked.

"Good. Very good, after only — half a dozen tries? See what you've done." The saint put fingers to his own ear.

Anders did the same, and laughed. I finally let the giggle burble up and covered my mouth with my palm to hide it. Pointing at me, he said, "You were hiding something, I knew. Shit, these really are horse ears." He covered both with his hands.

"They're even grey," I said. And they looked soft as Nipper's.

He shot his horse a sidelong glare. "How is it I didn't notice?"

"Because they are correct. When the charm is true and well rooted, the form is as the function requires. Thus, there is nothing unnatural about it. Remember how they feel, the acuity and the sense of location. Those will help you shape the charm without the horse for reference."

Anders lowered his hands and let the ears track for a moment, listening.

I had a sudden urge to touch them, but fought it back. I whispered, "How far can you hear?"

He whispered too. "The guards in the gatehouse are talking, but I can't make out the words. Two in the house. One's watching the approach, I think. That must be his boots on the stone. The shovels scraping are loud. And I know just where all the horses are in their stalls."

The gatehouse was outside and across thirty feet or so of space. As it was a nice day, the gatehouse door stood open when the guards were inside.

"If he masters the smelling as well, will he have a horse's nose?" I asked.

Saint Aleks nodded. "Add the eyes and the teeth and he'll be a horse-minotaur. The sum of a creature is more than its parts, but one must master the parts. It may look strange — shape-shifting is a less common skill, as kir goes — but it's a fine road to take."

"What are the common skills?" I asked.

"Battle kir is quite common. Healing," he said, with a nod to me. "A noble art, of course. Crafting, which shares roots with healing. Shape-shifters have made noteworthy elect, though. And saints. One must be careful of them." Aleks held up one hand and amended. "I say 'common skill' — in truth, nothing is common. Each kir-mage is his own mix of talents and experience, limited only by inborn potential and his own wits."

Watching Anders with his horse-ears, as he patted Nipper's shoulder and stepped out of the stall, I thought of the hawks' eyes that archers and huntsmen wore. They were counted as Saint Aleks' disciples, as home-builders, though there was much overlap with warcraft.

"Archers' eyes look much like a hawk's — is that all they are, then? A bit of shape-shifting?" I asked. Parselev had cautioned me not to needle with questions about Blessings; the saints did not speak about how they were made, and for many reasons.

Saint Aleksandr's thick brows perked up, curious, and he took a moment to weigh his answer. "In a way, they are merely another case of the form being as the function requires. That's a principle one finds often, in studying how things are made. It's true of castles and bridges as much as horses or hawks. Have you tried these ears under a helm, Anders?"

"They'd be a great help, I'm sure," Anders said. "Hard enough to see, inside those, let alone hear anything but a yell."

"Get comfortable with them, then. Keep at the nose as well. Till next week."

The saint shucked off his simple cote and braies and walked out, heedless as an animal of his nakedness. I turned to watch as he stepped out into the sun, and saw how his rukh's tail sprouted from the base of his spine. His whole body shrank as his substance flowed out into the massive wings, all those feathers. His back turned brown, his wings and tail barred, and his belly creamy white. With a leap and a jolt of kir, he launched.

I took a moment to see the transformation again in my memory, as a series of instants, then set it aside for later. Anders latched the stall's gate, beside me, brushing horse-hairs from his hands.

"Thank you for bringing me dinner on Saint-day," I said, "and for sitting with me."

His ears pricked forward, just like a horse's, and I couldn't help a silly smile. He smiled in return. "Are they so funny? Do I look a fool?"

"Fey, perhaps." On another thought, I added, "What of cat's ears?"

"One set at a time," he said. "These give me a enough to adjust to, as they are. I'm glad to see you out of bed. The rest did you good."

I nodded. As I watched, one of his ears began to flick, as if trying to throw something off, and kept flicking until he scratched it. I had to set my teeth on my bottom lip.

"I meant to ask what we spoke about — fevers blur my memories."

"You worried about your mother," he said. "And your siblings, and cousins, and neighbors. Whom you listed, but I don't recall their names now."

Anders leaned against the gate but I didn't notice until I thought of touching those ears again. That and my feverish chatter brought a blush to my cheeks. "I'm sorry to have bored you."

"Mother drilled me on her side of my lineage," he said with a shrug. "Ask me to recite it, next I'm ill."

I smiled, noting it, and in glancing down my eye caught on the wedding band I wore. Frida's; it was her inheritance from her mother. My smile drew into a purse, uncertain what to say now. "I'll see you on Saint-day, then?"

His ears turned toward me, alert. "You will."

I couldn't resist any longer; I reached out and stroked one ear as I shifted to go. It was just as soft as Nipper's. And though my touch startled him, I only smiled as I walked away.

The feel of velvet lingered on my fingers all day.

CHAPTER 4

The crescent garden behind Castle Kaltkern was cool, still, despite the warmth of the sun; it lay in the castle's shadow for much of the day and crusty heaps of snow hid from spring along the base of the wall. Both the rose bushes and the apple trees were budding as the Spring Moon waned to a thin crescent. The Field Moon was only a few days off.

Kiefan lay on the bench under the central apple tree, both hands on his head.

"Dame Kate, m'lord," his squire Gregor announced, hesitating at the gap in the ring-wall of juniper. "M'lord?"

I trotted to his side as Kiefan propped himself up on one elbow. Frowning hard against the pain, he waved his free arm toward Gregor. "By the door. Not to be disturbed."

Kneeling, I put my hand to his forehead and could almost see the knotted kir without calling. "What happened?" I murmured. "You've been well enough, all moon, that the once a week kept you." The hard little knots fought me, clenching when I pried at them. I'd gotten in the habit of shaping a hook from my kir to speed the untying, but they resisted that too.

He sat up further, wrapping me in his arms, and laid his head against mine. That sufficed for the contact I needed; I hugged him back. And the knots did loosen, a wee bit, as he breathed and his silver crown-band pressed into my skin.

"Kiefan?" I nudged him. "What's wrong?"

He had to clear his throat. "The Arceal army divided. They've a good thirty thousand, at the river, and more still marching up. They divided and sent half their troops eastward, up the Felsherz. Ten miles upriver, in the dark of the night, they laid down a ready-made bridge and began to cross this morning." Kiefan's grip on me tightened. "The split was made at the rear — they can't have seen, from across the river. Arcea's flanking with five thousand knights and centaurs, and infantry coming behind them. I sent word to Father and Tomas as soon as the watchmen reported it, but —"

I hushed him; his knots were tightening before my eyes. The anguish on his voice put a sudden lump in my throat. It clung despite my trying to swallow.

Kiefan merely breathed for a few moments. "The Engls have the flank, but they've been camped with little action for a week now. Unprepared. Three days ago, Arcea captured a party of our Rangers and put them up on the river bank. Crucified them. One of their elect stood catching arrows until sundown to be sure they suffered. After dark, my father called up the archery captain — he has heat-sight, too — to put them from their misery. They have to marshal the Engls quickly, find a defensible field wall or hilltop or those centaurs will cut right through."

I hushed him again. "They'll be ready," I whispered. Hoping to distract him, I asked, "What would you do?"

He began to rattle off formations and numbers. I freed little clusters of kir-whorls, one at a time. After a while, Kiefan trailed off again.

"A rider came from Knapptal," he said. "No sign of Caercoed yet."

"M'lady Leix promised to set out on the Equinox. It's only been a moon since then."

Kiefan lifted his head from mine, grey eyes lost in distant thought. My connection broken, I took his hand to finish the job. His kir answered my call for reinforcements, and arrowed toward what remained of his headache. As I worked at it, his hand came to rest on my growing belly.

"I need to —" Kiefan paused, thinking, and then nodded to himself. "I need the Rangers sweeping the east, ambushing Arceal scouts whenever they can. I must send word to Vysokov and the northern line at Kernweise. I need half our garrison out to support a retreat if — thank you, Kate." His focus came back to me, at the end.

I pulled one last tangle of kir free. Then I met his eyes. "Gladly. I haven't been much of a physician to you, of late." The truth of that needled me; I saw him once a week, across the table he'd taken me on. Each week, there was less time for chatting afterward. The war had hardly begun, and I wondered if I'd see him at all in a few moons. Much as that ached, it seemed likely.

"Thank you for that too," he said, and looked down at his hand on me, on the baby. "For clearing my head, both ways. May I? May I see the little one?"

That made me smile. My simple yellow dress was one that Ter Holly had given me when my clothes grew too tight. She said that a set of maternity clothes had been passed from Ter to Ter for years, and this one showed the wear in its oft-adjusted seams. I said, "She's still tiny and —"

He called my kir, whole-body, as strong and stable as I did. That startled me a little; I hadn't known he could. Our baby was still a little thing, curled up snug enough to seem smaller than my hand. The kir was tricky to pick out unless one knew of it, being small and wrapped in layers of my own, but I pointed Kiefan to the little bundle. One could make out the meridians threading through arms, legs, along the spine, now.

"You can tell it's a girl?" Kiefan murmured.

"Not till she's much larger. Or he. When did you learn to call kir?"

"Captain Aleks and Saint Woden shifted the focus of my training." His hand stroked across the curve of my womb, as my swirling colors faded. "I've no knack for healing, but I got the trick of calling up the patterns." His hand slipped around my belly to my back to tug me closer. "You'd never said you could see beneath clothing, thus."

My hand against his chest stopped him. "I stole no peeks of you," I said, feigning prudery by tipping my nose up. "So I expect —"

His kiss cut me off. I meant to keep it a simple one, but he pressed for more and I gave in. He let me take a breath after a few deep kisses; by then my hands gripped his black tabard for balance as my mind was slipping into a haze of longing. At this close range, I noticed the silver rank rings, rather than brass, strung on his epaulettes. How he must be keeping his knight's crest tidy with the same lavender shaving soap he always used. And he hadn't had his hands on my butt, as he did now, in more than a turn of the Shepherd moon.

"M'lord," Gregor called, "Captain Rostislav says there's news."

Close to my mouth, Kiefan murmured, "I miss you."

My heart quavered. "I miss you too."

He let go. I sighed as I settled on my heels to let him stand and go. I saw more of Anders, of late, in his half-days off on Saint-day. Father Duty was harsh; I'd heard that often but hadn't known the truth of it.

Lonely, I returned to my feverish and wounded, and a master who still hated me.

———————————✠———————————

The king's army split as well, we were all told at the status meeting a few days later. Arcea's flanking cavalry met a force ready to defend itself in an orderly retreat rather than an unprepared camp of Englic armsmen. Duke Seagrace and his army withdrew northeastwards, intending to block the way to Vorspitz. King Wilhelm came north, back to the safety of Wodenberg's walls, with what remained of the southern army.

Arcea, already divided, pursued both. The dark mass of monsters and men fought their way across the Felsherz to find the earthworks abandoned and flattened into the field they had been raised from. The enemy marched up the Southbound Road barely a day behind the king.

The foulburg stood largely empty, all its peasants and craftsmen and merchants sent north. Now it was scraped clean for good and all, and its last few families brought inside the city walls. Wodenberg's gates stood open, for the moment, but from the castle battlements the armies outside clarified into divisions as they neared — armsmen and archers on foot, knights on horseback — with banners and flags and a distant rumble of drums and trumpets. Seven thousand men, Duke Seagrace and Saint Qadeem having taken the lion's share toward Vorspitz.

Kiefan pointed out the king's banner and those of the barons, of various companies. He also knew some of the smaller dots of color in the distance, banners in the enemy army. Arcea had called on Suevi lords to strengthen their ranks, some of them blood kin of Queen Mercia and thus of Kiefan too. None of that meant much to me, though. I was going over the hospital's preparations in my head.

The next day, the first of the Field Moon, the king turned to face the enemy with his back to the city walls.

Word had come up from the gates, by way of the quartermaster's teamsters, that the king had arrayed his men on the uphill side of the southern fields. As he prepared to fight, the supply train continued to retreat into Wodenberg along with the army's baggage and the camp followers.

The gates still stood open. I could see them from just outside the Order's campus gates, looking down River Road. The hospital was, in truth, enjoying a bit of a lull, as many of our typhus patients had recovered and the entire staff had suffered through it as well. A few of the Ters and Thers stood with me to take in the view.

"Where was your husband posted?" I asked Ter Holly. Her husband was on the City Guard, as an armsman.

"He's on the Patch Tower, thank the Father," she said, pointing toward the eastward wall. That tower had earned its name for the distinctly white patch in its granite. "But I sang the Mother's benediction to him this morning. In case he must…"

From the castle came a distant shouting and the wagon-drivers on River Road angled their oxen to the sides of the street. The voices resolved, along with drumming horses' hooves, into "The prince! Make way!" as the company trotted downhill. Kiefan rode fully geared for battle, his helm waiting on the pommel. His black-bay warhorse, Pip, pranced at the column's head, trailed by Gregor on a sturdy palfrey with the lances and shields. Saint Woden rode beside Kiefan, dressed in mail and an unmarked black tabard. Two standard-bearers followed, one for the prince's banner, one for the city's, and then a dozen of the Prince's Guard — fully half of them — including Captain Rostislav.

But none of them were Anders. He had the stables to see to.

Kiefan would be safe enough on the wall. The southern fields were — a mile away? Far from the fighting. Kiefan wouldn't leave the city, I told myself as they descended River Road.

Small in the distance, the two banners and the knot of horsemen came to a stop in the middle of the open gates. He wouldn't ride out there with only a dozen knights. And Saint Woden. Would he?

I turned away, swallowing hard, not wanting to know if he did or not.

"We'd see more from the bell tower," Ther Adalslav said. "We could see over the wall, I'm sure."

The thought twisted my stomach. I didn't even look up at the stubby bell tower that guarded one side of the Order's gates. "We must be ready for the wounded," I told them, and started back to the hospital. They followed with a little grumbling.

Krepkin had sent the ambulance down to the wall early on, when we first heard the king meant to give battle. It was late morning now, and no word from them or Parselev.

I busied myself seeing to the final preparations. As our typhus wing had emptied, we'd moved out the patients who needed less tending — broken limbs or dislocations — and my invalids' floor was rather lacking in invalids. Soon, I had nothing to do but fuss at the fire and wait for news.

Thunder cracked once, twice, turning all heads toward the mountain. Then, silence.

The waiting dragged on. Krepkin ordered us all to the noon meal, saying if we were needed, the gatekeeper would call. I went simply to have something to do, and only ate a slice of buttered bread. My knotted stomach wouldn't allow anything else.

I'd begun to think the war would be a dreary procession of meetings and arguments with Krepkin — nothing like the awful night at the lamia fount, which I'd feared. Now the war pressed close, breathing on my neck. Like an overbearing dance partner, and me in dread of his hands wandering on me. I breathed a laugh at that. Not that I'd had to fear such a thing, since Anders became my dance partner.

Meinrad sat down on the bench opposite me, without a word, and began shuffling a deck of cards. Heima appeared, asking if I'd heard from Parselev. I hadn't. She sat down beside me and tapped the table. Meinrad dealt her in.

"Ott-stagi," he said, "Sets only, trumps double, no Shepherds. Master? We need a fourth."

Krepkin joined us. It wasn't a very fair game for Heima, playing with three memory-Blessed, but my poor luck compensated. By the second round, I wasn't even paying attention. I was waiting for shouts from arriving ambulances, for thunder on a clear day, for —

We all perked, save Heima, when we felt kir move. So much kir that, even at this distance, we could track it across the sky.

"That would be Saint Woden," Krepkin said, "replenishing his disciples."

"All of them?" Heima asked.

He nodded. "The Trinity did that several times, in the Englic campaign."

"Does it mean we're winning?" she asked.

"It means the men were tiring. When the Traitor sprang his trap —"

"Physicians!" came the shout at last, from the dining hall's door. I dropped my cards and ran.

Ambulances, finally. One stopping before the hospital door, one just clearing the campus gate. I pulled myself up to look into the bed and saw a layer of men in mail, feathered shafts jutting from them. Their panicky eyes stared back at me, their chests heaving in pain.

"What news?" I asked. "Orderlies!"

I stepped aside as the Thers unlatched the wagon bed's gate and reached in for the wounded. The driver told me, "Elect's bringing his infirmary in. They're inside the walls, set up in Sinnmach Square, to triage the wounded for you."

The wounded were armsmen, all rained upon by arrows with three-vaned fletchings. Two vanes grey or brown, one black, I noted. Parselev had sent a sample of one of those; they were diamond-headed and barbed. Each man's kir rose at my call and I sorted both wagon-loads into the care of nurses, for the lightly wounded, or to surgery.

Striding back into the hospital, I followed the second-worst-off patient into my surgery cubicle. The worst-off had gone into Krepkin's cubby, and was already under his knife. Our ground floor was for stitching and bandaging those who didn't need a cot upstairs, or for those who wouldn't survive the trip up.

Ther Adalslav, my surgical assistant, broke the arrow off short and eased the patient's mail tunic off over the stub. The man was conscious enough to help, but struggled to move his right arm. The shot had taken him just below the collarbone, angled near straight down from above.

When the second orderly tossed his mail on the floor, the patient weakly tried to reach for it. "Please, don't…"

"You'll get it back," I told him. "Lie down on the table."

His gambeson tunic untied and off, the patient obeyed. It was a warm enough day that he hadn't worn a cote underneath. I touched a knockout charm to his head and then untied a bundle of boiled tools. The second orderly gathered up his things.

Checking my memory for the alignment of the fletching vanes in comparison to the arrowhead, I cut into the armsman's shoulder. His kir danced for me, and his meridians pulsed. With a blunt-headed probe in my left hand, I made sure to draw the meridian aside. I could feel the artery pulsing against the probe's iron nose. Blood pooled in my cuts, but I followed the damaged kir down to the barbed arrowhead. My scalpel scraped alongside its sharp tips.

Putting my blade down, I grasped the shaft and with the probe's help I eased it out. The arrow had nicked his lung; a few little bubbles welled up in the blood. Calling my kir, I knit a tiny patch of a charm and slipped my pinky finger into the flesh to place the pattern.

His lung's flesh shifted and sealed. "Blood-stop," I murmured, and Ther Adalslav unraveled one over the incision. I daubed out some of the puddle with a clean rag. He handed me a needle and catgut and I stitched the armsman shut one layer at a time. I used wool thread to close his pale, sweat-crusted skin.

Adalslav had left a cleansing charm and bandage for me and gone to see about the next patient. I had this one ready to be helped upstairs when my assistant returned carrying another mailed armsman, this one with an arrow skewered through his bare thigh. "Tore the hose off — nothing else would do."

Thus, the afternoon sped by. Arrows in shoulders, in thighs, through arms, one unfortunate who'd caught it in his left butt cheek, all the shafts angled from straight overhead. Men with beards, or clean-shaven, faces tear-streaked or set like stone against the pain. Discipled by Woden, save a handful with Aleksandr's strength Blessing, but all born too poor or without enough skill for knighthood. Some wore mail shirts. Many settled for boiled leather.

One of my patients was an ambulance orderly, struck in risking too much to drag a wounded man clear.

The ache grew from my feet and worked its way up to my lower back. The baby, small as she still was, might as well have been a brick. When a lull came, I leaned against the surgery table and sighed. I put a hand to my ache, but had no kir left. Twice emptied, even — I had taken a charm-hand's, halfway through.

I looked up when a mug of tea was held into my line of sight. "How has Ther Adalslav proved himself?" Parselev asked, with a smile.

Relieved beyond words, I threw my arms around him and got a brief squeeze in return.

"Gently," he said. "Heima near broke my ribs. Stannis looks sour as ever, so you must be holding your own. Tell me everything."

———————————×———————————

When Anders settled on the bench beside me with a trencher of community-meal pickings, I caught a whiff of him and looked up from the gravy-slathered bread I'd been about to bite. His eyebrows rose. He'd shaved off the stubble below his Blessing ridges, and his pigtail was tied fresh and neat. I leaned a little closer and inhaled again.

"We're to wash on Saint-day," he said. "I've been known to obey."

"Is that rosewater?"

"Gatter took back the stables. It was either hope for a turn in a kitchen tub or pay at the bath house on Arbor Street." Anders took a bite of mashed potatoes. "They keep the water hotter on Arbor Street."

When Anders had been washing with the plain stuff the stables used, he'd still smelled faintly of leather and horses. Now that was drowned out by roses. "And scented soap."

"Theo paid for that. He was washing up too."

"I suppose he makes a habit of that?" I asked, thinking of what Alice had said about Theo Kaufmann. Anders' friend was a steady patron of the whores.

Anders shrugged. "He'd likely spent the night on the Street. I was on duty at the inner gate until the midnight bell."

I'd gotten in a bite of bread as he spoke. "How is it they have you on guard duty?"

"The King's Guard was trimmed a bit, in doing their duty. Captain Aleks let it be known they're considering applicants, but —" Anders shook his head. "I'll not apply for that."

"You still have charge over some horses in the stable, though?"

"That never needed me there daily. Gatter knows his work. So it's guard duty, and escort whenever the prince rides out. In mail all day, if not the helm too, shield on your back, sun or rain. Will spends his nights holding rust at bay."

Poor Will. "With any luck, he can give that job to his own squire, once he's knighted."

Anders shook his head. "He doesn't mean to ask Woden for knighthood."

"No? Mustn't he, if he's to be Baron Rossweide?" My voice lowered as I turned uncertain. I looked for the memory of someone saying titled nobles must be knights, but got nothing clear.

"King, yes, duke or margrave, yes. Barons receive a touch of leeway. And better an unknighted son suited to the job than some distant cousin. Or a bastard not of the blood. Will counts himself discipled by Saint Aleksandr," Anders said. "He trained to please his father. And because I did it, perhaps."

We ate in silence for a stretch, working through potatoes, roasted spring onions, and pastries filled with egg and cheese. The Order's kitchen offered only herbal teas, now, as they'd run out of small beer.

Our arms brushed, now and then, and we traded a snippet of smile back and forth. Easy and simple, two friends sharing a meal. It left me warm.

Anders broke the quiet as his trencher neared bare. "The Guard in my squad have been asking, since it's more than odd now — why I've no token on my helm." He paused, risked a glance at me. "I said I didn't need one, I was only tending the stable. Not riding escort."

He left it there. "But now you are," I said. He'd never worn a lady's token, so I wasn't sure why he brought it up now.

"It needn't be anything special — any kerchief would do."

He wanted —? My token. His wife, and a lady. Neither title would jump to my mind easily, still. I breathed a chuckle without meaning to. "One of mine? I never wear a kerchief."

I still wrapped my braid in a bun, most days, but sometimes I gathered it up in the crespine that Frida had given me. The close weight of it on my neck, and the band across my head, still felt odd.

"If it's a physician's favor, a bandage would be fitting," he said, and smiled with a twist. "Should I need one, it would be quite convenient."

I couldn't help smiling at that. But our supply of bandages was already walking out of the hospital on wounded men, and rarely returning. "Surely you could buy me a kerchief that would do."

Anders' smile dropped away. My heart dropped with it. He shifted back, then turned to what was left on his trencher. I barely caught his mutter, even so close to him. "If you don't wish me luck, then best to do without."

"Why wouldn't I —" I'd stepped in something, that was clear. "Of course I wish you luck. Not that you need it, but if you think my wishes will help…" That wasn't what he wanted to hear, though. He didn't look up until I touched his arm. Such blue eyes, and so quick to retreat from me. "Mother gave me a wimple, but it draws so much attention to wear one outside Engl Street. It's a nice, light green and it'll look fine on your helm."

He pressed his mouth in a line, then asked, "Have you worn it?"

I'd hardly unfolded it. "Must I have?"

"It's meant to —" Anders put up a hand to fend it all off. "Pay it no mind." He got up from the bench, taking his cup of tea as he went.

"Anders —" An edge of pleading wormed into my voice. I wanted a chance to mend my mis-step.

But he wouldn't look back.

CHAPTER 5

Sinnmach Square lay where River Road crossed Wallside Street, which ringed the inside of the city wall. As one rode in the city gates — shut and barred, now — one crossed Wallside Street and bore right onto the hard-packed oval. In the center stood a stone platform where announcements were made and criminals received their floggings. There was a stone post with a large iron ring at the top, for that.

Mostly, it served as a mustering-yard for traffic. As it sprawled the width of the block between Wallside Street and Low Street, the Kaufmanns' dry goods shop made the fourth side of the square.

Half of Sinnmach Square was under tarp now, as there'd been time to raise the infirmary's tents. Fresh straw covered the dirt. Two surgery tables stood at the far end and the handful of cots were currently empty, as there'd been time to move the patients up to the hospital as well. Kettles of water stood in the coals of the infirmary's perpetual campfire and simmered just off the boil.

Over it all, anchored on the dry goods shop and the whipping post, hung a triangular sheet of green kir. It was oddly hazy, when I stared up from underneath, but a dozen Arceal arrows were embedded in it.

"Woden lent some aid," Parselev said as I frowned at them. "I'd never spun such a large shield. Hadn't realized we were under attack until Ter Ida fell. This arrangement is otherwise like Ansehen, as you see — mark the arrangement well."

He went on to describe how the tables, cots and tents could be unloaded from wagons, where patients would arrive and be sorted, the flow of ambulances, and in the talking we slid into how I had handled the invalids' floor, how I'd managed with Krepkin, and how the baby had treated me thus far.

"My strength is creeping back," I answered Parselev. "Perhaps a little focus, as well. If not for my Blessing, I'd be of no use at all. Still, I got through the readings you left me. And I did try a little spinning. I managed a kir-shield the size of my palm, on a short stalk. It was indeed more stable."

"Good. You've tried drawing kir from someone, without the charm-hand?"

I nodded. "It would not come, still." I had tried to pull kir from a feverish archer, to see if I could.

"Give that time. A little test for you, then. Call the kir here." Parselev gestured toward the dirt and straw underfoot.

He'd asked me this, before, and nothing had ever answered. "What am I to call?" I asked, a bit irritated to face this after admitting I'd made little progress on other skills. "Straw is dead. Its kir won't answer me."

"Not the straw. Call the living kir."

"But —"

"Call it as you would call heat from the snow on Starknadel."

I opened my mouth, but that thought stopped me. I closed my mouth, remembering how the icy wind had sucked my warmth from me. Wondering how strong a pull I'd need to take it back.

Parselev stroked his beard. "Call it."

That hollow howl echoed in my ear when I put out a hand and demanded that the patterns rise. And for a flickering moment, it answered. A light sheen of whorls lay upon the straw, upon the corner of the stone platform, over my own hand before me. Not my kir; it was a skin atop everything, invisible until that moment.

"You asked why we must boil the bandages, the scalpels. You asked why cleansing charms must be used. You asked where the antagonizing patterns in the sick and abscessed come from."

"And you said I would see, someday," I murmured, staring at my bare hand.

"When you were strong enough. Life is all around us, unseen, unknown, seeking to feed on us as we feed on livestock. And to speak of the sick, you did well with the typhus."

My wonder faded into a grimace. "Four new patients arrived this morning."

"It will worsen by —"

The trumpet in the gatehouse cut Parselev off, one long blast followed by a pattern. Enemy at the gate, I knew; the captain of the watch had described the major alarms at the first weekly meeting. Through the high window, a man hollered, "Clear the streets!" and the cry was taken up below.

Parselev drew me further under the kir shield by one shoulder. "Physician of the floor," he assigned me, and went to see to the surgery.

I fell into the routine. Though I hadn't seen these nurses and orderlies in a moon's turning, they were all old hands and we set about readying the infirmary. Meanwhile, a messenger galloped up River Road toward the castle. The ramparts above filled with armsmen and archers. Crews swarmed to the massive catapults, one atop the tower on either side of the gate and those on the nearest towers along the southern wall.

Many houses along Wallside Street had two floors and peaked thatch roofs. The city wall, smooth and seamless like the castle's, stood a little taller. At the top, between the crenelated parapets, it was wide enough for three men to fight abreast. Saint Aleksandr had pulled the walls from the stone below the earth, as he had Kaltkern, and they had never been breached.

Another tune came from the trumpet, one I didn't know. From the castle, a deeper-throated trumpet answered. The bell tower in the Order began to ring at a steady pace, a more familiar alarm that raised my pulse further. There'd been a little traffic on Wallside Street and River Road; they were empty now.

I stood by the fire, which was stoked up well and the kettles boiling, as my gaze leaped from the catapults on the gate towers to the men on the walls. Three ambulances arrived, the horses skidding and struggling to slow from a downhill trot, and swung into Sinnmach Square.

"Under the shield!" Parselev waved them closer. Crossing to me, he said, "They're marshaling archers on River Road, so they mean to return volleys. Do not stray." He pointed up at the shield and its arrows.

"The king! The king!" I heard the shouts only a few moments before the company of banners and black-garbed Guardsmen arrived at a canter. Many banners, and I spotted the prince's among them. The warhorses kicked up dust in skidding to a halt, and shunted to either side of the gate. All the riders wore full gear, helms included. The king's bore a simple gold crown around its brow.

Atop the tower, an officer yelled the order and the catapults thrummed, sending loose shot over the wall. The crews were at them in a heartbeat to winch the long arms back down. I looked back to the royal company at the foot of the towers and saw half the horses standing with riders, half without.

"I must…" I began, looking about at the rows of cots, the stacks of bandage rolls waiting. The nurses and orderlies stood waiting, too, watching the wall as I did. Waiting for someone to bleed. "Should the orderlies be in the gate towers?"

"When the rhythm's set," Parselev answered, though that only puzzled me.

"Is Saint Woden here?"

"His concern, not ours." Through his hand on my shoulder, I felt kir pulse into me and my next breath came easier, deeper. "Take a little more."

"But you —"

"Drew all I could hold from the Pool this morning. Don't worry."

The catapults, once reloaded, shot again. The tower's trumpet announced something new and behind me, on River Road, orders were shouted.

From the tower came a scream: "Cover! Cover!"

A black cloud rose over the city wall, peaked and began to fall. My feet froze as the arrows plunged toward me, hissing, striking the kir shield and shivering from the effort. They thudded everyplace else, on wood and earth. Then men scrambled up from under their shields, on the wall, and resumed their work. I realized the enemy had largely missed; our archers were further up River Road.

From the road came an order: "Loose!" Our smaller flock of arrows answered, cresting lower over the parapet above the gate itself and vanishing.

And again: "Cover! Cover!"

The cloud rose more sharply, this time, and fell onto the wall and towers. Screams followed. But still, the moment the storm passed, they were up again. Most of them. Our archers answered, as well as the catapults.

"Orderlies!" Parselev shouted. "When their next volley falls!"

Thers were ordinary men, most of them Saint Aleksandr's disciples, who'd taken an oath to serve the Mother and Father through serving others. No armor, not a sword among them. When the next cloud of arrows rose over the wall and thudded down, our Thers sprinted for the nearer gate tower with their sling stretchers. They made for the open door and vanished inside.

Those of the royal company who'd stayed with the horses were out of the saddles and holding the animals close to the lee of the towers. There was a space in the shadow of the gate itself where arrows weren't falling, and they'd sidled into it. Impossible to see if Anders was among them — I couldn't make out the details on their tabards at this distance, and there were a few dappled greys among the horses.

There should've been another volley, but it didn't come. Someone shouted, "Elect!" behind us and my teacher's hand left my shoulder. I turned, spotted a wagon-driver with an arrow-studded friend slung on his shoulder. My frozen feet thawed; this was something I could help with at last. And our Thers would be back soon enough —

A thud against the city gate shook the earth. Then a second. Lower and heavier than any thunderbolt. Horses screamed. My mind shot back to the earthquake at Ansehen and my blood turned to ice. The third blow shuddered the massive timbers and I looked to the gate towers, searching for cracks, for falling stones. A clutch of the warhorses bolted across Wallside Street, torn loose from their knights.

Our enemy knocked. Like a giant.

Thunder answered thunder. Lightning struck, danced white-hot as a knot of brilliant kir landed on the parapet above the gate. The man within was only a faint silhouette, and further vanished in the glare as lightning swirled around him. Kir arced from the mountain above, massed into a brilliant wall before Woden's hand, and slammed down upon the enemy. The earth shuddered and wood tore, rumbled in collapsing.

After-spots whirled in my eyes, but I saw a squire running, half across Wallside Street already, chasing the fleeing warhorses. Gregor — paying no heed to the arrows peppering the ground and the danger.

"Loose!" the archery officer hollered, and a volley launched over the wall. Woden stood above the gate, his hair nearly parted by the low arrows, and folded his arms across his chest as he surveyed his handiwork outside.

"Kate!" A Ter tugged at my sleeve. The orderlies ran across Wallside Street, carrying wounded in slings, on their shoulders, however they could. Arrows struck near the heart, arrows skewering shield and arm together, men trailing blood as they came.

Their kir sprang up eagerly for me and I pointed one toward Parselev's surgery table. Others could survive the ride to the hospital. A few only needed a clean bandage to stop their bleeding.

I saw to an archer who'd taken an arrow clear through his calf muscle; extraction was simply a matter of breaking the shaft and pulling it free, but the hole needed a quick blood-stop and stitches. It had missed his artery, thankfully. And soon as I knotted the bandage, the man was on his feet, pulling his boot on, and hobbling back to the gate tower. I didn't try to argue with the fierce determination in his hawk's eyes.

The arrows kept falling. A Ther carried up an armsman with a shaft through the nape of his neck, just inside the collar of his mail shirt. His arm hung ominously limp, but I checked him. "Gone. Put him to rest," I said, nodding toward the short line of corpses along the wall of Kaufmann's shop.

"No! Dame Kate —"

"He's gone."

"He was talking!"

I pointed toward the line of dead. The man in the sling between the next two Thers was hazy from agony but alive, and he needed me. Parselev was still busy, so I sent him to the second surgery table. I snatched up a tool bundle and my medicine bag. They'd ripped the sleeve off his plain-spun cote when I arrived for a closer look at his wound.

A blade had cut through his bicep, clear to the bone. An arrow would've skewered.

My fingers found his artery and pinched it. I knew how to do this; finding the matching half, I coaxed and stretched the ends together and joined them. His meridian still wavered, though, and it took some close hunting to find the fibers that made up the rest of it.

He'd lost blood, too, and breathed harsh and shallow on the table. "Charm-hand!" Meridian-fibers in one hand, I put out my other and someone took it, one with a Blessing nub. I sucked the offered kir down, spinning it to blood as it flowed through me, and channeled it into my patient's artery. It was only a little, but his heart's beat strengthened. His face gained more color.

The remainder of my own kir went to mending his meridian. Someone had put out a needle and catgut for me; I looked up toward Parselev's table and Ter Biya smiled to me. Once the muscles were stitched, I gave over the skin stitches to a nurse and went to triage more fresh arrivals. Fewer arrows, I saw, more slashes. Stabs. I looked up at the wall.

Woden still stood above the gate, cloaked in twinkling green, and though there was sword-fighting on the ramparts I knew there was nothing to fear. We would turn them back from our walls.

Parselev dressed as plainly as any of us, most days, but for the parley he put on his silk cote. The tomato-red one, which was a bit old-fashioned for being knee-long. And he fussed at me, actually fussed over my plain brown dress. I didn't know what he thought I would wear; I had this, the older yellow one, or my Solstice dress.

"Put it on, then," he said, shooing me toward the screen in the cottage's corner. "Qadeem wants you to see this meeting."

"It won't fit," I told him, putting both hands on my bulge. "You said this was an empty formality."

"Standing before the Voice of Arcea's Empress is the same as standing before her. The housemistress will have something — I'll send a runner up."

For all his worry about my clothes, we rode down to Wallside Street in a humble wagon along with baskets of bread and cheese and some crates. I hadn't expected Theo Kaufmann would be driving. He'd seemed too fine for such things, when I met him at Solstice. His tabard bore a white wheel for an insignia, indicating the support branch of the army, and his brasses marked him captain-general — to the City Quartermaster himself. Anders teased him for it, but the position was no idle thing. He did wear a snowy white cote fit for Solstice under his everyday tabard, as the Kaufmanns were too rich for anything less, but watching Theo drive a humble wagon made me reconsider the oily first impression I'd gotten at the banquet.

I sat with my shawl over my head to keep the dust off. Parselev leaned close, because of the wheels' rumbling, and told me, "Watch the negotiations, take note of all that's said. It's a sort of dueling, with words, and you're sure to see more of it. But stay close to Kaufmann, as well. I must stand by the king."

I nodded, trusting that I would learn something my saint deemed necessary. The week had begun with the first attack on the city gate, and now it ended with the enemy wishing to talk. A strange thing to ask for, I thought.

The Gatekeeper Tavern stood on Wallside Street, a few blocks from the city gates, facing a blank stretch of the walls. Before its wide-open double doors, on the flagstone stoop, the royal party stood in loose conversation as they waited. King Wilhelm wore his ornate crown, his sword in a jeweled sheath over black silks, and his cloak lined with gold; Kiefan, the silver crown with amethysts that he'd worn for Solstice, and stark black and white. Both Captains of their personal Guard stood with them, spit-polished. Captain Rogen of the City Guard and the southern army's captain-general stood in the party as well.

I changed into the dress that Housemistress Wenda had sent down with the royal party — servant's blacks, but silk rather than wool. Slithery stuff. It caught on my hands whenever I touched it. Even in black, it was glossy and pretty. With my medicine bag on my shoulder, I drifted around the cluster of men, looking for my place to stand. Parselev had been drawn into the center, speaking in hushed tones with Kiefan and the king.

Eventually, I found my way to Theo Kaufmann. For a moment, it was far too awkward as I kept thinking of how Anders had warned him away from me when I was tipsy. He narrowed one eye at me, cocking his head. "You're to be my witness, then?"

"Witness?" I wasn't entirely sure what he meant.

"They keep a memory-Blessed by me at their parleys. You'll see why — we're useful, but not entirely trusted, after all. Kaufmanns have too much Suevi blood, I suppose. More than most." Theo cast a glance at Kiefan; Queen Mercia was Suevi herself, true. The king had fallen in love with her during a visit to Suevia and carried her off, the story went.

"Have there been many?"

"Half a dozen, that I've been to myself — they're like dances. Poses struck to impress. Though with knives up every sleeve." He paused, mid-breath, after saying that and glanced at me sidelong. "I should apologize, Physician. I frightened you, at Solstice? Or, if it seemed that I threatened you, I apologize."

Theo added a bow for good measure, and seemed sincere enough. "I did feel threatened," I agreed.

"I'm an insufferable ass when I'm drunk," he said. "As Anders can tell you. And for love of him, I beg your pardon."

Fair enough; I accepted with a solemn nod.

Wallside Street was blocked off to either side by the mounted knights of the King's and Prince's Guards, and the wall's parapet above was full of archers. Among them, in an unmarked tabard, was Saint Woden. I had spotted his bearded face among them. He kept his kir hidden tightly away, so that there was no chance of the enemy sensing him so close by — unlike when he'd made his appearance during the first attack.

Stories had it that the Spanne outside had been littered with Arceal corpses after his arrival. Woden's blazing kir-ram had struck down a swath of enemy soldiers, smashed a few houses, had made even the elect who'd pounded on the gate three times retreat in haste. A few scaling ladders had gotten to the wall and an Arceal saint had tossed a squad of minotaur soldiers up onto the ramparts, but the knights of the City Guard had cut them down. We'd turned them all back.

The archers on the wall shouted down at last and we all straightened to attention. On the parapet, Saint Woden's kir bloomed and my eyes were pulled to it even as I clenched my own kir tight to keep it from answering his call. A trickle of green kir-light rolled down the sleek face of the wall in a wandering line until it struck a node and flared bright. Spiderweb rays shot across the wall, arcing to meet each other, and the saint's door opened. The granite irised, gaped wide, and a company of mounted envoys rode in with hardly a glance up at the amazing doorway. Behind them, the saint's door closed and Woden folded his kir away snugly.

The Voice of the Empress rode at the head of the company, on a white horse, the gilt edges of his lamellar cuirass catching the sun nicely. The purple cloak was handsome, and exotic as his brown skin. His lobster-tail helm bore no crest, but instead a short, projecting arm from which fluttered a narrow, white silk banner. Written on it, in black brush strokes, was his title.

He dismounted in the middle of Wallside Street. "Even now, your saints will not parley, la? We came not for such insults, King Wilhelm. Do we not offer to end all this now?" His voice carried well, and his Alemannic was polished despite the odd cadence. His smile was bright white. "No more need die, if sainted and elect meet in single combat."

The king said, "Let me offer you refreshments and then we will talk of how this will end, deSvello Antonin." A pair of servants brought out a table and chairs from inside the tavern and swiftly set them up on the flagstone stoop. White cloth, wooden trenchers and cups followed, setting places for two. "Let me offer you my hospitality." With great deliberation, King Wilhelm unbuckled the royal sword-belt and passed his weapon to Captain Aleksandra. Then he reached out both hands in welcome.

More of our guests dismounted and flanked the Voice as he came forward to clasp the king's hands. Two of the officers in gilt lamellar cuirasses, red cloaks and red-crested helms were brown-skinned and dark-haired Arceal like the envoy deSvello. The third was Suevi, though, fair in coloring and much like us — wearing mail armor and a great helm, and further distinguished by the walnut-brown sash he wore as a baldric. A rope of braided gold thread glittered at his shoulder, tying his baldric to the epaulette. He lingered in clasping Kiefan's hand with intent eyes, for a moment.

None of them wore a sword, though, and they'd come with only a small, armed escort; they put themselves at our mercy. The dozen mounted Arceal knights stood in crisp lines on Wallside Street. Their lamellar was not gilt, but each wore a heavy red cloak with a golden eagle on the back. Their lobster-tail helms sported fierce, narrowed hawk-eyes along the crowns and a beak in front, and the crests were golden feathers. Each held a heavy spear in one hand, its butt set in the right stirrup, and each wore a sword, but they were heavily outnumbered and watched by archers on the wall as well.

Theo moved to quickly set the table with provisions from his wagon: fresh bread, honey, butter, and preserves, and a block of sharp cheddar as well. Two Suevi men, having swiftly unpacked the panniers on their horses, brought Arcea's side of the refreshments: a glass bottle of olive oil swirling with spice seeds, a jar of pickled black olives, onions, and peppers, a basket of soft rolls. A kettle of hot water was brought out when they set out fine porcelain cups and a teapot. As soon as the water hit the tea leaves, I could smell the rich spices. They'd brought their best.

My stomach growled. I was missing the noon meal for this.

The king sat, as did this deSvello Antonin, and their advisors stood behind them. For the king, that was Parselev and the captains. Kiefan hung back, watching but not involved. Theo withdrew smoothly, as did his Suevi counterparts, as the talk began. I drifted with them, as my teacher had wanted, when Theo moved further to the side and broke into a grin. He pulled the older of the two Suevi men into a quick hug and pats on the shoulder.

Theo saw me coming and switched from Suevi back to Alemannic. "Master Eadgard Bídon, my mother's brother," he said of the man he'd embraced. Turning a little further, he repeated that in a lower voice; Kiefan joined us, hands clasped behind his back. Captain Rostislav trailed just behind him, hand on his sword, eyes flicking to the dozen Arceal knights — though they might as well have been statues on horses for all the attention they paid.

Bídon was gone grey, but a few streaks of ashy blond lingered in his hair and beard. His eyes, in a deep-lined face, were bright and yet sad as he looked at Kiefan. The younger Suevi was brown-haired and a bit coarse-featured; he kept his brow ever furrowed as if in thought.

"The other is Abrecan Dennode," Theo said. "One of my uncle's associates."

Kiefan nodded to them both. "Herr Bídon, it's good to finally meet you. Wodenberg will not soon forget all you've done." The older man dipped a shallow bow with his eyes shut. Kiefan asked, "Is there any news?"

Bídon spun out a list of names and numbers, and I soon gathered that these were gentle-born families with command of knights and armsmen. Those that could be relied on, and those whose loyalty was less sure. He went on to specify those who were in the army outside our gates — few, and all of uncertain loyalty. "He chose his lackeys with care," Bídon said. "Our general is no fool."

Dennode, though silent, pursed his mouth and shifted from one foot to the other.

Kiefan nodded when Bídon finished. "Are you certain of this one?" he asked, and looked to Dennode.

"My cousin, m'lord," Bídon replied. "Theo met him —"

"It is true, then?" Dennode broke his silence. "That rumor of old. The last princess of Suevia, spirited off and made a queen in Wodenberg?"

He met Kiefan's cool gaze with a suspicious one. I hadn't heard anything about Queen Mercia being a last princess, but that held my ear well.

"The color of his eyes is sign enough," Bídon answered, voice low.

Kiefan's grey eyes? They weren't common, true. Blue and green were.

Dennode folded his arms across his chest, face held carefully neutral. His mouth quirked to one side.

I saw only a flash of kir, heard a hiss and then blades broke loose with a yell. Captain Rostislav fell from Blessing speed onto the paving-stones in a splash of blood. Dennode danced back, an impossibly long, white blade in his hand swooping up from a low guard as Kiefan sprang at him and they both blurred again.

A sharp, hollow crunch and Dennode landed on his back, sword clattering from his limp hand. A shockwave of kir burst from him along with the spray of blood. Kiefan lunged over him, sword ready if he should move, but the freed kir was sign enough; he was dead. His chest had staved in like a smashed box.

And in a heartbeat, the fair skin and brown hair melted away in a twinkle of kir to reveal dark curls and tanned skin. My blood ran cold for a moment. A cambifax? Here? Not in a fable to frighten children?

I nearly had a chance to exhale, but shouted orders in Arceal and hooves thundering all around caught it in my throat. Swords rasped from sheaths and someone yelled "Hedge!"

On the parapet above, an archery officer hollered, "Ready!"

Hands grabbed me and I found myself pressed between Kiefan and Theo when a louder voice boomed through the noise.

"Hold! Hold!!" King Wilhelm stood with sword in hand, the table flung aside against the tavern's face. Captain Aleks flung deSvello face-down on the road and put her boot on his back. Bared swords hung at ready on all sides; the Arceal knights circled with horses' rumps in the center, our Guard wedged between them and Kiefan, the unarmed Arceal officers facing Parselev's kir-lit hands. The warhorses jittered, held on hard reins a moment after being spurred.

"What treachery is this!" The king looked to Captain Aleks and she yanked the Voice up by the shoulders.

"I knew nothing!" deSvello put up one hand, to swear. "My life to the Empress, I have no part in it!"

I heard a burbling cough, despite the shouting that ensued. Captain Rostislav. He lay on the street gasping; I landed on my knees beside him, reaching into my bag for a blood-stop. "Elect!"

Dennode's blade had caught him low across the throat, cut through his windpipe and enough veins to flood the wound. The blood-stop clotted the lesser bleeding. I called his kir and pinched off the largest cut vein. Captain Rostislav convulsed with the force of his cough, the blood foaming red from his windpipe. Drowning. I wove a charm and swept it through his lungs, scraping off the blood, and with one hard heave he threw it all out in a clotty mouthful. He near retched as well as it splattered onto the road.

Part III: Embers on the Wind

He drew a harsh but clear breath. I'd spent some kir earlier to cleanse a deep abscess, and had none now for the captain's vein. The break in his windpipe hissed as he panted; he had a little kir left but I'd need it for a cleansing charm. There weren't any in my bag.

"Charm-hand?" I asked, looking up. Only knights, around me, easing back from what would've been a massacre. They glanced down at me with worried faces — Theo and Bídon stood by me, to be sure I wasn't trampled by hooves, and Kiefan was in the argument around the envoy — as they sidled back to their original formation, but none were charm-handed.

My teacher stood watching, too, with arms folded. He reached out one hand. "Take it."

I took his hand and called. The kir swirled in him, deep and strong, but didn't come. I called harder, not wanting to fail with so many eyes on me. It swirled again, coy.

I was its master. Strong as the howling wind on Starknadel. I demanded it.

The kir, as if it had lost interest, barely stirred.

My held breath slouched out of me.

Parselev spun the charm through me, sending it down my arm and into Captain Rostislav. The captain's windpipe knit shut and his slashed throat closed before my eyes. He fell limp as the pain faded, eyes sliding shut for a moment, and then levered himself into sitting up.

My teacher pulled me to my feet by my hand. "It was good —"

"Let him keep his head," Kiefan announced, striding back. "He can return this one."

DeSvello sat on his knees before the king, hands spread and empty, his fellow officers kneeling with him. Swords surrounded them, held by King's Guard.

Kiefan set his boot on Dennode's ruined chest, bones crunching further, and tore the man's head off with a hard twist. He slung it and the Voice caught the bloody thing in his belly, was knocked onto his ass by the impact.

King Wilhelm kicked him for good measure. "Get out of my city. You! What did you know of this?" He pointed, with his drawn sword, at Kaufmann and Bídon. "Captain!"

Rostislav had the old man thrown down on the street in a heartbeat. Theo blocked the captain's attempt to grab him — and stopped his second swing with the ease of a strength-Blessed. But then he showed both empty palms and dropped to his knees on his own.

"I knew nothing, Majesty," Theo answered. "Neither did my uncle."

"You would say so."

"I swear it," Bídon shouted, from the ground. "My life to the Empress." His raised, empty hands trembled.

Kiefan shook blood from his boot and stepped toward the two of them. At a nod, Rostislav hauled Bídon up by a handful of cote. I sidled closer, too, as voices lowered.

"How much did the cambifax know of the royalists?" Kiefan asked, switching the conversation to Alemannic.

"I've hardly seen him since we left Temitte," Bídon said. "The fever of the camp, I thought. Much of what he heard, I said here."

"That may be enough, though," my teacher said. A kir-vine shot from his hand and snatched Bídon from the captain's grip. "No more risks, for now. Be loyal to the Empress, however you must play-act it."

The Suevi officer near the king scrambled to his feet. "Majesty —" He met Captain Aleks' blade, leveled at his throat, with only a flinch. "The old man's no threat to Wodenberg."

Parselev spared him a glance and let Bídon drop. "Only another lackey of the Empress, Majesty," my teacher announced.

The king flicked a hand, dismissing it all.

"Be careful, Uncle," Theo murmured.

"My love to the old fox." Bídon winked, and then asked Kiefan, "Send me off harshly, m'lord?"

Kiefan pulled him up by the collar and shoved him toward Captain Rostislav. "Put that filth on a horse!" The captain took the lead and hauled him off to the waiting palfrey without letting the old man catch his balance.

Once the saint's door closed behind our guests, it was a little easier to breathe. I ventured back to the headless corpse for another look; a cambifax, a monster I'd heard of in stories of the Winter Wood that the Shepherd banished bad sheep to. Cambifaxi were liars, deceivers, not like honest shape-shifters who only took animal forms. The body looked ordinary enough, from what I could see. I'd thought they were soft, gooey things whose touch made your skin crawl.

Several pairs of boots joined me around the mess.

"Woden would've torn all their heads off and thrown them over the wall," Parselev said.

"In that, perhaps I'm not so much his disciple," Kiefan replied. "Even the head of our best informant in Temitte?"

Parselev made a vague noise and bent to pick up the blade the cambifax had dropped. Not so long as our knights', perhaps, and no cross-guard to speak of. Slender and elegant. Its sallow tint gave it away.

"Bone?" I asked.

"Yes, bone. Not his, to be certain, but they can slip by even the closest inspection."

"He turned my blade with it." Kiefan put out a hand, and my teacher passed it to him. "A strange thing."

"One must be careful of shape-shifters," Parselev said, echoing what Saint Aleksandr had said. "The Empress trains them well. Not even a whiff of kir off him, though he must've been elect. Kate, I must teach you how to spot hidden elect and saints." Then he looked to Kiefan. "You harvested him? Anything of use you can glean?"

Kiefan's head tipped. "Harvested?"

"And why would Woden tell you of that?" Parselev shook his head with a grimace. His sigh was more a growl. "At the moment of death, the mind's kir loses its grip on the body. As does all the kir, but it's the mind's kir you must call. Put a hand on him, if need be, but draw it out. Claim his skill, his power for yourself."

"Why would Woden keep that from me?" Kiefan asked. "For all his driving to strengthen me? I'm his own blood."

Parselev muttered, "So was Prince Wolfgang. It's because the control of knowledge is the control of people — mark that well. And next you face an elect, don't fail to claim your due."

CHAPTER 6

"Saint Cambifax was a shape-shifter, so ancient that he had forgotten his true form. The Empress claims that he trained her, and she calls her creatures by his name," Parselev had explained to Kiefan and me, after the King's Council met to lay out the full events of the parley.

"Most shifters, like Saint Aleksandr, prefer animal forms but the cambifax are infiltrators and assassins. They take human faces, and hide their charms well."

"If Saint Woden had joined in the parley —" I said.

"Saints do not parley with envoys, in war. They speak only to saints, and they do not use words."

I had repeated, for the King's Council, all that I witnessed in Kiefan's meeting with Bídon and described the Blessing-sped duel that followed. It had been a bone dart, flicked from under the shifter's skin and shot at Kiefan's eye, that started the attack. Only in finely sliced memories could I see the throw, Kiefan's twitch aside, and the cambifax's arm stretching to spring the impossible sword. Captain Rostislav, to his credit, had been first to move in Kiefan's defense and taken a slash across the throat.

"My anticipation piqued the moment he hesitated," Kiefan had said. "Nothing clear, but enough that I was at speed when he struck. I'd have been dead, without the saints."

I kept returning to how the bone blade had shot from the cambifax's arm, its point emerging from the heel of his hand. If one could hide a sword in one's arm, what of one's elbow?

"Kate?"

Anders' voice broke me away from it. He stood beside me, balanced on one foot with the other set just above his knee. Distracted by the disastrous parley, I couldn't manage the Tree Pose so well; Anders had focus to spare on noticing that I wasn't even trying.

"Only thinking," I said. I couldn't help remembering his horse ears, though. They were far more fitting to him than hidden darts and swords. He was no monster of the Winter Wood, no spy or assassin.

I put the thought aside and followed the disciple's dance, in a minimal way, trying to focus on the grass under my feet. Mud was finally giving way to green, in the courtyard. Birds sang in budding trees. Spring, at last. As I spent my days in the hospital, it was good to be out in the sun on Saint-days.

And my mind kept slipping back to the impact of Kiefan's fist on the cambifax's chest, splitting the breastbone and caving in the ribs. Crushing the heart against the spine.

"Is it the baby?" Anders asked, once the Ther gave us leave from the disciple's dance.

"The cambifax," I said.

"I wish I'd seen that. Captain put me near the back. I was fighting to stay awake and missed all three heartbeats of excitement."

"Why? Nothing exciting about —" I frowned, folded my arms. I'd been only a yard from Kiefan when the dart was thrown, and it had been Theo who pulled me back. Though as we had no speed Blessings, by the time we two knew what was happening it was over.

Anders waited for me continue, but I didn't. "It's been dull up at the gate house," he said. "But I mustn't waste my kir practicing horse-charms, so there's only card games and drills to pass the time."

"Keep to the horse-charms," I said, voice lowering. "That thing came to kill."

A frown creased his brow and his hand brushed my shoulder, meaning to comfort but awkward in its uncertainty. Anders hadn't done more than touch my hand since our wedding kiss and I had kept the same distance.

The courtyard swirled with chatting whorls of nurses, orderlies, and the half-healed patients who could come out for the dance and to set up for the communal meal. Anders tipped his head toward the lone maple in the center, away from the bustle. I didn't much want to be overheard, so I walked with him to its leafless shade. The maple's twigs were red with sap, overhead, and its buds bulging.

Anders stepped close. "If you think I've any interest in shifting to another human form," he said, "I don't. If I can choose between another man's face, or four hooves and the strength to race the wind? That Arceal shifter chose poorly."

"A knight who is a horse?" A faint smile picked up the corner of my mouth. "A strange cavalry that would make."

He shrugged. "Wars don't last forever. I can be a knight without a cavalry."

On that thought, I remembered. "My bag." I'd left it on the bench under the maple, a few steps away. I had it untied in a moment and dug around inside for the smallest bundle.

Returning to him, I unspooled the runty bandage — most of ours were a yard long, but this one had seen better days and had been cut down to only two feet — and loosely skeined it. "I've used this one myself," I told him, "several times. It was easy to remember for being so ragged at the ends and getting worse with each use. I finally cut it down and re-hemmed it for you."

I took Anders' hand and put the linen strip in it. I'd asked around for what the proper words were so that I wouldn't bungle this again. I hummed the chorus of the Mother's benediction, which told the soldier that whatever he must do for duty, he'd be welcomed home. Then I said, "Please keep this so my hopes and prayers are close by you. Never doubt that I am hoping and praying for — your safe return."

The last part had to fight its way out as Anders' eyes met mine. There'd been much giggling about how much more one could give along with the token and the benediction, and I could see they were as much on his mind as mine. My heart quavered in my chest. His hand closed on the bandage and my hand, our fingers threading between each other.

No smile in his eyes as he leaned just a little, only a gentle, lulling focus. A brief touch, lips to lips. I knew that look; I'd seen it in Kiefan's eyes.

Fear jabbed me, and I flinched. Looked away.

Anders touched his lips to my forehead, where my Blessing ridges broke the skin. He squeezed my hand in his and took the token when he let go. "I'll wear it proudly, m'lady."

The day after the weekly meeting, Parselev and I rode down to the infirmary in one of the ambulance wagons. With us came half the hospital staff, as there would be work to do. Rain had lingered for a couple days, keeping the enemy from attempting to storm the gate again and allowing the infirmary in Sinnmach Square to be emptied. Neglected a little, as well. The kir-shield had kept the rain off, but we still meant to be sure that the cots were dry, the blankets aired out, and the surgery tables scrubbed. We had until noon to prepare, perhaps a bit longer, I had been told at the briefing.

Since the first attack on the gate, Arcea's army had set to constructing half a dozen trebuchets around the city walls from the West Tower to the East. Those towers marked the outermost curve of the walls, the point where on either side the slope became abruptly steeper, the earth too thin for trees, and the city walls moved back toward each other as they climbed up onto the Rückenstein that joined the castle's promontory to Mount Woden.

The trebuchets' wooden skeletons rose around the edge of the Spanne, the bowshot-wide meadow that lay between the city wall and the foulburg. I had seen them from the castle's roof, and Kiefan had explained the mechanisms to me. The enemy meant to break through the city walls.

"Saint Aleksandr raised them, surely he could mend them?" I asked.

"Not in six places at once. We'll even the score on that, though."

Saint Aleks was not even in the city; he had much to see to in the north. Spring was well settled on the Englic coast, now that it was mid-Field Moon, and the western mountain passes needed watching. They were still choked with snow, but if the Empress ordered troops through them, they would try to obey.

Saint Woden, alone, had sketched today's plan to the King's Council, using a broad map of the city to draw the lines of movement. The king had sat in his chair by the fire, deliberately silent and frowning. Kiefan had stood, hands clasped behind his back, nodding as his saint gave orders.

When noon came, the three companies of armsmen had arrived but the knights had not. There was some laughing about waiting for the horse-boys when the three captains came to the infirmary to ask Parselev about how the ambulances would be deployed. A squad of fifteen armsmen and their lieutenant was assigned as escorts for the three ambulances, to keep them safe.

The trumpet in the gate-tower blew and my pulse spiked a painful rush of blood into my head — but it wasn't an alarm. I didn't know the pattern it blew.

"They're asking where the knights are," Parselev told me. "Caught in final arguments, most likely. King Wilhelm cannot be pleased about this."

"It seemed a fair plan, as Saint Woden explained it. Why would the king argue?"

"Because he hasn't yet learned that all children die. I hope he will not need to."

That stopped me in my tracks. For a moment I saw something of my teacher's age, even though he appeared a bit younger than the king. My hand went to my belly and stroked it, thinking of the babies I'd seen buried. I felt mine kicking, some mornings, but that was no assurance of anything. My voice fell. "That must be a terrible thing."

Parselev's hand covered mine, pressed gently and the baby's patterns pulsed up. "Not so terrible when the child dies asleep, silver-haired and wrinkled. You've a good, strong baby, Kate. See to that first."

The sketch of the plan was to sortie from the city gate in two parties. One would turn westward and destroy the half-built trebuchets as far as the West Tower. The other would turn eastward to attack one trebuchet, and would draw the enemy's attention away from the westbound party so they'd be certain to destroy all three along the western wall. To be sure they had Arcea's eye, Kiefan would lead the eastbound sortie.

He came, late, with all the Prince's Guard and another four squads of knights as well. Half were to be escorts for the westbound sortie, the rest his own. The lot of them took some work to organize and there was the allocating of a wagon's worth of oil casks to be done.

Our infirmary had been ready at noon. The sun was off its peak now and we'd taken up a card game on my surgery table. Now we left off; one of the Ters began singing and we all joined in. It was a good thing to do, giving the men another benediction for their courage.

I watched the knights, scanning until I found the grey dapple whose knight wore a double linen-bandage tail on his helm. Will trailed behind him on foot, securing extra shields behind some of the riders. There was no shortage of squires, Anders had said, but Will had trouble saying no when asked to help.

Soon enough, they were assembled and unbarring the gates. Strength-Blessed men made quick work of it; the portcullis was half up when they pulled the inner doors open, and they began drawing the bars on the outer door before it was fully lifted.

At the head of the formation, as the outer gates cracked open, Kiefan brandished his sword and spurred his warhorse up on its hind legs. The men cheered to answer him, swords raised. A swoop of the blade around and up, catching the sun, and they roared again. The door opened, out onto the Spanne and the foulburg, as their voices chanted in the rhythm set by Kiefan's sword. His warhorse spun around and plunged toward the enemy.

My voice trembled to a stop and I clenched my hands together. Both of them out there, charging into the enemy's teeth… my stomach turned over, knotted itself.

"They're in the Father's hands," Parselev announced, gesturing for us to see to our work. "Soon they'll be in ours."

That proved true. Half a company, fifty armsmen, stayed to block the gate, but left a gap for our ambulances to come and go. Men trickled back to us, some with arrows, some gashed by swords. I was to be a surgeon, today, with Ther Adalslav to assist me and Krepkin's apprentice Meinrad to manage triage. I extracted an arrow from deep in a man's liver. With care, I stitched each of the holes left in the layered coils of a man's stabbed gut. Adalslav helped me work the shattered, jutting ends of a thigh bone back into the flesh and held them in alignment as I spun enough kir to keep the knight from the Shepherd's shadow.

"Charm-hand." I reached out and a hand touched mine, gave me kir. "Who's next?"

"They're cut off. The gate." Ther Adalslav pointed. I had been so focused on the bone-setting charm that I hadn't heard the roaring and crashing.

Giants, I thought at first, for they loomed over the armsmen by head and shoulders. They wore lamellar armor and helms crested with great tufts of red hair; they stabbed down at the armsmen with heavy spears longer than ours. It was when one reared to lash with his hooves that I knew they were centaurs.

The armsmen made a shield-wall against them, bristling with blades, and the archers above could not miss. But those heavy spears smashed through shields, piercing the wall, and the arrows peppered into their lamellar mattered nothing. The one that did fall took an arrow in his helm's eye-slit, a hard shot even for hawk-eyed archers.

The monsters surged forward, through the gate, pushed from behind by their brothers. Smashing over our armsmen, shields against shields. Trampling. Breaking through. Charging.

"Elect!" My voice tore free. He looked up from his patient's guts. "Meinrad!"

Meinrad had seen them too; he whistled to the ambulance driver who'd been about to head up to the hospital and the man twisted, pulling the horses to a stop.

"Behind the wagon!" Parselev ordered, pointing. I felt kir arc to him, from some far distance, and he poured it into his patient. Ter Biya picked the man up and hauled him away. Patients who could, struggled to their feet, reaching for their swords. I threw a glance back and saw centaurs pouring through the break in the armsmen's formation.

An armsman with a bandaged thigh struggled on his cot. I grabbed his hand and pulled, got him to his feet. He drew his sword and charged the oncoming enemy with a yell. I turned, watching him go, and —

Hooves. Roaring. Shouting. The noise struck my ears, set my heart racing, and the din faded as fear seized me. Centaurs charged across Sinnmach Square, dripping spears high, their lamellar tunics and blankets spattered with blood, in a wedge pointed straight at our infirmary. They cut through the handful of wounded men in their way. Pounded straight at the Elect standing between them and us helpless disciples.

I threw myself toward him, suddenly furious that he'd face them alone. My kir rose to my hands. If I could touch one, I could kill even a monster. I could — I made a shield of what kir I had and threw it to him, spinning out a thin tendril to keep it connected to me as it went. Catching it, my teacher tethered it to his hand as he shook out his own kir into weapons.

Parselev threw a crescent Shepherd's knife and the lead centaur collapsed mid-pace. "Elect!" the second roared, lunging with his spear. The rest yelled it too. A green glow rose on the lead spear's black head, trailing sparks. Parselev's second kir-blade flew through his chest. Carried on his speed, the spear stabbed even as the monster fell.

He struck my shield and the flash of kir on kir tore through my arm like a hot knife. His weight knocked me off my feet as my shield unraveled. The black spear point burst through my teacher's back as if seeking me as well.

Part III: Embers on the Wind

I felt him call for kir, but I had no more. It arced to Parselev from far away, from the nurses huddled behind the wagon, and swirled around him in green folds. Another crescent knife shot out and dropped a third centaur.

The second spear took him through the ribs, and white-hot sparks crackled from its edges as the monster blasted kir through the blade. Parselev sank clawed fingers on the shaft and power shot back up at the centaur, tearing the monster's meat from his bones, fingertips to shoulders to head in a cloud of blood.

I must've been screaming, but all I could hear was the arcing kir.

He turned, my teacher, my second father, his grey hair falling to white. His face sinking into wrinkles. His true age claiming him as his life unraveled under a third spear-strike — but his eyes blazed and he reached for me. Shouting. I was deaf, frozen, but knew what he wanted. Not to let them take him.

Rage and defiance jolted me free of the paralysis. I grabbed his thinning hand and demanded his kir.

And all vanished in a golden blaze.

CHAPTER 7

The world spun and heaved in waves. My feet were in the air, nothing under me. I flew like a banner by an anchor at the back of my neck.

My eyes opened and I saw the city gates, standing open, and the towers. Arrows hissed down toward me. And the Spanne's fresh spring grass stretched as the gates drew away.

A dun centaur had me by a handful of my dress, racing down River Road outside the wall.

I screamed from the depths of my soul. I thrashed, scrabbled at the centaur's lamellar blanket, kicked and got tangled in his hind-leg for a moment. Pain burst across my back. He nearly stumbled, but shook me loose and then slapped my head against the breastplate across his horse-chest. The world spun, fading toward darkness.

Which street we turned down, I missed, but I didn't slip away entirely. I still screamed. My fingers found the thick, hard hand gripping my dress and I reached for my kir. Nothing. Parselev had drained me. Through the hand I'd grabbed, I called to the centaur's kir.

It stirred, at first, but then he clenched it tight and I heard him snarl at me from over-head. Looking up, I saw the dark eyeslit of his helm pointed at me, the grille cut in the face a steel-toothed grin. Strength drained out of me, leaving only cold terror.

I gulped a breath and looked away. The centaurs slowed, now, shouting and brandishing their bloody spears. Packed earth below gave way to grass, and I glimpsed an array of tents around a campfire. This had been a garden plot beside a prosperous home.

Horse-bodies milled in a ring around the fire, with more whooping and rough slaps in congratulations. My centaur held me up above the press, and I was cheered as a prize.

"Red Hoof! Red Hoof!"

The chant rose, in Arceal, spears pumped in the air. My centaur lowered me, my feet finding the ground and my back pressed against his horse-breastplate. Across the gap and the fire, I saw both the banner posted beside the camp's central fire — a black centaur with red hooves, on a white field — and the two centaur officers howling with their squadron. I guessed they were officers; the edges of their blood-spattered lamellar scales were gilt, as the Arceal envoy's had been.

A hand grabbed my breast and pulled. I twisted and tried to shove away. The bay-and-white paint centaur beside me laughed and groped my other breast. My captor shuffled back, turning, and pulled off his helm to smack the paint with. Both were horse-faced; nose and mouth drawn out into a bit of muzzle, flaring horse-nostrils, and horse ears pinned back. Growls turned to sharp snarls, showing oversized teeth.

"No pigging on captives!" the paint snapped.

"Touch her not, Stel! That elect did reach to her, la."

"His bitch, fool, and whelp too. Saints will wish it dead, and I've the gear to do it."

The paint yanked my arm and my dress tore in the dun's hand. Pain jolted across my shoulder and my knees buckled off balance, dropping me to the ground beside the paint centaur. Where I got a good look at a stallion-sized cock eager for action.

I screamed, lunged away and clawed at his wrist. He laughed and grabbed me in both hands, heaving me in the air level with his half-horsey face. His tongue snaked out at me, glistening, and my stomach knotted up its fear into convulsive hate. The centaur's kir sprang up at my call, blooming across his vast, intricate patterns, twisted into a blade and slashed across his prime meridian between human head and equine heart.

His eyes bulged, then rolled, and he dropped like a sack of rocks. I landed on my ass, crying from the pain, and rolled onto my back toward the campfire. The ring of centaurs surged up with a shout, spears in hand. Looking up at them, my Blessing called back that glimpse of the paint's pattern, all his glorious whorls and meridians, and the beauty knocked the breath from me.

And the terror.

"The saints claim her!" one of the officers bellowed, over the voices and hooves. "The saints claim her! Their questions afore —"

A fearful shout, in the voices, and crashing steel. Centaurs turned as best they could in the close quarters, defending with their spears, and skittered toward the fire as they were pushed from behind. Their hooves, red indeed, advanced on me; I heaved to my feet and felt heat at my back. Searched for a gap but saw none. Trampling, or the fire.

I saw a steely blur slice the arm from a chestnut, followed by his head despite the helm. The iron bucket, gashed and spewing blood, thumped at my feet. Over the falling chestnut leaped a black-bay horse, his knight throwing up his shield to deflect the dun centaur's spear. Twisting in the saddle, the knight stabbed into the lamellar, putting half the length of his blade into the monster's human belly. The dun fell to his knees, screaming.

Shepherd-moon crest, silver epaulette rings — Kiefan twisted back, leaving his sword in the centaur, and reached to me. I grabbed with both hands. He pulled me up and I landed between the pommel and his lap. My arms latched around his neck and I was safe again.

Pip spun nimbly and Kiefan pulled his sword from the dun's gut. On Kiefan's left, a black warhorse and Captain Rostislav, by his rank brasses. On the right, Nipper bulled against a centaur's rump and Anders slashed across the exposed hind leg.

"River Road," the shout went up. "River Road!"

I pressed my face against Kiefan's tabard, fingers digging into his mail through the wool. Pip moved under me, and Kiefan turned. Steel crashed on wood, close by, but I clenched my eyes shut. Pain throbbed in my arm, my head, in my hips and legs, dull and far away. I was out of kir. But our baby was safe between us and Kiefan would get me home.

"Swords!" someone shouted. "Swords!"

"Run them down! Break through!"

My eyes could just peek over Kiefan's shoulder as he rode. Near a dozen knights followed us at a trot, three abreast. Sound ebbed back into my ears through the pounding of my heart: waves of shouting, the slap of swords against shields, Kiefan's breath harsh inside his helm. Under me, Pip broke into a long-legged pace and leaped over something. I glimpsed a man cowering behind a square shield, pressed up against a cottage wall as the column rode by. One of the knights left off beating his shield to swing at him in passing, knocking him to his knees. I heard screams as I lost sight of him under following horses.

The houses on either side fell away into sunlight. On River Road, the knights spread out fast, swooping around and picking up more speed. Behind us, a wall of Arceal infantry shields, square and solid, spears bristling, filling the broad street. It was a straight ride up to the gate and safety, though. I turned, straining over my shoulder, to see home.

Ahead, a wall of Arceal infantry shields, spears bristling, filling the broad street. Beyond, the city gates stood closed.

My pulse shot up again and my mind went blank.

"West!" Kiefan yelled. "West!" They all shouted it.

The knights leading angled to the left, toward the corner of the phalanx, and twisted in their saddles to be ready on the right. Anders, on my right, pulled a little forward; the prince's standard-bearer, riding just ahead, had only his sword to defend himself with. Captain Rostislav slipped around, too, so that Kiefan and I would be furthest from the infantry on the outside.

My neck ached, but I couldn't look away as the column clipped the wall's corner. Swords knocked spear-heads aside and the horses charged, chests crashing through the square shields. One slipped and pitched headfirst into the close-packed infantry, throwing the knight to his death but tearing a gash in the line. Anders deflected a second-row spear up across his shield and swung into its owner. The impact rocked him in the saddle but he ripped through, sword coming up crimson. Whoever Nipper landed on wasn't sufficient to stop the big horse. Pip slipped and skidded under me, regained his footing, and charged on.

We plunged off River Road onto the Spanne. Kiefan kicked Pip and the horse accelerated across the grass with the rest. A half-built trebuchet, burning, marked the trail of the westbound sortie. Corpses lay all around it. And as we passed, men ran out from between the cottages and set their feet at ready, drawing back bows.

"Archers behind!" someone yelled. "Cover!" Kiefan's shield shifted on reflex, to cover his back.

A few of the enemy fell with shafts in them. On the wall above, our own archers lent us aid. But the rest of the enemy loosed, and shields rang from the strikes. A knight just behind us caught a shaft in his shoulder with a yell. Beside me, Nipper leaped over a horse fallen and tumbling across the grass. Behind Pip, other riders angled hard to miss the stricken horse and knight. My heart tore, watching them fall behind.

We passed a second burning trebuchet.

Captain Rostislav shouted, "Hold the saint's door!"

From the tower, a trumpet blasted out a cavalry withdrawal. I turned around again to see. Near the last burning trebuchet, the westbound sortie took their leave of Arcea and fell back through the wall. The enemy had mustered a phalanx of infantry there, too, and the knights beat against their shield wall while our armsmen retreated through the saint's door. Warhorses skipped backwards as their riders slashed off enemies, fighting their way free to withdraw as well. Archers loosed from above with hawk-eyed accuracy to cover the knights. Once free, they cantered for the opening in the wall. The Arceal infantry hunkered behind their shields, hiding from the arrows.

"Hold the door! Tell Woden!"

Could any of them hear us? They had to see the prince's banner. They had to.

I gripped Kiefan tighter. Over his shoulder, the dozen knights behind us had dropped to ten. Beyond them, kir blossomed intense and bright, pulling my eyes to River Road and a few distant forms. Kiefan tensed under me, feeling it too, and he twisted to look.

One form raised a hand and slung a little sun after us. White-hot, it spread out long wings in an arc as it swooped across the Spanne. Its reach brushed walls on either side as it gained faster than any horse could run.

The true Shepherd's knife could clear a battlefield, Parselev had told me. My scream strangled down to a tiny "No!" as I grabbed for kir.

"Father's fucking mercy!" Kiefan pulled kir too, his call strong and clear.

The scraps nearby shot to us like arrows. Kiefan had a little left too and I felt him spread it out in a sheet, echoing the shield he threw across his back again. In a heartbeat, I knew it would save us two but all around us would die.

I reached through Kiefan, into his charm, and spun a thin vine from the shield. Pushed it off his actual shield and pulled it up in line with the kir-blade; at the prodding of a strange memory, I focused the kir down to a curved bow counter to the Shepherd's relentless culling knife.

The hind-most three knights and horses, running all-out, dropped under its edge. One somersaulted fully, her rider limp as a rag doll. I pushed my shield harder, past the four following closest, and felt my vine thinning to the verge of breaking. It would unravel if that snapped. The Shepherd took one, two, three more, ignoring armor, training, Blessings, and prayers. Without a sound, they slumped an instant before their horses fell dead.

The Shepherd's knife hit my thin shield, flexed across its bowed edge, and both shattered in a shower of stars. The blow struck my arm numb to the shoulder. All four horses behind us shrieked in terror under the spray of sparks and ran harder with their knights cursing.

Stone clattered under Pip's hooves. The wall shot by and filled my view. Behind the last four knights, the saint's door snapped shut. I pressed my face back into Kiefan's shoulder, his arm tight around me. Pip slowed to a canter, swinging around wide.

Noise crowded around, little more than a windy rushing in my ears. I vaguely felt Kiefan shift under me to raise his sword high. My mind was full of blood and light, the breaking kir-blade, Parselev's eyes and the leering centaur's. Kiefan's mail pressed circles into my numb fingers, solid and real. The pulse in my throat raced ahead of my heaving lungs. Safe. Home. My baby safe inside me, kir swirling happily when I checked.

Pip slowed to a trot, then a walk. Kiefan's arm left me to sheathe his sword and a little noise twisted out of my throat. His arm returned, squeezed me close. "You're safe," he said, close by my ear.

A hand closed on my arm, tugged, and the paint centaur's leer flashed in my eyes, then his cock. I screamed, but fought the panic back. I'd struck that monster down. Dead.

"Don't touch her!" Kiefan slapped the hand away. Then he yanked his helm off and hissed, "I pulled her out of that hell. Not you."

"M'lord!" Gregor called, over hooves trotting up alongside.

Kiefan tossed the helm. "Take this. And the shield. Find the Elect, bring him right away to see to Kate."

Parselev. Stabbed. Dying. Centaurs howling for his blood. My eyes flooded and sobs clawed through my clenched throat. And in the same instant, I saw myself glassy-eyed, horrified, reaching for a hand I held out. Pain. Horrible, ripping pain… my throat was raw, but I screamed again.

"You're safe. We're safe, Kate. Safe inside the wall." Kiefan's breath caressed my ear as I sobbed. "The Elect will be sure you're well, you and the baby."

The blaze of my teacher's kir echoed in my eyes. A million patterns crammed and piled till they were a blinding sheet. My Blessing ridges throbbed in my scalp, aching.

"The Elect's dead, m'lord," Gregor said.

"What?" Pip came to a stop. Kiefan's voice fell off. "What happened here?"

"The men saw it all. They felt the shockwave, they said, and the Elect fell into dust. The centaurs grabbed Dame Kate and ran when the armsmen charged them. Those that survived pulled back to the Order."

I opened my eyes over Kiefan's shoulder and saw the city gates, the towers, knew we stood in the junction of River Road and Wallside Street. He was looking at the infirmary, the dead centaurs. Gregor, on a palfrey beside us, grimaced at the disaster in Sinnmach Square.

On the other side, a few steps back, Nipper shook his head. Anders sat with eyes fixed on me, mouth pressed in a hard line. His helm rested on the cantle, a streak of blood across its face. His grey horse ears twitched, and the corners of his mouth sank into melancholy. Looked away. Then he shifted a little. Nipper turned, flicking his tail, and jogged back down Wallside Street.

"Kiefan!" The king, a-horse, trotted to catch up with us. Face twisting in anger, he shouted louder. "Kiefan!" As the prince turned Pip, the king's voice dropped one notch. "Woden's approval does not give you leave to go haring off across the foulburg! Half the trebuchets stand untouched! They're certain to put a hole in the wall, with so many!"

My hands started to tremble, working Kiefan's tabard between my fingers. For me, he'd left off his mission?

"Your Guard's two dozen of our best and you waste half of them — if this is some camp whore you've —"

Kiefan's voice cut a cold line. "You'll not speak of her as anything but Dame Kate. I hared off to steal her back from Arcea and I'll ask no-one's forgiveness for that."

I peeked; the king's stern face was dark with anger. "You'd best explain to the saints why she's worth the whole city."

"Because I love her." Kiefan tapped Pip and turned him up River Road.

A sob twisted out of my throat. The city was too much. A dozen knights was too much. Six of them mown down behind us without a drop of blood. Too much, for me.

The tremble in my hands had spread to my whole body when Pip crossed the Order's courtyard to the hospital. My sobs fell directly into Kiefan's tabard, rolling out now that I was too tired to fight. I managed to loosen my grip on him only to wipe the tears away. I tried to tell him he shouldn't have left off his mission, but it came out in a twisted whine.

He touched a kiss to my forehead as Pip stopped before the hospital door. "Hold on," was all he said, and swung down from the saddle with me still clinging. Rather than setting me down, he adjusted his grip to my waist and knees.

"I can —" Orderlies bustled around an ambulance, helping fresh patients out, and we were drawing eyes.

He ignored me. With a nod to Gregor as he took Pip's bridle, Kiefan carried me through the open doors. "Who has charge here?"

One of the Ters answered, "Physician Krep — Dame Kate! It's Dame Kate!"

Feet came running and faces blurred past as my eyes welled up again. Wounded filled the hall, and the nurses came to gawp at me instead.

"Are you hurt?"

"He's in surgery — call him out!"

"Meinrad was just here, he'll be less sour."

I put out my hand to try to stop their fussing. "Don't. I'm well enough." Low in my back, the weight of my baby was rapidly turning to pain. My dress was sodden in a streak between my legs, and I recognized the smell; I'd lost control, from fear. Blood smears had soaked from off Kiefan's tabard where I'd clutched him. "I just need to clean up. Some willow tea. Charm-hand?"

Ter Holly reached to give me hers, and the kir washed into me warm and comforting. "The Elect's cottage, m'lord," she told Kiefan, pointing out the back door. "Heima will see to her."

He carried me across the hospital, past the surgery cubicle where Krepkin stood wiping his hands and pursing his mouth. Dread weighed down my stomach as Kiefan crossed the green herb garden; my head turned toward Parselev's cottage.

His cottage... he was gone.

Gregor ran ahead to open the door for us. I heard sobbing cut off sharply and saw Heima leap up from the bench, her eyes going wide. She wailed even louder, rushing to clutch my sleeve, and though her face was full of anguish she fell to her knees babbling in relief.

"Let me —" I had to hold her. Kiefan kept an arm around me to keep my weight off my throbbing legs as I folded down onto my knees to hug Heima. It ached, but she clutched at me and set me to crying again, too.

My eyes were drying out, though, and starting to itch. All my strength had gone with the tears. I held her against my shoulder, as much for support as comfort. "Let me up," I said, stroking her back. "I'm filthy and covered in bruises..."

"Bruises?" Heima put me out to arm's length, seeing me for the first time. "Oh, Kate, oh dear, you're... oh, m'lord!" She'd looked up at Kiefan.

My voice rasped in my throat, too. "Is my other dress clean?"

That clarified her. "Yes. Yes, I'll fetch it. And some tea." Heima pulled herself up and Kiefan lifted me easily by one arm around my waist. Her eyes went liquid again. "You're hurt! The baby?"

"No harm done," I said. My knees stabbed pain when I tried to stand, and my hands still shook.

"Hold on," Kiefan murmured, steadying me. I couldn't resist the chance to snuggle close under his arm and obey. Safe.

Heima hovered a moment more, hands out to catch me, but decided he could hold me up. She went to find my spare dress and shift in the folded laundry.

"How are you so calm?" I breathed, with a tired chuckle. Not the slightest tremble in his hands. I clenched mine, trying to still my nerves, and set my kir to mending my sprained knees and wrenched hip.

"All Woden's kin have steady nerves," he said. "Keep talking, though. The moment all quiets down, I'll drop and sleep like a rock. The morning after Ansehen, I woke covered in dried blood and mud."

Blood and sweat and horse rolled off him in a haze, but I caught a whiff of his lavender soap under it all. "You didn't soil yourself, at least."

His voice drifted, tired, and he shifted his grip on me. "The latrine's a vital part of preparing to ride."

"Here's your dress and shift." Heima brought them to the table, and turned to the kettle. "I've enough for tea and a little for you to wash with. When m'lord leaves." She threw Kiefan a glance, at that.

"I'll only go if Kate gives me leave."

My heart swelled in my chest, wanting him to stay. To talk, smile, hold me. And then my swollen heart sank under knowing he couldn't.

I straightened on my feet, testing them. Just aches, now. And the fatigue. When his arm lifted from me, my skin prickled goosebumps in fright. Exposed. Weak. My hand found his, gripped it.

"They said — the men said that Mechdan fell to dust. When all his kir broke free? Did he? Is that how he died?" Heima poured hot water onto mint leaves in two mugs.

My voice stumbled in my throat. I couldn't bear to tell her what the spears had done to him. "The blast knocked me cold," I said. "I didn't see."

"They said you were both gone. How did you rescue her, m'lord?"

"I broke off my sortie, outside the walls, and chased down the centaurs who carried her off. We slaughtered them at close quarters and I took her back."

But we had no elect, now, and the city walls would be broken. "Why leave off your mission?" I asked. "The trebuchets —"

"Do you think I'd leave you at Arcea's mercy?"

"Lost in the foulburg, and you found me?"

"And would do it again." He fixed me with serious, grey eyes. His hand fell to my belly, and his voice to a whisper. "To my last breath." Tears squeezed out when I shut my eyes. When Heima offered Kiefan one of the mugs, he declined with a shake of his head. "Will you be well?" he asked me.

I still felt raw, even after charming my pain away, but I nodded. The prince took my hand, kissed it — tearing at my heart — and took his leave. I stood in my teacher's cottage hugging myself, staring around at all Parselev's things.

Heima clucked her tongue and shut the open door, breaking my gloom. "Let's clean you up."

I peeled my wet dress and shift off and washed up with a small tub of warm water. Heima fussed that I'd lost my hair-pin and my braid hung loose, and she cooed over the bruises darkening across my lower back and thighs. I had spent my kir on the deeper damage, and left the rest to run its course.

My hands lingered over the stretch marks that streaked across my growing belly, for a moment. The baby's kir pulsed, safe inside layers of me.

"He's well?" Heima asked, my clean shift in her hands. "Thank the Mother," she said when I nodded. "It was Mechdan who told me I'd never have babies of my own. He asked me to come to Wodenberg and be his consort, as my husband had no use for me. He was always so kind to me."

I smiled, sad. "Kind to me, too."

She passed me my dress and laced her fingers together as I put it on. "He wanted you to have this. All of this, even the furniture and the pots."

Her sadness made me grab her arm as she collected my dirty laundry. "It's your cottage too," I said, making sure to meet her eyes. "I won't turn you out of your home, I swear."

Heima smiled, under her drying tears. "I'll be your keeper if you wish, Dame Kate. Till you're settled."

"Thank you."

I hauled myself to the bed by the fire, still aching, fatigue settling in. Willow tea would see to the rest of my aches — if I could find my medicine bag. My memory brought me the last glimpse I'd had of it, when I put it under the surgery table's feet, down in Sinnmach Square. Dropping down on the straw mattress, I heaved a sigh. The pillow caught me as the world faded again.

CHAPTER 8

I woke in a sweat, later that afternoon. My brain was a tangle of images: open wounds, diseased skin and shattered bones. Charms for every one crowded me in a jumble. I climbed from the bed, still sore and tired, needing to pee and hardly able to find my way for all the charms. Heima's hands caught mine and she steered me.

Then she plied me with willow tea — an ambulance driver had returned my medicine bag — and broth. She left the cottage door open and a steady trickle of Ters and Thers came to see us, to clasp my hand or hug Heima, and offer some little story about Elect Parselev. They excused my dazed face as the shock of losing my teacher. They weren't wrong.

My mind cleared slowly. I climbed the stairs to the office, stood there and looked at his empty chair in the midst of the books, papers, and herbs. The last messages to arrive before the siege was laid, from physicians in Prohzgrad and Kernweise, still lay atop his desk. His quill and ink pot lay to one side, waiting for him.

This would be mine, he'd said. The books, I was sure I could claim. The correspondences, the organizing of faraway Order hospitals and seeing that each town had a physician... I shook my head. Too much.

I picked up the ink pot and quill, descended the stair. The abbot had brought a funeral sack and it lay empty on the kitchen table, waiting for the honeyed oatcakes Heima was baking. Parselev had loved them; one would go in the sack. Inking the quill, I carefully wrote 'Mechdan Parselev' on its side, then wiped the point clean. With a candle's melted wax, I sealed the ink pot. Once cool, it and the quill went into the sack. He would want them, even at the Shepherd's Hearth.

Heima sat by the window, sewing my torn dress. More well-wishers knocked at the door. A royal messenger came, wanting news of me. For their majesties, he said, but likely he meant Kiefan.

Though I did little, my aches put me back in bed and I lay sorting out my memories of the attack, Parselev's death, the rescue, cataloging them and putting them away so they would trouble me no more. My memory of the Shepherd's knife pursuing me across the Spanne melted into another, very like it, in which I put up my hand and a broad, strong arc of kir spun out to break it. It wasn't a difficult charm; the size and the range were the challenge.

Beside me, a knight flourished his sword and shouted, "Wodenberg!" Across a broad meadow, the blue-painted enemy was coming with spears raised, shouting as they ran. Engls. I knew them from my father's stories. The knight flashed me a grin, and for an instant he was so like Anders that my heart stumbled. But he wore a silver prince's band. His hair was darker.

Elect Wolfgang, the king's younger brother, the memory told me. And he had —

Strong kir, nearby. My eyes popped open, looking on the darkened fireplace and its dim coals. Moonlight poured in the open window, dimming and brightening as a shadow moved through it. Boots scraped softly on the sill, kir glowed, and a silhouette alit before the hearth.

Tensed, I drew a slow breath and called my kir. Only a little answered; no fresh ration, thus it wasn't midnight yet. A dozen small charms raced through my mind, unbidden — little kir-needles, meridians to tweak and cause agony without killing. I'd never done such things. I'd never learned such charms. They were Parselev's.

The man straightened and turned to me, sketched in moonlight but I recognized him by his collar-long hair and beard. And by how he prowled, rather than walked, toward the bed. Saint Woden. I sat up and pushed the light blanket aside with a question forming on my lips.

He blurred and my jaw was in his iron hand, pulling me to my feet. I squawked, grabbing his arm for balance, and tried to pull away. Behind me, Heima stirred on her side of the bed, making a questioning noise.

A spark flicked from his finger and she fell back, snoring.

Ignoring all my pulling and twisting, Woden plucked my kir and it bloomed, only a spark as I was nearly drained but sounding a complex chord that hung in the air. A little green glow lingered in the back of the saint's eyes, eerily like the lamia at night.

Pulse throbbing hard, I whispered, "What, m'lord? What do you want, in the dark like this?" Who would hear me, if I screamed? He was our saint — who would stop him?

Woden let my jaw go, though he still loomed over me. "What did Mechdan tell you of binding?"

I blinked. "Of our disciple's bond? I read a little."

"Of binding elect."

There had only been the one page in the book he'd assigned me, and a few mentions of the Pool. The rest was children's tales. "Little, m'lord. I know what the stories say."

Woden smiled, and I mistrusted the look of it. His hand was on my arm and I was dragged halfway to the door in an eye-blink; I planted my feet to fight him but he yanked me off them. Through his hand, I flicked out my bit of kir in a needle, striking his meridian hard at the elbow. I wrenched my arm from his grip when the pain loosened it.

And suddenly was on the floor, my head spinning, blood in my mouth. I gasped a breath and felt two teeth fall onto my tongue. Woden towered above, kir falling in a nimbus around him. Sudden weight pressed me to the floor.

"Someday Qadeem will learn to teach his disciples respect."

The door banged and a shadow fell on me. "This is my disciple. I'll teach her as I please."

I looked up from the floor, the pain in my jaw tearing a hole in my mind. Tears rolled down my face. Saint Qadeem's cloak dragged across me as he shifted from straddling me to standing full before Woden, not cowed by the inches and muscle the man had on him. The weight on me lifted and I raised myself on trembling arms.

"You took so long in laying your claim, any would think you meant to leave her rogue," Woden said.

"Let there be no questions, then. She was my elect's choice blessed, and she will take his place."

Woden withdrew a fraction of a step. With a glance to me, he said, "You drew the kir, then, for the shield you put up against the Shepherd's blade. Kiefan was too drained, he said."

On my knees, I spat the two teeth out, getting a handful of blood too. "He drew it," I lisped. "Each time I've tried, it's fought me. Kiefan spun it and I —" What the proper term was, I didn't know, and the pain wouldn't let me find it.

Kir gushed through me and I gasped again; two bright threads snatched the teeth from my hand and set them back into my jaw. The pain faded.

"See to your own disciples," Qadeem said, folding his arms. "If I find she's ready, she'll be properly bound and acclaimed as my elect. We can make two of it, if the prince is ready."

A frown settled on Woden. "He wasn't able to draw on command." Still, he moved to the door. "She's a fierce one," Woden said, over his shoulder as he opened it. "Good."

My head still spun a bit. I'd as soon skip the chance to impress him further.

"Gentle Woden." With a flick of kir, Saint Qadeem shut the door behind him. Putting a hand on my shoulder, my saint knelt beside me. "May I sound you?"

I nodded and he did it, ear cocked to all the notes that rang. "I felt the blades Mechdan took. I felt him die, and came quick as I could. Know this, Kate — in his last moment, he thought only of giving you all he could. You were a daughter to him. He's glad you harvested him, surely, but I am sorry it had to be thus."

Of all the heartfelt sympathy from that afternoon, what I saw in Qadeem's black eyes touched me most. Tears thickened and I wiped at them.

"You'll need time to make sense of so much. It may feel like madness, taking in your first harvest, but you will always be yourself. He is gone, but for what you gleaned." Standing, he offered me his hand — long-fingered, uncalloused — to help me up. My aches were gone, all of them, I found. Qadeem said, "Let us walk. Bring your cloak against the chill."

I reached for my dress, the light-spun, yellow one, and pulled it over my linen shift. "It's a warm evening, m'lord. This is enough."

He smiled. "It's never truly warm in Wodenberg. Come."

By how he kept his light wool cloak wrapped close, I had to believe he thought it cool. Outside, the full Shepherd and three of his Flock shone in a cloudless sky. Qadeem walked and I trailed a step behind out of habit; he beckoned me closer and I obeyed. We crossed the herb garden toward the chapel gate, rather than heading for the main gate. This rear gate was latched on the inside, but his kir-vines swung it open for us and shut it behind us.

We stood on High Street, near the Great Chapel. Few were out so late at night, but Saint Qadeem drew up a bit of kir and cast a green hush sphere around us, the same that my teacher had used for privacy when my pregnancy was discovered. My memory showed the charm to me.

"Only as a precaution," Qadeem said as he began to walk toward the castle. The hush sphere followed, centered on him. "Woden returned to the fount and Aleksandr is in Rukharbor. I must ask something of you, once again too much and too soon. But it must be done as the enemy is at our gates. Will you be bound as my elect, Kate?"

I blinked. He was only a few inches taller than me, and at his serious tone and closeness I felt a queasy shift in my stomach. "Me? Why?"

"So that you may draw from the Pool, even if only at limited range, should the worst come to pass."

"But I haven't drawn kir from anyone, yet."

"If that's true, then you sleep undisturbed by Mechdan's memories and charms. Do you?"

My feet slowed for a moment. "I called the kir for the shield, then?"

Qadeem's brows rose. "Did you?"

Even in my perfect memory, I wasn't certain. Pressed up against Kiefan, fear blazing through my veins — "I can't say, m'lord. But why?" I asked again, the question I'd wanted to ask for so long bubbling up at last. "Why me?"

"What's done in the heat of a moment may not be fully mastered for some time yet. Ordinarily, Elect are acclaimed when they can draw kir at will. But we've need and you've done well when asked too much of, before."

"No, why a peasant girl, m'lord?" I dared look him in the eye, in asking. He was still warm olive brown, even in the blue moonlight, and his hair black as the night. Browner and blacker than Arceal men, even. "Why did you disciple me?"

He smiled and gathered his cloak close as he answered. "Often, the correct Blessing is a matter of aligning the child's discipleship with the talents he already shows. Your husband, for an example, being of Woden's blood already had an affinity for the sword. He also has a skill with animals which would blossom regardless, so for Blessings he was claimed by Woden.

In certain cases, the correct Blessing is a matter of encouraging talents that are less dominant. You would be hard-pressed to make Woden see that scholarship runs in his blood — likely he'd blame it on Seaxneat's, brought in by the queen — but Kiefan is and ever will be bookish by nature. Thus he was pushed and pushed harder than I thought wise, in truth. Blessing-days of royal blood are always marked by much disagreement."

Qadeem paused as we turned the first rising switchback that led to Castle Kaltkern's outer gate. "In the last instance, a Blessing is given entirely for the chances it will put in a child's path. We have given hawk's eyes to children with no inclination toward the hunt, we've given craft-hands to those with no trace of art, and on occasion we've given memory Blessings to otherwise quite ordinary peasant girls. Perhaps not entirely ordinary." He nodded to me as he modified this. "You were clever to begin with. Spirited. But given your sounding, even on your Blessing-day, need was to get you out of the foulburg and into the Order. That was why I discipled you. If Aleksandr, you would still be there. If Woden, you'd face a far harder road than you did. As it was, I nearly lost you once."

Lost me? The only time I'd been — I stopped on the road, stunned. "You killed the piglet!"

He shot me a grin, then put a finger to his lips. The rim of the hush-sphere passed over me, clammy and tickly as cobwebs. I shivered, but braved crossing it again and trotted to catch up.

"You knew I was betrothed? And to keep me at the Order...?" It seemed too ludicrous, a saint lurking about a peasant pig-sty to murder a piglet. Though it did explain the spotless corpse. Krepkin's accusations echoed back to me and I put a hand to my belly. "Have I disappointed you, m'lord? Betrayed you?"

A glance, looking down. "All knowledge, all experience, has value. Few things can match love and children in forcing lessons upon you. And if an unexpected child is such a betrayal, I have a treacherous past myself. What else must you know before answering me, then?"

We neared the outer gate; two Guards stood just outside watching us approach. "What must I do, as your elect? And what of the baby?"

"Your child is untouched by either binding, mine or the Pool's. In truth, the child of an elect or a saint often has little skill with kir at all." The hush-sphere fell away as we drew near the Guard. Qadeem called up a small sphere of kir that glowed warm and bright. It lit his face, but didn't shine much further.

"Saint Qadeem!" Both knights dropped to one knee in obeisance. "We did not expect you."

"I am only here briefly, sirs. Please convey to the watchtowers that there's no need for alarm — but the walk to the gate was quite sufficient. You may note that I have a guest, but not her identity."

"M'lord." The guards retreated into the gate tower.

Qadeem reached a hand to me and I hesitated in taking it. There was more for him to tell me.

"My elect must put truth and reason first in their minds," he said. "They must not fear knowledge or experience, but pursue them. As Mechdan often said, they must not look away. They must answer my questions fully and truthfully, when I ask. They must work with both Saint Woden and Saint Aleksandr, but they are not beholden to either." That, he raised a finger to emphasize. "Your first loyalty is to me. I will teach you, I will see you blossom to your fullest ability so long as your strength is mine and your loyalty holds true. And you must support me in battle, if need be."

"Battle?"

"The Empress did not send her lackeys for a tea party." Qadeem turned to the southward view, across the city, the wall and the army beyond. "There are saints in that camp. Do not doubt it. They will kill me, if they can, and you. As they did Mechdan."

"They said he fell to dust, after his kir broke free."

Qadeem nodded. "He was a hundred years past any natural death. It's always thus, for the old ones. I felt him die, as I told you, through the bond I am asking you to take. It is a deep and intimate thing, and not easily broken. We often spoke, without words, through it. In truth, I've no need to feel childbirth again," he said with a smile, "but it's a small price to pay. Will you be my elect, Kate? You must choose a saint." He must have seen my next question, because he answered it. "If you decline, Gentle Woden will put the question to you with force and his way with elect is very different from mine. But this is no time for rogue elect to be roaming the street."

Gentle Woden. The man had knocked two teeth out already. I didn't want to learn what more force would be, but I took Qadeem's hand honestly. Not from fear. "I owe all that I am to you, m'lord," I said.

Kir surged and the ground suddenly dropped away. Wind battered me for a moment, forcing my eyes narrow, and I felt a bit of kir drape across my face. The wind vanished and I looked down. The castle's battlements passed below as we soared across. Then we began to fall, and my grip on Qadeem's hand tightened. Thick stalks of kir shot toward the ground, and we slowed. Shifted in the air. We dropped behind the castle's back wall and between the two watchtowers, slowing on more kir.

My feet touched grass in the crescent garden, and I could breathe again.

"That is one way to fly. Aleksandr is the best at shape-shifting, of us. Perhaps you would prefer his way?"

My heart was still pounding, somewhere up in the sky. My smile was open, as I laughed. "That was amazing."

Qadeem chuckled. "Come."

He led me into the castle and down two flights of stairs, deep into the mountain's stone. Qadeem spun a kir-lamp in his hand, and held it high enough for both of us. The stone here, as in all the castle, ran smooth and seamless, though with a shallow groove at hand height. After a fork in the hall, we came to an unlocked door and an empty room behind it.

I'd felt the kir since before the fork. In the bare room, it was close by. Strong. Far stronger than the little fount the lamia claimed; the wall it lay behind held my eyes. There was no doubt in my mind where it was. But the wall was flat and blank.

"The Pool is behind the Door," Qadeem said, standing just before the wall. I joined him, and put up my hand to touch its smoothness. His caught me by the wrist. "The Pool is an outcropping of the fount at the mountain's summit. If Arcea reaches the Pool, they have the fount. If they have the fount, all is lost. You must defend it," and he slowed, fixing me with dark eyes, "with your life. Don't touch the Door, only hold your hand still. It will nip you."

Qadeem left my hand an inch from the Door, and I held it steady, though I was less than certain I was able to truly defend such cryptic things. Kir sparkled up into his fingertips. It arced through my hand and into the stone, and the light sent a spiderweb's worth of slender lines blooming out from the point. From within, it glowed on its own, brighter and stronger, and a sudden pain bit my palm. I felt a little blood trickle, but then Qadeem healed the wound.

"The Door knows you now, and will permit you to pass. It will only allow those it knows to pass. Do not return here without me until after your baby is born — it knows you, not your baby. I will get you both through, this time, but if you try alone the Door will take the child."

My saint took my hand and stepped into the wall. It rippled, like water, but otherwise gave no sign of his passing. From his hand, kir flowed into me, into my womb. He tugged. I closed my eyes and stepped.

Cool weight enveloped me, thick and strong and resolving into something alarmingly like teeth dragging across my belly. My saint's kir fended them off of my baby. Then it broke away and I was free. I opened my eyes.

Kir hung thick as humidity in the grotto. The Pool glowed, warm and inviting, glittering where bubbles broke the surface. Its light gently brightened the otherwise empty room, easy on my eyes even after the dimness of the hallways outside. Overhead, the roof arced a little, allowing plenty of headroom.

Qadeem led me to the shallow side of the Pool. The granite underfoot was textured into fish scales, and the small lip around the edge was worked in the shape of a wriggling serpent. My saint stepped in, leather shoes, cloak and all. I was barefoot; the water was warm, and barely covered my feet at first. Steps took us down to waist deep and a submerged landing. The Pool was so clear, I could see where the shelf ended and the water turned dark with depth. The glittering bubbles rose from there.

"Kate." Qadeem still held my right hand, I realized. In his left, he held a small knife of kir. "Make a blade."

I called, just a tiny, faint call, and kir rushed into me till I nearly glowed on my own. I formed it inside my fingers, then slid it out in a shape just like the scalpels I used in surgery.

"Many prefer a ritual, here, in this wellspring from the Mother's heart, to invoke the Shepherd's judgment and impress the severity of the bond upon the elect," he said. "I will tell you plainly. There are precious few things saints and elect can rely on, in the war of the founts. Through this bond, we will have each other. We may lose all else. But this will remain. Will you take the bond?"

My resolve wavered at the thought of losing all. "I mean to help defend my home. If I lose all of that…"

"I will offer you no empty promises. Nothing is certain but death, even for saints. This has been my home for centuries. It took me in and made me welcome, and I will defend it to the last hope. Will you take the bond?"

I supposed truth was better, even if harsh. The kingdom would have an Elect again, and two when Kiefan was ready. We'd be stronger against our enemy. "I will."

"Open your meridian, not your flesh." He held out his right arm and called his kir up; thicker and denser than any I'd seen before, his bright meridian ran through his arm to the heel of the hand, then branched out to the fingers and thumb. He sank his kir-blade into the center of his palm, on the middle finger's branch, and slit the meridian open to his elbow.

By how his breath turned harsh, I didn't need to guess if it hurt. I set my jaw and pressed my blade into my right palm. The thickness of my meridian, there, was no more than fine knitting yarn. My cut wobbled a little, as the pain gnawed on my focus. Along my arm, the meridian grew thicker and easier to follow. When I reached the elbow, my entire arm throbbed and tingled, and tears had filled my eyes again.

Qadeem's palm pressed to the pit of my elbow and the sudden shock weakened my knees. But I grasped his arm in return and steadied in the sloshing water. His meridian pulsed alongside mine, his hand dark against my pale skin. He called not on my kir but on my meridian, and its answering shift felt like my soul drawing out of my skin.

"Call me, Kate."

Fingers tightening on his arm, I focused on its bright, open line and called. It only shivered in reply. Gritting my teeth, I thought of Starknadel and demanded the dense kir come to me. Tight-knit as it was, I could feel it refusing to flow. For a heartbeat, I thought Qadeem was resisting, in order to test me.

He must have seen it on my face. "It isn't me hindering you — but neither will I help. I will not force this. You must take it yourself."

"I haven't mastered it, as you said — why did you think me ready?" It came out such a whine that my face burned hot for having said it.

His eyes lost all softness, all trace of their kindness. "You took the first step on instinct, and haven't fully fledged yet — true enough. But you are my disciple, Blessed with my memory, and you are held to a higher standard." His raw will transfixed me, and the spark of fear that shot through me left a defiant fire in its wake. "Now remember the moment you harvested Mechdan, and do it."

The moment flicked back to me: rage and resolve, with a trace of howling, cold wind.

Qadeem's meridian seared into mine, hot and throbbing and deep — and when my mind leaped to the moment I'd slipped my fingers across my clit and succumbed to the ecstasy Kiefan pounded into me, my knees wobbled and folded. Water on my face slapped me back to reality. I spluttered and flailed back to my feet, my saint's grip a solid anchor to help.

"Careful of the deeps," he said. I'd tumbled toward the dark end of the Pool. "Steady. Intimate, as I said."

I stood, sopping wet, my dress clinging to me, a little stunned by his shift from fierce back to kind. But I chuckled at the understatement. And then I asked, as I thought of it, "Would you feel that through me, as well? If I — did you see what I thought, then?"

"Only if you thought of…" A smile flickered past, but faded quickly. "Strong feelings leach through, but your thoughts will always be your own. And the bond can be tucked away as one's kir can." His grip on my arm loosened. "Ready?"

Curious, I lifted my fingers from his arm. I hadn't noticed the sleek-corded muscle I'd been clinging too. Qadeem raised his hand and a ripple of gossamer red stretched from his meridian to mine. The arm's-width of gauzy kir curled onto itself, descending to my palm and his as it went. Spinning itself into a fine meridian, it faded.

/ ? /

I felt the question, rather than heard — it tickled up my arm to the kir in my chest. I reached, in my mind, to the palm of my hand and felt the invisible meridian there, still.

/ hear me? / he sent. An echo of hearing, not a word, and a sense of self.

I tried to gather up certainty and push it into the meridian. / yes /

"Good. It needs practice, like most things. Now, the fount's binding." Qadeem raised a hand over the black, bubbling depths and from far below rose such a mass of kir that my breath caught in my throat. Water overflowed the Pool's lip as it rose up, twisting to a point as it went. Overhead, it bent to come to its master's hand, tiny stars lighting up as the point twisted finer into yarn, then thread. The stars squeezed out and fell around me. He took the thread in his fingers.

The tip glistened like a steel needle, long and sharp, and a spark spat off it. "Were you a saint, you would do this yourself and draw on the fount wherever you were," Qadeem said as he tugged the neck of my dress down. His fingers brushed aside Anders' necklace to clear a stretch of my breastbone over my heart. "This is a gift, then."

His gift was a hot stab through my heart, needle-thin, clean through in one thrust. Heat flushed out through my meridians, easing to the familiar warm tingle of kir. Like another meridian, I could feel the bond through my core. Pulsing slightly, even, with something like joy and eagerness.

"It's only a small bond, and limited in range. The full binding is much deeper."

I managed a weak smile, rubbing the spot on my breastbone. "Does it hurt more?"

Qadeem shrugged and, hand on mine, called up his pattern to show me. For a moment, I saw it all: his own thick, kir-rich patterns, the dense red fans of disciples' bonds on his fingers, my larger bond in his right palm, and three heavy green braids of kir knotted around his heart. One led down into the Pool. The others faded into the distance.

"One pays prices that are worth paying." He let his kir fade, then tucked it away. "I must not linger. It took far too long to negotiate the lamia's fount and Duke Seagrace needs me back come morning. We are hard pressed, out by Vorspitz, and still no sign of Caercoed. No need to tell anyone you are bound, yet. I cheated you out of a proper graduation once, but I will see you get your due acclaim as my elect. I promise you that. Keep your charms quiet — Arcea does not need to know of you. Let them think we are weak, for now. It's not a secret that keeps well, but keep it so long as you can."

"I will. The lamia's fount? Why did you go there?" I had so many questions, and only the freshest one popped out.

"All founts are connected. Guarded by those who own them, but connected. A safer way to travel than by air, when there's Arceal saints about." We climbed from the Pool dripping, but after a quick charm we were dry again. With a sidelong smile, Qadeem asked, "Would you like to fly home?"

CHAPTER 9

There were no more steps to climb today than yesterday, but I'd lost most of the night's sleep and the baby felt heavier this morning. Reaching the top, I took a deep breath.

The invalids' floor was nearly full. It had been all but empty when I left with Parselev yesterday; he'd healed the patients down to only light wounds, mending two dozen a day or so long as his focus held out. Now that would be my duty, though I wasn't sure I had the stamina for so many. The Pool was eager to give me the kir, though. Now I knew why he'd stayed here more than not. It was close to his source.

How many ambulances had gotten in through the city gates before they closed? In my memory, I spotted one that had been retreating with the westbound sortie through the saint's door. How many left behind to the mercies of Arcea's crucifixes?

Ter Gudrun, senior nurse of the day shift, spotted me and stood up from a patient's bed-side. I smiled and nodded to her as I went first to the peg-boards at the head of the stairs. Wooden chits with numbers, on one row of pegs, listed the order of priority in giving out healing charms come evening. Chits with names inscribed, on the other rows, indicated which Ters and Thers were to be on duty as nurses, orderlies, or in ambulances. Two of the Thers normally in ambulances were not listed. I glanced up and down the rows of beds to check for them, touched by dread.

"Dame Kate?" Ter Gudrun asked, at my elbow.

"I didn't mean to be so late," I said, turning from the shift-board. "Heima thought I needed a second day's rest, but I may lose my wits if I must be cooped in the cottage. Were Arnwald and Boris wounded yesterday? Are they here? Oh, there's Boris."

He was at the end of one row, by the fireplace in the far wall. As I looked, Meinrad spotted me and began to stride down the aisle between the feet of all our cots, folding his arms as he came. Behind him, Krepkin glanced up from checking a splinted arm, but paid me no mind.

That didn't bode well, but I asked Ter Gudrun all the same. "What's the current status?"

She laced her fingers together. "Begging your pardon, but I'm not certain if I should say."

"How would the physician of the floor not need to know?"

"You've been dismissed from the post," Meinrad answered for her. "It was part of the morning's announcements."

I considered that. "Krepkin dismissed me." Meinrad nodded, grim but determined. I asked, "He thinks that wise, dismissing one of the six physicians inside the city walls?"

Ter Gudrun said, with a sidelong glance at Meinrad, "There's to be a graduation on Saint-day."

My shoulders twitched, as it hardly mattered. "You've earned that," I told him. "Did Krepkin give a reason?"

"Not when he made the announcement." Meinrad shifted on his feet. "He's senior physician in the city, now. In the whole Order. He can —"

"Let him explain himself, then," I said. Looking past Meinrad's shoulder, I asked. "Will you explain yourself, sir?"

Krepkin's arrival was a chance for both Ter Gudrun and Meinrad to retreat. "Certainly the clever Frau Bockmann can suss out the reasons herself," Krepkin said.

"Frau? You haven't the authority to strip me of —"

"The abbot has confirmed my authority in matters of the Order's physicians and healing services. If Saint Qadeem wishes to take up the matter, he will do so when he is next here. Until such time, you are not needed here, Frau Bockmann." Krepkin pointed toward the stairway and the front door.

"You can't hope to run this hospital with three — four physicians, even, once you've graduated Meinrad." My voice slid toward a snarl on the stupidity of it all. His first chance, even after all I'd done, and I was out on the midden heap. "I don't expect friendship, but I know you're no fool. After all your talk of the horrors of war, you hobble yourself with so little staff?"

"Lehrer would be glad for a pair of hands," Krepkin said, naming one of the free-lance physicians still within the walls. "If you wish to help, inquire with him. Good day, Frau Bockmann."

I folded my arms to match his. "I am still your equal in title and you could do the simple courtesy of —"

He jabbed a finger at me, lip curling. "You are a fish-blooded peasant whore and you'll —"

A shove sent Krepkin tumbling, startling me as much as him. He fell with a cry. Anders stepped between us, hand on his sword. "You'll keep a civil tongue, old man, when speaking to my wife."

Krepkin spat from the floor. "Challenge me, then. Strike me down on the dueling field, if that will make you more of a man." He rolled himself onto his knees. "I've duties to see to, elsewise."

I had my elect's bond tingling in the palm of my hand, but I knew that meant little. Without the acclaim or the saint at hand, Krepkin wouldn't believe such a thing. And I wasn't wasting my breath on him now. I'd had enough of trying to please the old man.

"It's no matter," I told Anders, turning away. "I'm not welcome here, so I won't trouble Physician Krepkin."

I took a step toward the staircase, casting a glance to either side along the invalids' floor. The nurses and orderlies watched in grim silence. Ter Holly chewed at her bottom lip. When I took the first step down, I sighed and closed my eyes a moment. Fish-blooded peasant… few stooped to calling Engls such names. I hadn't heard that since I was a child.

Behind, Anders' boots followed me down. "Kate?"

Not needed here. The king would have something to say on that as the typhus culled men. There were deaths every day, in the hospital. More in the city, from what we'd heard. The wounded always took priority over the ill, and we had enough wounded to spend all our kir on with more waiting for tomorrow.

I had the Pool to draw on, now, but if Krepkin was so determined to have me gone, then gone I was. There'd be other ways for me to use my training. Other ways to serve Father Duty. He could explain himself to Saint Qadeem.

Reaching the bottom of the stair, I strode for the rear door into the herb garden. Anders caught up. "What do you mean, that you're not welcome here?"

"Krepkin dismissed me," I said, stepping down onto the garden path. "He believes he can —" The kick in my belly cut me off; they still took me by surprise.

"Are you well?" Anders stepped in front of me, hand on my shoulder. He glanced down when my hand went to my stomach.

The baby fluttered like a trapped bird. "She startles me," I said. "She kicks as she pleases."

"You didn't say the baby'd quickened." His hand moved to touch me, but hesitated. "Is he —?"

"You want to —?" I risked a glance up at him, anger draining away into a muddle of emotions. "I didn't think…"

Anders' brow quirked. "You thought me cold-hearted?" Lightly, he let his hand rest on the swell.

"No, only…" I shook my head and left that be, before I made it any worse. The baby kicked again, and I slid Anders' hand closer to the spot. "She's still small. Maybe you can't feel that?"

"A little quiver."

We waited, and the baby obliged with another flutter. That close, I could smell a trace of blood on Anders, still, under the leather and iron. No rosewater soap from Arbor Street, this time. "What brings you today?" I asked, voice low. "It's not Saint-day."

"To see that you're well," he said, with a glance that turned into a longer look. So close, such blue eyes. His strong hand under mine.

My stomach fluttered, and it wasn't the baby.

"You were swept off with hardly a word. The rest of us had to face the king and Saint Woden to answer for losing half the Guard out there. Thank the Father they didn't hand me over to Woden."

"Half." My heart sank yet again. "But why would they hand you over?"

Anders took his hand from my belly and shifted back, looking away. "It was my fault."

"Yours? You —" I stopped, the moment's image of Anders with his helmet off in my mind.

"I heard you screaming." His wry-twisted smile was an apology. "And Kiefan heard me. He gave the order, but…"

He'd heard me. That was how they'd found me — how Kiefan had. And then he'd… said nothing. While I'd been clinging to him for comfort, Anders had been facing Gentle

Woden. I swallowed the tightness in my throat. My hand found his. "It's not your fault. Doesn't it mean they agree, if they didn't blame you?"

Anders considered the beaten dirt path. "You don't turn on your brothers, right or wrong. But Rostislav will have something to say, next I'm reviewed."

I squeezed his hand to get him to look up. "Your fey ears saved my life." I offered a smile and he echoed that, but it wasn't right. It wasn't enough.

"We're even, then, for the lamia bite?"

"You were even on that when you saved my place here," I said, free hand going to the lamia-tooth necklace. "I owe you a debt. I owe you..."

Our eyes met, and mine jumped to his lips. Before my next thought, I kissed them. Just a soft, dry touch that lingered a heartbeat. Then the next thought hit and brought the memory of Kiefan's gentle hands, his warm chest spooned against my back. He loved me. Needed me to be strong. I withdrew to arm's length, hands still clasped in Anders'.

"Just a kiss?" he murmured. "Not what you offered him?"

My breath slipped away. I had only snuggled under Kiefan's arm a little while, but Anders had no reason to guess that. That he'd think me the sort — "A kiss is more than he got, sir."

Anders' smile vanished and he took a step back with eyes downcast. "I'm sorry, m'lady. I'll —"

That was wrong too. I snatched his hand before he could escape with the wrong idea. "No. Thank you," I told him, wanting to force it into his ears. "I'm sorry. I should not have done that. Don't apologize."

He hesitated, watching me fidget and let his hand go. "You can do as you please."

My stomach hollowed out at the thought, so sudden that I clutched at straws. "You know I love him." I told my hands this, as my fingers twisted around each other.

"Yes." A single, flat word. He took a deep breath and withdrew another step. "The watch captain gave me leave to check on you, not spend the morning. Till Saint-day, then?"

"Saint-day," I faintly agreed, and didn't watch him go. The muddle was too much as it was.

Three of the armsmen that the ambulance had brought in during the sortie had died in the wagon bed. It was no longer my concern, but Ter Holly told me while emptying her spleen about Krepkin, the next morning. That was not so unusual — the drivers and the orderlies wanted to save all they could, and would choose the worst off when loading the ambulance. Some would arrive dead or too far gone to save with anything short of an elect's strongest charms. We simply could not mend every gravely wounded man in the city, even when we had Parselev's wisdom in addition to the Pool.

And while the ambulance made its way to the hospital and back, some other wounded man waited bleeding, or was killed, or had to be left behind when the battle lines shifted. In the sortie especially, any wounded who couldn't walk or be put in the ambulance had to be left to the mercy of the enemy.

We buried what bodies we had on the second day after the sortie. They were bundled in plain woolen shrouds, each with a sack of gifts from their brothers in arms, and sent to the Shepherd's Hearth with ale and song. Then the shovels came out to see to the rest of the work.

For the lost dead, the send-off came on Saint-day. The saints' high table before the icons was covered in funeral sacks, each with a name carefully inked along the side. Too many. None of the knights who'd fallen in Kiefan's sortie could be brought home to bury. Arcea had stripped the bodies and dumped them in the Spanne for the guardsmen to see as crows and vultures did their work.

Part III: Embers on the Wind

And at the top of the pile of sacks, my teacher's.

The Grand Chapel was full for the communal funeral feast, but the sight of so many funeral sacks left me too heart-sick to eat. I excused myself from Anders when the abbot finished his homily. I didn't much want to return to the cottage, but it was the only place for me to go.

From boredom, I began going through Parselev's papers. Krepkin laid claim to all that was related to the Order's physicians, and sorting that from the more personal and the more general would take days yet. The documents went back decades.

I was deep in it when a knock on the front door below caught my ear. "Kate?" Anders called up. "A patient to see you."

"Krepkin dismissed me," I said, half my mind on the letter in my hands.

"But not the castle," Captain Rostislav called back.

That was true enough. I put the mess aside and came downstairs. Anders had invited the captain and another Prince's Guard — introduced as Sir Garrick Fechter — in to sit at the table. Heima was still at the funeral feast, so I offered them tea.

"You aren't castle staff, Captain," I said as I moved the warm kettle closer to the fire. "You should be seen in the hospital."

"The prince's endorsement is enough," he said, "and I know who saved me when I was trying to breathe through a cut throat." Captain Rostislav shot Anders a smirk. "I'd have sworn fealty, that moment my lungs cleared, had she asked. A lady never looked so beautiful."

Anders feigned a backhanded swing, but said, "Next I haul your drunken ass home, I'll take your wife's invitation."

Sir Garrick, beside the captain, laughed and fell to coughing. He did look a bit flushed and had a touch of feverish sweat on his brow. My medicine bag waited by the door; moving it to the table, I unlaced its flap. And I shot Anders a sidelong glare, as I did, since a wife ought to.

Quietly, he said, "I jest, of course."

I only raised my brows. A moment of that, and he added, "No, she hasn't offered. I'm sorry."

I let him go, on that much. Not that it was any of my business, truly. "When did the fever set in?" I asked Sir Garrick. I'd watched enough typhus to nearly guess it myself; they came to us when the rash broke out, as the fever worsened.

"Four days ago, m'lady."

As I had expected. His face was warm under my hands, his cheeks scratchy where he hadn't shaved. His kir showed me the pain in his joints, the vigorous, jittery dance of a fever and the odd patterns of the chest rash. Sir Garrick wasn't much older than Anders, who at twenty was the youngest of the Prince's Guard. Both had gotten into the Guard on their prowess at the jousting tournament. Garrick didn't wear a wedding band. How his blonde curls — if his knight's crest was any indication — and green eyes had failed to land a wife, I couldn't say.

"Did you wash today? As Saint Qadeem asks?"

"Just a basin bath, m'lady," he said.

I nearly asked if he'd eaten, he was such a lanky thing, but I held that off. Drawing from the Pool, I used some kir to repair certain points in his pattern's off-kilter dance. Then I poured them all cups of tea when the kettle whistled. That was when Captain Rostislav confessed to having a bit of fever himself.

"Most likely typhus," I said, cupping his heavy-jawed, Russe face in my hands.

"Well, it is all over Arbor Street," Anders commented, overly casually, "and you've spent enough nights there." His captain threw a glare and Sir Garrick nearly choked on his tea.

"Typhus is?" I cared more about that than what the captain was up to. Calling his kir, I saw a fever but no joint pains — and a streak of antagonizing patterns along his arm. "You're wounded, sir?"

Captain Rostislav pulled up his right sleeve to reveal a long cut that wasn't even bandaged. The wound should have been stitched. Now it was full of crust and inflamed. "You were on Arbor Street right along with us, Anders, how is it you've escaped? We lucky dozen who passed under the Shepherd's knife and lived. A wild night that was."

There had been only a couple nights since the sortie, so they'd been prompt in their celebrating. I pulled on my bond to the Pool and it trickled warm kir into my core. I didn't need much; it wasn't a large abscess, but tapping the Pool was easy.

"I only kept the bar tab running," Anders said, meanwhile.

Focused on spinning my charm, it took a moment for me to catch that. I looked up from the walnut-sized glow in my palm. "If you say so."

"Where did you find a wife so cool-headed? I'll have to start telling her about —" The captain's voice hitched when I lay down the shaped charm over his wound. The abscess broke into loose kir and flesh knit over it.

"I trust him," I said, intent on guiding the fine lines of kir that made up the muscle in the captain's forearm. I pinched his skin shut and it mended in little puckers that settled down flat. "You should've had this seen to," I told him.

He shrugged. "I looked in Physician Lehrer's shop while we were on Arbor Street, but he had far too much to see to already. And there was drinking to do. This had stopped bleeding — was only a little slip of a spearhead up my sleeve. I've had worse."

I picked up my tea mug for a sip. "Lehrer has a shop on Arbor Street, then?" I asked. "I thought he was on Low Street."

Sir Garrick answered. "He was by the Südwand Market, but that's closed up for now. What shops there are have moved into King's Market."

That was at one end of Arbor Street and its typhus. Arbor Street also lay on the east side of the city, where the three remaining trebuchets would be nearly finished by now. The king had said they'd put a hole in the wall. The infirmary in Sinnmach Square would be of little help if the hole were in the east wall.

Captain Rostislav tried to ruffle my calm with a story about Anders on Arbor Street, but I only freshened their mugs from the brass teapot. At one point, Anders corrected him, "That was Theo, and she's working as my mother's housemaid now, in truth."

"Sweet Alice? Is that why she's not in town?" The captain seemed genuinely disappointed, but then cuffed Anders' shoulders. "Getting it for free, then? Shepherd didn't shear you too close, did he."

"If you felt shorn after your wedding, it wasn't the Shepherd. And if you haven't settled your debts with Alice, I'll be collecting on her behalf." Anders cracked a couple of knuckles with a leer.

Captain Rostislav laughed it off, but took his leave then. Sir Garrick, whose ears had been beet-red throughout, mumbled an apology to me before he slipped out the door. The captain leaned closer as he passed, and pretended to confide in me. "Should Father Duty take that one, don't fear your bed will be empty long, m'lady. The Guard takes care of their own."

No playful thing, this time; Anders truly cuffed him, or he meant to as Rostislav wore an anticipation Blessing and dodged the first swing. Anders' speed landed the second. Both bristled, but held off anything further, though their knuckles were clenched white.

I struggled to keep my voice steady. "You're married, sir." Even after all I'd seen, the suddenness of the speed took my breath away.

Captain Rostislav straightened his tabard and went, trading a glare with Anders. The darkness lingered in his face even after the door closed.

"You don't need to… feign jealousy," I told him, voice low. "He meant nothing by it."

Anders took a deep breath, then kissed my hand good-bye for the day. I squeezed his fingers and got a scrap of a smile from him before he went. Then I sat down to think about Physician Lehrer and the east wall, and how to bring my idea to Krepkin.

I had never been to Arbor Street. It ran from King's Market to the East Tower in the city wall, and true to its name boasted many a rose arbor. Some houses were only cottages, some big enough to be taverns and inns, but all had a bit of garden and roses. The early blooms were starting to scent the air, as we were past the full of the Field Moon, and the pink was a striking splash against the whitewashed houses.

By law, all houses of prostitution were whitewashed. There were many stories as to why Saint Woden had put down so many laws to create and regulate the Arborguild for prostitutes. They were to be checked by a physician on equinoxes and solstices — Parselev had only seen those with difficult illnesses, and as I walked those charms popped to mind.

Four days and I was still sorting through my teacher's vast store of charms and catalog of horrors. They sprang up at the oddest times, now that their numbers grew thin.

The day was cloudy but I smiled as I walked along Arbor Street looking for a square or a large enough garden or someplace to squeeze an infirmary in.

Krepkin hated me, but could still see reason. Parselev's infirmary had done excellent triage on the wounded, immediately seeing to those who wouldn't survive the trip to the Order and skimming off those who only needed a quick bandage. If Arcea set its mind to coming through the east wall, the infirmary must be on the east side. Even with his newly minted Sir Meinrad Frieberg, physician, Krepkin could not spare more than nurses and orderlies for an infirmary.

I could be of help, and I wouldn't be in his hospital.

Alice had told me enough stories that I almost knew the street: the small cottage owned by a grey-haired lady who would tutor young hopefuls, the three-floor home where Alice and four others had split the rent, the bath-house that leaked steam and whose roses were already in full bloom, the rowdy Lady's Kiss Tavern where the largest parties were held.

That last caught my eye. The front was quiet, this early in the morning after Saint-day, so I crossed the street to investigate. A small stable stood in the back, as did a large garden of trellised roses that barely budded as yet. A flagstone patio for guests took up much of the space.

I noted it, and continued down the street.

On the whole, the gardens were small and the houses close — not cheek by jowl, to be sure, but even where small streets crossed Arbor there wasn't as much room as we'd had in Sinnmach Square. From all the stories I'd heard, I had thought it a bigger place.

Ahead, Arbor Street joined Wallside Street and off to the left the East Tower stood watch. Looking to the right, I found the Patch Tower and its odd "patch" of lighter granite. Catapults waited at ready on both, and City Guard stood watch. I'd walked the length of Arbor in no time, it seemed.

Closer, across my line of sight, a grey dappled warhorse scratched his neck against the side of a horse shed. All of the cottages had such a shed, two walls and a bit of roof for a horse to stand under while he waited with his reins tied. A handsome black stood at the far end of the shed, turned away from — Nipper, I had to confess. I recognized his dapples.

My feet slowed as I looked to the cottage; the door stood open, dark against the whitewashing. The obligatory roses climbed the walls, a haze of young green leaves and buds.

Anders stepped out, in the same off-white cote and dark green hose from yesterday, his sword and belt in hand. He looked back into the house, one hand out in surrender. His tabard hit him mid-chest and he caught it.

He retreated another step from the tall woman who came to the doorway, hands on both hips, and dismissed him with a sharp word and a laugh. A graceful, elegant woman who could nearly look him in the eye. When she turned to look behind herself, her honey-brown hair swung long and free — and that was what tightened my throat the most. More than how easy she stood on her own door-step in just a pink linen shift. The only sop to my pride was that she was even less blessed in the bosom than I.

Anders pulled his tabard over his head and my heart stumbled in my chest, realizing he was about to turn...

He froze, the white knight's-horse sigil falling into place on his shoulder. Staring at me. My fists clenched on the strap of my medicine bag. My heart, in my chest, clenched tighter. It may have been lack of air, as I couldn't breathe.

Theo Kaufmann breezed through the doorway, fully dressed, breaking our line of sight. Anders snapped back to the mistress of the cottage. She had spotted me, gave me a long look and then back to him. He was retreating, by then, looking away with one hand to his eyes. The horses were glad to be going, by how they perked up. Theo had the blanket on his black already. The lady turned and slipped indoors.

I turned and started walking. Quickly. My head was an empty cavern until I passed the next cross-street. Then I had to admit that if I'd agreed not to ask, I shouldn't be surprised where he spent his nights. Saint-day was his only time off, after all. I'd been stealing kisses, hugs, and pettings from Kiefan on back staircases once a week.

No business of mine. Anders had as much right to kiss someone as I. What part Theo played was no business of mine either, especially if he were paying the tab.

Still, it stung.

My feet took me, eventually, to Lehrer's small infirmary in King's Market. There was some bustle in the market, even in the midst of the siege; a scattering of stalls were occupied by craftsmen and merchants, and shopped at by the wives who'd stayed with their husbands.

The only way I could speak with Lehrer about where to put an infirmary was to help him clear his front room of fevers and abscesses, so I did. I was glad for the work, in truth. It kept my mind off Anders.

CHAPTER 10

Meinrad was sent in my place, to the weekly meeting — Freiberg, that is. As he was a physician now, I should address him correctly by family name. He'd stopped shaving on his graduation day; the few days' worth of reddish stubble did add some years and authority to his face. That did not help him, though, when the abbot introduced him and Kiefan glared up from the city map on the Council table.

"Dismissed Kate? Who?" He all but growled it.

Freiberg flinched, nearly dropping the mug of tea Housemistress Wenda had given him.

I stood just outside the door, before the two King's Guard. I had not been summoned by the Council and therefore could not enter. Likely they would have let me in on habit, but I didn't try. I could see most of the room from the door, and if told to leave I would. I wanted to petition the king concerning the east-side infirmary, though, so that Krepkin would be held to supporting it.

His Majesty was less than intrigued by Freiberg's replacing me, and waved for all to sit.

As the reports began, Kiefan spotted me at the door and was quickly out of his seat again. The king tracked his path and noted me. By how easily his eyes slid off, I wondered if anything had come of Kiefan's declaration that he loved me. I hardly dared ask, though. I remembered to curtsy as my prince came to the door; he offered his hand with a formal flourish, and escorted me to a chair. I whispered a thank you. My ankles had been starting to complain.

Saint Woden, standing at one of the windows, measured me with a narrow eye and my heart quivered in my chest. What did he know? I gathered my kir close, held it snug in case he meant to sound me. My bond to Qadeem tingled in my palm, and I wondered if Woden could see that.

Saint Aleksandr had stayed on for this meeting, and stood with a grey-muzzled hound leaning against his leg as he conferred with the city quartermaster. He seemed to pay me no mind.

I made my request toward the end of the meeting, and the king nodded. As final decisions were made, Housemistress Wenda carried in food for the meal and set about preparing portions. It was far less than usual, though.

"Arcea's forced another parley," Kiefan told me, leaning against my chair's back. "We're leaving right away. They've captured Brunnenberg and some of his officers, and want to know what they're worth to us."

The king's battle in the foulburg, just before the gates closed, had meant to cover the withdrawal of a small force up onto the slopes of Mount Woden. They'd been harrying the fringes of the besieging army since then, and rumor said crucifixes sprouted in the foulburg squares every time Brunnenberg had to leave wounded behind.

"Where will your new infirmary be?" Saint Aleksandr wrapped a little meat in a crust of bread as he asked me. The hound watched his fingers closely, fidgeting and anxious.

"On good advice, it seems Südwand Market has the space I need. I'm told it's closed down?"

"Good advice indeed. You'll set up soon?" He bit off half the treat and chewed.

I nodded. "Today, m'lord. So there's time to move the cots before there's trouble."

"We're to meet Arcea at the Patch Tower," Kiefan said. "Let me bring you down, as we can't go up to the roof today."

Saint Aleks frowned. "How did they come to dictate the site? A trebuchet stands before that tower."

"Father declined to open a saint's door, thus they announced they'd crucify the men before the Patch Tower. Will you be with us, m'lord?"

The saint tossed the rest of his bread and the hound caught it mid-air. "There's movement in the pass near Vysokiled that I must see to." He scratched at his salt-and-pepper beard, wrinkles crinkling around his eyes as his thoughts distracted him. He turned to Saint Woden. "I've surveyed the applicants, claimed mine. There's a dozen for you, by my count."

The other nodded as he wiped crumbs from his hands. "I will see to it tonight." Woden took a second measure of me, by eye, as Saint Aleks took his leave. Gruffly, Woden said, "You've large footprints to fill, and little time to do it in. I don't doubt we'll know soon enough how well-placed Mechdan's confidence was."

That didn't sit easily on me. But then the king was ready to leave and Kiefan offered me his hand again. Horses waited in the castle yard. Kiefan called for a spare and a palfrey was brought from the small royal stables alongside the castle. I asked for a messenger, meantime, and sent word to Ter Holly to meet me at Südwand. Kiefan gave me a boost into the saddle, but I caught him wincing when I put my weight on his arm.

I didn't even ask; I held out my hand.

He smiled. "Only bruises. Woden's sure I'll draw kir again, as I did under the Shepherd's knife. If I've enough reason to do it."

Taking my hand, he kissed it and went to mount his own palfrey.

Patch Street branched off River Road and angled across the eastern city, finally meeting Wallside Street just off-center of the Patch Tower. There, near the wall, it cut across one end of the Südwand Market. I dismounted at the tower, leaving the horse with the others under the eye of the King's Guard. Kiefan, with two of his Prince's Guard, was to remain at the foot of the tower to listen and send suggestions up with a messenger boy.

"The king wishes your advice?" I asked him as his father started up the stairs inside the tower.

"How could I advise the king?" Kiefan feigned a bewildered shrug. Then, with a melancholy smile, "The war I've been negotiating between him and Mother has been harsher."

For appearances' sake, I curtsied and asked, "By your leave, m'lord?" He dismissed me with a deep nod and I went to see about the marketplace.

It wasn't so large as the King's Market, and humbler. And empty, as promised. The booths were small; one cot each, I thought as I stepped into one. Whoever had put the walls and roofs together hadn't worried overmuch about straightness or flush lines, but the shed was sturdy enough. Underfoot, the dirt was firm, scattered with weeds. The booths ran in close rows for a distance, but on the Patch Street end was a circle large enough for wagons to turn about.

A call caught my ear and I trotted out to wave to the lead wagon. A second wagon followed. I'd spent the morning seeing that we had bundles of clean bandages, a bottle of witch hazel, and jars of herbal extracts, as well as orderlies, and nurses ready to hop into two ambulances for the trip down to Südwand. Krepkin easily gave over the staffers who liked me best — Ter Holly, Ther Adalslav — or who needed the most watching, but I wasn't going to let him ruffle my feathers today.

I sketched the plan to them, and we unloaded one wagon. That one drove off toward Sinnmach Square to fetch the surgery tables and the first few cots. One Ther could stay behind to take down the tents. It didn't look like rain today, but… the kir-shield. I looked up, thinking of Parselev's shield which still hung over the Square. It could be moved here, but where to anchor it?

There wasn't a whipping-post in the market, but I thought the kir-shield could be strung across a good swath of the stalls and the wagon circle. It would be lower. And we would be —

I turned to the wall, just across the triple-wagon-width of Wallside Street. My memory flicked to the city gates creaking open as Kiefan's horse reared, his sword catching the sun. I had put the darker memories away, but that one was enough to purse my mouth.

We would be very close to the wall, if it were breached. If centaurs cut their way through again.

They were using the loud-speaking charm, up on Patch Tower's flat roof; I could hear them start with introductions and veiled threats. On the tower roof, a row of King's Guard stood against the crenelated wall. Behind them, the king held well back with Captain Aleksandra beside him. The catapult was winched back, loaded, and ready to shoot as well.

I hoped King Wilhelm could keep this Brunnenberg and his men from crucifixion, but I had no say in that. I paced around the market, measuring out my infirmary, as the Arceal envoy — deSvello, I recognized his voice — regretted how the king continued to decline offers to marry Kiefan into Arcea's duchies. It was, apparently, a great honor.

Meanwhile, we picked out a line of stalls for the infirmary: those furthest from the wall, up in the corner of Südwand against Patch Street. I sent Ther Adalslav into one of the houses across the way to look around, and he returned with a good trestle table on his back. There were large iron pots that had been left behind, he reported, so we borrowed those too. It was the saints' work; no shame in it. I noted the house, to make amends to them later.

The wagon returned with surgery tables and cots. My Thers wouldn't let me carry anything, because of my pregnancy, and after a little friendly teasing I left them to the work. The kir-strengthened voices had turned sharp, over on the Patch Tower, and I glanced toward it. Kiefan paced in a slow circle on the street, looking up at the roof.

Kir blossomed, for an instant, so bright and strong my eyes were riveted to the blank wall between me and its source.

Fire struck the Patch Tower, flashing across its roof, and the loaded catapult burst into flame. Horses on the street spooked and ran. Men screamed, burning arms flailing. Ter Holly screamed, beside me. My jaw had fallen open. Then, as the smoke rose off the tower and the catapult burned, a man surged to his feet with sword raised to catch the sunlight.

"Wodenberg!" Even across the distance, I heard the king's shout. It was answered by dozens of voices as men scrambled up on the tower, on the walls where they'd ducked.

A heavy crack of stone on stone cut through them. Then a second. Third. A steady barrage. The seamless city walls glowed in a patch, mid-way up the smooth face. Spider-lines of kir shot out, arced around and returned. Under my feet, I felt kir move, like blood through a vein, from the Pool to the wall. When the spider-lines swung around, they strengthened and the central node absorbed them. It pulsed like a heart.

The ground began to quake. My own pulse shot into my throat as the tremor strengthened and houses creaked all around me. Began to tear, like trees in a high wind. The kir-lines in the wall faltered, losing their way, as stone shots — from the three trebuchets, it had to be — hit again. A dark crack appeared across one of the paths. The earthquake eased.

My arm tingled, alive. / ? /

It startled me out of my daze. / attacking! / wall! /

/ help / strength / breathe! /

Extra kir flowed up my arm from Saint Qadeem, though I'd taken all I could from the Pool while loading the wagons this morning. It tingled under my skin, threatening to overflow, but I held it tight and tucked it away. I'd need it. The king lived, and the men rallied around him. Kiefan, at the foot of Patch Tower, shouted orders. Sent riders off, up to the Rückenstein barracks and into the city. That put strength in my voice.

"Clear both wagons! Rangle, you're first ambulance!" I pointed the driver of the emptier wagon toward the Patch Tower. As I looked toward it, a black cloud of arrows rose on the tower's left and plunged down onto the parapets. That steady beat of stones on the wall at the tower's right was so strong as to put a shiver through my breastbone. The wall's charms still fought, though, its kir-lines pulsing.

And then the earth shook again. A beam gave in the house across the way, and its thatched roof collapsed. I grabbed a booth wall to keep my feet and felt it shivering under my hands.

The crack on the wall widened, breaking across a second kir-line. Interrupted, they couldn't return to the node and it was fading before my eyes. Drawing less kir through the underground vein.

Our second cart horse bucked in the traces, squealing. Ther Adalslav tried to catch her bridle, but she thrashed away from him and fought the bit. "Get down!" I shouted over the creaking of wood. "Let her go!" The quake eased again, thankfully, but the cracking and tearing went on. Another house tumbled in on itself.

The driver tumbled from the seat as the horse started to run, charging across the market into a flimsy booth stall. She knocked it down, but stumbled and fell on it herself. The wagon tried to tip on its side, but hung up halfway. Two of my Thers ran to catch it and see if the mare had hurt herself.

Meanwhile, Rangle's wagon returned, its horse white-eyed and skittery but holding. I pulled myself up into the wagon bed, with a boost from Ter Holly, and knelt beside the knight. King's Guard — the four-starred shoulder of his tabard had survived — and he must've been at the front when the fire hit. His gambeson, under the mail, had caught at the shoulder and burned to the skin before they'd managed to put him out. His flesh was charred across a swath that stretched onto his arm. He lay with eyes glazed, limp.

"Get his mail off?" Ther Adalslav asked, thumping across the wagon bed.

I glanced over at the second patient, an armsman with an arrow in his back. "His. Break the arrow off," I said with a nod. "Put him on the surgery table."

The patterns on the burned knight slowly fell into chaos as his heart struggled. I lay my hand on his ruined skin and called my memory for charms. Parselev's store supplied many related to burns, flickered terrible images past my eyes. I spun up patterns for the damaged lung, the meridian that ran into his arm, and laid them down first. His deeper whorls steadied.

I reached to the Pool for more kir, and felt it reaching back, wanting to give, but the line of kir strained to bridge the distance. It thinned as it came, down to just a thread. Only a drop of kir reached me.

Short range, as Qadeem had said. I wasn't even outside the city walls yet.

Krepkin's strategy served me well; I chose a few small junctures of the knight's pattern that were important, and strengthened them. He would have to last until the hospital, for more. As I climbed out of the wagon, I told Adalslav, "Put him on a cot and tell Holly to watch him closely."

The arrow-struck man awaited on my surgery table, panting, pale with fear, but relieved to see me. Adalslav had left the fletching for him to hold, so I could see what manner of head it had. The man gripped the table and screamed through clenched jaws as I cut the head out and stitched him up.

I heard hooves on Patch Street as I handed off the needle to Ter Edith to finish. At the head of the cavalry formation rode Saint Woden, flanked by the company's captain and the standard-bearer; the banner was a white winged horse on a black field. They streamed past, a hundred grim-faced men on warhorses. A wall of iron mail, helms and black tabards. All strangers, but perhaps I'd meet them soon enough.

The crack on the wall was widening under the steady barrage from the trebuchets. Another heavy thud, and another crack opened, spread — and a chunk of stone fell away. Just a little one, but my heart sank to my feet. I felt kir moving outside the walls, streaming in and pooling; there must be a saint out there, drawing from the Arceal founts in Suevia. Arrows still rained down on the battlements, but King Wilhelm was easy to spot. He was out on the wall, over the crack, with a glimmer of green shield protecting him. It must've been Captain Aleks' doing; she was close by his side, as were his remaining Guard. Squads of our archers returned shots on either side of the king, taking their toll on the trebuchet's crews.

Newly arrived knights filled the junction of Patch Street and Wallside Street; one of my ambulances had gotten through, but the other was blocked in. "Ter Holly, see to the triage. I'll return soon. Tell Rangle to find a second way down to the tower!"

Trotting down to Wallside Street, I slipped through the orderly rows in making my way to Kiefan. A strong hand caught my arm when I was a dozen steps from him. "Hold! Your name and business!"

I didn't recognize the King's Guard. "Dame Kate," I answered before another voice cut in.

"Sir, let her be. The prince will see her." Gregor took my other arm. The Guard frowned, but let me go.

"You're hurt?" I asked. Gregor had a bandage around his head, and his red hair seemed angry about it. "What happened?"

He blushed. "Fell off my horse. M'lord! Dame Kate is here!"

Kiefan turned, silver rings on his epaulettes catching the sun. Saint Woden spared me a glance over his shoulder. I stepped into the gap between them. "I've set up just on Patch Street," I said, pointing. "Can the wagons be let through this corner? Will we be in your men's way, over there?"

"Pull back another block," Kiefan said. "Two would be better."

"They're out of range," Saint Woden said. "They'll be well enough. Be ready to pick up and run, when they come through the wall."

"When? When will it be?" I asked.

He twitched one shoulder. "I can open a saint's door, but the walls belong to Aleks. I can feel the charms unraveling on this stretch, but I can't say how long it will be — they have two saints out there, and likely some elect as well. The attack on the walls is a diversion, so they mean to invite themselves in. Keep your eyes open and listen for the retreat horn. Do you know it?"

I nodded. But Kiefan said, "Move your infirmary back two blocks now. Out of harm's way. And when you hear the retreat, don't stop until the Order's gates."

"The further the wounded must go, the more they bleed," I told him. "And the more die. If m'lord says we're safe enough, we'll stay until we hear the retreat."

His face turned serious. "I'm ordering you back, Kate."

There were too many dead men arguing for me to stay put, though. "My saint told me to aid the Trinity," I said, nodding toward Saint Woden, "and I mean to."

That stiffened Kiefan's spine. "I am your —"

"Do not argue command on the field." Woden cut him off. "Strike her down, or move on."

Kiefan shut his mouth, with a grimace and a hard look shot at his saint. "Listen for the retreat," he said.

I took that with a curt nod and trotted back through the ranks of knights. Woden's orders sent some southward and I dodged my way through their lines as they turned their horses. Northward, on Wallside Street, I glimpsed a block of armsmen marching down from the Rückenstein. I was going to need more ambulances, and —

The ground jolted, rather than building up slowly, and I stumbled to my knees just at the market's edge. In keeping with the set pace, I looked up just before the next trebuchet struck and saw a round shot-ball punch through, leave a gouge in the Südwand's flimsy booths where it skipped, and stave in the side of a house. By the angle, the shot had come from off to the north. All three trebuchets were aimed on the one spot; thus, the steady pace.

"Mother have mercy," I breathed. I looked up to the sky, hoping for a rukh among the clouds. In vain.

The quake faded again, and kir struck the wall — gently. Splashed, almost, in bright green drops. It landed in the hole, which was in truth a stubby tunnel through a slab three or four yards thick, and my eyes caught a bit of its sparkle as it puddled. The sparkle faded, though. More was tossed in, and did the same.

My mind flicked to the lamia's kir fount, its splashing, sparkling water. Then to how water, once it seeped into cracks and gaps, could freeze and break even stone. Parselev's memories of kir ramming through solid doors brought me the rest of the answer.

"Cover!" I broke into a scream, kir strengthening my voice. The remaining mounted knights on the street startled, and their warhorses shied. "Cover! Get down!"

My other ambulance was just starting up Patch Street from the tower; I screamed to the driver, to anyone who could hear, as the mass of kir outside the wall focused down, knotted tighter and tighter, so strong I could all but see it through the wall. I spun out my kir in a little shield — only enough for myself — and curled over my baby.

Kir seared into the wall, seeking out the seeping puddles, and exploded. Fire poured in on its heels. Rock struck my shield, knocking the air from my lungs. The earth shuddered under the barrage. Stones smashed through house walls. Burning men fell like stars, with the gravel. Squealing horses stampeded, some crashing as they were struck. Another heavy blow bruised me, even through the shield, and a limp, burning body tumbled off to my side. A rock big as a sheep smashed into the middle of Wallside Street, half burying itself.

I squinted through tear-filled eyes and gritty lashes. My nose was full of acrid powder and smoke. A plume still lingered at the wall, falling away slowly. Blue sky showed in the gash cut through parapet and wall, and the faraway houses across the Spanne.

CHAPTER 11

The dust pushed away in a sphere around Saint Woden. He stood before the gash in the wall, kir-cloak thick and strong. Fire ignited in his hand and he slung it out into the enemy. The answer was swift; a massive pool of kir bloomed, split in two and struck him, one smashing through his shield and the second ramming him across the ruined street and the burning Südwand, through the solid wall of the house beyond and then through more walls still.

My arm tingled. / !? /

/ !!! / A silent wail was all I could send.

A shiver shot up my arm to my shoulder, into my head, and my Blessing ridges suddenly chilled in my flesh. My eyes tingled in their sockets. Loaf-sized rocks fell fast and thick. I held onto my kir-shield and ran through the chaos, mind blank but for Kiefan and the pounding of my heart. Riderless horses thrashed on the street, dying. Their knights lay crushed and bloody. Men afire tumbled in broken heaps. There was no air in my lungs, but I couldn't hear my own screams.

/ Kiefan! /

/ breathe /

I stumbled against a knee-high chunk of stone and clutched it for support, looking up as the dust plume sank further, revealing more of the hole and the ragged stone teeth fringing it.

I pushed panic through my bond. / broken! /

/ I see / help / strength / breathe! /

More kir flowed up my arm from Saint Qadeem, soothing me. I breathed. The screams of the dying horses, of the men, cut through my ears afresh.

Kiefan lunged through the wreckage, the falling gravel, and the cloud of dust, to snatch up one thrashing, burning body from the street. I landed on my knees opposite him, unraveling my shield and spinning its kir as a candle-snuff charm. The flames chewing at the silhouetted moon sigil died.

King Wilhelm, his gold band bright against charred skin, opened his eyes and clutched his son's tabard. His breath rasped harsh in his throat, gurgling. I felt kir alight on the broken wall; Kiefan felt it and leaped to his feet with a snarl. I glimpsed a soft-bodied Arceal man, and the guardsmen he swept away on either side, a moment before blazing kir poured from him.

I threw myself over the dying king, over the child in my belly, and heat slapped the air away. Fire roared up to either side, rippling under the blast. My skin cringing in the oven-heat, I looked up.

Kiefan stood silhouetted by the white-hot glare, kir-shield braced in both hands against the onslaught. Stars fell as his charm broke under the onslaught, and he re-knit it at Blessing speed. The blast broke across the shield and rushed to either side, just clear of his father's body, setting ablaze anything it touched as it splashed and spread like water.

Body. The king lay dead under me, smelling of roasted meat.

The attack stopped. Fire puddled and burned — but snuffed out as a call pulled the kir from the flames. I had to grab my own kir tight to keep it. Kiefan slung it all back, with a raw howl of rage, in a bolt of lightning. Thunder cracked, too loud to hear, and the afterimage of the strike seared my eyelids.

For a moment, the parapet was empty. Then the Arceal elect leaped up onto a merlon, grinning and shedding sparks from his robes. He dropped down from the wall and landed easy as a cat on green stalks of kir. He put out his hand and a sword flew to it.

Kiefan blurred into Blessing speed with a flash of green-charmed steel, streamers of kir from dying men rising to his call.

I heard a cry. Saw an arm reaching from behind a dead horse, a sword in it, toward the blinding duel shifting in and out of Blessing speed. A tendril of kir lashed out from that fight, snatched a stone; it struck Kiefan across the head and the elect dove into his moment's falter. Kiefan parried the blade, shoved into the strike and threw the enemy off.

I gained my feet and dashed across the burning wreckage. A smoldering horse had shielded someone from the oven-blast, though what looked like a blackened scrap of wood sticking up was actually the remains of a leg from the knee down. Captain Aleksandra stared up at me, her chest heaving, clutching her sword. I grabbed her free arm and a handful of tabard and pulled; she wasn't pinned under the horse, but she was heavy in that mail. She kicked with her good leg, to help. I planted both feet and threw my baby-heavy hips back for leverage.

Kiefan called for more kir, and without a thought I let mine go. He took it all in a green arc, snapped it out in a clap of lightning that threw the elect against the city wall with arms splayed open. Kiefan punched the man between the eyes. The elect's skull split like a pumpkin, splattering red rinds. A flash of light broke from the ruin, leaped to Kiefan's fist and rushed up his arm. He stumbled back as the rest of the kir broke free in a shockwave across the burning street.

The corpse shrank into a wrinkled old man as it slid down, leaving a thick red streak.

Wind shifted and smoke rolled over me, stinging my eyes. I coughed and tried to put up a little shield, but I had no kir. The market and the houses around it roared, pouring smoke up into the sky. Captain Aleks and I sat in a patch of the street blasted to cinders by the elect's attack. And she — "Father's bloody balls," I muttered, calling up her patterns. Her eyes had gone glassy from pain. She still breathed, her heart still beat, but her hipbone had shattered and chaos seeped up her leg from the burned ruin below her knee.

/ please /

I felt Qadeem on the other end, his worry, and another ration of kir poured in through my hand.

/ closer / Pool /

Yes, but they needed me here. My hands on Captain Aleks' cheeks, I drew up a memory of the proper pattern of a hipbone to match the Captain's — wide, sturdy, notched by child-birth — and began to knit the pieces together. Embers floated down on the breeze, catching my eye for an instant and my charm wobbled. With a hiss, I tried to ignore the heat licking at my back. I had to focus. The Captain wouldn't suffer as Ilya had.

Some bone shards had shifted in her flesh; one of Parselev's memories prodded me to lay my hand on her stomach. Pressing my hand gently helped coax the fragments into place. Under a wash of extra kir, her bone was willing to sketch itself together. Not healed, but enough to work with.

Captain Aleks twitched and her lips moved, skirting the edge of consciousness. With a touch to her cheek, I sent her back to sleep for a little while more. That was the last of my ration, though. Blood massing in her belly had come from a jagged bone edge cutting into her gut. She could survive the trip to the hospital, if — I looked up hoping to see an ambulance somewhere near, somebody to help. Closing my eyes, I felt for kir and found two puddles nearby. I turned my mind to them and called.

They came. Enough to strengthen my patient. I sealed her bleeding and re-spun the pooled blood into a bit of fresh, channeling it into her veins — another charm that Parselev supplied me. The remainder I sent down her ruined leg, thinking as I did of the frost-bitten toes I had treated over the winter. Around her knee, the flesh still fought for life. Under my charm, the roots of muscles shook off their damage, the tendons around her kneecap strength-ened. I followed the damaged meridian through the struggling kir-patterns of her burned flesh, strengthening it as much as I could and clearing away patterns that spread chaos. The core of her bones clung to life even past the point where they were laid bare and blackened. With the last of my kir, I twisted the meridian's end into a knot mid-way down her calf.

That was one of Parselev's tricks too; I hadn't seen that before.

The captain's eyes blinked into focus. "What happened? Where's —?" She stopped as she took in the burned horse nearby, the blackened rubble.

A shadow fell across me. Ther Adalslav, my surgery helper, and a second orderly stared down at me wide-eyed.

"Dame Kate," Adalslav said, blinking, "you took my kir. And Ludo's, too. Are you — you must be —?"

"The Captain needs careful handling," I said, getting up. "They need to cleanse her burns, up at the hospital. Do we still have an ambulance?" That got them moving.

"Rangle's up Patch Street, if the horse is holding." Adalslav gestured into the fire. I saw Ter Holly and Edith trotting down to join us.

"Good." To my Ters, I said, "Take him up to the castle." I pointed to the king's body. "Gently. I'll meet all of you at the Order when I can."

They went where I pointed, and I caught a moment's shock when they saw the gold band. But strong, good nurses that they were, they picked him up and carried him as best they could. Nobody else on the street lived. I scanned across the blackened ruin again.

Kiefan stood before the dust-choked rip in the wall, where Woden had stood before, a broken shield on his arm and a sword in his hand. Breathing hard. A tremble in his sword hand. His call for kir tugged at me, but I had none. Wallside Street was full of smashed, blackened corpses.

Outside, I felt kir massing again. Two saints, Woden had said, and more elect.

Kiefan's shoulder was hard as rock under my hand. "Fall back," I said, by his ear. "They need you." I looked to either side to be sure; knights on the south, armsmen on the north, uncertain what to do. "They need orders. Let me find Woden. I didn't feel him die, did you?"

Some of the tension melted from him, at that. "No. Father?"

"Going to the castle," I said.

"Good."

I opened the door. Inside, by the light of broken windows and the burning roof, I saw Saint Woden sprawled on the floor amid the wreckage. A trestle table had been smashed in catching him, and he looked rather worse off than it did.

When I touched his face, his head snapped up with teeth gritted and eyes feral in pain. His kir coiled to strike but hesitated even before "M'lord!" burst out of my mouth. His snarl eased. I put my hand to his forehead and called his patterns.

As when Qadeem had shown me his pattern in the Pool, densely packed whorls and brilliant meridians were all I could see when Woden let his kir answer me. I had to squint to pick out the patterns. All his bones had shattered in the impact, from the back of his skull to his hips, but that wasn't enough to kill a saint.

He had the kir. I had the charms he needed. Woden let me steer; I never doubted that I did no more than guide his hand. Still, when he sat up he looked me in the eye as an equal, if only for a moment. He gave me a slow, solemn nod.

"Take what you need," he said, holding his hand open. As I drew kir off him, he asked, "You can shield?"

"Some."

He sprang to his feet and his iron hand closed on my wrist. "That's all you need do. Come, before they kill Kiefan."

I was dragged out onto Patch Street at Blessing speed. There, I had only a moment to take in the chilling sight: a spreading mass of minotaurs and soldiers streaming onto Wallside Street. Woden launched us both into the air, over their heads, and as wind tore at my eyes a mass of kir bloomed in the midst of the invaders. Two star-cloaked saints stood with an elect between them.

Kiefan snapped around from shouting orders to his company of armsmen when we landed. Woden grabbed my shoulder, turned me toward the enemy saints as kir focused. On reflex, both my hands shot up and a thick little shield spun out as the blast of kir-fire lashed at me. The heat seared through my palms, but the stuff splattered off the shield to either side. Some of it bounced back onto the Suevi armsmen forming up on Wallside Street and set them on fire.

The blast stopped, thank the Mother.

Kir moved behind me; when I looked at Woden and Kiefan, I glimpsed the gossamer red of a saint's bond winding itself from elbow down to palm, on each of them. Woden looked Kiefan in the eye with a stern frown. "You'll be bound to the Pool before nightfall. Survive that long." He turned toward the invading saints. "Rakkar!"

The brown-bearded one turned, raised a hand and beckoned Woden with narrowed eyes. Our saint sprang, low over the infantry's heads, and rammed the enemy head-on. The second saint, a willowy woman, dodged to one side as they flew past and landed on a cushion of hapless Suevi men.

I looked back to Kiefan, so full-charged with kir that it hung in a cloak about him. Wallside Street, as it rose up the slope northward behind him, was full of armsmen who were, starting from the rear of the formation, marching into the side streets on some flanking maneuver. The nearest line of them stood with their shields overlapped for what protection it could offer.

"Kate!" Kiefan shouted as he drew his sword. I glimpsed the Arceal elect — lean, braided red hair arcing from under his helm, glittering gilt splint mail — as he landed before me with a kir-wrapped longsword gripped in both hands, kir-shields glowing on both arms. Kiefan's back appeared between us; steel crashed on Kiefan's wooden shield and the bottom third shore away cleanly.

His shield. I threw my kir onto it, knitting it out. I pinched at the pattern where knots should be, but the kir slithered and wouldn't obey. I played out the tendril thinner and lighter, letting it be only a tether, not a support. Thus, it could be far longer. It stuck, following the shield as Kiefan danced aside, feigned a low swing and blurred into Blessing speed. Sparks flew as kir struck kir, and I felt the jolt through my arm. The two of them spun through attacks, blades shining and skirling, snarling in rage as they worked their way across the road. My shield cracked under each kir-enforced blow and I re-knit it quickly.

Behind them, lines of red-sashed Suevi armsmen poured onto Wallside Street. They headed straight for Patch Street with only the barest glance as they ran past the duel. I saw why when one of Kiefan's deflected blows slung off a broken kir-blade that cut through them, dropping two men before it unraveled completely.

Kiefan lunged with his shield, catching the elect's shoulder, and the man stumbled back. Both men lapsed out of speed. The longsword swung around wildly, and Kiefan deflected it upward, then stabbed at — nothing. The elect rolled up onto his feet a yard further back, and leaped smoothly over the moving stream of armsmen.

Beyond the enemy soldiers, in the midst of the ruined market — and the freshly burning city, and the co-mingled roar of combat — the other Arceal saint took note of her Elect's alighting and turned to face us. She stood tall, cloaked in kir, her blond hair blowing on the hot wind that eddied from the fire. I couldn't see much of Saint Woden's fight with the one he'd called Rakkar, but I could feel it in the roiling power beyond. A kir-ram shot past her, crashing into a burning house near me and Kiefan. Flaming wood exploded across Wallside Street.

She raised her fist, and a brilliant point of light blossomed in it.

Kiefan had spent most of his kir in the duel, and I was too far from the Pool to call it. He raised his shield — with mine still on it — to be sure I was in its shadow.

The saint dropped to one knee, slamming her fist into the road. A shockwave rumbled through the earth, passing under Suevi feet harmlessly. It struck my shield like an avalanche, snapping it, threw Kiefan off his planted feet, and sent me skidding across the dirt on my back. Behind us, the remaining line of armsmen collapsed behind their shields. The world spun with black stars for a moment. My eyes blinked open on cloudy blue sky, though it wobbled a bit.

Movement. My eye caught a bit of white arrowing down, stooping, stars trailing from barred wings —

A raptor's scream, and the impact rattled my teeth, even a dozen yards away. I shot bolt upright and pain wrenched me over on my side with a cry.

"Kate!"

I only had eyes for the massive wings slashing in wide sweeps, trailing blood off their kir-sharpened feathers. A bull's head flew, streaming. Kiefan's hand grabbed mine and his kir flowed into me; my eyes cut to him, helm lost, on his stomach and straining to grip my fingers. "Take it," he gasped. "The baby?"

I put my other hand on my belly and soothed the few tangles I found there first. The baby was still small, in my womb, and well cushioned. The rest went to my broken ribs, to take the edge off. Kiefan's patterns told me he had just as many breaks in his. He lunged to his feet, fought for balance, and with a yell charged into the confused Suevi armsmen.

"No!" I cried, reaching after him.

The rukh rose on powerful wingbeats, screaming, talons bloody, and kir arced down from the fount to him. It passed through Saint Aleks and struck the jagged edges of the wall's gaping hole. The charm-lines lit up, golden against the grey stone, tracing out a sinuous web studded with starry nodes. Broken lines surged toward each other, flashing when they met across the gaps.

The wall rumbled, but it was no earthquake. The wound began to heal, inch by inch.

Woden, broken free of the Arceal saints, raised a sword wrapped in lightning and bellowed. "Wodenberg!"

Kir rose to him from the blazing houses. It came in a rippling, billowing mass that twisted down to fat coils sparking with heat and twined around his sword, following the blade into his arm. Flames sank as their strength ebbed. The thickening smoke choked them out for good. Woden blazed golden, on the verge of igniting himself, and all the kir shot from him, in thousands of straight lines, to his disciples — which I wasn't, but a surge of strength put me on my feet. My yell was lost in all of theirs. I let what kir I had spin up in bright knots in either hand as the nearest Suevi armsmen spotted me.

Half of them paled in fear; the other half put up their shields and yelled, "Elect!"

The word was the same in both our tongues. And my resolve wavered, looking at all of them; they'd call my bluff, and I didn't have so much as I was pretending.

A vine of kir lashed out, wrapped around my waist, and plucked me away. Kiefan was yanked up out of his one-man grand melee, as well, though he kicked and fought it at first. Saint Woden dropped us on either side of him, in the middle of the ruined, smoking Südwand Market. A handful of knights and their winged-horse banner trotted to join us.

Saint Aleks still hovered over the healing wall — draining the fount, by how the arc of kir thinned. A rind of stone had filed in the base of the gash, perhaps a yard high. A second arc, reaching from Rukharbor, joined in. Under him, unnoticed, passed a troop of minotaurs falling back along Wallside Street before the mounted knights. On Patch Street, the Suevi armsmen retreated from our own armsmen. Those at the rear, hearing shouted orders, turned and began to run. Not routing, but breaking up into squads and running.

Kiefan's moment to catch his breath snapped as he took command. "Does Rogen have the line set? Runner! Gregor, where's Pip?"

Saint Woden put out a hand to steady him. "I've given orders. The men can handle this."

"Where are the saints? I didn't feel any of them die."

Woden nodded. "Aleks nearly accounted for the woman, but that Elect put up a fine defense. He and Rakkar pulled her out."

That hung in the air a moment. Then I had to ask. "Rakkar, m'lord?"

"Saints have long memories." He turned to look down at me, eyes narrowed. My sore ribs still heaved, my head still wobbled a bit unsteady, my crespine was lost and my braid hanging loose. But I met his gaze. The saint sounded me, belling out my kir and its chord.

My brow furrowed. "I've been told that's rude," I said.

A smile crinkled his eyes. With a glance to include Kiefan, he said, "At last, a fine pair of elect."

CHAPTER 12

When we turned from Patch Street onto River Road, Kiefan reined to a stop and quietly asked me, "Father?"

I'd been put on a riderless warhorse, and Kiefan rode close by on Pip in case the horse tried to give me trouble. The question tightened my throat. He didn't know. I opened my mouth, but nothing came out. I closed it again.

My silence turned innocent worry, in his eyes, to slow dread. "Kate — you sent him to the hospital? Mended enough for the journey?"

Woden had ordered Kiefan to the castle, to take command there. He thought I should be turning toward the Order's front gate to see to the king. A squad of knights, under a lieutenant, rode with us as an honor guard. They waited, likely wondering what the delay was.

I turned my warhorse uphill and kicked her up to a trot. After a heartbeat, Kiefan followed and caught up alongside me. "Kate! Tell me! Is he —?"

My eyes blurred with tears for him. Through my clenched throat, I managed to say, "He's not at the hospital."

Kiefan stared, then kicked Pip harder. He led the way at a canter up the switchbacks, my mare puffing to keep up and the guard stringing out behind us.

The guardsmen at the outer castle gate came out as the horse neared. "The king!" one called, "Make way! The king!"

"No, I'm —" Kiefan's voice cut off mid-shout. And he urged Pip up to a run through the castle's outer rings.

My heart twisted in my chest. When we flashed through the inner gate, I pulled the reins hard as Pip scrabbled to a stop in the gate-yard. My humble ambulance wagon stood there, a black cloak covering the one body inside. Six King's Guard ringed it with naked swords held point-down to the stone. Half the castle staff stood in a group at a respectful distance, looking up from sobbing and hugging each other.

By tradition, only blood kin could give word on what to do with a body, and so the king waited on the prince's return.

Kiefan all but fell from Pip's saddle. I nearly tangled my skirts on my mare's pommel in trying to follow him. He ran to the tail of the wagon in a flurry of "No, no, Father, I —"

And froze there, hand raised to pull the shroud from his father's head. I caught up with him as the hand began to tremble. I put my arm across his shoulders and laid my forehead against him, my eyes swimming in tears. He shook under my hands.

"Father, I need —" he murmured, half lost. Nobody heard it but me.

Then his back stiffened, and the pain vanished. Kiefan wiped at his eyes, making a streaky mess of the dust and blood across his cheekbones. He glanced around, as if looking for what to do; I caught his hand in mine and squeezed. His eyes were still thick with tears when he looked to me.

But his voice was steady as he began giving orders for the chamberlain to prepare his father for the funeral. To me, "I've only slight wounds, at worst."

"If you don't need me, I'll go," I said, "but you should wash up before Saint Woden —"

"I need you," he said. "Stay. Watch captain?"

"M'lord?" A lieutenant of the King's Guard dipped in a quick obeisance; the watch captain was merely the man with charge of those on duty in the gatehouse. Behind him, Anders was one of the three gate Guards standing at stark attention. His eyes were fixed on me. Tension thrummed from his eyes, stunning me for a heartbeat.

"These men are under your command as relief," Kiefan said, gesturing at the squad we'd brought. "Find Rostislav and tell him the king is dead. Captain Aleksandra is gravely wounded. He will act as Captain of the King's Guard for the time being. He can expect the saints to return soon — and must have the Guard assembled."

"M'lord." The watch captain put his fist to his chest and trotted off to obey.

I followed Kiefan across the yard to the west wing door, where Housemistress Wenda intercepted him. She all but tackled him in a fierce hug, and he clutched her in return. "Will you see to Father? I must clean up."

"Yes, of course. The laundry room." She pointed through the doorway. And in turning to go, she caught my hand and leaned close. "Stay with him."

The laundry was just off the kitchen, full of warm, humid air and the smell of lye soap despite the open windows. Women's voices cut off when Kiefan strode in. "Out, Fräuleins. See to Wenda in the yard, she'll need you. Bring a change of clothes to the door here, but I'm not to be disturbed." His voice rose to follow them as they scurried out, leaving their scrubbing behind. "And send Gregor!"

He strode into the sunlit room, putting a hand to his head, as I closed the door and leaned against it. King of the laundry, I couldn't help thinking as he stood among the wide tubs. Dishes of soap stood ready, and there were large kettles on the fire; surely they knew tricks to get blood out of wool…

Kiefan's hand shook as he pulled off the silver prince's band, and it clattered to the floor. He drew a long, trembling breath.

He'd been steadier when he was moving. I took his hand and tried to sound sure of myself. "Let's get this mess off you. And let me see you."

He peeled off the sooty, bloody layers one at a time — the sword, the tabard, the mail, a quilted gambeson even on a warm day like this. Sweat-soaked, as were his linen cote and braies under it all. The gash on his head, from the rock, had clotted, but the blood had left a red trail through everything; with a little charm, his skin knit shut. His palms were burned red in a ring pattern, from clutching his father. Some bruises showed through his clinging linens. Those were easy enough to mend.

I cleared a rinsing tub and topped it with hot water while he stripped further. I didn't peek. Some trembling still lingered in Kiefan's hands when he stepped into the tub. Crossing his legs, he settled about waist deep. A double handful of water washed a good swath of the dust off his face. His hands lingered over his eyes again, with a deep sigh.

"Soap." I held out the dish and he took a handful of the soft stuff. I sudsed his back for him, rinsed that off, and washed the blood from his scalp wound. Then I unlaced his braided blond crest and combed the hair out with my fingers. A little soap for that, and a little more for his neck. The skin there fought my attempts to scrub, he was so tense. I put more pressure on the knotted muscles around the Blessing ridge on his spine, kneading with my soap-slick thumbs.

Kiefan wilted under my hands with a sigh. Forgetting about his washing, he leaned into the massage.

A knock at the door, and Gregor looked in. Kiefan gestured at the piles of mail and clothes without looking up, and murmured to me, "Don't stop."

I kept going, working across his shoulders as best I could. Gregor took the dirty things and left a bundle of fresh clothes on one of the three-legged stools.

"Headache?" I asked Kiefan.

"No... feels like a head cold. And a fever dream. That elect — his name was dePenna Cavo. He knew speed and anticipation, but in a completely different way from my Blessings. And he knew —" Kiefan put up his hand and a vine of kir shot out, snared his boot, and brought it to him.

"Elect Parselev knew that too," I said, massaging my fingertips across his scalp. He let the boot drop and leaned into my hands again. "I haven't tried it, though."

"You harvested him?" Kiefan twisted around, water sloshing. "You're elect? Why didn't you — why hasn't Saint Qadeem come to bind you?"

I wasn't much good at keeping secrets from him, it would seem. "He did. He said to let Arcea think we're weak, not to say anything just yet. He'll acclaim me later. You can keep that secret, can't you?" There was still a little blood by his ear. I wiped it away with my thumb. Light wounds they'd been, indeed; the real wound was to his heart, even though he and his father had clashed.

Kiefan pulled me into a kiss, hand at the back of my head. His tongue slipped against mine and then water sloshed as he shifted around, sat up in the tub. One damp hand stroked down my sides, over my hips, and then with both hands on my butt he lifted me into the tub. My feet caught on the rim, a moment, then splashed into the warm water.

"What —?" My breath caught.

"Kate —" His voice was thick, choked. "Stay?"

Tears in his eyes when he looked for my answer. Need. I wanted to hug him tight, draw the pain out of him, but I could only do half that. His strong arms squeezed, a little too tight in his anguish. My skirts dragged in the water as I shifted, trying to find footing. Kiefan shifted his grip, hoisted me a bit higher to straddle his lap. A half-firm cock brushed across the hollow of my thigh.

That startled me. "Now?" I whispered, throwing a glance at the door. "Here?"

His mouth found my throat, and his teeth brushing across my skin sent a chill down my spine. "Always," he whispered back. "I need you."

———————————✝———————————

The sun lingered, this late in the Field Moon; as long as the preparations took, the sky was still light when Kiefan knelt before Saint Woden and Saint Aleksandr.

The wooden dais had been pulled out into the middle of the hall and Woden, towering even taller on it, wore royal black and gold silks, the ornate jeweled crown and the royal sword. It was his crown to bestow, after all. The saints' land, the saints' people, and he the first among our Trinity. Kiefan came in only his mail, boots with knight's spurs, and a belt but no sword; simply a knight who wished to claim the crown.

Clean and dry and a little red around the eyes — his sobs had finally broken loose, against my shoulder, after his need had run its course. That tryst was a memory to keep, so raw and primal that my cheeks warmed at the thought.

The chamberlain recited, from a book, the long bloodline from Woden's eldest son, one Kiefan Weissberg, through the line of kings, and two warrior queens, to this Kiefan. After the claim of blood, the chamberlain read the claim of prowess, from Kiefan's earning knighthood to his decisive charge at Ansehen, his high ranking in the tournament, the assassin's attempt, his recent fledging to the rank of elect and binding to Saint Woden.

I had felt the Pool swirl when Kiefan was bound to it, pulling my eyes toward the floor. The thought of him cutting his meridian open to be joined to such a harsh saint — born yoked to the plow, as Kiefan had said. Best put your shoulder into it.

I stood in the line of senior staff, as physician of the castle, along one side of the great hall. The candelabras were lit, to supplement the light through the open doors, and the banners of all the noble houses of Wodenberg looked down on the ceremony; my eyes went to Seagrace's white rukh on blue and grey, in particular. Traditionally, all the nobles would attend a king's coronation. Traditionally, all three saints would as well, and there would be a week's feasting, a special jousting tournament and a great hunt in the forest of Mount Woden.

But the kingdom was invaded, the city was under siege and there were only we staff, servants and Guard to stand witness, and a crowd of city folk watching from the castle yard. There were precious few King's Guard left, as well as only nine of the Prince's. They stood against the opposite wall, at stiff attention, watching the recitation.

Except for Anders. His eyes were on me, steady and intense; my throat tightened when I found him in the line. I'd been wearing my old yellow dress, when I came, and now I was in a simple, dark red one that Housemistress Wenda had found. Because it was nicer, for the coronation, I meant to say if any asked. Though also because the yellow one had tried Kiefan's patience by clinging to me, wet and stubborn, and…

Anders stared, no doubt guessing something closer to the truth. Not that it was any more business of his than his night on Arbor Street was mine.

Perhaps he was as surprised by the sting as I had been. That made me look away, guilty — I didn't mean to sting him. No friend would. He knew that, surely. He knew where my heart lay. And as he'd proposed this arrangement, he had to be ready to keep to it.

"One claim to the crown has been laid," Woden said, his voice carried by the hall's quiet and not by kir. "Are there any others?"

Kiefan's back was to us all, kneeling before the dais. Woden folded his arms and scanned the entire hall as if there were more than one possible counter-claim. King Wilhelm's younger brother Wolfgang had pressed his claim when the old king died. Woden had chosen the elder brother. But Kiefan's nephews, in Rukharbor, were too young, and his cousin the duke had lost one foot in battle. Several, in the hall, stole sidelong glances toward the only one who could lay a claim on the crown.

Anders' stare broke, at last; he closed his eyes and kept silent. Gave up his claim to the crown.

"Kiefan Weissberg." Woden turned his attention back to the claimant. "You wish the authority and privileges due the king of my land?"

"I do."

"You wish the treasures and the comforts due the king of my land?"

"I do."

"Know, then, that this authority, these privileges, treasures, and comforts are given only in exchange for the defending of this land, its people, and we three saints who are bound to the founts of Wodenberg. Know that in exchange for the crown and sword, this land, this people and we three saints will require your strength, your seed, your very life, if need be, to defend Wodenberg."

A moment's pause, to let that sink in. Its weight settled on me, deepening into dread, and I nearly touched my belly again. The baby fluttered inside, innocently. Parselev had said my baby would have a claim to the crown, even as Anders' child. I wondered what my teacher had told Saint Qadeem. If Woden knew the truth.

"Do you claim the crown and sword of Wodenberg?" Woden asked the knight before him.

Only the slightest hesitation. "I do."

"Stand." The saint lifted the crown from his head with both hands; the light caught on the rich blue and green tourmalines set in the openwork band, ran along the facets of the irregular finials — they were mountains, in truth, gold silhouettes of the peaks that flanked our long valley.

He placed it on Kiefan's head, atop his freshly braided tail. Woden unbuckled the jeweled sword-belt next, held it and the gilt sheath up. In the sword's pommel gleamed a milky-white stone, like the full Shepherd moon. That was handed over and Kiefan wrapped it twice around his waist, buckled it.

Woden placed a hand on each of his shoulders. "I name you Kiefan Weissberg, king of Wodenberg, disciple of the Trinity and my first bound elect in twenty years. And long overdue! Wodenberg, you have a new king!"

Kiefan turned and Captain Rostislav whooped first, followed by hearty cheers and applause. I joined in, but my heart ached at the sight of Kiefan wearing that crown, his face so still and controlled.

Fighting tears for his father, still, I knew.

The laundry room was likely our last tryst. That fell on me like a sudden load of bricks. Until the baby came, my heart amended. Hoped. After that — he'd marry. He'd have the war. I'd have an infant and my duties as an elect. Dread of all Parselev's correspondences falling to me added to my despair.

My eyes blurred. He loved me. He deserved love, he —

Woden's voice rose. "King's Guard, Prince's Guard, present!"

I pinched my nose, drawing off tears at the corners of my eyes. Sniffed my suddenly runny nose. Focus.

In unison, they stepped from the wall and formed up in the middle of the hall. There were meant to be fifty of the King's Guard, but they had been reduced to twenty-some. Only nine of the Prince's remained. Captain Rostislav stood at the combined formation's head.

"It is tradition to allow any who ask to resign from the Guard to do so, when a king is crowned," Woden said.

My memory flicked back to Anders' mention of resigning when he could, and I set my teeth on my lower lip. Could he, in the middle of —?

"As we are besieged, your service is still required of you. The remaining Prince's Guard are now promoted to the King's. Captain, administer the oath to each and new tabards will be provided. Current King's Guard, stand down." That said, Woden turned to murmur something to Saint Aleksandr.

The twenty-odd King's Guard stepped back into their places along the wall, crisp and precise. I found Anders at third from the end of his line. He squeezed his eyes shut, jaw clenched, and he swallowed so hard I could see it. Captain Rostislav began with the rightmost, who happened to be Sir Garrick, and recited the oath to defend the king's person from harm, obey his orders, and defend the kingdom.

Queen Mercia hated Anders, that was no secret. My mind wandered to the day of Ilya's funeral, when she had wanted him flogged for imagined slights. But he'd endured that some years, as a Prince's Guard, so surely it would be no worse as a King's. Unless there were some other reason…

"Sir, you will answer!" Captain Rostislav's voice cut to an angry yell.

Anders stood with hands clasped behind his back, eyes fixed on the distance. "I will not," he answered.

"You refuse the oath?"

He only repeated, "I will not."

As the captain turned to look to Kiefan, Saint Woden said, "Stand aside. This is your duty, knight, not a request. You will take the oath and abide by it."

Not only was a line cleared from the saint to Anders, the Guard on either side of him sidled away too. "I cannot take the oath, m'lord."

Green kir lashed out and Anders fell to all fours with a grunt. He sat up on his knees, hands well away from his sword, open in surrender. Woden told him, "You have one breath before you die."

Anders turned his head to look Saint Aleksandr clearly in the eye. "If m'lord will hear me out?"

My breath had stopped, I realized when Saint Aleks raised a hand to stay — and Kiefan stepped close to Saint Woden, speaking too softly to hear. By the grip Kiefan held on his new sword, and by the frown gathering on Woden's brow, he was telling them —

Both saints looked to me. My blood froze.

Woden closed his eyes, pressed them with thumb and forefinger for a moment. Then he took a deep breath and said something curt. Aleks and Kiefan turned aside, giving Woden clear sight of Anders.

Who still waited on his knees. Wool tore; kir shredded Anders' tabard from neck to waist. His lieutenant's brasses clanged off the stone walls and went skittering. Black rags hung from his belt.

"I'll not have insubordination in this castle. You will report to the Captain of the City Guard," Saint Woden said. "Get out of my sight."

In the silence, I could hear Anders' spurs clink as he stood and walked out through the double doors. The stunned audience outside fell away to let him pass, but a murmur followed.

My jolt of terror faded on wondering what Kiefan might've said in Anders' defense. I turned to the saints again, as Aleks invited the people to say their good-byes to the king, and only just caught Kiefan being quick-stepped out, hauled by a fistful of his tabard's shoulder. Woden shot him a dark growl as the doors into the side dining room banged open under a kir-vine's shove.

That chill returned, knotting my stomach. Kiefan had told something of the secret, and why Anders couldn't take the oath. His wife loved the king and carried his child; could Father Duty ask so much? Anders might've had his pride stung, but I'd seen the look on Woden's face on my father, when my youngest brother had earned a hiding behind the chicken coop. I wove my way through the housemaids and stable-boys behind me, making for the double doors.

Shut, now, but I heard voices rising beyond. Breaking into anger. Gentle Woden, Qadeem had said, and that put my hand to the latch to open the door.

"I will not simply forget her and you cannot —"

Kiefan's shout twisted into a harsh rasp and he pitched over backward, arched stiff as a bow. Woden watched him fall, and thrash. The saint spread his right hand. His fingers flexed and Kiefan convulsed on the floor, retching.

"No!" I was halfway to him before I realized it, kir rising to my hands. A shield, a healing, a —

A vine struck me and I tumbled sideways, feet over head. Pain shot through my shoulder, twisting a shocked squeal out of me.

"Kate!"

I landed on my back, breath knocked out. Upside-down, Kiefan wrenched up from the floor, splay-legged, and fought some invisible grip to throw himself on Woden. A flick of the saint's hand, and Kiefan flew across the room, landed on a dining table and scraped hard across it in falling off the far side.

I rolled and came up on my knees as Woden strode to me. So close to the fount, I drew all the kir I could; I gathered it in my hands, uncertain what he meant to do. Woden came with deliberate, heavy steps, hands behind his back.

/ Woden! /

It was all I could put through my bond: my fear and the looming thunderhead of him.

/ respectful / hold your ground /

Hold my ground? My teeth throbbed in remembered pain.

"Don't you touch her!" Kiefan appeared between us, skidding to a stop from Blessing speed, both hands on the moon-pommeled sword. Ready to draw. On his own saint.

A chilly stare. "I meant to help her up." Woden put out one hand, simply.

Kiefan offered me his, and I took that one. I wrapped my arm around his, close to his side, and kept my kir in hand. Whatever Woden had done to Kiefan, I didn't mean to let him do it again.

"You did rightly, in seeing her married," Woden said, as if all this had been a civil conversation. "Now see to your duty and forget her until the child's old enough to train."

"I will never forget her," Kiefan growled back. "I know my duty, but you can't change my heart."

Woden fixed Kiefan with another glare. "Your foolishness will make you weak, and then there will be a winnowing." The saint walked away, done with us, and pulled the half-open door wider to leave.

Kiefan hugged me. "Are you hurt? The baby?"

"Just a few bumps. Did he hurt you? What —?"

"I'm well enough." He put his forehead to mine. "So long as you're well." How his crown had stayed on through all that, I didn't know. Whisper turning fierce, he repeated, "He can't order me to abandon you."

He meant it, I knew, but… "You've your duty. King of Wodenberg."

CHAPTER 13

When I opened the cottage door the next morning, steeled to see what Father Duty would require today, the morning mist was lifting. I turned back to Heima, unwrapping my wool shawl and tossing it on the table. "I won't need this, I think. Don't bother fussing at Krepkin about the allowance, he'll only dig in his heels. I'll try to speak to the chamberlain about what's due to me." And see if there was any word of Anders; he'd vanished after stalking from the hall.

Heima shook her carving-knife at me. "Krepkin owes you the proper measure of food. He owes you your post back — Father's beard, you should be the one dismissing him, now that you're elect!"

Even a mild curse was so odd, from her mouth, that I nearly missed the second part. "Elect? Who said I'm elect?" Saint Qadeem had been right; it wasn't a secret that kept well.

She sliced the bread loaf as she answered. "Ther Adalslav said you took his kir from three yards away. Ther Ludo says the same. So you must be elect. Everyone on campus knows, that's certain. You'll be bound, won't you? You wouldn't go rogue."

Cruel, rogue elect were a staple villain in children's tales, along with kir-bred monsters and other kobolds of the Winter Wood that the Shepherd banished unworthy sheep to. "I am no rogue," I told Heima, returning to the door. "Saint Qadeem bound me."

From the back of the hospital, Ter Holly waved and came trotting across the herb garden as I stepped out into the sun. "Dame Kate! Don't go yet!"

"Is he ill?" I asked. Her husband had taken an arrow during the attack on the Patch Tower, but being Englic he'd gotten little more from Krepkin than witch hazel and a bandage.

"He's well enough. The Captain is asking for you."

"Why would she? I'm sure Krepkin will see to her, and I've better things to do than duel with him over —"

Ter Holly put a hand on my arm. "She begs, Dame Kate. Please see her. She said she'd drag herself out of bed and chase you if you won't." She set her teeth on her lower lip. "She's halfway to doing it already."

If the Captain set her mind to it, she would, from what Kiefan had said of her. "For a moment, then," I said, starting with Ter Holly to the rear door.

Captain Aleksandra was out of bed, when I reached the top of the stairs. She rested in a chair by the peg-boards — "She's only catching her breath," Ter Holly cautioned me — dressed in cote, braies, and tabard, her dark hair neatly shaved to a knight's crest between her speed and anticipation Blessing ridges and the long, braided tail hanging free. Under the light linens, it was clear enough that she'd bound up her generous bosom and that caught my eye. Perhaps Kiefan liked what the baby had done for me, but my breasts ached often enough.

The Captain still had her blackened bones, as well. Her leg had been bandaged at the remaining charred flesh, but the two shin bones and her fused ankle remained.

"Dame Kate —" she said, trying to rise.

I held up a hand. "They'll be quite able to remove that, and you've nothing to fear from gangrene while you're here. The master carpenter can turn you a peg-leg in no time."

Across the invalids' floor, Mein — Freiberg, I corrected, had spotted me and was striding over.

She stood, one-legged, to look me in the eye. "Don't let them take it. They meant to, last night, but I insisted they use that kir on one of the fever-struck."

"The flesh is gone," I said, voice dropping. "The bone barely lives. It will rot."

"I asked for her." Captain Aleks shot a glare at the approaching Freiberg before he could get a word off. "If you'll not keep me whole, I'll be treated by a physician who will." Returning to me, she lowered her voice. "I cannot be laid up in a sickbed for weeks when we've a young king, a gutted Guard, and Arceal dogs inside the walls."

Freiberg retreated, shaking his head. Ter Holly still hovered, biting her lower lip, watching me for a signal to fetch something.

"He's elect now, he can defend himself," I told the Captain. "You trained him well — and he loves you. He was relieved to hear you're alive."

"He needs counsel," she said, fixing me with blue eyes. "He needs steadying. He needs a cooler head beside him because Saint Woden? Father bless him, but he's where that temper comes from. And Rostislav?" Captain Aleks' eyes rolled, with a shake of her head. "I cannot be hobbling around — I will not let him put me to pasture as a cripple. I must have my leg, Dame Kate. I must walk. He needs me."

I knew the temper she meant, in Saint Woden. Then my mind flicked to Kiefan lunging up from the grass at Anders, after losing the final joust. My gaze sank below her knee, where the bandage marked the transition from flesh to char. She leaned, so as to hold it just off the floor, and as that was a simple pose from the disciple's dance she held it easily enough. Still…

"Have you put weight on that?" I asked. "Did you hop here from your cot?" Hers would be the empty one, I assumed, searching along the row to find it.

"Some. I can hobble."

"It must've been agony." Where the lesser meridians were burnt away, she'd feel no pain, but in the lingering end of the main line there'd be pain aplenty.

"No worse than childbirth. You'll learn."

I'd heard such assurances often enough. I gestured for her to sit, and carefully lowered my growing bulk to the floor. "I saw child-birthing marks on your hips when I healed you."

"Yes, twice. Two girls. Good, strong girls, but no —" Cutting herself short, Dame Aleks put a hand on her knee, above the ruin. "Can you mend it? Elect?"

I put my hands on the bones, calling up her kir. "No. The flesh is gone." My memory brought me a whole leg's whorls and meridians, the muscles and tendons that lay under the skin, the bones as they ought to be. Some other corner of my mind asked, "Ter Holly, could you bring us a little tea?"

The meridian had retreated further as the core of the bones died. They would be attacked by the antagonizing patterns that skinned every surface, as would the dead flesh that hadn't been cut away yet. It was happening already, I could see; it was only a matter of time. The only way to save it all, short of a permanent charm like a Blessing, would be to cover it in skin.

Parselev had seen arrowheads, broken off and healed over, as blank spaces within the dance of a body's kir. That gave me something to think about as I sat there, sipping a cup of rose hip tea, studying the leg. Ter Holly had undone the bandage so I could see the few finger-widths of half-burnt flesh above the worst of the damage. There was still muscle there, the roots of her calf. And skin.

It was too much, to spin an entire calf. Even the centaurs, masterful as they were, were created by subtraction from a horse and a man. I had seen their full patterns, and that was clear. They also made clear that flesh was far more malleable than I had ever thought.

I used both hands to encircle Captain Aleks' calf, just below the knee, and cobbled together an image of what I meant to do from a dozen fragments of memory and some ideas. I fixed that in my mind, to remember it of itself. And I called kir.

Mine, the Captain's, and the Pool answered — this close to the castle, a steady trickle of warmth. Combined, it was a bright and eager mass needing firm guidance. I focused on the image of what I meant to do, and the steps needed to do it. The layers. Green and gold light rose around my fingers, sparks knotting up where the kir concentrated tightly to loosen up her flesh.

Squeezing gently, I drew my hands down her leg. The living muscle shifted as it stretched, pushing aside dead flesh which fell away under my fingers. A hand's-breadth down, I squeezed a little harder where the muscles needed to make their joins to the bone. Out of place, to be sure, but they could reach no further. The flesh knew how to become the proper tendon, and I could sculpt the proper root in the dead bone; I could feel that as I fed it more kir. The skin knew how to stretch, to follow. My hands kept sliding, drawing it along, and in my mind I reached higher up her leg for more skin.

I heard a pained growl through clenched teeth, distantly. The meridian struggled to keep pace, but it had some stretch in it as well. Just above the ankle, it could go no further. The skin strained, too.

Our own Blessings came to mind — protrusions of horn thrust through the skin, rimmed by cuticle. I reached into her skin and asked it to make a cuticle and extrude a layer of fingernail over the massed ankle joint. More kir, from what the Pool was still sending.

When I took my hands away, the end of the living peg-leg was grey and smooth, like a lamb's budding horn. The skin above strained, its pores running long and angry red stretch marks ringing her to the knee and beyond. All had been cleansed underneath, though, so no rot could spread. Further up, Captain Aleks pulled hard breaths, sweating, as she stared down at what I'd done.

I reached for my mug of tea and took a swallow. It had cooled. Just to the side, I spotted Ter Holly, kneeling with both hands over her mouth, and I twisted a bit further to look across the room. They all stared, patients and staff alike. Freiberg. And Krepkin.

The old man met my eyes for a moment, then turned away.

I had nothing to say to him. When I started to heave to my feet, Ter Holly was quick to help me. I had half a mind to collapse in a cot, but there was work to do. Turning to Captain Aleks, I said, "Spend this day abed, at least."

She managed a smile, through her panting. "Till noon?"

Likely that was the most she could stand. I waved her off.

"You should rest," Ter Holly said, still holding my arm to steady me. "You look so pale."

I reached for the Pool again and it answered. It had been so feeble last night, after Saint Aleks drained it, that I was heartened by its eagerness. The baby fluttered, too. "Thank you, but I'll —"

Kir blossomed, somewhere, strong enough to tug at me. I turned, frowning, as it wasn't anybody in the hospital. Or in the Order's campus; it was someplace west — and below —? I called it, for a clearer direction.

It vanished.

Saint Aleks had said he'd felt something odd along the western wall. But the saint had flown after the coronation, to scout the passes of the western mountains and return as quick as he could. I would have to bring it up when he did.

My Südwand infirmary was a heap of cinders. A swath of the southeastern city had burned before Woden turned his attention to it, and word was that smoke still lingered in the streets and ash sifted down on the breeze.

I found Ther Adalslav in the wagon yard outside the hospital, helping unload the wounded. He wasn't quite welcome inside, as he'd been my assistant. After watching them a bit, I joined in and soon found myself in charge of a half-dozen Blessing-strong Thers. That suited me. There was work to be done.

The ambulances found wounded in the southeastern city and brought them back as they could. Nobody knew for certain where the enemy squads were, where they'd hidden. Our drivers went carefully, only sure they were safe once they crossed Captain Rogen's line at River Road.

Arcea's diversionary attack at the wall had ended, and with it the arrows. Many of the wounded I saw were stabbed or slashed. A few were knights who'd fallen from dying horses and broken their bones, but it was the blood dripping from the wagon beds that haunted me. Every drop difficult to replace. My trickle of kir from the Pool kept me able to mend what I could, but blood-spinning needed far more. These wounded were often drained of their day's ration and my Thers needed theirs for their Blessings.

Wagon after wagon rolled across the Order's courtyard to me.

The wounded came ashy-faced, half dead, begging me when I leaned over to check their patterns. I told the ambulance orderlies about arteries and veins, I told them they had to choose men who were bleeding, but bleeding not so badly that they'd die during the trip. Men who'd had to wait for a second ambulance were, when it came, too far gone when they'd have been savable earlier.

Our orderlies were Thers, former shepherds or wagon-drivers who knew nothing of anatomy or meridians. They'd sworn to serve all the children of the Mother and Father; they saw pain and couldn't be so hard-hearted as to say no.

I would have sent Ther Adalslav with them — he knew better, after working with me — but I couldn't lift these armored men from the ambulances myself. He, Ther Ludo, and the others carried the wounded into the hospital and I didn't mean to set foot in there.

Ter Gudrun came out, once, to ask if I would help with the surgeries. As the senior nurse surely had more pressing duties, I knew who had sent her. I declined, telling her I was already trying to help by educating our ambulance orderlies.

I was also mending an artery here, clearing bloody lungs there. Seeing that men would keep their limbs and their strength.

Later in the afternoon, when the lowering sun ripened to orange, the fighting slowed in the southeastern city. Krepkin found time to come out himself. A towel in his hands, he dried between his fingers and in the creases of his knobby knuckles as he strode from the hospital door to where I stood waiting for the next ambulance.

"Elect Bockmann, would you kindly take your proper place in the Order's medical facility?" His voice held to a carefully neutral tone. "The surgery and the invalids' floor await your inspection and command."

My little knot of Thers, all of them taller and stronger and older than I, looked to me expecting this would mend all. But after so much triage and knowing there'd be more tomorrow, Krepkin's surrender meant little to me.

"It's kind of you to ask," I said, with a nod, "but please, keep your command of the hospital. I'll do the most good if I'm out with the ambulances, in truth. They don't know how to triage in the battlefield, and it's too much to ask of untrained men already weary and sore."

Krepkin's mouth worked under his white beard, and his bushy brows knit together. "Do you think Elect Parselev would wish a pregnant slip of a girl put so close to harm's way? I'll send Meinrad, if someone must go."

"I'm far more able to defend myself than Physician Freiberg," I said. "I am an elect, after all."

"What do you know of combat, then?"

A harsh laugh burst out of me. "Saint Woden took me into the fray himself, sir. I will be on the next ambulance. Captain Rogen has the bulk of the enemy bottled up, they are saying, down by Wallside Street. They've enough archers with heat sight to be sure nobody will creep out in the dark."

"If you must be on an ambulance, it will be in the morning," Krepkin said, annoyance turning his voice stern. "Eat, get off your feet and wash up."

"I will only —"

"Did you not tell me to keep command of this hospital?" he asked. My mouth drew into a purse, not much wanting to answer that. He folded his arms across his thin chest. "My ambulance staff are under my command, are they not? I will not have them exhausted, hungry or filthy. See to your own care and packing your memories away. The siege has not lasted even one moon yet — we must be ready for more."

I was near dead on my feet. I couldn't entirely feel my feet, in truth. He was right, there could be many moons of this yet to survive, if Caercoed didn't reinforce us. To agree, I nodded, and he turned away with a grumble under his breath.

"Krepkin," I said, and he paused. "You were right about not being ready for this. For war." He turned, considered me for a moment. "Nobody is ever ready, in truth."

———————✕———————

"They were bottled up, Captain Rogen said last night," I said. "They couldn't get out."

The archery sergeant spread his hands in surrender. "Wasn't my watch, m'lady. Just rolled from bed and buggered down from the Rückenstein myself. These minotaurs of theirs are damnably strong, to hear tell. Ballsy as bulls with cow-fucking on the mind." He hooked his thumbs in his belt, scanning up and down the street.

Our ambulance driver had caught up to a lieutenant's squad of armsmen on Baker's Street and they'd been quick to tell us to stop, stay here, and had left a hand of archers plus Sergeant Kartemann to keep us safe. They tracked a band of minotaurs last seen coming this way, westward from the "bottled" area toward the city gates. We'd pulled over at the corner of Baker's and a narrow side street, in front of a bakery, to wait for word.

Houses here stood close by each other, two or three floors tall and their thatch green with moss. Craftsmen worked on the ground level and lived just above; here in the lowest part of the city, they were tailors, cobblers, bakers and butchers. Peasants, but more respectable than the farmers and laborers — and Engls — outside the walls.

The five bowmen were City Guard; they all wore tabards with one star on the right shoulder, the white hawk of the archers on their left. As I watched Kartemann, his yellow hawk's-eyes flicked to and fro, iris adjusting constantly, and his translucent inner eyelid blinked sideways.

"They called you down off the wall, for this?" I asked. We'd been sitting for some time already, and I was wishing Ther Adalslav had brought his deck of cards.

Kartemann grinned. "Those that came in with the king — Shepherd see him home — are south-landers. They need us just to find the fucking latrines around town. Couldn't find a few hundred Arceal bastards if they bent over and got cocks up their asses. All the Guard are out for this one."

"Knights, too?" I'd still had no word from Anders — he'd reported to Rogen, but the City Guard had little reason to answer a mere physician's questions.

"And pleased as piss to get their asses back on horses. Not much call for those on the walls. Nice capper after the fun they've had these few days — heard how one of those tight-assed Prince's Guard got himself kicked down the hill?" He laughed at his own joke.

I hadn't said anything, but the story of Anders' expulsion from the Guard had torn through the city faster than the fire. Adalslav and Ludo both looked up, and our driver twisted on his seat.

Kartemann was pleased to have an audience. "Turns out it was him that ran the cav ragged all winter on account of they 'weren't up to par' or whatever shit that was." He tossed a look to one of his archers, who snorted to agree. "His balls have been in a sling, you can believe that. Then again, if he really is a mule it don't matter so much."

Mule? Anders?

The archers laughed. "He gave Rotmann back fairly last night," one of them added. "Mule's got a kick, at least."

Kartemann snorted. "Saw that shiner. Course, on Rotmann that's an im —" He cut himself off with a hiss and a raised hand; in the sudden quiet, I heard it too. Voices and pounding, coming closer. A tangle of yelling and wooden slapping and deep-throated bellows.

"Get this wagon around. Get some distance," Kartemann ordered, pointing; the noise was heading for Baker's Street ahead of us. "At ready! Ebur, your line in front." Three archers knelt with bows ready, and the other three stood behind them.

When the cart-horse balked at having to leave the patch of weeds he'd been eating, Adalslav jumped down and took him by the bridle. I climbed up in the wagon bed and knelt at the sideboard as we swung across the street in turning.

Minotaurs. I'd never seen one, alive.

From a side alley, the City Guard lieutenant was the first to trot out, spot the archers' formation, turn and shout orders to those following. They piled out, a bit too quick and jittery for an organized retreat, but half a dozen of the men turned in the middle of the street and stood fast, overlapping their shields to form a wall. A gap in the middle let the rest of the squad pour in, some at more of a run, some trailing blood.

The snorting and bellowing grew louder as a few more men skittered backwards from the alley, their shields and swords guarding. A spear lashed out, gouging the shield of the last man and he stumbled under the blow. The other two broke to either side at a run as the minotaur charged out of the alley, spear plunging into the fallen Guard as he came.

My eyes caught on the black horns, then the massive, tawny bull's head. The monster bellowed, lips peeled back from horse-sized teeth. His helm moulded close around his head and the horns, but did little to stop the two arrows that struck his neck under its rolled edge. A third took him in the chest, through the black, iron lamellar.

Sergeant Kartemann and the two standing archers shot the second minotaur to charge headlong from the alley. That one crashed down too, hoofed feet kicking. The two last Guardsmen circled behind the closed, ready shield wall.

"Stop!" I called to our wagon driver. We were a good block behind the archers' line, and there were only the two minotaurs dying on Baker's Street. The impaled Guard screamed but faded fast. There were wounded men toward the rear of their little shield wall. "They need us."

"Wait on their call," Ther Adalslav said, looking up at me from beside the wagon. "We should keep —"

The collective roar of the Arceal minotaurs tore our eyes back to the archers and the little shield wall. In a wedge the monsters charged out, heads lowered, their leader holding his spear crosswise to strike across the shield wall. He hit and threw five of the men back into the second line — and the second into the third — on the force; the crunch of wood and the yells cut through the bellowing. Blood spurted where a horn found flesh.

Kartemann's archers placed their shafts with care, but in a few heartbeats I saw the rumor was true. One arrow, even at this short range, even in the neck, didn't stop these monsters. One in the leg, where it wasn't covered by an iron greave, might make them stumble. The hide below their knees, where their feet had pulled out into hind legs and hooves, was thick and shaggy but vulnerable.

If I'd been braver, if I'd run back and thrown up a kir-shield —

The minotaurs' heavy spears crashed through shields and men bled. Swords stabbed back in return, too quick, too accurate to be deflected. The bulls' voices broke in pain. The arrows took their toll as they doubled up. I saw the moment the tide turned for certain; the lieutenant leaped through a gap in the shield wall and with one Blessing-fueled swing chopped through a bull's thick neck and spine. His sword snapped, or he'd have beheaded the beast.

"Break off!" The Arceal command was belled by the minotaur's voice, but I knew it.

The rear of the squad swung away from the archers and retreated downhill, protected by those who still fought. What side street they vanished into, I didn't see, but the last few minotaurs fell to cover their escape. The lieutenant yelled for eyes on them, and three armsmen sprinted to follow. The officer stood with chest heaving for a moment, shaking off the fight, and took in the remains of his squad, his broken blade, Sergeant Kartemann, and us in the ambulance beyond.

He raised an arm and gestured for us to come. I slid off and trotted down the slope as the wagon swung around again.

As I passed, Kartemann called, "Oh Fräulein, I've sprained my pinkie…" and his men laughed.

A few who'd taken spears still breathed, but not for long. Ther Ludo picked up one man and his guts spilled out of the gash in his belly; the armsman screamed at the sight and fainted.

"No!" I shouted when Ludo began to carry him to the ambulance. "Give him to a friend to watch. Take that one." I pointed to the Guard with a gash in his shoulder. I could repair most of that in the ambulance.

I knelt by an unconscious man with a dented helm and pried it off him. His head seemed well enough underneath, if coarse-featured. Calling his kir, I saw the crack in his skull, the bleeding inside. His only injury, it seemed, but one that would turn fatal with time.

"What do I do, m'lady? Father's coming to." I glanced up at the young armsman and saw the resemblance between him and the gutted one, who was mumbling and starting to twitch. Father. My stomach twisted.

"Adalslav, take this one," I said, pointing to the head injury. Standing, I crossed to the gutted father and knelt down to check him. He bled out the puddle he lay in and leaked yesterday's meals; the stink wouldn't come off his son's gambeson for days, I knew. Only a cleansing charm could get it out from under my fingernails.

I put my hand on the dying man's face and reached down his prime meridian to a spot just above the slash. With a little of his kir, I cut the meridian so he would feel no pain. This far from the Pool, I couldn't spare any if I meant to save those in the wagon. "Say your good-byes and stay with him until the Shepherd comes," I told the son. "I'm sorry."

Standing again, I surveyed the wreckage. Thirty armsmen, maybe, had stood against two dozen minotaurs at a cost of eight dead and five that I could help. Another six needed only a clean bandage to press to their wounds, but I only had three to offer. I wiped the cuts down with witch hazel and told them to keep clean as best they could.

"Kartemann." I raised my voice as I returned to the ambulance. "Where's the cavalry?" Climbing up, I glanced over the shoulder wound and the other injured, gauging kir and timing.

"Wallside Street, before the South Bend. What about my pinkie, m'lady?" He held one hand up, wiggling the finger with a smirk.

His brown hair was tied back in a sloppy tail and his beard wanted tidying — cleaned up, he might be attractive. I blew him a kiss. Kartemann slapped his hand to his heart, stumbling back with a grin. I waved his theatrics off and sat down beside the gashed shoulder as the ambulance started uphill.

CHAPTER 14

When the ambulance turned past Sinnmach Square onto Wallside Street, my gaze lingered on the arrows still stuck in Parselev's kir-shield overhead. We'd never had the chance to move it. I remembered him smiling, selecting a book from his shelf and passing it to me. The patient look he'd give me when I doubted I could do what he asked of me. How he'd said, "Majesty, she's my finest student," that night in the chapel. And I missed him.

It seemed a hundred years since he'd died, but it was not even two weeks yet. The baby kicked inside me and I stroked my belly.

With the aid of my teacher's lessons and some of his own memories, I had trepanned a hole in the head wound's skull to drain the blood before its buildup harmed the brain. A little pinch of kir and the bleeding had stopped. Krepkin would stitch the scalp shut over the hole. The man should survive with little trouble.

All five of the men in the ambulance would be well. Still, I thought of the dead armsmen on Baker Street and how my mother had wept when she learned that my father had died.

Along Wallside Street, warhorses stood close to the city wall with their knights dismounted and waiting for orders. City Guard, all; though the Guard was largely armsmen and archers, there were perhaps a hundred knights in the ranks. Captain Rogen had told us to report to Lieutenant Tritter, who would be by the Guildhall the minotaurs had barricaded. I scanned the faces as the ambulance rumbled by, but in truth it was easier to check the horses for Nipper. I'd know his dapples on sight.

Further along, we came to a second squad whose knights were mounted still. There, I spotted Will Bockmann bent over a horse's foreleg caught between his legs, checking the hoof while the knight stood by. Will's brown hair, shaggy as it was, hung past his eyes and he didn't look up as I passed. The horse wasn't Nipper, but I spotted his rump a little further on, in a group of other rumps.

Lieutenant Tritter, a knight wearing sergeant's brasses, and his hand of knights stood at the formation's head. Anders held the reins for the officers' horses as well as Nipper's — a page's job, if not a squire's. He wore a plain City Guard tabard over his mail, and his horse's ears. One flicked toward the ambulance briefly as we approached, but he didn't look away from the Cobblers' Guildhall another half-block down Wallside Street.

Mule, I saw, though I disagreed; mules had bigger ears.

The sergeant had a nasty black eye and Kartemann was right. The man wouldn't have looked any better without it.

"I won't be the one to explain to Saint Aleksandr there's a fire in the city again," the scar-faced lieutenant was telling Sergeant Rotmann when we came within earshot, "and neither will Captain Rogen. Either we flush them out here for a charge or we send in more men." He grimaced, eyeing the steps to the Guildhall's closed double doors where the blood was still fresh. Holes in them looked to be the work of minotaur spears. On the upper floor, the window shutters stood just ajar enough to see movement inside; they watched us as we watched them.

Our driver stopped a few yards short of Lieutenant Tritter's group, close enough to be noted but not so rude as to interrupt.

"A good squad could flush them out, sir," Anders said. In glancing up at Tritter, he noticed first the ambulance and then me. He looked away quickly, fidgeting with the reins.

"Mules should keep their mouths shut," Rotmann growled.

"Is that the mule volunteering?" Tritter asked. "You think a good kick will take those doors down?"

"Give me a hand of knights and I'll clear the building, sir."

"Those minotaurs can gut you through the fucking door — perhaps you missed that part?" Rotmann jerked a thumb toward the blood on the Guildhall steps.

Anders fixed the sergeant with a hard look. "Strength isn't worth a piss if you can't connect. Sir." That touched some nerve and Rotmann turned red.

"Enough, mule. A few shots from one of the catapults would do the job," Tritter said. "Rocks through the roof and they'll come out to play. Ambulance, you'll be needed after that. Stay — this is where the action will be." He tapped his horse forward a step and reached to take the reins from Anders.

"Sir, they could just go out the back and into Weber's squad," he said. "Those alleys are too close to swing —"

"Rotmann, you're in charge till I get back. It's Kunster on the wall today, isn't it?" The lieutenant looked down at Anders. "Don't let the mule wander off." He tapped his horse up to a walk, apparently giving the matter no more mind.

After him, Anders shouted, "Three crescents says I can clear the Guildhall before the catapult gets a shot off."

The lieutenant stopped his horse. A chuckle ran through his squad as he weighed the offer. Then he twisted around to look back. "I take payment out of your horse if you don't."

"And my widow gets the rest." Anders threw a glance at me, and every man in earshot looked. I had been searching the knights for any sign of the wounds that had left the blood on the steps, in vain — the lieutenant's plan was sound enough, to my ear. Far more sensible than charging into a Guildhall full of minotaurs, and thus I'd been paying Anders' claims little mind. Their collective eyes nearly stopped my heart with the realization that the officer was actually going to take this bet.

"Anyone volunteers, you'll be the Mule's Hand and we'll stitch you your own banner," the lieutenant announced and tapped his horse up to a trot, aiming for the gatehouse towers where the watch captain would be. The volunteers came, laughing and joking about it; all young knights, none older than Anders and one of them Englic as well.

"He honestly means to —" I looked to Ther Adalslav, but he only shrugged. "Anders!" I yelled, leaning further over the sideboard.

He explained his plan in low tones, by how they each nodded, and he pretended not to hear me. He couldn't not hear, with Nipper's ears on him. The largest of the men got some extra instructions, and nodded as well.

"Anders!" I called again as the hand of five gathered their helms and shields from their horses. Anders took a moment to pat Nipper's head, stroke his neck, and I was out of the wagon bed by then. I didn't bother raising my voice as I strode toward him. "You can't mean to go in there, even with five men. What in the Father's name —?"

I stopped when I felt kir move; Nipper shook his head, shifting away from Anders' hand. He looked to me, then, just one look, and the charm had drawn his face out into a bit of muzzle to accommodate two horse's nostrils. Complete with a grey-dappled fuzz like Nipper's. Strange as he looked, an eerie echo of a centaur with a pig-tailed crest of flaxen hair between his Blessing ridges, it was his eyes that held me. It was the sad cast on his resolve.

Anders clicked to Nipper, a command I didn't recognize, and tossed the reins at me. I caught one of them, startled. He trotted after his hand of knights, settling his shield on his arm as he went. I moved to collect Nipper's other rein, leaning away quick when he eyed me.

I thought of kir-blades, of kir-shields, but none of it would help him now. I turned away deliberately from the distraction the largest of the five knights put on in the middle of Wall-side Street — a barrage of Arceal insults, some rushes at the closed doors — and I didn't see how Anders got his men inside.

I looked up at the wall, instead, watching for the orders to turn the catapult and unleash it on the Guildhall. It took four men with strength Blessings to pick the machine up and rotate it on the circular tower roof. My heart sank as they set it back down. The artillery-man set about checking the aim and making adjustments. Lieutenant Tritter, to guess by the glint of brasses on his shoulders, leaned through a crenel to watch from above.

For a bet. I didn't believe for a moment Anders did this for a few silver crescents; it was only how he'd goosed the lieutenant into agreeing. Even if they were paying him back for the grief he'd given them in training, this was too rash a stunt to prove... what? That he wasn't their mule? To earn a sergeant's brasses and his own hand of men? He'd have me widowed for that? First the King's Guard and now —

I heard the crash of wood behind me, the bellowing of minotaurs followed by Rotmann ordering the charge. Nipper's head picked up and he fidgeted on his feet, looking around for Anders. I tried to grab his bridle and he snapped at me, though it was half-hearted. He wanted to go, to join in.

Nipper's ears had earned Anders the nickname, when it was in truth a clever and useful charm that only a fool would ridicule. If Saint Woden hadn't stripped Anders and sent him off to these louts... he would have killed Anders in the great hall for refusing to swear. There was little doubt of that. Anders knew full well what refusing Woden meant. And still declined a post on the King's Guard. His cold, grim stare from across the hall flicked past my eyes. Accusing. When last I'd seen him, on Arbor Street, he'd been stunned to see me. Caught in a crime.

Ther Adalslav, watching the scene from the wagon, looked to me once as the noise began to die down. Whatever he saw, he slid down out of the wagon and gestured to Ther Ludo to follow.

Three crescents for charging headlong into close quarters with Arceal minotaurs, where he'd be stabbed or gutted or —

Anders' hand grasped Nipper's reins above mine. I turned on him, snarling through my teeth. "You're no fool, so why? You're no fool or hound for glory or gambler — your life, for three crescents?"

He'd dropped his ear and nose charms. "What's it to you? Nipper's worth far more than that. You'll get the balance." Cold, narrow eyes.

It was the most absurd thing to ever come out of his mouth. I hit a new octave. "Money? You think I want your money?"

Anders leaned closer to snap back. "And my mother will never turn you out, so you can slip away and comfort the king whenever you please!"

This was about Kiefan? My volume dropped back as a few knights rode by, but my rage kept the edge on my voice. "As we agreed to? You suggested this! I've kept up my end! I don't care what you were doing on Arbor Street — what's it to you if I —"

"So you did fuck him." Anders' lip curled.

"And you fucked a whore. What of it?"

His voice rose. "I slept on the damn hearth!" And he drew back, looking away with a hard frown.

My anger cracked. "You — what?"

"Süssie's — I sleep better without the snoring. Rostislav is loud as a thunderstorm."

Confusion steadily washed away my fury. "You spend nights in a whore's cottage for the good night's sleep? Why?"

He snarled. "So believe I fucked her, if you please. It gave you leave to dash —" His throat cut off the rest, and he clapped his teeth back together.

I raised a hand to fend this off. "Why?" I gestured toward the Guildhall, trying to get back to that.

And he returned to, "What's it to you?" This time, he heaved a sigh.

"It's my husband? It's my baby's home and family? I thought you..." My hand went to my belly, echoing the memory of his there when the baby kicked. The flutter in my stomach made my throat tighten. What had I thought?

Anders grimaced, closed his eyes. He clenched Nipper's reins in his hand. "He'd take care of you, if you let him. A knight's widow and child? It would be charitable. Honorable. And you'd be happy."

He turned and led Nipper away without a glance back. Left me stunned.

I didn't let our driver take me back to Lieutenant Tritter's squad; we collected wounded from the City Guard's armsmen, who whittled at the barricaded squads of Suevi soldiers near the bend of Tailor's Street. That came to an end when the Suevi asked to discuss terms of surrender, and the afternoon was spent in negotiations between their lieutenant and Captain Rogen.

I stewed. In Parselev's office, I fell to sifting out the Order-related records that Krepkin had wanted; it kept my hands busy while my mind fumed over Anders. If he wanted to sleep on a hearth in Arbor Street, well, he could do that. He wasn't required to fuck the woman. That was his choice. I threw down a leather-bound book on a stack and it began to tip. As I caught them, my memory flicked back to Theo walking from the whore's — Süssie's? — door toward the horse shed. The two horses there.

The whore, paid for already. Theo's whore. A small thing to let his friend sleep on the hearth, perhaps, if he didn't want any part because… that thought squirmed up stronger, this time, and found words. Because he was married now. Because…

I put papers down, covered my eyes.

"Don't laugh," Saint Aleksandr had said, and I saw those horse ears sprout on Anders again. His surprise made me smile all over again, in spite of myself.

Then, the moment I'd seen him over Kiefan's shoulder after the disastrous sortie, those grey ears twitching as the hope drained from Anders' face. The kiss he'd taken with my token. The one I'd given him. And then catching him at Süssie's gave me leave to dash — his hopes? His heart?

He loved me. Mother Love have mercy. I dropped into Parselev's chair, eyes blurring, and gripped the arms with whitened knuckles.

He'd known. He'd known all along and this had been a plan. Kiefan might have my heart, but he had his duty, his honor, the entire kingdom now. Anders had all the time he could need to smile and tease and talk of bone-setting and horse ears and teach me to dance and… now he defied Woden and took fools' bets. He'd see me widowed?

That angry stare, from across the hall. Dashed hopes. And my memory cut to his slamming my door the morning after Solstice. "Don't trouble yourself, m'lady."

Dashed twice.

What could I say to him? I never meant to hurt him. He was my friend, my dear friend, and…

Eventually, I began sorting papers again because staring at bookshelves fixed little.

I still didn't know what to say to Anders when I went to the hall to eat at sunset. Ther Ivor probably ought not to feed a dismissed physician, but the old cook ruled the kitchens as a king in his own right, and didn't fear Krepkin. Over a cup of watery broth, fresh oat bread and roasted spring onions, I heard about the report of smoke spotted in the east. Below Vorspitz, the hawk-eyes on Kaltkern's watchtowers said.

Half of Arcea's army had chased Duke Seagrace and Saint Qadeem eastward, and there had been no direct word from them since. When he'd come to bind me, Qadeem had said only that they were hard pressed.

I went to bed thinking of Caercoed, of Lady Leix and Lorcana, Captain Mohra and the "interrogation" that I had endured. Their swords-women had acquitted themselves well in sparring with Kiefan and Anders, but to think of them facing centaurs and minotaurs... I lay awake beside Heima, my mind casting women in the place of the armsmen who'd fallen on Baker Street.

Thinking of Captain Aleksandra and her ruined leg. Thinking of the dying armsman and his son, and how my father had slipped away while my duty kept me elsewhere. For weeks, I'd known I could have saved him. Parselev had told me, eventually, exactly how many men had died that day and if I wished to punish myself it should be for failing all of them.

"We don't cheat the Shepherd of his sheep," my teacher had said. "We only bargain for more time."

My memory went back to the lamia's fount, sparkling ruby as Anders bled out. Even then, it had been beautiful. Its kir beckoned, twinkling. And it moved, sliding across...

I jerked awake in the dark cottage. Heima wheezed beside me, deep and even. No movement in the shadows, but they were deeper now that the Field Moon had only a few days left. Only the Flock shone overhead, waiting for the Shepherd to rise near dawn.

Cautious, I called for kir. The Pool answered, as did Heima's. Nothing amiss.

With a sigh, I lay back against the pillow. I resolved to send a message up to the castle to tell Saint Aleksandr, if he were there, about these passing traces of kir. And as I was awake, I might as well get up and join the abbot's disciple's dance again.

I still didn't know what I'd say.

"Stop here." I tapped the shoulder of the driver beside me when I spotted the City Guard's banner on River Road. The line of armsmen holding the road had contracted as the remaining invaders were pinned down in the south city; it only spanned a few blocks now. "Captain Rogen!" I called when I spotted the three brass rings on his epaulettes.

And the bald head. Sir Radulf Rogen, Captain of the City Guard, walked over to my ambulance. He was a tall man, hatchet-faced, head shaved entirely rather than keep a knight's crest between the brief ridges of his anticipation Blessing. He gave me the same once-over he always did, as if my pregnancy might disappear or I might let his disapproving frown change my mind about riding in ambulances.

"Is Lieutenant Tritter's squad still engaged?" I asked. "Did the Suevi men surrender?"

"They were selling us a pile of shit," he said, and then turned aside to hear the report of a messenger on a puffing horse. He waved the man on toward the castle and told me, "Follow along. Tritter says he's got them on the move, but damned if he can do anything right unless there's money on the line."

He shouted a few orders to his men and mounted his horse. A hand of knights peeled off the standing ranks to escort us along Low Street at as brisk a walk as our wagon horse could manage. Captain Rogen drew alongside my side of the driver's bench.

"Any new word from the watchtowers?" he asked.

"Last word was that the remains of Suevi cavalry and some centaurs reached the camp here, ahead of their retreat. Duke Seagrace pursues them — Saint Qadeem's flare last night signaled a victory."

Captain Rogen nodded. With a sidelong frown, he asked, "You knew I was sending you down to Tritter this time?"

"I need to speak to someone." My own brow creased as I hunted for words. Still. He owed me the worming charm. He'd sworn fealty on our wedding day and I demanded he stop this foolishness. He was to be as careful as any other man with a pregnant wife, and if he was only sleeping on the hearth in Arbor Street... Parselev's cottage had as good a hearth as any.

Would that stop him? Without breaking his heart again, weeks or moons from now? Tell him I wanted him there, my friend and…

He deserved love, as much as Kiefan did. Deserved a wife who loved him. Perhaps I should be the one taking fools' bets.

The houses along Low Street ran as close and tall as on Baker's; sound carried off their shake-shingled faces from fighting ahead. Craning to see around a bend in the road, I glimpsed a few warhorse rumps. Captain Rogen and his knights moved ahead to shield us, but from the driver's bench I could still see.

Tritter's squad of fifteen was down to ten, and on this street only three could ride abreast. They all moved at a slow walk, as the combat was moving. Standing up on the wagon, I got a better view; mounted Guards driving Suevi armsmen backward along Low Street in little charges against their patchwork shield wall. The horses pranced and lashed their hooves on the shields. Knights swung down hard on helmets and came away with bloody blades. The armsmen below blocked as best they could and got their jabs in on the horses, but when one knight fell back another took his position.

Still, there were a good number of Suevi. Far behind, across Low Street, a line of archers waited with bows ready. The more the Suevi retreated before the knights, the easier the shots for the archers. They waited for the knights to disengage, though.

Lieutenant Tritter rode to the captain. "We've got them in range. Drive them closer, or break off and let the hawks feather them?"

"Let the hawks have them."

I checked the five horses at hand, as their Guard were all helmed; none were Nipper. One was, though, a bay palfrey with Will Bockmann in the saddle, and his sleeve — "Will? You're hurt? Let me see that."

Tritter put two fingers in his mouth and whistled three loud blasts. Will glanced from the skirmish line to me, startled to hear my voice, and then looked down at the blood and torn cloth as if he'd forgotten.

"It's nothing," he said, pulling at the hole so I could see.

I had my medicine bag open already, and reached for cleansers and a cloth. "It's not nothing. Let me see that."

"Nipper nearly got me. It will keep, truly. Anders!" Will stood up in the stirrups to yell across the handful of yards to the skirmish. Knights, falling back, turned their horses aside down an alley and out of the archers' sight. Two by two, and then one more broke off. The knights around me turned their horses as well.

Nipper lunged back at the shield wall — gathering, now, into a solid line — and Anders stabbed down over a steel rim, metal clashing. The stallion danced back when a sword jabbed from the wall, tossing his head. He circled back, prancing and working his bit. There was blood on his chin.

"Break off, mule!" Tritter hollered. "Break off or we'll let the hawks have your fool ass too!"

The ambulance driver coaxed the wagon dray into backing up a few steps so we could get off the street as well. I wobbled, grabbed his shoulder for balance. I wanted to shout too, but wasn't sure it would help.

The Suevi armsmen inched forward at the ends of their shield wall, bowing in the center around Anders. Nipper spun around and kicked, putting a man down; another tight spin and Anders was hacking the hole in the wall open. Still, they closed around him.

"Shit!" Will kicked the palfrey and drew his sword. "Anders!"

My mouth fell open for a second, and then the ambulance began to turn off Low Street. "No!" I climbed into the back to keep my view of the skirmish. "No, no… Will!" I scrambled over Ther Ludo without seeing him, then Adalslav, and I slid off the end of the bed as Will kicked his palfrey harder and brandished the sword. He had no shield, no armor.

Nipper turned when the circle began to close behind him. Will yelled as he bore down on the shrinking gap. I heard arrows hiss, and a few Suevi at the edge of their formation fell.

"Dame Kate! Get off the street!"

Will's sword clanged off a helmet and the palfrey shied from the noise. Then screamed when a Suevi blade thrust into its ribs. The palfrey stumbled as Will swung again. Nipper bulled through the ring of men, snapping his teeth. I lost sight of Will for an agonizing heartbeat as the palfrey's hooves thrashed. Arrows struck again, coming thicker now, and the Suevi fell one by one. Nipper fought clear with a heave, and Anders had thrown down his shield, I saw, to haul Will up by one arm. Trailing blood.

Hooves pounding, Nipper pulled away, arrows hissing down behind him. He bled himself, from a cut on his flank. A few of the armsmen gave chase, out of bloodlust, but the hawks feathered them. Will's legs thrashed against the street, trying to keep from dragging as he pressed his free arm against his side.

"Ludo!" I screamed back at the alley as I ran to meet them. I reached for Will as Nipper reined in beside me, still hot and eager to bite. I slapped his nose away with a bit of kir-shield on my hand. Anders hoisted Will further up, to his feet, but his brother's knees buckled and he tried to choke back a cry. I caught Will's other arm across my shoulders and then Ludo was there to help.

Blood gushed from Will's side, under his black tabard and plainspun cote, all the way to the ambulance. I climbed up in the wagon bed beside him and called his kir up as I pulled the torn cloth open. No stench of stabbed gut, but too much blood; his liver had taken the point of a sword and it had twisted in pulling out. I pinched off the bleeding first and called for memories of the liver's patterns. And the gallbladder. I could smell bile.

Officers were shouting in anger nearby, but I hardly cared. The ambulance began to move as I reached into Will's side to patch the gash on his gallbladder. He screamed under my hands, and Ther Adalslav pinned him down. Anders leaned over the sideboard and caught Will's hand in a firm grip.

"You'll live. She's going to heal you," he told his brother. "She'll heal you."

A liver was a dense thing, full of interlaced kir patterns. Inch by inch, I mended the wound and called the Pool for more. It answered, trickling down to me drop-wise and then quicker. I looked up to see we'd gotten back to River Road, with Anders and Lieutenant Tritter and Sergeant Rotmann and the remains of the squad escorting my ambulance.

"Forget those sergeant's brasses now," Tritter snarled at Anders, leaning close to point. "You disregard again and I'll see Saint Woden hears of it!"

Anders slapped the pointing hand away and I caught a moment of blurred speed that ended with a crack that knocked Anders against his cantle. He came up wincing as he squeezed his jaw.

Anger flashed past me, but no time for that now. I looked back to Will. His color was good. He hadn't lost too much blood. The wound was down to only the cut skin and notched ribs. With some herbal extract and a cloth, I cleansed those and opened his cote further for the stitches he would need. We turned through the Order's gate and I breathed easier.

Then I sat up straighter in the wagon bed when I spotted Saint Aleksandr standing in the middle of the courtyard, under the budding maple tree, head cocked as if listening intently. He must've gotten my message.

CHAPTER 15

"Dame Kate," Saint Aleks said when I joined him under the maple tree, "you say you've felt kir nearby?"

"Briefly, but twice now," I answered, glancing back at the hospital's doors. Ludo and Adalslav carried Will inside for his stitches, and the lieutenant's knights stood waiting for me to return. Captain Rogen, in anger over the sloppy withdrawal, had assigned them to escort ambulances as punishment. The ten of them were glaring and growling as they used the brief stop to see to their horses, but Anders was paying them no mind.

He was down off Nipper and approaching Saint Aleks and me slowly, drawn to our conversation but uncertain.

"Where, and when?" the saint asked. I pointed and told him, realizing as I did that it made for a line pointed toward the western wall. My stomach shifted in dread.

Aleksandr let his kir unfold, then, dropping around him in a cloak, and I felt him call to the kir in the earth around me. It answered, that faint sheen over all things that I had managed to call once myself, and also the kir below the surface. Alive, all of it, I realized as I looked around my feet at the layers of patterns. All the earth was alive, under the grass, as far down as the stone. Except for — and I frowned, feeling the gap for a heartbeat.

Beneath my feet, a lake of kir blossomed and the ground began to shake. I stumbled, fell on my ass, and heard wood cracking all around, loud as thunder. I felt Saint Aleks' counterstrike, canceling out the earthquake at its source, but the earth tore open across the courtyard. It gaped like a mouth, lips crumbling into the chasm as it widened. I clawed away, lunging to my feet and reaching for the Pool as I turned.

My blood ran cold; centaurs charged up the earthen slope from below, tearing the dirt with their hooves, with spears and shields ready. They roared as they came, triumphant, and I was a helpless peasant girl again, staring at the glint on the spearhead rising over me. Dimly, I heard the Order's bell tower ringing the alarm.

Nipper rammed the centaur's shoulder and Anders' sword took the monster through the ribs, lamellar scales screeching against his blade. As the centaur collapsed, I snapped my kir-shield up and pushed it out further and larger to shelter Anders. A second centaur dove to the side, scraping across my shield, and I felt an echo of his weight on me. My feet un-frozen, I skipped backward as best I could, glancing over my shoulder as I went.

Earthen walls reared up shoulder-high, rumbling, and I fell again as the ground under my feet pulled into them. Nipper danced, eyes rolling, and some of the centaurs stumbled. But I saw why, in a heartbeat; Saint Aleks stood under the half-tipped maple tree, hand on the earth. His walls encircled the courtyard and the split-open maw to Arcea's secret tunnel. The centaurs were cut off from the Order's buildings and from the wounded, as well as from the front gate. Lieutenant Tritter's squad formed up into a wedge and circled around to attack the monsters.

But then I felt kir, deep and strong, rising from the earth's mouth.

Anders kicked Nipper toward the centaurs' open flank and I spared him a glance, but my eyes were pulled back to the saints. That battle elect with the red braid leaped up first, alit on the torn rim of the ground and launched himself at Saint Aleksandr — who swatted him aside, mid-air, with a flick of a kir-vine. The enemy struck the earth wall with a metallic crack and bounced.

Three Arceal saints arose from the maw to face Saint Aleks: the tall, blonde woman, the fierce man with the braided beard, who Woden had called Rakkar — I'd seen both at the broken wall — and a third. Arceal, by his tanned skin and dark, slicked-back hair. As was the Elect by his side, a woman with her long black hair braided and wrapped in red ribbons. They wore somber silk robes in formal Arceal style, wide-sleeved, double-breasted, closed by a pair of large buttons along one shoulder, and belted with tightly wrapped leather.

I drew my kir-shield closer, denser, around me. Qadeem had told me to help, but I didn't know what Aleksandr would want of me. Where was Woden? Reaching for my binding, I twisted my fear into thoughts as best I could.

/ they're here! /

/ where? /

He did it again, the cold tap into my Blessing and my senses. I sent my answer.

/ home /

Calm flooded me.

/ breathe / fight / will join you / soon /

Qadeem was closer, if it were true that the Duke's army was coming. How close?

The glint of sun on metal caught my eye, and that was my only warning; the red Elect's two-handed sword crashed down on my shield and the kir on his blade sliced through. The charm unraveled swiftly and in my panic I merely pushed. Kir-vines thrust me back a good yard and my feet struggled to keep up. I tripped again and put up a shield on my hands as I fell, for he was still on me, cutting open my new shield Blessing-fast, his sword a blur as it swooped down for the kill.

The impact took him from the side, a crunch so hard that I felt it, and Saint Woden didn't even pause to harvest the Elect's kir. He launched off the smashed corpse with a roar, lightning lashing across the courtyard at the two saints closing on Aleksandr. The shockwave of the red Elect's dying rushed past and I glanced at his face, under the open helmet. Age sank onto him as his heart flickered out.

Then, my saints. Kir roiled in heavy ropes, gouts of stars burst — and a by-blow smashed across the yard into a centaur, crushing him against the earth walls. I lunged to my feet, re-spinning my shield, and spotted Saint Aleks surging up. He lashed out with one hand — a cougar's paw, rather; he'd half-shifted to tawny cat — to rip away the willowy saint's shield and leaped at her. She ducked under him, throwing him to the ground. Thick arms of earth grabbed him, or tried to. He twisted, lashed, broke free.

A ball of kir spiraled up in her hand, ready to strike, and that was when my little Shepherd's knife sliced through her prime meridian at the waist. I stared at my own hand, stunned that such a thing had flown from me.

The saint's mouth fell open in surprise. Her kir caught her, mending the damage in the blink of an eye. In that eyeblink, her stomach tore open under Aleks' claws. Shredded flesh sprayed. He ripped into her throat with his cougar fangs. Devoured the bright star of her kir, through the blood. Then the entire sun broke free from inside her.

I fell under the blast, tumbled, blinded for a heartbeat. Horses screamed. In an afterimage, I saw a centaur stab his spear through a warhorse's neck and into a knight. Woden slung a thunderbolt and the Arceal saint turned it aside with one hand; the lightning roared past me into the earthen walls. The heat of it seared me as it tore apart my kir-shield. A hand jerked me away, pulling me up against mail, a black tabard. His free arm clapped me close, sword at guard.

Smell of leather. Horses. Anders.

The Arceal elect shot a thin vine of kir. It cracked Woden's shield as her saint's spear rammed in behind it. Impaled by one shoulder, Woden slammed into an earthen wall, pinned.

In the same moment, the bearded Saint Rakkar pounced on Aleks, who rose from his kill trailing heavy curtains of kir. He flung up a fold, for a shield, and Rakkar's charmed sword carved through it in an explosion of stars. Following through, Rakkar punched into the tear and a spike of kir thrust from his arm, stabbing through Aleks high in the chest. Claws laid Rakkar's arm open to the bone, but he hardly flinched.

Woden howled as if stabbed himself. Lightning sizzled through his bond, but it skinned over the Arceal saint and vanished. A pair of spears flew. Woden sliced both mid-air.

I felt Anders draw breath to yell, under my arms. I grabbed for my kir and threw it in a simple blade at Rakkar. It clashed off his shield as he stabbed his sword into Saint Aleks as well. Stabbed, and twisted. The kir tore from our saint as he snarled, bloody-toothed, and crumpled.

What little kir I had left sprang out in a small shield on my palm, arm held up against the coming blast.

Again, the sun burst across the courtyard. Anders and I stumbled back, but between the two of us kept our feet. The loose kir answered my call and I brimmed again. Spots still danced in my eyes as Anders tore away from me, his wordless cry agony in my ears.

Rakkar reeled back from the falling cloud that had been Saint Aleks, kir-shield dropped for the moment, and Anders flew on an eye-blink of Blessing speed. His champion's sword skewered the saint through the chest, cross-guard slamming against breastbone, blade jutting nearly two feet from his back.

Rakkar's arm snapped out, catching Anders by the throat. Dark eyes blazed with green kir as the saint lifted my husband up, hand tightening, fingers digging in. Anders thrashed in agony. I threw another Shepherd's knife with all I had; it cut the saint's fresh-spun shield. He spared me a glance. And a toothy grin.

Kir landed between us, then Saint Qadeem with his pale cloak snapping down hard. Three white-hot stars shot from his hand, curling in different paths toward Rakkar. Rakkar swung Anders as a shield, and the first star veered aside. He parried the second with the charmed sword in his other hand, shattering both. The third found Anders' blade, from behind. It set the sword afire and Rakkar screamed as kir crackled through his chest and a brilliant tear opened around his wound. The first star darted in and struck too, turning the sword to blinding light. Rakkar's harvest arced to Qadeem's hand, bright and strong.

Half a heartbeat; I pulled kir and threw it, in a shield, before Anders.

Against Rakkar's explosion, I saw Qadeem silhouetted, arms spread to accept the kir. The shockwave stopped at him, roiled and twisted into his splayed hands, and the rest of the kir dropped, returning to the earth. He staggered, fell to his knees.

/ vastness /

Qadeem's harvest echoed through my bond, and it felt like my skull cracking open at the touch of a mighty wind. I pushed my bond away; where was the enemy? Anders? My eyes struggled to focus, and I charmed them back to clarity. Thus, I saw the hand that grabbed a handful of Qadeem's dark hair and pulled his head back to put a blade through his throat, and I struck before I thought.

Hand. Arm. Their structures flashed through my mind, into the charm.

The hand on the sword flew apart, skin flayed flat, each muscle, artery and tendon blooming out in perfect array, as far up as the elbow before the owner's kir clamped down hard and stopped me. The charmed blade tumbled from the skeletal hand, as there was no flesh to grip it. Woden's gaze turned on me, blazing kir and blood-lust — and outrage.

Woden. My heart stumbled in my chest.

Qadeem shrugged him off, though there was enough kir behind it to toss a warhorse aside, and gained his feet. With a flick of his hand, he undid my charm and reassembled Woden's arm over his bones. The bloody hole through his shoulder closed. They exchanged a hard stare. Woden dipped his chin, curtly, and my saint returned the nod.

I managed a blink, my heart still too confused to know what to do. Woden. Not the Arceal saint.

Around me, the remaining centaurs roared back, surging up, and in a panicky glance around the courtyard I saw only blood and corpses — Nipper off to one side with another un-mounted horse — my saints and the Arceal with his elect. Those two looked calm and unruffled as if they were awaiting introductions and tea.

A yell answered from Aleks' earthen walls; Kiefan landed atop an intact stretch, closely followed by Captain Rostislav, and dropped down inside the courtyard. Kiefan hit the dirt at Blessing speed and carved through the first centaur mid-waist, turning as he went to take the second's arm off at the elbow. King's Guard poured over the wall, fresh and eager.

As they tore through the monsters, Saint Woden and Qadeem exchanged a word. Woden folded his arms across his chest and stood fast where he was with his gaze fixed on the invaders. Qadeem strode to face the Arceal saint.

I trotted to catch up, wanting the meeting to be equal. I met my opposite's dark eyes with as much resolve as I could manage after seeing one of my saints turn on the other and then as quickly ignore the moment.

"Gauvail," Qadeem said, inclining his head.

The Arceal saint returned it. "Qadeem. The Empress sends her best."

A tiny pause. "One should not flatter oneself."

Gauvail's eyes narrowed. "The first round goes to Wodenberg. Well done." He turned, then, and walked down the earthen ramp. His Elect followed two steps behind.

I glanced to Qadeem. He simply watched them go, his cloak shifting in a stray breeze. "The first round?" I asked.

"Yes." He took a deep breath and pressed his fingertips to his forehead. Then he turned to survey the ruined courtyard — the partly shattered earth walls, the maple tree which had broken under one blast or another, the half-collapsed roof of the dormitory that I hadn't noticed before. Softly, Qadeem said, "I'll do the best I can, old friend, but this will ever be your city."

Kir moved through him. The ground shuddered again and the torn mouth slowly closed. Aleks' walls sank, spreading to help fill it in, but when all settled the courtyard was lumpy. A furrow ran where the gash had been, and the grass was torn everywhere. Nothing could be done for the maple tree, sadly. And —

"Anders," I breathed, scanning the tangle of bodies, my pulse surging in my throat. Thers ran from the hospital to pick through the fallen, looking for survivors, and Freiberg was among them to charm the worst wounds. But none of the fallen had Anders' flaxen hair. Nipper and the other horse were caught. Kiefan stood shouting orders by the broken tree. Qadeem drew up a knot of kir and knelt down to spread the charm over a fallen knight.

Woden knelt where Aleks had died, clenching fistfuls of dust to his face. Hands trembling.

Anders had to be here. The shockwave of a dying saint was powerful, but — but how would I know? I'd been a handful of yards away, for each death, and shielded. He'd been at arm's length. The shield I'd thrown to him had been ripped apart. The same could've happened to him. He could've gotten his wish.

A pit opened in my gut.

No, he had to be here. Somewhere.

My memory brought back the image of Anders, held up by the throat, and which way Saint Rakkar had faced. I turned for another look across the rumpled grass there. The wall had been shoulder-high, to me, protecting the open windows of the dining hall. If he hadn't been thrown against that…

I looked up. The second floor of the dining hall was the orphanage, pressed into service for recuperating sick and wounded. Its windows stood open, too, to let in the spring day. One storm shutter hung half free, its window frame partly smashed.

Inside, up the stairs, down the hall and I was calling him. A nurse stuck her head out of one room. "M'lady? We were about to send for someone, if it's finally over."

I pushed past her, the other nurse, and the few curious patients. Anders looked up from the cot he sat on, his back stiffening as he tensed. Wary, of me. Bruises streaked his throat and his left arm hung askew at a dislocated shoulder, but it was me he feared.

My eyes hazed with sudden tears as I dashed across the tiny room, falling to my knees as I threw my arms around his shoulders. "Don't you dare," I hissed in his ear, meaning to be harsh but my voice turning to a squeak through a tight throat. "Don't you die, don't you leave…"

Anders' right arm tightened around me as he drew a ragged breath against my neck, the tension melting out of him.

———————✤———————

Captain Rogen came in search of the survivors of Lieutenant Tritter's squad before I had them all mended. The three men, plus Anders, were expected on horses and at duty in the southeastern city soon as they were able. As was Will, stitched and bandaged and good enough to ride.

Healing under the eye of my saint, even though he didn't say a word, was nearly as wracking as the first time I'd spun a charm while Parselev watched. I worked carefully.

Anders settled in Nipper's saddle and turned to find me; I watched the last of the wounded testing his ankle gingerly, not sure if he believed it was well and whole again, and only caught Anders in the corner of my eye. He kept his sober face for a couple heartbeats once I met his gaze, then gave me half a smile.

It infected me, despite my nerves. He broke into an honest grin, warm as the sun. "It's Saint-day," he said, "but Captain won't give me any time off. Might I see you at the next funeral feast?"

"You will," I promised.

Captain Rogen led the ragged remains of the squad across the courtyard toward the Order's gate. Left behind were the six dead men, the corpses of two dozen centaurs, and a handful of wounded King's Guard. Sergeant Rotmann, who'd taken a spear through the chest, had loaned Anders his sword in repayment for all the harrying he'd endured.

The champion's sword that Anders had run through Saint Rakkar had crumbled, leaving only the hilt and a few inches of blackened steel above the cross-guard.

Saint Aleks' defiant snarl, through a cougar's fangs, as the second blade rammed through him, lingered behind my eyes. A deadly game, Parselev had told me, that they all play, even the ones that seem gentle.

Woden's raging eyes, when he stopped my dissection charm… I shivered.

/ rest / wait / Parselev's home /

How Saint Qadeem encapsulated my teacher into a feeling, I didn't know but I recognized him instantly. Over-busy, detailed, but comfortable.

In the cottage, Heima had left the fire banked and a kettle on the warm hearth-stones. I poured myself a cup of water from it, though it wasn't warm enough for tea, and sat at the table to sort through the day's memories. They all needed putting away, starting with Anders' refusal to fall back from the Suevi armsmen.

I'd left the door open, to let the light in, and when a shadow blocked it I looked up.

"You are, indeed, a fine student," Saint Qadeem said. "Killing that piglet was the wisest thing I've done in years, it would seem. I've spoken with Physician Krepkin about your — differences, and what's to be done."

Qadeem took a seat opposite me, and I couldn't help tracking him; I dreaded, without doubting, that he'd send me back into the hospital.

"For now, the Order is quite able to administer itself," my saint said, though. "Mechdan took on the work when there was a need, years ago, and it suited him."

I couldn't help a smile. Not all physicians were part of the Order, that was true, but I'd heard so little of them and it seemed that Parselev had some tie to every last one in the kingdom. "I'm not bound to the Order, then?"

"You're bound to me. If the Mother and Father wish to lay a claim, they must see to it themselves."

"This has been my home, though..." My gaze slid over to the stairs and the office above.

"The cottage does belong to the Order, and is for its own. If you wish to stay, I'll speak to the abbot."

I thought of Heima, and then Frida's warm smile. "No, let Heima keep it," I said. "How long I'll stay, I don't know. But it should be hers."

"Inquire with the accounts-master as to the elect's stipend. He will disentangle it from the Order's finances. Remain the royal physician, for now, and keep me informed. As my bound elect," Qadeem said, slowing to make a point of his words, "you are in the service of the kingdom. We protect the kingdom, so that it may protect us in turn. This is the duty of the elect and the sainted."

Woden's knuckles in Qadeem's black hair, the charmed sword of golden light — I had to look away from my saint, from his intent dark eyes. "We protect each other?" I asked. "You avenged Saint Aleksandr, but..."

He took a deep breath. "As I said, there are few things a saint can rely on. We had a pact, the three of us. The day would come that only two would remain, we knew that, and we swore to remain bound by our oaths in memory of the third. Neither of us wished it to be Aleks who was lost. That much, we agree on. Woden is many things, and among them he is a man of his word."

"He tried —" I bit my words back when Ther Ivor walked in through the open door with hands full of food, smiling and humming under his breath. Heima followed, carrying a pitcher of small beer and a bowl of spring salad to go with the warm sausages, bread, and a small pot of soup.

"Here we are, m'lord, Dame Kate. Something I put together quickly," Ther Ivor said as he arrayed it on the table between us. Heima added her burdens and went to fetch two of the ceramic bowls she kept in the cupboard. "I know you're fond of salad, m'lord, and we just had some lettuce coming in. I only tossed these with some onion and a little cider vinegar."

He tossed the greens again — lettuce and dandelion leaves, croutons, thin-sliced onion — and put it in the bowls for us. Pleased with that, he poured us cups of small beer while Heima looked for her soup ladle.

"There. If I may, m'lord?"

Qadeem nodded. "Thank you, this is perfect." To me, "Seagrace's cooks do what they can, but I'll not miss this chance."

Ther Ivor hurried back to his kitchen. Heima brought the soup ladle and stirred the soup. "I'll keep this warm by the fire," she murmured, taking the pot by the handle.

Between bites of salad, Qadeem switched to perfect Englic and told me, "Were Woden in my place, I'd have done the same."

My piece of bread fell from my hand into the salad. I wasn't sure which surprised me more, the tongue or his words.

Quietly, he said, "I was weak, for a few heartbeats. That is the time to strike, if one is ever to strike. And that is how some saints survive and others do not. So long as I am not weak, Woden will keep his word. I knew that when I took the oath."

The salad was fresh and tender and tangy from the vinegar, but that dropped far from my mind. My saints were strong, the cornerstone of the kingdom, and we were to trust them with our lives, I'd been told. I'd believed.

"You accepted my bond, Kate, and you struck in my defense in that moment of weakness. You have nothing to fear from me." Qadeem paused a moment. "So long as your loyalty holds."

My loyalty. "And Kiefan?"

"Each saint has their own way, with elect."

He said that quietly, with a faint frown, and I took that for disapproval. I ate a few more bites, thinking of Kiefan's late arrival with the reinforcements. And what came next. "M'lord, you knew his name," I said, just above a murmur.

Qadeem's dark eyes met mine across the food for a moment.

"And Saint Woden knew the other man. Rakkar."

He finished his salad first. Heima brought the soup to fill his bowl, and I quickly cleaned mine out as well so she could fill both.

"There are, perhaps, a hundred saints in the world at any time. The number cannot be said for certain — disguised, saints may walk among us unseen. I walked thus, myself, for many years before I came to Wodenberg. Few as we are, saints' paths cross and we don't forget each other."

"You've seen Arcea?" I asked.

Qadeem's gaze sank into the distance. "I have met the Empress herself. And yes, I knew Gauvail. Rakkar, rather less. I declined to join their ranks, and here I am fighting them instead. Which I must return to, so enough talk for now."

We ate in silence, for a while. My baby kicked in my belly and I was hungrier than I'd thought. The sausages were mealy and the soup a bit thin, but it was a richer spread than Ther Ivor could put out for the general meal-times and I had a cup of small beer as well.

"Far better fare than in the Duke's camp," Saint Qadeem said, as if to agree with me. "They will need me again. We're in pursuit of Arcea's infantry, driving them toward the encampment here. Look for us within a few days."

"Lady Leix arrived?"

He smiled. "And was as welcome as a warm spring day."

On the last day of the Field Moon, the portcullis creaked and groaned as it rose. The city gates rumbled across the paving stones of River Road as strength-Blessed men pulled them open.

I watched, a little behind Kiefan on the platform in the center of Sinnmach Square. Captain Aleksandra stood at his right hand with Lieutenant Rostislav — he'd accepted that demotion, knowing he'd have her job someday — to back her up. Kiefan wore black and gold silk, the jeweled crown and the moon-pommeled sword. The whole King's Guard was arrayed in the square to receive our guests, and the City Guard kept those city folk who wanted to see at the edges of the square.

Banners came through the gate first: a kingdom banner of Mount Woden silhouetted by the full moon, on black, Duke Seagrace's white rukh on parti-colored blue and grey, a few baronial banners, and the Caercoed banner: two mountains framing a full Shepherd moon, on pale green. They came in their armor, cleaned up and presentable after forcing Arcea to retreat or be pinned against the city walls. Duke Seagrace led the column flanked by his highest officers and Margrave Leix Gwatcyn.

Duke Seagrace's grin faded as he saw who waited on the platform. He stopped his horse and swung down from the saddle, then didn't wait for the rest to join him. Crossing to the platform at a long lope, he took the steps in one stride and dropped onto his knee before Kiefan, fist pressed to his chest.

"We had no word," he said, and the pain on his face was achingly honest. "I would've come sooner, Kiefan, had I known your father had —"

Kiefan held up a hand. "You did precisely what you ought. That you brought our reinforcements and lifted the siege will not be overlooked."

"Majesty, may I give you my fealty?"

It should have been given within heartbeats of Kiefan's coronation. "That will be seen to. Your deeds are oath enough, for now. Get up." He reached, pulled his brother-in-law up into a fond hug.

Over Kiefan's shoulder, Duke Seagrace noted me and his eyes darted over the others. Looking for Parselev, most likely. I kept my spine straight and chin up. I wore the dark red dress again, and I'd netted my hair up loosely in a new crespine that Heima had made for me. This shift from physician and student to senior castle staff and bound elect needed some time to settle on me, yet. I wished Parselev were there.

As he released Kiefan, the Duke said, "The siege cost us dear, I see. May I present our friend, to shine some hope on matters?"

Margrave Leix Gwatcyn took her cue to step up and clasp Kiefan's hand, squeeze him briefly across the shoulders as well with a grin. Caercoed knights wore mail, too, a knee-long tunic of it over a matching quilted gambeson in dusty beige. Greaves protected her shins, below. Her sash belt was bright red, tied snug around her hips to carry a sword, and wrapped in gold braid. Fringe hung heavy from the dangling ends. Her helm, under one arm, was crested with red as well. A few more strands of grey amid the brown, perhaps, but her hair was bound up snug and her eyes bright as ever.

Two steps behind her, I was glad to see, stood Captain Mohra with her helm under her arm and her free hand resting on her sword. Ready to translate, if needed.

"We did come, quick as we could," m'lady Leix said in Arceal, her smile raising faint crow's-feet around her eyes. "Late snows tried to slow us. Your man in Suevia is a fine ally, though. 'Twould be remiss of me to forget him."

"I never doubted you, m'lady. This is the Captain of the King's Guard, Dame Aleksandra Rytsarova."

M'lady Leix clasped the Captain's hand. "Shall be as a sister to me, no doubt."

"Lieutenant Rostislav Loshadsky. And you know Kate already. Pardon — Elect Bockmann."

She nodded again, and for me there was another smile. "Strength in your coming blessings, Elect."

I whispered thanks to her, feeling my cheeks warm a bit.

"What word from the Voice of the Empress?" Kiefan asked.

"At first, he noted their reserves in Temitte," Duke Seagrace said. "Both soldiers and kir, he was careful to mention. It would be no large feat to bring them to Ansehen before Solstice."

"Two of their saints are dead, and three elect," Kiefan told him. "Even they can't put too brave a face on that."

"With Qadeem's help, we accounted for two elect as well," Seagrace added. "Still, there can be more."

Kiefan's voice lowered. "Saint Aleksandr is gone. As is Elect Parselev. But we have two elect now — myself and Kate."

Seagrace grimaced, with a sigh. "Their wisdom will be sorely missed."

M'lady Leix put her hand on Kiefan's arm. "'Tis dark news, a saint's passing. At Saint Sabh's instruction, I've brought Elect Tannait. She stands outside the gates, of respect, to await your saints' invitation. She offers her skills, however we may need them."

"She will be welcome in good faith, with thanks to both your saints." Kiefan pressed his hand on Leix's. "Arcea will return in force, then? We will need to call Vysokov down from Prohzgrad, and the northern reserves must move south."

"If we strike soon, we can force them to fall back further," Seagrace said. "Thin their ranks so far as we can before those reinforcements come. And bring Caercoed's strength to bear on Suevia's flank."

Kiefan nodded. "We'll make it safe for my brides to cross our southlands. If they'll accept a king in place of the prince my saints promised."

The margrave smirked back, and arched an eyebrow. "Many maids would, 'tis no doubt on that. And you'd tempt many a wedded wife as well, if 'tisn't too bold to say."

I bit my lower lip, sneaking a glance toward the mounted honor guard of Caercoed knights who'd followed the margrave through the gate. They all sat at attention, though, too well disciplined for such distractions. Captain Mohra kept her face straight as well.

Kiefan's hand had been promised before I even met him. I had no business being pained by that.

"My saints would have that alliance bound and sealed as soon as we're able," he said.

The margrave pursed her mouth for a moment. "Suevia is no small risk for the noble blood this binding requires. As you say, your southlands do crawl with Arceal monsters. Elect Tannait will pass word to Saint Sabh when 'tis clear the enemy's contained, and we'll see how best to seal the alliance."

"We must force Arcea back to Ansehen," Duke Seagrace said. "Across the Felsherz, somehow — all thirty thousand of them…" He grimaced. "Might we have half that number, now?"

"Only by the grace of m'lady Leix. We must catch them in disorder, in this retreat." Kiefan put a hand on each of them, though. "But first, come up to the castle and be welcomed properly. The siege is lifted and that deserves celebrating."

CHAPTER 16

Saint Woden found me at the disciple's dance. The Warm Moon was good as its name from its first night; so warm that even in the pre-dawn dew, I could stand barefoot on the lumpy grass of the courtyard and feel my center of balance. Even with my eyes closed in reflection, I knew where Woden waited by his kir.

I was more sensitive still, it would seem. He neither wore his kir openly nor had it hidden away.

When I opened the cottage door, Anders and Will still slept on the hearth, wrapped in bedrolls. Heima had only just woken, in the bed she shared with me. She blinked at my guest and pulled her dress on a little quicker.

Woden took two steps across the wood floor in his heavy boots and Anders was half on his feet, reaching for the sword leaning against the mantle. He hesitated when the saint stopped and tossed a sheathed blade to him. Anders caught it and stood, letting the bedroll slide away.

"You refused the King's Guard," Saint Woden told him. "You risked five lives for a three-crescent wager. You disregarded a direct order to fall back. Turn that tabard in again — I'll not have you serving inside these walls."

Though he'd said little, I'd thought Woden had come to speak to me; I turned from the table where I had just opened the tea box with my mouth falling open. Will, awake on the hearth, sat up looking from one of them to the other. Anders only stood with the sword in hand, face darkening.

Some men might've tried to explain. He flung the sword back at Woden and grabbed his boots; he'd slept in his clothes.

"The captain of the Rangers expects you," Woden said, and that gave Anders a moment's pause.

"For target practice?" Anders tossed off, and in storming from the cottage got as far as within reach of the saint.

I only heard Anders' back thump against the hearth-stone and the boots tumble to the floor; I didn't see Woden clap a hand to his chest and throw him until I checked my memory. He threw the sheathed sword harder, this time, but Anders still caught it.

"To train for scouting. You're a cambifax, handy with a sword, and you can pass for noble if you try."

Anders bristled. "I'm no cambifax, I'm —"

"You're one of mine and you'll do as you're told. Aleks had his own way with pets, but you're my disciple and my blood and you'll be of use to me or I'll do the Shepherd's culling for him." Woden's voice grew in the little cottage. "Get some wood-craft. Learn the bow."

"The bow? Me?"

"You'll see why you're there, if you've any wits. I've four others to sound out and ten thousand archers to re-bind — that's only this side of Lake Neva. Don't think you're a precious pet any more."

Kir flicked and my own slipped out to my hand, primed by my nerves. I heard only a faint echo of the chord that Anders' kir gave off, as I wasn't part of the sounding, and couldn't be sure of its length or complexity.

"Now come outside and show me your edge. I'll tell you what you're holding." Woden looked to me, in turning toward the door. "Stand down, but not far. He may need your charms."

Anders left his boots and followed. He glanced first at the sword in his hand and then me. I knew as little as he did, though. The Rangers were the army's finest scouts, its border patrol and secret messengers. Two steps behind, I joined them in the herb garden with my kir at ready. I doubted those were blunt training swords.

Woden spun and the sword at his belt hissed; Anders blurred and when the sword's sheath hit the flagstone path he was two steps back in a solid middle guard. The morning light gleamed on the blade, brighter and clearer than any sword I'd seen. Woden pressed the attack and steel whistled, rasped around and somewhere in the blur I felt Anders shift from giving ground to taking it. The saint slowed to a high guard a step back from his beginning.

"Aleks could make anything," Woden said, calmly whereas Anders' breathing was quick and sharp. "He took a fancy to swords for some years, and asked me to try every one for him. Iron swords. Pewter. Bronze. Stone, could you believe? A sword of pure quartz. Brass, one of them, mated to steel. Pretty, but no improvement. There's things you'll do for a dear friend, even after years of suffering the most ridiculous confections. And he —"

His voice stumbled, and Woden turned away, swinging the blade wide with a gusty sigh. Anders slipped after him, near silent on bare feet, but the saint shot around, deflected his stab and rushed in with a snarl. Both blurred for a moment and Anders stumbled back, out of Blessing speed, with a torn sleeve but no blood.

Woden chuckled. "Fair try, boy. Aleks would not approve."

"I didn't learn it from him."

"How's the blade?"

Anders flicked its hilt over his hand in a circle, and it flashed in the strengthening light. "Near disappears in the hand."

"He came around to more reasonable things, after all the foolishness. That's one of his better efforts. He'd want you to have something to remember him by." Woden sheathed his own sword. "Have you drawn kir?"

Anders lowered the bright blade from guard. "No, m'lord. Not yet."

Woden's eyes narrowed. "If you think you can keep it secret, you won't."

"If I'm such a liar, would you want me for an elect?"

"All shape-shifters lie, in their way. Rangers' captain. Report today. There will be eyes on you."

I wanted to ask how long Anders would be gone, but Woden walked away. No more needed be said, it seemed. Anders watched him go a moment, then picked up the sheath. The bright blade snicked home.

I caught his free hand and he startled. "Be careful," I said, with what I hoped was a stern look. "They're sending Rangers to the southern hills, to be sure Arcea doesn't smuggle elect or saints in. Even if they don't…" There were watch towers in the hills, home to small garrisons cut off by Arcea's remaining army. The southern hills were behind the enemy's line.

Anders' teasing smile flashed past, but turned sober. "I will. I don't mean to — leave."

That pinched my heart and my hand moved to touch him, hesitated, and I hugged him. Only for a moment. He squeezed back and let me go. We walked back to the cottage, my gaze fixed on the ground as Kiefan's demand echoed in my memory: if you touch her…

Did I dare touch him?

A week later, Saint Qadeem called me from my field infirmary to the command pavilion.

Duke Seagrace and m'lady Leix had forced the Arceal army to withdraw from besieging the city, but it had taken some days of harrying and moving divisions to catch the enemy on poor enough footing to attack outright. Arcea had retreated further after that battle, leaving behind thousands of dead, and had its back to the Felsherz River.

I had spent that day assisting Physician Brauer in her infirmary, and then withdrawn with the wounded to this camp closer to the city. Kiefan had insisted, and Qadeem had agreed with him. Not that I had put up so much of a fight. My baby was coming to six moons along, and seemed to have taken up square dancing.

I got one such kick as I approached the rear of the command pavilion, and when I wobbled one of the King's Guard swooped in to catch my arm. I murmured thanks and he nodded, then stepped aside to let me pass. Wincing from further wriggles in my belly, I walked in slowly. Kiefan had called me to one meeting, just before the battle, and the place was still... strange, to me.

The main space had been cleared, save for a craft-handed secretary's writing table and a few stools near it. The camp-steward steered me toward one of those, and I was glad to sit. Woden and Qadeem stood facing the pavilion's front entrance with their arms folded, Kiefan pacing to and fro before them with his black cloak billowing. He slowed when he saw me, focus softening, but then had to smile and nod and pay me no mind. Duty, here. Captain Aleks and some of the King's Guard were there, too, a pair of captains-general and Seagrace's field marshal, but it was a thin array for a strategy meeting.

/ ? /

Qadeem sent back to me: / watch / learn /

At the main door, a Guardsman leaned in and said, "He's arrived." Kiefan stopped and turned to face the door with one hand on his sword. His cloak fell still.

The Voice of the Empress, deSvello Antonin, strode in through the sun-drenched entrance. He wore his gilt lamellar and purple cloak, but the helm with the trailing white banner naming his rank was under his arm. The Voice flourished a bow to my saints and king, with his free arm stretched to the side. His brown skin was lighter than Saint Qadeem's, and while deSvello's cropped hair was dark, it was not black. As before, he wore no sword. Two gold-and-red hawk-helmed officers escorted him, taking only one step into the pavilion before standing at attention.

A call tugged at my kir; I felt my pattern rise, briefly, and glimpsed the patterns in all those around me. There was something odd in deSvello's pattern. Something complex in his head — something like a Blessing.

"And I am as you see me, Saints," the Voice said, in lilting Arceal. "At last, you will hear the Empress' offer yourselves?"

"Lest you doubt our resolve, Empress," Qadeem replied, in the same native lilt.

Beside me, the secretary's pen scratched as fast as they spoke. DeSvello's gaze passed over me, in taking in all the faces in the pavilion, and came back for a moment; I must have seemed an odd addition to the proceedings, plainly dressed and pregnant as I was. But he went on to Kiefan, who stood silent.

"And we must meet a-foot?"

Kiefan's hand tightened on the hilt of his moon-pommeled sword. "The king of Wodenberg does not sit on his ass."

DeSvello smiled. "A young, eager king, then. And elect, the Empress does know."

"While you've spent many elect of your own, already." Woden rumbled, just loud enough to hear. "Say your piece."

The Voice dipped his head. "Wodenberg has proven itself fierce in the field. Strong and able, and worthy of greater consideration. For the Empress would have such as you for allies, not mere conquests. Wodenberg should take its place at her side, wedded to pure Imperial blood. Its knights will be known as the most fearsome for a thousand miles — above even centaurs and minotaurs."

A heartbeat's silence. "We will be no ally of yours, Empress," Qadeem said.

DeSvello looked to Woden, but got only silence. "And you refuse Arcea's colleges? Place for your craftsmen among her guilds, too? Equal —"

"We will be no ally of yours," my saint repeated, louder. "For you do hear me, Seraphine."

Another heartbeat's silence. The Empress could hear him? That Qadeem knew her name as well made my stomach shift, unsettled.

"For you would force your people to suffer, Woden?" deSvello asked, shifting his attention to the other saint. "How many thousands are gone, now?"

"And how many more, if we become your slaves?" Woden answered. "You cull the gifted as your own. You destroy the Order, deny the Shepherd's authority. Murder all who rightfully rule."

The Voice took a step closer to the center of the pavilion, gaze so fixed on the saints that Kiefan might have been invisible. His voice dropped and took a harsh tone that wasn't his at all. "I offer you claim to founts, as to all allies. Weigh that against one drop of your blood, thinned in the river of time."

My skin prickled. The Empress had heard, and answered.

Woden strode to loom over deSvello, every muscled line tensed to strike. "I submit to no saint. This land is mine by blood and by kir and I will not sacrifice my kin — who are as my own sons —" he snarled, pointing at Kiefan, "to save my life."

My breath caught in my throat. The baby quivered in my belly, and I put my hand on it.

DeSvello, to his credit, did not so much as flinch, though he did take a prudent step back. He murmured something, as well, and I could only catch that it was some further offer. Kir crackled in a green line down Woden's arm to his hand.

"Get out," he answered. "We will not speak again."

Taking another step back, deSvello bowed. He looked up at Woden, and past him to Qadeem and Kiefan. "Remember that I offered you mercy," the Voice said, still in that harsh tone. He withdrew with his two officers.

I managed to exhale. Through my bond, I felt calm from my saint. Woden, still angry by the knit of his brow and the sparks of kir around his knuckles, turned and extended that hand to Qadeem. With an equally stone-set face, my saint crossed to clasp his forearm.

"In Saint Aleksandr's memory, we will defend this land," Woden said, "these people who love and serve us, to our last breath."

"We will," Qadeem replied, with a sober nod. "In his memory, for the love he bore for them."

It was Captain Aleks who dropped to one knee in obeisance first, fist pressed to her heart and eyes bright. The others did the same, even Kiefan, and I slipped off the stool to kneel too. I had put away my memory of Saint Aleks' terrible death, but it still ached.

"Your loyalty humbles us," Qadeem said, looking around the pavilion. "Thank you. We must confer with our Elect, now, alone."

A general murmur of "M'lord," and they left us four in the pavilion.

I drew closer to my saint, hands clasped, still not sure why I'd been summoned. Kiefan drifted closer to Woden.

"The Voice does an elect's work," Qadeem said, with a glance at both of us, "though he is not elect himself. In his skull is a structure like a memory Blessing, which is bound to the Empress. She may see and hear through him, as I may through Kate."

That caught Kiefan's ear and raised his brows.

"And she may feed him words, as any saint can an elect. We knew you should see what will be expected of you — there will be need for you to negotiate for us, when the meeting with Caercoed is set."

Kiefan nodded, at that. He paused a moment, pressing his lips together. "Is there some offer Arcea could make, that you would accept?"

Woden shook his head. Qadeem answered, "The Empress does not wish peace. She wishes control. We are past the time any parley will bring peace. Alliance with Caercoed will strengthen us, we will drive them out, and then we will see whether there will be peace."

"With their backs against the Felsherz, they may prove hard to push," Kiefan said.

"They'll retreat across the river. Without their crafter saint, they cannot easily raise earthworks here. At Ansehen, they've been doing that for two moons now — and their supply line will be far safer. They can wait for reinforcement at their leisure," Woden said.

"And we must maintain our army to keep them bottled there." Kiefan grimaced. "To be sure they don't cross the Neva and ravage Russe."

Woden nodded. "We need the threat of Caercoed's full strength attacking Suevia to hold off this army's reinforcements. Then we can pry them out of Ansehen." By how he glanced at me, that was all said for my benefit; true enough that I had little knowledge of strategy. It sounded sensible, though. Woden put a hand on Kiefan's shoulder. "Give them a push across the river, though. Don't let them think they can slip away easy."

A crisp nod. "M'lord."

"M'lord," I echoed.

"No, Kate, you should return to the city." Kiefan's hand moved toward me before he could think. "It's too much danger for you."

"For me? How was the siege less dangerous?"

He amended, with his hand still raised to fend off my objections, "For the baby."

I opened my mouth to say a few aches wouldn't stop me from serving, but Qadeem cut me off. "Return to the city, Kate. I'll remain with the army."

And he fixed me with firm, black eyes until I looked away and nodded. Disappointed, yes, but with a little relief. My back still ached from yesterday's work.

"Keep my grandchild well," Woden said, voice low. Then he told Qadeem, somewhere close to teasingly, "And keep my young king well, if you can."

Qadeem chuckled. "As if he were your son, indeed. Old friend." He said that with an oddly measuring look to his fellow saint. "What did the Empress offer you, at the last?"

Woden cast a glance about, with his mouth twisted to one side, to be sure we were alone before he answered. And he switched to Arceal. "That Wodenberg would be mine alone." He snorted. "Too much work! Lacking Aleks, we're chest-deep in duties. Not a moment to ourselves, anymore."

My saint chuckled at that, too, but it reminded me too much of that moment Woden had put a kir-blade to Qadeem's throat. "Zina," he said, abruptly, the smile dropping away.

Woden threw up his hand. "Zina, mercy, I'll —" He sighed. "I'll tell her something. Enough, now, there's much to see to." He clapped Kiefan on the shoulder again, and called for the camp-steward.

/ go / take wounded home / leave at dawn /

I nodded to Qadeem, at his instructions, and took a few steps toward the pavilion's rear door. My feet slowed and I looked back to Kiefan. There'd been a story, in the general news, that he'd taken some minor wound in yesterday's battle. Surely it had been seen to; he showed no sign of pain, or even a bandage under all his armor. I caught him looking to me, his mouth twisted a bit. Worried? Wanting me to stay? But he was bound by duty. We both were.

I had to go. Had to trust that Qadeem could keep him safe — and that Father Duty would keep Anders safe, among the Rangers scouting our dangerous borders.

DISCIPLE, PART IV
salt in the wound

AUTUMN'S PROLOGUE

The baby loved riding. She wiggled and twisted in my belly whenever Buttercup settled into her long, easy walk and I swayed in the saddle. I'd thought rocking would soothe a baby to sleep. I'd need to find some other way for her.

Her. I set my teeth on my lower lip as the horse carried me home along Five Pasture Road. I hadn't checked the baby's kir since the Warm Moon. Now that she was bigger, it would be easy to suss out a girl from a boy.

In truth, I'd been afraid to look. It was only my fancy that I called the baby a girl. My daughter would still be put on a horse; she could still love riding. But no sword would be put in her hand, no shield. No command to charge the enemy line. Not like her father.

Unless she were born to it, I knew, and that sank my heart. She could easily be Kiefan's daughter and a disciple of Saint Woden as well.

Baron Reinhardt Bockmann had been recalled from his duties on the eastern slopes of the mountain after Kiefan finally set the place and time to formalize Wodenberg's alliance with Caercoed. There would be trade agreements to underpin it all, matters of lumber, beer, furs, and horses. Kiefan needed the baron's expertise, as well as what hoofed stock he had that would make worthy gifts for favored guests.

M'lord Bockmann had sent for his family from the north, and once she was home Frida had come in full force to move me from Parselev's cottage to the upstairs room that had belonged to Anders. She'd brought Will, who was complicit in this plan, and a wagon — though of course I did not own so much as to need an entire wagon. And while Parselev's books and papers were mine, the cottage was still the best place for them. Genteel as the baron was, he did not have enough bookshelves for it all. It was unlikely anyone in Wodenberg did.

The alliance parley with Caercoed would begin with the Leaf Moon. We were now half-way through the Fruit Moon and high summer; sweat trickled down my back as I rode. The baby kicked, lively and strong, still a moon and some from being in my arms.

I hadn't seen Anders since Saint Woden ordered him to report to the Rangers; I could only hope he was keeping himself safe. Not indulging in any foolishness like his attack on the guildhall full of minotaurs.

I'd hardly seen Kiefan since our saints refused the Empress's last offer. Harrowing stories had trickled back from the front line: the hard fight to push her army back across the Felsherz, of the attacks on their supply line by Margrave Schutze and brave companies of hill-folk. The remaining Arceal saint seemed loathe to fall back to their safe, fortified camp at Ansehen, but mile by mile he did. Early in the Summer Moon, the tide had turned enough that Kiefan rode back to the castle with the Arceal standards and banners he'd been so set on capturing. Those now hung above the great hall's mantle with the other trophies he'd taken from Arcea.

What happened to our lost standards, I didn't know.

I'd stayed in the city to assist Saint Woden should he need me. I hadn't so much as seen him. Rather, my days were spent on patients at their homes. Typhus lingered in the city, along with more usual ailments. A few pregnancies, and as I'd first learned medicine from my mother's midwifery, those came easily to me. Other ranking families with mercantile interests had been recalled for the trade negotiations and had dared bring their families. Some of the guild-masters, too.

They all had aches and fevers, and given the choice between the overworked city physician in the marketplace or the king's own — who was also Saint Qadeem's bound elect — well, what choice was that?

Now I rode home on Buttercup to Baron Rossweide's manor house and its barn, to Frida's warm smile and Alice's cooking. My friend had taken to the role of housemaid with more joy than I'd seen in her face in years. When the orphans returned from Prohzgrad, she meant to reclaim Magda and find a husband.

But as the horse clopped across the yard from the open gate to the barn, Will wasn't there to meet me. He wasn't in the near pastures, and the barn was quiet when I rode in. Nipper looked over his gate, as he always wanted to see who came and went. When I put Buttercup in her stall, I spotted an unfamiliar pair of horses in the stall next to hers. The buckskin reached his nose toward me for a sniff, reins trailing from his bridle; the bay only spared me a glance.

Visitors. I ran a hand over my hair, wispy and loose in its braided bun — even bundled in a crespine, my hair against my neck was too warm — as I crossed to the kitchen door. Perhaps it was only Reinhardt's courier. He'd been expecting a report from the captain-general who'd been left in command of Rossweide's garrison to guard against Arceal scouts and looters. I opened the door into the kitchen.

"He's shit with a bow, your pardon m'lady, but a saint with the horses. Oh?" The man talking turned, hands on his hips, as the door creaked. The glimpse of a brown tabard edged in black was all I needed.

"Anders?"

He was in my arms before I even finished, scooping me up in a hug. I slid back down. I was heavier than he expected. Rosewater soap overlaid horse and leather; he was freshly scrubbed, smooth-cheeked, and grinning as he squeezed me. He stole a quick little kiss, since he could.

A warm blush bloomed on my face. "You're home? For how long?" I asked, retreating a step with his hands in mine. At a glance, he looked well, even better than well.

"You can keep him," the Ranger said with a wave of one hand. "Mother's tits, man, you left this girl waiting for you?"

The Ranger was Englic, judging by his hatchet nose and freckles, not to mention the accent, and a sergeant by the single rings on his epaulettes: dark, plain iron, not shiny brass. Rangers wore nail-studded brigandines rather than mail. The straight line it made of their shoulders was further accented by the brown-and-black tabard, which bore no insignia. All uniforms made men look a bit taller, broader-beamed, stronger, but these turned them mysterious as well.

Beyond him, m'lord Reinhardt and Frida sat at the table, where a bow and quiver lay. Will stood with a mug of small beer in hand, and Alice tended the fire. Hilly sat in the rocking chair with her doll, curled up and shy.

"Sergeant Smithtree," Anders introduced him. "The most demanding bastard south of Lake Neva."

Smithtree snorted. "You keep up your practice. If you can't hit a moving tree by the time you're called back, I'm letting Voislav at you." He clapped a hand on Anders' shoulder in passing. Despite the clutter of weapons on the sergeant, he moved silently: a sword on his belt, a second blade a good foot long across the small of his back, and a quiver and bow over his shoulder.

He had a knight's Blessing, speed ridges breaking through his scalp far back on his head and running down his skull to the spine. The sandy blond thatch was cut plainly and short, having never been shaved for battle. Anders still had his flaxen knight's crest, of course, and the rest grown in enough to color his scalp.

"M'lord, m'lady." Smithtree turned at the door to bow to Reinhardt and Frida. "Mother and Father keep you. If I may?"

Reinhardt nodded to dismiss him. "Safe travels, Sergeant." When the door clicked shut, m'lord folded his long arms with careful precision. "When I left, you were Master of Horse for the Prince's Guard and a lieutenant," he said to Anders in his cool, even tone. I'd come to know that meant to tread carefully. "How is it you're a green Ranger scouting the southern hills, now?"

Anders' hands tightened and his eyes darted to mine. Anxious. Looking for…? I laced my fingers between his, hoping it would help.

"I declined the King's Guard," he said, facing the baron, "because it would be impossible to avoid the queen as she wishes. You know how tricky it was as merely Prince's Guard."

Fear of the queen had little to do with it, but that sounded fair enough.

"Thus you left Nipper behind with Will?" Reinhardt mused, stroking his tidy brown beard. "They issued you a horse?"

"Courier stock, crossed with mountain ponies. Something Vysokov's been developing, I gathered." Anders' grip eased as they slid into the common cause of horses. "Tough and canny, but they could stand for more speed."

"And the gear?" M'lord indicated the bow on the table. "How'd you cover that?"

Anders' voice tightened a notch. "Put against my pay. As Kate had her own income, I put it all against the gear. I've cleared the debt."

"That's not your sword."

"I lost mine in the siege. This was a gift."

"Stolen?"

Anders' hand clenched mine, but his voice stayed neutral. "Saint Woden gave it to me, m'lord."

"And I saw it," I said.

Reinhardt's jaw shifted and he took a sip of tea.

"Which did they give you first, the bow or the knife?" Will asked.

"They gave me the laundry first," Anders said. "Let me say a proper hello to Nipper or he'll be in a pique." He strode for the door and into the barn, towing me by the hand.

Alice threw me a wink and a grin from the hearth. My stomach abruptly unsettled.

Smithtree had gone and taken both his horses. Nipper, spotting Anders, whickered and bumped against his stall door eagerly. My hand slipped free of his grip as he trotted to greet his horse. My gaze lingered on his sword and the long knife across his back, as the sergeant wore.

My hand went to my belly, big as it was. "The Ranger squads were only called in for new orders." I'd asked the captain myself. "How long do you have?"

"The baron requested my leave," Anders said as I reached the stall door beside him. He stroked Nipper's neck, scratched behind his ears. "He needs a trainer — the only stock we have now is youngsters. Half-taught. If they're to be gifts they'll need some manners about them. I'll be needed through this parley, most likely. I might've let on I'd like to be home for the baby's arrival, as well."

I couldn't help smiling. "I'm ready for that myself."

"Is he well?" Anders' voice lowered a little, glancing to my belly.

"Lively. She seems well enough."

"She?" His brows perked.

I shook my head. "I don't know. I haven't looked since the full Warm Moon."

"But you could. Why not?"

I had watched m'lord Reinhardt and his younger son, who was ten now, in the rear yard with wooden training swords. Sometimes Will joined them, gentle Will who'd ridden into a line of infantry to help Anders get free and been stabbed for his trouble.

The words stuck in my throat at the thought of a sword in my baby's hand.

"You rode Buttercup?" Anders asked, voice soft. When I nodded, he crossed the aisle to her stall. "Mother gave you my room?"

I exhaled, glad for the change in subject. I followed him and put my hands atop the stall's gate. "Yes, but Ein decided he's too old to sleep with Hilly anymore. He's a big boy and wants to room with his brother. I've been sleeping in the nursery." The bed there was big enough for three children — plenty of room for me, my belly, and a five-year-old.

"She's still afraid of the dark?" Anders unbuckled Buttercup's bridle.

"Someone's told her too much of the monsters in the Winter Wood."

"That wasn't my doing," he said. "She's half afraid of me as it is."

"I told her how many lamia you slew in the Winter Wood, how you took their fangs and made a necklace for me." My hand went to it, thinking of her wide eyes and how carefully she'd touched the teeth. "That helped a bit."

Anders hung up the bridle on a nail and paused. "It was the Winter Wood, wasn't it?" he murmured. Then, with a sidelong smile, "My bed is my own, then?"

"Yes." I watched him unbuckle the girth and take Buttercup's saddle off. There was a cheer in his eyes, a little tuck at the corner of his mouth that I hadn't seen since... "Ranging agrees with you?"

He shrugged with a smile. "Much to learn and little to distract. They gave me that buckskin because he's a biter. Once we'd set that straight, he let me study his patterns as I pleased. I thought it would spook the men, but as it turns out there's a shifter or two among the Rangers. Not much more than dog's ears, but they didn't glance at me more than twice even with the horse nose. Smell, they don't use much, but I got in a deal of practice. When they weren't trying to beat archery into me." He began brushing Buttercup down.

"You're to hit moving trees, the sergeant said?"

Anders nodded. "I can only hit trees that stand still. Not always, but often enough for them to fear me." He shot me a fierce glare, and I couldn't help chuckling.

I leaned against the stall gate, watching him work across Buttercup's bay hide with even strokes, and the smile lingered long on my face. It was good to have him home and his cheerful self again. My smile faded as those last days of the siege trickled back to me, along with what I had realized: he loved me. The summer had given me no answer for that yet.

———————— ⟶ ————————

Anders led the way on Nipper, at an easy jog. I followed on Buttercup, still uncertain.

Why city physicians kept shops to see patients was simple to understand; one would have on hand whatever was needed, and one could be sure of its cleanliness. While talking to Frida about it, Anders had been drawn in and said that I should put together a list of what I'd need for a shop of my own and a guess at how much it would cost. As it was only a daydream, I'd composed it as an ideal little hospital of my own and applied my father's prices to the carpentry. The herbs and extracts, I knew the value of. Reinhardt had helped estimate the rest.

It came to a ridiculous sum: twenty-three silver crescents, which was nearly a gold crown. That did not even include rent on a shop big enough for such a thing.

Now we rode down from the baronial manor houses into the upper crust of Wodenberg. Master crafters and other wealthy families had their homes here. The houses stood large but close together, and their attached workshops were for gold-smithing or paper-making. All of this above Arbor Street was called the Reichang, for the wealth of its occupants.

Anders turned onto Scribe Street and the houses stood shoulder to shoulder, as they did in poorer parts of the city, but they were fresh-painted, handsome, and backed by healthy stretches of garden. I heard wagons, oxen, and men whistling as we passed a long stretch of houses all painted the same light ochre. We turned a corner onto a side street, and the wagon yard bustled behind the ochre houses. A stockade wall enclosed it all, and its broad gates stood open. Half a dozen wagons stacked with barrels waited in the yard as the first few rumbled out onto Scribe Street and turned toward River Road. The passing wagoners noted us, with a glance for Anders and a nod and a touch to their wide-brimmed straw hats for me. Within the wall, I saw that the ochre houses were joined by a long stretch of high porch. Across the gap of the wagon yard ran an equally long warehouse with three sets of double doors.

"Sir Anders!" a man bellowed over the noise. I saw him waving from the high porch. Then he snapped his fingers and pointed at us. "Boy! Look sharp!"

Anders waved and shouted back. "Is Theo in?" He caught the boy's eye before he got too close to Nipper and pointed him toward me and Buttercup.

"He is! Come on in."

The dust roiled up thick from the wagon wheels, and the hot sun was enough to get me sweating. Air seemed scarce in the wagon yard. The boy had Buttercup's bridle, but with all the noise and the weight of the baby… I hesitated.

Anders' hand touched my knee. I looked and he raised both hands.

I unhooked my knee from the pommel and slid down; he caught me in something of a hug and put me down. "Thank you," I said, near his ear.

He smiled and gave me a little squeeze of a hug. His hand found mine and held it, perhaps to see if I'd let him. I did. The dust made me squint hard, and I could feel it sticking to my face. Wiping did little good.

"Hein will call a servant down," he said, tugging me toward the steps.

We climbed up to the long porch, level with a wagon bed, crossed the creaky stretch of planks to a rear door of the house. Just inside, a servant met us in the foyer with cups of cool water and damp towels to get the dust off.

"Anders?" Theo came around the corner and burst into a smile. He pulled him into a brief hug with a thump on the back. Turning to me, he took my hand and bowed over it. "Elect Bockmann, an honor."

I acknowledged him with a deep nod. Saint Qadeem had explained to me the peculiar rank of elect at length; I owed no more than a nod to anybody but a king or a saint, and only if I wished that much. Still, the fine herringbone weave on the red cote Theo wore spoke of money, there was always something butter-rich and golden about him, and a nod seemed such a little thing.

"Please come in. There are chairs in the office. Never make an expecting lady stand, Anders. Shouldn't make her ride, either — you're still coarse as a stableboy, it's the Father's own truth. You ought to have held out for better, Elect."

"I'm well enough," I said and started down the hallway he indicated. I hoped the office would be sufficiently obvious.

Behind me, I heard the thump of a fist on a shoulder. "You didn't even send word you were in town. Last I heard, you'd been kidnapped by Rangers?"

"I've only been home two —"

"And no word?" When I turned and caught him feigning a moment's anger, Theo slid easily back into a smile. "Your pardon, Elect Bockmann. No harm done." He picked at Anders' green cote, straightening it.

Anders mimed popping his shoulder back into joint with a wink. I fought down a smile.

"Call me Kate, please," I said. "He says you've been friends since you were castle pages?"

Theo clasped his hands behind his back and walked alongside me. "Since he called me a lazeabout and a coward, so naturally I punched him in the nose and it all got confusing after that."

"I pinned you and you screamed like a girl for mercy."

Theo only shook his head with a grimace and gestured me through the door of his office. One wall, floor to beam-timbered ceiling, was paper. Ledgers, invoices, inventories, all. His desk was equally covered in tidy stacks, and a space was hollowed out for his quill and ink and such things. A side-table kept the tea service away from the mess. A small brazier had been shoved into a far corner for the summer, and chairs for guests were scattered near the sunny window.

I took the chair furthest from the sun. The servant brought me a cup of tea. Real black tea from Arcea. I sipped it slowly.

"I would invite you both to celebrate Anders' return, but we've the king's hospitality at Vorspitz to see to." Theo dropped into the seat behind his desk with a sigh. "Baron Eismann can't be expected to entertain a king and two queens at once. How safe the road is, none are willing to say — would you know anything of that?"

Anders considered, shifting to sit crosswise in his chair. "This side of the Felsherz is safe enough."

"I'd feel better if those brandy wagons had an escort." Theo jerked a thumb toward the wagon yard.

Anders only spread his hands. "Rossweide has me for horse-training. And there's the late foaling." One hand swung toward me.

Theo nodded, but his mouth still quirked to one side. He took a sip of his tea and dismissed the servant with a nod. "If there's service I can be to you, Elect, in Vorspitz, you have only to ask," he said. "Or any aid to your child. Traveling with fragile cargo can be difficult."

"We mean to go slowly in any case." This much of my father-in-law's plan had been laid out already. "I'm here, though, on Anders' advice."

I explained my thoughts on a physician's shop and sketched out the list I'd composed. Theo listened with chin in his hand, nodding, asking how much space I'd need and whether I'd inquired about the subsidy all physicians drew from the Order. Anders sipped at his tea and sat with one ankle on the other knee. He fell to picking at the dirt ground into his boot's seams as Theo and I diverted into the prices that physicians charged for services.

"Those rates are from down-slope, though," Theo told me with a flick of his hand, "and those are mere physicians, not elect."

"Does that matter?" I had to ask.

"The king's own physician is worth a bit more than some common herb-brewer. And an elect... well, you can steal a man from under the Shepherd's knife. Everyone knows that."

I opened my mouth to object — dead was dead, and nothing to be done about it, even for saints — but Theo threw a look at Anders and I was sure he knew something of what had happened at the lamia fount. What Saint Qadeem had said about letting people wonder echoed in my memory.

"You say I should charge more," I said. "Elect Parselev charged nothing at all."

Theo nodded. "He had no children and no rent to pay. No husband with a half-tame warhorse and a habit of breaking lances on friends."

"At least I didn't drop it," Anders said.

"Rent?" That was the part my ear caught on.

"There's a house just up the street that would suit you," Theo said. "It's been standing empty about a year now, but I can have it cleaned and bring in carpenters to rearrange it to suit you. You're going to need about a crown and a half, all told, and I can set the rent at," and here he tipped his head to consider, "two crescents a moon, which is a pittance for the location. I can loan you the crown and a half, if that's what you want, and I'll lower the repayment to two crowns sixteen crescents as I'm still soft in the head from that foul hit."

Anders snorted into his tea mug.

"But." Theo raised one finger. "I'd rather give you three crowns — not a loan — and let you pay me one brun of every five you earn, instead."

Three crowns? Not a loan? And one brun of five, if I were charging...

I still figured on that as Theo leaned over and clicked a latch by his foot. Metal clinked and my eyes caught on three disks of solid sunlight that he dropped on his desk. Casual, as if they were of little matter. I'd never even laid eyes on a gold crown coin before.

"Theo," Anders chided.

Theo spread his hands. "I never bluff. Though you're right, that's too greedy. With this stipulation: after twenty years, the obligation expires and if I wish to re-invest — or if my children wish to, should, Mother forbid, the Shepherd call me home — we will discuss the matter afresh."

Was that such a difference? "How is that less greedy, sir?"

He hesitated. "For if it's left open-ended, and... well, true, not all elect live so long, but I'm sure you will, m'lady."

So long as... Qadeem's words echoed back to me. Parselev had been a hundred years past any natural death. I looked to Anders beside me, sound and well and picking at his other boot now. Next Saint-day, I would turn seventeen. After the jousting tournament, he would be twenty-two.

Twenty years wasn't so much, truly. Thirty-seven was not so old — m'lady Frida was forty-one. Or in twenty years I might be as dead as the red-braided Arceal elect who'd nearly killed me.

My mind reached for something less bleak and came up with Theo's wife, pregnant at the winter Solstice. In twenty years, the baby would be grown. "Your children? How is your wife?"

Theo's creeping uncertainty at my silence broke into a smile. "She's well. As is our daughter, Mina. They're in Prohzgrad, still, with Father and half the family. Using money for firewood, it would seem."

Anders' eyes perked up from his boot.

"I meant to tell you, next I saw you," Theo told him. "I didn't hear until the siege lifted and you'd vanished." He looked back to me. "That house is only up the street a few doors. Are you well enough to walk that far?"

Heima looked up from the fire when I knocked on the open cottage door. In the late summer heat, the sun-drenched herb garden swaddled me in the scents of marjoram and sage. Shadowed and cooler, my teacher's home was just as I remembered it. Perhaps a little tidier, without him or me for Heima to clean up after. She looked up from her sewing at my knock.

"Kate!" She spread her arms and came to hug me. "How are you? So big, now! It must be nearly time."

"Soon," I said. She noticed the wagon in the herb garden, Will on the driver's seat, and the open Chapel gate we'd driven through. "I've come for the books."

Her brows rose. "You've someplace to put them?"

"I'll have a shop on Scribe Street above King's Market." I didn't mean to grin, but it crept across my face. I couldn't help it. Heima's eyes went wide and she hugged me again.

"Would you like some tea? I just cut some mint. Good morning, sir."

She said that to Will as he joined me at the door. I introduced him and she curtsied. "Let me get upstairs while you make the tea," I said. "This will take so long, I should work as we drink."

Parselev's office waited as I'd left it. I had sorted out enough of the Order's documents to satisfy Krepkin before I moved out; that job was not finished by any measure, though. I sat in my teacher's chair, caught my breath, and set to clearing the desk first.

Will, being a quicker reader than I, sorted papers and books into those related to the Order's official business and those not. They needed further sorting into those written in everyday Alemannic, those written in scholarly Arceal, and those written in Parselev's native Russe, which neither of us knew. The Arceal papers I had to check, as Will spoke little of it.

The loose sheets were mainly letters. The books, which I took more interest in, came in several sorts. Those in Arceal were anatomy texts, encyclopedias of medicines, and compilations of essays. The Alemannic books were written in Parselev's hand and contained lessons of his own for those he couldn't teach in person — many of them charms, kir techniques, or his own experiences with unusual conditions. None of his books were in Russe, thankfully.

Will carried armloads down to the wagon as I sorted through a group of bound volumes of Order-related correspondence. Those would go to Krepkin. There were also the herbs and the jarred extracts to consider, the powders and the seeds. Will kept trudging to and fro. Books and jars and bottles. Heima brought up the pot of tea and forced us to stop for a bit, and I know he was glad to sit and drink a few cups.

She told us that a few siege orphans had been brought in, children whose fathers had been killed and whose mothers had died of typhus. Heima was glad to be taking her turn in the orphanage; she loved helping raise those children. She told me Ter Holly and Ter Edith were well and my surgery assistant Adalslav oversaw the ambulances now.

Afterward, there were more books for the wagon. The two sides of the office had three shelves apiece, and I had fully cleared the lowest thus far. Significant holes had been made in the middle and top. Behind the books, the plank shelving was bracketed to support struts at regular intervals and the back left open to the thatch roofing behind. As the roof slanted toward the peak overhead, behind the shelves was a varying amount of space. I had thought I would find things fallen and lost in the back, and thus I had started at the floor — but there were no such, it seemed. Parselev had been careful.

One stretch of the middle shelf held a multi-volume Arceal bestiary that distracted me for some minutes with its detailed drawings. When Will returned and asked what to carry out next, he broke the spell. I took the entire set from the shelf, stacking it against my arm, hoping I would have time to read the descriptions and wondering if Kiefan —

Behind the books, this stretch of shelf between two supports had a back.

I hesitated, frowning. I handed the bestiary to Will and he left.

Clearing away more space to the side, I stuck my head in. Behind the support, a bit of wall enclosed the space between the shelf and the thatch. It was a cache. I straightened, looking for a latch, a seam, anything that might open it. Nothing. I found the dovetailing that held the corners together, and it was fine, solid work.

It must be charmed, then. I brushed my fingers across the wood, lightly, and called for kir. Nothing, at first. I gritted my teeth and demanded it show itself. A tiny bit stirred, in the

294   Part IV: Salt in the Wound

corner, just a little pin. Too small for most to find. I pinched it, and it unknotted. Something clicked and the dovetailed corner popped away. The side panel near the thatch twisted out of place under my fingers and came free. Inside the cache were a few leather-bound books, all in my teacher's hand, all in Arceal. One held me with its multi-colored diagrams of Blessings — not only what showed through the skin, but all of the structure hidden below as well. Page upon page of near-identical sketches, and the only differences were the red lines that knotted and stretched and danced across the Blessings.

My teeth settled on my lower lip as I flipped through the series illustrating a charm-hand Blessing, sussing out what they were without trying to read the text. Parselev had charted the flow of kir through various Blessings as they were used. And he'd drawn them out from his memory, finely sliced moment by moment.

He'd told me not to question our Blessings or study them. That saints guarded their secrets closely. Jealously.

Will's feet on the stairs startled me. I pulled out the books — I nearly dropped one when the kir wrapped around it pulsed in my hand — and closed the panel. When he reached the top, they were just four more books among dozens.

CHAPTER 1

This time, the pain was enough to stop me mid-sentence. My audience of elders, all with questions about their arthritis or constipation, waited expectantly for a heartbeat or two.

"Oh, that was a contraction," Frau Nebel said. "I remember that feeling."

"Best be getting home, then."

"Someone should go with her."

"Send to the Rossweide's for her husband."

Nods. "Abbot Lev!" Several of them called for the Reichang Orderhaus's abbot, who was assigning the day's duties to his Ters and Thers.

"I can walk myself," I told them, for what it mattered. "They're still far apart."

It mattered little. "We've a new lamb on the way! Send the boy up to fetch her husband."

"He has work to see to," I told them. Anders was up at dawn, with Will, to work the horses. "I'll be home in the time it takes him to come down."

Frau Nebel, who'd been a widow twenty years, shooed the others back. "Elect Kate is quite able to care for herself," she announced. "Wish her well and bake a treat for Lambing-day." The frau smiled, wrinkles fanning around her watery eyes. "And envy m'lady Frida the new little one she'll have for the spoiling."

That set them to chuckling. The abbot came to check on me, having been called, but he was willing to trust an elect to walk herself home along quiet streets. The summer heat had broken, finally, and the Grain Moon had glowed through cool pre-dawn mist when I walked to the Reichang Orderhaus each morning for disciple's dance — the daily dance being the domain of the elderly and the pious, gentle enough for even those ready to foal. It was a pleasant start to the day, as I couldn't sleep through the dawn anymore, with a bit of chatting before I walked home in time for breakfast.

The Shepherd still hovered on the horizon in the dawn, a few days past his full and three of his Flock high overhead. Mist huddled behind trees, blurring out the traces of autumn yellow in the leaves, as the sun warmed the air.

Anders trotted Sprite on a lunge line in the roadside pasture as I walked with my hands tucked in my armpits. She was a petite black with four white stockings and a star on her forehead, very pretty, and that was fortunate as she was a mischievous thing. She knew all the whistle and click commands Anders gave her — I had picked up most of them myself — but she didn't always care to obey. He had a long whip in his hand, but Rossweide horses never needed such a thing once fully trained, m'lord Reinhardt had explained to me. Anders only used it to keep Sprite's attention.

Another contraction stopped me at the kitchen door for a few deep breaths. My saint's bond tingled in the palm of my hand, on the verge of opening, but I squeezed it shut. Saint Qadeem would suffer enough once my labor set in. Though perhaps I should warn him. Once the contraction passed, I focused, and the red strand glowed in my mind's eye.

/ baby / tonight /

After a moment, a warm feeling like a hug flooded back.

/ strength / will be close by / correct? /

In that, he meant whether the baby and I were positioned and prepared. My answer was rather muddled by reluctance to admit I still hadn't checked the baby's kir.

/ check / That came through as a clear order.

I opened the kitchen door with a sigh. He was right. My stomach was growling, though, for its morning oatmeal.

"There she is," Alice said, glancing up from her dough-kneading. "She does want her breakfast after all."

"You're late!" Hilly hopped off the end of the bench and glared at me.

"I'm late. Is there any porridge left?"

"I was going to eat it," she said, crossing her arms over her chest.

Frida looked up from her embroidery by the open window. "Let Kate eat her porridge."

Hilly scuffed her foot, but left my bowl on the dining table. When I crossed the room to it, she threw up her hands to stop me. "No! You're supposed to do it!"

I was to reach for things with kir-vines, for the practice and the strengthening. A dish of oatmeal porridge was heavy for me, and my grip was clumsy as a toddler's. Hilly wouldn't miss any chance to watch me try, though.

"Not today," I said, sitting down on the bench.

"No! You're supposed to do it right!"

"Not... today." My voice hitched as another contraction cramped across my belly. I reached across the dining table for the honey jar. I knew all eyes were on me, so I said, "Yes, it's starting."

I heard Frida put her work aside as I dolloped honey into my porridge. Her hands touched my back, kneaded down low and over my hips. "This always helped me," she said. "Hilly, fill the kettle and put it on the hearth."

A little foot stamped, but she obeyed. "Thank you," I murmured between mouthfuls. Frida joined me on the bench.

When Alice set the dough to rise, she toweled her hands off. "Won't you send down to Physician Lehrer and ask if he'd come, at least?"

There weren't any midwives to be had inside the city walls, and little need for them. Those who did went to Lehrer or Krepkin at the Order, or called me.

"Mother did teach me a thing or two," I said for the fifth time in as many weeks, adding, "I'll not have a man play at midwifing me — the two of you know more than he ever will."

Alice had her daughter, and Frida had given birth seven times. She'd only lost two babies, both to swift cradle fevers. "I only need some extra hands."

"Won't it be difficult to —" Alice outlined a belly with her hands, "see how well it's going?"

"I'll see the kir." My hands ran over the vast curve as my muscles tensed again. Breathe, my Mother had always been saying when she attended a childbirth. I breathed through the pain.

Frida's hand returned to my shoulder, stroking. "You said you hadn't been looking at the patterns?"

Alice, sitting down on my other side, frowned. "You haven't? I would've checked on Magda every day, if I could. How long has it been?"

The contraction eased. I kept eating. "Three moons."

"Three!" Alice cuffed me on the back of the head. Barely a tap, but she knocked my bunned-up braid loose. "And put your crespine on, or get out that wimple like a proper lady. Mother have mercy, Kate, I thought you were the sensible one of us." She went to check the fire and threw me a frown as she went, bottom lip drawn under her teeth.

I scraped my bowl clean with my spoon. "It sounds foolish, I know, but..." I trailed off into a sigh. It was time to look. "I know. Enough."

Closing my eyes, I called my baby's patterns. They spun up in a rainbow storm, whirling between the curves of my arms. Head settled well between my hips, facing correctly, arms wrapped close, legs bundled together. I could count fingers and toes, see the dense clustering of organs in his torso — a boy, yes. My son. Kiefan's son.

"He's perfect," I whispered.

Frida pulled me close, her arm across my shoulders, and her head touched mine.

"It's a boy?" Alice asked.

I could see Kiefan before the opening city gates, sword raised to lead that fateful sortie outside the walls. Smelled the blood and bile as I reached into the gash in Will's belly to mend him. His screams, thrashing under my hands.

"How do you let them do it?" I asked Frida in a thick whisper. "How do you let them put a sword in your baby's hand?"

She touched a kiss to my forehead. "You know that he will only fight to defend, to protect, because you raised him well," she whispered back. Her voice was as tight as my throat felt. "Because you know he's a good boy, even when he's... " She managed a sigh. "Even when no one else sees it." I got a firmer kiss. "Thank you for seeing."

That was a knife between my ribs. I took the pain in silence, preferring that over any hint that would make her question my marriage. I did see it. I knew he loved me. I saw it in each little kindness now, and every one tore at me.

Kiefan had said he'd kill Anders if he touched me.

Frida leaned back, her hand lingering on my shoulder. "Couldn't your son be a disciple of Saint Qadeem, though?"

"I'd expect he would be," Alice said. She always spoiled her own eavesdropping thus. "Carpenter blood will out. Meaning no offense, m'lady."

She smiled, touching her flaxen hair. "We Kaltegrasen are from so far north we're nearly Engls ourselves. That's no insult." Hilly crawled under Frida's arm, always wanting a cuddle if there were hugs to be had, and Frida hoisted the five-year-old onto the bench. "Kate's having her baby today."

Hilly eyed my stomach, brow crinkling. "But you promised to stay."

That caught me off guard. "I'll stay. Until we must leave for Vorspitz."

"No! You promised!"

Frida fixed Hilly with a stern eye. "Mind your temper. You're a big girl — almost six! And you'll be a big sister now. You must set a good example for the baby."

She grabbed handfuls of her pale green dress and twisted them. Her frown darkened. "But it's cold now," she muttered.

I thought I saw her meaning. "You won't have to sleep alone."

Her anger eased, but she still doubted me. Frida picked Hilly up bodily and settled her on one hip. "We need to wash some laundry today, but first we'll tell Papa and the menfolk. And we need the rest of the baby things from the loft. Do you want to go up there to help Papa?"

Hilly shook her head; she was afraid of the dark loft above the second floor. As Frida carried her out the other kitchen door, toward Reinhardt's office, Alice returned to hug me. "I know why you worry. No baby of mine would be picked by Saint Woden, boy or girl — but you'll see. We'd best have a book ready for when this one's born."

I managed to smile at that much.

<hr />

"My father made a birthing stool for Mother. I didn't think to ask for it before she went north." I paced the kitchen, sweating though I wore only my shift, Frida walking with one arm around me. After the laundry, the day's meals, and all her duties, I hated to make her walk with me but she wouldn't sit down.

"You hardly expected to need it," she said.

I regretted that my mother wasn't here and didn't even know of her grandchild. Whether she'd even reached whatever little town on Lake Neva she'd been sent to, I didn't know. I'd been so eager to forget my father's humble cottage, my mother, and all of Engl Street in favor of the Order and Parselev and the saints — and now I wished that I had just one little piece of father's handiwork.

A carpenter in King's Market had made me a birthing stool, a crescent of wood on three legs high enough for a midwife to reach beneath. Or he'd sworn he had; I suspected his apprentice had made it, even though the stool looked solid enough. I wanted the one that ought to have been mine, as the eldest daughter.

I stopped when the next contraction set in, closing my eyes. Even calling my kir through the hard clench of my muscle was too much to ask. I felt my saint's bond throb in my hand, transmitting my resolve along with the pain. Qadeem was nearby. He'd come if I needed him.

As it eased, I checked my pattern against my mother's measure of a woman's full opening. "Almost there," I murmured. My back hurt. My shoulders felt knotted. My ankles ached from pacing. "Let me sit."

Alice had put out a meal at sunset, but only Reinhardt, Will, and Hilly were eating. Water was all I'd wanted, and plenty of it. Ein nibbled at his food and watched me closely, perhaps on the chance I might burst. Anders only fidgeted, his knees jittering under the table when he likely ought to be pacing with me. Frida had to be as tired as I.

"You should rest," I told her. "You've been walking…"

She hushed me and steered me by one elbow. My stool waited before the hearth. The next contraction came on as I toddled toward it, and I tried to keep breathing. My tired legs wobbled but I fought it, not wanting to lean on her further. I reached out for balance. A hand caught mine, strong and steady. I dropped onto the stool harder than I meant to, and the rear leg shifted in its socket, settling a little shorter than the others and nearly tipping me over.

"That fucking bastard!"

Anders knelt behind me, shifting his grip on my hand. His shoulders against my back stabilized me. "I'll kill him in the morning," he promised. "Rest a bit first."

For a moment I resisted, but then his cool hand brushed sweat from my forehead and I didn't care. His shoulder was strong, and I got in a whole deep breath of rest before the next contraction. I tensed against him, then braced, and he shifted closer to give more support.

Each time the pain eased, he had a cup of water at hand. Frida took his place now and then to knead my knotted lower back. Anders soon learned enough to take over that job for his mother. After each contraction, my head lay limp on his shoulder as I heaved for breath. So much work. I thought each one was the last I could manage, but they kept coming.

"You're open, Kate," Alice said. "Are you pushing?" I picked my head up; she knelt between my knees, my shift bunched up around my hips. I'd lectured them on the signs all afternoon.

It was well into night now, I realized. The fire crackled under a pot of hot water, and a washbasin waited, rags soaking in it. Anders held both my hands in his, and I dimly remembered bracing against his grip through the last few contractions.

Reinhardt had gone to see to his ledgers in his office. Will sat braiding a new leather whip in the firelight, behind me and to the side for politeness' sake. At the hearth's corner, Ein sat transfixed, though he looked a little green around the gills. Hilly slept, curled, in the rocking chair.

Here it came again, and from somewhere in my gut came the urge to push. All day, I'd been getting to this part; I knew what happened from here, and I could do this. Strength surged, lifting me up off Anders' chest even as my hands gripped his. Barely a chance to breathe between the contractions, it seemed now.

"Your pattern, Kate," Frida nagged. "Check your pattern."

"I'm well, I'm well."

"You didn't look," Anders said, and he was right. So I called, so tired that only a patch of me answered. The wrong patch. With a groan, I slumped against him. He hushed me, gave me a sip of water, and then he called up my pattern strong and clear. "What do you see?"

I saw a head wedged through my hips, straining them hard — just as I'd seen dozens of times. "He's coming."

My son was coming, bit by bit.

Snarls clawed out through my clenched teeth when each contraction peaked. Anders told me to breathe, keep breathing, his words on my ear, his scent of leather and horse in my nostrils. My own blood and sweat too.

I felt a wet cloth on my groin and saw Frida pass the washrag back to Alice. "Get the towel. He's almost here, Kate."

"Almost," I breathed and pulled a few more lungfuls as it came on again. I braced against Anders' hands again, bearing down hard, hissing through my teeth, and when something came loose the shock of it knocked my elbows from rigid to feeble. He caught me, and then my grip steadied.

"Just a few more," Frida told me with a broad smile. "A few more and he's in your arms."

Anders' cheek pressed against mine, squeezing my hands. Both of us sweat-slicked. How long had he sat with me? Bracing me, encouraging… I glanced down at my hand in his and saw red crescents behind his knuckles. From my nails. My heart ached.

The next contraction rippled through me. I put his arm across my chest and he held me firm against his shoulders. I leaned into his grip, pushing. Felt the baby sliding free. I panted when it passed and fell limp in Anders' arms.

"Oh, look at him!" Alice cooed.

"Yes, there you go, take that breath," Frida clucked and I picked my head up from Anders' shoulder. Ein was up from the hearth, on his toes to crane over his mother and Alice, his eyes wide.

My mother had slapped babies' rears to be sure they were lively; my son was silent. "Is he…?"

Frida stood with the towel-wrapped bundle in her arms, and the moment my eyes found the egg-shaped little head I could see nothing else. "He's perfect, just as you said," she told me from somewhere far away.

He squirmed in my hands as I took him. Anders let me go so I could lay the baby on my chest, his little head against my neck. Damp and warm and pink. His eyes opened for a moment, blinked, and one fist unfurled into a tiny flower. Anders' finger came up under his palm, and his hand curled around it. Then he twitched away, wanted to wriggle in the towel but thought the better of it and stilled again with his eyes closed.

The fingernail gouges on Anders' hand caught my eye again. I covered them with my palm, heart aching, and drew his arm close. He hugged me, squeezing up tears into my eyes. "You stayed," I whispered. "The whole time."

"The least I could do," he whispered back, and touched a kiss to my cheek. Even softer, he added, "For my wife and son."

My hand found the side of his head and I pressed his cheek to mine. Tears broke loose. Anders hushed me as I sobbed, holding us both snug against his chest. A tear or two of his own might have slipped in. It was all I could do to breathe through the crushing gratitude.

The contractions continued, milder now, to force the afterbirth out. Alice asking how long it should take brought my mind back to the moment and my training. I rattled off the steps, my voice weakened by the tears, and checked my patterns. My emptied belly collapsed with each contraction. The afterbirth, peeled from my womb, crept outward.

My baby's eyes were open again. His hand lay over my heart; I picked it up on my fingertip and stroked my thumb over his velvety skin.

Anders reached up, startling me, to clasp the hand that Reinhardt offered. "The Mother's seen fit to set her discipline on you, and I know better than to argue with a mother," Reinhardt said. "Past is past?"

"Past is past." Anders nodded.

There was cutting the cord to see to, and then Will took the afterbirth and a shovel out to the far pasture. I pried myself off the stool — my ass felt permanently creased — and away from Anders. Cold air hit my sweat-soaked back. Trembling, I knelt beside the washbasin with my baby as Alice poured in a little more boiling water. Frida held a soapy washrag at ready as I checked the temperature.

"I'll wash him." She reached with her other hand.

"I can do it." I put the dirty towel aside. Chubby arms and legs, a round little tummy, pudgy cheeks… I had many hands helping me wash him. He kicked, wriggled, and started to cry. Alice stroked his cheek, cooing, but he didn't want to be wet, didn't want to be soaped. Once he was clean, Frida had the swaddling blanket ready.

I took it from her and wrapped him myself. Snug and warm. That quieted him. Laid against my heart again, he dozed right off.

"You should rest," Frida said, holding out her arms to try again. "It's late. You must be exhausted."

Her eyes were fixed on her grandson, so far as she knew. Let her dote, Anders had said, it will make her happy. And she was right, I was wrung out. I needed washing myself.

He stirred when I passed him to Frida and she hushed him. Alice tracked the passage, and no doubt she'd get a cuddle in soon enough. "A little more hot water?" I asked her, and she fetched the kettle again.

I squatted by the basin — wasn't sure if I could stand, in truth — and Alice let me lean on her. She helped me wash the blood and sweat from below my belly. It still pulsed, was still

300

swollen, but it had come down a good deal already. I still bled, but only a trickle and my kir patterns were strong.

My cramped legs fought my attempt to stand. Alice caught me on one side, Anders the other. "Bring the baby?" I reached for him. "Where's the cradle?"

"I'll bring him," Frida promised. "We're all worn out. Anders, be sure she gets to bed."

<hr />

I slept past dawn for the first time since my teacher had died.

My baby fussed in his cradle beside the nursery bed. As I sat up, wincing when my sore hips and knees protested, Hilly stirred behind me.

"What's that?"

"It's my baby." The cradle was an oval basket big enough for two babies, but my little one lay well padded on a folded lambswool blanket. Once cuddled against me, he quieted down to a mutter.

Joints popping, I hauled myself up from the bed. Blood oozed down below, but I had my flux rag on. I could mend that once I was awake. My stomach grumbled, reminding me I'd missed dinner last night. The house was quiet when I listened for feet and voices. Hilly had dozed off again.

In just my shift, I slipped out of the nursery and down the stairs with my son. I drew myself a cup of water from the barrel by the door and went to check on the overnight porridge by the low coals in the fireplace. The smell of it set my stomach to growling again.

My baby whimpered, too. "Are you hungry?" I whispered. "Let's try it, then."

The rocking chair waited by the hearth, so I sat down and untied the drawstring neck of my shift. Newborns didn't always want to nurse, I knew, but now and then they did. He nuzzled around a bit, but that seemed to be enough and he closed his eyes again. I sat in the chair with him a while, stroking my fingers across his cheek, his scalp where his thin down was all but invisible, and his little ears.

Porridge, my stomach insisted. It would need two hands, though. Getting up, I lay my son on the dining table, dozing in his swaddling blanket, and crept to get a bowl and a spoon. I only took my eyes off him to lift the lid from the porridge pot and scoop out a big dollop.

A soft scrape of socked feet on the stairs and then they padded down quickly. I twisted around as Anders crossed to the table in long strides. He bent over, teasing the blanket open a little. "Good morning," he whispered. "You're a quiet one, then. Good."

I stood with my porridge, and Anders glanced at me with a smile on his face. Full-dressed already, but for his boots. His flaxen knight's crest hung loose to one side, wanting a combing and a tie.

"He's awake." Anders picked him up and I tensed for a heartbeat, but he did it right. He steadied the little head and gently lay the baby against his shoulder. "He'll need a name."

I brought my porridge to the table. "Wilhelm?" I asked, voice low in case anyone else was awake. That was traditional, for both Alemanni and Engls, to name a boy for one grandfather or another. But it raised a question, too. "There was no King Anders." It was an odd name in this part of Wodenberg.

"No. As the baron wouldn't have me named from his side of the family, it was up to my mother's kin to provide a name. Sir Anders Kaltegrasen, baron of Schwarzbaum."

My baby drew me to Anders' side, and the chubby little cheek made me stroke its curve with my finger. Firelight caught a sheen of golden stubble on Anders' neck, reminding me how close I was — but I lingered. Laid my hand on the breathing little bundle. Wilhelm?

"I'd rather call him William," I murmured. It was the Englic version of the king's name, but had lost favor after the conquest. "King Wilhelm was your father, though."

Anders looked up from watching my son sleep, his smile soured by disdain. "The man was no father to me. He hardly so much as looked me in the eye. Couldn't face his own shame, even when I was champion of the joust. Don't honor him for that." The baby twitched, and Anders' tone softened. "What about your family?"

"Father's name was Edward," I said. "My mother's father was Rafe."

"Rafe?" That caught Anders' ear. "There was a year we went north, to the Kaltegrasen estate. I was twelve, perhaps? My Blessings were still fresh. I met my grandfather and spent the whole summer riding horses bareback with my cousin. Rafe. Nothing but stony hills up there, covered in sheep. We made a game of charging down into flocks and scattering them and caught a lot of belt for it. Best summer of my life."

By how pensive he turned on that thought, I said, "Rafe, then?"

"Sir Rafe Bockmann."

"Physician," I murmured, heart quavering.

"Perhaps. We'll see how he does on a horse first." Anders smiled, but I couldn't return it. He turned serious again, drew me close and touched his forehead to mine. "He won't be riding to war tomorrow."

I knew that was all years off. Anders' hand shifted from my shoulder to my hair, combed into my loose locks. His breath on my mouth, so close, just shy of a kiss — my head turned aside, into his shoulder, and I hugged him. Heart trembling in my chest.

Kiefan might kill him for touching me. I couldn't bear to see that.

CHAPTER 2

Qadeem came to check on me and Rafe before noon that day. He smiled when he lifted my son — sound asleep — and called his pattern. My saint saw what I'd been so glad to see: Rafe did not have Kiefan's flawed prime meridian in his egg-shaped little head. He'd never suffer those terrible headaches.

I asked for news of the Arceal army, but Qadeem would tell me nothing. He sent me back to bed, to rest.

I charmed my womb, mended the bleeding, and combed out the painful tangles of kir. It resisted when I pushed its pattern toward the small, tidy thing it should be — and my teacher had told me it was best to let a womb take its time. So I did. The charms cleared away much of my pain, though, and the next morning, Saint-day, I felt well enough to go to Rafe's Lambing-day.

Which caused some fuss. Mothers of only two days past did not go, were not expected to; they stayed a-bed with the midwife to nurse them.

"I am Saint Qadeem's elect," I said to Frida's objections. And I pulled my shoes on to go.

My father-in-law would hear nothing of walking to the Orderhaus and hitched up the wagon. I was still tired, even after a day abed cuddling Rafe, so I was willing enough to sit on cushions in the wagon bed.

My disciple's dance companions had gotten word around, and it seemed half the city knew of the elect's baby. They'd come to the Reichang Orderhaus with their dish for the communal meal and what sweets they could cook from the limited provisions in the city. Lambing-days were always an occasion for sweets, and there'd been few in the city since the siege began.

The disciple's dance was soon to begin when we arrived, and I'd never seen the chapel so close to full. I took a place near the back and set my baby's cradle on the floor at my feet. He'd wailed all the wagon ride down, not liking the noise or the vibration, and now he fell sound asleep. I drew stares, heard murmurs, but they didn't question my presence. Perhaps because I was an elect now.

The gentle stretches and twists the dance led me through were worth it. I felt my spine click back into alignment, and my hips too.

After the dance, I picked Rafe up and settled him against my shoulder. Frida had washed him that morning and dressed him in a sturdy linen bunting of dark Rossweide green embroidered with white horses prancing around the hem. "All my babies wore this for their Lambing-day," she'd said with misty eyes.

She joined me now, slipping her arm into mine. Anders took his post at my other side. And we started for the table of honor together.

It took some doing, though it went quicker than it might have. Lambing-day was the official arrival of the flock's newest member, when the baby was presented to the Mother and the Father, the saints, and the entire community. Habit was that small children and elders could meet the baby before the official receiving for a chance to coo a bit more.

Frau Nebel took pride of place and was first to kiss Rafe's head. "Beautiful! May the Mother keep you strong, dear, and bless you with more lambs."

There were a few children who wanted to see the baby, touch his hand, and give him a kiss. Frida answered their questions while I quieted Rafe when he began to object to it all. Some of the older men interrogated Anders about the siege and the summer — trying to suss out truth from the rumors, most likely. He had worn his Ranger's tabard for that reason. Still, they doubted that he'd submitted to the Father's and Mother's disciplines for good and all.

"Is it true then, Elect, that the Rangers took him on?"

I spared the grey-bearded knight a sober nod. "I heard Woden tell Anders to report to them myself. And his sergeant praised his service when he was released for the parley."

"For the parley? Not…?"

He didn't care to speak whatever rumor was afoot. "Yes, the parley," I said. "The king expects us there."

That caught a number of ears and prodded out several startled gasps, but I wasn't going to linger for tiresome questions. Yes, I was taking an infant to Vorspitz. I was an elect and I had my duty to saints and kingdom. I quickened my pace and they parted for me.

All was ready for the communal meal when I reached the steps up to the table of honor. The full-length icons of the Mother and the Father stood just behind. Between them, our saints' triple symbol: the anvil, book, and sword. Frida stopped at the table, beside the abbot, with her hands clasped together.

Anders and I crossed the last few feet with Rafe. Both icons were finely painted on pale wood, the Mother kind and smiling, the Father stern. Each stood with one hand on their ancient, primal selves, the Father his ram and the Mother her ewe.

My little lamb squirmed against my shoulder as I dropped to one knee with my husband, my fist against my heart in obeisance. I stroked my lamb's back when he twitched in his sleep.

"This is my son, Rafe," I said, voice low and cracking with sudden emotion. "Thank you, Mother. Thank you, Father. Please keep him strong to serve your saints."

Mother Love smiled, understanding my fears. Father Duty knew I would do the right thing.

Anders took my baby and laid him on his knee. Rafe's eyes opened, piqued by the change, but he didn't cry. Only looked up at the raftered roof far overhead.

"This is my son, Rafe. I swear, Mother, he will be my son. I swear." Anders' voice trailed off for a moment, his eyes closed. I tried to swallow the lump in my throat. "Thank you, Father. Please keep him strong to serve your saints."

He stood first, cradling my baby — ours — in one arm. I slipped under his other as we turned, wanting to hug him for that promise. But there was one more introduction to make. They all stood watching us, smiling, eager to hear who our baby was.

Anders cleared his throat and took a steadying breath. "This is our son, Rafe Bockmann, the Shepherd's new little lamb. Will the Flock help us teach him the wisdom of the Mother and the Father?"

Our son. My arm, looped across his back, squeezed him as the applause began and his grip tightened on me. I looked up, eyes wet again, not wanting to let him go, and he looked down —

And he kissed me, a simple, gentle touch that lingered a heartbeat too long and weakened my knees. When our lips parted, I didn't dare breathe or think.

Mother have mercy.

A faint rumble of hooves outside caught my ear for a moment, breaking the spell. Abbot Lev came first to greet Rafe and kiss his forehead and I should've thanked him, but I looked for the horses. Who...? Anders' eyes slid toward the chapel's open doors and the approaching hooves, narrowing. The riders stopped just outside the doors.

Kiefan appeared in the doorway, looking back toward the horses, and a cold knife plunged through my heart. I flinched from Anders in sudden fright; he wasn't to touch me. The smell of hot blood on Kiefan's tabard filled my nose. Centaur blood. I'd sobbed on Kiefan's shoulder as he carried me home to the Order, reeking of blood. Their iron lamellar had parted like wool under his sword, no match for Blessing strength. Even before he was a bound elect.

Had he seen? The goodfolk in the chapel raised a cheer for their king, which turned his head toward them. Kiefan stepped in, Gregor appearing behind him with a couple bundles awkwardly in hand.

No surprise that word of my labor had gotten to the castle, and of course Kiefan would want to meet the... his baby. His son.

"Give me the baby," I murmured to Anders, reaching without looking. Rafe twitched against my shoulder as he settled.

The cheer faded as the crowd knelt in obeisance — the elder members needing a helping hand — from those closest to the door when Kiefan entered to Anders beside me. I lowered my chin in a deep nod, swallowing a nervous lump. No sign of anger, though. He hadn't seen Anders touching me.

"Majesty!" Abbot Lev stood from his obeisance first. "We're honored, but what brings you to Reichang?"

Kiefan's spurs clicked on the chapel's stone floor as he crossed to the table of honor. His fur-lined cloak belled open; he wore no sword, and only a moon-crested black cote. Not even his gold crown-band. His blonde stubble below his Blessing ridges was near as invisible as my son's down, and his braided knight's crest had added another twist in length. Long enough to rest on his shoulder, now.

"I wished to see that my sister elect is well, Abbot," Kiefan answered. He pulled off his riding gloves as he came. "To see that my newest nephew is well. I would add this to the sweets."

His squire Gregor passed a covered iron pot in a rope sling to the abbot. He raised the lid; I smelled apple-sauce cake, with a maple syrup glaze. Still warm. "We're honored," the abbot repeated, and he went to put it on the table.

Kiefan's gaze never left the bundle in my arms as he drew close. His polite smile dropped into wary curiosity tinged with disbelief for a heartbeat, and then he locked that away behind a crinkled brow. "I meant to arrive earlier," he muttered, the frown deepening to a glare — at Anders. "I meant to find Kate at home, but the house was empty. You dragged her out of bed —?"

"No, I —"

"You think she's weak?" Anders cut me off, his voice low as well. "Don't insult her."

Kiefan's spine stiffened. "I think she deserves all the rest and care she wishes," he growled. "You chose duty over her. Don't walk in here —"

"No." I shifted between the two of them. "He came to see that we're well."

Kiefan's whisper lost its edge. "I came to meet my son. I've that much right."

Anders leaned away, holding his tongue behind a pressed-firm mouth.

I shifted Rafe from my shoulder to my arm. He was awake and staring with muddled-blue eyes. Kiefan reached, hesitated, and put his hand on Rafe's chest. Found his little arm, his hand, and stroked a calloused thumb over Rafe's palm. Kiefan leaned in and kissed our baby's forehead.

"You'll want for nothing, little one," he whispered. "I am not my father. I will not abandon you." Kiefan touched Rafe's delicate scalp, his cheek, and my baby's head twitched toward his hand.

"Do you want —?" I tried to whisper through a heart-choked throat. I shifted Rafe toward Kiefan.

His brow shot up, and he took a sharp breath as his hands moved to agree. "May I?"

I passed Rafe to him. Kiefan put a hand under Rafe's rear, the other under his shoulders — and his little head dropped sharply when he came off my arm. Anders hissed an angry breath and reached to catch him, Kiefan bristled and glared, and Rafe lay against his shoulder before my hands could move.

"Father's beard!" Anders all but spat it.

I felt kir shift when Kiefan called Rafe's pattern, to be sure he was well. "My son's no fragile thing," he hissed back.

"My son," Anders said with a bitter twist.

"I've every right —"

I had my hand up, my kir gathering to — distract them, I hardly knew how yet — when the crowd turned suddenly. Breaths caught and they all dropped in obeisance again. Saint Woden filled the doorway. Arms folded.

Kiefan looked, and his hands tightened on Rafe's soft body.

Woden had told him to forget about me and the baby till Rafe was old enough to train. The saints took little interest in children before their Blessing-day, but he had called my baby his grandson that day in the command pavilion. Surely he didn't mean to…

As Woden crossed the chapel, hands clasped behind his back, his gaze shifted across the three of us, then to the baby and back to me.

It was all I could do not to snatch Rafe away with kir-vines and further tie him to me. Saint Woden would not touch my baby, not sound him, not lay any claim. There was no danger of that until Rafe turned twelve. He had come in curiosity, or to remind Kiefan of his duty. Surely.

My chin had to tip up as Woden drew close; his smile was faint and shallow. "Elect," he said with a nod. "A son. May the Mother and Father keep you strong for him. Should he need anything, ask. I look after my own. Bockmann." The saint looked to Anders, who rose from his obeisance. "Walk with me. Your captain reported..." The saint's voice lowered as they went.

Kiefan breathed a sigh. He took a deep lungful of Rafe's clean, soapy smell and passed him back to me. "He's beautiful," he murmured. "Wilhelm?"

I met his grey eyes. "Rafe."

A crease of frown. "Rafe?"

"My grandfather's name." Kiefan looked away, still frowning, so I went on. "Anders says the king was too ashamed to even look him in the eye. Should that be honored with a name?"

Quietly, "No. And Anders wasn't the only son pushed aside by my father's duty. I will do better. If I must be an uncle, Rafe will have the best uncle in the kingdom. I'll find a way, whatever the saints require." He shot a resentful look toward Woden. Turning a little further, he beckoned Gregor, and the squire hurried up to hand over the cloth bundle. "Something for Rafe."

It was tied with a bit of red ribbon. I tucked it under my arm and saw Woden returning with Anders as I did.

"Baron Rossweide tells me you've a young mare fine enough to gift to the Crowns of Caercoed," the saint said. "We'll need two."

Anders nodded. "Then Sprite will be ready as well. M'lord."

"See that she is." Woden drew up and took a heavy breath. "You shouldn't have come," he told Kiefan. With one hand, he flicked away unspoken objections. "Your next defiance will not go unanswered. And if you think to take after your uncle, Elect Wolfgang, I may well come to regret," and he paused to put weight on that, "my choice of king."

Kiefan bowed his head, sober, and turned to follow his saint in leaving. Bustle returned around us when Saint Woden told the crowd to see to the meal that was waiting. Anders and I stood silent in the midst of it as we watched the two go. Rafe slept, drooling on my shoulder, blessedly untouched by it all.

⁂

The newborn-sized cotes Frida had put on Hilly and Ein were snug on Rafe from the beginning. A week later, they were only growing snugger. Both had been spring babies, so the larger cotes she had were summer-weight linens. As the Grain Moon waned and the chill strengthened, Frida and Alice set to sewing woolen buntings for him. Those were simple enough, but Frida had a fine hand at embroidery and wanted them to be handsome enough for him as well.

I took Rafe outside and laid him on a blanket in the sun, then wedged the distaff of linen fiber under my armpit and spun with the help of a drop spindle. Frida found most embroidery thread not to her standard and made her own. I needed the practice at spinning.

Alice joined me, sitting on the grass beside Rafe's blanket and peeling and slicing apples for the cake. We left for Vorspitz in only two mornings, and Frida meant to serve a treat tonight.

In the pasture, Will rode Dove and Anders was on Sprite. Dove was a lovely young mare, mild and sweet, born black but half-turned to white. She knew all of the gaits and commands a Rossweide palfrey should and was sure to be a gift to the Crowns of Caercoed. Sprite was more interested in chasing butterflies, in Nipper and his companions two fences away, or anything that wasn't doing as she was told. Anders had his hands full keeping her at a trot and matching Dove's paces until she decided to listen to him.

I pinched the flax fibers between my fingers, letting the drop spindle twirl as I played out the thread. My kir, in my hand along with the linen, spun out with it. Fatter than the thread by how it felt, but thinner than anything I'd managed yet. When I held the progressing end tight and wrapped up the spun thread onto the spindle, I took the kir back into my hand to do it again.

My kir must be tight and solid when I threw it out too quickly to think. Thus it could firmly grasp a thing and lift it, as I'd seen others do. The charms I'd inherited from my teacher could show me how, but without the skill I couldn't —

"I'll sleep in the nursery with Hilly," Alice said, of a sudden. My fingers faltered and made a slub on the thread. "My little room will be cold soon enough, even by the kitchen. We can hold off the night monsters. Go back to Anders' bed."

Frida had given Alice the sick-room just off the kitchen for her own. It was a tiny space, but it had a small bed and shelves for her things. I wound up the good thread and worked at tightening the slub. "He has work to see to," I told her with a nod toward the horses. "Waking four times a night will make him fussy as Hilly." I hadn't been to a morning disciple's dance since Rafe was born, as I needed the sleep. Hilly's temper was short as a weasel's.

"Mustn't have that." Alice chuckled. "When Rafe's sleeping better, then. Or when it gets cold enough."

I'd need a new excuse by then. Or... my mind shifted, uneasily. Would Kiefan be married? Would Anders still —?

A puffed breath on my ear startled me. I dropped the spindle and distaff in whirling around. My shield spread from my palm, putting a layer of green between me and... Saint Qadeem.

"Mother have mercy," Alice gasped, fumbling for the paring knife and half-peeled apple she'd dropped.

"Fair reflexes," he said with a smile, "for one without speed. But you had no warning. Had I been an enemy, you would be dead."

He'd tucked his kir away so well that I could no more sense him than I could Alice. Yet when he let it free, it was simple enough. I took a deep breath to slow my heart's pounding against my breastbone. "Do I wear a shield forever, then?" I let it unravel.

"Some do. I came to speak of hiding, and of finding the hidden." Qadeem's fur-lined cloak puddled around him as he crouched beside Rafe's blanket. He stroked one chubby cheek, his fingers dark beside my baby's pale skin. Rafe's head jerked toward the touch. Qadeem switched to Arceal. "And to see the little prince."

I grimaced and bent to pick up my spinning. "So everyone knows, then?"

"Mechdan told me and no others. The affection between you and the king is plain, but most believe the rumor that he spent Solstice with an Arbor Street lady he met at the bonfire. They say this is Anders' son. Don't despair yet." He stood and crossed his arms, as he often did for my lessons. "Show me your kir-vines, firstly."

I flicked my hand, spinning out a finger-width of kir, and snatched up the last unpeeled apple beside Alice. She flinched when it rose beside her, but then smiled and ate the curling peel from off her paring knife. I tossed the apple and caught it in a coil of vine, then brought it to my hand.

"Good. The bowl?"

Thinking of the strong, tight linen thread, I looped my vine around the ceramic bowl and lifted. It rose from the grass, its weight pressing on my mind. Alice tossed in another apple slice as I drew it past her. Halfway to me, it wobbled and I spun a second vine from my other hand to steady it. The bowl reached my hands, but my pulse throbbed in my throat.

"Your practice has served you well."

"I have a stern taskmaster." Hilly wouldn't let me pick up anything unless it was by kir-vine, and she didn't like my excuse of some things being too heavy.

Qadeem smiled. "And perhaps you wish to fly?"

That was true enough. One needed to lift one's whole self to fly without wings. "Someday."

"Continue to reach, then. Have you any questions on that?"

"No." Parselev's secret books crossed my mind. I had looked through them all, committed the pages to memory, but hadn't had time to read yet. I trusted that my teacher had his reasons for hiding them. I'd mixed them in with the other books on the sawdust-strewn floor of my office-to-be, and it wasn't likely any of the carpenters would touch them. The oddest one, which was tied shut with strings of kir, was upstairs, under the nursery room bed.

Qadeem held up his hand and drew kir to it, little by little. "As to finding the hidden then. You feel my kir now, and I feel yours. All people and animals can feel kir in sufficient concentration. What we sense, precisely, is loose kir. You know loose kir from that which is shaped and bound in patterns."

I nodded. The green glow in his hand tightened, ignited into a spark, and Alice looked up suddenly from peeling the last apple. The spark bounced in his hand and he tossed it from one to the other; she smiled at that, as she had no idea what we spoke of. We still used Arceal.

"You do not feel your friend's loose kir, her daily ration, unless you call it. Loose kir soaks into patterns, as water soaks into soil. A small amount, and the soil seems no different at first. A great amount, and it becomes mud."

Mother had tended a few herbs by our chicken coop, watering them in dry spells. I saw the thirsty earth drinking in the water, for a heartbeat. "If Alice had so much kir, then I would feel her?"

Qadeem raised a finger, and the spark hovered above it. "As one's skill blossoms, one can hold far more kir. Alice is —" He appraised her heat-sight patches with a glance; she'd heard her name and met his eyes with raised brows. "She has little gift for kir. Fräulein?" Qadeem switched to Alemannic. "Would you assist?"

Alice tossed apple and knife in the bowl and stood, brushing off her butt. "I'd be glad to," she tipped her head with a hint of smile, brown braid hanging free, "assist you, m'lord."

He looked up from diffusing the spark into a green ball, one eyebrow cocked. Alice only smirked. My eyes rolled in spite of myself.

"Your hand?" he asked, putting his out with the cloud hovering around his palm. Then he took it back for a moment. "Have you touched a Trinity symbol for re-binding?"

Saint Aleksandr's disciples had gone without kir rations since he died, unless they'd been re-bound to Woden or Qadeem. Each Saint-day, the unbound could put a hand on the anvil, book, and sword and their bond was re-made.

"No, m'lord, I haven't yet. I'm sorry. It slipped my mind on the Lambing-day," Alice said.

Qadeem ran his left thumb across his fingertips and I saw a faint ripple of the red disciple-bonds there. Hundreds, if not thousands. He reached with his pinky finger, touched the tip of hers, and drew it back slowly. Finer than spider silk, a trace of kir followed. "You'll have your rations again, each midnight. Now, to illustrate."

He opened his handful of kir over her palm, and he poured it into her. It flowed across her skin in a mist and her pattern rose to meet it, shining through her dress as it absorbed. More and more. Alice's eyes widened. The surplus fell from her in a cloak, rippling bright green and dropping to the earth where it vanished. Qadeem withdrew from her hand, and it ran off her a while more, trailing into rivulets and then drops, like water.

Still, Alice was bright-eyed and grinning. "If I knew that charm, I'd have been the richest lady on Arbor Street." She laughed. "What do I owe you, m'lord?" She watched one last drop fall from her hand, caught it with the other. It only gathered on the back of her second hand and fell again.

"I will keep you in mind." He slipped her a narrow, sidelong glance and she smirked again. Then he returned to Arceal to tell me, "Those who cannot hold so much kir are no threat to you. And those who can may hide the kir in their patterns rather than leaving it free and sensible. If they do it well, leave no scrap free, they will seem harmless. Still, there is a way to spot the elect and the sainted."

My mind went to Saint Woden's pattern as he lay wounded in that burning house, and the moment in the Pool when Qadeem had let me see his. "Your patterns are so much denser."

"Yes. And hers —" He turned to Alice, but she had bent to pick up the bowl of apple slices. He paused to let her stand, rather than calling her pattern up butt-first. She didn't even notice, it seemed, when the colors rose on her skin, shining through her dress. "Hers are ordinary. Yours run thickly, now that you are elect, and mine, as you saw, run thicker still. You know that you can hold more kir now than you could before — you're sleeping less as well, yes?" Startled, I nodded. "Kir never sleeps. It will keep you young as well. Practice calling patterns without touching your patient, if you have not."

"I can, at close range."

Qadeem nodded. "Increase that. It will serve you well in protecting our kingdom and our allies — which is your duty, Kate." He put weight on that. "Protect the kingdom, we saints, and yourself. You need not be the aggressor. Leave that to Kiefan and Woden — though if they need your aid, give it wholly. And keep an eye and an ear open, always. Report to me often on the parley's progress. I've long had a net laid in Wodenberg to watch for danger, but such news comes to me after many changes of hands. You are my eyes and ears now."

I shivered at the memory of Qadeem tapping my Blessing. My eyes crept toward Anders in the pasture — not so far away, I was startled to see. He stood at the fence, off Sprite with her reins in hand. Watching.

"There are matters in Vorspitz you should see to, as Kiefan will be occupied. A few youths to be sounded, to check their progress. If a physician asks you to mend a patient, do it if you can. Beware…" Qadeem strolled toward Anders as he told me this, but stopped now and glanced behind us. Alice had gone into the house. My saint continued in Englic, which Anders couldn't understand. "Do nothing to anger the lamia, should you see one."

Odd, that. "Baron Eismann has said they're distant. Not troubling the upslope villages. We killed so many on the mission, their numbers have dropped."

Qadeem nodded. "You killed many — let us say that lamia are discipled wolves. You killed many disciples, true."

My mind seized that and blurted out a thousand questions. I hardly knew where to begin.

"There are blessed and elect. Few, but they shepherd their brothers. And they watch for danger in their kingdom, as we do. Aleks was the one who spoke to them for us, and it's a matter that must be broached when…" Qadeem drew a deep breath with a glance at Anders. "Perhaps a new shifter can be of aid, when he's able. So long as the lamia harm no one, turn a blind eye."

"But they're monsters, shaped by the kir they drink," I said, though my memory was quick to remind me of their cleverness, their ambushes, and all Ulf had said. They knew about bows. Weren't afraid of fire.

"Kir makes monsters?" My saint only raised a hand to his black hair, where Blessing ridges would run if he had any. His brows rose. My mind tripped on that and dropped all its thoughts.

We reached the fence. I glanced back at Rafe, who lay on his blanket wiggling now and then. Anders sketched a bow to my saint, who asked, "You've a question?"

"If I may, m'lord. Saint Woden sent me to the Rangers to ride with the few shape-shifters in Wodenberg. He cannot offer me any guidance in that — but you, m'lord, you slew that saint who murdered Saint Aleks. Kate's said there's a way to take charms, in death, and so I thought you might have... harvested is the word?" Anders trailed off, fidgeting with Sprite's reins in his hand. The mare had noticed a patch of clover and tugged as she reached for a mouthful.

"I harvested Saint Rakkar," Qadeem said with a slow nod. "He was, himself, rather over-loaded in that moment. Not only with Aleks, but with Haladi whom Aleks had just harvested. In such situations, there is always a loss. Even a saint's mind can only catch a finite volume at once. In the time I've had to absorb all of that harvesting, I believe I caught a great deal of Aleks. Not all, sadly, but some of it is shape-shifting. I've meant to try it, as I've never been a shifter, but there is much to do now that Aleks is gone. Woden claimed his archers and the strength-Blessed, but that left all the crafters..." Qadeem waved it off with a hand. "You, however, yes, I will show you what I can. Kate, you have enough to keep you until we next meet."

I supposed it was. "And I will report nightly." Blessed and elect lamia still circled my mind, though. Was there a Saint Lamia?

After a moment's wait, Qadeem smiled and told me, "A little privacy if we may, Kate. Shape-shifters and clothing do not mix well — Aleks may have been unconcerned by such things, but I was raised differently."

My cheeks warmed a bit at that thought, but the image stuck; Anders...

"M'lord," I murmured, bobbed a curtsy, and went to collect my baby and my spinning.

CHAPTER 3

I wore Rafe in a sling as I rode, which kept him at hand for nursing. Alice rode beside me, clutching the pommel of Pal's saddle much as I had on my first day riding. Will led us with the baronial banner of Rossweide braced against his shoulder, its long swath of dark green rippling in the breeze. The white horse, rampant on the field, was crowned with an arc of seven stars, for the Flock moons. Reinhardt and Anders followed us, managing the strings of horses expected in Vorspitz and the wagonload of luggage.

I'd brought my teacher's kir-bound book, and while I didn't expect to be able to open it, I had thought there'd be moments I could read pages from memory. Mastering diaper-changing in the saddle took some practice, though, even with kir-vines to assist me. By noon, I was able to hold Rafe in vines alone of sheer necessity while I reached for a clean diaper in the saddlebag on my right. Alice struggled to catch the ones that slipped my grasp, or fetch them from the weeds. She was soon an expert at mounting and dismounting on her own.

Once Rafe was clean, he wriggled and complained though nothing was wrong. As I'd guessed, the gentle rocking of Buttercup's pace didn't soothe him. He needed close cuddling to sleep at all, once he'd worn himself out. Then nursing. Whereupon he wet his diaper again.

When we stopped at noon to eat and rest, I dozed off within moments from being so worn out by it all. For all my healing skills, my strength still hadn't recovered from childbirth.

Humbled, I climbed into the wagon bed and rode cushioned by horse blankets. Rafe still cried, but changing him was easier.

The checkpoints we passed through were more an annoyance than a reassurance. The villages along the road were silent and empty, and had been since the last evacuations at Spring Equinox. Many had been burned down in the summer's fighting between Seagrace and the half of Arcea's army that pursued him nearly to Vorspitz. Around us, the oat-fields grew only grass and wildflowers. Cisterns hadn't been mucked out and were full of reeds and slime.

Camps of local armsmen, perhaps a hand of knights and archers, kept watch for trouble — Arceal scouts or looters, officially, but in truth it was packs of feral dogs and a scattering of fey-touched who'd been abandoned by their families that the armsmen dealt with. They were bored and wanted to trade news at length once m'lord Reinhardt showed his orders to their officer. An elect was of particular interest.

I didn't wish to be of particular interest; I wished a clean, sleeping baby. Even an elect had little power over that, it seemed.

Rafe dozed at last and I tried to as well, but Alice wanted to know what Vorspitz was like. She rode alongside the wagon, hanging on my words as I told her what little I'd seen during the mission. That led into more stories of our trip up into the mountain pass. Since Margrave Leix Gwatcyn had brought a full Caer division, two thousand strong, of knights and archers to Wodenberg's relief, the true story of Kiefan's mission had crept out in scraps here and there.

I hadn't spoken much of it. Ilya's death still stung me, as did what had become of Ther Boristan, and Bjorn, and Ulf, who had been killed unseen. It all ached, still, and dwelling on my failures darkened my mood further. Once Alice stopped trying to pry stories out of me, I lost the rest of the afternoon to remembering Kiefan and Anders' duel at the jousting tournament, and to ruminating on how it would play out if Kiefan knew that Anders loved me. No good could come of it. That was clear enough.

<hr />

The inn's main room was dusty, the air a bit stale. A pair of doves fled when Alice and I opened the front door; they flew up the stair toward whatever open window they'd come in by.

"Still, well enough," Alice said. That was true; this was the first unburnt, un-ransacked village we'd seen all day. She carried the kitchenware pack to the hearth and set it down with a clank.

I followed with Rafe and the diaper bags. We'd need to get some quick scrubbing in, or we'd have little to wrap Rafe in tomorrow. Leaving him, in his cradle-basket by the cold hearth, I emptied the dirty-diaper bag into one of the buckets we'd brought. Thanks to a judicious cleansing charm, it didn't smell too badly. Will brought us water in the second bucket. Alice and I knelt on either side — I with a pained wince, as I was too tired to charm the aches away — with a handful of soap apiece, just as we had on many a laundry day on Engl Street.

"So alike, so different," Alice said in Englic as it was an old saying. "You an elect now, and riding to see the prince married to some… disciple of Woden. Fair enough, I suppose."

I scrubbed and said nothing. Married, yes. Never to be truly mine. Squeezing suds from one diaper, I ducked it in the rinsing bucket. The cold well water numbed my fingertips.

Alice shot me a sly look. "All those days in the Winter Wood, you must've seen much of the prince. The king."

I'd seen him drive himself to passing out, I'd seen him stand over me with sword bared, snarling back at the lamia. My memory flicked past that moment he'd first kissed me, his heavy-lidded eyes a nose-width from me. I wrung the wet diaper tighter, wishing it was the ache in my heart dripping out.

"Does His Majesty have any of what Anders' got?"

Alice smirked when my face flushed hot. "What —?"

"Bathed every Saint-day, didn't he? Even you must've been tempted to steal a peek. Your play-act at being the good girl, that's well over, so don't claim you weren't." She shooed it away. "There was a rumor that the prince came down to Arbor Street once, but nothing ever came of it. Ludmilla keeps a betting pot for brothers, you see, on who's the more blessed. And who's the more skilled with it." Alice laughed as she rinsed a diaper. "It needs a chance at sampling both, though, and the prince never gave us that."

I stared at her across the bucket, my brain flailing for the calmness to merely make out Kiefan to be Anders if she pressed for details. But the thought of Anders in Kiefan's place, sprawled naked on the feather bed, dim-lit by the low fire, that Solstice night...

"I got my bruns back when I moved out, of course, used it to pay —" Alice caught herself for a heartbeat, then laughed again. She put up a hand. "Yes, I put a bet in that pot after a dalliance with Anders. That was damn pleasant, but it was only business. And if you mean to talk of blessings —"

"No," got out of my mouth. "Stop there." I didn't want to know, I didn't want my mind comparing them any further, mixing them together, dwelling on their kindness or kisses. Or blessings.

Alice frowned, raised her shoulders. "I made no secret of it. And it's nothing you haven't — well, true, you've little to compare him to."

"I don't need you bragging —"

Her voice rose. "Bragging? You've always asked me about the work, Kate, don't play at prudish with me!"

Will looked up from laying firewood in the hearth, but he spoke no Englic. Thank the Mother.

As well he didn't know what I shouted back. "It's prudish to take offense at him with another woman?"

She leaned across the bucket. "I've not touched him since I gave up the work, and I'll swear it to Mother Love."

"No need — I don't wish speak of it is all!"

"I sussed that on my own. M'lady." Alice glared. She flung another diaper into the rinsing bucket. "If you take offense at every woman he's fucked, you'll hardly leave the house!"

"He hasn't —" I barely caught myself. Not Kiefan. Anders. Yet it still stung me. Why? I fumbled for a retort. "Name me one! And not a whore."

"Brynhilde Kaufmann." Alice added a flippant sneer and resumed scrubbing.

Theo's wife? I saw her again by the Solstice bonfire, glittering richly and pregnant. Four or five months along, so that must've begun before I'd even met Anders. He wouldn't do such a thing to his friend, either. I pushed it away with a shake of my head.

"Give me truths, not rumors," I said, meaning it to be sharper than it came out.

Alice snorted. "It's a rumor mill, not a truth mill." She washed in silence.

I scrubbed too. Was the sting in my heart for Anders?

Anders walked in, Mother help me, with an armload of half-rotted, year-old firewood from the inn's woodshed. We both tracked him. When he dumped the wood by the hearth, he shot us one of his teasing half-smiles as he went to fetch more.

Why did that sting?

Alice's hand found mine, in the sudsy water. "I'm sorry," she murmured, still in Englic. "I spoke in anger. It's only that I'm jealous, sometimes."

I met her eyes and knew she meant it. Regretted my snipes. "I spoke in anger too. Rafe worked me hard today. And my ass hurts."

"He's quite the little lord," Alice said, arching her chin. "Thinks he has every lady 'round his pinkie finger?" She broke her arch tone for a moment with a sly grin. "Perhaps someday — but not now, sir!"

Rafe whimpered and we went running all the same.

The next day, late in the afternoon, we rode into Vorspitz and it was just as I remembered. Arcea hadn't reached this far during the siege. We passed the small Orderhaus first, perhaps a quarter mile from the middle of town. The Felsherz River lay flat, nearly a lake, and much of the town ran along its northern bank. A large tavern, the Riverman, sprawled between the road and the water, welcoming all comers into its bustle and noise. Two handsome houses stood across the street, distanced from each other by a wheel-rutted road with generous, grassy shoulders. Sod-roofed long-houses in the old style stood scattered along the river shore, some with docks and small fishing boats. A landing for the rope ferry lay beside the tavern.

Above the town, the river tumbled down some modest rapids, and Baron Eismann's stockaded keep stood atop the hill. The road ran past his gate and continued upward, past smaller cottages, into the mountains. His stone watchtower loomed above the trees, square and strong.

As we rode past the tavern, men came out to see us. Theo found his way to the front in time to call to Anders, who waved in return. Reinhardt led us up to Baron Eismann's gate, Will riding beside him with the Rossweide banner rippling.

Kiefan met us at the gate with Baron Eismann to one side and the duke of Alemannia on the other. Duke Adalrich Haken was the son of King Wilhelm's younger sister, Kiefan's only cousin, and was said to be a quiet and gracious lord.

He'd been anything but, last I saw him. That had been while all hands pinned him to the surgery table and I sawed his crushed foot off just above the ankle. He'd lay in agony on the battlefield most of the afternoon with his meridian ruined — the foot was lost already, and the need was to stop his bleeding, cauterize the wound clean. Even Elect Parselev had been too exhausted to risk a charm. I'd done what a physician must.

M'lord Haken leaned on a carved cane inlaid with bright bits of quartz. He wore two boots, but hobbled when he came to greet us alongside Kiefan — who'd been sparring, to guess by his armor and the sheen of sweat. He kept a proper, kingly face, though, and offered us a formal greeting.

Baron Eismann also bowed and welcomed me, followed by his wife and family. The baron had seemed grand when we dined in his hall, and now he was only a man. His wife had been kind to me, and his eldest daughter — I'd seen Anders kiss her. She kept her eyes averted now, didn't dare look at me it seemed.

"Caercoed's not yet arrived," Kiefan told us, "but there's a squad of Rangers seeking them out in Suevia. Surely you're tired from the road. Take your ease tonight and we'll welcome you properly with a feast tomorrow."

I thanked him, and then had to see to quieting Rafe, who squalled in the sling at this interruption of his nap. M'lord Reinhardt invited Kiefan to see the horses, and I saw most of the men drift off. Save one.

"Elect Bockmann." The duke offered me a bow and reached out his hand. I let him take mine, and he touched a kiss to my knuckles. "I believe I owe you an apology, m'lady."

A duke bowing to a peasant-born girl and apologizing. Perhaps this would become ordinary, someday. "You spoke in agony, sir, and I have already forgiven the words," I told him. "I hope that my handiwork has not pained you any further."

"Certainly not. I thank the Mother and Father each day that I live to kiss my wife and watch my daughters grow. Please, be welcome in my barony of Eispitzen."

As the sun was quickly setting, Eismann called for a horse and saw us to our quarters. Ours was the fine house across from the tavern, the one with the longer barn and a broader apron of fenced pastures. It belonged to one Herr Eburhart Schäfer, who met us at the door in a deep obeisance. His son knelt beside him. Schäfer owned the largest flocks and herds in Vorspitz, leasing hundreds of acres of pasture from the baron to graze them. He was a broad-boned man, softened by middle age, with a nose that had seen some breaking and cheeks pocked by scars. Missing a couple teeth when he smiled.

He welcomed us to his house. "It's nothing fine, m'lady Elect, m'lord Baron, not what you're accustomed to I'm sure," he said, bowing, "but it's yours. I've sent my wife and the girls to her mother's so there's room for all. I'm at your service, me and my boy Trauger, my housemaid Hilda, for whatever you need. I've worked with horses some and laid in a good store of hay and oats if you'd like to see."

The house's central space was partitioned into a receiving room in the front and a master bedroom at the back. In the receiving room a fire crackled on the hearth and a blonde-wood dining table with cushioned chairs stood before that. Horned rams' skulls and antlers from deer and elk hung above the mantle. All of it good and well crafted, but small and dark to my eye. I'd been quick to grow accustomed to the Bockmann's city manor and all its glassed windows, it would seem. A door to the right led into the kitchen, a small cottage with a sunken firepit in the center, and a smoke trapdoor in the thatch above, where Hilda tended the pots and pans.

Alice looked to me. "Ah, we're home again."

It was just like the cottage I'd grown up in, lacking only my parents' bed and the loft overhead for me and my brothers.

Out the left-hand door from the receiving room was the barn. Upstairs were two small bedrooms, one claimed by Schäfer and his son.

"This can be our nursery," I told Alice when we looked into the other. "Bring up your bags too."

She'd unlatched the small, shuttered window to find it looked out onto the pastures behind the house. Frowning, she turned back to me. "Not Anders?"

I shrugged, hoping it looked casual. "He still wakes so often at night. Anders needs his sleep if he's to have Sprite polished. Let the menfolk have the master bed downstairs."

I took a wailing Rafe from Alice and laid him on my shoulder as I untied the drawstring neck of my shift. "Go, catch some of that apple ale before it's gone," I said, waving toward the keg on the far side of Eismann's kitchen. A strength-Blessed servant gently tipped the massive keg to fill a few last steins. "It's delicious."

She didn't need telling twice. I sidled the shoulder of my pale green dress off and Rafe's screams trailed away when his cheek brushed against my breast. That was what he wanted, and I'd been far too slow in coming. Not that the banquet in Eismann's great hall was so entrancing; Anders and Reinhardt had been drawn off by Theo to engage with a handful of other trade-invested men. Some sort of verbal duel, it seemed, full of numbers and dozens of specifics.

I turned from watching Alice guzzle a stein of ale, cheered on by two of the stable-grooms, and strolled from the busy kitchen. Sensibly, it stood a few yards from the nearest wing of the keep, and once I stepped off the well-worn flagstone path outside its door, all was peaceful and quiet. Wisps of cloud high above hid some of the stars, but the Flock moons shone bright. The day had been warm, and it wasn't so chilly yet as to see my breath.

Rafe sucked firmly, my hungry little boy. He'd suffered a bit of fever this morning, likely from the traveling, but with a few little charms he was well again. Nursing would bind my day up badly as my duties grew. Perhaps Rafe would take some pap to stretch out his feedings. His screams when I was late would wear on anyone and I didn't envy Alice.

My eye caught movement and I turned back toward the kitchen. Kiefan stepped off the flagstone path and crossed the grass, warm light from the doorway catching on his gold band. I smiled. "You escaped."

"It was not easy." He put a hand on my arm and looked to be sure none watched us. We drew further around the kitchen-cottage, into the gap between it and the stockade wall. Deeper in the shadows. I put my hand out, brushed across the mud-plaster wall, and set my back to it.

Kiefan's hand on my arm slipped up to my cheek, tipped my head and his kiss, sudden and deep, squeezed a whimper from my throat. His tongue, his whiff of lavender soap, tore open a yearning I'd half forgotten. Gently pressed against the wall, I wished I could put both arms around him. I had to settle for clenching a handful of his cote, at the shoulder.

Rafe wiggled between us, and Kiefan looked down. He slipped a finger across Rafe's open hand, and my baby gripped in return.

"I meant no disrespect to your grandfather," Kiefan said, his voice low. "Rafe is as much his blood as my father's. I only wanted to see you, and my son, and know you're both well." He tugged against Rafe's grip as he said it. My baby's hand opened and his arm dropped to his side as he relaxed into his work. "I've missed you," Kiefan murmured.

There'd been some letters, far too limiting for what needed to be said. I'd doubted myself, as Anders and I settled into our comfortable routine. I'd worried what I'd say to Kiefan in this moment. Feared, even, that he'd sense it. Smell Anders' kindness on me and how it made my heart quiver.

And all this was a heartbeat too long for me to answer; Kiefan put his forehead to mine. "What do you fear?" he whispered.

My breath caught in my throat, at that. "I'll miss you more once you're wed," I managed to answer. It was part of the truth.

He wore his lamia-tooth brooch on the shoulder of his black silk cote, perhaps to remind everyone why the monsters hadn't sung in the forest all year. It was the sparkling cote from Solstice, I realized with a blink. I'd helped him peel it off over his head.

Slim chance I ever would again, no matter how much love lay between us. He was here to find a pair of Caer brides, after all; it was his duty. They'd know they had to share him, and weren't likely to share him any further. Even if he were so lucky as to find twins that he got on well with…

"Stay, tonight."

He touched a kiss to my neck, just by my ear, and a shiver shot along my spine. The memory of his hands on my skin, his mouth — but my heart stretched, strained in my chest. It was well snared by Kiefan and dragged toward him, but felt the pull of another hook.

Anders. His little touches. How he kissed my cheek in the morning. How he'd always take Rafe when asked and walk him to sleep. Anders loved me, he surely wanted more, and to lead him on — and lie to Kiefan — was more than I could bear. I had too many lies already: my lies to Frida, to Alice.

Rafe, tangled in the middle of it all, had his own hooks in my heart. "I have a new lord," I whispered in kind, "and I must attend him four times nightly. I have a saint and duties to him. As do you. Once the Caer ladies are here…" I had to trail off on that thought. Kiefan deserved love.

"They are not here yet. It's been half the year since we had a night together, or even a book to share, and —"

"I found something." It popped out of me, a ray of sunlight through a thundercloud. "A journal that my teacher wrote himself. It begins when your father marched north from Kernweise into Englia with his army." I had stolen enough time to read the first pages of the kir-bound book yesterday.

Kiefan drew back to arm's length, his hand on the wall by my shoulder. "Father told me of those battles, to explain the strategies and the mis-steps." He frowned as he remembered. "It was a more difficult campaign than expected. Elect Parselev wrote of — the healing? Wouldn't he have simply remembered it?"

"I've read a few pages thus far, but he's not mentioned any wounds. Mainly, he describes how the army was harried the moment they crossed into Englia."

That brought a frown to Kiefan's face. "Harried? Through the forest?"

"He calls it the Tiefwald?" That was the name Parselev used in the book. I knew it as the Stormbreak, from my parents.

"Father never mentioned harrying."

"They seem sure the Englic army will meet them, but it hasn't thus far," I said. "I've looked through the pages — I could bring the book and we'll read it piecemeal?"

I forgot, for a moment, where we were. Kiefan's grey eyes met mine, and he kissed me again. "Bring the book," he said, close by my mouth. "To dinner, some evening, with the baby?"

He wouldn't forget me. It was a cold knife, that moment's despair. I didn't want to be let go, truly. This would kill me; perhaps I should take Rafe, ride up to the fount, and make a hermit of myself among the lamia.

But then I'd have nobody to read the journal with.

"I'll bring the book. When I can. And you have your duty to find your brides."

Kiefan nodded, with a sigh. I lingered until Rafe finished nursing, both of us cuddled snug and warm in Kiefan's arms. Safe.

CHAPTER 4

The first Saint-day of the Leaf Moon passed. Rain fell on leaves mottled by gold and orange. I woke before dawn and joined the local abbess and her staff for the morning disciple's dance. They were surprised to have me, made me welcome, but kept their distance. When I returned to Schäfer's house for breakfast, Anders and Will were out, in the rain, on the horses.

There was little to report to Saint Qadeem; it was good to see m'lady Leix and Elect Tannait again and to meet the few officers of m'lady's Tadhlon Guard who had come for the parley. Her company had leave to withdraw a distance from Wodenberg's army, to set up a camp on the south bank of the Felsherz and enjoy a few weeks of well-deserved rest. Duke

Seagrace had charge of the main army, now settled into something of a siege of the Arceal forces in Ansehen.

Kiefan faced a backlog of judicial cases dating from before the spring, matters that Duke Adalrich could not settle, which largely meant disagreements with the Order or between noble houses. There was the matter of a water wheel mill broken during a bad spring's flooding some years ago and never repaired, and a land inheritance twisted by generations of gifting, selling, and pledging. Though Eismann and the duke were perfectly polite, neither would budge in these cases and it was for the king to settle them.

A number of men had come to petition the king for a release from service to the army. It fell to me to verify the ailments they presented as reason — badly clubbed feet, palsies, and the like — or heal them, if I could. That was not what they had expected, to be sure. Of them, only the simpleton brought by his father to be excused from duty walked out with it.

I put that one's pattern aside for further study.

Perhaps it was nothing exciting, but it broke the routine of nursing and diapers. The next day, I walked up under a surprisingly warm sun and nodded to the gate watchmen as I passed through. The square, field-stone keep that enclosed Baron Eismann's great hall rose to a crenelated top, windowless until the second floor. On either side, wings of split timber and mud plaster housed the family and the guests. Eismann's watchtower made half of the gate-house, and the barracks and stables were against the stockade wall.

Today, five men stood in the gate-yard, wrists bound and ankles hobbled, ringed by armsmen. Kiefan stood before the keep's doors with the duke and the baron, flanked by King's Guard. Heads turned as I slowed, took in the prisoners' dirt and bruises, the wagon to one side with its gate down to display the ironwares inside, and a few silver cups and bowls placed prominently.

"Elect Kate, please join me in hearing the accusations against these disciples," Kiefan said. "Perhaps you could remind them of the saints' law regarding such things."

I crossed the yard to stand beside Kiefan, clasping my hands and hoping that how I clenched my fingers wasn't too obvious. "Saint Qadeem has ordered that the accused must be presented to his lord along with the evidence of his crime before punishment is judged upon him," I said. That was common enough knowledge; the law was centuries old. "Is there some question of that?"

"These men, five disciples of Saint Aleksandr, are accused of looting. They were captured near Brennanbaum by the lieutenant," Kiefan nodded to the officer, who was one of those I'd met on the ride to Vorspitz, "who found prosperous houses broken into and pillaged. The accused were captured with their stolen goods." That was the wagon, sure enough.

"They asked to be judged by Saint Qadeem's elect." Kiefan looked to me as he said this. "That one says they're disciple of Qadeem now."

It was likely true. My saint had taken on Aleksandr's craft-Blessed as his own. But I lowered my voice. "It's a matter for the king as well as the elect. The saints are of one accord on their laws. You hardly need me to make a judgment in this." There seemed to be little question of it, either.

"M'lady, I spoke only for the chance to ask mercy." One of the younger men hobbled forward and dropped to his knees before me, head low. "We're poor shepherds, nothing more. All our flocks were lost to hoof and mouth rot, this summer, and we've gone hungry since. My wife wastes away, my children starve."

A second, even younger, threw himself down, saying, "My mother's long widowed, m'lady, and my little brothers —" The rest piled on after him, the older men kneeling silently with sad eyes.

My heart ached at the thought of hungry children, and I touched my saint's bond to ask what to do.

"You." Kiefan pointed to the one who'd started it. "Do not lie to the saints, on peril of your life."

His jaw dropped. "M'lord, I wouldn't —"

"You are a liar." Kiefan said it as a simple fact. Picking up the youngest, the widow's son, by the scruff, he put him on his feet and pushed him to one side. "You tell the truth. You —"

The third man, under Kiefan's cool, grey stare, trembled and babbled.

He passed the third man over. "And you?"

The two older men, who'd held their peace, shifted on their knees. "We did it, m'lord. Poor and hungry, is all. Was only for getting greedy that we were caught."

Kiefan nodded. "They speak the truth."

/ mercy / if honest /

"M'lady, please! I speak true!" The first man shuffled closer to me, anguished. "Mercy! If my wife's widowed, how —"

Steel rasped and the man's head came away in Kiefan's hand. He kicked the body backward, gushing out blood, and threw the head into the spreading pool. The babbling man fainted, the widow's son screamed, and the older men went white as snow.

"Do not lie to the saints," Kiefan said, and it carried in the deathly silence.

I stared, stomach knotting. Lying to the saints was a dire crime, but — "He has a wife! Children!"

Kiefan only wiped his blade on the accused's cote and sheathed it.

"No, m'lady," one of the older men said. "He doesn't. He had a charmed tongue, though. Most thought."

My stare shifted to Kiefan. There were no charms for mind-reading, so far as I knew.

"The saints' law sets the punishment for looting at flogging and branding with the thieves' mark," he said.

"Saint Qadeem wishes mercy for the honest," I was quick to tell him. "Were your flocks lost this summer?"

The men nodded.

"If your Orderhaus has been poorly provisioned, that's a matter the saints wish to know of," Kiefan said. "Last year's harvest was to support us all."

"Our abbot fears it may not be enough, m'lord, and rations us," the eldest of them said. He risked a glance up when Kiefan eyed him.

Gauging his honesty, however he did it. "The north's harvest is coming south," he said, letting his harsh edge fade. "I saw the numbers before leaving Wodenberg. Trust our saints, protect them and they will protect you. Baron Eismann, these men are to suffer a flogging for breaking the saints' law. Their wounds are to be cleansed and tended, but not healed. They will remain here, in the Order's care, until they are well. Chamberlain! Draft a message for their abbot that he's not to starve his flock. The saints will not have it."

The man who'd fainted struggled to sit up and the widow's son sidled in to prop him up. All of them eyed the growing puddle of blood with dread. I gestured for the guardsmen to help the prisoners up and get them away from that.

———————————✕———————————

I dressed Rafe in the bunting that Kiefan had given me on my son's Lambing-day. The golden, quilted lambswool was plush and warm, roomy enough for an infant to grow into over the winter… and fine enough for a prince. Embroidered white lambs cavorted over dark green grass, along the hem. The seven Flock moons, with their names, were beaded in fresh-

Part IV: Salt in the Wound

water pearls across the torso. I tied the quilted cap on, too, and laid Rafe in his basket next to Parselev's secret journal for the walk up to the baron's hall.

I didn't miss that the bunting's seams showed some wear. I suspected I ought to give it back as a Lambing-day gift, when Kiefan became a father again.

Kiefan met me at the door. "The dress suits you well, Elect." He took my hand and kissed it, lingering just a heartbeat.

"M'lady Frida insisted, at Equinox," I said. She'd given me two dresses, a green one with embroidered roses and this buttercup-yellow one with daisies. "There's more important matters…" I turned toward where the looter had died; the gate-yard dirt was still dark with blood.

"He meant to play on your kind heart," Kiefan said, stepping back through the great hall's door. I followed. "That was bad enough. That he lied when questioned…?" He shook his head. "The journal. That, I want to talk about. And might I… hold the baby?" His voice dropped to a whisper.

Rafe had fallen asleep. "When he wakes," I said, "and after I change him."

"I've never changed a diaper."

I caught the laugh before it escaped and covered my mouth.

"Gisella's boys were born in Rukharbor," Kiefan said. "I didn't meet them until years later."

We walked from the hall by a side door. Baron Eismann had given us the use of his family's smaller dining room, near the kitchen, for a private meal at a small table. Tapestries hung on the split-log walls, depicting summer hunts and family banquets. One servant attended us, carving the herbed roast mutton and dishing up creamed potatoes. He fetched an extra candelabra to improve the light for reading. I glanced under the table to be sure a chamber pot was there, as I'd told the baron there must be. Rafe slept on as I set his basket by my chair and sat down.

Kiefan opened Parselev's journal to the first written page, as the servant placed the brass candelabra on the table, and began to read. While I cut my meat and ate, I crept through the words at the top of a new page, in my memory.

Our servant brought us bowls of pickled cabbage-and-radish slaw and topped our ale steins. "Shall I stay, Majesty? M'lady?"

Kiefan glanced up, turning the first page already. "Leave the pitcher. Give us some time — we'll call if we need anything."

Quiet fell after he shut the door. I ate slowly, as I read from my memory.

"How many pages have you finished?" Kiefan asked.

"Twelve."

"This part about my uncle, here." He tapped the page and put the book down to see to his food. "My father rarely spoke of him. Yet those who knew him say he was a fine knight and commander — Aleks served on his Prince's Guard, after she won the jousting tournament."

I suppose it should've been no surprise. "Captain Aleks won the tournament?"

"And rode in the Englic campaign. Shaved her first crest for it."

"Yet they never speak of him?"

Kiefan glanced across the table at me. "No, he died in it. Saint Ethmund killed him and Woden avenged him."

Prince Wolfgang had been Woden's bound elect. After him, Parselev was the only remaining elect in Wodenberg for twenty years. In the glimpse I had of the prince, through my teacher's memories, he'd looked something like Anders — that same easy charisma, the twinkle in his eye. I would've liked a glimpse of Saint Ethmund as well, after all my parents had said of him, but I hadn't found one.

"I hope Parselev wrote about that," I said.

Kiefan nodded, absorbed in the book again. We talked of the harrying, then, through the swath of forest that covered southern Englia. Kiefan had ridden through it on his journey to Rukharbor. Even after Saint Aleksandr had cut a good, clear road through it, the Stormbreak was still dark and unsettling.

"It was as much a Winter Wood as what we suffered," Kiefan said. "Half of me waited to hear lamia singing at night."

Beyond the forest were marshes, Parselev described, where the Englic baron in King Wilhelm's pay had led them into the muck — and turned traitor. The Englic army pounced on them, and it had nearly been a slaughter.

"No place for knights or horses," Kiefan said, which was borne out in what my teacher had written. "Father said..." He trailed off as he read the mention of a battle-field meeting that ended in shouting between the king, the prince, and Woden.

The part that had given me similar pause was my teacher's mention of his student, Physician Krepkin, whose brother died in the Englic traitor's trap. Parselev lamented how deep Krepkin's hate of Engls ran.

Kiefan's brow furrowed, and he kept reading. "You've caught up to me," I told him. "Give me time to follow along."

Kiefan took a pull of his ale and began reading aloud from the next page ahead of me. Parselev had been attending to broken limbs on the day after the first battle. In the command pavilion, one of Saint Ethmund's elect had come to discuss whether any terms could be reached — there had been some question of whether the saint might agree to join in our Trinity's pact and share his fount.

The command pavilion burst into a fireball. Parselev reached the spot in time to hear Woden cursing the Englic elect and see the death-blow. Orders were roared to carry the man's head back to his escort and drive them off, flag of truce be damned. Wolfgang, his loyal elect, obeyed.

It was King Wilhelm, singed and shaken, who told Parselev how Woden had lost his temper over Saint Ethmund's demands.

Kiefan put the journal down and looked at me, across the table. "My parents were young when all of this happened," I said. "My mother told me she was terrified that my father would be conscripted and have to face the Blessed knights after they slaughtered one of our elect under a flag of truce. She never said any more than that."

He set his teeth on his lip for a moment, then drank some more ale. "It's no surprise it happened, though," he said, voice low. "I met with the Voice of the Empress twice, after driving them across the Felsherz. Had Woden been there, my pavilion likely would've burned as well." His brow furrowed and he set the stein down. "I earned those headaches fairly enough and still had to reason with him after."

"He gets so angry?"

"I didn't dare say half of what he wished me to, to deSvello. Some words will only make the enemy dig in his heels and fight harder. My mother taught me that." Kiefan picked at his dinner a bit more. "I negotiated by my own gauging of what might persuade, and then argued it out to Woden through the bond. Then had to take the edge off with whatever drink was at hand." He looked up, across the table. "Would that it had been you there."

A knock at the door; our servant returned with dishes of warm, candied apples and a full ale pitcher, and found we'd hardly touched our steins. Rafe stirred in his basket, gurgling. When I looked down, he waved his hands at the dangling ribbon-ends — I had made a rose of the red ribbon that bundled Kiefan's gift and tied it to the basket's handle. I reached down

Part IV: Salt in the Wound

and picked him up; likely he'd be wanting to nurse soon. For now, though, he was bright-eyed and his view of the dining table from my lap held him mesmerized.

The servant spared my baby a kind smile as he cleared away my empty trencher. He poured small cups of cherry wine to go with the sweet apples and left us again.

One thing Kiefan had said was still caught in my ear. "Your own gauging?"

He was smiling at Rafe's wondering stare and sat up straighter at my question. "Since my binding, that's been shifting. My anticipation Blessing always warned me of danger, always guided my hand in battle, but now it's noting deeper things. People wear the truth on their faces. I only never saw it before, it seems."

I'd just taken a mouthful of the candied apples and drew my spoon out slowly. The soft, sweet fruit went down quickly so I could ask, "As with the liar?"

He picked up the journal again. "As with the liar."

My spoon slowed for a moment: Kiefan might see my affection for Anders. Mother Love help me.

I set that aside as best I could and ate the little bowl of apples, then scooped out some of the syrupy juice on my finger for Rafe to taste. He wriggled and squeaked happily, so I gave him some more. Kiefan began reading aloud again, a page that began with Prince Wolfgang asking Parselev to mend the stringence that Woden had laid on him for taking two women to bed when he had a wife at home —

Kiefan meant to smile across the table, but I was frowning when he looked up. "Strin-gence?"

He blinked. "Yes, that's an odd word — Arceal does that sometimes. Ignores its own rules. It ought to be — here, come see." He dipped his finger in sauce and began to sketch out the words on the tablecloth. I got up and circled round to see, though it wasn't what I'd meant. True that it was an odd word, though.

Kiefan wrote out a few examples of rule-obedient constructions and a few that weren't. Then he put an arm around my waist and pulled me closer, baby and all. I leaned over with a smile. Graced him with a brief kiss, but then I had to turn more serious. "I meant: is that what Woden did to you? At the coronation?"

A nod. "I spoke too hastily, and he chastised me with it. You haven't angered your saint yet?" He tried to chuckle at that, but at my blank look it died in his mouth.

"No." I leaned back on my feet. Kiefan's smile vanished. I asked, "Has he done it since?" I stood there looking into his grey eyes, dread spreading from my gut. "Lambing-day?"

He stood, still holding me with his eyes, and cupped my cheek with one hand. "Pain will not change my mind. He demanded I seal this alliance — which I will. But he cannot change my heart."

The words ached. I kissed him, and he pressed deeper into my mouth. His tongue on mine, mercy, and… Rafe farted, loud as a goat braying. We both startled, then broke into giggles. Rafe whimpered as he did when he was about to cry, and that was the end of the kiss. I hushed him, rocked him.

"He'll be needing a clean diaper," I said. I returned to my chair to collect the clean one from under his blanket, as well as the chamber pot. "Have you ever seen that done?"

"Tell me how, and I'll do it."

And he did. The king changed a diaper, and did a fair job. Once Rafe was pinned up again, Kiefan lifted him — careful to hold his head properly — and sat our son in the crook of his arm. I put away the dirty linen. Rafe muttered and whimpered, still.

"What else must I do?" Kiefan asked.

"He's hungry." The buttercup dress laced up the front, from the waist, so I undid that as I returned. My shift underneath had a drawstring neck. An extra hand helped me ease that out far enough to reveal a breast. I shooed Kiefan away with a smile and reached for Rafe.

He let me settle my baby into nursing, but that helpful hand found rest on my hip. Kiefan sat in his chair and tugged me closer. I sat on his knee and sure enough, his arm slid around my waist. His chin rested on my shoulder, his chest warm against my back. I lay my cheek against his head with a sigh.

I missed his arms. That morning, waking spooned against him…

"Stay tonight," Kiefan whispered. "One night, as a family."

My free hand covered his at my waist. I wanted to say yes. The aches and stretch marks of childbirth had faded; I was tired from waking at night to nurse, but kir kept me strong. "But it would be no secret," I whispered back. "The baron's servants would know. Alice. And… Qadeem felt my labor through the bond. Parselev's death. Can ecstasy leach through as well?"

"Woden doesn't deny me my hand."

"You would lie?" It came out in a fierce whisper, my fresh memory of the beheaded looter flicking past. I hadn't thought I needed to carefully put it away.

Kiefan only gave me a sober, silent look. "I swore my duty and my kir to Woden's aid. My strength, my seed, and my life to the kingdom. Not my heart."

I looked him in the eye. "You deserve better than the duty-marriage your mother and father had. Not lies and shame. Give these brides a chance to win you over, at least. A chance for a good marriage." A moment's sadness in his eyes, and he looked away again. "Give them a chance," was all I could say, stroking his cheek. "I'll always love you. You must marry, but it need not be a misery."

"Must I?" He murmured that, a passing thought. Then he kissed my cheek. I hugged him tight. "I will give them a chance," he said. "Because you asked."

Rafe had dozed off in all our talking. I drew him from my breast and shifted to lay him on the table; Kiefan cleared plenty of room for him. When I sat back to tie up my dress, he caught my hands and stilled them. His breath against my neck sent a prickle across my skin.

"Kate…" He cupped my breasts, hugging me against his chest. "Perhaps…?"

My pulse throbbed in my throat, under his lips. What other chance would we have? "Gently?" I whispered back. "Quietly?"

CHAPTER 5

"Rider approaching!" On the watchtower, an arm pointed eastward, upriver. "A Ranger!"

"At last, word of Caercoed." Kiefan nodded to Baron Eismann, who barked orders to his men. Soon enough, the rider galloped through the gate and kicked up dust in the gate-yard in swinging around to slow the horse. The Ranger scout swung off his saddle easily and dropped into obeisance before Kiefan.

Caercoed's royal envoy had been attacked in Suevia, the man reported, by a well-armed scouting party that refused to honor their flag of truce. The Crowns had been ambushed by archers on a narrow trail.

The Rangers had come upon the scene to see the final mopping-up of the Suevi men by the Crown's Blades. "As fierce a Guard as Majesty's own," the Ranger said, adding a nod to Captain Aleks. "Begging the captain's pardon for saying so. They should be crossing the high ford soon. Here by mid-afternoon, Majesty."

At last. It had been two days since the looters were caught.

Kiefan nodded. "See to your horse and rest. Well done."

All our men of note were summoned to meet the Crowns: Theo Kaufmann, the Brauers, Reinhardt. They likely had all been in the Riverman Tavern's common room, arguing about their Caer counterparts and how to negotiate terms with them. Reinhardt always left those meetings in time for Alice's dinner, and he saw to it that neither Anders nor Will stayed on for the drinking and dancing in the tavern.

I tapped my saint's bond, hunting for how to identify the Caercoed crown without words. I could only think of the guards-women cheering during my drunken interrogation, of their laughter and the rollicking dance.

/ they're arriving /

I felt amusement through the bond at my impression of them.

True to the Ranger's word, in the middle of the afternoon the call came from the watch-tower. "Riders approaching! Hundred-fifty, plus a squad of Rangers! Caercoed's banner and the Crown's Blades!"

As elect, I stood beside Kiefan in his jeweled crown, Duke Adalrich, m'lady Leix, and Elect Tannait between the king's standard and Leix's. Ranks of our armsmen on foot and knights on horses flanked the stockade gates, standing at attention. M'lord Reinhardt had sidled his way into a spot near Baron Eismann, just to my right, and brought Anders and Will. All the men wore their black uniform tabards, the insignias marking out the variety of divisions: cavalry, armsmen, provisioners. Anders, in his Ranger's brown, stuck out among the black. He and Will waited silently, fidgeting.

Hooves rumbled at a walk, and the Ranger lieutenant turned off the road into the gate. Behind him came the squad, all with right fists to their chests to salute us. The lieutenant took position off Kiefan's right and his men went deeper into the gate-yard, out of the way, as the Caer rode in.

Two standard-bearers led the royal escort. Caercoed's banner was a wide-armed Mother Tree on a blue field, two crowns side by side over the leafy peak. The Crown's Blades' was a circle described by seven swords. Behind the banners, I glimpsed two women in white, bright green sash belts tied high under their bosoms, as Leix had said the Crowns would be.

The armsmen and knights snapped to sharper attention, on either side.

Behind them rode a handful of civilians, then Caer archers in a column three wide, and knights behind those. The standard-bearers stopped a few yards from Kiefan and the horses pranced delicately to either side. Kiefan stepped forward, the breeze catching his gold-lined silk cloak, and I put as warm and unworried a smile on my face as I could manage.

They weren't twins. Both were brown-haired, but the women in white clearly weren't twins.

Kiefan shot a sharp glare to the Ranger lieutenant. The hawk-eyed man nodded toward the column, further back.

"'Tis for me to apologize," a woman called as the false Crowns bowed in their saddles to Kiefan and coaxed their horses aside. Through the loose knot of civilians, one of the archers rode up into the gap between the standards. A few horse-steps behind came a second.

"One cannot be too careful," the first Caer said in Arceal. She swung down from the saddle, in the same beige woolen cloak, leather hose, long gambeson tunic and mail as any of the archers. A loaded crossbow hung on the saddle, alongside a quiver. Her dark brown hair was braided in two tails, and her green eyes sparkled as she grinned at Kiefan's easing frown. The Crown had picked up a sunburn on the road. Both Crowns.

The other wore a polite, shallow smile. Her eyes were on our knights, our banners, me and Kiefan. Not until she found Leix and Elect Tannait did they soften.

"Majesty, 'tis an honor to present Ceelin and Ciara Crierwy, tenth Crowned by Saints Sabh and Conbarre in the shade of the Great Mother Tree of Caercoed." Leix bowed to her queens as she recited.

Duke Adalrich stepped forward. "Honored guests, may I present King Kiefan Weissberg, second of his name, lord of Alemannia, Russe, and Englia, and bound elect of the saints of Wodenberg."

"Well met, king of Wodenberg." The word did not roll easily for her, but Crown Ceelin managed it with a smile.

"Well met, Crowns of Caercoed. We are indebted for the loan of your valiant Margrave Gwatcyn and her Tadhlon Guard. Had she and her knights not come to our aid, we might still be besieged in our castle. I cannot praise her highly enough for all she has done, and for the kindness she showed when my companions and I stumbled from the mountains into her home."

M'lady Leix colored, faint lines crinkling around her eyes when Kiefan added a bow to that praise, but it was the simple truth and she had earned it.

"We know well the valor of House Gwatcyn," Crown Ceelin said, pleased by Leix's blush. Then she threw her arms wide and hugged the margrave tight, pattering in Caer as she rocked on her feet. When Ceelin released her, the second Crown, Ciara, embraced her with far more reserve but just as tightly.

"Your rangers did find us in good time," Ceelin said in the meantime. "Beset by Suevi dogs despite our flag of truce. Your lieutenant swept us under the watchtowers and through your smuggling pass with nary a missed step. We would see him rewarded." She pulled off her riding gloves one at a time, and the hands underneath were smooth and pale. "'Twas fortunate we had Leix's descriptions of your Blessings. Else 'twould've been alarming to meet —"

A bump from her horse cut her off as the bay sidled none-too-subtly with neck stretched, ears perked, nostrils wide and whuffing, to my right — toward Anders. He stood with arms crossed, looking at the ground with a grimace as the horse approached. Will elbowed him; we were all looking now.

Anders put a hand on the bay's nose, clicked, but a Caer horse knew no such commands. It nudged closer, insistent. He gave in and reached for the purse on his belt. His treat-purse. I knew what it was before he got it open. Quartered apples, for training. He'd been working one of the younger horses this morning.

Crown Ceelin laughed when her bay took the treat from his hand. A few steps and she caught the reins, tugged the horse away. It had other ideas, though; Anders had another bit of apple still.

"'Tis hard to resist a sweet, true," she said. My stomach shifted at how her head tipped just askance at Anders. "You were not in the squad. Must've remembered, had you been." She spoke low enough that I barely picked it out over Ciara's talk of the insignia on the Suevi ambushers. He offered her a polite bow.

Anders' eyes slipped to me just as I was wondering if I dared interrupt a Crown. "I am the lowest of apprentices as a Ranger, m'lady," he told her in Arceal. "More danger to myself with a bow than the enemy."

She smiled. "'Tis better to have a — sword in hand, true."

"My sister is tired, certainly." Crown Ciara's voice gained a notch in volume. "'Tis a long road we've taken."

"Join us for a banquet tomorrow, dear guests," m'lord Adalrich said, "a proper welcoming and proper introductions."

"On the morrow, then." Ceelin turned her smile on him. She cast one more look to Anders as she climbed back into the saddle.

I would be at the welcoming banquet, no doubt. If Anders came as well — I set my mouth in a firm line and waved dust from my face as the riders turned about in the gate-yard to ride down to their host's house.

I supposed I would see the truth of his resolve to be my husband, if the Crown were half the flirt he could be. We still had our agreement, and he could spend his nights as he chose. I would honor that. But if any woman thought him a mere plaything, even a Crown, she would be wrong.

———————————✕———————————

For three weeks I had charmed and soothed my womb back to its place. My aches had passed, and I was nearly as I was a year ago. Save that now I was lumpy.

"Not so snug," I murmured when Alice laced the back of my new best dress — pale green, a light shade of the Rossweide color. Frida had embroidered rose vines around the neck and cuffs and hem with her own hands.

"Show them off while you have them. The Mother didn't bless you there." Alice meant my breasts, though they seemed little more than udders now. "You look lovely, stop." She shooed my hands away from trying to smooth my belly down. "Men don't want to worry they'll break a skinny little thing. More meat on your bones is a good thing."

"Loosen it a little," I said, reaching behind my neck to untie the lacing. She objected. My voice rose. "No, do it. I'll not be packed in a sausage skin when —"

When the ladies of Caercoed swept in, confident, laughing — brassy, as Ulf had called them — to claim Kiefan for a husband. Lumpy me, with the fussy baby, and the milk-drooling udders, would likely have to be out nursing half the night. Perhaps their Crown would tempt Anders as well, since I'd not — was too afraid —

"As you like it," Alice said, tying the looser laces at my nape. "Saggy and wrinkled."

"Saggy?" It stung.

"Fussy? Whatever's nibbling at you, it's not a hungry baby and simmering bone broth all day. I'll try the pap on Rafe to give you more time at your duty, but I'm sure it'll mean nothing. Broth pap or water, it's just as well."

"Use the broth," I told her, buckling my belt high across my hips.

Alice put up a hand as she brushed by me. "Water pap was good enough for us, the Mother well knows. And half the work."

"Oh, it's the work then?" Alice knew the work when she took it on; complaining now was far too late.

Alice turned, just outside the door. "Pardon, m'lady, but a wet-nurse wouldn't be so difficult. Unless m'lord's too particular for low-born tits." Then she went downstairs without letting me get a word in reply.

Low-born? As if I — and a wet-nurse? My mouth twisted, along with my stomach, at the thought of expecting a girl little different from me to move her baby aside and feed mine too.

I coiled up my hair with a grumble, netted it in a white crespine and let it rest heavy against my neck. Lumpy. Fussy. And I had two Crowns to speak politely to. Pap or wet-nurses were likely not something of interest. War, perhaps. Soldiers and elect. Caercoed had more elect than Wodenberg, I'd gathered, and I wondered if their people had more skill with kir.

The banquet might be a good chance to see their patterns, in truth. I could call a bit of their pattern when they were close. I needed only a glimpse. Practice had mapped out the gradual shift from the common, un-gifted's pattern to those with a disciple's level of skill to the truly Blessed. Captain Aleksandra was one such, to judge by her pattern.

"Kate, they're waiting for you," Alice called from downstairs.

My eyes focused on the pasture outside the open window, where Nipper and the wagon dray grazed. "Coming." I picked up my little eating knife from the bed and buttoned the sheath onto my belt as I went. My hems trailed on the steps as I descended to the receiving room.

The menfolk looked up at my shoes scuffing on the wood and the conversation paused a moment. Anders stepped up to take my hand near the bottom and touched a kiss to my knuckles. Herr Schäfer wore walnut brown, the rest dark Rossweide green surcotes over bleached-white cotes and black hose. Reinhardt's bore the rampant horse and its crown of stars, in Frida's fine needlework, and he was all the more dignified by wearing it.

"I can't believe such a pretty young frau is an elect, m'lady," our host said, fidgeting with his straw hat in both hands. His son Trauger, by the fire, stared at me.

"You're very kind, Herr Schäfer," I replied. The two of them all but groveled whenever I spoke, as if I were some deadly beast in their midst. "I'm still not quite myself, since the baby," I said, hoping I'd sound ordinary enough.

I caught Alice's brief grimace and regret needled me. Fussy, yes, she was right. Pulled in too many directions. When I could, I'd apologize to her.

Horses waited in the barn, saddled and ready. Afternoon sun slanted through the barn doors; this meal was meant to run long when discussions began in earnest. War and soldiers and trade to be covered. Marriage to be considered. Dancing. Perhaps Kiefan would like one of these ladies at first meeting, and perhaps that would be well. If he smiled, if she loved books, if they —

"When you ride back, you can leave her in her stall. Don't worry yourself about the tack. I'll see to it in the morning," Anders told me as he double-checked Buttercup's cinch. As he always did for me. So kindly.

I blinked. Buttercup shook her head, ears perking as Reinhardt tapped Dove and walked out of the barn. He and Will cast looks back over their shoulders. Anders waved them off.

Why wouldn't he be home till morning? Chilly fear coagulated in my gut. "If you wish. If you'll be…" I grasped for some way to say it. "Tempting the Crown's horse?"

He chuckled at that. "I'd forgotten all about those. The Caer horses mustn't expect treats from me. They might demand I be hired as their trainer." Anders grinned, and I echoed it despite my melancholy. "I mean to be home early, with Will, to see to the chores. Abed when you get in, unless you don't stay."

"I don't mean to stay all night," slipped out of my mouth before I thought. "I don't know, in truth."

"Might I ask you to dance, though?"

That put a true smile on my face. "Yes. You must, in fact." I put my foot in the stirrup and climbed up. My knee hooked over the pommel, I spread my skirts out while he shortened the stirrup for me to keep a foot in.

His flaxen knight's crest was long enough to be a true tail now, though he still didn't braid it. My fingers combed into it before I knew they meant to. Anders looked up, expecting something, but I had no words to say. Only a muddle of worries and longings.

"Pardon," I whispered, and looked away.

It surprised me to recognize the musicians in the manor's great hall. They had played at the castle for Solstice.

"I had them knocked on the head, tied to horses, and rushed over," Theo told me with a frown. "M'lord Eismann had thought the louts in the tavern sufficient! And the duke was rightly more concerned with settling the Crowns' escort into sufficient camp close by."

If it was true, they seemed none the worse for such handling. The lutist tuned while the drum and flutes played a little ditty; the hall wasn't yet ready, but Theo had pulled me inside for the formal greeting line.

Kiefan owned the room, standing in the center and listening to a dusty courier's report with the blue stones and jagged gold mountains of the royal crown catching the afternoon sun. He wore Woden's moon-pommeled sword, an old-fashioned, knee-long surcote in blackest black and whitest Shepherd moon framing Mount Woden; he trailed the gold-lined cloak from his shoulders. New, un-scuffed boots with gold buckles rather than laces. Gregor stood just behind him, a dark red shadow with ginger hair.

"Elect." Duke Haken reached for my hand. "Excellent, Kaufmann, and we will remember your diligence." He nodded pointedly toward the musicians.

"M'lord." Theo bowed in turning me over to the duke.

My hand hovered in midair a moment, unclaimed, and Haken caught me. His cane tapped smartly on the floor and he bowed. I curtsied, as he was so graceful — and looked so fine in a somber red brocade and the black elk sigil of the duchy, his brown beard trimmed short and his knight's crest slicked down between his anticipation ridges.

"If I may, elect, do not honor to me. You have the advantage," he said, voice low.

"I'm sorry, m'lord."

With a smile, "And do not apologize. You need explain yourself to none but your saint." Duke Haken escorted me across the great hall, cane tapping out the slow cadence.

Kiefan dismissed the courier with a nod and looked to the two of us. "A report from Vysokov," he said. "The queen has returned to Wodenberg, and my sister and her sons are with her."

"No further word of trouble near Tochki?"

"No. Are the guests waiting?"

Duke Haken beckoned Baron Eismann from the double doors. His shadow fell long in the slash of golden sun as he trotted across his own great hall to us. I had thought him imposing when I sat at his table as a mere physician. Now he seemed harried, uncertain, his brow always furrowed by worries. More grey was in his hair.

"The guests are here," the baron confirmed. At the word, he turned to his chamberlain at the door. "We will begin!"

Behind me, I heard the pages and kitchen maids scramble out the last dishes of butter and platters of fresh bread. The best wooden trenchers were out for this meal, for certain.

M'lady Leix strode in first, in her full officer's regalia: knee-long, dust-brown tunic, the red and gold sash belt at her waist, red-sheathed, gold-hilted sword, black hose and boots and riding gloves, her red cloak billowing behind to show off the twin-mountain crest of Gwatcyn writ large across her back. Beside her came Captain Mohra, her belt simple black leather and her cloak mottled green.

"'Tis for us to see to the introductions," Leix said, clasping Kiefan's hand briefly. I reached and she took mine as well, with a smile. "And to answer what questions I may."

She didn't notice that I checked her patterns, just of curiosity; the margrave had no kir-talent. Captain Mohra only nodded to me, and was too far away — but I knew her to be a Blessed, by her ease with languages. I'd seen her spar with Kiefan during our mission and suspected she had some charms for combat as well.

Leix announced the first guests through the door as they strode into the hall. "Teleri Eoghan, Captain-general of the Crown's Blades and bound elect of Saint Conbarre. Her captains Aisling Ceffyl and Fionn Helwyr."

The Crown's Blades wore blue uniforms, rich, expensive blue, even the Captain-general's cloak with its crown of seven swords worked in silvery thread was blue. Teleri Eoghan stood tall, nearly able to look Kiefan in the eye, and I'd have known she was elect without the announcement. She made no attempt to hide her kir. Her sandy blonde hair was cut short, like Captain Mohra's, and her eyes hazel-brown. I didn't see the captain on her right, as the one on her left piqued my curiosity.

Captain Fionn was a man, the blue uniform tunic cut as a cote instead. Willowy, perhaps, by Wodenberg standards, but when I called his pattern I was sure he could hold his own in any fight. He was a blessed.

Elect Teleri and Kiefan held each others' eyes for an overly long moment, spines stiff, faces blank, saying nothing. Leix had introduced us all in Caer and doubtless included his own rank of elect. I wasn't worth her consideration, it seemed. Captain Fionn was more polite; he felt me call his pattern and his eyes narrowed, but when he heard me introduced he bowed.

"Shall be a chance for sparring some morn," m'lady Leix said mildly in Arceal, and Teleri turned her head at last.

"I would have it no other way," she said, "after reading your account of their swordsmanship. Needs must see for myself, ere my saint asks for word on the truth of it." A curt order in Caer and she led her two captains aside, to be escorted to their seats by the baron's chamberlain.

"You've men outside the kitchens?" Kiefan asked.

M'lady Leix smiled. "Boys are not required a stint of service, but may volunteer. 'Tis an honorable way for a man to earn a dower, should his family not afford one. Some do forget to marry, though." Turning, she glanced at the next guest crossing from the doorway. "Her Grace the Duchess Faola Taircoeden of Henffyrdd."

The duchess paid no mind to Leix's bow or Captain Mohra's; her eyes were fixed on Kiefan. Her lace overskirt trailed a few inches behind her, and she held her golden skirts in one hand as she curtsied. The sash belt under her bosom was rich brown and tasseled at its dragging ends. Grey diluted her red hair and lines bracketed her mouth, but she moved with grace and her eyes were sharp. Jewels sparkled here, there, and everywhere, on her fingers, in her hair, looped around her throat.

"The duchy of Henffyrdd does nominate its scions for the king's consideration," m'lady Taircoeden said, in elegantly accented Arceal. "My vested heirs, Davnait and Sorcha, are fifteen and trained in every grace and skill. For Henffyrdd's control of Eryr Pass, 'tis first among the duchies of Caercoed, both for war and for trade. And you know already the honor of our leal house, Gwatcyn. Father willing, my daughters have reached Arforddinas and may be here on two weeks' notice. We await your word, Majesty." She curtsied again, as deeply as before.

"Duchess Taircoeden," Kiefan murmured, nodding in return. When she swept away, he looked to Leix.

"She is my lady," Leix answered his unsaid question, "and I am her sword-arm."

"Do you know her daughters?"

A nod. "Do squire for noble houses at far sides of Caercoed, and do it well. Full elegant as their mothers. The image of them, twenty years past."

I kept a firm grip on my resolve. Perfect they might be, and redheads as well, but they were not here.

Leix looked to the door, took a fresh breath. "The ladies Míde and Una Lanfuar, vested heirs to the Duchy of Dheathain."

They were Kiefan's age, petite and far better blessed in curves than I, their strawberry blonde hair curling and waving to their waists… I looked away from the frothy pink lace over lighter pink gowns, knowing what they would say. Vying for his hand as well. White ermine trimmed their long, trailing hems, apparently a poor enough fur for such a job.

"Our mothers do nominate us, their heirs, for the king's consideration," m'lady Una said, rising from her curtsy. "'Tis an honor to meet you at last, Majesty. And so fierce you are, as the Margrave Gwatcyn said."

Even her smile was petite and soft. I clasped my hands behind my back and knotted my fingers together.

"Fierce?" Kiefan asked in return.

"None of the Rangers wore their hair thus," m'lady Una said, with a nod to his knight's crest. "'Tis why, to make the ridges all the stranger?"

"And yet the handsome braid," m'lady Mída noted to her sister.

"Knights shave their hair to a crest before riding into battle," he answered, "to prove they've served the saints with their swords and blood. It's a great honor to be crested."

A faint frown on Míde's pale brow. "And you've done this?"

Kiefan settled his hand on the moon-white pommel of his sword. "When Arcea first thought to attack us, I led the charge against heir hidden reserve of centaurs. We broke their ranks and spoiled their attempt to flank my father."

Silence. The twin duchess-heirs glanced at each other.

If they expected Kiefan to cook and change diapers — I bit back a smile. I had to bite hard.

M'lady Una spoke. "Majesty, 'tis peace we do wish to speak of. We hope that we may." They curtsied and swished away to be seated.

"Dheathain is an ancient and honorable house," m'lady Leix said without prompt. Yeethane, she pronounced it, and my mind flicked to the map of Caercoed I had seen in Leix's study. It was near the middle of the kingdom, with no piece of the coastline. "'Tis a land of deep forest and… deep tradition."

Kiefan must have heard the care she took in her words, too. "May I rely on your honesty, in private?"

Leix looked to the door, where one Crown stood with arms folded, bathed golden by the lowering sun, waiting for her sister. At a glance, it seemed to be nothing, but then a thought needled me. I had left Anders out in the gate-yard. With Reinhardt and Will, true, and I didn't yet know one Crown from the other for certain.

"I should not speak ill of a duchess, Majesty," Leix replied. "Nor her vested heirs. I leave the politics to Lorcana."

At the door, the second Crown joined the first. Both stepped into the hall, and as they passed from the sunshine their gowns fell from golden into snowy white, billowing in gentle layers of gauze. Their bright green sashes trailed with their skirts, tied high and snug to dish up matching bosoms. Out of their uniforms, one Crown was clearly the softer, the other the more slender, and they were not yet thirty but I didn't think it far off. The white gowns accented their elegantly fair skin under the dark brown braids coiled and piled atop their heads. A healer must have cleared up those sunburns. Gemstones set in gold crusted snug around their necks and wrists and glittered in their diadems. Emeralds, all of them, winking dark green eyes. Darker than the Crowns' eyes, and richer than Wodenberg's jewels.

Leix recited their introduction again, adding a list of notable areas in Caercoed and a decisive battle against Arcea to their honors. The teenaged girl shadowing them, wearing grey and green, was their handmaid Bévin; she caught my eye for being as ginger-haired as Gregor. Then Kiefan's introduction rattled along, and I dared call the nearer Crown's pattern.

Crown Ceelin, the softer of them, did not notice. When she twitched her skirts aside with her left hand, I noted she wore no wedding band. Caercoed held the same tradition, I knew; m'lady Leix wore one. M'lady had said her brother was the Crown Consort, and so the Crowns must be unwed... but yet said nothing of marriage. It seemed they would be as obvious a candidate as Kiefan — not that I wished to see Ceelin flirt with him any more than with Anders.

"You've met our duchesses. 'Tis only those we could gather in the time we had. There's well-born pairs a-plenty in Caercoed, but by tradition the Crowns do not marry. And well that is," Ceelin said with a smile.

"Needs must be settled here, though, if we're to seal this alliance." Crown Ciara nearly interrupted her sister. "Margrave Gwatcyn came to your relief with our blessing, but at her own risk. 'Twas made clear: a treaty with agreeable terms, a marriage well and proper, and Wodenberg has Caercoed's full alliance. We shall withdraw, with Gwatcyn's troops, unless there's both."

"And the remaining members of your party?" Kiefan asked. I cast a glance toward the duchesses seated at table behind us and saw they'd separated to opposite ends.

"Minor houses concerned with trade. Some will bring matters of interest to you, doubtless, but for now the question is to the whole alliance," Ceelin answered. "A question of strategies and soldiers. Come, tell us your victories over dinner and we'll share our own."

CHAPTER 6

Word came to me in the midst of the third course — elk, a full haunch crowned with the head and antlers — and I whispered, "Rafe needs me," in Kiefan's ear as I pushed my chair back. I had the seat at his left at the high table. The Crowns sat on his right. He'd been telling them, and the duchesses beyond, small parts of the siege, more parts of driving Arcea southward, and would sometimes turn to me to check on details.

Which had been a distraction from Duchess Faola. Henffyrdd was, intriguingly, where Caercoed's physicians learned their craft. It was a guild, rather than an Order, with its mother house in the shadow of the ducal castle. We had fallen deep into talk of military medicine, ambulances, and training. Much as I wanted to hate m'lady Faola, I found myself sorry to have to leave.

As I crossed the hall, I passed one of the low tables and caught one eye in the midst of the lively discussion between the Rossweides and Theo on one side of the table and the two Crown's Blades captains along with a pair of Caer merchants on the other. The topic was surely horses, but Anders saw me pass and stopped mid-sentence. He mimed cradling Rafe in one arm, and I nodded.

Nurse, burp, and diapers. Nurse, burp, and diapers. My leash was short; I mustn't stray far, or for too long. Even though I slept less since I turned elect, his night feedings wore at me. And now I'd left an interesting chat, and a trencher of tender roast elk, for another shift as a cow.

Alice waited in the gate-yard, where the other half of the banquet was underway. They had rougher tables, perhaps, but they encircled a hearty fire, the chamberlain carved a roasted buck for them all, and the tavern's band was playing bawdy songs. The Alemanni half of the banquet sang along; the Caers didn't know the words, but they liked the tune and the steady supply of ale.

"I did try," Alice said, sullen. "I gave you as long as I could, but he won't take the pap. M'lord will have none of such poor fare."

I took Rafe from her, sorry again for the argument. He knew me, and his cries faded. "Thank you for trying. I know you're as tired as I. Stay, eat. Tell them I commanded you to eat some venison."

That brought a smile back to her face. Cradling Rafe in one arm, I loosened my neckline and, after a moment's hunt, spotted a quiet space to one side of the manor's front door. Servants carried platters to and from the kitchen's side door at one end of the manor, so the half of the house away from the kitchen was far quieter. Rafe waved his hands as we left the fire behind, his voice rising.

"If you'd take the pap, you could've stayed by the fire," I told him, perhaps sharply, as I scooped out a breast for him.

Rafe looked up at me, alert as if he understood, and then smiled.

A beautiful, innocent smile, and my irritation melted away. He wiggled in time with the singing, still grinning, and I had to hush him. "Easy, now. There'll be time for dancing when you're older."

He latched onto my nipple quickly enough; it was sundown and he wanted his dinner. I stood, watching the servants pass to and fro as he nursed, looking up at the golden, rippled sheet of clouds. Patches of blue still showed. Perhaps the rain would hold off.

"Elect Kate?"

I turned toward the great hall's doors. "Elect Tannait," I said in reply. She'd tucked her kir away, as had I, and for a heartbeat I wrestled with whether to draw mine up.

"You've a lovely child. So precious, when so new," she said with a smile. "'Tis a joy none forget."

Rafe was plumping out well with all the nursing, and he wouldn't doze off unless it was on someone's shoulder. Mine, Alice's, Anders', he didn't much care so long as he was cuddled. "He's a sweetling, even with all his demands," I said. "You have children?"

Elect Tannait drew closer, arms folded across her chest. Her silver hair was bundled up loosely and pinned, but the faint lines on her face spoke of a younger woman. I wouldn't have hazarded her age. "Three," she said. "Grown now, of course, but ever precious. Wedded, too, did I hear?"

When I said, "Yes, wedded too," Elect Tannait nodded. Her mouth pursed to one side, though, and she looked away. "M'lady?" I asked.

"Did marry that knight? 'Tis brave to saddle yourself thus, so young," she answered. Her voice turned kind. "Love him while he's here. Treasure him ever after."

My mouth opened to ask what she meant, but my memory flicked back to Parselev and what he'd said of children dying silver-haired and wrinkled. Surely he'd had to bury his children's mother too. I thought of seeing Anders old and grey someday; I was an elect now and would have to bury him. My heart dropped to my feet, so sudden that I wobbled.

Tannait caught my face in both hands. "Do love them while they're here," she told me again, in a severe tone. "Husband, children, all. 'Tis nothing certain but death, even for elect and saints. You were but a disciple when I sounded you, but now an elect. The Mother's blessed you. And the Father."

My brain fumbled for words. "It was the siege that forced it."

She nodded, letting me go. "'Tis often thus. You and the king both. Good that Wodenberg has more elect, but 'tis a job with much to teach." Her voice lowered. "And Arcea is a harsh teacher. You know something of that?"

I nodded, as did she. She eased me away from the shock, I could see, by drawing me back to the work at hand. It was kind of her. Rafe's pace slowed at my breast and I rocked him a little. Tannait tucked her hands in her armpits.

"Our saints do know it, and 'tis for us to see to the work behind our alliance." She raised her chin, canted her voice more formally. "Elect, I've leave from Saint Sabh to swear we mean you and yours no harm. We came in good faith to enter this alliance. We've two elect and no shape-shifters. Can you say the same?"

I touched my bond, felt it open in my palm under Rafe's feet, and asked Qadeem.

/ yes / only two / no shifters /

/ none? / I sent a memory of Anders' horse ears.

/ not elect / not relevant /

"By leave from Saint Qadeem, I swear we mean you and yours no harm. We came in good faith," I said. "We have two elect. No shape-shifters."

"And so many blessed. 'Tis disquieting to see an un-gifted knight match speeds with a gifted one. Or turn aside the swing of a minotaur easy as a child's." Tannait hesitated, eyelids flickering. "Kate, my saint wishes to speak directly."

/ speak? /

The answer came in the cold tingle of Qadeem tapping my Blessing. I wondered if Tannait felt the same touch from her saint.

/ possible / sphere /

I knew Parselev's hush sphere charm; I drew my kir into a tight knot in my hand, spinning it into whorls, and the moment before it shrank tight enough to spark I puffed it open around us. Just high enough to clear our heads.

"'Twere warnings aplenty, yet you asked our aid last. Nearly too late," Tannait said. "Why?"

Through me, Qadeem heard and prompted me to answer. "We knew you took little interest in the world beyond your borders."

"Have you such interests? Englia was let stand many a year ere you moved on it."

"Arcea's eyes began to turn north, and we knew they would come. We did only what we must to claim Englia's fount. No slaughter save those who attacked us, no forced bindings." There was more in the meaning I felt from my saint, and I struggled with it a moment. "As they do... Arcea?" My questions flowed back through the bond. He may have felt, as well, that this wasn't the story I'd heard from my parents.

/ another time /

"And replacing your fallen brother?"

"Saint Aleksandr cannot be replaced. We will continue as we are."

"You do trust Saint Woden still?"

"I know his rules." It was a curt reply in my mind, with much unsaid. I squashed my questions down. A pause followed, then I was prompted to ask, "I speak for myself, to you alone. What of your sister?"

"I speak for myself, to you alone, and will do nothing to harm my sister. We do remember you, Saint Qadeem, from your wandering days." Tannait's head tipped, whether her curiosity or her saint's I couldn't say. "Needs must know now, which part of Arcea 'tis you hail from."

It was a thought I'd never dared let do more than flit across my mind. An impression of deep, close green, humid and scented, came through my bond. His sadness tinged me. I had no words for it, though, and it took a moment for Qadeem and I to work out the answer. "Arcea counts my homeland part of its south. It was a kingdom once. I am not Arceal. Never."

Tannait nodded. "Only two elect you have, though."

I felt a nod, so I did. "Young and strong. What will you give?"

"This one, and four more when our divisions march south."

"Battle elect?"

Tannait's eyes cleared. "I am a jack-of-all-trades, m'lord. Shall add two battle elect and two crafters — which have ever been our strength. Saint Sabh does ask, you bring one battle elect and a healer?"

I felt a nudge from Qadeem, and a bit of a blush warmed my cheeks. "M'lord says I may be a flesh forger."

Tannait's brows rose. "'Tis a high skill, that."

Movement caught my eye; Kiefan's squire Gregor hesitated at the green skin of the hush sphere. I beckoned him in and he came, flinching when the cobwebby surface slid across his face. Rafe had dozed off in my arm. I shifted him up to lie against my shoulder and cover me — and held him with my other hand so I could shake out my tired arm.

"M'ladies." Gregor bowed briefly to each of us. "His Majesty and the Crown ask you to return. It's an important matter."

/ go /

"Shall continue this," Tannait told me as well.

I released the hush sphere and the kir fell away. "Let me hand off my baby," I told Gregor, tugging up my shift underneath Rafe. The boy blushed bright red, even at just a glimpse, and was quick to withdraw.

<hr />

The musicians struck up a slow square-dancing tune as Tannait and I followed Gregor into the great hall. Most of the guests were assembled in groups of four; in the center, Baron Eismann and his wife led to show the steps. The Caer must have known a similar dance, or else they were quick to pick it up.

The other half of the baron's square was Crown Ceelin and Anders. She held her skirt with one hand and slid across the floor to take his hand with her other. I knew what he said without hearing the words, because he'd taught me this dance on our wedding day.

Bow, turn to one side, turn to the other… I tore my eyes away from her glittering emeralds and gold to Gregor's dark red cote ahead of me. By the hearth, a clutch of chairs had been dragged from the high table — which two serving-men worked at clearing — and Gregor led Tannait and me around the dancers to the chairs. I set my eyes on them.

They waited for us, Kiefan and Duke Haken, Crown Ciara and Elect Teleri, with two chairs free and steins of dark oatmeal stout for all. Kiefan paced before the fire, cloak rippling, and Elect Teleri stood behind Crown Ciara's chair. A hush sphere covered the chairs and the hearth.

A chill shivered around the roots of my Blessing; Saint Qadeem still watched. I looked to the Caer in particular as I crossed to an empty chair, so he would see them. The Crown noted and tracked me with a narrowed eye until I sat and reached for an unclaimed stein. The stout was thick and hoppy, a good harbinger of the winter beers to come.

"The Crown and I spoke of Arcea's campaign thus far," Kiefan said, slowing to a stop before the fire. "Their use of centaurs and minotaurs, of the native companies they sent from the south — and the Suevi lords they enlisted. Suevia is a problem for both Wodenberg and Caercoed."

"We've held our two passes against Suevia nigh on five hundred years," Crown Ciara said, "at great investment that has proved itself time and again. Likewise, our coast is well patrolled. No Suevi has set foot in Caercoed but by our permission in all those years. Perhaps 'tis trouble for Wodenberg."

Qadeem prompted me to speak. "And you had no alliance with Suevia before its conquest?"

The Crown's brows rose, at me. "No. Peaceful neighbors, 'tis true, but no wedded alliances. The saints sought no such, ere Arcea demanded one, and 'twas our saints who were proven right in that."

"'Tis no small thing we propose," Elect Teleri said. She looked to Kiefan, brows creased. "Our kingdom is as we wish it. Free of foreign men and their arrogance."

"Not all men wear the same stripes," Tannait said, though perhaps she spoke for Saint Sabh. She took the chair beside Crown Ciara, hands folded neatly on one knee.

Qadeem nudged me. "Still, you came to our aid."

"When Arcea came for Suevia, my grandmothers did close the southern passes," Crown Ciara said. "We drew our line in the sea and watched the kingdom fall. 'Twas not long ere they came knocking at our door, and we choked the passes with blood. Thus, Caercoed earned a treaty and a marriage with Arcea. 'Twas ill-fated, though. Badly ended. 'Twas knowing they will come again that we sent you aid, that we are here now despite the danger of the road."

"And knowing that if Wodenberg falls, you will face our knights as well?" Kiefan asked. I wasn't sure if he spoke for Woden, though; the rest of us paused, blank-eyed, a moment before speaking and he did not.

Ciara sipped her beer; it was Tannait who answered. "Once the report on you came from this elect, yes."

Outside the sphere, a new dance must have begun. A quicker one; I caught a glimpse of white gauzy layers and Rossweide green, close together.

/ focus /

I took another swallow of stout and tried to put it from my mind.

Kiefan had paused to check with Saint Woden. "I have been told there was old blood between Wodenberg and Suevia," he said. "At first, we held back because of that. Too long, and when we did ride south, Arcea could not be stopped. The slaughter could not be stemmed. Arcea claimed they purged all of Saint Seaxneat's blood to the fifth degree — but that was not true."

All three of the Caer cocked eyebrows at that. Kiefan held my gaze away from the dancers. Behind him, the fire popped and logs shifted, settling.

"Suevia's king was the saint's son, as he made a habit of keeping his bloodline fresh. The king's youngest child, Mercia Aethelings-dóhtor, was a babe in arms entrusted to her mother's kinfolk and hidden until she came of age. Arcea watched for her, though, by report of any grey-eyed girls. They pursued her throughout Suevia, meaning to kill her. But at Temitte, by secret arrangement, she was kidnapped by a prince and carried north. To Wodenberg. She is my mother."

A heartbeat passed. "The grey-eyed king of Wodenberg," Tannait said. "Blood of the Eald."

"Wodenberg has one ambition, then?" Crown Ciara asked.

"Our kingdoms can drive Arcea from our neighbor," Qadeem answered, through me. "Kiefan's claim to Suevia's throne is strong. The people would accept him."

Tannait and Elect Teleri exchanged a glance. "And once doubled, would Wodenberg remain as good a neighbor?" Teleri asked.

"We will stand between you and Arcea," I said. "Allies."

"And how shall we divide Suevia?" Crown Ciara asked, setting down her stein.

Qadeem sent me a complex thing to piece out. "Your ships would roam free —"

"Land," the Crown said curtly. "The piedmont below the Iawyr, so far as —"

"Suevia is ours," Kiefan said, and I caught a twitch in his shoulders, the wince in his brow. "You want us for a shield, then pay for the gear."

Ciara's brow lowered. "I'll not send women to die for a man's glory."

"Glory is a fool's game." Kiefan spat it out, then closed his eyes a moment, clenching his jaw. The tension ebbed. When he spoke again, it was calmly. "The Caer brides I choose will be queens of Suevia. You'll have your claim, by blood, to play out in time."

"Our blood did lay claim through thirty years' war at the passes," Elect Teleri told him. "Caercoed shall have her safe distance from southlanders."

"As will we — all of Suevia between our borders and Arcea."

"And are southlanders yourselves," Crown Ciara snapped. "'Tis disaster each time Caercoed crosses the pass to parley." She turned her head toward Elect Teleri and added something in Caer.

Kiefan bristled at that. "If you'll not do us the courtesy of speaking —"

"I speak as I wish. Not as pleases a boy," Ciara shot back. Kiefan's brow furrowed deeper.

Qadeem's irritation drove me to my feet. "Our enemy is at our door," I said, before there was any more sniping. "Our enemy lost five elect and two saints in one summer, and needs only re-group before attacking again. Which of us can spare that? This alliance is our hope, and it must be set before the Empress' second round begins."

I hesitated, remembering the enemy saint conceding the first round to Wodenberg in the ruined courtyard. With my bond open and Qadeem's emotions flowing free, the words came easy but they were not entirely mine.

/ good / he told me, more privately / don't resist the bond /

"What do you know of it?" Kiefan asked. My eyes went to him, and I saw Woden for a heartbeat. It chilled me.

/ sit / silence /

I obeyed.

Duke Haken rose from his chair, leaning on his cane, with his stein in hand. "Let the pages freshen our drinks," he said, with only a little nervous tremble. "The chamberlain's been trying to catch my eye — the sweets are ready, I'm sure. We've much to think on, Majesty. Highness." One to each of them, and a slight bow too.

Elect Teleri's hand twitched and the hush sphere fell. Music flooded in, the last round of a rollicking couple's dance. The dance floor had thinned to only the bravest, and the rest stood clapping and singing along. Crown Ciara left her chair, murmuring in Tannait's ear and then Elect Teleri's.

Gauzy white and dark green swirled by, beyond the line of onlookers. And a glimpse of Ceelin's breezy grin. Beautiful and free. I took my stein for another drink, clutched it in both hands, and forced my mind to wondering about Arcea's second round. Little luck with that.

"Kate." Kiefan's hand caught my eye; I took it and stood as he kissed my palm. In his pattern, a fresh headache throbbed along his Blessing ridges. The knots hadn't had time to tighten entirely, and I picked them apart.

"They aren't so eager for this alliance, then?" I murmured.

"It's a slow dance," he murmured back. "A game." Kiefan's eyes cracked open. "What troubles you?"

My heart stumbled in fear. I wanted to be the one dancing with Anders. "Everything," I murmured, so close to a lie that it needled me.

"We will find how to make this alliance stick." Kiefan put his hand over mine, on his cheek. The last tangles of his kir tumbled free. "Thank you. Let me think a moment, before they're at me again."

Thank the Mother. I picked up my stein and drifted away, looking for the various Caer in the audience. The band wrapped up the last few bars and the dancers tumbled to a halt, laughing. Through a gap in the ringed audience, I saw Crown Ceelin leaning on Anders' arm, flushed and grinning, raising a fist in triumph at finishing the dance. I'd never made it through the whole sequence of that one, as it got too complex for my feet halfway through. The audience cheered her and the handful of other couples.

She caught Anders with her free hand and planted a kiss on his cheek. He drew away, a smile twisting into one of his teasing smirks, and then stepped back to flourish a bow. Crown Ceelin curtsied in return, smooth and elegant despite that her pulse had to be rushing.

My heart quavered and I turned away. Kiefan, by the fire, looked up from the settling logs as one of the petite pink twins drifted across the floor toward him. A smile broke across his face — mere politeness, perhaps. Or genuine? She held out her hand and he accepted.

"Ice-treats! Maple or raspberry!" the baroness called from the barrel of snow by the door. She scooped bowls-full to be topped with syrup or preserves. Pages hurried the treats to the table, four precariously in hand at a time. The dancers' audience dissolved in a rush. They eddied around me, happy and chatting.

A hand touched my shoulder, slipped across my back. "Don't let yours melt," Anders said, near my ear.

I looked up into sky-blue eyes, and the corner of my mouth dared perk up in hope. At last, a chance. "You must ask me to dance, sir."

He smiled. "The very next one, m'lady."

Ceelin had to find another dancing partner and was late to begin; I took that little victory, tucked it in at the top of my memory. I wanted to follow it with a dance with Kiefan to avert any suspicions, but the twin duchesses and then m'lady Faola all must have their turn. Chatting and smiling, each of them. I didn't miss how his eyes tracked me, though.

If he liked any of them, had I any right to be jealous? Seeing his hands on them stung. Anders, close enough to hug, but I didn't dare — all of it hurt. After a few dances, his chores in the stables needed seeing to, and I had little wish to stay.

I found Alice with Rafe, laughing on some garrison knight's knee, and that added another pinch atop the stings. A simple thing, for her to sit on a man's knee. She had little to worry about. Grabbing my baby from her, I waved off her questions — I hardly cared what she did just then — and went home with the one boy I was certain of.

CHAPTER 7

My Ranger's name was Sigmund, and he arrived promptly at dawn. Anders was securing the diaper bags on Buttercup's saddle when he dismounted in the open barn door.

"Have you home this afternoon, m'lady," Sigmund told me, tapping his fist to his chest. "Weather looks to be fair enough."

He was an archer, hawk-eyed, and wore his brown hair tied back in a tail. A local man, I'd been told, who knew these hills as well as his own hands. It was only half a morning's ride to Kaltenbach, so I'd have the rest of it plus half the afternoon to see these difficult illnesses the physicians in Knapptal had brought up, and then a ride back.

Bringing Rafe with me was a mercy to Alice, I suspected; I didn't know when she'd come to bed, but she still smelled of oatmeal stout. Likely she'd had more fun than she ought. Though whether Kiefan had —

"Kate?" Anders stood holding Buttercup's stirrup for me.

I blinked; they waited for me. I climbed in the saddle, Rafe rocking in the sling across my chest. A tap and she ambled after Sigmund's gelding, settling into her easy walk. Rafe, briefly interrupted in his nursing, latched back onto my breast.

"Such a little one, Elect?" Sigmund said when he got a look at my baby. "If we're needing to stop often, might not be till noon that we arrive."

"No need to stop," I told him.

He took me at my word. Sigmund led me up to the north ford across the Felsherz and tracked his way down to the road — there was no marking for the ford, as the ferry was meant to be used. The beaten road wound under golden and orange trees, all but a tunnel that filled with showers of leaves when the wind gusted. The smell of woodsmoke faded with Vorspitz, letting a faint trace of moss creep up from the forest. We passed a wagon stacked with firewood, pulled by two shaggy ponies whose master walked alongside them. He raised a hand to wave and we returned it.

Birdsong, bursts of sun, and a cool breeze. Once Rafe slept, I closed my eyes and took a deep breath. Peace, out here, on my saint's business to help the sick. No Kiefan, no Anders.

Which brought them crashing back to me, of course, them and this tangle I'd gotten myself bound into. It was the woman's fault, in all the stories, the helpless woman who'd pine while a good man and an evil one fought to marry her. Never a story where one loved books and the other made a kind husband. I'd get no help —

Kir. My head perked toward it, off in the wood, and I pulled Buttercup's reins. She stopped.

I called, wide and strong, and around me patterns sprang up: the horses, Sigmund, birds in the trees, and two shapes a dozen yards up the mild slope on my left. They sprang up and fled; I glimpsed four legs as their patterns faded. Ratty tails.

Lamia.

One had used enough kir that I felt it. Which meant it must be strong.

"M'lady?" Sigmund twisted in his saddle. "Trouble?" He'd strung his bow and nocked an arrow in the two heartbeats I'd looked away from him.

They ran, rather than attack. Perhaps they knew what the strength of my call meant. "I think not," I answered him, and tapped Buttercup.

Soon enough, we found the Shepherd's Crook tavern and true to its name the pens alongside it were full of sheep. Yearly, shepherds sold off their wares here and the day wasn't far off. Word had gotten out that I was expected as well, and the crowd spilled out onto the road; I was greeted with a cheer.

Knapptal's senior-most Physician, whose name was Bjorn, had collected those he'd been nursing along for some time and brought them in a wagon yesterday. I handed Rafe to a cluster of fraus to tickle and coo over while I went to work.

Since I came to Vorspitz, I'd healed a dozen such things close by the town. I'd checked on all the kir-gifted children Qadeem pointed me toward. None of it had been overly difficult. But today, after a morning's ride alone with my troubles…

The clubbed foot jerked under my hands, the man's kir fighting me as I coaxed his joint into its proper alignment. When I cleansed a young girl of scrofula, the abscess on her neck burst open when I had meant to neatly lance and drain it; that was nasty ichor, but harmless. My audience of simple shepherds did not even know I was fumbling. They thought it all miraculous, the saints' work.

/ was better / apprenticed /
/ breathe / focus / Qadeem replied.

He sent me another ration of kir as well; I needed it.

The frau with the goiter came to me next, bobbed a nervous curtsy. Her husband stood with her, wringing his felt cap in both hands. It looked like she'd swallowed an acorn squash, and it had caught in her throat.

I breathed. I focused. I took a cup of small beer.

By the look of her patterns, the physician had tried to patch her thyroid but it had grown too large for him to heal altogether. Tangled whorls of kir clogged the swollen flesh. I called up a memory of a healthy thyroid, two little wings of dense swirls that lay against the wind-pipe. My kir, called to my hand at her throat, glowed green and then yellow as I knotted it down into the proper patterns. Dense and tight. Busy. Stars ignited in the haze, eager to do the work.

The extra flesh would need to —

My charm slipped my fingers, splashed onto the goiter and its confused pattern danced into its proper arrangement. All those whorls, over and over, unraveled into a single massive organ, and I felt patterns rush from it into the frau's blood.

She jerked, cried out, and fell. Her face flushed red, then all her skin. Sweat broke out. I followed her down to the floor, put my hand back to the goiter. Fever so hot I could feel it there. Her heart galloped, beyond panic. The frau heaved and threw up her breakfast as I reached into the massive thyroid, cutting its pattern free. Too much, far too much, and still pumping out patterns; a chunk of it came away in my hand and I threw it aside. She screamed now, between heaves. I could see her pulse in her throat, it pounded so.

Her husband clutched her shoulders, wild-eyed. I raised my free hand and demanded his kir; it arced obediently, raced along my arm into his wife, to repair the damage. I sluffed away more, ripping its pattern apart, until she had near the right amount. I soothed her heart as much as I could before it burst. Her skin, I had to stretch over the rip I'd made. Never would a woman be so glad to have her jowls put to use.

The fever still burned. I called for compresses, for a cool drink, and my audience was quick to obey. The frau lay gasping for breath, her husband wiping away traces of vomit on her mouth and whispering that it was over, she'd be well now.

When I was sure of that myself, I sat down beside her and took a deep breath.

I'd nearly burned my father's cottage down once. After Parselev apprenticed me, I so loved studying at the Order that going home for solstices and equinoxes became a terrible chore. Two days without books or lectures. I even missed the extra work foisted on me by the jealous apprentices. Every time, I worried that something would keep me from returning to my master. Foolish, perhaps, but it haunted me. In my misery, I'd been so careless as to spill a bowl of melted tallow near the fire, and it had caught. Flames had puddled across the straw-covered floor.

Kiefan and Anders were just as distracting. I'd driven Anders to despair once already and wouldn't do it again. Kiefan expected me... much as I loved him, we both had our duty. There must be some way we could see to it without breaking both our hearts. I had the ride home to work on what to say.

I had to, I knew now. Knew it in my bones. I needed my focus.

Meantime, there was more work to do. I told my audience to throw the hunk of goiter into the fire before one of the dogs ate it and took ill. They'd suspected it was dangerous and kept their distance, and that settled it. Into the fireplace it went.

Part IV: Salt in the Wound

The last patient was a boy, Blessed with a charm-hand, who'd been out gathering mushrooms when he met a bear. He'd run in a panic, tripped and fallen onto a stick. His right eye had been gouged. Physician Bjorn had cleansed the wound, and that was all he could do for the boy. He'd also stitched him up when the boy sliced his own leg open chopping wood. Cleansed his burns when he brushed too close to an oil lamp. Having a blind side was dangerous.

I held his eyelid open and considered the healed socket. It was a mass of withered flesh and scar. His patterns told me that the muscles still lived, though their lack of work left them weak. The slender meridian at the back lay unused but whole.

"This will hurt," I told him. "Is there a belt he could brace himself with?"

There was. He bit it while I used my thinnest scalpel to cut the remains of his eye free and fished out the mass with my little finger. My audience watched with breath held, completely silent. Outside, I heard the sheep baaing amongst themselves.

An idea hit me. "Bring me a sheep. Healthy, but not valuable." This got me a young ram, confused but placid enough. "Hold him still."

Animals never liked being touched with kir; the ram scrabbled against the dirt floor as I studied his right eye's patterns. He had golden eyes, and his pupil was a line rather than a dot — but the size was right, the muscles similar...

My memory went back to the centaur I'd killed, and my glimpse of his astounding pattern. They were man and horse united, both alive despite that the man must have been separated at the hips and the horse at his chest. Surely one little eye could move, alive, from a sheep to a boy.

I called the kir from half a dozen of my audience and made it quick. A scoop of a kir-blade, a delicate pluck with a slender vine, and the ram hardly had time to scream and thrash before his eye arrowed into the boy's socket. My charm swirled around, calling the muscles to root and the meridian to join, for blood to flush through. With the boy's other eye for comparison, I adjusted the patterns in the sheep's — little pinches here and there, looking deep into their dance.

He blinked when I stepped back to cleanse the sheep's wound and stop the bleeding. The boy tracked me with both eyes, one brown, one golden and strange. And he smiled.

I nearly wasn't allowed to leave the Shepherd's Crook; drinks had to be offered to my health, to thank the saints, to praise the Mother and the Father. They wanted to serve up a feast in my honor, and there I had to decline. I only did the saints' work. When Rafe was returned to me, he was wrapped in a cobweb wool shawl of fine lace — but nobody would claim it when I asked. The one-eyed ram belonged to the boy's father and he wanted to pledge his entire flock to me. I escaped with only the ram in tow, his halter roped to Buttercup's saddle.

The whole afternoon's ride back to Vorspitz, I hunted the words I'd need for Kiefan and Anders. They were elusive things. I had a little worked out, when Sigmund left me at the barn again.

Alice came out to meet me and drew up short at sight of the ram. "What happened to this poor thing?"

"Me." I passed Rafe to her. "He needs changing. Herr Schäfer would know what to do with One-eye — is he here?"

Buttercup went into her stall on her own, to wait for Will or Anders. I took One-eye the ram by the lead rope and walked him down to one of the sheep-sized stalls.

"Schäfer won't be back until dark." Alice patted Rafe as he began to cry. She turned to go and remembered, "M'lord Reinhardt hasn't been back, either — ask him if he wants any of the stew? He's over at the Riverman. I'll call Will in after I see to Rafe."

I owed Alice for all my fussing; one little favor was easy enough. Leaving One-eye with a double handful of hay, I trotted across the road to the tavern. It had been shuttered and dark when I rode out in the morning, and now its doors stood open to let in the pleasant day. The Riverman's common room was nearly as large as the baron's great hall. A small stage in one corner was for the band. Half a dozen tables and a herd of chairs scattered across the space, but the men were by the hearth. And women, I saw as I crossed the room.

"Elect!" Theo spotted me and raised his cup. "Here's my latest investment," he told the rest. "Elect Kate needed capital to open herself an infirmary and I'm in for twenty percent."

They thought that a good investment, by their nods.

Theo introduced the three Caer ladies, as I already knew m'lord Reinhardt and Herr Radulf Brauer. The Caer wore fine, damask-woven wool tunics, well-used riding leathers, and sash belts striped in brown and white. Each took my hand and bowed low over it — did not kiss in fealty, but it was kind of them to honor me as I wasn't their saints' elect. I did take the chance to peek at their patterns, though.

Frau Branwen and Frau Pryderi had little kir talent. The younger woman with the torn left ear had a disciple's worth of gift.

"Síochana Cainwen," Theo said as I touched her hand, "acting margrave of Myrddin — and is it lieutenant?"

"Lieutenant of the Northern Horse," she said, her Arceal thickly accented. "Elect Kate 'tis, truly?"

Theo put a hand on my elbow and the other on hers, steering us gently away from the others. "The margrave has an interest in Englia," he told me, then he looked to her. "I over-heard you last night, m'lady. I meant to approach you. I meant to ask you to dance, in truth, but you were well spoken for."

She shrugged that off. Like many of the soldier Caer, m'lady Síochana — See-o, with a throat-clearing "ch" — wore her tunic short and her brown hair shorter. Though not in uni-form, she wore her belt across her hips waiting for a sword, and I was finding it easy to spot a knight's poise these days. "I mean to renew the trade lost when Englia fell," she said. Focusing on me, she went on. "Myrddin lies on the north coast, above the... Dragon's Fangs, 'tis your name for them?"

I nodded; they were a string of islands and treacherous rocks off Englia's coast.

"Generations bound us to the Engls. 'Tis a deadly crossing, true, but bold ships made it and were welcome in our harbors. All ended, twenty-odd years ago. My mother has not forgot-ten." M'lady Síochana's blue eyes added to the spark in her voice. "I would petition the king to allow ships to pass again — we have crafters, now, who would aid in cutting the channel deeper. Safer. A lighthouse on the Wyrm-spear, perhaps. Trade over-land must walk a long road, to Myrddin — 'twould be a great boon to merely sail from Rukharbor. Great profit."

Theo leaned closer to my ear. "Great incentive to invest, if there's any worry of finding the gold for it."

"You'd find an ally in Duke Seagrace, I'm sure," I said, a bit infected by their spirit.

"Seagrace, 'tis a fine bloodline. She's in the king's retinue?"

"No, he's engaged with the army. You should've brought this up at the welcome." I hadn't seen her in the great hall. "How is it you weren't introduced?"

M'lady Síochana's mouth twisted as she looked away. "'Twas no place for a mere mar-grave, then. 'Twas for the Crowns and the marriage. Next banquet, though. May I ask after you, Elect?"

"Margrave Gwatcyn was in the hall — this would've been a welcome proposition," I said. Something all could agree on, perhaps.

"House Gwatcyn is close to the Crown's heart. And well deserved. The captain-general —" She smiled, a touch of pink on her cheeks. "I should be proud to meet her. 'Twould've been improper, though."

"Ask for me if you like, but I'm sure Theo can find you a chance to petition."

She bowed her head. "My thanks, Elect."

I took my leave, then, with my head full of the sea-tales my father told me as a child.

CHAPTER 8

Next morning was Saint-day. I woke in the grey hush before dawn, when the light of the near-full Shepherd's setting cast an ivory pall on the dark. A few crickets sang, and the birds still slept. Alice breathed deep beside me, her dark braid snaked across the pillow. Rafe lay between us, on his back, swaddled and cozy warm.

I slipped from under the blankets. My brown dress hung from a peg, waiting. Pulling it over my shift, I buckled my belt low around my waist and settled my eating knife on my hip. We'd left the shutters open a crack, despite the frost, and I peeked out at the sky. The Shepherd loomed behind the western mountains, its light picking out straggles of cloud among the stars and the Flock.

I returned to the bed and scooped Rafe up to my shoulder. He only twitched a little; I kissed his fuzzy head, took a lungful of his scent.

"Wisdom, Strength, and Kindness," I whispered to him, naming the three Flock moons that were always in the sky. "They're faithful to the Shepherd. His favorites."

The bedroom door creaked a little when I left, picking up my shoes as I went. In sock feet, I padded down the stairs and crossed through the open kitchen door by the dim light from the sunken hearth. After a glance to gauge the strength of the coals, I went to the wood pile by the outer door and picked two sticks in my free hand. Went back for some kindling. Schäfer's maid Hilda kept stools and benches to work from; I sat on the stool closest the fire and began to stoke it up. The branches slipped and rattled. Rafe stirred in my grip, whimpering.

I hummed my mother's lullaby as I fed the twigs to the strongest coals. The words came, half-formed, to my mouth as a few flames crackled up. It was a sad song, as lullabies are, about when Kindness was lost in the Winter Wood. The Englic words, the smell of smoky thatch, the chilly nip in the air, and the humble seat — for a moment I saw my parents' bed against the wall, lumpy blankets and all. The words caught in my throat.

This would've been my place, if not for my Blessing, my gift, or —

A pale figure at the inside door startled me.

"You're here?" Anders whispered. In only his cote and long braies, he was wool-white. Over one arm he carried his clothes and boots.

"Saint-day. No morning dance," I whispered back.

"Ah. I wouldn't know of such things." He smiled as he crossed to an empty bench, set down his clothes except for the walnut-brown cote. "Once a week is enough for me."

"You're awake early," I said as he pulled the cote over his head. Rafe twitched again, and I stroked him with my free hand. The fire crackled up, eating the twigs.

"Work to do." Anders leaned over to take a stick and add it to the fire before it ebbed. "We're to give m'lady Leix a gift, as well. So a third horse must be ready."

"Is Sprite behaving?"

He stood and snugged his cote's lacings under his arm, tied them. "When she wishes to. Shade is the best of those we brought, but he hasn't learned the crosswise paces. There's rumor of a hunt, too, which will need all the horses. You'd best be on Jenner for that."

"Not Buttercup?"

"If someone takes a tumble, they'll need you. She won't keep up for long. Better for someone more intent on a party than a hunt. Theo, perhaps."

I smiled as he pulled on his hose legs. "You tease him so."

The boots came next. He tightened the laces along the outside, wrapped the long ends twice just below his knee, and tied them snug. Rafe wriggled, nuzzled my neck, and began to wake. The fire had strengthened, so I went to fetch more wood.

Rafe burbled against my shoulder. I tossed a quartered log down by the hearth and lifted my son in both hands. "Good-morn, sweetling. Your fourth Saint-day now — what shall we do this time? We'll go to the disciple's dance at noon. You'll get to see everyone during the meal, I'm sure. You were everyone's favorite last week. But what to do this morning?"

He turned his head, and it lolled to one side. Anders leaned in to kiss his chubby cheek, and Rafe's mouth gaped open. Meaning to smile, I was sure.

"Come and watch the horses," Anders said.

"He loves the horses." I settled him back on my shoulder. "He always kicked when I was riding."

"Of course he did."

I looked up; Anders' flaxen crest hung to one side, loose, and a smile tucked up the corner of his mouth. His hand touched my arm and he leaned closer to kiss my cheek. I turned against his scratchy stubble to kiss him back and slipped one arm around him. A squeeze, warm and close, smelling of horses.

Love him while he's here. My throat tightened, of a sudden. Anders' arm loosened, but I kept my grip on him. He hugged me again, easily persuaded, and nuzzled against my temple in place of a question.

So easy to kiss him, if I dared, to be the wife he should have. I wanted to, Mother have mercy. If only Kiefan had seen something in the duchesses. If only he'd sounded more glad to try —

Anders' mouth touched mine, gently tipping my face up. My breath caught, my heart skipped a beat in fear. I pulled back, my arm around him stiffening to an arm's length. He went still, tracking me with the calm, unruffled gaze he used on skittish fillies.

"I'll not put you in danger," I said. Until I knew Kiefan could be content in a marriage.

Anders' gentleness shifted to resolve. "I'm not afraid of him."

I heard a door open; Will was awake. "Let him find a bride," I got out before Will shuffled into the kitchen. He tossed out muttered greetings, rubbing his eyes.

Anders shot me a measuring glance before he cuffed his brother and started up the talk of horses. It would have to do until we had another chance to talk. Rafe gurgled against my shoulder, fussed a little. "We'll watch the horses this morning," I told him.

————————✗————————

Alice joined me at the split-rail fence once breakfast was well underway. She brought me a chunk of bread stuffed with cooked egg and I ate it one-handed, the other holding Rafe against my shoulder. He sat on the top rail, leaning back against me, head lolling to and fro as the horses trotted up and down the pasture.

Will rode Sprite, and she was eager to learn this time. He and Anders had piled up some spare logs for the horses to jump; the mare loved jumping. The blue roan gelding, Shade, was reluctant to try. Anders had coaxed him into cantering around to the pile and jumping it once, but on the second try Shade skewed aside and jolted to a stop.

"A hunt, they said, night before last?" Alice asked, leaning both arms on the top rail beside Rafe.

"It hasn't been announced yet. Were you a-bed before midnight, after the banquet?" I asked. She'd been tired the next morning.

Alice smiled. "Oh, certainly. But then I had to walk home, which was rather less fun. Still —" She caught me pursing my mouth to one side. "I know what a pessary is. Now."

My memory flicked back to Sir Rostislav, then captain of the Prince's Guard. He'd come along to Vorspitz as Captain Aleks' right-hand lieutenant. "Certainly Sweet Alice knows pessaries. Aren't you a housemaid?"

"Sweet — you know about Rostislav?" Her mouth twisted. "When have you been tending the gossip mill?"

"I have my ways."

She chuckled. "Kate Carpenter, mysterious elect of Saint Qadeem."

I stuffed the last bite of bread into my mouth and chewed. Shade swung close by the fence in a rush of blue-grey hide, dark leather, and Anders' smile. Rafe let out a squeal, whether delight or fear I wasn't sure — it fell into an uncertain whimper. I held him with both hands, kissed him, and wrapped the end of my wool shawl a little tighter over him. That quieted him. Frost still lingered on the grass, and the air smelled a bit like snow. Green had gone from the trees; it was only gold and burning orange or red, now. Beautiful, but a warning of winter to come.

"Good morn!"

The handmaid waved. Crown Ceelin walked just before her, green cloak wrapped over a pale golden tunic and green hose. They followed the fencing from the wagon-rut road between our houses, a few steps ahead of Elect Tannait. The pastures behind their host's house were dotted with tents for the Crown's Blades. Our men and horses had an audience each morning. Most of the royal escort camped outside the town, though.

I took Rafe from the rail and curtsied for the Crown. "Fetch m'lord Reinhardt," I told Alice. She bobbed and scurried into the nearest door. Louder, I answered the hail. "Good morn, Crown. Good morn, Elect Tannait." Whether I should greet the handmaid, Bévin, I was not sure. Elect Teleri was coming too, in her dark blue uniform, though with no great rush.

"'Tis told me 'tis Baron Rossweide I'm to ask of these fine colts?" Crown Ceelin put an arm on the top rail of the fence and looked over at Sprite and Shade. "Each morn, I see them at work and admire their lines."

Tannait wore grey, several shades of it, with her hair loose. Something in how she began to speak but then clamped her mouth shut gave me pause. She crossed her arms and gave it further thought, whatever it was.

"My father-in-law breeds fine horses," I said. "Palfreys, couriers, and warhorses."

"Breeding 'tisn't so important. Conformation, temperament, training, those set a colt apart. Striking color is a fine thing as well." Crown Ceelin tracked Shade as Anders brought him around toward the log pile again. This time, he hurdled it easily enough.

Blue roan was not so uncommon, as far as I knew. "I'm sure m'lord would be glad to put a horse through its paces for the Crown," I said, which seemed a reasonable reply. I glanced toward the kitchen's door and was glad to see Reinhardt pinning on a cloak as he came. "Here he is."

Teleri joined Ceelin at the fence, and I saw Crown Ciara walking over with another handmaid in tow. Ceelin only had eyes for the horses, it seemed. She hardly looked when Reinhardt dropped to one knee beside her.

"You do me great honor, Crown," he said. His Arceal was rusty, but fair.

"'Tis been a joy to watch your pastures each morn, Baron, ere I'm dragged off to such tedium."

Reinhardt stood, head still bowed. "If Crown would care to, the black mare and her sister —"

"I've more interest in colts, sir."

By how she narrowed her eyes and surveyed the options... no, it wasn't colts exactly.

"The gelding's a good horse, but the mare is much finer."

Crown Ceelin cast a glance toward Sprite and Will. "That one — yes, shall be fine in a few more years." But she returned to Shade and Anders. With a sigh, "Oh, say he's not a gelding, please."

Reinhardt paused, frowning.

Tannait caught my elbow. "Elect," she murmured, with a tug.

"I deal in horses, good Crown," Reinhardt managed to say, with emphasis.

Ceelin grimaced. "The horses, then."

Teleri's eyes followed as Tannait drew me a few steps away. "Elect, if I may."

I lowered my voice. "Call me Kate, m'lady, you know that."

Tannait nodded, still distracted by her thoughts, and took a deep breath. Folded her arms. "When the margraves and I did question you at the Crowned Leaf," she said, "'twas asked whether you must go, should your lord order you to his bed." When I nodded, she continued. "Your answer missed the mark, in truth."

I'd been drunk by that question. "True."

"Would you answer it now?"

In the pasture, Will started Sprite on her slower paces. Anders sat on Shade, off to the side. Not suspecting, perhaps. "We are as bound by the Mother's and Father's teachings as you. No lord should order it, and any maid should refuse it."

"But being foolish sheep, all might stray."

And Ceelin's eyes were straying to Anders, clear enough. How much a habit the Crown made of that was little business of mine, but I recalled something else Leix had said. "The margraves' brother Oisin is the Crowns' Consort — is that why Caercoed offers duchesses for this alliance? He's their husband?"

"Oisin is Ceelin's consort," Tannait's tone slipped toward lecturing. "Crowns do not marry. They do serve to mediate betwixt the noble houses, the common people, the saints, the southlanders. Needs must remain unbound, must renounce any blood tie and serve at the pleasure of all. Too much displeasure, and Crowns may well be replaced."

"A consort is not a husband, then?"

Tannait shook her head. "He may be dismissed — though as a practical matter, 'tisn't likely once there's children at hand. Oisin's father to the princesses, and 'tis in the raising that a man's a father."

"And father in blood...?" It seemed an odd thing to say.

She twitched one shoulder. "They take after their mother. Perhaps his blood, perhaps not. Ceelin does invoke oíche-te as she pleases — which does bring me to you, today."

"Oíche-te." A strange word. "And whether I must go, if ordered to my lord's bed?"

Tannait began to walk, in slow steps, along the fence and I went with her. "'Tis a tradition from the Crowns of old. She can summon any man for oíche-te. Or capture him in battle. Mayhaps he's kept one night, mayhaps he's kept as a surety of his family's obedience — 'tis one night, in these days." She put an emphasis on that. "Before we were united, oíche-te was both leash and threat. Long ago. No need to send Crown's Blades to serve the summons now."

She said it with a dismissive smile, but I didn't echo it. Where this led seemed clear enough, and it chilled me. "You've come to ask if Anders will go, if summoned for this."

"Leix did insist — she's distraught that she did tell Ceelin he was a free man, ere she knew you'd wed him. Did say he left a gift in her stable-mistress, and 'tis well known southlander men will gladly dally, married or not. 'Tis for me to set the matter straight, ere Ceelin settles her mind."

I shifted on my feet, in a moment's unease. What Anders had done with Leix's stable-mistress was little business of mine, but now… "He's married," I told her, voice low. "Bound by the Mother's discipline."

Bound, but we had our agreement. Our agreement, but he'd dared kiss me and I dared want more. I wanted, and as elect, I had a high rank. I spoke for the saints. Whether it was for me to refuse the Crown something, or the elect of our allies-to-be…

Tannait's voice dropped as well. "'Tis one night. Another tie in the binding of our kingdoms."

"I will not send him — if it's me who receives the summons." I wasn't entirely clear on that.

"Shall be him."

I had to swallow a lump when my answer came to me, but I said it. "It's for him to answer, then. If he declines, if you send Blades for him — I will take my husband's side."

One should fix one's eyes to show certainty. I hoped Tannait was convinced; my stomach was tightening in my belly at the thought of a fight. What I'd do, I had no idea, but Tannait accepted my words with a deep nod.

We walked back in silence. My stomach slowly un-kinked.

At the fence, Crown Ciara and Reinhardt were deep in discussion; in the pasture, Crown Ceelin was in Sprite's saddle and had her leaping over the logs with Shade two steps behind. "Open the gate!" she shouted, and as soon as Will pulled it aside she kicked Sprite. The mare streaked out and tore across the grass toward the road. Anders pulled Shade around and followed, flat-out. The Crown's whoop faded in the distance.

Sprite's spirit might be a good match with the Crown's, for all their worrying about her manners.

The abbess divided the crowd into an easy disciple's dance led by her inside the Chapel and a challenging dance outside — which she asked me to lead. Daily attendance had improved me, true enough, but it surprised me all the same.

So I did all of my favorite sequences, and my partners were mainly knights, archers, the handful of Caer who joined for curiosity. I called the transitions in both Alemannic and Arceal, with added advice in the latter. A few Caer dropped out, but more stuck it through.

When I dismissed them, the Crowns announced they would bring over their cook's near-finished dinner as a contribution to the communal meal, if given time to do so. That earned them applause and gave Kiefan time to announce the hunt in three days and then call for sparring swords. That won the audience's favor too.

Kiefan called Gregor out to spar, and for a moment I hoped my disciple's dance had helped clear his head. But soon enough, I could see the audience was too much on the squire's mind. The Caer knights' squires and the handmaids were his age, and his cheeks held a red blush to rival his hair throughout. Kiefan kept at him to watch his balance, but he attacked more in desperation than confidence. The giggles started in the audience.

Gregor over-reached and Kiefan knocked him down with only a light swat. Kiefan put one hand to his brow with a sigh. Gregor would've been as happy for the earth to swallow him, I was sure.

"Let the poor boy back to the kitchen!"

It got a moment's laugh. Gregor slumped, face buried in the grass. Kiefan poked him with the wooden sword as he strode past. "Get up."

He tossed his sparring sword to the taunter: Míde Lanfuar, one of the pink duchesses-to-be. She caught it, if clumsily. Kiefan jerked his head toward Gregor, who was up on his knees. Her sister Una shoved her into the ring with a laugh. Míde smirked and hefted the sword as she walked across the grass. Gregor stood, slow and downcast, and combed his hair back from his eyes as she came.

Míde stopped an arm's length from him, cocked her head — Gregor had begun a growing spurt, and had three inches on her — and stabbed at his gut.

Gregor sidestepped, despite the surprise.

She pressed the attack, and even I could see she wasn't particularly good but Gregor still struggled. When he merely avoided her, nothing she did could touch him. His wavering kept him from getting through even her sketchy guard, though, until she began to tire. Gregor knocked her off-balance in sweeping away her blow, and when she wobbled, Kiefan yelled:

"Now!"

"But —"

Her stick cracked into Gregor's jaw, splitting his lip, and he went down. The Caer whooped and Míde raised the wooden blade, triumphant. Then she tossed it down beside Gregor and returned to her sister, grinning.

I set my mouth in a line and went to see if he'd lost a tooth. Kiefan crouched beside him.

"But? But she's a girl? How would a steel blade have left you?"

He didn't want to answer, but mumbled, "Maimed, m'lord."

I put my hand on his chin and turned his face to me. One tooth loose, which I rooted back in place. A good deal of blood from the gashed lip. A tear streaked through it, either from the pain or the humiliation.

"Let him keep the cut," Kiefan said, standing.

Gregor pulled away from me and stood, collecting the sparring swords as he went. I wished there were something I could say to help him. As I returned to take Rafe from Alice's arms, the audience raised a cheer; Leix had taken the sparring swords from Gregor and stood in the center of the ring, offering one with a smile. Captain Aleks was elbowed by a King's Guard on either side, and at last she unbuckled her sword belt and passed it to Lieutenant Rostislav.

Leix tossed her the blade. I knew the two were evenly matched in kir-skill. They were nearly of an age as well, though perhaps Captain Aleks was a couple years closer to forty. The captain's dark knight's crest, braided and free, hung to her waist; she'd first shaved it for battle at Kiefan's age. I couldn't help thinking she looked far fiercer than m'lady Leix. I hadn't seen the margrave's swordsmanship, and Captain Aleks did have the peg leg to hamper her, but I worried a little.

I felt Tannait's kir draw closer; she'd wound her way through the audience from the cluster of Caer. "'Tis your work, the leg? Bold."

I smiled, glad it was an easier topic than earlier. "It fits her."

Captain Aleks attacked without hesitation, driving Leix back a few steps. I felt kir move in the margrave. Green spikes unfolded from her free forearm and she caught the captain's sword, tangled it for a heartbeat. Leix's blade slapped against Captain Aleks' side.

The crowd cheered. Aleks stumped back, grinning, and crouched into a middle guard. Leix took a slightly lower guard, leaning back with her spiked arm held where a shield should be. Hush fell, knowing the gloves would come off next.

Captain Aleks attacked at Blessing speed, and if the peg leg slowed her at all I wasn't expert enough to say. Leix, to her credit, met the onslaught and slipped aside of much of it. Wood cracked twice, then a third time as they parted. Leix patted her upper shield arm.

"I'd be dead soon enough, if un-armored," she said.

Aleks touched her thigh. "And I wounded. The score is even, sister. Let's leave this to the puppies." The audience called for more, but the ladies bowed out. The crowd's voice turned to a cheer when Elect Teleri strode into the circle, wooden sword pointing across at her intended.

"Best we stay," Tannait said as Kiefan strode out to meet the challenge. "'Tis ever thus, with battle elect — put all else aside, they must know who's the stronger." Her voice rose. "No kir! You spar as friends! Let us draw you dry."

Teleri shook her head. "Let it be a measure of the pup's control. I'll not let a kir-blade slip. My word of honor that I'll only defend."

Kiefan bowed over his blade. "Likewise, m'lady. On my honor."

Tannait grimaced.

"Kiefan is good as his word," I said. "He won't use any kir-blades."

"No saint would risk the loss," she said. "Not of so seasoned an elect as she."

The two of them circled, their kir shaken out into glowing cloaks around them. To my side, Theo was collecting wagers and giving the coins to Anders for safeguarding.

"Elect Teleri… has much experience?" I wasn't sure how to ask.

"Forty-odd years."

A brief blur, a crashing of wood, and one blade flew free only to be snared by a kir-vine and returned to Kiefan's hand. The crowd's breath caught, collectively.

Teleri didn't look even forty-odd, let alone older. Her sandy hair and face were untouched by age. Unlike Tannait, who wore her grey-white boldly. She caught me looking. "I'm eldest of the family, yes. 'Tis wise to make that clear, in ways. You will learn of that."

They darted together again, sparks trailing from cloaks, and Kiefan lapsed out of Blessing speed with his sword tangled deep in kir-vines; he lost it and it flew away. The audience ducked as it landed among them. He dove in as Teleri swung around, her guard seeming open, and I caught my breath, thinking of the cambifax's crushed heart. Hard cracks of wood on kir, and a vine shot out seeking the sword. But it hesitated in the air, over the crowd.

"Can't, ere you see it," Tannait murmured, and that was true enough.

Kiefan darted back and Teleri let him, holding her blade in high guard and grinning. He kept both fists up, an oblong plank of kir-shield on each forearm.

"M'lord!" Someone threw the sparring sword into the ring. His vine shot toward it, but was struck aside by Teleri's; she snaked around his, yanking. Rather than lose balance, he charged. She caught him on her shoulder and threw him onto his back, hard enough that I felt the impact. Her sparring sword's point at his throat.

His sword hit and bounced, as he lay panting through clenched teeth.

Kiefan's kir-vines snaked up her blade, her arm, to her throat at Blessing speed, slamming her chin with the force of a fist. He had her down and pinned for half a heartbeat, and then he flew sideways through the air. He crashed into the ring of onlookers in a tangle of limbs. Teleri rose to her feet, slow, perhaps with a wince, blood streaming from her nose.

"Enough!" Tannait shouted. Then, at a mutter, "End this foolishness."

I put Rafe in Alice's hands and ran to the mess. I got there in time to catch him on his feet again — I put a hand to his chest as he got sight of Teleri again, a feral snarl on his mouth. "No." My kir knotted on my hand, ready to do anything I asked, and the focus of it there gave him a moment's pause.

Kiefan's eyes cleared. He took a deep breath and closed them. Then, with a grimace, turned to help me with the bruised and battered.

CHAPTER 9

Next morning, two Crown's Blades joined the disciple's dance. They took spots near me and I translated for them; in halting Arceal, they thanked me. We walked back to our guest houses together, but they were content to keep quiet, and I let them get ahead of me. We left brown tracks through the fragile dusting of snow, and streaks where the corner of a cloak dipped through the powder. My breath billowed, catching pink rays of the rising sun.

Kiefan was to go riding with Míde and Una today, and I was expected for an early banquet and the conversations afterward. Perhaps Suevia would come up again. Perhaps oíche-te. That made me grimace.

Kir surged and vanished. My feet stopped, eyes locking on the distance, skin prickling. I stood reaching for the door into my host's kitchen, which put the wheel-rut road and the Caer's house at my back. The two Crown's Blades continued to their front door, ignorant of the flare.

Somewhere down the rutted road, someone had tapped a fair mass of kir. More than a day's ration. Far more than that little charm I'd felt the lamia use on the road. I touched my saint's bond.

/ felt kir / large / lamia? /

Qadeem sent me a second day's ration, through the bond. / check / aid nearby? /

/ no /

The birds had only begun to sing on the way home; dawn warmed the cloudy sky and the snow twinkled on the grass.

/ careful / There was worry buried in his warning.

No sign of movement so far as I could see down the rutted road. I began to walk. The rail fences to either side were open enough to betray anything slipping behind them. On my right, a few early risers in the Crown's Blades camp tracked me. A few horses grazed in their furthest pasture. Perhaps Tannait or Teleri were awake already and had felt it.

I strengthened my voice with a little kir. "Ask Elect Tannait to join me!" I pointed along the road. One of the Blades saluted and trotted toward the house.

I'd feel better with her on hand. Or, better yet, Kiefan.

The memory of the flare in mind, I tried to judge the distance. It'd been on the Caer side of the road, I was fairly sure, and when I passed the last corner fencepost, I thought I must be close. Beyond the pasture, ferns and young trees sprang up alongside the road. The patch of trees ran for a couple hundred yards and stretched up and down the slope to either side. Further down, I could see the face of a sod-roof cottage and hear faint baaing from a sheep-fold.

Birds sang. Chilly wind breathed through the branches, showering me with snow-flecked gold and orange leaves. Water burbled close by. A stream ran through, that was what the trees had sprung up around. It cut deep through the earth, down to the rocks, and hid inside the steep banks. I stopped on a stubby bridge of fat logs so packed with dirt that grass had sprouted.

Nothing and nobody. I called kir and felt only a little ripple from back along the road; Tannait raised a hand in greeting behind me. Standing on the bridge, I folded my arms and grimaced. Wished for Anders' horse ears, for an archer's hawk eyes. I might try stumbling around in the brush, but I was no woodsman to catch a hiding shadow. And in all honesty, if a lamia able to use such kir lurked here, I'd as soon not anger him.

I turned back and walked. "Did you feel a kir-flare?" I asked Tannait, when I drew close. "'Twasn't you, then?"

I shook my head. "It was out here, it seemed to me."

"'Twasn't either of us. I felt no arc, so it must've been a charm. One that left little trace. I saw nothing overhead," Tannait said, looking up at the empty sky. "Would tell us if you've rogue elect afoot, yes?"

"We don't have such things here." Rogue elect were dangerous things; the selfishness of refusing to serve saint and kingdom was proof enough of that. "There are lamia, though."

Her eyes widened. "So close by? You did say they'd not trouble us."

"No trouble's expected," I said, and I was fairly certain of that. What charm a lamia could've cast, what it meant to do, I had no idea.

Tannait surveyed the trees. "'Twould fit, as I felt nothing, saw nothing — a stealthy lamia, creeping away. Needs must be sure, though. If 'tis gone, 'tis well. If not, 'tis a spy. Do probe that side." She gestured toward my left.

That was a chilling thought. I called up my kir and focused it with care, in part to see what she did. Tannait pointed toward the trees and thrust out a long vine of kir, shooting it through brush and around trunks. Sparrows burst from one bush; a sapling trembled when she hit it.

I did the same, spinning out as far as I could. The vine sent me each little jarring hit, when a bush shuddered or I hit a tree. We snaked our vines through the patch, the kir obedient to the paths our eyes traced. Blue jays exploded from their hiding places, screeching, and squirrels fled. How far I could reach surprised me; I saw bushes shake thirty feet away, and —

A woman leaped up with a shriek, goosed by Tannait's vine. She spun toward us and her face lit up. A rapid string of Caer rattled from her, pointing uphill and deeper into the trees. Tannait answered and trotted off the road toward her. Over her shoulder, she translated into Arceal. "Did see something in the trees and hid from it. A wolf, she thought."

I followed, holding my skirts up in one fist. A lamia looked enough like a wolf, certainly. "Who is she?" I called after Tannait.

"'Tis a stable-hand. Ealga." Tannait asked something of her; the woman was halfway to the edge of the trees. Ealga held up a bucket. "Did fetch water from the stream, for the horses."

When we reached her, Ealga pointed to where she'd seen the beast — green eyes in a black shadow — and the way she'd heard it run. She was a plain enough Caer, brown hair tied back in a tail, her knee-long tunic coarse and brown with a sash-belt to match. Both of those were well stained with saddle-grease, and her knuckles were crusted with dirt. When dismissed, she slipped through the knee-deep ferns to the pasture fence. Bending double, she stepped through its wide-set beams and brought the bucket with her. The horses raised their heads and came for a drink.

Tannait and I sent vines through the trees where the lamia might've taken up a new hiding spot. We walked further uphill, calling kir and searching, but the monster likely felt all our poking about and had run for whatever home the lamia had.

Mind-weary, foot-weary, and truly hungry, we came to that conclusion at near the same time. Half the morning spent, but little to show for it. Walking back, Tannait told me, "Did know of Wodenberg's fount on the mountain, and that at Rukharbor — 'tis a third, then, not far. Needs must tell my saint."

Qadeem sent me a nod, through my bond, and a caution that I passed along. "Saint Lamia guards his fount well. I have been there myself and seen it. My saint warned me to do nothing to anger the lamia, to stay away from the fount now that I am elect."

Tannait nodded, with a faint smile. "'Tis a shame they've such a taste for our flesh. 'Twould make fine allies."

Rafe's screaming put some speed in my tired feet as I approached the kitchen's outer door. Alice and Hilda looked up when I opened it. Rafe lay in his basket, a few feet from Alice. I swooped in to pick him up.

"You leave him? Crying?" Once his little head was against my neck, his wails dropped. "How long have you ignored him?"

Alice put a hand to her ear. In Englic, she asked, "Pardon, m'lady?"

Anger spiked through my worry. "I'll not have you neglecting him!"

"Neglecting?" She rose from the stool, gesturing at a small bowl of pap on the workbench. "You'll blame me if your baby won't take pap when you simply vanish one morning. Nary a word, and all's my fault?"

"I'll do my best to keep Father Duty's demands to a schedule," I threw back. Rafe nuzzled at my neck, searching. With my free hand, I loosened my neckline. "Perhaps the two of you should speak on it."

"No, no, I'll not imply it's any trouble." Alice threw up a hand. "Three men bent on ruining all their knit hose in the saddle, a babe too fine for pap, and the saints' right hand — no trouble at all, in a peasant hut that's put on wealthy airs —"

She kept to Englic at least, and Herr Schäfer's maid didn't hear that. "We're guests here," I told her while I got Rafe settled at my breast. "Do you hear yourself? Putting on airs? Must we pardon Herr Schäfer for not being a baron?"

"Then pardon me for not nursing Rafe." Alice dropped onto the workbench with a sigh. Beside her was a pile of sewing to be done — hose, worn to raveling at the thighs.

"Pardoned," I said. "Is there any breakfast left?"

She picked up one leg of hose. "Only the pap."

My stomach ground. Picking up the bowl, I drained it. And then I considered the little puddle that gathered at the bottom. "Might be your cooking's spoiled me, but I'd fuss at that, too. Throw together one of your shepherd's pies, next he's hungry."

I meant it teasingly, but wasn't sure she'd take it thus — until she snorted. "The Orderhaus sent a boy to ask after you," she said. "You were to tutor the apprentices?"

"Yes." I grimaced and tried to guess how much of the day I had left. "And then another banquet tonight — quickly, sweetling, quickly."

Rafe was gulping as fast as he could, as if I might disappear at any moment.

Part IV: Salt in the Wound

I rode up to the manor late, on Buttercup who'd been left saddled in her stall. The afternoon waned into evening, helped along by thickening clouds overhead. A stable boy ran out to take Buttercup and hold up a hand to help me; I was already sliding off the saddle and only nodded to him. Late, late, late.

I nodded to Lieutenant Rostislav, who held the great hall's door for me, and strode toward the high table. It was the bottom of a long U of tables, as there were a full complement of officers and merchants on hand.

In the center of the high table, Kiefan's chair stood empty. But then I found him, leaning over m'lady Míde's shoulder to pour small beer into her stein. Smooth and precise, he stepped to the side and did the same for her sister Una. They both smiled up at him, and when he moved on whispered to each other. Kiefan crossed the gap behind his empty chair and inclined his head to Duchess Faola in inquiry. She nodded, and he topped her stein as well.

I took my seat on the duchess' other side as he crossed back to fill Crown Ceelin's upraised stein. My place was set with a bare, wooden trencher and empty stein.

"'Twas an interesting ride this morning," Duchess Faola said, leaning close to my shoulder. "If you care for talk of hunts in Dheathain. Did mean to wait on you, and heard some business proposed. There was even talk of Englia."

I looked down the high table; the two white-gowned Crowns sat at the end so that the marriage applicants might work at charming Kiefan. He passed the beer pitcher to a page and snapped his fingers, pointing toward the serving platters by the fire. The boy scrambled to fetch them.

"How is it the king is…?"

"Caer tradition," the duchess said. "The duchy of Dheathain has two passions: the hunt, and tradition. A husband needs must be a worthy host and serve at table, whatever other talents he has."

"Since I served as a page," Kiefan said, leaning over my shoulder and nearly startling me off the chair, "and I remembered how Leix's husband and son did it, I offered to try my hand."

"'Twas your hand, and arm, they did twist into this."

He piled my trencher with roasted pork and potatoes cooked with apples and onions. "Father Duty calls knights to serve," was all he answered to that. There was a sweet onion gravy to cover the food, which Míde called for more of while he had the bowl and dipper in hand. I watched him cross back to spread more on her meat. I caught how deliberately she elbowed him, too, and how he dodged just out of the way.

"Unsubtle, m'lady."

"Your father taught you well," Una said.

That got a snort from him. "My father taught me the sword and the lance." Kiefan handed the sauce bowl back to a page and took his own chair at last. The baroness was quick to fill his trencher and another page his stein.

"Our meal's not finished," Míde told him, flicking her hand. "You insult your guests, not waiting on their needs."

He paused between swallows of small beer. "The king eats when he pleases."

She chuckled. Her sister snorted. "King is a southlander word. Husband or consort."

I hadn't known that; I hesitated and a saucy chunk of pork slid through my fingers. Kiefan's brow creased under his plain gold band. Duchess Faola put a hand on his elbow and leaned close. I barely heard her.

"'Tis youth, Highness, and shelter from the world. Dheathain is… remote and old-fashioned." She nodded to emphasize that, and her voice rose a little. "My girls are not so ignorant. They've been to Suevia, they know something of others' ways. They know you'll have far greater duties than serving at table. They will have their own to see to, in the duchy."

Interesting as Duchess Faola was, I wished she'd brought her daughters. Faola had said the girls were squired to other noble houses and served at opposite sides of the kingdom. There'd been no chance of calling them home before the Crowns set out for Wodenberg, but with some luck they'd be in Arforddinas now.

"You'll expect them at home often?" he asked her. "How would we manage their time between your duchy and my kingdom?"

"Mayhaps 'twill require securing that pass you crossed. Or mayhaps they'll go by Suevia, if there's peace, and bring a trade caravan in their wake. Summer in Wodenberg, winter at home."

"Perhaps." Kiefan nodded, and his gaze shifted to me.

My heart ached and I looked away. He'd promised to try. Hardly his fault if one pair was a poor match, the other absent, and the Crowns not in the offering.

After several more bites of potato and apple, I dared look for Anders at the lower tables. He sat with Theo, laughing over some story Radulf Brauer was telling. Scanning further, I found Reinhardt and Will sitting near the three Caer ladies. Margrave Síochana sat at one end of the three, quiet while the other two had out paper and quill to jot down something Reinhardt explained. Síochana watched the high table. Kiefan, in particular.

Both Crowns stood from the table. The other Caer were quick to leave their meals and stand as well. The rest of us did the same, of respect. "Our gratitude for your hospitality," Crown Ceelin said, raising her stein. The Caer ended every meal with a toast. "And for the fine service." She looked to Kiefan with a smile.

He accepted it with a nod, despite what the twin duchesses had said.

I raised my stein with them and drank. Ladies Míde and Una wisely made no further comments on the service. Once the Crowns and the Caer left the tables, the rest took their leave to follow. Back to negotiations, soon enough. I stole one last bite of baked apple and wiped my fingers on the tablecloth, then slipped from my chair to catch Elect Tannait.

She turned as I approached, brows raised. Teleri, hovering by Crown Ciara, looked as well. "No sign the lamia returned?" I asked, voice low.

"Nothing. Did stay, on the chance it might," Tannait said.

"Do often have lamia wandering your streets?" Teleri's voice neared a growl. "'Tis no matter for guests to worry on?"

"Their numbers were thinned in trying to kill me, Kiefan, and Anders. They'll not trouble us, so long as we don't trouble them."

Still, she frowned. "Do let them live at all? Rukhs, 'tis one thing, but lamia?"

"If you wish to question our saints on that, do it yourself," I told her.

Teleri let it drop and went to take her place by the Crowns. Tannait lingered a bit more. "Caercoed has rukhs?" I asked, curious.

"Our north-most fount is home to a few. Selkies, more commonly."

That caught my ear, but Crown Ceelin beckoned Tannait over for a word. I took another sip of my small beer and looked back to the high table. Kiefan leaned against it as Síochana explained something to him with one hand raised to punctuate. Her short, brown hair was drawn back from her face and held under a simple beaded band. That her left ear missed a chunk mattered nothing to her, apparently. I wondered how that had happened. Her tunic seemed plain enough — nearly a uniform — but I knew a single-color damask from seeing it on Theo Kaufmann. Kiefan nodded and spoke, getting a smile from her and some manner of admission.

Was that a hint of a smile on him?

Motion caught my eye as Leix moved closer, alongside me. "'Twas an interesting proposition the margrave brought," she said. "Most gave up trade with Englia as lost, when the spring ships never returned."

"You know her, then?" I asked.

"Not well," Leix said, folding her arms. "Cainwen inquired after Tiarnan's hand when he turned sixteen, but we declined. Needs must. 'Twas never a rich holding, and once Englia was lost 'twas worse. Her last mother has lain ill for years, left the governing to the young singleton — another tragedy, that. Her twin died in the cradle. Fools murmur about curses." She shrugged to dismiss that. "I've heard most of her through the army, in truth. She's a year and some into her stint, and distinguishing herself with the Northern Horse."

Síochana leaned closer to Kiefan to confide something and he chuckled, told her something that brightened her smile further. He looked to me and then she did too. My brows rose, wondering what it was. He'd lost his near-permanent frown; they both stood at ease and smiling.

Hope and ache tangled each other in my throat.

"How is it she's not one of the nominees?" I asked Leix, sidelong.

She chuckled. "A threadbare margrave? Should a king stoop so low? She's betrothed as well. 'Tis a son of a small house, but a rich one. As good a match as she could."

Kiefan beckoned me with two fingers. With a nod to Leix, I went.

"You never told me Englia married into Caercoed," he said.

"How should I know of that? I was born in Wodenberg." I looked to m'lady Síochana.

"'Twas my grandmothers' mothers who kept a ship's captain for a long winter," she said. "The next year, daughters and a son were born. He wanted to take the boy with him back to Rukharbor, and 'twas the death of their love. I've dreamed of seeing it, someday. Rukharbor. Englia, too. It must be a lovely place."

My memory flicked to the descriptions in Parselev's war-journal. "I'm told there are long stretches of cold marshland," I said. "The snow lingers through the Spring Moon."

"Rukharbor is striking — the cliffs along the coast, the fount tumbling into the sea. On a hill above the city, there's a whale carved into the earth," Kiefan said.

Síochana nodded at his description. "Keto the guardian. You've seen him?"

"I was there last autumn. We collected Duke Seagrace and his knights and brought them south for the king's jousting tournament."

"Oh? Jousting?"

"Do the Caer —?"

She twitched one shoulder. "'Tis a full lance, you use, twelve foot? Caer prefer a glaive, in truth."

Kiefan stroked one thumb across his chin. "Nasty. Six foot?"

"Eight. No tournaments with that. Sport dueling, though."

I backed away slowly as they followed that vein, my mind muddled between hope they'd continue and melancholy that he looked at her with such a smile. I slipped off once I was far enough.

When I stood in the hall's doors, ready to follow everyone down to the party Theo had just announced and looked back, they were still there. Still talking. In the gate-yard, Anders waited for the stable boy to bring Buttercup and Jenner.

I set my teeth on my bottom lip, daring to wonder.

The hand-drum thumped and the lute sang over the rhythm; I tapped my foot and spun with skirts in hand. When I came around, the outer ring of dance partners had shifted and my new match bowed to me.

Kiefan added a wink, which nearly made me laugh. My two beers hadn't worn entirely off yet. I offered my hand on the beat, he took it and we traded places — he stole a kiss from my cheek, as was allowed — and we spun back to each other one step at a time with the beat as well. He offered his hand and we switched again. I stole the kiss back, as was allowed. Pirouette again and I had a new partner.

I suspected Anders had asked the band to play "Ducks in the Mud" as a joke on me.

Baron Eismann was too polite to steal a kiss when I danced with him. When Will's turn came, he did, but I didn't give it back; I wagged a scolding finger at him. Anders, next in the circle, cuffed his shoulder. One more shift and one last turn with my original partner, who did steal his kiss. And got it back. The band finished with a flourish, earning a round of applause.

They'd also earned a round of beer, in truth; they'd played half a dozen dances in full. I'd danced with Anders for most of those, and each time I sat one out he needed reclaiming from Crown Ceelin. The woman paid me no mind, glares or smiles, so I did the same.

Kiefan and Síochana had come to the Riverman last and they were still lingering close all those dances later. Their hands touched, now and then, and there was no mistaking they meant to stick together. I even dared think he was not watching me closely and I could linger near Anders without much danger.

The twin duchesses glowered over their hands of cards from a small game table by the hearth.

Anders caught my arm and passed me his half-full stein. "You look thirsty."

I took a swallow of the rich stout, getting mostly the creamy head. I had to lick that off my top lip. "Did you ask them to play that?"

He smiled. "I've no idea what you mean." Then he confessed further. "I see why you like it, though I'd never have thought you such a flirt."

I raised my nose. "It's a test of one's composure, sir." Then I pulled a longer draught.

Anders took it back to finish it. I leaned against his shoulder as he did and scanned the clusters of people. The entire banquet had come, and perhaps the Riverman was a better place for conversations. Even Crown Ciara seemed warmer, almost at ease, with a stein in one hand and her other arm wrapped in Elect Teleri's. The tavern's main hall was full. We'd barely had room for the dances.

Anders... he took such care with me, perfectly polite and yet letting his hand linger here, a smile twist there. Was he thinking of that kiss the morning before this, as well?

The sun had set some time past. "Rafe will want me," I said, turning toward Anders' ear. He nodded, handing off the empty stein to a barmaid.

"Theo!" Anders raised a hand to our host, across the hall, to take our leave.

"No!" I heard him even over the rumble of voices. Theo cut across the clots toward us, golden among the dark uniforms. He put a hand on each of our arms. "No, no, no, you can't leave. We've hardly gotten started."

"The baby," I said.

"The baby." Theo spread his hands, tossed his head. "The guests will be most dismayed, sir. If m'lady must leave, so be it, but you must stay."

"Good night, Theo." Anders shot a sidelong glance. I leaned a little to follow it, and wasn't surprised to spot Crown Ceelin. Watching us.

"Creep out quickly, then," Theo said, with an affectionate cuff. To me, bowing, "Elect Kate, an honor to have you here."

"And a fine party it was, sir," I replied. "Please, continue."

Through the double doors, we escaped into the frosty night of a near-full Leaf Moon. Anders wrapped an arm around my shoulders; I'd worn just my shawl when the day was warm. We had only to cross the street, though. I cuddled close, inhaling his woolly, horsey scent. Wondered if his skin smelled the same.

My heart quivered. Tonight? Kiefan and Síochana — perhaps? She was betrothed, though, and not a candidate. It would be a terrible risk to kiss Anders again. I knew what a kiss could lead to.

Anders opened the door for me. Inside, Reinhardt and Alice sat at the table, still teaching Herr Schäfer and Trauger to play ott-stagi. "Let me see to the horses," Anders told me, and kissed my cheek good-night. I kissed him back, and my hand found his of its own accord. Squeezed briefly.

Perhaps a bit too tipsy, still. I pressed my eyes shut to focus as I stepped into the warmth and pulled the door shut. "Rafe's asleep?" I asked. His basket sat on the table beside Alice, blanket rising and falling as he breathed.

"Mother let some mercy slip," Alice said. "Perhaps we'll sleep a little more tonight."

"Not now you've jinxed it."

"Where's Will?" Reinhardt asked, throwing a trump card into the game.

I hadn't thought to look for him. "Still there, most likely."

"Fetch him back — he's had enough by now. Send Anders."

M'lord had strict ideas of how much one should drink, dance, or take ease. I hadn't wondered for too long why he and Anders had come to butt heads over nearly everything. I pushed open the side door and went to give the orders — though a corner of my mind thought perhaps there'd be a delay. A kiss in the shadowy barn, perhaps hands wandering…

One lantern burned in the stable. The flash of a pale grey skirt caught the corner of my eye. I whirled toward it, kir rising to my hand, and the Crown's handmaid froze with eyes wide. Bévin, that was her name. Then she bolted, the heavy barn door creaking as she shoved through.

I turned. Anders stood before Jenner's stall, the lantern in his hand. Brow furrowed, even in the dim light. His eyes met mine, but he held his silence.

"Why…?" My faint tipsy haze melted away; my gut knew why the Crown's handmaid came here. Anders' summons. My voice lowered, strengthened. "Did she bring a message from Crown Ceelin?"

His head tipped. "What do you know of it?"

"What was your answer?"

He unlatched Jenner's stall. "I told her I have chores to see to." Hanging the lantern on a nail, he closed the gate and spoke to the horse.

He'd said no. Tannait's jest of sending Crown's Blades to serve summons — a jest, surely. They wouldn't dare attack a family — at night — when all were in the tavern tipsy and dancing —

I strode back into the main room. "Get your sword," I told Reinhardt. "Anders', too. Alice, fetch Will back. Quickly."

"When we finish this hand," my father-in-law said, focused on his cards. Alice frowned up at me, piqued by my tone.

I tightened it further and shifted my kir to my right hand. "Sir, I am the bound elect of your saints and I said get your sword."

That tore his gaze up to my glowing hand. Alice scrambled from her seat and trotted out the door; Reinhardt stood, knees popping, and touched his fist to his chest. I leaned on the door sill to watch Alice go, and looked up and down the empty street. The Shepherd's light dimmed behind a cloud, then strengthened. I called kir and got only responses from behind me and faint echoes from the Riverman. A heartbeat later, Alice dragged Will by one wrist through its doors.

When I turned, Reinhardt stood with a sheathed sword in either hand, precise as the cut of his beard. "M'lady."

"Did Will bring his?" I asked.

"No."

Will had shaken off Alice's grip and grumbled as he shut the door behind the two of them. "I'd have come, no need to grab me."

"Take Anders his sword and help him finish." I pointed Will toward the barn. To Reinhardt, I said, "Sir," and beckoned him.

At the outer kitchen door, he gave me a brief sketch of how two dozen Blessed knights might attack a house with only two swords and an elect inside. It sounded grim to me. He didn't ask why I wanted to know.

Across the wheel-rutted road, the upstairs windows of the Caer house glowed. A campfire burned among the tents behind it. No sign of trouble.

Perhaps I had read too much into Tannait's words. Returning to the table, I found Anders sitting, with his sword on, shuffling the deck while the other four watched. "Deal for poker," I said, sitting down beside Alice. "Seven of us, so make it Flock's poker. Seven hands, and if there's no trouble — we'll try to get some sleep."

I wasn't sure if I would, though.

CHAPTER 10

Anders was out on Shade when I walked back from the disciple's dance next morning. The blue roan trotted easily and at a silent command wheeled around tight and burst to a gallop, dark tail streaming. I looked over to the Blades' camp and sure enough, those standing by the campfire watched. I couldn't quite make out their faces, but all wore the dark blue uniform.

I wanted to tell him — last night, he'd asked no questions. He was no fool, and surely knew what Ceelin wanted, if not why. I still wasn't sure what to say, and the disciple's dance hadn't been able to clarify me. The abbess had asked if I was well, the balance poses gave me such trouble. But Anders didn't come in for breakfast and there was no chance to try.

Walking up to the manor, I struggled with how to tell Saint Qadeem. I'd reported the general conversation with Tannait, and he'd indicated that he knew the tradition. He'd said no more, though.

I kept my silence for now.

Frau Branwen, Frau Pryderi, and Síochana stood next to Kiefan, smiling. Paper and inkpots waited on the high table, and a craft-handed secretary trimmed a fresh point on his quill. Kiefan beckoned me over and caught my hand, kissed my knuckles.

"So early?" I asked, with brows arched. His knotted kir wasn't in its usual place; it clustered behind his eyes.

"Kaufmann's party ran late," he murmured.

"'Twas well bargained," Frau Pryderi said with a smile. "Theo did acquit himself well, and we shall present these terms to the Crown."

The secretary copied from a much scribbled-on and beer-stained sheet of paper, which also looked to have been stepped on at some point.

"Once it's readable, I'll be the judge of that," Kiefan said.

"Do recall the matter of the lighthouse?" Síochana asked. He nodded, taking a mug of hot mint tea from a maid with a tray of them.

"M'lady?" She offered me one. "Your cloak?" The maid draped my cloak over her arm and offered tea to the Caer ladies.

Kiefan watched the secretary's quill bob, reading over his shoulder, and added a few points of his own in quiet words. I'd seen him steal a kiss from Síochana during "Ducks in the Mud." She'd stolen it back. I wondered just how late the party had run, and why.

The doors opened, letting in thin morning light. A Caer in gambeson and mail, riding leathers, and cloak strode in, gloved hands fisted and shoulders tight. Her long brown braid swung free over one shoulder. Crown Ceelin. Trailing by several steps, her sister followed with arms crossed, Elect Teleri by her side with kir loosely ready. Tannait, dressed for riding as well. Two more Crown's Blades.

Kiefan circled around Síochana to meet her. "What —"

"We ride." Crown Ceelin planted her fists on her hips, lip curled. She barked out orders in Caer, and the three ladies stiffened, then grabbed up their draft of the terms.

Ceelin returned to Arceal. "Soon as all's ready, shall be off, and should any follow we'll not hesitate to defend ourselves. Am I clear?"

A pit opened in my stomach.

Síochana met Kiefan's eyes as she passed, her mouth pressed tight, and she followed her companions out the door.

"Leaving? Crown, last night we came to terms on —" Kiefan raised a hand, but Ceelin threw up an arm to stop him and the Blades' swords cleared their sheaths in a blink. At the door behind them, the King's Guard drew as well. Kir gathered in my hand and I saw Teleri and Tannait stiffen in response.

"Hold!" Kiefan's voice cut through the noise. "A word, please, m'lady. To explain. We were friends last night."

Ceelin glared, shifting her weight on her feet. "The Crown was insulted last night."

Kiefan looked to me, Mother have mercy. I clenched my teeth shut and focused on the two elect rather than meet his gaze. "If anyone has insulted you, m'lady," he said, voice low, "give me a chance to set it right before you abandon all hope of alliance. We have common cause, and common danger in standing alone. Too much is at stake."

Her shoulders eased a little. A gesture from Teleri and the Blades sheathed their swords. "You have 'till next morn to repair the insult and offer apology. Only 'till dawn, and then we ride," the Crown said.

Kiefan's brow lowered. "It will be done. Tell me his name, and I'll give his orders personally."

I knew it before she said it. "'Twas Anders Bockmann."

My hand clenched, drawing my kir back. He'd said no to Crown Ceelin, and now —

Kiefan's voice rose, toward his Guard at the door. "Bring the Rossweides. Drag them, if need be."

"She has no —" I growled through my teeth.

His eyes had gone stone-cold. "Argue with Woden."

Two of my teeth throbbed in my jaw, remembering Gentle Woden. I closed my mouth.

Kiefan's tone softened. "M'lady, might I offer a token of good faith? An apology for this misunderstanding?"

Crown Ceelin stepped back, arching her brows. "Mayhaps."

"I'm told you've admired Baron Rossweide's horses. They're the finest in Wodenberg. Take two that please you."

She had to fight a smirk, and fight it hard. If she asked for a pair of colts...

"'Tis a noble gift," she said. "The stockinged black and the grey, then, if the Baron and his kin will deliver the mares themselves."

"Before noon, m'lady."

"Shall trust Wodenberg's honor, then. And take its true measure from this." Crown Ceelin turned and led her escort out the doors, through the King's Guard on either side with hardly a blink. The pit in my stomach shifted in watching her go, and I couldn't have said whether the Caer would ride in the morning or not. Not for want of Anders' honor — but did she truly think this would do in the place of seduction?

As they took their leave, I opened my bond and sent what I could make clear thoughts of to Qadeem. Much of it was anger, though.

/ Woden's disciple / Father Duty / then husband /

When he felt the stab of that, though my bond, Qadeem sent more.

/ if he's yours / none can steal /

I clung to that. Another thought came to me as horses rode into the gate-yard outside. I caught glimpses of Reinhardt, of Shade's blue roan head, through the open doors. "They would abandon us over one slight?" I muttered to Kiefan. "Will a marriage be enough to hold them in an alliance?"

"Crown Ceelin doesn't play the game so well as her sister — perhaps there was a slight, but I saw it's little concern to her. This is a play-act, an excuse to make demands," he said. "If Anders was fool enough to give them excuses, then he can mend it. If there was a slight at all. I saw none given last night, and we were at the Riverman until near dawn."

"You've no idea what she wishes, then."

"It's Anders. Must I guess?"

That twisted my mouth. Ever ready to believe the worst of him.

Reinhardt led, Will on his right, Anders on his left. The baron dropped to one knee, fist to his chest, and they followed. At a nod from Kiefan, they rose.

"If not for Caercoed," he said, "Castle Kaltkern would still be under siege — in the best of situations. The Father only knows what might've come of their saints tunneling under the walls had they not been pressed by Seagrace. Had Saint Qadeem not been close enough to come to Woden's aid. If not for Caercoed, thousands more would lie dead now." He looked Anders in the eye. "You insulted the Crown last night. Do you deny it?"

Anders' gaze shifted to the distance, and his face went blank. Reinhardt's eyes closed, jaw clenching, his hand tightening on the pommel of his sword. Ruined, all the bridge-mending Anders had done since he took the Father's Discipline. I didn't doubt that.

As there was no denial, Kiefan went on. "You will do whatever the Crown requires, before next morning, to make your amends. If Caercoed rides from here offended, withdrawing their support and severing this alliance, you will answer to me." That got another moment to sink in. "And then you will answer to Saint Woden. Baron Rossweide, you and yours will deliver the stockinged black mare and the grey to the Crowns before noon."

M'lord Reinhardt dropped to one knee in obeisance, closely followed by Will. Anders stood, blank as a wall. His fist went to his chest, accepting the orders. My jaw clenched tighter, holding back the anger until I had words for it.

"Dismissed."

I knotted my kir into a hush sphere and threw it up around the two of us. "You have no right to make a whore of him! The Mother's Discipline binds him and he said no as he ought to."

If that surprised Kiefan, it was for less than a heartbeat. "What's it to you who he beds? Let the Crown keep him, if she wishes."

"He's my husband!" It flew from my mouth in shock, before I could think.

Kiefan's voice lowered as he leaned closer. "Leave him, then. Bring Rafe. Wenda would love to have a baby in the castle again."

My mouth fell open for a heartbeat. In the castle? As his mistress? "Woden would —"

"Woden knows he cannot game with the Crowns — your own teacher was witness to how he negotiates. After all his raging through my bond that first night here, he slammed that shut and left me to it. He'd do no better with Arcea. Woden needs me." Kiefan's surety was so rooted that my own faltered. "And I need you."

I looked away, heart sinking. Grateful, of a sudden, I hadn't kissed Anders last night. He'd see it, as he'd seen the lies —

Kiefan's head tipped and my throat tightened. "What's it to you who he beds?"

Soft, almost a whisper. My mind groped for a safe answer. "I swore the same oath as he. Duty says I must be his support, however I can. He told the Crown no."

"Duty to the kingdom trumps." Kiefan took a deep breath. "One night at worst, Kate. How hard could she ride him, truly?"

He walked from my hush sphere before I unraveled it and went to see what the secretary had copied. Done with the matter, it would seem. Miserable, I took my leave.

———————✕———————

He avoided me.

Sprite and Dove needed washing, which took both Trauger and the maid Hilda going to and from the river for water. I walked the barn with Rafe on my shoulder, watching the horses turn sudsy and then glossy from water. Anders brushed the mares down with long, sure strokes. Reinhardt braided their tails with deft fingers. Will rubbed the tack to a shine. Rossweide green saddle blankets, with saddles atop that. Anders tightened the girths and polished the brass stirrups a bit more with his sleeve.

He never once met my eyes, even in passing.

Three men made short work of it all. They were beautiful horses, true enough, they all were — Anders had explained the details of why Sprite was finer than Shade, and why Jenner would never be more than a courier, but they were all equal to me.

Then the men went to groom and dress themselves as well. I lingered in the barn, trying to work out a question for Saint Qadeem.

/ might keep him? / this tradition? /

A pause. / unlikely / old things fade / were pale / when I saw them /

I hesitated, searching for what to say.

/ hard question /

/ ask /

/ wise? / good allies? /

/ needed /

The only answer ever given, it seemed. My jaw tightened.

/ why? / enemy asked for parley / peace /

/ no / no binding / The concept he sent me for Arcea was one of muggy heat and fear.

/ binding? /

/ too much / we must speak / report / sundown /

Rafe twitched on my shoulder in his sleep. I stood in the barn's open doors, looking out across the fenced pastures and little wanting to trade it for Castle Kaltkern. Selfish of me, to want one man for books and stolen moments, one man for home and hearth.

I had to hope Anders pleased Ceelin enough that Kiefan could pick a Caer bride who pleased him — so that I might love my husband while I had him. A bitter twist, that.

The word echoed in my mind. Love Anders. I'd always liked him, ever since that day he freed my foot from the stirrup. An echo of the gratitude I'd felt when Rafe was born washed through me, pulling the corners of my mouth down in melancholy.

My menfolk came into the barn smelling of soap, fresh-shaven, and dressed in their finest greens. Reinhardt took both the mares' reins and led the way. Will walked at his right hand, both of them clear-eyed and determined to do well.

Anders trailed behind and I caught his hand. In his surprise, he forgot himself and our eyes met. "Whatever happens," I whispered. "Come home."

Perhaps I ought to be more angry, but I feared for him. He saw the truth, I hoped, in my eyes. Some of the fear in his melted, I saw.

His hand was strong, but I could take a hard squeeze without wincing. And then he stole a kiss, such a kiss...

I sat by the kitchen hearth, still heart-sick from it, when Alice returned late from the market. Hilda hadn't yet come to help start dinner, and I had knocked down the bread dough for tonight's meal and set it out for its second rising. When Alice spotted me she rushed from the doorway to kneel beside me.

"It's all over the market — did Anders insult the queens? Is he —?" She put her hand on my arm, eyes widening at the melancholy on my face.

"He's gone to make amends." My voice cracked, and I had to clear my throat.

"With the gift horses?" She'd seen the preparations; she'd set out some cold mutton and bread on the table for a noon meal before she left. I nodded. "I didn't mean to be so long," Alice said, holding up one of the skeins of dark green wool in her basket. "It took some hunting to find the right color, and then the questions! Theo Kaufmann and Radulf Brauer were worked over for all the rumor mill could get from them. They wouldn't let me go without a good squeezing — I told them you've made a good man of him."

She expected that to help, but it only made my mouth purse to one side. She did the same, and crept closer on her knees, and put an arm around me. "What must he do to make amends?"

I breathed a laugh. "It's Anders."

Alice frowned as she stroked my back. "He's a fine flirt, but sweetening an angry queen's a tall order for any —"

I laughed more honestly. "She's been flirting with him since the moment they arrived." True, Alice wouldn't have seen that. I'd have thought the rumor mill would tell her.

She paused. "Oh, so the queen's angry that it was only a dalliance?"

A frown creased my brow as I tipped my head to stare at her. Alice took her hand from my back, leaned away.

"You can't be shocked. It's been how many moons? One night, Kate, surely the saints can spare you one night to dally with your own husband. A man can only go hungry so long."

"He's not like that," came out of my mouth — the truth, which I had to follow up with a limping half-truth. "Since Rafe, I don't want —" I got tangled in how to explain.

"Not like that? Not a man? Don't try to say you've forgotten. Father's bloody balls, Kate, I haven't forgotten and it's been years." Alice threw up her hands and stood. "He's puppy-struck for you. Just put out your fool hand," she told me.

My fool hands. I put one on each elbow. "He told Crown Ceelin no," I said. The front door opened as I finished. "That's why she's angry."

Reinhardt and Will appeared in the doorway. "Anders stayed to explain the mares' commands," Reinhardt said, his words clipped.

I only nodded to that.

The Order's apprentices had expected me for more tutoring; I didn't go. I took Rafe outside to watch Will carry water to the pastured horses and worked at hoisting my baby with kir-vines. My focus wouldn't let me lift more than a few dry leaves. I was listening for horses' hooves. His voice. Anything to know that he was well and home.

Love. Without his flirting, without a single book of d'Ovio Alain's essays…

At sundown, I reported to my saint that Anders had stayed. Qadeem sent a nod and asked no more.

It was Alice who asked, "Are you well?" in Englic when I'd sat watching the cook-fire for some time. She and Hilda nearly had dinner ready, and the menfolk sat at the table in the receiving-room. Rafe slept in his basket cradle, freshly nursed.

"I will be, when he comes home."

We ate roast mutton with potatoes and onions. Afterward, the cards came out again and we dealt poker rather than ott-stagi so that six could play. We gambled for stories rather than coins, wherein the holder of the worst hand must tell something true at the request of the winner. Alice would always demand something far too personal, I knew from our games as children, and I begged the Mother silently that I not lose to her.

Sometime after Hilda left for the night, Anders came in by the kitchen door. His dark greens and the cloak melted into the shadows as he crossed the kitchen, and he emerged into the front room looking much the same as he'd left. Quieter, perhaps.

I was up from my chair and reaching for him in a heartbeat. He intercepted my hands with his own, stopped me at arm's length with his mouth set in a grim line. Then he kissed my knuckles, lingering. I cupped his face, called his kir as I did with Kiefan. No harm done, that I could see.

Though I did catch a whiff of brandy.

Alice stood, putting down her cards. "There's mutton —"

"No, don't trouble yourself," he said. "I'm going to the Riverman. Ola will draw a hot bath for a few bruns. Perhaps a stein with Theo, and I'll be back. I only meant to say that I'm home." He took my hands from his cheeks, squeezed them.

"Don't be out late — they might still have the hunt in the morning," Reinhardt said.

Anders nodded. He let my hands go and left through the front door. The Shepherd was full tonight, but the sky must have clouded over, for there was only darkness to see when Anders stepped outside.

When I went to bed, I lay awake waiting for the door to open again. Losing last night's sleep had taken its toll, though, and I didn't hear Anders return.

———————————✚———————————

The morning was dark, but I heard no rain. I stirred up the fire, as I always did, pinned on my felt cloak, and left through the kitchen door. When I turned from latching it behind me, the sight stopped me in my tracks.

A crest of trampled, dead grass ran between the wagon ruts, which were dusty brown. The huddle of pale — my brow furrowed as the outstretched arm gave me reference to grasp it. A woman lay half-curled between the ruts, back to me. Naked and pale, streaked with angry blotches.

I ran. Too white, she was too white. A long brown braid, hanging in one rut. Her legs were splayed open to show off the streaks of dried blood on her thighs, on her ass.

The scream stabbed my ears as I dropped to my knees beside her. At the Caer house's side door, a maid dropped the slops bucket, her hands paralyzed. I called kir, got nothing from the body. The shoulder was cold under my hand. I turned her, spotting bruises on her forearms, her cheek.

Ceelin. Short hairs made a curl by her ear, that was how I knew her from Crown Ciara. Nose broken and the blood long dry. Four dark, angry streaks on her throat. Scratches on her breasts. Staring.

The screams shifted from one throat to another, and I looked up. A Blade stumbled, wide-eyed, when she saw her queen's battered face, and shouted a word. The second Blade behind her turned and ran into the house, shouting too.

Blood had settled along the side Ceelin lay on. That happened only after some time, I knew. How long had she lay out here? When did she die? How? The house was full of Blades, two elect, and I'd been just across the street.

"Father's fucking mercy!" Anders' hand snatched my elbow, yanked me up; I stumbled and fell against him.

The Crown's Blade pointed at us with her sword. "Away!" she snarled in Arceal. "Away!" Behind her, a window shutter opened upstairs and Bévin stumbled back, hands covering her mouth. From the door, Elect Tannait shoved her way through the wailing maids. She wore no hose, and her hair flew uncombed. She froze, jaw dropping.

Anders dragged me, willing or not. "No! I must see —!" He ignored me. "Anders, we need to know!" I glimpsed Reinhardt and Will in passing, and Alice inside the kitchen door as we went. Anders shoved the door shut and hauled me across the kitchen. His sheathed sword was in his hand, likely grabbed on reflex. Rafe's cradle was by the kitchen fire; I saw him wiggling under a blanket.

I planted my feet and twisted in his grip. "What're —"

"Kate." Anders let go finally, voice dropping as he stepped close. "I swear, Kate, I never hurt her. I swear. On my life, my honor, my love —" His knuckles brushed my cheek and he bit his lip.

His eyes were a knife through my heart. "Of course you didn't," I whispered back.

Kir bloomed, brilliant, and the door crashed inward. Teleri's sword led, wrapped in green kir, her eyes lantern-lit with fury. Anders drew, dropping the sheath, and I threw out a shield before him, wide enough to split the kitchen. She snarled and slashed it open, blurring through the gap at Blessing speed. Anders met her, and sparks sprayed where their swords met. I spun out a kir-vine, twined her ankle and threw my weight back to pull —

The ram struck me square in the chest, knocked air from my lungs, slammed me through plaster into stone, and pain exploded across my back. I fell. Black whirled through my head and a strong call pulled at my kir. I clutched it, heart snarling. But I felt its hammering falter through the roar of agony. Kir shot into me through my bond, throwing my eyes open with a gasp.

My spine broken, my ribs shattered. The gush of kir turned under my mind's hand, whirling into patterns and sweeping the pain away. My eyes focused. My ears cleared.

My baby, screaming.

I leaped from the floor. Launched through the hole in the wall, and Tannait bending over, her hands on my son. My rage struck before thought; hands, arms, their structure down to the bones, flashed past my eyes. Skin flayed from muscles that bloomed out, curling red as rose petals, tendons and veins flaring wide, pale bone stripped to the shoulders — my baby fell from her ruined grip and she stopped my kir with hers. I only had eyes for the bundle and reached for it with two vines.

A blow knocked me sideways to the ground. Kir looped around my throat, choking. I tore it away, lunged up on my knees and twisted kir to lash back.

Rafe shrieked as he flew, a kir-vine launching him across the room, and my mind went blank. I was free; I dove to catch him. My vines wrapped around him, brought him safe to my hands.

At the kitchen door, Tannait clutched her ruined arms with a cloud of kir as she retreated. Her eyes rolled wild in panic despite her thick shield. Behind her, Teleri dragged Anders on his knees, wrists bound. He struggled to keep me in sight, screaming, but I could barely hear him: don't fight them, Kate, don't…

He vanished behind a wall of blue. Teleri turned, kir-charmed sword at ready to cover the retreat. Tannait stumbled past her and was caught by a Blade. The woman fought a horrified shudder at the ruin of the elect's arms.

My throat tightened. I hugged Rafe close. He was sticky with sprayed blood, his face screwed tight and red in wailing. I laid him against my shoulder, calling his patterns to be sure he was unhurt.

/ !? /

/ … / ruined /

/ coming /

I had no more thoughts than that. They had all fled. There was shouting outside, Alemannic words as well as Caer. Duty. I gained my feet, breathing hard, head spinning from the blows. I'd torn a hole in the wattle-and-daub kitchen wall and struck the fireplace beyond. Anders' sword lay, bright and clean, on the packed-dirt floor.

Rafe's basket burned bright and tall. It had been bumped partly over the fire-pit. My heart quavered, numb as it was.

Will appeared in the doorway, breathing hard, taking in the toppled benches, the fire, the hole and — Alice, huddled against the wall, sobbing and shaking.

"Are you hurt?" I reached for her, striding across the kitchen.

She leaped into Will's arms, clutched him for dear life as she gaped at me. He backed away, too, shifting her behind him. "Are you?" he stammered.

I looked down at my dress, saw kir-stars twinkling in my green cloak — and blood. My cheek throbbed, cut open, and I wasn't sure what had done that. "Only a scratch," I said. "Alice?" I offered her Rafe. She cringed, unable to blink.

"You — you —" she whispered.

"Alice, it's me."

"I saw —" Her head shook, a terrified tremble. "No, no, you can't —"

Kiefan was coming, I could feel his kir. I set my mouth and walked past them; they were glad to give me room. The Caer house was shut up tight now, the upstairs windows cracked only enough for an archer and crossbow to see out. Baron Eismann's armsmen were forming up in a line in the main street and along the rutted road, their shields lapped over each other. The camp behind the house was empty; the small barn was shut up, too, and likely full of Blades.

Crown Ceelin's body was gone, taken back by her sisters. Along with the man she'd last been with.

CHAPTER 11

"Those shutters are sturdy," Eismann's captain told Kiefan. "Might get through them, might not. Their archers will get shots off, most likely, before we can put them down." He jerked his head at the upstairs windows of the Riverman, now full of our hawk-eyed bowmen.

"Only two doors, you said?"

"Front and side. Barn's separate. Not a house we'd want to storm, given a choice."

"Pray the Father we have a choice."

I'd repaired my wound, changed my dress, finally calmed Alice enough to look me in the eye again, and now stood waiting for Crown Ciara as promised. The sun was well up and peeking through breaks in the cloud. Our wide ring of armsmen had settled to kneeling behind their shields.

Through my bond, I gave a clearer report to my saint.

/ any could strangle / man / strong woman / who else hates? /

I had no answer. Or, rather, I was the one with best reason to hate Crown Ceelin, more so than Anders. I would not have strangled her, though. I'd beat her with harsh words, but nothing fatal.

The front door opened. My heart dared stir. The armsmen shifted aside to let Kiefan, Captain Aleks, and me pass through to the gap between our line and the house. Captain Aleks moved in front of him — she wore her mail, and he'd declined to have his fetched — but Kiefan put a hand on her shoulder.

"Let me speak."

She frowned, jaw clenched, but stepped aside.

Likewise, Crown Ciara put Elect Teleri behind her. M'lady Leix stood on her other side, grim-faced. The Crown wore her riding gear, ready to leave as she'd threatened. Red rimmed her green eyes. Her hands clenched in fists.

"Withdraw and let us pass," she said, just above a seething hiss. "We cannot quit this place too quickly."

"Release the knight you took," Kiefan replied.

"Shall leave him for burial, nothing more."

Fear prickled every inch of my skin. My kir gathered in my chest. I felt Teleri's rise in answer, saw her eyes widen.

"If you've stolen one of Woden's Blessed and murdered him without cause —"

"The bastard did slay a Crown," Ciara snarled.

"In a house full of Crown's Blades?" It burst from my mouth. "With two elect under your roof, and a third across the street?"

Elect Teleri snapped back. "Strangling needs no kir. Nor beating. Nor rape."

"In silence?"

"If her mouth were sealed."

Crown Ciara's face clenched as the words tore past her.

"He does not know any such charm." As soon as it was said, I knew what Teleri would answer.

"Shall claim he knows nothing of the sword, if need be."

"Shall deal to the killer as such are dealt." Ciara fought the raw edge in her voice. "House Gwatcyn shall withdraw and escort my sister home to the Mother Tree. We leave at noon, when the remainder of my Blades come for me, as they've had no word from us this morn." Three-quarters of her escort had camped outside Vorspitz, for lack of room for the horses.

"You will present the proof of this knight's crime before you take your justice. By order of Saint Qadeem, no disciple is convicted without the proof laid before his lord." Kiefan's voice rose.

Ciara's lip curled. "So keep your saints' laws for your own. We owe you nothing!"

"Kill Woden's knights without cause and we are at war, Caercoed!" I saw muscle clench in Kiefan's neck and jaw. "And you will not leave here alive."

Her anguish snapped into defiance. "My daughters will avenge me."

Qadeem nudged me, through my bond, and I nearly jumped in surprise. "Did you see her killed then?" I shouted, and glares became frowns. "She could not have lay out all night unseen, but he left your house long before midnight. Didn't he?"

Ciara held her stony silence. Elect Teleri answered for her. "'Twas the stable-hand that admitted him after midnight. Believing he was welcome, as he'd been in the afternoon."

That sank my heart, but my mind still scrabbled for hope. Theo. I turned toward the Riverman. It was shut up tight, save for the archers in the windows.

"Present your witnesses," Kiefan said. "Bring them to the great hall at noon and let them speak. If not, we set fire to the house and the barn. Your Blades will not save you." He turned and strode back through the line of armsmen, followed by Captain Aleks.

/ gentle Woden /

/ where are you? /

/ there / before noon /

Across the gap, my eyes met m'lady Leix's as she turned to follow Ciara into the house. Leix's grimace deepened for a heartbeat. Then she turned away to hear something the Crown said and nodded.

Theo. I had to find Theo.

"I was a-bed early last night, and not to be disturbed," Theo told me with a shake of his head. "A man can only go hungry so long before he makes do with what's at hand."

That twisted my moment of despair into a sour frown. He caught it as he sipped his mug of mint tea and frowned back.

"I speak for myself — why? You've —" He hesitated when I stood from the table with a sigh.

"You didn't see him, then? He meant to share a stein with you."

Theo put down both his mug and his quill. "No, I didn't see him. Ola! Was Anders here last night?"

The housemistress looked up from sweeping under the tables. "Which one's that, m'lord?"

"Knight's crest, white-blonde, charm the horns off a goat?"

"Ah, that one." Ola nodded to herself. "Took a long bath, yes. Didn't see if he stayed afterward."

"What's he gotten himself into this time?" Theo asked, with such innocence that I stared. A heartbeat of that, and his perked brows shifted into alarm. "He's the one they snatched? Father's bloody fucking balls…"

"They think he killed the Crown."

Theo started gathering up his papers and ink, shaking his head. "Mother only knows if I can help, but say the word if I can. Fechter! Are we all stuck in here?"

The guard at the Riverman's door shook his head. "Just the Caer, sir."

———————————✕———————————

"Majesty? A message from the watch post at Südenteich."

The courier dropped to one knee, holding up the sealed paper. Kiefan took it, glanced at the message. Frowned, but then nodded. It was a town across the Felsherz, I knew, halfway to Ansehen. "Wait on my reply."

"The Captain says your guests are at the gate as well."

"Early," Kiefan muttered, echoing my thought. The great hall's doors stood open to the intermittent sun, and it wasn't quite noon. "Dismissed."

My knuckles whitened as I clenched my threaded fingers on each other. Gregor waited with the jeweled crown in hand; Kiefan traded his plain gold band for it, settling it over the crease in his scalp. He'd dressed for this, kingly in black and gold, jewels, and the lamia-fang brooch.

Alice had brought up my pale green dress and my baby to nurse, and I'd sent her home afterward. If this turned badly she didn't need to see such things again.

Eismann's company of armsmen left a broad aisle for the Caer to approach the keep from the stockade's gate. Crown Ciara paused on the sill of the doorway, her fine white gown lit by the sun for a moment. Her crown gleamed in her dark bundle of braided hair as she stepped inside. King's Guard lined the hall in full mail and helms, each with a hand resting on his sword.

Likewise, the Crown's Blades were ready with mail over their rich blue uniforms. They carried their helms, though, and marched with heads held high, as if they were not surrounded and badly outnumbered.

Teleri prowled at the head of the column, her kir wrapped around her in a cloak. Tannait, beside her, wore a fine, golden dress with long sleeves that bulged over the wreck I'd made. No mere physician could fix such a thing — though they'd managed to keep the flesh alive and tucked her hands into the sleeves to hide the naked bone. I could feel the kir knit into her arms from here. Her face was serene and alert.

In truth, I wasn't sure how to repair it myself. I flicked my memory through Parselev's charms. He'd never done such a thing to a living creature, from what I found. It had been a party trick, just as he had done it at my wedding.

Crown Ciara stood a couple yards from Kiefan and me — and Duke Haken, in his mail and black tabard — and folded her arms. "As you summoned, Caercoed has come. This morn, we did find our Crown murdered, by Sir Anders Bockmann, left naked in the street to shame her and her people. Do you deny it?"

I would, but she addressed the king. My stomach roiled at the charges, because somewhere the true killer slipped away from us. The beast was loose in Vorspitz, doing as it wished, while an innocent man was dragged away — if they'd hurt Anders, if they'd killed him… my heart shivered in my chest as my eyes darted to Tannait. I clamped my fear down.

"I trust the messages we've carried between you and your remaining Blades were delivered as promised."

She drew a slow breath before admitting, "'Tis satisfactory. Do you deny the charges?"

"I see no accused."

"'Tis a surety against my safe return."

"Is he alive?" I asked, and it came out harsher than I expected.

Her cold gaze slid to me. "Mayhaps your butcher should stand down, Wodenberg."

Behind her, I saw taut nerves in stiff spines and knots of kir at ready in all her Blades. Let them fear. Some corner of my heart was glad to sink its teeth into that.

Kiefan's voice lowered a notch. "Present your evidence, Caercoed."

Crown Ciara drew herself up another inch, if possible, just as I felt kir approaching. We four elect looked as one toward the door, and what landed there was a knot powerful enough that even the least gifted felt it.

Cloak fluttering around him, Saint Qadeem arced over the column of Blades and alit in the gap between Ciara and Kiefan. The King's Guard dropped to one knee in unison, fists pressed to their hearts in obeisance. The ermine lining flashed white as Qadeem swept his cloak over his shoulders; Ciara retreated a few steps behind the shields Tannait and Teleri spun out.

His black hair and close-cropped beard sparkled with raindrops, and his cloak as well. He surveyed the Caer with a glance and offered them a deep nod. "Peace, Elect Tannait, Elect Teleri. Crown of Caercoed. I am Saint Qadeem, guardian of Wodenberg, and I would not see further bloodshed today. Let us resolve this. Elect?" He held out both brown hands to Tannait.

The shields unraveled, the kir was tucked away. Tannait hesitated, as it was clear she couldn't touch his hands.

"You've taken grievous harm in service to Father Duty," Qadeem said.

She took a step toward him, and his kir spun out across the gap. The sleeves writhed, then loosened, and two mended hands emerged as they ought to. Her eyes shut and she dipped a low curtsy to him, her head bowed.

"Saint Sabh does thank you. As do I."

"Let it not be said that Wodenberg is ill-equipped against its enemies."

"Having sounded your messengers, we expected no less." Tannait looked to Kiefan and I as she stood. Serene, still. Chill.

I had thought her a friend, or near enough to one. Doubtful there was any of that left.

Tannait held up a hand for a heartbeat. "Saint Sabh requests safe passage, Saint Qadeem. She would speak directly."

"Once we've rooted out the killer, it will be an honor to meet Saint Sabh," he said with another deep nod. "It's by my rule that there must be evidence presented before judgment is passed. Make your case, Crown of Caercoed."

He took Duke Haken's place beside Kiefan. At a barked order from Captain Aleks, the Guard stood and resumed their watch on the guests. Crown Ciara summoned Bévin, her sister's maid, to tell her story.

The girl trembled, eyes locked on our saint, as she stammered it out. She had carried the summons of oíche-te to Anders, and he had refused. He had appeared as part of the gifting of the mares, and Crown Ceelin wished him to instruct her on the horses' gaits and commands.

"Reluctant, Highness," she answered when Ciara prompted her for his attitude.

"'Twas resentful, you said."

"Yes, resentful. But did go, as asked. 'Twas nightfall ere they returned."

The Crown nodded. "Dismissed. Elect Teleri?"

She turned toward her Captain of the Blades, who stood with sword-hip cocked. "In the stables, we spoke a moment as he saw to the mares' unsaddling. Did tell him to leave it to our own and he wasn't pleased by that. But he left."

When Elect Teleri finished, a pause. Which lengthened into a silence. Crown Ciara clasped her hands, clenching her jaw, and took a breath to speak.

"This stable-hand you spoke of?" Kiefan interrupted her thought. "Let her give her accusation."

Poison in her green eyes. "She's not been seen since morn."

My heart leaped. My second thought tempered my hope; Kiefan said it aloud.

"None have left your house since morning."

Qadeem broke his silence. "You have a cambifax, Crown."

A shape-shifter. In human disguise. All the pieces fell in place in a heartbeat: the murder, the accusation, the stable hand — the kir flare. Where we'd met the monster ourselves, wearing a face Tannait knew, who pointed us toward some figment as a distraction. My jaw hung open. I closed it.

And the creature must still be in there. In a different face.

Tannait pulled kir from the three closest Blades and threw herself out the open doors. Guards drew, Blessing-quick, as she cleared their heads, but at Qadeem's order the men let her pass. Whether they could've caught her, I wasn't so sure.

/ changed face / no flare? / I sent to Qadeem.

/ small change / no flare / animal to human / flare /

"Your elect risks much, going alone," Qadeem said aloud. "Should you need our aid, you have it."

"'Tis our eldest," Teleri said, "and able."

Kiefan returned to the main question. "You have no case without this stable hand. Sir Anders left after sundown, irked perhaps but in peace."

"Shall bring his confession, if 'twould suffice."

Kiefan's brows rose as a chill shot down my spine. "You have his confession?"

Ciara's eyes narrowed. "Soon."

My kir surged with my pulse. An order to hold arrowed through my bond, and though it made my teeth grind I obeyed. Kiefan looked to Saint Qadeem, and I caught a nod exchanged. Puzzlement skittered through my anger as Kiefan beckoned Ciara closer. What did they agree to, what...? They had to be torturing Anders. For nothing.

The Crown came slowly. Stiff with mistrust, but she came.

"You've a cambifax among you," Kiefan said. "Do you question a saint?"

"Arcea's feared murderers — and yet I live. Does your saint question that?" She held her hand out to Qadeem, chin high, and he called her patterns. She had no kir gift; she couldn't be the cambifax. "Should Tannait bring proof of a cambifax, 'twill suffice for me. Ere that, shall have this knight's confession, and my justice."

Just above a murmur, Kiefan asked, "What would you offer?"

She spat out a laugh. "Offer? When 'tis I who's wronged?"

"You cannot ride. Your southern passes are snowed in now and you'll lose half your knights at best. I cannot let blood spill cheaply. I've no wish to storm the house or burn it, but I will."

"Attack and he dies first." Ciara said it, but with little edge to it. Kiefan nodded.

/ hold /

My teeth might break for clenching my jaw, but I held my kir in a fist.

"Or mend this, winter here, and nurse some hope for our alliance."

Her lip curled. "No alliance. None without justice." The glare she shot at Qadeem dared him to disagree. "Give it, and mayhaps we'll talk of alliance, ere spring's thaw."

Kiefan sighed. "Bring this confession in the morning. Sunrise," he said. "Or else bring a worthy offer."

I stood frozen, focused on my breathing to keep from bursting. From bursting the Crown, splaying her like a great crimson flower — Qadeem sucked away my kir through the bond, despite my grip on it. And so sudden that I flinched, so strong that the other two glanced toward me when they felt it move.

My face flushed red. My saint's dark eyes were on me; I looked down at the floor.

Softly, Crown Ciara said, "We will." She stepped backward, chin held high. I tracked her from under lowered brow, my jaw clenched till it ached. They withdrew without turning away.

I hissed through my teeth. "A worthy offer?" Turning on Kiefan, I snarled, "A worthy offer!?"

"The entire kingdom hangs on this." He'd gone chill as his granite eyes. "Fighting for him will kill thousands."

"You ordered him to her bed!" I pointed out through the door. "After he obeyed, you abandon him? After all I owe him —"

Anger uncoiled in his voice. "You owe him nothing!"

"Nothing? You'd have me defy my teacher — the elect —?"

"I would have for you. If you'd given me the chance." His voice rose.

And mine did too. "And Saint Woden?"

He leaned closer, seething. "For the woman I love?"

My heart quailed. "I had to stay, to serve the saints — and when Parselev was killed —"

"You threw it at me, already decided. That you'd marry him." Kiefan spat that last word. "Every moment I see you beside him gnaws at me. Him standing in my place, smiling at my son — and you'd attack the Crown before her own elect? Over him?" His hand jerked toward the doors and the gate-yard.

My anger rallied. "He held your son and called him his own. Before the Mother and Father, before the flock! He's not done one thing that wasn't good and honorable, and if he dies in the place of a fucking cambifax because you stood by — from jealousy — Shepherd help me —"

Tears tripped me up, clenched my throat.

I saw the pit open in Kiefan's stomach, Mother have mercy. His voice fell. "You love him."

The tears slid away when I squeezed my eyes shut.

"You promised he was only — and you lied to me?" His voice started to rise, then broke down to a fierce whisper. "What else was a lie? The baby?"

I slapped him. He flinched.

"I never lied!" I took a trembling breath. "Did you think I'm made of stone?" It grated through my throat. "Do you think I mean for you to be? When I saw you with Síochana, talking, smiling — I was glad. So glad that you might be happy. I love you but if you can be happy with her… for so long as she lives…" My next breath shuddered. The anger had sunk into a grinding ache. "Can't you wish the same for me?"

I dared look up. He'd clenched his mouth in a thin line and shut his eyes. When he cracked them open, they shone.

"Saint! Majesty!" A shout from the door. "The Caer!"

"Father's fucking mercy," Kiefan muttered, pressing the heel of his hand to one eye.

Saint Qadeem swept past us, cloak trailing — I'd forgotten he was there — and beckoned the runner over. "Report!"

"A deserter from the Caer house, m'lord. Broke from the barn and ran for it."

My saint's voice sharpened. "Which way?"

"She'll not get far — one of the archers struck square in her back. They're looking for the body now."

"They're dead," Qadeem corrected, making the runner gape in surprise. Turning, Qadeem pointed to Kiefan. "With me. We hunt. Kate, there's proof somewhere. Find it, and you'll save him without shedding blood."

Kiefan tossed the silk cloak to Gregor, and Qadeem offered his hand. When Kiefan took it, they launched through the doorway fast as an arrow, angling upward to clear the stockade gates outside. The aisle of King's Guard dropped to one knee, half in respect, half in surprise.

I wiped at my eyes, glancing at Gregor. The poor squire blushed dark red. He'd heard it all, most likely. Captain Aleks and Lieutenant Rostislav, at the heads of the two aisles — well, we could trust them if they'd heard it. I had more important things to worry on.

CHAPTER 12

Proof. The stable-hand who'd claimed she let Anders into the house at midnight was missing, but she was a cambifax and had now fled the Caer house. Somewhere, the true stable-hand was most likely dead. My memory flicked back to the kir-flare, when the cambifax had woven its new form. The body must be well hidden, as Tannait and I hadn't found it.

I surveyed that stand of trees in my memory. The stripe ran from the wheel-rutted road up the hill for miles. It should be someplace near where we'd met the woman. The sun was past noon.

And the Crown meant to wring a confession from Anders.

My eyes fell on Theo Kaufmann, who stood chatting with Eismann's chamberlain. That buttery softness about him made me hesitate a moment, but if he were truly Anders' friend... "Herr Kaufmann? I need your help."

He took his leave of the chamberlain with a nod. "Anything, Elect."

"Kate," I corrected him with a smile.

He returned it. "And Theo, please. What help can I be?"

I tipped my head toward the door and we walked. A page caught us at the sill to return our cloaks. I pinned mine on as I told Theo we must search a stretch of trees for a body. He didn't precisely look eager, but he was too much a friend to drag his feet. He asked whether I were certain the corpse would be there at all, and whether we should get more hands to help.

All Eismann's knights and armsmen were stationed around the Caer house, keeping watch on the Blades outside Vorspitz, or at their usual posts. The King's Guard assisted to stretch their numbers further.

When I asked about those in the Riverman, Theo shook his head. "Brauer's no friend of Anders' and the Caer ladies are under guard."

That turned my feet toward home. As I suspected, Will and m'lord Reinhard had finished the morning chores and everyone was at the table for a bite to eat. I explained the search I intended.

Will stood from the table at once. "I'll help."

"Sit." Reinhardt snapped. "You'll not risk your life for him."

"Sir —"

He cut me off. "I've taken too much disgrace on his behalf, for Frida's sake. Why you married him, I'll never grasp. If this monster is out there, I'll not risk my son." Reinhardt folded his arms.

Alice hugged Rafe and backed away till she reached the wall, staring as if I might strike him down for daring speak.

"Father —"

I held up a hand to stop Will. "Don't. Don't argue on account of me." Theo followed me out the kitchen door, and I muttered as I went. "For all the carrying on about what Anders' reputation, nobody ever speaks of what he did."

Theo caught up alongside me. We walked on grass, as the wheel-rut road was lined three deep by armsmen fencing the Caer in. "Do you wish the full list, or only the most memorable?" he asked. "I saw a good portion of it."

My feet slowed as I looked up at him. He was no knight and he had no ridges, perhaps that was why I thought him buttery-soft. Yet he and his family had long served the saints in gathering intelligence on Arcea as a merchant. They'd been friends since both were pages in the castle, Anders had said.

"Gossip is no use to me," I said. "I want truth."

He tsked me. "Gossip's near as valuable as gold and silks."

I shrugged. "I'm peasant-born, sir." Then, my voice lower, I asked, "Was it so bad?"

A pause. We reached the end of the line of armsmen and walked on toward the trees. "Frederika Bügel hung herself because of him. That was no gossip."

"Was that the worst?"

"There were some questionable pregnancies. A betrothal ruined. Carousing that ended badly."

"How badly?"

"A squire drowned in a horse trough, for being so drunk. I don't recall that night so clearly, in truth, but I don't see how they hung that one on him. He's always made himself easy to hate, though." We stopped on the grass-tufted footbridge and looked up the hill. "These trees? I don't see any crows."

"Nor vultures," I agreed. The patch of trees, now half naked of leaves, held only bird-song and small rustlings. "It must be hidden somehow. Can you sense kir?"

Theo grimaced, uncertain. "When Saint Qadeem arrived, I felt that."

He had little gift with kir. I spun up enough kir for a hush sphere, in my hand. "Do you feel this?"

"It's a little… warmth?"

"You'll need to be close. Look for it, too. A touch of green somewhere. And it should be somewhere near that pasture." I pointed as I stepped off the rutted road.

My skirts and cloak caught immediately on blackberry brambles and juniper bushes. Wrapping my clothes closer, I plowed into the gentler ferns. "Easy to hate?" I asked.

He spoke carefully as he tromped through the brush. "Anders was always larking through sword drills, saddle training, a grin on his face and a quick joke no matter what you said. Showing off every heartbeat someone had eyes on him. Lured us all into his hare-brained capers, but then something would go wrong, he'd give the Queen a fit and we'd all catch hell for it."

We drew close to where we'd flushed out the stable hand. Ealga, that was her name. I stopped, looked around the lumpy ground, the deep-banked stream, and called kir. No answer. Theo drew his sword and poked through the denser brambles.

"And you called him friend?" I asked.

"It did make for a lot of fun, between the extra chores we earned. There was always someone willing to take those for me, for a few bruns." He ducked under a low branch to venture closer to the pasture. "Was always an odd thing, though, that they let him in the castle at all. The Queen couldn't stand the sight of him. The King never took note of him. Who wanted him there, I never knew."

Woden, perhaps. Or Saint Aleks.

We wandered away from each other, searching windfalls, fern-cloaked dips in the slope, and the steep-banked stream. A pair of rabbits burst from the brambles nearly under my feet, and I stumbled against a white birch with my heart racing. Theo stepped across the stream by way of a stone in the center and searched the other side.

I called kir every few yards, but that was only in hope there was a fair mass of kir woven into hiding it. That wasn't likely, as I would've felt that much kir moving, but I needed the hope. The sun crept westward without a care and there was still more to search. Perhaps I ought to look closer to the road, as well. Surely there'd been too much risk of being seen for the cambifax to murder this poor woman there. But who knew how far the thing had moved before it spotted us and hid?

"No luck?" Theo called across the stream.

I straightened, back crackling. I hadn't been to the disciple's dance in two days, and my shoulders felt tense. Sore. "Not yet," I called back. The shadows were gathering. We had gotten some ways past the Caer pasture, well up the hill.

"Might it —"

When he didn't finish, I turned to look. Didn't see him for a moment.

"Kate!" Theo stood and waved.

Eager, I splashed across the stream and tore through the bushes, weaving my way to him. An old stump of a bigger tree had been overgrown by juniper, and its spreading branches sheltered a little hollow. Over the hollow, a faint green glimmer. Theo poked it with his sword, but the blade slid off the surface. Inside, the shadow of the juniper obscured a vague shape with two human feet.

"Only kir cuts kir," I said, spinning up a little blade. A slice and the charm unraveled, sinking into the earth. My stomach turned over and knotted at the smell it freed. Theo turned away, hand over his face, and I heard him retch.

The bugs skittered away at first, but not for long. Her sunken eyes and open mouth lured them back. She lay naked, curled up, belly swollen as if a few months pregnant. Pallid white skin, but shadowed purple-black where her blood had settled. The smell lurked around her, not too strong now but I doubted I'd forget it soon.

"Is that her?" Theo managed to choke words out once his stomach was empty.

Her face had sunken, but it was her. "We need to take her back. We'll need..." I stood, glancing around at the saplings.

Theo unpinned his cloak. "They can bury her in it, after this," he muttered through his teeth.

The corpse slid into the cloak, flopped, and a pop let some more gas free — that's when I retched.

Theo had a handful at either end, by the time I cleared my stomach, and with his strength Blessing he carried her easily enough across his back. She wasn't too wet, thankfully. I brushed off any beetles that found their way out, or tried to. One got up into his hair and he dropped one end of the bundle in trying to swat it. The body nearly spilled out.

Part IV: Salt in the Wound

We drew eyes, needless to say, as we hauled the proof to the Caer guest house. The lieutenant on duty met us at the front, lantern in hand as it was near dark now.

"Elect Kate? Do you require… anything?" He wasn't sure he wanted to ask, by his face. Perhaps because of the whiffs of rot.

"Find Kiefan and bring him here," I answered. Saint Qadeem was on his way; I felt his kir in the distance. Or I hoped it was his.

"His Majesty?"

"Yes." I might've frowned at him. The lieutenant bit his lower lip and snapped his fingers at the sergeant nearby. The man scrambled into a run up the hill toward the stockade.

Turning to the guest house, I looked up at the slivers of archers visible through the window shutters. I put a little kir in my voice. "Crown, come out and hear my case for his innocence."

The door opened before I finished. The armsmen behind me tensed in a rippling rattle of steel. Elect Tannait stepped out, still in her golden dress, and lit a kir-lamp in her hand. The green glow below her chin made eerie angles of her face. I walked halfway, and she joined me in the middle of the gap. Theo followed, dropping the bundle with a moist thump.

Tannait couldn't help crinkling her nose. "A moment while the Crown prepares," she said, voice low. And then she simply looked at me, her restored fingers slowly twirling the glowing ball of kir.

Her hand, which had flown to pieces under my anger. She'd been taking Rafe from harm's way, and I'd struck on instinct. I wanted to apologize, but I'd acted only in defense. They had burst into my home, laid hands on Anders and Rafe. Still, I owed her something.

"Thank you for saving Rafe from the fire," I murmured.

Her mouth pursed to one side. Some distance away, we both felt Saint Qadeem drop from the sky and alight on the road, but neither of us broke eye contact.

"Young elect oft forget their shield when attacking," she murmured back. "That charm — 'tis formidable, yes, but had we leave to kill? Teleri would've gutted you and been glad to claim it."

It was true; I hadn't shielded myself. Even saints forgot their shields in the heat of combat. Saint Aleksandr had leaped on the Arceal woman when her attention lapsed. I dropped my chin in a slow nod. "Thank you."

Qadeem joined us, and in turning to bow to him I spotted the messenger sergeant trotting into the Riverman. Seeking Kiefan there? I wondered for a heartbeat, then remembered. Síochana.

"Elect Tannait," my saint said.

She offered a shallow bow. "Saint Qadeem."

"Will the Crown hear the proof of this knight's innocence?" He folded his arms. The kir-light caught his pale woolens, the ermine in the cloak, and tinted them green.

"Shall come. Was the cambifax dealt with?"

"Two archers and a hand of armsmen, killed without a mark. No mere elect, this. The Empress has a new shifter saint, or —" Qadeem's brow lowered for a moment and he left his thought unsaid. Movement in the house caught his eye, though, and mine.

Crown Ciara stood in the doorway with her tall blue shadow, Elect Teleri. As they came, m'lady Leix appeared but did not follow. The lamp in her hand showed me the grim set of her face.

"What foul gift is this?" Ciara's nose crinkled.

I spun out a kir-vine to pick open the folds of the cloak around the corpse's head. Theo stepped back, glad to leave it. When I nodded to him, he took it as a dismissal. "Your stable hand," I told the Crown. "The one who accused my husband, I believe?"

She looked to Teleri, who tipped her head to consider. Tannait raised the kir-lamp higher and the light fell better on the sunken face. A beetle scuttled across the cheek.

"Fetch the physician," Teleri called to the house, and Leix disappeared from the door. "Might be her."

"'Tis the one we met," Tannait said with a glance at me.

I nodded. "I'd wager she went to fill her water bucket at the stream. The cambifax attacked and murdered her with kir — there's no mark on the body."

The armsmen rattled as they let Kiefan through the line. He joined us at the corpse's feet. "The accuser?" he asked.

"This one accused nobody," I said. "She's been dead near three days. The woman who accused Anders was a cambifax, lying to cover the murder it committed. He's innocent. That's why he hasn't confessed."

The Crown met my eyes at that, and I wasn't much more than a beetle by the glare she gave me.

My jaw tightened. "Stop torturing him and let him go."

"I'll have this one's identity confirmed ere I let any man go," she said.

"This is Ealga," Tannait said. "And 'tis true, she's three days dead. Teleri?"

The other nodded. "Three days, or near enough."

Ciara's chill face did not so much as twitch. Her chin rose an inch. "I will not stay here. My sister's death must be avenged."

"We will take your blood-price from Arcea together," Saint Qadeem told her.

She drew a harsh breath and lashed a few words of Caer under her breath, then bolted toward the doorway. Elect Teleri called after — softer words than I expected — and trotted to follow her. In the door, a brief confusion as the Crown charged through, then the elect. Their physician emerged, bewildered.

Tannait said, "Shall release the prisoner. Ere midnight. The Crown…"

"Whatever you require to prepare the body, ask," Kiefan said. "You cannot ride for home so late in autumn. You must light a pyre?"

She grimaced. "True, we cannot ride. 'Tis pyres we'll need for these two. Needs must impose upon a new host, as well. This house — we cannot stay."

"We will find a place," Kiefan said.

"Give us a day to mourn. 'Tis no small thing, to be stripped thus." Tannait looked down at the physician, who crouched over the corpse. She pattered out a little Caer and got a nod in reply. "Shall care for our own. Thank you for finding her. We sleep best in the shade of a Mother Tree — the lost may never find their way to the Shepherd's fold."

———————————×———————————

The dark deepened. I went home to take off my green dress — the smell clung — and wash. My stomach was too stunned to eat, but Rafe wanted his dinner. His smiles, his warm clean scent, kept me from pacing or climbing the walls. He was my peace. I sat before the fire in the front room while the others ate, in my old brown dress, cradling my son as he nursed.

My little cuddle-bug. Once he finished, he dozed off and I laid him in his cradle.

I returned to the line that stood watching the Caer house's front door; Saint Qadeem nodded when I joined him. Theo was there too, arms folded. After some time, Will came as well. The two of them fell to quietly talking about the hunt that had been missed, and whether it might still happen.

Through my bond, I felt pride. I looked to my saint.

/ found truth /

I nodded. Truth was a fine thing. I wanted Anders back. By midnight, Tannait said. What could take so long?

They argued, perhaps, with the Crown. She was angry, of course, heartbroken over her sister, wanting someone to blame. Someone to hurt. Tannait would keep her word, though. She understood I'd only struck in defense and didn't hate me for it. Surely.

It came to me suddenly: healing. They'd broken him and… I tensed on my feet, focusing on the door again. My memory flicked through Parselev's charms, turning up entirely too many ways to hurt without serious damage. I pushed them away.

My feet nearly carried me to the front door to kick it down myself. No. It would be an attack.

/ patience /

I grimaced. / apologies /

When their door opened, we all startled. Two Blades walked Anders out, his arms across their shoulders; Will and Theo hurried to meet them. In handing him over, Anders teetered on his feet for a moment and stumbled forward with a pained gasp. Will caught him on one side, Theo on the other.

"What happened?" Will asked.

"Anders?" My voice came out tiny. His hair was slicked down, wet, and his clothes damp. His pattern rose at my touch and I bit my lip. "Don't try to walk."

"What did they do to you? Mother of love —" Theo hoisted him higher, half carried him back to Saint Qadeem. Will helped.

"Hot bath." Anders' voice scratched, hoarse. "Don't know how I survived."

Qadeem had a hush sphere ready. "Did the Crown speak, before freeing you?"

My hand on Anders' chest, I sent my kir down to the worst of it: his ankles. The physician had healed what she could, but two broken ankles were much to ask of a blessed. I set my teeth on my lip as I smoothed away the remaining cracks and carefully re-spun the swollen ligaments.

"Didn't see her," Anders said. "Elect gave the order. Did see — something." Anders coughed, cleared his throat. "A shifter. I was in a daze, but the kir woke me. Saw the last of — her face shifting into place. Watched her strip a dead guard of her uniform, put it on. She cut up the body and hid it — they kept me in the root cellar, plenty of barrels about."

"Did she see you?" Qadeem's eyes had sharpened.

Anders nodded. "She sounded me. Studied me. She said it was a shame no one here could train me properly. Then she stood guard and didn't say another word."

"Did you warn them about her?"

He grimaced a moment, then shook his head. I looked to my saint. He stared at the Caer house, sliding his teeth over his lower lip. A blink, and he was back with us. "That was a bit of bad luck, drawing her eye," he told Anders. "True, Aleks should have been your teacher. Take care. Shifters have many enemies and cling to each other all the tighter — do not trust her. She would make a cambifax of you." He said that slowly, sternly. "You are one of us, whether you take animal forms or human, and you will always be welcome here."

He waited until Anders nodded, accepted that.

"Go home." To me, "Mend him well."

His ankles were healed, but there was more to do. Theo and Will didn't let him walk, they hauled him back to our house. Reinhardt and Alice were up from the fireplace the moment the door opened.

"Bed," I pointed at the door into the master bedroom. "Dry clothes."

They carried him in and eased him onto the bed. Alice put a candlestick on the wall sconce as I sat down to take his boots off. They were laced but not tied. His ankles underneath were newly scabbed where the rope had chafed. Theo took his leave, clasping Anders' hand. Will pulled off the other boot. The damp hose, too, which still smelled faintly of dirt and urine.

"All of it?" Will asked.

Anders, heaving up to peel one cote over his head, answered, "I can manage."

Alice caught Will's elbow and tugged. I glanced up from charming the rope burns off his ankles as she dragged him from the room. She shot me a stern look before she closed the bedroom door behind herself. I focused on my work.

"Did they —?"

My words dropped away as Anders peeled off his damp under-cote. Fresh, stippled bruises striped his arm and shoulder, crossed his back as well. One on his neck, under his ear. All on his left side. I'd seen it in his kir, but on his skin…

I whispered. "Who did this?"

Anders closed his eyes. "The Mother laid her discipline on me," he rasped.

I shifted onto my knees to lay my cool hand on the angry stripe across his throat. My kir soothed it, righted his pattern's tangled dance. Anders leaned into my touch with a sigh. I coaxed him into lying down as I mended the second. Straw in the mattress crinkled under my knees when I sidled further alongside him. His hand went to mine on his face, and he turned to kiss my palm.

"Shh." I managed that much through my knotted throat. I let my charm spread, and my fingers followed it across his shoulder, over his hard-chiseled bicep. The bruises scattered before me, fading. Rope burns on his wrists unwound, released him. I let my hand fall to the mattress and leaned, half over him. He'd turned a little blurry through the tears in my eyes.

He stroked my cheek, and a bit of a smile tucked up the corner of his mouth. My heart thudded in my chest, caught in a tangle. Earning rope burns of its own. Home at last, safe and mended —

I kissed him. A simple touch, at first, but I lingered. Then his fingers combed into my hair, and his tongue plunged after mine. I met him with a whimper. His arms pulled me down against his chest. I broke from his mouth to catch a breath, heart pounding, and he met my eyes.

Hope. A touch of fear. A tear ran out on my lashes and dropped onto him. I followed it for another kiss, deep, thorough, everything he deserved for his patience. His hands stroked over my curves, slow and firm, pausing to knead where he liked. My skin throbbed in the wake of his touch.

He liked my breasts. My hips. My butt.

Anders let go to lean up; I let him turn me on my side, then I rolled onto my back with my fingers threaded over his Blessing ridges to keep from breaking the kiss. Shifting onto his elbows over me, he nuzzled my head aside and took a deep breath of my hair. Nipped at my throat, which wrenched another whimper from me.

"Anders —" I whispered, wanting to… I had no words for it. Apologize?

He rose up on his arms. "Stop?"

My grip on his ridges, at the back of his neck, tightened. "No."

His smile made my heart soar. But he sat up further, which confused me a moment — he grabbed the hems of my dress and shift, pulled. I was quick to help shimmy them up and shuck them off. He slung them away without a glance.

Then he was in my arms, warm and solid against me. Kissing me, urgent and deep. My legs slipped over his hips and he ground against me. Hard. As eager as me. I slipped my hand between us, under the loose lacing of his braies, and gripped him. He pulsed, groaning low in

Part IV: Salt in the Wound

his throat. My breath quickened, shallowed, my wanting tinged with worry. Fear of anger, the echo of swords rasping from sheaths.

"Anders," I whispered again, even softer.

His mouth hovered over mine, breathing my air. "No — don't wake me," he whispered back, and my heart twisted in my chest, tearing itself.

"I love you too."

A little sound from his throat cut me further, and then his mouth was on mine and he took me. Deep. My head reeled and I gasped for breath. Anders shifted up onto his hands, but he couldn't let my mouth go; he ground against my hips, I felt his forearm clench under my hand, and dear Mother how he spurted in me. My nails dug into his skin.

The breath he let go hit my mouth in a guttural gasp. He pulled deep breaths. I did too, pressing my cheek to his. His horse-smell was faint, scrubbed over by sweat and lye soap.

Anders breathed a laugh.

"Mm?"

"I can do better," he whispered with another weak chuckle. He dropped his head onto the mattress. Muffled, "I promise, I can do better than that. Give me a second chance?"

Such a notorious lover, and he'd lasted only a few heartbeats. A giggle shook me, caught behind my grin. He laughed against the bed and rolled onto his side to hug me close. I squeezed him back with a sigh. And then giggled again. He cut me off with a kiss.

His second try was amazing.

CHAPTER 13

My baby's cries woke me; I heard the bedroom door creak open and they grew louder.

"Kate?" Alice's voice was thick with sleep.

Anders had blown out the candle. I drew some kir to my hand and focused it into a little star over my finger. She shuffled over, squinting in even that gentle light. Rafe quieted when I shushed him, and once in my arms he stilled too.

Alice pried her eyes further open and leaned past me to look Anders over. He lay on his back, hand tucked under his head, and since I'd pulled off the covers in sitting up the kir-light traced out a fine stretch of chiseled muscle. She touched my shoulder and brushed her finger twice across her cheek — old Englic code for chiding — but she added a wink. I tugged the blankets to cover him, shooed her away with a smirk and a feigned glare.

She smiled and retreated. The door creaked shut behind her.

"What was that?" Anders murmured.

I lay on my side, propped on one elbow so Rafe could nurse. "Only teasing."

"Did she know?"

Dark fell when I unraveled the kir. "No. She was beginning to notice, though."

Anders rolled against my back, his arm settling across my waist. His hand found Rafe, rested on him. A kiss on my shoulder. I tipped my head against Anders'. Warm and close, we three, tonight.

"In the morning…" I said it before I knew how to finish it.

Close by my ear, he murmured, "It's only another morning."

I felt his hand move on Rafe, stroking him.

"They'll know."

"Why would they think anything of it?"

He was right, but I couldn't help thinking of the near-fight in the cottage kitchen, of the oath demanded. Kiefan's jealousy.

"If he learns —"

"How?" Anders' cheek shifted against mine. "Unless you tell him?"

"He's neither blind nor a fool. A touch, a kiss, a stray word…"

"Kate." Anders' whisper turned sober, by my ear. "Be my wife. No bargains, no secrets. Just a husband and wife."

My heart choked me. "He'll kill you."

"He might try."

"He's Woden's bound —"

"Do you love me?"

"I —" It was strangled in my throat.

"Do you trust me?"

"Don't —"

His fingers covered my lips. "Yes or no."

I had to swallow and breathe deep a few times. "Yes. But don't fight him. He'll cut you down. Please."

"I've never wanted a fight from him. If he wants to risk one, that's his choice."

Anders had beaten Kiefan at the jousting tournament, but that had been without kir, without Blessings. And before Kiefan blossomed into an elect. A duel between them, close enough to the Pool that he'd have a steady stream of kir — the fight might run long, but it could only end one way.

I'd seen Anders' patterns. He was a strong blessed, true, but not an elect.

"I asked Kiefan to give the Caer a chance," I said. "I asked him to try to find a bride he might be happy with. So that perhaps we —" I put my arm over his, across my waist, twined my fingers in his. "But now, if there's no alliance, no marriage — and he still wants me…" The pain in Kiefan's eyes when he accused me of loving Anders. Anguish. "I can't bear to break his heart. I can't bear to break yours." My voice sank to a bitter whisper. "I'm such a fool."

Silence. Anders sighed, against my back. "It's not a mortal wound."

"If there were still an alliance with Caercoed, if he were marrying," I spun out, aloud, "if he were marrying that Síochana, and happy with her…"

Rafe had stopped nursing and half-dozed with my nipple in his mouth. I saw to that with my free hand, my mind skipping through possibilities in search of a hope. Saint Sabh had asked to meet with Qadeem. Perhaps.

I tipped my head against Anders'. "I want to be your wife. No bargains. I want Kiefan happy with his wife and willing to let me go. Give me a little more time?"

His arm tightened around my waist. "If it will make you happy," he whispered back.

The Caer funeral dirge rang in my ears as I walked through the stockade gate. I'd stood beside Saint Qadeem at dawn, to welcome Saint Sabh when she soared down from the sky and alit with casual ease. She was a small woman with long, dark hair streaked by one lock of bright white. She might not be beautiful, but the traces of age across her brow and cheeks lent her an iron dignity. Only a slow nod was exchanged between the saints; she was here to bless her dead, oversee their pyre, and counsel the remaining Crown. Then, perhaps, to discuss the situation.

Kiefan sent a messenger down to summon me, mid-morning. The Voice of the Empress would arrive by noon. I carried my baby indoors from watching Anders working one of the yearlings on a lunge line to put my hair up and see what I could wear. My green dress was still wet from its scrubbing.

I was just as glad to put walls between me and the raging pyre, the high, mournful song. It reminded me of the lamia howling in the night.

Here, in the gate-yard, Kiefan and Gregor and a handful of boys drilled with sparring swords. Spotting me, Kiefan left off and patted his squire on the shoulder in passing. The wooden sword in hand, he joined me near the manor's double doors. Duke Haken stood there, leaning on his cane and watching the drills. I smiled and nodded when he offered me a bow; I clasped my hands before me and tried to look no different than I had yesterday.

A passing jolt of fear and I checked my kir patterns for bruises, any sign of Anders' nipping on my neck. Nothing.

"I shouldn't raise a sweat when deSvello's on his way," Kiefan said, "but if I spent another day sitting, my spine would lock in place."

Whatever the Voice was coming to say, I didn't relish yet another round of disagreements and nit-picking. "I didn't know talking could be so much trouble."

He twisted a smile to one side. "We needed that hunt. Kaufmann's party was a great help, but the hunt would've broken up the ice further."

"Perhaps we can salvage it," Duke Haken said. "In a few days, if the weather's fair?"

I knew little of hunting and didn't see the attraction, but Kiefan nodded. "Though it may be only us and Eismann riding. The Crown will refuse, and then Leix must refuse as well."

A thought struck me, turned this into a small chance. "Would the ladies at the Riverman be free to ride with you?"

Neither man had an answer, at first. "They're subjects of their Crown," the duke said, dubious.

"M'lady Leix is an officer on duty and must obey," I said, "but the ladies?"

"Síochana's on leave from the Northern Horse." Kiefan pressed his knuckles to his mouth, considering. "Perhaps they could hunt with us."

"Better not to bring them trouble," his cousin said.

To counter that, I said, "There's no harm in asking, surely."

"What of the duchesses, though?" the duke asked. "The twins? M'lady Faola?"

"M'lady Faola, perhaps, but not —"

Kiefan and I both looked up as kir dropped from the sky in a thick, braided vine. Saint Qadeem rode it to the ground, alighting on both feet. The boys in the yard and the guards around us dropped to one knee in obeisance. Kiefan and I bowed.

"Not late, good." Qadeem nodded. "No rainclouds this time. Knapptal will be made as comfortable as possible for the Crown. Smuggler's Pass is ankle-deep in snow and Schutze had little to report."

"Ciara sent a rider this morning," Kiefan said, voice low, "ordering Leix's knights to break camp. She still means to withdraw them for the winter."

"And it's a long winter ahead," Qadeem said. "Don't lose hope yet."

"DeSvello's wasted a ride up here. I'll not sit through another of his lists of vague promises from the Empress." Kiefan paused a moment. "Woden's opinion is that sending his head back in a box would keep them from thinking they can push to the city gates and besiege us again before the snows truly start."

My saint did not so much as glance at him. "We will hear their offer."

Hooves on the road outside the gate. The guards there moved to attention. The boys scattered from their training, and Gregor trotted to take his post behind Kiefan. The Voice of the Empress rode in first, the white banner painted with his title trailing from his helm and across his purple cloak. His escort was small, only a few of the eagle-helmed Arceal knights and a petite lady perched sidesaddle with skirts flowing.

Deep, dark eyes on the lady. Knife-whetted cheekbones. Walnut-brown curls, and skin the clarity of perfectly steeped tea. She was wrapped in high-collared gold silk and tawny furs. Kiefan tracked her — I tracked her, I confess — as the white palfrey pranced to a halt.

A strong call from my saint, and kir-patterns glowed: the riders, the horses, the invisible skin over us all. None batted an eye, as they had nothing to hide. The knights and Voice were blessed, to judge by their patterns. None a saint, and thus not the cambifax.

DeSvello dismounted and bowed low. "Mine is the honor, Saint Qadeem. Much have I heard of you."

"We trust you carry sober news from Ansehen?" Qadeem's Arceal matched the Voice's native accent.

"Indeed. Our Empress is loath to be ignored, la."

"Your Empress knows what has passed here. Let us not play at that." Qadeem paused as the lady slid from the saddle into a guardian knight's hands. Once down, she dropped to her knees and laid her face on them, arms spread open in supplication toward my saint. "Truly, a maiden of the blood. Come, dearest, and take ease."

The lady stood as gracefully as she knelt, her dress still spotless. She kept her gaze averted, but still watched us closely.

"This servant is Clarilunes Graziana, blood of the third degree. Thus would the Empress welcome her new kin," deSvello said. "For we have brought you a new proposal."

In the great hall, the Arceal were matched knight for knight by King's Guard headed by Captain Aleks. A noontime meal was set out for us at a small table by the fireplace. Qadeem sat opposite deSvello, and Kiefan and I opposite each other. M'lady Graziana swished to stand at Kiefan's right shoulder, which flustered Gregor. She shot him a chilly stare and he backed off, letting her take command of filling Kiefan's stein. She poured a perfect head onto his beer on her first try.

The terms spun out over cabbage-and-radish slaw, then hot omelets wrapped around sheep's-milk cheese. No vague promises, this time: tea, silk, and steel would drop to set prices. Tariffs on our timber and beer would be cut in half. The army in Ansehen would withdraw and camp on the meadows below.

Kiefan couldn't hide all his surprise, but each time m'lady Graziana reached to wipe his eating knife with a napkin or to refill his stein his hope cooled a bit. He was surely right, too. These generous numbers would come with a hook. M'lady Graziana, for her part, served with silent grace, her dark curls bobbing. Gregor stood back with his lower lip under his teeth, eyeing the Arceal knight who guarded her.

When deSvello finished laying out the details, he took a few bites of his cooling omelet. Saint Qadeem had said nothing yet, and cleaned his trencher. So had I; the baroness was a good cook.

"For singing and art, Caer beauty is known. Passionate is their blood. Quick to anger. They shall turn on you in the twinkling of an eye," deSvello said, with a particular look to Kiefan. "Their kingdom beyond the mountains is fair, and deep rooted in fertility charms. Their coast runs long, rich with every creature of the sea. Women, lovely and strong." The Voice paused, again, to let the thought linger. "They do not guard their mountain border, as it's rarely crossed."

Kiefan leaned back in his chair, leaving the last few bites untouched. M'lady Graziana was quick to clear the trencher away. There'd been talk of invading Suevia; as fair to talk of invading Caercoed, I supposed. True enough that they'd turned on us.

"For good reason, it's rarely crossed," Kiefan said.

"For want of a clear pass. Lacking the saint to clear it, la." DeSvello gestured for his trencher to be removed. "Little force would take their western provinces, sweep east with ease. And keep those lands, once they've broken."

Qadeem finally spoke. "This is your tempting, then, fine trade and Caercoed for the taking. If we wed you."

The Voice met my saint's gaze, dark eyes to dark eyes. "Should the issue be persuasion — removal, if need be — there shall be aid offered. She would say: all may yet be forgiven, lost lamb."

A soft snort from Qadeem. In Alemannic, he murmured, "Don't pass that to Woden."

A tray of sliced apples and pears arrived, and m'lady Graziana swiftly arranged some in a whorl on Kiefan's trencher. I reached for one of the uncut pears in the center, then nearly dropped it when Saint Qadeem stood.

"Your duty is done, Voice. Go, now."

"My Empress would have her answer."

"She has her answer, la."

DeSvello stood, eyes narrow, and spat out the command to leave. M'lady Graziana took Kiefan's hand of a sudden and pressed her forehead to it for a heartbeat before scurrying after the Voice and his escort. Captain Aleks and the Guard saw them out to their horses, leaving us with Gregor and one of the baron's maidservants.

Kiefan broke the silence. "Twenty-five thousand are in Temitte at this moment. More than our reserves. Without Caercoed, if deSvello's offer is reasonable —"

"Their offer is for us to stab our neighbor in the ribs," Saint Qadeem said, sitting again, "while they rape her from the south."

That gave Kiefan a heartbeat's pause. My stomach shifted; I hadn't seen it that way.

"If we take and hold Tadhlon and Myrddin, we could protect them from Arcea. They're the only two houses to show us any kindness," Kiefan said.

"If we stab our neighbor, it leaves us without a knife in hand. Arcea does not ally. It swallows." Qadeem bit a slice of apple and chewed it. "It swallows the unprepared."

There had to be a story. "Will you tell us why you say that?" I asked.

He pressed his mouth in a line and ate another few slices before answering in Arceal. "Rasila was a rich land. Green. Warm." He smiled thinly, bundling his ermine cloak closer. "Peaceful enough. I was twenty years a bound elect when Arcea offered us friendship, alliance, marriage into the Empress' bloodline. At first, they took our scion's hand in marriage. Then they culled our gifted for training in Arcea itself — from which they never returned, for, I later learned, most were forged into monsters. They watched our elect for signs of ascent and stole them away. Bound to the Empress."

My head tipped. Bound elect, stolen? Saints could be bound?

Qadeem smiled, seeing my questions. "Yes," he answered, "they can. Kiefan could tell you things of the binding that I don't mean to inflict on you, Kate. I've always trusted more in the velvet glove than the iron fist."

"Were you bound to the Empress?" I asked.

"Some elect ascend when they kill and harvest. Some go quietly. I was able to hide it for some years, before they caught scent of me. It played well into the Empress' plan, to come for me in force and wipe away the last traces of Rasila's kingdom in the balance. I thought my —

saint would turn on me, but…" He paused, putting something difficult aside with a sigh. "I went north. I knew that somewhere, the stand must be made against the Empress. For years I wandered before a small kingdom in a cold valley took me in. They had a saint who was warrior enough to prepare his people, and one who was crafter enough to advise me in creating new organs for the body. Ones which harnesses kir."

"Blessings." Kiefan turned a slice of pear in his fingers.

Qadeem's gaze was lost in the distance. "Rasila is all but forgotten now. Consumed and long since digested by Arcea. They need farmland and they need kir founts to feed themselves. They need disciples to flesh-forge into monstrous soldiers. The Empress controls all through her bound saints and elect. She is ancient, herself. Her claim that Saint Cambifax trained her may well be true. I doubt she even remembers her true form now." He scratched his bearded chin. "I was little more than a fool in her shadow."

Who could make my saint seem like a fool, I couldn't imagine.

"How do we win, then?" I asked. "How will there be peace?"

"Take Suevia back first," Kiefan said.

"Yes." Qadeem stood again. He had said all of that in Arceal, which left Gregor and the maid ignorant and lulled; he startled them awake. And he returned to Alemannic. "Come. We must pay our respects to the dead. One more lesson in negotiation, I think. Father knows you won't have any from Woden."

In the pasture, a column of fire roared. Part of the fence had been taken down to cart in the wood, and the Crown had been laid atop the tall bier they had built. I'd seen her white gown bright in the sun. The stable-hand had been placed on a lower shelf, at her feet. And a third body, as well — the unfortunate Blade who'd been guarding Anders, I had to guess.

Saint Sabh stood with Crown Ciara at one hand and Elect Tannait at the other; shorter than either, but clearly in command. She wore her glittering kir as a sash belt for her white gown, and her lock of white hair had been braided. Ciara wore white, as well, with a filmy black veil of linen sweeping from crown to fingertips.

She asked no leave of her saint when she saw us; she simply turned and walked away.

M'lady Leix introduced us properly. Elect Teleri moved into Ciara's place so the meeting was equal, saints with two elect apiece. Behind the Caer, the funeral pyre roiled in the chilly breeze. Heat lifted loose hair, rippled cloaks. It smelled of burning meat and grease.

"Which parts of Wodenberg has Arcea offered you?" Qadeem asked simply.

A corner of Saint Sabh's mouth tucked up. Tannait answered for her. "Englia, and so far south to Lake Neva as we can hold. And you?"

Kiefan breathed a laugh, though the sound was lost in the fire. Qadeem said, "The western provinces. We have a particular eye on Tadhlon and Myrddin. It's meant as a compliment, Margrave."

M'lady Leix's jaw had gone slack, but she recovered with a frown.

Sabh spoke in a smoky contralto. "'Tis a poorer deal for you — our western provinces have no founts."

He nodded. "We will demand control of one of the southern passes, then."

"Fair, that." Saint Sabh gestured for a handmaid to bring bergamot tea for us all. "'Tis a shame to be conquering each other when 'twas looking to be a fine alliance."

"It would be a fine alliance indeed," Qadeem said. "Our king's negotiated well, or so I've heard. Despite his youth."

"Youth was mentioned, I believe." Saint Sabh cast a glance to her elect, Tannait. "Done well with his numbers, yes, and in the sparring field as well. 'Twas less clear how our nominees fared. Mayhaps that's how we've come to a state of war?"

Qadeem looked to Kiefan, who took a few breaths to find the right words. The duchesses stood not far away, partly watching the pyre and partly eavesdropping. "The ladies each bring persuasive offers," he said at last.

Crinkled brows at that, and pursed mouths. "If 'tis to be damned with faint praise, we've little choice then," Sabh said.

"If I may, m'lady, the Crown has made clear there's to be no alliance," Kiefan said. "She's sent orders to withdraw Tadhlon's knights. Did she not act with your blessing?"

Her white braid shifted as she nodded. "We have ever taken comfort from the strength of our border guard — our mountains — and how little we need of the southlands. 'Tis grief you bring us," she said with a sidelong glance to the pyre, "when we meet. Caercoed would withdraw, then, and see to its own. We need nothing of yours, Saint Qadeem. Though." Saint Sabh considered. "Give the noble houses of Caercoed their favors, their tie to royal blood, their chance to drive Arcea from our doorstep, and they will accept your alliance. We do listen, when our people bring their choice in one accord through the Crown. And if she resists, shall deal with her as they choose. If 'tis merely persuasive offers, though, 'twill do little to fire their hearts." Saint Sabh turned her head one way and the other to survey the Caer — nobles, servants, and Crown's Blades — who stood near the fire. "Which would you defy a saint for, young king?"

Kiefan hesitated, opening his mouth and then closing it. Then he looked to me, across Qadeem's back, full of longing.

It still stung, still ached, but I hissed, "She made you smile." I sent a silent plea to Mother Love as well. When I turned back to Saint Sabh, her brows were up, her eyes on me. But she said nothing.

"M'lady, the margrave of Myrddin came seeking trade across the Dragon's Fangs," Kiefan answered, "but —"

"Myrddin!" The saint's voice carried on kir. A moment later, Síochana saluted at m'lady Leix's side. It had to be her Northern Horse squadron's uniform that she wore: a pale blue tunic cut short over black hose and boots, a thick leather belt double-wrapped across her hips for her sword, and a touch of gold braid to mark her rank.

Her eyes crept to Kiefan. He'd snapped to attention with her, though I don't know if he realized it.

"'Tis a small house, Cainwen of Myrddin," Saint Sabh said. "Not the best of leverage. Not the most persuasive of offers, surely."

Kiefan steeled himself to look the saint in the eye. "Far more persuasive than the others, if I may disagree. And I'm told she's made me smile, which is said to be a rare thing. However, the margrave is betrothed and bound by her word."

"Myrddin?" The saint looked to Síochana. "'Twould be bound by your word, or be a queen of Wodenberg? That is the offer, true?"

"If she would have me." Kiefan raised his chin, the fire catching on his gold band and the braided knight's crest pinned under it.

Her voice trembled a little. "If 'tis you, sir, the crown matters little. If I may be freed of my word, yes, I would." The corners of her mouth tucked up. "I'm told 'tis rare for me, as well."

"Be freed, then, and let it be a love story that's told in Caercoed. Come your wedding day, we shall be allies for good and all."

"Kate." Kiefan caught my arm, tugged me aside. "I didn't mean for you to see that."

"See — Síochana? You think me jealous?" I put my hands on his face, to be clearer. "She made you smile. I want to see you smiling. Why do you doubt me?"

The kitchen in the Caer guest house held only their cook and his apprentice, busy at slathering sweetbread dough with apples, walnuts, and honey, rolling it and flattening it out for another application. Neither likely spoke a word of Alemannic. Outside, the pyre held all attention.

Kiefan put his hands over mine, eyes downcast. His sadness still pinched my heart, made my mouth twist. "I can't bear to think of you hating me. I had to bargain with the Crown — you see why, don't you? It was the only thing she wanted of us. Anders' life was the only trump card."

A hot needle of anger made me bite my lip before I answered. I took my hands from Kiefan's cheeks, threading my fingers through his. "I stopped them. I proved he was innocent and they released him." Patched up and scrubbed clean, but free and whole.

"You do love him." Barely a murmur.

I couldn't deny it outright. "He's been so good to me."

Kiefan's grey eyes met mine, sharp. "I want to be the one who's good to you, Kate. I still want it. I will always want it to be you beside me."

"I will be beside you," I said, and could say it truthfully. "As an elect, as a friend, as one who loves you. Loves you dearly." My throat tightened, halfway through, but it got out.

"One thing, one damn thing I've wanted for myself after all Father Duty's yoked me with, and he denies me you as well." His fingers clenched around mine, so tight it nearly hurt. "I should've been the third son, I should've been the one of little consequence."

"The Father gave you a lady who makes you smile," I offered.

He looked away. "Watching you marry him — I clung to trusting you, Kate. Else it would've destroyed me. Will you wait a little longer for me?"

"Until the day they both pass of old age," I murmured. Kiefan's eyes sharpened at that. Hope. I squeezed his hands again. "Give Síochana a chance to make you happy."

Kiefan put his forehead to mine, nodded. "If you won't leave me."

"Ever beside you," I murmured.

He glanced toward the cook, and then the kiss caught me unawares. Just a simple one, like our first, but lingering. Then we parted, both heartsick and misty-eyed.

CHAPTER 14

Saint Sabh flew over the mountains by the light of the just-off-full Shepherd and his Flock. The Crown departed in the morning. Three jars of ashes rode lashed to Dove's saddle.

Ciara refused an escort, but a squad of Rangers rode out before them to scout the road ahead. The men risked crossbow bolts in their backs, as the Crown had glowered under her mourning veil at the sight of Kiefan and ignored his well-wishes, but they went.

Leix had her orders to see to her knights' withdrawal to Knapptal. "'Twill be better wintering below a castle than in open fields," she said of it. "The better rested for the spring's sport."

"All you've done will not be forgotten." Kiefan reached for her hands, and she clasped his with a smile. "If I may, one small token." He nodded toward Will, who stood holding Shade's bridle.

Leix grinned. "A fine gift indeed! Needs must decline the squire, though." The blue roan was handsome in new black tack; Will blushed charmingly. "If I can, shall come for your jousting tournament. And for the wedding," she promised before she rode out.

Síochana and her two companions remained at the Riverman. Kiefan rode out hunting with them, his cousin the duke, and a handful of woodsmen; I stayed in Vorspitz preparing for the ride home and healing any who asked, so far as my kir stretched.

Saint Qadeem joined me for a cup of tea before he took his leave. "We must resume your lessons," he told me. "You've prepared a shop in the city, you said?"

"It should be ready and waiting." I nodded. "The carpenters were nearly finished when we left. It should have enough bookshelves for all Parselev's collection now."

He smiled. "He would be glad of that. Though when you move his books, there's a few to watch for. He may not have mentioned them to you. Mechdan had a great command of his Blessing, and a fine hand for art as well. He documented the Blessings in sketches — their function. For, as he said, while we saints know them all, anything might happen. Wisdom is lost whenever a saint dies, and only a fool would believe he'd live forever."

Qadeem's smile faded into sober thought as he said all that. "I consented to his making the books, but they're not to be mentioned to Woden. Find and read them. There is much you should learn, still, and Blessings are one of them. There's no need to limit yourself to one."

He took a sip of tea as my mind went to my teacher and how he'd pulled apart Kiefan and Anders at Blessing speed, that day in the cottage kitchen. That must have come of his studying the Blessings. "I did find those books," I said, "while moving the library. I'll read them next." It would mean putting aside the Englic war journal, but I hadn't had the time I'd wanted for that — or for Kiefan's thoughts.

"Good. And if you've improved enough with your kir-spinning, perhaps we'll try flying?"

He knew I wanted that. I resolved to keep at it; I could lift a twenty-pound flour sack with my kir-vines now, but that was still a little thing.

And I had to ask: "What of the cambifax?"

"Be watchful. Check who you will — it is your right. The cambifaxi hide best when they take short-term faces. Beware strangers. Watch for lapses in those you trust; that is a sure warning. Cambifaxi learn what they can of those they replace, but cannot know all. Your shop will give you a useful eye on the city, you'll find. Folk will bring you news if you ask."

That was likely true enough; Parselev had always listened to patients, wagon-drivers, couriers, anyone who wished to speak to him.

"There's much to watch for, and a dose of caution is wise. But do not let fear rule you."

"But the cambifax could be among us now, or anyplace in the kingdom."

"And ever could be, if one wishes to think thus. Some saints and elect kill any shifter they meet, for fear — or any gifted who hides their nature. They live in terror of stumbling on that one kir-mage with a deadly quirk they cannot defend against." He smiled again. "I prefer to take the challenge to be the one with the deadly quirk."

My mind caught on one part. "Cannot defend against?"

"There's no knowing what your enemy might do. All kir-mages are different, within the limits kir sets."

"Line of sight," I said, thinking of Kiefan reaching for the sword he couldn't see, and his kir-vine hanging in the air aimless. "And what kir you have or can draw — there are other limits?"

"Do the Engls still invoke Saint Ethmund's blessing?"

"Those who remember him." There'd been some blessing songs sung at my wedding. "It seems foolish to me, as he's long dead."

Qadeem freshened his mug of tea from the pot. "Ethmund could not hear them, even alive. One cannot surpass one's senses."

I frowned. "But Anders' horse-ears —"

"Are far sharper than his own, true. Cat's ears are sharper still. But no ears can hear whispered prayers across a hundred miles. Nor shouted pleas."

In stories, saints saw all, heard all, knew all. Qadeem's chilly touch through my bond and my Blessing echoed back to me. "Unless you hear it through my ears. See through my eyes."

Half a nod. "When I look through our bond. That's a quirk of mine — of your Blessing. Woden cannot, I know, and must rely on what his elect report. You're my trusted eyes and ears. A valuable asset and a threat to any elect or saint." He paused, tea in hand, to fix me with a serious gaze. "Know your worth, Kate. Do not sell your life cheaply, if you must sell it."

My stomach shifted inside me at the memory of Tannait's arms. "I'm a healer, first."

"Which matters nothing," he said. "You saw how Mechdan died. You were nearly cut down yourself, that day the saints invaded. Do not hesitate to strike if you see danger. They will underestimate you, as you're a young and pretty girl — use that to your advantage." Finally, a bit of a smile broke the severe tone. "There's some who would kill you on jealousy alone for that. Mark your pattern well at this age, so you can maintain it as you choose."

Which unleashed a new torrent of questions, but my saint had duties of his own to see to. "I have Blessings to give, and a new elect, possibly. One of Aleksandr's," he said. "I will look for you in the city when I return."

It was good to be home. Frida caught me in her arms and squeezed tight, rocking me, as if I'd been away a year rather than just of a moon's turning. She'd had word of when we'd be home and had a fine roast of venison ready, potatoes, and this year's kraut on the side. The whole house smelled of pickling, in truth, which made me smile. If my mother could afford the salt to pickle a few barrels of kraut, it had been a good year and the winter wouldn't be so hungry.

There was word, too, that Anders was to report to the Rangers no later than the morning after the jousting tournament ended. For two weeks of evaluation, the message said. He frowned at that, and took out the bow he'd brought home from his training. He'd done a little shooting in Vorspitz, late some afternoons, but not much.

I could see why riding horses had won out over archery; a bow was an ornery thing in his hands. Ulf and Bjorn had made it seem easy, during our mission, to put a shaft between a lamia's eyes.

That night we arrived home turned dramatic, of a sudden, when Frida told Hilly that she'd need to go back to the nursery. As the nights were cold, she and Ein had been sleeping with their mother. But Ein was glad to be sharing a room with his brother Will again, and m'lord Reinhardt naturally wanted his own place back.

This was cause for tears and a little wailing about snowy monsters in the dark, until I told her Alice wanted to move into the nursery to sleep safe from the monsters too. That helped.

I caught a mischievous glance, across the table, from Anders. And returned it.

Alice laced me into the snow-white shift and helped me pull down the light, amber dress over it. Unlikely that any would notice I wasn't laced so snugly as the last time I'd worn this.

Queen Mercia had returned from Prohzgrad weeks ago and she announced a welcoming feast the day after Kiefan rode home from Vorspitz with his three Caer guests. Her invitation, as recited by the messenger, was quite precise; I was expected, as were the Baron and Baroness Rossweide, and their heir. Ein was expected to serve as a page. Alice would come to watch Rafe. Hilly was eager to spend the night with her friend down the street under the care of older siblings who weren't going to the feast.

"I'll find someone to share a beer at the Black Knight," Anders said, with a shrug. "Sound out who's expected at the joust this year and what these restrictions everyone's a-tizzy about will be."

I rode Buttercup through the castle gates with Alice close beside me on Pal, a bit ahead of the rest. A stable boy took both the horses when we dismounted in the inner gate-yard. Alice trailed a bit; she'd never been to the castle itself. Never closer than the midnight bonfire at the guest house on Solstice night. There was a separate meal for attending servants in the smaller dining room, so she took her leave with Rafe on her shoulder.

As the King's Guard pulled the great hall's doors open for me, I stepped in alone. I was announced and a page took my felt cloak. Three musicians played lutes and a flute while standing in the middle of the U of long tables. Many people had returned to Wodenberg, but not all; it was a far smaller gathering than Solstice had been. I did not, at a glance, see Kiefan, but m'lady Síochana and her two companions circulated with the castle steward, Herr Vogt, to translate their Arceal as needed. She wore her uniform and sword and chatted with Theo by the fire.

For a dozen heartbeats, I didn't know what to do. I rather wished Anders were there.

Then the Rossweides were announced behind me, and Frida caught my elbow. "Come and meet the ladies."

She introduced me, though I remembered their names from Solstice, and luckily Alice arrived as summoned to hand over Rafe. Frida had her heart set on showing off her grandson. He was awake, bright-eyed even, and had them all fawning in a heartbeat. Her glowing eyes, her smile, all pinched at my heart; he wasn't her grandson, not truly. Perhaps she'd love him the same even if she knew.

"Is it true?"

I turned toward the whisper, from a frau not much my elder. Svetlana Sahnen, wife of a local baron. She'd had a few cups of the apple ale, by the glint in her eye.

"You married him? Sir Anders?" Svetlana asked. When I nodded, she pressed my arm with her hand. "I'm so sorry." Puzzlingly earnest in that. "It must be terrible."

"Pardon?"

Her blue eyes went wide. "To suffer such an outrage — and with the Queen of Caercoed?" She mangled the name. "When you've such a fine little boy? He's so precious." Svetlana turned to sweetness, blew a kiss at Rafe as he changed hands. Then it was back to an eager-eyed whisper. "And then she was murdered!"

I nodded, since it was true. "He didn't —"

"And they took him! Such a fight, they said! You must've — did you? You're the Elect." Svetlana remembered who I was and retreated half a step, caught between fear and wanting the story.

"A house destroyed, they said?" One of the other fraus joined in, on my other side. "Was it your doing, Elect? I can't imagine —"

Svetlana chuckled. "Walden tumbles a queen, he'll have a door slammed in his face. They can keep him if they please." Then she pressed my arm again, softening. "Your pardon, Elect. It was so brave of you to face them down for him. When he'd hurt you so."

"You do the Mother proud," the frau assured me. Then, lower, "Don't let him go unscathed for such a thing. Time that boy was properly housebroken, and surely an Elect can do it."

"What did you do?" Svetlana's grin widened, thinking there was something juicy. "What punishment?"

I hadn't gotten a word in edgewise yet, for all my taking a breath to speak and being cut off. But now I got a pause, and rapt attention. I wasn't about to tell them of the broken ankles or the beating, that Crown Ciara had done the Mother's work — which he hadn't even deserved, given that he'd all but been ordered into Ceelin's arms.

Let them wonder, as Qadeem had said. "He's been disciplined." I took a sip of my ale.

Their minds went to work behind their eyes. "He's met his match at last," the frau declared.

"Don't be jealous," Svetlana teased back.

"Ladies! If I may?" Theo arrived with both hands raised, flourishing a deep bow to us without spilling his ale. The fraus all turned with smiles and nods.

"Perhaps you've heard a rumor the elect will open an infirmary in the Reichang — it's true. The shop stands on Scribe Street. Tomorrow, come and greet Elect Kate for a welcoming party after noon, if you would. We shall have a little music, a little cider, and the elect will appraise your health without charge. Just this once."

He got a small chuckle from a growing audience, and then a clamor of questions. Raised brows from me; this was news. I'd been to the shop to check the preparations and they were nearly done. But not quite.

"What was this?" A new voice cut through the noise, and silence followed it. All fell into deep bows and curtsies. "Elect...?"

The queen trailed off as I curtsied to her. "Majesty," I said.

"Kate, is it?"

"Yes, Majesty."

"Bockmann." She said the word, despite her reluctance. "Yes, there was some fuss about an Englic girl." She analyzed me, my golden dress, my crespined hair, my necklace. Her mourning veil, under her plain gold band, lent deeper shadows to her grey eyes. Harsher. Her head tipped. "Have we met?"

"No, Majesty," I said, truthfully enough.

She folded her arms, nodding to herself. "I've seen you before."

I fumbled for an answer. "I attended the winter Solstice with my teacher, Elect Parselev. Perhaps you saw me?"

Theo and his audience had fallen back, I noticed. Frida, Rafe in her arms again, had turned away, though she stole furtive glances. A friend anxiously plucked at her arm to retreat further. One faced Queen Mercia alone, it would seem.

"Perhaps." Her gaze lingered, though, on my white-and-amber dress.

Cold fear stabbed me. This dress had been tossed atop a chest beside Kiefan's bed when the Queen had walked in and nearly caught me. She had no memory Blessing, no Blessing at all as she was Suevi, so surely the Queen couldn't remember a small thing... that had set off her first fit in years...

"Majesty, if I may, Elect Kate and I have a business endeavor to discuss." I could've kissed Theo for interrupting. He dipped to one knee to the queen and reached for my hand. I let him take it in a high, formal carry.

"Very well, then, Kaufmann," she said. "Odile, shouldn't Kiefan be here by now?" Her handmaid stepped up beside her with a nod.

I exhaled as Theo led me away from the fireplace where the guests had clotted. "Thank you."

"Her Majesty isn't so frightening if you're precise," he said. "So I've learned. The welcoming tomorrow. I have everything arranged."

"Aside from telling me of it."

"Yes," he allowed with a nod, "aside from that. By noon everyone inside the walls will know where your infirmary is, have no doubt. News of something for free makes for excellent conversation. It will be no trouble, will it, to merely appraise one's health?"

The shop was close enough to the Pool that I could draw a trickle. Not so much as in the Order's hospital, but enough. And merely looking at kir was a simple thing. "It will be no trouble. But next time —"

The band played a final chord and fell silent; the chamberlain called, "Goodfolk, attend!"

Kiefan stood behind the high table in jewels, silk, and his uniform tabard with its gold ranking rings. The queen stood to one side with hands clasped, her daughter Princess Gisella beside her. To the other side, our Caer guests.

He introduced them, beginning with Fraus Branwen and Pryderi, and they bowed to the audience in turn. When he came to the last, he put out one hand. She came to take it, shoulder-high and properly formal. "Kindly welcome Síochana Cainwen, the nineteenth Margrave of Myrddin, lieutenant of the Northern Horse cavalry of Caercoed. M'lady is as fine a knight as I have met and an excellent shot in the hunt — she felled a bull elk before my eyes. We feast tonight on her generosity."

That with a stern glance to a knot of older men that included Reinhardt. Those who'd want to see proof of her mettle, perhaps.

Kiefan swept the golden cloak aside to drop to one knee, still holding her hand with formal grace. He put something small in her palm, covered it with his other hand. My throat tightened, suddenly. "If Síochana would honor me with her hand in marriage, our kingdoms shall be united against our common enemy."

She answered him in accented Alemannic. "Let our kingdoms be united, then."

He stood and gave her a brief kiss — or not so brief, which the audience cheered. I looked away, toward the floor, taking a deep breath to fight the growing ache. If the closeness of their embrace meant there'd been some sampling of the wares already, it was none of my concern. He would be happy. I would be happy. We both deserved that.

I wished Anders were here, again. My hand went to his necklace.

Kiefan finally got a chance to speak. "The first day of the Snow Moon, Wodenberg and Caercoed seal their alliance. I call for a royal hunt to celebrate!" That got a cheer and a raised fist from Síochana. Her other arm was around him, and his arm across her shoulders. "I was advised to cancel the jousting tournament, but I call the kingdom's best knights to compete as part of our celebration!" A bigger cheer for that. "And join us now in celebrating our betrothal, goodfolk. Wish us well."

We feasted on the bull elk, in his roasted glory. My teacher's place at the head of the second table was mine now, and I presided as best I could over the steward, my in-laws, and a scattering of others. Chatting was rather far from my mind, and the beer I drank with the meal only drove me further into melancholy. When Rafe demanded his dinner, I moved to a chair by the fireplace for not wanting eyes on me just then.

I did not stay for the dancing; Alice followed me without much comment, perhaps because I couldn't manage even a smile for a little story she told about one of the maids. Bundled in my cloak, against the cold wind, I rode straight home to the Bockmanns'.

Anders came out to let us into the barn. Alice took Rafe to warm up in the kitchen. I swung down from Buttercup's saddle and stood holding her reins for a few minutes, still haunted by that betrothal kiss. In the dim light of the one lantern by the kitchen door, it was easy to picture. The two of them in his bed, cuddled and cozy. As I had been.

A hand took Buttercup's reins from mine. Anders didn't say a word, only led the mare into her stall. I followed him, knowing he'd unsaddle her and brush her down. That ritual had a peaceful rhythm to it.

He left the gate unlatched. I stood with my hands on it for a moment, then slipped inside. Hardly any light got into the stall from the lantern. He could unsaddle Buttercup by touch, by how leather slithered and brass clinked. My eyes adjusted slowly, picking him out by his light woolens. The horse, by her curves catching the dim light. I might've lit a little kir, but the close, warm dark soothed me.

Anders came and pulled the gate shut. The brushes were on a shelf near me, and I thought he'd reach for them. Fingertips brushed my jaw and I looked up, a little startled, to catch Anders' kiss. In parting, I caught a gleam of light on his eyes. Something like a question hung in the air.

I whispered, and that seemed too loud. "I didn't expect it to hurt." My throat tried to strangle the words.

He kissed me again. Firm and deep. His arms around me, squeezed the pain from my chest. He reached lower, picked me up by the butt and pinned me against the wall. The impact forced my breath from me. His hands, searching for my skin under the amber and white — I wrapped my legs around him, or tried to. Too much skirt in the way, tangling me.

A bit of a growl on his breath, and he dropped me onto a mass of fresh straw in the dark corner. My felt cloak was thick enough to cushion the pokes, though the stuff crinkled fiercely as he kissed me and found his way through my skirts. I had a grip on his belt, to pull him closer, but he broke off the kiss and sidled down, pausing to find my breasts in the dark and nip them. I let him go, my knees weakening and my breath quickening as he sidled further down, for I'd already learned what this meant he'd do.

CHAPTER 15

"The cot still hasn't arrived," I told Theo when he declared the shop finished. "And a door, here." I sketched my finger around the open frame in the bit of wall sectioning off my library and office from the rest of the upstairs. Theo and Anders, standing in the open space beyond, surveyed the fresh boards walling off the thatched roof. The peak in the center was amply high for both of them to stand, tall as they were.

I drew the heavy canvas sheet off the pile of Parselev's books, which nearly filled the little library's floor, and found the cloth's corners to fold it up. Good to have an extra length of the stuff; downstairs, canvas partitions sectioned off spaces without being so inflexible as walls.

"I'll speak to Adal on it," Theo said, turning toward the stairs down to the kitchen. "He's sure to be here — he never passes up something for free. Though I didn't think you needed an appraisal." That, he aimed at Anders.

"I'm only here for the cider." Anders waved him off. "She can vouch for my health, I trust." I caught the wink he threw at me, and my cheeks may have colored a bit.

Theo chuckled. "Still, it's fine work?" He gestured toward all of it before he descended.

"It's good work." I tossed the folded canvas onto my new writing table, which stood under the shuttered window. I'd be able to look down onto Scribe Street, if I wished. The shelves bracketed onto the sloping roof, to either side, were good and sturdy. I would need some strongboxes, true, but it was a good start.

"We could," Anders said, leaning against the doorframe, "invest in a couple beds for up here. Lamp-stands, a few chests, partitions."

"A couple beds?"

He stepped back from the frame and shrugged, casual. "Rafe will need one, when he outgrows the cradle."

I considered the upstairs afresh; through all the other worries, I hadn't thought of living here. Not as a family. It was perhaps a little larger than my father's cottage, in truth, even without the ground floor. And the small root cellar. Anders went to the window at the back of the house, twin to the one above my writing table, and unlatched the shutters to look down on the bit of grass in the back.

"I mean to plant herbs," I said. There might be room for a chicken coop, as well.

He nodded. "It's too small for Nipper. He'd have to stay there, if he can." My father-in-law didn't charge us the full amount for Nipper's feed, stall, and care, but the warhorse still ate more than I'd imagined an animal could.

Out on the street, a flute and a drum struck up a tune. From downstairs, Theo called, "Elect, if you would join us?"

"I will," I called back. "All that furniture, though? Pots and pans? Crockery?" I asked as I crossed the open space to join Anders at the window. "It runs to some money." Parselev had left me all that was in his cottage, true, but I wouldn't claim it unless Heima had no need of it.

"You still have a whole crown," Anders said. "And we can beg a few gifts, I'm certain. Throw a housewarming. A second one."

I turned and tried to picture two beds, some partitions, a toddler playing in the square of sunlight the window threw. "Someone will need to watch Rafe, if you're off ranging and I'm... being an elect."

Anders smiled. "It's more that we'll need to drive Mother away from Rafe with sticks, if we want any time alone."

"M'lady Kate, you've customers," Theo called again, more urgently.

"Don't leave the window open," I told Anders, and went downstairs. It was chilly outside, even at noon, this late in the Leaf Moon.

At the foot of the stairs, which was just by the back door, a bit of kitchen remained of what the shop had come with. The hearth in the stone chimney was deep and had an oven built into the side as well as its iron crossbars for hanging pots. The shelving was old, but the kitchen table and its benches were new. A canvas partition would section off the gap between the chimney and the far wall, but that stood to one side for now, to let people through.

Those who could brave their way past the surgery table on the other side, that was. The sturdy thing, bolted to the floor, its blood groove draining into a crockery bowl below, wasn't something most had seen before. Neither was my assortment of iron tools around the new, shallow fireplace that masons had cut into the back of the chimney. I'd be able to heat-cleanse and cauterize, though, should I need my kir for greater things. Or if I should be training an apprentice who would need to know how.

In the front, by the door onto the street, more partitions hid my surgery from those waiting or walking by. Most of my mending would happen there — the small charms for fever or wounds. Now it was filled by a handful of fraus with children near to hand.

I met them all, heard their names, where they lived, what they did, checked their patterns and told most that they were well. They walked wide-eyed past my surgery table, hearing that it was for mending the gravely wounded, and into the back where the wagon with the kegs of cider waited.

Before mid-afternoon, my memory had peopled most of the Reichang with names and faces. "This was brilliant," I said to Theo when he handed me a cup of cider during a lull. Children were dancing to the music in the street while their mothers chatted. Those menfolk who'd been drawn in as well stood with Anders just inside the door, deeply analyzing the jousting hopefuls.

"Drawing interest aids you, which aids me," Theo replied, draining his own cup. "Sensible, not brilliant."

I still had one gold crown of the money he'd given me, and a handful of bruns, and though I could well pay my rent from that my gut didn't want to part with the bright, heavy coin yet. "Might I be a little late with my rent for Hunter's Moon?" I asked. It was due on the day before the moon began. "I don't know if I'll earn enough to cover it, in the few days left."

"I think you may." His eyes narrowed, but then he smiled. "It's no trouble. Send it over whenever you have it. On the second, I'm sure."

"That's kind of you," I said. Secretly, I wasn't sure how many days I'd have the shop open — Kiefan had re-instated the weekly meetings in preparation for spring, and I was expected. There was to be the royal hunt in Mount Woden's forest as well, and the joust. "Next time you wish to promise off my time, ask me first. I have little enough as it is."

Theo nodded, his smile bemused. "Easier to ask forgiveness than permission." He moved to put his cup on the surgery table but hesitated just shy of the blood groove and didn't touch it.

"It still serves as a table," I said, meaning to tease him.

He shooed that away with one hand. "No table, that. I hope I never lie on it. If I never see this room again —" He turned to ward off the saws, the cauterizing irons, the trepanning drills, neatly hanging from nails driven into the chimney stone. A bit of a shudder. "If you invite me in, I'll circle round to the back door if I may."

"This is all for healing," I said, taking another swallow of the cider. "Not harming."

My front door opened and a lady filled it, a baby on her cocked hip. Theo brightened, spreading his arms. "There you are! I told you to come at noon. Where've you been with my little sweetling?"

"We had a fitting," his wife Brynhilde answered, "so we all came afterward. Here."

Theo lifted his daughter, tossed her, and she laughed. "Mina, this is Elect Kate," he said, carrying her over. "Elect, Mina Kaufmann. She'll be shrewdly investing her money here in no time, you'll see."

Mina was as bright-eyed a six-month-old as anyone could ask for, sunny-haired, blue-eyed, healthy as a horse. Her mother had brought her circle of wealthy ladies, those who'd returned thus far, and their littlest ones. Well-fed toddlers, all — I'd have thought them a year older than they were.

Frida arrived, driving the carriage with several neighbors from Five Pasture Road to wish me well and be assessed. With all those who came, that day, I did see a few who needed healing. One sickly child had a fault in his heart, right in the core of his prime meridian. An archer of the City Guard came, a woman with hawk's eyes who had been hit on the head during the siege and couldn't focus her left eye. Krepkin, at the Order's hospital, hadn't been able to mend it as Blessing eyes weren't like ordinary ones.

/ true / Qadeem replied, when I asked. / book? /

I hadn't yet read through all Parselev's notes concerning his diagrams. "Come back tomorrow," I told the archer, "and I'll mend you."

She was glad to hear that and left with a smile.

Not long after, the growing joust debate in the front reached a loud point and Anders threw up one hand. "All right! Let's make this clear, then!" A hush fell as all eyes turned to him — my front room was nearly full, though the surgery table still commanded a respectful margin.

"I've competed in the joust three years running," Anders said. He'd only put up one hand because Rafe dozed in his other arm, drooling on his shoulder. "Since I was knighted after defeating my master — in fair combat, if you think this comes of fear." He pointed to a couple of the men, knights by their bearing. "Three years competing, and not once defeated. Not once. I leave the joust an undefeated champion."

"Leave?" That was Theo. "Who will I bet on?"

Laughter. "It's not a matter of these restrictions this year — they only mean to keep men whole for the spring, not nursing broken legs. I've no quarrel with that. Father Duty's put me with the Rangers," Anders said. "Mother Love's saddled me up and no, the bit didn't sit well at first, I'll confess." He raised a hand to that and got more chuckles. A glance upward. "But I'll not fight the bit, Mother." The hand went to pat Rafe. "An inside betting tip? This one, in eighteen years: Sir Rafe Bockmann."

He picked Rafe up from his shoulder, and though it got some half-grumbling noises from the gamblers, the ladies were all smiles. Rafe began to whimper and then cry; I went to claim him and he settled again.

Later in the afternoon, my guests shifted; the families took their leave, and the ladies of Arbor Street arrived. They came in fine dresses, embroidered and beaded, hair woven elaborately and pinned with jewels. Ludmilla, the grand dame of the Arborguild's mother house swept in at the head of the column and took command of my front room.

She looked me square in the eye. "Elect Bockmann, it's an honor to meet you. Might we welcome you to the Reichang?" Her voice dropped, and her smile condensed. "I'm sure there's much we may discuss."

/ excellent source / treat well /

From each of the ladies, I learned a trade name and a true name when I checked them for illness. They confided in me, in hushed tones, past pregnancies that confirmed the wear I saw in their hips, the drinking that explained the sickly livers, the fevers that had caused the scarred wombs. Save for one.

"May I ask your pardon, Elect?" Despite that Süssie had several inches' height on me, she kept her eyes downcast and regretful. "If I could take my appraisal on another day, more privately?"

She fidgeted with the end of one brown, red-ribboned braid. Smooth, graceful fingers that had never suffered hard work — many of the ladies were peasant-born, I could guess by the marks left on their bodies, living in more finery than they could have expected otherwise. Süssie was far softer, and pretty enough.

"I suppose —"

"This one's well." Theo laid a hand on her shoulder, leaning close with an easy familiarity I hadn't seen when he took his baby from his wife. He grinned. "Truly, I can vouch for her."

I couldn't help glancing to where Brynhilde stood, with Mina in her arms, chatting with Anders over a cup of cider. Oblivious, by all I could see. "Perhaps you shouldn't, while she's —" I cast a pointed look at Theo's hand on Süssie's pink woolen sleeve.

His brows rose. "Who?"

Süssie ducked from under his hand. "Yes, love, and you should be more discreet," she chided, voice turning husky in its softness. "I'll not trouble you, Elect. My apologies."

"If you wish more privacy, come whenever you like," I said as she retreated. The lady before her had suffered poorly healed old breaks in her arms and ribs, but she had refused to speak of them. From Süssie, only a quick nod. I frowned at Theo. "You should be more discreet. Wouldn't an argument now harm our business?"

He shrugged, mouth twisting. "With Brynhilde? She has no reason to complain." No anger; he said it as a simple fact and then went after Süssie. His wife didn't notice.

Anders did and leaned to watch them through the front door. A glance to me. Perhaps my frown was what brought him over. It was puzzling enough to crease my brow.

"Did you —?" he asked, voice low.

"He's your friend, I know, but he seems so callous of his wife," I murmured. My memory flicked to Qadeem's warning to beware of oddities. "Is he always?" As I watched, Brynhilde called after a friend of hers, crossing the room to join her.

Anders opened his mouth but thought twice before answering. "In truth, Brynhilde and Süssie get along well enough."

That was odd as well, but I took his word on it. He offered to fetch me more cider, and I had more customers to check.

The ladies stayed until sunset, questioning me on my rates for both healing and creating new item-bound charms. I wondered about that until my memory sifted out a number of novelties from Parselev's collection. The ladies sang along with the flute and drum as well, and they incited a round of "Ducks in the Mud" out on the street. When they climbed into their carriages again and drove off, it marked the end of the day.

I lit a handful of kir and searched through the books for the volumes on Blessings. Partway through, the thought struck me that I could as easily move books onto shelves as I looked, and I chuckled at myself. When I found them, I turned directly to the hawk's eyes and leafed slowly through the sequence, lingering on some that illustrated complex whorls of moving kir. I could picture the flow from loose kir in the wearer's daily ration into a charm, woven by structures within the Blessing.

According to Parselev's notes, the eyes were indeed simply hawk's eyes, made man-sized, and the charms eased the use of them. They had something to do with helping the archer gauge distance, the wind, and even anticipate the target's movement to a degree. Not so much as the true anticipation Blessing, though, he'd written.

Organs to create charms, indeed. Was digestion a charm, then, performed by one's stomach?

"Will there be enough shelves?" Anders asked, leaning against the doorframe again.

I blinked, looking up. It was full dark, now, and the only light was my kir-lamp. My stomach growled, wanting to work its charms. "Yes, I think there will," I said. "I needed to check on something, for that archer."

"Did I surprise you with the talk of furniture?"

I closed the book and picked up its mate. "A bit. The Order was home for so long, and then your mother was so welcoming, that I hadn't thought of moving out. Then again..."

Books in hand, I met him at the door and he let me by for a toll of one kiss. "Then again?"

"I'm not so good a cook, and there'd be laundry to see to, and sewing." I lingered, close to him, and smiled. "You may regret moving out. Or wish for a better wife."

His hand caught mine. "And you for a better husband, once the Rangers learn a bow's useless to me and take their tabard back."

We both made faces at each other and laughed, which ended in a tight hug. Then a walk home to Five Pasture Road.

Strange to watch the jousting tournament from the royal pavilion, standing by Qadeem as my teacher had. He and Woden presided over the contest, small as it was this year, with most of the actual jousting removed to minimize injury. Elect Tannait rode from Knapptal to attend, along with m'lady Leix and a few officers that included Captain Mohra. The infirmary ran under Ada Brauer's command; many of the faces were familiar, many smiled and waved to me, but there were new apprentices as well.

Anders did not even watch. "The sooner I go, the sooner I'm back," he'd said, and he'd reported to the Rangers for his two-week evaluation before the joust began.

After the four days of the joust came a week of hunting, and I had to leave my baby behind to ride with the royal party. Never more than one night camping afield at a time, but when I came home each time Rafe was colicky and refusing the wet-nurse's breast in addition to the pap.

Kiefan and Síochana, though, were all laughter and good cheer. That brought a smile to my face.

There was little time to see customers in my shop — though I did mend that archer's eye, which was a savory challenge. Qadeem gave me only the slightest help, implying through the bond that I could suss this out myself.

And I did.

I wouldn't charge for such a thing — it was the saints' work and Qadeem had put into law that no price would be put to one's life or service to the saints. It was not to be bought and sold, it was to be done.

Smaller things, fevers or wounds, I did take payment for. That came as a trickle of bruns or bartered goods. Came the second Saint-day of the Hunter's Moon, and I didn't have the silver crescents to pay my rent. Reluctantly, I sent the gold crown back to Theo and he made change for me. The pile of silver was still handsome and I locked it away, meaning to keep it for truer emergencies.

One day, I felt an echo of Qadeem's pain in opening his meridian to bind a second elect. The man was a crafter and a Russe, as Saint Aleks had been — the Russe had a skill for crafting, by Qadeem's opinion — and much needed. I couldn't glean his name through my bond, but he was riding to Rukharbor before the snows deepened. There, he'd assist the new elect that Woden had taken and bound to the northern fount. That was Dame Pirra, the knight Kiefan had bested in last year's joust.

/ fallow field / harvest comes /

I could feel relief in what Qadeem sent.

Near halfway through the Hunter's moon, the Rangers returned my husband and agreed that a bow was useless in his hands but he was tolerably good at tracking. Particularly with his horse-nose and horse-ear charms in effect. Other wood-craft skills were a mixed bag for him, though his talent with animals served him well there.

Saint Woden looked Anders up and down, likely sounded him, asked if he'd drawn kir — no — and told him to keep training over the winter. There'd be uses for him come the spring offensive.

There were uses for him in training young warhorses, in the meantime. And uses for him in our bed, or in the hay, or the recovery cot that finally arrived and took its place under the stairs in my shop. It was the only bed to be had there.

Alice teased us constantly, and I had to bite my tongue each time. The ladies on Arbor Street would never resolve their bets on Kiefan versus Anders so long as only I knew the answer. One was a bit more blessed, true, and he meant to be gentle and sweet but hunger got the better of him sometimes. The other…

I had never felt so worshipped.

My fluxes had not yet started again, but I checked my pattern in any case.

Qadeem stole several afternoons for flying lessons. It was still troublesome for me, despite all my straining to lift heavier things with kir-vines. He showed me how to braid the vines as he did. That helped and I was able to push myself up off the ground by nearly a yard. The strain of it set my brain to throbbing in a heartbeat, though, and my vines unraveled under the pressure, dumping me on my butt.

It wasn't much to call flying.

I could see the density of Qadeem's vines, that was simple enough, but just as kir had been unruly in my hands when I was struggling with my first lessons, it would not do as I wished. Yet. If my skill blossomed far enough, it would come just as simple whorls and sparks had. And as knotting charms to make them permanent had, after much practice.

"With each set of talents comes a set of failings," my saint confided in me, after I was reduced to tears of frustration. "Woden's lightning bolts? Deadly, yes, and frightening and commanding, which is even more useful than their deadliness. I have no idea how he throws them. Turning them aside, I can do. But striking with one? Years, I spent trying. I found my way to liquid fire in the process, but no lightning bolts."

"But flying…" I sighed, thinking of Saint Aleksandr and his brown-barred feathers.

"Have you tried shape-shifting?" Qadeem must have thought of him too.

I brought it up with Anders, and we finally exchanged my bone-setting charm for his horse-worming charm. He got the knack of it quickly enough, even if we didn't have a broken bone at hand to work with. Trying to explain how to build his horse-ears charm left him stumped, though. Showing me left many questions unanswered.

Qadeem took Anders aside for a few more lessons on shape-shifting, but I was not invited to those.

I meant to try some shifting, but as the Hunter's Moon waned to a crescent, I needed to earn my rent. That none could be sure when I'd be in my shop worked against me, that had quickly become clear. That several of those I did heal could only pay in a trickle of bruns was another problem. I was sure Theo would be willing to arrange something, though. The silver crescents could pay for beds, chests, pots and pans, perhaps a chicken coop too. The idea had a hold on my mind.

CHAPTER 16

The very last day of the Hunter's Moon, I set out my lantern on the iron hook at my shop's front door, signifying I was open for business. It was the usual signal among shopkeepers. Taking a broom, I swept the front out quickly. I hadn't gotten to my shop for a couple days and a little dried mud lingered from the melting muck that had been tracked in when I was last open. We'd had another hard freeze since then, and a dusting of fresh snow overnight.

These short days of early winter, the sun was only just up. I'd woken in full dark that morning, nursed Rafe, and then gone to the disciple's dance before dawn. Anders had come down the stairs before I left and kissed me when he took a milk-full and happy Rafe to cuddle.

He was up as early as I was, these days. I paused, memories flicking past my eyes. At Vorspitz, the horses had gotten him up. Now there was no rush. Odd.

A knock at my front door and it opened. "Good morn." Theo smiled as he stepped in. Clouds of breath puffed around him. "I was glad to see your lantern out."

"Good morn. Had you been looking for it? Are you well?" I swept toward him and he stood aside to let me clear the dirt out. I shut the door, clicked the latch.

"Yes, I'm well enough. It's not a matter of healing that brings me, in truth."

I'd been about to invite him back to the fire, though in his fine, fur-lined cloak I didn't imagine he was too cold. But his words caught me. "Is it the rent?"

"I fear it is." He gripped the seams of his cloak in gloved hands, wrapped it closer around him. Theo offered a sympathetic grimace. "I allowed a late payment last rent, but I cannot this time."

"Come and warm up." I beckoned him through the gap in the partitions. "I meant to speak with you after one of the weekly meetings," I said as we walked to the kitchen in the back, "but there was hardly a chance. And you missed the last one."

I'd started a small fire, put a kettle nearby to keep warm. "It's the preparations," Theo said, pulling off his gloves and reaching toward the heat. "Provisioning the king for so many feasts and celebrations takes every wagon I have. And every spare brun — in truth, I'd not care if you paid mid-moon again but all my coin is leveraged for brandy and ham and cabbage and now I must find more to cover the honey. For the cakes. The castle needs it tonight, for they'll be baking till dawn."

By tradition, whenever a royal wedded the castle gave away honeycakes to all the city. I remembered eating one when the princess married Duke Seagrace; a wagonload had come down to Engl Street on the duke's orders.

Theo's eyes looked a little hollow, from all his work and worries I supposed. "You need to rest, from the looks of you," I said. "I do have some coin — I can pay you the cut we agreed on. And…" I bit my lower lip, thinking of the silver.

Earnestly, "Anything you have would help."

It was for the honeycakes. I couldn't deny some peasant girl her first honeycake.

"Let me get it," I said and climbed the stairs. The door had been installed in my library wall, though I hardly closed it. My wooden money box acted as a bookend for now and the band of kir locking it shut glowed faintly green. Breaking the charm, I opened the box and took out two of the silver crowns, then counted out the bruns I owed Theo.

For a moment, I had to check my memory to be sure of the number. Twenty-seven bruns, a little more than a crescent. I took a third silver and only two of the bronze coins instead.

I looked at the space against the chimney, where I meant to put the bed I meant to buy, as I passed. There was still money for it.

Descending, I found the hearth empty. Surely he hadn't gone — I heard a clink of iron and rounded the chimney looking for the sound. Theo stood with my trepanning drill in hand, pinching the twisted bit between his fingers. He pressed the tip against the pad of his thumb.

He glanced up. A guilty smile. "I'm being nosy. My apologies." Theo hung it on its pair of nails. "Only checking the workmanship, after what we paid for all this." Theo nodded toward the surgery table, the other tools. "Is that —?"

"Rent, and your profits," I said, handing him the money. "It was the joust and the hunt that kept me away. After the wedding, I'll see to the shop more and pay you early for Bitter Moon."

"I don't doubt it." He smiled. "Thank you." When he turned to go, he hesitated and asked, "Will you be at tonight's feast? It will be as fine a spread as tomorrow's, I promise."

"I must earn my keep," I said, shaking my head. "The wedding feast will be glorious enough, I'm sure."

It was a good day, in all. One of my patients paid me with a bag of dried mint leaves for tea, and another promised a pair of wooden spoons as soon as her husband whittled them. I'd read through more of Parselev's notes on Blessings when I could.

The sun leaned toward the west, already thinking of his bed, and the lamp on the table near the front door fought the early shadows. The flame rippled in drafts; I needed drapes for the shutters in addition to furniture. I poked at the lowering fire with my kir, gauging whether the coals were safe to leave, and thought of how Saint Woden had pulled kir from fire to kill it.

I called kir, and the coals glimmered with it. Parselev had told me that kir was like heat when I was an apprentice. Not the flame, but the warmth. I drew the bit of kir, and it wafted up like a breath of steam to my hand. The coals died.

Hooves sounded faintly on the street and then the door opened. "Kate?"

I hopped up, trotting to the front. "Anders? What's wrong?"

He breathed a little hard, face cold-nipped, and his hair windblown from riding with his hood down. "This note," he said, holding up a sheet of paper. "You need to see Theo. Now."

"He was just here this morning. I paid him, there's no trouble. What does he want?" And if he wanted something of me, he could have simply come and asked. I was only up the street from his home.

"This's from Brynhilde," Anders said, straightening the sheet and bringing it to the lamp. "Not him. A messenger delivered it, but Mother didn't think anything of it till I came in from the barn."

The penmanship was scratchy, hurried, and I worked out the first few words. "Theo is not..."

"Theo is not well," Anders read for me, far quicker. "This past week and some, he's not been himself but I thought it the strain of supplying the castle. Today, when I told him I felt old and ugly, he kissed me and pressed me to the wall. He meant to have me, right there, and I was so shocked that I froze. He noticed, he changed his tune and let me go, but — he's not well, Anders. Could you ask the elect —"

"You said we must watch for lapses," Anders looked up from the letter.

"Comforting his wife is a lapse?" The message made little sense as it was.

He took a breath, hesitated, folded the letter and squeezed it in his hand. "Theo didn't marry for the usual reason. He has no interest in women."

That seemed unlikely. "He has both a wife and a whore." My memory flicked through all I'd seen of Theo since we first met, as well. "You warned him off me at Solstice. You thought he might've hurt me."

"Süssie's not a woman."

She was tall, true, far from blessed with curves... and had declined a pattern check. My mind stumbled over that as Anders continued.

"He flirts to keep up appearances. When he gets drunk enough, sometimes he tries — well, it never goes well, and if the girl won't agree to buggery, it can go quite badly." Anders' voice fell. "He's not Theo."

I'd heard of buggery. From Alice. More important than that word, though: "Cambifax."

His touching my tools after shuddering at the thought had been my only warning.

"If it's killed him —" Anders took a harsh breath, hand settling on his sword hilt. "Let me help you kill it?"

"The thing is a saint," I said, and touched my bond.

/ cambifax / in the city /

Alarm poured back to me. / find / track / warn Kiefan and Woden / coming /

/ where are you? /

I had a brief impression of the crumbled walls of Ansehen falling behind as Qadeem flew. A second ration of kir warmed me.

"We find it first," I said, aloud. Gathering up my kir, I hid it away. I could draw more from the Pool, if I needed. "Your day's ration?"

"Untouched."

"Theo's home first?"

Anders' hand tightened on his sword as he nodded.

Jenner trotted down the street toward the Kaufmanns' wagon yard — which stood quiet. Empty. Anders slowed the horse at the broad, open gates and scanned the vast space before we entered. The warehouse doors were shut. The thin blanket of snow was all but destroyed by wagon wheels and feet, reduced to only an edging about the corners.

"Hein?" Anders called for the foreman. He stopped Jenner by the steps up to the wagon-bed-height porch and I slid off the pommel. "Hein?"

The house's rear door opened and a manservant looked out. "Sir Anders, good day. Theo didn't mention you'd be by."

I trotted up the steps. "Is Theo here? Or his wife?"

He ducked a bow to me. "The frau's here, yes, Elect. She didn't feel well enough for the feast."

"Where is everyone?" Anders pounded up behind me.

"The men put in so much work preparing for the marriage, sir's given them the night off. Please, come in. I'll tell Brynhilde you're here." The servant gestured us through the door. I checked his kir — he was a charm-hand and had the loose, quiet pattern of an un-gifted man — and strode into the foyer.

I stopped. Anders crashed into me. "What?"

"Kir." I looked up, through the ceiling toward it. Just enough to feel through the layer of wood. "What's upstairs?"

The servant hurried past us in the hall, turned and bowed. "Sir's room, frau's room, the children's — is something wrong, Elect?"

"Children?" Dread seeped in.

"Sir's brothers and sisters, m'lady. And the baby."

Anders brushed past. "Call Bryn — that's Theo's room you're looking at, Kate." He motioned for me to follow and drew his sword. I followed, sneaking out a little kir into my hand.

"We're not to go in sir's room," the man called as we found the stairs up. "The door's been locked all week!"

"Bloody fucking balls," Anders muttered, slowing at the top of the stairs and peeking around. "Bryn's room is at the other end, and his brother's has been empty for moons. If this turns into a fight —"

"Don't charge in," I hissed.

He slipped into the hall, sword at middle guard, but all was quiet. The door was locked indeed, with a knotted string of kir. A slender red line stretched from it into the distance. It trembled when I touched the knot. "He'll know when I break this," I said. "He's not here." I was fairly sure of that. Something about the angle the thread shot off at told me it was reaching a fair distance.

"He's hiding something, though. Not letting the servants in?" Anders stood before the door, ready. "Open it."

I sharpened the kir on my finger and cut the knot. The red line snapped away. Lifting the latch, I shoved the door open and called all my kir to my hand.

The charm inside rippled at my call, and I knew it: a hush sphere. A flick of my sharp finger and it unraveled, fell away — and the smell strengthened. Death. Blood, piss, and shit. Anders swept in, sword up, despite my warning, but found nothing. I followed, and the body on the bed put speed in my feet.

Theo, limp, tied to the bed frame. Blood-stained gouges had been raked into his chest, then left to scab and fester; I could see the hot swelling, and there was sweat on his brow. He'd lost a nipple. Around the breastbone ridge of his strength Blessing, the flesh was dug to the bone, as if to see how deep it went.

"Theo!" Anders slapped his cheek. No response, though he was alive. "He's burning, Kate. Dob!" He went to the door, shouting for the manservant.

The mattress was deeply stained — it would need burning along with his braies — but I put a knee on it and leaned to touch Theo's face. Sunken and pale. His jaw hung slack. He barely breathed. When I called his patterns, I saw why he hadn't simply broken free of his bonds; the lines of his Blessing had been cut. The digging at his breastbone had severed them from that central locus. I set my teeth on my lower lip and started with the wounds. Scratches, by how they ran in fours. Some older than others. He'd been tortured.

"What's been — Mother's mercy! Theo!" Brynhilde burst in the door with a shriek. She circled the bed at a run, skipping over where the filth had run onto the carpet. "Water, Dob!"

Theo twitched under my hand as I laid new patterns over his wounds. Flesh moved to knit them shut. Fever had a strong grip on him; it was in his blood. His arms, having been tied up above his head for so long, were half starved. He'd lain here for days. The cambifax must've brought him some water, some food, or he'd have died. Not that he was far from it.

Anders cut him from the frame with his sword. Brynhilde wrestled the ropes off, revealing raw, bloody rings. Tears streaked her cheeks as she pattered to him. Apologizing. Asking what happened, and Anders answering her.

I focused on his blood, seeking knots of invading kir-patterns. Soothing away the fever. His eyes opened, at last, bloodshot but focused.

"Why did he torture you?" I asked. Brynhilde and Anders fell silent, turning to me.

Theo's throat had been screamed raw. "Everything. Schedules. King's Guard. The castle."

Dob, the manservant, passed me a cup of water and I coaxed Theo up onto one elbow. His wife was quick to help when he hissed a breath through clenched teeth.

A few swallows and he answered further. "How thorough the gate inspections are. Who can be bribed. The castle's layout. I — he didn't hurt you? The baby?"

Brynhilde stroked his hair. "No. I'm so sorry, I thought it one of your..."

"Where is he?" I asked, looking to Dob. The man stared, ashy-faced, his hands shaking. The housemaid at the door didn't look much better.

Part IV: Salt in the Wound

"He didn't say, Elect," Dob answered. "But he left after — he wrote some letters, after noon tea, and then he left with all the wagons."

"He gave everyone the day off," Bryn said, frowning. "What wagons? Who drove?"

Dob's face went slack in bewilderment. "The drivers — don't know which exactly, their hoods were up. Tarp-covered wagons, six or eight of them. Sir said if anyone else came in, they had the night off."

Gone to the castle, no doubt. My stomach should've been sinking, but it only twisted inside me. My eyes were full of the silvery skin that had stretched across Theo's scratches, thinking of an Arceal saint loose in Castle Kaltkern. With men. Near the Pool. If they reach the Pool, they have the fount and all is lost, Qadeem had said. I drew kir and it trickled down, warm, strengthening my resolve. They were all looking to me for what to do, even Anders.

"I tried," Theo whispered, "but my strength is gone. These ropes are nothing, the frame's only wood."

He'd been soft — a week's starving had melted the butter from him — and ordinary without his Blessing. It was too much to tell him, just then. I checked his patterns once more, to be sure the fever was broken, and stood.

"He went to the castle," I said to Anders. "My duty's there."

"The feast. They're all in the great hall."

Anyone with a drop of royal blood was a target. "And the Pool."

CHAPTER 17

Dob would ride to the City Guard with the alarm.

/ coming / strength / clarity /

Qadeem sent calm through the bond, but my mind was already far too clear. My pulse pounded in my neck and there was a bit of tremble in my hands. The ride up the switchbacks to the castle gate never seemed so long.

I jumped when the castle's trumpet blew, loud and long. The general alarm. Jenner skittered, but Anders clicked, steadying him. Kicked him to keep going up the steep slope.

The portcullis was down. Jenner puffed hard breaths, circling away from the bars and a whiff of blood. I slid down and put my hands on the close-set grid, straining to see past the wagon parked to block the view. An arm in a mail sleeve, limp on the ground.

"There must be a way in." Anders looped Jenner's reins around one bar, looking up at where the iron vanished into darkness above.

I looked up at the gatehouse towers, the crosswalk over the gate. Smooth, seamless granite, and not a man to be seen. It was twenty feet to the lowest crenel, or more.

Focus. They needed me. Kiefan needed me.

I massed my kir, braided it, and thrust against the ground. Put my hands up, straining as the gate and the wall rushed past me. Spotted the crenel, a bit of sunset-red sky between the stone merlons, and my hand latched onto it. Kir spun from my other hand and I threw it up into the crenel, thinking of a hook. It held, and half my weight hung on my mind.

Gasping hard breaths, I got my feet onto the smooth wall and pushed with kir. Nothing for purchase; I gained only an inch. I threw my kir-hook higher, over the merlon, and pulled. Another inch. Letting go with my hand, I put a second hook on the merlon and heaved again, bringing my legs up. My foot hooked into the crenel. My knee followed. All those mornings at the disciple's dance served me well. I slid sideways through the crenel and fell onto the walkway. Panting. Head throbbing.

"Kate!"

Anders stood below, both hands raked into his hair. I spun a rope of kir and threw it down to him; he made it look easy, pulling himself up, while I braced against his weight and hooked myself to the merlon across the way for good measure.

The gatehouse was empty. In running across the gate-yard, we passed eight King's Guard in pools of blood. Four Arceal knights wearing brown cotes over their lamellar cuirasses, as well. Cloaks with hoods to hide their tanned skin and dark hair. Stabbed, slashed, all. Fresh blood, still warm on the cold ground. One Guard had lost his shield arm and bled to death. Anders stopped to shake the limb loose and settled the shield on his own arm; he was in plain clothes, no mail.

Those were the Guard for both the first and second gates. Past the second, the bonfire was a welcome break in the quiet — but the bodies sprawled around it stopped my heart. Common folk, some King's Guard in black tabards, and a few Caer officers in dust-brown uniforms. One fallen man had dropped his stein of ale.

I slowed, but Anders snatched my arm. "Don't stop!"

Gritting my teeth, I called their kir. It answered, which let me take a breath. "They're alive."

Anders kept running. "Too early to be drunk."

"Doped?" It was all I could do to keep up with him past the guest house, through the garden, and up the slope to the third gate. Why drug them?

No kir needed, I realized. No spike that Kiefan might sense.

And those guests had no saints' blood to speak of. All of that was in the castle: Kiefan, his sister, his nephews, his crippled cousin the duke…

I felt kir flare in the castle, a slender arc streaming from far away. Thinner than a saint's — Tannait. My heart leapt. Tannait had come with m'lady Leix to witness the marriage.

Anders' sword rasped free and he snarled, pulling my eyes back. A lone Arceal knight at the inner gate turned and ran toward the open grand hall doors, shouting as he went. My legs flagged as we crossed the gate-yard; Anders pulled away, hounding him. No bodies here, no Guard. The silence was all wrong. The horn should've kept blowing, calling up defenders. There should've been —

I crashed into Anders' back, at the doors of the great hall. Two Arceal knights, plus the one we'd chased, turned and lapped their shields into a little wall, kir spinning out to further shield them. Yelling in the back of the hall, from six more knights, and a sudden bellow from the minotaur in the center as he swung around toward us. The tawny beast wore black iron lamellar and red wool, held a heavy-bladed sword in his massive fist. His horns dripped blood.

My stomach dropped.

Blood covered the floor, the red pool strewn with hacked bodies. The tables overturned. Duke Haken lay on a scattering of his own guts, sword under his limp hand. Knights in mail and black tabards, cut nearly in half. A young girl, barely old enough for Blessing. Faint screams poured down the great stair from the second floor.

And then the high-pitched squeal of a child upstairs steeled my nerve. Kir lit up, further above, and a pulse from the Pool arced up to answer Kiefan's call.

From the side door into the west wing, a cry of "Wodenberg!" and Captain Aleks charged out with sword and shield, half a dozen Guard behind her. A green kir-ram shot over their heads and scattered three of the Arceal knights. The minotaur turned away from me and Anders, lowered its head, and counter-charged.

"Kate!" Anders jerked his chin at the stair. He spun out a kir-shield atop the one he wore, and a blade charm slid down over his sword.

Yes, despite my fear. The Pool filled me, in an eyeblink, and with a touch I filled him too. "Go," I told him, and he swooped into the line of three at Blessing speed.

I shoved against the floor at an angle and flew across the high ceiling, brushing through the dusty, hanging banners. Throwing out a column of kir, I caught myself at the foot of the steps and launched again, away from the startled enemy knight there. Up to the landing. Then again to the space before the King's Council door. Far faster than running.

The child's scream cut off suddenly, and a small corpse flew through an open door, struck the stone wall with a sickening crack. The little boy fell in a heap. William, the older of Kiefan's nephews. On my other side, a woman screamed and a heavy thud silenced her.

Below, the ruckus of combat. Above, hooves pounding, more bellowing, and Kiefan pulling kir. He was alive and fighting.

I flew up the stairs to the third floor. The minotaur standing before the smashed door into the king's suite turned, shifting his heavy, charmed sword to point at me. Behind him, two bloody heaps of guts and mail. And a dead monster, thank Father Duty.

The noise fell away. Kir rose to my hand in a half-moon, its curved edge sparking as my mind honed it to a cutting blade. I threw. The minotaur knocked it aside, and the two charms cut each other in a burst of sparks. I pulled more kir, braided it, and threw it in a ram as his blade swung back.

I struck between his mottled horns and knocked him back. My arms were shocked numb by the impact, and I slid despite my well-braced feet. He tripped over the dead Guards and fell. I rushed to the door — some tiny corner of my mind squeaked for a shield and I threw one up — and whipped off another kir-blade. It flew awry but struck his leg, severing the meridian.

A scream in the room yanked my head around. I glimpsed a minotaur, fallen on one knee, and Síochana swinging down for the kill. Its horn caught her in the belly. Gored clean through as her swing threw her against its head. Her blow missed as the beast lunged up and slung her off against the wall. She left a red stain in falling.

"Sío!"

Kir crackled around Kiefan and struck the minotaur he faced in a full-body ram of rage. The monster fell back, splaying to keep its balance. A blur of steel flew through its sword-arm. Kiefan caught the freed limb as blood spurted and slung it with Blessed strength into the second minotaur's head as the beast gained his feet. Bone shattered. I all but heard the neck crack on Síochana's murderer.

Steel struck my shield, and I tumbled into the room. My half-lamed minotaur pulled himself into the doorframe by one hand, the other clutching the sword he'd clubbed me with. Yellowed teeth bared in a grin. He spun his kir out in a fresh blade charm — and I put up a hand, pulled from the Pool. It lit my hand in a nimbus, curled around my palm, and bent into a crescent blade. The Shepherd's knife slashed through the bull's head at an angle. The monster dropped.

When I looked, the dis-armed minotaur's guts slid across the floor. The other twitched and Kiefan struck him with the limp arm, then stabbed through the iron lamellar. Panting, he dropped the hunk of meat. Then the sword.

"Sío…" He fell to his knees, scooped her up from the floor. "No, no…" Her white shift, Caer-short, was all she wore, and it dripped crimson from the waist down. Kiefan's pale under-cote picked up the stain quickly.

I stood, gasping deep breaths, my stomach grinding. Wanting to vomit. Somewhere below, kir roiled and knotted. Enough to draw my eye, through all the floors of castle stone between us. "Kiefan, the Pool," I said. A second flare of kir, and a long, thick arc reached into the bowels of the castle from far away. "The cambifax!"

He looked up, anguish clouding his eyes. "Woden," he whispered, straightening as if something had caught his ear.

"Duty," I told him, though my heart twisted and I wished I could let him grieve.

He looked down at Síochana again, then laid her on the bloody floor. Then he stood, wiped his bloody sword on one white leg of his long braies, and his grey eyes had gone cold.

"Duty."

There was nothing to be done for Kiefan's dead kin on the second floor. He faltered for a heartbeat when he spotted his nephew lying broken, but I grabbed his arm and pulled. One Arceal knight spotted us and hollered, but he was nothing. Two saint-sized stars of kir boiled up from the Pool chamber and one streaked after the other into the great hall.

Hardly any noise from there as I leaped to the landing. Fear stabbed me; there should be shouting, fighting, if Anders and Captain Aleks — I rushed to the railing to see.

The leading saint, afire like a golden comet, flew the length of the hall and out the front doors. A lightning bolt shot after and caught it as it crossed the sill; the thunder slapped my eyes shut for a heartbeat, numbed my ears. The invader's kir vanished, like a snuffed candle.

I leaped down. What I saw opened a pit in my stomach as Kiefan and I landed in the hall; knights in black tabards, one sitting among the dead with a hand pressed to his side. The minotaur, hacked to a ruin. Blood and piss thick in the air. One knight standing, and that was Captain Aleks. She wobbled when she spun, sword at ready.

My mind emptied. "Anders?" My voice rose to almost a scream. "Anders!"

Black tabards, brown cotes, colorful dresses, blood all the same color — I spun, looking for him on the floor, and nearly tripped. Saint Woden alit beside the Captain as she helped the wounded Guardsman to his feet. But Anders wouldn't be wearing black —

"Kate!"

I turned toward his voice and ran. He caught me in his shield arm, clutched me close. Alive. Sticky wet, but alive. Blood streaking his flaxen hair, but unhurt. His lips didn't have any blood on them, thank the Mother — I couldn't kiss him deeply enough, even with both hands raked into his hair —

A roar and Anders threw me aside, sword flashing up. Steel clashed and kir sparked. I fell on my butt and gaped as Kiefan pulled kir from the Pool and let it swirl out in a green cloak. Teeth gritted, all but frothing. Anders' eyes widened for less than a heartbeat, and then a snarl curled his lip. Kiefan lunged at him, slipping into a blur, and Anders met him head-on.

A scream tore from me and I lunged, shoving a shield between them. It split under Kiefan's blade, saved Anders from a strike.

Kir looped around my waist, yanked, and threw me at Woden's feet. I slashed away the kir-vine and threw another shield, meaning to knock Kiefan and Anders away from each other. Woden caught it, snapped it in mid-air. He loomed over me, kir-blade to my throat. "My elect. My winnowing," he growled.

For a moment, my heart shrank in terror, wanted to grovel. Then fury flared.

/ don't! /

Part IV: Salt in the Wound

Its harshness, through my bond, snapped me back.

Kiefan shore the top four inches from Anders' shield in one swing. They'd both lapsed from Blessing speed, their kir burning off fast. Anders fell back a step, throwing away what remained of the shield and holding his sword, Saint Aleks' sword, at high guard.

The Pool answered Kiefan's call, brimming him again.

Anders was nearly spent. Tears flooded my eyes. No, please Mother, Father, no —

The call pulled at my kir, and with a gasp I let it fly. All of it, full as I was. It arced to Anders, and he struck, the charm rippling across him as he went. Muscle pulsed in his sleeves, his shoulders deepened, his neck thickened and furred with grey dapples — ears pinned back, muzzle lengthening as he lunged past their tangled blades — and Nipper's teeth sank into Kiefan's bicep. Flesh tore when he pulled away.

In shock, Kiefan stumbled back on the defensive. His shield arm swung limp, blood spattering, but his kir spun out in a shield on his sword arm. He caught Anders' next swing on his sword, sent it across the shield and threw his arm wide, ruining Anders' balance.

I surged against Woden's hold, pulling more kir from the Pool, as their swords blurred around, skirled, and Anders threw himself back.

The point of Kiefan's sword thrust just below Anders' breastbone, jutted red from his back near the spine.

Anders' blade, reversing in an arc, pulled a crimson stream from Kiefan's throat.

My scream tore my mind in two.

Woden's binding burst under the force. I flew. Blood spewed as Kiefan dropped to his knees, eyes wide. His head lolled, held on by only spine, and I caught him by his braided crest. My other hand clutched his throat, kir rushing into the gap.

I felt the blow coming, Gentle Woden's kir-blade, to kill me for defiance. A heavy shield sprang up around me and the strike burst against it. A braided vine lashed, and Woden fell back with a furious roar. The air crackled and lightning struck; I felt it slam past, drawn to Saint Qadeem's hand and shunted into the earth along a slender thread. Thunder rebounded off the stone walls and slapped me twice. My ears rang.

Qadeem's hands lit with blazing stars, the same that had killed Rakkar. Kir-amplified, he shouted, "Neither of us can hold alone. Don't be a fool!"

Woden stood with kir cloaked about him, stars dripping, eyes narrowed. Then he flicked it away. Qadeem bristled a heartbeat longer and let his fires fade.

Kiefan gasped a breath through his rejoined windpipe, under my hands. The torn meridian in his arm pulsed, freshly re-knit to stop the bleeding. I poured blood into his sealed arteries and felt his struggling heart steady. It was enough; I dropped him and turned to the second disaster.

Corpses, all around, Qadeem standing with arms folded, and Kiefan pressing at his ripped arm on his knees.

"Anders?"

His sword, blooded, had fallen on a dead Arceal knight. In all the gore, any of it could have been Anders'. Where —? How —? My chest heaving faster, fear growing, I reached the open doors. Kiefan's moon-pommeled sword lay just outside, part of a crimson trail.

No, no, he'd die in a heartbeat! "Anders!" I screamed and tripped over the sill in trying to follow the trail.

Kir flared, and a rukh launched itself through the inner gate. Or something like one; its wings were black, though white flashed on their undersides. Its head was featherless, puny. A rukh-sized vulture. Silhouetted against the last gloaming on the clouds, I saw a body in its talons. Two legs hanging.

I stumbled to my knees, mouth falling open.

"Seraphine!" Qadeem's voice carried on kir.

The vulture-rukh screeched in reply and gained altitude. Heading south with its prize.

"No..."

My chest pumped, fear roiling into disbelief and into anger. Anger condensing into rage. I was on my feet and running back into the hall, not caring what I stepped on. Woden stood with arms crossed, looking down at Kiefan, likely disappointed they hadn't covered the walls with each others' guts —

"You let them fight!" ripped from me as a kir-vine jerked me to a stop two feet from the saint. Qadeem sucked my kir back through my bond before I could shape a knife from it.

Woden spared me a cool look. "I'll not rely on weaklings in battle."

I slung an arm around to fight the vine, and another caught my arm. "I could've stopped them!" I snarled, lunging against my leashes.

"Better to let them scheme and poison all around them with their hate? Rather than one clean duel?"

His calm face. All I wanted was to put a kir-ram through that calm, disdainful face. Qadeem drained me as fast as I pulled from the Pool. "So they could kill each other?" I screamed. "Who'd wear your fucking crown then?"

"There's always another claimant." Woden clapped a hand on Kiefan's bloody collar and yanked him up, turning away from me. Ending the discussion.

Kiefan's eyes hit mine as he was pulled along, such a muddle of alarm and denial that my anger faltered. He looked away, pain winning out. Hurt, but alive by my hand, when Anders... I crumbled over my knees, strength draining away in my tears. The sobs heaved out, my mind full of Anders lying dead, bled out like the knights in the hall, stooped over by a monstrous vulture.

Qadeem's gentle hand stroked my back. "Strength, Kate. There are lives you can save, still."

CHAPTER 18

Lives I could save. In a glance, I didn't see it. Kiefan stood, trembling from the effort of it, with Woden and Captain Aleks. Lieutenant Rostislav and the third surviving Guard prodded the Arceal dead to be sure. The two remaining enemy knights had surrendered and lay, hog-tied, on the grand stair's landing.

I called kir in the hall to see who was alive.

Kir answered, bright and clear, huddled against the wall behind a fallen Arceal knight. Dense pattern. Tannait. I turned, and saw Woden's head pick up like a scenting hound. Grabbing my skirts, I rushed across the floor to get between them. I turned to face Woden, jaw set.

Qadeem had said that so long as you didn't show weakness — I saw Woden's eyes slide toward where Tannait hid, then back to me. Beside him, Kiefan only glanced and looked away again.

"Go raise the portcullis," Woden told him, deliberately disregarding me. "Are your men fit for that?"

"Once my arm's bandaged. And if Kate could see to Rostislav's wounds," Kiefan gasped between deep breaths. His shield arm still hung limp, the bicep ripped in half. Still bleeding, slowly.

I picked my way to Tannait. A bit of green shield sprouted over her, and she levered herself up on one hand. Blood clotted in her silver hair. Her chest heaved. She pointed at me, kir focused in her fingertips, and her teeth gritted.

"Don't," I said, spreading my hands. "Tannait —"

"I aided," she hissed. "'Twasn't my fight, but I aided your knights."

"I know. I saw. Let me help you."

"I'm not dying," she growled.

That might be true, but if she could've healed herself she would have. "Please."

Tannait's hand trembled. She let it drop, and I took that for permission. I rolled away the dead knight with both hands and touched her shoulder.

She'd known how to stop the bleeding, and her dense, energetic kir-patterns resisted the damaged dance around the wound. Where the chaos normally would have spread, rattling the prime meridian and destroying the entire body's pattern, hers struggled to maintain its proper dance. Weak as she was, she'd have been easy prey for anyone who wished to claim her kir. Perhaps she'd even have died eventually.

I mended her in a few dozen heartbeats, taking care as my mind was half-dazed and wandered back to Anders, the spray of blood from Kiefan's neck, the vulture-rukh's black wings. When she sat up, Tannait whispered thanks to me and looked around the ruin of the hall with grim eyes.

"Margrave Gwatcyn dined beside me," she said. "'Twere split when the minotaurs charged."

My heart sank again. I bit my lip. Qadeem, appearing beside me, offered Tannait his hand to pull her up. She accepted. "Let's find her then," he said. "Kate, the servants must be somewhere. Perhaps wounded. They won't take well to a brown face just now."

A few had died in the hall. The rest were barricaded in the kitchen, armed with butcher knives and brooms for staves. Housemistress Wenda hugged me in joy, then began barking orders to the rest. There were two who'd been slashed while running from the hall, and those were easily healed. As I nodded to accept their thanks, a smaller body crashed into me, clasping my waist.

Ein. I dropped to one knee to hug him, a little surprised that he let me. He was always so intent on being as strict and proper as his father. He didn't ask me about Anders or the blood splattered all over me. Wenda gave the younger pages orders to draw more water, and he was soon off to obey.

"To keep them away from the worst of it," Wenda told me, sidelong. "The hall?"

I nodded. "Butchery."

———————————✕———————————

The last night of the Hunter's Moon, there was no Shepherd in the sky. Only the Flock of seven little moons. Frost had already fallen when I lit a kir-lamp in my hand, wrapped my cloak — despite its stiff patches of dry blood — closer, and walked out of the castle. I crossed the gate-yard, following the dark spots of Anders' blood to a patch by the gate-house. Then, nothing. He'd met the cambifax here.

Fought it? Died at its feet?

The streaky patch couldn't tell me.

"He lives," Saint Qadeem said, joining me with his ermine snug around him. Hood up. Nobody else wore the white fur, though, lining a dun-colored cloak. "She would not have stolen a corpse."

"Seraphine?"

He nodded, and walked through the gate-house. I followed.

"You recognized... her?" I asked.

"Giddha-rukhs are crueler than Wodenberg's osprey-rukhs. She's alone in mastering their pattern, so far as I know." Qadeem looked to me, sidelong. "The Empress."

Here? Didn't empresses lounge on cushions, wrapped in silk...? I pushed that away. "What will she do to him?"

He didn't answer as we passed the guest house. Teams of men from the upper city were rousing the drugged revelers as best they could, and taking inside those who slept too soundly. The bonfire had settled in its neglect. We walked through the middle gate and down to the outer yard, where the City Guard was busy laying out the dead. The wagons the enemy had arrived in served now for their corpses. Messengers sprinted past into the stables, claiming horses to ride into the city. I stopped to ask about Jenner, and he was brought. With his reins in hand, I kept walking with my saint, out the opened gate and down the switchbacks.

Partway, Qadeem said, "That depends on what he does."

Another long pause as we rounded a turn. A messenger trotted by on a dark horse.

"What might she do to him?" I asked.

"Kate —"

"You say you know her. You've seen what she does." Pleading crept in, despite fighting it.

His voice sharpened. "Nobody knows a thousand-year-old cambifax who's survived every plot, every machination of building the greatest empire in the world. Nobody knows the Empress. I survived her, I escaped her, and that's more than most — perhaps that's why she came to see to this herself. I bruised her pride, three centuries gone."

He hated her, by the bitterness in those words. "What did she do to you?"

The answer fought its way out. "Something like what Kiefan's suffered."

Kiefan's blood on my hands, the gape of his cut throat. I'd cheated the Shepherd of him, full and fair. "I should've..." But I couldn't say it. The terrible wound, the blood, when Anders' would hold for a moment longer. So long as he didn't pull the sword out.

"You did what you must," Qadeem said. Another pause, while we walked down River Road. "How did you get free of Woden?"

"The bonds broke." That was all I knew. "He would've killed me for healing Kiefan?"

A grimace. "He keeps only the strong."

"If you'd been a heartbeat later..."

"I've been far too late twice now, by my count."

He thought of Saint Aleks, I was sure. Which brought my mind back to Anders and his shifting into horse-form. His pulling kir from me — easily, knowing what he meant to do with it. Not the first he'd done it, I would guess. "Did you know he was elect?"

"I saw the density of his pattern at our last lesson. I warned him that Woden doesn't tolerate rogue elect in his kingdom. The bond is not something I will force, and he was not my disciple to claim. Had he asked, I would have."

We walked in silence, angling off River Road toward Five Pasture Street. Questions boiled in me, pressing on my throat. Eventually, I got one orderly enough to ask. "Might the Empress trade? Prisoners? Ransom?"

The answer came softly. "You're not likely to see him again."

It dug into my heart's fresh wound, all the same. My feet faltered, stopped. My knees weakened as the night dissolved into tears. Qadeem caught me when I wobbled, hugged me close against him for support. Hushed me when the sobs came again, rough as broken glass in my chest.

After all the crying, I still had to walk home. He moved to put me in Jenner's saddle, but I shook him off. Walked. Eyes burning, ribs sore, I walked. They were all there, awake, worried, full of questions, but one look at my face and they handed me my cuddle-bug, let me upstairs to collapse on Anders' bed. To breathe his scent on the blankets and sob while my saint tried to explain.

<hr>

No honeycakes, the next day.

I returned to the castle in my embroidered green dress, because the people were afraid and needed to see their saints and elect, alive and strong. I went because Frida's grief and my own were too much for one house to contain. I couldn't breathe, for the weight of it.

They were all laid out, Kiefan's closest blood, on tables under the gaze of the Mother and the Father's icons. His sister, his nephews, his cousin. His cousin's daughters. Each bundled in a warm woolen shroud.

The queen knelt by the votive table, hands clasped in prayer to the Mother, sobs shaking her thin shoulders. She was only a pale shadow inside her black veil. After taking the drugged ale with dinner, she had gone to her rooms to lie down, leaving her two Queen's Guard on duty in the great hall. They'd been cut down in the initial attack.

Captain Aleksandra told the story, having seen it from the castle roof with the half-dozen Guard she'd led into the hall. They'd spotted Arceal knights taking the outer gate — from within the castle. Echoing up the stairwells, they heard the slaughter in the great hall. The captain had ordered the alarm blown in the watchtowers and organized the men she had. When they reached the foot of the west stairs, they'd met Elect Tannait, wounded and alone. Together, they'd mounted their attack just as Anders and I had arrived.

In places of honor, m'lady Leix and Síochana lay with Tannait and the few Caer officers to stand watch. Captain Mohra kept one hand on her lady's body and let her tears flow. She'd been at the bonfire, she'd been drugged along with the others, and likely would never forgive herself.

Woden and Qadeem stood on the platform, above the high table where the princess and her sons lay. I stood to my saint's side, Kiefan to his, at far corners. That was well, for if I had to look him in the eye a rage might seize me and I didn't — no, I had a fair idea what would happen.

He'd started it. He'd attacked Anders. I should've let him bleed out, let his head fall back and break his prime meridian at the neck.

This man I loved with all my heart.

After the abbot spoke for the dead, a miserable hush followed. There was a funeral feast laid out, but nobody wanted much. It ought to have been the wedding feast.

"You have questioned, I am sure," Qadeem said, and all their eyes picked up with a little hope, "why we saints refused all Arcea's offers of alliance and marriage. Questioned privately, for you are good, loyal folk. Perhaps you think that had we accepted, such as this would never have passed." He gave that a moment, but nobody would admit to that yet. "This day would've come twenty years later, but it would run just the same. It would've come while the royal heirs were groomed in Arcea's courts to take the throne after their parents' slaughter.

After their kingdom's saints were murdered and its founts claimed. I have seen it done. I have seen many things Arcea has done, and I stand against them. Will you stand with me?"

Nodded heads, a general murmur in agreement.

Kiefan hopped off the platform and stalked toward them. "Do you stand!"

Their spines straightened, voices cleared.

"They sent their knights, their monsters, their greatest saint — and yet we stand!" Kiefan stabbed the air with one hand, the other gripping his sword. He wore a bandage under that sleeve, I could tell. Krepkin's work, that and the tidy, pale scar around Kiefan's neck. The black-and-gold cloak rippled as he paced. Voices strengthened in the crowd, especially the men's.

"Arcea sent minotaurs to slay women and children and drugged men — as a measure of their own cowardice! And well that they should fear the whole men of Wodenberg. The Blessed knights, the chosen. Who will not treat with murderers."

In the heartbeat's pause, their voices answered.

"Who give no quarter to monsters!"

Louder. Kiefan drew the sword and pointed at the double doors, southward toward Suevia. "Father Duty, witness my oath on the grave of my kin — Arcea will pay blood for blood, fire for fire, and Suevia is forfeit!"

Woden thrust up a fist. Steel rasped as swords joined in the oath, pointing southward to the enemy with a yell. My heart burned in my chest, from rage at more than just the enemy. Tainted with memories of the siege, too. I clenched my fists over my folded arms.

Kiefan sheathed his sword and the crowd followed. "Now we see our dead to the Shepherd's Hearth. A fresh round of ale!"

That got a cheer. Kiefan turned, brow still furrowed with anger, and took a deep breath.

"We need Caercoed," Woden told him.

He nodded, settling his hands on his hips. "I ride for Knapptal in the morning."

DISCIPLE, PART V
cold solace

CHAPTER 1

REOWAN

It wasn't the Winter Wood, that was for certain. Anders slitted his eyes open. The Shepherd's Hearth would include a hearth, surely. No, he saw a lamp in a sconce to one side, a dark, drape-shrouded window on the other. The smell of lamp tallow was all too familiar, and it was much too quiet to be the Hearth. Wasn't it one long banquet there?

Just his luck if it turned out the Shepherd kept a sober, proper household.

Someone shifted, with a sigh, and a chair creaked. Anders let his eyes settle shut, listening. A faint clicking of knitting needles. Kate didn't knit, that he knew of. His mother preferred her embroidery, if she had time to spare.

Not dead. Not at home. Where? His memory was a jumble of swords, the burn of fatigue in his arms, an awful pain in his chest and creeping blackness.

Cautious, he raised his eyelids again. A woman sat knitting near the lamp, pausing to count her stitches and then yawn. She wore a kerchief over her hair and her skin was coarse, loose around her jowls. Creases and worry lines. But ordinary enough.

"Frau…?" he whispered. Her gaze snapped up, needles stopping. "Where am I?"

"Safe, safe," she whispered back. "Sleep."

Anders' hands curled under the blankets. The woman's thick accent was Suevi. And what he felt in his hand made him blink, too. It was a handful of silk. Someone had dressed him in silk. Father's bloody balls, what happened?

The minotaur, roaring as it swung around with its huge fucking blade trailing blood —

Arceal knights, in the great hall. Bodies strewn across the floor. His breath hitched when pain jabbed through his chest. He looked down and glimpsed a sword's moon-white pommel stone, a scant few fingers' widths of blade between the hilt and his cote. A memory.

He ought to be dead.

Anders' heart pounded, his hand crept under the covers, searching for his sword. The bed was empty, but for him, and the silk — he sat up on one elbow, and white silk caught the lamplight. A broad purple stripe slashed from his left shoulder downward. An Arceal robe. He'd seen them in Temitte, those times he'd gone as a horse-wrangler with the Kaufmanns. Officials wore them. All purple belonged to the Empress, he knew that much.

"Sleep," his minder said, putting down her knitting. "You are safe here. Lie." She fussed the blankets back up, tucking him in.

Anders lay down, sinking into the feather pillow. His nerves jangled, miles away from sleep. Wherever he was, this was nowhere he wanted to be. His minder was the first thing to be rid of.

"Tea?" he asked the woman. "To help me sleep?"

He pulled the puppy eyes on her. Anders hadn't used them on a woman since — but her mouth quirked to the side and she nodded. With a final pat on the blankets over his heart, she went to the door and left. Anders slid out from under the covers a heartbeat later, landing soft on socked feet. A glance down; he wore a thigh-long Arceal tunic and baggy trousers, all white with purple-trimmed hems. Under those, his own cote and braies. When he checked inside the silk, he saw bloodstains on the wool. No time to wonder about that now.

Outside the door, a hallway lit by one lamp in a sconce. He heard his minder's heavy feet on stairs, to one side. It was a back staircase, narrow and empty. He pattered after her, matching her pace, alert for danger.

Nipper's ears would help, but he had no kir.

Voices, from below. Speaking Suevi — a good-morning, Anders recognized that much. He pressed his back to the wall at the foot of the steps and risked a peek around the corner. He saw a kitchen, and a good-sized one. Two cooks kneaded bread dough as they chatted with Anders' minder. He noted the doors he could see, starting beyond them, moving his gaze past the tables and wash-basins closer to —

A gust of cold air warned him and he ducked back. A page-boy hurried in with an armload of firewood and some kind of complaint. He left the door open, in going to dump his burden by the hearth.

Anders slipped around the wall and out the door before his nerves could warn him not to. He put his back to the outside wall beside the door and then thought to lean easy. Pretended he had a reason to be there.

His breath billowed in the cold. Above arched a dark blue sky clotted with grey clouds. Stars. Flock moons. His gaze dropped toward the horizon, finding only a trace of early dawn, and in so doing he saw the stables.

They lay across a gate-yard, a good twenty or thirty feet of open space. His back was against a tall, stone manor house — bigger than a manor. Nearly a castle. The stables were a horse-palace to match; anytime else, and Anders would be asking if he could get work there. High walls joined the manor to its stables, and to one side stood a full gate with tower and guards. A second, smaller gate by the stables was clearly for informal comings and goings.

The two red-tabarded guardsmen on duty leaned on their spears and watched whatever was outside the open gates. Late in the midnight shift. They'd be tired. Bored. Only the earliest birds were about, so far before dawn.

Beside him, the page-boy shut the kitchen door from inside. Anders pushed himself off the cold stone wall and strolled. Never mind that he wore only socks, and there was an inch of mashed snow in the yard. He did this every morning, just walked from the kitchen to the stables. A wiser man would've gotten a cloak, but he was on duty. Nothing unusual at all.

Through the stable gate rode a trickle of guardsmen, clattering hooves and shouting greetings. Complaining about the cold. One stable-groom came out to meet them, and held the officer's horse by the bridle as he swung down.

No worry of Anders', any of that. He was fighting shivers when he stepped onto straw-covered flagstones through the stables' side door. Horses whuffed, scenting him. He fought the urge to greet them back, then put his back to wood and crept past their stalls. Ahead, the newly arrived guardsmen were off their horses. Most of their words were too quick to catch, but Anders didn't hear any alarm or anger. The guards moved off, leaving their half-dozen horses for the stable-hand to tend.

The man led the officer's mount into the dim stable, turning to put her into the first stall. Anders ran past, caught the reins of a horse standing near the gate, and swung up into the saddle in one clean motion. The horse startled a bit, but he pulled its head around and tapped his heels. The horse jogged out the gate, with a huff, and wanted to slow to an amble.

Anders tapped, clicking, and the horse grudgingly agreed to trot along the manor's outer wall. The street let into a broad city square, right before the very gate and tower he'd been looking at from inside. He checked the sunrise, turned the horse's head to north, and kicked hard. It snorted, skittered a couple steps.

"Run, damn you!" He tried Suevi, what little he knew.

The horse broke into a canter and plunged down the northward road. Hooves quieted to thumping when the square's paving-stones gave out, but the close-packed houses still rang with the noise. Shuttered windows and shake-shingled walls blurred past. A man on foot, carrying a faggot of kindling, didn't even look up in the heartbeat before the horse flashed by.

Anders gripped the front of his silk robe; it was a double-breasted thing, buttoned at the shoulders, and ought to be belted to hold the flaps shut. It wanted to fly open, and the wind was cold enough already. He couldn't feel his toes, in his wet socks, as it was.

A smaller square gaped around him for a moment, but the street continued northward. If it had been River Road, he'd be at the city gates — how big was this damn town? Anders risked a glance back, but there was no sign of pursuit from the manor-castle.

Kate. She'd been there, in Castle Kaltkern's gore-covered hall. A landslide of memories broke loose: finding Theo half-dead, storming to the castle with Kate, the carnage of the wedding-eve banquet.

Anders blinked, and saw gates ahead. A city wall, full as high as Wodenberg's but made from stone blocks. Two towers and open gates. Guardsmen, four of them, turned as they noticed him. One put up a hand. Expecting Anders to stop?

No sword, no weapon but the horse. They had spears, and likely archers in the tower. Anders' grip tightened on the reins and he pushed the perhapses aside. Running them down was all he had.

The guardsman's companion shouted something, and Anders caught "Empress" — it was the same word as in Alemanni. The raised hand changed to a dismissive wave, and they paid him no further mind.

Empress. The purple stripe.

His horse was puffing; Anders let it slow to a trot once past the gates. A broad Spanne ringed the city walls, and then the houses returned. Not so tight-packed, but thicker than outside Wodenberg. And for a moment, to the east, he glimpsed — water. Broad, flat, and catching the pre-dawn light.

Father's bloody balls, where was there a lake so big? Anders looked to the sky again, counting the Flock moons as they winked in and out of the clouds. Seven. No sign of the Shepherd. It was the first morning of Snow Moon, surely. How had he be so far from home so soon?

The horse dropped to a walk, and he let it. His hand shifted from holding his robe shut to pressing flat, sliding up to find the base of his breastbone. The flesh there ached under his hand. Bloodstains on the wool underneath.

Run through. He ought to be dead. When he blinked, he saw the snarl twisting Kiefan's face, that final stab Anders knew he couldn't dodge — and, in the same heartbeat, knew that he had the fucker. Steel through his chest, but he'd felt the pull on his sword's tip as it cut through Kiefan's throat.

Cold, cold satisfaction in that. His jaw clenched, breath turning harsh under an echo of the rage. Kate was his. She loved him. He'd fucking earned that. And she'd — she must have —

His fingers dug into the silk, remembering the sword hilt in his grip. Darkness swirling. The pain of trying to breathe, looking up when Kate rushed with kir in her hands — to Kiefan.

His breath caught in his throat again. The same anguish hazed his eyes. Him. She'd gone to him first.

Something surged in his left hand, burrowing into his palm and burning up his arm. The air in his lungs wrenched out in a startled scream. His arm twisted and the muscles clenched. Pain shot through his chest. In his mind's eye, his arm's meridian ran in a bright red line that reached past his palm and into the distance.

/ where are you? /

The anger in the question slapped him like ice water. Anders clutched the saddle's pommel with his right hand, clung with both legs, and gasped for breath. The pain washed past, spreading an ache down to his toes. It left raw confusion in its wake.

/ WHERE ARE YOU? /

He gritted his teeth, but the agony ripped through his body, clenching every muscle for a heartbeat. A yell fought its out in spite of that. The pain released him as suddenly as it struck, and he sent his answer back through his meridian.

/ FUCK YOU /

The answer was a raw blast. Anders felt himself tip, convulsing, and the pounded dirt road caught him. His stomach wrenched itself in a knot and heaved up what acid it had. Black stars crowded his eyes, his mind, when the pain roiled on and on. Skimming the edge of passing out, he could only clench his eyes shut and thrash.

It kept swirling long after it eased. Eddies of pain kept his head spinning as he lay breathing. That hurt, too. The fresh bruise on his head throbbed; so did his joints, as if he'd sprained every one. Anders risked opening his eyes.

His horse had wandered off a few steps, to nibble on a patch of snow-dusted grass just off the road. Dawn was coming. So were a few pairs of feet in worn shoes. There was a gabble of Suevi voices that his jumbled ears couldn't begin to understand.

Anders tried to sit up, and found he couldn't move. His limbs were stiff. Shivers fluttered through his muscle, trying to work their way free, but couldn't. The meridian joined to his left hand pulsed in a steady, slow beat. Far slower than his heart pounded as he struggled against the binding. No idea how to fight it, but he raged.

/ hush /

And who the fuck was that, sending ideas through his meridian — for a moment, he thought of Saint Aleks, how he'd said meridians could be cut and spliced like —

Wondering voices turned to alarm, and the feet skittered away. Above, something shrieked. A harsh, rough call, as from a massive bird.

Anders' heart burst into a full gallop and he wanted to scramble — but he only shuddered a little, still paralyzed on the frozen ground. A shadow fell over him, terrifying as the Shepherd's own, and black wings brushed the snowy ground. The horse bolted. Leathery, yellow hands with long fingers and heavy, nightmare-black talons alit.

Memories rushed back. Agony. The blade sliding through his body, falling away. His strength gushing out, hot, onto the ground. No. No, Shepherd have mercy — Kate hadn't come to save him —

The paralysis eased and Anders scrambled to his knees, staring. Shuddering from the cold. The monstrous vulture's red head cocked. And it shifted before his eyes, wings thinning, legs lengthening. He kept his eyes on its, saw the yellow irises shift to brown. The face spread out into cheekbones, beak shrinking to a nose, and dark hair sprouted. A beautiful woman, with skin delicate as milk-laced spice tea. She put her hands on her hips and frowned at him.

Little matter that she stood naked, in the middle of a village road, on mushy snow with her breath clouding around her head.

One of the bystanders pulled off his cloak and held it toward her, voice quavering as he said something about saints. She cast him a glance and a curt reply. He backed away, bowing low.

Anders got his feet under himself and lunged — and fell on his face with a cry when the pain shot through his arm again.

"For I will not chase you further, today," the woman, the saint, told him in Arceal. She spoke with a native lilt, too. "This is my stringence, and you shall feel it when you disobey me."

She walked to him on delicate feet. He managed to sit up, trembling from the cold, from the pain, from half-remembered terror. That she was a little thing, trailing a braid of black hair thick as his arm, that her lush curves would've whetted his appetite anywhere else — that was all a lie, he knew in his bones. She was far more than she appeared.

"Such work to save you from the Shepherd, and you race back to his arms? You judge in haste, Anders."

"I serve my saints," he gasped out. "I'm discipled by —"

"You are elect, and bound to the Empress."

His resolve steadied, in rejecting that. "I am a Blessed knight of Wodenberg. Proven in battle. I belong to Saint Woden." He had his knight's crest as proof, loose and straggly from melted snow but proof.

The Empress stood over him, without even gooseflesh from the cold. "And what did he give you, for your service? Blessings? A sword? Your sounding does tell it truly; you were as born to the sword as to the saddle. Woden only gilded a lily, with his claim. What you truly need, la…" She crouched down, looked Anders in the eye. "That is a true shifter, to teach you art."

His chest ached where he'd been stabbed. Anders shifted away from her, pulse pounding in his throat. "Saint Aleks taught me. He showed me how to work it out myself."

"Saint Aleksandr," she said, overly patiently, "was a mere stonecutter with stars in his eyes. He did harvest his shifting charms, or I'm a scullery whore."

Anders straightened, bristling in Saint Aleks' defense, but the Empress held up one finger in warning. The bond in his palm tingled. Anders shut his mouth.

"Do not waste my time, sir. I am empress of eight kingdoms. I take few apprentices, and spare not my enemies. But mayhaps there is one man in Wodenberg worth sparing. And what, at home, draws you?"

Kate's name leaped to his lips, and froze there. Her hands, glowing with kir, catching Kiefan as he fell. Stemming the fountain of his blood. Anders' eyes closed as the pain in his chest stopped his breath. The sword had hurt, too.

When his eyes opened, they swam with tears. "I have…" Kate had said she loved him. But not even a glance at his mortal wound… had their nights together been a lie? Pity?

"For they left you to die," the Empress said, voice softer. "And I did mend you, then. Saw your worth and bound you, Elect."

Left him to die. And now they were finally rid of him. Anders' heart skipped in cold terror; how happy was Kate, now that he was gone? This vulture had plucked him from the Shepherd's shadow, done what Kate wouldn't…

"Stay, and you will master your gifts. Which none understand as your own kind do."

There'd been none in Wodenberg who could teach him; Saint Qadeem himself had said as much. Since Saint Aleks was killed, Anders had largely been left to his own devices. He met the Empress' eyes, and she was all the world had left for him to choose. Because without Kate…

With her betrayal tearing a ragged hole in his chest at each breath, Anders nodded.

The Empress touched his shoulder, and his aches melted away. The cold vanished. Kir flooded in, lifting his head with a deep, cleansing breath. She stood, and a small blade spun out from one hand. His knight's crest, she gathered up in the other. With a slash, it came away and she held the handful of flaxen hair before his face. Then dropped it.

"For you are mine. Come home."

CHAPTER 2

KNAPPTAL

Fresh powder churned in clouds behind the horses, billowing in the company of their breath. Above, the rich blue sky held not a scrap of cloud. Pines and bare maples reached across it, offering scant shadows in the glare. Full sun on snow forced Kiefan to keep his eyes narrow. If not for the trail the Rangers had cut, they'd be stumbling their way through the narrow valley and falling into the stream under the white blanket. In winter, cold water could be the death of a man.

"Spiegel Lake!" The Ranger sergeant pointed ahead.

"Thank you, Father," Captain Aleksandra said, riding beside Kiefan.

Kiefan tapped Nail up to a trot, after the sergeant, and she followed. Gregor had been watching the crows in the trees; he caught up a moment later. More King's Guard followed, Elect Tannait with the surviving Caer, and some pack horses carrying their grim burdens. A pair of Rangers brought up the rear. It wasn't far, from Vorspitz to Knapptal, but Baron Eismann hadn't liked seeing Kiefan go with so little escort. It was rugged land, thinly peopled. Anything might be in the hills.

Lamia, wolves, or Arceal soldiers worried Kiefan little. He'd hoarded his kir and tucked it away well. If he should find an enemy elect out here, or a saint — there were scores to settle. Blood for Arcea to answer for.

Tannait would stand with him, he was sure, if they met any such. She'd spoken less, this week's ride, whereas she'd been at ease before the attack on Castle Kaltkern. But she and Kiefan woke before dawn and made a habit of seeing to light chores about the camp together. They'd fallen into some conversations. Talked of elects' practicalities, like waking early, and their duties.

Yesterday, during the snowstorm, they'd spoken of mountain passes. The storm had brought back much of Starknadel to Kiefan's mind: wind keening through the trees, ice prickling his face, oilskin tarps snapping and straining. Tannait had over-wintered in Eryr Pass, when there was an Arceal army camped below it, and they'd compared the foothills there to those in Wodenberg.

The narrow valley fell open. Broad Spiegel Lake lay still as a mirror, true to its name. Ice rimmed the sky's reflection, but hadn't blotted out the deep blue yet. On the north, the Eispitzen reared straight up from the lake's shore, a forbidding white wall. One tall marking-stone stood where the road turned to follow the lake shore, its white crust of snow half obscuring the ram's head carved in its face. The Ranger sergeant touched the ram's burnished nose as they rode past.

Kiefan looked back along the line of riders as Nail swung around the curve. Tannait rode at the head of the Caer, gazing across the lake toward the mountains and her home beyond them. For all their chatting, she would say only that the twin saints would decide what was to be of the alliance, without a marriage, and the Caer would wait on their saints' word.

Arcea had its army well dug in at Ansehen, and might be thirty thousand strong now. Breaking them was much to ask of the twelve thousand men remaining from the summer's fighting. Even with Vysokov's reserve, they'd be less than twenty. Arcea had still more army waiting in Temitte, as well.

Wodenberg needed Caercoed still. Thus far there was only trouble and death between them, though: m'lady Leix and Kiefan's bride-to-be, shrouded and tied to the horses, and Crown Ciara's own sister murdered not two moon-turnings past. There'd been the ridiculous negotiations about Anders.

Yet another mess left to Kiefan for mending. As always. He grimly hung onto the hope he could offer some advantage, pay some price that would rebuild the alliance with Caercoed.

Ahead, Knapptal's watchtower rose sharp against the blue. Its mate stood across the lake. A keep huddled at the nearer tower's base, and a handful of shorter towers as well. Castle and town held the flank of a hill that jutted into the lake, watching the narrow pass that the lake spilled through. The hill — nearly a mountain, in truth — was one of several that fell off sharply in cliffs and landslide-scraped slopes into Suevia.

The company rode past clusters of sod-roofed cottages and humble piers where small fishing boats lay, put up for the winter. Wind rose, rippled the Spiegel, and made Kiefan pull his fur-lined hood lower. His gold band caught the cold all too well and held it against his skull; he'd rather not ride with it on, but they'd make Knapptal today. A fore-runner had left at dawn to announce them.

Margrave Schutze ought to be ready. For the guests, if not for the news they brought.

The morn after the storm dawned clear. Clear and cold. Elect Teleri knew the mirror-lake would freeze, and those who'd wagered on sooner days for its full covering would take heart. These boys did bet on everything, to stave off boredom.

"Two words more of Alemannic, today," she told Ciara as she filled both their tea mugs from the pot. "'Freezing' and 'setting.'"

"The Shepherd's setting?" Ciara took her chair with one socked foot tucked in the other knee. She wrapped her dressing gown tight; cold as she was, she never tied the belt.

"'Twas rising ahead of the sun. I learnt 'rising' yester-morn." Teleri reached across the table to rake Ciara's mussed hair back from her face, and smiled when her Crown did. "They call the Flock after the Virtues, here."

"Yes, certainly," Ciara muttered into her mug, clasped in both her hands, and drank deep. Till the Crown finished her first mug of tea, Tel knew it best to expect little answer.

The door opened, held by the Blade sergeant on duty, and Bévin carried in a tray of breakfast, trailing delicious steam. Rónan had sent up hot porridge and a good scramble of eggs and onions. Teleri returned the iron teapot to the hearth's coals and sat across the small table from Ciara.

Bévin perched her tray on the table's corner and laid out the plates and bowls, the little honey pot. "Word's for clear weather, m'lady," she reported to Teleri. "'Twill be a day for training?"

Tel nodded as she sat. "Tell Fionn it shall be archery."

Bévin went. Ciara ate her egg scramble with a spoon, then moved on to the oat porridge. Teleri watched her, how her brown hair fell in a loose tangle over her shoulder, how her gown slid open at the neck to allow a peek of green silk. This peace would end soon enough. Tel ate too — the oats, if none else. Or half the oats, with a spoonful of honey.

/ word? /

Conbarre stirred, at the far end of the bond. Teleri felt a touch of cold wind, a whiff of salt water. That was enough for a pang of homesickness.

/ soon / prepare to sing /

Teleri pressed her lips in a line. Needs must sing dirges, again. Thank Father Care for Tannait's life; losing their eldest elect would've been a heavy blow.

She picked up her plate of egg scramble and scraped it onto Ciara's. Fetched the teapot and poured more. Archery, today, before all's focus broke on the news that rode with the king. Wasn't so far for word to come, but yester-morn's storm had surely slowed it.

Feet, on the stairs, in a rush. Teleri tensed and Ciara looked up; the sergeant on duty pushed the door open again for Bévin. The maid arrived breathless, her grey gown's hem wet from trailing in the snow.

"The king comes," she gasped. "M'lord does ride here."

Ciara's green eyes lost their morning haze. "When?"

"Mayhaps noon."

"My uniform. The gown for the welcome feast."

Bévin trotted to open the clothes-chest and lay them out. One of Ciara's day-tunics waited at the foot of the unmade bed, the plain white bed-curtains parted around it; she began to put it away.

Ciara scooped up the second helping of eggs. "Dreary place for a bride's-moon," she said between bites. "Likely he wants to talk of conquest all winter — pity, for Síochana. Though likely she's of a mind to join in that."

Teleri took a deep breath, a last sip of tea, and stood. Clasped her hands behind her back, over her sword-belt; she was in Blades' blues, as always. "Needs must give you word now, my Crown," she said, canting to the formal. "Bévin, you must leave us. Pass word on of the king's coming."

"Elect." The maid bobbed a curtsy and went, closing the door behind herself.

Ciara's brows rose. "Tel?"

"Conbarre did wish it held." Teleri stuck to reporting the news. "'Twas sent through my bond, as sent by Tannait." It would be vague, for all that. And yet: "'Twere attacked, ere the marriage could be sealed. A slaughter in the castle itself. Síochana among the dead."

Ciara's teeth clenched, by how her jaw tensed. "Elect Tannait?"

"Lives. Aided them as she could."

"And he rides here."

Silence.

/ coming / told her /

Conbarre sent a nod.

"What say the saints?" Ciara's voice grated through her teeth.

"Prepare to sing."

"No, Tel —" She cut off her own retort, then took a sharper tone in anger. "Again, yes, again we must dirge and burn, and what will the saints have of us now? More blood wasted… wasted! These southern boys, what have they ever brought Caercoed but blood and dirges?"

Teleri looked away from her Crown's angry green eyes, remembering the red creeks of Eryr Pass and the battlements on fire. The blood Arcea had brought, years ago.

"Shall give word when 'tis given." She said it quietly, for it was nothing.

Ciara exhaled. Picked up her mug and finished her tea. "A little training, early, ere we go mad for being cooped. Then we shall remain in the barracks."

Margrave Schutze had given the Caer use of the barracks, inside the castle walls. They were large enough to house all the Blades in only half the building, and they'd blocked doors, raised quick-work walls to see they had privacy. Rooms a-plenty, officers' quarters for the gentle-blooded, and a mess hall besides — generous, and fine hospitality. Margrave Gwatcyn's Tadhlon Guard camped in a village not far off, well sheltered by forest.

"Needs must greet the king," Teleri said.

"If you must." Ciara rose, tossing off her dressing-gown. "I shall not leave the barracks, and none shall enter."

Light shifted on the green silk shift as her curves moved under the glossy fabric. Teleri blinked, and sent her gaze back to the fireplace. "For certain, he'll wish —"

"And you've my answer. No more of our blood for these southlanders, Elect."

———————————×———————————

The castle was the Spiegelwache, properly. More often, the Wache. It was older than Castle Kaltkern, and smaller. The watchtower, a square keep buttressed against it, and walls enclosed barracks, stables, and a barn. Low towers guarded gates onto both the road and a bit of private lakeshore with two docks. Saint Aleksandr's hand showed in the stone blocks he'd smoothed together for strength, in the fish-head whimsies worked into lintels and frames.

Knapptal came out to see when the Ranger sergeant rode ahead announcing, "The king!" They lifted children and pointed, then waved. Yesterday's storm had filled the streets ankle-deep and a wagon or two had cut fresh ruts. The farmers and woodcutters had been out banking snow against their cottages, and their children had played in the drifts.

Kiefan rode with his hood back, returning their waves.

The guards at the gate knelt in obeisance when he rode through. Inside, the greeting party did the same. A squad of Crown's Blades stood in formal lines to one side, and with them the three Caer duchesses in fur-lined cloaks. Elect Teleri's kir drew Kiefan's eye for a moment. She nodded, her short, sandy hair tilting forward, and he returned it.

No Crown Ciara, though.

"Welcome, m'lord and king." Margrave Schutze came to take Kiefan's hand when he swung down from the saddle, and knelt again. "Your Ranger arrived this morning. We are honored you've come to spend your wedding-moon on the Spiegel. And m'lady —?"

Sir Bjornhardt Schutze was a blunt and single-minded man; his wife had likely given him his words. He raised his head from kissing fealty on Kiefan's hand and looked at the rest of the party for the first time. Kiefan's anticipation Blessing piqued to tell him: pride, mixed with nerves. Schutze found Captain Aleks, then the Caer women in turn, as he searched for the matching gold crown-band. And did not find it.

Instead, two pack horses bore wrapped corpses tied to backboards.

"Majesty?" Confusion and the beginnings of alarm; they'd had no word, plain enough. His wife spotted the bodies, covered her open mouth and put her other hand on her daughter's shoulder, tugging her closer to whisper in her ear.

"We were attacked," Kiefan said, loud enough to draw all their eyes away from the two pack horses. Schutze stood, already stiffening in outrage. "The night before my wedding, Arcea smuggled knights and minotaurs into the castle. And a saint as well. Drugged our ale and slaughtered all they could." The gasps and murmured prayers punctuated the story well. "My bride fell in battle, fierce as any disciple of Woden. Margrave Gwatcyn was also slain, hampered by the drugged ale. Her friendship will be sorely missed."

He turned to Elect Teleri for that part. Captain Mohra stood by the Blades, translating his story into Caer. Their faces were cast in stone, fixed by anger. The Elect, though… she had known, by the grim twist to her mouth. Little anger, he saw in her, but resolve and a touch of dread. Not what Kiefan had hoped for.

"I have sworn before the Father that Arcea will pay blood for blood, fire for fire and we will take Suevia back from them," he said.

"Majesty, may we swear with you?" Schutze nearly interrupted in his eagerness. Kiefan drew his sword and repeated the oath, the margrave and his officers joining in. "The Wache stands ready for your command," Schutze declared.

Kiefan nodded. "We've much to discuss. And much I must discuss with the Crown of Caercoed. Is m'lady well?" He looked to Elect Teleri.

In Arceal, she answered, "Our Crown does not receive guests today."

Schutze frowned. "She was out to practice her archery this morning — she's well enough to —"

Kiefan raised a hand. "It's been a long ride and we lost yesterday to the storm."

"Of course, m'lord. Take your ease, and please join my wife and I for dinner." He bowed, sweeping an arm toward the lady, their daughter and three younger sons.

The boys were rusty-haired and blunt-faced, like their father. The girl, Haralda, a young reflection of her mother, wore her straw-blond braid wrapped around her head. Blue eyes wide and blushing pinker than the cold could account for. Her mother nudged her to curtsy and she did, her fists clenching on her dove-grey skirts for dear life. Awed, his anticipation read.

Kiefan's eyes lingered. Perhaps it was the wrapped braid. She didn't have memory Blessing ridges. When she glanced up and caught him looking, she looked as stunned as Kate when he'd first told her to be quiet as they rode out of the city.

He flicked that memory aside before it stuck. "Might I have a warm bath before dinner?" he asked, pulling his gloves off finger by finger. "The storm kept us from observing Saint-day properly."

"At once, Majesty," Schutze's wife answered.

CHAPTER 3

Teleri read over Ciara's shoulder as she wrote, the next morning. "Should you?"

She inked her quill afresh. "Oisin may spend his days as he pleases, but 'tis time the princesses saw less of him." Her voice lowered as she scratched the last few words. "If he wishes to pout, he may go home to Tadhlon."

"He'll not leave his girls."

"No." Ciara signed her name. "But neither is he my Consort."

"Who shall serve at table, then?" Oisin had been Ceelin's darling, true enough, but there'd been no ill will between him and Ciara. Even with Ceelin only ash in an urn now…

"Think you there'll be need for any? The girls will dine with him, and 'twill be you and I alone."

"Shall be banquets —" Teleri put a hand on her shoulder, meaning to comfort.

Ciara sighed. "Without Ceelin? Truly?" She shook her head. "Mayhaps those should move to the guest house, as well."

Teleri leaned, put her cheek to Ciara's. The Crown still felt her sister's shadow, it seemed. With another sigh, Ciara turned her head to kiss Tel's cheek and set about folding her letter. "Who might we send with these? 'Twill be a hard ride to the coast."

A tap at the door, and Captain Fionn stepped in. He saluted. "The king's squire, m'lady, waits to arrange your meeting with the king."

She shook her head. "I'll not meet the king."

The captain nodded, crisp, and went. Ciara warmed a bar of green sealing-wax in the lamp's flame and smeared a blob onto the letter. "No word from the saints yet?" She glanced up at Teleri.

"'Twill be tonight. Needs must dine together, with the duchesses." Tel looked to the door Captain Fionn had shut. Took a breath. "'Twould be best to hear the king out, and so leave his feathers unruffled when we ride."

King Kiefan wouldn't be pleased by further refusals. He seemed wise enough, for a southerner, but what Tannait had witnessed in the castle's great hall — he was young, still, and had his passions. Better not to lump him with all those southerners who'd brought misery to Caercoed over several generations.

Ciara put the sealed letter in her writing-box and closed it. Standing, she took her riding-cloak from the hook by the door and wrapped it around her shoulders, stabbed a golden pin through to secure it.

There'd be no speaking of it, clearly. Teleri took her own Blades-blue cloak as she followed.

"Sir, the Caer are riding out."

Kiefan looked up from his small, silver mirror. He checked his finger for blood; the nick had clotted. Leaving his shaving kit open on the corner table, he took the hand towel and wiped off the last traces of lavender soap as he followed Gregor down the hall. Margrave Schutze's council chamber stood at the front of the little keep, and its window looked onto the gate yard.

Gregor unlatched the shutter and Kiefan opened it. Horses waited below. Ciara, by her green cloak, led the way out of the gate — riding Dove, if he recognized the grey correctly. Elect Teleri followed with a hand of Blades. One led a pack horse by the reins, bearing one of the shrouded bodies.

"They take m'lady Leix for her soldiers to mourn," Gregor said, beside him. "I asked Captain Mohra," he added when Kiefan glanced at him with raised brows.

"How is she?"

"The same. Wouldn't meet my eyes more than a flicker."

"That's a good detail to note." Kiefan latched the shutter, let the curtain fall shut. "That's a sign of guilt, most often."

Gregor fidgeted, clasped his hands behind his back. "She needn't be, not to me. I drank the ale too. I'm as guilty."

Kiefan put a hand on his squire's shoulder and steered him toward the door. That night had left Kiefan so numb — the slaughter, the madness — that he'd said nothing when Gregor appeared with a washbasin and towels. Hardly noticed him while trying to scrub the blood from his own knuckles. "I'd rather you were drugged by the bonfire than dead in the great hall. Much better to have you alive, for it's far too difficult to replace you," Kiefan said.

"Sir?" Gregor's feet slowed, once in the dim hall. The only light here fought through the shutter over the archer's slit.

Kiefan's voice dropped. "You've been a better squire than you know. Perhaps not in sparring, but…" He nodded. Then smiled. "And in Vorspitz, you heard far too much to keep you anyplace but here."

Gregor's ears turned red. "Captain Aleks spoke to me of that, m'lord."

He nodded again. "Certainly. Though she hardly needed to."

"Who would I tell?"

Kiefan breathed a laugh. The boy's country-bred honor… "You're the king's squire. My father's squires never paid for a drink, so long as they gave the news. Be worthy of my confidence and you'll never lack a place."

He could nearly look Gregor level in the eye, and the squire wasn't yet sixteen. A faint line of frown flickered around his blue eyes, a question in his mind.

"Ask it," Kiefan said.

"It's true you attacked Sir Anders?" Just above a whisper. "Was it because of Elect Kate?"

For a heartbeat, he felt the resistance on his blade as it thrust through muscle, scraped ribs. And the sudden chill in his throat, his strength melting away. The battle-rage lifting. Because Kate — no, that knotted Kiefan's throat. Because Anders had — no. The scar prickled in his skin. Struck silent, Kiefan began to walk, and Gregor fell in beside him.

When he could speak again, Kiefan returned to matters at hand. "Tomorrow, I will ask for the Crown myself. Likely they'll be readying the pyres — perhaps she'll let me say goodbye."

Gregor barely hesitated at the change in subject. "But what if the Crown won't receive you?"

He grimaced. "It could be a very long winter. I'll seek the duchesses out, if need be."

"Which would you marry, now?"

"None. I'll not be stabbed in the heart again. Twice will do for most men, but yet here I stand. I must sound out the possibilities with the Crown, and salvage this somehow."

"Shan't be taken well," Tannait murmured as they sat to dine, "however 'tis said."

Teleri nodded. "They don't remember."

A touch of smile. "You hardly remember — were but a squire."

"Nightmares do keep it fresh."

"You sleep, still?"

A fond smile tucked up the corner of Teleri's mouth, thinking of her last good sleep. "When my Crown permits it."

Tannait chuckled under her breath. Then, sober, "How will she fall?"

Tel waited until Rónan's apprentice finished heaping smoked sausages and kraut on her trencher. "Shall side with us."

The meal passed in sober silence, though Rónan and his apprentice did try to chat. Ciara's eyes were distant and she only nodded. Míde and Una Lanfuar of Dheathain whispered together now and then, and cast many a glance at the two elect. Faola Taircoeden of Henffyrdd, alone, took up Rónan's banter and smiled.

All else had eaten and been sent out to the Spanne to stack wood for the pyres. Grim task, that. Tonight the two dead lay under watch, wrapped with fire-warmed bricks to hold off freezing.

After a dish of Rónan's pound cake with honeyed apples, Tannait, as the eldest elect, took up her after-dinner brandy and stood. They all stood with her. "Our thanks for your

Part V: Cold Solace

meal," she began, bowing her head to the cook and raising her cup, "and for your constant service. Our thanks for warm hearth and dry roof, sisters in arms and the wisdom of saints."

All agreed, and sipped the spiced brandy. Ciara and the duchesses sat. Teleri clasped her hands behind her back and stepped to Tannait's side at the end of the table, settling into a parade rest. As eldest, it was for her to give the message and for Tel to support.

"Morn after Equinox, we ride for home. Unless the snows forbid it. Shall cross by way of Eryr Pass into Henffyrdd and behind us the battlements will close. Shall be sealed, and the garrison withdrawn. Elect Teleri and I shall call down the landslides — both outer and inner."

Duchess Faola put down her spoon, face gone blank. The Dheathain twins still picked at their pound cake, but watched intently. Ciara nodded, silent.

Tannait continued. "The inner battlements shall close as well, for good and all. In riding to Arforddinas, shall do the same for Dwyncraig Pass." That pass belonged to Lancynnes, duchy of the southern coast. Likely they'd be dismayed as Faola. Or nearly. "Caercoed is done with the south," Tannait said. "Long have we seen to our own and needed naught of them, and thus it shall be."

Míde spoke first, of the twins. "Needs must wean ourselves of Arceal tea, then?"

"Trade may still pass through Arforddinas and the southern ports. On Caercoed's terms, as she sees fit. As our army wanes, our navy waxes."

Duchess Faola slowly wiped her mouth with her napkin, and placed it by her trencher. "Much as I love my cousins of Lancynnes," she said, with equal care, "how 'tis they've earned such stranglehold on trade?"

No idle thing, that. Lancynnes and Henffyrdd had sealed an ancient feud with marriage, but that was only a generation in the past. It had been a relief, then. Teleri shifted on her feet, knowing the two duchies held the greater share of the kingdom's wealth and power. If made enemies again over this seeming favoritism, it would be a great loss of strength.

"All duchies shall be needed in support of our ships. 'Twill be a border to guard, still, as well," Teleri said. "Henffyrdd will ever be a power in Caercoed."

But the duchess' mouth pursed. Still displeased.

Una stood first, brandy cup in hand, and her twin with her. "Dheathain shall do its part, saints, and gladly. Our ranks run deeper than ever before. Mayhaps we know little of the sea," and she smiled when she admitted it, "but in lumber and shipwrighting, we will be of aid."

Ciara raised her cup. "'Twas no doubt Dheathain would stand with us."

Which put all eyes on Duchess Faola. Teleri knew her from the battlements of Eryr Pass; perhaps more an overseer than a marshal, but the duchess was no stranger to the blade. And far more seasoned than the others. After a life's service, the saints asked her to cut her duchy's own throat in sealing the pass.

"Five years ago, 'twas in Eryr that Arcea did turn back," Faola said. "Turned by our glaives and crossbows and the skill of our engineers. And now our ranks swell with all those born in the twenty years' peace, come of age for their stint of service. Yet Conbarre and Sabh wish to seal both passes? As if we're weak, afraid?"

Teleri remembered it, and it was true enough. Arcea had come with little warning, and Faola's duchy had faced them all but alone. By the time reinforcements arrived from the northern provinces, Henffyrdd had done the worst of the work already.

"True, there's been many a pregnancy in the first half of the peace," Ciara answered as her brandy was refilled. "This parley alone has cost us a Crown and two margraves — setting all else we've suffered aside. What have we gained? A few tariffs reduced? 'Tis a calamity each time Caercoed hears out these southerners. 'Twas when we parleyed with Arcea direct, and 'tis again now."

"Henffyrdd, mayhaps you remember the marriage of alliance with Arcea," Tannait said, looking to Duchess Faola. It had begun the twenty years' peace, but the marriage lasted only ten. "How they meant to steal away the children to Arcea. Raise them by their own ways."

"We remember also," Una said. "'Twas our aunts who suffered for it."

"Saint Qadeem knows Arcea's ways, and 'tis likely they planned for us what passed in Castle Kaltkern." Tannait nodded toward the Wache's keep, where the king now waited.

"Treacherous," Teleri said, as it seemed a good moment for it.

Míde added, "Fickle, these southern boys." Her sister snorted in agreement.

"'Tis a young king they have." Faola folded her arms across her chest. "If 'tweren't so narrow-minded —"

"Weak. Easy-led by a threadbare margrave with ambition and a grip on his balls." Míde spat that out. She pulled a quick sip of brandy. "'Twas right, what the Voice said at that night-meet. Might cross the Dragon's Fangs and take Rukharbor for our own. With its fount."

Faola shot back. "Shall need Myrddin's ships for such."

"Myrddin's margrave lies years ill and has lost her heir," Una returned. "None would stop us."

Silence, for a heartbeat. Knit brows, hard mouths. Caercoed's duchies had ever been quarrelsome, had needed Crowns to temper and balance and redirect. Little surprise they fell to old habits when hearing sour news, as Teleri had feared. She sent her sinking heart through her bond.

/ not well /

/ remind / the enemy /

Ciara put her cup down empty again. "The saints do wish us to seal the passes, and 'tis well to be rid of these southerners," she said. "Even Englia."

"Turning our backs on Suevia was how we came to have Arcea at our doors," Faola said.

Una chuckled. "Oh, you do remember that?"

"'Twas the days of the Winter Wood —" Míde began with a storyteller's lilt, and fell into a snicker.

"I do, in truth, remember," Teleri said, irked by the twins' mocking. "Did squire to Crowns Mor and Slaine, and served them at Dwyncraig Pass."

They fell silent, at mention of Ciara's grandmothers.

"They did seal the battlements to Suevia when Arcea came, and held them when that dark tide did first crash against us. 'Twas thirty years of war ere the parley and the failed marriage, and we elect remember it all. None here have truly seen blood, children, trust in that. We must protect the kingdom."

Mother, let them hear the truth of it.

Faola clenched her fist. "But we are far stronger, now. 'Twould cower behind walls and landslides? Brick up our doors and, trapped, turn on each other?"

"Should Arcea scent disunity," Tannait said, in even tone, "'twill tear us to pieces. Turn one side on the other as did the Crowns of old. Did keep us weak, for too long, with that. We must be one in this."

Another silence followed, restless, of sipped brandy and empty dishes of sweets.

"The old Crowns — 'tis true, that Crown Mor did call the son of Henffyrdd for oíche-te and keep him as a surety?" Una asked. "Kept him till he declined to leave? No weakness, keeping Henffyrdd at heel thus. Might do it again."

Faola's jaw shifted. She did have a son, Faolán, who was of age. Precious things, sons. An oíche-te was only a night's dallying these days; keeping him as a surety would hearken to the old days, when such things were less pleasant.

Teleri kept her answer low. "'Tis true. But angered many as surely as it kept the duchess in line, and near ruined the peace with Lancynnes."

"'Twas a wily move," Tannait said. "Made knowing Henffyrdd's power, and needing its strength. As do we now — in peace."

"No danger of Faolán being taken so." Faola meant it as a subtle barb at Ciara. It struck. The Crown stiffened in her chair, brandy-muddled eyes sharpening.

"Were Ceelin still afoot, 'twould be." Míde was in agreement with the duchess on that. "'Twas a fit ploy for the Crowns of old, to braid all together in feud or folly. To Slaine and Mor." She raised her cup again. "Last of the great Crowns."

"'Tisn't —" Teleri was cut off by Tannait's hand on her arm. The duchesses spun into tales of the Crowns of old and their conniving. Ciara grew stiller, colder, by the moment, from anger.

At a murmur, Tannait said, "An oíche-te might keep Henffyrdd close. Might make this boy a consort, since Ciara cares little for the one Ceelin kept. Sabh presses — needs must be certain where they stand."

"Shall stand against strangling their merchants with closed passes," Teleri hissed back. Meantime, the duchesses got their teeth into Ciara, in bantering about Ceelin, and knew it — and Tannait would hold her back — "The Crown wishes no consort. She has a beloved."

Teleri caught Tannait's moment of un-focus as Saint Sabh sent her answer. "Hearts may heal more than once. The kingdom abides, past any one beloved."

Saint Conbarre felt Teleri's anger flare and sent caution.

/ if / not must / peace /

"— and the king's face when Ceelin declared the insult!" Míde slapped the table, laughing. "They danced to our tune quick enough."

"'Tis a young king they have," Faola asserted again. "Fierce, true, but could yet be led to our aid. By the balls, or elsewise."

Míde twitched one shoulder. "Had we a Crown who'd —" and caught herself.

Ciara's eyes were cold as emeralds, glaring at her.

But the duchess didn't fear that. "Where might Dheathain best throw its weight? The princesses —"

Ciara's chair rumbled. She shot to her feet and stormed from the table, the mess hall. Teleri bit her lower lip and gave chase.

"Cici —"

"I'll not go back!" Ciara shoved her door open, ignoring the Blades' salute, and slammed it behind herself.

Teleri caught the door on her arm, and followed. "Must you ever let them bait you?" Behind her, she closed it and leaned on it.

"Must they ever bemoan my failing to be Ceelin!" Ciara pointed back toward the mess hall. "The Crowns of old? Those that kept us splintered, feuding, till Granny Mor's day? They spin tales when Arcea's blade lies on our throat? 'Tis for me to face that, given their support!"

"'Tis you who bemoans." Tel said it plainly, knowing she'd still not hear it.

Ciara shook her head. "'Tis her they mention in one breath with the Crowns of old. 'Tis her their eyes light up for — and I, the poor dull sister, I'm to be endured. Dheathain would throw in with the princesses? Her girls? 'Tis no baiting, 'tis an honest threat." She threw up her hand and then raked it into her loosely braided hair. "There's more love for them than me. They have her spirit."

Teleri crossed the room, reaching for her other hand. "As do you. Show it to them."

She began to reach, then turned away. "Show them how I whine?"

Ceelin had called it that, to pique her twin, and it had stuck hard. Teleri stepped close to Ciara's back, putting a hand on her belt. "'Tis no more than she ever did, in truth."

Hand on hers, Ciara sighed. Reached for Tel's other hand, brought it across her waist for a hug. Let her Blade squeeze a little air from her, even. "And a stain on our dignity," Ciara murmured.

Her mothers had woven that pride deep in her; it had never taken in Ceelin. The younger twin had ever run afire, unstoppable, and the elder was left the sober and thoughtful one. The one who felt the sting of every disappointment that fell near her. Teleri touched a kiss by her ear, pressed her cheek against Ciara's.

"'Tis your dignity alone, now."

"And matters nothing to Dheathain," Ciara breathed a laugh, "what use for dignity, among inbred back-wood —"

Teleri hushed her. "Speak no ill of your people."

"No great thing to cast aside a Crown. Needs only a bit of poison or treachery. Granny Mor and Slaine did ascend, thus. Dheathain would back who they please, for only the lark of taking Myrddin and reaching for Rukharbor." Ciara's hands stroked over Teleri's arms as she spoke, as her mind turned to the paths before her. She needed little guiding through the brambles of politics, Teleri knew. Never had. "And Henffyrdd — 'tis bitter medicine, true, but they and Lancynnes needs must take the draught. They're wedded houses, surely they may share in the ports' trade."

This, though... Teleri took a deep breath and spoke low. "Bitter medicine is never loved. The south's strength must ever be on a Crown's mind."

"All the north would love to see them drink it."

She nodded. Even quieter, she said, "The saints ask much of you, to hold them together in this." She began to release the embrace, but Ciara gripped her hands, pulled her close again.

"And if I cannot — will you remember me?"

Foolishness. "Shan't hear such talk, Cici." She meant it to be stern.

"I served. Ceelin could barely hit the target, but I earned a place in the archery lines for my stint... and they remember her for tumbling some blonde. How can I hold them together?"

True enough that Ciara had served well. Teleri had spotted a young archer, at the trials that summer day, but hadn't known who she was. Tel hadn't seen the princess since she was girl of ten. She'd crystallized into as strong and bright an emerald as any in Caercoed's crown, in those years. Equal skill with both crossbow and long, to her credit. Not the finest archer in the land, but more than worthy enough to qualify. She'd been in harm's way while her sister worked in the supply lines.

And yes, few thought of that when it was Ceelin's brash spirit in the room. Together, the sisters could've persuaded the duchies that the saints' call to seal the passes was wisdom: Ciara negotiating, Ceelin charming.

Ceelin was gone, though, and Ciara did not know her own strength.

There'd be war in Caercoed, whether with Arcea, Wodenberg, or among the duchies. That was certain. One Crown's life was a small thing to take, in any of those fights. They'd have to face an Elect to do that, but anything might happen on a battlefield. Anybody might fall.

"If 'tis me the Shepherd takes first —"

"No." Ciara's grip tightened.

"— mourn me for a moon, and —"

"No. No other."

Tel buried her face against her neck, inhaled the scent of her hair. Violets, faintly. Lilac. "You're too young to say that, even now." Exhaling, she let the ache ebb away. And any talk of dying. "Sealing the passes will strain all. 'Tis the reed you must be, not the oak."

Ciara's softness hardened, her back straightening under Teleri's embrace. "Our saints are in the right. The duchies must see it." She set her hands on Teleri's arms and was released.

"But watch the wind," Tel said, with earnest force. "One eye to its direction."

A nod, at least.

CHAPTER 4

The wind was a knife; Kiefan turned his cheek to it before it could tug off his fur-lined hood. Still, it sliced at his nose and mouth, pulling the cloud of his breath into a streamer. He took a lungful of the wind. Damp enough for snow.

When it ebbed, he turned back to the view down onto Knapptal's main street. The gatehouse tower was his alone, as none of the guard wished to brave the wind. From here, he could see along the lake shore, northwards, to the village where Leix Gwatcyn's knights and archers camped.

As Tannait had said, they brought their commander to the pyre at dawn, singing their dirge.

It came faint, at first, with the wind. A shiver gripped him a moment — it was something like the lamia's song. Long, high notes. These wanted to be screams, though, they wove along a raw edge and then fell into harsh melodies.

Their procession joined the main road half a mile off, led by the Gwatcyn standard of mountains and moons. They came in their mail and swords, in perfect formation, marching as they sang. Six carried the pall. Gwatcyn's red cloak, wrapped around her, flapped in a tail when the wind picked up again.

Kiefan covered his eyes with one gloved hand. Drew a hard breath, though it shook. Dead, now, his only friends in Caercoed. Leix had always been ready with a solid strategy, always ready to argue with Seagrace but never made a fight of it. Her defensive, sword-tangling kir-spikes had taken him unawares in their first sparring, and he'd been trying to work them into his practice since. Not that there'd been much time for that.

And Síochana… her lessons…

Below him, closer voices joined in the dirge when the melody began anew. Kiefan put his back to the merlon and slid down to sit on the cold stone. Pressed his hand to his eyes, to crush the tears out all the quicker. His chest trembled, on the edge of pain in fighting the surge of memories.

Sío's blood on his cote, her mouth hanging slack as her head lolled. Dead, all of them, lying in blood in the hall. And Kate, running to — him, that fucking bastard who haunted Kiefan's every day, she ran to his fucking arms and —

Kiefan slammed his fist into the stone, and pain in his knuckles split through the rage. He was here, alone, in the cold. Not there, afire with hate, running through the bastard — the man — Kate loved —

He'd never so wanted to doubt his anticipation Blessing. Only a fool would.

/ let poison bleed out /

Kiefan wiped at his nose and drew a hard breath through it. Held it, exhaled. The tears kept coming, despite that. Too strong to deny. Sío, dead. Kate, worse, alive and so furious she'd refused to look at him during the funeral.

She hated him. He fought the sob that tried to claw its way up his throat.

/ let it bleed /

He dropped his head against the stone and breathed, let the fist around his heart loosen. His tears slid out and the silent sobs wracked him as the dirge grew louder. A week's stoic silence, he'd held. A week's festering, and now the abscess drained. Left him empty, resigned.

The voices reached the Spanne, below. Sío lay on the bier already, wrapped in her blue-white lieutenant's cloak. Still wearing the ring he'd given her, the silver band set with a green tourmaline. Something from the jewel cache, something he'd seen as a boy while his father told him the family stories.

His mother had wanted it back. But it was Sío's, freely given, and he'd seen that she kept it.

When his breath came even and quiet, he stood, lifted the trap door and descended. The pyre stood in the center of the Spanne, a long bier of firewood that the two bodies lay upon, head to head. Bright red and pale blue. Gregor followed, a few steps behind, as Kiefan walked toward them. So did Captain Aleks; they'd waited for him at the gate. Kiefan's hand settled on his sword.

The Crown's Blades made a ring around the mourners, facing outward with their hands on their swords as well, ignoring the cold wind rippling their blue cloaks. Inside, Gwatcyn's soldiers stood at attention with the duchesses, Sío's business partners, and the Blade officers. And, in white and green, Ciara.

She held a torch, guttering in the breeze. The sun was only just up and warming the clouds that skittered overhead. It would take most of the short winter day to burn the dead.

"Caercoed!"

Ciara turned, raising the torch higher. Elect Teleri folded her arms, beside the Crown.

"We would honor the dead with you," he said.

Just to touch Sío's hand once more, even cold and stiff. Say one last goodbye to her, and to Leix one last thank-you.

"'Twas many a chance after you failed them. What more have you to say?" Ciara asked.

"That I will avenge them." He stopped at the ring of Blades, in a gap between two — whose hands gripped their sheaths tight, kir at ready for a quick-draw. His anticipation Blessing piqued, telling him to stab left first, then cut back at speed to block on the right.

Ciara's voice went flat. "With such prowess as Wodenberg brings, 'twill indeed. Your castle lies gutted by one squad of Arceal?"

Aleks muttered under her breath.

"We would avenge the Crown as well," Kiefan said as Ciara lowered the torch toward the kindling. "The Empress stole from us both."

She paused. "'Twas my sister. See to your own." Then, touched the oil-soaked rags and sticks. Fire crackled up, spreading fast where lamp oil had been splashed in a ring around the stacked wood.

His sister Gisella was bundled safe and warm in her shroud, in a royal grave. Or, perhaps, sitting at the Shepherd's hearth with her father and her sons.

Kiefan raised his voice, over the flames. "We must seal the alliance, Crown. There are still —"

"No." She didn't shout, but the word was clear. Ciara stalked to the ring, snow clotting around the hem of her white gown. Torch held to the side, at something like a low rear guard. "Nothing. Wodenberg has nothing Caercoed wishes. 'Tis clear enough?"

She wore her dark hair in braided loops, to shelter her pale neck. Gold and emeralds in her crown winked in the clouded sun. Anger in her green eyes, not unlike Kate when —

"Sir Anders Bockmann," he said, as a simple fact.

Ciara's head tipped, eyes narrowing. "What of him?"

Her heart would jump to what she wished the most. "I ran him through."

Silence. Measuring him, as his mother did when she questioned his word. Kiefan kept his breath smooth, low, and his gaze steady. It was the truth.

"His head on a platter would be a fine gift, but shan't sway me." Ciara turned and resumed her place at the pyre. There was another dirge to sing, as the fire thickened over the dead.

Kiefan stood and watched, the cold seeping through his boots and woolen socks.

———————×———————

At dawn the next morning, Kiefan crossed the gate-yard to the double doors at the Caer end of the barracks. The Blade on duty rapped a pattern on the iron-bound wood as he approached.

"You think they'll say yes today?" Gregor asked, fighting to match his pace.

"Not likely."

"And you'll let them say no?"

"Little need for a second war." He felt the kir inside the barracks move to the door.

It opened when he was four steps off. Elect Teleri walked out, past the guard, folding her arms as she went. Elect Tannait stood on the sill, hands clasped.

Captain Aleks had reported on the aid Tannait gave in the great hall. Seagrace had said that over the summer she'd lashed blasts of wind across enemy lines, breaking their focus just as his men struck their first blows. She'd shielded entire squads from enemy kir-fire and turned it back on the Arceal soldiers.

Still, she was no battle elect. He looked to Teleri. Their one sparring had goaded him to work his kir-ropes harder too; she'd been far stronger and nearly made a puppet of him. He'd known her stances, though, seen how similar their styles were. And her willingness to grapple had whetted his appetite too. Woden had noticed, in their weekly sparring.

It was Tannait who broke the silence. "'Twere not invited, Elect."

"What must I do to earn an audience?"

"Shall be no audience. We ride, the dawn after Equinox. Nothing more."

"The Crown won't ignore the danger — Arcea will march on Caercoed, soon or late. Your saints know that." He leaned a little, to sight down the hall behind Tannait, but two Blades backed her with crossbows in hand.

"'Tis our saints' concern."

Not made for war, perhaps, but she had an exceptional poker face. Or else she was every bit as calm and certain as she appeared. Kiefan turned his head; Teleri watched with sharp, hazel eyes. "Not saints of war, either of them. That's clear enough," he said.

The shift in her eyes was small enough he wasn't sure he'd seen it. She agreed, his Blessing noted. She knew her saints' faults. She was too much a warrior not to, if she'd been Elect and Captain of the Blades for so long. Cowering behind mountains was not the only answer Caercoed had.

He threw out a possibility. "You mean to take Suevia for yourselves?"

"Needs must ask you to leave, Elect," Tannait said.

Teleri loosened her arms, settled one hand on her sword. The set of her jaw told him there was a chink in the armor there. Disagreements. There'd been talk of Suevia, or talk of war at least. And she was far from eager.

"Tomorrow morning, then," he said. It would be a slow game, and no hurrying it.

"If you must."

"'Tis an augur," Teleri said when the door latched behind them. "Did see how he watched me? If he brings kir to bear, he'll read minds."

"None read minds," Tannait murmured. "'Tis a battle elect, as you said, with fine instincts. Kir makes an augur of him, it can not improve upon it."

"And should trust his instincts — the boy's a racehorse loaded up as a mule, or near enough." Tel threw a hand up, helpless. "A crown will snap many a spine, with its weight. I'd see him unleashed only for the chance to cross swords."

Tannait's brows gathered. "Needs must find you fresh students." When the other sighed, she went on. "Every five years, sure as the dawn, Tel. You grouse for finer students, or orders — 'tis battle you want, all of you. Elect of war."

"Elect of gardens."

"Each to their own."

"Indeed, and 'tis well."

"Fionn!" Tannait called down the hall as they went. "Needs must be sword drills, 'twould seem."

The captain called back from a side room. "Gladly, Elect."

They reached the door into the mess hall, which smelled of egg scrambles and fresh oatbread, near ready to serve. "He will come to watch," Teleri mused.

"Doubtless. Let Ciara weigh her choices, if he persists." Tannait's voice fell further as she met Teleri's eyes. "'Tis true, we have no saints of war. Mother Strength forbid we disagree with them, but the kingdom must abide."

"Might I have your advice in the sword as well, Elect?"

Teleri watched her Blades' forms, their footwork in particular as the snow was rough and well crusted. It would be a day to see how they fought while sliding. She waited on Ciara, whose boot-lace had broken and Bévin was fetching a new one.

Duchess Faola had knotted her greying red hair tight under brass pins and borrowed a Blade's quilted blue gambeson. She carried a wooden sparring sword at her hip, stuck in her belt, and wore knitted wool gloves in the cold. Something of the ease learnt in her stint of service lingered, still, in her poise. Mayhaps she'd not be too much a trial.

And likely she wished the practice for more than an elect's advice. Teleri measured that, as well, and nodded. "Show me your primary forms."

In her eye's corner, she noted Kiefan crossing to the gatehouse, that fumbling squire of his in tow. Margrave Schutze followed as well, with a leather-bound book under his arm. The king's attention was on the Blades as he went, and he caught sight of Ciara when she strode from the barracks to join the practice. At the gatehouse door, he stopped to watch.

Teleri glanced back to Duchess Faola and touched her ankle with the point of a sparring sword; she was mis-aligned, though not badly. "You remember much," Teleri said.

"'Tis hard to forget. These disciple dances brought much back." Their hosts' routine of simple forms drew several Caer to the Orderhaus weekly.

"Needs must remember those," Ciara said, pulling on her gloves. "Mayhaps not for nightly devotionals, but 'tis some use for them I'm sure. You'd join us, Duchess?"

"If I may." Faola stood and saluted with the sparring sword. "'Tis wisest to practice ere one needs such skill, and 'tis sure that I shall."

Fionn and Aisling were sufficient to oversee the rest; Teleri signaled and put out a hand to coax her two charges a bit further from the ranks of Blades.

Ciara went easily, though with a light frown. "Shan't be my doing," she said.

"Needs must apologize for my words at dinner, Highness," Faola said, and bowed deeper. "'Tis a relief, as a mother, that you'd not stoop to claiming my son as hostage. Or for oíche-te."

Ciara stopped, one hand on her hip, and pointed with her sword. "I'll do as I must."

"As will I, should —"

"Start at Disciple's third sequence." Teleri nudged them further apart with her wooden blade. "Ciara, take the northern stance." Time enough for chat after practice. Tel nudged Faola's foot, again, toward better position. Fitting to give her the southern stance to start from. A quick check of Ciara, a nod when her elbow was, for once, high enough. Progress. "Begin."

They traded slow blows, side-stepping and lunging, their footwork fair on the lumpy snow. The duchess was indeed more limber than most her age, though her reflexes had slowed with time and lack of practice. Teleri tapped her elbow when she took the wrong pose and it was a heartbeat before she righted it. When finished, they flourished the swords and listened to Tel's advice.

They repeated the third sequence, doing better. She then gave her students space to catch their breath — and talk, as Faola surely meant to do. It would be wise to hear her out.

"You expect to march on Dheathain, then? Will they drive you mad so quickly?" Ciara asked. No great leap to think thus.

"Three moons since we left home — do you love their company?" Faola breathed a laugh, and Ciara pursed her mouth against smiling. "Had we no common cause, and not been so far afield, I'd have left you to them. But we're cooped here, standing on each others' toes. 'Twill be the same if we seal the passes. I mean no treason by it, truly." She looked to Teleri.

The duchess spoke truly; this party had grown distant, rather than knitting together. "Speak freely, m'ladies." Saint Conbarre need not hear of every word spoken.

"Dheathain does grate," Ciara said.

"Grate by their rigid minds and surety the world's a small and simple place." Faola drew closer, voice low. "Proud of their pure blood — 'tis inbreeding, in truth. But so long as their eyes look beyond our border, they've much to bend their minds to. If locked in with them, 'twill be they who find some slight to turn against the south. Naught from Henffyrdd needed, nor Lancynnes. Shall defend ourselves, when attacked, and 'twill be war."

Ciara grimaced. She knew the tales of the last civil war in Caercoed as well as Teleri did. Saints Sabh and Conbarre had withdrawn their elect, ordered all their discipled to stand down, and many had. But many had taken sides as well and with the ranks of un-gifted had laid waste to much of the kingdom. There'd been smaller feuds since, mostly between Henffyrdd and Lancynnes, but none of the discipled would serve in such battles.

Sabh and Conbarre were no saints of war; they had little stomach for killing their own, even in rebellion.

Faola continued. "Spring past, I did muster eleven thousand to begin their martial stint. As did Lancynnes. Our full strength, we two, would best this army we hear Arcea is massing to invade Wodenberg. We are strong, Crown."

Teleri knew the numbers. As did the saints, but that would not persuade them to war. Her heart sank as the duchess laid out truths.

"If we turn on each other, 'twill cost much. And should a new saint ascend?" Faola nodded. "A saint of war?"

They both looked to Teleri, who straightened her mouth quickly. Held her silence. There were ever rising stars, ever the possibility of a saint ascending. The last, some fifty years past, had gone a-wandering rather than linger in Caercoed. Teleri had thought him a bold and romantic thing, being young at the time. Now, she thought him wise. Little room in the world for new saints, had they scruples against murder.

Ciara looked up at the overcast sky, beset by those truths. "Disciple's fourth sequence," Teleri said, to give both time to digest it. Ciara's focus was off, Faola knew less of the fourth sequence, and Teleri often stepped in to tap them into correct alignment and poise.

"What does the king offer?" Ciara asked her when they finished the sequence.

"He says only that he would speak."

"But the saints wish no alliance."

Teleri nodded. "You did hear what they wish."

"Mayhaps 'tis best to see all that's in the game," Ciara said. "One meeting, he'll have. One."

CHAPTER 5

He wished Kate were there, difficult as that was. He remembered too clearly the hard clench of her jaw, her nails digging into her own palms, when she stood at the far corner of the dais. Refusing to look at him.

Anders had sworn, he'd known full well — but it mattered nothing now. Nothing. He shoved that away before it could drag him into a mire.

Kiefan wrapped his belt twice and buckled it, the familiar weight of Woden's sword settling into place. He hadn't brought the silken, beaded get-up or the jewels; his simple black cote with the moon sigil would do. The plain gold band was more comfortable than the crown in any case. And a black wool cloak, enough to cross from the keep to the barracks.

Ciara had granted one meeting. Must keep his head clear, and wring all he could from it. Woden had only nodded and left it in his hands.

Gregor handed him the black leather gloves, too. He took them with a nod, and walked out of the guest room. Passed the two Guards on duty, and he pretended not to notice when one of those followed too. Thumping half-time to his pace.

"Off duty for the afternoon," he heard Captain Aleks tell Gregor.

Kiefan pulled the gloves on. "I've nothing they want. Not likely they'd keep me," he said.

"Even so, I'll not have you in there with only a squire at your back."

The corner of his mouth pulled up. Better not to argue. She'd order an afternoon of drills and sparring — with her. Down the stair to the second floor, past the open door where the margravine and her daughter sat embroidering by the fire, down the stairs again and movement caught his eye.

The girl stood at the railing above, watching him go. Only a glimpse of her, but his Blessing caught the look on her face. Awe. Same as last time he'd caught her watching. He had little time to worry about a girl's puppy crush, though.

Crossed the hall and out into the brilliant snow. A fresh inch had fallen, in the night, and now the sun was out. He pulled his cloak closer.

The Crown might have any reason for changing her mind. She might mean to see how much he'd offer. She might mean to laugh at him. Grim as it would be to ride home without aid, he must be ready to do it. He could still stop at the Tadhlon Guard's encampment and speak with the captains, if nothing else. A deathly slim chance, that, but a chance.

A Blade opened the door for him: one of the few men, in mail and hooded cloak. They traded a glance in passing and Kiefan's anticipation saw nothing. If anything were afoot, he was innocent of it.

In the briefing room, Crown Ciara waited with both elect — and the duchesses in their finery. Faola, in gold and brown, Míde and Una, in pink and white. The Crown in white and green, elegant and royal even without her emeralds. The elect were little surprise, but the duchesses were less than welcome.

Ciara stepped forward to greet him with a nod. "King Kiefan of Wodenberg, be welcome." Her dark brown hair hung loose, accenting her pale skin. He wondered if she knew what it meant, here in Wodenberg. Crowns did not marry, true, but in letting her hair down she accented it.

He nodded in return. Captain Aleks bowed, behind him. "It's gracious of you to hear me out, m'lady. Though I'd thought we would speak alone."

Ciara slid toward the arranged chairs and side-tables, her feet hidden under the gauzy layers of white. "'Tis for nobility to have its say in the kingdom's matters, surely?"

Interesting. "It's for nobility to obey the saints."

She took one of the high-backed chairs that had a cushion on the seat. His was the other, and the plain chairs were arrayed to the Crown's side. Captain Aleks and the elect stood at attention, silent. There'd be no memory-Blessed or craft-handed secretary to note the meeting; that was at once reassuring and unsettling. Perhaps Elect Tannait could recall as well as one of Qadeem's disciples.

The handmaid in grey brought small beer and honey-glazed oatcakes. Ciara took one bite of hers and set it aside. She turned an arched brow on him; she expected little, that was clear enough. His anticipation piqued, just a tiny pinch, drawing his eyes to hers. A hard gaze, despite her calm. He'd come to think of that as a warning of venom, in all the training his mother and father had given him.

Míde and Una wore the samev marks of disdain as always, but this time they meant it to hide their curiosity. Faola took a more open interest. She'd always piqued more at trade, during the talks in Vorspitz.

"What burns to be said, then?" Ciara asked as the duchesses sampled their tea.

The Crown was not one for chatting. "Last we spoke, tariffs and the like were agreed on. Those did not bring me, though. This alliance has always been a matter of soldiers first," Kiefan said.

"I bring Caercoed two marriage nominees to complete our alliance. Firstly, the duke of Russe has a daughter and she is his heir. By which I mean that she is a disciple of Saint Woden and will seek knighthood — next year, most likely, when she is eighteen. Her name is Nadya Vysokova. If she were to set foot in Caercoed, none would doubt she belongs among you. Secondly, Duke Tomas Seagrace of Englia. He was made a widower in Arcea's attack. I am certain Elect Tannait would speak well of him, as he did of her."

"We're to buy a horse without laying eyes on it?" Una's mouth twisted. "'Tis a fine old trick."

Elect Tannait broke her silence. "Duke Seagrace is a fine commander, well loved by his soldiers, and no more short-sighted than any man. Of an age with Crown Ciara, I believe, and had two sons to his credit?"

Little William, lying broken in the hallway — Kiefan nodded.

"'Twas the worst if it," Tannait said, voice soft, "those little boys."

A pang of sympathy in Duchess Faola's grimace, and she leaned on her chair's arm to edge into the discussion. "This young knight — has she seen battle?"

"She rode with me, and her father, when Arcea thought to slip a small army through our southwest passes. Squires do not go into battle in Wodenberg, unless there's great need. Nadya stood as an aide in the command pavilion."

Faola nodded, settling against the chair back as she thought on that. Míde and Una whispered together, mouths curled in disapproving twists. Little doubt what their objection would be. Ciara studied her cup of small beer, but was only feigning disinterest.

"Do tell how 'tis you now speak of dukes and daughters?" Una asked. "Did risk the road through Suevia for a royal marriage and its advantages."

"Saint Woden sent me to regain Caercoed's aid. He did not speak as to how."

The twins pursed their mouths, reflections of each other. Elect Teleri shifted on her feet, brow crinkling. "Surely 'twas meant to be as before, m'lord," she said.

"Negotiations are my concern." Woden was as glad to leave it to him entirely, thus far.

"But 'tis for nobility to obey, in Wodenberg," Ciara said.

"It's for elect to serve the kingdom."

She set her cup on her side table. "And so you rode to Knapptal to offer us lesser blood for our support. Despite that nothing could be sealed ere spring, when you mean to see to your revenge. How do you sweeten the pot?"

He met her hard eyes. "Plunder."

"Land," she said.

"Suevia cannot be divided. They are one people, and its throne is mine through their saint's blood." This was the sticking point, true enough.

"A fount. Reowan's."

There were two in Suevia: one at Temitte and one at Reowan, the capital. They were more precious than the land itself. "Founts are not given lightly, nor shared."

"'Tis nothing you're giving," Ciara's tone sharpened. "The same words as Vorspitz — trinkets of trade, vague talk of Suevia when you haven't half Arcea's army —"

"We strike fast and early. We flank them." Kiefan leaned toward her, intent. A glance to Teleri, to include her. "Scatter the camp in Ansehen and drive straight into Temitte. Caercoed meets us at their gates and we can take it without a siege. Strip its riches. Then Reowan."

A snicker from the twin duchesses. None of them knew of the royalists in Suevia, those who supported Kiefan's claim to the throne and would see him on it. He couldn't tell them without the surety of an alliance.

"They shan't be taken unawares," Teleri said.

"More trinkets," Ciara said, shaking her head. "You think us girls to be bought with jewels? 'Tis little more to say."

"If it must be..." Kiefan took a deep breath, and not for showmanship. Woden would take a price from his flesh, but — the great hall had stood half an inch deep in blood. And the fount in Englia was a small trade for two in Suevia.

"Must be more than southlander promises, which change with the wind." Ciara crossed her legs, frowning, her mind shuttering up before his eyes.

"Rukharbor."

Brows rose on all of them. The city itself, even with its good harbor, was a little thing. Iced in five moons a year. Hedged by rocky islands, whirlpools, and shoals. It had a fount, though.

When the thought had a heartbeat to settle, Kiefan continued. "Shared among four saints, in peace."

"While you claim two in Suevia?" Ciara's smoothed brow furrowed again.

"Needs must prove 'tis your saint's words you speak, if 'tis founts you wish to offer." Elect Tannait spoke quietly, but with authority.

"Enough." Ciara stood from her chair, chin held high. "I've more gainful matters to pursue."

"M'lady, hear me out." Kiefan stood, close to her; Elect Teleri's arms unfolded, her poise shifting. Her kir coiled.

"I have. 'Tis enough. We came for the terms offered, and you've lowered them. Caercoed does not haggle as fishwives do." Ciara's aloof — his mother, that was who she reminded him of. That was what made his stomach shift toward bitter.

It tainted his voice. "If it's royal blood that means so much, then invoke your oíche-te. Don't think you can keep me as a surety, though."

Hardly a blink, no trace of a sneer. "You've nothing I need." It was a simple fact that Ciara spoke. "Leave, sir."

Lost, quick as that. She'd hear nothing he said further, his Blessing warned.

It would be a long winter.

Teleri drew an easier breath when the door closed behind Kiefan and his captain. No need to doubt his honor — but Tannait had known a battle-rage when she'd seen it on him, in Castle Kaltkern.

"A little boy reaching for the plate of cookies," Míde said, with a snort. "'Tis a slap on the fingers he'll earn."

"Highness, 'twould be a fair match of this duke's daughter and my son," Faola said.

Ciara still stood, her arms folded. "The saints did give their instructions, and once again 'tis clear why. Southlanders offer only half a fount, though surely they'd wriggle from under it in time. Trinkets for our strength and blood. They think us as bewitched by jewels as their sheltered ladies."

"We might strike, still," Una said, gesturing with her cup of small beer. "Strike Rukharbor, take it in full. 'Tis speed this king wishes? While he plays in the south, we show him speed and strength in the north."

"Would you have agreed, for a fount?" Faola asked.

Teleri answered that. "We need no founts from them. The saints have instructed us, and hold to it." 'Twas a quick answer when she'd asked through her bond.

"'Tis only more wasted wind," Ciara said with a sigh.

"Oíche-te." Míde snorted again and drained her small beer.

For once, Ciara agreed. "They do think their pizzles bewitch us, as well."

The twins chuckled, but Duchess Faola only stroked her chin in thought. After a moment's silence, she said, "We might take Rukharbor, Highness, even without the saints' aid."

Caer facing Wodenberg's knights without elect, with thinned ranks of Caer blessed — "The cost would run high," Teleri said. "Don't rely on the support of your own blessed, when the saints order them to stand down."

"Shall choose for themselves. But with the Northern Horse and the ice-boats, mayhaps we cross the Dragon's Fangs soon after Equinox, well before any would think to look for attackers. They know the ice, those seal-hunters."

True enough. A few letters slipped in with those Ciara had already written, and word would get to Seliolan well ahead of the Equinox. Dheathain could move support, as well — send their snow-troops, on skis.

"We have our instructions. Shall seal the passes," Ciara said. "Speak no more on it."

<hr />

Knapptal's small Orderhaus looked onto the lake. Its classrooms, dormitory, orphans, and hospital all fit into one longhouse of massive, split logs chinked with river mud. The chapel stood to one side, large enough for the flock that could make the journey on fair Saint-days.

Kiefan's arrival had added another dozen to a flock already swelled by curious Caer. The abbess had sent up to ask if the Elect might lead an early disciple's dance for those who wished a challenge. He'd agreed before the failed meeting with Ciara.

The second day after that talk, frustration still dogged him. Those who'd come — his own Guard, several of the Blades, local knights and squires — suffered through a more grueling dance than they could've expected. Those arriving for the easier dance with the abbess walked into a warm, sweaty chapel.

Kiefan slipped outside, knelt down and washed his face with snow. Another double handful he slicked over his head, melting as it went and shredding across the short burr of hair below his Blessing ridges. Dripping into his layers of wool.

"Did break a sweat merely watching." A pair of worn, brown boots crunched through the calf-deep snow beside him. Elect Tannait wore grey, as she often did, hose and a mid-thigh tunic with embroidered green knotwork, a black sash tied under her bosom. Her silver hair hung loose, shoulder-long, and the breeze fingered through the strands.

"It cleared my head," he said. "I had thought Elect Teleri might come."

Tannait twitched one shoulder as he stood. "'Tis never far from the Crown, and she'll come with the meal."

If she came at all, this Saint-day. The Crown hadn't left the barracks since their meeting, nor let her Blades out to spar. When she did, Kiefan meant to haul out the Wache's squires for sparring as well and see what might come of it. But that might be in vain if Ciara would truly hear no more.

"If I may, Tannait," he said, fairly certain he could speak plainly. Her brows only rose, so he continued. "After all you told me of elect, of the… conflicts of duty, I count you a friend."

Faint smile lines crinkled around her eyes. "In all I know of you, 'tis an honor to be counted."

He looked down, a little surprised to be smiling. More sober, he asked, "May you tell me why your saints withdrew their alliance?"

Tannait folded her arms, but also looked up at the sky in considering. She turned, tipping her head for him to walk with her. He did, folding his arms to tuck his bare hands in his armpits. After a couple steps, she spoke. "Caercoed will see to itself, and shut its doors."

"All its doors?" He frowned. A thousand other questions leaped to mind, but it would be too much to ask. Elect must guard the kingdom's secrets as much as its founts.

"'Tis what they wish."

"The Crown only met with me for amusement, then?"

They neared the front of the chapel, by the road. Horses with Blade-blue saddle blankets stood breathing clouds and shaking their manes, and a few Caer moved among them, unloading saddlebags.

"No," Tannait said. "As was said, the noble houses do have their say. 'Twas to take stock of all at hand."

Duchess Faola couldn't be pleased, if her trade in Suevia was to be lost. And if the duchesses had say in — swaying the saints? What power did the Crown have? "Might they persuade your saints otherwise?" he asked, feeling it was a risk to ask. Tannait had proven slow to anger, though.

"'Tis no small game afoot. And meddling will earn hate faster than love." She threw him a firm glance.

Rounding the chapel's corner to the front, he glimpsed Crown Ciara, for a moment, before her Blades shifted into a ring around her. That message was clear enough. Tannait's mouth had twisted, regretful, and likely she looked for something to say.

"I'll not trouble the Crown," Kiefan said, with a nod. "Would you tell her that?"

She returned the nod.

Cold and dark, each morning, when Kiefan woke. Kir sleeps little, Woden had said, and the longer one steeped in it, the less one slept.

Something of a curse, when there was only a further muddle of unclear, useless — Kiefan had had to get out of Castle Kaltkern, he couldn't stand to be there a moment longer once the funeral feast ended. Knapptal had proven little better, thus far. Only more frustration, closed doors, and less space to himself.

A disciple's dance each morning began to seem a fine idea, save that only a fool would walk out into frigid darkness and knee-deep snow to the Orderhaus. He'd have to do it himself, perhaps in the margrave's great hall. Though not this morning.

Kiefan bundled the blankets back over his squire after slipping out of bed. He brought up enough green glow to his hands to find his clothes in the dark without waking Gregor. A light sleeper — he had mischievous brothers, at home.

Even through socks, even through the bearskin carpet, the stone floor was cold. It needed boots to ward that off. Kiefan slipped out and down the hall, thinking of Schutze's collection of books in the second-floor council chamber. He'd meant to take a closer look at them for some days now.

The night-lamp flickered on the staircase as he descended. On the council's door-sill, he brought up more kir and knotted it down till it ignited. The green cloud made a ball around the bright yellow point, suffusing the light gently. Tying it off, he set it in the bowl of an unlit lamp on the writing-table and began looking through the books.

Many were ledgers, or books of military tactics that he had read. There was a copy of Woden's book of law, with loose sheets of notes added. Then Kiefan found a cluster of interesting books at the end of one shelf. One was the Schutze family history, tracing back nearly as many generations as the Weissbergs. They had always been lords of the Spiegel and these rugged hills, and were a fair mixing of Alemanni blood with Suevi. The next book was a history of battles and blood-feuds around Knapptal.

That one he put aside for another look. Kiefan drew the next volume, and it was a compendium of stories. Some were familiar, like the Red Hunter's Revenge, though with different details and a nastier ending. Some he'd never seen before. And some were about the saints — Woden's exploits, going back to when he was newly ascended. Aleksandr's feats, which must've come third- and fourth-hand from Russe. Some of those details were jumbled or wrong.

And some stories of a saint named Vitur.

Kiefan sat down at the writing table and tipped the pages toward the lamp. The ink was brown, watery, and the language old-fashioned. There were drawings, though the people stood oddly, awkwardly, and all was flat. Houses were far too small and children were merely small people. Horses looked like dogs.

No craft-hand had made this. Though why one would let an un-crafted illustrate a book — if there were any craft-handed to be had. Kiefan flipped the book shut, running a thumb over the old leather. The first Blessed were chosen after Saint Qadeem joined in the great oath of Wodenberg. Some ten generations past.

He hunched over the book, knuckles against his mouth, studying the pages all the closer. Who was Saint Vitur? How long ago had this been? Had Woden known him? Been his elect? Kate would love this.

The stab of pain took him unawares. Kate.

Kiefan had said it twice, that she loved… him. Anders. The sadness, the anguish in her eyes had kept him hoping he was wrong. That she was only fond of him for being kind, not that she — kissed him as she did in the blood-drenched hall.

The knife Kiefan felt in his gut that moment, knowing Anders had fucked her, had torn the last shreds of reason from his mind. Sío dead, everyone dead, and Kate lost as well.

Kiefan covered his face with both hands, pressing his eyes. Nothing could've stopped Sío from fighting beside him when the minotaurs kicked the door in. She'd been nothing like Kate, and yet he'd dared to hope they could make a marriage work. Sío knew the sword, horses, and taught him what pleased her in bed…

Let her make you happy, Kate had said. He looked down at the book, lying open. She'd asked why he couldn't wish the same for her. Rather than resenting what must be done. Demanding oaths. Like a fool.

His heart sank, too weary to fight it anymore. In his rage, he'd stabbed her husband. Kate hadn't let him bleed out, hadn't harvested him, but her anger at the funeral had all but set his anticipation afire with warnings. Next he saw her, she might gut him with a charm, but he feared she'd do it with words. And be right to. He'd well earned her hate and well deserved it.

Woden had been right: in trying to keep Kate, he'd turned jealous and reckless. Weak. And driven her away, with his son, in the bargain. He'd been a fool and would pay for it the rest of his life.

Schutze had paper and a quill; Kiefan pushed the book aside and reached for those. The inkpot was only half full and the quill wanted trimming, but he began writing before the words slipped away.

He ought to saddle Nail and say it to her face, but his gut knotted in fear. Not yet.

Around dawn, Gregor interrupted him. "M'lord? Are you hungry?"

Kiefan looked up, the quill hesitating. He sat up, wincing when his clenched shoulders shifted, and saw the thin light seeping through the shuttered window. With a deep breath, he took stock — breakfast, yes, that would be good. Once he finished —

He frowned at the sheets, turned them over. Two pages, covered front and back. Much of it scratched through and rewritten.

Useless, all of it. Trying to explain the unforgivable.

Kiefan picked the sheets up and ripped them. "I'll be down shortly," he told Gregor, standing up and tearing the pieces smaller.

Gregor nodded, but lingered to watch. Kiefan picked up the kir-lamp and tossed the bits of paper in the lamp's bowl, where they soaked up oil quickly. Un-knotting the kir, he took it in hand and focused it down to a spark charm. It dropped into the lamp and lit the paper. Fire flared up, bright and strong.

"Is a courier on hand?" Kiefan asked, sitting back down and pulling out a fresh sheet. He wrote something short, quick, and signed it. "I have something that must go to Wodenberg. Where's the sealing wax…?"

"I'll ask m'lord Schutze," Gregor said.

CHAPTER 6

Kiefan's mind cleared the next day when the courier rode out with Kate's letter among the others in his saddlebag.

Caercoed had no use for him, but she must wait for Equinox to leave, and that was three moons off. He had a spring campaign to plan.

Margrave Schutze was quick to throw in his aid. On the office table, they spread out maps of Knapptal and the Spiegel, of the river valley below in Suevia, and of the hilly, cliff-studded line that formed Wodenberg's southern border. Schutze called in the captain-general of the garrison, Hochwald, and the lieutenant of the local Ranger squad, Klippe. Schutze's steward, Koch, rattled off numbers and served as a record-keeper. Gregor and Hochwald's squire stood to the side, all eyes and ears.

Schutze's garrison had near two thousand, largely armsmen and archers but all locals who knew the hills. The hundred or so knights posted there were a mix of natives and Alemanni from deeper in the kingdom. Klippe had his squad of fifteen Rangers and was sure he could put together another fifteen woodsmen who'd make good scouts, given a week or two. More, if given more time.

From the south end of the Spiegel, a river dropped through a steep gorge and into a valley. Suevi called the river the Dúnforst-éa, and it bent westward until it met the Neva at Temitte. The first town of any size on the Dúnforst-éa was a watchtower garrison called Langsceadu.

"They've good woodsmen," Klippe allowed, with a nod, "but they've no Blessings. Our hawk-eyes can scout from twice as far, and they never miss."

From Knapptal to Ansehen, a crow would fly some forty miles. On foot, across the hills, it was further. A thin road ran along the wall and the watchtowers that Saint Aleks had raised along the border, connecting the string of pearls. On the southern slope, in Suevia, the hills were wild — too thin for farming or even much grazing, though there were villages here and there. The road from the Suevi watchtower to Temitte was the only one of any size.

"Thaw starts at the Equinox, most years," Captain-general Hochwald said. "Meltwater creeks spring up all along the hills, the ponds fill. The Spiegel rises," and he tapped the map where Knapptal Hill's flank curved away from the lake, "and the shore road floods a while. The men could get through, afore that, and slip through the Notch. With some help from the woodsmen, they can go light on supplies."

They all nodded and stood looking at the map in silence, measuring the distances again and the little figurines set out in estimate of the Arceal camp at Ansehen.

"Damn ballsy," Hochwald said, "if it works. But no way to signal when we're in position."

If they had two elect — if Kiefan hadn't stabbed one — it would be simple. Another penance to pay. "I'll ride with you, and I will send word to Saint Woden."

"Into Suevia?"

"Majesty —"

Honest shock dropped their jaws. Kiefan put up a hand. "Once in sight, we'll work out what's best — striking at their supply train, at a reserve they might've hidden, or creep up to attack from the rear."

"We'd only be two thousand," Hochwald said.

"With much surprise, if you're stealthy." Schutz frowned. "If you're not the man for it, name a better one."

The officer's pride snapped his spine straight. "I go where you do, m'lord. And where you go, Majesty."

A tap sounded on the office door. Gregor stepped to open it and Schutze's daughter Haralda looked in. "M'lords, may I offer refreshment?" She raised a pitcher of small beer; the housemaid behind her carried steins.

Schutze grinned. "And a good time for it, sweetling. Talking's thirsty work."

Haralda bobbed a curtsy and the men cleared one end of the table for the cups. Kiefan stepped aside to let her pour, and weighed Seagrace's army against the Arceal camp. Surprise was their only advantage in this.

"That — is the enemy?" Haralda asked, and he realized she'd been trying to pass him a drink. She tilted her head to see the map properly. "Father said they were at Ansehen, as is Duke Seagrace?"

"Yes," Kiefan said, putting his hand on the stein. Her timing in interrupting their quick-scrambled meeting struck him, for a moment. No cambifax, surely… his fingers touched hers on the stein, and he still hadn't taken it. A quick call of her kir-patterns, to be sure.

Only a girl, and not even sensitive enough to notice. One staring, now, with a mix of awe and hope. "My thanks, fräulein," he said, taking the drink.

A bright smile. She handed out the last two to the squires and turned back to the map. "Papa says the Neva Lake is larger than the Spiegel," Haralda said, still beaming. "Is it so great? Have you seen it?"

"I've hunted along its western shore." Kiefan tried to make it gruff and focused on his drink.

"Hunting?" Her eyes lit brighter. "Papa took us to hunt turkeys, in Hunter's Moon. I shot two."

Gregor, fidgeting with his untouched beer on her other side, broke in. "M'lady's a fine shot. I saw you on the archery range. Last week?" He quailed as she turned on him, startled. They both blushed, on the same cue.

Mother have mercy on them both.

"You watched me? Did m'lord see, too?" A quick glance back at Kiefan, and then she asked him, "Have you tried our range, m'lord? Perhaps you'd — train, sometime —?"

Schutze tried to break in. "Don't pester m'lord, Haralda."

Her eyes were full of hope and that stung Kiefan. Puppy love was the last of the things needed, this winter. "Your father and I have much to discuss, fräulein," he said, turning his shoulder to her.

Haralda needed a small nudge, still, but she went with eyes downcast. Gregor tracked her, his lower lip pulled under his teeth. He still held his full stein of beer. Two puppy loves, a fine disaster in the making.

"Keep your mind to the task," Kiefan told him. "A broken heart's of little use in war."

WODENBERG

When my eyes snapped to focus, I was already sitting up in bed. Moonlight outlined my latched shutters, on the wall beyond the foot of my bed. I put out my hands to either side; one found the brick chimney, gone cool for the night, the other found Rafe.

Warm and sleeping.

I breathed a sigh. My pulse slowed. An echo of the nightmare flicked by: Kiefan twisting his moon-pommeled sword as he ripped it through Anders' chest, Anders cutting him open low across the stomach, hacking each other to bits heedless of their spurting blood and tumbling guts.

I held my breath as tears gathered in my eyes. My nerves jangled in my flesh, twitching in my arms and thighs.

The same, every night. Snarls on their faces. Set on destroying each other.

Rafe was a snug little bundle; I picked him up and cradled him close. I wrapped the top blanket around me as I slid off the mattress. There'd be no getting to sleep. I'd lain awake night after night, jittering from the nightmares. Pacing helped. And climbing the stairs.

My socks scraped on the steps. The shop was cold and silent. Moonlight seeped in; the Snow Moon was full, and the sky clear. A few days in Frida's house without Anders and I hadn't been able to stand it. Rafe wasn't her grandson and my marriage had been a ruse. At first. In my hearth, the coals still glowed red. I paced across my kitchen and back, with Rafe asleep against my shoulder.

Watching Frida weep with little Hilly clinging to her skirts, Alice sniffling and wiping at her eyes as she tried to cook — it had broken my heart afresh every moment I was in the house. M'lord Reinhardt had the decency to keep his voice low and spend his days with the horses, thank the Mother. Will had gotten his tears out and came home drunk one night, which earned him a stern look from his father but he'd only done it the once. Ein had glowered and huffed, impatient with it all, young enough that he nearly said what the baron was too wise to. M'lord Reinhardt had caught him by the ear and hauled him out to the barn just in time.

Frida had burst into tears in any case.

She hadn't wanted to let me move out. I'd said I needed to work, to be busy, here in my shop. And I'd packed my few things and gone despite her protests.

Today being Saint-day, Frida had driven out with the wagon and caught me in my lie. I hadn't opened the shop even once in four days. There were only some heels of bread on the table, and some water in the keg, as I'd hardly opened the door save to let the water-carriers in.

I kept pacing, stroking Rafe's back. Dear Frida, setting a pot of oats and water on the hearth to cook while she bullied me into washing and combing my hair. Shoving me down on my knees to scrub diapers in the tub she'd brought. Telling me the news as we did. Putting a bowl of hot porridge before me and playing with Rafe while I ate.

She'd wanted to drag me to the disciple's dance and the meal, but I had diverted us onto sweeping, dusting, and discussing what furniture I needed to make this a proper home. And where I might get the curtains I needed for the drafty shutters. Frida had left at sun-down after extracting a promise that I'd visit her each Saint-day.

"I will not lose both of you. Or Rafe," she'd told me with an uncommonly stern glare.

Both of us. My throat tightened. My memory brought it back, unbidden: the point of Kiefan's sword tenting the back of Anders' cote, tearing through, glinting red with his blood. The vulture's black wings taking heavy strokes through the air.

Lost him. Because Kiefan — and Woden wouldn't let me —

Rafe's arms twitched against my chest. I hushed him, stroked him, but he was waking. Time to nurse. I sat down at the table and untied my shift's drawstring neck. Rafe cooed, picking his head up for a moment, and looked around.

"Nothing to fuss about," I murmured, working my neckline down. The dim moonlight glinted on my son's mouth when he smiled at me.

My little sweetling. I kissed his fuzzy head. Rafe threw his hands up in glee and grinned big as he could. I kissed him again. He wriggled. He loved this game, he was a darling little — prince —

I clutched him close, my throat knotted shut and tears bursting out. Sobs shook me. Kiefan's name tried to crawl out, but got twisted into a raw noise.

The blood, Mother have mercy, the blood that had sprayed from his slashed throat.

Rafe mewled against my neck, confused, then cried.

"I'm sorry, I'm sorry, shh." I shifted him down, lay him alongside my breast. That stopped his crying. He latched on easily and nursed.

I looked around my kitchen as he did. Frida had left the porridge pot and a large bowl covered by a towel; there was a chunk of ham in there and some onions. Those needed some bread and a few pounds of oats to fill them out into meals. Maybe a few eggs, too. I had money up in my office.

Those could all be had in a short walk down Scribe Street, but my bones grew tired at the thought of it.

Rafe still woke twice a night, but I was getting even less sleep than that.

It was time to put away the nightmare of two men I loved killing each other.

That needed taking my memories firmly in hand, studying them closely to note all their awful details, and then they could be folded up like blankets. Put into the great trunk of my mind's Blessing and the lid closed.

The dreams would end. I never dreamed of the lamia on Starknadel, of Elect Parselev's death, or the breaking of the city walls. I'd put those away.

My thumb stroked across Rafe's cheek as he sucked. He needed me strong and well. And it was cowardly of me to hide in a shop when the city needed healers. Needed its elect. My saint's bond, in my right palm, had lain quiet since Qadeem went north to Rukharbor. He had duties to see to.

So did I, as his bound elect.

I took a deep breath and closed my damp eyes. Called the first moment of that awful night at the castle to be inspected.

KNAPPTAL

Hardly dawn yet, but Síochana's two companions meant to get an early start and so Teleri brought them the packet of royal letters to hide in their baggage. And a purse of silver, to aid their passage. The ladies knew cold-weather travel, they were veterans of the trade roads, but they still faced a long trek through Suevia to the coast. They didn't speak of how they'd get to Arforddinas from there and she didn't press.

As Teleri took her leave of the ladies Branwen and Pryderi, she caught a glimpse of Una's pink skirt as the door down the hall closed behind her.

Hardly odd, save that it was Duchess Faola's door. Unlikely she would've invited either of the twins to her room — no love would be lost, if there were war between their duchies.

Teleri crept down the hall. At Faola's door, she pressed her ear by the crack. Mumbled voices, three of them. No sound of argument or struggle. With a little kir, she made a cup around her ear and that helped.

"— next we're at the Two Lanterns. 'Tis much on our minds."

Tricky to tell Míde from Una, by voice, but Teleri suspected the second.

"Idle talk," Duchess Faola said.

"Need not be. Has been done afore." That was Míde, ever the blunter weapon.

"'Tis something to blame on southerners, if 'tis done sooner," Una said. "Shall sway Iâtreth and Seliolan."

Both were northern duchies, one on each coast. Seliolan included Myrddin, Síochana's margravate. Both duchesses were cautious, but ice-hard in resolve once won over.

"Anger won't sway such as them, so easily. Even for murder." Faola said.

"If Eryr Pass is sealed behind us, you've lost," Una replied.

"Shall be sealed with or without a Crown — or do you think to account for two elect as well?" Faola's voice fell to a hiss. "Don't be fools. Eryr is lost. 'Tis Dwyncraig that might be saved, and shall bring Lancynnes to us without question. To you."

Teleri's fist pressed against the door, kir glowing in her knuckles, and only by discipline did she keep her breath even. The elder duchess was right. If she said more of where or when they'd turn traitor…

"Needs must have the north," Una said. "To stand against the saints as one."

"Three duchies united, 'tis miracle enough."

"Needs only a drugged ale and a snowdrift overnight." Míde muttered, at the edge of hearing.

"'Tis what we've come to?" Faola turned angry. "This? Ciara's right enough, 'tis been a disaster."

A moment's pause. "If we only had Ceelin," Míde said. "She'd bring these southlanders to heel."

"Must do with as we're dealt," Una said. "Do think on it, Faola, if 'tis —"

"Say no more 'til we're among ignorant ears."

Blades and Caer went to the tavern on the main road, the Two Lanterns, in small groups now and then. Only a few words of Alemannic were needed to buy ale. Teleri hadn't noted if the duchesses had gone together in the week past. Needs must watch them closer.

"Shall look for an eve no Blades mean to go."

"And 'tis much to digest. Let me be till —"

Not much longer talking, by the sound of it. Teleri backed away from the door, unwinding her charm, and looked for an excuse. Crossing back to the merchants' door, she opened it and asked, "Did I give you silver for the road?"

Their baggage was ready, and they'd been about to call for the stable-hands. When Míde and Una slipped from Duchess Faola's room, Teleri had a saddlebag over one shoulder and was offering to take a second. It made a fair scene that she'd been helping them prepare the whole time and hardly noticed the twins at all.

Once she'd carried the baggage down to the stables, Teleri took her leave.

/ treason / plots / murder the Crown /

It was only two heartbeats' wait for Conbarre to respond, but it felt longer. Teleri passed what she knew, as clearly as she could. She reached Ciara's closed door and stood before it, waiting for instructions.

/ fools / seeking war / seal the passes /

/ will invade / by sea /

/ our elect / our disciples / will not /

Teleri's jaw clenched; no saint of war, Conbarre. She chose her message carefully.

/ would obey / no killing Caer / will rally / against outsiders /

Especially if the southerners had murdered both Crowns. Details mattered little in such things. In the pause, Tel sent more.

/ will arrest / will protect /

/ watch / report / protect / seal the passes /

Her anger flared. / must stop them! / now! /

The bond came alive in her palm, a jittery pain shooting through her fingers, muscle clenching and shuddering as it climbed to her elbow. Teleri's breath hissed through her teeth.

/ no more dead / never by Caer hand /

Hardly the worst stringence she'd gotten, but Conbarre convulsed her hand for long, painful heartbeats.

/ do not! /

Did expect an answer, as well. Teleri clenched her left fist and cleared her mind of anger. None could lie through the bond.

/ will obey / protect /

The stringence eased, leaving the muscle shivering under her skin.

/ will bury her / serve daughters /

And always took a parting shot. Teleri had seen Crowns buried, had lost lovers to the Shepherd. Her own twin was ten years dead, at a fine old age.

"In time. But not soon." She pressed the latch and went in.

The bed's white wool curtains hung open, on Teleri's side, and she went to the gap knowing what she'd find. Ciara lay sprawled across the mattress, as she did when alone, the blankets kicked off to her feet. No matter how cold, she kicked off the blankets. Her lamb-swool shift barely covered her butt, and the bare leg she'd thrown toward the open curtains was a strong temptation.

Tel sat, though, softly crinkling the hay-stuffed bed, and reached toward Ciara's elbow.

She pounced, grabbing the arm, and climbed up it to Teleri's shoulder. Her wicked smile drew an echo from Tel, despite it all. "Did wish you back to bed, and you came," Ciara whispered. Her dark braid, wispy from sleep, slid over her shoulder and trailed on the mattress. She inched closer, intent on Tel's lips.

She leaned, touched a quick kiss and put her forehead to Ciara's. "Needs must tell you, first."

A faint raspberry. "'Tis snowing, again? Must I order —"

"The duchesses wonder how best to murder you."

Ciara's eyes widened and she sat back, alert as a cat. Teleri told her, word for word when prodded for details. Ciara gathered her legs under her as she listened, her face a calm mask carved from whitest shell.

"Ceelin," she murmured, when Teleri reached that part. "No, they'd not murder Ceelin. She could do no wrong."

Tel's throat tightened, but she went on to the end. Quiet lingered after her words. Ciara looked down at her hands, picking at her nails.

"What would they have me be? Ceelin?"

Tel's arms ached to hug her close, but she answered instead. "Would have you take their side and put their argument to the saints."

"You're certain?"

"They would keep the passes and attack our neighbor, rather than seek safety. 'Twill rally many who wouldn't see the passes sealed."

"Mayhaps I'm no fit Crown for them." Ciara's hands fell still. "Etain and Eithne are better loved, for their spirit. If they come for me —"

Teleri snatched her close, squeezed her tight. "Must come through me, first."

Ciara's arms latched around her in return, stronger than they looked. Her ribcage trembled in Tel's grip, but no sobs came. Teleri held her Crown, loosening her arms a little, until she could speak again.

"What say the saints?"

"To seal the passes."

Ciara sighed against Teleri's shoulder. "Needs must stand under the Mother Tree and face them."

"Shall listen, if the people are united. Ever have, before."

"If 'tis to be me, with five duchies at my back… if I must be Ceelin…"

Her mind went to work. Teleri held her, gently now, one hand slowly stroking her back. Best not to interrupt, only stay close. Willing as Tel was to storm the duchesses' quarters with sword and kir, to murder them for their plots, she'd face her saints' justice for it. Her word alone was slim reason to arrest them, and it would unsettle their duchies further once the passes were sealed. All would see Ceelin's sour twin using her lover's power, in that.

Her mind strayed to Conbarre's pinch: will bury her. Teleri kept a bag of mementos among her things. A bone brooch, a hair-pin, a seashell, and the like. Small reminders of those she'd loved. What she'd add to it for Ciara — her heart sank at the thought, but she'd done it before and surely would again.

Ciara was young, still, not even thirty. With safekeeping there'd be many long years yet.

"Tel." Ciara's voice was steady, but soft. "If I asked. If 'twere — would you stand with me, if the saints order you to withdraw?" She sat back, looked Teleri in the eye.

Decades ago, Tel had led a company on a night raid into an Arceal camp. She'd gone against orders on a hunch soon proven wrong. The disaster had cost her the whole company. A hundred Caer. Conbarre had seen to Teleri's discipline herself, with full stringence and a whipping delivered by the icy sea itself.

Strong as Tel knew she was, the memory still made her gut tremble. Conbarre would not kill her own, true, but she'd wished for it. Defiance needed dire reasons, to be forgiven.

"'Twould cost me much. More than you know," Teleri answered.

Ciara's hands tightened on hers, knuckles whitening. "I'll not ask you to, then. The duchesses — would Suevia satisfy them? In place of Wodenberg?"

Suevia was larger, richer, had two good founts fit to match Wodenberg's. And it was fiercer defended. "Needs must have a bold plan for that. King Kiefan means to take their throne, and has their old saint's eyes to anchor his claim."

"He hasn't the swords to take it outright. 'Twas what you said."

"True, he hasn't. He'll not do it without us."

Ciara's mouth twisted to one side. "Had Ceelin taken him for her precious oíche-te rather than that blonde, made a consort of him… but never a thought to tactics, from her."

Teleri watched her face sink into calm again as she weighed thoughts. Her own heart quavered in suspicion. "You might take him for consort?" It came out a whisper.

A hard stare. "Shall have none but you."

There'd been a boy, once, when Ciara was a young archer serving her stint. He'd been killed by Arcea below Eryr Pass. She'd not turned her head for a man in seven years since. Didn't for this handsome young king, either.

Still…

Ciara kissed her, firm and slow. Lips close to hers, she whispered again. "None."

A pang shot through Teleri's heart. Her hand found the hem of Ciara's shift, on her hip, and brushed it aside. Ran her sword-hardened hand across the smooth skin underneath. Cici's mouth delved into hers, soft but insistent, forcing her to yield. The mattress crinkled as Teleri lay back.

CHAPTER 7

WODENBERG

I opened my shop. I'd told each of the vendors I would, when I went from stall to stall in the King's Market buying supplies. Each one had said they were glad to see me and they'd pass word. They cooed over Rafe, asleep in his sling, and slipped little extras into my basket. Another egg. Two biscuits. The drapes I'd ordered for my windows were stitched up in just a couple days and those slowed the drafts considerably.

Surely word did pass, but the weather was cold and the snow knee-deep. Little reason to leave the house unless there was need.

A middle-aged housemaid knocked on my door one afternoon. "Word has it you're doing business," she said as she shuffled into my curtain-walled foyer. "You've saved me a walk down to Lehrer's, I hope. Laundry, you see. I spent all morning on it, day before last, out in the washing-shed, and it's…"

I'd called up her kir-pattern as I shut the door behind her. "…it's set off your chillblains," I finished when she stopped to glance over my canvas curtains. Little wonder she shuffled, by the swelling in her toes and knees.

The woman turned, eyebrows flying up. "Why, yes. How —?" She chuckled. "Ah, pay me no mind. You're the Elect. I need some mustard oil for the poultice, if you have any."

"I have some," I said with a nod. She had more aches than the chillblains, in her ankles and lower back. An afternoon's scrubbing on your knees at a washtub would do that. "Two bruns for a vial — or I could mend all your pains for five."

She tracked me as I circled around her. As we were alone, I didn't invite her to step behind a privacy curtain. The woman's mouth fell open but she had to think on her answer a few moments more. "I'll be scrubbing again at Goldkraft's tomorrow, and the floor won't be any warmer. If it's the same to you, Elect, might I take four bruns' worth of oil?"

I poured some into a little jar she'd brought, from the supply I'd inherited from Parselev. While I was in my office, Rafe began to fuss; he'd been asleep on the bed. I picked him up in passing and carried him down on my shoulder. He promptly fell back to sleep. The housemaid smiled, crinkling her face with cheerful lines, when I returned.

"You've a baby! So you're not here alone after all?"

That caught me off guard. "Only myself and Rafe," I said. I passed her the stoppered jar.

A crease between her brows shifted her smile to worry. "I'd heard you were wed — your pardon, Elect, oh…" She covered her mouth with one hand. "Castle Kaltkern?"

I still held the jar out to her, but I looked away. The ache blossomed, seeping easily through my chest. "I lost him, yes."

She took the jar, and my hand, in both of hers. "So many killed, that evil night. Shepherd see him home, m'lady."

"I — he was taken," I said, because it wasn't true. Qadeem had said Anders was alive.

"Taken?"

The memories were safely tucked away, but my eyes still brimmed with tears. My throat knotted up and I shook my head. The housemaid murmured at me sadly and pressed her coins into my hand. She retreated out the door. Its latch didn't quite catch, and it stood just ajar for a moment.

A timid knock, and it swung open again. This woman came in with a dozing toddler on her hip, a lock of hair hanging from under the kerchief around her head, the hem of her apron wet and dirt-stained. She didn't have a cloak, only a wool shawl; she must be a servant's wife, or a laborer's.

"Elect — Kate?" She shifted on her feet, glanced toward the closed door behind her as if someone might see her. "I heard — that you mended Inga's eye."

Inga had been the archer whose hawk eye had lost its focus after a blow to her head. "I did, yes." At a glance, this woman seemed healthy enough. She was pregnant, in fact, though not showing yet.

Her voice dropped, and she sidled nearer. "It's my husband."

I lowered mine, too. "Trouble with his eyes?"

"No. Well, some nights, but — it's the drinking. If I can bring him to you, might you mend that?" She grimaced, hefted her daughter up to snooze on her shoulder. "He's a good man, truly. He never hits me. Never. Nor Tilly. But his drinking — it's put us in debt. I've gotten some work thread-spinning, but I must hide the money or he'll drink it."

I was nodding as she spoke; I knew this story. "You must speak with your abbot, then, on how to put the Mother's Discipline to him." Surely she knew this already. "Have you?"

"I can't." It brought tears to her eyes. She fell to a whisper. "I've wronged the Mother too. I kissed…" She shook her head. My gaze slipped to her belly. She went white, and put her hand to it. "Please don't, please, Elect, don't tell…"

My heart twisted in my chest. I leaned close to her, searching for the right words. It wasn't for me to fix any of this; my teacher had warned me on that. "Tell the abbot that your husband is a drunkard, and he's putting your marriage oaths at risk. How are you to raise strong lambs, when the collectors take everything to cover his debts?"

She sighed, and I knew despair when I heard it.

A knock at the door. "Elect Kate?"

The woman stepped away from me. "Come in," I called back.

When the door opened, she bolted out past the messenger. He flattened himself to let her by, and watched her go with a frown. Then he stepped in. Under his fur-lined cloak, he wore a black tabard with the white wheel of the support division embroidered on the shoulder. A messenger's bag hung at his side.

"A letter for you, Elect." He unbuttoned the bag and fished out a folded, wax-sealed paper.

My heart thudded as he held it out, and my hand reached of its own accord. Took it from him. Knew what I'd see before I did: my name, in Kiefan's clean hand, above the wax.

He'd written.

My fingers fidgeted at the clean-cut edges of the folded paper. A small thing, once folded in three. It couldn't be much. Though he could write fine and small, when he put his mind to it...

I blinked. "Thank you," I told the messenger, who was waiting for my leave. "If this is all, then go."

He went, closing the door carefully behind himself. I followed him to it, and put my hand on the latch to be sure it was shut. My nerves jittered in my arm, my hand, on the cold iron. Kiefan had written. Had something to tell me, after...

What chance was there that he'd found another book of d'Ovio Alain's essays?

I put my back to the door and sighed as the drunkard's wife had. No, it must be something to do with... Caercoed. Perhaps he'd found a new bride, but why would he write to me of that? Kiefan wasn't one to gloat, even if m'lady Faola had somehow spirited her perfect daughters to Knapptal.

But then, I hadn't thought Kiefan would attack Anders in a blind rage.

Anders. The kiss I'd given him, unthinking. I had put the memory away, but there'd been such anger in that moment Kiefan would've struck me down, too, if Anders hadn't pushed me aside.

I looked at the calm, clear writing on the letter. Kiefan had found words for his anger? Had he seen the truth with his augury: that I loved Anders — and that he deserved it? My hand tightened on the paper. Anders had been there when Rafe was born and every morning after it. He'd called him his son, rocked him to sleep, kissed him even when snot dripped from his little nose.

That set my heart in grim determination, and I broke the seal. If Kiefan wrote to me in anger, he'd get the same —

"I covered two pages, trying to explain, but it means nothing. I could not bear to lose you too and I know that now you are lost to me. By my own hand. On my life, I swear I never meant to hurt you."

I threw it down, and clenched my fist. Hurt me? No, but he'd fully meant to run Anders through, and he had. And Woden, Shepherd damn him, had let them fight. Sooner see them both dead than let me — tried to strike me down, too, if Qadeem hadn't —

When I could've healed both! Fools, the lot of them! There'd been no time to think that I'd just cheated the Shepherd of Kiefan, full and fair, when I turned to see to Anders...

...and he'd been gone.

I slid down the door, my butt hitting the cold floor. Tears tumbled down my cheeks when I blinked.

Gone. Anders had to know I could save his life, but he'd stumbled away to —

Lost. Both of them.

"I could not bear to lose you too." I heard the words in Kiefan's whisper.

He'd taken the first swing. If Kiefan had been standing in my shop to say that, I'd have slapped him.

Instead, I sat and cried.

———————✕———————

KNAPPTAL

The courier returned the day before Solstice; nine days to Wodenberg and back was as fair as one could hope for, in such snow. He brought word from the Queen, Steward Vogt, and the quartermaster — nothing from Kate. The man swore he'd put the letter in her hand himself.

"Did she read it? Did she say anything?"

The courier hesitated, looking to one side. "She saw the seal, m'lord, and she thanked me. Said I could go, so I did."

Her name had been over the seal. She'd know his handwriting. Couldn't doubt who it was from. Did she read it, or throw it in the fire?

Kiefan hadn't truly expected an answer, but it ached all the same.

Solstice morning, he rose in the dark and padded barefoot to the kitchen. It was far warmer than the hall at this hour and the baker was always up to see to the day's bread. The floor was wood rather than stone, as well. By arrangement, once the baker filled the oven-pots with risen dough and set them on spiders over the coals, Kiefan could loosen his joints before the fire until the bread smelled delicious.

Some mornings, a disciple's dance of stretching and focus. Today, he brought a sparring sword and began with the first stances a boy learned. Years had burned them past his thinking mind and into instinct, where the speed Blessing dwelled. Done slowly, they let his joints shake off the night's sleep. He stepped through the entire series: basic guards, sword-drawings, and slashes.

Then, at speed, feeling the kir tingle along his ridges, his spine. No need to stop; he flew through the attack sequences, the master guards, into the grapples. Years' worth of training blazed through him in a few dozen heartbeats.

When he hit the end, on one knee with sword thrust defiantly upward, his lungs heaved. In his mind, Captain Aleks cuffed him and told him to slow for breath before he got dizzy and fell into his enemy's sword.

The baker sat watching at the farthest prep table, two pageboys staring in awe beside him. Hochwald's squire, too, and one of Schutze's sons. Haralda — doe-eyed, Mother have mercy. Gregor's attempts to talk to her were hopeless and her parents' words were water on a duck's feathers.

Kiefan avoided her as best he could all day. He'd promised a training session with any garrison knights who wished it, and an evaluation for squires who meant to ask for knighthood in the new year. He gave advice, corrected stances, and led them through challenging sequences that few un-Blessed enemies could survive.

"You can best even minotaurs," he told his students as a squall dropped fat flakes around them. "Strong, yes. Tougher than a man. But easy to anticipate, and speed will save you — Blessed or otherwise."

The knights who came were ambitious sorts, eager to learn. Some of the squires needed only a little more polish to be ready for promotion. One had meant to present himself to Woden at the King's Joust, but hadn't been able to make the trip; once they'd sparred and Woden gave the nod, Kiefan put the oath to him.

A good day's work, for once. It kept his mind off Kate's silence.

___

Part V: Cold Solace

REOWAN

Anders stood beside Laurent on the flat roof, holding a towel and waiting for Empress Seraphine's return. Though the sun glared down from a clear sky, it gave no heat. Fresh snow lay thick on the beach, on the branches of the twisted salt pine that held the Empress' roost aloft beside Reowan's fount. A good breeze from the sea would knock the branches clear, but all was still as yet.

The fount at Reowan, the largest in Suevia, glittered beside the salt pine. A six-foot column of murky quartz enclosed it, and the kir-laced water twinkled as it gushed over the rim. A pool around the base caught the water and let it out to run down the beach to the rocky shore. Waves claimed it there. A driftwood throne stood in the center of the pillar, looking down on the carefully groomed sand. Around the open-air courtyard, the three sides of Castle Áering stood, guardsmen walking the ramparts and keeping warm in the towers.

It had all been Saint Seaxneat's before Arcea invaded and murdered him.

The dead saint's guardian sphere still enclosed the column, throne, and pool. Green kir crackled along the webbed strands at its surface. It would gather a knot of kir on its surface when it sensed a threat, a knot bright and tempting enough to distract anyone. It was a lure, Seraphine had told Anders, and she'd left the skeleton in the sand as a warning of what the knot did.

The skeleton had no skull.

Anders ignored the knot of kir the guardian was offering him. It made the sphere look like an enormous eyeball.

Laurent was no threat; the man had no gift with kir. He was Seraphine's body servant and executed his duties with the rigor of a captain-general. Two glances, when Seraphine had first brought Anders to her tree-nest, had been enough for them to suss each other out as men of the sword.

Laurent was made of old brown leather, grey horsehair, and had the charm of a crabapple. But he had the Empress' trust. And her bed, when she took the time to visit it. The saint never actually slept, it seemed. Today, Laurent stood with the steel spine of an old soldier, ignoring the cold.

Anders kept his cloak sensibly shut — the foolish thing was purple silk lined with white rabbit. The full robe he must wear, as Seraphine's servant, was more foolishness. White silk with the purple stripe, ankle-long and prone to flapping. The only reasonable things he could wear were woolen braies and partway decent shoes.

He'd kill for a good pair of riding boots.

The green glow in the fount's quartz column dimmed as a shadow rose, and Seraphine broke the surface beside the driftwood throne. She smoothed her black hair back with both hands. Submerged steps brought her up to the throne, trailing bright water from her purple silk robe — which clung to her curves jealously.

Seraphine leaped from the fount to the flat roof, easy as a cat. Laurent was quick to shake out the towel he held; she unbuttoned her robe at each shoulder and shrugged out of it. With a little kir, she flung the water from the silk. Laurent, meanwhile, wrapped her in the towel from shoulders to hips.

Anders took his position behind them both and wrung out Seraphine's fat braid of black hair. Why she wore her hair thus, he'd guessed when he first saw it, and confirmed each time he did this; it wasn't simply hair, in truth. Seraphine had shape-shifted to masquerade as Theo, in Wodenberg, and her vulture-rukh form was larger than this little woman's body as well.

The braid hid a tail of sorts. Surplus flesh that she didn't wish to part with, while in this form, or to wear as fat. Anders hadn't learned the trick of it yet, but simply knowing it could be done had set his brain to simmering.

"Musaad is here," Laurent said. He slung his wet towel at Anders, took the dry robe from her and held it up. "News, with your lunch."

Seraphine nodded as she put her arms in the sleeves. Anders held up her braid to let the robe slip underneath. He used both towels to squeeze a little more water from her hair before she was fully buttoned and ready.

Anders had been a page in Castle Kaltkern, like most knights in Wodenberg proper, but he'd never had to attend the queen with towels. Thank the Mother.

Stairs led down into the tree-home; it was a cozy, lush nest of a few rooms, full of carpets and silk drapes. Seraphine went directly to the parlor. Saint Musaad stood waiting, looking out one of the unshuttered windows at the sea's restless waves. He turned as she entered, dipping his head in a bow.

Suevia was his, at Seraphine's pleasure. The man was darker-skinned than most Arceal, had hair that was truly charcoal black, and stood as tall as Anders. He seemed rail-thin under his red silk robe, but that was deceptive. Saint Musaad carried a bit of gold, sometimes silver, in his spider-fingered hands, kneading and shaping it as if it were a bit of clay. A faint glimmer of kir lubricated the metal — hardly enough for a spark charm, but yet solid gold twisted in his bare fingers easy as bread dough.

Anders slipped across the parlor, beneath the saints' notice. Blythe stood by a long-legged brazier, in the slate-tiled corner of the parlor, managing a small pot and kettle. She checked the ceramic teapot on the small sideboard and shot a glance at him. He moved it to a silver tray, alongside two cups and a small honeypot, and brought that to the dining table.

Musaad and Seraphine took seats opposite each other, going over the day's news point by point. He'd heard reports from various officers stationed around Suevia. She had come from Arcea itself, where she'd spent the morning speaking to various ministers. Anders paid it little mind, setting out cups and pouring spiced tea for them. Seraphine liked hers straight. Musaad took a half-spoonful of honey.

"This young king of Wodenberg —" Musaad said, but cut himself short when Seraphine raised a hand. He took a sip of tea rather than finish.

"Trouble not my servant with news of those who failed him so." She glanced at Anders as he set the teapot and honey at the center of the table.

He lied a little. "It's no trouble, m'lady."

Still, she turned the conversation toward southern things. Anders returned to the sideboard for bowls of hot soup, full of shredded greens and bits of sausage. Though it took only a moment, when he turned back Laurent had moved the teapot and honeypot to opposite sides of the table and adjusted the teacups to their owners' right hand, rather than directly before them.

Again. Anders shot him a half-hearted glare. He placed the first bowl before Seraphine, then laid out the linen napkin and spoon — half hoping Laurent would correct him and give him an excuse to punch the ass. Seraphine never said a word against Anders' table service. He'd been good enough for the Elect's table at Solstice banquets.

He served Musaad and then set out warmed rolls and butter. Laurent moved the bread basket. The two saints ate their light luncheon and shifted to a language Anders hadn't heard before. In time, Musaad took his leave of the Empress and saw himself out.

Seraphine wiped her lips with the napkin. "At dawn, I saw you on the roof," she said with another glance at Anders. "You call that the disciple's dance?"

He nodded. "I needed the stretch, m'lady." Saint-days in Suevia were odd things, and twenty-odd days without a proper disciple's dance had left him far too tense.

"You have proven yourself worthy as a servant. Sparring, this afternoon, and use all you've learned."

Anders' hopes rose; Seraphine had let him out of the tree-home only a few times, and never near anything larger than a table-knife. He'd tested her leash and gotten his fill of stringence within the first week.

"Laurent." She tipped her head toward her favorite. "Take your measure of him and be done with glaring."

"You won't — m'lady?" It got out of Anders' mouth before he caught it.

"For I have the Solstice tithe to inspect, and more. The beach is yours, today."

Seraphine stood and walked from the parlor. Anders lingered at the table, the empty teapot in his hands. Sparring and shape-shifting on the beach. In clear view of the soldiers in Castle Áering.

He'd taken all his lessons here in the tree-home, with only Seraphine to see. Or, now and then, Laurent or Blythe.

Strangers, staring and muttering. Gauging his every fumble and twitch.

Blythe took the teapot from his hands. "I thought you'd leap at the chance," she said in Suevi.

Anders had paced the tree-home's one hall many a night, too jangled and trapped to sleep. He'd sat on the roof, staring at the restless sea with tears streaking his face, lost in visions of how happy Kate and his mother were now that he was gone. He'd perched in all the windowsills, fighting the urge to test Seraphine one more time and earn a convulsive dose of stringence.

Now the thought of climbing down the tree and crossing sparring swords with that ass —

Laurent leaned into the parlor and sneered, "Coming? Or turning pussy, boy?"

CHAPTER 8

The snow was ankle-deep, and virgin but for where Blythe and Laurent had cut a trail to one of the castle doorways. Anders crouched by the rill of fount-water, just outside the guardian sphere, and called it to him. Kir rushed up, warming and soothing.

Laurent brought two wooden swords and two bucklers, tossed one of each at Anders. He settled them in his hands and kicked at the hem of his Arceal robe with a grimace. Hadn't fought in a skirt, before. Damn thing was too long. Woden's maidens all wore cotes and hose, sensibly enough. But at least he wouldn't need to worry about it tearing when he shifted.

"What forms do you start —"

Laurent lunged straight for Anders' thigh; anticipation pegged it as a feint and speed made his own limbs a blur. Anders caught only glimpses of what he did at speed: one moment, Laurent's wooden blade thrust above Anders' shoulder, the next the old soldier was reeling back to regain his balance. Anders eased into a middle guard rather than press the attack. Laurent recovered and circled him.

"Blessings, they say?" Laurent snorted. "Shall see."

He slid in, using some liquid style Anders' anticipation didn't know — and got a hit. Anders barely caught a second blow with the rim of his buckler. Had to give ground as the attacks continued. When Laurent let him go, he felt a couple bruises taking root.

Anders glanced up at the battlements and saw a row of helmeted heads. A few guards, in red tabards and white baldrics, loitered at one of the tower doors. Watching. Laying bets, likely, on the Empress' old favorite and her new pet.

Best give them a good show, then.

His anticipation caught on to Laurent's style over the next few skirmishes. Anders collected his kir, knotting it into pattern, and then took the attack. Let the charm spread over him as he lunged in close. The world turned louder, smells razor-sharp, and his center shifted. Horse-form stole a few inches from him, in truth, and the neck was heavy. His sword dropped below Laurent's. The new power in his legs surged in a well-grounded line toward —

— and his shoes slid, awkward. Anders stumbled face-first. Speed caught him, and he skittered away before Laurent's blade crashed down where he'd been.

Anders kicked the damn shoes off. He planted his hooves, Nipper's hooves, wide on the snowy sand. The shape-shifting had moved his knees, his heels — hooves were, in truth, toes — and he took a moment to feel the grip of them in the sand, the differing traction.

Laurent gave him no more than that. Feinted right and his blade caught on Anders'. Horse-strength made bulling through easy; Anders kept tight rein on his speed, to be sure of his balance in lunging past Laurent's buckler. Nipper's neck was heavy, but the reach it lent was worth it. He got his horse-teeth on the old soldier's ear. Just a nip, but enough to draw blood. Anders' hooves plowed through the sand to catch his balance and yank him back when Laurent's wooden blade shot for his ribs.

The old soldier skipped back, shaking his head. Blood scattered from his ear. He gave Anders a twisted smirk. "For nobody expects such reach, do they."

Anders' reply came out in a horsey harrumph. He nodded. The surprise, when he'd pulled it on Kiefan, had been its only value. In truth, that had been a desperate lunge; with his three Blessings, Kiefan had had the advantage. Their duel wouldn't have lasted another two heartbeats. Shock, a lucky bite on Kiefan's arm, and Anders had cut him across the throat. A perfectly elegant, mortal wound.

Laurent readied for another skirmish, but Anders hesitated. Looked out at the waves splashing against the rocks that hemmed the beach. Salt tingled in his horse-nostrils.

Even with the sword through him, he'd had the strength to stagger away. Kiefan ought to have been dead when he hit the floor. Kate had gone to the worse wound. That was all. Her simple honesty, her unwavering strength, all that he loved — snapped back into place in his heart.

Laurent's shoes cut the sand, loud in Nipper's ears. Anders let his speed flow. Block left; block right; head butt. Laurent staggered backward, fell on his ass. Anders snorted. One of the guards at the tower door whooped and demanded his money from his friends.

Anders let the charm go, and his flesh slid back into place. Laurent picked himself up, dusted off powdery snow. "M'lady won't like that." He gestured at Anders' head.

Anders ran his hand over the ridges of his Blessings. His knight's crest had reappeared, after so many days of shifting back to a uniformly close-cropped head of hair.

"First round's on me! Join us, sirs!" The victorious guardsman strode across the beach, grinning. He put out a hand to clasp Laurent's. "It was a fine fight. I thought for sure I'd lose the bet, but then —"

His words stopped when he turned to offer Anders the same clasp and nearly took his hand back. Nearly. Anders took the last step between them to accept the handshake.

"So it's true. You're Alemanni," the guardsman, the sergeant, said. "One of those Blessed knights."

Anders twitched one shoulder. "Bound to the Empress," he answered in his rough Suevi, though his throat tightened halfway through. Bound and trapped.

"A drink at the bonfire?" The sergeant jerked his head toward the side of Castle Áering that faced the city.

That only made it worse. "I'm not to leave the castle." His bare feet were freezing rapidly in the snow. "Some other time."

Laurent took the offer, though, slapping the sergeant's shoulder. Anders found his shoes and crossed back to the salt pine alone. The guardian sphere tracked him, suspicious, with its giant eye. He paused at the fount's trickling overflow and looked up at the green knot of kir.

Could Seraphine see him so easily? His fingers pressed against his palm, where her bond lay quiet. He knew next to nothing of that, save that pain and orders came through it. Anders' gaze crept to the lumpy snow over the skeleton. Its ribs poked free of the white blanket.

Bound to her. A pet. He'd doubted Kate for one broken moment and sealed his own fate. His next breath came hard, harshened by the cold and the salt air. A small fate for a knight who'd always been cast aside.

Little trace of him left behind, as befit a bastard. One grieving mother. Perhaps a widow — no, surely Kate missed him. Rafe would never remember, though. And the other babies would never know. The stable-mistress that he'd been told he left pregnant in m'lady Leix's household. Theo's little girl, if she was his doing. And Theo would miss him, or at least his usefulness.

His string of broken hearts, his championships at the King's joust… soon forgotten.

Anders ran his fingers into his knight's crest, clenched them. Surely Kate had looked for him, had meant to draw the sword out and heal him. Surely she mourned.

But she was better off without him. She had Kiefan to comfort her. That gnawed at his heart, but Anders shoved it away. She deserved happiness. She'd said she loved him. She'd wanted to be his wife, without secret arrangements. Lying in bed with her cuddled against his chest, warm and sated… and he'd doubted her. Taken Seraphine's offer.

Like a rat, the pain chewed on him.

He looked down at his bare feet, which he couldn't feel anymore, and guessed how far he might run before Seraphine struck him down again. He couldn't cut her bond; he'd tried. He looked up at the roof of the tree-home, gauged how far a fall it was. Or wasn't. Then he came back to the guardian sphere's deadly offer.

But it was hers to order. Everything here was hers, bred, bound, and yoked to the plow. Everything but…

Anders turned and faced the sea. It lay under an afternoon sun now, as Solstice day was so short. The lines of waves glittered amber as they marched to the rocky shore. Ice rimed the jagged stones. His numb feet took him from the snow across the line of sea-wrack that high tide left. Left marks on the patches of slick sand among the rocks.

He paused and let his shoes drop. Seraphine had him, owned him, by her power and by his own word. The only freedom was out there.

Anders ran across the rocks, feeling the gash one left in his foot, into the water. Cold as ice, for a heartbeat, and then he felt nothing. Waves pushed at him but he plowed through. Waist deep. The first shuddering shivers gripped his guts, nearly knocked him down.

/ foolishness /

He didn't answer her. Chest deep, he pressed on. A wave slapped his face, and he clenched his eyes shut against the salt. Didn't need to see to keep going. His sodden robe weighed him down, though the waves still shoved —

Something gripped him, pulled him off his feet and ducked him. Anders thrashed on reflex, but his arm struck only sand. He called kir, and only his own pattern answered him. No hands on his ankle, nothing nearby. The sea's riptide pulled him out into the deeps.

Helping him. He willed himself still. Drifted in the water, his lungs aching for air. Slowly sinking.

/ won't work /

Seraphine sent no pain, though.

Anders' head spun as he sank. Water pressed on him. The moment would come that he'd have to breathe. The moment he'd drown. Serenity touched him and he let his air go, bubbling out and rising away.

The cold seawater was a knife through his chest when it came.

His eyes opened, saw grey-green-blue, and squeezed shut again. Agony. Struggling for breath, getting only more cold.

/ it cannot kill you /

Bright kir reached down to him. Anders hugged his arms close, curled up. Kept sinking. Convulsing, now, vomiting water and taking in more, his mind full of black stars and yet clinging to consciousness. His kir-patterns throbbed as they fought to hold to their dance, the red lines of his meridians burning in his mind's eye.

The reaching kir waited, keeping to its offer. Rescue.

Suffocating agony ripped at him. His pattern held, clinging to what scraps of kir he had. An eternity with lungs full of water, and another eternity ahead —

He could only think of Kate, in his arms, and Rafe in hers, nested and warm.

Anders reached. The kir twined around his wrist and pulled. His head broke the surface and the force of his retching knocked him back under. Seraphine snared him with a second kir-rope and reeled him up. He sucked in air, edged with a ragged scream.

Her arms wrapped around him, and he felt kir surge as they flew. Anders coughed from deep in his gut and heaved out more seawater. Every breath was a dozen icy razors. The cold shuddered through him, and Seraphine's arms felt hot as flame.

/ kir? /

/ you wished suffering / suffer /

They landed on the tree-home, Anders knew that much through the haze of pain. He focused on breathing. There was nothing else in the world but breathing. Kir swirled around him, and warmth burned at his skin. It was only more pain, engulfing him like the sea.

It took ages, but that sea receded.

/ why? /

Anders opened his eyes. He lay against Seraphine's throat, wrapped in her arms, his legs tangled in hers. He lifted his head, still trembling a little. She was full as tall as him, though lean, and they were both bundled under down quilts in her bed. An oil lamp burned in one of the sconces. Her face was rounder, plainer, and her short black hair fanned on the pillow. She wore a shift, but it was a thin, silky thing. He was naked.

Ought to move. Get out. But she was very warm. Feverishly warm.

Seraphine pressed him back to her skin. "Why, then?"

The breath he took didn't hurt. "Any horse will go mad, locked in a stall. Alone. Trapped." His voice was rough, though. Salty.

Heartbeats passed under his ear. "And shifters are ever alone. All shall turn on you, mewling of deception, of lies at your core. None understand us. We earn only their fear."

Kiefan's stunned, terrified eyes —

"Already, you know more of shifting in swordplay than Woden could teach. Not even a full moon, and you held your own with an old master. For I did watch you spar." Seraphine combed his damp knight's crest back from his face as she spoke. "What a cambifax you should be. My master himself would have taken you for his elect."

Cambifax. The memory of Theo, stinking of shit and dying of fever, turned Anders' stomach. He pushed away, sat up under the heavy quilts and turned his back to her. "I'm no sneak-thief. No murderer. Not when I have the — freedom, the truth of animal senses. I won't."

His back prickled gooseflesh for not knowing how she'd answer defiance. He tensed when fingers touched the cuticle alongside his spinal ridge, traced the line where the speed Blessing broke through his skin. She found her way down to the last nub, just above his butt.

Anders closed his eyes and ignored his cock's curiosity.

"Yet I cannot loose you from your stall as you are," Seraphine said. "Even here, far from Wodenberg, enough know what your ridges mean. And even if your accent fades, you are too flaxen for a Suevi. They would arrest you in the street. If not attack."

He cared little about that, but held his tongue. Her fingers left him, thank the Mother.

"I will not hamper their vigilance, la. And yet there is a way. For you can shift your crest away — only change it to brown as well. Darken your eyes. I will un-knit these Blessings and find you place in the governor's stables. For your love is horses, I know."

Anders' throat knotted. He twisted, caught Seraphine's hand in both of his. "No, please. M'lady, let me beg — don't take my Blessings." His voice fell to a whisper as he fell onto his belly and kissed her hand against the mattress. Pressed his forehead to it. "Whatever you —" He caught himself just short of that trap. "There must be some other way."

He turned her hand over and added another kiss, lingering on her palm.

The bedroom door opened and Laurent startled back, nearly dropping the lamp in his hand. Then his jaw dropped, for a moment; he clapped it shut, but his eyes glared at Anders in silent outrage.

Seraphine turned her head on the pillow. "I shall join the banquet at my leisure. Send for Blythe and my gown." She gave Laurent a heartbeat to obey and said, "Make no assumptions, la. Fetch a robe for Anders."

The old soldier set his face, bowed, and went.

"Must I wear those robes?" Anders murmured.

Seraphine's brow creased. "My purple will keep you safe here. You must hide your Blessings, if you keep them. Change your colors. Then be free within the city walls."

"The stables?"

She nodded, taking her hand back from him. "My word, and you may work. And spar with Laurent, still. And shift. If it must be animals for you, let me train you in something rare."

Horses. The smell of hay and manure, apples and leather... the familiar strokes of brushing a horse down, of pitching straw. If he must be trapped and doomed for a fool, it would be some comfort. Anders took a deep breath. "I'll change my colors. And wear a hat."

Seraphine sat up and caught his knight's crest in her hand. He closed his eyes as she cut it off.

"For you are mine," she told him again. "You owe Woden nothing."

———————————✕———————————

Part V: Cold Solace

WODENBERG

/ ready? /

I stepped out from under the pavilion in Castle Kaltkern's gate-yard and looked up. The peak of Mount Woden, snow clouding off it in the distant wind, still glowed faintly pink in the fading sunset.

/ yes /

Even so far away, I felt an echo of the call. Two saints, drawing up such a mass of kir from the fount atop the mountain — and winding it into such a knot — that I felt it an eye-blink before it ignited. Green light flared at the mountain's peak, like a candle flame springing free. A beacon calling the sun back to start the year anew.

There was one small advantage to having to come to the castle so early for Solstice. I wrapped my lace shawl, which was far warmer than it looked, snug around my shoulders as a cold breeze rippled over me. The gate-yard's bonfire hadn't been lit yet, and outside the protection of the pavilion it was an icy, clear night. Only the bravest guests were out by the stack of wood — squires, mostly, waiting for the saints to come.

Kir alit on one of the castle's corner towers, and a white-hot star blazed to life. All heads turned as my saint drew back and pitched the knot of kir-fire. It shot across the gate-yard and struck the stacked wood, splattering into a constellation. Fire bloomed, swelled, and then settled back. A little warmth rolled across me, and I smiled.

"Yes, much nicer."

Queen Mercia could be quieter than a mouse, I'd been quickly learning. She'd joined me without a sound. Though she still wore her black mourning veil, and a modest diadem now that she was only the king's mother, the corners of m'lady's mouth were tacked upward rather than down.

"If only Kiefan were here," she murmured, looking up at the mountain. "And Gisella. They always loved the beacon."

For all that I'd wanted to hate her, for how she'd treated Anders, for her demands on Kiefan, Queen Mercia's melancholy always tipped me toward pity.

Saint Woden lingered to meet the squires at the bonfire; Qadeem crossed the gate-yard to join us. He offered the queen a polite nod and then turned to me. "The tears have slowed, I hope?" He murmured it in Englic.

The queen withdrew into the pavilion; the castle chamberlain was organizing the guests into a line to meet us, and it would be cruel to make them wait in the cold.

"A little," I answered my saint as we moved under the canvas. "Opening my shop did help, but I've only had a few customers. Though — why Englic?"

I asked that as we took up position in the center of the pavilion, I on Qadeem's right, a space for Woden and then Queen Mercia in a chair. The last of our greeting party joined us, trading rowdy hand-clasps with the squires as he came. The eldest of the lads, maybe sixteen, had a grip strong enough to get an approving grin from Woden. And a clap on the shoulder.

"Saints and elect have their secrets to keep," Qadeem answered me, "even when they don't. Is Rafe well?"

I smiled, despite myself. Frida had stolen him from me, in the gate-yard, as soon as she had given me a hug and a kiss. M'lord Reinhardt had assured me he would keep Nipper through the winter, so long as he could use him for a stud in the spring. Rafe had been squealing happily, through that, but I'd caught all the words.

"He's happier to be here than I am."

"The people are glad you're here," Qadeem said, with a nod toward our first announced guests. The master goldsmith, his wife, and squiring-aged son dropped to one knee in obeisance before we two saints, one elect, and the king's mother. Each of the guests looked to me, and I wasn't sure what to make of their expressions. Perhaps it was gladness.

As they moved on to make way for the next family's introduction, Qadeem asked, side-long, "You didn't get a new dress?"

I wore my pale green one, which Frida had embroidered with roses at the neck. "This one still fits." I wasn't foolish enough to wear my amber one again.

Woden snorted. "Dresses aside. What of Terekhov?" His Englic was accented, but clear enough. He broke into Alemannic to greet one of the City Guard officers and his wife when they were introduced.

"His map of the shoals on Rukharbor's west side will prove valuable," Qadeem answered. "We've decided on the line to build the sea wall upon."

"Don't tell me he was lunatic enough to walk the shoals during Snow Moon."

"Mother bless him, but he's a Russe."

My new brother elect, Terekhov, was a crafter like Saint Aleks had been. Stone-crafting, along with some skill forging metal. What that all meant, I hardly knew — perhaps it was like how I shaped flesh.

"Pirra has Rukharbor's garrison well in hand," Qadeem added, between guests. "The men adore her."

Woden grinned at that. "And what've you done, Kate?" He looked to me, over Qadeem's head, with his brows raised.

"I, well — there was a nasty burn last week." I doubted the chillblains and fevers I'd seen would measure up to much beside a sea wall and managing an entire garrison.

Woden twisted his mouth, looked away a moment, and switched to a language I didn't know. I suspected it was Russe. Qadeem answered him, at some length, and they both nodded.

To me, Woden said in Englic, "Be ready tomorrow. I'll collect a general readiness meeting after noon. Spring will be coming soon enough."

"M'lord," I said.

The chamberlain announced Duke Tomas Seagrace and his captain, and the freshly wid-owed duke knelt in obeisance. When he looked up, his eyes were red-rimmed; he'd come to visit the graves of his wife and sons, on leave from the army that kept our enemy bottled up in Ansehen. He'd missed their funerals, had never had a chance to say his good-byes.

"King's Council, tomorrow, after noon," Woden told him, still in Englic. "Give a gen-eral report on what the spring will require."

"M'lord." The duke answered crisply, in Englic, and saluted.

"I was in Rukharbor this morning. Your cousin sends her love and sympathies," Qadeem told him, meaning Elect Pirra. "They held a funeral in the Sea Chapel for Gisella and the boys, and sang all the old hymns for them."

Duke Seagrace's eyes clouded, at that, and pain twisted his mouth. I knew the hymns, I'd heard them sung whenever we held a funeral on Engl Street. My father and mother had said that the dead couldn't find their way home without the song to lead them. I'd seen Princess Gisella and her little boys, bundled in shrouds — innocent victims of the Empress' attack — and nobody had sung for them because Alemanni didn't —

I took two steps and hugged. Seagrace clutched me tight, and I felt him shudder, fighting a sob. "They'll find the sea-grass path," I whispered to him. The path to the Hearth atop the sea-cliffs.

He nodded, and then he abruptly let me go. Put me at arm's length, looking away as he wiped at his eyes. Blushing. There was grey in his chestnut knight's crest, now, earned in his long months at war. His captain, beet-faced, studied the ground.

"Bless you, Elect Kate," Seagrace murmured. "Your pardon. M'lords." His voice steadied quickly as he saluted again. "By your leave?"

I'd embarrassed him. Queen Mercia ignored the whole scene with a blank face. My own face burned; I retreated to Qadeem's side and blinked away my damp eyes. Saint Woden dismissed the duke with a curt nod.

I wanted to apologize. My saint's bond tingled, in my hand.

/ don't regret / heal /

KNAPPTAL

Once washed and shaved and dressed in his best blacks, Kiefan had to face the abbess' traditional homily about the season of Mother Love. It was, word for word, the one the old abbot in Wodenberg had given through much of Kiefan's childhood. He could nearly recite it himself.

Last Solstice night, with Kate — until the beginning of this moon, it had been his warmest memory. All that had come of it had gone badly, but the night itself he'd never regret. His son, he'd not abandon. However much Kate detested him now, Kiefan knew she'd see reason. Best for Rafe to receive the prince's training due him: swords, books, and all. Kir, if he had a gift for it. Someday he might kneel before Woden and ask for the crown. He must be ready for it.

As for Kate… in stories, a heart could hibernate for years while waiting for its true love. A cock, though, couldn't manage a week. Father Duty's discipline was difficult to keep even when there was little pleasure in scratching that itch alone.

At last, the abbess finished. Kiefan raised his stein of winter bock. "May Mother Love keep us kind," he said, first in Alemannic and then in Arceal for the Caer. He turned to Crown Ciara, standing beside him, and nodded. She returned it.

The guests, three long tables full of them, echoed his words and drank. Margrave Schutze called for a toast to the king's health, and more followed. Kiefan offered one for their guests, and Ciara did the same for gracious hosts.

When she'd walked in, a cloud of formal white bound by green, sparkling with gemstones, how she'd passed words to the duchesses at her sides had piqued Kiefan's anticipation. Something was afoot among them. She'd hardly said a word since she took post at his left. Elect Tannait was her escort and guard this time. Elect Teleri was nowhere to be seen. Odd, that.

Sidelong, he looked for more hints but Ciara was serenely smiling. He'd meant only to glance, but lingered a heartbeat more; she was pretty, true, and elegant. Her dark hair made her skin paler, despite a scattering of freckles. Her wit, he knew, had a fine edge. Though her passion did run counter to her reason, from what he'd seen, and what the Voice of the Empress had said still lingered.

They'll turn on you in the twinkling of an eye.

She nearly caught him looking; his anticipation warned and he turned further, gesturing for the page to top off his stein.

When they took their seats for the feast, Ciara leaned a scant inch closer. "'Tis Mother Strength, in Caercoed. Winter's harshness must be endured, and in the spring the hard work of planting. Come the bounty of summer and autumn, 'tis Father Care's season for sharing and joy."

"No duty, in Caercoed's summer? No war?"

"Surely 'tisn't war each year in Wodenberg."

"Training, even in peacetime. Teaching the children."

She looked him square in the eye, head tipped just a hint. No guile in her face. "You've harsh saints."

"It's a harsh world, m'lady."

Ciara drew her mouth to one side, for a moment. "Needs must apologize, m'lord," she said. "'Twasn't right to deny you a last farewell. I was angry, still, and failed Father Care."

Her hand touched his, curled around and squeezed. Her eyes looked for his — and his Blessing piqued, warning. Kiefan took his hand back, though slowly enough not to offend. He nodded. "I'm glad you said that, m'lady."

Good words, but there was a plan behind them.

The food arrived, the first piping-hot chicken pie served in an iron dish before Kiefan. He cut it, as it was to be shared, and the pages served out heaping spoonfuls of crust and meat, peas and onions, all in thick gravy. After that came fresh lake trout with pickled slaw, and then roasted venison with turnips.

On his right, Margrave Schutze apologized for the humble fare until Kiefan ordered him to be silent.

Ciara asked about the trout, and embroiled the three of them in talk of ice-fishing, then hunting — which Kiefan knew far more of — and then when to use spears in the hunt rather than bows. This saw them through the venison course and came to a halt when the pages brought out several long rolls of pastry covered in chopped walnuts and honey.

"'Tis walnut logs! Just as Rónan makes." Ciara broke out in an honest smile.

Tannait leaned over her shoulder. "Did ask him what you'd love. All were sworn to secrecy on it."

Ciara took up her stein and stood. "You honor me, Margrave Schutze, and I shall drink to your health." She got much agreement to that, once translated, and then she said, "Now cut them, or 'twill drive me mad."

Walnuts and honey were worked into the pastry, and after a few bites Kiefan knew he couldn't finish it quickly atop a Solstice feast. Ciara seemed in a fairer mood, whatever purpose she had, so perhaps some hope for spring could be kindled. A loan of Tadhlon's soldiers, as they were here already, at least.

"I hope you'll not think so ill of us, m'lady, tomorrow," he said.

"'Tis persuasive." She nodded toward what remained of the walnut log, after being served to the whole table.

"It's long moons until Equinox, and we're nearly snow-bound already. Best to see one's guests smiling at Solstice," he said.

She sat back with her cup of apple brandy in her hands. "Winter Court, at Castle Adhalon, teaches much the same lesson. Must make the best of snow-binding, or pay a heavy price. Look to those at hand." Hers went to his arm, lightly. "Spend the time wisely."

"Plan for spring. Train and read." Kiefan leaned back too, as an excuse to shift his arm away from her. His mother only touched him to fuss, to criticize; how Ciara piqued his anticipation brought that to mind. Another reason for caution.

The corner of her mouth perked up. "And flirt."

"Pardon?"

She nodded toward the second table, where Haralda sat among knights' wives. The girl straightened, when Kiefan looked, and blushed. She smiled, so eager that he looked away.

Kiefan took a swallow of the brandy. "I've no need of moon-eyed girls," he said, quietly. Shouldn't have met her gaze, in the gate yard when he arrived. Shouldn't have given her anything to daydream about.

"No need for love?"

"Need for a winter's hibernation," he said. "Perhaps there's wisdom in the Crown not marrying — and yet you would have Síochana marry me?"

Ciara swallowed another bite of pastry. "Making families of kingdoms, 'tis a strong symbol. A Crown is ever a go-between, a mediator, and cannot be tied to any one."

"No matter, then, whose child your heir is?"

One shoulder twitched. "My heir is my child. 'Tis rarely any doubt who bore you. More weight lies upon who helps raise my heir."

"You have a child?"

"A twin's daughters are as one's own. 'Tis the same blood."

Blood and heirs. A murky thing, stripped as Kiefan was of nephews and cousins. If he died in the spring, there'd be many knights with equal claim on the crown. As Woden had said, there was always another applicant.

Ciara watched him, just off a predator's intensity. "I find myself short on blood," he said.

"Surely the Shepherd welcomed them home."

She touched his arm, again, and he held off the urge to jerk away. Perhaps it was not entirely a lie. Letting her play her new tune would make her plan clear. If the Caer were so quick to turn against, perhaps they might turn toward as quickly.

Kiefan nodded, let out a melancholy smile that was honest enough. "Surely he did."

CHAPTER 9

WODENBERG

I knew where Rafe and Frida were, during the banquet, by the knot of mothers and girls milling about the far table. The Rossweides always sat at the furthest, humblest table at Solstice, so as to keep Frida from having to face Queen Mercia, but this year they drew attention. Rafe was the only baby to coo over at the banquet this year.

And it was a smaller, quieter affair. Perhaps half the size of last year's. The braised beef was just as fine, though, and the bock as free-flowing — I sipped at mine. Though there was little danger of my repeating last Solstice.

Difficult not to dwell on it, but I tried.

Parselev's place at the head of the elect's table was mine now. I presided as best I could, with one eye on the far table and my baby. Little by little, the bock eased my nerves. Our desserts were honey cakes, this year, and I sighed for a moment remembering the fruit tarts and Anders doctoring mine with brandy. But then I put that aside and ate a few bites. I was too full, again, for more than that.

When the servants began to clear the tables away, it was good to stand up. The musicians, who'd been playing softly as they strolled around the banquet, made their way to chairs at one side of the hall.

"Might I ask you to dance?" Theo Kaufmann offered me a smile with his hand. "I meant to, last year."

"Strange how you went about it," I said. I passed my half-empty cup of brandy to a page boy and asked, "Tea?" He nodded and went to fetch it.

"I presumed you were one of his passing fancies." Theo drew closer, voice dropping. "Wrongly, true. And since then you've learned far more of me than you wished, I'm certain. No game's afoot tonight. I only ask for fear the matchmakers will stiffen their resolve and try to pair you up."

Theo's imprisonment in his own bed had gone largely unknown. His health had recovered, but a darkness lingered in his eyes. A shadow of pain. Saint Woden had re-knit his strength Blessing and told Theo, directly, that he'd face no ill will for having confessed so much under torture. The scars remained, though.

"That's kind of you," I said, with a smile. "I trust your hands will not wander, sir?"

He raised his brows, innocent. "I have a reputation to maintain, m'lady."

I knew the secret he and Süssie kept; his beloved whore of Arbor Street was, as Anders had said, not a woman. Yet Theo worked at a reputation of being nearly as much a rake as him. Theo's hands would wander, I would smack them away, and it would all be for show. I put my hand in his, fearless, and he held it shoulder-high, as was formally proper. The musicians struck their first chord.

"M'lady!"

The woman waved to catch my eye. I hesitated a moment, and my memory fetched her name. One of Frida's friends — and she carried a bundle, squalling through the rising music. That voice, I knew in my bones.

"We tried to tempt him with honey cake," the lady said with a smile, "but he'd only take a few crumbs."

My sweetling, as particular as ever. "Your pardon, Theo." I took my son with both hands, and his screaming lowered in a heartbeat. "My lord requires me to attend him."

"I shall fend for myself, then," Theo said, with a gracious bow. "M'lady?"

Frida's friend startled when he offered his hand, and turned pink. "Certainly not!"

She huffed off, but Theo shot me a wink. I smiled as I sidled the shoulder of my dress off, and turned away from the dancers. A few steps toward the wall, and the blazing fireplace, and I was well clear of them. Rafe wriggled with the music, smiling now, and eagerly looked for my breast.

It was a square dance, and I knew the tune. Anders had showed me the steps for this one. I hummed along with the melody as Rafe nursed, and drifted closer to the warm hearth. Some of the elder guests had settled here, in cushioned chairs, to chat and appreciate the dancers. The abbot nodded to me with a smile. Krepkin was here, and he'd been polite to me all evening. Queen Mercia, too.

I stroked Rafe's cheek as he nursed. My little baby, three moons on — growing so fast and full of smiles. So like my younger brother, in wondering at the world. In fussing little, save for those things he would not compromise on. Such as me. Rafe looked up, just then, and that illusion faded for a moment. No carpenter's child, this.

"Such a lovely babe," Queen Mercia said, leaning in from one side. "Your son, did I hear?"

I caught myself mid-flinch, in surprise. "Yes, my son. Rafe."

"Rafe, ah, that's very... Englic. He's so fair. You'll need to keep him out of the sun."

My son's hair was still only a thin layer of down, and couldn't even hide the tracery of a blue vein under his pale scalp. He was finished nursing, too, and I didn't much want him to linger. I shifted him to my shoulder, closer to the queen, and hoisted my dress back up.

"Hello, sweetling." I could hear a smile in Queen Mercia's voice. Rafe wriggled. "Yes, you certainly —"

Her sudden pause caught my ear and I turned. The Queen's smile melted under the pall of her veil, and her eyes turned harsh. Locked onto mine, so like a lamia that my skin prickled. Grey eyes. Kiefan had gotten his from her, clearly.

So had Rafe. The murky blue had drained right out of his irises over the last week or so. I'd never seen the like of it; most babies took far longer to settle on their color.

"His eyes." Mercia's voice carried a touch of gravel. "All my babies' eyes went grey before their third moon. It is the mark of Saint Seaxneat."

A shiver shot down my spine. My dress in place, I faced her with both hands on Rafe. I'd survived lamia, centaurs, far worse things than her.

Her voice cut through the lutes' polite song. "You were the girl in Kiefan's bed, last Solstice." Heads turned, among the bystanders watching the dance floor. Queen Mercia's voice kept rising. "He let me think it was some whore from Arbor Street — but I have a grandson? And you kept him from me?"

The music stopped. Firelight, from behind me, danced on the queen's wet eyes. She held out both her hands, gaze fixed on Rafe. My heart pounded in my throat as I clutched him. He burbled, blithely innocent, and I felt drool seeping through the shoulder of my dress. She wanted him. The queen, the castle —

"He's my son," I said, glancing to Saint Woden. He watched. Not far enough away for me to feel safe.

"I have buried so many babies. Please." The queen's voice trembled. It tore at my heart, the memory of the two little boys buried with the princess. The graves of two brothers Kiefan never met. When I blinked, and my eyes swam a moment with tears, the queen was two steps closer. "Please."

I let her touch Rafe, and her agony turned to wonder. She took him, gently, and held him up with a smile that brought back much of her beauty. My son gurgled and kicked his legs — he liked being held aloft.

Queen Mercia cuddled him against her neck, against the black veil, and cooed. "Such a handsome prince you are, yes, my little golden boy."

I trailed close as she turned away from me, rocking him gently. My eye caught on the queen's handmaid beckoning one of the Queen's Guard closer. "Majesty," I murmured, "it was wiser not to tell you —"

She paid me no mind and kept walking. "So late at night, we must get you back to the nursery. Tuck you in, warm and snug."

The queen turned toward the grand staircase and "Majesty!" burst out of me. I raised my hands. If she got Rafe upstairs, into the royal nursery... no, he was my son. Then a prince, if he must be. Not theirs yet, not Woden's. Mine.

She stared at me, a perplexed frown creasing her brow. "I can see to him, Svetlana."

Trailing her black skirts, she swept toward the staircase. My heart leaped into my throat. "No! Give him back." I caught her by one thin shoulder and spun her around; she hissed, hands turning to claws on Rafe's dark green cote, and I flinched back. Then I steadied. "He's my son."

"Nobody will take my —"

/ gently /

Kir blossomed, strong enough to draw her gaze. "Mercia." Qadeem, star-studded cloak rippling free, swept between us. "When did you last see Kiefan?"

She blinked. My hands itched to touch my baby, but I closed them into fists. Trusted my saint. And watched her like a hawk.

"I — when he rode for Knapptal," the queen answered. "The morning after the funeral. He should've stayed, just a day or two. So soon, and it's near mid-winter. It's not safe. But he won't listen to me, not any more." Her voice fell into misery as she went. "He's grown so. So like his father."

"I'm glad my elect's son could comfort you," Qadeem said. "She needs to tend him; pass him back."

The Queen's two Guardsmen had sidled around behind her, hands clasped behind their backs as casually as they could manage. And Woden had moved closer. That kept my pulse jittering. He'd looked at Rafe, true, but he'd said nothing. All my fears that he'd lay claim to my son had been only that. Fears.

Queen Mercia lifted Rafe from her shoulder with a fond smile. "Yes, he's been a comfort, this sweetling." But her eyes caught on Rafe's and her lip curled. She clutched him with a snarl, lapsing into Suevi. In the harsh words she shot, I heard "Arceal" aimed at my saint. She backed toward the staircase and I drew my kir to my fingers. Qadeem put out a hand to stop me, his face impassive despite her insults.

"Father's fucking mercy, woman, he's not your baby." Woden's kir-vine slung over my shoulder, looped around Rafe and hoisted him straight up. Mercia startled, her grip faltering, and then she groped after him with a scream. My baby shrieked back, half thrilled, half frightened.

My own kir-vine wrapped around Woden's; he left it to me. Rafe looked down at me, eyes wide, and wriggled in joy as he flew to my hands.

The queen launched herself at Woden with an outraged scream, but her Guardsmen caught her. She kicked and clawed at them, shrieking in Suevi. I had my baby in my arms again. He smelled of warm wool and honeycakes, and nothing else mattered. The screams faded as the queen was dragged away, and silence fell. Near silence; voices murmured.

I dared peek at them over Rafe's shoulder. The audience for our little drama.

/ bravely /

That set my teeth on my lower lip. I straightened. Qadeem stood beside me and I was his bound elect. Not a peasant girl or an Arbor Street whore. Mother of the king's son. Little by little, silence fell in the hall as the audience watched me.

"Each of you is charged to keep the secret," my saint told them. He put a brown hand on Rafe's back. "To keep this child safe from Arcea. They will kill him, if they can."

Heads dipped, fists touched chests, in obedience. When they looked at me again, it was with level eyes and respectful nods.

"Music!" Woden broke the silence, bless him. The flutist picked up a new tune, and the lute and drum joined in. My audience's attention wavered, tracking Woden as he returned to a knot of officers and fell to talking again. My next breath came easier.

But who I saw cutting through the onlookers shook my courage to pieces.

Frida caught me in her arms, Rafe and all, and hugged me. "I'm sorry —"

She hushed me.

I had to confess it, though. She deserved the truth. "Master would've sent me away, but — Anders was so good to me. I love him, I do, Mother's mercy but —"

Frida hushed me again. "Let me see my grandson."

"He's not." It tore at my heart all over again.

She fixed me with another of her stern looks. "He is." I handed Rafe over and she kissed him.

<hr/>

KNAPPTAL

In good time, the banquet gave way to dancing and then the dancers made their way to the roof of the keep. Cleared of snow, it was the same size as the hall. A bonfire blazed in one corner, drawing the older guests to it. The lutist checked the tune on her strings, once she'd settled on her stool, and her companions on flute and drum played a little ditty in the meantime. Pages offered cups of brandy to those who'd been dancing too much to drink.

The half-moon rose at midnight, marking the new year, but there was still time for a few dances. Kiefan declined another brandy; he'd gone through a few in the course of conversations about the spring and the more immediate plans to scout the Suevi side of the border. Margrave Schutze owed his wife a dance before midnight, as he'd said when they climbed the stairs to the roof. The Caer ladies had been willing to dance with the wives of those men Kiefan had monopolized, and that had been interesting to watch. But now he was likely to be needing a dance partner himself.

"Majesty?" A small voice caught his ear. Haralda looked up at him, fidgeting with her loose hair. "Don't you have — a dance partner?"

He spotted Ciara, knotted close with the three duchesses and speaking in Caer. Further away, Gregor stood with a couple of squires.

"Might you do something for me?" Kiefan asked. Haralda nodded. "Ask my squire Gregor who it was he wanted to dance with. Don't let him just mumble, he does that sometimes. Make him tell you."

Surely it was too transparent for even a young girl — but no, she went. She knew the other two squires by how she slowed and straightened her shoulders in resolve. Twisting up her courage to ask.

"What ploy's this?" Ciara asked, taking a sip of brandy. She slid across the stone, skirts trailing.

"He's shy of girls." Kiefan turned away as Haralda addressed the squires with all the pomp a fourteen-year-old could muster. Gregor would see through it instantly.

"And you're not, or so I was given to think — and yet you've not danced, tonight." Ciara put her cup on a passing page's tray. "In Caercoed, 'tis well for the lady to ask." She put out her hand, expectant. The flute and drum stopped and the lutist strummed a few chords as a final check.

Time to resume the game. He took her hand, carrying it at shoulder height, and they strode to the head of the dancing line. Eyes tracked them, no doubt. The duchesses, the local officers, and — "How is it Elect Teleri isn't here?" Kiefan asked. "Is it wise to dance with another kingdom's elect?"

The band played the dance's introduction; something slow, as they'd ended with a spirited one in the hall.

"Teleri does see to our security," Ciara said, "as 'tis been troubling, since we left home."

The dance began slowly, but picked up in tempo after a few rounds through the steps. Then the musicians shifted directly into a partner-swapping dance and increased the pace again. Kiefan made his rounds through the ladies one by one, bowing to each when the steps called for it and getting more smiles and winks than he expected.

In the end, he was returned to Ciara, now bright-eyed and grinning herself, for the last round of steps. For a few moments, it was only a dance on a cold night under the stars. The music ended with a flourish and she fell against him with a cheer for the band.

Back to the game. Kiefan joined in the cheer, steadying Ciara by the elbow. Subtly putting her back on her feet and off his shoulder.

"'Twas a fine dance!" She turned to him, breath billowing as it caught up to her. "'Twas wise to study it in Vorspitz."

"I had meant to say that you didn't dance, that I had seen." Which made it likely part of her ploy. To get close, perhaps. To speak privately, away from Elect Teleri?

"Needs must study the steps, as 'tis different from ours."

Ciara's words slipped from his attention when he caught sight, across the roof, of Elect Teleri. Arms folded, feet planted, brow lowered, kir tucked away so he'd not detect her; Kiefan wore his openly, as he had nothing to hide.

His anticipation told him the obvious: not to turn his back on her.

"The moon rises." Ciara pointed in the opposite direction. "Ah, they did distract us! Shame on that lutist."

On cue, the musicians began again, playing the Sun-caller's lament. Ciara tugged at his arm and Kiefan turned halfway, reluctant to ignore his Blessing. Around them, the song was taken up; usually, he sang along, but he kept one eye on Teleri.

Didn't miss that Ciara had slipped herself under his arm, either. That was the game, then. Her Elect had not known of this, that was clear enough, and did not like it at all.

"'Tis a song for the sun?" Ciara asked, close enough he could hear her under the singing. He nodded. "We do the same." Her voice lowered. He felt her breath on his ear, warmth rather than the cold breeze. "'Tis a kiss after, as well?"

Kiefan met her eyes, saw careful cheer, a glaze of hope — and anxiety, buried in their depths. A kiss, yes, and most likely the Caer spent the rest of Solstice night as many in Wodenberg did. As he had, last year.

Little different from his mother and all the girls at court, after all. Ciara was smarter than such things; that made the souring in his stomach all the worse. "I first kissed a girl, at moonrise on Solstice," he said. "I was fourteen." Everyone thought that part of the story sweet. "She meant to get in my bed, as well, but my mother saw through that and set us both straight. Twice a year since, every Solstice, one girl or another tried her hand at it." All but Kate.

Ciara's shallow smile faded, dropping the pretense.

"None succeeded." Kiefan shoved her off, just enough to catch a few eyes. Raised his voice a little. "You think me a fool, then, to be led by a pretty face? I took manipulation with Mother's milk, and if you think to out-do her you must be far more subtle. No second chance — whatever your ploy, I'll have no part in it, Crown. And you've insulted me as well."

She might've been carved of ice. His anticipation noted that she'd bolt, given the chance, but her pride was stronger. Small blessing that few nearby spoke Arceal; his tone had caught their attention. Kiefan stalked past her, cutting through the last bars of the song. Voices trailed off as heads turned in surprise. He pattered down the stairs, taking a cup of brandy from the tray a page was carrying up. "See I get another," he told the boy, and swallowed a mouthful. "In the council chamber." Books would do for company, tonight.

"Yes, Majesty."

———————————✕———————————

Teleri knew Ciara fought the urge to run, that she trembled with the effort of it. Once Kiefan was gone, she stood with chin high, trapped under the eyes she'd drawn. It would be too cowardly to run now.

Tel pushed off the wall, strode through the gawpers and snatched her by the elbow. Ciara stumbled, but caught herself near the stair. She planted her feet, swung around and —

A twitch of kir jerked Teleri's head back, dodging her slap. Ciara glared like a cat.

Like a child. Teleri took her arm and pulled her down the stair. Let her hiss and fuss if she wished, and fall down the stairs as well if she wouldn't keep up. All her talk of aiding the margrave's guardsmen, how this would be as fine a target for Arcea as the wedding slaughter — Teleri had slipped away to collect that moonrise kiss, for the good luck it brought. And had found her love tucked under another's arm. Playing at something.

"Shall unhand me, Elect!" Ciara pulled free in the banquet hall, where a few silver-haired Alemanni still lingered by the fire and servants cleaned up. All heads turned, though none knew Caer.

Teleri's fists went to her hips. "Shall explain yourself! How you came so near to kissing — Mother's tits, Cici, you've all but slammed doors in his face!"

"'Tis his charm, Tel." Ciara put fists to her hips as well, cocked her head in sneering. "I've seen my error and once he's a chance to, 'tis simple to cast his spell on me. He'll sweet-talk me of two divisions from Henffyrdd and Dheathain, and the Tadhlon Guard as well."

If she hadn't laid it so, Tel would've thought her mad. Even so, her jaw hung for a heart-beat. "For a kiss?"

Ciara's eyes rolled. "A hush sphere, Tel." With that in place, she lowered her voice. "Does ride from here with Tadhlon, true, and attacks Temitte as he wishes. Shall entangle all Arcea's ranks, draw garrisons from Reowan to strike back — to crush, doubtless. Meantime, our ships move on Reowan's harbor. Land a force and attack. We take the city as Wodenberg draws the brunt of their army. Once we've the capital, and the fount, shall clean away what's left of both."

A bold thing. "But send no divisions to aid Wodenberg."

She nodded. "They sail to Reowan."

Good chance it might work. Safe to trust Wodenberg would fight fierce, and might wound Arcea's army deep before they fell. The treachery of it was a bitter thing, but the prize... "Send ships through the Dragon's Fangs for Rukharbor?"

Ciara folded her arms. "Needs must focus our strength on Temitte. Think you the saints will keep the passes open for two new founts?"

"With two more for the taking." Those at Rukharbor and Mount Woden would cost no little blood, but... Teleri had to nod. Still, that bitter lump of the treachery shifted in her gut. It uncoiled and spread unease. "For a kiss, you'd do this?"

She looked away from Tel's gaze, shifting back. "A play-act of seduction, lure him into a true oíche-te as of old — send him off with Tadhlon and promises to salve his pride. 'Tis worthy of the ancient Crowns. The pink twins did pounce on it straight away. Even Faola called it sly."

Excuses, and no more. Teleri's voice lowered as her unease became an ache. "Cici. Do mean to fuck him?"

Ciara bit her lip for a moment. "'Tis little worry, Tel. Shan't deign to even kiss me."

"You'd keep this from me? Give me no say? Haven't I —"

"Did need three days' convincing, myself," she spat. "And liquid courage, as well. Did have an odd idea you'd not like it, and 'twould've destroyed any hope I had. I'm no Ceelin, I —"

"No. I thought you more loyal." It was ever Ceelin, after all the years, all the encouraging, after she'd gone to her pyre. Couldn't leave her shadow.

Ciara stared, eyes wide. "Thought — what?" Her voice climbed some notches.

"I'm not Oisin, to stand by meek while you're fucking —"

"'Tis only oíche-te! Shall save —"

"Whatever the price, 'tis still a whore!"

"You think 'tis what I want?"

"You think he'll forgive an oíche-te of old? That merely Tadhlon will salve such wounded pride?" Teleri flung up an arm, toward the stairs at hall's rear.

Her disbelief twisted into sarcasm as her arms folded across her chest. "Wish me fawning under his hand, then? As Ceelin would?"

Teleri's lip curled. Hardly more than a teenager, sometimes, and she ever hoped the woman within her would — "Don't play the fool at me. He'll not lay a hand on you."

"'Tis for you to decide, then?"

"If seven years your consort means so little, 'tis for you still being a child!"

That struck home; her lip trembled — rage, or pain, or… "'Tis why I said nothing." Her voice fell, chilled to ice. "Do think you own me."

"Do think you need a spanking, at times!"

Ciara broke into a snarl. "You'd spank me for fearing I'd lose you in this?"

Teleri's mouth opened, but her throat clenched shut on the words. Not now. Not like this. She closed her eyes. Heard shoes scuff; Ciara broke through the hush sphere and escaped to the gate-yard. Tears blurred the world, when Teleri looked after her.

She murmured, half broken, "Have lost me, wish it or not."

Schutze's night watch knew Teleri, despite that they shared only a few Alemannic words, and they let her walk the wall. On the keep's roof, the bonfire crackled on, fed by the abbess and a dozen of her pious who meant to keep watch for the sun.

All with any sense were in their beds, lulled by drink or a good fucking.

Teleri knew the night watch, she'd stood it oft enough as a knight. Never cried through one, before. Never suffered the twisting knife of knowing her words put love near death. There were new things to suffer, even at her age.

Each time she reached the gate-house, she meant to go in and join the card game by the brazier. It would calm her, ease her, even without common tongue. Each time, she hesitated, knew who she ought to be speaking to, and turned her feet around for another circuit.

Boots fell in alongside her, old brown ones. Tannait matched her pace in silence, as they rounded behind the keep.

"Do know you'll lose your post when we bring her home," Tannait said.

That pain seemed a small thing, now. "Did earn it, in failing the Crown." Teleri hadn't asked what Tannait's penance for Ceelin's murder would be; it would be something as dire.

"Might be you're sent far. So long as Conbarre wishes you there. Mayhaps you'll not see Ciara again."

Teleri's throat thickened. "Mayhaps 'tis best I don't."

Tannait looked up at her, stern. "'Tis what you wish to think, standing at her grave?"

They walked in silence, and reached the right-hand gate-house.

"Mark this day; I've silenced Elect Teleri."

"No rush to think on it," she returned. "Shall ever be regrets, at a lover's grave. No matter what befell." Turning on her heel, Teleri walked. Tannait kept with her, silent for some distance again.

"Do remember the moment you knew you'd bury them all."

She said it as fact, for it was. Tel had stood by younger elect when it hit; 'twas best medicated with the strongest liquor at hand.

"How many were in the Mother Tree's shade?" Tannait asked.

"My mothers. Father. I did see the silver on my twin, did see the wrinkles on her face. Triese lasted a decade more, but…"

Shame stopped her. Tannait said, likely guessing the truth, "Does make one draw back. Take up what shields we have, to keep them away. One makes rules, dictates terms, says: 'I know this, 'tis best for all.' 'When did you outlive your lover, little one?' For we are the elect, and they are children, here and gone with the morn. True?"

Teleri stared out across the lake.

"'Twas what I did." Tannait shrugged. "Did decide who left, who stayed, when all was ruined. How 'twas to be. And he dared defy me? Dared cling to my girls —?"

"You do well to have no consort since," Teleri murmured.

A sidelong look. "You know less of me than you think."

Teleri frowned in return. Twelve elect in Caercoed, and she knew them all well. Or so she thought.

"Ciara is a woman and her life is her own. Her body is her own. Furthermore, she's Crown of Caercoed and needs must see to her duties. 'Tisn't for you to order her, save in the name of the saints." Tel hadn't received Tannait's stern voice in some years.

"I have no claim on her then? Needs must wait on her fancy, like a pet?"

Tannait's voice sharpened further. "You are bound by the saints, an elect of Caercoed. What claim does she have on you?" They stopped on the wall.

Only Conbarre had claim, by oath and by kir. Could strip Teleri, banish her, harvest her if she willed. Or could lavish her with every comfort, in trade for loyalty.

Ciara had Teleri's heart, but wounded hearts did heal in time. Time Ciara might not have.

"You would love, and be loved." Tannait's voice softened at last. "Not as a pet, but as a woman. How best to do that?"

CHAPTER 10

Solstice needed a day's recovery, for most. Next morning, Kiefan swung into Nail's saddle. No gold band, no ranking on his tabard, nothing to mark him king but Woden's moon-pommeled sword. Mail, helm, and the plain shield of an ordinary knight. Captain Aleks and the two Guard she brought wore borrowed tabards. They mingled easily with the hand of Knapptal-native garrison knights. A hand of the local Rangers and their lieutenant would lead the scouting foray; they knew the borderland well.

Sir Eburhart, one of the garrison captains, barked orders to the squires checking the saddlebags and called, "Move out, then, while the morning's young! Gar, you take —" before catching himself. He cast about over each shoulder before he found Kiefan, not far off his side. "Pardon, Majesty," he boomed, and a grin split his thick brown beard. The man sported an impressive black eye as well. "Old habits run deep. Ready for your command."

"Then move out, while the morning's young. I put the riding order at your discretion, sir."

They rode through the gate, past the salutes of the watchmen on duty and the Guards that stayed behind. Outside, the Spanne's expanse of virgin snow had been broken by a tall snow-fort on Solstice morning, and signs of battle still scarred the drifts. All was bright and clear, this morning, only wisps of cloud breaking the blue overhead. A sharp wind, but fitful.

Kiefan pulled up his hood with mittened hands and tucked folds of his cloak between his thighs and the saddle. They'd make Suevia before noon, he'd been told.

Gregor rode alongside him, bundled and silent. Kiefan had sought his bed before dawn, after reading the book of local tales again, and his squire had not been in it. A cold bed had been a fit end for Solstice night, perhaps, but he'd not had a chance to ask where Gregor had been.

At a brisk walk, the party turned southward. Two Rangers trotted ahead, two lingered behind for a rearguard. Sir Eburhart consulted with the lieutenant and then tapped his buckskin horse to draw alongside Kiefan. Knapptal's shops, fine houses, and lake-shore docks passed quickly into humbler cottages. Few were out — a wood-cutter here and there, children playing in the snow — but those who saw them waved.

"There's a question to be settled, Majesty," Sir Eburhart announced. "It's become a matter of money among the men, or I wouldn't trouble you."

"It seems you bet on everything, sir," Captain Aleks commented from behind. Small wonder she could hear that, with such a voice on him.

"The men value each other all the more, bound by debts." He grinned again. "Majesty, it's a wager on you we must resolve."

"If you'll call me Sir Kiefan."

"Sir." Eburhart dipped his head. The knights ahead had drawn back a bit, meaning to overhear while they watched for trouble. It was a serious bet, then.

"There's two stories told, sir, of how you came by that scar." Eburhart indicated his neck. "Both told by your own men, so we'd not question either save that they're not agreeing."

Kiefan twisted in his saddle to cast a frown at his Guard; it hadn't been Aleks' doing, and he knew better than to ask. She had Sir Garrick in her sights, though, and the knight offered a few protests before falling silent under her glare.

Garrick hadn't been on duty that night. He had little business telling stories.

The neck scar was a silver line now, clearest when it cut a stripe through Kiefan's morning stubble. For all its dramatic sweep across his throat, the wound on his shield arm had been more trouble, and was scarring up thick and jagged. That had gotten less healing, and he'd shooed away physicians once he could flex the muscle through the ache. In all his sparring since then, he'd made sure to carry a shield and put the arm through its paces.

Neither was a scar he'd want to tell the story of. But eyes were on him. "How do they disagree?" he asked.

"Some say — and I'm partial to this one myself, m'lord — it was the monster-saint herself that cut you. A terrible slash of her claws, and it cost her all but the one. Maimed, she flew away screaming on black vulture's wings." Sir Eburhart's gestures made it all the more grand. "A fine prize, the talons you cut off her. Must be hideous things."

Kiefan smiled in spite of himself. Gregor stared, from his other side, in frank bewilderment.

Eburhart waited a heartbeat. "Sir, don't say —"

Kiefan gestured for more. "The other story, first."

He was already disappointed, though. "The other story's only that one of the minotaurs dueled you. Last and fiercest of them, a huge beast with white bull's head and great, black horns. Its sword, heavier than any man could swing, dripped with innocent blood." Eburhart slid back into embroidery easily enough. "But no match for our king; you ran the monster through and gutted it, and only with dying luck did it catch you as it fell."

The mention of a white bull set Kiefan's teeth on his lip for a heartbeat — too close to Anders' unnerving attack with a grey horse's head. Dying luck was unsettlingly close, as well. But watching Eburhart tell the tale piqued nothing from Kiefan's Blessing. It was all the story he knew.

Nobody had seen the whole duel but Kate and Woden. Kiefan had thought himself sure on that. All else in the hall were dead or —

Then his stomach dropped. Elect Tannait. Not a word of it, not one hint she'd slipped since then. She had no reason to change the story of it, though, and no reason to keep his secrets for him. Someone else had told this.

"I've lost my bet, sir?" Eburhart asked.

Kiefan glanced at the garrison captain, tucking away his new worry for later. "I like the first story better," he said, "but sadly it was the minotaur." No need to say the minotaur had been horse-headed. "I have the sword, and true it's a brute."

That made a good diversion, describing the grim trophy they'd taken from the minotaur that Captain Aleks and her handful of Guard had hacked to pieces in the bloody hall. It hung above the fireplace, in tribute to the captain. A knight would need a strength Blessing to use that sword all day. It was short enough for close fighting, and the edge was impressively sharp.

Those garrison knights who weren't native had earned this quiet post after service in the southern army with Kiefan's father. Some of them had battle trophies — minotaur swords or helms, centaurs' mail horse-blankets. They'd been telling their own stories and showing off their prizes.

The armsmen and archers here hadn't yet seen Arcea's monsters themselves. Lamia didn't wander this far from their fount. Something else to worry on: how their first battle with such would turn.

During a lull in the talk, the sunlight caught Sir Eburhart's black eye again and shone on the swelling. Kiefan had to ask. "Which minotaur punched you, then?"

He barked a laugh. "It was a mighty battle."

One of the knights ahead threw back over his shoulder, "It was two girls," and got a round of laughs.

Eburhart threw up a hand, suffering it all. "I meant to help — Father Duty will vouch for me. After moonrise, I made my way back to the barracks — alone," and that deserved special emphasis, "with no luck for the year." More laughs, at that. "And near our end of the barracks, our end mind you, I find a pair of Caer ladies. Together. Up against the wall, and —" He didn't have a word for that, it seemed, only a vague wave. "It would be a crime before the Father, leaving two ladies in such need. How could any knight walk by? I was honor-bound to offer whatever aid I could."

A pause, to shake his head. "Would you believe the redhead punched me and —"

"The blonde punched you." It was Sir Garrick who spoke up. "The redhead threw you down."

"Knocked the breath clean out of me."

"Broke a rib," the knight up front added.

"Physician said it's just a crack." Eburhart put a hand to his side. "Might walk straight again, if the swelling in my nuts eases. Took four men to pull the wildcats off me."

"Four Guard," Garrick amended.

The next pause gave Kiefan a chance to catch his breath, from laughing. Wildcats, yes, he'd earned the scratches that Sío — that hobbled his mirth. Still hurt, in a wash across his chest, to think of her. Sío. Kate…

"Such spirit in those ladies, and the pretty ones?" Eburhart sucked a breath through his teeth. "Stay away, boys. Not a word to be said, once they've set their minds. Might as well be stone walls. You've been polite, m'lord, you've asked and waited and that queen of theirs wouldn't even look at you. Carved from ice, that one. Saw her at the Two Lanterns, when they'd first arrived, wouldn't dance with any man. Not even Adal, and he can get any woman in town on his knee with two winks. She ought to be knocking on your door, m'lord, that —"

"Enough," Kiefan said, and he stopped. "The Caer are guests here and they've suffered enough for it."

Eburhart fell to a mutter. "Your pardon, m'lord, I didn't mean to offend."

Lake Spiegel lay under a blanket of snow and the wind picked up twisting clouds of powder from its flat expanse. The road left the fishermen's cottages behind, the woodcutters' and the pigherds' too. It narrowed from two-wagon width to one, and the forest closed in along their right. In truth, the road was more a theory than a certainty; towering pines and naked maples on the right, a few yards of willows and snow made lumpy by brambles between the road and the lake. The wind had carved drifts in it, then it'd been churned by the forward Rangers' passing, but else-wise it was merely an ongoing gap in the trees. One they'd been cautioned several times to stay on, whatever happened.

Riding two abreast, Kiefan looked to Gregor, who'd said little thus far. "Did you dance with Haralda?"

"Yes, sir." His words were as limp and hopeless as his face.

A bad night for everyone, then. "She stepped on your feet so much?"

"No, sir, it was that when the dance came back around she'd switched places and I ended with…"

A different partner. When he didn't finish, Kiefan grimaced. "Did your Blessing aid you?"

"It was a jumble. I couldn't get anything clear off her. I could hardly get the steps right, when I was dancing with her. Once the gavotte started, I got better — don't think I stepped on any feet."

"Once you were changing partners."

Gregor nodded. "My focus slips so much —"

"When you think less," Kiefan told him, "the Blessing runs clearer. Trust it. Perhaps I must goad you out into every dance, to keep you moving while it does its work."

His voice fell to a murmur. "I'd need a dance partner." Red crept into his ears, oddly enough.

Kiefan watched the red spread, and when Gregor happened to meet his eyes it flushed out faster.

"You kept dancing?"

Gregor stumbled over some words, and it led into, "The musicians played the lament, then a few happier songs. No more dances."

And yet he'd been missing till morning. And was as red-faced as he could be. "If it's anything I'll be hearing about…" Kiefan let that dangle, not sure he wanted to risk a guess.

"I — don't believe, well, or I didn't think by how — no. Sir. Most likely."

Kiefan sighed.

Gregor wilted further in the saddle. "A poor knight I'll make."

"Woden judged you able to defend the kingdom. He doesn't waste his time with the weak." Kiefan drew Nail to a stop, as the column halted.

A tree had split and fallen into the road. A man or horse could duck under it, near the trunk, but just as well to clear it now. Axes were pulled from saddle loops to cut the trunk free of the stump. Kiefan swung down from the saddle and after a few minutes' planning he found two good branches to take the fallen half by. One of the garrison knights had a strength Blessing as well, and did the same on the other side. A shout from the men; the tree was loose. Knee-deep in snow, they braced their feet as best they could and pulled.

Kiefan felt the lines of kir strung through his flesh pulse. Muscle tingled in his arms, his thighs, as the Blessing drove them hard. Bark dug into his skin, even through the mittens, and the heavy branches bent with a slow groan.

Something was caught in the snow — and snapped, suddenly, dumping Kiefan as the whole thing slid. A cheer went up. Another good pull and they hauled the half-tree out onto the lake. Ice groaned under them as they trotted to shore and cracks shot out. They might've cut the tree up, but the day was short and there was far to go.

Little clutches of huts passed for villages along the lake shore and had names like Krachzen or Windschlag. The last of them was Schweinfuss, where a squat tower stood between the river bank and the road, more a stone platform for two catapults than a lookout. The road wound down a sudden hillside, beyond the redoubt, through thin saplings that had sprouted since the first half-mile was last cleared of trees.

Kiefan looked back to the Wache, which wasn't so far; their road had followed a pocket of the lake. The trebuchets on the Wache's walls could support Schwienfuss with light shot, given a little fine-tuning of their aim.

A trail split off the road and climbed away from the lake. Knee-deep snow ran under tall, close-ranked pines. Stones jutted from the hillside, big as wagons. The pines' lower branches, long dead, reached toward the trail — spindly, black hands. Brush lurked under the snow, and the horses jittered when they stumbled into thorns. Slow going.

The Rangers' tracks led on until they crested the hill and found the signal tower. It was another short thing, no more than a stone shed with a broad iron bowl for a roof. The firewood in the bowl was covered by an oilskin, which had been freshly cleared of snow. This was the last point one could see the Wache from; the lookout itself was around the hill.

The two Rangers stood in the snow by the signal tower, with their horses and the fur-bundled sergeant on duty at the lookout. The sergeant made his obeisance and reported, "Lookout Point's clear, Majesty. Leave the horses, let them rest."

Along the hilltop, the pines thinned. Rock broke through the knee-deep snow. The hilltop itself narrowed, climbed, and a thin sheet of snow clung despite the wind's best efforts. Kiefan's cloak billowed as its hollow whistle rose, and he pulled the fur-lined wool closer. A whistle became a howl and his stomach tightened. Starknadel. Naked rock and snow, wind and flying ice needles. Panting for every breath, even when sitting still. His pulse quickened.

The sergeant led them onto a point of bare granite. Looking south, Suevia rolled out in a lumpy rug. The Eispitzen mountains reared up to one side, brilliant in their white blankets and wreathed in clouds. Knapptal was a rocky knot of rugged hills, a spur of the mountains that stabbed into the valleys below. They turned their bare faces south, guarding Wodenberg. By Ansehen, the hills were lower, crusted with grass in the summer, and Saint Aleksander had raised a wall to supplement them — which had cracked and crumbled in the earthquake.

Near a year and a half gone, that. Kiefan looked toward Ansehen, where he'd first faced Arcea's monsters himself.

Dúnforst-éa, the river, twisted through the narrow gorge below and rolled into Suevia. "There's the watchtower. See the smoke?" The sergeant pointed. A moment's scanning, and Kiefan picked out the faint column of grey, then the pale, granite tower in the valley below. It stood in a crook of the river, protected on two sides. Taller than the trees, certainly. Fifty feet? Ten miles off?

"Can you make them out?" he asked.

Two of the four rangers were archers, hawk-eyed, and one nodded. "Movement on the tower, m'lord. They're vigilant. Never catch us, though."

"Eburhart, where's this trail you spoke of?"

The garrison captain had a map, though with the wind it needed three hands to hold it. He traced with his finger and then pointed out the landmarks in the valley — a rocky point, a long cliff face, a glimpsed lake — along the Ansehen-bound path. The Ranger lieutenant added a few details about the spring runoff from melting snow; where the creeks would spring up overnight, which ponds overflowed. Muddy hillsides were a danger all their own. Rocky ridges would be their best way through.

Suevi scouts rode out in the spring, from the watchtower, to check on the few villages, to watch for smugglers, and to creep their way up through the hills for a little spying of their own. There'd been a handful of times, the Ranger lieutenant said, when the Rangers had attacked Suevi scouts — and only twice had been attacked themselves.

"If we've a force, we must be sure they see nothing or don't live to tell," Kiefan said. His eyes returned to the granite tower jutting from the dark pine-tops. "They can't see us from there?"

"It's twelve miles, m'lord."

"May well have Blessed of their own on watch."

They all stared at the tower a few heartbeats, and then Eburhart rolled up his map. "The trailhead's not far from here, m'lord. Might find it, even in the snow."

They took their leave of the sergeant of the watch and found the trail; it branched off half a mile downslope and meandered across the hill's brow. Not much more than a gap in the trees, but a trail. Slogging back uphill through the snow was enough to wind any man, and when they re-joined those minding the horses it was a good time to eat and drink a bit. Overhead, the sun winked through clouds — puffy, grey-bellied, and racing at a good clip.

When they'd finished the cold ham and bread, the Ranger lieutenant looked up at the stream of clouds. "Best head straight home, m'lord. Stick to the road." He eyed Kiefan. "Ulf Waldgrun got you over Starknadel and back, I hear. You know what to do."

Kiefan nodded. "Stay close," he told Gregor, Captain Aleks, and his two Guards. Sir Garrick and Sir Waldemar watched the thickening clouds with a frown. Storms rarely rolled in without warning in Wodenberg proper. The watchtowers always sent word.

They rode down, careful and slow, seeming to hit every bramble they'd met on the way up. A roof of pine boughs hid the sky, but the wind came up and glimpses of grey showed through the swaying treetops. When they reached Schweinfuss and turned to follow the lake shore, a thick blanket lay close above them. The wind was cold and damp; snow coming, and no doubt.

CHAPTER 11

Five miles to the little knot of cottages called Krachzen; they sped up to a high-stepping trot. Powder blew up in their faces, southbound with the storm. Kiefan took quick stock of the column — two garrison knights just ahead, of the five, and two behind. Eburhart riding alongside Captain Aleks behind him, and Garrick and Waldemar behind them. Gregor on his left, watching the sky. Crows flew above, cawing.

The Rangers and their lieutenant scouted somewhere nearby, but they could handle themselves.

Snow joined the powder, secretly; the wind eased for a moment and it still fell. Then rose again, breathing through the trees, and rose further. Kept rising. Kiefan turned his cheek to the blowing ice, pulling his hood across. Nail stopped, sensibly, and lowered his head.

He checked his left. "Gregor!"

Only a shadow in the thickening wall of snow. "M'lord!"

"Don't move!"

The wind kept climbing, howling now, and wood cracked nearby. Deep ripping in the trees and the rush of branches falling. And still the wind climbed, the snow thickened. A horse bumped against his leg, close by, and a hand groped for Kiefan's arm.

"I'm here." He reached and caught it, knew it. Aleks.

"Gregor!" she called. "Damn, did he move?"

"Captain?" The voice came from his left, a couple yards off. "Are you there?"

"Garrick, you were to stay close!" she yelled back.

Trees ripped under the wind's hand. Even through the wool and fur, quilted gambeson and two cotes, Kiefan shivered. Eburhart cuffed his shoulder from behind, then Captain Aleks'.

"Dismount," Eburhart called over the wind. "We'll freeze. Your squire?"

Kiefan swung down into knee-deep snow. "I'll lead. Gregor!"

Faintly, though the grey-white curtain billowing on the wind, "Here!"

Kiefan had kept his kir tucked close, hidden. He loosed it now, all of it, let it unfurl in a green cloak around him — one the wind couldn't touch. Leading Nail, he stomped through the snow, free hand before him to shield his eyes. Captain Aleks kept one hand on Nail's stirrup and the other on her horse's reins.

A few steps and Gregor should've been there. A few more. The wind had eased from its peak but the snow still fell thick enough to hide the trees hemming the road, narrow though it was. "Gregor!"

"Here!" He stumbled out of the curtain, leading his horse. "She wouldn't move."

"She's got good sense, then. Aleks! We have Eburhart?"

She looked. "Yes. Garrick and Waldemar too. Drawn to you."

"Good." Not all the men would be sensitive enough to feel the kir, but any help in a storm. "We can still make the town — bring Eburhart up front! Walk with Nail. Hold his bridle." That, sternly, to Gregor, who nodded.

"What of the others? The two up front vanished," Gregor said.

"With any luck, we'll meet them on the way." There were the two who'd been behind Garrick and Waldemar, as well; natives knew what to do, Kiefan had to hope.

The wind screamed up to a new pitch to disagree, and Kiefan leaned into it with eyes squeezed shut. Its icy knife found the tip of his nose beyond the hood's hem and sliced through it. Wood in the forest gave again, in a cascade of cracks and rips.

When it eased, Kiefan patted Gregor's arm and began walking. His squire shifted his hands to Nail's reins, then the bridle, and fell in alongside with his own horse. Eburhart came up on Nail's outside, stamping through the snow, and joined Kiefan.

"Two steps left," he said. "I'm tramping on brush. Edge of the road."

Kiefan took two steps left, and the line of horses and knights shifted with him as they went. The wind eased a little, let the snow fall in rambling lines. The view cleared to a few dozen yards.

A tree lay across the road, a big old maple freshly torn off at an angle. Its forked trunk blocked even the view ahead, for being nearly as high as Kiefan's head.

"No moving this grandfather," Eburhart said, trying to peer between the trunks. "Gar!" he shouted. "You hear me?"

"Around, then. On the lake side?"

"The water never stops underneath, m'lord. I wouldn't lead a horse onto it before Bitter Moon."

Falling through would be deadlier than anything in the forest could be. They had bed-rolls and more food, but only the fallen tree for shelter. Had to reach the village. "Only three miles more," Kiefan said. "We go through the forest."

Wind whirled up again as he followed the maple's trunk toward its stump. Eburhart shouted for the others to bunch up closer, follow the tree. He lingered behind to be sure all were still in line, and to bring up the rear.

Kiefan found the edge of the road at a sapling half-pinned under the maple. He had to swing around, and meant to angle back as soon as he could. Grandfather Tree had pulled down several neighbors, though, and finding a gap wide enough for the horses meant weaving further from the stump they needed to get around. The wind came up again, blowing the snow crosswise through the trees, hanging curtains of it between the dark trunks.

Kiefan gritted his teeth. If he lost sight of the way back to the road, it was a big, empty forest.

"There." He spotted the fresh-broken stump at last and quickened to a jog. Nail did the same, and Gregor who still held his bridle, and —

It was Garrick who hollered. Kiefan whipped around to see shapes falling, horses stumbling at the sudden weight on the reins, the snow seeming to swallow them all whole. Wood cracked, tore. Horses squealed. The wind threw snow in his eyes and he squinted but still ran back, trying to see.

The snow gave under Kiefan's feet; he felt it crack, he sank hip-deep in the drift, and then it all began to slide. Nail squealed in fright as he stumbled, Gregor shouted, and the wind shrieked in pure glee. Kiefan flailed and his arm struck wood. A branch tried to stab him and snapped against his mail. The sapling shifted under his weight; he hugged it with both arms as snow shoved past him. Faint yelling, somewhere below. Horses shrilling.

"Kiefan!"

He looked up, saw a hand. Nothing under his feet, nothing but the tree he hugged and a hand attached to Gregor. The squire had a grip on a sapling, one slim and limber enough to wrap around his arm and pull over.

Kiefan swung a leg up onto his tree, then shifted a hand to Gregor. "Just hold!" A man in mail was too much to pull. Nearly too much to hold, in the time it took Kiefan to get his feet under him, on the tree. It shifted again, threatening to tear free at the roots. Kiefan crawled onto the top of the massive boulder and now the wind had dropped again, he could see what they'd done. They'd walked onto a fat lip of snow leaning over the sheer drop of a cottage-sized boulder. It had broken under their weight and dumped horses and men over the side.

Twenty feet below, the horses thrashed. Eburhart was up and helping one to its feet, shouting orders to the dark-cloaked knight with him. Only Nail and Gregor had escaped the tumble.

"Any hurt?" Kiefan called down.

"Haven't found them all!"

"There must be —"

Kir unfolded. Nearby. Kiefan straightened in a heartbeat. Less; his speed kicked in. Anticipation crackled, looking for danger. Gregor froze, beside him, staring.

Softly, "M'lord?"

He couldn't feel it. "Kir," Kiefan whispered. "Elect. Or a saint." He called to the kir, felt it shift, then the return call stirred his own. A quick pluck of his saint-bond, and Woden sent an extra ration without question. "Stay out of this," Kiefan murmured to Gregor.

Drawing his sword, he stalked through the drifts. Snow blew sideways, whirling and rippling. No question where the kir was. A falling lump of snow piqued his nerves onto razor's edge for a heartbeat. Grandfather Tree's broken stump came into view. Snow fell thicker, through the gap it had torn in the canopy. Beside it, a doubly-cloaked, hooded figure: dark wool and green kir. Nearly tall as Kiefan, light build —

He recognized Teleri a heartbeat before she twitched her hood back. Quick-draw, his anticipation warned. Kir-ropes, at this range. He kept his sword at middle guard, centered, neither aggressive nor defensive.

Not chance, meeting here — all but alone —

Anticipation surged, speed flared; closed the distance; dropping under her guard; pressure on his blade telling him the next move; kir wrapped around his free wrist and he struck back, kir-shield slamming her full body. She stumbled, lapsing from speed, and her rope around his wrist became a leash. He yanked, lunging in. Her blade knocked his aside. The kir melted in his hand. She tumbled over, despite the snow, came up on her feet and charging.

Their blades scratched again and some corner of his mind noted that her blade wasn't charmed. He threw himself backward from the kir-spikes on her arm and called for a little dagger of his own. The kir spun out in his palm and he threw; not his best weapon, but it sparked and sliced through her kir-spikes when she knocked it aside.

She pounced at speed; defensive; his blade found nothing; she tackled him mid-chest and they tumbled in the snow, ropes of kir lashing, binding, choking. His sword tore from his hand and impaled a sapling. Blinding light burst from Teleri, and a heartbeat's worth of summer heat — it snapped his kir-rope, knocked the wind from him, and she punched him square in the solar plexus.

Kiefan grunted, pain breaking his focus. She grabbed his chin, leaned close and snarled. "'Tis for humiliating her, you dog-fucking bastard."

He pulled a hard lungful of icy air, brain spinning around to — humiliating? —

His anticipation piqued on the incoming blade, and her kir leaping out to block it. The blow still knocked her off and she spun up to her feet. Snow tangled her legs, but she blocked the next swing. Then she was on the attack.

Kiefan lunged up, slinging out a kir-rope to yank his sword from the sapling. Gregor gave ground, on full defensive, turning three blows before Teleri put a little speed in her attack. She struck him across the temple with a fist of kir and he stumbled backward into the snow.

Speed put Kiefan between them, blade shoulder-high and close; not a good start for more sword-play, but he suspected —

Teleri met his eyes. Made no move for a few breaths. "'Tis a game Ciara would play with you," she said. The wind whistled again, ruffling her short, sandy hair, and she pulled her hood back up. "She cannot say it, though. And your insult at Solstice? I'd gladly give you more bruises, but…" A tip of the head, for emphasis. "'Tis a game for her life, this. Cost her that, and we will cross swords for good and all."

He was fairly certain he could spare a glance back at Gregor; he lay shaking his head in the snow, fumbling for his dropped sword. Ought to give him a lashing for disobeying, but he'd done well.

"We move," he said, dropping his voice. The wind nearly drowned him out, but Teleri nodded. She backed away and he followed, both sheathing their swords. They stepped around the torn trunk of the fallen maple tree. Snow cut across his face, even in the lee of the windfall, so Kiefan pulled up his hood as well.

"It's no game I play for my kingdom," he said. "If the Crown wishes a game of me, she knows my price. Alliance."

Teleri's mouth twisted, but she nodded. Whether she liked it mattered little, only that Caercoed would keep its word. "Shall have your soldiers. Needs must be a play-act for the duchesses — the Crown seduces a young king, takes him for oíche-te, casts him aside. Wounded, by preference."

"No less than seven thousand, half knights, a quarter archers."

"Tadhlon's camp, three thousand dispatched through Eryr so soon as we reach it, two more to follow from Dheathain."

"Seven in addition to Tadhlon's camp."

Teleri's eyes narrowed. "You can feign tears?"

Not easily. "I must spin my own story from our little play-act. Take no offense if the words reach your ears."

From around the broken stump, Gregor called, "M'lord! Where are you?"

"Stay where you are!" he threw over his shoulder. "All's well!"

"Mayhaps Dheathain will agree to commit three thousand. Needs must convince the twins you come to oíche-te innocent and take the soldiers as a sop," Teleri said. "Whatever tale you need, spin with care."

Her words tasted sour, by her face. And Ciara was pretty enough, but… "They must see a seduction — what's the truth of it?"

A little anger wiped the sourness away. "Shall be no feigning the oíche-te. If you think to lay a hand on her afterward, 'twill be at risk of your life."

Kiefan met her eyes. "I've no need to bring my heart to bed. But if she thinks to cry rape the next morning…"

Teleri's mouth twitched. Mirth, his anticipation read, which piqued his suspicions.

"No fear of that," she said. "Only play your part."

"What is that, in oíche-te?"

A chill smile. "You sent a knight to it without question."

Danger, his Blessing warned. Kiefan lowered his voice further and had to lean closer to be heard. "If Caercoed thinks to keep me hostage…"

"On my honor, you'll walk from it the moment 'tis finished. If you doubt me, then see to Suevia yourself."

But his anticipation Blessing latched onto something in the back of her eyes. She'd resigned herself to — this? Half on instinct, he said, "Ciara didn't send you." Teleri drew back, that resignation he'd glimpsed turning to caution. "Saint Conbarre?" he asked. No, his Blessing said. "On whose authority do you offer this, then?"

No flicker of fear or hesitation in the elect's eyes. "On my honor, bound by my word before my Mother Strength and your Father Duty, I offer this and 'tis upon me to deliver. So long as you maintain your side."

Anders hadn't suffered, by what Kiefan knew, from the oíche-te. Something lurked in this. Teleri little wished to see her Crown bed a stranger, for any cause, that was clear enough. She saw this the lesser of evils, though, Kiefan's augury suspected.

He set his mind's hand on his bond, but hesitated. Knew his saint's replies already: could he see this through, and to do it. Kiefan dared wish he'd been bound to Saint Qadeem, now and then.

If only Kate were here, she'd help lay the tangle straight. The ache of that pulled his mouth into a grimace.

If the Crowns notched their bed-posts and counted it worth six thousand knights, then it was a small price for a king to pay. Kiefan nodded. "Before Mother Strength and Father Duty."

"We never spoke, though. I did go to the Two Lanterns for a peaceful drink. If pressed, I saw the cloud-bank and did mean to warn you." Teleri cocked her chin at the blowing snow. "Take care, a storm's coming."

"Kind of you to say." Kiefan took a step back.

One last nod, and she gathered kir to launch herself skyward, despite the snow and wind. Kiefan took a deep breath, settled on a brief story, and trotted back. Gregor stood by the broken rim of the snowbank, waiting. "Are you well?"

Kiefan nodded. "Only a bruise, on you?" It was darkening on Gregor's temple. "That was well gotten. No more telling me your Blessing doesn't speak — no," he said, stopping Gregor's objections with a raised finger. "You stood against an elder Elect and lived to tell. If any question your valor, I'll correct them."

Gregor's voice lowered. "Did you kill her? Why'd she attack you?"

"There's much Elect aren't to speak of." He'd said this before, and he got a nod. "The matter's settled. Don't speak of it. Can I rely on you?"

"M'lord." Gregor stood a little straighter, a little taller.

"Good. On to the next problem." Kiefan leaned over the edge of the cottage-sized boulder and looked down on his horses and men below.

Kiefan collected all their kir and made a clearer beacon of himself; in time, they found their way around and up to the road. The horses were bruised, two favored a hoof, and Sir Waldemar had broken ribs for having been pinned under a horse in the snow.

The afternoon grew dark, through the blanket of cloud and the gusting snow. Slower, now, but not letting up yet. It might well go all night.

"Could clear a space, string up bedrolls for tarps," Sir Eburhart said, sketching out the shelter up against the fallen maple tree. "A bad night, but not so bad as some."

Calls in the distance caught their ear, and they all shouted back. From the storm came, at a trot, the rearguard garrison knights and two of the Rangers. "I knew it was m'lord!" one of the knights declared. "That'll cost you a hot dinner at the Two Lanterns, when we're home." He cuffed the hawk-eyed ranger with a grin.

It settled Kiefan, too. "Two miles to Krachzen," he said. "Waldemar, on your horse. You'll carry the kir-lamp."

They walked it, though the snow was inches past their knees. The green lamplight turned the snow fey, and its whorls seemed to beckon. Kiefan's mind turned to the stories Housemistress Wenda had told him at bed-time, if he begged hard enough — the dark stories of the Winter Wood, its kobolds, lamia, and the rogue elect who preyed on lost sheep.

No terrors in those, anymore. Though he'd not faced kobolds yet.

He looked up into the pelting snow and whispered. "Shepherd, lead your lambs back to hearth."

Wenda had always sung that lullaby after the stories, to help him sleep. Not that it had, but he'd pretended well enough.

Krachzen was only half a dozen lumps in the snow, but there were five horses sheltered between the cottages. Pounding on the doors roused the few men, and it was a humble peasant hearth the Shepherd put Kiefan at but he'd not complain. Warm water to drink, some more bread and ham from the saddlebags, and glowing coals to set his cold, wet feet close to. The chickens, he had little experience with. One stole a good chunk of bread before he got wise to them.

Smoky. Dark. Faces rose from the shadows only in passing near the fire. Kiefan couldn't say how many of the glinting pairs of eyes were children and how many sheep-dogs. One was a girl, though, with a long braid. That gave him pause.

Kate had grown up in a cottage thus. She'd left it for the Order, for Elect Parselev. And when she'd fallen pregnant —

No. She faced no danger of returning here. Not now. Saint Qadeem would see she and Rafe were comfortable. Kiefan shifted his feet before the ring of hearth stones, repeating that to himself. Though had she not stayed for the siege, she wouldn't be elect now. Lacking that guarantee of the saints' attention, she might've vanished, baby and all, into the north.

If Anders hadn't married her.

That settled heavy on Kiefan's shoulders. There might be no mending all he'd broken, now that Anders was gone.

Still, he must try.

Bundled in bedrolls, he and his men slept on a packed earth floor, safe from the hollow wail of the Winter Wood.

CHAPTER 12

Kiefan hadn't seen Sir Eburhart since the blizzard; trotting across the broad gate-yard, he caught the captain's eye with a wave. Eburhart grinned and boomed out a welcome. "Sleeping warm enough, m'lord? I heard the Red Hunter's horn out there, I'll swear it till my grave."

The Red Hunter's prey felt a chill they couldn't drive off, it was said. "Not so warm as you, if you've made amends with those Caer ladies."

That got an enormous laugh, and the guards on gate duty joined in. Eburhart was captain of the watch, for the day. "No, no, I'm not fool enough to face them without a squad at my back." He waved a hand toward the barracks, where archery targets were set up. The Crown's Blades were stringing longbows and paying no mind to the guards at the gate. With them were some of the Wache's ladies, those who hunted with their menfolk. And — yes, Ciara was there, in ordinary green and brown woolens. The duchesses too.

Just as Kiefan had watched for.

"They're fine archers," he said, as an allowance. "I've hunted with them."

"I'd not doubt it," Eburhart agreed. "They hit those targets well. Perhaps they'll teach m'lady and the fräulein a secret or two — but not their stubbornness, for m'lord's sake."

He said that as Haralda raised her bow and tested its draw. One of the Blade captains adjusted her stance a touch.

"Surely the fräulein's as good a daughter as any could wish for."

Eburhart twitched one shoulder. "She's followed their ice queen about like a duckling. Every archery session, the fräulein's running out with her bow. M'lord's lenient with her, and she's a fine girl, mind," he was careful to make that clear, "but my sister went astray, at her age."

"Ice queen, truly, that might be harsh. Any ice will thaw, given a chance."

"I'd not lay money on it —"

"You wouldn't?" Kiefan turned to the captain, brows raised.

Eburhart snapped up the bait before his eyes. As did the two guards behind him; fresh sport was always welcome, to bored gate guards. "Are you suggesting to try it, m'lord?"

"Suggesting? Fail to melt the ice queen, and I march on Temitte alone in the spring." He added a thin smile.

The big man's mirth faded to grim. "Your pardon, m'lord. No light matter, as you say."

"So heavy as to need lightening. A wager on my chances to sweeten her? If you think I have any."

"Word has it you stung her fierce on Solstice night," one of the guards said. "M'lord."

"I must be sweet enough to mend that, then, and leave her warm enough to forgive that there'll be no marriage," Kiefan said. "I'm good for whatever you lay, sir."

Eburhart thought a moment, and named a fair amount of silver. Likely more than he could pay when he lost.

"Raise that in a pot, and I'm good for it," Kiefan told him and his grinning guardsmen. He started toward the archers, turning to point back at them. "Schutze will hold the coin till we settle."

"It'll make only a humble funeral for you," Eburhart called after him, adding a single laugh.

True enough. Kiefan's coming drew eyes, and a half-dozen Blades stepped out into a line. He spread his arms, hands empty. Still, they tightened their line as he neared, hands shifting to the swords at their hips. Ready.

"I would make amends," Kiefan announced in Arceal. "Caercoed, I spoke in anger and I would make amends. It was a pleasant evening, until brandy and talk of war turned my mind to darker things."

Behind the line of Blades, Ciara stood with her strung bow tucked under one arm, checking the fletching on a pair of arrows. Beside her, Haralda leaned close and whispered something. She looked up at the girl and shook her head, whispered back.

He went on, not doubting she could hear him. "It's bad luck to see Solstice moonrise without a kiss. Worse to anger Mother Love at the start of her season — and as any man I've angered the Mother enough."

And the Mother needled him still, with thoughts of Kate and whether she'd read his letter.

No hint of understanding, in these Blades' faces; none knew Arceal. Ciara graced him with a cool and level gaze. Haralda looked from one to the other, starting to turn pale from holding her breath. The Crown gave a command, and the two Blades before Kiefan stepped aside. He went slow, cautious, and needed no play-acting for it. One sword against a dozen, and archers at arm's length.

Saint Woden believed he had a talent for negotiating; this would be a true test.

Ciara put a hand on her bow, level with her chin. Stood her ground as he drew close, closer than was polite. She tipped her eyes up to keep their gazes matched. Silent.

Still his move, then. "Caught in that blizzard, I had a taste of what ill luck might cost me in the spring. It's a poor leader who shirks his duty to his men. In luck as well as skill. Though I must confess," he said, lowering his voice as he leaned closer still, "it was the kiss I thought of most."

He felt her breath, hovered close enough to kiss her, if — but she was cool-blooded, indeed. Hardly a pique from his anticipation.

"Little can mend the ill luck you dealt yourself," she said simply, as if he were at arm's length.

"You'd keep what was dealt you?"

"A kiss in an archery range won't mend it."

Kiefan eased back. "Perhaps an evening re-made? Dinner, musicians, a dance. Waiting for moonrise on the rooftop. An evening as it ought to have played out."

"Mayhaps. Needs must think on whether I'll let such as you kiss me." Ciara took up her bow and returned one of her two arrows to the quiver at her hip. "Shall send word." She turned toward the target, fitting the arrow to the string.

Haralda, her suspense melted into heartbreak by the scene, needed a nudge to stand aside when the Crown raised her bow. Ciara drew the arrow back to her cheek, sighting the target.

Kiefan leaned close to her ear. "Soon?"

She missed the target entirely. When she shot him a glare, he smiled and retreated.

He caught Haralda's tear-rimmed eyes as he turned away and pressed his mouth in a firm line. Best to break her heart cleanly. It would heal faster.

———————✕———————

Kiefan's anticipation piqued the moment Haralda appeared with the steaming soup tureen. Her scattered anguish, so plain as she served the replacement Solstice dinner, had steeled into resolve. That she'd ordered pages away to take over serving had been unsubtle, but she'd been content to throw pained looks and bite her lip.

Haralda's glare was fixed on Ciara's back; no doubt who her target was. Kiefan slipped from his chair and set his face cold and hard. Her focus slipped into confusion as he put a hand on the tureen to stop her, well short of the table.

"This stops. Now."

Her blue eyes flooded. Her face flushed scarlet. Haralda dropped the entire tureen and fled.

Mother Love forgive him.

Kiefan returned to his seat, boots splattered, Ciara tracking him with startled confusion. He said nothing and returned to the smoked sausages and turnips the soup had been meant to accompany.

They'd managed a little conversation, but it had lapsed and stayed down despite the soup. Not much was said until they'd finished and climbed the stairs to the keep's roof. Then Ciara brought it up.

"What befell the soup?" She crossed from the stair to the crenelated wall, to look out on the frozen lake.

Kiefan followed, pulling his cloak snug about him with one hand; one of their guards moved to shut the trapdoor. She'd brought two Blades and he two Guard. None spoke any Arceal, but his men could be counted on to gossip.

He joined her at the gap between two merlons. "She meant to spill the soup on you," he answered.

"Meant to?" Ciara glanced up at him, brows perked. He nodded. "'Twas a rumor you read minds," Ciara said.

"Rumors have their uses."

"A shame. You might've told me what I'm thinking now."

Kiefan half smiled. He leaned against the merlon, facing her across the crenel. Bits of impatience, he saw, a little shivering, and the occasional anxious twitch. "You're thinking it's a fit night for the Bitter Moon. That as it's but three days old, the Shepherd won't rise until near dawn and that's a long, cold wait."

Cold indeed. Breath hung in the air and drifted away as tiny clouds, rather than vanishing.

"Mayhaps 'tis to see how you offer to warm me." Ciara leaned against her merlon likewise, arms crossed under her green cloak.

"Perhaps you don't plan to wait so long for your kiss."

She wasn't eager for it, his Blessing cautioned. "'Tis been a pleasant evening, sir, but not so pleasant I wish to linger under frostbitten stars."

Overhead, the sky was clear. Six of the Flock moons wandered among the stars, grazing. Dinner had been... no, Ciara was right. Not that pleasant. Two days' wait for her to agree to this, a day's preparations, and he'd found his interest worn away by rumination. Her wandering focus and weak smiles told him she felt much the same.

"A change of luck and we'll return to the hearth, then?" Kiefan asked. Meaning to seem casual, he leaned away from the cold stone.

Ciara tipped her head. "In truth, you're not so superstitious."

She did play the game well. He stepped closer, dropping his voice, and told her two bits of truth. "I'm not. But Síochana did give me a taste of Caer women and — it's hard to forget."

Fear, his anticipation whispered. A touch of knowing she must do this. Kiefan's resolve wavered a heartbeat, then accepted it; let her break first, slap him, storm away, if she hadn't the courage. He leaned down, caught her lips as she looked up, kissed her. Simple, lingering to see if she'd return it.

Her palm pressed against his chest. Kiefan leaned back and gave her a heartbeat — swooped in again and paused just short. Nose alongside hers, inhaling her breath, waiting for a slap. Nothing. Fear? He stole a second little kiss, though it pinched at his pride that she might fear him.

"Suffer no more than you wish," he whispered.

Anger sparked in her eyes. "If you think to play —"

Kiefan put his finger to her lips. Soft lips. "Teleri told me."

Her brow crinkled for a moment. "And you kiss me?"

That struck him odd. "Feigning a seduction would be tricky without kisses."

Still, her hand returned to his chest and pushed him back. "Did agree to feign, then?"

Teleri hadn't confessed to her part, clearly. "Caer knights in trade for kisses, a little bruised pride — hardly a chore."

"Kisses and what more?" She had her resolve well in hand when she met his eyes.

"What more do you wish?"

Ciara looked out at the lake. Flock-light washed her face pearly white, but sank her dark hair into the stone's shadow. Easy enough to kiss. That was true.

"Shall need a few more meetings," she said, voice still low. "Am cooped in the barracks and needs must escape. The Two Lanterns, mayhaps? And something for my Blades — sparring does lose its shine, two moons on."

Kiefan was on her track by the time she finished. "Larger than sparring, then, your Blades, my Guard, the garrison — and the Tadhlon Guard. Perhaps a game of war?"

Her brows rose. "A game of war. 'Twould be well. And 'tis snow a-plenty for fortification. Ammunition." She looked to their minders, who watched with alert calm. Not catching a word of it. "Meeting, to lay the parameters, will play well in the game."

He nodded. "And a night at the Two Lanterns, if you wish."

"A night?" she echoed, voice fading with her thoughts. "Needs must be a night, true."

"Your oíche-te." It was a slippery word to say.

"You did agree to that? A bruised pride?" Ciara's eyes narrowed, checking him for a reaction.

He twitched one shoulder. "I'll spin a tale of my own from it. Take no offense, if it reaches your ears. We only do what we must here."

Regret, his anticipation saw. "Suffer no more than you wish." She returned his words to him.

Did she think herself to be suffered? Kiefan caught her chin gently in his hand, and kissed her deep. Felt her tense, but then return it — yes, a fierce tongue on the attack, a nip at his lip as she retreated. Kiefan drew a deep breath, Sío's ghost touching him once more. Ghosts, ashes, and ice were all he had left in his heart now that she and Kate were lost to him.

A dalliance with a pretty, if razor-edged, queen was a small thing to ask. Might make the best of it, even.

"There's nothing to suffer," he told her.

Ciara put her hand on his, at her chin, and Kiefan caught a moment's vulnerability. "Another place, another time, mayhaps we…" She pressed her lips shut, then took his hand from her and it was back to the game.

<hr/>

WODENBERG

I was explaining to the armor-maker's son that this was why Arbor Street whores were required to be examined by physicians four times a year when I heard the shouting outside my shop. My head turned; it was coming from the wrong direction.

Faintly, through my back door, "Elect!"

"Come." I spared my patient a beckon and led him through my curtains past my surgery table, then through my small kitchen. Two weeks since Solstice, and there'd been little more than a few small burns and fevers to tend. Those patients had scuttled in and out quick as they could, too, as if they didn't want to be seen.

The armorer's son didn't want to be seen either, but his rash was nasty enough to change his mind.

I opened my back door to find a man on the three steps that led down to my patch of rear yard, carrying a woman in his arms. All the houses backed onto a stripe of snow-covered grass, which was patched with herb gardens, chicken coops, and dotted with outhouses. I recognized him; Adalev Trüberde and his wife Linde. They'd come to my housewarming party with their baby boy.

"Elect, please!" Hoarse, now, Adalev held her up and she lolled. Eyes bleary with pain. She reached, feebly. On her trailing skirt, pinned under her legs, I saw the blood.

"Help them!" I stepped out of the way, pulling the door open. My patient shook off his shocked surprise and reached to help pull Linde in. "The surgery table." I went to draw the curtain aside for them.

Between Adalev and the armorer's son, the bleeding woman reached my table in a few heartbeats. They lay her on it as I lit two lamps and moved my kettle to the small fire on the surgery's side of my chimney.

"I came home and found her on the floor," Adalev told me. "She was well this morning, well and strong."

It was just after noon now. "Come back tomorrow," I said to the armorer's son, and he retreated out the front door. "You don't know how long she's been bleeding?" I asked Adalev.

"No." He had her hand in both of his, despite the bloodstains. Her head turned toward him, in a daze. "Linde, love, the Elect will mend you."

"The baby…"

"And the baby." He kissed her hand, fervently.

I pursed my mouth and took a slow breath. Linde's pattern told me the story. I put my hand on her belly and stopped the bleeding with a little twist of a charm. "You have a baby already?"

"Yes, we have a son. A good, strong boy," he said.

"Go and see that he's well. And bring her a clean dress."

Adalev blinked, confused, and then horror dawned across his face. "I didn't think to check — right away, yes, I'll be back in a heartbeat, love." He kissed her forehead.

Linde turned her head as he rushed out. My kitchen door banged behind him. I tugged at her skirts, working them upward. Her voice was thin and tired from having bled so much. "The baby's gone."

I nodded. "I'm sorry. And it must come out. Sleep a little." I touched her cheek and a knockout charm sent her beyond pain.

A bit still lived, in truth; a patch of the afterbirth was still attached to her womb. The rest had come loose and was a dead, blank mass in the midst of her swirling kir-pattern. I poured my kir into her hips, loosening her muscle and bone to match that of a woman in labor. Linde's flesh struggled to obey; it wasn't ready for that, but it opened as best it could. I reached inside her with a narrow kir blade and gently, carefully, scraped it across her womb.

Anything left behind would rot.

It came out in a ragged mass, trailing clots. I dumped it into the basin below the blood groove's drain. Then I spun a cleansing charm over her and soothed all back into place. Her womb tried to make a scar where the child had died, but I untangled that before it could settle. Then I straightened out her skirts, fetched cups and my tea-box, and poured hot water over mint to steep. Linde's easy breathing quickened as she began to wake.

Adalev charged back in with the baby, Gerhart, in one arm and a bundled yellow dress in the other. Calling voices trailed him, but came no closer than my kitchen door. "Linde? Linde, love, I'm here. Ger's safe."

Linde looked toward his voice, and her eyelids fluttered. He put down the clean dress and took her hand in his; her son, six months old and bright-eyed, stuck his fingers in his mouth and muttered around them. She tried to sit up, but was too wobbly for that. Her husband put his arm under her shoulders and helped.

"Easy," I said, but she leaned on him and he looked sturdy enough for it. I passed Linde a cup of tea. She took it in both hands, with care.

"Thank you, Elect Kate, I didn't know —" Adalev said.

"The baby was already gone." I cut him off. His face fell. I met Linde's tired, but determined, gaze. "I saw to it that you're cleansed and whole, and I saw no reason there won't be more lambs in your future. You need to rest, now. My mother was a midwife, and she would stay with the mother the first day or two, see that all was settled. So if I may, I would do as much for you."

Ger was already reaching for his mother's teacup and she was too tired to dodge him. Adalev retreated a step and Linde leaned on her arm as she drank. "Hush," he said when Ger objected. Adalev turned sheepish for a moment. "If you think it best, Elect, but if I may — my mother might come up and stay with us —"

"Lev," his wife murmured, voice turning even wearier.

"You must finish that bolt, or we'll never afford this." He leaned close to mutter that, but I still heard it. They were weavers, they'd said when they introduced themselves, or she was at least. A guild member, which was quite respectable.

But they need not worry. "You've served the saints, and you'll continue to," I told him, more than her. "That is payment enough. Qadeem puts no price on a life."

Linde's eyes teared up, at that. She reached for my hand, and I let her hug me as best she could. "Thank you, Elect. You've no idea…"

"Kate," I said including Adalev in that with a smile. "You can call me Kate." Once Linde had settled her weary head on my shoulder, she had to pry herself off. Then Adalev gave me a quick squeeze too. Anxious, perhaps, but the gratitude dampening his eyes was sweet.

"I'm so sorry," he said.

It seemed odd. "Why?"

"That you — well, what they say. Your husband was killed at the castle. And it's been so melancholy to see you here, alone as you are. With your own little boy, aren't you? The…" He didn't finish, but surely he meant to say "prince."

My heart quivered. "Yes, my son. Rafe. He's a little younger than Gerhart."

Adalev smiled, like the sun breaking through clouds. "A playmate! Finally, love, a child Ger's age. We were first back after the siege, and all the rest are still in Prohzgrad. It breaks my heart, how quiet the streets are now. I grew up just three blocks over." He pointed and kept rattling on for some time about the neighborhood. Linde smiled to herself as she finished her tea. "I can't believe — oh."

He paused when she patted his arm. "I think I can get up now, love."

"Here." I put out my hands to take Ger from him. I heard my front door opened and voices in my antechamber worrying about Linde. "Help her change out of that dress. I'll reassure the neighbors. And maybe sir would care to meet my little boy? Share his toys?"

Ger was entranced by trying to poke his fingers into my braid, which I'd wrapped around my head. Adalev helped Linde off the surgery table, holding her so close and gentle in her trembling weakness that I smiled in spite of myself.

Finally, I'd done something right. Something that mattered.

———————⚔———————

KNAPPTAL

At last, a week flew by. He broached the idea of a wargame to Margrave Schutze, brought it to the garrison and the Rangers, and then Kiefan met Ciara at the Two Lanterns for several pumpkin ales, a formal challenge and acceptance, and a few line dances.

One kiss, at the end of a dance. Ciara nuzzled his cheek, breathed against him, and then backed away with a teasing smile. All saw it, and the gossip mill ground it up eagerly.

Next day, they met in the Caer barracks' briefing-room: the garrison captains, the Tadhlon Guard captains, Blade officers, elect, the duchesses, Margrave Schutze, Captain Aleks, Kiefan and Ciara. Rules were laid down, translated every which way, and written as well. No blades were to be on the field, not even eating knives. The weapons were to be snow, not ice, and dagger-length pine boughs with their needles still on. A hit to the head was a "kill," and the dead were to remove themselves as quick as possible.

Kiefan and Ciara would serve as targets to capture. The Tadhlon camp had already put a week into its snow fortifications and would be attacked by the garrison and Rangers. After some wrangling, they agreed to begin at noon, in three days' time.

Each duchess had command of a sector of the camp and had much to discuss with the various captains. Schutze, Sir Eburhart, and Klippe the Ranger lieutenant likewise needed to plan with their officers and took their leave of the crowded room once all was agreed upon and recorded by the craft-handed secretary.

Kiefan stood just outside, listening to Schutze's strategy, and saw Ciara leave on her own. Schutze was a veteran and needed no help; Kiefan sidled away as sketches started to be drawn on scrap paper. Sir Eburhart caught the movement and glanced, then took a breath to question.

Kiefan put a finger to his lips, tipped his head toward Ciara walking down the hall.

Eburhart grinned and held his peace. Kiefan went.

Ciara turned a corner and climbed a stair. He followed; she heard his feet and turned, partway. Hesitated a moment.

"Might we speak in private?" he asked. "On how our game will play out?"

She smiled. "Come, then."

Up the stairs and down a short hall; she had the captain-general's room, the largest in the barracks. A small table and two chairs before the hearth were stacked with loose papers and a few ledgers. Quills and ink pots waited, neatly arranged. Trunks stood against one wall with clothes laid to air out on their tops. And the curtained bed filled much of the space.

Ciara went to one trunk, lifted its lid and fished out a glass bottle of clear liquid. Anxious, his Blessing noted, drawing his eye to her small hesitations, the sharp movements. "I've no tea to offer," she said, to apologize. "Your apple brandy is good, as 'tis the ale. Your beer's rather bitter."

"Only the winter stout," he said as she crossed to the writing-table. "If I trouble you, only say the word. Your consort made it clear she'll cut my throat if you wish it."

He knew it was a poor jest, but Ciara breathed a laugh. "'Tis only men who are consorts." She found two small glasses and pulled the stopper on the bottle. "I have no consort — women are merely beloved."

Kiefan approached slowly, hands behind his back, as she poured. "No consort? Ever?"

Sadness, there. Ciara held out one glass to him. "Nearly, once. Lorcan. A fellow archer, when I served my stint in the army." Kiefan took the drink, and she considered the one in her other hand. "Arcea killed him, in a — skirmish. Scouting parties, a chance meeting below Eryr Pass. A little thing, hardly enough to report." She sighed and threw the drink down. "Near eight years ago, now. Teleri meant to comfort me at first. But then stayed."

"On little things our lives turn." Kiefan said it as he thought it. Kate's story of the dead piglet. Síochana's quick choice to ride with the Crowns to Wodenberg. He'd never have met either otherwise, and never would've questioned that duty came before love. Never resented the yoke he'd been born to wear. He swallowed the alcohol, took the burn in his throat with a deep breath.

"'Tis revenge you wish, in Suevia," Ciara said, pouring a refill for them both. "Revenge for your slain kin. Honest enough. But what more? Did come here saddled with more."

He set his teeth on his lower lip, weighing his reply. "I must strike back, must — face enough enemies to let my rage slip its leash. Must be the Shepherd's culling knife, for a time. For my sister. For Síochana. For — others as well."

"His culling knife may turn in your hand. Near claimed you in your own hall, I did hear. 'Twas the rage of a broken heart, clear enough."

Tannait had seen it all, then. "Twice broken, in a dozen heartbeats. And when the Mother and Father see fit to deal their justice to me, it will be welcome." He watched the low fire in the hearth-grate as he said it, then took a sip from his glass. Better the Mother's wrath than Kate's.

Ciara, beside him, looked up from the fire. "Do all have our crimes gnawing at our guts, so long as we leash them close by our side. 'Tis best to let them slip. Confess that we've —"

She didn't finish and took a drink instead. Kiefan said, "Blood on our hands."

"Poison in our hearts." Her voice fell to a murmur. "That we stood by our dead sister and felt only anger. No tears, no anguish for her, only anger for her foolishness, her eternal headstrong, bright-eyed idiocy —" Ciara's sharpening tone ended in a wince, and she hissed a breath between her teeth. "And leaving me such a ruin, surrounded, far from home — no, not a tear. Never. 'Tis a blessing she's gone." She threw down her drink and glared at the fire.

It explained the anger his anticipation had caught when everyone spoke of mourning in Vorspitz. She'd trusted him with that, so he must offer as much. "I'll shed no tears for the man I ran through," Kiefan said. "He knew I love — her — and paid it no mind, thinking — that he could steal her away and laugh? I ran him through and never felt such satisfaction."

And felt it again, in dim echo. It ebbed as he went on. "But I owed him much, in truth. She loved him, and I took him from her. When I face her —"

Kiefan shook his head and looked down at the glass. Drained it.

"'Tis penance for both of us." He felt her fingers on his Blessing ridges, along the cuticle where they broke from his scalp. "I must become my sister. You must lose something dear, to know her pain. You'll be captured, then, in the snow-battle and submit to a true oíche-te? Tradition did loose its teeth with the years, but 'twill be renewed with you."

Her touch was gentle. Kiefan met her green eyes. "You think you can get your teeth in me with this?"

Ciara only dipped her chin, and her certainty pinched his resolve with a bit of fear. The memory of fields strewn with dead men steeled him, though. He nodded in return. Then he asked, quietly, "I'm to be your penance — for your archer so disappointed you that you foreswore all men?"

Her head tilted, considering. "I've never thought poorly of him. 'Twas no fault of his, in truth."

Kiefan risked half a smile. "The penance is in suffering an ignorant southlander, then?" She chuckled at that, so he went on. "Síochana tutored me — and meant to teach more —"

"Shall serve you well, someday." Ciara smiled. "Go, and we shall meet on the field of battle."

CHAPTER 13

"The Alemanni do come!" Teleri stood on the ledge, her back to the ramparts, facing the Tadhlon knights. "They think 'tis a game of war with shy girls and spineless boys!"

They surged up with an angry yell, raising their pine switches and home-made caithdo racquets. Two moons could not pass without Caer forming caithdo teams and gaming in whatever meadow was at hand, and Tadhlon was well equipped for that. They'd lashed together branches into Y-shapes and woven baskets of bark strips betwixt the arms — and from all any knew, the Alemanni had nothing of the like. Any child in Caercoed could sling a snowball with a caithdo racquet.

"'Tis a wonder we've stood against Arcea without them, they think!"

She grinned when they roared louder. Teleri looked over her shoulder at the close-packed pines. 'Twas half a mile to the village where the road did end, and they'd done a fine job creeping thus far. One company did march toward Tadhlon's snow-fort openly, but 'twas their Rangers in the wood to beware.

"You've your orders and your duchesses — shall lure these southlanders in and show them battlements! Their king will charge in for certain, and shall be captured for our Crown!"

Teleri yielded the ledge to Eithne Croícruach, Tadhlon's captain-general, as they cheered. Tel crossed through the fortifications to the command pavilion in the center. Stacks of snowballs waited around its canvas walls, and Crown's Blades stood at ready with their pine switches. No mail armor today, only the quilted blue uniforms for warmth. Ciara paced around the map table, eying the enemy tokens placed around their sketched battlements.

She wore a Blades uniform as well, with her royal green sash belt, her braid bunned atop her head. A caithdo racquet in one hand, to fidget with. Captain Fionn stood with her, his arms crossed.

"Near noon," Ciara said when Teleri ducked under the low door-flap. "Needs must begin, or I'll worry this to pieces." She waved the racquet.

"Tadhlon's not even a defensive wing, but 'tis a fine bit of engineering," Tel told her. "They're eager to plaster some faces."

Fionn grinned, but Ciara only circled, tapping the snow with the racquet's head. "Needs must do this, Tel, or the duchesses…"

She left that hanging, with a grimace. Teleri stepped closer, leaned on one hand on the table beside Ciara, and lowered her voice. "Gentle it, then. Even Granny Mor did not put the Henffyrdd boy to such an ancient oíche-te. Clear the pavilion, make his draught less bitter."

But Ciara's mouth was set in resolve. "They wish a Crown of old, and they shall have her."

A yell, and snowballs pounded the canvas wall. Teleri put Ciara behind her back — Fionn did the same — and when a Ranger burst in Tel nearly dropped him with a kir-blade. He threw a pine switch, though, and she knocked it away. Caught his wrist as he brought up a second, twisted him around and onto the snow face-first. Cuffed him across the head for a "kill," and leaped up as a second Ranger stumbled in and fell, peppered by snowballs.

Five of them, a full hand, and they'd taken four Blades. Outside, the roar on the south battlements meant it had begun at last. Teleri did feel a smile spread as her pulse quickened. Too long without battle, far too long. She caught Ciara by the waist and kissed her.

"Shall bring you your prize," she promised. "If it cost me all, shall bring him."

Ciara kissed her back. "Whatever passes, you are my beloved. Never doubt."

"Never." Teleri let her go and snatched a pair of snowballs as she trotted for the west side. Kiefan might think they hadn't noted the squads creeping toward that wall. They'd be the ones surprised.

———————————⚔———————————

The snow fort boasted as sheer a wall as Castle Kaltkern's, six feet tall if you stood in the ditch before it, and caked with ice. Battering it had cost five men already. Merely getting to the wall was a trial; the Caer on the battlements had Woden's own arm for throwing snowballs. Kiefan had caught one on the shoulder and felt it even through his wool layers.

Shields were proving valuable, whether wooden or kir. Kiefan waved his three Guard and Gregor closer and they lapped their shields. "With me!" he shouted, and a dozen more knights formed up. Covering fire was readied. With a yell, they charged.

Balls thumped on the shields, but only a few. They waited for openings to take their shots, cleverly. The rim of the ditch was nearly invisible, and tripping had left many men open to strikes from above. Kiefan gauged it well and landed on his feet. Turned his shield edge-on and kept up the charge; rammed the wood through ice and snow till it stuck. Then yanked his arm from the traces and crouched in its shadow.

Sir Garrick fell with snow in his knight's crest. He leaped up, snarling. "I'll not be —!" The second took him square in the face, and blood gushed from his nose.

"Die with dignity," Kiefan told him. "And get clear."

On either side, the squads who'd made the run chopped at the snow fort with shields, their companions protecting them as best they could. Kiefan pulled his shield from the wall and did the same, crouching so Gregor could hold his kir-shield overhead. It was a good sign that he could spin one, even a sloppy, wasteful one, so young. Kir burned through Kiefan's muscle and the hole deepened fast. The shouting overhead shifted, sounded more like rapid-fire orders.

There was a second layer of ice in the middle, damn them. Kiefan let his strength flow and broke through it. Sweat on his brow. Beside him, Sir Waldemar widened the hole and scooped loose snow away. Snowballs thumped on the shields protecting them, faster and harder.

Kiefan glimpsed light through the wall, and shoved his shield's rim through into air. Dragged away snow as he pulled back, and Waldemar yanked him aside. A snowball shot through the hole, hard enough to break any nose.

"Push me!" Gregor shoved his kir-shield into the hole and braced both arms against it. Kiefan stood, passed his own shield to Waldemar, and grabbed his squire by the waist. Rammed him through, widening the hole.

Overhead, a suspicious chopping sound. The Caer shouts gained a rhythm. Snow began to crinkle, moving under pressure — and began to fall out of the wall as the burrowing sapped its strength.

Toppling the whole — "Through!" Kiefan yelled. "Go!"

Waldemar blinked, but then plunged through the hole. The mouth gaped wider. Kiefan shoved his shield before him and crawled through as the avalanche fell from above and the wall crumbled around the hole. A couple Caer women tumbled past, yelling. Snow buried his legs; he kicked and hauled himself from under its weight. Free, he rolled with the shield over his head. Took a hit right off, when he came up low. Crashed into someone and slung them down on reflex. A ball hit his side as he spun around with his pine switch in hand; he laid into the enemy at Blessing speed, his anticipation keeping him ahead of them.

Snowballs struck the Caer down, too, thrown through the half-collapsed wall. All those in the ditch were lost, by the game's rules, but they'd opened the battlements. Kiefan's reinforcements swarmed up from the trees with a roar.

The Caer fell back, orderly, to either side. Kiefan threw up his shield when one slung a snowball with a Y-shaped stick. It thwacked hard; that was it, then. Must capture one of those.

Inside the battlements, ten feet or so of open field and then a second, four-foot wall. Stacks of snowballs everywhere. In a week and a half, they'd done all this. Kiefan ducked another missile. He swooped to one stack and returned fire.

The first armsmen over the broken wall rallied to him with a yell. "Wodenberg!"

"Ware the flanks!" He pointed them to either side, where the Caer re-grouped on the intact ledges. They lapped their shields into walls —

With a blood-curdling scream, the Caer artillery struck from behind the second wall. The ball that hit the back of Kiefan's shoulder nearly knocked him down. On wooden shields, it sounded like thunder. Kiefan added his shield to the phalanx and hunkered down.

"Fucking wildcats!" The man beside him panted from his running.

Ciara's royal standard, the crowned tree, stood proud inside the wall, though. Victory was close. Let them work, if they wished to capture him for Ciara. Kiefan took a deep breath. "Over the wall!" He surged up into the barrage. "Over the wall!"

The men charged with him, taking up the cry. Kiefan pulled ahead of the line, throwing the snowball in his free hand, and —

His foot plunged through the thin crust of snow, the canvas underneath, into a ditch. Face-first, he threw out his hands and pushed with all his kir. A shield hit his back and a man fell past, then another. Kiefan threw an arm and a leg over the narrow walkway between two ditches and hauled himself up; pulling his kir back, he spun it in a shield to ward off snowballs. Tossed his wooden one away. Cheating or not, his anger was straining at its leash and that four-foot wall wasn't stopping him.

Some armsmen had skidded to a stop at the edge of the hidden ditches. They held together in a phalanx, back to back under a barrage from all sides.

"With me!" Kiefan shouted, and their heads turned. Eyes focused, confusion falling away. "Over —"

A kir-rope lashed out and whip-cracked on Kiefan's shield, shattering it into green sparks; Teleri drew it back and shouted a new order. Kiefan pulled kir and it shot to him from either side to raise a new shield. He charged, eyes fixed on her, men at his back.

"Over the wall!"

She fell back, vanishing for a moment before he leaped up, boosted by kir, to the crest of the wall. His boots bit into the thin rim, but it held. The nearest Caer fell off her ledge with a surprised shout. Her sister swung at his chest with her Y-stick; he caught it, twisted it from her grip, and flung it away in an eye-blink.

Kir looped around his neck and yanked. He fell, tearing at the rope, and lashed back. In the same moment a strong pull yanked at his kir. Kiefan clenched, pulled back. A stick-slung snowball struck his ear, wobbling him a moment, and he lost more kir when his grip faltered. Snowballs pummeled him, and the rope dragged him to his knees.

Not choking, but relentless. He sat on his heels, pulling deep breaths. Hands open. By the rules, he was dead. The rope at his neck slid away, accepting his surrender. Got too far ahead of his men, and now they'd fought to the wall only to see him defeated. He shook his head as his father's lecture on controlling battle-rage echoed in his snow-filled ear.

But it played well in the game.

Fresh kir-ropes snared each wrist, pulled his arms further apart, and the sudden, strong pull through them made Kiefan snatch his kir close. They threw him down, on his back, and hands tugged at his tabard. Feet still free, he twisted under their weight, against the strength of the kir-ropes, and heaved up again. Tannait, holding one rope, intoned in Caer. Teleri, on the other side. Both fought him for his kir.

The Caer knights got his belt unbuckled, yanked his crested tabard off and held it up with a triumphant howl.

"Are claimed for oíche-te." Tannait finally switched to Arceal. "Yield, or be overcome."

Teleri strode close, shoving him onto his back with a second kir-rope. "'Tis the role you did choose," she told him, kneeling. At the wall, a Caer officer held up his tabard to prove they'd won. "Give over your kir and 'twill be done all the sooner."

She'd given her word he'd walk from this. Kiefan let it go. "You did this for Ceelin's oíche-te?"

Her mouth twitched to one side. "Ciara does invoke the old ways. Abide it, and suffer only bruised pride."

Bruised pride. Whatever she required, he could survive it. They thought him one of their meek kitchen-boys, or some brutish southlander...?

He meant to stand, but the two elect dragged him by the kir-ropes into the pavilion. The open flaps dropped shut behind him, and his eyes saw little at first in the dimness. On his knees, he waited for his eyes to adjust. Logs burned in two braziers, tinting the air with smoke, and most of the faces they lit were familiar. Duchess Faola, poker-faced, and the twins, Míde and Una — their smirks needed little translating. The Tadhlon Guard's captain-general, Cróicruach, who'd been Margrave Leix's right hand, and three of her senior captains. The two Crown's Blades captains who reported to Teleri; the man's name was Fionn and the woman's... Aisling? Their physician, too, an older woman with bemused eyes. The dark uniforms blended well into the shadows.

All watched him, save one. Fionn stood at casual attention, studying a log burning in one brazier.

That was what unsettled Kiefan's stomach.

Ciara stepped from behind her captains, folding her arms, and eyed him. Pale and chilly as the snow outside, despite the firelight and her warm, dark braid knotted atop her head. She gave a curt command.

Captain Aisling drew a dagger as she moved to obey; Kiefan threw himself back, against the ropes, and pulled for kir. None came. They'd all been drained, save for the two elect who held his leashes. They planted their feet against his struggles, and Tannait spun up a little ring of lightning on one finger. Flicked it at him and the jolt turned him to jelly in their grip. The captain caught him by the collar and slashed open the ties on his quilted gambeson. Kiefan thrashed, willing his legs to kick, but had little strength for it. Pushing his gambeson open, she cut his woolen cote underneath from neck to hem.

They all watched, impassive. The captain paused to trace the dagger's tip across his breast-bone ridge, her brow crinkled in curiosity. Someone tossed out a comment and she grinned, caught his braided knight's crest and tugged it. That got a few laughs. Captain Aisling slid the knife-tip under the tied lacings on his braies and lifted the waist away. She leaned, with narrowed eyes, to peek.

He resisted the urge to head-butt her, with a blade that close to his crotch.

She undid the slipknot, rather than cut it, and untied the lacing for his woolen hose, too. Stood and backed away; at a word, Teleri and Tannait dragged him across the packed snow toward a low, narrow pile of rugs. It pulled his braies down along the way and Kiefan managed to get his knees under himself to slow that. They tossed him, on his back, atop the pile and knotted the kir-ropes around two long tent-stakes. Likewise for his ankles, though with some slack. He set his feet on the ground to either side of the rugs and closed his eyes. Chilly air prickled gooseflesh across his chest, his belly, tightened his balls.

Penance. Would it please Kate to see him thus? Punished for how he'd hurt her?

Ciara recited some complex stanzas in Caer, and he looked. She handed her green sash to her handmaid, and pulled off her Blades-blue gambeson. Her snow-white shift rippled as she crossed the pavilion, and her breasts shifted underneath. When she bent to slip her braies off from over her dark hose and boots, they bumped against the light fabric.

The lilt of Caer, the flickering light, his upward view teasing him with a glimpse of pale skin under her short shift… Kiefan's pulse shifted below his waist, despite the chill. And the audience. Ciara stood above him, hands on her hips, and tilted her head to look him in the eye. Without kir for his Blessing, he saw only a calm resolve.

She threw a leg over, straddled him, and set a hand to either side of his chest. Leaned close, whispering in Arceal. "'Twas the enemy's favorites the Crowns did claim for oíche-te. Husbands, fathers, sons — willing, unwilling. Mayhaps they'd allow a bargain for their release. Mayhaps they'd keep them for a pet. A lap-dog, to trot out on his leash."

Her neckline hung loose, and he had to pull his eyes away from her shadowed breasts. "A king of Wodenberg is no lap-dog." He tugged on the tent-stakes, to gauge their strength. They were sunk deep. "You think a few ropes will leash me?" The words came easy, as they were true. Bruised pride, they'd said. They were up against that wall already.

"All the more challenge, collaring a wolf," she replied, leaning closer. Her breath smelled of brandy, and a taste of that would help.

"I bite." He reached for her mouth, nearly caught it before she flinched back.

Ciara nodded and the kir-ropes took up their slack. Pulled him to stiffly spread-eagled over the low hump of carpets. "I'll not keep you." A sneer crept in as she straightened upward. "No more than a bed-ornament. Pretty enough to fuck, and no more."

A laugh, and Míde said, "Make a gift of your ornament, dear Crown?"

Ciara ran her fingertips along Kiefan's center line, throat to chest to belly. "'Tis my toy, now," she answered as she went. "Do claim him." Her hand stroked firmly across his cock and it surged in reply.

Kiefan's fists clenched, pulling hard on the kir ropes as she wrapped her fingers snug around his shaft. The hem of her shift teased him; his hands could be under that, pushing it up to cradle her breasts and tug her down to him. Her nipple in his mouth, her pale throat for kissing, his hands gripping her ass —

The stakes weren't even budging. Ciara settled onto her knees over him, and warm flesh touched his cock. She pulled her shift up around her hips with both hands and moved against him. A hot cleft stroked across his erection, on a touch of wetness. His breath deepened, skirted close to a groan.

The sound cracked her eyes open a heartbeat, then she closed them again. He saw her knuckles clenched on handfuls of her shift, the tense set of her jaw, as she ground against his cock. Determined, not eager. A little damp in her cunny, true, but not wet. They were all watching, and she was tense as Gregor at sparring practice.

"Let me go," he whispered, and her eyes slitted open again. "Make this easier —"

Teleri leaned from behind to kiss Ciara's cheek, then nuzzled alongside as her arms circled around her Crown. A sharp glare as Ciara leaned against her, tension melting. Teleri mouthed one word. "Mine."

Her hands cupped under Ciara's breasts, kneading gently. A kiss to her ear, the corner of her jaw, soft and slow. Kiefan breathed a groan, his cock throbbing against Ciara. Teleri leaned further, kissed the corner of her mouth and she turned, kissed back. Tongues sliding — and mercy, she was slicking up now. Kiefan dragged at his bonds, begging for an inch of leverage, anything to thrust against her with.

No, he had to watch them kiss. Teleri's hands wandering over Ciara's curves. The torture of her grinding on him.

Ciara rose up, her hand sliding to clench around his cock again. She glanced down, curious as his foreskin slid back under a gentle brush of her thumb. Then she looked to one side and said a word. Someone stepped from the circled audience and touched Teleri's hand to receive a bit of kir.

The Blades' physician. Kiefan's head cleared a moment, wariness driving off the lust. The physician twined out a charm, a tight green thread, and reached down to apply it. Kiefan's breath caught when it looped around the base of his cock, his balls, and pinched tight. Very tight. Knotted itself.

No escape.

His pulse picked up and he twisted his wrists in the kir-ropes. He whispered, "Ciara, on my honor, you don't need —"

Teleri cuffed him with a bit of kir. "Dogs don't speak."

Ciara straightened higher, drawing his throbbing cock upright, and slowly impaled herself. Teleri laid her hand overtop as she sank, whispering in Caer, hushing her when a little moan worked its way through her throat.

Kiefan forgot all about the ring-charm; she was tight and wet and oh, mercy, for a free hand to touch her...

His eyes locked on where his cock disappeared behind Teleri's knuckles. The shadow of dark hair on Ciara's crotch. She sank deeper onto him, her hips twitching. Not a proper thrust, not what he wanted. Still, he ached and throbbed from watching. Ciara's head lolled back to let Teleri nip her throat. Her back arched and she took his cock to the hilt at last. Gasped a breath at that, and put her hands down behind herself. Rose up and thrust down on him.

Kiefan felt her cunny grip and let his head drop, eyes closing. She fucked him, slow as she liked, Teleri at her clit, orgasm gathering like a storm.

His strained toward bursting. The ring around his cock held it at bay, frustrating it, and the pressure rose toward pain. He picked his head up, looked again, and saw Tel's fingers framing Ciara's cunny lips around his cock as she kissed her — it exploded out of him with a savage moan. Took half his strength with it. Ciara's breath caught, her spine straightened, and she ground down hard on him. A few more hard thrusts and he felt her come, like a pulsing fist on his cock. She bucked in Teleri's arms, her head cradled against her beloved's shoulder. It passed, as storms do, in trailing bursts of sighs and shudders.

Kiefan's head dropped against the rugs again, his limbs loosening. His pounding heart slowed, with a few deep breaths. After a few more, Ciara stood. Teleri kept a hand on her hip, forehead pressed to Ciara's temple. Close and warm. A little color lingered on Ciara's pale cheeks. Perhaps a hint of a smile, too. She stepped off him, turned toward her audience to speak to them.

He let his eyes slide shut, waiting for the kir-bindings to release. The ring-charm still pinched, and his still-mostly-hard cock ached. It wanted to be unleashed a moment, to re-group —

The thump of boots landing on either side of him knocked his eyes open. Míde grinned, slow and smug, as she gripped his cock, squeezed it.

Kiefan's teeth clenched, and he hissed, "Don't —"

She leaned down to snarl at close range. "Did think 'twas a nice cup of tea and a dozen women to worship your cock? Shall know your place, boy."

He rose, straining against the bonds. "I'm no plaything of yours!"

She slapped him, hard enough to sting. He lunged back, so much as he could, with a growl. Míde only snorted, smirking. She thrust down onto him, well wetted already. Kiefan's groin tightened, his limbs clenched. The ring-charm gave him no say in the matter.

Míde rode him smooth and hard; had she been anyone else, he'd match the pace. He strained against the bonds, showing her his teeth, as he growled in Alemannic. "Pray these bonds don't slip, bitch."

She hovered just above his reach, smug. "Speak Arceal, coward." Míde slowed, drew off him to run her fist over his length with a smile, and slide him back between her lips. "'Twould make a fine whore-dog with that," she told him. "Ten silvers a night, easy. But I'd stake you in the town square, let every Dheathain have her fill. Did think you'd turn your nose up at me, for a threadbare margrave?"

He fixed her with as icy a glare as he could manage. "If we meet again, I'll rip your head from your shoulders."

And held her eyes until she looked away. Míde's fucking slowed, stopped, and she stood abruptly. Brow furrowed, she set her hands on her hips and glared down at him — snatched the Y-stick leaning against the table, swung —

Tannait's kir-rope snared it just shy of his head, pulled it from Míde's hands. She spat in Caer and Tannait snapped an order. The duchess yielded, with muttered curses, and returned to the circle of witnesses.

Kiefan worked against the bonds again. The ache in his cock had drawn into a knot at the base where the charm bound it. Anger threaded those familiar lines from his eyeballs along his Blessing ridges — another headache taking root. Tannait knelt beside his head, a cup in her hand. She offered the brandy, but he turned away from it.

"Let me go. Bruised, as you said," he said.

Tannait brushed stray hairs from his brow. "Close your eyes," she murmured. "Endure this."

Kiefan looked up at her, a pit tearing open in his stomach. She offered the brandy again, and he took a swallow. Raw stuff, military issue. It burned in his throat, a good match for the dread.

Una straddled him and stroked his charm-bound cock, her hand gentler than her sister's. "Close your eyes," she repeated, at a whisper. "I'll be quick."

Kiefan clenched his teeth and looked away. His cock wasn't so fussy, despite the creeping pain from the ring; her warm cunny drew his blood back. Treacherous thing. She took her pleasure with sighs and light fingertips tracing across his chest. Halfway through, the pressure in his groin knotted tight enough that she drew a second orgasm from him, but it was as pleasant as a sneeze.

He lay still when the next came, whispered soft Caer words in his ear, and needed only a few hard thrusts and tickles of her clit to climax. His cock found its strength again in her grip, and pressure gathered slowly behind the ring-charm. Unwanted, now, but growing nonetheless. He stared at the brazier off to the side and gave it no help. The next woman only ground against him, leaned down to breathe close to his neck. Touched his Blessing ridges, stroked his braided crest and the plain gold band he wore for a crown. Savored him, and left him with a raw stripe along his cock.

A burning log shifted and dropped sparks onto the ceramic plate below. No need to see these Caer's faces; if the Tadhlon officers so much as flicked an eyebrow at him, while under his command come spring — that shut his eyes and roiled his gut. But he'd have the Tadhlon knights and archers to command. And more Caer coming as reinforcements, if Teleri and Ciara were good as their word…

He set his jaw, ignoring the fresh-sprouting doubts.

His cock throbbed, wanting an excuse for release.

Another woman straddled him and stroked her hand along his length. Gently. Sore as he was, that was enough to tear a weak spurt out of him. The ring-charm held him, still, and a needle of pain shot through. His headache broke into full flower, hot pain spreading across his skull. Kiefan bit his lip, breathing harsh to keep from whimpering. The Caer hushed him, by his ear, and touched a kiss to it.

"Yes, 'tis wrong," she whispered, and he knew her voice. Fingertips stroked his cheek. "A beautiful thing, tied down and broken. Beautiful, even so." Duchess Faola tipped his head when his eyes opened, studied him. Her hand lay on his cock, unmoving and cool. Then she straightened and stepped away, demanded no more from him.

Tannait offered Kiefan another sip of brandy and called up his kir-pattern. She held up her hand when another moved from the ring toward him; he heard disappointment in the other's words, and felt a wash of gratitude when Tannait waved her off. The physician came instead, and loosed the charm. Agony washed out into his groin, clutching his throat tight. Soothing kir followed, mercifully.

The kir-ropes unwound at last and Kiefan lay limp, merely breathing as his head pounded. His shoulders popped when he reached down for his braies. Sitting up sent a stab of pain through his skull; a fierce one this time, and no Kate to heal him. He'd need a bottle of brandy. Two, perhaps.

A hand was offered, strong and thick-knuckled. Captain Fionn looked down on him, sober-faced while the women stood whispering and smirking. Kiefan took the offer with one hand and kept a grip on his clothes with the other. On his feet, he tied his drawstrings by memory. The captain slung a cloak around his shoulders, to cover the sliced cote and gambeson.

In broken Arceal, he said, "Now make a meal by sun-down if you still think us weak men."

Kiefan looked him in the eye and twisted his mouth to one side. Shook his head; he'd not doubt the mettle of Caer men. Captain Fionn nodded and took him by the arm — that first step made Kiefan frown in concentration, but it grew easier. Ciara stood by her map-table, considering a pile of papers, re-dressed and apparently paying the whole matter no further mind. Teleri waited at her shoulder. Kiefan stopped, across the table from her, and she glanced up.

Regret in her eyes, but she looked away quickly. She barked out a name and Tadhlon's captain-general stepped forward, snapped to attention. She rattled off a series of orders and received a crisp reply. "This camp, 'tis under your command," Ciara told Kiefan, "ere the autumn equinox dawns, so long as you supply it with provisions and materiel. These are yours as well."

Selecting several documents, she rolled them together and took a stick of wax from the lip of an oil lamp to seal it all with. She handed them across the table. Kiefan brushed his thumb across the cooling lump of wax, considering the two thousand knights and archers he'd gained.

On his back.

"Your men have pledged a ransom," Ciara said. "Six kegs of pumpkin ale, ten hams, and a dozen young men of loose morals — 'tis sufficient, I suppose. Shall accept it. Captain, deliver him to his escort."

CHAPTER 14

"'Twas excellent for spirits," Croícruach said as they strode down the hall from the barracks' front door. Fresh from the Tadhlon camp, the captain-general still had snow clinging to her hose as far as her knees. "Mayhaps should be cavalry movements, next we game with them? The horses do grow idle."

Teleri flanked Ciara on her left, opposite Croícruach. "Likely we might arrange another," the Crown agreed. "Something in co-operation, rather than opposing."

"No chance of taking prisoners, then?"

Teleri shot the captain-general a stern look. Ciara answered, "No need. Shall remember well who's leashed him."

Croícruach smirked. Tel weighed whether they'd survive the spring, when Wodenberg's reinforcements never came. The game was set: Kiefan believed he had an alliance, the duchesses believed he'd been hoodwinked, Ciara believed she had their united support and the offer of conquering founts in Suevia to avert the saints' anger when they realized the passes had not been closed.

All that remained to be told was that Teleri would ride with the Tadhlon Guard, both to add to their strength and to shield them from Kiefan's anger. She'd given her word on this, and meant for him to hold it to her alone.

Much could still go awry. And Saint Conbarre would take her price in stringence, doubtless. So be it.

At the mess hall's door, the noise and chatter of half the Crown's Blades at table greeted them. Ciara dined with them oft enough, and wished no fuss made of it. This time, though, they fell silent when their Crown appeared in the door. A scrape of boots and benches, and all stood at attention. Teleri found the duchesses among them, also standing.

Ciara paused in the door, raising her chin. Accepted the honor with a nod. "As you were." She strode across the floor toward the duchesses, looking for the cook, Rónan, on the way. He was swiftly assembling trenchers of meat and greens, snapping at his apprentice to be quick.

Tel allowed half a smile. There was only one bit of news in the barracks or the camp: Ciara had let her sister play her games, be a trinket to please the eye, but now the southlanders had been put in their place by a true Crown. Their king had come bound and willing to endure oíche-te for a scrap of Caercoed's strength. No pleasant night in a feather bed either, but the harsh old way. There was a breath of rumor that the king had feared an attack on Rukharbor if he refused. Some suspected he'd been less than willing.

The more rumors, the better to hide the truth.

When Ciara arrived at her table, the head had been cleared for her along with a place for the captain-general. Míde rose to take her hand and kiss it in fealty, with a grin. "'Twas good sport, Highness. Shall we hunt again?"

Teleri remained by Ciara's shoulder as she took her seat. "Mayhaps," the Crown replied. Rónan brought two fine trenchers of ham, cabbage, and warm bread with a flourish. "'Tis been remiss of me not to ask after Donnán and — how was your second brother named?"

Míde's grin faded. Una, beside her, grew still. "Banan, Highness."

"Banan. Have their voices dropped yet? 'Twould be well to see how they hunt. Surely boys are taught such, even in Dheathain?"

Tel caught a pleased glint in Duchess Faola's eye as the twins sat, making polite excuses. Boys were bed-ornaments in Dheathain, and yet were soft spots in their kin's hearts. All would guard their mouths closer, now that their menfolk might face a true oíche-te. The promise of a strong Crown confronting the saints on their behalf kept their thoughts from murder. They must wonder what part the elect did play, having aided the Crown thus far.

Came the day Ciara learned what was still for Teleri to do on the kingdom's behalf... well, that would be soon enough. Teleri meant to enjoy what remained of this winter, and treasure it.

Gregor itched with questions, clear enough, as there was no hiding the ruined gambeson and cote from him. He bit his lip, though, and brought Kiefan fresh paper, ink and quills for writing orders. It would need another courier to carry them to Castle Kaltkern. A ride up to Vorspitz and a visit to the new duke of Alemannia would be well, too. Woden had made his choice from among a half-dozen second cousins, and Kiefan hadn't yet met the man.

/ have reinforcements /

/ good /

That was all Woden needed on the matter. The truth of the oíche-te, his doubts, Kiefan kept to himself. He wrote out an order for the Klippe, the Ranger lieutenant, to send word through the Suevi resistance: be ready in Temitte, after the equinox. No need for Caercoed to hear anything of that.

Kiefan had asked Schutze, Sir Eburhart, and the betting pool to meet him at the Two Lanterns after the day watch changed to night. Time slipped away, though, and he wasn't in Nail's saddle until the last gloaming had faded from the clouds overhead. Gregor rode alongside him, at a trot down Knapptal's main road, eager to get there and resolve the matter of the bet.

"What rumors are there?" Kiefan asked, as they angled toward the lake's shore. The tavern's namesake lanterns hung lit, one by the street door, one on its dock.

"I said nothing." Gregor was quick with that. "It was Garrick, I think, who said you returned in a borrowed cloak."

The King's Guard had been waiting to see him safely back to the Wache. A whole bottle of brandy to break the headache, to get to sleep at all, and Kiefan hadn't woken so late since his father was killed. He'd laid in bed a few heartbeats still feeling those kir-ropes on his wrists, though.

In the Two Lanterns' great room, every chair was filled — and emptied, when they stood to greet him. Eburhart cuffed his shoulder, gentle as a bear, and steins were raised to wish Kiefan health. "Sit, sit, you're all fresh from duty," Kiefan told them, over their voices. "Half of you, that is."

They chuckled; less than half were guardsmen, in truth. The rest were curious garrison soldiers, townsmen, or the local whores. Margrave Schutze held up the purse of money that Eburhart's men had pooled and it got a cheer.

"How much?" Kiefan asked.

"About ten crescents, it came to."

"So little?" He looked to Eburhart.

"I seeded the pot myself!" The big knight put up a hand to swear to it. "A whole crescent. Seems word got around the garrison and many thought —" He looked to his lieutenant for the right words. "Thought you spoke in jest, m'lord. All your Guardsmen told us was how sober and honorable a commander you are. Never darkened the door of a whorehouse, they said."

Good that they didn't know of the once his father's Guard had taken him to Arbor Street for a proper breaking-in.

"It was a matter of the kingdom's defense, though," Kiefan said, taking the light purse from Schutze. It jingled in his hand, mostly bruns. "Did you think I jested in that?"

"Of course not, m' —"

"The wager was to thaw the Ice Queen." The most buxom of the whores spoke up. She leaned on the bar, letting it support her blessings for better display. "I threw in a crescent, m'lord, as you've not graced us with your company. You'll tell us the true story, won't you, of what passed in the Caer pavilion? Who wins the bet?"

That was what they'd been waiting for, by how heads turned, ears all but perked like horses'. Kiefan smiled, shook the purse again. A lifetime under his mother's hand, his father's — in truth, sobriety and honor came easy to him. Though Kate had struck a deep nerve, skipping past his armor and flesh like a kir-knife. Now that she was lost to him, honor seemed a cold and empty road to walk. It was what he'd been dealt. And he'd driven Kate away himself.

None needed know of the kir-ropes, the ring-charm, or that it had left him with little appetite. Let them see the proofs and think what they wished.

Kiefan opened the purse and poured it onto the bar before the tapped kegs. "An ale for the house," he announced, "with my winnings." When the cheer roared up, he leaned close to the innkeeper's ear, told him to send up to the castle for whatever more it came to.

"Proof!" the whore cried through it, and several voices joined her.

He had the sealed papers in his own purse; Kiefan held them up. "Marching orders for Caer knights and archers, to be under my command come spring." They were copies of those written to the Tadhlon Guard, and more from the duchies of Dheathain and Henffyrdd. Signed by Crown, duchesses, and affirmed by both Elect.

"How many?"

"When do they march?"

"Six thousand." Kiefan answered the first. "And Tadhlon marches with us in the spring."

"The pavilion!" The town's whores banded together to raise the cry. When the men's voices fell back, the buxom one demanded, "Your wager was to sweeten the crown, m'lord. You've not won yet!"

The armsmen and archers weren't so willing to challenge him, not with free ale being pulled from the tap for them. Kiefan's Blessing caught their eagerness, though. Rumor of a borrowed cloak, to hide his disarray… hounds with the deer's scent, all of them.

Kiefan had the cut cote bundled tight and tucked under his belt. He tossed it to the woman and it half-unrolled in the air. She caught it, turned it, found the shoulder seams and held it up with a laugh. The cut gaped open. Her nearest sister caught the raveling edge of the cut and crowed. "Bit of a hurry, m'lord?" she called, over the growing noise.

He only smiled, left it at that. Didn't miss how the buxom one bundled the wool to her nose and took a deep breath. She shot him a sly look.

"They let you alone with their queen?" Sir Eburhart boomed.

"Not at all."

The innkeeper put a stein of ale by Kiefan's elbow and set out several more for his wife to distribute. Good timing; Kiefan picked his up and leaned back with deliberate ease to take a swallow.

A gale of laughter. "Left them smiling, m'lord?" one of the whores asked.

"As many as I could." He told his ale that, but they still heard him.

The buxom whore sidled closer with a smile… but the thought turned his stomach, in truth. Mother Love only knew when he'd get that appetite back. Kiefan kissed her cheek, whispered in her ear to keep the cote, and took her hand from his thigh. Caught Gregor by the shoulder and left the men to their merry ale and story-embroidering.

WODENBERG

"I'm confident in Physician Brauer's leadership of the army's infirmary." I looked across the faces of the officers, on the right-hand side of the King's Council chamber, as I said that. They'd been the most unsettled by hearing I wouldn't be leading the infirmary myself. "I will be where I can be of most use to the army."

My teacher still loomed large in their memory, though, and he had always been in the surgery when the army marched.

I rattled off the status of the infirmary's preparations and watched our craft-handed secretary scratch it down as quickly as I spoke. Beside me, Saint Woden shifted in the King's chair, before the crackling fire, and tapped one finger on the arm-rest. When I finished, I took my seat again.

Woden had called the first preparation meeting just after winter Solstice, and re-convened us on the same day in the Bitter Moon. He'd told us when we began that Caercoed would lend us aid. Nothing more.

A bit odd, perhaps, that I had no urge to ask him for more.

Official report was that Kiefan would ride to Vorspitz, then along the Felsherz, and surely he'd be home before Equinox but when exactly… I pressed my mouth in a line and turned my mind to my duties. There were more than enough of those. Readying the infirmary. My patients. My own preparations for spring. Letting people bend my ear as they needed; simply being the elect, it seemed, meant I ought to know how they should solve their problems. I found myself reciting bits of the Mother's and Father's catechism to them. Which they ought to know already.

Theo Kaufmann stood, next, to report on the logistics of supplying an invasion of Suevia from the army's stockpiles in Wodenberg and Prohzgrad. As the Kaufmanns had long held one of the king's charters to do business with Suevia, Theo knew the road to Temitte well. He had cousins in that city. And after how the Empress had tortured him, stolen his face and then his closest friend, he was grimly set on repaying her.

His health had recovered, but darkness lingered in his eyes. I hadn't meant to replace Anders as his friend, but in healing his wounds, knowing the secret he and Süssie kept — he was easy to talk to.

The meeting finished before noon and as the others chatted and gathered their papers, I heard Woden rumble. "Kate, with me."

He left his chair as if on a mission; I blinked once and followed. He had kept his distance since the day Arcea invaded the castle. He'd been curt, but proper, and I hadn't missed that he watched me closely. Surely he had something like the anticipation Blessing, though I doubted he could read me as closely as Kiefan did.

That he thought me — dangerous enough — gave me pause.

Woden led me down the east wing's hallway toward the stairwell and he had long legs. I quickened my pace.

On the stairwell's second-floor landing, Woden unlatched the window's shutters and looked down. His kir, already strong enough to draw my eye, tightened further and he stepped off the sill. I leaned out, guessing what he meant to do; far below, the practice yard lay between the castle and its curtain wall. It was a short staircase below the ground floor.

That was rather further than I'd been able to boost myself on my kir-vines. I'd tried to repeat my trick that got me over the castle's portcullis, and I'd managed to touch a second-floor window, but this was further. Below, Woden landed and moved aside, looked up.

I knew better than to make him wait. I pulled more kir from the Pool and stepped off the window sill.

My skirts fluttered up against my clenched fists. I focused my kir in a shield and threw it at the ground; I jolted in the air and the charm cracked under my weight. Focus slowed its unraveling, and it slowed me. A second kir-vine, thrust down, let me land with fair dignity. Behind my eyes, my brain pulsed with something like a headache.

"You've anger and spirit," Woden said. He had a buckler in his hand, and tossed it to me. I caught it. "You should know something of how to survive, as well."

Bucklers were small things, just a circle of wood with a handle and an iron rim. They had always struck me odd. Why not use a larger, safer shield?

"Make a kir-shield to match that." Woden pointed as he went to the doorway into the castle. I wasn't sure if I needed the buckler's handle or if the shield charm could simply be attached to my left hand. While I shaped the charm, he looked inside and picked a wooden sparring sword from the rack.

Woden swung the sword, loosening his shoulders as he returned. "In battle, he who spends out his kir first dies," he said. "Kir-shields will stop a blade. They'll break a charm, but be broken in turn and the kir lost."

I nodded. Sometimes I could snatch a little back as it fell away, but the stuff was intent on rejoining the earth. This would be a good lesson, I knew, however difficult.

"No need to waste kir to build a large shield. A buckler will serve."

"Or those — bracers?" I asked, putting my hand to my forearm. I had seen Kiefan use simple bars of kir there to deflect blades.

Woden nodded. "Those require some confidence. Small steps, first. Set your feet." He set his own, and I echoed him. With the wooden sword, he tapped my foot and I adjusted. A touch to my shoulder, my arm, and I recognized this pose from the disciple's dance. Woden set me at something like a middle guard, my left shoulder and leg facing him.

"Give the enemy a small target."

He slashed at me. My first instinct was to stop his swing, which numbed my arm — though he put no real effort into his blows.

"Easier to deflect than stop."

Turning his swing upward came to me first, and then he hammered at me with the same swing over and over and over. I blocked, the movement clarifying in my mind. Sweat rose on me, despite the cold air. And then Woden reversed and swung from the other direction. It was a different move, different muscles, and I began to ache.

"Make your enemy doubt himself." Woden stopped at last. "You're a slip of a girl — one quick stab and move on — but no, you surprise him. What else are you hiding? Fear kills on the battlefield."

My hard breath smoothed as he spoke. His words rang true enough; I had frozen in terror, a few times, during the siege. I would've been easy to kill.

Saint Qadeem stood by the castle door, his ermine cloak wrapped close and his hood up. His kir, approaching, had distracted me and earned me a bruise on my forearm. "You've more instinct for it than your teacher," he told me. "You'll need this, on the field, and more."

Physician Brauer would head the infirmary because I meant to ride with the ambulances and do whatever I must near the front lines. I had expected Qadeem to tell me no, for Woden to laugh it off, for someone to stop me, but — instead, more lessons.

"I should shield the ambulances?" I asked, to be sure.

"If you can. Likely you'll have greater worries," my saint said. "There'll be no objection to your healing men, but this campaign will need more of you."

"Come on Saint-day morning, and I will tutor you further," Woden said.

"I have duties on Saint-day," I said, with a shake of my head.

"The day after, then. For now, something to eat." Woden moved for the doorway. In passing, he jabbed at Qadeem. "And get this thin-blood inside before he freezes."

"I survived Rukharbor this long," he replied. My saint had been on the north coast since Solstice, working with both his new crafter elect, Terekhov, and Woden's Elect Pirra. The two of them would have charge of protecting the city and its fount, come spring. That came some weeks later on the north coast than here, but they might be on their own for the entire summer.

"As much snow in the air as on the ground. And yet the fresh mustering of reserves is willing to drill in it. Englia continues to prove its worth." There was a subtle barb in that, by how Qadeem aimed it at Woden.

He gave only a raised brow, sidelong, in return. "Numbers?"

Qadeem gave them, and Woden reported our own. I had thought him impatient, through the meeting, or distracted, and his accuracy startled me. As we climbed the stairs, they peppered through a list of towns and numbers, moving up the eastern side of the kingdom and down the western, comparing counts of men, horses, and supplies. Dates were given. They shifted into Russe briefly, which pinched my pride but it wasn't my place to interrupt.

I saw they were aiming for the smaller dining room in the east wing, and I waved over a maid to ask for a meal to be brought. She curtsied and ran for the kitchen. I opened the dining room's doors ahead of the two saints and they kept right on talking as they walked through.

They trailed off, a few steps in. Woden flicked out a tendril of kir and dropped a tiny star of a spark charm on each candle wick. Qadeem drew up a ball of kir in one hand and twisted it down into a brilliant orb; he tossed it onto the wood stacked in the fireplace and it splattered, white-hot. The firewood burst into full flame so hard that the pile slipped a bit.

Woden switched to Arceal as the fire crackled and settled. "We must attack Ansehen after Equinox. The day after, if we can." He looked to me and I stepped up between the two of them. "Best to have you both there before."

On my other side, Qadeem asked, "You've found a wet-nurse?"

"Yes. Rafe is quite fond of her."

My saint nodded. "Have you thought of some new dresses?"

I blushed, hot, in surprise. Had he been watching when I stopped to look in Frau Schneider's window? The shutters had been open, to let in the light, and the lovely fabric laid out on her work table had given me a pang of longing.

"I have enough dresses, m'lord," I said, voice low.

"You need another formal gown and three more plain dresses." When I frowned, Qadeem asked, "You have two of each?"

"Yes, but I've put the amber one away and —"

"Two formal gowns, then." Which was even worse, but he raised a hand to stop my objections. "You represent this kingdom, Kate. We are thrifty, yes, but not poor. If you need coin for it, the chamberlain will see to that."

The chamberlain would do little, from what I knew. "He hardly dares speak to me," I said. Qadeem frowned, and then I had to explain. "Queen Mercia dismissed me as physician of the castle, and ordered him to stop my pay. He won't cross her, none of the staff will, until —"

"Father's bloody balls," Woden growled, "that woman's lost her mind again." He stalked from the fireplace with such a frown that the page boy carrying in a basket of fresh bread nearly dropped it in fright. Woden stormed past, ignoring the boy's obeisance.

"M'lord, don't!"

He drew up, looked back at me.

"Don't... she's only..."

Woden strode back, brow still knit. I took a step back as he leaned close. "Don't? What did you think I mean to do? Hurt her?"

I bit my lip, staring up into stormy blue eyes. He smelled faintly of leather, and something like fresh-cut grass. And he was twice as big, this close, twice the mountain. "I don't know, m'lord." It came out at a whisper.

"You have served me, and Qadeem, and this kingdom well. You will have your due so you may be strong and well equipped to serve at need."

My voice strengthened a little. "It's no trouble, m'lord, truly. My shop's income is fair enough."

Woden straightened, giving me more room to breathe, and he considered me for a few heartbeats. His voice kept its stern edge, when he continued. "I know it seems too much, at first. More than you deserve. Clothes for every day of the week? Bread and potatoes and meat? Every single night?"

That struck a secret chord in me, and my eyes widened. Some days, I couldn't believe I could still afford ham or eggs. They never seemed to run out. Woden knew of that?

He saw, nodded. The corner of his mouth tucked up. "Have you let someone see to your laundry yet?"

He truly knew. I breathed a laugh. "My neighbors keep trying to."

"Let them." Woden's strong hand squeezed my shoulder. "Don't forget what it is to sleep hungry and cold. But don't feel guilty that you aren't. The Shepherd spreads his gifts as he will, and we defend his flock. Whether it's a carpenter's daughter, or a whore's son, or —"

He looked to Qadeem and I did too. My saint smiled. "A scribe's son."

"Oh, a rich boy then."

"A street-corner scribe, and I joined him there so soon as I could write. There were five younger ones to feed."

Nearly on cue, a platter of warmed roast arrived, with fresh-boiled potatoes and gravy to go with our bread. Housemistress Wenda brought it, with a smile, and we sat down to eat.

CHAPTER 15

We'd had heating charms for the journey through Starknadel's pass; those had been wooden bars the size of candles, carved with swirling flames and painted red. There were hundreds of blood-stops and cleansing charms and knock-outs in the Order's hospital, each one a piece of bone or wood or antler. Dozens more circulated in Wodenberg and the countryside, passed down as heirlooms.

Not only healing or heating — many sorts of charms could be bound to an object. Any could use them, once they learned the trick, and any could push their day's kir into a charm to recharge it. They were rare, and valuable, because only elect and saints could make new ones.

I held a shaft of bone cut from a cow's femur. It was fresh, still full of marrow, and heavy. Three more pieces waited on the table; one had already been charmed, so that I could see how it was done.

"Pack the matrix tightly," Qadeem said, prodding an errant strand of my kir back into the bone. "The more kir it can hold, the longer it will boil."

There had been no new boiling charms made since my teacher died. As it was now late in the Ice Moon, maple sap was running and syrup season made the issue urgent. Boiling charms, which were the larger, stronger cousins to heating charms, stretched out supplies of firewood and lowered the cost of the maple syrup everyone loved. When the bone was properly sealed in glaze by a potter, they lasted decades but did break now and then. Or someone wished to add more kettles to their business and thus needed more boiling charms.

I had bound an apple-sized sun into the center of the bone and the rest would contain the matrix that absorbed loose kir to fuel the charm. Threads... I thought of tight threads as I spun and they came. Near fine enough for sewing, after all the practice I'd put into such things.

On the floor, Rafe sat entranced by the green tendrils of kir flowing from my fingers and twisting around the bone shaft. He'd forgotten all about his rag-doll horse.

"Good." Qadeem sat across my kitchen table, arms crossed on it. "Knot it off."

I twisted, tied, and let the kir go. The bone hung in my mind's eye as a bar of dense-packed whorls and knots. It would need careful glazing and firing by a guild-trained potter with heat-sight, to keep the bone whole as the protective shell encased it. Then it could sit in a merrily boiling syrup-kettle over and over.

Five silver crescents, there in my hands. Furnishing my shop to live in had run to some money, and I'd be glad to have it.

Qadeem freshened my mug of tea. "Arbor Street has been asking for charms, did you say?"

I smiled against the mug as I sipped. "Bound to leather. Will that take a charm as well as bone?"

He shook his head. "It's the structure of bone and wood that make them so suited to it. Antler and teeth less so, but better than a fleshy thing like leather. Simple charms, for that."

"And stone?"

"Only master crafters can charm stone." Qadeem said it, and then smiled. "It's Aleksandr's secret, how he charmed the city walls. I'll not tell."

Someone knocked on my kitchen door. I got up from my bench and Rafe craned his neck to track me; he tipped backward and I caught him. Picking him up, I went to the door.

"Good-eve!" Adalev and Linde smiled. He held up the covered pot in his mittened hands; she had little Gerhart on her hip. They'd been wonderful neighbors; they often fed me, and Linde was Rafe's wet-nurse. The first he'd deign to nurse from.

"Come in!" Stepping aside, I let them in. Slushy snow trailed from their shoes and cloak hems. The warm weather had held these past few days, but when I glanced up at the sky behind them I saw only grey. I leaned against the doorsill and took a whiff. Cold and damp. Snow. "Looks like the melting won't keep," I said as I shut the door.

When I turned, they were both on one knee in obeisance, trying to put fist to heart despite the baby and the hot pot. Qadeem turned on the bench to acknowledge them. He was even more bundled than we were, in thick woolen cotes and a quilted vest as well. White fur peeked at the top of his boots; he wore light colors, as he often did.

"See to your burdens," Qadeem told them, with a nod. "Don't drop either of them." His eyes narrowed. "Trüberde, was it? Linde?"

"M'lord, you honor me," she murmured, standing. "How is it you remember me?"

"You were presented as a master of the weaver's guild," Qadeem said, as if that were all the reason needed. "Your husband?"

"Adalev, m'lord," he answered. "And our son, Gerhart." Ger was nine months old now, and had brought his rag-doll Doggy. Its head was deep in his mouth.

"They've been kind to me," I said as I returned to the table.

"I hadn't seen you at King's Market," Adalev said, and then added, "m'lady." He took his wife's fabric to various tailors' shops and saw to such things while she wove. "We thought you must be too busy, or perhaps — but you've m'lord to attend to. We didn't mean to interrupt. Here." He put the pot on the table.

"Sit," I told them, going to my shelves for bowls. "The teapot is about empty, but —"

"Oh, we couldn't impose. We won't trouble you. Please don't bother," Linde said.

I turned with four bowls in my hand and they'd already backed up to the kitchen door. "It's no bother," I said. "It's your dinner, too."

Linde had her free hand up to fend me off, her smile weak and worried. Gerhart stared at Qadeem and chewed on his Doggy. "Simple enough to warm up a little ham at home," she said. Her son pointed, thrusting his arm out. She caught his hand and pulled it down.

Adalev opened the door and she scurried out; he bowed to Qadeem, and then added one to me as well. "We're sorry to disturb you," he said as he pulled the door shut.

My saint only looked to me, one finger against his mouth. The covered pot waited on the table, smelling faintly of cheesy cream sauce. Rafe gurgled, his brow knotting; he'd seen his friend, and now Ger was inexplicably gone.

I hushed Rafe and brought the bowls to the table. The pot was still warm, but not so hot that I couldn't lift the lid. Potato and cabbage gratin, with diced ham atop. Linde was craft-handed, and everything she made was fine work.

"Good neighbors indeed," Qadeem said. He slung out a kir-vine to pluck the kettle from the fire, and refilled the teapot. I spun one, too, to take my serving spoon from the shelf. It unnerved people to see me do that so casually, so I rarely did.

"Linde had a miscarriage just after Solstice." I put Rafe down near his Horsey. "They've been keeping watch over me since then. If not them, then —" I gestured vaguely toward the front of my shop, meaning the houses across the street. It hardly mattered. "They're not sure what to make of me."

"Since Solstice?"

I spooned out bowlfuls of gratin. "They've decided I'm a widow of sorts. Most still think Anders was killed that night, in Kaltkern. Frida still grieves as if he's dead."

Most were struck silent when I told them Anders had married me knowing my baby wasn't his; it was a noble thing, both in duty and love. Perhaps I'd choked the rumor mill with that. Two moons on, they all treated me gently and didn't speak of Anders at all.

"The neighbors bring me food, send their maids over to offer to wash my laundry. They check on me to be sure I haven't set the place afire or fallen into ruin."

My voice trailed off. I put a bowl before Qadeem, and fetched him a spoon with a slender kir-vine. He only watched my face. "You are their elect."

My mouth twisted. "Not some frail widow." I was strung between resenting their worry and loving them for it. "They should save their charity for those who need it. I've enough money from charming fevers and setting bones. Even before Woden cleared that up…"

It was a lot of money, in truth, once my stipend from the castle returned. I'd allowed myself the glee of picking out fabrics for new dresses at Frau Schneider's shop but it still left me uneasy. Made me feel all the more petty for being angry with the queen — it was only extra money. Dresses I didn't need. Woden had been right in it feeling like too much.

I sat down with my own bowl of gratin. I stirred the ham bits deeper into the potatoes and cabbage.

"What troubles you now?"

The frustration of a long day spent circling from one office to another — and darker things — burbled up. With it, the thought I'd had. "She wanted to fuss over money, when I could kill her with a thought?" I grimaced when I said it, and then amended. "I shouldn't think such things."

"That can't be the only time you've thought such."

I blinked. Qadeem's brows rose.

"If she had taken Rafe up the staircase, Solstice night, what would you have done?"

The moment flicked through my mind again: the fluttering panic rising in my throat, my hands itching to take my son back. The queen's pleading still haunted me, though. It was true — she'd buried too many babies. I wanted to say that pity would've stayed my hand.

"I don't know," I had to murmur.

A moment's quiet. I risked a glance across the table at Qadeem; his black eyes had shifted to the distance for a moment. "Such moments are precisely when you must be thinking whether killing the queen will solve problems or create them," he said. "Which would it?"

I stared. Kill the queen?

He put his chin on his hand and raised his brows, expecting an answer.

The solutions came easily enough. "It would stop the slander. She's fed the rumor mill lies about Anders all his life, so near as I can tell. And she wished me to beg her for a dozen crescents a month that's mine as the kingdom's elect?"

He gave me a curt nod. "Slander and money. Not her bouts of madness?"

My voice fell. "I pity her for those. It would be a mercy, I suppose."

"What problems would killing her create?"

My mouth closed. "It may upset… someone?" I wasn't certain whether Kiefan would be so sad to bury his mother, in truth. "Why do you ask? I don't mean to kill her."

"But you could. 'Should' is little shield against anger — with a thought, you could kill your way through this city tonight, and who could stop you?"

Those pattern checks I had done, all the names and faces, flickered through my memory. Some of the City Guard were truly Blessed, I knew. Three, working together, could likely do it. "Some officers of the Guard might. You would. And Woden." I saw what he meant, though. How many dead before a saint stopped me?

"No elect of mine will lash out in anger." Qadeem said. "We may yet need Mercia to strengthen Kiefan's claim to Suevia, so do her no harm."

Needed her for her eyes, which marked her the granddaughter of Suevia's dead saint. On the floor, Rafe flung his Horsey down and it slid away. He reached, and then looked up at me with those same grey eyes. Kiefan's.

Leaning over, I picked him up and set him on my thigh. "Another prince of Suevia," I murmured. I kissed Rafe's downy head, remembering Kiefan spooned against my back. The warm smell of his bed. When mine was so cold and lonely now.

Qadeem nodded. "I'm sorry."

"You must think me such a fool." My voice struggled out of my throat. "So blind. So tangled — if I'd been stronger, if I'd — Master never should've sent me —"

His brown hand covered mine, and I dropped my spoon to feel his palm against mine. A simple thing, but it felt like the first true touch I'd had since that awful night in Kaltkern. My eyes flooded.

"There was no avoiding each other, in this city." Qadeem's words came soft, but firm. "Three young disciples with such soundings? You had to meet, and you had to see past all the trappings each other wore. That was one reason we sent you across the mountains. In the snow, there was no prince, no bastard son, no peasant girl. Only disciples."

It rang true. I pressed my eyes with my free hand, took a deep breath.

"We had to show Caercoed that one elect was not all we had to offer," he said as I blinked my eyes clear. "It was dangerous. All three of you might've been lost. The risk of broken hearts seemed small, next to that."

I had to chuckle at that. "You knew they'd break my heart?"

"None know. There's no prophecy in kir. A bout of lovesickness, like all fevers, strikes you down but then passes." Qadeem squeezed my hand and let go. Rafe reached, patted the tabletop, and he offered his hand to my son. "Little danger that any would say I'm wise in the heart's ways. But broken hearts do mend. Yours will, Kate."

Rafe patted my saint's fingers, then wrapped his little hand around his thumb. I knew it was right, I knew my pain had eased to an ache, now. After putting my memories of the duel away, I had yet to touch them. But I didn't fear to, anymore.

"Kiefan wrote, while he was in Knapptal," I said. The image of it flicked past my eyes: the sealing wax, the paper, his name below the message. After a few moments' ache, I recited it. "I covered two pages to explain, but it means nothing. I could not bear to lose you too, and I know that now you are lost to me. By my own hand. On my life, I swear I never meant to hurt you."

It made my eyes well again, but I got it all out.

Qadeem ate a couple more spoonfuls of gratin. "Are you lost to him?"

"I need to know if Anders is alive or dead." When he quirked his mouth to one side, I put up my free hand. "I cannot answer until I know."

"Dying is a simple thing, near the Empress. He might be anyplace in the empire, if he lives. Perhaps there will be some word from our contacts in Suevia, in the spring. Or at Temitte." On that thought, he said, "You must learn your part in claiming a fount. And you must set all aside — all —" with a raised finger, for emphasis, "of your pain to take your place in the army. Do as Kiefan orders, so long as it does not compromise your duty to me. Will you do that?"

Kiefan, standing with his drawn sword pointed at Suevia. Knotted in cold anger and resolve, though he didn't once look me in the eye. I'd seethed, waiting for him to slip, for Woden to give me some excuse… but no, only a dull, throbbing ache now. He'd seen his bride killed, his family slaughtered, and then me kissing Anders; how much could Father Duty have expected him to bear?

To Qadeem, I nodded. "Broken hearts mend slowly," I murmured.

"They do. Let Mother Love do her work while you do Father Duty's."

We both ate, then, and scraped out our bowls. Rafe wanted his own dinner, and I saw to that while Qadeem sent the dishes and spoons to the washing-bucket on a vine of kir.

"Now that Caercoed is with us, there's a true chance of taking Temitte," he said. "So long as they haven't brought a full dozen elect up."

"A dozen?" The number made me blink.

"With the five they've lost already, it would be more than they'd expected to spend on a small kingdom — but not difficult. We shall see what the Suevi can do to aid us in that. If we can put Kiefan on the Eald-stol, there will be far more to draw on in resisting Arcea. They called Saint Seaxneat that: the Eald, the Ancient. He was, true enough. One of the elder saints I've met." Qadeem's eyes sank into distant memories.

I looked down at Rafe's grey eyes again. "And he kept his bloodline fresh?" I asked. "How is it everyone in Suevia isn't grey-eyed, then, if it's so strong in the blood?" Any child might have his father's eyes, or his mother's, but for it to pass so cleanly from the queen to Kiefan to Rafe was a strange thing.

"It holds for five generations," Qadeem answered. "Rafe's children will have grey eyes, and then it will be gone."

"It's a charm, then?"

Qadeem's head tipped as his mouth twisted. "In all honesty, I don't know how he did it. There was nothing like a charm to be found in any of Mercia's children — I looked, when they were babies. I saw Kiefan's flawed meridian, but nothing else amiss."

I knew already that Rafe didn't have that flaw; he'd never suffer those headaches, whatever Blessings he received. "And how do the Caer saints cause all girls to be twins?" I added to the questions.

"I could lay a bet on that, if need be. Seaxneat's grey eyes are more subtle. He was a flesh-forger — a shame that his wisdom is lost to us. Perhaps you'll suss it out yourself, one day. I wasn't surprised by your swapping of the sheep's eye; that was well done, and trickier than you know. Such a thing will die, without the right charms."

"It will?" I straightened on the bench.

"I asked after the boy in Knapptal and he's well. Next you do such a thing, I'd like to see it." Qadeem rubbed his chin, scratching his short, black beard. "Perhaps you can tell me what a centaur breeds, if he mounts a mare."

A laugh burst from me at the thought. I began to answer that, but as my memory scanned through that centaur's pattern again the words faded in my mouth. Centaurs weren't a matter of stitching man onto horse. Neither were minotaurs simply pieced together. "And what of minotaurs?" I asked. Where that centaur might've killed me, if he'd raped me as he meant to, a minotaur was — I cringed a little, but in truth they were only men.

"You might learn." Qadeem said it, and focused on me. Sober. His voice dropped. "If we fail, Kate, if Seraphine…" A pause. "She may give you a chance to live, if she knows your talents. You've no royal blood to force her hand —" He saw my grip tighten on Rafe. "It's much to ask, I know. It will break anyone to see their child slain." Qadeem set his teeth on his lip for a heartbeat. "But that can mend, too."

My heart ached, at the sadness in his voice. "She killed your family."

He took a deep breath; he picked up the gratin pot's lid and set it carefully in its place, with a little scrape. "Twenty years a bound elect, as I said, when Arcea came to Rasila. Bound elect and my saint's consort, father of three brilliant, beautiful children. War was not our strength; when Seraphine offered us marriage into the imperial bloodline, we agreed. Our eldest, our daughter, was our offering. Her two babies were in their teens, and little seen for all their schooling in Arcea itself, when the slaughter came." Qadeem looked toward Castle Kaltkern. "I had been hiding my ascension for years. Where I saw Arcea draining our strength and yoking us to the plow, Reema saw prosperity and luxury. We'd argued, we'd all but stopped speaking over it. When I saw all of my children, my grandchildren, murdered, it broke me. I near destroyed the city in hunting down the monsters that did Seraphine's dirty work. She came for me herself."

He looked away, shaking his head. "I can remember every day for hundreds of years, save for those. A haze hangs over them. I harvested two of her elect. Reema… turned on Seraphine, to give me the chance to escape. That was the end of Rasila for good and all. My head cleared enough that I had the sense to go to ground, to hide my kir and take passage as a caravan's physician."

Wind leaned against my home, and the walls creaked. It whistled through the chinks upstairs; I knew about those, and still had not had time to find them. We both looked up toward the whistles. Qadeem stood.

"That storm's arrived, then." He went to my window, pushed aside the drapes, and unlatched the shutter for a look as the wind ebbed. Dark had fallen, outside. "A little more winter, then," he said as an eddy threw snow past him.

"It's a little mercy if it isn't ice," I said.

"True." When he'd latched the shutter again he asked, "Might I stay a bit longer?"

Rafe was finished nursing and was dozing off. "As long as you wish." I drew my shift's neckline up, thinking nothing of what my saint might see, and tied the drawstring snug at my neck. That was when the next thought reached me. "Where should you sleep?"

He twitched one shoulder. "I sleep little."

"You must have a bed — on the mountaintop? At the fount?" My brow creased, trying to imagine it. "If it's snowing here, it must be a blizzard at the peak."

Qadeem nodded as he returned to his seat opposite me. "Yes, yes, and yes. Often it's snowing there when all is sunny here. And one can fly in a storm, but it has its risks. I've bounced off enough rocks up there, had to straighten this…" He pinched his sharp-chiseled nose, mimed twisting it. I smiled with him.

"You do live up there, then?" It still seemed unlikely.

"Saint Aleks had free rein, when he created our dens." Qadeem's smile turned fond. "A pack-rat's den. The man kept every last thing."

"Wouldn't you rather live in the castle?"

He looked to the fire, which had settled a bit, and considered. "Solitude has its attractions. You know something of that already." He nodded to indicate my shop. "Even if one has a family, it's no simple thing to live with — anyone, when there's so much duty to see to.

The nightly kir-rations. Choosing Blessings. I haven't had a family since… Rasila, in truth. I kept a wife and children, during my wandering years but…" He pressed his mouth shut, for a moment. "I should not have. Not until my wounds had healed."

I couldn't fathom the wound of seeing my children and grandchildren killed; the wreckage in the great hall had been terrible enough. "How long does it need? Mine has scabbed, thus far."

"Don't pick at it," he answered, and feigned a stern look. "Kiefan's likely to return within a few weeks, and wounds or no the kingdom needs both of you."

"I only hope whichever Caer brides —" I frowned, realizing that nothing had said which of the duchesses he'd chosen.

"His marriage is his concern. You say you must know if Anders is alive or dead — yes, look for him. Sift for word of his passing. But you may never have a clear answer. Meantime, your little one may be a man next you look at him. Don't cheat him of love — and don't cheat yourself." Qadeem made a point of that. "I wasted thirty years, a good woman's life, and let five children grow up with hardly a warm word from their father. That's pained me far more than loving them and mourning them ever could."

Elect Tannait's words came back to me. "Love them while they're here, treasure them ever after." I hugged Rafe tighter against my shoulder. He was sound asleep and drooling. I got up to put him in his cradle.

Anders and Kiefan were elect now. We might live a century, or we might be killed by the Empress this summer — and that was my first duty. Defending the kingdom, all its good people like my neighbors, defending my saint and Woden too, even if I still foolishly itched to slap him with a kir-ram.

When I returned to the table, Qadeem had the other two shafts of cow bone waiting. "Shall we finish these?"

CHAPTER 16

REOWAN

The silver, ripple-scaled snake twisting through the low hills was still the Neva River to him, but the Suevi called it the Ildra-éa. Alongside it lay a road, broad and white in the noontime sun, the caravans of wagons little more than creeping toys from this vantage.

Anders banked to follow the river's curve. Thermals still gave him trouble, and they didn't rise from water. Banking without a tail had taken practice. His feet, trailing behind, were too narrow to offer the delicate precision that Seraphine's black fan of feathers did. Neither was he so aerodynamic, as he was still half human.

Looked like a half-plucked chicken. But he was in the air. He pumped his wings to catch up.

Muscle burned in his chest and as soon as he could glide in her wake, he did. Anders' breastbone had thrust out like an axe blade to accommodate a rukh's flying muscles — that breast meat so tasty on a chicken — but it was still barely enough to keep him aloft. This flight was his longest yet, and it would be a fight to reach home.

Not home, not truly. Seraphine's home.

Docks cluttered the Ildra-éa and barges slid among them. Clusters of houses became towns. Walled pastures, as there were few fields here, shrank to gardens. The Éa-stípel loomed ahead, a six-sided tower anchoring the great city wall of Reowan at the river's edge. Salt tickled the deep nostrils above Anders' beak. Only a mile to go.

The sun's glare on the water spread as it reached the marshlands on the south side. Broad and lazy, the river met the sea. The silver band of reflected sun shot out to either side, lost at the horizon. Reowan stood proud at the junction.

Anders took a deep breath and beat his black wings to catch up again. He angled down when Seraphine did. Twenty feet over the shingle roofs, she leveled off and took one strong stroke of the wind. White flashed on her wings' undersides. Anders worked harder and still slipped behind. Burning muscle became aches. He'd grit his teeth but the beak didn't have any.

He wouldn't crash, not out in the city. He could feel the fount ahead, calling him. Tugging.

The pair of them went flying often enough, but the giddha-rukh and her bird-man still drew eyes. When they flashed across the great square before the governor's palace, all faces craned upwards. Anders glimpsed the banners and flags; spring Equinox, today, and the festival was well underway.

First Solstice and now Equinox, so far from home.

Áering, the castle on the shore, rose to meet him; he'd lost altitude. Anders threw all his strength into gaining a few more feet of height, the effort ripping out a harsh cry. A guardsman on the ramparts ducked as Anders just cleared the merlons. Between the towers, across the roof, over the inside battlements and at last he could glide downward over the groomed sand behind the three-sided castle.

In the embrace of the curtain wall, the quartz column of the fount glowed and twinkled. Seraphine alit on the tree-home in the twisted old salt pine, shifting back to human form so smoothly that she landed on small, bare feet.

Anders collapsed onto the deck, feet-first at least, rolled to a stop, and lay panting. His lungs, huge in his reshaped chest, pulled air hard. But he'd made it. A ten-mile flight without begging to rest.

Soon enough, his panting slowed. His pulse evened out. Then he let the charm unravel.

Feathers melted together and his wings shrank, thinned. Fingers re-emerged, drawing back to their proper lengths. His chest flattened and his shoulders spread; rukhs had little in the way of those. The beak fell back as his face broadened, returning to fully human. And his hair reasserted itself after having been muddled into pale not-quite-feathers.

"Doubt not. Your stamina does improve, la," Seraphine told him. "Further and further, and —"

He looked up as she swooped across the roof with a hiss, and winced when she grabbed him by the hair. Kir twisted near his head and she sawed at the handful. It came free, and she thrust it in his face.

"Again? How oft must I say it? You owe Woden nothing." She threw his knight's crest down, and it scattered on the breeze.

He'd been growing his hair out evenly when he shifted, but today the crest-and-stubble had come back. Anders took a breath to blame the fatigue of the long morning's flight, but

512

Part V: Cold Solace

something in his gut shoved that away. He closed his mouth instead. For moons he'd hidden what he was in exchange for a little freedom. Equinox was a day for honesty, for balancing one's accounts, and he didn't have it in him to lie.

"I am a Blessed knight. I rode into battle and lived to tell — nothing changes that," he told her in Alemannic, for what extra defiance that lent. He risked meeting her gaze, as he shifted onto his knees.

"You rode in his service, trained to the sword. Which any man with an arm might study. What was his gift? Three moons in my care, and the sky is yours." Seraphine's dark eyes sharpened, cold as a vulture's. Laurent wrapped a purple silk robe across her shoulders, careful to slip her heavy braid aside first.

Anders turned his eyes to the wind-scoured deck. Laurent shook out a white robe with purple trim for Anders, but he put up one hand to refuse it.

He felt Seraphine's chiding, through his bond, with a touch of disdain. She turned away, slipping her arms into the wide sleeves of her robe.

Laurent draped the white one over one arm. It nearly vanished against his own white, purple-trimmed sleeve. "Sir will go naked, then?" he asked, in Arceal.

"Bring me a cote. I need to see to the stables."

"This is no working-day for you," Seraphine said, over her shoulder.

"It's Equinox. I have accounts to balance." Anders stood, raking one hand through the ragged mess of his crest. His Blessing ridges scraped across his palm, comfortingly familiar.

"Equinox accounts? How quaint. So long as you return before the banquet." Seraphine faced the sea, her mind turning to her many bonds. Their flying lesson had begun early, run long, and she had much to check across her empire. Later, there would be ministers to meet with.

Anders' time was his own during that. A precious bit of freedom.

"Blythe," Laurent called, standing at the head of the stairs. "Bring cote and hose." He descended, the white robe over his arm, throwing a measuring glance back at Anders as he went. Laurent was tall enough that he was half down the stair before the floor cut off his gaze.

Let him mistrust. Anders could trounce him in sparring.

Anders paused beside Seraphine, looking out at the rolling sea. The constant rhythm kept him awake some nights, left him restless and searching. Salt and seaweed on the air had lured him down to the stony beach between the towers, where he'd lost an afternoon crouching over tidal pools and tearing his shoes on the sharp rocks. He hadn't been down there since.

He trotted down the steps, wanting to get away from its noise, and met Blythe coming up with his clothes. Anders took them from her in a smooth swoop of one arm. At the bottom, he turned toward his small bedroom and caught a glimpse of her watching him go with a smirk on her face.

She'd never miss a chance to get an eyeful. Ten years his elder, softened by babies and ease of rank — a mouse in the front room, likely a wildcat in bed, he'd put money on it. Or would have, a few years ago.

Before Kate.

Anders pulled the linens on, then the fine-woven woolens. Cote and hose, not one of Arcea's shapeless silk robes, and sensible red and brown rather than the white and purple of the Empress' servants. It wasn't his day to work in the stables, and he hadn't been sure Seraphine would let him. The chance to see the horses made the next part easier.

With a little kir in his hands, he raked his fingers through his hair. His crest evened out and darkened. His eyes tingled. The woolen arming-cap he kept on a peg went on over his Blessing ridges but he left the strings untied and hanging. Spring had come early this year, and the snow was already gone. Hardly any need for a cap to keep his ears warm — but that was their deal. He hid his ridges.

The governor's palace was a stone-walled compound just short of a castle. A fortified front gate, a gate-yard and a grand stone house stood to one side. Its stable filled the other side of the square wall, and had its own small gate for receiving messengers and wagons. Nobody there knew he'd been the one who escaped, the morning Seraphine had returned from Wodenberg.

"Didn't expect you," Eldwin, the officer on duty said, reaching out a hand to clasp Anders' as he passed. "Working Equinox too? Couldn't come up with a pissant excuse?"

"I'm only here to balance," Anders answered.

Eldwin's brow creased and he snorted. "Balance? Only grand-mams worry about that. Grand-mams and deep-wood hicks."

Anders had picked up Suevi quickly, but it was enough like Alemannic that he always slipped into old habits and marked himself a northerner. His story, in the stables, was that he came from the hill country around the headwaters of the Dúnforst-éa — a week's walk past nowhere, so far as Reowans cared.

Arcea had disbanded the Order after the conquest of Suevia. No Ters or Thers served the people here. The Mother and Father weren't spoken of. Seraphine was all that mattered.

"All things equal, on the table." Anders turned in passing, spread his arms as if laying it all out. "Merry Equinox to you." Eldwin and his fellow gate-guard only shrugged and turned back to watching the street.

There was more bustle in the stables than Anders expected. A wagon stood just inside the gate, full of barrels branded with the local brewing guild's seal. Horsfald, the stable-master, had the wagon-dray by the bridle, checking his teeth. Two messengers waited for horses, and Cys was just leading out the two-socked brown for the first of them. The boy hardly spared Anders a glance in passing.

Halfway down the barn, Trinket looked out of her stall and blew a raspberry. "Home already?" Anders went straight to the mare, stroked her cheek and then her neck. "Glad to see you, pretty girl. Yes, you're the prettiest here." She'd been claimed by the governor's son, on Anders' last working shift, to go duck-hunting in the delta marshes. Spring had come early, and the ducks as well.

Trinket's grey dapples were darker than Nipper's. She had a broad white blaze, where he had only a little star. But she was a feisty girl, and she'd known at their first meeting that Anders would scratch her neck if she nibbled on his sleeve.

"Had a nice run in the fresh air?" he asked, hands slowing to rest on her warm hide. "Out in the grass and the sun?"

Reowan was a far larger city than Wodenberg, and much more crowded. Grass grew where it could, wherever feet and hooves hadn't pounded the dirt hard. Whenever the sea breeze ebbed, the smell of shit and rot crawled up to nose-height. The salt pine was the only tree Anders had seen since he'd woken with his cote still blood-crusted where Kiefan's sword had run him through.

Anders put his head against Trinket's and breathed her scent. "Would you take me out there?" He slipped into Alemmanic, in a whisper. "How far could you get me? Before…?"

Fool to think it, even. He'd learned how to pinch his bond shut, but Seraphine was too… clever, or else prescient. It hardly mattered which. She owned him now, and there was no escape. Equinox meant war was marching back to Wodenberg. To Kate. And not a damn thing Anders could do.

Trinket looked up as feet approached; Horsfald's thick hand cuffed Anders' shoulder. "Here even on Equinox? I should fire the rest. You and I can run this stable ourselves."

"I came to balance," he answered. "I owed Trinket some scratching. I owe you my thanks."

The big man huffed a laugh. He reached to pat Trinket too, stepping past Anders to reach her. "Balance? Out in those hills, they may keep the old ways but don't —"

Horsfald's head turned when Anders pulled off his arming-cap, then the big man threw himself back. He stared at the ridges.

"Bloody beard, Andwear, what —?"

"Anders," he corrected. "I owe you the truth, and the right name. You've been kind to me."

He still stared. "You're Alemann. From Wodenberg. But your reference came from Áering —" The old man's jaw dropped. "You're the new pet! Pardon, sir, I didn't mean —"

"Little matter. May I balance, in the old way?" Anders put out his hand.

Horsfald clasped it. Voice low, he said, "Nothing is owed, brother lamb. Shepherd see you home."

It had the worn feel of an old saying. Anders nodded. "Shepherd see you home."

He walked out, with his cap back on, and met Cys on the way in. The boy raised a hand, expecting one of those quick clasps the Suevi traded. Anders cuffed him, Blessing-quick, across the head and the boy stumbled with mouth dropping open. "What was that for?"

"You left all that tack to be polished." Anders turned on his heel. "That was your chore."

"I forgot!"

Anders waved the excuse off and kept going with a grin. Balanced.

From the stable's gate, it was a short walk to the front of the governor's palace where the plaza was full of music and dancing. Peddlers with push-carts lined the road, offering meat pies, ale from a keg, or trinkets. Cloth flowers and ribbons for girls' hair, in particular, though Anders spotted a few caps hanging over the lip of one cart. He took the brown one and switched the arming cap for it while the peddler wasn't looking.

Suevi knit caps came to a point, which was to be folded over to one side at a fashionably jaunty angle. Anders' arming cap had kept his ears warm and his ridges hidden, but it was a dull thing. Especially for Equinox.

"Suits you well, sir, for three sesterces." The matron added a warm smile.

He had that in a small purse under his cote. That had been something else he'd learned; there were few pickpockets in Wodenberg. Once paid, he was sure to go unnoticed through the plaza — by guardsmen, at least. Surely ladies seeking a dance partner would notice him.

The platform in the center of the plaza had been scrubbed clean and decked with garlands. A band of several drums, flutes, and dulcimers led the festival from there, and the dancers swirled before them, running ten deep in places. A collection of booths alongside the platform had been taken over from the usual clerks by a rogue kitchen; chickens roasted on spits, the smell of potato soup wafted from a kettle, and they were doing brisk business. Rimming the plaza, more push-cart peddlers hawked their wares.

Suevi songs were different. Their dances had a few different steps that could trip you up. Anders watched at first, as the partners wove back and forth, turning and bowing in time. They smiled, they frowned in concentration, they danced, they were not so different from good-folk in Wodenberg in that. They meant to enjoy the day, away from their duties to Suevia and Arcea.

The song ended and the dancers cheered. Anders scanned the milling crowd as the next song's name was called out. There. A lady led an older man to the benches around the edge of the plaza; he was red-faced, laughing, but needing her help. Old enough to be her father.

Anders was there when her father landed on the bench with a gusty sigh. "A dance, m'lady?" He offered his hand. To the man, "May I?"

Her surprise melted into a smile. Her father gave his blessing, and they were off. It was a slower dance, but had some tricky footwork to keep Anders careful. Good for easing him into the festival. Next song, he had a new partner and a quicker pace to keep up with. Dances began to run together; the band was large enough that its members traded off songs to rest, and the dancers simply found their way out to food and drink as needed.

There was a core of those who meant to dance the day away, and Anders worked his way into it. He paired with a girl barely old enough for budding breasts — but she had all the easy grace of a yearling filly. Then a woman with callused hands and a plaited straw wreath around her head, who was not so graceful but loved every heartbeat of the dance. A tea-skinned Arceal lady, dark hair braided and looped, who met his eyes so sharply that Anders was sure she recognized him despite the hat and his brown eyes. She said nothing, though, and stole a kiss when the dance's steps gave her leave to.

At the end of that song, Anders let go of the Arceal lady's hand a moment and was grabbed by a new one. The woman responsible shot him a teasing grin when he startled — most Suevi girls weren't so bold — and then he laughed when he saw why. She wore a pointed brown cap, too.

"We must dance, then," he said, with a bow.

"We must."

She stayed with him, even though the band worked up to its fastest dances to wear the crowd out. When Anders missed a step, she began warning him when the next change was coming. The plaza began to thin out, which gave the dedicated core of dancers more space to show off and that suited them just fine. His partner laughed in his arms, giddy with the speed, and her blue eyes glowed. The band's barker called out the last turn of the floor and it flew by all too fast.

When the music stopped, the cheering boiled up in the gap. Anders heaved a great breath and whooped with them; his lady laughed again and leaned on his arm. He hadn't noticed how dry his throat had gotten in all the fun. They'd come to a stop a few strides from an ale peddler.

"Thirsty?" He pointed. She nodded, still cheering the band — they'd earned it, true enough.

The peddler drew them a cup while Anders fished out the sesterces. He stepped to one side, out of the way, as he took the first taste. Its sourness curled his lip. Sour and thin. His dance partner reached for it and he passed the cup.

"It's piss," he warned her. "Street ale. Over-priced and watered down."

She took a swallow and shrugged. "But it's drunk in good company." To return it, she sidled closer, under his arm.

Anders' brows rose. Her blue eyes held his, her smile turned up at him. His hand had found her firm butt all on its own, and she gave no sign of minding that. Might steal a kiss. Wanted to, for a heartbeat. Four moons of starving, after the feast in Kate's arms...

It ached all the more. He looked away from her gaze, groping for kind words to turn her down.

An angry shout; a hand snatched the lady's hat and slapped her with it. Her brown hair tumbled free, shoulder long. Anders had the man's wrist in his grip, his arm twisted, before the next word was out. The speed took him by surprise. Snarling, the man put his weight into a lunge. Anders slipped aside and let him crash into the next peddler's cart over.

His lady caught Anders' arm, rattling too fast for him to follow, and then dove past him to pull her man up from the ground. The peddler threw in a few curses as she apologized. The attacker shot Anders a heavy glare as he gained his feet. Anders shifted his weight to a more ready stance, clenching back his kir; it wanted to lash out. Everyone was looking, their faces turning alarmed and confused.

"Graeme, come. It was only a dance, and he was a gentleman. I swear it!" The girl dragged on his arm as he eyed Anders. He shrugged her off and pretended to straighten his cote. Then Graeme grabbed her by one wrist and hauled her away, cursing under his breath.

The audience lost interest, turned away with no sidelong looks, no half-hidden smirks over this juicy bit for the gossip mill. Anders was just another face here. Far from home. Alone. All his accounts that needed balancing were well out of reach. He leaned against the wall between the two peddler's carts, not wanting to rattle them off even as they came to mind. There was money he still owed: a tab at the Black Knight tavern, old debts on Arbor Street. He'd sworn to his mother that he wouldn't make her cry again, and owed her much for breaking that.

Kate, he owed his love to. Rafe.

Kiefan, he owed…

Anders pushed off the wall, his mouth set in a line against the smoldering bile in his gut. He'd lost his cup of ale, but it was barely worth drinking in any case. The afternoon grew old, to guess by the angle of the sun. He crossed the plaza to the governor's main gate, weaving through the crowd with little care for who he bumped on the way. The captain of the watch knew the password he gave, and sent him on through.

CHAPTER 17

Seraphine maintained a guest suite at the governor's palace. Blythe had laid out Anders' robe on one of the trundle beds; he was pulling off his cote as he crossed the lush bedroom to it. Blythe looked up from re-sewing one of the seed pearls on Seraphine's dark banquet gown and smiled to herself. He stripped to his linens and picked up his white robe. Wide purple stripes, at the cuffs, the hem, and along the bold sweep of the right-hand flap.

"You've been sweating. Fresh linens, too," Blythe said. "Shall I get them?"

He'd dry off by the time the food was served. Anders slung the robe around his shoulders, arms through the loose sleeves. Button the left flap inside the right shoulder. Button the right flap outside the left shoulder. The golden disk, etched with the Empress' sun, shone against the purple stripe. Damn hem knocked around the top of his ankles; adding his belt and blousing the robe out a little got him another inch or two higher. There was a purple silk cap, to replace the brown one.

Blythe looked up again as he pulled his shoes back on, and tsked.

"Didn't see enough of me this morning?"

She knotted her thread. "A pleasing scene is joy for all."

If she wanted to play, he could turn those tables quick enough. He could kiss her on the way out. Could goose her. Most likely, she'd shoo him off, perhaps slap him, and drop the game. If not, Seraphine's bed was two steps and a sweep of the silk curtains away. He could find out if she was a wildcat or not.

Mother have mercy. His fey streak had slept sound for a year and a half and now its teeth were back in him as if it had never left.

Anders steered well clear of Blythe, in leaving.

<hr />

Seraphine was not in her usual sitting room, taking her afternoon tea; she was in the governor's grand hall. That took some finding, as Anders had only been to the palace a few times. The governor's staff had little time to direct one of the Empress' servants, what with the banquet to have ready by sundown. He reached the hall frowning from the pinches of annoyance.

Anders took in the scene in a heartbeat, and put his back to the wall beside the servants' door to wait on her notice and orders. He set his face to bland. Queen Mercia had taught him how to note everything while staring into the distance; it was a vital skill if you wished to avoid her notice and yet dodge the slap aimed at your cheek if you failed.

Three straight lines of young Suevi stood at stiff attention before the steps up to the high banquet table. Twenty-some of them, looking to be twelve to fourteen in age, boys and girls in an even mix. All wore short, Arceal-style robes with baggy trousers. Some sweat in fear, others stared at the garlands of pussy willow and forsythia hung along the walls.

The Empress, in purple, slid silently through their ranks with her thick braid trailing behind her. A step behind that came Saint Musaad. He worked another bit of gold behind his back as if it were bread dough.

"And these did score highest in their examinations," he said, in Arceal, as they reached the front row.

Seraphine sounded them as she walked the line, by how their kir stirred. Examinations governed all, in Arcea; they found the kir-gifted and those with other talents, they could set a child on the road to education, or they could turn him out for common labor. If one were an Arceal citizen, passing the examinations could earn government office, power, and salary.

These youths were Suevi, though. They were the country's quarterly tithe in kir-gifted.

"Now a dozen combat-gifted here, good, for I lost my elite minotaurs in Castle Kaltkern." Seraphine paused before one tall, sandy-haired boy. He'd had some sword training, by his stance. "Mark this one thus. Shall turn Blessed."

Blessed minotaurs. Anders glanced to the tall boy, tried to picture him with the tawny bull's head of the monster that had stood in Kaltkern's bloody hall. The beast had taken the head clean off Stanislav, the poor bastard. When Anders fought clear of the four Arceal knights at last and stabbed the monster in the back, it had swung around so fast Anders needed speed to duck. The pique of warning from his anticipation had saved his neck.

Only a scratch, his stab through that iron lamellar, but the distraction had let Aleks strike its thigh well. Even fallen, the minotaur had fought hard.

"We must replenish centaur ranks, as well. But Chale would try new hybrids, he did say," Musaad said. His long fingers flicked behind his back and a knob of gold twisted down on a slender thread. Reeled back up, as quickly.

"Chale would ever try new hybrids." Seraphine sighed. "Shall need to focus his mind, should he think frogs might serve my army. Send him half these. I'll waste no more than that."

The tithed children came from all over Suevia, and had either mastered poker faces or knew no word of Arceal. Not one flicker of fear in their eyes at the chance of being made into frog-men.

Seraphine looked down the rows one last time. "None shall be even elect, la. None at Solstice, as well." She pursed her mouth and switched to Suevi. "Many of you are chosen for elite training. The rest will serve lesser functions. For all, equal chance of citizenship. Serve your fifteen years and join us."

Had that minotaur stood and smiled in pride when he heard he was chosen? Had he been as proud when he woke in the body of a monster? The things had men's eyes, still, broad-set over a muzzle. Always rage and hate burning in them, that Anders had seen.

Seraphine's hand flicked as she crossed the hall to the grand stair; Anders was quick to follow at the summons. Musaad walked beside her, speaking that language Anders didn't know. Seraphine answered likewise.

Her beasts, those minotaurs. And the centaurs. Her bound saint. Her pet Blessed knight. She thought nothing of leading them up to her bedroom. Once there, she dropped her robe without a care to change into her jeweled gown, giving orders all the while.

She was more deadly naked than Anders was in full battle gear.

There was no running. So he held the Empress' pearl-spangled gown for her to step into, like a good servant, and pushed the gnawing despair deep into his gut.

* * *

Empress Seraphine received her banquet guests with Saint Musaad on one hand and the governor on her other. Anders and Laurent stood a few steps behind her, at ready for anything she might need.

Most guests were ministers and nobles. The few officers, Anders took note of, sifting those who'd gone soft in command-pavilion leadership from those who still had their sharp eyes and knight's prowl. They noted him, in turn, knew what he was likewise, but they said nothing of it.

Anders tracked one such captain-general and the pretty wife on his arm as the last guests stepped forward for introduction. Those were a set of three, to break from the stream of couples, and at a glance none were Suevi. Dark-haired, dark-eyed, two of them tanned.

"Elect Liandro, good," Seraphine said with a nod to the elder of the two men. "You shall ride to Ansehen, execute him in command of the infirmary for incompetence and take that post." Turning to the woman, a knight by her stance, the Empress said, "Elect Carina, Saint Gauvail expects you in Temitte."

That left the younger man, the pale one who kept his hands behind his back. An aggressive profile on that one, like the hard line of a sword. And a hint of training with the blade, Anders' Blessing noted. Seraphine paused a moment, considering him.

"Elect Titos."

A quick bow. "Indeed, Empress."

"Melantha's new binding. Ellerene, yes?"

"Born of Aktipoli."

"She gave no specialty for you."

He managed a smile. "I have proven equal in all, thus far."

Titos' kir twitched when Seraphine sounded him. She listened, then nodded. "Your hand."

He held it out. A thick blade of kir sprang from Seraphine's hand and she caught his saint's bond in the other. It fought the blade, shining brighter red as she bore down. It snapped in a flash that left a green afterglow in Anders' eyes.

"Musaad, claim him," Seraphine said. "You will be of use here, Elect Titos."

Saint Musaad flicked a little kir-knife out and opened the meridian on his left arm with one slash. Titos wasn't quick enough for him, and the saint cut his open as well, then grasped his forearm. Anders felt an echo of the harsh call from the saint, yanking the elect's meridian into a bond with his own. Titos flushed red, closing his eyes a moment, but then steadied. Musaad drew his hand away and their joined meridians stretched, winding down to cords that joined them hand to hand.

Anders' fingers twitched against his right palm. His brow lowered. So that was how she'd bound him.

At a nod, the three Elect went to their seats at the Empress' own table. Titos, by his careful poker face, was resigned to his fate. She turned to her seated guests and raised her hands, the pearls gleaming against the dark silk of her long gown. "May the celebration of Equinox begin, dear friends."

Anders' seat in the banquet was at a humble table. So far as the governor knew, Anders was the Empress' favored servant and apparently that was sufficient explanation. The ministers and minor nobles Anders sat among took little interest as well.

The cockfighting ring thrown down in the middle of the banquet floor was ample distraction. Servants dished out trenchers of fresh spring greens and the soft rolls that the Suevi liked so much while the duel-master called out the first two roosters' litanies of success. The birds did their best to drown him out with their crowing.

Anders had been down to the cockfighting ring by the river a few times. It was out of his way and lacked in young ladies, so it hadn't held him for long. The cocks' initial strutting, feathers standing out in ruffs on their necks, and the quick lunges with their claws, were interesting enough but once one bird was down there was little to see.

He knew what blood looked like and didn't need reminders.

The early lettuce and dandelion salad was good. It had thin-sliced onion and a scattering of shaved cheese, too. He reached for his stein, took a swallow of ale to wash — and nearly spat the sour mouthful out. With a wince, he swallowed it.

"Mercy," he muttered, looking into the stein. Red. Red vinegar, or near enough. Bad as the street vendor's, only stronger. This had to be a jest. "Girl!"

A servant girl carrying a pitcher of the stuff came. "Yes, sir?"

Anders held up his stein. "Get me some of the brown beer." That was fair stuff, if in need of more hops.

"Sir, this is what we are to serve."

"Whatever barrel-dregs you have, I'd rather drink them."

Her brow crinkled, looking at his stein. "The brown ran out two days past, sir."

Mother have mercy. "A pot of tea, then." His voice had to rise, over the screeching roosters. Anders tossed the ale on the floor. "I won't drink this piss."

A few faces turned. The girl blushed. She bobbed a curtsy and ran. Anders thumped his stein on the table and shot a glare at the man across the table, who looked stunned.

"I'd drink it if you won't," he said.

"I'll send you a barrel of my mother's vinegar, as well, " Anders said around a mouthful of bread. They were afraid of crusts in Suevia, it would seem. Crusts and decent beer.

The crowd cheered when the black cock knocked the brown one down, got its claws into one wing and tore. A few hard pecks and the dark bird's beak was red. The brown cock thrashed, a few feathers scattering, but fell still. The winner was held up by its owner for more cheering.

Down on the river, one could cross the street from the cockfighting ring and get a cheap bowl of yesterday's losers, stewed with onions.

Anders finished his salad and reached for — his stein was still empty.

"Would you have mine?" The young wife beside the vinegar-lover nudged her own stein with an uncertain smile. She had a baby on her knee, perhaps a year old, who gummed at one of the soft rolls.

Anders' warmest smile and a gentle tease leaped to ready, all too easy, and nearly slipped out. The baby, with his halo of blond hair, caught the words. Rafe. But no, she was no Kate: a heavy bosom, freckles, hair tucked away under a veil. Anders closed his mouth. His throat twisted shut for a moment, wishing Kate was there, warm against his side and smelling of herbs.

Two page boys brought platters of roasted duck, saving him from having to answer. In a heartbeat, both drumsticks had been claimed. Anders leaned over with his eating knife to slice off a breast and got it back to his plate. A spoonful of crisp-fried potatoes were added to his trencher. Anders snapped his fingers, and got a second. Those were good, he knew. He snagged the mustard pot from the middle of the table.

His stein was still empty. "Boy!"

One of the pages pulled up short.

"Brown beer, or a pot of tea." Anders held up his stein. The boy frowned, confused, but nodded and went.

Perhaps a visit to the kitchen would get more results.

In the ring, a fresh pair of roosters came out of their sacks, crowing. The white one flapped his wings as he was held up, proud of his list of victories. Anders craned to see the first pass; these two were fierce, and got right into it rather than dancing first. He went back to his duck and potatoes.

A thick hand landed on his shoulder. "If you would explain, sir, the trouble?"

Anders looked up and turned to straddle the bench; the man was grey-haired, bearded, and barrel-stout but not soft. He noted Anders' white-and-purple robe, the purple arming cap, with a frown, but then replaced that with a smile. A shallow one, as befit his rich woolens and silk, and the gold chain around his neck with the heavy sigil of some minor official. "I've been told you've refused my ale?"

He was responsible for the awful stuff, then. "I did. I would have something worth drinking with this fine banquet."

"This red ale, fresh from my cellars, is well blended and judged the finest in the land, sir." The greybeard took a pitcher from the page beside him and reached for Anders' stein. "If I may explain its —"

Anders put a hand on his arm to stop him. "No need. It would be poured out on the street in Wodenberg, I know that quite well."

Folk watched, eyes wide. Let them.

"Wodenberg?" The man's brows rose. Color flushed his face. "Breówan has been under the Empress' commission for three generations now. I'll not be insulted by a servant."

As if Arcea knew anything of beer. Anders rose from the bench to lean over Breówan. "You're serving her piss and I won't drink it."

That got a snarl. "We'll find some brew you may carve with a knife, since cups are such trouble for Alemanni."

He thought a good stout too rich? "You wouldn't know fine beer if —" Anders' hand came up to point, but Herr Breówan flinched and swung to slap him away. Anders slipped aside of it easily and cuffed the old man, which knocked him back a step.

Benches scraped, boots hit the floor, and a kir-rope looped around Anders' raised arm. The rope pulled his arm up, away from Breówan. The saint-bond in his right hand tingled in warning.

/ peace /

Anders spread his raised hand, relaxing his arm. The kir released him. Anders stepped clear of the bench and Herr Breówan's chin rose, expecting more trouble. A son of his, given the fair likeness, rushed to his side with fists clenched.

"There shall be no disagreements in this hall, sirs," Saint Musaad said, from the high table. "Resolve the matter, la."

All eyes on Anders. Strangers, all of them, or near enough. In that moment, he didn't want a single friend. This was no place he wanted to be and nothing he wanted part of. He flicked one hand across the other sleeve, brushing Herr Breówan from his mind, and stalked out of the grand hall through the front door.

The guards posted there made no move to stop him.

Anders didn't bother to pull the door shut behind himself and strode across the gate-yard. His anger wavered a moment, but clearly Seraphine thought nothing of it. She had no need to, after all, he was leashed to her like a dog.

Too much stillness, too much standing and watching with only his thoughts circling and knotting into anger. He needed a sword in his hand, or reins, and to break a sweat. That would clear his mind. It always did.

He passed through the main gate and crossed the plaza. It had darkened with nightfall, and the large tavern across from the palace was the new center of music and good cheer. Light spilled from its open doors.

No. Not there. Anders turned away from it, taking the street toward Castle Áering.

CHAPTER 18

The Shepherd would not rise until midnight, but four of the Flock moons shone and that was enough to find his way down the middle of the street. Craftsmen's shops and merchant stores lined this road, closed now to let their owners join in the celebration. Áering's tall towers loomed above the rooftops and the castle gates stood at the end of the street. The pale granite caught the faint moonlight and shone chilly blue. Anders' breath misted in the cool sea-breeze, the last lingering hint of winter.

His needed a sword, a real one. Laurent would attend Seraphine all night, so he needed a partner as well. And steel was not something Seraphine let him have. Nothing more than his eating knife.

A shame he'd lost Saint Aleks' sword in stumbling from Kaltkern's hall. That had been a lovely thing. Quick and bright.

His feet slowed as memories of the hall flicked back. Jolts of blood and fear; the moment he'd known the four knights he'd faced were Blessed. Feeling his anticipation slip as his kir ran out. One knight had tripped on a corpse and lost his mental grip on his kir; Anders had

Part V: Cold Solace

ripped it from him. Gotten the upper hand, in that heartbeat. The last one had screamed as he gushed.

And then the fury in Kiefan's eyes, and his own anger surging to meet it. His, Kate was his — he'd earned her, fair and honest. Damn anyone who thought they'd take her.

He stopped in the middle of the street. Anders put a hand to his brow, massaged it. Three moons since this had last welled up, three moons of working to master his shifting and caring for the governor's horses. Sleeping alone, his dreams of Kate the only lingering pain. It had been enough.

Too much time alone: no Kate, no Will, Theo, or his mother…

Anders walked again. There would be swords in the castle's gate-house, two or three spares in a rack. He'd seen them often enough.

Feet scraped behind him. Anders cocked an ear and they broke into a run, coming up fast. He spun around and his anticipation piqued: down. The speeding blackjack smacked his hat away, and the man nearly lost his balance in the swing. The second man caught Anders' arm and punched him in the kidney, so deep that his head spun. Still, he lunged away. The first man grabbed his other arm and cuffed him across the head with the stick.

They dragged him off the street in two heartbeats. Anders got his feet under himself at the edge of the alley and twisted in their grip. Kicked, and connected with the blackjacker's knee. He stumbled with a yell. Anders threw his weight into the second man, to pin him to the wall —

Pain burst across his head. On the ground suddenly, rolling on his back, three shadows over him and the fourth rising. His eating knife was in his hand for a moment and then in someone's ankle. Its owner tried to bite back a scream. A boot caught his hip. A blackjack struck his arm, numbed it. Anders ripped through the ankle, the hamstring, and slashed at a shadow. Light contact, maybe a cut. Anticipation had nothing, in the dark; he couldn't see their tells. Cursing, shouts — one landed on him, heavy as a horse, and a blackjack clubbed his shoulder. Anders felt the joint pop out.

With a snarl, he pulled their kir. They had only scraps, but it was enough with his own stash. Nipper. The pattern poured out across his head, his shoulders, stretching his flesh to match. His shoulders shifted, the loose bone falling into place. Anders lunged at the man pinning him, an easy reach with a long neck, knowing just where his head was by his breathing.

The man screamed. Blood in Anders' mouth. He wrenched to the side, rear hooves cutting into the dirt for leverage, and threw the man away. A second jumped on him, but Anders surged up with a warhorse's strength. Nose and ears told him where all four were, and despite the dark he slashed across one's belly. Blood turned the little knife's grip slippery.

"The charm!"

Anders threw off the man on his back, kicked him with one hoof. He hit the wall with a crack. The last one standing lunged, smart enough to feint and get in close. Anders slipped aside just in time, on his speed. He felt a knot of kir, and a knife cut across his side. Shallow, just a scratch. But then the charm lashed out of the blade.

Raw pain ripped through his spine, and he saw his own whorled kir surge and jitter madly. The ground caught him again.

Kir blossomed in the alley, brilliant gold and green. A curtain of it passed over him, heavy as iron, and four screams rose — then vanished in a crunch. The kir dropped into the earth, and darkness resumed its place.

Anders blinked, panting, and the stink of blood and shit filled his horse-nostrils. He hissed, puffed to clear his nose. Tried to sit up, but his arms trembled. Every muscle shivered from that stun charm. Turning his ears, he heard dripping. Quiet breath. One person approached from the mouth of the alley.

Seraphine lit a single kir-flame as she squatted beside him. Anders propped himself up on one hand, still blinking to clear the afterimage of the flash. The stench came from four large smears on the walls, his nose told him. He let the charm unravel and the smell faded. His shoulder ached, but he'd popped that one so often that it barely troubled him.

"A nasty thing," she said, holding up the knife. "For this may kill near anyone. The Breówan are not to be crossed."

She showed it to him in her hand, and then her flesh rippled around it. Took it in, drew it under her skin and toward her body. Seraphine held her arm out straight as it passed her elbow and vanished into her depths. Then she settled back, elbows on her knees, pearly gown winking as she moved.

Anders glanced up into her eyes. His gut tightened. "I deserved it," he said, looking down. "After —"

The wash of pain through his bond jolted the air from his lungs in a gasp. It passed just as quickly.

Seraphine's head tilted, her brows rising.

"I was a fool, back —"

She struck him again, long enough that his spine arched and he nearly tumbled backward. Anders fell onto his elbow, panting, and risked a glance up. Stillness. A calm mask for a face, her dark eyes deep-shadowed by the green light in her hand.

"I'm sorry." He dropped his head onto his arm. "You should've let them —"

The stringence convulsed him, face-down on the dirt, and his stomach heaved up its contents. His heart shuddered in his chest. Black stars whirled through his head. She drew the pain back and let him gasp, but the rest of him lay stiff on the ground.

"You shall not waste my time," Seraphine told him. "These moons have I invested in you, my elect. How many days?" She leaned closer, over his ear, voice falling to a hiss. "Woden gave you so much? Aleksandr? Neither. I offer you the sky. Power. Three times have you turned fool, and that shall end. By midnight, choose your fate."

His knotted muscles eased, trembling, aching. Anders propped himself on both hands, then wiped at the vomit on his cheek. Kir shifted, the candle-flame winked out, and when he looked up Seraphine was gone.

The sand in the courtyard around the fount was cool; it spent the afternoon in the castle's shadow. Anders trudged through the soft stuff, skirting around the fount and its sphere. The traces of kir in his core thrummed as the guardian sensed him, and the ghostly green orb lit. Its dense web of meridians pulsed as kir raced along the lines, blinking to stars at each junction. The kir found its way to a knot near Anders, shifting to track him as he walked. Growing. Tempting.

Anders didn't look at it or the lamplight in the tree house's window. He gripped the sword's hilt, jangled it in his hand to feel its balance. A decent blade, good enough for going through his forms.

Anders crouched at the rill of kir-water trickling to the ocean and soaked up a full ration. His lingering aches eased. His robe stank of vomit and blood, so he unbuckled his belt and stripped it off. His cap was long gone. The breeze raised goose-flesh on him, but braies would do once the exercise warmed him.

His brown-hair charm had gone with the shift to half-horse. Anders stood and faced the sea in his true skin, flaxen knight's crest hanging to one side across his Blessing ridges. He considered the line of rolling waves breaking on the dark rocks, the dim Flock-light picking out the incoming swells, the rich spray of stars beyond the clouds overhead. The Shepherd, half-waned, would rise from the sea come midnight.

He brought the blade up before him, to salute the horizon, and began with the simplest forms.

Ease crept in with the rhythm. His bones knew this. Lunges, parries, deflections. Set combinations that had been drilled into him for use at speed, when the sequence would be over before he fully thought of it. Combinations that he'd devised on his own.

He felt kir move past the fount, and the guardian twinkled in greeting. Anders looked, then let his arm lower.

Seraphine. She'd taken off the gown and came in just a pair of braies. They hung low on her generous hips. She pulled an arc of kir from the fount and spun it into a sword that matched his; it looked too large, on a little thing like her.

She stopped, faced him from a few feet away. Her heavy braid trailed behind her, on the sand. One hand on her hip, she raised the blade in a salute.

Anders had sparred with Captain Aleksandra, but she tended to be fully dressed. And taller.

He saluted in return and took a middle-guard stance. Kept his eyes on hers, his anticipation already piquing faint warnings.

She came fast, smooth, and tricky. Anders managed to deflect her to one side and slipped inside her guard at Blessing speed, meaning to feign a punch to her jaw — but kir flared and a man's pale hand caught his, twisted his wrist, and slung him aside.

Theo, un-scarred and well. Skinny, perhaps, as she hadn't the flesh to fully match him. Anders caught himself, dumping his inertia in a spin, and a snarl boiled up from his core. "You've no right to wear his face."

Seraphine smiled. "Come and take it."

He lunged, and knew all the more it wasn't Theo. He was never so nimble. Anders felt his blade connect, just its tip across Seraphine's shoulder, and the wound flashed red for a moment. Then it vanished. She nearly got him back, but Anders danced back a step. Out of reach, he circled and attacked.

Seraphine knew the sword well enough, and she was fast. Wounds meant nothing, though, and after a few more useless cuts, Anders stalked away from her. She still wore Theo's face; she knew it was a goad, and that alone angered him. Marred his dueling-clarity.

"We are not finished, la," she called after him.

Anders stopped. Perhaps she wasn't finished. But he was finished with this game.

He turned and sped back, throwing a stab square at her heart. Her kir-blade shot up on cue to block, and he let his sword tip to one side as he lunged to spit himself on —

Her kir-blade unraveled as it struck his chest. Seraphine twisted aside, pulling kir in a thick arc, and slammed Anders to the sand. Ropes yanked the sword from his hand. Seraphine shifted back to her curvaceous, tanned self and stepped close to his hip. Kir cloaked her, studded with stars, and pinned Anders from head to toe. He could breathe, but nothing more, under the weight of her mind. She folded her arms under her breasts.

"A lesson," she said, "on healers, crafters and shifters. Should one write a letter, and let slip the wrong word, one might write over it, re-shaping the letters. Thus do healers mend the body, by writing over the damage."

The fount's kir arced still, dancing green and gold in the dark, striking her chest and setting her aglow. From her, it washed into Anders, filling him to capacity. Running over. He never felt so awake and alert, the world all but sharp-edged in its vibrance. The cool sea-breeze felt like ice on his skin, prickling all his hairs.

"When clay grows dry, a potter takes water and does knead it in. Thus, it becomes soft again. Thus do crafters make pliable even stone and steel."

The kir pouring from Seraphine twisted, and Anders felt his flesh turn supple. He knew it from shifting his form, but he couldn't cause it over his full body. Not yet. It must be what melting felt like, but he couldn't move his head to see himself. His heart quickened, wanting to see, yet afraid to. He tried to steady his pattern but the wealth of kir flooded on. Seraphine kept speaking, bathed in green light.

"Shifters do both. We are crafters of our selves. Thus, we are rare and fearsome things, reminding all that we are merely clay." Seraphine squatted beside him, looked him up and down. "Shall I read your future?"

A knife of kir spun from her hand in a slender blade. Anders felt it touch his chest at the top of his breastbone, felt it slip through the layers and then the parting — his heart thudded in his ears, his breath tightened, and Mother have mercy she cut on, past the bone, to his navel. Pain roiled somewhere in the back of his mind, drowned by panic and the heady strength of the kir.

The sea breeze reached its fingers into the line. It had no business there.

He screamed, though it was trapped in his mouth.

Seraphine's little fingers spread his chest open. Air caressed his core, his gut, the inner curve of his ribs.

Eyes clenched shut, he screamed.

Her voice carried over the chaos in his mind. "I see this is the end of your foolishness, or the start of your breaking."

Tears made cold streaks from the corners of his eyes. Anders' screams broke into a sob. Seraphine waited. The first clear thought that came through his terror was a lamb, gutted and skinned, its carcass on a butcher's block as he rendered it into roasts and steaks.

Shepherd, have pity.

Seraphine looked him in the eye, and the pinning weight on Anders' head lifted. He breathed hard, his mind a blazing tangle of fears. Still, she waited. It cleared, slowly. The pain rose and the chill itched on the verge of a shiver. Anders swallowed and searched for words.

"Do not think to charm me," she said. "Your sort, I meet often. Smiles and warm words for all, but never do you show your true face. Thus, you will be such a rose in my garden — that secret core you hide. A shifter may lose himself in another body. You won't. All your life, already, you've been a cambifax."

"I would be a horse, or a vulture, but not another man." Anders' voice rasped after all his screams.

"Be woman, then." Seraphine said it as a simple fact. "Your choice is this: be a secret no more, my bound elect and student of Cambifax, la. Crested, if it please you." She spared a twist of her mouth for his hair. "Take friends and lovers as you will. Your life is here. Or refuse me. Be broken at your core and re-made, weaker, true, but still for my use."

Anders' throat twisted shut, but anger won out. "This is my choice? You stole me from my home, my family, and call this a choice?"

"You remember not, then? When I asked what they did to earn your loyalty — as I stemmed your bleeding — you said: nothing."

He stared up at her. There'd been blackness after he drew the sword from his chest. She might say anything. "Qadeem told me not to trust you."

Seraphine smiled, warm. She put a hand over Anders' spread ribcage and it creaked shut. The cut remained, though. "Qadeem. Such ideals, such lofty thoughts he spun out. Children often spew such, before they learn the truth. It's well that he has taken on responsibilities. Perhaps he has matured at last, and seen that there is only what you can do and what you cannot. There is no should."

"I never said it," Anders told her, "because it's not true. Kate earned my loyalty. She judged me fairly, she trusted me, she stood by me. And she loved me." His throat tightened again. "I swore to the Mother and Father to be her husband."

Seraphine's lip curled, and she leaned closer. "You swore. To the Mother and Father. And when did you last meet? Ever? You swore to two painted boards — what can they do? What can I do?"

Her hand slipped between the halves of his breastbone, and his beating heart felt fingers. She stroked it as it quickened. "No, no, don't…" His whispers trailed off, strangled by terror.

"I am your saint."

His eyes closed, surrendering. Begging Kate for forgiveness.

"Say it."

At a whisper, "You are my saint."

The hand left him unhurt. "If you wish to be a husband, you shall be. Arcea has a thousand girls within its walls. Surely one will suit you."

His stomach sank. Arcea was a long way off, though.

Seraphine ran her finger along his cut chest, and it knit shut obediently. Kir drained from him, down to what his core could keep. His flesh settled, firmed again. She shifted from her crouch to sitting cross-legged beside him, and eased the binding weight on his body.

The half-Shepherd peeked above the horizon behind her, swollen as if with sea-water.

Anders sat up, looked down at his chest. Not even a thin scar remained. The breeze tickled his skin and he shivered; he looked to Seraphine, struggled with the thought for a moment, and moved to curl up beside her. Laid his head on her thigh. He felt the muscle tense, suspicious for a heartbeat, but then her hand rested on his shoulder and she relaxed.

"Begin work on faces, and I'll train you further on your animal forms as well," she said. "You shall master one full shift, I believe. I have read it in your sounding. But you must choose which: horse or rukh."

The face-shifting was what pinched him with dread. "Do you mean to make me spy on my own, in another face? Kill for you?"

Seraphine breathed a laugh. "I am no fool. You'll not see Wodenberg again." Her fingers brushed locks of his crest from his face. "We will push from Ansehen and strike east for the little fount. Woden will think me eager to lay siege. No, I saw his weak spot. So soon as my army turns east, you and I turn southward. To Arcea. Your home is there, with me. Musaad and Gauvail will see to the war."

His fear eased, a little. Mother, keep Kate strong. Keep Rafe well. If he dared hope they would survive, if she could be happy with Kiefan… Anders sighed. He would be far away, hoping to never hear that she'd been killed.

He murmured, "Thank you," and turned his head to touch a kiss to Seraphine's thigh, through the linen braies. Her breast brushed the back of his head. His hand lay on her knee, near his kiss, and he lingered a moment on a thought — a possibility.

Seraphine snorted. "For you believe you're stallion enough for me?"

Challenge in her voice, but if she could drive Kate from his mind… Anders sat up, just behind Seraphine, and shifted again. Nipper's dark nose was velvet-soft; he nuzzled her cheek with his lightest touch, his smallest whuff.

A laugh broke her face into a grin, and the sly glint in her eye stirred his own fey streak.

KNAPPTAL

Morn after the Equinox, Teleri woke to dawn's grey light caught in the bed-curtains. It was later than she usually woke, as they'd been late to bed and later to sleep. She rolled, found Ciara blanket-less and cool-skinned, and cuddled against her back. The silken night-shift slid under her hand, scraping where her calluses caught the delicate stuff. Tel laid her head close by her love's hair, breathed her faint spice. Closed her eyes a moment more.

Tannait had been right; once all was done and settled in his mind, Kiefan had made plans to ride despite the snow. She'd gone to tell him what more he needed to know of the plan, and to give him the twin-charm she wore. That was a saint-made charm of two parts. Each half was bound to a bit of carved bone knot-work strung on a leather thong, and when one released the charm on one necklace its kir shot to its mate around the neck of someone else. No matter how far. Only a small amount, so it needed a sensitive wearer, but it signaled well.

Kiefan had meant to return for equinox, to ride into Suevia with his flanking soldiers. Now he didn't need to. Just as well; Ciara worried afresh on the matter of not sealing the passes, of confronting the saints under the Mother Tree, and little needed Kiefan in that muddle.

Teleri's hand stroked across Ciara's belly, lingered for a heartbeat. She leaned, touched a slow kiss to Ciara's neck, and rolled away. Pulled on her boots and rose from the bed, reaching for her blue uniform. Buckled on her sword-belt. Opening her own iron-bound chest, she fished out her half of the twin-charm and tied it around her neck, then slipped it under her clothes. Deeper down, she found a small leather sack with a knotted drawstring, and loosened the tie. Inside, small things clinked: a hairpin, a brooch, and the like.

Ciara had given Tel a pair of soft leather shoes with small brass buckles shaped like maple leaves, and they were in the chest as well. They were meant for the once or twice a year Teleri had no reason to put on boots, and though near seven years old the shoes were still new. She cut one little buckle off with her knife, kissed it, and added it to the sack. Knotted it tight and took it, dropping the chest lid softly. A rucksack waited, half-hidden beside it, with all she truly needed. Teleri stuffed her mementos inside as she went.

In the mess hall, she found her Blades preparing for leave-taking. "Aisling." Teleri beckoned her senior captain aside. "You shall take command of the Crown's Blades. Do charge you with seeing the Crown home safe — to Gwyrddinas, not Castle Adhalon. Needs must ride direct to the Mother Tree. 'Tis her command and my request, as your past commander." She took a breath. "Never meet the Crown more than half-way, when she turns stubborn. Shall hear reason, when her ears clear."

Sorrow creased Aisling's eyes, but she held to attention. "'Tis an honor, Elect. Needs must say — you'll be sorely missed."

That pinched Teleri's heart harder than it ought to. She nodded, clapped the captain on one shoulder, and strode from the mess hall with her rucksack. Two steps from the door, she met Captain Fionn and put out a hand to catch him. Pulled him into a fierce, brief hug about the shoulders. "Work them hard," she told him. "Keep at the Crown's sword-work."

"What?" He frowned a moment and then it melted into dismay. Teleri put a finger to her lips and walked on.

In the Wache's gate-yard, horses waited in rows. All the Crown's baggage, all her companions', made its way onto pack-mules. Teleri went to the stables, where her gelding waited, and saddled him up. It was good to do it herself, this time.

When she led him out by the reins, Ciara stood in the open stable door with arms folded. Spring sunshine made an angry silhouette of her.

"Did mean to melt away, as the snow?"

"Meant to find you, ere I reported to my new commander," Teleri answered. She approached the door and Ciara held her ground. "Did lose my command when I failed my Crowns, Cici. 'Tis right. Conbarre agreed Aisling is best for the post. She'll see you safely home."

"Saint Conbarre did order you to — stay? With Tadhlon? Or —" Ciara's grief twisted her mouth when Teleri only looked at the reins in her hands. "Or 'tis your choice, to leave me sooner?"

"'Tis for me to ride with Tadhlon, to flank the enemy at Ansehen. And on to Temitte. 'Tis for me to stand between them and Kiefan, when he knows he'll get no further aid. Or mayhaps Mother Strength has her own plan. I've not served Caercoed fifty years to see it torn asunder by duchies and made weak for Arcea to invade. Conbarre does as she believes best. 'Tis for me to do as I believe best, as well." Teleri braved meeting Ciara's damp eyes, to tell her more. "I did learn, over time, that broken hearts do heal. Wish it, or not. I do hope, if we meet again, you've forgiven me."

Ciara hugged her tight, and took a hard squeeze in return. "Would have you with me, Tel," she whispered, throat tight. "Needs must be a Crown of old... do need you ever at my back."

Teleri put her at arm's length, by her shoulders. "Seven years, I've tried to say it. 'Twas ever in you, waiting to flower. Not a Crown of old, but Ciara Crierwy. Needing no Elect to be her shadow. Go, beloved, and fear nothing."

A kiss. Ciara went, her hand lingering in Tel's until their fingers slipped free of each other. Teleri watched her walk away, one last time. Tannait moved in from the side, having waited her turn.

"Mother Strength guide you. Father Care bring you safely home." The elder Elect gave an ancient benediction. "Fare you better than I, dear sister."

Teleri narrowed her eyes, with a smile. "'Tisn't such a danger. Eryr Pass isn't so far."

"True, but I'm to call down the landslides before the battlements and seal the pass." Tannait folded her arms, kicked a pebble away. "If I'm to be stopped, needs must be struck from behind ere I begin. Mother grant they not split my skull in the doing."

"Mother grant," she agreed. "And Father grant that Saint Sabh forgives you for it."

Tannait embraced her, for a moment, and in parting took Teleri's chin in her strong hand. Looked up with a stern eye. "Am honored to have known you, Elect Teleri."

"Am honored you did teach me, Elect Tannait."

There'd be no forgiveness from Conbarre, when the truth was out. When the passes stood open, the Tadhlon Guard gone missing, and her own Elect the plotter of it all. Rage would pour through the bond until Ciara made her stand at the Mother Tree, backed by the duchesses. Might not end, even then.

So be it. Ciara would live, and rule.

Leading her gelding, Teleri walked through the Wache's open gate alone. Rogue.

DISCIPLE, PART VI
fount's crucible

CHAPTER 1

I'd known I must face Kiefan, in time, but Equinox came without word from him.

A hush spread through the chatting around me. I hardly noticed until Alice cut off her story mid-sentence and stared past my shoulder. Frida, sitting beside her, set her teeth on her lower lip. I twisted on my seat; the menfolk had carried my kitchen table and benches outside into the sunny afternoon so we could watch the children run and shriek while we drank small beer.

"Elect Kate?" A fourteen-year-old boy in a red royal messenger's tabard stood at the mouth of the narrow alley between my shop and my neighbor's. His horse stood two steps behind, its reins in his hand.

I shifted Rafe onto my shoulder and stood. "Yes?"

One of the fathers hissed an order and even the little ones screeched to a halt on the grass. Alice's daughter Magda ran screaming in delight a little further before she realized nobody was chasing. My family, my few friends, half a dozen neighbors, all looked from me to the messenger as he unrolled his list of announcements. The hush deepened to silence.

"By order of Saint Woden and His Majesty the king, Elect Kate is to accompany Duke Vysokov's reserve forces to the king's camp at Straussweg. Duke Vysokov departs next morn." The messenger surveyed my guests and asked, "Baron Rossweide?"

My father-in-law stood. "Rossweide is ready."

The boy read the official message in any case. "By order of Saint Woden and His Majesty the king, Rossweide will muster its garrison and report to Captain-general Steif, to replenish the city garrison and remain under his command until further instruction. Theo Kaufmann?"

Theo had incited this Equinox party in my yard. "Here."

"Expect further orders." The boy rolled his messages up and bowed to me. I nodded to dismiss him.

My neighbors murmured, exchanged glances. Alice circled the table to be the first to hug me good-bye and said, "They just had to ruin Equinox, didn't they."

Linde put a hand on my arm. "It'll be no trouble," she said, heading off the question I meant to ask. She was the only woman I'd found who Rafe would nurse from. "Gar will be glad to have a brother until you're home."

Frida had gone to her husband and son first, grateful that they'd be staying here; I was next. "Mother Love bless and keep you," she said while she squeezed me with both arms. When she loosened her grip, she kissed Rafe.

"I know you and Linde will keep him safe," I said, wanting it to be true. If things went badly at Ansehen, if Arcea laid siege to the city again — I steered my mind from what might happen. Saint Woden's war-craft, I trusted. Qadeem's wit, I trusted. And all my preparations for this were well made.

"Keep yourself safe. A warm hearth waits for you here." Frida put one hand on Alice and one on Linde, to include them. Linde was still rather overwhelmed by the force of Frida's kind attention each time it turned on her, but she smiled bravely.

Frida began to sing the Mother's benediction, and within a few words all the others had joined in. I didn't sing along; it was for me, for m'lord Reinhardt, Will, and Theo who moved to stand with me. The baron listened with his chin lowered, eyes shut. He must've received this benediction several times, in his life.

My eyes misted. I was going to war and they loved me enough to sing. Most of them sang the friends' verse. Frida stepped closer to take her husband's and son's hands and sing the mother's verse to them. When they finished, each came to wish us well. M'lord Reinhardt clasped my hand with a sober nod. Even Theo's wife Brynhilde, with their little girl Mina on her hip, did the same. My neighbors assured me they'd watch my shop, dust it weekly, and remind Linde to send word to me about Rafe.

When Will came, I gave him a quick hug and did the same for Adaliya — the young lady who Frida had found foolishly unattended during the Solstice banquet. Her father was one of the Russe barons riding with Duke Vysokov, and she was a squire herself. I didn't doubt she'd earn her knighthood. Adaliya and Will had much in common and she had turned up for many Saint-day communal dinners at our Orderhaus despite the long ride from her father's camp.

Frida pulled Adaliya away for a hug, as she'd be leaving with her father, and Will leaned close to my ear. "Should I ask her?"

"You think I can give advice?" I teased him back. They were both of an age with me; how did I know any more of love than they did? "It would thrill your mother."

He considered, mouth pursing. "I'll ask Father for the bracelet. If he agrees, I'll approach her father tonight."

As the heir, he had claim to the Rossweide betrothal jewelry. Anders had made my lamia-tooth necklace because he couldn't offer me any such. My fingers went to the fangs at my neck, thinking of him.

Rafe squealed just by my ear and threw his arms up. "A word, first, sir, with your mother," Theo said, stepping around me as Will moved off. Rafe thought Theo was great fun; he'd toss Rafe as high as he dared and catch him. My son was fearless. "Where do I send your baggage? To the infirmary, with the command's, or will you make your own arrangements? Kaufmann teamsters' rates are quite reasonable." Theo added a smile.

I'd have a chest of clothes and herbs, but — "Baggage?"

"Tent, camp bed frame, mattress, linens, a home-wares kit, grooming gear… do you have a horse?"

"Yes." I had discussed it with Reinhardt over the winter, and the buckskin gelding named Jenner was mine. He was young, quick, and tough; he'd been slated for courier service. Since Woden had said a few stern words to the queen and the castle chamberlain, I could draw extra money for such necessities.

"And a groom for it?"

There was that. "Send it over to the infirmary," I said, though I was less than certain.

Physician Ada Brauer had spent the year running Duke Seagrace's infirmary in the field. I had joined her briefly during that first large battle after the siege broke, and it had been sufficient to show me that I was only needed for the worst of the wounded. I had earned my keep as a surgeon as well, but she and her staff were well settled into the job. I saw no reason to meddle with Brauer's infirmary.

I'd gladly heal the wounded, but Woden's ongoing shield tutoring and Qadeem's lessons were enough to tell me that they didn't expect me to spend much time in the surgery this summer. Still, it had been my teacher's infirmary. It tugged at me with memories of the first battle of Ansehen, a year and a half gone now.

"How big a tent?" I asked, thinking of the little one I'd shared with three Ters when I was Elect Parselev's apprentice.

534   Part VI: Fount's Crucible

Theo shrugged. "A fair size for one. And fitting for an Elect, but I expected you didn't want anything elaborate."

"Do I need a tent at all?"

"Yes. Truly, it won't make you feel cosseted." He raised a hand to emphasize that. His voice lowered. "If my Papa taught me anything, it was how to match the wares to the customers. When the order came down I put aside a sensible but sufficiently fine kit."

I frowned. "An order come down?"

"From the castle, early in the moon. From the saints." Theo's wife Brynhilde joined him with Mina sound asleep in her arms. I thanked her for coming, she wished me well again, and as they turned to go, Theo told me, "I'll be leading the baggage, most likely. Look for me."

I nodded, glad to hear it. Over the winter, he'd been very kind in checking on me — and not in the way my neighbors did. Theo could carry a conversation. All on his own, if need be. Brynhilde was more reserved, but polite. Despite how well I'd come to know them, their marriage was still a strange thing to me. She and Theo spoke easily, but rarely touched. He doted on Mina but it was Süssie — who was, as Anders had said, not a woman at all — that he loved. Süssie bound herself up in a tightly laced bodice to create what mild curves she had. Never the slightest shadow of a beard on her, and her eyebrows were immaculately plucked. If anyone else knew her secret, I couldn't guess.

But even odd sheep were part of the Flock, so long as they served the saints.

Will and Adalev, Linde's husband, carried my table back into my kitchen as the neighbors dispersed. I had packing to do and Rafe's things to put together for Linde to take. My son gurgled on my shoulder as I followed my table indoors. I kissed his cheek and the sun-warmed smell of him stopped me for a heartbeat. Six months old, now, and he was finally sleeping through the night. His eyes were every speck as steel-grey as Kiefan's. His hair floated, even without a breeze, so wispy and pale it was still invisible against his scalp. I took a deep lungful of his scent and kissed him again.

"I'll miss you most, sweetling."

<hr />

Word had come a few days before Equinox that Kiefan had joined Duke Seagrace's camp at Straussweg but I had still thought he would come home before beginning his campaign. I had thought he'd want to see me, I realized as Jenner kept pace with the infirmary wagons. Perhaps he didn't.

His one short, melancholy letter was tucked away at home: he hadn't been able to bear the thought of losing me, but believed that he had. I didn't doubt that he'd never meant to hurt me but neither did I know what to write in reply.

It would seem there was no new queen to root our alliance with Caercoed. There'd been no word of what had been agreed upon in Knapptal, only that there'd been play-battles waged with snowballs.

Some corner of my mind wondered if Kiefan were now consort to the Crown. That didn't fit him, though, unless it was purely a formality. A duty. What business of mine his heart was now… I wasn't certain.

I wasn't certain of several things between us. Was I lost to him, as he said?

That would need seeing him, talking, learning Anders' fate, to know — but I was far from eager.

It was a dewy morning, warm even for this late in the Slush Moon. Days had been running warm since mid-Ice Moon despite the occasional snow squall. The slush itself was all but gone now. Under Jenner's hooves, the Southbound Road squelched. Dozens of supply wagons and hundreds of hooves kneaded even its hard-packed surface into mud. Past the stone walls to either side, the grass-matted fields blushed with new green. Weeping willows along the Neva's shore glowed golden in the sun, already beginning to bloom. In the cattails red-winged blackbirds sang and showed off their colorful shoulders.

Straussweg had been a tiny village a few miles north of Ansehen. It was three days' walk from Wodenberg proper, at an army's pace. The town had been burned when Arcea's army first marched north through it and further destroyed when they retreated south through it. Only the village's well remained, it was said. Duke Seagrace had made his army's headquarters there this autumn past when Arcea had finally retreated behind their newly built fortifications around Ansehen.

Vysokov had invited me to dine with him, when we laid camp last night, and it had been a pleasant evening with his daughter and heir Nadya — also a squire, intriguingly enough — and the barons whose companies made up the reserves. One of those was m'lord Lesnikov, Adaliya's father.

At table, Lesnikov had asked me what I thought of Will and whether he would inherit the barony of Rossweide. I'd answered that the youngest brother, Ein, was still two years from his Blessing and it was not for me to guess whether Saint Woden would make a disciple of him. Then I'd told the story from the last days of the siege of how Will had charged, alone and un-armored, into the closing circle around Anders and helped him cut free of the enemy. He'd taken a serious wound and I'd managed to patch him. That had earned some approving nods.

M'lord Lesnikov had been glad to hear that, as his daughter had blurted out a yes to Will's proposal and kissed him before Father could answer properly.

That night, I'd charmed the ache from my breasts. This morn they still felt heavy but not so stiff as yesterday. I'd laid awake on my camp bed far too aware that I was alone. Spring peepers had replaced Rafe's even breathing, and were louder. When I woke, early as always, there was no baby to nurse and no morning disciple's dance. Only men's clothing to put on as if I were back on that first mission once again. Hose were just as tedious now as they'd been — but I had to admit it did make for easier riding. And these fit better. Bless Theo and his good eye for sizing.

On cue, Theo rode by and asked me to dine with him and the teamsters tonight, and to tell them the story of the mission across the mountains. I agreed. With a smile I tapped Jenner to follow Theo's horse. Theo had been complaining about how slow the army was to move out in the morning. His teamsters kept a far tighter schedule so as to minimize delivery times.

His wagons carried barrels of salt pork, jerky, oat flour, and sauerkraut from the northern half of the kingdom. Clothes and boots, quivers of arrows, swords and shields too. Seagrace had perhaps twelve thousand knights, armsmen, and archers camped outside Ansehen.

And a king to lead them.

CHAPTER 2

Welcoming cheers rose as men trotted from their humble tents to line up on either side of the road. The standard-bearers, with the duke's and the barons' banners, rode before us and the evening breeze rippled the heavy fabric. Russe's black bear on a red field led the way.

Half the barons' banners involved a bear, as well, whether black, red, or brown, crowned by the seven Flock moons or the crescent Shepherd — the other half paid tribute to the western mountains many Russe hailed from.

Duke Vysokov rode with one hand up to accept the men's welcome. I settled in near m'lord Lesnikov, grateful that he was a reserved and quiet man. The duke had nudged me to wave back to the men but I didn't want their cheers. In my well-worn, fur-lined cloak and men's clothes, my blonde braid wrapped around my head, I felt little like an elect or a leader.

But we heartened them and that was good.

The main body of the reserves had split off the road some ways back with instructions of where to camp. Theo had gone with them to deliver his wagons to the quartermaster. Ada Brauer, who'd returned with us after a moon's leave to see her family, would be taking charge of the infirmary on her own — I was expected in the command pavilion.

We drew up before that group of tents set between the Southbound Road and the Neva's banks. I saw Englic blue and grey, and the king's black, snapping in the breeze atop the tall tent-poles. King's Guards kept the awning-shaded approach to the pavilion's entrance clear as we drew up and men kept coming to cheer us.

I was glad to see the Guards were four I'd trained in pattern-checking over the winter. A fair number of the King's Guard were true blessed-level knights, I'd learned in sounding those who wintered at the castle. They'd all learned the pattern trick easily enough and could check for unexpected elect or saints approaching the king.

Sounding them had also made something else clear; the chords their kir sounded shared certain notes. In truth, they were all quite similar. As the saints used kir-sounding to choose their disciples and Blessings, perhaps that should've been little surprise. What had caught my ear was that my own sounding included a couple of those notes. Which brought to mind the night of my binding when Woden had called me fierce.

Now here I was. Riding to war.

I swung down from Jenner's saddle when the others did, sufficiently lost in the muddle of barons that I thought myself secret for a little longer. But a squire cut through the bustle and took Jenner's reins for me, then put out one arm to invite me toward the front. I had to blink in surprise.

Gregor must've grown three inches over the winter. And it wasn't all height, either. The surety in his eyes and dare I say the grace of his invitation — I had to smile. I also had to walk to the front alongside Duke Vysokov. I nodded, to thank Gregor, and joined the line before the three men waiting for us under the awning.

When I'd first met Duke Seagrace at the jousting tournament, he'd seemed far younger. A year's campaigning had put grey in his chestnut knight's crest and cut lines into his brow. He'd visited the graves of his wife and sons, at Solstice, but hadn't stayed long. His easy smile looked to have died with his family.

From him, my eyes skipped over Kiefan in the center to a man I didn't know. He wore the rampant black-elk-on-white of the duke of Alemannia and he had the leathery face of a knight who'd been years in the saddle and the outdoors. His crest stood only an inch taller than the grey-frosted thatch of dirty blonde on his head. It was losing ground as his hairline receded.

Beside me, Duke Vysokov dropped to one knee, fist to his chest in obeisance, followed by the rest of his company. Save for me. I met Kiefan's eyes for a heartbeat and curtsied. He dipped his chin, slowly, in return.

That much was easy enough to survive.

"You made good time from Wodenberg," Kiefan told Vysokov. "Join me at table to discuss the situation with Saint Woden. The enemy's preparing to push out of Ansehen." He turned, in a sweep of black cloak, and walked into the command pavilion.

Vysokov stood, beside me, and ran one hand across his bald head as he often did. "Back to Father Duty's land even earlier than last year," he muttered, with a glance at me. "M'lady?"

They all looked to me, waiting, so I went first. Lamplight inside the pavilion clustered around a map table set up with carved horses, armsmen, quivers of arrows, bits of crenelated wall, and tiny wagons. Around the rim of the table wooden trenchers were laid out with cups of small beer. Saint Woden sat on one of the three-legged stools, considering the map while he chewed on a heel of bread. With his kir tucked away he was only one more tall, bearded knight among the others.

Duke Seagrace gestured us toward the table, or me in particular. "Please sit, Elect."

I took a stool opposite the square table from Kiefan. According to the map, the Arceal army had raised a wall to hem in the north side of Ansehen — there had been none when last I was here. Attacks could only have come from the south, then. Ansehen's south wall, studded with towers and a heavy gate, rimmed the lip of a steep slope down toward Suevia. Much of that wall and the towers had broken and fallen in the earthquake that the Arceal Elect had summoned before Saint Woden killed him.

A page offered me bread from a basket. The next filled my trencher with a breast of chicken and fresh spring greens. I tore into the chicken and used the bread to catch the grease. Kiefan let us eat for a while, picking at his own dinner and leaning back with an ear cocked when messengers brought news to him. Gregor stood behind Kiefan's shoulder, ready should he need anything, and at his other was Herr Vogt the memory-Blessed steward to be a record of it all.

Kiefan stood and broke the silence. "You have all received word concerning our new duke of Alemannia. Saint Woden selected Captain Gunther Stahlmann, who is the youngest son of my grandfather's younger sister." He slowed, in reciting that, looking to the duke for agreement. More certain, Kiefan went on. "Sir Gunther is a veteran of the borderlands and has served with us since the first battle of Ansehen. It will be good to restore him to his proper seat, even in its current state."

The castle had suffered in the earthquake and then been burned when Arcea first invaded us last spring.

"In consulting the royal family tree Woden also considered each of the applicants to the kingship, should there be need before my son, Rafe Bockmann, is able to make a claim."

That stopped the vague clatter of men in mail eating. My grip on my bread tightened; a few of the men glanced at me sidelong.

"The rumor's been in camp since Solstice, I'm told," Kiefan said, taking in the roomful of them with a calm stare. "Mother and Father willing, my son will prove worthy of the crown. But we are at war and a choice has been made." Kiefan looked past Duke Vysokov's shoulder and raised his voice. "Captain Konrad Tolokov?"

"Majesty?" The man who stepped forward and put a fist to his chest was the captain of the duke's personal guard, perhaps thirty years old. He'd served the duke since he earned a high ranking in the king's joust as a young knight, from what I'd heard.

"We are second cousins through another of my grandfather's sisters, I'm told. Saint Woden has judged your claim to his crown the best and you will return to Wodenberg to take command of the castle. Pick a captain for your Prince's Guard and the rest will be waiting for you there. Aleks took the liberty." Kiefan nodded to his own Captain, at the edge of the lamplight.

Sir Konrad froze a moment, his mouth falling open. He looked to Saint Woden, who only nodded. The knight dipped to one knee in obeisance and said, "I will leave immediately, m'lord."

"Leave in the morning." Woden broke his silence. "Take a seat at the table."

As Sir Konrad obeyed a page brought another trencher and food for the newly minted heir. He cleaned his plate with the speed of a man who was always expected back on duty.

I took a slow breath as all settled and it seemed that Kiefan didn't mean to say anything more about Rafe. My son would have no claim to the crown unless he earned knighthood, but then he'd outstrip any array of second cousins.

"Before I brief you on this," Kiefan said, gesturing at the map, "there's also the matter of Caercoed. The Crown and I came to an agreement regarding their support and no more need be said on that until after Temitte. We have Lady Leix's Tadhlon Guard and one of their battle elect flanking the enemy on the south side of the hill country."

He leaned over the map to draw his finger across Wodenberg's southern border from Knapptal to Ansehen. "Schutze reported that they left the morning after Equinox but they have not yet signaled us that they are in position. When they do, Saint Woden will send up a flare when we are ready to attack. However." Kiefan held up one hand. "Arcea began making preparations on Equinox rather than celebrating. They will be ready to push out of their fortifications soon." He put his hand on the carved bits of wall placed on the map; word was that the Arceal reserve had labored all spring in raising that wall, while we were besieged. "Thus, the orders I sent you to lay a quick camp tonight. We move into position tomorrow. If you would, Gunther?"

Kiefan sat as the new Duke Stahlmann of Alemannia set out more black figurines to represent our added relief forces. According to the map, our camp was half a mile from Ansehen's new fortifications. M'lord Stahlmann moved them into position before the walls, straddling the Southbound Road. He explained as he went that Arcea had raised a quarter-circle of earthen wall with a stake-filled ditch before it, and then built three trebuchets for added defense. There were two gates, one on the road and one at the corner where the earthworks didn't quite meet the half-ruined tower at the end of Ansehen's southern wall. The river buttressed the other end of the earthwork.

Our main force would make two blocks of armsmen and one of cavalry, which would be in the center and on the road. Our knights would feign a sloppy formation and disarray, enticing Arcea to attack them and then follow when the knights pretended to retreat. The armsmen to either side would engage any other Arceal companies as seemed fit — and here m'lord Stahlmann sketched out some possibilities with the figurines.

"What of the center?" Duke Vysokov pointed to the golden horse figurine that had advanced between our armsmen to represent the enemy cavalry.

Kiefan's voice rumbled, nearly like Woden's. "Those are my Lambing-day gift. I will see to them."

My throat tightened.

"Those may well be centaurs, m'lord." The duke frowned.

Kiefan nodded, the lamplight glinting on his golden band. "Woden will be with me. And our cavalry will swing around and follow me in."

M'lord Stahlmann finished the plan by pointing out the reserve forces and the two companies of archers who would be available for support as needed. Duke Seagrace would have the command pavilion, to gauge the needs as the battle progressed, and Duke Vysokov would lead the reserves.

"Elect Kate," Duke Stahlmann said, with a nod to me, "will support the left flank with defensive charms, though if she's needed she will do as she must." As I stared at the lines, rearranged to the beginning of our theoretical battle, I couldn't think of how I could shield so many men at once. "Our main concern is the trebuchets," m'lord said, perhaps guessing my worry. "Arcea has two elect for certain and they may load the artillery with any manner of things. Saint Woden's said he's confident you'll save many lives."

Thus, all my shield training of late. I met the saint's eyes and perhaps a little of his confidence wormed its way into my heart. When Arcea first broke the city walls, I'd shielded Kiefan while he fought that red-haired Elect. The crack of stone shot on the walls and the rumbling earthquakes crossed my mind, unsettling my confidence. I touched my own saint's bond in my right palm.

/ stop flying stones / ? /

Qadeem sent me an image, a simple drawing of a trebuchet slinging a stone into the air. Its path was traced in a red line, and a contrary line of kir in green struck it from below halfway across its arc. The stone flew off at a wild angle.

My head tipped, curious, as the sense of that clicked into place.

/ kir? /

/ vines / strike hard / keep your kir /

It would take a hard blow indeed to turn a large rock and likely the hit would numb my arms —

"Elect Kate?"

I blinked and looked to the voice. Kiefan. My heart stumbled in my chest when I met those grey eyes. He nodded, to one side, and I looked up; Gregor stood there, holding a bundle for me. A bundle of mail and a quilted gambeson, bound in a leather belt.

I took a breath to ask but it died in my throat. I closed my mouth and took the heavy bundle. The mail smelled faintly of oil, familiar from — I pressed my lips in a line. Clearly, I was to wear this. Further proof of what my saints needed of me.

"You'll have a hand of my Guard, commanded by Rostislav, for further protection," Kiefan said. "He can advise you on how to wear that, as well." When I nodded he turned back to the dukes and barons.

"After we break their army here, we march hard for Temitte. Caercoed pledged six thousand more to march from Eryr Pass after Equinox. The city cannot stand for a long siege, cannot pack in the twenty-five thousand soldiers they have on hand; they must face us in battle. If there must be a siege, our contacts among the Suevi royalists will be of great help inside the city. We will take Temitte by Solstice." Kiefan laid out a second map, of Suevia, behind the line of enemy figurines. He ran his finger along a river. "Over the summer we will strengthen our line along the Dúnforst-éa. Gain the people's support. Next summer, Reowan."

Heads nodded around the table. Duke Vysokov held up his cup of beer. "Reowan."

They all tapped cups and echoed him, then drank. I could only think of Rafe and how old he'd be by Solstice. Surely I could be home for the autumn Equinox, before he turned a year old. If not I'd have to sleep alone for far too long — and last night had been no easier than the previous.

Around the table some numbers were bandied about and some complaining about muddy roads. I gave half an ear to it while running my fingers over my new mail tunic, until the dukes stood from the map table and began to take their leave. The barons and officers followed suit, at a leisurely, chatting pace. The meeting was over and I'd survived on silent politeness with Kiefan. Thank the Mother.

I stood as well, cradling the bundle in my arm. Surely they'd given me a small, light tunic but I couldn't imagine running in such a thing. I'd need to sleep well tonight. Physician Brauer had told me where the infirmary was and my tent ought to be near there. Jenner would want his feed and a brushing.

"Elect Kate, stay. Sirs, if you would see to your posts?" Kiefan asked.

I stiffened my spine against the chilly touch of dread. He wanted to speak after all. I could do that. I'd faced worse.

He still sat, across from me, with one elbow on the table. He nodded when Seagrace told him he'd be off with the vanguard before first light. The pavilion cleared quickly; even the steward and the pages left once they'd cleared the trenchers. Woden stood looking through the wallet of documents that Vysokov had brought. Captain Aleksandra lurked by the pinned-open front door-flaps. Gregor stood beside her when he discreetly herded the last of the captains out.

"I'll return after midnight, after the kir-rationing," Woden told Kiefan, stuffing the papers back into the wallet. "We can do our own scouting then."

He walked out, patting Captain Aleks on her shoulder as he went; she followed on that summons. Which left me nearly alone with Kiefan. I'd thought I had a hundred questions for him, some sharp, some anguished, but now I had only the familiar ache that had settled in after my tears ran out.

"Can I rely on you, on the battlefield?"

Kiefan spoke quietly, watching me. Gauging me with his truth-sense — Qadeem had called it augury. I would've told him the truth in any case. "Yes."

"Can I rely on your advice, should I need it?"

That he even had to ask needled my heart. "Do you doubt me?"

I watched him in return, thought I saw an ache in him too. Or perhaps I only wished I did.

"No," he answered. Kiefan stood, setting both his hands on the table. "Is Rafe well?"

I nodded, my son's scent haunting me. "Strong and healthy."

"How — what is he —?" Uncertainty was an odd thing to hear from Kiefan; my brows rose. He looked away. "Who is he like?"

"I would've brought him to the castle if you wished to meet him." What Qadeem had said of not denying Rafe love had stuck with me. If Anders was gone, it wasn't for me to push away Kiefan if he meant to take Father Duty's role. But Kiefan hadn't come home for Equinox and the meeting I'd been steeling myself for had become this instead.

"I had to see to —" He cut himself off with a grimace and sighed. With stronger resolve, he asked, "Do we agree that he should study at the castle? Books, riding, the sword?"

I could teach Rafe to read. His uncle Will could teach him to ride. Much as I wanted to deny Rafe would ever need a sword, it wasn't likely I could stop his learning. Anders would have done the same as Kiefan, in that.

"Yes," I said.

"If this should go badly, Woden will want you and Rafe to live in the castle. Captain Konrad has a fine reputation but I do not know him." The emphasis Kiefan put on that drew my eyes to his. "He has sons of his own."

A chill tickled down my spine at that thought. And worse. I felt my jaw tighten, to match Kiefan's, and I nodded. "If this should go badly —" I had to chase the words; they scurried away from the thought of Kiefan lying dead on a battlefield. "It will be the Empress I must protect him from."

Something too grim to be a smile pulled at one corner of his mouth. "If she threatens you, I'll ride back from the Winter Wood itself."

I'd seen that iron in him before — when he put me on Puck that last day of the mission, when he locked away his grief beside his father's body — and in that heartbeat I didn't doubt that he would.

Gregor moved so quietly, he startled me when he laid a shaving kit on the map table and unrolled it. The razor and the silver mirror caught the lamplight as the dark leather fell flat. He said nothing, only picked up the mirror and polished it on his sleeve.

That set both our minds back to the matters at hand. "There will be nightly meetings," Kiefan said, "over dinner. Things you should know. We'll expect you at sundown."

"Is there a morning disciple's dance?"

Kiefan nodded. "Abbot Shaw."

"Shaw?"

"Yes, Tomas's abbot." Kiefan meant Duke Seagrace; the abbot was plainly as Englic as I was. "I don't get to every one but they're vigorous."

At the pavilion door, the entire King's Guard was gathering with Captain Aleks, to judge by how many four-starred tabards I saw. They meant to do the ritual crest-shaving, it would seem, which could mean razor wounds in the infirmary tonight. I retreated a step from the map table, my mail in hand. "Finish the shaving before the drinking begins," I said.

A thin smile. Kiefan inclined his head. "Physician."

At the infirmary, I got a brief update from Physician Brauer: some pneumonia, some flu, frostbite had not been much of a problem, and the Englic men were slowly learning to wash on Saint-day. They smelled rather better than I remembered from the siege.

Ter Biya, who had been my teacher's surgery assistant, was glad to see me and wanted to know everything about Rafe. I drew an audience of Ters and that set off rounds of baby stories. When I finally left the infirmary I was smiling and sleepy.

My modest, circular tent stood off to the side of the infirmary's stables. All the other sleeping tents had been in place for moons and they were surrounded by foot-beaten paths in the grass. To give me some quiet, the Thers had pitched my tent out of the way. The low, waning Shepherd and the six Flock moons overhead lent enough light to find the door-flap and slip inside.

I lit a little kir-lamp in my palm. A heavy, circular rag rug covered the grass. My camp bed stood just to the side, its straw mattress covered with my pair of wool quilts. They still smelled faintly of home. My chest of clothes stood to the other side. I'd packed some jars of willow bark, alum-root, and goldenrod, as well as a box of dried rose-hips for tea and a few books. The dagger I'd worn on the long-ago mission was in there too.

The bundled mail and gambeson clinked when I dropped it on the rug. Sitting down on my bed, I pulled my bone hairpin and let my braid fall down my back. Beyond my canvas walls, horses faintly whickered and puffed. The peepers were further away on the riverbank.

My hand was on my necklace, rubbing across the gold wire wrapping the lamia fangs, and I hadn't noticed. The oil from the mail lingered on my fingers, smelling of — both Anders and Kiefan. That ached.

Anders in the claws of that monstrous vulture.

Kiefan riding through the Winter Wood. At the Red Hunter's right hand, perhaps, allied in seeking vengeance. It was an old fable that the Hunter would aid in a righteous cause. A story for children. I'd seen such things, in my saints' service, that I wasn't sure fables were only fables.

I curled my hands into fists with a sigh. Maybe I could get some sleep tonight. I might face my first battle in the morning.

CHAPTER 3

There'd been a stretch of woods along the Southbound Road, but it was gone now and the stumps had bleached to grey. The houses we passed were piles of thatch and broken wood; many had been burnt. These had been fields and pastures, before the war, and fieldstone walls snaked up and down the hills. When we topped the last hill, they were easy enough to see across.

Arcea's new wall ran a good six feet high, behind the ditch they'd dug the earth from. Their trebuchets stood cocked, looking like herons bent over backwards. Beyond that, some of the town's houses were intact but many were burnt wrecks. Only two towers of Castle Ansehen's four still survived.

Seagrace's vanguard had stopped at the raised platform his men had built a prudent distance from the closed front gate. A pair of hawk-eyed archers kept an eye on the enemy from that aerie. The duke's rukh banner flapped in the cold, damp wind. Grey clouds rushed by overhead, warning of rain.

Wodenberg's black banner rode down the gentle slope ahead of me, its full Shepherd moon brilliantly white behind the silhouette of Mount Woden. Kiefan and Saint Woden rode with it, escorted by the King's Guard. Then me on Jenner with Lieutenant Rostislav and his five men in tow at the head of our long column of cavalry.

Getting me into the saddle while wearing the thigh-long mail tunic had taken some work. Working by memory, I'd gotten the gambeson laced up over a light linen cote, then the mail, then double-wrapped the belt over it — which had eased the weight of the iron surprisingly well. Rostislav had seemed confused to be nodding in approval.

But hoisting me up on Jenner's back had required a heave-ho and a few minutes of panicky scrabbling for balance as the weight of the tunic pulled me askew.

I got a little ahead of my guard; Sir Rostislav trotted his warhorse to catch up. "If not the Black Knight, m'lady, then surely Saint-day dinners?" he asked to renew our haphazard conversation.

"Yes," I had to admit, "I never miss a Saint-day. It's far more convenient to bring a baby to than a tavern. And his grandmother must see him weekly."

"The flock cannot be neglecting you at your own Orderhaus. Surely you don't dine alone there."

"What concerns you about how I spend my days, sir?"

He'd been circling around how much time I spent alone for the entire brief ride from the camp. It would seem it troubled the lieutenant that I was well settled into my routine of patients, baby, and sleeping. My memory brought me a scrap from the siege, when Sir Rostislav had said that were I widowed I wouldn't be alone for long. Perhaps that was it.

He tried to shrug it off. "Any should be concerned for a young lady alone. No widow should suffer —"

"I am not widowed, sir. And how an Elect spends her days is in service to the saints."

My sharp words turned a few ears in the line ahead of us. The lieutenant dipped his head, accepting the chastisement. "My apologies, Elect."

Kiefan led us directly to the front and the duke next to the watchmen's platform and standing on the Southbound Road. Seagrace greeted us from his saddle and described the situation. I let Jenner walk a bit further, close enough to hear but not part of the conversation, and looked back along the road.

The cavalry turned off to begin forming up in a hay field. Each company's banner led them so it was an array of green, brown, and grey flags finding their way into place — or not, since they had orders to feign disarray. The horses stitched on the fabric were white or black, some winged, some silhouetted by the Shepherd moon or accompanied by a ram, to represent Father Duty.

Many of the fieldstone walls had been ruined already but not all. Warhorses carrying knights in full armor were not jumpers and thus having to knock down more walls slowed the deployment. The knights got off their horses to work at it, which made their disarray quite convincing.

Behind the knights came the armsmen with their own banners. They had less difficulty getting to their assigned areas; they just clambered over those walls that remained.

On the earthworks, a dark smudge of Arceal soldiers watched us.

More and more knights and armsmen. I catalogued my gear again: my dagger, the contents of my fully stocked medicine bag. My kir was knotted away and secret for now. Messengers came and went around Kiefan, confirming that Duke Vysokov was taking position on the other side of the hill as agreed, that the camp behind us was being loaded into wagons, that the infirmary had reached its place by the river and was setting up. The hawk-eyed men on the raised platform reported movement in Ansehen: centaurs and minotaurs forming up in the main square.

The morning wore on and men kept coming. Nearly twelve thousand of them, Alemanni, Russe, and Engls, all Blessed by our saints. No amount of checking or fidgeting could fill the time. I wondered if this were as harrowingly dull for them as for me.

By best estimate there were thirty thousand behind that earthwork wall.

A squad of Rangers crested a hill to the east, rode across the fields, and brought the first real news of the day; they'd caught a Suevi hunting party, killed most of them, and now delivered the two survivors to Kiefan. Most of the papers found on the bodies were maps of the immediate area.

Kiefan glanced over those, then eyed the two men kneeling with their hands bound behind their backs. He asked something in Suevi and it nearly made sense to me; their tongue wasn't far off ours. Their muttered answers were some claim of ignorance. I didn't need a translator for that.

"Take them to Vysokov for questioning," Kiefan said, passing the satchel of papers back to the Ranger sergeant.

"Hunting fresh game for their officers, most likely," Duke Stahlmann said.

"You weren't to be letting them out of their walls." Kiefan included both dukes in a stern look.

It was Saint Woden who spoke in their defense. "The nights have been overcast. Those were hill boys, by their accents. They won't know much but keep them alive."

And then I was back to watching armsmen march down from the top of the hill and turn — to the left, now, as the right was sufficiently full. That had been a moment's excitement, when the standard-bearer with the green-fish-on-grey banner had turned in a novel direction. Lieutenant Rostislav, beside me, and his men talked about a skit that a small circus troop had put on last night, laughing over the routine again. They'd had a very clever pony, I gathered, who outwitted them at every turn.

Distantly, I heard a click and a creak and someone yelled, "Attend!"

A stone ball arced into the sky with deceptive ease, followed by a second and then a third. I pulled Jenner around — "The left!" I wasn't even in position. My kir flushed out from hiding, to my fingertips, and —

"Don't tip our hand." Woden's raised palm drew me up short. I looked up at the shots; they were already falling. Well short of our front lines they hit the turf and tore up strips, bounced, and rolled to a stop.

Duke Seagrace spared me a smile. "We built the platform beyond their range, Elect Kate."

The three balls lay in the grass, one before each of our three formations. Each was bigger than my head.

"If they're ready to begin, then to your posts sirs," Kiefan said, "or m'lady." He drew his sword and tapped Pip to a trot. Off the road and across the grass, and the disorderly knights took up a cheer when they saw him. Woden followed, nearly anonymous in mail and a plain black tabard, and then Captain Aleks with the King's Guard.

The left, then. Jenner carried me off the Southbound Road and across the front of the formations. Rostislav and my hand of knights kept pace. My eyes stayed on the trebuchets as we went. Their long arms, which had thrashed to and fro just after loosing their shots, were now reeling downwards. I imagined I could hear the creak of the ropes under strain.

Our left flank was headed by the green-fish banner. The men were all Engls; I could tell by the hawkish noses and freckles under the open-faced helmets. They wore boiled leather breastplates, carried heavy-headed spears and rectangular shields. Eyes tracked me and Jenner as I trotted down their line.

"Must you be Elect, Fräulein?"

I stopped Jenner near the officer beside the standard-bearer; the company's captain by the brass rings on his epaulettes. His Alemannic was terrible so I answered him in Englic. "Bound to Saint Qadeem. Were they finding their range with those shots?"

He grinned. "It's true then, boys! We gave the saints an Elect and a pretty one!" When his men cheered, he answered me. "Might be, m'lady. They've tested their artillery before, though. Did that when they put them up back in autumn. We're out of range."

Overhead the clouds thinned a bit and the sun braved his way through. The trebuchets stood ready and waiting to shoot again. It made little sense.

/ ? /

/ distraction? /

Qadeem's reply seemed fair enough. But their gate across the Southbound Road stood shut. No sign of a sortie. The six-foot wall and the distance obscured much of the goings-on beyond; we were perhaps a thousand feet out. I could feel no concentrations of kir and nothing unusual answered my call. And over on the far left —

"Lieutenant?" I pointed toward the side gate, at a faint reflection on flat surfaces. Were those shields?

Rostislav turned his horse and frowned into the distance. "Father's bloody beard, they're up to something."

"Those're shields," one of the other Guard said. Sir Waldemar, my memory supplied.

They were outside the earthworks. That gate was open and they were building a wall of lapped shields to protect an avenue behind them. I saw movement but it wasn't until they advanced beyond the end of the growing shield line that I saw the shape of them and knew.

Horses? No. Centaurs.

Kir flared, pulling my head back to the wall and the nearest trebuchet. That same click, that same creak, and the thing's long arm lashed up faster, slung its stone harder, and in that heartbeat I knew what I'd see.

My kir coiled in my hand. Jenner stepped forward, obedient. I tracked the shot but as it arced down my eye lost its gauge of the distance. My kir-vine thrust up from my arm and I felt the range through it. The hit shot up my arm to my shoulder in a numbing jolt; worse, the stone popped upward over my head and crashed down. Men screamed, in the thud. I saw it bounce and strike one in the hip, throwing him down. In a line, two more fell. There was a red mess where it had first hit.

Mother have mercy, my first duty and I failed.

And I felt kir flare again at the center trebuchet.

"Elect!" Sir Waldemar pointed as the machine began to move.

No time. I kicked Jenner to a run and the buckskin pulled away from my Guards' heavier warhorses. The shot arced through the grey sky toward the knights. Still feigning disarray, they scattered underneath it.

Kiefan waved me past as I rode. Kir flared at the third trebuchet. Its click and creak were lost in the beat of Jenner's hooves but its arm swung up and slung its stone. I pulled Jenner to a stop before the right-hand armsmen formation and searched the grey sky for a hurtling grey rock.

There. I braided my kir-vines from my other palm, pushing with all the fierce will I'd had when I launched myself up over the castle's portcullis that horrible night of the slaughter. My blow hit the ball across its face and the force skidded across my arm. It spun and veered downward, gouging the grass.

Behind me the entire line of armsmen roared in joy. My heart leaped.

/ again! / Pride came through my bond.

I cantered Jenner back to my Engls; one eye on the re-loading trebuchets, one on the formation of knights as I passed. Kiefan shouted orders, pointing with his sword, so it was Woden who waved me past again. The knights must've dodged the shot in their show of disarray.

Under the green fish banner, the sight of one man down and groaning in agony made me pull one foot from the stirrup to dismount. Lieutenant Rostislav caught me by the ankle as I swung, though, and his grip nearly unbalanced me.

"They're coming, Elect," he said, nodding up the line. An ambulance wagon was coming, its horse at a trot, through the gap between the armsmen and the cavalry. "Let them do their work. And they're about to —"

The enemy loosed the right-most trebuchet first. I kicked Jenner to a gallop and in passing caught a snatch of Kiefan snarling something bloodthirsty and the knights howling in reply. No time for that. As Jenner slowed, I struck the stone ball aside. Pain spiked through my arm but faded.

Pip reared up and Kiefan swung his sword high; when the horse came down, he launched into a run. The knights roared in unison and hooves rumbled. I stared as they followed him. This wasn't the plan. Kiefan meant to charge the wall? Through trebuchet shots and surely archers once they were closer?

I caught a glimpse of the trebuchet shot that fell among them as they rode past me. Horses' screams cut through the men's voices. And further away, another shot hurtled toward my Engls. I struck for it, over the knights' heads, but it was too far to reach. It smashed through their ranks, skipping off bodies.

Father's bloody balls.

The fallen horses made a further mess of the knights' lines as they cantered after Kiefan, but they finally passed. One thrashed on the ground, broken and screaming. The second was only twitching, and the man trapped under him flailed weakly. An unhorsed knight tried to lunge to his feet, but collapsed with a cry.

Jenner didn't want to get close. I called their patterns while he jittered and shook his head. The knight half-pinned under the dying horse was dying himself. A third man, in the grass, lay dead where he'd been thrown.

"Stay down!" I ordered the crippled knight, who was trying to get up again. His knee was a ruin. I spared a glance to the trebuchets — half-cocked already — and swung down from my saddle. "Warn me!" I told Rostislav before he could object.

I heard Sir Waldemar shouting for an ambulance as I touched the dying knight and struck him unconscious so he'd feel no pain. I stole his kir too. The crippled one I pushed down with one hand and spun up a charm to piece the end of his femur back together under his smashed kneecap.

"Elect, what does he need?"

I told the Ther, "Brace his knee. No surgery, just a splint and maintenance."

"They're ready!" Lieutenant Rostislav shouted.

What I'd managed would have to do. Ther carried the knight to the wagon to lie with the wounded Englic armsmen as I climbed back into Jenner's saddle. Once there, I turned my gelding toward Ansehen and walked him to where the front line had been. I stood in about the middle, between the two blocks of armsmen. Of the knights, I could only see a line of horse rumps and tails cantering toward the side gate and that shield wall.

Click. Creak. Two catapult arms slung up, nearly synchronous, and their shots flew free. One to either side. Trying to force me to choose.

My jaw tightened in anger. No failing this time.

On either side, my Guards' horses skittered back when the kir gathered in my hands. I pointed to each shot and struck, lashing out my anger in dense whips. Pain forced a hiss through my teeth when they hit. The round clay pots burst and their oily innards caught the flames from their burning wicks. Fire splattered down on the damp grass. A little reached the front lines and the two-white-rams banner on the right smoldered a bit, but all was quickly stamped out.

They cheered me as the trebuchets winched back again. The center one waited, still ready.

A mass of kir lit over on the left and shot up in a flare bright as the sun. Despite how much flew up, scaring off the low clouds as it went, so much more blossomed at its origin that it drew all our eyes.

Kiefan's knights were still riding, over by the side gate, swinging around to attack the centaurs pouring out across the open pastures. The kir-bloom — and the massive golden arc that came to Saint Woden's call — was near the gate, at the root of the Arceal shield-wall. Light flashed. I heard thunder.

"Elect!" Sir Waldemar pointed me back to the earthworks.

They launched more fire-pots to either side of me. As those flew I thought I felt a flare of kir at the center trebuchet. Through the din of roiling power by the side gate, I wasn't certain.

My left shoulder felt a knife of pain, when I struck at both pots at once. The one on my right slipped past and crashed onto the Alemanni ranks, splashing burning oil across a dozen men and setting the grass ablaze. It was a long way to pull kir, but I fixed my eyes on it. The knight beside me lost his as well, with a surprised gasp. Flames fell to smoke and smoldering, which the men could stamp out.

I gripped my throbbing shoulder. My head ached at the same pulse. Distantly, I heard Rostislav shouting a report for Vysokov to a messenger and Sir Waldemar directing the next ambulance. Through all that, I heard that click and creak again.

"This one's for you, Elect," the knight I'd drained said.

The dark pot arced through the sky, well ahead of the next pair of shots. "Back!" I shouted and spun out a flat shield over my head and Jenner's. Braced it on both my hands, to spread out the impact and spare my aching shoulders. My Guard skipped their horses back half a dozen steps.

I felt the kir just before it hit. White-hot kir-fire tore through my shield, spread like water, lighting all it touched. Jenner squealed in terror. Fire ripped across my gambeson arms, under the mail, struck my thigh. Heat enveloped me, blooming hot as a summer day and blinding as the sun. Jenner ran, screaming.

Terror wiped my mind clean for a heartbeat and on reflex I pushed it all away. Kir swirled around me in a nimbus, free — and I took it, hot at it was, for my own. And I pulled on the reins. Jenner fought, twisting his head to one side, and jolted toward a stop. Then he decided to be rid of me and I had to hang on with both hands. I whistled to him, loud as I could, trying to tell him to be still. He bucked and thrashed.

I put my hand on Jenner's neck and gave him some kir. The gelding slowed and that let me tighten my grip with my thighs. I whistled again, clicked the all's-well signal, and he jounced to a stop.

In time for me to see fire-pots hit my armsmen. And see the new column marching down the hill behind us, headed by a red hawk banner. Our archers were coming to help.

CHAPTER 4

"We're to advance under your protection, Elect, and slow those trebuchets," Captain Blick told me.

"How many?" Archers trotted out to fill the cavalry's gap far quicker than armsmen, but the stream of them still reached to the crest of the hill behind us.

"Two thousand, Elect."

At bow range, Arcea would return shots, and my widest shield… "I won't be able to protect them all," I had to admit.

Captain Blick nodded. "The sooner we start, the sooner we stop those fucking things."

"Elect!"

I turned as the new trebuchet volley loosed and tapped Jenner to walk ahead of my line. Pain ate at my focus, but I lashed the fire-pots from the sky. No more kir-fire surprises; those would cost their elect a good deal of kir.

Rostislav drew up beside me. "Are you well enough? Do you need kir?"

My quilted gambeson was burned to the elbows, but the fire hadn't reached my skin. A swath of my right thigh throbbed. That pain was what I had to focus through. "Well enough," I told him.

Behind me, the standard-bearer and Captain Blick advanced. Archers didn't keep such neat lines as knights or armsmen but they all had their bows strung and arrows nocked. I rode ahead of them, at a walk, with my King's Guards clustered around me. Two thousand pairs of yellow hawk's eyes were unnerving, when focused on my back.

Click. Creak.

I'd be hearing those in my nightmares, no doubt.

All three trebuchets hurled at my archers, all double loads of fire-pots. My joints counted them off: two on one side, two on the other, and then the center pair were too low when I struck them. Flaming oil sprayed across the ranks, catching two of my knights as well as the archers. I put up my hand but the fire ignored me for a heartbeat.

Focus.

Burning released kir, Qadeem had told me. Thus, it was free in the flame and could be taken. It came to my hand warm and eager and circled for a heartbeat before sinking into my flesh.

We drew closer to the stake-filled ditch and the earthworks. The dark smudge behind the wall resolved into helmeted heads, shoulders, here and there an arm as someone gestured. Too far for faces, though. I watched the trebuchets' heads draw down below the line of the wall and the counterweight basket on the near end rise. One corner of my mind wondered how they'd adjust for our shorter range.

A shockwave passed over me, weakened by the distance but it snapped my head around toward the side gate. Someone had died, an elect or a saint — kir arced, again, to Saint Woden. It splayed out, and the size of it kept my gaze on the side gate. That had to be a full Shepherd's blade. He lived, at least. But who had — was Kiefan —?

"Company halt!" the captain behind me shouted and the order echoed back from his men.

I put my worry aside. We stood four hundred feet, perhaps, from the wall. "Captain!" I twisted in the saddle to look for the man. "Are their archers readying to shoot?"

Rather than answer, the captain sent a man up to stand beside me. He surveyed the enemy for a moment, then looked up at me with golden hawk eyes. "They're gathering on the wall, Elect, but not ready yet. Could be more behind, too."

I had the better part of two kir-rations left, but I knew I couldn't knit a shield wide enough to protect more than a few hundred archers. "They'll shoot in a mass, as we do? And what's your name?"

"Most likely. Baldwin Harke, in your service, m'lady."

"Take aim!" the archery captain shouted behind us.

To my saint, I sent an image of a kir-vine lashing across a cloud of arrows, as a question. He answered quickly.

/ bladed vine /

That was an impression of sharpness, as in my little Shepherd blades.

/ speed /

Pages from one of my teacher's books flashed past; his diagrams of the speed Blessing in use. Or, what parts he could fit onto a page at once. The charms in that raced from brain to spine to muscle too fast for even him to parse out.

The progression of red ink lines hung in my mind. In my core, my kir rippled, spun into threads that echoed the patterns across my shoulder and arm.

"Loose!"

Two thousand shafts hissed behind me, rising over my head in a dark cloud. I looked up as they flew and a few droplets of rain fell on my face. Their archers loosed as our arrows poured down.

I spooled out a long vine of kir, drawing my mind across it to whet a knife-edge into its pattern. Anders had said one needed to know the action before one could do it at speed; this was nothing so complicated as sword-fighting, but I focused on sweeping my arm across the cloud. What effect our arrows had, I didn't see for tracking their answering volley. Behind me, the captain ordered his men to take aim again.

Range was easier to guess this time. The arrows passed the mark I'd set and I felt my arm tense — and suddenly it was slung over to my other side and the kir-vine snapped back into my hand. The arrow cloud burst in a wild array of splinters for thirty feet to either side of me. Fletching and arrowheads scattered, largely harmless. Some shafts had escaped me, though, and I heard scattered cries of pain.

"Loose!" the captain ordered. A fresh swarm of arrows shot up.

"Baldwin, the enemy?" I asked.

"We cut a fucking swath through them, m'lady."

"Ready!" our archery captain shouted again and arrows rattled from hip-slung quivers to nock against bowstrings. A few more drops of rain struck me.

Thunder cracked and fire exploded by the left-most trebuchet. I hadn't noticed that houses were ablaze over there. A patch of arrows shot up, from between the left and the center, and after a couple heartbeats a patch from over on the right. Our captain shouted orders to aim half our hawk-eyes to either side as I spooled out another sharp-edged vine and swatted down the Arceal arrows.

Few of them reached my archers. All of ours reached them.

In the center, a click and a creak and as the long trebuchet arm swung up, kir snapped out and smashed the fire-pots in its sling. Fire streamed and tumbled down onto their own wall.

Over my shoulder, I shouted, "Archers, hold!" If Kiefan and Woden were near the center trebuchet, I didn't want to add our arrows to their troubles.

We waited. The Arceal archers didn't answer our last volley. A vague ruckus came from Ansehen but nothing definite. Ambulances reached us, at last, and I dismounted Jenner to help them. I drained off my kir quickly, charming men who'd been hit by arrows — but I took theirs in payment. I left cleansing and bandaging for the infirmary and mended only what was worst.

The stream of their pain wore at my mind. I pushed it aside. These men had counted on me for protection and I did all I could to mend them. My teeth clenched, over their wounds, as the ambulances drove away with them. Kir was not the matter; I had to ration out my focus. The haze of fatigue was creeping in and healing charms tried to twist under my hands. Stubborn patterns resisted me. The day wasn't over yet.

I returned to Jenner and heard Lieutenant Rostislav's report of what we knew of the enemy. One of my Guard had dismounted and Baldwin sat in the saddle, craning his neck to see. Fire had spread, in Ansehen, even though a light rain was falling now. As I watched, kir arced across the sky overhead, green and gold, to answer Saint Woden's call.

All three trebuchets stood with arms straight up, out of the action. It was past noon, I was sure, though without the sun it was tricky to judge. The terror of advancing and our attack gave way to waiting for some sign or word of orders. Light rain thinned to a drizzle. My archers unstrung their bows and protected the strings with oilskin.

Messengers rode up from behind us, asking for news and trotting off with our reports. It was the rider who came from the left, the side gate, that caught my eye first. Then, the man's face — it was Sir Garrick, one of the King's Guard.

His brown horse was so splattered with red I'd think it a pinto, but the animal seemed unhurt. Sir Garrick was, himself, slowly dripping from one shiny-wet boot, and his mail glistened. I didn't think it was merely well oiled, given the coppery stink rolling off him.

"Elect Kate, Saint Woden commands you to advance to the gate and open it," he reported, saluting. "He wants the elect who's been giving you such trouble. Alive, by preference, but if not…" Garrick shrugged, just as I could imagine Woden had.

"Are you well?" I felt I should ask, though Sir Garrick didn't show any pain.

"A few bruises — oh, this?" He glanced down and his brows jumped. He hesitated with his mouth open. "Best to come in the front gate, m'lady. Truly."

———————×———————

The elect who'd given me such trouble — my archers that was, and the armsmen before them. And the pot of kir-fire. My thigh still tingled with hot needles where it had touched me. Poor Jenner had burns of his own, which he kept trying to lick.

A chance to repay that.

I told Captain Blick to do as he saw fit and he scattered his men in clumped squads to approach the wall. Several came with me, trotting ahead, sweeping to either side, their bows at ready. Now and then an Arceal head appeared over the wall and caught a shaft above his nose. Our hawk-eyes rarely missed.

But it wasn't any sort of real resistance, that was clear even to me.

"Let us go first," Lieutenant Rostislav hissed as we drew close to the gate. "Throw us over and we'll open the gate."

One of our oak-solid knights in full mail was far too heavy for me to lift. I bit my lip as we drew up to the double-doored gate. It was solidly made, six feet tall and level with the earth walls. Iron bars had been nailed across its beams for further strength.

Two hands of my archers crept right up to the gate and crouched on either side at the grass-fuzzed shoulders of the wall. One sergeant caught my eye and mimed boosting a man up to the top. I nodded, but held up one hand for him to wait.

I stopped Jenner a dozen yards from the gate and slid from the saddle, landing heavy thanks to my mail tunic. Rostislav and my guard were quick to follow but I didn't want to argue with them about who would go first. If that elect were here, if anything waited inside, I'd have to be quick. The gate stood, darkened by the rain, still so new that only faint streaks of rust ran from the nails across the iron bars.

My hands trembled but I had to do this. I was the only useful thing I could toss over that gate — assuming I could manage it with the weight of my mail. Woden needed me to do this, to help him and Kiefan. To protect the kingdom. Rafe.

/ breathe /

Fear must've leached through my bond. Qadeem sent me another kir-ration.

Rostislav got wind of my plan by how I fought to steady myself. "No, don't!"

I thrust kir against the ground and leaped. My boots found the top of the gate, narrow but strong, and I perched for a moment, crouching, to scan around. I wobbled, flailed one arm, and thrust down a kir-vine to steady myself.

The southbound road cut through Ansehen, as I remembered, and the center trebuchet stood just to the right. Charred ruins and foundations were all that remained of the buildings here, offering plenty of cover —

One arrow hissed by my ear. The other struck my chest, like a punch, and my rage lashed back. I saw blood burst into the air beside a blackened chimney.

Shield. Stupid. My pattern was whole, though; the mail and gambeson had stopped the arrow. I ripped it out.

"Bastards!" The first archer boosted onto the wall by those outside drew back and shot. Another scrambled up beside him.

More arrows flew. Two hit my fresh-spun shield. The gate. I jumped down and put my hands on the heavy bolts barring it shut. Bracing my feet, I pulled. The wooden bolts didn't budge. I yanked on them but they didn't even rattle in their seating. In rage, I lashed at it with kir-vines. Bolts fused to gates, iron hinges welded, all of it useless to me.

That elect was a crafter, posted to charm the trebuchets. He'd fused the wood together.

Rostislav landed beside me and arrows thumped into his shield. "Turn and fight!" he yelled, muffled by his helm.

I swung around and saw a line of armsmen charging us, their shields roughly overlapping. A kir-vine shot from my hand, just an angry fist of it, and punched one in the face. The blow woke that knife of pain in my shoulder but he went down. I slung the vine leftward and down low, tripping half of them at a full run.

Sir Waldemar dropped down beside Rostislav and the two of them met the remaining armsmen. Not for long; Blessed knights made ordinary men look fierce as sheep.

Their archers thought they were safe twenty feet away behind fallen house-beams and rubble. They'd shot the archers who'd first leaped onto the wall to defend me — I saw three of them down, studded with Arceal arrows. My bladed kir-vine reached those cowards, cut them, sent them running if they survived.

With my Guard around me, I moved on the center trebuchet. Calling kir-patterns, I spotted another Arceal archer meaning to snipe at us. I flushed out a knot of soldiers when I stabbed him with a kir-vine. They retreated from the cover of burned rubble and I caught a glimpse of them: two tanned Arceal bow-men, a pair of armsmen, and between them — somebody's mother? A mousy, soft woman — the elect.

"Their elect!" I shouted, and ran with a fresh shield ready before me.

But they didn't shoot; the five of them ran from me. I chased. Rostislav shouted behind me. The tall shell of a shop-front gave them a corner to slip around. I called kir, strong as I could, and caught the last one's pattern as he broke into a sprint.

I chased but my legs turned wobbly within a few paces. The damn mail was getting heavier. Gritting my teeth, I pushed on. I'd seen some of Ansehen's streets, long ago, and I recognized their route through the burned shops. They were going for the wall. Launching myself, I leaped over the low ruin of a shop and landed, panting, in time to spin around and face them.

The armsman in front skidded in surprise and fell to his knees. My kir-vine shot at the elect and, soft as she was, she knocked it aside. It struck the second armsman and arrowed through his chest, destroying his heart and prime meridian without breaking the skin. He fell with a rattle of lamellar armor. Her kir snaked through the earth to my feet. Something cold and strong grabbed my ankle. It snicked my shield-charm, unraveled it as her two archers drew back and loosed.

My arms flew up on their own but at such close range, armor meant little. One arrow skewered through my forearm, tenting the mail sleeve before my eyes. The other hit my gut.

Kir roiled in me, twisted by rage into a charm — a body's full pattern flashed through my Blessed memory — and shot back. The archers' bow-hands blossomed, skin flaying off followed by muscle, tendons, arteries. Sleeves burst open as their arms unraveled, flew apart in a cloud of blood and meat. At the shoulder, their leather jerkins held together but the blood still flew. Their terrified eyes the moment before their faces bloomed —

Braided kir landed to one side, then the other, and the tiny street blazed with golden light. Woden slapped aside the last armsman — the man fell in a rag-doll heap — and snatched up the elect by her neck.

My knees wobbled and gave out. I landed heavy. The jolt hurt. A vine of kir-laced earth still held my ankle hostage. My hands went to the arrow in my gut, trying to focus on my patterns.

"Kate!"

Kiefan's hand covered mine. His arm circled my shoulders and pulled me into a thick, coppery reek of blood. My eyes flew open, stunned by the smell, and I put up an arm to fend him off. He knelt beside me, face lightly smudged with red — and dripping from the neck down.

Saint Woden spun out a heavy knife of kir and sawed against the elect's right hand. Red flashed and something broke. Her saint's bond?

"The arrows!" Kiefan's snarl sharpened as he went. "You were to keep her safe!"

"M'lord, we —" Sir Waldemar was closest by.

"You left her out here!"

"No!" I put up my arm, slapped Kiefan with the arrow through it by accident. "They never left me. Let me…"

I still bled and the burn from my stomach was spreading. Eyes clenched, I bore my will down onto my unruly kir-patterns. They knew I was too tired to truly force them, though, and they only wobbled around the steel arrowhead.

"Pull it out," I said.

"Take my kir." Kiefan's hand clenched mine.

"Pull the arrow!" I ordered him, eye to eye. The ghost of worry in his eyes fled and he bit back his objections. He nudged my fingers from the shaft. A short, strong jerk, and the head tore out. He'd gotten my medicine bag open and he pressed a wad of clean cloth onto the wound. That was enough for the bleeding. I worked at knitting my stomach shut.

"Stop fussing and let her up," Woden said, above us.

"I'll not have her suffer," Kiefan snarled back. "She wasn't ready for the front lines."

Woden chuckled. "See her handiwork, over there. You. Captain Aleks is…"

My stomach mended, I reached into my medicine bag for a blood-stop charm. A second one, and a cleansing charm, were good enough for my skewered arm. Kiefan pushed my sleeves up, snapped off the arrowhead and pulled that shaft without prompting.

He stank of gore and sweat. He left red smudges on everything. Fatigue had laid shadows under his eyes; I had them myself, I was sure.

"Drink," Kiefan told me, voice low. He put a small water-skin in my hands. "Mend yourself. We aren't done yet."

"I can't risk healing charms," I murmured back.

"If I could I'd let you sleep. Even here, surrounded by enemies."

I leaned against his wet shoulder with a sigh, too tired to take care what I said. "It's safe enough to sleep here."

CHAPTER 5

"Renata," the Arceal elect answered when Woden demanded her name. She was a small woman, tanned face soft with age, her curly brown hair watered down by grey. She looked more the sort to slip extra honey into your oat porridge than to be overseeing the trebuchets at Ansehen. On her knees, hands bound with kir, she kept her eyes on Woden's boots.

Better those than the two archers I'd ruined. They were already drawing flies on the rain-dampened street.

"Look at me," Woden commanded in Arceal, and she looked up. "You know who I am."

"Saint Woden of Wodenberg, la."

"If you doubt us, you'll be taken to the east gate to see what we deal to our enemies, and how else my elect will defend their people." Woden pointed at Kiefan, and she looked to him. Then her gaze slid to me and she looked away with a shudder. She shook her head.

Just as well. If she'd broken free and tried to fight, I could hardly light a spark charm for all my bone-weariness and pain. I only managed to stand beside Kiefan, despite the weight of my damn mail tunic, by force of will and the strength of another kir-ration from Saint Qadeem.

"Wodenberg does not force binding," Woden told Renata. "Neither do we cast aside those willing to serve. Consider what you can offer and where your loyalties lie now that you're rid of your saint's bond. But do not take too long."

Renata looked up at him, her teeth working against her lower lip. "Does Wodenberg value crafters?"

He folded his arms across his chest. "Saint Aleksandr was a brother to me — one that Arcea murdered. His skill was without price."

"Will you tear elect from their forges, conscript them as wood-smiths?" Renata cast a sneer toward the trebuchets. My tired brain tried to wrestle with the image of this soft, mousy woman working a smithy.

"Only if they wish it," Woden said.

"Might be I have something to offer, la."

Our saint looked to Kiefan, who gave a nod; she told the truth. "Will you be bound?" Woden asked Renata, putting out one hand.

Her brows rose. "Or die?"

"If your saint will not bargain for you."

Renata's voice fell to a mutter. "Little more than a hound to its master."

"We will speak on what might happen."

Woden touched her forehead and she slumped unconscious; on his instructions two of my King's Guard pulled her up and carried her off for safe-keeping. Once she was away, the saint turned to me.

"Will he hear?" he asked. I took a moment to check my bond, and nodded. Qadeem's touch shivered through my Blessing. Woden said, "Kiefan broke a division. Twenty-third, I think the standard said. Half of them routed into our cavalry lines. Half routed into the town and threw the seventeenth division into disarray. A number of companies have surrendered already. One battle elect is dead, one crafter elect captured. It remains to be seen if they'll need another Shepherd's knife to convince the rest to surrender. There may well be more elect."

Qadeem's opinion came to me and I said, "He wishes you to allow the officers to negotiate for the lives of their men."

Woden didn't think much of that, by the set of his mouth. "Centaurs and minotaurs, perhaps they'd bargain for those, but the Empress won't give a pip for the enlisted. And we can't feed them. We expect word from downslope soon, as well. Take stock of our men outside the walls and tell Vysokov to bring up the reserve." That was for Kiefan. My orders were, "Patch what you can on our men. Check these Arceal for blessed — most make officer, but not all."

Rostislav had an arrow in his shoulder; shot at close range, it had punched through his mail and gambeson. Once I'd cut that out and stitched him, he was all but tied to my side by Kiefan's stern glares.

He stood watch while I gnawed my share of a rack of half-roasted beef ribs. We had worked our way deeper in Ansehen, where the houses were still intact, checking kir-gifted prisoners and flushing out small knots of misplaced Arceal armsmen. A kitchen had been abandoned with pots still boiling on the fire and the meat still roasting. My Guard and I had the food readied, as well as we could, in what seemed a few heartbeats and we fell to without hesitation. A hand of hawk-eyed archers who happened by helped us finish off the huge pot of mashed potatoes with roasted garlic.

Kiefan found me again soon after that. Word had come from Rangers sent down the hairpin road into Suevia and we were to ride with an escort to meet the Caer. Kiefan had found a bucket of water and washed his face, and his hands, clean of the drying blood. Its brown-red still dulled his mail, though, and stained the white-moon sigil on his black tabard.

The rest of the King's Guard were with him as were the horses who'd been waiting outside the gate. Several strength-Blessed men with axes had gotten that open at last.

Boosted back in Jenner's saddle, I rode beside Kiefan down the Southbound Road. His Guard and the squad of Rangers escorted us. Ansehen had been a fine town before the burnings, before the earthquake. I couldn't help thinking it was ashamed to be seen in such a state. The stone wall that ran along the lip of the hill was Saint Aleksandr's seamless work, high as the city walls around Wodenberg — where it still stood. The Southbound Road had run between two towers and a gate but those were only piles of rubble on either side now.

Past the ruined gate, we rode into the wall's afternoon shadow and curved through a paved mustering-yard on our first of many sharp corners down the hill. Bare stone stood on our right for much of the way as the road snaked its way down. On the left was an open drop down to scrubby trees and a brackish, stagnant lake caught at the foot of these hills. When enough rain fell, it overflowed and fed into the Neva.

The road was wide and well tended. Brush lining the way was putting out green buds and a long stretch of dandelions on the right-hand slope greeted us when we rounded one sharp corner. Blue jays called — but so did crows, perched by the dozens on what few trees there were. Overhead, the clouds were breaking up and forgetting about rain but the wind was still chilly and the hill's shadow cooler still. Vultures were circling, too.

Ordinary vultures, even though their wings flashed white on the underside just like the monstrous one that had carried off Anders. I touched my necklace again, murmured a bit of a prayer to the Mother.

Halfway down, we met the Ramsbridge. Two four-horned stone rams bigger than bulls guarded the bridge with their heads lowered in challenge. Even though storms had worn and pitted the stone, the four horns stood fearsome: two curled out sideways, two rising in a V. Their stone bridge joined one hillside to another above the brackish lake.

When I'd first crossed it, Elect Parselev had told me that this bridge was saint-made — but far older than Saint Aleksandr.

Kiefan and I looked up at the first pair of rams, and then the pair at the far end, as we passed between them. "Father Duty, lend me wisdom," Kiefan said. That left me thinking of the duty I'd done already today; it was afternoon now and still plenty of day left for more. My first battle. I'd never thought to fight in one, or to kill men.

On the lower hill, the Southbound Road ran a little straighter but just as steep. Below, Suevia came clearly into view.

The Neva river churned down through a bed of rocks, frothing white, and stormed on for some miles more. Thin, rolling pasture stretched for some miles, too, studded with the faces of grey rocks among the grass. We'd fought Arcea here over a year ago, on the apron of pasture that the brackish lake flooded when it rained. Now rows of tents covered it — but many of them were on fire — and mustering-yards of supply-laden wagons stood to either side of the Southbound Road. They waited alone.

Against the angry river's bank, a mass of men was hemmed in by a thin hedge of Caer.

Tadhlon's twin-mountain-and-moon banner stood in the road, accompanied by two squads of Caer knights. Captain Mohra Fionmaen, who had first found us when we descended from Starknadel's pass and who had come with m'lady Leix to break the siege, rode out to meet us. She still wore her brown hair boyishly short and her scout's uniform of browns and greens, but her smile had thinned under the weight of losing m'lady Leix.

"Be welcome, King of Wodenberg," she greeted us in our own language. "Be welcome, Elect Kate. Might I lead you to Elect Teleri and Captain-general Croícruach?"

We walked our horses into the Arceal camp, our standard-bearers at the front. Captain Mohra told us their journey across the Suevi side of the hills had gone well. Slowed by mud and avoiding tiny villages, but quickly enough. The Rangers assigned to scout for them had seen to it they passed in secret. Teleri had spent this morning learning the lay of the camp before signaling their readiness. When Woden's flare had gone up immediately, the Tadhlon Guard attacked.

"Did catch these boys entirely unaware," Captain Mohra said. "'Tis their supply line's depot and their reserve force — ten thousand Suevi."

"Thirty thousand in Ansehen sounded like an uncomfortable crowd," Kiefan said. "It isn't so large a town. Twenty above, ten below, then."

"With surprise, we did drive them to the shore and gain their surrender. 'Tis a fine start to our alliance."

The Suevi command pavilion was still decked with their division standards but the knights who stood at the door were Caer: Tadhlon's dusty-beige gambesons under knee-long mail shirts, red cloaks and full, crested helms. They saluted us.

"In the pavilion," Mohra told us just before we dismounted, "only elect or those drained of kir."

"You've captured another elect?" Kiefan asked. She nodded.

The King's Guard and Mohra stayed outside. Inside, at the map table, Elect Teleri looked up and grinned. With her stood a broad-faced, grizzled knight with a scar across her cheek; the captain-general saluted us. On the carpeted floor, wearing only braies, hands bound behind his back and a burlap sack over his head, knelt their prisoner. The afternoon sun streamed in through pinned-open flaps and all of the chests in the pavilion had been dragged into the pools of light to be opened and half-emptied.

In one long stride, Elect Teleri crossed to the prisoner and yanked the sack off his head. "'Tis ill fortune for you," she told him. "They did send their butcher."

He was Arceal, tanned a little browner than most and dark hair cropped short. His gaze shot straight to Kiefan and his bloody mail.

"Not him!" Teleri barked a laugh and pointed at me. "She's the one to fear."

Teleri had called me a butcher, after what I'd done to Elect Tannait. I kept my face serene as the prisoner eyed me, his brows crinkling in puzzlement. Let him wonder. I touched my saint's bond and Qadeem saw him as well.

/ know? /

/ many elect / Qadeem sent that sense of muggy heat and fear by which he meant Arcea.

Kiefan paced around the prisoner, looming over him with a frown. "Name?" he asked in Arceal.

"DePesci Liandro."

"Assignment? Your saint?"

Elect Liandro looked at the carpet under his knees.

"Consider what you're worth to your saint. Consider what awaits you as an enemy of Wodenberg, as an invader of my kingdom," Kiefan said.

"So think you, when I've set no foot in your frozen wasteland?"

Kiefan leaned closer, hissing, "You're pawn to those who murdered my family. This blood doesn't begin to pay the debt owed to Wodenberg." He gestured at his stained tabard.

"When you refused all overtures, kidnapped royal blood, incited rebellion —"

"We incited nothing. My mother was marked for death," Kiefan snarled back. "We rescued her from the likes of you."

Elect Liandro, staring up at Kiefan, echoed faintly. "Mother? Oh, la. The grey eyes, as she said."

"Suevia's throne is mine by blood."

He dismissed that with a shrug. "By blood did the Empress take it. Suevia's throne is hers."

"The Empress will pay blood for blood, for those she murdered."

"For you will conquer us? This little gang of boys will best Arceal might?" A laugh lurked around the edge of Elect Liandro's words.

Qadeem sent me an image of the Arceal saint who'd stood unruffled in the Order's courtyard, despite the wreckage and death. "Gauvail," I said aloud, and the prisoner's head snapped to me. "You speak for him. His bound elect."

Elect Liandro's chin rose, considering me. "Qadeem. Thus our third round begins?"

I felt a nod, so I did. My instructions came as well. "I'm to take him up to Ansehen," I told Kiefan in Alemannic. To Woden, specifically, but I wasn't to say that.

Kiefan nodded. "I will see to the Suevi officers' surrender."

<hr/>

Once knocked unconscious, Elect Liandro was easily tied to a saddle and delivered up the hills. By then, dusk was settling. What rainclouds remained were painted scarlet by the lowering sun. Flock moons rose, one at a time, tinted ruddy orange. They winked among the clouds, wary of the battlefield below.

Ansehen still teemed with men; there were thousands of prisoners to disarm and organize. What would become of so many Arceal men, I didn't know yet. I was too tired to care much. Saint Woden had dismissed me to rest once he'd cut Liandro's saint-bond and that had been all I'd wanted to hear.

I needed to catalogue the day's slaughter, fold up the memories and put them away before they could haunt me. The arrow hole through my arm and the burn on my thigh still throbbed. My stomach growled again despite the beef ribs and potatoes. My lonely camp bed was just the thing for my bone-weariness and gnawing headache, once this mail tunic was off.

Lieutenant Rostislav and my hand of Guards still shadowed me. One had been killed in trying to follow my chase of Elect Renata; he'd met two Arceal knights and as I'd accidentally drained him of kir, earlier, he'd had none to fuel his Blessings. That Guard's blood was on my hands, both for his draining and for my haring off without warning and making him chase me. Sir Garrick had taken up the empty post.

I turned Jenner away from the armsmen and archers, the knights and their horses, that seethed around and through the open front gate. That was too much noise and bother just now. At a brisk walk, I led the way toward the side gate. All was silent, this way, but for some wing-flapping and caws.

Rostislav hurried up alongside me. "We should go out the main gate, m'lady. This's far out of our way."

"But quieter," I said. "It's not so far — the infirmary's set up by the road, they said."

"I'll see you go through untroubled," Rostislav said, leaning closer. "M'lady… please, let's go out the main gate."

"Corpses and crows don't frighten me, sir."

We passed into a half-burned neighborhood that still smelled of smoke. And death: blood and shit. Here and there, embers glowed on exposed rafters. Shadows deepened, strengthened by all the soot, but I still noticed the bodies. Jenner slowed and stopped, snorting. I tapped him and the gelding took a few careful steps.

Sir Garrick moved to my other side even though the road was narrow. He watched the cross-streets, hand on his sword, his usual lanky, gawky self remade as a sleek predator by his blood-stained armor and tabard. Even the ash-blond curls in his knight's crest couldn't touch that.

I drew out a globe of kir and lit it; the diffuse green glow reached far but made no heat in my hand. A squad of crows rose from a dead centaur just ahead, harsh caws punctuating the flapping of black wings. There were not so many of them, in truth. Crows roosted at night and most had gone to their rest.

Jenner stopped again and the warhorses were quick to do the same. Rostislav's tossed his head and wanted to back up, but got a stern order to hold. Under more clicks and taps, the horse reluctantly advanced. I kicked Jenner, but he wouldn't move until he was in the middle of the warhorses.

Beyond the centaur, two more corpses sprawled, one headless, the other's belly cut open. A vulture looked up from that as we passed and judged that we wouldn't trouble him. He returned to his work.

"With respect, m'lady," Sir Garrick said, "it will be worse at the gate."

We reached a solid carpet of men who'd fallen, while running, without a mark on them. Beyond them the street narrowed to a meandering path through the dead but the stink of blood eased. The warhorses walked a bit easier, picking their way through, and Jenner took his courage from them.

"Tell me what happened," I said. These were Woden's doing, the work of a Shepherd's knife. The memory of the one that had chased me and Kiefan and Anders along the city walls was safely put away and couldn't haunt me.

"When we saw how much of the Arceal division had gotten out into the fields," Sir Garrick said, "m'lord Kiefan sent the knights to stop them a quarter mile down. He rode toward the gate with only we Guard and Saint Woden. He paid no mind to their archers. When we neared, Kiefan dismounted and ordered us to stay there until summoned. Captain Aleks refused. He snapped at her with such venom — and Woden told her to stay, as well. Kiefan walked toward the Arceal shield wall… sword and shield, wearing his kir. No more. I feared for him at first. But after the first few… I laughed at the slaughter — Mother Love forgive me — and once Woden joined in…"

Garrick didn't need to say more; we were ten yards from the gate, but had to stop. Our horses would go no further. They only turned their heads away with ears pinned back when urged on. Those who'd been cut down bloodlessly by the Shepherd's knife ended here. Beyond, the carpet lay thick: meat and innards. It took some staring to pick out the limbs, the torsos, the heads. Centaurs. Men. In the green light of my kir-lamp, their blood was black.

Everything was black.

CHAPTER 6

And yet, in the morning fresh dew fell, sparrows sang, and dandelions opened to the sun. Even those that had been trampled; they were tough little flowers.

I looked across yesterday's battlefield as the sun rose, having already stretched my limbs at Abbot Shaw's disciple's dance, and walked into the infirmary to check its rows of patients. There were a few badly broken legs that were too complex for even Physician Brauer to fully set, so I saw to those. Ter Biya put some salve on my burn and bandaged me. As I left, a handful of armsmen arrived carrying three of their companions who suffered belly cramps and the runs.

Outside, the sparrows fell silent as flocks of crows and ravens circled down to the feast laid out for them. Vultures came, too, bullying their way through with dark wings spread. All night, living Arceal soldiers had been herded into the stone-walled fields under guard. Thousands of them, and hundreds of centaurs and minotaurs as well.

/ find Woden / Qadeem's image of him included the mountain that bore his name, the touch of cold stone. It fit him.

/ sick / wounded / was my reply. They needed me.

/ will remain / Woden /

I fetched Jenner from the stable and rode to the command pavilion. There I found our saint and all three dukes listening as the army's quartermaster, with Theo Kaufmann beside him, reported on the supplies captured thus far and the preparations to distribute bread and water to the prisoners.

"Give them water," Woden said, "but hold back the bread until I've spoken with their captains. There's been no sign of the Voice, yet?"

"No, m'lord. Nor the gentle-born lady we were to look for."

The Voice of the Empress, deSvello Antonin, had been with the army all the summer long. Perhaps he'd left with Clarilunes Graziana, the bride that the Empress had offered Kiefan.

"Word from the Caer?"

"His Majesty has sent for Kaufmann to organize the supplies available in the camp, I believe." The quartermaster indicated Theo. "I have no specifics beyond that."

Woden nodded. "Go, then."

The quartermaster and Theo dipped in obeisance and went. Theo smiled to me as he passed and I was glad to see him well. Woden stood from his camp chair, drained his cup of small beer and passed it to a page.

"Assemble two squads of archers and send them to me at the prisoner pickets," Woden told Duke Seagrace. Then he turned to me. "Qadeem will have his say, yes, so come along."

I felt thin amusement through my bond.

Woden took a roan mare and Duke Vysokov's daughter Nadya for an aide, and led the way. We turned off the Southbound Road and cut across fallow fields, finding our way over the tumbled stone walls to the intact fields used to pen our Arceal prisoners. The captain who had charge of guarding them, an archer Blessed with heat sight as well as hawk's eyes, trotted to meet us with his lieutenant beside him.

"Captain Eadulf Saltgrass, m'lord," he said. "Three tried to escape, overnight, but we shot them, m'lord."

"Good. Bring me their captains." Woden glanced across the two occupied fields. "Looks to be six thousand men — there should be six captains."

Captain Saltgrass sent his lieutenant, muttering the orders in Englic. "Drag those tight-assed bastards, if you have to." He turned back to Saint Woden and said, "Right away, m'lord. What else can I offer? We've some hot chicory on the fire."

Woden declined and walked his mare along the stone wall until he could sight across both fields. Archers and pairs of armsmen dotted the perimeter. More armsmen waited further to the side to catch any who ran the gauntlet of arrows. The two squads of archers he'd asked for joined us, and Woden set them in a staggered array to either side of us.

The four surviving captains were brought. Woden met them face to face; Nadya held our horses. Even in plain clothes, the Arceal officers were leather-tough men with hard eyes. They wore their grey hairs and scars as badges. All had to look up to meet Saint Woden's gaze, but none shrank from that — even when he let his kir unfurl and hang in a starry green cloak around him.

Each spared me a glance, a faintly suspicious frown, and kept half an eye on me as they focused on Woden. They were too wise to overlook even a slip of a girl, if a saint wished her at hand.

/ let them speak /

But Woden didn't need a nudge from me. "You acted to spare your men last night," he told them. "Be as wise now. I will have no slaves in my kingdom. There's no ransom the Empress will pay for armsmen and mere knights. Renounce her —"

"Never!" The eldest of them spat at Woden.

He slapped the captain and the man's head spun much too far around. He fell in a heap. "Renounce her and serve me as mercenaries until the war is ended." Woden finished with the same calm he'd begun with.

A moment's silence. "None renounce the Empress," the second captain answered him. "We must refuse." He was the brownest, of them, with the blackest hair. Black eyes, as well. Like Saint Qadeem's.

/ yes / sadly /

Rasila, he'd said his homeland was called. Long part of Arcea's empire. Of course there'd be countrymen of Qadeem's among the Empress's soldiers.

"You choose the Shepherd over service, then?" Woden asked as kir massed in his hand. It ignited and kept growing.

The Rasilai captain stood at attention, fighting a shudder of fear. "There's no Shepherd to fear. Only the Empress."

Woden's ball of kir writhed, knotting, and spit out stars that circled the little sun. It was big as an acorn squash, now. It held all our eyes with its golden brilliance: the captains, the prisoners, the guards. Our saint stepped back, pitched it, and the curved scythe-wings flashed out on either side to match the width of the field.

The Shepherd's culling knife cut through the captains near the neck and raced across the prisoners. They fell like harvested oats, bloodless and limp. The first few rows were too dumb-struck to move; those behind them screamed in terror, fell on their faces, ran for the walls. Some stood proud to meet their deaths.

A pit opened in my stomach, but I did not look away. As my master had taught me.

Beside me, the archers shot those who ran. And those who sat up after the blade passed. Woden slung a whip-crack vine of kir after the Shepherd's knife, as it reached the far end of the fields, to snap the charm. It broke into a cascade of stars and the earth took its kir back. Else-wise, it would have traveled on and on, cutting down all it crossed until it met someone brave enough to hold up a charm to break it.

At a command, the squads of archers beside us climbed over the stone walls and checked the fallen. Huddled, weeping prisoners got a point-blank arrow to the heart.

My hollowed stomach turned sick. I clenched my teeth and fought it.

Woden's heavy hand landed on my shoulder. "There's no honor in it," he said, rumbling softly. "In Arcea, surrender means slavery or the gladiator pits for the poor bastards in the shield walls. But there will be no slaves in Wodenberg while I live, and I won't call killing a sport. There were too many to feed and too much the enemy to trust them. Pray the Father that the Suevi have more sense."

Once woken, Elect Renata took in the small tent, Woden and I, and Elect Liandro lying unconscious on the other bedroll with a glance. Woden's hush sphere pressed against the canvas walls around us. Her gaze came to the low table and the humble meal last. She knelt beside it and ate the fried egg, drank the water, then started on the bowl of oat porridge.

Woden told her about the master-smith's forge in Ansehen, which had caught fire and then stood gutted for the better part of a year. Arcea had used a smaller forge near the ruined castle, as they'd only needed to shoe horses and mend armor.

Elect Renata nodded; she'd seen the master forge and mourned it. When Woden asked what she'd need to get it running again, her eyes lit. He mentioned that the master smith himself was only a day's ride away in the city, and he would be a fine assistant. By then she'd already been won over.

Renata told us that the heavy strikers — as Arcea called its centaur- and minotaur-based divisions — had received orders from the Empress to capture our secret fount in the Eispitzen. By which she meant the lamia fount; likely the Empress had sensed it while she was in Vorspitz to murder Crown Ceelin.

Woden chuckled, at that, but said nothing. A thought goosed me; I took a breath to ask if there'd been any word of the Empress bringing a prisoner from Wodenberg. But Woden nudged Elect Renata about Suevia's founts and the moment passed. She told us all she knew about the layers of protection around them. She'd never been given complete access to either fount but she'd seen much of the one in Temitte. It was protected by a spherical guardian charm, and a castle around the charm, and a city around the castle — not unlike the Pool in Wodenberg.

/ mountain fount / unusual / pool was made /

I had forgotten that Qadeem was listening. / how? /

/ before me / before Woden / Qadeem left that teasing bit of history hanging.

Elect Renata renounced the Empress of Arcea and asked to be bound. Woden did it, then said she'd be a better fit for Saint Qadeem — he agreed, through me — and he'd re-bind her when he arrived. Woden gave her some freedom under hand-picked guard until then. She was eager to start cleaning out the ruined master forge.

"Such as her need to be busy," Woden said as we walked to the command pavilion. "They need to know their value."

"I cannot imagine her working a forge. She hasn't the arms for it." Saint Aleksandr had been a bear of a man, intimidating until you saw the deft care he took with all things. Him, I could see pounding steel on an anvil.

Woden smiled. "For elect and saints, forging does not need a hammer. Aleks could pull a sword from the furnace as women pull thread from a hank of wool."

That widened my eyes, but Woden only nodded to the King's Guard at the pavilion's entrance as one of them pulled the door flap open for us. "Saint Woden and Elect Kate, Majesty."

Theo Kaufmann stood with Kiefan by the map table; both looked to us, as did Gregor who stood by the side-table where a pitcher of small beer and extra cups waited. Theo and Gregor both made a brief obeisance.

"Making arrangements? You're certain of him, then?" Woden asked.

Kiefan nodded. He waited until Gregor had handed us cups of small beer to answer. "Lucan Scyfe, captain-general of the thirty-first division, mustered entirely from Suevia —" he added that for me — "will do as we ask. So long as we reward him well. He claims it's loyalty to his house, he wishes to see it restored, but what he wants is money. Land. Possibly a particular woman." Kiefan shrugged that off.

"It's much to trust any man with, let alone an enemy," Woden said. "Safer to put them under the Shepherd's knife."

"They're ten thousand fully trained and equipped Suevi," Kiefan said. "Scyfe was on his knees before I entered the tent, to ask how they might be spared."

"How he might be spared."

That sounded likely enough, to me. I sipped my drink, savoring its tangy bite.

"He's little use without them. There's twenty-five thousand or more in Temitte rather than here — our alliance with Caercoed made them cautious, as we hoped. With the Tadhlon Guard and Caercoed's aid we may match that. We must leave our wounded here, plus a thousand as a garrison and to guard the monsters," Kiefan said. "Another ten on our side is no small thing."

A moment's silence followed. Likely Kiefan and Woden had laid out the plan through their bond, and needed say little on it. "Scyfe is willing to fight for us? As mercenaries?" I asked. "Would they turn on their own people?"

"It would be too much to ask them to attack fellow Suevi," Kiefan said. "I don't plan to ask Scyfe to attack even Arceal soldiers, at first. Only that when the time is right, he do nothing at all."

Woden's interest perked, at that. "Not to open doors for us?"

"I open the doors." Theo spoke up at last. He had been fighting to keep quiet, I knew. "Scyfe will grease the hinges, perhaps."

"For that," Kiefan said, "it must be someone we trust."

Theo went on. "My uncle is quartermaster of the supply depot — I thanked the Caer for not killing him — and so long as he escapes along with Scyfe's division, I can be just another of his foremen." Theo's mother was Suevi, and he had blood kin in Temitte. He spoke the language with a native accent. He knew the city well. "Once he and I are there, we can open whatever doors you need. Whatever gates."

"Herr Bídon has sketched out the military camps around Temitte," Kiefan said. "He was there two weeks ago. Scyfe will tip the scales for us. His allegiance will persuade other old houses to join our cause. That's worth his price."

Woden considered for a few more swallows of beer, and then nodded. "The plan is for the Suevi to escape tonight?"

"Yes. To give them lead time on us."

Part VI: Fount's Crucible

An early dinner followed, made slow by many reports on the day's work. I sat on Woden's left, Kiefan on his right, at the table carried in by the kitchen crew for the meal. All three dukes joined us along with some captains-general; those who gave their reports stood before the table and were given refreshments off to one side.

It was a great deal of men and foodstuffs and equipment to hear about. Save for the news from the infirmary, it had little to do with me — and that report had me eager to go and help them. Since the morning, men had trickled in with fevers, stomach pain, and flooded bowels. I'd seen dysentery before and I'd suffered it; it had swept through the foulburg when I was young.

/ after / be my ears now /

So I stayed, ate roasted river trout, and tore off bread to dip in the bowl of olive oil. There'd been barrels of it in the supply camp, and the cook had added sliced garlic cloves. It was a strong temptation to stay, on its own, but duty tugged me toward the infirmary.

Spiced Arceal tea marked the end of dinner. I sat reviewing what I knew of bowel diseases with both hands wrapped around the warm tea mug while the dukes and captains began to move toward the door flaps.

Saint Woden stood, so Kiefan and I did too. "Qadeem will arrive by morning," Woden told us. "You'll have whatever aid I can give from the fount. And I'll see you next in Temitte."

"M'lord," I murmured, dipping my head. Despite how long he'd been away in Woden-berg, my saint knew more of Arcea, the Empress, and how she guarded her founts. And, he'd told me through the bond, Woden was too cautious to leave the safety of his founts and kingdom to anyone else. He'd come to Ansehen to see the enemy thrown out and now he'd resume his place atop his mountain.

Woden swept the dukes and captains out with him to give them final orders and advice. Captain Aleksandra and Lieutenant Rostislav were among those. They hadn't spoken at dinner, but had stood guard at either end of our table.

"Rostislav asked if he may tie you to your horse, next time he must guard you in battle." Kiefan leaned against the table, picking up his mug of tea.

I frowned at him for a heartbeat, but then that knight's death cut me afresh. "I didn't mean to drain him — I'll take more care, if I must pull kir again."

Kiefan's head cocked, curious. "He said that you went haring off into a trap and strung the men out in a vulnerable line, in chasing you. One dead and two wounded."

I hadn't asked how Rostislav caught that arrow in his shoulder. My mouth twisted to one side, guilt needling me further. Still standing by the table, I picked up my mug. "I will take more care in that, too. And he should correct me if I'm being foolish. I don't know anything of the battlefield. I suppose that was a trap, as he says." I'd caught them off guard, it seemed at the time.

"He's gotten the idea it's dangerous to anger you. Some assurance may help him in that." Kiefan caught me in a sip of tea and I spluttered. "Dangerous?" He meant the two archers, true, but that seemed a little thing to me now. "I'm not — I'm no battle elect." My voice fell off as the kir-lit carnage at the side gate came back to me. "Not so dangerous as you."

He hesitated, then put his mug down. "You saw that?"

"I meant to ride out the side gate," I said. Kiefan kept his eyes on his tea. "My horse refused." I'd had to ride out the front after all.

Silence hung between Kiefan and me. I watched his hand, by the tea mug, even his knuckles and nails clean of blood now. Memories of where else that hand had been flitted by my mind. The blood didn't rest easy, alongside that.

"It was a terrible thing to do," I murmured.

He was slow to answer that. "But my mind is clear. All the — smoke — the rage. Burned off now."

Rage. I had put those memories away but I still knew what they were. "Rage for the murders?" Afraid to hear his answer, and I asked nonetheless. Rage at Anders. And...

"For many things."

The ache twisted into pain and I needed to hear it, of a sudden. That he was angry, still, that he would be polite to me for duty's sake but that was all.

"Me?" I asked.

Silence. My heart quavered in my chest, waiting for the merciful blow. I wanted to sit down in case my knees weakened any further, but I set my hands on the table and steeled myself.

Kiefan took a step back from the table, folded his arms across his chest, and took a deep breath. "You've more right to hate me than I you," he murmured, eyes downcast still. "I hurt you. I've done little but hurt you, it seems. The shame of that is more —" He stopped to swallow. His voice turned rough but he looked me in the eye. "If it would mend that, I would do anything you asked of me."

Tears blurred my eyes. He'd hurt me, yes, but it wasn't all he'd done and I didn't hate him. But if I said that aloud, Kiefan would... hope. I'd spent a long winter alone aching over the loss of him and Anders, knowing I had been a fool and hurt them both. I wouldn't do them any more harm.

I must be polite with Kiefan. Say nothing until I knew if Anders was dead.

But my winter would've been far worse, if not for Kiefan.

When my silence stretched into several heartbeats, he shifted, looking away, and drained his mug of tea. "Clear that away," he told Gregor, gesturing at the tea service. "Get the training gear. A few rounds, before the sun sets."

"You hurt me," I said. Kiefan froze, looking to me. "But Rafe?" I shook my head. "He's been my sunshine and my hope, and you —" I had to stop and fight for control of my voice. "He reminds me of my younger brother, Leyman. Quiet and alert. Fearless. Though Ley did turn out a troublemaker — and he wasn't so particular as Rafe is. Rafe will not be persuaded once he's set his mind. But his smile, when he's happy..."

When I looked again, Kiefan had drawn a step closer. We stood facing each other, a yard apart, and it seemed we were matched in not daring to get any closer. Too perilous.

"I wanted to come, to see Rafe," Kiefan said. "I had duties and — I don't wish to be my father, but he set duty first. In all things. And I could not face you, so soon."

It had been a long winter. "It isn't soon anymore."

"No." Kiefan took another deep breath. "Is it late?"

Perilous, to ask that. "We have our duties," I said.

He nodded. "Duty."

Silence, again, looking at each other and unwilling to break off as we needed to.

Kiefan murmured, "Good night."

The echo of his first kiss made my breath catch. But I answered, "Good night," and escaped.

CHAPTER 7

Saint Qadeem arrived in a most unusual way. On a horse.

I trotted to the command pavilion from the infirmary, my skirts in my hands. Mud got on my hems anyway; a light rain had begun before dawn and the morning was a dismal grey. When I arrived, Qadeem was just drawing up at the awning-covered entrance on a muddy brown palfrey. The King's Guard dropped to one knee in obeisance as he swung down from the saddle; the royal courier alongside him went ahead into the pavilion. One Guard caught his arm, jerked him to a surprised stop, and checked his pattern before letting him pass.

Qadeem smiled at the sight of me and put up an arm. A brief hug made me smile too. He was so warm, as always, under that silly fur-lined cloak. It was never a nice enough day for him.

"How does it go?" he asked before he released me. "With Kiefan?"

That tempered my cheer. "Gingerly."

Qadeem's hand lingered on my shoulder. "Rafe is well. I checked on him before leaving." He looked toward the pavilion as Kiefan appeared in the doorway and bowed. "A risky attack, sir," Qadeem said. "Thank the Father it worked. Or perhaps the Shepherd."

"The Shepherd kindly lent me his culling knife," Kiefan answered. "There's a kettle on the fire for tea, m'lord, and Gregor's fetching something to go alongside it."

Qadeem put that aside with one hand. "I'm well enough for now. Let young Bern have it — he's ridden all night. Where's this elect?"

"At the master forge. A horse for Kate!" At Kiefan's order, one of the pages handed the courier's reins off and ran for the stables.

I rode with my saint into Ansehen, telling him about the dysentery as we went. Physician Brauer had sent out Ters to see how many men truly had it; they were reluctant to come to the infirmary even when they were weak from the fever and thirst and saw blood in their leavings. It was coming on quickly and strong.

"It was waiting for us in Ansehen," Qadeem said. He looked up at the grey blankets overhead. "This rain will make it worse."

We rode past the creeping column of men on the Southbound Road. Wide as the switchback road and the Ramsbridge were, it was slow going to march an army along them. Captain-general Scyfe and his division of Suevi had slipped away in the cloudy dark when the night watch dozed off at their posts, and had stolen a few unattended wagons of their own supplies. He'd have two days' lead on us by the time we were ready to follow.

Elect Renata seemed to pay no mind at all to the steady rivulet of water falling from a broken beam in the master forge's roof. Other drips made puddles on the floor, but none were over the furnace. Her four guards clustered in a dry spot out of her way, playing cards. They sprang to attention when Qadeem stepped into the charred doorway and then they dipped in obeisance. He dismissed them.

She came up short and stared a moment. "For you must be Saint Qadeem, la."

"And you are Elect Renata." He answered her in that same Arceal cadence. I followed him through the doorway — the door was a heap of half-burned boards outside — and looked up.

She had braced the worst of the roof beams with a piece of another, creating a pillar in the middle of the shop. Qadeem asked and she gave us the complete list of what she'd done thus far to clean out the forge and organize. The shop's table leaned but it bore the array of tools she'd dug out. A sack of charcoal and a pile of wood near to being charcoal itself waited for the furnace to be ready.

"Its mortar needs repair. For which I must have kir."

"You would be bound?" He said the words slowly, giving them weight.

She put out her hand for Qadeem to cut Woden's temporary bond. "I renounce Empress Seraphine, who tore me from my saint." Elect Renata's voice rose. "Who gave me to Gauvail for a toy. I would be bound to one who respects craft. Loves art."

Qadeem and Saint Aleksandr had shared many of the Blessings that gave craft: the craft-hands, the heat-sighted, the strength-blessed. My saint's particular love had been scribing and drawing but there was much overlap with carpentry, architecture, and stonework. With Aleks gone, he had become the saint of nearly all Wodenberg's crafts.

"My elect must put truth and reason first in their minds," he told Renata, as he'd told me at my binding. "They must seek knowledge and experience, answer me truly and fully when I question. They must aid me in battle if needed. You must aid Saint Woden as well, but your first loyalty is to me. Your second, to your sister and brother elect." Qadeem indicated me.

Renata nodded. "My saint, my siblings in binding. And Saint Woden."

"So long as your strength and loyalty are mine, I will see you blossom to your fullest. Though I suspect…"

He sounded her, and through my bond I faintly heard the strange, rich chord her kir sounded. It hung in the air, and then faded sooner than I had expected.

"Your saint did train you well." Qadeem fell back into Arceal cadence.

Renata nodded, the lines on her soft face deepening. "Saint Chale gave much —"

"Saint Chale?"

She nodded again, paying his sharp tone no mind. Renata put out her right hand again. "I would be bound."

Qadeem spun up a kir-blade in his hand. "I do not force the bond. Prepare yourself."

He cut his meridian open — I felt my own ache in sympathy — and she cut her own. I noted that saint's name, Chale, as the bond was made. He must be a crafter saint.

I felt kir move between my saint and my new sister elect. "Mend the forge," Qadeem said.

Renata put her hands on the stone hearth and kir seeped into the mortar. I moved closer, curious to see how she did it. It mended as if it were flesh. I was the nearest to the sack of charcoal when she wanted it. I heaved the sooty thing up with kir-vines and she dumped it into the fire-pot. With a handful of kir-fire, she lit it to an instant blaze and stoked it into a neat pile with her bare hands, heedless of the growing heat. Renata lay a shaped bowl of kir over the fire and I felt its heat rise further. We called in her four guards and set them to working the bellows.

She'd found the pieces of a broken dagger in the wreckage. It had rusted as well, after a year's weathering. Renata buried it in the coals and I caught a faint glimmer of the kir protecting her fingers.

"Crafters are wonders to watch," Qadeem murmured, stepping beside me.

"Can you mend a blade, thus?" I had to ask; from what little I knew, a broken blade was only scrap metal.

He didn't answer. Renata had selected a pair of tongs from the several on the table. She fished half the dagger out by its hilt and set the tongs into a pair of holes in the hearth. The broken blade stood upright, glowing dull red. She plucked the rest of the blade from the fire and set the broken edges together. Heedless of the heat or the blade's edges, she leaned into pressing the pieces together. The blade slid through her fisted hand, from point to hilt, and I felt kir roiling. Golden embers sparked off and sank into the hearth.

The dagger stood in the tongs' grip, bright, clean and whole.

"As smoothly done as any I've seen, la," Qadeem said. Renata passed the mended blade to him. "But we shall need some time to fully supply you — though there may be materials here still. Can we rely on you to repair blades? Armor?"

Elect Renata's smile turned proud. "Surely, my saint."

"If you recall aught of the founts, tell me."

I saw my chance to ask. "Did you hear anything of the Empress bringing a prisoner out of Wodenberg?"

Her dark eyes, sunk in her soft face, turned to me. "A prisoner? She flew over Temitte, for I felt her pass. The orders came later. Nothing of a prisoner in them, la."

"When did the order come?" Qadeem asked.

"Before Solstice. And Gauvail did send me north then. Arkho was here, commanding. Liandro was sent after Equinox." Renata spoke slowly, stoking the burning charcoal with one hand. "Might I fetch the iron bars in the shed? Could draw some wire, here."

Little need to tell Saint Gauvail, or his elect, of the Empress' prisoner. Perhaps that was true enough. But someone must know — or else I'd have to ask the Empress Seraphine herself.

———————✠———————

It was not all so wondrous a day as Renata's blade-mending. Elect Liandro would not even speak to Qadeem, once woken from unconsciousness. He snarled about my saint being a traitor and a fool, and tried to steal my kir twice. He tried to pull from the men outside the little tent; Qadeem struck him with a kir-vine that coiled around the prime meridian in his throat and set him thrashing in pain.

"I gave you chances," he said, standing over Liandro as he screamed curses. "Kate, come and see this."

I did not flinch, though I wanted to. I caught Liandro's hand as the agonizing fit eased, to see the charm Qadeem spun. It was a thread of kir, which he sent wriggling through the patterns of Liandro's mind.

His eyes flew wide. "No." He breathed it at first. "Don't — please! I'll —"

The thread turned and wove like a slender worm, drawing its loops snug as it went. One little pinch cut his words off, mid-syllable. I glanced up at my saint, uneasy; his gaze was chill and intent, as unshakeable as Woden. Liandro twitched on the braided rag carpet each time another cluster of patterns was bound.

Qadeem looped the ends of the kir-thread together and melded them. He stepped back, so I did too. Liandro lay limp and staring. Breathing.

"Stand up."

The elect obeyed, if slowly. His head gradually turned, surveying the tent with dim eyes. I thought of a very old man I'd met, once, simple as a child and barely aware of what went on.

"Sit." Qadeem pointed at the bedroll. "Stay." He took me by the arm as Liandro moved to sit down. "To undo it, only cut the thread," he said as we left. "He can be watched, thus, by anyone and used to bargain with Arcea if they'll have him back."

———————✠———————

The field below the switchback road flooded. The rain stopped, overnight, but the next day was still wet. Cold wind blew the clouds away and left us all raw and wishing for the heavy woolens that had been packed away. And feverish, cramping in the belly, and bleeding. Half the camp had dysentery now.

I felt a touch of it myself, but no more than a little pain and unpleasantness. My patterns fought the disruption of the infection and a pulse of kir cleansed the antagonizers away.

"No elect, no saint, dies of illness," Saint Qadeem said. "Only violence."

Miserable as dysentery was, most men were strong enough to endure it so long as they had river water to drink and something to eat. The worst off would stay in Ansehen with a physician and some Ters. They'd be part of the guards who'd keep watch over the five thousand disarmed centaurs and minotaurs — and Elect Liandro — who'd be bargaining chips should we ever face the Voice of the Empress across a negotiating table again.

There was talk of setting the prisoners to clearing the rubble and cinders in Ansehen to keep them busy in the meantime.

By the end of the second day, our army joined the Tadhlon Guard below the hills and was organized for the march to Temitte. The city was three days away.

Elect Teleri and Croícruach joined our dinner meeting, replacing Duke Stahlmann who was to stay in his ruined castle of Ansehen. By meal's end, talk had turned to the mud.

"Did pitch camp on the rise, for that," Croícruach told us. She'd also told us to call her Eith. "Your Rangers did know straight off 'tis often flooded. Surely they told you?" She stamped one boot on the carpets, which squelched.

"It's unwise to set the command pavilion on the camp's outskirts," Kiefan answered. "It's an invitation to ambush, if we did."

"Wet feet, 'tis an invitation to ringworm. I'll sleep better without itching — keeping one hand on a sword's little new." Eith slathered preserves on her bread and took a bite. For sweets after dinner, we had preserves of those fuzzy fruit Arcea traded in. Peaches.

I was glad for the spiced tea to warm my hands on. "I ordered the infirmary moved, for that," I said. "The wet aids the dysentery as well."

"'Tis only sensible to sleep dry," Eith said. "Now, if only 'twasn't alone."

"I've no complaints," Duke Vysokov said, with such dryness that it took a moment to catch the jest. His duchess was quartermaster to his reserve force and had given her report with the others during dinner.

"Fortunate one," Elect Teleri chuckled. She raised her mug of tea. "To hearth and home."

That was easy to drink to. "Hearth and home." I tapped my mug to Saint Qadeem's, on one side, and Duke Seagrace on the other. Despite the wound of his lost wife, he took the joke and the toast well.

"Must make do, then." Captain Eith looked down the table toward me. "Shall be aught to sample of Wodenberg's camp dogs, Elect?"

I didn't quite catch her meaning. "Pardon?"

"It's warm enough to sleep alone." Saint Qadeem spoke for me, and I sussed it out then.

"I haven't sampled," I said. "Though not for lack of offers."

The number of heads that turned toward me brought a blush to my face. I'd worn my kir openly, my first few days in camp, after so many took me for a fresh face among the camp followers. Watching their cheerful flirting turn to shock and frightened obeisance, begging my pardon, had given me no pleasure. And when an Englic armsman caught my hand, kissed it, and declared that I must be the queen of Arbor Street — with such confidence and a handsome face that he stopped my breath a moment —

Better to wear my kir than to feel such hollow hunger again. I'd survived the cold winter alone. I was stronger than that.

/ trouble? /

I shook my head when Qadeem glanced at me, but I doubted I convinced him.

"Might find something, though." By how Eith's gaze roamed the table and the King's Guards standing just by, she might do her shopping right here. "Did take some looking, but 'tisn't so odd now. Your Blessings."

"We seem odd to you?" Kiefan put a subtle emphasis on both ends of that.

Elect Teleri cut her captain off. "The work of saints, 'tis ever mysterious," she said with a nod to Qadeem. "But on first sight, unsettling."

"Which was little accident," Qadeem said in reply.

"Not so unsettling as Arcea's beasts," Captain Eith said, shooing the thought away with one hand. "No longer men, those."

"But they were, once," Qadeem said.

That caught many ears, of those who understood Arceal around the table. But then, they'd never seen the kir-patterns of a centaur — or a minotaur, as I had that afternoon with my saint. We'd spoken to one of their officers. The men they'd been could still be seen in what they'd become.

My saint went on, scanning across those who'd looked toward him. "Yes, they were men. Each one taken as a tithe from his homeland, for he showed some talent with kir. Each one trained with the sword and further chosen by the Empress. Given to Saint Chale to be forged into something new."

I perked at that part: the saint Renata had been trained by. I felt a sober nod from Qadeem through my bond. His talk of the Empress sparing me for my flesh-forging talents flicked back to mind.

"You know this saint?" Kiefan was quick to ask.

The answer did not come as quickly. "I knew something of him. Enough to say this: he loves his art above all else. All else. He does not see monsters in what he makes. And if you talk to these centaurs, these minotaurs, you may not see monsters either — as you have seen beyond the Blessings." That, he directed toward Captain Eith and Elect Teleri. "Which are, themselves, yes, a bit of flesh forging. As is what Elect Kate did to mend Captain Aleksandra's leg. It is in the doing that a talent is healing or is monstrous. It is never simple."

Silence followed. I felt the weight of that, of a sudden. The peg leg I'd made for Captain Aleks, and the boy's replacement sheep eye, had been to help them. Perhaps some would be frightened or call it monstrous. The minotaur's rumbling, gravelly voice had been a man's despite his bull's muzzle, twitching ears, and the horns. He'd said little of where he was from and stuck to what was expected of his men if they wished to be treated well.

"Even a talent for killing?" Kiefan asked.

Qadeem gave him a thin smile. "It is never simple."

"What do they do if there's no war?" Duke Seagrace spoke up from my other side. "The centaurs and minotaurs?"

"They serve for life. It's their oath. Those left maimed may be laborers. Many fight in the gladiator pits until they die there. Few options, but the Empress sees that they are busy."

That turned the talk to gladiator pits — there was one in Temitte, it would seem. My thoughts lingered on my sheep-eyed boy, though, and the minotaur's dazzling pattern. An eye seemed an innocent thing in comparison. And simple. How one could put a bull's head onto a man —

For a moment, I saw those two archers' faces the moment my charm hit and pictured each piece hanging in air. Waiting for something new to be added.

My blood ran cold.

CHAPTER 8

It was a slow start.

Qadeem roamed the line on a grey mare, wearing a black tabard with the king's full-moon crest and keeping his hood up. Those men who'd been in Seagrace's army last year knew of him but much of the reserves did not and might take him for Arceal. I kept close, easy to overlook in dark brown cote and hose.

We marched through a small town, not much different from any small town in Woden-berg, that stood empty but for some chickens and barn cats. Captain-general Scyfe had doubt-less warned them we'd come and they'd done the wise thing. Perhaps they thought they'd returned to find their homes stripped, perhaps burnt, but Kiefan had made his orders clear to all the captains.

There was to be no looting unless leave was given. No trouble made unless trouble was offered, and none were to touch the Suevi women. On pain of Woden's full law.

Once moving, the army marched well enough. We reached the town of Batresten around noon and stopped to rest. Rangers reported that the burg-meister's walled manor was barri-caded and archers in place in the watchtower, but else-wise the town was empty.

"Perhaps fifty," the Ranger sergeant said when Kiefan asked how many were inside. "Some hold-outs barricaded in farm houses as well, given that their stock's still in the barn."

"Pass word to take note of them," Kiefan told him. "So long as they don't follow, leave them be. Aleks, bring a squad or two."

Gregor sprinted to fetch Kiefan's warhorse, Pip. I shifted toward Jenner but stopped when Qadeem shook his head. Duke Seagrace and Vysokov waited with us until Kiefan rode back. By then, the army was picking up to resume the march.

"They listened to me," Kiefan said, "but no more."

"To do more would invite Seraphine's anger," Qadeem told him. "A king upon a throne is far more convincing."

The afternoon warmed and that was welcome enough after the cold rain. Qadeem and I talked and spun charms; he taught me some words of Suevi and we drew Kiefan into that lesson as well. He'd learned it from Queen Mercia. From there we slid into Arceal, which my saint spoke with a native's cadence. I tried to match it, and had to add a "la" to each thought to get it right. It took far too much thinking, though Qadeem said it was simple enough.

Word came that a lieutenant had caught some of our men raping a Suevi woman. The smile dropped from Kiefan's face in a heartbeat.

"Where?"

"A mile back, Majesty. They've been disarmed, bound. The woman's hurt so they've sent for a physician."

"We'll see to this now," Kiefan said. "Gregor, fetch Dobro. Kate?"

I rode with him and some Guard, and his standard-bearer, a mile back and off the main road. On a beaten-dirt patch by a river-fed cistern, some squads of armsmen clustered around the five rapists. Physician Leafwell stood holding the woman's hand, his eyes closed in focus. Her plain dress was torn at the shoulder and a bruise was darkening on her jaw. Tears streaked her face. When she saw the king's banner, she cringed and Leafwell steadied her with both hands and kind words.

Kiefan swung down from Pip and strode over to the kneeling men. "Which of you began this!"

He loomed over them; two were quick to accuse a third, who denied it. The fourth swore it was the youngest of them. It fell into an argument quickly enough.

Kiefan watched it all, saying nothing. I was down off Jenner by then and I crossed to Leafwell and the woman. She watched the men snarling with innocent worry, not understanding a word. I offered her a smile, when she noticed me, but she was too bewildered to return it.

"Anything I could mend?" I murmured, to Leafwell.

"I stopped the bleeding," he said. "Her bruises?"

Lucky that Qadeem had taught me the words I needed. "May I?" I held out my hands to the woman. She meekly put hers out, uncertain whether to look at me or the argument amongst the men. Her bruises were simple enough to untangle.

"Enough!" They fell silent at Kiefan's command. He pulled two aside by their shoulders, dumping them on their backs. A third he took by the chin and demanded, "Did you rape her?"

"No, m'lord."

"Liar." He tossed him with the other two. "You?"

The grizzled man cowered lower to the ground. "No, m'lord."

Kiefan nodded, and turned to the last. "Did you rape her?"

"No, m'lord."

He was thrown over with the other guilty men. "Prepare them for Dobro." Kiefan pointed at the cluster of them as he walked away. He turned and glared at the one innocent man. "You. Keep better company."

The man shook like a leaf.

The Suevi woman saw Kiefan coming and jerked her hands from mine. Leafwell caught her, hushing her but gripping her sleeve tight. I grabbed her other arm and tried to calm her too but she cringed and fell to her knees, hiding her eyes. Perhaps it was his gold crown-band, perhaps the Blessing ridges bared by his fresh-shaved knight's crest.

He spoke gently in her own language, and she stilled. Mumbling, she answered his questions; the men had snatched her from her farm-house and she worried her husband was hurt. By Woden's law, she had the right to see her tormentors flogged and marked, and she nodded when offered that.

Dobro, the army's seneschal and sometime executioner, meted out a dozen lashes for each man. He cut the rapist's rune into each one's right forearm and poured ashes in the wounds. Leafwell bandaged them; I rode with Lieutenant Rostislav and a few King's Guard to return the woman to her home and mend the nasty lump on her husband's head.

I stayed awake until midnight to ride out of camp with Qadeem. He doubted any word would reach Temitte ahead of us, but this nightly duty of his couldn't go unnoticed. He chose a far field, not yet plowed, and stood in the mud. Looked at the Flock moons scattered above. The Shepherd, only two days into the Spring Moon, wouldn't rise until nearly dawn.

I held our horses by the bridle, clicking to them that all was well.

Qadeem's pull tugged my remnants of kir to him and the massive arc that answered from Wodenberg's founts blazed golden in the night. I squinted into the cloud of stars that swirled around him, gripping the horses as they tried to skitter backward. Through the glare, I saw his hands silhouetted as the kir swirled down into his skin. His patterns surged up, spinning rich and strong. The meridians followed, warming from red to white and drowning out the swirls with their strong, bright lines. The red disciple's bonds pulsed at his fingertips, in heavy fans, and with each pulse Qadeem's light faded.

I felt my daily kir-ration arrive, warm and refreshing.

His nimbus fell to a green glow over his skin and then he tucked the last of it away. When he looked to me, a bit of kir shone in the back of his black eyes. "Here I must stay," he told me, "else I'll tip our hand, doing this too close to Temitte. Your third day's march will end in preparing for battle. After I distribute that night's kir, I will come to join you. Take the horses — I'll be quicker on my own."

Our second day's march went much as the first: slow to begin, many men still weak with dysentery, but sunny and warm. Word came in the afternoon that a squad of our Rangers had found signs of Arceal scouts, tracked down and dispatched them. Later, they reported they'd met a messenger and would bring him so soon as they dealt with the spies who'd been following him.

The messenger was sure to be word from Captain-general Scyfe and Theo. I waited with Kiefan in the quickly set-up command pavilion as evening settled into shadows, along with our dukes, Elect Teleri, and the Caer captains. The map-table stood in the middle, its figurines set up according to what we knew of Temitte. There were, our scouts had confirmed, twenty-five thousand men camped near it. Thirty-five, now that Scyfe had rejoined them with his story of escaping us.

When the Rangers rode up, Captain Aleks and Lieutenant Rostislav stopped them at the door for pattern-checking. The Ranger sergeant offered an obeisance and the messenger dropped onto one knee beside him.

"Row Bídon, Majesty," the stranger said in fair Alemannic. He seemed ordinary enough, brown-haired and blue-eyed, as tall as Theo and sharing a slight resemblance. "Cousin to Theobald. It's an honor, m'lord, to meet the heir to the Eald-stol."

"And I am grateful for the risk you've taken, Herr Bídon. Gregor, tea for our guest."

Bídon unlaced his boot as he knelt and pulled out several folded papers. Standing, he traded those for a mug of tea and Gregor brought them to Kiefan. He took the papers directly to the map table and began adjusting the figurines. Bídon recited the numbers as Kiefan went: precise counts of armsmen, knight and centaur cavalry, archers, and minotaurs. We all moved to the map table to watch.

"Ten thousand Arceal across the Neva," Kiefan said, adding another cavalry figurine. He spoke in Arceal, so that the Caer would understand. "The Ildra-éa, as they call it."

"It's always been prime campground for armies." Bídon fell into Arceal as well. "When word came, they started building trebuchets here." He traced his finger along the far riverbank, across from the Southbound Road approaching Temitte. "Day and night, they've pressed to build them."

"Ten thousand native Suevi on the east." Kiefan shifted figurines to the opposite side of Temitte. "Camped on the Dúnforst-éa."

"Leaving the least of sites for Scyfe." Bídon tapped a broad meadow half a mile from Temitte's walls, an awkward distance from either river.

"That's well," Duke Vysokov said.

Kiefan nodded. "Scyfe will do nothing to stop us. We engage here." He tapped the Suevi camp on the Dúnforst-éa. "It must be quick. Saint Gauvail must think Scyfe has turned to engage us. And we must stop Arcea from crossing the river."

Two wide bridges crossed the Neva — the Ildra-éa, Suevi called it — one within the city walls and one just north.

"Both are charmed to crumble if unleashed. The how of it is above our reach, Majesty."

Kiefan glanced through the other pages and added smaller figurines in the city itself; the fount's castle and the city walls had its own garrison.

"If Scyfe will let us slip by," Duke Seagrace said, reaching in to move some of our black figurines, "we can see to the bridges and assault the main gate before it closes. Might avoid a siege entirely, with luck."

"While the Caer reinforcements engage the Dúnforst camp." Kiefan nodded again. He looked through the pages again. "When did the Caer descend from Eryr Pass?"

Row Bídon glanced up from the map with a frown. "Caer, sir?"

Kiefan met his eyes, frowning as well. "Six thousand Caer. Soon after Equinox?"

He didn't see Elect Teleri straighten and step back from the map table, her hand on Captain Eith's shoulder to tug her away as well. A tickle of suspicion shot down my spine; on my other side, I saw Captain Aleks tense with a similar thought.

"Majesty, no word from the north," Bídon said in honest confusion. "All is quiet."

The men turned to the Caer. Teleri held her arm across Captain Eith, who stared at her Elect as confused as Bídon. Kiefan stepped from the table and Duke Vysokov was quick to fall back from between them.

"Elect, have you some way of hiding so many soldiers?" Kiefan's voice skirted the edge of an accusation.

She met his gaze, held her silence for a long moment. "Do speak your mind," she said.

His voice dropped. "They aren't coming."

My breath caught, stunned. Teleri's arm dropped onto her sword. As did Captain Eith's. Their two captains turned backs to theirs, ready for trouble on all sides. Captain Aleks, Rostislav, Gregor, all tensed in a metallic whisper of mail but Kiefan's stillness held them back. No kir moved, not a glimmer.

"Do you deny it?"

Teleri held her silence. Please, Father, let her speak. They must be coming.

"You knew. You knew she lied." Kiefan's growl was worse than a shout.

"'Twas my lie," Teleri said, voice even. "No others'."

"The Crown's offer —"

"My offer," she corrected. "I did bring you the terms and name the price."

"And you know what I paid!"

Cold jolted through my heart at that snarl. What could they have —?

I only caught Captain Eith's scrap of a smirk when I checked my memory; kir burst and the six feet between them was nothing. Kiefan's blade skirled off Teleri's and she threw him off with a kir-ram before I could sling a shield between them.

"No, me!" she shouted over the rasp of drawing swords. "'Tis for me to pay this! Tadhlon knew nothing. Nothing! You shall not harm them."

My shield was a sheet of green between them: four Caer in a huddle, Kiefan with Gregor on one side and Aleks the other. Vysokov had fallen back, sword in hand, and on my side was Duke Seagrace. Rostislav stalked behind me to flank the Caer. I had no idea why Kiefan had made such a leap to treachery from Caercoed, or what he'd paid for this, but I would aid him as best I could.

When Kiefan held off a heartbeat more, Teleri went on. "Do have the Tadhlon Guard. Do have me for an Elect. Do have your own support, as a surprise."

"You think that fair payment for —" Kiefan cut himself off. I wanted him to say more, but he didn't.

"'Twas more to pay for than you know." Her voice lost its forceful edge. "I did swear my life to protect Caercoed and did swear my love to protect its Crown. I've done both. You do what you must, king of Wodenberg. Only let Tadhlon go, for Leix's memory."

I hadn't felt Qadeem's touch over the pounding of my pulse and his sending startled me. / mercy / on my way /

"Saint Qadeem asks you to spare them," I said. It was no small thing, this betrayal, but clearly there was more to it than soldiers. That Ciara might have made a consort of him flicked past my mind — but would that cut him to the quick, like this?

"For Leix, for all she did for me, I will spare you." Kiefan pointed his blade at Captain Eith. No trace of a smirk on her now, only a white-knuckled grip on her sword's hilt. "Next you mock me, you die. Elect. If you're here honestly to shield the Tadhlon Guard, let Aleks bind you to the prisoner's picket. Run, or harm her, and I will hunt you to the Winter Wood itself. It holds no terrors for me any more."

Teleri spread her hands, dropped her sword, and stepped away from the knot of Caer. Captain Aleks strode to her and unbuckled her belt, picked up the sword and sheathed it. They met eye to eye for a moment, sisters of the blade, and the Elect dropped her chin. Aleks took her arm and escorted her from the pavilion.

"Go," Kiefan told the Caer captains, then returned to the map table. His brow furrowed deep as he leaned on it. Pain, I knew. "All of you, out."

Lieutenant Rostislav sheathed his sword and gestured Captain Eith toward the door flaps. They went, and the two dukes fell back as well but looked to Kiefan for further word. He rubbed his eyes with thumb and forefinger rather than give them anything. It was Gregor who moved to see them out.

"Gregor, brandy," Kiefan said, and that decided me.

"Don't be drinking tonight," I said as I circled the map table. "You'll need a clear head."

His cheek was scratchy under my hand. I meant to turn his head toward me but he resisted. So I called his pattern as he was.

"Don't." Kiefan's hand took mine. "Kate —"

I didn't need to touch him; that was habit. His headache pulsed along his Blessing ridges, same as ever, and I twisted a firm hook of kir into the knots. "I'm still your physician, Majesty," I said.

"Majesty? I'm —" Kiefan threw my hand down, yanked the gold band from his head and slung it away.

"What —?"

"No!" He raked both hands into his braided crest, clenched. "No mercy, Kate. I did this. I led our best men out here to their deaths. Then Arcea will — destroy —" Kiefan swung an arm out to include the whole camp, Wodenberg beyond, and then caught both my hands in his. He leaned close, voice dropping as he fought the words out. "Get out, Kate. Leave tonight. Go straight home, take the baby, and run."

A knot of kir-whorls tumbled free, but I forgot the rest. I stared at him. "You think I'd abandon —?"

"Let me get this right!" Mother have mercy, there were tears in his eyes. "I cost us an elect in Anders, I led what's left of our army into the Empress' arms, I've failed you at every turn, Kate — let me do one right thing. You must be safe. Both of you."

My throat knotted under the force of his words. And in the same heartbeat, I knew he was stronger than this. My hands cupped his face. I fixed him with my eyes. "You keep us alive," I whispered, fierce as I could. "You're the elect that Saint Woden looks to for aid, Kiefan Weissberg. Ciara's betrayal will not stop you."

His focus snapped to me. He drew a harsh breath. Truth was in my eyes; I knew he saw it.

My fierceness couldn't hold, though. "You failed me. I was a fool." I nodded. And I leaned away before the flitting urge to kiss him circled back around. "We have our scars now. And we have Rafe."

Kiefan nodded. Gregor set a bottle of amber brandy on the map table and two cups beside it. He looked to Kiefan, one hand on the stopper. "Leave it," Kiefan murmured. "Check on Aleks."

Gregor went. Kiefan turned back to the map table, tracking over the figurines. When I called his pattern again, the swirling kir whorls — a blizzard of thoughts in his head — forced a bit of a smile on me. I tugged at the remaining knots of pain.

"We cannot lay siege," he murmured. "We cannot expose the men to their artillery. We must engage the Suevi ourselves." Kiefan tapped the eastern camp, on the Dúnforst-éa.

"Saint Qadeem is coming," I said as the last knot loosened.

Kiefan put his fist to his chin. "Not yet. Tell him not yet. He must stay a secret."

/ not yet / new plans /

/ listening / am near /

"The fount is all that matters," Kiefan said. Gregor appeared in the door flaps but before he could speak Kiefan ordered, "Fetch Bídon back. And the dukes."

The bottle of brandy went untouched.

CHAPTER 9

It was well past dark when Kiefan left the pavilion and Qadeem prodded me to follow him. Just outside, Captain Eith perked up at the sight of us; the King's Guard nearest her put out an arm to stop her. "Majesty? A word, on Elect Teleri."

Kiefan waved off the Guard. "Say it."

"'Twas two days from Knapptal, she did ask me to bind her to her horse. Told me she'd take ill, but not to stop. Gag her if need be, but ride on." The captain looked to me; she knew I was a healer. "I've seen many a sickness, but 'twasn't. A palsy, mayhaps, but no Elect suffers such. 'Tis true?"

"So far as I know," I said, honestly enough.

"Convulsions?" Kiefan asked her. "Rigor and agony?"

"And vomit. But no fever," Captain Eith said with a nod. "And did pass by nightfall."

Woden had stood over Kiefan, his right hand clenched in a claw, watching him writhe and retch on the castle floor. Punishing him for hiding the truth of my pregnancy on the day of his coronation. That anyone could suffer that for a whole day twisted my gut in sympathy.

"That changes matters," Kiefan said. "Thank you." He strode off toward the prisoner's picket with Gregor in tow. I wanted to ask more but trotted to catch up.

When I got alongside Kiefan, I whispered, "As Woden inflicted on you?"

"Yes. Stringence," he whispered back. Then, with a frown, "You never disagree with Qadeem, even?"

I shrugged but it was too dark to see that. "What would we disagree on?"

The picket was a pair of wide-spaced, deep-set stakes that held the prisoner's chained wrists well spread. Captain Aleks stood beside Teleri, who had settled onto the damp grass. The nearest campfires were some yards off and the men sitting by them pretended not to watch what little there was to see. Above, clouds winked out a Flock moon here, another there.

Aleks straightened as we neared. When Teleri only looked up, the captain kicked with her peg-leg and I heard the whack from some paces off. "Get up!"

The elect got up, pulling on her chains to steady herself. Kiefan drew up a hush sphere in his hand, puffed it out wide around us all as he stopped a mere foot from Teleri.

"You've gone rogue. Your deal didn't even have your saint's backing," he spat. He took her right hand and I felt him call the kir. Her patterns spun up, just in her palm, and there was no sign of a saint's bond.

I was closer to her left, so I checked her other hand. Nothing. "She cut your bond? How have you gotten kir?" I asked.

"Do have some Blessed and discipled among the Tadhlon Guard," she said. "'Tis simple enough to skim."

"You lied to your captains, you led your sisters here with no hope of reinforcement —" Kiefan's lip curled as he leaned closer. "Are there any you've not lied to yet?"

Teleri's calm never rippled. "Elect Tannait does know the truth of it all."

My heart sank at the thought of that wise elect turning against her saints. "Is she rogue, too?"

"What's her part in this treason?" Kiefan snarled.

Teleri pulled her chains taut to answer in his face. Gregor bristled, hand on his sword. "We defend our land," she growled as Captain Aleks yanked her away by one chain. "Against all. Our own saints, if need be. Pray 'tis never passed to you to do the same."

A cold shiver touched me.

"The saints are the land," Kiefan told her.

"Are yet women, for all their power. Not all saints have tastes for war. Needs must defend our land despite them."

His tone eased at last. "You chose exile, then, in choosing your people over your saint?"

"No." Teleri tugged at her chains with both hands. "Choosing love and duty."

There was an ache in her words. I remembered her at the Riverman tavern, at Theo's party, with Crown Ciara's arm wrapped around hers. How they smiled and danced together. "You did this for love, did as she asked?"

Teleri only looked down at the grass.

"Caercoed has sealed its passes, then?" Kiefan asked. She gripped her chains in both hands silently. He drew closer, lighting a handful of green kir close by her face. "You led the Tadhlon Guard here to die. What honor's in that?"

The green light shone on her eyes; she did not even blink as it knotted down to a hot spark near her skin.

I didn't know Teleri so well, that was true. But I felt it safe to say, "Elect Tannait would not agree to that."

Kiefan drew the spark back, let it unwind into a heatless lamp. Teleri stared into the distance. "Elect Tannait might say there must be sacrifices," he said, "but no, she has more honor than to send two thousand to die without a word in it. Captain Eith knew nothing of this, that's clear enough." When there was still no response, he asked, "Will you fight alongside them?"

Her eyes came up. "You cannot stop me."

Qadeem nudged me. "Will you be bound?" I asked.

"No. Honor that, and I aid my sisters in whatever you order. 'Tis them I owe a debt to now."

He sent a nod. "Saint Qadeem will honor your wish," I told her.

"Let us take Temitte, then," Teleri said. Her eyes narrowed, looking to Kiefan. "'Tis a plan, surely, that brought you to me at all."

———————————×———————————

Row Bídon rode back to Scyfe's camp outside Temitte with word of the plan. Qadeem, having listened through my Blessing, had agreed to his part in it. Saint Woden, Kiefan said, had given his advice at the first idea of it and would stand ready.

My hands shook for much of the third day's march, knowing what we must do. Steal a fount from under Arcea's nose.

Kiefan's anger at Teleri, the price he'd paid for this broken promise — that bit of a smirk from Captain Eith — clung to my mind. Why wouldn't Kiefan speak of it? Through my bond, I asked Qadeem if there'd been stories from Knapptal. He was slow to answer and gave me only a sense that I knew all I needed.

That, I disagreed with but I did not press for more.

Perhaps Crown Ciara had taken Kiefan as a consort, if only for one night in that oíche-te Anders had been put to. Thus, there'd been no talk of marriage. Perhaps he'd liked her more than he expected, and now the betrayal stung all the worse. But would he call that a price? Why would it amuse Eith?

I chewed on the gristly problem, or perhaps it chewed on me. Better that than the plan for tomorrow.

If he cared for Crown Ciara, though, if he hoped to see her again — or had, before this — then I could be content as his friend and fellow elect. It would be a burden off my mind. That was why I settled Jenner in alongside Pip soon after the army finished its noon-time rest.

Kiefan glanced at me, sidelong, expecting me to speak some moments before I had the words.

"In Knapptal," I said. "You gained Caercoed's aid without a marriage?" I glanced up in time to catch his grimace. "You gained a promise of aid."

"Yes." He had to search for words as much as I. "Foolish of me to trust, perhaps. I'll not blame m'lady Leix or Síochana for my failings, but…"

My thoughts went to Crown Ceelin and her manipulating, but I put them aside. "You must've found common ground with Crown Ciara, then? Some manner of — arrangement? The Crowns do not marry, but they do take consorts."

Kiefan looked at me then, eyes fixed despite the sway of Pip's striding. The sun caught on his gold band, back in place despite that he'd flung it off in doubt. But he said nothing.

I tried another tack, venturing closer to what I wanted to hear. "If you mean to see her again — often —"

"If we survive this, Kate, we are —" He caught himself, put up one hand. "If we survive. Let's see to that first."

He tapped Pip and the warhorse lengthened his stride. Across the hole he left, I saw Sir Waldemar and Sir Garrick. They noted me with polite nods. I tugged on Jenner's reins to angle him closer, remembering that they'd gone with Kiefan to Knapptal.

Sir Waldemar was closer. He was a man of middle age, one of those who'd long been on King Wilhelm's Guard with Captain Aleksandra. There was a sprinkling of grey in his brown beard, but age hadn't softened him yet.

"You rode with Kiefan to Knapptal," I said. They both nodded to that. "You know, then, what arrangement he reached with the Crown?"

Sir Waldemar's brow furrowed under the force of his brows rising. "We weren't privy to Majesty's negotiations, Elect…"

"Not the conversations," I allowed, "but you must've seen the two of them. How often they met?"

"The Crown refused him." Sir Garrick leaned past Waldemar as he fumbled for an answer. "She'd not see him at all, at first."

Given how she'd left Vorspitz with her sister's ashes, that rang true. "But they must've talked. They must've agreed to this, however false it is now."

"They did speak after Solstice," Waldemar said.

"After m'lord laid the bet." Sir Garrick threw that out and smiled when my brow crinkled. "He bet half the garrison he could sweeten the Crown into aid — I joined the pot on his side." Garrick was careful to make that clear. "It did seem a long shot, but m'lord's not one to fail the task before him."

"Sweeten?" I echoed. "Truly?" He'd seduced Crown Ciara? Kiefan?

Garrick cast about for an answer. "Grief may drive a man to strange things and m'lord had his share. That was clear enough."

"And he did this?" I needed to hear it said, not only guess at it.

Sir Waldemar shrugged. "He had proof."

That widened my eyes. "What proof?"

The knight's cheeks colored, above his beard. "Well, it — she, well —"

"The Elect's no tender maid," Garrick said, swatting Waldemar's elbow. "She tamed Sir Anders. The Crown was hungry enough to cut m'lord's cote off him. Or perhaps the other ladies in the pavilion helped in that."

Oh. I remembered Crown Ciara in her snowy white layers of gauze, bound by the green sash under her bosom, twinkling with gold and emeralds. She'd slid across the floor without effort, chin held high. Would she be so passionate? The Voice of the Empress had warned us the Caer were hot-blooded… Captain Eith's smirk flitted through my memory again. Sampling the camp dogs, indeed.

Garrick went on about a drinking celebration in Knapptal's tavern but my gaze turned ahead to find Kiefan among a few knight captains. The King's Guard had no reason to lie to me, but Kiefan as a seducer didn't fit him.

Not when he'd written me that anguished letter from Knapptal.

I asked no more on the matter, though. We had surviving to see to, as Kiefan had said.

We split on the Southbound Road late that afternoon, two miles from Temitte. A road branched off toward the east and that was where we took leave of Elect Teleri, Captain Eith, and the Tadhlon Guard. I held out my hand to Teleri and she took all my kir; Qadeem had sent me enough to fill her.

"If 'tis for me to die," Captain Eith said, "shall be under a heap of Arceal corpses."

"No less," Teleri said, agreeing. Looking to Kiefan, she nodded. "The bridges will fall."

He nodded in return and she tapped her horse. The Caer rode in loose formation, their banners furled and wearing cloaks over their mail. Not that two thousand could be anything but a division — our Rangers had been out hunting enemy messengers, and while word could still get through, with luck it would be vague. The towns we marched through were shuttered but there were always some folk barricaded in a stockaded house or a watch tower. Surely more in hiding, watching us pass. They'd left fields part-plowed and seed for the planting; they'd not go further than they must.

There'd been another flogging for rape and one for looting, but on the whole we'd left little mark on Suevia thus far.

Kiefan sent one of Theo's senior wagon-drivers who spoke Suevi well to Scyfe's camp and he returned with word. Scyfe had orders to find Wodenberg's army and attack it, but would not. Theo had his new instructions, would be ready for us at dawn, and had named a meeting place. The wagon-driver attested that the camp was well settled and showed no signs of readying for attack. Several Ranger squads reported there were no Suevi scouts trailing us.

A greedy captain-general we could trust over the Crown of Caercoed, it seemed.

"But you said I've improved so!" Gregor barely held off whining.

"You have. It's no small thing to squire for Captain Aleks," Kiefan told him, stern. "You keep her well and whole."

Aleks cuffed him from behind, across the head. When he swung around, she grabbed his wrist and twisted his arm to tip his ear down lower. "Keep yourself whole or I'll thrash your ass at the Shepherd's Hearth," she growled. With a shove, she let him go and stalked past, her peg leg thudding. "Boy! Come." Gregor jittered, fighting two urges, but followed.

Kiefan heaved a breath, setting a hand on his sword. "That was the worst danger of this," he said. "Thank the Father we survived." The dozen King's Guard around us laughed.

Captain Aleks hadn't been pleased that she must stay behind with the rest of the Guard, but surely she knew she was too much an oddity with her peg leg. She'd draw too many eyes and questions.

Abbot Shaw stepped into the uncomfortable moment and recited the first few lines of the Father's Challenge. The men fell into that easily, answering Father Duty's demands with firm, rumbling cheers. I lingered on the edge of that, too unsettled to join in.

The command pavilion was already down and dawn was just warming the horizon to yellow. The horses' puffs made only wisps of cloud in the dewy morning. I stood patting Jenner, wearing one of the dresses Qadeem had so insisted I buy — a fawn-colored, lightweight wool with little kir-whorls embroidered in green around the neckline. I kept my wool shawl wrapped close to hold the chill off. My disguise didn't allow for the mail tunic and I was glad to go without the weight. But also uneasy without it. Qadeem went unarmored as well, but he was a saint.

The knights wore their gambesons and mail, their scuffed riding boots and swords, but no tabards or black cloaks. The colors would give us away. Kiefan went without his crownband and I couldn't help noticing the crease where it usually sat. Their knights' crests and Blessings, they'd hide under their bucket helms. My low ridges might go unnoticed in my hair — I'd braided loosely, for that, and wrapped it around my head.

I fidgeted with Jenner's bridle, wishing for the weight of my medicine bag on my shoulder. Something for my nervous hands to grip.

Qadeem touched my shoulder and he gave me more kir. "Clarity," he told me, voice low. "Trust your instincts. You are, in truth, far more a fighter than Mechdan ever was."

I thought of the notes that my sounding shared with all the knights — signs of fierceness, perhaps. My teacher's sounding had been gentler, that day I'd heard it in his office. "But he died fighting."

"Defending those he loved. As he ever did. I would not have agreed to this, Kate, if it were him beside me."

Rostislav, on his horse already, caught my eye as he turned toward me. "The lieutenant might disagree on how well I fight," I said, hoping to make a joke of it.

He heard me. "Only stay close, m'lady," he said. "Hard enough to chase a lamb through back streets without archers sniping at me."

Saint Qadeem smiled. "She's no lamb. It will turn deadly to stay too close, today." He pointed a look at Rostislav, and then all the dozen Guards. "Keep that in mind. Your duty is to defend against swords and arrows. That's danger enough."

They took it as an order. We were ready once I was perched on my saddle in the skirts, and we rode from the camp in silence. It had been even simpler than the camps on the march; most had slept on the ground, wrapped only in their blankets, rather than put up tents. We'd left the wagons and baggage behind yesterday with some of Vysokov's reserve to guard them.

Villages ringed Temitte; the crossroads came often enough and the houses lay thick enough that they crowded out the fields and orchards. We slipped past shuttered taverns and lines of shops, noted only by bakers who looked up from their morning bread-kneading as we passed. Their open doors spilled out warm light into the lingering shadows.

I couldn't help looking as we passed, wanting that simple life inside. Thinking of home and Rafe, my little sweetling. And Anders.

The road led us toward the city and just when it seemed there'd be no more pastures to separate the villages, the houses ended. Acres of grass spread out across the road and on it camped Scyfe's ten thousand.

Sentries moved to block the road. Kiefan tugged Pip to a stop and raised his helm to give the password. We rode through, the sentries' eyes tracking us for being curiosities on a dull morning. I caught their interest, in particular.

Lathe-and-wattle cottages, with thatched roofs, clustered in the middle of the camp-ground rather than a command pavilion. Kiefan led us to the longest and widest of them — a warehouse — and as we approached a figure stepped around a two-horse wagon and raised one hand.

Theo. His uncle was with him, Eadgard Bídon who had brought the refreshments to the brief parley during the siege of Wodenberg. He'd unwittingly brought that first cambifax with him and it had tried to murder Kiefan when it saw his grey eyes, when it knew he was the heir to the Suevi throne.

Kiefan dismounted and caught Theo's hand in a clasp with a brief nod. Bídon, in doing the same, dropped to his knee and touched his forehead to Kiefan's hand. Then stood, his deep-lined eyes damp.

"The uniforms," Theo said, pointing to the wagon bed. He wore one of them himself. Rostislav and his men were quick to hand them out. For a little while, there was only the rattle of leather and mail as they pulled on the green tabards and the brown sash baldrics, then buckled their sword belts over-top. There was a green shield for each, as well.

I was beckoned to the wagon beside Theo during all this. Qadeem had climbed up into the wagon-driver's seat and settled himself. He was dressed plainly and had given up his fur-lined cloak for a simple brown one.

"When all begins, Theo, you and your uncle take the horses and go. I see you've made an officer of yourself," Qadeem said, noting the tasseled white braid that secured Theo's baldric to the epaulette at his shoulder.

"M'lord will be my second, as his Suevi is good enough. You and Uncle bring the wagon. Uncle has a few Arceal teamsters and you can pass for that. Few Rasilai are seen this far north. We go to fetch a fresh payroll, as Scyfe's was stolen by those Alemanni dogs. Kate —" Theo looked me up and down, considering. "Let your braid down, at least. I brought a couple caps. Wear one of those."

I pulled the pin from my wrapped braid and gave it to him. Looking to Qadeem, Theo asked, "Might there be a reason you'd let a maid ride in your wagon?"

Qadeem smiled, a flash of white. "Must a man explain such things?"

Theo caught the jest before I did. "Perhaps explain why she's not on your lap, then."

It struck me funny for a moment and a handful of men closest by laughed. But I blushed at the same time; I hadn't thought of my saint thus, though he'd said himself he'd raised two families. He didn't seem older than his mid-thirties, as no grey salted his midnight hair or his close-cropped beard. And he certainly wasn't unpleasant to look at.

"You must have my ár?" Kiefan asked, walking up from the rear of the wagon. He spotted Theo's white braid and said. "Oh, lieutenant then?"

"Yes, sergeant." Theo tossed Kiefan a brown, tassel-ended braid. "The rest of you, do not speak. And don't pay anything much mind, we're only escorting payroll. Temitte's no den of thieves."

"When Kiefan dismounts," Saint Qadeem said, scanning across us all, "do the same. As I said, you're to guard against swords and arrows. Some of you saw the Order's courtyard, that final day?"

A few of them had followed Kiefan over the earthen wall to finish off the centaurs, and nodded.

"This will be far deadlier. Saint Gauvail's talent is in putting his strength through kirvines." Qadeem flicked out a little tendril from his hand, as he spoke. He whip-cracked it at Sir Waldemar's face, getting a flinch. "I knew him, yes, he was a young saint when I first met the Empress. It was Gauvail who broke Saint Aleksandr's city wall. Do not stand between us."

I had put away the terrible memories of the wall exploding, the fire, the screaming horses and the dying king, but my throat still tightened.

"Father, keep us strong for your duty," Kiefan said, his voice rough. The Guards echoed him.

"And the Shepherd will honor those he takes," Qadeem added. "If you've any accounts yet to balance, forgive them now."

That pinched me; my gaze shot to Kiefan before I could help it, and Mother help me but our eyes met. Caught in the same tangle. I closed my eyes and asked the Father to keep safe all those I'd left at home — Kiefan and Anders, too.

I climbed up on the wagon's open gate and sat with my legs dangling. I leaned my elbow on the sideboard as Qadeem whistled to the horses and they started off. Theo, riding Jenner, circled around to me and he handed over a knit green cap that came to a soft point on top. I pulled it down over my memory Blessing ridges.

"Tip it." He mimed bending the point to my right, so I did, cautiously. "No, the other way. You're not a ruffian. Good. Cute as a gnome." Theo gave me one more smile, this time with worried eyes, as Jenner picked up his pace. As he passed, Theo touched my arm and told me, "Anders will see the Father keeps you strong."

Anders. My fingers went to my necklace, hidden under my shift's high neckline. I had to push that ache away, though, and review all we'd gleaned from Renata in preparing for this. And all Qadeem had told me of what we must do to steal a fount.

CHAPTER 10

It wasn't noon yet when we reached Temitte's main gate on the Southbound Road. As Theo carried written orders from Captain-general Scyfe, we skipped the inspection line and the captain of the watch saw to us himself.

He and Theo traded exasperation, judging by the shrugs and head-shakes that punctuated their words. A lesser sentry looked over the side of the wagon at the loosely-folded tarp and the handfuls of rope and spotted me sitting on the end. He blinked in surprise. I smiled, set my chin on my hand, and meant to look cute.

That needed checking with the captain and I heard Qadeem add something that got a laugh. Lieutenant Rostislav, who was bringing up the rear with Sir Waldemar, tried to feign boredom but kept eyeing our audience. The long line of impatient wagon-drivers was not wishing us well, their frowns said. Many of the wagons were piled with housewares, I noticed. Small faces looked out over sideboards here and there.

They were peasants running from our army, hoping to get inside before the attack.

Rumbling on the packed dirt, our wagon passed through the city gates. They loomed as tall as Wodenberg's, a layered portcullis, gate, and portcullis as ours was. The towers were square and made of stone blocks rather than seamless.

A whistle caught my ear and the captain of the watch jangled his coin-purse at me with a suggestive leer. Mother have mercy. I managed to smile instead of rolling my eyes.

Inside, the shops began immediately and I watched a familiar market-street bustle as I rode by. This was Saint-day, as it had been on the day we attacked Ansehen, but the Suevi honored the Empress instead. We knew that Suevia was overseen, currently, by a saint named Musaad and Gauvail was here as well because of the invasion, but Empress Seraphine was the only saint honored in Arcea.

Qadeem had told me all Arcea's saints were bound to her the same as elect were bound to saints. It was her strength, cunning, and will that kept saints bound, whereas no elect had the power to cut his own bond. Qadeem, Woden, and Aleksandr had taken their great oath as equals, trusting honor and common purpose, rather than domination, to hold them together.

Elect Renata had said that so far as she knew Empress Seraphine had spent the winter in Reowan, the capital city where a fount stood on the ocean shore. But that was all she knew. The Empress came and went as she pleased. She might be anywhere.

Temitte's castle was called Willefreá. That sounded like a woman's name to me but when we turned a corner into sight of it, Willefreá was as bluntly strong as any man. I twisted, leaning on the sideboard, to count the towers. It seemed a simple box on the face, but inside was a narrow, deadly gap and a second wall with its own gates and towers. Inside that, the guardian sphere enclosed the fount itself.

Eight towers. Perhaps it seemed ignorant to merely wall in the fount, Qadeem had told us, but in truth the courtyard was a killing field. All eight towers and the inner wall could defend the fount.

Qadeem drove the wagon up to the closed gates; another half dozen sentries met us there. Theo brought out his orders again for inspection. Two Suevi guards in grey tabards and yellow baldrics spotted me in the wagon and one barked an order with a flick of his hand.

I hopped down with a smile. The men converged to shoo me off and that drew the attention of a couple more. I held my smile, tipped my head, and wrapped the end of my braid around my hand as I looked the younger of them up and down.

I'd studied every scrap of memory I had of Alice flirting.

The younger one's brows rose and he smiled back. Some words I nearly recognized were tossed about as two more guards drifted over. Something about the afternoon. I tipped my head and put a finger to my lips while I considered the new pair, too.

My heart pounded in my chest. I must do this. The moment they knew who we were, they'd try to kill me and Kiefan and all the Guardsmen.

Kiefan dismounted, over by the wagon, and all our escort followed suit. That was the cue.

The elder of the guards wasn't impressed by my flirting and grabbed my arm to push me away. I felt his scrap of kir answer my call and it twisted under my will. Slashed across his meridian. His eyes rolled up and he fell. Before he landed, I stabbed kir-vines through the other two's necks and they died without a sound.

It was the fourth, the one who'd smiled at me, who made me hesitate a heartbeat. He was pulling his sword in alarm when kir blossomed, behind him, and the castle gates flew to pieces. Whole beams, crossbars, nails, iron plates, all burst into the air, streaming overhead and crossing the square in a heartbeat. They rained down on the shops behind us.

The guard tracked it all, jaw going slack. He never saw the kir-vine that dropped him.

A heavy green arc of kir lit Qadeem at the gate. I ran to my place at his side as the dozen King's Guard took up position in the gate's frame ahead of us. He strode after them, spinning a sheet of kir across the frame overhead. The twin portcullis gates dropped a few inches and stuck in the barrier.

I drew kir and threw a shield atop half our Guards' wooden shields. Kiefan gave shields to the other half. Archers massed on the inner wall ahead of us; Suevi armsmen with spears were running to form up on either side.

Saint Qadeem pulsed kir at the blank stone wall we faced; if we wanted a gate, it was clear on the other side of the inner ring. The grid of charms within the wall pulsed in answer and his black eyes tracked all the glowing lines as they faded.

I spun a shield for myself and stood before him. Kiefan was to cover our backs.

A second pulse, and the charms lit again. "Aleks, what do you see? Where's the weakness…?" Qadeem's murmur barely reached my ears as the archers loosed on us from above. Four arrows struck my shield. A charm-tipped one broke it.

One more pulse and my saint lapsed into Russe, a pattern of words that matched the pulses of the wall's charm nodes — "Down!" he ordered. I fell to my knees.

I glimpsed three streams of white-hot kir-fire braiding as they shot toward a node low on the wall. It struck, blazed, and punched through with a crack. A fresh arc of kir burned my retinas, despite my arm across my eyes, and I didn't need to see the kir-ram that smashed the inner wall. It brushed past my mind like a charging bull.

Castle Willefreá shuddered, stabbed through the gut. Men stumbled as the ground shook. A cloud of gravel fell on us us, forcing my eyes shut despite my fresh shield. When I looked up a gash in the wall poured out dust like blood.

"Through!" Kiefan's shout carried on kir and he was at the front to lead his Guard. The few Suevi armsmen who still had their wits charged to meet him and the first splash of red came from a man's side bursting open — seemingly on its own — as Kiefan blurred with speed.

Qadeem's hand on my shoulder pulled me up. I raised my arrow-studded shield and we ran. The Guard held open a short corridor for us to the fresh hole where crumbling rock still rained down amid a cloud of dust.

Behind, Qadeem unraveled the overhead barrier. The two portcullis lattices dropped hard.

I scrambled over broken rock and through the gash, shield over my head, calling for kir. Falling rocks bounced off my shield. I could feel the fount, ahead, feel its tug — and the guardian answered me. Golden threads glimmered through the haze of granite dust, twinkled and strengthened as I cleared the worst of the broken stone.

Looming from the dust cloud, the guardian sphere was a spider's web of glimmering kir. A knot of it grew before me, strong and warm. Making a massive eyeball of the thing. It saw me.

Men gave a battle-cry, to my side; a squad of Suevi armsmen charged from the nearest tower door. They were in a tight knot, shields lapped, spears bristling; I cut a crescent Shepherd's knife and threw it. Shouting, half of them dove to either side. The blade caught one mid-chest and he fell. The rest, stumbling, fought to keep their balance.

One brushed against the guardian sphere. Kir flared and struck; his head exploded in a cloud of crimson steam. Under the mail tunic, flames tore up through his gambeson. His helm rang off the far wall like a bell.

"Arrows!" Two of my Guard charged past and carved into the nearest of the Suevi armsmen, drawing some of the archers' arrows — but at that range, their mail and gambesons could stop the shafts.

I threw up my shield. One arrow was charmed and cut through it; I swung my arm and knocked a dozen from the sky with a kir-vine. As the archers nocked and drew, I lashed again and a few fell before they could shoot.

Kir arced again, to Qadeem, and he threw a web of kir over the last of the doors into the central courtyard. Then he swung around and cleared the battlements from tower to tower with a blast. The remaining archers scrambled to re-group. Behind us, Kiefan and his Guard held the gash in the wall.

Qadeem strode toward the sphere, brown cloak twinkling with kir-stars. I trotted to catch up. The eye-spot adjusted to meet us, growing larger as the charm-lines drew more kir from the fount within. He looked up, the strong light rimming his face, each lock of his hair, and raised his hand. I slipped in front of him, and held up my own. It trembled. My skin prickled to gooseflesh as I felt the fount's strength crackling across the sphere's surface.

Kir blossomed above; my shield spread over our heads before I could think. It split with a glassy crack and exploded. Pain slashed across my hand, my cheek, as shards and hot sparks fell.

The sphere rippled as the saint met it, dropped through, and landed knee-deep in the fount. It lit, silhouetting Gauvail from beneath. He wore black, as he had in the Order's courtyard when he watched us kill two of his companion saints. The Arceal-style robe and his slicked-back hair made hard, harsh angles of him. Stars swirled up around him, ready to strike. Behind us, a second blossom of kir — but that was for Kiefan to see to.

The saint's eyes burned green. "Qadeem."

"Gauvail."

Qadeem reached over my shoulder and put his hand to the sphere's deadly eye-spot. Kir flared, white-hot, sizzled in a blazing spiral around his arm — and poured from his elbow where the grounding line dropped to the earth. The same he'd turned Woden's lightning with. The smell of fresh-mown grass billowed up.

/ touch /

That man's head had popped like —

/ trust me /

I put my hand atop my saint's, and within that same heartbeat saw the truth of what he did. As the kir-fire tore through his arm and the grounding-charm, it burned. Qadeem spun the grounding line at blinding speed and held his flesh immobile under the scalding blast. Fire could not gain any foothold against his focused will. Thus, he needed me to defend him while he bled the fount.

Also, he had three arrows in his back from when a charmed shaft nicked his shield, but such things couldn't kill a saint.

Near the end of that heartbeat, Gauvail lashed out a vine studded with stars, braiding down tight into a brilliant needle as it came. Woden's training held; I thrust out a buckler on a vine and tilted to knock it upward. It shot through the guardian sphere toward the castle battlements.

The second, right behind it, speared through my buckler, my vine — sent a stab of pain up the length of my arm — and through both our hands on the sphere's face. It shot past Qadeem's ear, singeing his hair. He didn't even flinch. My mind reeled in agony. I clutched Qadeem's hand to keep from losing contact.

A dark patch in the sphere's web was growing under his palm. As the fount drained, the guardian lost its strength, and where it was weak, I could attack through it.

/ clarity /

I clung to my saint's bond. My Blessing caught the moment of the needle's passing, sliced it fine, gleaned the thing's pattern, and its image hung in my mind.

The grassy smell thickened as the kir-fire bled on and on through Qadeem's arm. It scraped at my lungs, harsh and bitter.

Gauvail pulled kir from a distant fount and the arc found him through the guardian sphere, coiled around his long arm, and blasted at us. Thinning, stars igniting, twisting down to a needle —

My fear snapped to anger and I struck through the hole under Qadeem's palm. The needle's pattern flashed past my eyes. Its point unraveled, each thread, star-knot and whorl blooming outward. Like the archers' arms. It splattered through the sphere's web, warm enough to sting but far from deadly, and sank eagerly to the earth.

A flash of pride, through my bond. It was all the thought he could spare.

The harsh, grassy air was making my head spin.

Behind the fount-blast flew a tiny charm. I blinked, recognizing it: a spark charm. My brow crinkled.

The spark flew between the lines of the web and the grass-scented air burst into flame. I screamed on reflex. Heat billowed, skimmed over my flesh, and my terror flashed back to anger. My kir. It spun, came to my free hand in a heady mass, and I slung it back at Gauvail.

/ no! /

My blast hit the intact web, outside Qadeem's weak spot; the guardian flared and it struck through the trail of kir to my hand. It snarled into Qadeem's other hand, clamped hard on my wrist, and shunted through a second ground into the earth beside me.

I gasped a breath. My hand felt afire. Qadeem shot me a hard glare that echoed what I felt through my bond.

I had time to blink. Then I saw why.

The dark spot on the sphere was growing faster, now that two streams of kir poured out into the earth. Founts had their limits, after all.

Gauvail crouched in the fount, kir gathering around him in a nimbus. Another arc reached him from some faraway fount, pouring down stars.

/ ready /

I sent back a nod. My throat tightened, knowing what came next.

Behind us, kir lashed and arced. I had a heartbeat to hope Kiefan was beating down that Elect and wonder if it was the girl with the dark braid who'd stood beside Gauvail in the Order's courtyard.

The guardian sphere crumbled into a cloud of golden spider-silk.

Gauvail's kir-ram crashed past like a brick wall, even as Qadeem diverted it up over his shoulder. I heard stone break, behind us. My saint pounced past me before I blinked; I dove after him and slung a bladed kir-vine at Gauvail's knee.

I cut his shield, the jolt numbing my arm, and it burst into sparks before Qadeem's braided kir-fire flashed from his hand. Light burst and the stars that scattered blinked to black in my stunned eyes. The fount roiled as if golden serpents thrashed in its depths and the ground trembled. Kir-fire flew, arcing up toward the battlements.

Behind me came a second flash, and a shockwave of kir. My heart skipped a beat, but I didn't dare turn to look. I spotted an arm in black silk and lashed out my vine again, Blessing-quick.

I felt it connect, with a crack of bone — and agony exploded through my gut. A spear-head jutted from my belly, and a hand's width of shaft. Kir flared behind me and I twisted, throwing up my hand. It struck my half-spun buckler and both charms shattered.

I glimpsed a long, dark braid, black silk, and a bloodthirsty grin. Gauvail's elect. A long, green knife of kir spun from her fist as she lunged to stab me. I stumbled back, legs weak, and put up my arm as if I had a buckler. In the tangle, I grabbed her arm to keep the knife away but lost my balance and pulled her down with me. I screamed as the spear thrust further through my gut. Twisted.

The elect dove aside to miss it, came up on her knees beside me with the knife raised. I pulled kir and the roiling fount answered feebly, sent me only a mouthful.

A sun broke free inside the fount. Her scream vanished in the blast that threw her across the courtyard. I caught some of the kir, clutched it close. My poor eyes saw only blackness and bright spots. I gasped for breath, mind a whirl of pain and noise.

Then I cried as I gripped the spear's shaft, adjusted a little, and rolled hard onto my back. It slid, I pulled, and it came through. Toppled. I lay there gasping for breath.

Kir. I could focus enough to stop most of the gushing blood. Up. The courtyard tipped and I caught myself. The quaking had stopped.

Qadeem? Kiefan?

The fount blazed, a sun trapped beneath the earth and glaring through a pinhole. A man stood in the glare, hands spread. A dozen thick tendrils pulsed into visibility at a call so strong I had to grab my kir. He spun up a blade and slashed through them.

Stumbling away from the fount, falling to his knees and then all fours, I spotted —

My feet put me at Kiefan's side in a heartbeat. There was blood on him; I called his pattern and saw a wild tangle swirling through him, like a trapped blizzard. Amid that, I found the worst of the slashes across his side and put my hand on it.

Kir? I looked to the fount and cold terror jolted through me. Behind Qadeem rose a cruel-beaked vulture, wrought in gold kir, its wings spreading as he cut away the font's bonds. My jaw fell open, wanting to scream before it struck.

A green vine coiled around the monster, knotted on its throat, and yanked it down as Qadeem spun. The earth rumbled, again, then stilled.

From the battlements, a shouted word. Dozens of archers drew back their bows. I threw up a shield over myself and Kiefan. He panted under my hand and I heard him mutter my name.

An angry roar answered them and a sphere lit on the fount, shot wide and hit the stone walls with a crunch. It passed over me firm but harmless and I recognized it, knew whose force-sphere it was. Woden stood in the fount beside Qadeem. He strode to step over its lip, kir-cloak swirling brilliant around him.

"Stand clear!"

I felt the warning through my bond, too, and then the guardian sphere spun itself up around the fount again. Its web-threads pulsed where they met, rising faster as the curve shrank to a tiny, flat top overhead.

Kiefan's hand found mine on his throbbing wound and moved it to his cheek. I looked down, into his half-focused eyes, as he kissed my palm.

And I still loved him, Mother forgive me. I only wanted to protect him from all his pain.

Woden took a handful of Kiefan's tabard and mail, yanked him to his feet and sounded him. Through my fingers, still tangled in his, I heard the rich chord, all its fierce notes, and saw the blossom his kir answered with.

All I could think was how wondrously different Kiefan's sounding was from mine. How it hung in the air like mine. Though a heartbeat briefer.

"Bind the fount," Woden told him.

"I —"

"You harvested a saint, I felt it. Do it — if you can."

Kiefan?

Woden put out his free hand and silently ordered the fount to him. A thick snake of kir reared up from the pool, spun toward him and wormed its head into his chest. His fingers clenched, the only sign of pain he gave. The snake twitched and relaxed, then faded.

Kiefan closed his eyes to focus and I felt him pull. The fount shifted, but no snake came.

"Deeper," Woden said. "Reach deeper."

He tried, he furrowed his brow, but then closed his eyes.

Woden let go of his mail. "Still elect, then."

Kiefan grimaced and I got up to tell him not to —

"Kate!"

Next I knew, I was in the fount, Qadeem's hand on my belly. Warmth swirled through my veins, washing away the last of the ache. I looked up at his face, upside down, and he smiled. "See to your own health first, physician," he told me.

I'd been stabbed by — "Gauvail's elect!" I put my feet down, scrambled to stand.

"Must have fled when he died."

I looked around the courtyard for her, though I knew Qadeem was right. The doors were still blocked with kir, and the wall was still gashed. The battlements were empty, though there were archers watching from the towers' arrow slits. Six King's Guard stood with their backs to the sphere, Woden and Kiefan with them. Waiting for something. I must've lost a little time.

My voice dropped. "Kiefan harvested Saint Gauvail?"

Qadeem nodded. "We were tangled in each other tight, but he landed on the pool's rim and cut him clean in half. Took his harvest through the blade, it seemed."

"I should've been with you," I said.

"Your aid let me land the first blow. You fought well." He fixed me with a stern look. "Your unraveling his charm was beautiful."

I couldn't help smiling, at that praise. I gathered up some kir from the fount and waded to the knee-high rim. "I should see to the men's wounds."

Picking up my sopping skirt to step out, I noticed the rip where I'd been stabbed. A brand new dress, already torn and bloodstained. With a sigh I walked from the fount, dripping.

/ wait /

The guardian sphere shivered.

/ safe /

I put up my hand, hesitated just shy of the golden web-threads, but it didn't respond. Taking a breath, I walked through. My skin tingled, but no worse than that.

Sir Waldemar had two arrows in him but they were only shallow wounds. Sir Garrick suffered a nasty gash in his thigh but he'd gotten in the killing blow on the battle elect while she dueled Kiefan. He managed a smile as his brother knights cuffed him fondly for that.

Rostislav was not among them. I scanned across the courtyard again, picking out a brown tabard here and there, my heart sinking. And I saw, climbing through the rock-filled gash as best they could, a squad of castle knights. Their leader made it through first and strode halfway across the gap. His grey tabard was edged with gold braid, and his yellow sash secured at the epaulette by more gold braid. Behind him, the men fell into formation — officers all, by their color-coded braids. One set Castle Willefreá's banner pole by his foot and the fabric unfurled: a ram crowned with green stars, on a yellow field.

The captain-general raised his sheathed sword in both hands. "I would offer the surrender of Willefreá if you spare my men, lord Saint," he declared in Arceal.

"We will spare the castle and its men," Woden replied in kind. "Lay down your arms."

Mail rattled as they knelt and obeyed. The banner was laid, gently, on the dirt as well. As they surrendered, Kiefan crossed the gap in long strides and stood before their captain with one hand on his moon-pommeled sword. The men looked up, tensed in fear.

"Know that the king of Wodenberg, Saint Woden's bound elect, is who you owe your lives to. Look at me." He gave them a heartbeat to note his grey eyes. "My mother is Mercia Heathugrim Aethlings-dóhtor, saved from Arcea's swords as an infant. When you fetch Temitte's burg-meister to offer his surrender, tell him that the blood of the Eald has been restored to Suevia."

CHAPTER 11

I rode through Temitte — Theo had brought back Jenner — with the remnants of my escort, calling kir. Looking for Gauvail's elect, or any gifted who might still be in the city. There were few and all belonged to the city governance.

When the afternoon waned, I returned to Castle Willefreá. In the courtyard I paused a moment to kneel by our six cloak-covered dead and touch Rostislav's hand again. What had torn half his ribcage away, I didn't know. But I owed him my gratitude.

Qadeem sat on the raised rim of the fount, one hand in its water, his eyes closed. They opened when I sat beside him and he took his hand out, let the water drip off. The fount's subdued glow veered around a black burn spiraling across his arm where the grounding-line had run.

"Oh." I reached without thinking and he let me see it. The sphere's kir-fire had left a mark after all: a slender welt, skin-deep, from palm to elbow. Where Gauvail's needle had punched through my shield and our hands, he had already healed.

"The burn will fade," Qadeem said.

I'd have thought it painted on, if I hadn't known better. "His charm split my shield," I said, circling the spot on his palm with one finger, "but didn't break in doing that."

"Yes, that was Gauvail's deadly quirk. But you unraveled him just the same. As I hoped." My saint smiled and I echoed it. "Perhaps Kiefan can master such a thing, if he has the focus for it."

I'd thought Qadeem's hands soft, but they were long-fingered and felt full of wires. I hadn't noticed the sharp angles of his knuckles before. And my skin seemed pale, beside his.

"Strange?" he asked when I lingered over his details.

"So brown," I murmured. Arcea was well south of Wodenberg and its people tanned easily but not so dark as Qadeem. "Rasila must be far away."

He took his hand back with a thin smile. "There are far browner men than Rasilai in the world. Yes. Black, even." My surprise must've been clear on my face.

"Sheep come in many colors," Saint Woden said, folding his arms as he stopped a few paces from us. "I've not seen a spotted man yet, though."

Kiefan followed him, rolling a sheet of paper as he came.

"Surely somewhere," Qadeem said.

Woden nodded at the guardian sphere overhead. "You were right to convince Aleks to re-build our guardians. I see why."

I remembered the Pool, deep in Castle Kaltkern's belly, and its Door whose teeth had scraped over me as I passed. A trick like Qadeem's wouldn't work on it, clear enough.

"Did Seraphine get through to the Pool on the night of the slaughter?" Kiefan asked.

Woden shook his head. "I didn't give her time to study the Door. It took a bite of her." He put a hand on Kiefan's shoulder. "You have this in hand now. Win your people over. Watch closely for treachery — and opportunity. Should the Empress try to reclaim this fount, we'll be ready."

He stepped over the rim onto the knee-deep landing inside the fount. Qadeem put out his hand, as he passed, and they clasped briefly. "My thanks. You were at my back."

Woden flashed a grin. "And I'd thought you had eyes under that hair, till now."

That had been Woden's kir that pulled the vulture down. "That vulture. Was it —?" I asked.

"Seraphine?" Woden nodded. "But that one's more slippery than an eel. I couldn't get a grip on her." Woden raised a hand in farewell and stepped off the landing. The glittering water swallowed him. I craned my neck to watch him vanish into the black deeps and caught Kiefan leaning over the rim too.

"All founts are connected, like beads on a string" Qadeem told us. We looked to him as he turned, on the rim, bringing up one leg and setting his ankle on the other knee. "Guarded by those who own them, to be certain. This fount leads to Mount Woden on one side and Reowan on the other."

"The Empress is in Reowan, then?" Kiefan asked.

"She struck from there. Reowan's fount is a junction of three, as Rukharbor's is, and she may have traveled there from any of Arcea's linked founts." Before we could ask, Qadeem said, "Which of Caercoed's founts is linked to Reowan, I do not know." He paused a moment. "What news of our army?"

Kiefan sat on Qadeem's other side. "The burg-meister gave his surrender and ordered the gates opened — we just got in ahead of word of the Tadhlon Guard attacking the north bridge. Seagrace reports," he said, holding up the rolled paper, "that the Dúnforst-éa camp was taken by surprise but fought bravely. They were reluctant to surrender, but likely will now that the burg-meister has sent word the fount is taken. Scyfe kept his word and never moved against us."

"The bridges?"

Kiefan nodded. "Both broken. With luck, Elect Teleri will see our banner once it goes up over the city gates and creep from wherever she's hiding."

Quiet fell among us. The fount burbled, kir slowly rising from its depths to renew its strength. Yet the water never overflowed the rim, just as the Pool didn't overflow.

"Have you eaten? Either of you?" Qadeem looked to us on either side. "I will see to any news that comes. Take your rest. Sleep."

Kiefan stood with a tired smile. "Sleep? Here?" He looked up at the inner walls and towers. Woden's force-sphere had left cracks in them. That diverted kir-ram had smashed the corner off one tower. Lamps glowed in the windows above, now that the afternoon ebbed.

My little tent was far away, if it was set up at all. I did want a bed, though. "There must be officer's quarters here," I said. "Or perhaps Theo and his uncle…?" I wasn't sure I wanted to sleep alone in a strange city where Gauvail's last elect might lurk hidden.

"There's a dining hall, at least," Qadeem said, pointing us toward the nearest unsealed tower door. "One of their squires brought me some beef pastries and a spring ale."

Kiefan started toward the door and I followed. He turned, on word of the ale. "Is their beer fair?"

Qadeem pinched one eye shut, looking for the words. "Wodenberg's tastes run to… assertive brews. Moreso than Suevia's."

Assertive? "Tea would be enough," I said. A nice, hot cup to soothe me. "Tea and a safe bed."

"I doubt I dare sleep, however tired," Kiefan said as we crossed the courtyard to the tower door. He picked at his mail — he'd stripped off the brown tabard and baldric — and its rips. "It would be good to get this off."

I'd forgotten the hole in my dress; I'd been showing off my stomach to all and sundry. I put my hand over it and my other over the matching hole at my back.

Kiefan stopped on the doorsill. "Wear your mail tunic from now on. Twice, now, I've had to see you wounded."

There was no jest in his face. As if I faced more danger than he, in this war. "Twice, now, I've felt a shockwave and feared it was you."

We looked at each other, there on the sill. Feared. The word rang true now that I'd said it. I feared seeing him dead. Kiefan's hand rose, wanting to touch me, but hesitated. "I would not cause you any more pain, if I could."

My throat tightened, aching. "I know you never meant to."

His eyes closed, for a heartbeat, and his hand found mine. Warm. I squeezed it. Our fingers threaded together. We went in search of dinner.

I woke before dawn in the small squire's room I'd chosen. A humble thing, just a straw cot and worn wool quilts, but the door was easily locked with a little charm.

The hollow I'd made in the mattress was warm but when I rolled over I met chilly cloth. Alone. My eyes opened on the small sphere of kir I'd left glowing between my worn boots. Its warm green light, in this cool stone room, seemed as alone as I felt.

A bowl of stewed chicken and dumplings with Kiefan, across a simple table, had been a comfort. We hadn't spoken — didn't need to. Simply that he'd been there, un-pestered by messengers or officers, had been enough to warm me.

Kiefan met me at a pre-dawn breakfast in the castle's dining hall, where the Suevi men gave us wide berth, for a little more of our comfortable silence. Then it was off to our duties.

He had the burg-meister of Temitte and his staff, along with the city guard and officers of the surrendered Dúnforst-éa camp, to question and to lay down Wodenberg's terms to.

Temitte's town criers would give summons to all discipled and blessed in the city to report to the burg-meister and then Saint Qadeem. They had simple choices: be cut free of their saint and re-bound, or be exiled. Since all disciples were known and tracked in Arcea, any who did not report would be hunted down as presumed enemies.

I was expected out in the camps on the east side of the city to check the goings-on. And to get myself a change of clothing. Overnight, Captain Aleks had led the King's Guard into Temitte and saw that I had a full hand of knights for an escort. Sir Garrick, freshly promoted to lieutenant, inherited Rostislav's job.

"Kate!"

I twisted in Jenner's saddle. Theo raised his hand. His mare clopped across the town square, here before the castle's ruined gates, cutting through the wagon traffic.

"A moment," I told Sir Garrick.

"I've been checking my sources," Theo said, drawing up stirrup to stirrup. "Despite yesterday, there were a few drinking in the Weary Ox by the curtain gate last night."

He gestured toward the Dúnforst-éa. Across that river, a bit more of Temitte was guarded by a sweep of wall from river bank to river bank — they called it the curtain wall. Naturally, it had a gate on the Southbound Road.

"Freshly arrived from Reowan." That was Theo's point, by the emphasis on it. He put a hand lightly on my arm and his voice dropped. "They said that over the winter, the Empress kept some secret new pet in her roost."

A chill shot down my spine, widening my eyes. "Anders?" I whispered.

"It was a mystery at first, but the Empress said nothing and the city near forgot. Until Equinox. And then…" Theo hesitated, bit his lip. He glanced to the King's Guard who waited on their horses only a few steps away. His voice fell further. "Then she revealed him. A knight of Wodenberg, she said, the only one worth… salvaging… and her bound elect."

The burst of hope turned leaden in my stomach. My hands clenched around Jenner's reins. Bound.

"She meant to return to Arcea. With him."

My eyes hazed. Alive, but bound to the Empress and carried away to Arcea only weeks ago. I wanted to say he'd choose death over living on her leash, but I couldn't wish him dead.

Theo's hand clasped my arm and I shifted my hand into his. He understood some of it; he was as hurt by the news as I. His eyes were tender in sympathy. Mine stung. I blinked and the tears broke free.

"But he's alive," Theo said.

I nodded. "Yes." I wiped my face with my sleeve, let go of his hand to do a better job of it. "Thank you for telling me."

"Mother Love willing, maybe someday — as you're both elect —"

He meant it hopefully, but it twisted the needle in my heart. I took the reins in my hands, though I could hardly see them. "I have duty, Theo."

/ ? /

My misery leached through the bond. I sent back a muddle that included Anders and felt a hug. As when he'd told me I wouldn't see Anders again, and held me as I cried.

"Should you need an ear, Kate, only ask." Theo said that with earnest eyes.

I nodded. "Thank you." It came out in a squeak. I tapped Jenner and he carried me away. My knights followed, wary but keeping their silence. My tears came thick and fast for a little while and then trailed off. My cheeks were dry by the time I rode through the camp of the surrendered Suevi division.

It still ached, the question I'd put my finger on one winter night. Why hadn't Anders stayed? I could've healed him. Instead he'd... slunk off to die. Meant to.

He hadn't wanted my aid. I'd gone to Kiefan first because his cut throat would kill him first. Had Anders thought...? Perhaps he'd let Seraphine take him. If he was gone to Arcea, I might never know. Mother Love's teachings said little on how long one should wait for proof of a lost husband.

Qadeem's caution echoed in my memory: not to cheat Rafe of love, and not to cheat myself.

———————————✕———————————

Once the flood of news began, the entire tone of Reowan shifted. Anders had felt an echo of what had stopped Seraphine mid-sentence and made her hiss a breath through her teeth: a sudden lash of pain across the waist. She'd said nothing, only stepped into the fount and vanished. She had returned quickly, darkly angry and saying little but clearly there'd been a great loss. That alone was enough to put the city on its full war footing.

Anders kept his mouth shut. But if the Mother had any mercy, his training might have distracted the Empress from the war, might have given Wodenberg some small edge... in the depths of his heart, far from the saint's-bond in his hand, that made him smile.

In the mere week since he'd been acclaimed as Seraphine's elect, his shape-shifting had taken another leap. Far beyond what it had pleased her to dally with the once she'd called him to her bed. Once. Laurent was pissy as a jilted handmaid about that, despite that she had plainly told Anders to take lovers as he pleased and dismissed him. How it was Anders' fault that the old soldier couldn't scratch that particular itch for the Empress, he wasn't clear on.

But no matter.

First word from Temitte, by hard-pressed post rider, arrived the afternoon after Seraphine's abrupt sojourn. Saint Gauvail and Elect Carina, dead. Castle Willefreá, surrendered. Both river bridges destroyed, leaving ten thousand soldiers on the wrong side.

When Seraphine snapped her fingers, Anders followed her to the main gate out of the beach-side courtyard. Castle Áering, which embraced the fount with strong stone arms, had a killing gallery for a main hall. One might walk from the city square outside, through that hall, directly onto the sand before the fount — passing through charmed gates, under twin balconies of archers, and upriver of whatever kir-fire the saint in the fount poured down.

The Empress stood at the head of the gallery, the fount and the sea behind her, and held a martial court. Anders stood behind her right shoulder, wearing his ridges and knight's crest openly, as officers and messengers came and went. Blessed-level secretaries tracked numbers and wrote orders. City magistrates waited for word and gossiped in the corners.

Details of Temitte's fall developed. The field marshals who reported to Seraphine were angry enough to march that afternoon; when the army at Ansehen had broken, they had wanted to counter-attack. Elect Arkho had died and Liandro and Renata gone missing. Only the need to guard against a possible invasion from Caercoed had held them back.

Saint Musaad was on Suevia's north coast, near Dwyncraig Pass, to see about the truth of that.

Little surprise, to Anders, that Kiefan and Woden had carved their way through the army at Ansehen. By the reports, the two of them had unleashed upon a division of centaurs and left little standing. There was no answer, though, for what tugged at the corner of his mind: where was Kate?

"The enemy came bearing orders to escort a fresh payroll to the Thirty-first division, m'lady," the next messenger reported. "A dozen knights, two teamsters, and a camp girl."

Anders' brows perked for a flicker and then he wiped his face clean of hope.

"Which escaped from Ansehen, or so claimed. Whose command is the Thirty-first?" Seraphine looked to the nearest of the military secretaries.

He scrambled for the answer. "Lucan Scyfe, m'lady."

"His kin shall be found and executed. Their property burnt to the ground. And all shall know the why of it. What more?"

That order was written as the messenger answered. "One of the teamsters was a saint, disguised, and the girl his Elect. A battle elect aided them — one of the knights."

"How is the saint described?"

"Southern Arceal or Rasilai, m'lady. Saint Gauvail fought well —"

"If it please the Empress!" A shout came from the killing gallery's front gate, onto the city square. "Elect Fijolais requests audience!"

"Send her." Seraphine raised one hand and beckoned. The crowd parted.

Anders recognized her: long, dark braid, haunted eyes, black Arceal robe. Not much older than him. Fijolais had been the elect beside Gauvail in the Order's courtyard when Saint Aleks died.

Rage sparked in her sunken, red-rimmed eyes when she spotted Anders. He set his hand on his sword and met her gaze steadily. If she wanted a fight, he'd take whatever revenge for Aleksandr that he could. His anticipation had slight hints of what she might do, if she attacked.

Fijolais dropped to her knees before Seraphine and touched her forehead to the ground. "End me, m'lady, for I failed my saint." The elect's voice was raw.

A moment's silence. "For you are his broken little wildcat." Seraphine nodded. "You'd die? Let Gauvail go without vengeance?"

Fijolais' eyes tipped up from the ground, all but glowing with hate. "I would see them gutted. May I?"

Seraphine raised her arm and cut her meridian — and the elect was on her feet slicing her own to accept the bond. Eagerly. "For your vengeance," Seraphine said. "Then we shall find you a new saint."

"Order me, la." Fijolais pressed her forehead to the hand that bound her.

"Escort the tenth company, be their aid. I must see what Qadeem's wits have wrought here. A fine game he played, with a poor hand —" Seraphine cast a glance at Anders and snorted. "None to train what talent he had. Just one battle elect and a healer? Now this must end." Her voice rose as she said, "Musaad is recalled here to hold command. I go with the tenth to end this."

The hall filled with orders, questions, and Seraphine stood directing them. Anders clenched his right hand, pinching his bond tight for what it would help keep his roiling emotions secret. Kate was in the army with Kiefan and Saint Qadeem. Perhaps Seraphine thought Kate just a healer; Anders had glimpsed what she'd done to Elect Tannait's arms, in the brief fight when the two Caer elect came to arrest him. He'd seen her charge up the castle staircase into Father-knew-what danger, the night of the massacre.

That night was a taste of what would happen if Seraphine put her end to this war.

Anders knew what defying her cost: agony, paralysis, his innards laid bare to the wind.

He weighed that against Kate, dead. Rafe.

He took a deep breath and calm settled in.

Seraphine left the rest of the details to the officers and magistrates; she turned and crossed the sandy courtyard, closing the gates behind herself with two kir-vines. Anders followed, keeping close.

"Will I come with you?" he asked, keeping his voice steady. Neutral.

"Time you went south," she said. "Laurent will prepare the household. All will return to Arcea. For I will follow when this ends."

Anders drew beside her with a longer stride. "All the gains I've earned and now I lose a moon's training?" When she cast him a sidelong, unmoved glance, he laid out some truth. "I know what trying to escape would earn me."

"For you think you've gained much?"

There was a trap, there. "I thought you were pleased with my progress. That one night, particularly."

Seraphine stopped below the salt pine and its lofty nest, her mouth quirking to one side. "Shall we test your progress and its true-ness? Your stamina?"

Anders took a breath to flirt, but held it back. Seraphine smirked.

"He learns. Come with me, then, bound in your new form until the animal clouds your mind. For that stamina is what you shall need."

He dipped his head in a bow. "I'll be ready —"

"No need," she said. "You need bring nothing but a halter."

CHAPTER 12

"The Empress visits now and then, and requires a suite." The burg-meister of Temitte, one Kend Throsm, led us himself to the third floor of his manor. The first two were given over to record-keeping, meeting-rooms, and other official functions. He and his family lived in the garden-hedged wing adjoining. "It's kept ready for her. Would m'lord consider it?"

My report on our new Suevi prisoners and our dukes — I had brought Vysokov back with me, left Seagrace in command — had been part of a long afternoon's assembling of our status. I had witnessed it all for my saint, spending much of it trying not to think of Anders. The subject of living arrangements had come up after concerns about feeding our men entirely through the supply train from home, or on what we could reasonably glean here in Temitte. There were provisions stockpiled here for supplying Arceal armies but they'd been drained by the invasion of Wodenberg. Burg-meister Throsm was concerned about the spring planting and whether we'd seize the seed stock for food.

Kiefan would order no such thing, of course, but it touched a sore spot.

"I won't have the people thinking I mean to replace the Empress," Kiefan told Throsm as the man pressed the bright brass latch on a tall, dark-cherry door.

He looked up at Kiefan, brows raised over his watery old eyes. "If you end the tithe, fear nothing. Dress in purple if you wish and you will still be loved."

That had needed some explaining, how the empire put all its children through examinations to sift out the gifted and the skilled. Those with kir talent were skimmed off and claimed as a tithe for training in Arcea. One in ten children, the mayor had told us. Taken. Returned with all the habits of Arceal citizens and on their way to earning full citizenship — if they returned at all. Life in a provincial backwater like Suevia had few charms in comparison to the rest of the empire.

Burg-meister Throsm pushed the door open. Tall windows looked onto the city square and Castle Willefreá, and the afternoon sun glowed on the gauzy linen drapes. Two silk-covered couches made a corner before the fireplace and a dark table with matched chairs stood by the windows. Racks of antlers hung over the mantle, as did a torn and stained Suevi banner, and two tapestries filled the gaps between the bookshelves.

My eyes caught on their bindings. I missed my own bookshelves, back home.

Kiefan turned to the Guards behind him. "Tell Gregor to bring up my kit." Then he turned to the burg-meister. "Thank you, this looks to be the best place for me."

He smiled, pleased. "I shall send up a man to attend you, m'lord."

I ventured toward the bookshelves. Kiefan strode past me, looking up at the high shelves, and put his hand on the bindings. "Perhaps she's our enemy, but she cares for books."

They smelled of dust and old leather. When I drew one out, a few strands of spider silk glinted. "She may not have touched these much."

Kiefan took a fat book from higher up. "I'll gladly relieve her of them, then. The jewels in the treasury were fine, but…" He trailed off, leafing through the heavy pages. "This is on military engineering," he said.

"Herbs in this one." On the pages of my book were fine sketches of leaves, flowers, roots, seeds, all labeled with their uses.

"This is the plan Arcea uses for its trebuchets." Kiefan tapped one diagram and turned the book to show me. "Thank the Father they've abandoned those half-built across the Neva. With both bridges out, we'd need our own to stop their bombardment."

That had been the report, that the ten thousand Arceal across the river had withdrawn. "Qadeem said we could destroy them, so they retreated," I said. I thought of the Shepherd's knife Woden had mown down the prisoners with.

"Without an elect of their own — or perhaps they have orders. The next bridge across the Neva is at Singréne. They'll return. We must be ready." Kiefan put the book back and selected another, but he paused. "We've ten thousand we can trust. Engls, Alemanni, and Russe. Scyfe, trust so long as he's paid. Elect Teleri's loyalty…"

Hers was less certain, true. "The Tadhlon Guard paid for those bridges. Do you doubt the knights, the archers?" They'd lost hundreds, which was a good number of their company.

"Why send them to die?" Kiefan asked, holding up the book. "Caercoed was to seal its passes when the Crown returned. Their saints mean to make a fortress of their land. In itself, that's dangerous but they're no saints of war, as Teleri said."

It still felt true, so I said it again. "Elect Tannait would not send two thousand to die without knowing."

"She wouldn't," Kiefan agreed. "And if Caercoed sealed its passes, Suevia would know. That would've been the word, rather than all's quiet in the north."

I looked down at a portrait of an arrowroot plant. "The Tadhlon Guard might go home, then."

"You saw how both Crowns embraced m'lady Leix. They loved her. But Ciara ordered Leix's knights to ride with me, knowing she'd not send reinforcements as she pledged — sent them to die, surely, open passes or not." Kiefan frowned, put the book down, leaned on the shelf with a huff.

It made little sense to me as well. "They're passionate, deSvello said," I reminded him.

He snorted. His voice fell to a mutter. "Fey-touched. Fools. She thinks she collared me?"

Collared? I closed the herb book and took the one beside it. Anatomy diagrams greeted me, so familiar as to be soothing.

Kiefan straightened. His voice sharpened. "She sent them to be sure I'd march on Temitte."

My brows rose. We were in Temitte, yes, despite the lack of her aid. And thus not in Ansehen, or... in Wodenberg...

"Rukharbor."

Fear stabbed me, thinking of Elect Pirra and Elect Terekhov. When I looked to Kiefan, he stared at the distance, tapped into his saint's bond. I touched my own.

/ brother elect / safe? /

Qadeem paused a moment. / yes / trouble? /

/ lured here? /

I felt questioning alarm in reply.

"Woden says Elect Pirra is well. He's in Rukharbor now, at the fount," Kiefan told me. I relayed that to Qadeem. "Ciara knows how long a march it is from Ansehen to Rukharbor," Kiefan said, still chewing on the riddle. "Even on the Southbound Road. If she broke the reserves there, our army wouldn't arrive for a week or more."

"But she wanted you to attack Temitte," I said. "She wanted you believing you could take it." My stomach shifted, uneasy. "She sent you here to die, not Teleri."

Fire in his grey eyes. My heart shivered at the anger there; may it never be meant for me. He pushed off the bookshelf, strode across the room. "When the Empress strikes back and crushes me," he said, edged with a growl. At the door, he snapped to the two Guard posted there. "Fetch Vysokov. Seagrace. Teleri and Captain Eith. Scyfe. And the Rangers."

Gregor had just reached the top of the grand staircase, the largest of Kiefan's gear-bags in his hands. He stopped before the door to catch his breath as one of the Guards thundered down the wooden steps. Kiefan grabbed the bags from his hands.

"I'll need a mail tunic from the armory. We'll be under attack before mine's repaired. Go, see what they have." Kiefan carried the bags in, tossed them to one side. My mind was full of the wounded lying in Brauer's infirmary when he turned back to me. "If the Empress is here to kill me, where is she not? This wasn't to distract me from defending Rukharbor. It was to distract her from defending Reowan, where there's a fount right on the beach. And much as I love you Kate, Englia's a cold, miserable marshland. Suevia's a far finer prize."

I frowned at that part and didn't notice that he'd taken my hands in his. "We prepare for a siege, then?"

His eyes narrowed. "Ciara will not have Reowan."

I blinked, stunned. "But —"

"No rewards for betrayal. And not one more fount to fight us with," he said. Striding past me, he added, "We strike now and take it first."

I must've misheard all his worrying about how small our army was. I trotted after him, to the railing that looked down on the grand sweep of the staircase past the second floor, down to the great welcoming hall and the scurrying men there.

"How?" I put my hands on the rail and risked a glance at him.

"Vysokov," Kiefan called down to the duke, who looked up from the ground floor. "We ready to march. Scyfe, tell that stiff-necked ass he can swear fealty or see if his captains would rather string him up and double their pay under my command. I need Bídon here, too, and Theo Kaufmann."

Kiefan leaned against the railing to answer me. "Arcea has ten thousand who withdrew from the camp across the river. Ten thousand in Reowan. The smallest number of them we've faced since..." He shrugged. "We strike before she can call for more. And before Caercoed claims the fount."

"How many saints might she call, though?" I had to ask it. And, "Why not let Caercoed face the Empress at Reowan?"

His brows lowered. "Ciara will not profit on her betrayal."

This couldn't be a matter of six thousand soldiers, or of a night's dallying and disappointment. There must be far more, far deeper. My stomach shifted again, in dread. I didn't hope for much, but I asked, "Does Saint Woden agree with you?"

"On striking before Arcea reinforces her, yes. And letting Caercoed weaken her first." Kiefan considered that. "It's still the better part of six days' march to Reowan. Equinox is twelve days past now. Were there an army marching from Caercoed, there'd be word of it — it must be a small force. Or perhaps coming by sea. The ten thousand who withdrew from here —"

He let that hang but I had nothing to aid him with. I only hoped there wasn't an outbreak of sickness among the men, as there'd been after Ansehen. Dysentery still lingered in some of our squads. Whenever wounded took precedence for kir, the sickness gained ground.

"We must press to the sea, looking for an army to break before it falls back to the city there. My father did the same in Englia." Kiefan looked to me. "By any luck, did you bring Elect Parselev's war-journal along?"

I had, in fact. It was in my trunk.

"'Twas Margrave Leix I did swear to," Captain Eith told Kiefan, leaning back against the sofa's padded arm and setting her boots on the creamy silk. "'Twas the margrave that did give my orders and the margrave who did pull broken glass from my scalp after that night in Finn's Tap. The Crown sent me south on a goose chase."

Gregor poured us all mint tea on the low table nestled in the crook of the two sofas and set the kettle back on its trivet by the fire. I thought Kiefan would prod Eith for a clearer answer about where her loyalty lay, but he only waited.

She took a swallow of tea. "Don't ask us to fight our own."

"Never," Kiefan said. "I would ask you to guard the baggage and the supply line."

The captain looked at him across her mug. "You'll release us from the Crown's order to aid you?"

"If we take Reowan, yes. If not, you won't need my word on it."

Her mouth twisted, at that. The scar on her cheek caught the light. "I do not mock you," she said, raising one hand. He did the same, in agreement. "'Tis stern stuff you're made of, southlander. The baggage, then, and the supply line." The captain stood and saluted him.

"Be ready to cross the Dúnforst-éa tomorrow," Kiefan told her, standing as well. "You'll get your mustering orders."

Eith turned crisply and took her leave. Gregor saw her out past the door guards and asked the next guest into the imperial suite. This was why I'd stayed through a flurry of messengers and leafed through more of the books to pass the time.

Elect Teleri crossed the room with ease, hand on her hip where her sword should be. The guard had taken it from her when he checked her pattern. She wore no mail, today, only her dark blue Crown's Blades tunic and black hose.

Kiefan did not ask her to sit; he went to stand opposite her before the fire. I lingered on the sofa with my tea.

"The Crown marches on Reowan," he said.

Teleri folded her arms to match his.

"I will take it first."

She eyed him, for a couple heartbeats. "What has this to do with me?"

"You chose Caercoed over your saint, you said. Your life for the kingdom and your love for its Crown."

She said nothing, but her eyes slipped to me.

"Will you fight the Empress with us, to keep those oaths?"

"I'll do nothing to harm Caercoed."

"You don't deny the attack on Reowan."

Teleri's eyes narrowed. "Little sense in lying to an augur. I did deliver two ruined bridges as you asked. What more, now?"

"Your loyalty, so long as we fight Arcea."

"I'll take no oath to you."

"Woden would have you bound."

"He'll not touch me."

"We're not such fools as to turn our backs on a rogue elect."

Neither raised their voices but the threats were plain enough. I kept a firm grip on my kir, not wanting to set either of them off.

"Perhaps Qadeem?" I said it softly as I could.

Both chins jerked toward me. I put my mug of tea down.

"He'll not force a bond on you. He'll not ask you to harm your own. He only demands the truth."

Teleri shifted back, shoulders easing a little. Kiefan added, "It seems he doesn't even use stringence."

That got a disbelieving frown. Teleri set her hands on her hips. "Might I speak with Elect Kate in confidence? And Saint Qadeem?"

Kiefan's turn to frown. But he nodded and withdrew, crossed the room to the bedroom door in the far wall and leaned against the sill. I took his place opposite Elect Teleri, not sure what I could say that would convince her to join us. I opened my bond to Qadeem, to hear her questions.

"'Tis much I cannot say, that is truth," she said. "Caercoed has its secrets."

Qadeem sent a nod and more. "There's much we would not tell you of Wodenberg's secrets."

"Fair enough. Mayhaps you don't use stringence, m'lord, but you know its uses. We might swear on the Mother and the Father, but they've a poor record of stopping oath-breakers."

It took me a moment to piece out his answer to that. "When we met, I mended the harm done to Elect Tannait. Let that stand as a mark of my honor."

Teleri's head tipped, considering that. She was near as tall as Kiefan; I had to look up to meet her hazel eyes. After a moment, she nodded. "You do give your word to release me, when all's done? I would go home, Mother willing."

I nodded.

"Let it be done, then." Teleri looked down at me, cocking one hip. "'Twas a fearsome thing you did to Tannait. Near made our healer ill to look upon."

I grimaced. "And I'm sorry I struck in haste. She only meant to protect my son from the fire."

"'Twas the heat of battle. You're a fierce thing, far more than you seem." Her eyes turned shrewd. "Have they trained you? In proper arms?"

"Woden gave me some lessons in shielding," I admitted. On the chance it might help, I went on. "Perhaps you could show me more."

"Did forget your shield, that day. Your... king does not teach you that?"

Her pause struck me as a hint. I looked to Kiefan, who feigned taking no interest in us. Surely Teleri knew something, as the captain-general of the Crown's Blades, and if she loved the Crown, of what angered Kiefan so.

"What happened to him, in Knapptal?"

She drew back a bit further, her brows rising. But that passed quickly. "'Tisn't for me to tell your king's secrets. Nor my Crown's. M'lord." Her voice rose. "I do accept Saint Qadeem's bond on the terms we've laid. What's your plan for the Empress, then?"

It needed a day to extract us from Temitte.

The captain-general of the defeated Suevi camp was loyal to his Empress. His six captains, less so. They dispatched him and chose from among themselves a man named Glyman to lead. He agreed to fight alongside Scyfe so long as we would pay them well. That was another seven thousand able armsmen in our tally.

Temitte's main avenues were broad and accustomed to seeing armies march through. Moving so many men, horses, and wagons was still no small thing. It took much of the day.

I spent what time I could with my saint at the fount. Back to its full strength, it glowed now, the rising bubbles from the deep twinkling in the sunlight. Qadeem had pitched a tent for himself inside the guardian sphere. There was a lush room at the top of one castle tower, for a saint, but he meant to stay close to the fount.

He couldn't leave it undefended to come with us. I spent the morning learning Qadeem's grounding charm.

"It may be that the guardian sphere at Reowan is different," he cautioned, "but they were both made by Saint Seaxneat. Taken from him by Seraphine. That fount is stronger than this one. It will take longer to drain and may well strike harder. Should the fire catch, on you —" Qadeem grimaced, but continued. "Keep your pattern fixed in your mind. Your memory will aid you in that. Your Blessing," he corrected himself. "My memory."

I spun out the grounding-line from my palm to my elbow, quick as I could. Trying to bring that memory of the speed Blessing to bear — "Your memory. As you said earlier."

A nod. "You are Blessed with my memory and held to a higher standard." He'd said it at my binding, in the Pool. "Most saints must work out their own memory charms, but the Shepherd gave me mine. Yours will hold through pain and terror, regardless of your will. Trust it. Kate." Qadeem's voice turned soft. "Let the Caer face Seraphine and her saints. Three elect against one saint — perhaps, with luck. A long shot. But we know Saint Musaad is with her, if none else."

"Do you know him?" I asked.

He shook his head. "Only that he's Rasilai. It's a common enough name in my homeland." With a squeeze of my hand, he told me, "Be prudent. Let them exhaust themselves on the Caer if you can. I will be first to aid you, from below, when you attack the fount."

I rode over the Dúnforst bridge in the afternoon, among the rearguard. We left two thousand and Duke Vysokov to hold Temitte. Captain Eith and the Tadhlon Guard would follow, escorting the baggage and our supply wagons.

Elect Teleri rode with Kiefan and sat at that night's meeting after we'd marched a few miles past Temitte. I came, bringing my teacher's war journal — with a moment's hesitation, remembering when Kiefan and I had last read it in Vorspitz.

My bed felt all the colder, since the news of Anders. Now that I knew how far away he was.

But Kiefan and I read several pages after dinner and the nightly meeting. Gregor kept our mugs full of fresh tea and saw to honing Kiefan's sword otherwise. A Ranger sergeant interrupted us with a report.

I left the journal with Kiefan and went to my chilly bed alone. I smiled enough to warm it, though; it had been far too long since we'd shared a book.

Suevia, south of Temitte, gentled into low, rolling hills covered by oat-fields. Many had been partly plowed before the farmers snatched their families and fled from the word of us. That needled me with guilt; I knew there were only so many days for plowing and then the seed must be planted. Else-wise it couldn't be harvested before the autumn rains kept the men from the fields long enough for the grain to spoil.

Young leaves greened all the trees now, looking like mid-Spring Moon already. A few brave patches of violets were out with the dandelions. There'd been a trace of frost last night, when we'd gone some days without any.

I rode in the main body of our men. Kiefan went with the vanguard, which was mainly knights, and Teleri the rearguard of armsmen. Duke Seagrace rode with me and we managed bits of conversation about Englia in the morning. Came the afternoon flurry of reports, and there was little time for talking.

Our scouting Rangers met with camps of enemy men — clutches of armsmen and archers, a squad of knights — lying in wait on roads and in farmhouses. Clashes forced them to turn back; such a cache of men was too strong for a squad of light-armed Rangers. Attempts to slip around them fell afoul of quick-footed snipers in blinds, undoubtably local men who knew this land well.

Kiefan sent companies of armsmen to pin these camps down. Some camps numbered a hundred men and more, big enough to harry a column like ours. It began with one company, soon after our noontime rest. More and more were sent as the afternoon turned cloudy, drizzled a bit, and cleared.

Wounded Rangers were carried in by their companions; I stopped one who had two arrows in him and wouldn't have survived the ride down the line to the infirmary wagons. His brown Ranger tabard with its black border reminded me of Anders', with a pang. I put that aside; he needed blood to strengthen his heart, so I gave him enough to steady its racing beat. Then I cut the arrows free of the man's ribs and shoulder, stitched and cleansed my work, and sent him on for further wound-dressing.

"Mother bless you, Elect," his companion said, before he rode off.

That evening, the trouble was made clear on Kiefan's map table. The enemy made a hedge of men and kept our scouts from reporting on what lay beyond. Largely, that line lay ahead of us, east of Singréne, but there were some worrisome spots not far away. Those had the officers fretting over what might lie in wait for tomorrow's march. Ambushes? A larger force in hiding?

We'd gotten a good day's walking in. Singréne was only a few miles ahead.

"Likely that the ten thousand from Temitte have crossed the bridge already," Kiefan said. Singréne was a large city, straddling the Neva River — the Ildra-éa, on this Suevi map — where it met a river called Benn-éa. "The line is meant to shield them, clearly; they've not turned south for Reowan. Neither have they stayed in Singréne, from the Rangers' reports." Kiefan tapped an area of wide fields on the north side of Singréne, off the Southbound Road. "We'll see the lie of things when we reach here. Before we're in the city's trebuchet range."

I listened, but lingered around the edge of the officers clustered at the map table. Elect Teleri joined me there, which struck me odd. "Little in common 'twixt body-guarding and battle-field tactics," she said. "Saint Conbarre did trust that to the field marshals."

She and I ate much of the warm ham, pan-cooked cabbage, and biscuits put out for dinner; the men were too absorbed in their theories and fretting. After gnawing over the most likely plans, Kiefan dismissed them.

"Set your watches and get what rest you can." He had to order it, pointing at the door flaps. It was a light camp, out there, only bedrolls and small campfires. We'd all wake sore and chilly.

I might get in a turn through the infirmary, though, to check on those Rangers.

"Kate?"

I turned. Kiefan caught my hand, kissed my knuckles. Our old signal. I turned my palm to his cheek, called his pattern and found headache-knots. "May I, this time?" I asked it to tease him a little.

A smile. "Please."

His eyes closed as I picked at the knots — stubborn as ever — and his face eased. That drew a bit of a smile to me. Kiefan's braided knight's crest needed freshening. It wisped, even under his golden band. He could do that himself; I'd seen him braiding it once, during our long-ago mission. But of course he had other worries.

Only one knot remained when he murmured again. "Wear your mail, tomorrow. Promise me you'll be safe."

I set my teeth on my lip for a moment. "Only if you promise the same."

He sighed, opened his eyes. His arms slipped around me and pulled me close. My breath caught but then I hugged him back. His cheek lay against my temple; my forehead nestled against his neck. The scent of his mail's oil drowned out the lavender soap he'd shaved with. I could faintly feel his pulse. The simple comfort of it ached in my throat. Warm. Safe. For the first time since —

"Kaufmann told me the news of Anders," he said, voice still low.

My hands, at the small of Kiefan's back, gripped each other. I tried to swallow, dreading that he wanted me to answer — something. I had no answers. Why Anders had crawled away to die… why he'd let the Empress take him… what I could do to seek him out in faraway Arcea…

"I will never leave you, Kate." Kiefan's voice nearly caught. His arms twitched but he kept himself to a gentle hug. "I would make you queen of Wodenberg if you'll let me. Let Woden rage. I know what I can endure. I've been a jealous fool. I let Father Duty own me. That must end, I know, if I'm to have any hope of earning you back. On my life, I swear I mean to change. I will marry you or I will die alone."

That knife-pain between my ribs, spearing my heart, throbbed again. An old wound, now. I tightened my grip on him and he obliged until my ribs creaked, both of us breathing harsh from the pain of his words.

Without his jealousy, just the easy comfort of shared books and expecting no duty of each other — a queen or a farmer's wife, it mattered nothing to me. So long as it was Kiefan.

And so long as I was widowed, free of the wife-fealty I'd sworn to Anders. If he were truly gone, a traitor to our saints — but I still doubted that. Wanted to, despite that I'd turned to heal him and he'd been gone.

"If Anders is gone to Arcea, if there's no sign of him in Reowan," I said, my words tumbling out on their own. "If he chose the Empress and her binding…"

"She acclaimed him before her court — you believe it a lie?" Kiefan gave me enough space to meet his gaze.

My voice fell to a whisper. "I don't want to believe it's true."

He nodded. "And bindings can be broken, if she forced it on him."

"But if he's gone, then…" I had to swallow. "Ask me in Reowan and I will say yes."

Kiefan put his forehead to mine, kissed me. Just a gentle touch that lingered and then he let out an easier breath. I sighed, harder, and we both smiled in relief.

"Good night," he whispered and let me go.

CHAPTER 13

One of our Ranger squads disappeared entirely.

Two of the companies sent out yesterday were attacked in the night and routed to Father-knew-where across the deserted countryside. Messengers found only corpses and ruined camps.

Mid-morning, I felt kir flare in the distance. I sent word of that to Kiefan in the vanguard along with a reminder for those King's Guard I'd trained to check the patterns of all who approached him. Sir Garrick, still my lieutenant, had learned the trick of it and could check any near me. I warned Elect Teleri as well.

By then, she was atop a hill that overlooked the Southbound Road while it followed close by the Neva's shore. The hill narrowed the way and offered a fine place to attack from, so a company had been sent to hold it. Teleri had joined them. They'd watched the vanguard as it crossed the neck and now they guarded Duke Seagrace and me with the main army.

Word came back with the same messenger I'd sent to Teleri: centaurs spotted on our flank.

Duke Seagrace gave orders. I drew more kir from Qadeem and draped it around me in a cloak. Let me be the target, if they came, not these men. I angled Jenner to the edge of the road and stopped him there, watching and calling kir. But no attack came.

I had to catch up when orders arrived for us to form up in those fields Kiefan had pointed to on the map. It wasn't far past the narrow neck. Less than a mile. But we wound through a light, brushy forest and all eyes were on the trees. All hands on swords and bows.

The forest gave way to broad, open land with few stone walls. Farmhouses clustered in a few low spots. Singréne's gates, on the Southbound Road, were shut. Trebuchets on the wall stood ready. The wall looped long around the city, gave way to a bridge where it met the water, and became a wall again on the other side. The castle stood on a low hill across the broad Neva and well out of our reach.

Kiefan's vanguard had stopped at a cautious distance from the city walls. Seagrace's men marched off the Southbound Road and across the fields to form up in blocks. Scyfe and Glyman's Suevi marched off the other side, taking up formation between the road and the river.

I stayed on the road with Duke Seagrace and Kiefan. Teleri joined us, riding up at a canter ahead of her company of a hundred. "Did see three hundred centaurs, at least," she reported.

"When?" Kiefan asked.

"Some time past — did send word."

"Word never arrived."

And they poured out of the scrubby trees behind us. Centaurs pranced high in the front and Arceal armsmen marched behind them. The sun glinted on their iron lamellar. My stomach sank at first, and I had to remind myself we were strong here. They were only ten thousand. Our baggage and supply were safe on the far side of the narrow neck, protected by the Tadhlon Guard.

I watched them as more orders were given to adjust our men's arrangement. Teleri and her company rode to join the open flank. The fields were wide enough for cavalry charges and the centaurs took pride of place in their center. Across a bowshot's distance they faced us, chanting in a rumble of deep voices. Their armsmen made blocks to either side, matching us width for width. Half of them were Suevi, by their banners, and faced their turncoat kinsmen across the gap.

Noon passed before all was set. The day warmed and my mail tunic weighed on me. Scyfe rode up to confer with Kiefan and Duke Seagrace. I listened with half an ear; they seemed sure this was their entire force. This was bold of them, then, to face us like this. Unless they knew something we did not.

Teleri sent the news of a block of men and centaurs deploying along a string of low hill-tops off our east flank. Dozens of banners, the messenger said, and I knew that each Arceal banner meant a thousand men. They could only have come from Reowan, to march up on the southeast as they had.

Kiefan muttered a few curses. Scyfe went pale. This fight had evened out, of a sudden. "My men won't gladly kill brothers in arms," he told Kiefan.

"Then be slaughtered," he shot back. "Or fall back and be pinned against the city walls."

We looked to Singréne's closed gates and its trebuchets. We ought to be out of range. Scyfe spurred his horse and returned to his men with a grim face.

The army we faced began beating their shields in a rising thunder. Jenner fidgeted, not liking the noise, and I patted his neck. His turning away from the enemy gave me the first view of the trebuchets slinging upward, throwing small jars. I pointed, my voice lost in the din.

It stopped, so sudden as to stun the ears. When the small jars reached their peak they shattered. Kir-fire sprayed out over our men on all sides — not much, but anything it touched caught fire. Grass, wool, or flesh. Shouts and screams rose from the ranks.

"Guard, with me!" Kiefan drew his sword. "Archers' company! We must stop the rain! Kate!" He pointed his blade toward our Suevi allies.

It was on me to defend them. I kicked Jenner and he cantered off the road. I crossed the block of Suevi men with one hand up, pulling the kir from the patches of fire. It came it hazy clumps, streamed as it tried to catch up to Jenner, and quickly grew to a cloud around my hand. Their alarm stilled behind me. A glance over my shoulder and I caught them staring in slack-jawed awe.

Not a disciple or a blessed among them; I stole no-one's ration. These were only ordinary men.

At the end, I cornered and rode to the front of the formation. The river was less than a quarter-mile off but one last stone-walled field separated us from a row of dockside ware-houses. I knotted my cloud of kir down into stars and drew it into my core.

As I rode across the front toward Scyfe's banner, I heard the Suevi across the field chant-ing. The harsh words rumbled near to understandable — enough to unsettle my stomach. Violent words. Scyfe and Glyman were both at the banner, arguing by how they gestured, but they left off as I approached.

"Hold fast," I told them. "I can protect the men."

To test that, on cue, Singréne's trebuchets launched their next volley. My memory gave me Saint Gauvail's charm-splitting needles and my kir obeyed. I couldn't match the star-tight twists that he made, but they made good, strong darts. I shot them at the kir-fire jars on light threads of kir to be sure of their aim. Two, I struck before they reached their breaking-point and their fire fell short. The third burst and I threw a broad shield through the shower as men panicked and scattered below. Sparks flew as my charm and the kir-fire broke each other.

It cost me to throw so much at once, but the men went unharmed.

Qadeem sent me more with an unspoken promise to keep me as brim-full as he could.

"And can you knock arrows down the same, girl?" Glyman gestured toward the chanting Suevi. "Can you stop the fire as they cut us down? We were fools to come here, Scyfe."

Some of the captains near Glyman rumbled in agreement.

"We're trapped!" Glyman threw up his hands. "The wall, or the Twenty-fifth's spears? This boy king thinks we're only mowing-hay!"

I let my kir surge out, strong enough that even his eyes snapped to me. I strengthened my voice to carry with a little more. "He thinks Suevi men worthy of an Elect's protection. You're his rightful subjects and he means to be your king." Jenner jittered as I said it, unnerved by the kir, but I pulled him around to keep near the captains.

Across the field, kir flared in answer to mine. Its bearer walked from the front line across the field, cloak twinkling. A black Arceal robe, a long braid hanging past her shoulder — Gauvail's elect.

"Traitors." She put kir in her voice. Men muttered, behind me. "For traitors you are and I speak for the Empress. Those who wish to live shall lay down arms and serve as slaves upon her mercy. Or die today."

The muttering rose, angry. Scyfe drew his sword and shouted back. "I'll be a Blessed of Saint Woden before a slave in the gladiator pits!"

She struck, serpent-quick, and my arrow-sweeping reflex was all that caught the kir-needle inches from Scyfe's head. The charm broke, half blinding him with its sparks and spooking all the horses at hand. I kicked Jenner, which distracted him, and he pranced out a few steps from the line.

It was a fool's offer. "Death, or death as a slave?" I asked the Suevi on both sides, in Arceal, and I know they all heard me. "Or have the blood of the Eald for your king again?"

She lashed out three needle-tipped vines and I lashed back in reply. Two broke against my kir-vine. The third nicked Jenner's ear and he squealed, reared, and bucked. I threw myself off rather than fight him. Kir cushioned my fall. I was up on my knees as he ran.

The Elect strode closer, a thread of kir arcing to her from — not so far. I began to search for the source, but pulled my eyes back to my enemy. Shield, the echo of Woden's voice reminded me, and I spun out a buckler as I gained my feet.

"We have unfinished matters." She spoke from under lowered brows. A few yards of young spring grass separated us, between the opposing army-lines. Kir gathered in her hands, igniting to stars. "For I am Fijolais, ever the bound elect of Saint Gauvail."

I dreaded ever feeling Qadeem die through my bond. "And I am Kate," I answered her. The rest seemed foolish, but to tweak her I added, "Who unraveled your saint's charms."

She snarled and struck. From her shoulders, two needle-tipped vines of kir swooped in broad arcs. They shot for me from each side, too far apart to see. For a heartbeat, I was a frightened rabbit under her pounce. Then Woden's shield-lessons snapped my arms up against the sidewise blows, a second buckler sprouting from my free hand. A sting shot up both my arms when my shields broke.

I slung a little Shepherd's knife back at her with a hiss. It struck a third needle, halfway to me, and both burst into sparks. I glimpsed more coming, left, right, staggered, and caught the proud twist of her mouth too. That twisted my fear into anger. I pulled my kir-cloak tight around me, cut another knife with my mind and threw it square at her heart.

One needle struck my cloak, tore it, and I pulled at the sparks as they sprayed free. Some of them answered. Qadeem answered, too, and kir spilled into me as Fijolais' second needle — scraped by, only just missing. Her next two wavered. My Shepherd's knife slashed the kir on her upraised arm, broke her shield-charm.

I lashed, taking the attack with a bladed kir-vine. Fijolais' dark eyes flew wide and she threw herself aside of it, reeling off balance. It shot past her head. Through the vine, I flexed, as if an arm. My vine coiled, I reeled it back and it plunged toward her.

Three needles shot from her hand. Lighter, faster. I lunged forward, keeping my eyes on her, and made her look away from them to fend off my vine. The needles shot past me.

My vine dodged her clumsy swing, then darted in. I stabbed through her left arm at the elbow and her hand went limp. She screamed, her kir surging, and my vine shattered.

"Bitch!" I snarled, another little Shepherd's knife honing to a razor-edge in my hand. Those came easy, the oldest of my weapons. Harvested from my teacher.

I'd forgotten the three needles she'd missed me with. They pierced my back and wild kir jolted through me. My pattern blazed on my retinas, brilliant colors on black, and all I could do was clench it in place. I was suddenly on the grass, looking at clouds. Pain glowed from every whorl of me.

Fijolais blocked out the sky. Her good arm raised. Kir-spun dagger in her fist. My own fist shot up as hers plunged. I hit her solar plexus and surged up into her. Her blade stabbed the earth.

All I could see were her murderous eyes, all I could feel was pain — and her kir, as my hands found her neck. She stabbed down again, too close to miss.

My rage seized all the kir and the pattern of an entire body spun through my memory into it.

Fijolais blossomed.

Her structure, all its interlaced fibers, flashed before my eyes as they flew free. I saw her star behind her dark eyes, mine to harvest, and ripped it from her. The cloud of blood hit with her shockwave and I blinked.

Then I saw her eyes again. They fell out of her crimson skull onto me. Meat flew, scattered. The long rope of her gut. Her skin fell like a flag, pulled down by her braided hair. Lungs, heart, all the ribcage held, tumbled out with a splat.

My hands went limp and her bones toppled over. I stared down at her, panting.

I vomited.

/ clarity /

Kir strengthened me, curtained out around me safe and warm, but I came up trembling.

The Suevi armsmen, jaws slack in terror, backed away. Spears fell from their hands. They turned and ran, shoving their way through the ranks. Behind me, a roar surged up. Scyfe's turncoats charged after their fleeing countrymen, running by me first in ones and twos and then —

I raised my hand, knotting a star of kir in it, and lunged to my feet. The tide of them broke around me, around the slippery mess of Fijolais, and for a long series of breaths I only stood. Not able to think much beyond that I must stand or be trampled.

Dark memories swirled through my head. Fijolais' memories. The stink of sour beer, voices arguing, Father's belt against my back. No, her back. Her mother looking away, slack-faced, rather than fight for her daughter.

I pushed the darkness away, gleaning out her charms. The better memories of Saint Gauvail's tutoring her. He'd been firm but fair. Never broke his word, as her father had so often. She'd loved him for it.

The last of our Suevi rushed past me, shouting. My knees wobbled and I sank down. In the gap they'd left, I looked across the fields to Singréne's walls. Patches of fire ate at the grass and a few burned bodies lay smoldering, but on the walls beyond I could just make out the faces of those who'd watched me destroy an elect. The three trebuchets closest to me stood uncocked.

And Jenner was grazing as if nothing were amiss. I whistled to him and he looked up, then ambled over. My mail tunic was sticky with blood, my face dripping. The knees of my hose were a mess of bloody, muddy grass. Every joint ached, from the stun-strike that had put me down — a mild sort of lightning, from what I'd gleaned — as I pulled myself up into the saddle.

Scyfe's division chased the fleeing armsmen into the light wood, leaving a lumpy carpet of dead and dying. The centaurs, in the center, had not broken and the other Arceal wing held too. Seagrace's side of the field pounded their shields, working up their spirit for a charge. At their head, kir flared as Teleri raised her sword; their voices rose in reply. The block of men, their shields lapped and spears bristling, set off at an easy jog toward the opposing line of armsmen.

A block of our knights remained, opposite the centaurs. I turned Jenner toward them. The captain-general, posted by his banner, watched my approach, taking in my gore with nary a blink.

"I don't know what you did, Elect, but Father's bloody balls you're a mess. And you scared the shit out them." He spared a glance at the remaining enemy. "I sent word to his Majesty, asked him to rejoin us."

Blood dripped in my eye; I wiped at it but only made matters worse. If this captain wanted orders from me, I had none to give. "Are there any wounded?" I asked. Perhaps I could ease a little suffering before my mind lost all focus.

I didn't hear how the rest of the battle went until much later. That afternoon, I kept to what my hands could do alone. An ambulance let me climb into the back — alarming as I looked — and once they recognized me they let me stay there. I pinched bleeding arteries shut and stitched cuts.

Brauer's infirmary had found a fair enough spot in a small cherry orchard. They were part of Seagrace's army, not the baggage that we'd left behind, and had their own escort of a hundred mixed armsmen and archers.

Brauer looked at me once and threw a washrag. I caught it and was glad for something clean and wet against my face.

My mind cleared, slowly, as Fijolais settled into my memory Blessing. A cup of mint tea helped. It wasn't so difficult as when I'd harvested my teacher. There was far less of her, as she'd been much younger than him.

Late in the afternoon, a messenger found me; a command pavilion was up and I was expected.

Seagrace's men were in loose formations along a line, now. Our army had shifted to center on a village a quarter mile from Singréne's walls. The hill line that Arcea's reinforcements from Reowan had threatened us from was empty now. I saw a few company banners of Scyfe's men, but only a few.

We had commandeered a farm house, an old-style longhouse of split logs chinked with river mud. Inside, one met the fire-pit first; further back, a screen carved from golden wood sectioned off the rear of the house. Likely where the family slept. I knew this was a well-off farmer by the handsome trestle table and chairs that stood by the window. Duke Seagrace and Scyfe had a map laid out in the puddle of sunlight that fell through the window.

"Glyman's still out there," Seagrace told me as I approached the table. "Seems he's chased them…" He traced a line across the map with one finger.

"He didn't hear the regroup I sounded," Scyfe said. "We lost formation as the men scattered."

It sounded like an apology. "Kiefan is the one to tell, sir. Where is he?"

"Seeing that the Reowan force is retreating. They were bluffing — it was only one company."

"And bluffing well." Scyfe heaved a sigh. "The Empress would not empty Reowan for us. She made a fool of me."

Through the open door, the scuffing and snorting of horses arriving. "We must send out our trumpeters to call Glyman back — can you describe the signal to them?" Seagrace asked Scyfe, over the noise.

I turned toward the door as a knight filled it and only caught a glimpse of Kiefan before I was in his arms. He lifted me off my feet, clutching me tight, whispering my name. I could hardly breathe, for his grip. He kissed me, half a dozen touches that pressed deeper, each wanting more, each a sore temptation — and then we remembered our audience in the same heartbeat. I flinched back. He pressed his mouth shut.

Duke Seagrace didn't look as surprised as I'd expect, or else he had a good poker face. Scyfe avoided my gaze, smoothed out his furrowed brow with some effort. None of the King's Guard following Kiefan through the door even took notice, so far as I could tell.

Kiefan put his forehead to mine. "I felt the shockwave," he said. "I felt it, and — mercy, Kate, I'm sorry if I ever made you worry so. I'm sorry." That fell to a whisper.

I nodded. "Are you hurt?"

"A few scratches. Gregor — see to him first. Gregor!" He let me go as he called.

I slid down him to my feet, looking to the door. Captain Aleks stepped through it with Gregor's arm across her shoulder. The broken arrow in his thigh jostled as he hobbled along with her. I had a medicine bag, as I'd been working the infirmary, and I opened it with one hand, pointing to the nearest stool with the other.

Gregor wore a mail tunic but it only reached to mid-thigh. The arrow had sunk deep, hit the bone, and its barbed head was a dark shadow amid his wounded, swirling pattern.

"Give him something to brace with," I said, laying out my scalpel, needle, and catgut.

He didn't like that I stripped off one leg of his hose and shoved the leg of his braies up so far with little regard for what my hand might brush against. Some color rose on his face and he stammered out an apology.

I spared him a smile. "I've seen all men's secrets since I learned to check patterns. Steady, now. This will hurt."

He took it well, biting down on a leather glove for the worst of my cutting. I prodded aside a vein and eased out the arrowhead. Then, the curved needle to stitch up the wound layer by layer.

"Mark it with ash and it'll scar." Captain Aleks jerked a thumb toward the fire-pit.

Gregor managed a weak chuckle. "It's only an arrow."

"Fairly gotten in battle," Kiefan said, leaving off his conference with Seagrace and Scyfe to see how his squire fared.

I paused before stitching his skin and glanced up with my brows raised. Gregor shook his head and I finished. Catgut sometimes left a scar, as well, if the skin didn't take it well.

A call from the door drew Kiefan away, and then Captain Aleks. At the end, I knotted my thread, cut it, and put my hand over the line. A cleansing charm to be sure it would heal well. Kir seeped down through his whorls, tearing apart the patterns that didn't belong.

Gregor sighed in relief when I reached for a rolled bandage. "I can't help noticing," I said as I wrapped it around his ginger-haired thigh, "how you changed over the winter. Not just that you sprouted so. Your confidence sprouted, too."

"It's kind of you to say, Elect." He had blue eyes, and they turned hazy in thought for a moment. "I fell in love. Twice. But one — well, both were hopeless. I saw that on my own. And so much else happened — and now this —" Gregor shook his head.

"What did you see of Kiefan and Crown Ciara?" The words tumbled out before I fully thought them.

"That she wouldn't speak to him. He made a jest of it, laid a bet with the garrison officers, but it was no jest for him." His brow creased in a frown. "It's not for me to say more, m'lady. I'm sorry."

I nodded, though it was disappointing. Nobody would speak, then. Tying off the bandage, I patted his wound. "Gently, on this."

"M'lady."

We were both on our feet when Kiefan returned with a second squire in tow. This one carried a bucket of water. "Wash up and get some rest," Kiefan said to me, nodding toward the screened-off end of the longhouse. "Might well be trouble later on and one of us must be fresh. Teleri's bringing the essential baggage in, but it'll be light camp tonight. I must see if we can call those Suevi back."

He tugged me close by one hand and we both glanced to our audience — only King's Guard, this time. A brief kiss and he went. I sighed, stood there on my feet a moment to let the touch of his lips tingle on mine. And weighing another night in a bedroll on the cold ground against whatever was behind the screen. And whatever might happen, sleeping there.

Captain Aleks, Sir Garrick, and a few more King's Guard had carried over a bench from against the wall to sit by the fire-pit. Gregor, wounded leg cocked to keep his weight off it, lowered the teapot over the flames to heat faster. None of them thought anything amiss, by how they settled with muttered complaints and jokes. The water bucket stood beside my foot.

The hunger for warm arms around me gnawed at my gut. I picked up the bucket and carried it back, lighting a kir-lamp in my hand. Behind the screen, a final show of the farmer's wealth: a four-posted bed frame in honey-gold wood, its mattress covered by wooly blankets.

With a rag and the water, I washed off as much dry blood as I could once I'd stripped to my linen cote and braies. I scrubbed my knuckles and picked at my nails. My hair I let down, wiped off the flaking blood, and re-braided. The wool surcote and hose I put outside the screen with the bucket for a squire to see to. The sunlight on the kitchen table was fading, by then.

It was early but I slipped under the blankets and fell asleep easily enough. The flitting wraiths of Fijolais' dark history couldn't stop me.

CHAPTER 14

I drifted up to warmth. The mattress shiftedunder me, crinkling, and an arm slid over my waist. Kiefan spooned against my back with a sigh.

My eyes cracked open. Dim. Traces of light flickered; the fire was low beyond the wooden screen. I lay my arm over Kiefan's and my hand found his. Our fingers laced together. He squeezed me closer. His ear slid past mine and he touched a kiss to my shoulder.

All those lonely winter moons with only Rafe to keep me warm… I breathed a sigh.

Kiefan kissed my cheek next, lingered there. His hand slid up across my linen under-cote, slow and deliberate. I tugged him higher. His hand curled around my breast and the jolt of it caught my breath. My nipple was a tight peak when his fingers found it.

He leaned up on his elbow, pressing kisses to my neck, my cheek, and when I twisted toward him his tongue found mine. I let his hand go to touch his cheek, to find his braided crest above his Blessing ridges — no crown-band on him. Just Kiefan.

Our eyes met, glints in the dim light. His hand found the hem of my cote, slipped under it to feel my skin, to caress both my breasts, gently tweak them and make me shiver. My back arched. My butt brushed against his cock. Already eager.

I rolled over to kiss him, get my arm around him, let him pull my leg up over his hip and stroke his way from my thigh to my butt. My linen braies twisted in the rolling, and pulled further askew under his hand. I was too busy kissing him, lost in grinding against him, to worry much. My wandering fingers found the tie on his braies, pulled it loose, and slipped under the cloth.

Kiefan's breath caught, against my mouth. His grip on my butt-cheek tightened. Then he went for the tie on my braies — but it wasn't where it should be — and after a moment's fumbling I breathed a chuckle and pushed his shoulder. He tipped on his back and I followed, straddling him as I started un-twisting my braies.

He tensed, under me, with a hiss, and sat up suddenly. Nearly knocked me over.

"What —?" Had I leaned on a bruise? Pinched something?

"Sorry." He caught me by the arms. "I'm sorry, I —" He exhaled. Set his head against my shoulder for a moment, his hands shifting to my hips.

"Did I —?"

"No," he whispered. He nuzzled against my neck, took a deep breath of me. Then he found my braies' tie and undid it.

I nuzzled him back and called his pattern. Some bruise somewhere, some untended nick…? My hand found his cock again, meaning to distract him. He liked a firm grip, so —

His breath caught and he flinched, but then he steeled himself.

There wasn't anything amiss under my hand. "What —?"

Kiefan cut me off with a kiss and rolled me back to the mattress. "It's nothing," he whispered and another kiss followed. "Roll again."

Back to where we'd started, but this time his hand slipped under my braies and down to — make my breath catch and my back arch against his hard cock — and oh yes, Síochana had taught him a few things…

***

My clothes were drying by the fire. Captain Aleks turned as I crept out to claim them; she stood in the open front door. Through it, dawn was lightening the sky. The King's Guard posted outside glanced in around the sill. I snatched up my beige wool cote and held it to my chest; my linens were lightweight, for summer.

Captain Aleks only chuckled and told me, "The Guard isn't filled with lechers. And we know a thing or two of keeping secrets. Will you two finally be admitting to this?"

My cheeks warmed a bit. I found the hem of my cote and slid my arms into it. "How long have you known?"

"Housemistress Wenda and I have common cause. You're good for him, you know." Her hand rested on her sword as she watched me. She was in full armor already, early as it was, and her four-starred tabard and captain's brasses were immaculate. Her waist-long, braided knight's crest disappeared against the black.

My gaze went to the peg leg I'd crafted from her burnt bones and skin. "How has that been?" I nodded to it.

Aleks nodded. "Took some settling, but it's a sight better than being cripple." She raised her voice as Kiefan stepped into the firelight. "The abbot would have a word, on the coming Saint-day. We asked him to wait outside."

Kiefan tightened the last tie of his gambeson's tunic as he came. Gregor slipped past him, going for the mail laid out on the trestle table. He'd been in the children's mattress across the room from our bed, asleep — or feigning well enough. I didn't think we'd been so loud.

"I'll only need tea this morning," Kiefan told Gregor. He pulled his golden braid from the back of his gambeson. "Any word from Singréne?"

"Not yet. I'd like to see if Reinwin got through the night. He took a bad fall."

He nodded. "Yes, see about that."

"I'm going to the infirmary," I said, pulling on one leg of my hose.

Captain Aleks smiled. "Together, then."

———————————✕———————————

Physician Brauer was glad to see me. Much was uncertain this morning: the army might march, it might not; how many Arceal soldiers remained wasn't certain; several companies of our men, and their wounded, were still misplaced. Brauer's concern was that they'd have to move those wounded we had already. Some were too fragile to jostle around in a wagon bed.

I was required to give them the story of my duel with Fijolais, firstly. All the soldiers who could sat up to listen. They had only unstuffed mattresses to lie on — just sacks, really — and blankets to keep off the chill. Canvas had been strung from the cherry trees to keep the weather off, for what it could help. They were a rapt audience and loved the tale.

Captain Aleks had found her Guardsman among the worst off. I knelt on his other side and touched his pale face. By the breaks in his shinbones, he'd fallen from his horse. A charm had cleansed the gash the bones had made, it had been stitched, and a good splint secured him from knee to ankle. He'd come too late in the day for more healing than that.

I eased bone fragments back into alignment and knit them loosely. It would be much to fix all at once, but when I was done a wagon-ride wouldn't ruin the set of the bone. Sir Reinwin clung to Captain Aleks' arm as I worked — this was no painless thing — gritting his teeth and groaning. He asked if he'd lose the leg, many times, and I told him no.

Aleks cuffed him, the dozenth time. "And miss your chance for a peg like mine? Father's beard, boy, keep a grip on your balls."

She stayed with him while I moved on to another patient. He was an armsman and he'd taken a spear in the gut. His cousin had dragged him clear, he told me at a whisper. They'd hated each other for years, but his cousin had saved his life. Then he started to give me the long story of why they hated each other. I hushed him. The man had lost much blood, but he was steady enough.

The stitches sealing the rips in his gut were rushed, loose. Need had been to close him up quickly, before he bled to death. His kir patterns told me the stitches were leaking, here and there. It would be a long, hard journey to get him through the fever that would cause.

I pinched each leak shut, using the efficient little stitch-charms that Krepkin had shown me last year. A little more kir cleansed the infection that was already loose.

On to the next. They had six who truly needed me — more shattered bones and stabbed guts. There was a man whose arm had been cut clean off by a centaur. There was little I could do for him, aside from ease the fever he was already running. I lingered beside him, though, considering the pattern of his stump. They'd cauterized it, to seal the arteries.

"Oh, a shame, that," Captain Aleks said, at sight of the man's lost arm. "A hook, perhaps? Might you craft something for him?"

There was no spinning a new arm from kir alone. No bone to work with, but for the bit of forearm below his elbow. "Perhaps," I said, wondering if a bone hook with the muscles stretched and rooted to give it some use… though the meridian would be tricky…

"Your pardon, I must speak to Teleri about the supply line." Captain Aleks touched my arm before moving off. I nodded to her, glancing in the direction she went. Teleri crouched beside one of the cots, listening to a wounded Caer speak.

Brauer's worst-off six stabilized, I slipped out the rear tent-flap meaning to wash my hands. One of the patients had bled a little when I changed his bandage; the laundry would be back here, with ample soap and water. I spotted the kettles and Ters bustling over washbasins across the way.

The ambulance horses were on their pickets here as well, in the shade of the trees with grass underfoot. A man led a pony past them by a simple rope halter. He was ordinary enough, coarse-faced, brown-haired, familiar in a general way but I'd not met him before. The pony was so small I'd have thought him a colt but he had the build of a stallion.

And he stopped, oddly, and stood firm against the jerk of his man coming up short. The pony looked me square in the eye with ears perked.

I blinked. Grey dapples. A white star and a near-black nose. I knew those markings; my memory drew up the matching horse. My mouth fell open.

Anders' warhorse, Nipper. The pony was a tiny Nipper.

"Anders!" It flew out of my mouth as the pony squealed and bucked away from his man. He tore free and ran. I chased, but even a pony was faster than me. He dodged around a big, brown dray and scared a stableboy half to death. I half ran the boy over in my haste. Cherry trees flashed by, then ended. The pony looked over his shoulder for me and shook his head, slowed a moment. I gained on him. With a toss of his grey mane, he chose his direction and lengthened his stride.

Leaving me behind. I thrust my kir at the earth and bounded after him. The pony turned onto a road and galloped toward a handful of archers.

"Catch him!" I shouted, landing at an awkward run and leaping again.

Strange a scene as we were, two of the archers lunged for the pony's halter. He braked hard, twisted, and ducked under their arms. Once clear, he galloped again and swerved off the road toward a farmstead.

I gained on him. "Anders!" He had to hear me. Why run? Why —

Kir looped around my waist, mid-leap, and snapped taut. Pulled me from the air. I landed hard on my chest. My head spun but I scrabbled up on all fours and swung around to slash the kir. A second vine caught my arm, breaking and broken by my blade.

Teleri dug in her heels and reeled me back by my waist.

"No! Let me go!"

"Don't be a fool!"

The pony vanished into the open barn beside the abandoned farmhouse.

Gravel cut my knees. I swung around, letting my kir unfold, and slashed the vine at my waist. She snared me again in an eye-blink. "'Tis a trap! Think on it!"

Trap? Anders? "He wouldn't! No, he…"

"Do know that pony?"

"It's Anders. My husband." She likely didn't know. "He's a shifter."

Teleri squinted at the barn. "Then 'tis fine bait they laid out."

Bait. I looked to the barn. Off the road. Away from our camp. Alone. My heart sank. A trap. My hands dropped from the kir-vine binding me and it unraveled. The gravelly road under my stinging knees blurred and I covered my eyes with my hands.

Her boots crunched on the gravel. She crouched beside me. "I never failed my Crown, ere I failed Ceelin," Teleri said, her voice gentler. She took my arm and tugged. "Do know the look of a trap. 'Twas your man who was taken by the Empress, true?"

I stood. A trap for me? Qadeem had said the Empress might spare me but that was a long walk from laying a trap. No, Anders wouldn't be part of such a thing. "Come with me, then. Come and see."

"Walk into a trap laid for an Elect? And how do you know 'tis your husband? Not some spooked pony?"

"He's —" It sounded foolish to say. Teleri put her arm across my shoulders and steered me away, confident she was right. My voice fell. "The dapples. The white star."

"And did often lay traps for you?" She put her other hand to my near shoulder. "We return with a squad to see what's afoot. From afar."

───────────────✕───────────────

The pony crashed through the hush sphere's wall just inside the barn and tossed his head at its cobwebby touch. A pair of lamellar-clad knights sprang from each stall, charmed swords at ready, as he braked hard. He reared, lips peeled back from his teeth, and kir clouded out around him. The nearest knight ducked back when he lunged to bite.

Another caught his halter and the pony slammed his shoulder into the knight's side. He stumbled and the horse lunged to stomp on him — and was shoved back by the squad's lieutenant. He skittered back, found himself hedged in by three behind him with drawn swords. More men backed up the lieutenant.

The pony snorted and settled, tossing his head.

"Enough of that, enough." Behind him, the hedge parted for his handler. Breathing hard, he strode up to take the pony's halter with a hard jerk. "For she did recognize you, there! How? Tell me all and I may spare you — and her!"

The pony shuddered, head dropping, and his stomach heaved. His handler let the halter go as he fumbled back a step. The charm unraveled and he wobbled as his rear legs shrank at the feet and stretched at the thigh. Shoulders spread as his neck shrank. The dappled hide faded into flesh. His tail withdrew. Anders settled onto his knees and hands, still drawing hard breaths from the jolt of stringence.

"Secure. Find us a clear route back." The man's — Seraphine's — crisp order sent the knights trotting to obey. Laurent stepped from one of the empty stalls, a purple robe draped over one arm if the Empress should shift back to her usual body.

"Spare me? You swore you'd not make a spy of me — and you make me bait?" Anders looked up from under lowered brows. His flaxen crest hung loose, a mane of its own. "Those men would be dead if they tried to hurt her."

He had no right to be surprised, perhaps, but angry? Furious. It roiled in his gut, tangled in the pain of seeing Kate again, of being so unexpectedly close. And Seraphine's threat to cut her down where she stood.

"I asked nothing of you," his master spat at him. "You drew her eye! You ran!"

"You threatened to slaughter —"

Anders choked on the stringence, curling up on the dirt. Seraphine loomed over him, still a plain-faced man. "You were to do nothing. Shall thank me for the chance to save her life in leading her to our escort. Which you did fail. Now answer it: do you think to spy on me for Qadeem?"

The pain eased enough that he could snort out a laugh. "Thinking of home is more agony than you can inflict on me."

Seraphine paced a circle around Anders as he sat up again, arms trembling from the pain. He closed his eyes, seeing Kate with the sun dappling her hair, back in men's clothes as when he'd first met her. She'd hugged him that day he put her on Puck's back to escape. Innocently. Calling him a friend. He'd never told her what that had done to him.

He'd nearly led her into a trap, under threat Seraphine would kill her else-wise. Anders knotted that anger and pain together, clutched it tight even as he smoothed his face to a calm mask. A war, he couldn't stop. Quarrels between saints were too large a thing to wrestle. But some small corner of Seraphine's plans, he could block. Especially if it concerned Kate.

"Bait you are, when I demand it," Seraphine said, in her woman's voice. When she circled back into view, she was herself again, trailing her thick black braid. The man's clothes hung lose on her curves. Laurent moved closer, readying the robe.

She paid him no mind. "For if but one elect is worth saving, of your kingdom, perhaps it isn't you. A silver piece will buy a litter of battle elect. Shifters, rare things. But flesh-forgers, by what became of Fijolais? Precious."

Anders' throat tightened at the thought of Kate bound to Seraphine. Suffering her stringence. Though if she were here, perhaps he could protect her — for a moment he felt her in his arms again, cuddled against his side — but he shoved that thought away. "She won't be a pet of yours," he said. "You think us all puppies? Only hounds?"

Seraphine folded her arms across her bosom. "I am the hunted, pup. Each saint I bind would gladly murder me and gladly take my throne. So I winnow and must replace what I cull. For my pets do keep me alive. All who rule know it, even your boy king. Shall he live to learn of prudence? For a ruler needs both." She leaned closer. "But enough, now. You will turn south at last, with the household and see no more of this. You did show me your folk's weakness. All's well." She even smiled.

A thread of kir shot from her hand, struck Anders' temple, and though he threw himself back it wormed its way into his skull. He grabbed at it in horror but his muscle froze at a pulse through his saint's-bond. The kir-worm writhed through his brain.

"No — what —?" He jerked when the first loops tightened, and his anger was strangled. Eyes unfocused. "Please," he whimpered before she tied off his voice.

"Lead him," Seraphine told Laurent, her voice receding into a blur. "See that…"

CHAPTER 15

After we found the barn empty, Kiefan waited for us at the infirmary. I only walked past him. Surely he could augur all he needed from my face; he let me go without a word, and that was all I wanted. Brauer had little objection to my joining in the laundry. There was ever laundry to do: stained bandages, mattresses, the clothes stripped off the wounded. Few men had more than two of anything in an army, so the infirmary made an honest try of returning clean clothes to their owners.

Thank the Mother for mindless scrubbing.

In time, duty drew me back to the command longhouse. Kiefan had meant to tell me there'd been word of an old Suevi family marching to join us. They arrived in the afternoon, some two thousand men led by Galan Heathugrim.

He would have been a duke, had Arcea not abolished Suevia's lordships in favor of governmental offices. M'lord Galan and Kiefan were second cousins: Queen Mercia's mother had been a Heathugrim, a sister of his grandfather's. Naturally, he favored putting his kin on Suvia's throne. He knew of Theo Kaufmann, too, greeted him with a hand-clasp.

The men he brought were light infantry, trained in secret and loyal to the old house. More importantly, he had news of Reowan.

On the first of the Spring Moon, now eight days past, a fleet had left the southernmost Caer port, Arforddinas. Sleek, deep longboats all. Meant for war. Spring storms came often enough but even so they must now be close to Reowan and what Arceal navy docked there.

The city had been sealed after sending a few thousand soldiers toward Singréne. Word was that refugees filled the towns outside the wall and all their clamor for safety went ignored by Saint Musaad on the Empress' orders.

"That one's a cold fish," m'lord said. "Last word was that the Empress took leave of the city and gave him charge of this war. Musaad's her loyal dog and he won't disappoint her."

If Anders were her bound elect, how was he here? Escaped? Sent to trap... me?

I sipped my tea, Qadeem listening through me as Kiefan and Theo questioned m'lord Galan. He didn't know exact numbers of soldiers or navy ships in Reowan, such things were not spoken of, but he could give names of sympathizers to Kiefan's claim on the throne.

Talk of smuggling followed. I passed on Qadeem's questions as they came but said little myself. My mind had no reason to doubt the story that Seraphine had bound Anders and named him her elect, but my heart still said she must've forced it on him. Stolen him against his will because he was a shifter like her. He'd been wounded, too weak to fight. Surely he was chained to her side and dreaming of home.

I could've healed him. I would have. But when I had turned, he was gone.

And he'd been leading me to an abandoned barn alone. Anything could've waited inside.

When Teleri spoke up, she caught my ear. "Shall be three elect against this Saint Musaad, yes, but fount's a doorway for more. In truth, we won't know how many we face 'til we stand there. The Empress herself, mayhaps."

"The same's true of Caercoed," Kiefan replied.

Her shoulder twitched. "They've Saint Conbarre, most likely. Our sea-saint."

"We cannot know anything for certain before we see the city walls," Kiefan said.

M'lord Galan looked around the table at Captain Aleks, Theo, and toward the guarded door. "You haven't the men to take Reowan, m'lord. Even with mine."

That was when Theo said, "No, but we do have a good number of Suevi uniforms."

Ideas spooled out from there. The afternoon grew old and despite all the evidence in its favor, I mistrusted the idea of disguising ourselves as Suevi again. Kiefan heard my doubts, and Theo's certainty, and declined to commit fully either way. He gave orders to look into the uniforms and equipment for further discussion tomorrow. When m'lord Galan took his leave, I stood to go, too.

"Stay, Kate?" Kiefan set aside most of his maps, uncovering Parselev's journal from the clutter on the trestle table. As the last few Guard made their way out, taking Theo with them, Kiefan held the book up. "Might we read the last few pages over dinner?"

"There's much we should discuss," I said. "Aside from the journal."

Kiefan nodded as he opened it and leafed to the end. "This first, though."

I was glad enough to put the worries of the war aside for an evening. We sat at the clear end of the table and he read aloud while Gregor and the cook's boy brought dinner. Venison, tonight, with potatoes and spring onions and a little Suevi small beer from Temitte to wash it down.

Parselev had followed Woden and his elect, Prince Wolfgang, to Saint Ethmund's fount on the cliffs above Rukharbor. It had always been an eyrie; atop a finger of stone split from the cliff wall, the fount's water overflowed from a small pool shaped in the rock and fell hundreds of feet to the sea in a glittering spray. Rukhs nested around it, and Parselev had wanted to see those, study them, but instead they fought their way up. Ethmund had taken refuge there with his last elect.

The rukhs were his allies and theyfought hard.

My teacher was a gentle man, I knew, and he didn't write of the carnage. Only the sadness. Elect Wolfgang cut the noble birds from the air — and took terrible wounds, to be sure. Both he and Woden were torn and bleeding, and only Parselev's skill had kept them strong enough to continue.

Kiefan paused then. "The rukhs still nest around the fount," he said. "I'd hardly wish to make the climb even as a welcome guest."

"There won't be any rukhs at Reowan, at least."

"Only a vulture."

I ate, following on my memory of the page as he read on. The last of the rukhs tore Woden's eyes and my teacher needed some moments to mend that. Elect Wolfgang reached the summit ahead of them. A snarl had been all the warning my teacher heard before the last Englic elect pounced on him and Woden.

"It says only: I killed him. Mother forgive me, I killed and harvested him."

My teacher had told me he'd killed two elect, in his day, because he'd had to. I could see him grimace, disappointed, over doing his duty.

Kiefan turned the page and paused to eat a few more bites of venison. I got a little ahead of him in reading and a frown gathered on my brow as I went.

Parselev saw the flash, felt the shockwave of Saint Ethmund's death, as he and Woden reached the peak. Wolfgang stood in the fount amid the dusty cloud of Ethmund's remains. The wind carried that away. The elect turned, shaken by the harvest of an ancient saint, to face Woden and Parselev. He fell to his knees and put out a hand. A thick coil of kir snaked up from the fount to his heart.

I leaned back against my chair, mouth pursed. I trusted my teacher's word on it, but — "Your father said Ethmund killed Wolfgang."

Kiefan nodded. "Father knew no more, I think. He didn't see his brother die."

"Parselev couldn't have…"

"No. Woden killed Wolfgang. I read this last night," he admitted. "I wanted your thoughts on it."

"Read it?" I was too slow for my own impatience.

Kiefan glanced to be sure Gregor and the cook's boy were both out fetching us tea and our sweets, and read on. Wolfgang called up the fount's defense to stop Woden when he stepped forward; an icy, salt-rimed hedge swarmed up, slicing and crushing and freezing him in place. Our saint raged, cursed him for a traitor, and shouted for Parselev's aid. Likely he'd meant for my teacher to attack but instead Parselev struck the ice-hedge. It cracked, Woden tore free, and he fell upon the fledgling Saint Wolfgang.

That was the word he used: fledgling. "Fragile as a butterfly fresh from its cocoon," I murmured, remembering.

"Woden flung his body into the sea, piecemeal." Kiefan put the journal down as Gregor brought us a platter of small honey cakes. I gladly took one and a mug of spiced tea.

The last page was Parselev's admission that he'd been sworn to secrecy. He wrote this because the truth was more important. Saint Qadeem would agree, he wrote, and perhaps Saint Aleksandr would understand. But Shepherd help him if Woden ever learned.

He was likely right on that. Gentle Woden, as Qadeem had said.

We sipped tea and licked honey and cake crumbs from our fingers. Kiefan waited for me to speak first. "I'm sure it is the truth." I kept my voice low. "Woden's anger…"

"His own elect, though. My uncle, his own blood." Kiefan shifted in his chair. "When he picked me up, after I harvested Gauvail…"

I saw Woden's narrowed eyes, heard Kiefan's sounding again. "You're his faithful elect," I said. "You gave him Temitte when all seemed lost."

"And I didn't ascend."

"You didn't try to deny him the fount. Saints kill for founts, that's no secret."

Kiefan rubbed his eyes. "And why would my uncle — after fighting beside Woden through all the campaign — why try to claim it?"

"What should Prince Wolfgang have done? As a saint, could he give over his fount so easily?"

Kiefan shook his head. Neither of us knew the answer to that. "I've never thought Woden cruel. Harsh, yes, but the need is great. We must be strong to see to our duty. This is how he answers defiance. Rogues." He held up the closed journal.

And he meant to face Woden, if he must. "Don't defy him for me, if —"

"He can be reasoned with."

"You'll reason with him? Reason to me why we're marching to Reowan, first."

It slipped out unbidden but I held to it when Kiefan sat back in his chair, eyes narrowing. He didn't answer at first.

"To deny Caercoed a fount? Or revenge?" I wanted his reasons, I wanted him to lay it out in a sensible order — surely there was one. I didn't want to doubt him in that. "You aren't Woden, to lash out in rage. What happened in Knapptal?"

He looked down to the mug of tea in his hands. Took a deep breath. "I did what I must for the kingdom. My duty and honor are all I have. If not you."

That twisted my heart in a knot.

"I knew you were lost to me, after… I stabbed your husband."

"You swore off being a jealous fool," I said.

"Yes. I'll swear it again, whenever you ask." He breathed a laugh.

"I trust you to keep to that." Much as I wanted to be sure of that, my stomach still tightened and my fingers went to my necklace. Anders…

Kiefan's eyes sharpened, watching me. Reading me. He tensed in his chair, hand falling to his sword. "Is he here?"

My voice fell. "The pony I chased. It was him, I'm sure."

He frowned, but looked away. Smoothed his face with care before he spoke again. "He was in the camp? How?"

I spread one hand, having no answer.

"Teleri said that was a trap."

"It may have been. I don't believe he would hurt me —"

"I do not say this to slander him." Kiefan leaned on the trestle table, sober and serious. "He was acclaimed as the Empress' bound elect. Not any Arceal saint — the Empress herself. We need you here, Kate, not murdered in a barn or worse. The kingdom needs you, the saints. I need you."

It was true but in the face of Kiefan's bold stab at a city too big for us to take —

"And what happens if Seraphine takes you, cuts your saint's bond, claims you as her own? If she doesn't merely kill you? I can't lead an army. They won't follow Teleri gladly. And Qadeem will be alone in Temitte."

"If we wait even a moon's turning, she will have another ten or twenty thousand soldiers, more elect, whatever saints she can spare, here in Suevia." Kiefan tapped the table as he counted those off. "This is her lowest ebb. Even Qadeem agrees on that."

"But we must face Caercoed too?"

"We need only hold them off, not conquer the kingdom. When we have Reowan we will deal with them." Kiefan's hand clenched in a fist. I sighed, back to this thing he wouldn't speak of, this revenge he needed. He went on, voice low. "If you're right. About Anders. If he's at Reowan, alive and true to Wodenberg, and even though that means — you must say no to me —" He stumbled into silence.

Kiefan's offer to make me queen. I fought to take a deep breath without it aching. "If —"

He put up one hand to stop me, though he didn't look up from the table. Couldn't bear to see the truth on my face. "I will not ask. I would see you happy, whatever that must be."

I swallowed a lump. "Do you swear you'd do nothing to hurt Anders?"

Now he looked up. "I swear it, on all I hold dear."

Mainly me, by the weight of his gaze. "Do you trust that I love you still?"

That gave him pause. Kiefan's voice turned rough. "Would you be my queen, even then?"

"I love him. I cannot," and my throat knotted on it, for a moment. "I cannot choose between you. Do not ask me to. Better that I leave you both, take Rafe, and seek solitude."

We looked at each other for long heartbeats, across the table. I tried to swallow to clear the knot from my throat and sipped my tea. Kiefan's mail clinked, a whispery slither, and I tensed a moment but he only slid from his chair onto one knee before me. He took my hand in both of his and kissed it.

Looked up at me, his gold crown-band catching the candlelight. "I trust in your love, m'lady. I rely on it. And I will wait on your word, asking nothing of you. Or him."

I gripped his hands with both of mine, my fears draining away. "Thank you," I whispered. It was a small thing but it was all I could say.

⁂

My tent was in the cherry orchard near the infirmary. Kiefan had kissed me, gentle but deep, and let me go.

I walked back to the cherry orchard under the stars, my mind as aswirl with hopes and fears as on my wedding day. The picketed horses whuffed and shifted and I paused at my tent's door flap to look. Browns, bays, Jenner's buckskin standing out for being pale... no grey dapples. I ducked inside.

Foolish to think my heart's wound had healed over the winter, perhaps. And now I'd torn the stitches open.

/ hurt never fades? /

I felt a hug through my bond. / slowly / patience /

/ foolish / letting Kiefan? / I sat on my camp bed, lighting a ball of kir in my hand.

I left the last thought off; my saint had felt some echo of this morning through my bond, surely. All those moons alone, then one morning's love-making — one! — and there Anders was. I had not even a full morning to bask in the comfort.

/ what penance / balances it? /

That, I had no answer for. My fawn dress lay on my trunk, light against its dark wood. Returned, finally, from its repairing. I picked it up to check the holes the spear had made. The tailor had used kir to mend the cloth so there was no seam. No sign of the rips. A good scrubbing had gotten the blood out. I held it up by the shoulders. Like new.

Canvas rustled and I lowered it.

Anders straightened from ducking through the flap, letting it fall shut behind him.

My mouth fell open and then I dropped my dress to pull kir to my hands — here to steal me? To — ?

He fell to one knee, hands open. Empty. He wore no sword; his cote and hose were plain woolens. His hair fell across his Blessing, over a winter's worth of fuzzy regrowth below his ridges. And his summer-sky eyes — begging my forgiveness as he looked up at me.

"I'm sorry, Kate," he said. "I never meant to leave."

And he was in my arms, mine around his neck, in a heartbeat. A fresh sob tore out of me, raw and jagged. "Why?" That tore out, too. "Why?"

"She stole me." His voice caught.

"But —"

He kissed me but I needed an answer; I pushed him back. The Empress stole him, yes, and she was — I called his pattern. It swirled up. Blazing. Too dense to see. My heart leaped in terror and kir flashed to my hands — as a sharp thread of kir burrowed into my skull —

A shouted warning. Kir flared.

Kiefan was on his feet from the table, sword in hand, and two steps toward the door before it fully registered. Gregor leaped up from feeding the fire-pit. Sir Waldemar crashed headfirst through the heavy lintel, trailing blood and brains as he flew across and landed on the wooden screen. A gout of blood and an arm gone limp, sliding to the ground in the doorway, was all Kiefan saw of the kir-ram crushing Sir Readulf.

Kiefan waved Gregor behind him, opening the saint-bond to Woden. Fresh kir shot up his arm as —

Kate walked through the puddled blood in the doorway, her eyes unfocused. As if dreaming on her feet. A green collar of kir and a slender rope tied her to Anders' wrist. Kiefan's sword arm snapped up into a high guard.

No, not Anders. Something wearing his face.

/ she's here /

Woden's resolve made Kiefan's jaw clench and the twin lines of his Blessing spark with pain.

Anders melted before his eyes, darkening, black hair twining in a braid and reaching the ground. Turning into an Arceal woman. Behind her, a glimpse of black tabards and gold stars.

"Guard, stand down!" Kiefan ordered, harsh as he could while his gut was knotting itself. If they charged in here and were slaughtered — he must ration his resources. It was Kate they should rescue, if anyone. From this brazen enemy. He lowered his sword and steeled his voice. "Saint Seraphine."

Her chin dipped. "Elect Kiefan. Mark well." With two flicks of her wrist, she bound Kate's meridian to her own. The red line spun out from palm to palm.

/ she bound Kate /

/ steady / Behind that, duty threatened.

Father have mercy, let it not come to that.

"Woden. Qadeem." The Empress looked to Kiefan, then Kate. "Now you will hear my final terms. Wodenberg falls. Wodenberg dies in flame. This mercy, you might buy: Qadeem, surrendered to my hand, and I shall spare what common folk do not resist. Woden, surrendered to my hand, for one of your blood spared. These two elect are my trophies, and shall live so far as Reowan. There you may earn what mercy you will have."

Kiefan heard only silence through his bond when he relayed that to Woden. On his own, then. Not daring to show weakness. Heart pounding in his throat, Kiefan growled, "Why should I let you walk from here?"

Seraphine looked to the collar of kir around Kate's neck and it tightened. Kate's eyes flickered and her face flushed red.

"Your half-brother did tell me all, in time. What do you offer for her life?"

Damn Anders.

/ we dig in / fight to the last / Woden sent.

/ no / Kiefan gripped his sword one last time and let it fall. Kate's face was paling, her breaths coming in shallow gasps.

The bond tingled in his palm, warning of stringence.

/ cannot let her die /

Pain caught him halfway to kneeling, gnawing up to his shoulder and twisting the arm in a rictus. Knocking him down. Kiefan clenched it to his side with his good hand, and gritted his teeth. "My life, instead of hers. Empress."

Woden's wordless rage burned hotter than the stringence. Agony bloomed across his head, in familiar old lines.

/ love her! / Kiefan snarled back through his bond. / haven't you loved? /

Disgust answered, then silence.

Seraphine's shadow made Kiefan look up from his knees. Kate, on her leash, breathed easy and stared blankly. The Empress took his hand and cut his meridian with a lash of her mind. Kiefan cast his eyes down, flinching from the intimacy of the joining. Through the bond, she tore away his kir despite his clenched will.

"Your obedience keeps your lover alive," she told him. "For Qadeem has heard my message and I need her no more."

A pit opened in his gut, sucking down what hope remained. Kiefan lowered his head. "I will obey."

"We leave at once. Bring only a few retainers. Give your orders." Seraphine nodded toward the broken, dripping doorway. "Go no further than the lintel."

He stood. To Gregor he said, "Fill one pack." Kiefan glanced at his sword, mind flicking to the kir that Gregor likely still had, how fast he could snatch it — and steadied his nerves. Walked to the door.

Outside, Captain Aleks and two dozen Guard crouched in wedge formations on either side. It was Teleri, though, who stepped closer to the door and saluted. Aleks had, brilliantly, put her King's Guard tabard on the Elect.

"Captain," he said, then lowered his voice and spoke fast. "Kate and I must go with the Empress. Gather volunteers to accompany us. Seagrace must put this camp on full defense. Look for the first chance to retreat to Temitte."

His eyes were drawn to the walls of Singréne; there was at least one elect in there, spinning kir-fire for the trebuchets. That would be sufficient to slaughter Wodenberg's army, if used wisely.

"'Tis likely true she'll spare the good-folk," Teleri murmured back, speaking for Saint Qadeem. "Less that she'll spare Woden's blood."

When Kiefan passed that, Woden's reply was sullen. "He doubts her entirely. Chose your own way but he will go fighting."

"He knows. Kate's mind is bound with kir-thread. Cut it and she'll be free."

Hope rose from the pit of despair on white wings. Behind him, Seraphine said, "Enough." Teleri murmured, as she stepped away, "She must live."

Kiefan risked a tiny nod and turned back to the Empress.

CHAPTER 16

The entire King's Guard volunteered to escort Kiefan, unarmed and on foot, from the camp. Captain Aleks led them, standing proud on her peg leg, and Teleri hid herself in the ranks. There ought to be fifty of them but the war had whittled their numbers and now there were only about forty.

Seraphine drained their kir in an eye-blink along with all those who'd gathered at ten paces' distance to watch, the green haze of it streaking from each heart to hers in the night. It clouded around, knotting into stars and draping in a bright cloak. She glowed brighter than the waxing Shepherd moon overhead.

A rope spun out from her hand and twined around Kiefan's wrists, pulling them together. He clenched his fists and bit his lip.

"So, come," the Empress said, with a tug on the two leashes she held, and walked from the longhouse's ruined door.

Kiefan's head throbbed as he followed. Movement in the watching line caught his eye: Seagrace, without a tabard. Kiefan's anticipation warned he might give an attack signal; he spread his hands.

Any chance might come. A bit of kir for a blade to stab the Empress. To free Kate's mind and double their chances.

Attack now, and Seraphine would mow them down.

She led them toward Singréne's gates. Less than a mile by road, through pastures and one small cluster of houses. As they approached those Seraphine threw her chin forward — the only warning before a long beak sprouted from her face, her neck thinned and her eyes grew.

Kiefan froze and his leash grew taut. Seraphine stopped, though, cocking her vulture's head to either side. The nostril piercing her beak caught the moonlight.

Her call brought up his pattern, Kate's, all the Guard's — and he saw the creeping squad of men, likely archers, a heartbeat before white-hot fire broke the dark. A thatched cottage exploded, straw flying as the kir-ram struck. Men cried out, nearly lost in the crack and rumble. Collapsing, the cottage roared up in flames.

Seraphine's head returned to its shape. Her kir-cloak still glittered, untapped. Mildly, she clucked to Kiefan as she tugged the leash again, and walked on.

He looked back, once, hoping for — no, only fire. Aleksandra, five paces back, marched with a grim-set face.

Kate dream-walked beside Seraphine, still oblivious.

Soon enough, Singréne's gates opened before them, hauled back by a team of oxen apiece. A lone man stood in the middle of the street with a lantern, wearing the thinner kir-cloak of an elect. The soldiers on the walls above cheered once, twice, three times.

Seraphine put up one hand and they fell quiet. "I bring prisoners and trophies, as I swore to. Is all ready?"

Singréne's elect bowed. The Empress turned to face Captain Aleks and the King's Guard. "Divide your company. Half remain here."

Turning again, Seraphine tugged the leashes and strode into her city. The cheer rose again from soldiers and goodfolk lining the streets, leaning from windows. Nearly midnight, and they waved hats and held up torches. Kiefan clenched his fists again, his head throbbing with each surge of their voices. The lantern-bearing Elect led the way, likely the only kir on hand.

Kiefan cast a glance at Kate and trailed like an obedient hound.

The grinding of the gate closing caught his ear and he twisted around. He glimpsed half the Guard still outside, Teleri at the front line, before the doors closed. Seraphine tugged and he tripped, fell to his knees. The crowd broke into laughter, then jeering.

Kiefan's spine snapped taut at that and he dug in. She was only a short, soft woman but she yanked him off his knees with ease. Pain jolted down his second bond, convulsing Kiefan on the dirt as Seraphine dragged him. The laughter vanished in the roaring of his own racing pulse in his ears. He left his dinner on the street.

Hands touched him, pulled him up, and he saw Gregor's worried eyes.

Kir lashed. Kiefan lunged to his feet alone. "No!"

Gregor sat on the street, blood dripping from his nose, as Aleksandra reached him and paused to pull him up.

Another yank and Kiefan stumbled after the Empress. The crowd chanted an old Suevi child's verse about dragging a sheep to the butcher-shop. He gritted his teeth and walked, raising his head. Vomit-stained, now, but he still wore Wodenberg's crown. Whatever humiliation they required, he'd survive it. To keep Kate alive.

He'd heard of the Arceal gladiator arenas. Hadn't seen one, even in Temitte; no time. Its gates stood open and torches blazed, lighting the way inside. Three layers of stands rose on either side. At the end of the brief hall, after a heavy gate, stone steps led down onto sand. In the center of the oval, a wooden platform stood.

The stands were filling fast. Kiefan's feet slowed, remembering the first battle of Ansehen. Seraphine's first threats. She'd sworn Kiefan would die a gladiator slave.

"Up, up," Seraphine clucked at Kate, who fumbled a moment and then climbed the platform's steps.

Kiefan told Woden what he could through his right-hand bond. Alone, on the platform, with the Empress. Twenty Guard on the sands. Gregor climbing the steps with the pack on his shoulder; perhaps he'd slipped a knife in there.

/ kir? /

/ hush / Seraphine ordered and agony dropped Kiefan onto the boards.

The growing crowd cheered. Fingers knotted in Kiefan's crest and pulled his head up. "Behold, Arcea, your enemy here!" Kir carried her voice and a roar answered. "For I bring both Wodenberg's elect and its king!"

She didn't know — two more were in Rukharbor. Far away. He jammed that hope down lest she overhear it.

On his knees, bound, Kiefan watched the crowd as Seraphine listed his crimes against the Empire. Soldiers, his Blessing told him. Angry. Those along the wall rimming the gladiator sands were archers with strung bows. They wanted blood.

Little chance of surviving, even if Kiefan and his Guard had their swords and kir.

"I bring this trophy!" Seraphine shook Kiefan's head and flung him down. "I bring vengeance for the brothers they slew!"

The roar surged again. Behind him, hooves. Kiefan spun around on his knees. Minotaurs, heavy swords clenched in both hands, leaped the stone steps to the sand. His Guards bunched together at a shout from Aleksandra.

Unarmed. Helpless. He screamed, lost in the noise.

Rage surging, Kiefan pulled for kir. It blazed through Woden's bond, igniting as a bolt of lightning that cracked through the ranks of minotaurs. Half stumbled, a heartbeat from striking, and the Blessed knights counter-charged.

Powerful will seized Kiefan's kir in his core, tore it from him and clubbed him across the head with it. His face bounced off the boards. The world spun with black stars. A small foot dug into the small of his back and pinned him down with a spike of kir through his spine.

Minotaurs rallied, reinforced by more brothers. Their blades plunged, came up trailing blood, plunged again.

Kiefan dropped to his face but Seraphine pulled him up by his crest. "Watch, king," she hissed in his ear. "And you shall watch Kate's pain for your disobedience, too."

For a moment, he spotted Aleks tackling one monster and bearing it down. A second minotaur caught her braid, tore her off, and slung her across the sand. She tumbled, came up on her feet and cursing in Russe. Three of them turned, closed on her. She backed against the wall, chest heaving.

The crowd's cheering shifted to a chant, spreading quickly through the stands.

"Rape her! Rape her!"

Tears drowned his eyes. He clenched his eyes shut. Couldn't watch as the chant gave way to a bloodthirsty roar.

All was hazed, a muddle of voices familiar and strange. Faces were featureless moons with blots for eyes. The sway of a horse under him, comforting as a cradle's rocking. Orders he couldn't resist, or a hand taking him by the wrist to lead. This wasn't right, he didn't want to go, but there was no arguing. Words wouldn't come. His body wouldn't obey.

Then it all snapped to clarity.

Anders blinked, focused on the concerned brown eyes over him. Grey in the man's brown beard, lines around his eyes. A bit of kir fell away from his hand. "Who did that to you, lad? I've never seen the like," he said in Suevi.

"Where am I?" He sat on a humble bed, in a small room with an open window and an ajar door. Saddlebags lay to one side.

"The Greyhound's Rest, at Fersceá. Fever broke out here two days ago. They called me to —"

The door slammed open. Laurent snarled, "Who let you in here?"

"I knocked, and he —" The physician stood, turning, as he answered.

Laurent's eyes met Anders' and anticipation had him on his feet at speed; feint; fist cracked across the old soldier's jaw; took a hard blow to his ribs, knocking him off balance. Anders let himself stumble to the side, keeping his feet and falling into an aggressive middle guard. Minus a sword, though. Laurent, unfazed by the punch, drew his dagger and let it hover at his side.

Anticipation knew he'd be no easy kill. No speed. Anders had only a little kir and needed the anticipation more. He took a deep breath to soothe off the jitter that speed put in his muscle. Needed deliberation, instead.

Laurent waited for his move. "Might do this easy, yet," he said. "She doesn't wish you hurt."

"If she wants me out of Suevia, then this is where I need to be."

Anders feinted into Laurent's simplest line of attack and dropped under it. Caught the old soldier's thrusting knife arm and shoved it upward. Pain stabbed Anders, shooting up his arm to the hand gripping Laurent's wrist. His knuckles twisted deeper into the pressure point in Anders' side.

Anders kneed him in the gut. Twisted the knife from his hand, feeling a bone crack in the doing — but the old soldier punched him hard in the ear. The room spun. A clatter when the knife fell. Anticipation pinged, speed took hold; caught the next blow on his arm; grabbed, twisted; braced feet for strength; Laurent's head hit the wall and punched through the mud plaster and lathe. Blood sprayed when Anders yanked him out, threw him across the room to fall in a heap.

The dagger lay on the floor. Anders snatched it up and pounced on Laurent as he staggered to his feet. Pulled him up by his white-and-purple silk robe. He snarled through the blood and lunged. Anders jerked back and the punch missed his eye by a hair's breadth. The dagger's crossguard slammed against Laurent's ribs and Anders twisted the blade before tearing out. Shoved him away.

Blood gushed as he hit the wall, slid down. Laurent gasped for breath, hand against the wound. It frothed between his fingers. His tanned skin paled. Then his mouth twisted in a snarl again and he spit at Anders.

"Fuck you too," he shot back.

Outside, down the hall, a man shouted, "Shall I call the guards?"

Anders turned. In the doorway, half a dozen stunned faces. Strangers all but frozen in fear. The Suevi physician dropped onto the bed, staring and breathing hard in panic. He held up both trembling hands when Anders looked to him.

"I am the Empress' bound elect, on her business. This man had taken me prisoner. Where's Reowan?"

The man's voice shook as he raised an arm to point. "Thirty miles, by the post road. Mercy, please, I —"

"You've nothing to fear." Anders looked to the faces in the doorway. "Neither do you, so long as you let me go. Be on your way and say nothing."

Laurent gurgled out his last breath. One of the audience clapped his hand over his mouth and fled.

Anders knelt to wipe the dagger on Laurent's sleeve, then unbuckled his belt and took it with the dagger's sheath. In the saddlebags, he found a clean silk robe — white with a broad purple border, the colors of the Empress' servants. Short enough for riding. Anders pulled it on over his red woolen cote, buttoned the inside on the right shoulder, outside on the left, buckled the belt overtop and slid the dagger home in its sheath.

Those remaining in the doorway fell back when he strode out. A stairway at the end of the hall. He could hear horses outside. In the common room, a man looked up from sweeping and asked, "Is all well, upstairs? What was that ruckus?"

Anders spared him only a glance in passing. Through the kitchen, into the stables. The smell of hay and manure cleared his mind. Thirty miles to Reowan on the post road. It was still morning, by the light. How much time had he lost, since the barn?

It was the post road and he wore the Empress' colors. He could ride hard, change horses at each post, and get through Reowan's city gates on her authority.

Whatever Seraphine wanted him to miss —

When Seraphine extruded a cruel black talon from one finger and drew it across Kate's cheek, Kate flinched back, cried in surprise, and fell to her knees. It was the last thing Kiefan saw before Seraphine struck him unconscious.

He woke at dawn, drained of kir and chained spread-eagle to the prow of a riverboat. The weight of his armor dragged at his wrists and ankles despite the extra rope around his waist. He still had his Shepherd-moon tabard and crown-band, so all would know who he was.

He hung there with only the mist rising off the still water and the wading herons to look at and Suevi voices readying to cast off behind him. The boat cut away from the docks and followed the river southeasterly.

/ hungry? /

How he knew Seraphine from Woden — it was something in the tone. / thirsty /

Soon enough, Gregor came with a water skin and some soft rolls stuffed with cooked egg. His black eye and broken nose were swollen. "They let the rest of the Guard in," he murmured as Kiefan chewed. "Put them below-decks, in a cage. Slaves' pen. Garrick took command. Tel's with him."

He swallowed. "Kate?"

"Unchanged. They let me wash off that cut."

"Thank you." Kiefan looked down at the rippling, dark water. "Can you swim?"

"Fair enough."

"Better than me, then."

The rope bit into Kiefan's wrists and ankles, passing from ache into pain and then numbness as the day wore on. He murmured through his bond to Woden, plotting out possibilities. His saint meant to attack the fount at Reowan, Qadeem's aid or no. He wanted Kiefan's, though, and Kate's. Teleri, if it could be managed.

/ not beg? /

/ she will kill you / whatever I say / Woden answered.

Rafe had laid warm against Kiefan's shoulder, that night in Vorspitz. When he'd learned to change a diaper. Small and soft and full of possibilities.

He didn't bring Rafe up, though, only let the bond lapse shut after working over possible lines of attack. Whether Seraphine would keep him conscious or bind his mind like Kate, he didn't know. Likely if she meant to parade him about as a trophy, he'd be conscious. Likely, she meant to make playthings of the rest of his Guard in another arena somewhere.

That would force their hand, if Teleri had to defend herself...

A rustle of silk, behind him. "Kate's well enough," Seraphine told him. "Sits beside me quiet as mice under the canopy. She's a healer? Word was your one elect trained her."

"She's a physician, as he was," he said, throat dry and rasping. If she knew no more of Kate, he wouldn't tell.

"I've no need for more such. But there's ever use for healers. Would she see reason, or cling to her saint? If, say, I were persuaded to spare her."

Kiefan's throat tightened. Hope, and yet fear — what payment would this need? "What must I do?"

"There's little must. For I know Woden will not come for his blood's life. He will attack. He will expect your aid." Seraphine leaned over the side and Kiefan met her gaze. "You have a son with Kate."

He looked away, swallowed.

"Offered her son's life, would she see reason?"

Yes. Kiefan didn't doubt it. "Kate's reason is passed only by Saint Qadeem's. I must betray my saint?" He looked to Seraphine, saw it on her face.

"You must show me what their lives are worth to you," she answered. Then she left him.

They stopped at a river town for the night; the goodfolk turned out to see the captured, defeated enemy king who claimed right to the throne by the blood of Saint Seaxneat. He was dragged through the streets on a wooden frame to prove the Empress' power.

He spent the night unconscious again. The Empress, her trophies and her prisoners traveled on the next morning and reached Reowan's docks by noon.

Squads of the local garrison met them there to escort the remaining, kir-drained, King's Guard through the streets. Kiefan, bound and leashed again, stumbled after Seraphine with aching joints and a still-throbbing head. The blurry mass of cheering people waved hats and laughed when Kiefan fell and was dragged.

He could feel the kir, though. The fount. Like scenting baking bread from far away.

The procession stopped in a square before a wall and a set of gates and the crowd jostled so thick that Seraphine ordered them back. They receded, heads ducked low, and quieted too. Kiefan dropped to his knees, grateful for the moment's rest. Gregor brought the water skin and gave him a drink.

There was a courtyard beyond the gates, and a fine stone house. A single Elect crossed from the house's door to the gates at a trot, kir-cloak streaming, dropped to his knees before the Empress, and touched his forehead to the ground. When he sat up, Kiefan saw his face; like many Arceal men, his skin was tanned and his curls dark, but his profile was near as straight, from brow to nose to chin, as a hatchet blade.

"Bound for Castle Áering and we must leave one prize behind," Seraphine said. She passed Kate's kir-leash to the Elect, casting a stern look at Kiefan. "For surety of obedience."

No. Kiefan scrambled to his feet, the aches dropping from his mind.

"If the word is given, kill her. Else-wise only keep her."

The Elect bowed. When he straightened, he noticed the stray lock of hair that had worked free of Kate's braid and hung in her face; he combed it aside. And his brown fingers lingered on her cheek…

Kiefan took two steps, jaw clenched, but the warning tingle in Seraphine's bond stopped him.

She smirked and tugged on his leash. When he didn't move, Seraphine pulled him off his feet and dragged him. He scrambled to straighten up and keep his glare fixed on the Elect, across the square.

The last Kiefan saw, Kate meekly followed the stranger into the courtyard.

The haze lifted suddenly. I blinked, and the glint of light on steel caught my eye in the dimness.

A dagger lay hard against a man's neck, a scant foot in front of me. I'd never seen him before — Arceal in complexion, though with a stronger nose than most. Standing stiff, breathing with deliberate care, he clearly thought himself badly trapped. His kir-cloak offset the dimness. I was in a stable, somehow, my back against a stall's gate. The fist that held the knife, though, the arm — my heart was rising even before Anders twisted the man aside.

"Are you well?" he asked, voice low.

I wanted to hug him but his hands were full of the wary Elect. A glance down at my dress, my hands, and I found I wore a collar and leash of kir. A cut throbbed on my cheek. Once that was cut off and the wound healed, I felt well enough, so I nodded. "Where am I? Who is that?"

Anders switched to Arceal. "This is Reowan, and this is Titos, who I thought more honorable," he said, with a threatening shake. "If he hasn't betrayed us yet, I may spare his life."

Titos raised both hands. "I've said nothing to Musaad, yet. Need not." Native cadence, but with an accent I'd never heard before. My curiosity would have to wait, though. I was in Reowan, with an Arceal elect, and Anders had seen fit to... rescue me? He'd not hurt me. I'd been right about him.

"Why?" Anders demanded.

"For my saint is Melanthe, whoever the Empress does bind me to. I was lifted from a dock-snipe on her orders. Saved from that life."

I must've lost days, to be in Reowan. Last I knew, Anders... no, the pattern I'd seen was far too dense. A saint. The Empress, wearing his face. She must've bound my mind as Qadeem had done with Elect Liandro. Suspicion growing, I asked, "How am I here?"

Anders dropped the knife from Titos' throat and shoved him aside. Both hesitated, wary, but the elect took a step back. Hands still spread. "We've no quarrel if you tell Musaad nothing," Anders told him. "How is it Kate's here?"

"I know only to keep her or kill her if commanded," Titos said. "For the Empress gave her over to me, saying thus."

"I saw that much. Who else was with her?"

Titos wore a Suevi uniform tabard over a short Arceal robe, and a purple baldric. Sandals that laced up to his knees, rather than hose. More curious oddities. "Her other prisoner. A man like you, shaved up to the ridges. Wore a gold band. A small company of more under guard."

Kiefan, prisoner? "Where?" I asked.

"Bound for the castle?" Anders asked. Titos nodded to him.

"What castle?" Though I could guess; the castle around Reowan's fount. Why?

"Tell me no more of what you'll do," Titos said, taking another step back. "I've no quarrel with you."

At a nod from Anders, he left us. At the sunlit end of the stable's corridor, a broad-set man glanced up from splicing a rope when Titos passed. He glanced to Anders but paid us no mind.

"Horsfald is a friend," Anders said, of him. He returned to Alemmanic to go on. "I was just at Áering — they expect Seraphine with hostages but they're occupied with the harbor."

"The Caer fleet?"

"Someone's fleet. Horsfald always knows more, so I came here next. Saw you handed to Titos on a leash. Had my suspicions when you followed him in here meek and quiet, so..."

Mind-bound. Kiefan, captured. Here in Reowan. And Anders had somehow found me, freed me, or — was he? I plucked his kir, with a quick little hook that startled him, and called his pattern. It sounded a tangled, complex chord that lingered in my ears. Half his notes were the same fierce ones that all knights shared. The others strange, discordant. His pattern told me: elect. Strong and clear. Bound, at his left hand.

"It's you."

He snatched my hand, pulled me close, and kissed me, his tongue searching for mine. I hesitated, a heartbeat, and let him taste. "And it's you." Anders smiled as he said it — and he called my pattern, being no fool. It pulsed up, across my shoulders and arms, my bond —

Our breaths caught, at the same moment. Two bonds, one in each hand. My mouth fell open. "I have two —?"

"Don't." Anders clapped his hands over mine. "She must've bound you. Don't touch them. She snoops."

"She —?" The Empress had bound me?

Anders pinned me to his side, under his arm. "We'll get you free of her," he murmured. "Mind your thoughts. Keep the bond wrapped tight. She'll pry it open when she pleases, so give her no reason to."

And yet I must warn my saint, who could warn Teleri — where was she? What did she know? I put my hands to my face, pressing my eyes shut. Fighting to breathe evenly, to keep my panic from seeping through the bonds.

Anders' lips touched my forehead. "She doesn't know you're free, or that I am. If she has both you and Kiefan hostage, she's close to breaking Wodenberg."

My brain swirled with more questions but one thing stood clear: Kiefan. "We have Teleri, too," I whispered. "She took Qadeem's bond. Whatever chance we have, against the Empress, we need Kiefan to better it."

"He'll have a plan, at the least." Anders took my hand in his. "How fast can you run?"

CHAPTER 17

The guards at the gate fell back at the sight of the purple stripe on Anders' white robe — the Empress' colors. We charged through a gate, out onto a town square. I followed Anders; he turned down a broad avenue toward a tall, graceful castle. He outran me, too, even without his pony form.

I launched myself past him with kir, bounding down the street andscattering what little traffic there was. I didn't care. A cluster of guards stood at Áering's gate and saw me coming; they scrambled to make a wall of their shields, spears ready, shield charms knit out. The gates were still open behind them and inside I glimpsed heads turning. I landed before them, my own kir snapping down in a cloak.

"Stand down!" Anders yelled, skidding to a stop beside me.

"Elect?" The Suevi officer wavered. "But you —"

Kir arced from the distance to a spot behind him and a woman howled. "Wodenberg!"

A green blade cut through two men, dropping them. King's Guard tackled the rest from behind, bearing several down. Teleri snatched a sword from a sheath, tossed it to Sir Garrick. He stabbed the Suevi soldier he'd pinned and lunged to block one who'd drawn steel on a fellow Guard. I lashed at one about to swing and he fell. That Guardsman grabbed the sword from his hand.

The castle gates began to swing shut; two King's Guard turned and threw themselves against the doors. Teleri planted her feet and rammed it open with kir. I jumped the line of bleeding corpses and landed inside ahead of the knights.

Beyond, rather than a yard, the gate let directly into a great hall. Greater than any I'd seen. Skylights let in the sun. Balconies ran the length to either side, full of archers ready to loose on the floor. Huddled in the middle, made small by the space, the rest of the King's Guard. Hardly any.

At their center, Kiefan on his knees. The woman who held his head by one hand, her long black talons pricking trickles of blood from his scalp, one claw hovering in threat over his grey eye, could only be the Empress.

Rage and fear crashed together; fear won. I froze.

"Scatter!" Teleri shouted, beside me. The remaining King's Guard dove under the balconies.

With a snarl, Kiefan blurred from under her hand. I sketched half a shield charm, the beginnings of a kir-vine, and stringence stabbed through me. All vanished in a crackling flood of agony, behind my eyes.

Clarity washed through my right hand, Qadeem's, and kir with it. Not merely loose kir; it was a healing charm. On my knees, I blinked when the stringence lost its grip and saw a kir-ram throw Kiefan across the room, into the stone wall. He crumpled.

I lunged, lashing out a bladed kir-vine. It impaled Seraphine at the shoulder. She turned on me, eyes blazing, and my left arm went stiff in agony, racing into my chest — and met Qadeem's charm there. They smashed into each other over my heart.

The world tipped. Seraphine yanked me off my feet, by my kir-vine, and reeled me in. Fresh pain poured through my bond, up my arm.

/ together! /

I answered my saint with gritted teeth. The speed Blessing's pattern flashed through my memory and my own healing charm broke the stringence. Qadeem struck, a bright line of fire stringing from my right hand to the left and shooting out to Seraphine. My mind clear, I threw myself up from the floor, rage taking me. I saw her focus break for a heartbeat when Qadeem's attack howled up her bond. I threw a Shepherd's knife, its crescent slinging from my hand quicker than thought.

It passed clean through her, at the thighs. Seraphine's taloned hand landed on my right wrist and a starry blade flashed in her hand.

I screamed.

Worse than pain. She cut Qadeem's bond in a red flash. His stream of kir stopped dead. She yanked at my core reserve and I clutched it tight with a snarl. Her talons dug into my wrist, into my meridian. Her stringence jolted in from there and met my grip on my pattern. Washed over it, like water over a stone. I felt the pain sweep by but it couldn't touch me.

My anger knotted tighter. I clapped my hand over hers and twisted my kir, the full body-pattern flying through my memory Blessing into her —

Her dark eyes gleamed as she smiled. She let her pattern rise, in absorbing my kir, to show me. To blind me. Her body had no structure. Pattern so dense and saturated it was all but liquid. I stared into the sun, at her.

Despair stabbed me.

Shadows moved, closing around us, against the glare. She flashed out a sphere, heavy as iron, and I heard men scream. Felt kir spark against it, distantly.

/ surrender / live / she told me.

/ no! /

My teeth gritted. I hissed, demanding kir from her. It gushed into me, then hesitated as she snatched it back. I dug in my heels. Pulled harder, rage burning in my every whorl. Under the blinding mass, I glimpsed her meridians. A structure. I dragged harder and they slowly clarified. The kir twisted, bucked under our grip as she fought to make a charm of it. I unraveled it quick as I saw its pattern. My memory poured out its own patterns, counter-fighting to shape my deconstruction charm. Her talons sank clean through my arm, slick with blood. The agony only sharpened my mind.

Two of her fingers blossomed, slow as roses, revealing bone.

A kir-edged sword cut through the light of her, from shoulder to waist, through the faint line of her prime meridian. The charmed blade split her heart, and nearly stopped my own with the echo of the pain. Unleashed, my charm rammed into Seraphine and she unraveled. A brilliant star leaped free, up the blade to its new master.

Her blast struck like an avalanche. Blinding, burning white. My raised hand, into the fury, parted it to either side. I brimmed with kir.

I fell to my knees, gasping for breath, blinking to clear the spots. Dust fell around me.

The sword slipped from a slack hand — brown hair, a stranger's face, but it melted before my eyes. Returned to Anders. He toppled and I caught him with a vine. Pulled him to my bloodstained arms. He breathed, but stared unblinking.

I hadn't noticed that he hadn't followed me in. She'd have struck him down too if she'd known he was there.

Stone cracked and fell, pulling my head around. A portion of the archers' balcony collapsed. A few limp bodies fell with the rock and a few live men scrambled to safety. Around me, King's Guard lay dead, peppered with arrows. Some men were red-uniformed Suevi, with sword wounds. Blood smeared the walls, too, splattered impacts with crumpled bodies below.

Teleri surged up from under one balcony with a yell and lashed a bladed kir-vine across the opposite line of archers. Too stunned to duck, they fell dead.

"Wodenberg!" Kiefan's roar — my heart leaped — got a reply and he charged the closed double gates at the far end of the hall. A crack of light showed through them, bowed as they were by Seraphine's dying blast. Kir massed around him and punched the doors. Wood cracked, loud as thunder, and they wavered in their frame.

The beach and the fount were beyond. Kir roiled, out there, strong and angry. I tried to stand and agony shot through my back. My hand found an arrow. Two. A shout from the balcony, as new lines of archers notched shafts and drew. Teleri, falling back with a handful of surviving Guards, stopped behind me and spun up a broad shield. I did the same, covering the other side of the hall. The arrows struck and vibrated, feeling like needles in my hand.

"He lives?" She glanced down at Anders.

"Yes."

Behind us, wood cracked again and gave. The archers drew fresh arrows.

"They'll have charmed ones, to break a shield. Come." Teleri pulled up Anders by one arm, I took his other, and we hauled him toward the beach.

/ Qadeem! /

Our bond was cut, but I still tried. The silence was too much to bear.

Anders was near too much to carry, even once I'd mended my talon-torn arm and even with Teleri's help. Arrows thudded into our shields — Tel's was cut by a charmed one — and the Guardsmen shut the bent, weakened gates behind us. Kiefan helped wrestle the broken halves of the heavy crossbar into the iron hooks to hold it. Teleri spun out kir-ropes to further secure it.

Barely ten King's Guard survived. Garrick gave them orders. I didn't see Captain Aleks. They pressed against the inside walls, looking up. Archers on the battlements twenty feet above were firing out toward the water. Past the crackling guardian sphere and the two saints in the fount, bathed in its golden light. Beyond them the castle's arms, on either side of the sandy courtyard, reached down to the sea.

Anders found his feet, pulled himself up by my shoulders. I had to steady myself in the cool sand to help. The arrows in my back stabbed at me but I clamped off the bleeding. "Easy, easy," I said. He wobbled, still, in my arms. His mouth hung open, trying to make words. "I'm here. Are you…?"

I dared a peek inside his head, and had to squint. He'd harvested a thousand-year-old cambifax and brimmed with it all. But he didn't seem hurt.

"Musaad," he managed, voice thick. He waved an arm toward the saints in the fount.

Across the sand, the fount was a cloudy column of quartz. Green glow suffused up from the earth. The kir-rich water tumbled over its sides, twinkling, into a low pool around the base. A driftwood throne stood in the center, but there was plenty of room on either side for the two saints who lobbed balls of kir-fire out to sea. Flames dotted the water, out beyond the breakers. A twisted salt pine stood just outside the guardian sphere, a house built into its branches.

The guardian sphere saw me. It had four eye-spots, one for each of us.

"Is he hurt?" Kiefan swung past me, kir-covered sword at a high guard against arrows. But the archers above paid us no mind, yet.

"He harvested Seraphine," I said.

Kiefan threw a heartbeat's stare. "Not you?"

I shook my head.

Arrows hissed down from straight overhead. "Shields!" Kiefan yelled, spinning one for himself.

Anders lurched in my arms, meaning to do it too. Kir spun out on his left arm. "Up," I said, helping raise his arm.

"Got him." Garrick ducked under his other arm. He had an arrow in his thigh. "Get your shield up, knight!"

The order reached some corner of his mind; Anders straightened, eyes clearing a bit, and his arm shot up. The kir-shield was a match to his own. I let him go. Garrick half-dragged him to defend the remaining Guard. Something thudded against the barred gates and they rocked on their wounded hinges. The men threw their shoulders against it.

And kir came ashore. Kiefan, Teleri and I turned in unison, toward it.

The sea reared up and crashed against the tower that anchored one of Áering Castle's arms to the beach, washing men from its roof and pouring out the archery slits all the way to the sand. Green stars swirled with the water, spiraling down to a woman standing at the tower's base. Alit on her raised hand. From her side, three elect sprinted across the beach, their own cloaks unfurling in shields.

Beside me, Teleri's head rose another inch. Knowing them, perhaps; they wore long Caer mail tunics, plate greaves, spiky helms. Bright swords. The saint — Conbarre, dark-haired like her sister Sabh, with a broad stripe of white — held a golden sun in her hand. A tendril of the sea looped up, in a vine, to spin around it and shoot toward the guardian sphere.

One of the saints in the fount pointed. The sand erupted, glassy daggers spraying the three elect. Tearing through their shields. Kir lashed, met the seawater, and all burst into stars and salty rain.

"Kate, the sphere!"

Kiefan's shout knocked my wits loose. This was our chance. I took two steps across the sand and the arrows in my back stabbed again. With a snarl, I grabbed the shafts and thrust the steel heads out with my kir. I pinched off the bleeding and —

A heavy arm of the sea roared, braiding to a star-bright point as it swung around Saint Conbarre and struck the guardian sphere. Its webbed kir-lines flashed, fractured, and it sent back a white-hot bolt of kir-fire. Like thunder, the blast of steam threw me to the sand. I glimpsed Conbarre, hair a flying nimbus of fire, in the cloud. And saw her fall to her knees.

From the fount, one of the saints launched from the cylinder's edge, through the sphere, for the killing blow. A star-edged kir-sword sprouted from his fist.

Teleri flew past me with a howl. The three Caer elect braked hard, fell into a scramble backward from the unshattered sphere's edge. One was cut down in passing by the war-saint, her kir flashing out unnoticed. He arrowed for Conbarre.

He never saw Teleri coming. Her kir-vine rammed through his spine, then her sword fell on his neck.

She never saw the four kir-edged glass claws that burst from the sand and ripped clean through her — the motion echoing the sweep of the remaining saint's hand. Her pieces burst loose across the sand.

I put up my arm against the double blast of unleashed kir. Grabbed what I could of the loose stuff as I gained my feet again. I had to reach the sphere. Shepherd, give Tel a place of honor; I hardly had time to ask it, but I did.

The sphere crackled, the knot of kir it offered me whirling with power. It held my eyes, called me. Touch it. Grounding charm first. The line spun out from my palm, coiled over my forearm, dropped from my elbow, trailed across on the sand. My memory brought Qadeem's advice to me in his calm, steady voice. It had to contend with my racing heart, though, and the massive, deadly knot hanging before me. I'd seen the power of it through touching Qadeem. I knew what it could do to me.

My hand trembled as I reached. Beyond the knot, the saint in the fount swung around, his eyes blazing green. His skin was as brown as my saint's, his short hair midnight black, and I matched name to face; Musaad of Rasila, as Qadeem was.

I met his burning gaze and put my hand to the sphere.

White-hot fire flowed over my skin, spiraling along the grounding charm, burning it. I let my kir flow to maintain the line. Beside me, the ground trembled and the corner of my eye caught a glassy flash — and a steel one as Kiefan defended me. Focus. I had kir and the grounding charm was a little thing. My Blessing kept pace, pouring out the pattern over and over. More kir than I'd ever dreamed of streamed over my arm, the heat dragging its teeth across my skin. Kir lashed, loose sand sprayed over me, and Kiefan snarled something I couldn't hear over my own focus.

I was Qadeem's disciple and held to a higher standard.

Reowan's massive fount drained.

Through the sphere, I felt shivers. Blows. It truly was a sphere, despite that I only saw the part above ground. It guarded the fount from below as well. And saints beat against it, there at the junction of three ley lines.

I could feel them, a tiny part of my mind realized. That must wait, though.

My skin turned red, under the blazing kir-fire. Somewhere beyond, Saint Musaad thrust his arm at me and Kiefan's charmed sword broke my line of sight. I shut my eyes as sparks erupted.

Trusted him to protect me.

Spinning, spinning, and even a small charm nibbled its way through my store of kir. The sphere dimmed in a patch under my hand as the one at Temitte had, but —

Through the sphere, an echo of a thought reached my hand and shot up my meridian to my heart. I knew Qadeem's pride, even so faint. Then, an urgent request.

/ pull kir /

I set my teeth and pulled. Kir surged across the guardian's surface to my hand. The fire surged over my arm, cutting a black line, and I clung to my focus, to my charm. A scream took some of my pain with it. There'd be more, I knew. I was nearly out of kir and then the fire would take me.

The sphere's spiderweb of kir flickered, fading. Weak. I gritted my teeth against the hot agony eating into my arm and held my pattern firm. Qadeem was here with me, as he'd promised.

Something massive punched through, below, and shot up through the fount. My last scrap of kir spun into a grounding line and I yanked my hand from the sphere. My skin caught fire to the elbow. Kiefan's hand clapped down on mine, snuffing the flames. A second pair of hands caught me as my knees wobbled. I fell against Anders' chest.

We all saw the fount erupt in stars below Saint Musaad. A green blade rammed up, in his waist and out his back between the shoulders. A thick hand thrust from the water, catching the kir-star that broke free. Musaad's shockwave struck the dissolving sphere from the inside, lit its fractured web in a blaze.

I put my hand up to catch some and barely recognized my own flesh. Raw meat showed in a jagged, spiral stripe, and blisters dotted the rest. Kiefan pulled my hand down before I touched the sphere. Kir rose to his palm. I took it and steadied. Stood free of Anders, though the pain still gnawed at me.

Saint Woden stepped onto the rim of the quartz cylinder, wrapped in kir. The fount thrust a heavy coil into his chest; he called, and other bonds shimmered to light, leading off to all the saints it fed. Woden spun out a sword and sliced them off.

The sphere flickered and dropped at his command. I felt a moment's echo of fighting, still, below, and worried. Kiefan crossed the last few yards of sand at a run, hand raised. Woden dropped down to the shallow pool and clasped his hand, thumped his shoulder, grinning in victory.

"Your arm —" Anders shifted to see my wounds, putting out his hand. "I have a little left —"

"Rogue! And traitor!"

My eyes snapped up. Woden's snarl vanished behind a green cloud of kir, knotting into a fist as it shot toward us. Anders' sword swooped up, slicing through the charm. I stumbled, pushed aside as he spun up a shield and raised it.

Lightning struck it, tore through into his arm. Threw Anders across the sand. I flung myself between them, right hand up, and the second bolt struck me, raced down my grounding charm along the burned spiral and fell to the earth.

No. He wouldn't hurt Anders.

Woden cleared the pool and dropped to a crouch, on the sand, slung out his arm — Kiefan's kir-vine snared his wrist, jerked, ruined the aim of his Shepherd's knife. It flew awry, up through the castle. Woden snapped around in a blur and stars burst out once, twice, from breaking charms. Kiefan dropped to the sand with a ragged cry. He thrashed, from the waist up, in the grip of stringence.

Rage surged in my blood. Blessing-quick, Woden launched across the sand at me, at Anders behind me. I had a little buckler spun up, in my hand. His thick kir-vine looped out to swat me aside.

No. Every fiber of me hated, in that heartbeat.

My Blessing spun out the patterns strong and hard, unraveling his kir-vine before it struck, the fist behind it, every muscle and tendon of his arm — and he fought it, yes, he had an iron grip his pattern. My charm burrowed into his shoulder, though, and just brushed the heavy coil of the fount's binding.

Its structure flashed in answer to my pull. The binding spun loose, the coil ripped from Woden's chest and shot to my hand.

Like a bolt of lightning, one that turned under my hand and slammed back into Woden. Chewed through his chest, blossomed out every spindle of muscle, unwound the ligaments from his bones. His ribcage burst open, scattering organs.

And I saw grim pride in his smile, a thin moment before his face peeled away.

My harvest flew to my wounded hand, crackled up my arm to spiral around the inner curve of my skull. My Blessing soaked it up, letting no scrap escape. The shockwave flashed past me, a moment's thunder.

I clenched my fingers and the scattered pieces of Woden stilled in the air. Even the blood, in its millions of droplets. It wanted to turn to dust, I could feel the pressure of it on my mind. His pattern was evaporating with the unleashed kir and even my will could not stop it.

But I took one last look at Saint Woden.

And I let him go.

The fount's snake of kir sidled up my arm, like some pet, and I gave it a nod. It struck, a hot iron through my chest, but kir flushed into me and the pain vanished. All my pains vanished. In an eyeblink, I knew why the fledgling Saint Wolfgang had turned on Woden.

My life to that moment had been a dream. I was awake now. I'd rather die than fall asleep again.

The entirety of the Reowan fount snapped clear in my mind: the column, the node below, the sphere, the fighting at the ley-crossroads. Two beings, evenly matched.

/ protect / us /

The sphere crackled back to life at my command, kir shooting through its web. I'd drained the fount but it was regaining its strength quickly.

I heard screaming. Kiefan clawed at the sand, his voice trailing off ragged. He gasped for breath. He'd felt Woden's death through his bond; that was a pang through my heart. Kiefan pulled himself up on his hands and retched. Trembled from the effort of it.

I pulled kir and reached for him. My vine coiled around him, lifted him — gave him a moment's panic, but he saw it was me. With my other hand, I scooped up Anders. After the lightning strike and harvesting Seraphine, he was too wobbly to stand. A mown-grass scent and a whiff of smoke clung to him.

One to each side of me. My fount arced to me and I combed through Kiefan's pattern. Mended the severed meridian low in his back; he crawled up to his knees, clinging to my thigh. Tangled whorls tumbled free, easing his pain. Through my other hand, I soothed Anders' jangled pattern as much as I could. Seraphine still roiled in him, much for an elect to bear. He twitched, regaining some of his focus, and looked up from leaning against my hip.

Still elect. Both of them. And kir was gathering again, out in the sea.

"Kate." Kiefan raised his arm, cutting his meridian open with a kir-blade in his right hand. He looked up at me, longing.

My elect. I took my hands off them to open both my meridians. Kiefan took my left without hesitation. I offered the other to Anders, my mouth pressing into a line. He considered my right arm — it bore a red, spiral scar, frond-armed like the lightning that had cut it — took a slow breath, looked up at me as well. Did I dare ask? The rightness of what Qadeem had said struck me hard in that moment.

"I won't force the bond," I whispered. It must be made in trust.

Anders sliced a blade along his arm and gripped mine. The joining shuddered through both my arms under their strong hands. Their sleek muscle under my palms, pulses throbbing. But kir grew stronger, in the sea; no time to savor this.

"Caercoed's coming," I said.

CHAPTER 18

I had only a few heartbeats to take in our battlefield. The dead Caer elect and Teleri's bloody pieces lay on the beach. On the battlements of Áering Castle, the archers only peeked from behind the merlons. At the barricaded gate, the doors still stood, and our ten King's Guard still clustered under a few scavenged, upraised shields. Stunned by what they'd seen.

Kiefan lunged to his feet. "Rations, for them?" he asked me sidelong, and then he raised his sword. "Wodenberg!"

That broke their daze. Lieutenant Garrick in the lead, they surged up with an answering yell.

Woden being dead, none of them were bound. I wasn't entirely sure how it was done, in truth. For the moment, I spun up a sheaf of Fijolais' threaded kir-needles and tossed them out. With a little guidance, I pricked each of the Guardsmen and flushed out kir along the threads. They cheered louder, invigorated, and formed up under Kiefan's orders.

Beside me, kir swirled and I turned in time to see Anders' pale hair turn to a silver-grey mane. Nipper's head dipped to meet my gaze, ears pinned back, and Anders shifted on his feet to kick off his boots. Hooves, not feet, I saw, and his legs had changed angles, shortened, gained Nipper's heavy muscle. All of him had compacted, strengthened, in shifting to this unsettling horse-minotaur. He snorted, softer than I'd expect, caught my hand and squeezed it.

Still him, yes. He threw out a slim kir-vine and snatched up Teleri's fallen sword and shield.

Beyond the corpses, one of the Caer longboats swung broadside in the water. It had to be fifty yards out, yet, but its crew shipped the oars and snatched up their shields from the sideboards. Thirty of them climbed right over the side in full knightly gear.

And stood on the water, where it had gone still.

Once I saw that, I could trace out the path through the waves; water gone stiff with kir. Conbarre's two Elect climbed up onto the walkway, out of the sea but yet perfectly dry. Kir-cloaks trailed behind them as they stood.

The Caer charged the beach with a shout.

Kiefan and Anders exchanged a glance, a nod, and stood shoulder to shoulder a few yards before me. Brothers again.

I coiled kir in my hands but an instinct told me to wait. Something just below words. My head cocked, questioning it even as it noted that I was not in danger. Anticipation, my Blessing informed me by bringing up snippets of Woden's charms. It crackled as I looked across the formation of King's Guard, noting what they were likely to do — none of it a danger to me.

This was what Gregor had had such trouble focusing through? Small wonder.

Below the fount, I felt a strike against my guardian sphere, and its return blow. A second presence roiled through the kir, tangling with the first. Qadeem and Saint Sabh. I couldn't spare them more than a thought.

My elect blurred to Blessing speed, meeting Conbarre's elect. My knights strode to meet hers, their shields lapped in an orderly wall against the passionate Caer charge.

Behind them, Conbarre rose from the sea. Through a corridor in the fight, I saw her and the wave that rose with her. It swept over the black stone beach, loomed dark and taller than a man — and the speed came easy to me now, as did a full Shepherd's blade wide as the courtyard. It slung from me, left to right, slashing over my men to cut the wave's cresting head off. Kir unraveled with a flash. Water crashed down, still knocking knights off their feet.

Anticipation warned and it was right. I was ready.

Half the water bounced, coiled as it rose up again and braided itself down to a spark-shedding point. It swung over men's heads toward me. Like Gauvail's punch-blade. My kir met it and the sea-spike blossomed into a glassy flower as it unraveled. Harmless.

My speed flowed, under Woden's well-used charm; shot a dozen needles back, punching through the falling water; staggered them to dodge what defenses she had; a thicker vine in a perfect spear's arc, its knife-head plunging down at her.

She didn't have speed. Couldn't block it all. Six kir-arms sprang to defend her, knocking the needles away, but my spear crashed against her shielded skin. I felt the charm break against it; in that slender moment, I unleashed the lightning. It roiled along the breaking vine, jumping from the ragged whorls to her with a sizzle. Thunder cracked.

I felt the shock flash out across the wet sand, hitting the Caer from behind. And my men. Even the elect stumbled — and blood spurted where Anders' sword got under one's guard.

Steam rose from Conbarre and she pulled a thick arc of kir from her faraway founts, but she stood. Breathing hard. Behind her, a second longship bumped against the sea-path and knights began scrambling over the side. Her one remaining elect fell back, at guard, and Kiefan and Anders let her. The remaining knights of the first party joined them.

Kiefan was bleeding. A few of the King's Guard were down. I gave them all the kir they could hold, pulled more for myself too.

My guardian sphere struck, below the fount, and one entity fell away. The other skimmed close, setting the surface to tingling, and I felt —

/ ? /

— along with a faint impression of standing in the glowing Pool, clasping Qadeem's hand for our own binding.

He wasn't sure it was me. I sent back a nod. And a brief image of Conbarre, her reinforcements coming up behind her. I needed to break that sea-path.

Qadeem dared skim closer to the sphere's surface, to send his question. My guardian spat sparks, wanting to strike but I stayed its hand.

/ safe passage? / no challenge / on my honor / our trust /

My gut snarled at the thought. A saint, here? He'd try to steal my fount.

I knew his honor, though. I trusted him. And I needed help. Fatigue was taking its toll despite the rush of battle.

Conbarre had thirty fresh, blessed-level knights now. The sea coiled, behind her. I couldn't see its pattern through the wall-sized shield her elect held before them all, but I twisted together a handful of little Shepherd blades. Those were easy to make. I touched my guardian sphere.

/ allow this one /

Anticipation hinted at the weakest targets in the line of knights. I struck first, and hard; the dozen little blades fanned from my hand; weaving on threads of kir at my command. The first burst in cutting the shield, and the rest found targets. Cut through shields. The elect, to her credit, swept down a hand of them. A few found unprotected flesh and flew through meridians.

The survivors charged and the sea sprang over their heads to strike first.

I threw out a kir-ram to counter-strike.

At the corner of my eye, a familiar form leaped up, perched on the fount's high rim. Three stars of kir-fire hissed through the air from his hand. My ram struck first, the weight of the sea throwing me back off my feet. Qadeem's stars plunged down on Conbarre, so sudden that she froze in a moment's terror. Her elect leaped into the path, slashing the first star and taking the spray of kir-fire it released. Conbarre lashed across the other two stars, but they dodged, shot in — struck the column of water that sprang up around her. Exploded in steam and stars, dangerous but not fatal.

The water seized the smoldering Caer elect and the mass threw itself into the sea. Conbarre's knights felt her retreat and fell back, drawing into a clump.

"Hold!" My voice carried on kir. My remaining King's Guard obeyed.

I spun up a mass of kir and lashed it out. The Caer cringed, thinking I'd kill them, but I reached past and struck the sea-path. It shattered. The two longboats still circled but the rocky shore might hold them off.

"Wodenberg will give quarter," I told the Caer, in Arceal, hoping some of them understood.

Qadeem repeated it for me in their tongue as he crossed the sand, passing through my guardian sphere unharmed. The knights hesitated, considered their options, and laid their shields down. Then their swords.

Weariness landed on my shoulders. I took a deep breath and straightened them, though. I looked across the sea and saw all the plumes of fire and smoke where Caer longships burned. Musaad had been holding their fleet off. The afternoon was growing old and the castle's shadow reached out past the beach into the water. The fount twinkled, tempting me with rest.

Kiefan and Anders shifted to my side as Qadeem approached, their swords at low guard but wary. My anticipation saw no danger; I reached to them, on either side.

/ peace /

Their hands found mine. Kiefan dropped to one knee, wincing at the wound in his shoulder. Anders did the same, puffing hard breaths through his horse-nostrils.

Qadeem stopped a few yards off, crossed his arms, and nodded to my boys. "Well met, Elect. And I am — so very pleased to finally meet you, Saint Kate." A smile worked its way out, bright and infectious. "Saint Kate of Reowan. Welcome to the great game."

I told my Guard, "Bring me the wounded. All of them, whatever their allegiance."

Qadeem, true to his word, did not touch my fount. He drew his own kir and helped me mend the wounded. The gash in Kiefan's shoulder. Lieutenant Garrick had an arrow skewered through his thigh. One of the older Guard had caught a bad jolt from my lightning and his heart stumbled along just off its proper rhythm.

Kiefan led the opening of the gate and the killing hall was searched for survivors. They dragged a few men to me on cloaks, weak from blood loss, barely breathing — Suevi, but I was quick to put my hands on them.

"Kate!"

Kiefan's shout brought me running. He pulled a dead Suevi up and tossed him aside, crouching down beside the man who'd been pinned underneath to lift him by the shoulders.

Boy. Or man, I corrected as I dropped to my knees; it was Gregor. Deathly pale from blood loss. His heart barely shivered in his chest when I called his pattern. His lungs were tainted with blood from two arrow wounds. A third jutted from his hip. At such close range, in that hall, mail couldn't stop the shafts.

I forced them all out, with kir, heaved the blood through his mouth in a stream, and spun him a fresh supply. His color warmed. He breathed easy as the holes knit shut. Then his eyes flicked open.

"My sword's…" His hand groped weakly, searching. "Where?"

Kiefan glanced behind himself at the dead Suevi, who'd been run clean through. "Stuck," he told Gregor, "but you'll get it back. Easy, now."

"No, I…"

I touched him again and Gregor slipped into sleep. He needed it and I had other wounded to see to.

Captain-general Felstrang of Áering Castle needed some assurances before he and his officers would venture onto the courtyard's sand before the fount. What he'd seen me do to Woden, and to fight off Conbarre, had given him things to fear. I let Kiefan speak for me in that and stood two steps behind him with Anders at my side. He'd shifted back to fully human and taken off the Empress' striped robe; he wore plain woolens and had taken Teleri's belt and sheath for her sword.

Felstrang was an old enough man, silver-haired and leather-skinned, to have been a child when Suevia first suffered under Arcea's conquest. He was also old enough that Kiefan's grey eyes, that proof of Saint Seaxneat's blood, carried some weight. Once he'd laid his sword and the castle's standard at my feet, he signaled for one of the officers at the back to come forward.

I knew him immediately: Titos. Anders' hand went to his sword, beside me. Kiefan, catching his suspicion, shifted on his feet. They both had clear lines of attack, Woden's anticipation charm told me.

The elect knelt gracefully, touching his head to the sand before me. "Elect Titos, once bound of Melanthe," he said, looking up.

"Bound to Saint Musaad," Anders corrected. "But you didn't come to his defense."

Anger sparked in Elect Titos' dark eyes. "For I had no care to. I felt the Empress' passing through Musaad and refused to aid him. For I have no quarrel with Wodenberg. I shall not beg, Saint Kate. Do what you must."

Perhaps I ought to kill this elect or tangle up his mind and use him as a bargaining chit, for I wouldn't force a bond on him. His loyalties didn't lie with my enemy, though. By his name and his saint's, he wasn't Arceal.

Qadeem, knowing my question, leaned close to my ear. "He's Ellerene. A proud people, one of Arcea's first conquests."

I had seen the name on a map; Elleras wasn't far south of Suevia. "Give this man a horse," I said, breaking my silence. "Give him a few days' food. Ride now and do not stop. Tell your saint that the Empress is dead by our hands, and you were spared because we have no quarrel with your people."

He touched his head to the sand again and went.

After that, there was the matter of the governor to see to, of the Voice of the Empress, of the rest of the city's garrison — I left Kiefan to that with Captain Felstrang's aid. The castle's housemistress brought out a quick meal and the King's Guard devoured it all while on their feet. Though they had to be exhausted, Lieutenant Garrick declined to leave when I brought it up.

The housemistress also offered to tidy up the house in the old salt pine. I had to lift the woman up to the flat roof; no steps, no doors, no entry for any but an elect or saint.

Qadeem and Kiefan were deep in conversation with Felstrang and his officers when I glanced at them. I didn't ask Anders if he was tired, I only hoisted him up to the roof with me. It was flat and high, hedged on three sides by the pine's highest branches. The rolling sea lay dark, rimmed by fading red at the horizon. A few columns of smoke from burning Caer ships still marred the shining waves.

"It must be beautiful at dawn," I said.

Anders nodded. "This was her — nest," he said, with a glance at me. "Seraphine's."

"And she's gone." I slipped my hand into his. He squeezed it and led me down the stairs.

The color struck me first. In truth, the furnishings were simple, graceful, but every fabric was silk or velvet and dyed rich, expensive purple. Or blue. Snow-white was only an accent, an edging the cushions or hanging in heavy fringe from the bed-curtains. Perhaps it was a small nest for an Empress, but there was a coziness to it. And privacy.

Anders looked in each of the rooms — a sitting room, a washroom, a bedroom — but said little. He did introduce the housemistress, when we found her in the last, finest bedroom. "This is Blythe. She waited on the Empress."

The housemistress was a woman of middle age. Her cheeks flushed pink as she bowed to me, then Anders. I let her finish tidying the Empress' bed and went to the window to open the shutters. I could hear the waves sighing and sure enough the window looked onto the beach through a bristly screen of pine needles. Closing the window, I checked in the nearby wardrobe. It was empty and so was the trunk.

"Seraphine sent her household south a few days past, m'lady," Blythe told me as she smoothed the embroidered purple coverlet. Her Arceal was quite good. "Thus, all's empty."

My eyes passed over a silver mirror as I turned; I didn't look any different, for being a saint now. Blythe and I were alone in the room. "Anders?" I leaned to look out the door for him.

Blythe gestured toward the far end. "His room was under the stair."

"His?" There'd been a door there, but he hadn't checked that room.

She hesitated, turning cautious. "Yes, m'lady."

I found him there, wanting to ask why he hadn't said this had been his prison. But Anders lay atop the blankets of the bed, his boots still on, sound asleep. It was a small room; it pretended to be humble but the thick carpet hushed my feet and the mattress, when I sat beside him, was stuffed with feathers. I combed my fingers through his flaxen knight's crest, tracing over the lumpy ridge of his Blessing, my heart aching at the sight of him.

Above, I heard light feet on the roof. I called kir and knew it was Qadeem. Leaning, I touched a kiss to Anders' cheek and left him to sleep.

"You knew?" I asked, joining Qadeem on the seaward side. The near-full Shepherd peeked over the horizon, fat and golden. A cool, salty breeze blew off the restless water.

"Nothing is certain," he said. "You had the sounding to ascend but so much can go awry."

"As with Prince Wolfgang?"

Qadeem's brows rose as he glanced at me. He clasped his hands behind his back. "Mechdan did write that down, then?" When I nodded, he said, "It troubled him. Deeply. As it should."

"And he knew, too," I said as I thought it. Sadness touched me, in thinking of my teacher.

"Yes. He was determined to protect you so much as he could but to let your will blossom through adversity."

That put a new light on my stint in the hospital. But I had to return to the story of Wolfgang. "Woden murdered his own kin — and yet you trusted him?"

"To put a blade to my throat if I were ever weak. And to keep his word so long as I wasn't." Qadeem looked out across the sea again. "It was Aleksandr who held us together. Lacking him, with the three of you in the city —" Qadeem shook his head. "One of us was sure to be the last saint of Wodenberg. I wasn't entirely certain it would be me, even with you for an elect."

I folded my arms, tucked my hands in my armpits where the chilly breeze couldn't reach them. My skirts rippled against my legs. "Might Kiefan and Anders ascend, too?"

"No. If such a crucible as this couldn't make saints of them, they won't. Fine, strong elect to have." Qadeem turned his head to see my reaction when he added, "So long as they don't turn on each other."

I had Kiefan's word on that and Anders had said he'd never wanted a fight from him. The memory of their blood still twisted my gut. "Do you have advice, for that?"

Qadeem didn't answer quickly. I looked when the silence grew long and watched him stare at the sea. He turned to me, stepped closer, and dropped his voice low. Most tellingly, he switched to Englic. "I know you trust me. I trust you, by being here alone. But trust between saints is a far trickier thing than between a student and a teacher. We both have much to gain in being allies — we also still have much to learn of each other. Of trusting. In truth, I've told you little of myself. Strong as you are, you are still very young and giving me the teacher's role may well turn against us both."

That gave me much to wrestle with. I'd thought we were allies, true enough, and it had been easy enough to brush off the misgivings of letting him into my fount.

"You think yourself a saint of Wodenberg," he said. "You aren't, in truth."

Hearing it said sent a pang through my heart. I nodded. "In all of this, I wanted only to protect it. My home." I was the saint of Reowan, now. A sudden fear stabbed me. "You wouldn't deny me — Rafe —?"

"I'm wise enough to never stand between a mother and her child." Even the barest hint of a smile was a relief. "There's much you don't know of the saints of Wodenberg. All saints have their duties and we three were rather fools for duty. The daily rations. The Blessings. No other kingdom does such and I've learned why — it was much for three to shoulder. Before you wish to be a saint of Wodenberg, think of those you are saint of already." I looked to Áering Castle's towers, when he nodded toward them. "Half of Suevia, or more. A larger, richer land than little Wodenberg. What will you offer your people in exchange for their love and loyalty?"

Soldiers stood in the towers, walked along the battlements at a slow watch-man's pace. Suevi men. I barely spoke their language. Knew only a little of their ways. "They aren't my people."

"Not yet. You're Englic, you're from Wodenberg — but it's not so bad a fit, in truth. You do have their rightful king for an elect."

"He's king of Wodenberg, though."

A nod. "It's tricky. While I know the people of Wodenberg are fond of me, they will wish their king returned."

Fond of him, true, and that slid into place next to my fitness as Suevia's saint. Qadeem would ever be something of a stranger, in Wodenberg, with his brown skin and black hair. "We need to be allies," I said. "You need me, and Kiefan, and I need your advice."

Qadeem drew back, only an inch, but I felt a greater distance in his words. "Can I trust you not to bind my founts? Not to sever me from them?"

I turned to look at my own, glittering under the throne of Suevia as it trickled over the lip of the quartz cylinder. Deep within, green light glowed. Qadeem might step through my guardian and take ownership of it, himself, in a few heartbeats. Cut me from its warm touch. Leave me vulnerable.

As I looked at it, through my bond I felt a presence at the ley line junction below. A nudge against my sphere. My guardian knotted kir on its surface and spat it at the saint, warning him off.

"Do only saints travel through the lines?"

"Any others would be consumed," Qadeem said. "Ley lines run deep and long. Kate. You need more than my advice in this, but it's for you to realize what more. I don't doubt you'll suss it out for yourself. For now, I will give you my aid and you will owe me a debt. In time, we must speak of kings, and Wodenberg, and what I need. Do we agree on this?"

One of those things was in defending my fount, I knew already. That saint might've been Arceal, might've been Saint Sabh. The three lines made for too many possibilities. I was all but chained here, in truth, until I could be sure my fount was safe. Having broken through two guardian spheres, I wasn't so convinced it was. "We agree. May I ask for my first lesson?"

CHAPTER 19

/ ? /

I couldn't say for certain how I knew Anders from Kiefan, through the bonds. Something in the timbre of it.

I sat up in the fount; I'd been floating on my back, my mind creeping through the long tangle of Woden's battle charms. And his memories of learning them. I'd found my way back to his earliest one and the moment Woden had lashed out in hate at a man who'd started beating his mother in her own home. Which was a tiny, filthy hut even to my peasant eyes. Woden only remembered a vague stream of hate from the man's mouth, that Mama was a rancid old whore nobody would pay a fish head to fuck. The kir-whip he'd struck with was etched in his memory clear as day, though.

And his mother's terrified eyes when she saw what he'd done.

Woden hadn't lied about being poor and a whore's son.

I put my feet on the underwater steps that ringed the driftwood throne and climbed, trailing fount water. The moons lit the near face of the tree house, traced the twisted paths of the branches embracing it.

Anders was alone in there since Blythe had finished tidying and I'd hoisted her down. Likely, the mass of kir when Qadeem gathered and sent the daily rations had woken him.

/ here /

"Go," Qadeem said. He sat on the throne's steps, to one side. "Get some rest. You've done much today."

"Thank you," I murmured, and leaped to the roof on a boost of kir.

Kiefan was napping, in shifts with now-Captain Garrick, while keeping the governor's palace surrounded. Reowan's city guard, which was largely local men, had listened to Captain-general Felstrang and thrown in with us. The governor, the Voice, and half the garrison, all Arceal, were barricaded in the palace. Kiefan meant to give them until morning to weigh their options. Hoping they wouldn't note how strong their position truly was.

Especially if the other half of the garrison, outside the closed city gates, set their mind to rescuing them. But the situation looked to be holding until dawn.

/ here /

I sent Anders a hug as I padded down the stairs, dripping all the way. His sleepy surprise tickled back through the bond and then he returned the hug with an enthusiasm that made me smile.

/ can do that? / he asked.

/ yes / hug /

I stood in the door. His room had a westerly window and the shutters were closed, so there was little to see until my eyes acclimated. His kir was strong enough to find him, though. I took his hand and he shifted on the mattress. His arm wrapped around my waist and pulled me down, but I was sopping wet; he startled up, awake.

"What've —?" Anders breathed a laugh. "The fount?"

"Yes," I whispered, "it's very comfortable."

He pulled my wet dress up to get it off. "You're dripping everywhere. You'll get the bed wet."

"You've still got your boots on," I teased him back, reaching for his feet. "Did your mother let you wear boots to bed?"

My dress fell with a splat. Anders kicked off his boots — he'd never laced them, when he put them back on — and sat up. Found my mouth in the dark. My hands stilled on his woolen cote, too distracted by his tongue to pull it any higher.

/ missed you /

The raw ache in it pinched a whimper from me. My own longing washed back through the bond, along with my gratitude at being in his arms again. Anders hugged me tight, stroked my back, and slipped his hands over my wet shift.

"You'll catch cold," he whispered, tugging it up.

For revenge, I coaxed his cote off, too, but as I tossed it aside my joy sank into a muddle of worries. It was him, this time, and no doubting, but — Kiefan had given his word, but —

/ ? / Anders' cheek brushed alongside mine. His hands stroked over the curve of my hip.

/ he needed me /

My weary anguish went with it. It echoed back to me from Anders.

/ I needed too /

An impression of lust came, with a tangle of despair and fear, a sense of helplessness. Nothing he should ever have to feel; I kissed him again.

/ nothing / forget that /

/ nothing / forget yours /

He sent my thought back firm, with his hand on my cheek. I loved him for that. But there was more.

"He asked me to be his queen," I whispered. "After I heard you were her bound elect. When I didn't know if — or why — and he swore he'll do nothing to hurt you. Because he loves me. And now you're here, and well, and…"

That morning came back to me, unbidden, of Kiefan's fingers finding me slick and wanting, his mouth on mine as he stroked me to the verge of ecstasy. I pushed it away, but it clung.

Anders hushed me, likely feeling the struggle, perhaps more. "Do you love me?"

"Yes." I sent all my aching honesty with the word.

"You are his queen now. And mine. Our saint. What do you wish?"

I searched his eyes for a jest but saw none. "Peace. A family."

"And kisses?" At last, a smile. "Be his when he needs you. Be my wife, else-wise."

I breathed a laugh. "And forget the Mother's discipline?"

"It's twice the discipline, is it not?" He twitched one shoulder. "Next you speak to the Mother, ask her advice."

There was that. Some part of me had been waiting for the Mother and the Father to appear, to explain it all to me. Especially why they'd chosen me to guard their Flock. No sign of them yet. More danger that Kiefan and Anders would turn jealous, hate each other, and duel again.

"But if jealousy —"

"Do you love me?"

"Yes."

"Don't let me forget that." Anders lapsed back to his bond, rather than words. / all I need /

I kissed him. The need for air broke us apart eventually and then I really ought to get that wet shift off and it was silly to be sitting on top of the blankets when it was far warmer to be under them. Wrapped in him.

<hr>

Anders was an un-hurried lover and we were both tired — we dozed off and woke back to our play without truly noticing. The bond made a seamless shift of it, echoing warmth, longing, and then lust in a rising loop until we were grinding and moaning and clutching each other so tight that it skirted the edge of pain. My head spun so hard, at the climax, I grabbed the mattress to keep from falling off — impossible as that was. We collapsed and lay there panting.

/ very distracting /

I burst out laughing, a little hysterical, at Kiefan's dry comment. I managed to mash a sincere answer together.

/ so sorry / distracting? /

He sent me back a rumble to the effect of if I'd come over there, he'd demonstrate how distracting it was. I sighed a deep breath and sent him back a hug. A long one.

Anders rolled onto his back, beside me, and managed to chuckle as his breathing evened out. "I didn't know that would be so dangerous," he got out.

"Something to practice," I murmured. I groped for his arm and pulled it over me as I rolled onto my side. He obligingly cuddled up to my back with an agreeing purr.

Next I opened my eyes, a trace of morning light lightened the shadows. The feather bed and blankets, nicely warm, were tempting but I felt well rested. And —

A soft creak of floorboards pulled my gaze to Anders. He buckled on a belt, a sheathed dagger hanging at his side. Then he finger-combed his knight's crest back and tied it in a tail with a leather string. Ready to go, perhaps.

Save that he was naked.

/ ? /

Caught him, by the guilty look he cast me. I felt a muddle of things through his bond. "There's something I need to do."

I sat up, reaching for him. "And you thought to just leave? Like that?"

He took my hand but didn't come when I tugged. "It's no simple thing to explain."

So I went to him, naked as I was. "Try to."

"Seraphine... among her charms and the memories with them — or I think they're her memories... it's such a tangle..."

He didn't have a memory Blessing to help him, either. I traced my fingers along the downy fuzz below his ridges, calling his pattern. His mind still swirled, still a blizzard of whorls and sparks. No painful knots.

"The empire is tied to her throne." Anders' voice dropped to a murmur, as if someone might overhear. "Not to her face. I harvested her. I have — I'm her heir."

"No."

"I have to go." He whispered it, pushing my arms from him.

/ no! /

A flicker of Woden, of his stringence charm, crossed my mind and I snatched it back. I wouldn't hurt Anders. No. Even if it made him stay. Even if my heart burst of panic, which it was galloping toward.

/ will protect / all /

/ need you here! /

"I swear it, Kate," he said, dropping to his knees. Both my hands in his. "On all my love for you, for Rafe, I swear I can keep Arcea from our throats."

"By becoming the Emperor?"

His eyes met mine, steadfast. "No. If I leave now and reach Arcea before they put aside their differences, I can unravel it all. Seraphine bound her saints, bound the whole empire — I hardly have the words for it but I can see the whole knot. I know what to do. Do you trust me?"

He'd rescued me and killed his bound saint for me. The answer slipped through my bond without words. He blurred through my tears. My knuckles turned white, gripping his hands, but with a little ripple of kir they slipped from my grip. Anders strode from the room without a backward glance. Misery tore a bitter thought from me.

/ not afraid / my stringence? /

/ she taught me / worse things /

I heard his feet on the steps and trotted after him. "Anders." I climbed after him. "Anders. Only swear that you'll return. Please."

Kir rippled over him as I reached the roof. He faced the sunrise, his profile lengthening into a cruel beak. A dot of sky appeared through it: a vulture's deep nostril. His arms lengthened, his fingers fused and stretched. White quills sprouted, as they had on Saint Aleksandr, but when they unfurled the feathers were black. His shoulders vanished and his breastbone thrust out to anchor his wings' muscles.

He was only half a giddha-rukh, though. The feathers gave out across his chest, and though his legs were shorter, they and his feet were human still. Anders closed his eyes in focus and a small fan of quills rose at the base of his spine, unfurled into a little tail. He'd made his toys discreet, too. When his eyes opened, they were golden, set on a featherless head still topped by a flaxen ponytail. That made me smile, through my tears.

/ will return /

He couldn't speak in that form.

"You must. You need to teach Rafe to ride." I gave him all the kir he could hold.

Anders hugged me, fiercely tight, through the bond. Then he gathered his kir and rammed himself into the sky on it, less than elegant but he gained height with a few heavy strokes of his wings. The wind caught him, lifted him higher against the red-and-gold dawn, and he tilted toward the south.

That day was filled with the bloodshed of taking the governor's palace; they would not accept my authority, the kir-gifted among them would not be bound, and they would not surrender the palace.

I didn't wish to do it. The governor's wife and children, the servants, and a handful of slaves were inside and innocent of this. After Kiefan laid out the options, I had to agree that breaking down the main gate would be best. Not the stable gate, for that was narrow and worked to the defenders' advantage. With some kir strengthening my voice — to be certain those inside heard me — I gave my soldiers clear orders to spare anyone who laid down their weapons and surrendered.

One of Woden's massive kir-rams made firewood of the gate. I stood in the gutted frame with my arms folded, funneling kir to Kiefan and my new disciples among the Reowan city guard.

The Arceal resisters fell back into the palace but I didn't give them a chance to bar the doors. I'd seen enough by then; I draped my kir in a trailing cloak and walked up to the doors. The red-tabarded city guard on my side of the door-shoving contest felt me coming and scattered to either side. The doors slammed shut for an eye-blink and then I slammed them back open with a wedge of kir.

I walked into the palace's main hall, Kiefan a blurred swirl of steel around me. Dozens of lamellar-clad knights, with swords clenched in their fists and blood in their eyes, quailed and fell back. There was a dais at the far end and a grand, gilded chair on it.

One hand of men rallied and rushed at me, halfway down the hall. Two tripped over their own spilling guts when Kiefan swooped across their formation. The other three caught my kir-vine across their necks and collapsed in a rattle of steel. I snapped that kir back to my hand, spun it in a sphere, and poured more in until it ignited. Yellow light flooded the hall.

The dozen or so who'd drawn enough courage to yell and run a few steps all but fell over themselves in trying to scatter. They knew about force-spheres and there were stone walls all around them.

It wasn't one — though I'd harvested that charm from Woden — but no need for them to know.

I walked up to the governor's chair and swept it aside with that kir. Turning, I faced the hall. Kiefan stood on the dais' first step, his own kir-cloak glittering, bloodied blade at guard.

Swords began to fall to the floor.

After the soldiers surrendered and I'd seen to healing the wounded, I remained on the dais. The governor threw himself at my feet and claimed the resistance had all been the captain-general's doing. With far more composure, the former Voice of the Empress, deSvello Antonin, offered me his services as a negotiator.

For the time being, both could wait behind locked doors. There was much to do; Kiefan stayed by my side through it all, leaving the securing of the palace to Captain Garrick and the King's Guard. From this place, much of the governing of Suevia was done. There were guilds and courthouses and more, as well, and officials to oversee them all. I'd sent summons at dawn and some of them came to declare their loyalty.

It was nearly evening when Kiefan let on that I could do another saintly thing. Qadeem's question of what I'd do to earn Suevia's love had weighed on me and I'd found one answer. The sooner I could start, the better.

"If you give it until morning, we might find you something finer to wear," Kiefan murmured, gesturing at my simple, buttercup-yellow dress. "Look the part of a saint and queen."

I twisted my mouth to one side. "Better that Suevia love me as I am — a carpenter's daughter turned saint. You're their king, and welcome to it."

"I'm nothing without my saint," he answered, with quiet sincerity.

My teeth pressed on my lip for a moment. "Let me see the refugees." Taking a handful of my skirts, I stepped down from the dais. Kiefan dropped to one knee in obeisance, fist over his heart, followed by the sergeant Guardsman on my other side. A heartbeat later, everyone in the hall was on one knee as well.

Warmth crept into my cheeks but I kept my head high. I was a saint now. I put out my hand, at shoulder height, and Kiefan was quick to take it. "Herr Osric," I said as I walked, "if you would give me that translation?"

Herr Osric was a sympathizer to Kiefan's claim; Galan Heathugrim had mentioned him. Osric was a master architect and senior guild-member, a Blessed with a knack for wood-shaping and an excellent memory. He'd been taken as a tithe by Arcea, trained there for fifteen years, and been one of the few native Suevi to return home afterward. He'd asked me to cut his saint-bond take him as my own, so I had. And he'd been working on a translation of what I meant to say to my new people.

I wanted to ask Qadeem's advice on it but he guarded my fount. I'd felt a few nudges against my guardian sphere, through the day, and had to fight down the urge to fly back to the castle each time.

I stood before Reowan's city gates as they opened. Kiefan stood just behind my shoulder, naked sword in hand. Which piqued my memory. "That isn't your sword." Not Woden's moon-pommeled blade, given to the king of Wodenberg.

He shook his head. "It's back at the camp by Singréne."

Messengers had been sent but there'd be no word from there before morning. I hoped Duke Seagrace had survived.

Word had gotten over the wall, of the Empress' death, the Caer attack, and my claiming the fount. And of the governor's resistance. The other half of the garrison might yet try to attack but I meant to give them reason to leave peacefully — and take the governor and the surviving Arceal soldiers with them. Perhaps deSvello too; I had not decided.

Trumpets played a fanfare for me. I clenched my hands in fists.

/ strength / Kiefan sent to me, as Qadeem so often had. / together /

Outside, the end of the Southbound Road stood clear. Goodfolk packed it on either side, faces turned toward me and staring. They murmured as they took me in, plain yellow dress, hanging blond braid, kir-cloak and all. A knight and crowned king behind me, for an elect, and officers of the city guard further back.

Herr Osric had recited my speech and I gave it from memory. I told them the Empress Seraphine was dead, Saint Musaad was dead — and had to wait as cheers broke out in the crowd. Then I told them I was Saint Kate, lately of Wodenberg, who'd been only an elect but I'd ascended and claimed the fount. That I had two elect of my own, one of them the son of the Aethlings-dóhtor and rightful king of Suevia.

"You came here fleeing the army of Wodenberg," I said with my kir-strengthened voice. "I understand why — for I was born a carpenter's daughter and a peasant. But you have nothing to fear from Wodenberg's soldiers. Go home, see to your plowing and planting, return to your lives. If there is any more fighting, it will be because of Arceal soldiers. They are the enemy we both wish thrown out of Suevia."

The people cheered that, clapped. "The Empress is dead," I repeated. "There will be no more tithe taken from your children." The noise grew. "I wish to be your saint, Suevia, and I wish to heal what Arcea has done. Firstly, I'm told there's fever among you, out here."

Packed together, camping on the Spanne outside the city walls with little shelter, sickness had taken hold of these helpless goodfolk. The few physicians worked themselves to the point of dropping but the Shepherd had still claimed many. Especially children.

I put out my hands with a little kir in each. "Patience. I will see you all, one at a time. If not today, then tomorrow."

Kiefan wanted to follow me, I knew, but I told him to stay at the gate. I walked into the crowd, calling up their patterns as I went. There was no danger, only fevers and dysentery. A quick touch to a cheek, a pulse to cleanse their patterns, and they'd be well.

They wanted to press close; hands reached over the shoulders of those in the front line. I kept murmuring "Patience, patience," in Suevi, and made my way down the line. A baby nearly dead in her mother's arms took a moment longer. Her parents broke into tears when she woke, color flushed back to a healthy glow. The many voices became a gabble of begging and gratitude. They took up my name as a chant and melded it into a song very like the Sun-caller's Lament.

Tears streaked my face, too, but I kept touching, kept healing. I wouldn't look away from their suffering, as my teacher had said.

CHAPTER 20

A week passed. When I dropped into the chair opposite Kiefan, it knocked a weary sigh out of me. He chuckled into his cup, having just taken a sip.

"That is why you need a chamberlain, a steward, and a seneschal," he said. "Any business which they deem worthy of your time likely actually is."

I had questioned why so many officials were necessary. "All those, and my elect."

"Yes."

Our cups were filled with mead; Suevi beer was thin and mild, to my tastes. The berry-flavored mead was pleasant. We sat across a small table in the receiving-room of my comfortable suite in Castle Áering. The open windows looked down on my fount; its water twinkled in the castle's shadow as the evening faded. The sea murmured to itself as it ever did. Restless thing, always thinking aloud.

The quartz cylinder stood empty. I'd taken the driftwood throne off and moved it to the palace, where it had replaced the governor's chair. As the throne of Suevia, it no longer belonged to a saint. The carpenters' guild was building something for me to sit on in the fount for any state meetings I must suffer.

A ladder stood against the salt pine's tree-house. All of the purple, all of the Empress, was cleaned out of it now. That was being refurnished as well. For now, what little sleep I needed I took in this velvet-draped suite.

Kiefan spent his days in the palace commanding his new army of officials and magistrates. We saw each other often enough, but never like this. Never simply sitting together while Gregor and a page served us dinner.

"Seagrace has set up camp," Kiefan said. We spoke Alemannic for privacy. "He brought the full story from the burg-meister of Singréne; it seems the elect posted there merely vanished the night that Seraphine died. Likely called back by his saint."

Bowls of hot fish chowder and a loaf of soft oat bread were served. "I'm glad Seagrace is well, but abandoning such a city…"

"There are many saints in the empire, still. They'll each be snatching up what they can." Kiefan paused to try the soup. "Seagrace brought Aleks and the rest, too. So much as they could find." I felt gratitude through my bond.

Kiefan had said only that Captain Aleks and twenty Guardsmen were murdered in Singréne. I'd learned how through other sources and that the bodies were likely tossed onto a midden heap. I'd ordered them brought to Reowan for a proper burial in the newly rededicated Orderhaus.

"You've heard from Anders?" Kiefan asked.

I nodded. "He's well."

Anders always hugged me, through the bond, when he checked in. A bit of his longing seeped through, too. I missed him too.

/ you well? / I felt Kiefan touch me through my bond, like an uncertain hug. I blinked, cheeks flushing warm. Caught. Kiefan raised his brows a moment, to ask it again.

He'd been stealing what sleep he could in the Empress' suite, over in the palace. It had been quickly stripped of her, too, but he hardly minded the sparse decoration.

/ lonely / I sent back. Then I switched to words.

"There's been so much to see to. Dispersing the refugees. Summoning the old houses for their fealty. Talking of restoring the Order." Mother Love, Father Duty, and the Shepherd had been banished under Arcea. The Order had been subsumed into the Empire's bureaucracy. It might well return, if somewhat reshaped by Arcea's quirks — but I put that aside. / neglected you /

Kiefan looked down at his soup, twitched one shoulder. "I swore I would wait on your word," he murmured.

I sent him a warm hug, which brought out a bit of a smile. Then I asked him about the Tadhlon Guard; we had given them wood to burn their dead, especially Elect Teleri, seen that they were well provisioned, and released them from their orders to aid us. At last report they were near Dwyncraig Pass, which still stood open despite that the saints of Caercoed had ordered them closed.

What was happening, north of the passes, nobody was quite sure. The Caer war-fleet and Saint Conbarre had withdrawn to Arforddinas. The spring merchant ships, regular visitors here in Reowan, had not come yet.

There'd been one attack on my fount from the ley lines soon after my first day as saint of Suevia. Qadeem and I had turned it back. There'd been nothing further. He'd returned to Temitte and to Wodenberg to see to his own duties for a few days. That led to questions of what Wodenberg needed; a tricky thing, as it was for me to make peace with Wodenberg now, in truth. Yet my elect was its king.

Kiefan and I talked of such concerns as we ate. Spring greens followed the soup, along with herbed chicken in cream sauce. Then a bit of honeycake. The cook had learned of my weakness for it.

I sent a nuzzle through the bond, a memory of my cheek against Kiefan's. When I glanced up, I caught him blinking. Startled, perhaps. He sent back a bolder hug this time, something warm and soft that somehow reminded me of that after-Solstice morning I'd woken in his arms.

"Shall I bring more mead?" the pageboy asked softly as he collected our empty plates. "Tea?"

The pages were all shy around me, still, except for this bold one. I gave him a smile. "Neither. We're well enough."

Kiefan watched him go. "Once all's settled, there's knight training to see to," he said. "Even with Arcea's tithe abolished, even without Wodenberg's Blessings, we must still look for the gifted. Teach them."

I nodded; that was another tangled skein to be worked out. There'd be no Blessings in Suevia, not as we'd known them. Likely not in Wodenberg either, with only one saint remaining. I'd met a few of the physicians in Reowan —

Kiefan's desire brushed past my neck like lips with a hint of teeth. My breath caught, skin tingling. I imagined my hand sliding up his thigh, over fine wool and firm muscle, teasing... his smile twisted, eyes narrowing.

"I mean to see that physicians, especially, are well trained here," I said, standing from my chair. Playing at sticking to business. "There must be knights, of course, to defend the kingdom, but —"

His mouth cut me off, too hungry for playing. And he was right; solid in my arms, lifted on tiptoe by my butt, his tongue deep in my mouth — the feather bed was what we needed. Kiefan picked me up without breaking our kiss and knocked my bedroom door open with my feet in carrying me through. I pushed it shut behind us with a bit of kir.

The feather mattress caught us both with a sigh; pinned under him, I gripped handfuls of his white linen cote-sleeves. His sleek muscle moved under the fabric as he shifted to work my skirts up.

"Get this off," I whispered, when I could, and tugged on the linen. He sat up on his knees to shuck off his belt, then the sleeveless black cote over his linen one. I kicked my shoes off, my pulse throbbing in anticipation of...

Kiefan had felt it, that first morning with Anders. My hands slowed, bunching my linen skirts at my knees. Surely this would reach him. Surely he'd known it would happen, sometime.

/ distractions / careful / I sent. Kiefan untied my dress's laces at the neck and started to work them open. I put my hand on his to slow him and he stopped.

/ trouble? / he asked.

"Anders." His silence cooled me as it lengthened. Surely...

Anders answered, at last. Amusement trickled through his bond. / let it flow /

With a smile, I sent him a hug. When I opened my eyes, the smile fading, Kiefan waited on his knees beside me, half undressed. Our eyes met.

"I didn't wish to surprise him," I said, "as I surprised you, that morning."

Kiefan looked away, sitting back on his feet. I touched his hand on his thigh. He'd given a teasing answer, that morning when I apologized, and there was no lying through the bond. But.

"It did trouble you," I murmured. "Though you never said it." I had wondered but hadn't found the courage to ask.

He grimaced. "If your joy troubles me, then Mother Love ought to put me over her knee and beat my ass red."

"Don't." I didn't want any talk of beating, not there. My fingers curled around his hand; he squeezed back. I shifted up onto my knees, facing him. "I'm yours when you need me. I know you do. You've told me so many times. But you've never spoken of your own joy — and I've never..." That thought stopped me as it tumbled out of my mouth. Stung me. I eased the gold band off his head, tossed it off the side of the bed. Kiefan's eyes closed as I touched my forehead to his. Nothing between us. "Do you know how much I need you?"

Kiefan hugged me tight. His breath turned harsh. It took him a few moments to get his voice back. "My duty and my love," he whispered, "are one and the same. I couldn't ask for more."

Perfume from the towering, blossom-covered tree hung in the warm air. It stood before the Beauty Gate, its splayed pink-and-white flowers big as men's hands held out to welcome those select enough to pass the Blessed guardsmen.

A small woman, wrapped in a plain cloak, circled the grandfather magnolia and strode toward the gate with hardly a glance to the guards. The four of them tensed for a heartbeat, hands on the heavy swords at their sides. Their long, Arceal robes were white, the purple stripe a bright slash from left shoulder to ankle. Servants of the Empress. They knew her face and let her pass.

Anders kept his gaze set on the vast courtyard inside. Seraphine's black braid trailed behind him, heavy with the extra flesh he hid to match her height and size. He had the charm, from harvesting her, but not the control to do a perfect job of it. Naked, he'd fool nobody. But he could match her face, her hair, her height. Hide his hands inside the cloak and hope nobody looked too closely at the bosom.

This innermost sanctum of Arcea's imperial palace was no castle. Colonnades, rather than walls, flanked the Beauty Gate. Their polished, warm oak glowed in the sun. Clay tiles, on the narrow roof the columns held up, were painted gaudy red. The power here feared no attack.

As he crossed the first guardian sphere, inside the gate, Anders spun up an intricate key from kir in his hand. The sphere crackled around it, under his cloak, accepted the pattern and let him pass.

Those assembled in the sanctum courtyard felt the kir move and turned to look.

He kept his chin up, as she would, and walked to the fount. They were all here just as Seraphine's tally of bonds and debts listed. She'd had a memory-charm, something like Kate's Blessing, and so much had carved itself into his mind — but he was not insane and he was not Seraphine. Perhaps she'd been right about the strength of his core self; he'd harvested all she was and survived the strain of it.

He glanced from one particular saint to the other. Of the four arrayed around the fount, those were the keystones: Chale, father of monsters, and Dolorata, war-master of Arcea. Seraphine's right and left hands, and the two she'd known she must keep ahead of. They had their own lieutenant saints at hand and three elect apiece, all webbed in their loyalties to Chale or Dolorata. Who mistrusted each other.

Their eyes tracked him, knowing he was not Seraphine but her heir. This must be how a rabbit felt, walking a gauntlet of hungry wolves.

Anders reached the first of the three inner spheres. The great fount of Arcea was a flat pool, barely rippling where its spring fed the circular tub. A marble path led to the imperial throne in the center: a great, gilt thing of creamy marble carved into rukhs, lamia and dragons.

The sphere offered him a tiny eye-spot that would render him a greasy puddle if he failed. Anders slipped a pale hand from his cloak, brow furrowing as he twisted up the proper key-charm from Seraphine's memories. He held it to the sphere.

Its eye-spot unraveled and he stepped through. His braid just cleared the outer sphere as he met the second. It demanded a different key-charm, one that danced. Anders kept his breath steady, focusing as on the duel of his life.

Which he'd thought he had faced many years ago when his master demanded the chance to kill him for catching him abed with his wife. Anders had walked away from that duel bleeding but having earned his knighthood. Woden had bestowed it on the spot.

The third sphere was a subtle one. Anders touched the knot of kir it offered and knit it into shape, twisted and pushed it into the sphere's surface. He stepped through onto the marble dais. When he asked for kir, the fount gave it willingly, bond or no bond, for being so close by. Anders let his disguise fall as he turned toward the audience and swept the cloak wide to take his seat on Arcea's throne.

He wore only a white tabard under the cloak; he'd stolen both from the guardhouse at the outer gates of the imperial palace.

Chale watched with narrowed eyes. That one would miss nothing, not the hue of Anders' hair, not the Blessing ridges, not the double scar inside his right thigh if he caught a glimpse of it. Dolorata would know where Anders hailed from, too; there'd been Blessed knights captured, dragged to Arcea, interrogated by her and then… inspected by Chale. Seraphine had taken an interest in unlacing the charms embedded in their ridges as Chale sought the finer tendrils of the speed Blessing in their muscle. The screams had slid past her ears unnoticed.

The saints held their silence, waiting for him to demand their loyalty. Prove himself strong enough to fit them with bit and bridle.

Whatever temptation there might be to claim this throne and its riches, its power to turn the empire's attention away from Wodenberg, no delusion could hold against that truth. Anders was only an elect. He couldn't claim the fount under his feet, let alone two ancient and viperous saints.

But for a moment, he was emperor of Arcea — the bastard son of a minor king.

He stood, gathering his kir to be ready. "I am the third to claim this throne," Anders said, voice carrying on a bit of kir. It made the other saints and elect cock their heads, curious. But not Chale and Dolorata. "Some of you know that story. Seraphine is dead. I harvested her. This throne is mine by that right. But I am Sir Anders Bockmann, Blessed knight of Saint Woden, bound elect of Saint Kate of Suevia, and you can keep your damn throne. The Empire is no more."

Anders pulled the cloak-pin, burst out his kir, and launched himself into the sky as his black wings blossomed from both arms. The spheres let him pass and so soon as he cleared the third he pulled his wings in, letting himself fall. Sure enough, two deadly blasts of kir crashed into each other above his head. Brilliant stars exploded, pouring over the spheres. Anders rammed his own kir down to gain more height, pumping his wings hard —

A kir-rope snared his ankle. Leashed him with a jerk.

He fell, twisted, meaning to cut it, but saw the blast of kir-fire Dolorata's lieutenant shot at Chale. A flick of the saint's wrist and it unraveled, splattering, and his charm chewed its way up the stream in an eye-blink. The elect unraveled in a cloud of blood.

A glob kir-fire struck Anders' leash and severed it. He pushed again, hard as he could, and flew. Behind him roared fire, lightning, and blood. He cleared the tiled colonnade roof, passing through the outer sphere. Squads of guardsmen rushed to the Beauty Gate, Blessing-quick, and took no notice of a half-giddha-rukh overhead.

Anders heard an explosion, felt the wash of heat, as he crossed the true castle walls of the imperial palace, but he couldn't spare a glance back. Once over those, he caught a thermal rising off Arcea and let it carry him. Below, the clay-tile roofs shrank into patches of red, brown, ochre, tawny gold. They made for a lumpy carpet hemmed by a silver river on one side, a vast bay on another. Salt tickled his vulture's nose. So warm, here, though it was still only spring.

He turned away from the sea, toward home.

CHAPTER 21

I woke, as I often did, to a room dimly lit by the green glitter of the kir-fount and the first traces of dawn. This morning, the half-Shepherd moon lent some warm glow too. I left the shutters of my castle suite open, whatever the weather, so that I was never more than a heartbeat from my fount. That had been pleasant enough, all summer, but this pre-dawn of the day before the autumn Equinox was chilly.

Anders lay on his back beside me, one hand tucked under the pillow, breathing shallow and soft through an open mouth.

Midnight was my usual bed-time now and still I woke before sunrise. Being elect, he'd wake soon. When I sat up, folding the quilts back, he stirred. "Morning," I said, combing my fingers through my loose hair. I'd barely gotten it out of the braid before the lure of cuddling up to a sleeping Anders had pulled me in.

"Morning," he answered. His hand curled around my waist and he dragged me back. I chuckled; he did this every morning. My pattern whirled up, at his call, thick and bright — but not so thick as to hide what he wanted to see.

His little star, between my hips. Anders planted a kiss on my belly, then let me go.

I slid off the bed and flicked a vine of kir across the room to drop a spark on the candle by my bedroom door. That light was the signal to the night maid, Etha, that we were up, next time she looked into my suite. When she came in I was combing out my hair. She brought Anders' boots with her, clean and polished.

"I'll be at the palace by noon," Anders said as he stood from the bed to pull his hose legs up. "There's a handful more squires to test."

Etha laid down Anders' new uniform on the bed beside him; as Knight Protector of Suevia, he wore a red tabard and white baldric hemmed with gold braid and tassels. As Saint Seaxneat had never required his sons, the Aethlings of Suevia, to be knights, the Protector had ever served as chief guardian, champion, and military advisor to the king. The Protector also presided over Suevia's yearly cycle of jousting tournaments, saw to the testing of squires ready for knighthood, and had a hand in maintaining the top bloodlines of warhorses.

Kiefan needed no champion or advisor, but it was also a way to sift out future battle elect. Offering the post to Anders, complete with the chance to breed and train his own horses, had been a bit like asking a boy if he'd care to eat his favorite cake every day.

There'd been no jousting tournaments this summer because of the trouble; the first was to begin the day after next and Anders had been down to the tourney fields daily. Knights and squires were trickling in from all over to be tested and to compete.

And see the coronation tomorrow, on Equinox.

Anders pulled the red on over his white linens, buckled his jeweled sword-belt atop that. The blacksmiths' guild had offered him a blade as a sign of their fealty; it was elect-made, hidden away since the conquest and kept safe. With a smile to me, he left for the tourney fields.

Etha laced up my dress snugly. The chamberlain of the palace, Eadwin, had asked leave to consult with the master seamstresses on the matter of my formal gowns. My penchant for plain dresses, he'd never said a word about — only this. He was a wiry, silver-bearded man who remembered Saint Seaxneat and had proven himself priceless in wisdom and tact. So I had agreed and quietly bore the results.

The gown was silk, a shade of green that fairly matched a fount's glow. Embroidered white kir-whorls ran along the hems and clustered around the close neckline. My loose hair was bundled in a crespine of gold wire strung with green tourmaline beads. The jeweled headband I wore was gold, too, set with more small stones.

Fine stuff for today's formalities, but it wouldn't stop me from my weekly duty to the goodfolk. The palace staff expected me to inspect the guest accommodations as well before the guests themselves arrived. They were expected at noon, at the palace.

I sat on the windowsill when I was ready and swung my feet over. Caught myself on kir and soared. The cool, damp wind on my face, the rush of the castle beneath me — I would never tire of flying. Perhaps in truth it was bounding on long legs made of kir rather than true flying, but I'd not complain. I crossed the city in a few heartbeats and landed before the palace's open gates. The guardsmen there dropped to one knee in obeisance; I still couldn't help nodding to acknowledge them. Saints weren't to notice such things. It was their due.

The sick, the wounded, and the maimed waiting for me in the paved city square gave me obeisance as best they could. I walked from the gate, my silk skirt trailing in the dust, and called their patterns as they went. Suevia's first restored Orderhaus, here in Reowan, managed the supplicants, housed them, and brought them to the square once a week grouped by the worst off, the youngest, and the rest. That was all that mattered; money could not buy my healing and I passed over those with minor afflictions.

A man in rags, suffering scrofula. A woman whose moon's flux never ceased. A sickly child with a flawed kidney. Hernias. Ruined knees. Consumption. Whore's rash. Some patients had come alone, some with their families to help them. A week, some had walked or ridden in a wagon. Some days there were more than the square could hold.

It would need moving indoors as the winter neared. But for now, I crouched down beside a little girl and took her hands in mine. She'd been kicked by a goat as a toddler and her hip had given her pain ever since. I ended that and smiled when she did.

I worked my way across the square, from worst off to youngest to the others. When I returned to the gates the goodfolk honored me with a song — a tradition, Eadwin had told me — and I curtsied in return.

Eadwin himself waited for me at the palace doors, his knobby hands clasped behind his back, with a maid who set about brushing the dirt from my hems. "The guest chambers await your approval, m'lady," the chamberlain told me.

The first two floors of the palace were given over to offices and council chambers. On the third, the largest suite had been redecorated in Suevi green and white for Kiefan. The other suite had been re-purposed as a nursery. And where the governor had lived, honored guests would be staying.

I walked through the rooms, glancing over the furnishings. Particularly those meant for Queen Mercia. I hadn't known that the Suevi still told stories of the poor, orphaned princess — the Aethlings-dóhtor — and her narrow escapes from Arceal assassins. Her mother's kin, the Heathugrim, had risked much in hiding her until she was a beautiful young woman. The stories recounted the heroic sacrifices and her kindness and ended when she met a handsome northern prince who carried her off.

She was coming home, now. Saint Qadeem was bringing her to Reowan himself in a gesture of good faith and friendship to mark the beginning of the alliance between Suevia and Wodenberg.

I paused in the door of the finest suite, which would be Qadeem's. Unlikely he'd sleep much but it was proper for him to have one. The windows looked on the gardens behind the palace, which were a riot of late summer flowers.

"If I may, m'lady," Eadwin said, as he did when he must broach a delicate subject.

"Certainly."

"If there should be, say, an urgent message for Saint Qadeem at an odd hour of the night. Would it be possible that he'd be found in… other bedchambers?"

That gave me pause, for a moment. It still didn't sit easy, thinking of my saint — my former saint, thus.

Eadwin stroked his white beard. "I only ask as it's known that m'lady and Saint Qadeem are… dear friends."

Me? I blinked. "Not thus," I said, with emphasis. "He was my saint, my teacher. I do love him, but only as a friend."

My chamberlain dipped his head. "Of course, m'lady. I didn't mean to offend."

"Though —" A question stuck and I asked it. "Do I offend? Do the people think me —?"

He hesitated. "In matters of the bedchamber?"

"I keep a husband and a consort." I said it plainly, before I could flinch away from asking. "Does that trouble the goodfolk?"

Eadwin's mouth twitched as he thought. I looked out at the garden, at the laden cherry tree in the center, while waiting for his answer. "Saint Seaxneat kept consorts, often several at a time. He found them as he pleased, whether among the noble houses or in the countryside. Many stayed only a few moons, but a few lingered until they died of old age. Only his favorites ever bore him sons, though."

"The Aethlings," I said and he nodded. "Who ruled…?"

"Who led, in what roles suited them. The goodfolk loved them. Seaxneat himself was… a difficult man to love. He ruled well, though."

And had for centuries. As I might, with my elect. "So the goodfolk will call Kiefan their Aethling?"

Another nod. "It's the Aethling's crown that awaits him. The saint needed none. That crown passed from Aethlings to their sons, or to a new son of the saint's, for generations. If there's an elect wearing it, though… m'lady's son is of the saint's blood?"

"He is Kiefan's son." What of Rafe, then? He had claim to both Suevia and Wodenberg, as Kiefan did. "And Kiefan is my consort rather than my husband. I would not wish the people feeling belittled by that."

"It's not for any but Mother Love and Father Duty to chastise the saints, m'lady. The people love you for your kindness and, increasingly, your strength."

My strength. Once my pregnancy grew and they saw how scatter-minded I became… but other worries, first. I hadn't yet told anyone of the baby but Anders and Kiefan. It was only two moons along.

We returned to the gate-yard where the greeting party was assembling. Many were city elders and were inside the great hall to avoid the increasingly hot sun. The knights of the honor-guard, the Árheald, stood in neat lines pretending to be untouched by such things. Outside, in the square, a new crowd murmured and jostled for the best views of the avenue from the city gates. I made my rounds in the gate-yard and the hall of the elders, the officials, the soon-to-be restored nobles.

Anders was missing. / ? /

He answered quickly, with glee. / on my way /

If he missed this arrival, it wouldn't go well. I touched Kiefan's bond in my other hand. / ? /

/ city gates /

Faintly, I heard a cheer. I strode to the palace gates and looked, along with the hundreds of goodfolk. The cheer rippled down the avenue to us, spread out over the voices and they raised their hands in excitement. I let my kir-cloak unfurl and stood waiting. Elders and officials joined me, shading their eyes against the sun.

Banners came first: Wodenberg's black with the Shepherd moon, Suevia's green with the white ram and ewe restored to it. Knights riding escort, from both kingdoms. Then I smiled, glad to see Kiefan at last. He'd gone to Temitte to meet Qadeem and his mother outside the city walls and had been away better than a week.

Though the weather had been fair and the road was easy, I'd pestered him for updates. That had been nothing like the grueling summer of hearing only what Kiefan could explain through our bond, feeling jolts of his anger and frustration, sending him kir and hoping it was enough.

Field Moon had started well, with word that some of the youths collected for the spring Equinox tithe had been rescued. A captain of the guard in the border city Suthleá had mounted a rescue to keep the tithed from crossing the river into Arcea's clutches; his own daughter had been among them. But his Arceal superiors had attempted to arrest the captain and bloody riots had broken out.

Kiefan had gone to support those who'd accept me as saint. He'd taken Suevi soldiers, along with Scyfe and Glyman, and the rooting out of the Arceal divisions along the southern border had taken much of the summer. There were still rumors of warlords and renegade Arceal companies in the south but Kiefan had come home on a rising tide of success and hope. The noble houses, the guilds, the good-folk chanting in the streets, had all demanded a coronation.

Now he traveled with precious cargo. Not just his mother and my teacher.

Qadeem and Mercia rode side by side, the saint carrying her hand formally. The cheering rose to a thunder around her. She came with her head high, dressed in white and green, finally free of her black mourning veil — all but glowing in the triumph.

The banners and knights circled around to the stable gate; Kiefan dismounted before me and was followed by our guests. A small corner of me wanted to shove them all aside to see what other guests were among them — and where was Anders, mother have mercy? — but there were formal greetings to give.

Qadeem presented the Aethling's-dóhtor to me, and Suevia, as a sign of the good-will between our kingdoms. I spoke of the people's gratitude and confirmed that good-will. Mercia called this the most joyous day of her life, returning home with her son and grandson.

I dared crane my neck to search the stopped column that curled from the palace gates across the crowded square. I saw Anders on horseback and glimpsed grey ears. One of the elders discreetly poked me for having missed my cue.

"Dear guests, please take refreshments and rest before tonight's banquet to welcome the Aethlings-dóhtor home," I said. The crier would remind the goodfolk of tomorrow's celebrations and to balance their accounts for Equinox. I could clear out of the gate now and let the rest of the procession into the gate-yard. They came, leading their horses, and quickly filled the space. I could see... I craned again, climbed the two little steps to the palace's double doors in searching the milling horses.

I heard a cry, my only warning. Frida caught me in a hug. "At last!" she cried. "Oh, so long! Oh, look at you! So beautiful!" Frida put me at arm's length to survey the jewels, the gold.

Tears streaked her cheeks. I kissed them away on both sides, not wanting her to cry even if it was joy. "Thank you. Thank you so — for all you've done," I managed to say before the question I had to ask fought its way out. "Where's Rafe?"

"Kate!"

Frida let me go to turn and hug Kiefan. Tight. I took a deep breath of him, freshly scrubbed and shaved with lavender soap. "I missed you," I murmured, near his ear.

/ safe / warm /

I'd never have guessed he felt as safe in my arms as I did in his.

Kiefan gave me an extra squeeze and let me go. He still wore black, but with Suevi green layered underneath, peeking under loose sleeves and at his collar. His sword was Woden's, once again, its moon-white pommel under his hand.

His smile was his own as he kissed me. "I missed you."

"Where's Rafe?" I asked again. "He's gotten past his shyness?" Through the bond, Kiefan had told me that Rafe had clung to Frida when they first met. He'd only said that they were improving, after that, and the muddle of Kiefan's emotions had been difficult to sort. Save for a deep wanting to understand his son.

"Rafe's a sweetling. He loves everyone." Frida slipped her arm in mine.

"He was cautious at first," Kiefan answered me, "as befits a prince. But as he assisted me in my correspondence, each night, we developed a mutual interest in quills."

"Quills?" My brows rose, then crinkled together.

"The barbs must be carefully stripped before you cut the nib," Kiefan said. "It takes a great deal of practice. A great many feathers."

I breathed a laugh, picturing my son stripping a feather down to its spine with clenched baby fists. But he wouldn't be so small any more. He'd been six moons old when I left and now his first Lambing-day was in just a week off — my breath caught, finally spotting them.

Around the edge of the gate-yard walked a grey-dappled warhorse, tossing his mane each time he wanted to bite an unwary guest and was tugged back. Anders kept Nipper in line as they looped past the palace gates and as they went some of the officers called well-wishes. Nipper pranced to a stop before the open palace gates. Anders waved toward the crowd outside, got a dozen waves in return and a cheer for the Knight Protector. A small hand flew up to do the same.

My throat knotted. Rafe straddled the saddle's pommel, leaning back against Anders. The hand that held Nipper's reins also held him close by the chest, but I breathed easier when Anders had both hands back on my baby. At a touch, Nipper's stride lengthened and he circled to the palace's front doors.

Rafe was so big. My hands covered my gaping mouth. He was in black woolen cotes, socks, little leather shoes and oh, his hair was still downy-fine and so wild. Needed combing. It caught the sunlight and turned gold.

Anders stopped Nipper and grinned at my wide eyes. Rafe threw up both arms. "Gama!"

Frida reached to take him and kiss his cheek. "Papa took you riding! Such a big boy!"

"Papa?" Rafe echoed her, turning toward Kiefan. Waving, he repeated, "Papa…" Then he stuck his fingers in his mouth.

"Your Mama's so glad to see you," Frida told him, carrying him to me.

My hands flew from my face to reach for him. Rafe looked at me, his grey eyes innocent. "Give Mama a kiss."

That was his cue; he threw his arms up, I took him, hugged him tight as I dared. Rafe kissed me on the cheek, soft and wet. His arms, around my neck, squeezed as tight as he could. My heart wanted to rip from my chest to be closer to him.

Rafe decided when he was finished hugging and leaned away from me. Twisting, he found Frida and reached for her. I handed him back with some reluctance but he'd be mine again soon enough. Frida carried him into the hall where cider and honeyed oatcakes were on hand for refreshments. It was already full of talk and good cheer; Saint Qadeem stood alone in an aisle from doorway to dais, waiting for me.

He was just the same as ever, in woolens and a fur-lined cloak, and yet looked different. Perhaps I looked as different, too.

I walked toward the dais. Qadeem fell into step beside me.

The driftwood throne stood on the dais, pale and sinuous. A thin cushion on the seat bore the Aethling's crown, a heavy, braided thing clutching chunks of gemstone in its coils. A rugged thing, in contrast to the gentility of Suevia thus far.

"A good sign, that the people wish their king crowned," Qadeem said in Englic. "The people on the Southbound Road spoke only of your kindness and healing. And of the rioting in Suthleá, and of Kiefan's successes. Not an easy birth of a kingdom, perhaps, but not so hard as some."

"Would that there'd be no worse ahead," I said.

"There will be," Qadeem said, plainly. "Arcea unravels at the seams. There's founts to be taken if one has the strength. I'm the sole master of four, now, if the lamia fount can be said to be mine — I'm the envy of the world. A difficult job to have."

He needed peace with me as much as I needed his advice and aid. "It's not only Arcea that unravels," I said. "Have you had word from Caercoed?"

Qadeem's voice lowered. "I know Eryr Pass still stands open."

I nodded. "As does Dwyncraig Pass. The Caer merchant ships came late this year, and under a flag of truce. Duchess Faola, of Henffyrdd, and her cousin duchess of Lancynnes, sent a letter with them. They asked for peace."

"They asked, for themselves?"

"For Henffyrdd and Lancynnes, no more." There'd been mention of Duchess Faola's marriageable son and a younger pair of daughters of Lancynnes, but the most telling tidbit had been written separately. "The second note, wrapped within the first, was charmed with a spark to destroy both if it was cut by less an an elect," I said. "Crown Ciara is imprisoned. By the saints."

Qadeem shifted on his feet, pursing his mouth.

"Saint Conbarre ordered it. Caercoed is split in anger over it. Anger at their own saints." He nodded. "And the elect?"

"Must be split as well. It was Tannait who signed and charmed the note. She thanked me for sending Teleri home with her sword. The story swayed more to their cause."

"Never doubt," Qadeem said, "how much saints need their elect. Never doubt how badly you were needed in Wodenberg, or how we thanked the Shepherd for sending you."

That still touched me, despite that I knew I must be careful in my dealings. Even with Qadeem. He would expect no less of me. "And I thank the Shepherd for giving me a neighbor I can gladly offer peace to," I said. Adding a smile, I modified that to, "Once we've settled a few matters of land and kings."

He smiled too. "Indeed. No small matters, either. You must ask me to share Temitte and give over the land we rightfully conquered."

I stepped up to the dais, touching both my bonds as I went. They came at once, both my elect. Kiefan with a parting kiss to his mother's hand. Anders gave Theo's shoulder a fond cuff and left his friend at the palace door. I couldn't help smiling as they joined me on the dais. I stood before the throne and they dropped to one knee on either side. I'd never asked them to, but they'd made a habit of returning to that moment I'd bound them.

A page stood with a tray of fresh cider, waiting for his chance to pass out the cups. We all took one.

"You must ask me to share my elect and my son, and guard your southern border," I said. "No small matter."

"No." Qadeem raised his cup and his voice, switching now to Suevi. "First, a toast to the unity of Suevia and Wodenberg. To the blood of old saints and new." He nodded toward Kiefan, who returned it. Every cup in the hall was raised to join in. "To peace in the midst of crumbling empires and troubled neighbors. May we find it and keep it."

"May we find it and keep it," I agreed, and in unity we drank.

APPENDIX

CALENDAR OF MOONS

Each moon is four seven-day weeks, covering one complete turn of the Shepherd moon from new to full and back. The last day of the moon falls on the new (dark) moon. The full moon falls in the middle, and equinoxes or solstices tend to land on the waning half-moon. Once, moons began and ended on Saint-days, but the system is old enough that things have shifted — it pre-dates Wodenberg's saints by quite a bit.

Number	Moon	Event
1	Bitter	
2	Ice	
3	Slush	Spring equinox; Kiefan's Lambing-day on the 25th
4	Spring	
5	Field	
6	Warm	Summer solstice
7	Summer	
8	Fruit	Kate's Lambing-day on the 18th
9	Grain	Autumn equinox
10	Leaf	
11	Hunter's	Jousting tournament starts on the first; Anders' Lambing-day on the 11th
12	Snow	Winter solstice; a new year begins

LAMBING-DAY

One's Lambing-day is the first Saint-day after you were born. If you were born on Saint-day, you were Lambed on the next one. The infant is presented to the Mother and Father, and then the entire Flock of a given Orderhaus before the communal meal. Everyone greets the new lamb with a kiss. Traditionally, relatives and friends bring extra sweets for the meal.

Lambing-days are marked with sweets or small gifts, but they aren't significant until a child reaches twelve and is ready for Blessing by the saints.

ON RANKING KIR-MAGES

Laypeople

Nine of ten people have little or no gift for kir. Perhaps eight of those ten can learn one small charm if they set their mind to it, but no more than that. These folk can only feel concentrations of kir if they are very strong (as in a fount or a highly charged kir-mage) and close by. They can retain a small amount of kir if they are given it through a bond or they drink it from a fount's water. Any more than that will overflow and return to the earth.

Laypeople's overall kir-pattern is the baseline for comparison; on sounding, their kir gives a single, short note like a silver bell.

One in ten people cannot use any kir at all, and are not even able to activate charms bound in small objects.

Disciples

Six in a hundred people are able to master a handful of small charms, usually within a certain area of talent such as healing, combat, or crafting in a particular medium. For example, a low-level healer may know: blood-stop, cleansing, how to patch small areas of kir, and how to untangle pain knots. A low-level fighter may be able to sharpen their reflexes, briefly, strike with unusual force, and resist cuts and bruises with a skin-level kir-shield.

These six disciples can hold a bit more kir than laypeople, and the overall kir-pattern inherent in their bodies is a little denser, a little stronger. On sounding, their kir may give two notes, and will last a little longer. Two heartbeats, perhaps. The difference is subtle, admittedly. Advanced disciples — through skill or experience — may attain a full chord of three notes.

Blessed

Four in a hundred have the talent to be counted blessed. All of the Wodenberg enhancements are examples of one blessed-level charm — a true blessed would have two or maybe three such abilities, and a handful of lesser ones. At this level, the use of kir begins to creep out of the tidy groupings that people like to put kir-mages in. Someone who has largely focused on combat may, at this level, also show some talent for mending, or crafting, or shape-shifting.

The person at this level knows that kir charms are not simple formulas, and can be extemporized to some degree. How successful they will be at trying new things, making it up as they go, etc., varies. They will find their limits, sometimes disastrously.

A blessed, when sounded, will give three notes, maybe four, and sustain for as many heartbeats.

An example of the generalizing of kir ability is the Captain of the King's Guard, Aleksandra Rytsarova. In addition to her saint-given speed and anticipation Blessings, which gave her a head start to her full flowering of ability, she can shield herself with kir, charm her sword, and wields a full complement of "household" charms — spark, flame-snuffing, mending torn fabric, sharpening blades, etc.

Elect

The defining sign of an elect is the ability to draw free kir from other people (barring resistance) and to cast charms on others without touching them.

An elect has a deeper understanding of kir and it responds to him accordingly. Charms become large, complex things affecting the full body. They can collect and hold large amounts of kir, and diffuse it to avoid detection. Grouping elect becomes even more difficult, as they often have multiple areas of expertise.

It's often said that the only limits on a kir-mage are inborn ability and his own wit; the elect are in a position to truly explore the limits of that.

Because of their scarcity and power, politics and control play strongly in the life of an elect. Saints seek them out and bind them, offering training and a steady supply of kir in exchange for loyalty and protection. They often function as gate-keepers for the saints, and as such are the focus of all the kingdom's responsibilities — and luxuries — alongside whatever rulership there may be. Power corrupts, after all, and elect can live for centuries.

Saints

The pinnacle of mastery is both a gift and a curse.

Saints tend to say little about what they're truly capable of, but this much is known: a saint is one who can bind a fount to himself. Thus, the full power of one or more wellsprings of kir are always at his command. And therefore, saints seek out founts, guard them jealously, and surround themselves with kingdoms for further defense.

This is because a saint can be cut off from his fount if another saint severs the binding — which can be done at the source. A saint with no fount is far from helpless, but he's much more vulnerable.

Furthermore, saints target each other in order to harvest their accumulated wisdom and charms. This applies to elect as well — blessed are generally not sufficiently interesting to harvest — and further thins the ranks of the weak, insecure or slow-witted.

Exactly how many saints there are, in the world, cannot be said for certain as they can hide their kir and walk among laypeople undetected.

ON INHERITANCE IN WODENBERG

There are ancient customs in Wodenberg, to be sure, but as in all kingdoms the saint(s) have made modifications. Saint Woden recognized the old clans' claims to hereditary titles and estates, but he added certain requirements.

Firstly, that the holder of a hereditary title must have earned knighthood through Blessings and skill at arms, to the satisfaction of Saint Woden or the holder of a hereditary title.

Secondly, the holder must be currently capable of serving the saints in battle.

Thirdly, the holder must be able to document his or her blood lineage to the clan which held the title in antiquity. This serves to choose between equally qualified candidates — though the final decision is always Saint Woden's to make.

The list of hereditary titles in Wodenberg was simplified to baron, margrave, duke, and king. Certain lands and assets were defined as belonging to the current holder of the title alone, not to be divided among children or other heirs. Saint Woden ruled that no other military rank, government office, or title in the Order, is hereditary; they must be earned through skill or wisdom.

Because of these rules, a number of situations never happen in Wodenberg. There are no regencies, as children cannot have earned knighthood. The spouse of a title holder does not inherit the title or the title's estate on the holder's death. Spouses and children may inherit whatever other assets were articulated in the title-holder's will, but not the office itself.

The complex situation of Anders Bockmann

As an example, let's consider Anders' situation. His mother's pregnancy and his birth were recorded in the register of Saint Woden's descendants, since Anders is King Wilhelm's bastard son. He is also a descendant of the Kaltgrasen clan of northern Wodenberg, through his mother. She was the eldest daughter of the baron of Kaltgrasen before she moved south and married the baron of Rossweide.

Anders has no claim on the barony of Rossweide, as he is of no relation to the Bockmann clan. He might have inherited other assets from the step-father who raised him, but their many fallings-out have resulted in Anders being removed from the baron's will. What his mother might leave to him remains to be seen.

The Kaltgrasen barony passed to his mother's brother, upon his grandfather's death, and should the barony need an heir Anders would be a good candidate. That doesn't seem likely, as the current baron is in good health and has a family of his own.

Anders has a valid claim to the crown of Wodenberg, though: he has earned knighthood, is able-bodied, and is a son of the main line of Woden's descendants.

King Wilhelm has an elder daughter, Gisella, who married Duke Seagrace. She has no claim to the throne because she has not earned knighthood. Her two sons might press a claim, if they grow up and prove to be knights. They may also lay claim to the duchy of Englia, through their father's blood.

But, obviously, Kiefan is the primary claimant to Wodenberg's crown as he has been trained to the job of ruling from childhood, and is the legitimate son of both the king and the last living princess of Suevia. So long as he's alive and well, there's no reason to doubt Woden would pass the crown to Kiefan, should King Wilhelm die.

Thus, Anders is largely left to make his own name for himself.

ON FAITH

All people belong to a Flock — their neighbors, their kingdom, all humanity — which is led by the Ram and the Ewe. These alphas are more commonly known as Father Duty and Mother Love. They teach the Flock how to be good sheep so that the Shepherd will find them worthy when he comes for them.

Since the Flock is so large, it's naturally divided into smaller Flocks. Those are the kingdoms, which are led by the saints, who were given their kir-gift by the Shepherd to mark them as leaders. Kingdom Flocks are further divided into neighborhoods and villages, overseen by abbots/abbesses of the Order.

Rituals are determined by one's saints, heavily influenced by local tradition. In Wodenberg, Saints-day rituals are observed once a week; the more pious can observe them daily, or take the vows of the Order and dedicate their lives to service of the Flock.

Mother Love, the Ewe

The Ewe is all things warm and homey, gentle and nurturing, loving and healing. She teaches the Flock to care and forgive, to help and shelter one another. Community and sharing are encouraged in her name. The Mother's Discipline is marriage, which is more rigorous than it would seem: fidelity, the raising of children, giving one's support as a family to the Flock you live in.

The Mother is merciful, rather than stern, and advises seeking compromise whenever possible — whether it's a cheating spouse or quarrelsome neighbors. Colloquially, the running joke is that the Mother's teachings come easier to women, the Father's easier to men, and thus the two sexes are always a little at odds with each other. But one is to obey both the Mother and the Father, regardless of one's gender. Teamwork, whether at the level of families or kingdoms, is always the overriding concern. While there's sympathy for how one must compromise one's selfish desires for the betterment of all, it's what one is expected to do.

Father Duty, the Ram

The Ram oversees all one's duties: work, service, teaching, and generally the less pleasant things in life. The Father's Discipline is a month-long purification that demonstrates one's dedication to duty, and it requires equal doses of humility and perseverance as well. Taking Discipline is required for any squire seeking knighthood, any wishing to take the vows of the Order, or it can be endured to clear a debt of honor.

While the Father can be harsh and unforgiving, the sacrifices one makes for duty are noble and praiseworthy. Authority and power are implicit in observing Father Duty's teachings. One should know one's place, and know that all places have value. A Flock must stand together against the wolves and monsters of the world, not run willy-nilly and defenseless. Again, teamwork is paramount.

The Shepherd

The Shepherd gives life, the Shepherd brings death: sometimes merciful, sometimes incomprehensible, and never cheated. He is fair in his evaluation of his sheep, and they cannot hide anything from him. The Shepherd culls his flock, when he chooses, of the unworthy. He also chooses those to bring home to his fold where it's safe and warm. Those who are especially worthy with will have a place at the Shepherd's Hearth.

Sheep he isn't pleased with are banished to the Winter Wood, to wander forever.

The Hearth

Heaven is eternal warmth, companionship and hospitality. All the good things of life are there, and all those you loved who've gone before you. It's an eternal banquet around a well-laden table. But like most heavens, people catalog its wonderful things and then prefer to talk about the horrors of hell…

The Winter Wood

Hell, conversely, is cold, isolation, and wandering the monster-infested Winter Wood. It's well stocked with folklore villains: rogue Elect, kobolds, wild animals, kir-mutated beasts, and all the agonies of the cold. Since life for most goodfolk is cold and wild animals are often a concern, the line between life and the Winter Wood is far blurrier than the Shepherd's Hearth. Nobody stumbles into heaven accidentally, but the warning signs at the edges of the Wood are well known.

And, of course, everyone gets a little taste of hell each winter. They say that it's to remind the Flock to keep themselves worthy of the Hearth.

Heroes find their way to the Wood, sometimes, to rescue someone who's been stolen by a rogue Elect or kobolds. Lovers swear they'll fight their way back from it, if they must. Most are content to take care when they venture into a real forest, to avoid drawing the notice of the evils in the Wood, and be good sheep that the Shepherd would come and find if they're lost. Or, perhaps, send a hero to rescue them.

MILITARY RANKS OF WODENBERG

The officer structure is fairly simple, in Wodenberg; there are, of course, plenty of other functions which have particular titles and responsibilities such as quartermasters, captains of the watch, or masters of horse.

All soldiers wear a black tabard for a uniform, shoulder-wide, knee long front and back. Embroidered patches on each shoulder mark one's place in the army, and epaulette straps on the shoulders are used to tie on brass ranking rings. The patch on the left shoulder is for the branch of service.

Branches
Knights: white horse, rampant
Archers: white hawk, stooping
Armsmen: two swords, crossed, in white
Supply and support: white wagon wheel

The patch on the right shoulder is for one's affiliation. This can be one's lord, whether baron, margrave, or duke, a particularly famous company that has earned its own banner and insignia, or one of the Guard.

Affiliations
Duke of Alemannia: black elk, rampant, on white
Duke of Englia: white rukh, stooping, on blue
Duke of Russe: black bear, rampant, on red
Margrave of Knapptal: white ram's head on green
Baron of Rossweide: white horse, rampant, on green
City Guard of Wodenberg: one gold star
Prince's Guard: two gold stars
Queen's Guard: three gold stars
King's Guard: four gold stars

Ranks
Sergeant: wears one brass ring on each shoulder, commands a hand of five men.
Lieutenant: two brass rings, commands a squad of about eighteen (three hands plus sergeants.)
Captain: three brass rings, commands a company of one hundred or so. The number here can vary as companies are often drawn from a particular region or a part of a city.
Captain-general: four brass rings, commands a regiment of about a thousand. These are also organized geographically, and even more likely to be kept together for the camaraderie rather than split up for tidiness' sake.
Field Marshal: five brass rings. This is a particular and sometimes temporary position to assist and advise a young noble who's settling into his military duties. Field marshals are always experienced captains-general who have impressed the king with their service. The king himself keeps a few simply for the organizational assistance and as sounding boards for strategy-planning.
A baron generally commands a few captains-general, depending on the size of his holding, and may have a field marshal to assist. Barons wear six ranking rings and their crest embroidered, large, in the center of their tabards' chest.
There are only a few margraves in Wodenberg: Knapptal, Kernweise, and one in southern Englia. They command barons, and may have a field marshal to assist. Since they've always been a bit unusual, they don't wear ranking rings but do wear their crests.
The three dukes of Wodenberg command all of the nobles ranked under them, and may have additional field marshals to help keep it all straight. Rather than ranking rings, a duke wears a hollow bar of brass the width of each shoulder, and his tabard is embroidered with his crest.

The king wears gold ranking rings, his crown, and the crest of Wodenberg. He answers only to Saint Woden.

Rangers

Unlike the other branches of the military, Rangers wear an entirely different tabard: walnut brown, with a black border two fingers wide around the hems. Their ranking rings are iron, not shiny brass, and there are no embroidered patches.

Whether they're archers, swordsmen, or trackers, Rangers work in close-knit teams of either five, under sergeants or eighteen to a lieutenant. The one captain of the Rangers is rarely in the field, but would lead a small, elite team if he did go.

CAERCOED

Society in Caercoed is the result of a biological oddity: all female conceptions automatically split into identical twins within a few days of fertilization. This isn't accidental or genetic. It's a fertility charm implanted by the kingdom's twin saints — and that's a carefully guarded secret.

As a result, two-thirds of babies born are female. Given the slightly higher mortality rate for boys as infants and children, this discrepancy only increases as a given crop of babies reaches maturity. Twin boys do happen, though they're rare and considered quite precious.

Because of the imbalance in the sexes, women have taken the upper hand in Caer society. They have the wisdom and breadth of view necessary to work toward the collective good, whereas men are headstrong and selfish. Twin sisters can keep a man gentled, though, and focused on the important things in life.

Gender traditions

In the strictest of tradition — meaning upper-class, old-blood families — men are the keepers of home and hearth, and a young man has no need for anything not directly related to maintenance his house and home. Which is a broad range of subjects, but it does not include reading, foreign languages, math beyond simple arithmetic, or other intellectual pursuits. Men are expected to be morally strong, maintain the house physically and socially, garden and cook, see to the furnishings and the family's clothes, raise the children, and always be well groomed. As parents, they're expected to be the more indulgent ones, especially toward their daughters.

Also in the strictest tradition, a young woman is expected to be educated, confident, adventurous, and team-oriented. In the upper classes, her skills will fall into either the martial arts or some sort of engineering, whether civil or military. Humbly born girls are apprenticed out at twelve or fourteen to learn a trade or to study the higher callings in Caercoed — military, medicine, sailing. Mothers dispense wisdom and discipline, in Caercoed, because the world is a harsh place and bringing children into it is a great responsibility.

Naturally, with humbler roots come more flexible standards. Lower-class men are more likely to work outside the home as laborers or to pick up hunting and fighting skills. He's expected to give that up when he marries.

A boy of fourteen is expected to be actively learning home management from his father and putting together a dower to prove his skills. If this isn't an option, earning a dower of hard cash is an acceptable substitute. Men are not expected to serve in the military, but they can sign up and receive a modest salary.

At twenty, young women are required to serve a four year stint in the military. Marriage inquiries begin around this time, usually initiated by the parents. Courtships tend to run about four years with the marriages coming soon after military service ends. If children haven't started yet, they do then.

Marriage

The function of marriage, in Caercoed, is to clearly define inheritances, alliances, and ownerships. A married man cannot be turned out of his home or separated from his children except through divorce. Divorces are rare. Children born within a marriage have legal claim to an inheritance from both their parents.

Marriage is strictly defined: a set of twins marries one man. In any other arrangement, the man is only a consort.

Consorts

This is a much more casual arrangement than a marriage; these are often love matches that can cross class and legal lines, and aren't expected to last although it's considered wonderfully romantic when they do. So long as one is fulfilling one's marital obligations, having or being a consort is no fault. Though given all of a man's responsibilities, not many of them have the energy to be a consort as well as a husband.

A consort has no claim to the home, the children, or any possessions he did not bring with him. He could be turned out at any time, though society generally frowns on this if it leaves children fatherless.

Children

"Legitimacy" is not much of an issue, in Caercoed. What matters is who your mothers are and what they can give you in the way of advantages.

If your mothers are married, you are an heir to both them and their husband. If your mothers aren't married, your situation is much more fluid. Maybe you'll inherit something, maybe you won't. Best to strike out early and make something of yourself, on your own.

Traditionally, the children of one twin are the children of both. Sisters are expected to support each other fully and without question — though of course personality clashes are common. Girls who've lost their twin are seen as misfortunate, possibly unlucky, and lonely.

Boys, being almost all singly born, seem all the more vulnerable and in need of sheltering.

A VERY BRIEF HISTORY OF WODENBERG

An interview with Saint Woden

So you were born in...

Ansehen. I was born in a hovel on the waterfront, to a whore who miscarried or lost all others.

A rough childhood?

(shrugs) She drank. I was there only til Saint Vitur's people found me and brought me in for training. Which was late, perhaps, compared to those I teach now. I thought I'd be an armsman and that would be enough to support my mother — it was an Elect who taught me the sword, though.

Saint Vitur?

He was an old saint from the hill country. Shrewd, but set in his ways and stubborn. It was his undoing.

When did you get a sense of your abilities?

Soon enough. There was trouble aplenty in those days. Vitur claimed, you see, the fount at Temitte. The fount on the mountain belonged to Saint Jaroslav — the Russe — and we were all caught between Ethmund up in Rukharbor and Seaxneat down at Reowan. That's no arrangement meant to last long: four saints in so small a stretch of land.

When did war break out?

Not war so much as a long blood feud. Tit for tat. Jockeying for allies with the noble houses. Poaching gifted where we could. Sorties to take the lamia fount, which — Mother have mercy, those were worst of all. One good came of it: I met Aleksandr, who was then an Elect as I was.

Did you hit it off quickly?

(smiles) We shared a love of brewed things.

I suspect there are epic stories to be told there.

(he laughs)

Obviously, Saint Seaxneat ended up with both Reowan and Temitte's founts in the end.

In the end, yes. Jaroslav was a cruel man. Vitur was little softer — but his training has stood me well these hundreds of years, so I'll not speak too much ill of him. Jaroslav, though. He deserved what he got. It was right to help my brother Aleks in destroying him.

You unified the Alemanni and the Russe into one kingdom.

My son Kiefan married Aleks' daughter Svetlana. Those around us believed Wodenberg would not last. I know Ethmund and Seaxneat had a wager going for some time.

Who was the bigger threat, Ethmund or Seaxneat?

That old seabird was too odd to be a true threat. Suevia was ever the greater danger, and more so once the Empress conquered it.

Let's not skip over Saint Qadeem's arrival.

Certainly not. If we're speaking of odd birds. (shakes his head)

Did he seem as crazy as Ethmund?

One's crazy only if there's no strength behind one's threat. I'd been saint a hundred years when Qadeem walked into Castle Kaltkern, bolder than brass, to announce himself — and I've been able to suss out an enemy since I was a boy. Qadeem never needed to threaten. He simply wore his strength and knew that was sufficient. Father's beard, I can count on one hand the number of times he's so much as raised his voice.

So you respected him right off?

I knew how deadly he was right off. How capable. But I was ever the wary one. Aleks, he respected Qadeem. He was drawn to the riddle, as he loved to understand things.

Qadeem won you over in time.

(stares into the distance thoughtfully) I came to trust his honor. We had common cause in preparing for future invasions. But for many reasons the two of us could never truly be friends. Two dominant rams cannot share a flock. It was only through Aleksandr that we were brothers.

And now that he's gone?

(tips his head to one side) Now it's only a question of how long Qadeem and I will last.

TRAVELER'S TALE

An interview with Saint Qadeem

You traveled the world before you came to Wodenberg?

I traveled more than most do. When I fled Rasila I joined a caravan, then took service on a merchant ship as a healer. Having such skills made it simpler to travel — and being a saint made it far safer, so long as I was never sounded or pattern-checked.

And you didn't stay so long that your perpetual youth drew suspicion.

I was a man of middle age at the time. Perhaps a bit older. I let myself age some decades more before I began to manage my pattern more closely.

How far did you go with the merchants?

(*smiles*) So far south that I was as fair-skinned to those folk as Kate is to me. The port of call was a city carved into the cliff face above the harbor — the foot of the cliff eaten so far by the sea that ships anchored under the feet of the high dwellings. My employers did business in spices, ivory, and such things there, trading for northern herbs and goods.

Strangest thing you saw out there?

It was not human, the strangest thing I saw. In the deeps of the sea there is a lost fount. Our captain had meant to avoid it, and with good reason, but a storm blew us off course the night before. I was aiding in repairs when I felt the kir off to starboard. I knew no better — I called it in curiosity, and that was what set off the attack, not angering the Shepherd as my shipmates believed.

The dragons boiled up from the water in a tangle and shot into the air in all directions. My jaw fell open, I'll admit, watching twenty-foot-long, brightly striped serpents writhe through the air trailing kir-stars.

Is that what dragons are? Sea snakes?

Sea snakes with ruffs of horn and stretched skin about their heads, with stubby, clawed limbs, with fins at their flat tails to better swim through the sky. Their snake bodies were thicker than my thigh. And they do not like humans, let alone those able to disturb their fount.

They have that much in common with lamia, then.

And they are as aggressive, too. I was caught between being my shipmates' best defense and the fear I'd anger a greater dragon below if I showed my hand too much.

A Saint Dragon?

(*raises both hands to hold that off*) Sainted beasts are no light matter. The fight turned ugly. By its end, I was under such suspicion that I put off at the next port and sought a new ship. I chose one that traded in simpler things — olive oil and tea — and such trade was what brought me back to Arcea.

You missed home?

(*shrugs*) There was no home to return to. I'd gone grey by then and most had forgotten me. As I was content to be a mere herbalist, I was able to slip beneath the Empress's notice and find my way north slowly.

To Wodenberg.

I wished to have my revenge on Seraphine someday, and finding the right kingdom, the right saints, proved tricky. Saint Seaxneat trusted in his own strength. The twin ladies of Caercoed trusted their isolation. It was Woden who listened best to me, in truth.

Once you'd won his trust?

(*laughs*) Trust is a strange thing, between saints. For all his strengths, Aleksandr was perhaps too trusting and as Woden loved him as a brother he also protected him as a brother. I won Aleksandr's trust, and then proved to Woden that my honor would not let me twist that.

Are you saying that Woden was the only saint paranoid enough to believe a stranger's tale that an Empire would someday roll up out of the south?

Perhaps. (*smiles*)

INDEX OF CHARACTERS

Alphabetical by family name, then given name.

WODENBERG

Burrbreak, armsman and lieutenant of Duke Seagrace's army.

Kate Carpenter, Physician of Wodenberg. Student of the Elect, recently graduated to Physician.

Rafe, Kate's son.

Dob, manservant of the Kaufmanns.

Dobro, seneschal of the army. Dispenses discipline and executions.

Hope Dunlea, steward to Duke Seagrace.

Eburhart, knight and captain of the Knapptal garrison.

Edith, Ter of the Order. Nurse and a friend of Kate's.

Meinrad Eismann, knight and Baron of Vorspitz. Advises and provisions the mission. Has a wife and several children, including a teenaged daughter.

Garrick Fechter, knight of the Prince's Guard.

Meinrad Freiberg, fifth-year apprentice of Physician Krepkin.

Gatter, knight and Master of Horse to the King's Guard.

Gudrun, Ter of the Order and senior nurse at the hospital.

Adalrich Haken, knight and duke of Alemannia. Son of King Wilhelm's younger sister, and Kiefan's only cousin. Kate amputated his foot at the battle of Ansehen.

Hannah, student at the Order and Kate's bed-mate.

Baldwin Harke, archer of Wodenberg.

Harold, apprentice blacksmith. Kate was betrothed to him, briefly.

Heima, Ter of the Order. Elect Parselev's consort.

Hein, foreman of the Kaufmanns' wagon yard.

Hilda, house-maid to the Schäfers.

Hochwald, knight and captain-general of the Knapptal garrison.

Holly, Ter of the Order. Nurse and a friend of Kate's.

Ivor, Ther of the Order and master of the Wodenberg Orderhaus' kitchens.

Anders Kaltegrasen, knight and Baron of Schwarzbaum. Frida Bockmann's father.

Rafe Kaltegrasen, Anders' cousin on his mother's side.

Kartemann, archer and sergeant of the City Guard of Wodenberg.

Brynhilde Kaufmann, Theo's wife.

Mina Kaufmann, Theo's infant daughter.

Theobald "Theo" Kaufmann, prosperous dry goods merchant. His family holds one of the few royal charters to do business directly with Suevia. Anders' best friend.

Klippe, lieutenant of the Knapptal Rangers.

Koch, steward to Margrave Schutze.

Kop, Ther of the Order and hospital orderly.

Stannis Krepkin, Physician. Senior physician of the Order and director of the hospital.

Kunster, frequent captain of the watch on Wodenberg's city walls. Lieutenant of the City Guard.

Lauter, chamberlain of Castle Kaltkern.

Leafwell, physician of the infirmary in Duke Seagrace's army. Englic.

Lehrer, a free-lance Physician working in the city.

Adaliya Lesnikova, squire and daughter of a Russe baron. Accepted betrothal to Will Bock-mann before riding to war with her father.

Lesnikov, Baron of Russe and father to Adaliaya. Part of Duke Vysokov's reserve forces.

Lev, Ther and abbot of the Reichang Orderhaus.

Liese, Ter of the Order and infirmary nurse.

Rostislav Loshadsky, knight and Captain of the Prince's Guard.

Ludmilla, madam (guild-master) of Arbor Street.

Ludo, Ther of the Order and hospital orderly.

Gregor Malyshev, Kiefan's squire. Second son of a Russe baron on the north shore of Lake Neva.

Mara, a lady of Wodenberg.

Mudrysky, Physician. Senior physician in service to the Orderhaus at Prohzgrad.

Odile, handmaid to Queen Mercia.

Mechdan Parselev, bound Elect of Saint Qadeem, in service of Wodenberg. Physician of the Order. Attends the royal family as well.

Nebel, a widowed frau of Wodenberg.

Ola, housemistress of the Riverman tavern in Vorspitz.

Saint Qadeem, of the Wodenberg Trinity. Philosopher saint.

Gudrun Rabskov, Ilya's wife.

Ilya Rabskov, servant in Castle Kaltkern. Sent on the mission as a general handyman.

Rangle, Ther of the Order and ambulance driver.

Riker, warhorse trainer in service of the Rossweide barony.

Radulf Rogen, knight and Captain of the City Guard of Wodenberg.

Readulf, knight of the King's Guard.

Reinwin, knight of the King's Guard.

Rotmann, knight and Sergeant of the City Guard of Wodenberg.

Adal Rytsarov, a Russe knight.

Aleksandra Rytsarova, knight and Captain of the King's Guard. Prince Kiefan served as her squire.

Svetlana Sahnen, baroness of Wodenberg.

Walden Sahnen, baron of Wodenberg.

Eadulf Saltgrass, Englic archer and Captain.

Sasha, house-maid of the Bockmanns.

Eburhart Schäfer, wealthy livestock dealer in Vorspitz. Hosted Kate and her family during their stay.

Trauger Schäfer, son of Eburhart.

Schneider, seamstress of Wodenberg.

Bjornhardt Schutze, knight and margrave of Knapptal. Nearly died in the first battle with Arcea's forces.

Haralda Schutze, teenaged daughter of the margrave.

Gisella Seagrace, princess of Wodenberg and duchess of Englia. Kiefan's older sister and mother of two boys.

Pirra Seagrace, knight and cousin of Duke Seagrace.

Tomas Seagrace, knight and duke of Englia. Married Kiefan's older sister and has two sons.

William Seagrace, the older of the duke's two sons. Kiefan's nephew.

Sergeyev, Ther and quartermaster of the Order.

Shaw, abbot of the Order in Duke Seagrace's army.

Sigmund, an archer of the Rangers and native of the Vorspitz area.

Smithtree, a sergeant of the Rangers.

Alice Springlea, prostitute of Arbor Street and Kate's best friend.

Magda Springlea, Alice's daughter.

Staffwright, armsman and sergeant of Duke Seagrace's army.

Gunther Stahlmann, knight and Duke of Alemannia. Kiefan's second cousin. Chosen to replace the late Duke Haken.

Wenda Stark, housemistress of Castle Kaltkern.

Steif, Captain-general of the local garrison at the city of Wodenberg.

Süssie, prostitute of Arbor Street. Theobald Kaufmann's favorite.

Terekhov, bound Elect of Saint Qadeem, in service of Wodenberg. A crafter elect.

Konrad Tolokov, knight and captain of Duke Vysokov's personal guard. Kiefan's second cousin. Chosen as the heir apparent by Saint Woden, should Kiefan not survive the campaign.

Boristan Tolstyev, Ther of the Order. Personal secretary to the abbot. Sent on the mission to document events.

Tritter, knight and lieutenant of the City Guard of Wodenberg. Has a gambling problem.

Adalev Trüberde, Linde's husband.

Gerhart Trüberde, Linde's year-old son.

Linde Trüberde, master weaver of Wodenberg. Kate's neighbor.

Saint Vitur, an ancient saint of Alemannia.

Voislav, an archer of the Rangers.

Kleelinde Vollman, daughter of the margrave of Kernweise.

Nadya Vysokova, daughter and heir of the duke of Russe. Serves as a squire and aide to her father.

Olga Vysokova, duchess of Russe.

Stanislaus Vysokov, knight and duke of Russe.

Olga Vysokova, duchess of Russe.

Wachmann, Physician of the Order.

Waldemar, a knight of the King's Guard.

Bjorn Waldgrun, woodsman. Assigned the mission as a guide by Baron Eismann.

Johanna Waldgrun, Bjorn Waldgrun's wife.

Ulf Waldgrun, woodsman. Assigned the mission as a guide by Baron Eismann.

Weber, armsman and lieutenant of the City Guard of Wodenberg.

Kiefan Weissberg, knight and prince of Wodenberg. Third and only surviving son of King Wilhelm and Queen Mercia.

Mercia Weissberg, Queen of Wodenberg and Kiefan's mother. Born the Aethelings-dóhtor of Suevia.

Wilhelm Weissberg, fourth of his name, King of Wodenberg.

Wolfgang Weissberg, former bound Elect of Saint Woden in service of Wodenberg. Younger brother of Wilhelm and a prince of Wodenberg as well. He died during the conquest of Englia.

Saint Woden, of the Wodenberg Trinity. Saint of war.

Zina, Saint Aleksandr's semi-secret consort.

CAERCOED

Anwyl, servant of House Gwatcyn.

Bévin, handmaid to the Crowns.

Branwen, a merchant lady of Caercoed. Traveled with Síochana Cainwen.

Tannait Broic, bound Elect of Saint Sabh, in service of Caercoed.

Síochana Cainwen, acting Margrave of Myrddin and Lieutenant of the Northern Horse.

Aisling Ceffyl, knight and Captain of the Crown's Blades.

Saint Conbarre, saint of Caercoed.

Ceelin Crierwy, Crown of Caercoed. Younger of the two Crowns.

Ciara Crierwy, Crown of Caercoed. Elder of the two Crowns.

Ealga, a stable-hand of the Crown's Blades.

Teleri Eoghan, bound Elect of Saint Conbarre, in service of Caercoed. Captain-general of the Crown's Blades. Battle elect.

Mohra Fionmaen, Captain of the Tadhlon Guard. Translator and intelligence officer.

Aed Gwatcyn, husband to the Margraves of Tadhlon.

Aifric Gwatcyn, daughter and heir of the Margraves Gwatcyn. The wilder one.

Esgwen Gwatcyn, daughter and heir of the Margraves Gwatcyn. The more polite one.

Leix Gwatcyn, Margrave of Tadhlon and Captain-general to the Crown. Mother of the youngest set of twins.

Lorcana Gwatcyn, Margrave of Tadhlon. Mother of Tiarnan, Aifric and Esgwen.

Oisin Gwatcyn, consort of the Crowns and brother of Leix and Lorcana Gwatcyn.

Tiarnan Gwatcyn, eldest son of the Margraves Gwatcyn.

Fionn Helwyr, knight and Captain of the Crown's Blades.

Míde Lanfuar, co-heir to the Duchy of Dheathain. The louder one.

Una Lanfuar, co-heir to the Duchy of Dheathain. The quieter one.

Pryderi, a merchant lady of Caercoed. Traveled with Síochana Cainwen.

Rónan, on-staff cook of the Crown's Blades.

Saint Sabh, saint of Caercoed.

Faola Taircoeden, Duchess of Henffrydd. Mother of twin marriage candidates. Margrave Gwatcyn's liege lord.

Faolán Taircoeden, son of the duchess of Henffyrdd.

Davnait and Sorcha Taircoeden, heirs of the Duchess of Henffyrdd. Represented by their mother, at Vorspitz.

Tana, stable-master of House Gwatcyn.

ARCEA

Bréowan, master brewer and head of the Brewers' Guild of Reowan.

Carina, bound Elect in service of Arcea.

Saint Chale, bound saint of Empress Seraphine. Flesh forger and creator of Arcea's centaurs and minotaurs.

Clarilunes Graziana, blood of the Empress and marriage candidate.

d'Ovio Alain. Ancient philosopher of Arcea.

dePenna Cavo, bound Elect of Saint Rakkar, in service to Arcea.

dePesci Liandro, bound Elect of Saint Gauvail, in the service of the Empress of Arcea.

deSvello Antonin, Voice of the Empress. Her official envoy and negotiator.

Saint Dolorata, bound Saint of Empress Seraphine. War-master of Arcea.

Empress Seraphine, the saint and ruler of the Arceal Empire.

Fijolais, bound Elect of Saint Gauvail, in service of the Arceal Empire.

Saint Gauvail, bound Saint of the Empress.

Saint Haladi, bound Saint of the Empress.

Laurent, Seraphine's body-servant. Ex-military and extremely devoted to her.

Saint Melantha, bound Saint of Empress Seraphine, in service of Arcea. Saint of Elleras.

Saint Musaad, bound Saint of Empress Seraphine, in service of Arcea. Crafter saint, originally from Rasila.

Saint Rakkar, bound Saint of the Empress. Saint of war.

Renata, bound Elect of Saint Gauvail, in the service of the Empress of Arcea. Crafter Elect, specifically a blacksmith.

Stel, a centaur of the Red Hoof company.

Titos, bound Elect in service of Arcea.

SUEVIA

Eadgard Bídon, brother of Theo's mother. Royalist, and a spy for Wodenberg, in Suevia.

Row Bídon, merchant of Suevia, son of Eadgard Bídon and Theo's cousin.

Blythe, housemistress of Áering Castle, assigned to serve Seraphine.

Cys, a stable-hand at the Governor's palace.

Abrecan Dennode, Bídon's associate.

Eadwin, long-serving chamberlain of the governor's palace.

Eldwin, a guard of the Governor's palace.

Etha, one of the night-shift housemaids at Castle Áering.

Graeme, a Suevi man.

Glyman, captain of a Suevi division of Arcea's army.

Galan Heathugrim, would-be duke of Suevia and supporter of the royalist movement. Kiefan's second cousin, on his mother's side.

Horsfald, stable-master at the Governor's palace.

Osric, a senior guild-member of Reowan and royalist sympathizer.

Lucan Scyfe, knight and Captain-general of the thirty-first Arceal division. Descended from one of the former noble houses of Suevia.

Saint Seaxneat, of Suevia. He was killed by Arceal saints, in the conquest.

Kend Throsm, burg-meister of Temitte.

OTHERS

Saint Cambifax, an ancient saint and master shape-shifter. The Empress claims to have been his disciple.

Saint Ethmund, of Englia. He was killed in the conquest by Wodenberg.

www.ingramcontent.com/pod-product-compliance
Lightning Source LLC
Chambersburg PA
CBHW070535030726
47505CB00001B/45